Graham Masterton Omnibus

Tengu
The Devils of D-Day
Mirror
Charnel House

Also by Graham Masterton

Graham Masterton Omnibus

Tengu
The Devils of D-Day
Mirror
Charnel House

GRAHAM MASTERTON

timewarner paperbacks

A *Time Warner* Paperback

This omnibus edition first published in Great Britain by Time Warner Paperbacks in 200
Graham Masterton Omnibus Copyright © Graham Masterton 2004

Previously published separately:
Tengu first published in the United States of America by Tor Books in 1983
First published in Great Britain by Sphere Books Ltd in 1984
Reprinted 1986, 1988, 1989
Reprinted by Warner Books in 1993
Copyright © Graham Masterton 1983

The Devils of D-Day first published in Great Britain by Sphere Books Ltd in 1979
Reprinted 1981 (twice), 1984, 1985, 1987, 1988, 1990
Copyright © Graham Masterton 1979

Mirror first published in Great Britain by Severn House Ltd in 1988
First published in paperback by Sphere Books Ltd in 1988
Reprinted 1990
Published by Sphere Books in 1996
Copyright © Graham Masterton 1988

Charnel House first published in Great Britain by Sphere Books in 1978
Reprinted 1979, 1980, 1981, 1984, 1985, 1987, 1988, 1990
Reprinted by Warner Books in 1993
Copyright © Graham Masterton 1978

The moral right of the author has been asserted.

All characters in this publication are fictitious and any
resemblance to real persons, living or dead is purely coincidental.

A CIP catalogue record for this book is available from the British Library

ISBN 0 7515 3650 4

Printed and bound in Great Britain by
Mackays of Chatham Ltd, Chatham

Time Warner Paperbacks
An imprint of
Time Warner Books UK
Brettenham House
Lancaster Place
London WC2E 7EN

www.TimeWarnerBooks.co.uk

Tengu

Naval records show indisputably that the radio monitoring vessel USS *Value* was at Pearl Harbor on July 2, 1945, undergoing routine equipment repairs. There can be no basis whatever for your suggestion that the vessel was anchored at that time off the coast of Japan. Nor can there be any substance in your claim that the USS *Value* was connected with what you call the "Appomattox Situation." The Navy has no record of any file of that title or description.

SEN. NEILSEN (N.J.): Did you at any time prior to this ortie appreciate that you might have to sacrifice the lives f all but one of your fellow operatives in order to achieve a omparatively minor intelligence coup?

LT. COL. KASTNER: Yes, sir. I was conscious of the risks. I night add that my fellow operatives were, too. We were rained.

SEN. NEILSEN: Do you now believe that what you achieved was worth the loss of all those lives, and worth the political risks which Senator Goldfarb has already out-lined?

LT. COL. KASTNER: There was a possibility that it might have been, sir. I admit the net result was a disappoint-ment.

SEN. NEILSEN: A disappointment?

LT. COL. KASTNER: Not all such sorties are disappointments, sir. Appomattox was a good example.

SEN. NEILSEN: Appomattox? What was Appomattox?

LT. COL. KASTNER: I have just been given instructions that I am not to respond to that question, sir. It is outside the area of my competence.

SEN. NEILSEN: I think this inquiry deserves some kind of explanation of your remarks, Colonel.

LT. COL. KASTNER: I'm sorry, sir. I have been advised that any kind of response would be a violation of national security.

SEN. NEILSEN: Very well, Colonel. But I intend to take this matter further.

LT. COL. KASTNER: That is your privilege, sir.

MESSAGE RECEIVED FROM APPOMATTOX ONE, JULY 11, 1945

"We've located it, sir. No question about it. We've taken sixteen radio bearings and we have it right on the button."

"In that case (*inaudible*) immediately. I repeat, immediately. You will be picked up at 2125 hours on the 15th on the beach at (*inaudible*.)"

BOOK ONE
BURNED DOVES

CHAPTER ONE

When Sherry Cantor's alarm clock woke her at 7:27 on the morning of August 9 she had twenty-three minutes to live.

That was the most overwhelming fact of her morning. Yet it was the only fact she didn't know.

She knew that her twenty-second birthday was only three days away. She knew that in two weeks she was supposed to drive down to San Diego and spend a week with her brother Manny and his wife Ruth. She knew that she had a date to meet her good-looking new lawyer, Bert Dentz, in thirteen hours and thirty-three minutes for dinner at the Palm Restaurant on Santa Monica Boulevard.

She knew that her savings account at Security Pacific contained $127,053.62, and she knew that last Wednesday's *Variety* had dubbed her "most promising young video star of 1983."

But knowing all that was not enough. Knowing all that could not possibly save her from what was going to happen in twenty-three minutes' time.

After the alarm had woken her up, she lay on her emerald-green satin sheets in her small white California-rococo bedroom, under the framed black-and-white print of yuccas at Santa Barbara. She thought about the dream she had just been dreaming. It had been vivid, almost realer than real, as only early-morning dreams can be. She had imagined herself jumping rope in the front yard of the old white house in Bloomington, Indiana. She had

13

imagined the leaves falling from the trees like flakes of rust. She had imagined her mother coming to the door, and waving her to come in for cookies and milk. . . .

Sherry thought about her dream, and then let it warmly melt away. Bloomington, Indiana, was five years ago, and a lifetime away. She stretched on the twisted sheets.

She was a tall, striking girl with rich chestnut hair and a face that was uncompromisingly European. Her eyes were wide, and almost amber. She was wide-shouldered, big-breasted, and narrow-hipped. She slept naked, except for a small pair of blue satin panties, and her skin was soft and brown against the shiny sheets.

There was a faded photograph on the sideboard in Bloomington of Sherry's mother in a transit camp in Munchen Gladbach, Germany, in 1945. Except for the puff-sleeved dress and the headscarf, it could have been Sherry.

At 7:31, with only nineteen minutes left, Sherry sat up in bed and ran her hands through her tousled hair. On the bleached calico window blind, the first nodding patterns of sunlight shone through the fan palms in her garden, and made a shadow-play.

Somewhere outside, a radio was giving the morning traffic report. It was bad everywhere.

Sherry climbed out of bed, stood up, stretched, and stifled a yawn. Then she padded out of the bedroom and into her kitchenette. She opened the mock Oregon-oak cupboard and took down a can of Folger's coffee. As she reached for her percolator, a triangle of sunlight lit her hair, and then her shoulder, and then her right breast. The nipple was pale and soft.

While the coffee perked, Sherry poured herself an orange-juice and stood in the kitchenette drinking it. She felt hungry. Last night, she'd shared a bottle of tequila with Dan Mayhew, the curly-haired actor who played her unhappily married cousin in *Our Family Jones*, and hangovers always made her feel hungry.

She opened the fridge again. There were two Thomas's

muffins left. She wondered how guilty she would feel if she toasted one.

It was 7:37. She decided against the muffin. Dan Mayhew hadn't even been worth getting a hangover over, and so he certainly wasn't worth putting on weight over. Last week she'd seen him sitting in the studio commissary with a boy whose pale lemon ballet shoes and surfer's knobs hadn't exactly reassured her about Dan's essential virility.

It was 7:39. There were eleven minutes of life left. Sherry left the kitchenette as the coffee began to perk, and walked into her small bathroom. There were T-shirts and panties hanging to dry on a line over the tub. She looked at herself in the mirror, pouted at herself, and pulled down her eyelids to make sure her eyes weren't too bloodshot. Lionel—Lionel Schultz, the director of *Our Family Jones*—always went crazy if anyone arrived on the floor with reddened eyes.

"What do you think we're shooting here?" he invariably screamed. "A fucking Dracula picture?"

Lionel Schultz wasn't a gentle man. He wasn't much of a gentleman, either. But he had a perverse genius for soap opera, and for provoking believable performances out of inexperienced actors. It was Lionel Schultz who had shown Sherry how to develop the dumb, busty part of Lindsay Jones into a character of sweet and quirky sympathy. And he hadn't touched her once.

Sherry finished her orange juice and set her glass down on the basin, next to her cake of herbal soap. She stepped out of her panties, and sat on the toilet. She could hear the birds chittering in the garden, and the distant murmur of the freeways. She closed her eyes, and tried to think what she felt like wearing today.

It was 7:42. She flushed the toilet, washed her face, and walked back into the kitchenette naked. The coffee was popping and jumping. She picked up the folded-back script that lay on the counter, next to the Popeye cookie jar, and flicked through two or three pages.

LINDSAY (*sobbing*): Is that really what you think of me? After all those days and nights together? After all those things you said?

MARK: Honey, you don't understand. I had to tell Carla we were finished. I didn't have any other choice.

Riboyne Shel O'lem, thought Sherry. If anyone had shown me this script before I signed up for *Our Family Jones*, I wouldn't have thought it was worth turning up at the studio. I would have stayed as a waitress at Butterfield's, fetching and carrying white wine and cottage cheese salads for pretentious British tax exiles in tinted glasses, and been glad of the work. Who would have guessed that some treacly saga about some even more treacly family would have gotten off the ground for a pilot and two episodes, let alone for two series?

Even more amazing, who would have thought that a Jewish girl from Bloomington, Indiana, would have been picked out of hundreds of would-be starlets for one of the most noticeable roles in the whole drama?

There wasn't any question that *Our Family Jones* had cost Sherry the love of her live-in boyfriend, Mack Holt. Mack was lean and moody, with curly blond hair and a broken nose, and he could swim and ride and fence and dance like Fred Astaire. They had met one evening on the plaza outside of the Security Pacific Bank at Century City, when she had just opened her savings account with $10 her mother had sent her. The shadows of the dying day had been very Bauhaus, and he had crossed the plaza at that trotting pace athletes use when they're just on the point of breaking into a run. She had been putting away her bankbook; dropped her purse; and he had picked it up for her in one fell swoop. After such a meeting, he should have known she would make it in soap opera.

Sherry and Mack had lived for seven months on the second floor of a brown crumbling hacienda off Franklin Avenue, in Hollywòod. They had shared their three-room apartment with a lumpy divan, two fraying basketwork chairs, three peeling posters for the Grateful Dead, and a dyspeptic gas stove. They had talked, played records, made love, smoked Mexican grass, argued, gone off to work, brushed their teeth, and finally arrived at the moment when Lionel had called to say Sherry was fabulous, and just had to come down to the studio right away, and Mack, far more talented, but still parking cars for a living, had refused to kiss her and wish her luck.

From then on, it had been nothing but sulks, arguments, and eventually, packed suitcases. Sherry had lived for a while with a plain but friendly girl she knew from Butterfield's, and then taken out a mortgage on this small secluded bungalow at the top of a steeply graded dead end called Orchid Place. She enjoyed the luxury of living alone, with her own small garden, her own wrought-iron fence, her own living room, her own perfect peace. She began to think about who she was, and what she wanted out of her life, and all of her friends said she was much nicer since she'd left Mack, and much more relaxed.

To ease one of the more pressing demands of being single, Sherry had bought, through the mail, a pink vibrator. Most of the time it stayed in her bedside cupboard, next to her Oil of Olay and her Piz Buin sun oil, but occasionally there were nights when fantasies crowded her mind, and the Los Angeles heat almost stifled her, and she used it just to keep herself sane.

It was harder than anyone knew, being the most promising young video star of 1983.

With four minutes left, she poured herself a cup of coffee. She sipped it and repeated her lines under her breath: "Is that really what you think of me? After all those days and nights together? After all those things you said?"

There were three minutes left. One hundred eighty seconds of life. She crossed the living room with her coffee mug in one hand and her script in the other. The sun was shining through the loose-woven yellow drapes drawn across the French doors, and the whole room was suffused in daffodil-colored light. Her bare toes curled into the white shag rug.

"Is that *really* what you think of me?" she repeated.

Two minutes. She switched on the Sony television which stood in the corner. On top of the television was a sprig of poinsettia in a glass carafe of water. She had picked it yesterday evening, before she went out with Dan. On the wall behind the television was an original studio sketch for the Jones family parlor, signed by the artist. In a concentrated whisper, Sherry said: "After all those days and nights together? After all those things you said?"

A commercial for Santa Anita Dodge appeared on the television screen—a fast-talking man in a powder-blue suit and a Buddy Holly hairstyle. "When you bring the family down to Santa Anita Dodge, we'll give each of your children a free balloon, and your wife will be able to pick up a free voucher for hairstyling and a beauty treatment. That's guaranteed, whether you buy a new Dodge or not."

"Is that *really* what you think of me?"

One minute left. Thirty seconds. Fifteen. Ten. Five. Sherry turned away from the television to set her mug down on the glass-and-bamboo coffee table in the middle of the living room. Her telephone rang, although nobody ever found out who it was, calling her at 7:49:55 in the morning.

The noise was so shattering that she thought a bomb had gone off. Then she thought it must be an earthquake. But as she turned back toward the French windows, she saw both huge panes of glass bursting inward, so that the whole living room was filled with a blizzard of glittering, tumbling fragments. Next, the metal screens were ripped away, and the aluminum upright between the broken windows was smashed aside as if it were cardboard.

She didn't scream. She didn't even understand what was happening until it was too late. She raised her hands to protect her face from the flying glass, but the glass was nothing.

Through the wrecked windowframe stepped a short,

powerfully built man dressed in a strangely tied-up yellow robe. His skull was cropped down to a bristly black brush. His face was covered by a grotesque white mask, expressionless and evil.

Sherry tried to back away, tried to cover her nakedness, but a sharp triangle of glass sliced into the side of her foot, and her hesitation was fatal.

The man seized her left wrist in a grip so hard that it broke both her radius and her ulna. He twisted her fiercely around, and gripped her throat from behind. She gagged and choked, and tried to thrash against him with her legs, but he was impossibly strong.

Without a word, without even a grunt, he went down on one knee and pulled Sherry backward across his thigh. She felt a splitting pain in her spine that was so intense that she passed out. But she instantly regained consciousness and was drowned in scarlet waves of agony. The man was hurting her so much she couldn't even believe it was happening to her.

Her back broke. She felt it snap. She could see the combed-plaster ceiling of her bungalow, and the paper lantern with the flower patterns on it. She couldn't speak, couldn't cry out, couldn't move. It couldn't be real. Things like this didn't happen. She wasn't here at all. She must be someplace else. Asleep. Dreaming.

She could still hear the radio somewhere outside. It was playing "Samba Pa Ti."

Silently, the powerful man gripped the inside of her thighs. Her head was lying back on the rug now, and her hands were clenched in paralysis over her breasts. Her entire nervous system was dislocated, and she was already dying. The man let out a deep, suppressed *hmph*! as he pulled her thighs further and further apart, stretching every muscle and sinew. Through a haze of pain and disbelief, Sherry heard something crack in her groin, although she could no longer feel anything below her waist.

The man let her tumble from his upraised knee onto the

rug. He stood up, keeping a hold on the ankle and the thigh of her right leg. With deliberate care, he planted his black silk slipper on Sherry's pubic bone, to give him balance and leverage, and then he twisted her leg around as if he were trying to tear the leg off a chicken.

She was lucky she couldn't feel it. The ball of her thigh-bone was wrenched out of its socket. Then the skin and flesh were screwed around so tightly that they tore apart, in a grisly welter of burst arteries. The man gave Sherry's leg one more turn, and ripped it right away from her body.

He stepped back, and looked down at her. Her breathing was shallow with shock, and her face was already blue. Her eyes were clouded over. The man wiped his hands, first on his robes, then on the drapes. He didn't seem to know what to do next.

Sherry realized she was dying. She didn't know why. She could see the man looking down at her, and she tried to think how she could ask him. It didn't really matter, of course. Nothing mattered when you were dead.

Her last thought was that she wished she could see her home in Indiana just one more time.

The man in the yellow robe watched her die, his mask impassive. Then he walked back out the broken French window, and stood in the morning sunlight, still and thoughtful, as if he had just returned from a long and unexpected journey.

CHAPTER TWO

As Sherry was dying, Mrs. Eva Crowley was parking her slate-colored Seville Elegante on a red line close to the twin towers of Century Park East. She switched off the motor and sat in the driver's seat for a while, watching her pale blue eyes in the rearview mirror. Well, she thought, this is it. This is where my life is pasted back together again, or lost for good.

She climbed out of the car and locked it. Normally she never bothered, but this morning she felt the need for as many mundane rituals as possible—not only to keep herself from trembling with fear, but to delay the moment when she was going to have to stand face to face with Gerard and tell him: "Choose."

Gerard hadn't come home now for three nights in succession, and Eva Crowley had had enough. She had sworn to herself in the small hours of the morning, as she lay hugging her husband's crumpled pillow, that she was going to finish for good all the pain and humiliation of being a cheated wife. No more evenings with only Dan Rather, a bottle of Jack Daniel's, and her sleeping twin daughters for company. No more false sympathy when Gerard called from the office to say that work had snowed him under again, and I'm sorry, Evie, I just have to keep at it all through the night.

Today, Gerard Crowley, the self-made president of Crowley Tobacco Imports, was going to be forced to make up his mind.

As Eva walked across the plaza toward the entrance of Century Park East, her footsteps echoed on the concrete paving, and she could see a distant and severe image of herself in the glass doors, approaching with all the inevitability of her own fate.

She was a petite, slender woman, with ash-blonde hair drawn back in a bun. Her face was pale and perfectly oval, like a blanched almond. For the frightening and solemn performance which this day demanded of her, she was wearing a dark gray suit with a pencil skirt, and black stiletto shoes. She could have been going to a board meeting, or a funeral.

Eva felt breathless as she waited in the deserted lobby for the elevator to take her to the twenty-seventh floor. She began to bite at her pearl-pink nails, and then stopped herself. She hadn't bitten her nails since she was an overweight young student in New York, plain and agonizingly shy, and hopelessly infatuated with an overbearing slob of a business administration senior called Hank Pretty. Her life in those days had been haunted by slipping grades, headaches, and the vision of spending the rest of her years with a man whose body stank of sweat and whose mind had about as much charm and order as the morning after Mardi Gras.

Eva and Hank had fought. Hank had hit her. She had spat red blood into the rose-colored washbasin, and the whole world had seemed to be coming to a close.

She hadn't attempted suicide, though. Eva had never been the suicidal type. These days, she put on weight when she was anxious, eating too many taco chips and guacamole, and she smoked, too. But she had the painful strength to make appointments with her fears and face up to them, as if her fears were imaginary doctors with bad news about her smear, or phantom dentists with bicuspids to pull.

She sometimes wished she had no strength at all, and could readily sacrifice herself to Gerard's faithlessness without a struggle. But she couldn't, and wouldn't. She was too much like her father. Ornery.

The elevator bell softly chimed the arrival of the twenty-seventh floor. The doors rumbled open and Eva stepped out. On the wall in front of the elevator bank was a brushed-aluminum sign with the inscription CROWLEY TOBACCO IMPORTS, INC. LOS ANGELES—CHICAGO —MIAMI. She stood and looked at it for a moment, because she remembered the day it had first been screwed into place. Then she walked evenly along the corridor toward the tinted glass doors of the office itself.

It was a few seconds before eight o'clock. Gerard had always started work early. When they had first married, nineteen years ago, she had hardly ever seen him in the mornings. He had been out of bed and jogging along Lexington Road well before six, and she had only woken up at seven o'clock when the door of his Riviera slammed and the engine whistled into life. The kitchen would be left like the mess deck of the *Marie Celeste*—half-eaten crispbread, spilled milk, letters ripped open and left on the table—and there would never be any husband around to prove who had done it.

In later years, though, Eva had woken up earlier. Some mornings Gerard had opened his eyes, and she had been lying there watching him. He had mistaken her steady gaze for affection, even for adoration. In fact, she had been considering the empty and ungraspable nature of their marriage, and wondering who he really was.

She loved him. She had always known that. She wanted to stay married to him. But she had never been able to decide whether he loved her in return or simply used her as a hostess, and mother, and occasional bed partner. He always called her "Evie," and for three of their nineteen years she had protested about it. Then she had given up.

She opened the office door. There were decorative plants and white vinyl chairs, and a wide teak desk. There was nobody around. Eva waited for a moment, and then crossed the reception area to the door marked GERARD F. CROWLEY, PRESIDENT. She felt peculiarly numb, and her hesitation in front of the door seemed to last for whole minutes.

Here I am, she thought. *I've seen him so tired that he was weeping. I've seen him laugh. I've seen him sick, and I've seen him happy. I've seen every detail of his naked body. The pattern of moles on his thigh. The curl of his pubic hair. I've borne him twins. And yet I'm standing in front of his office door, almost too frightened to knock.*

She knocked.

There was a pause. Then his voice asked, "Who is that?"

In a dry, tight falsetto, she said, "It's me."

"Evie?" he queried.

She opened the door. The office faced east, and it was suffused with the milky light of morning. Gerard, dark and unshaven, and wearing a black shirt with the sleeves rolled up, was sitting behind his wide white desk. On the corner of the desk, her eyes wide with anticipation, was his receptionist Francesca, auburn-haired, tall, and dressed in skin-tight white cotton jeans and an olive-green silk blouse.

There was a silver cigar box on Gerard's desk. It had been Eva's tenth-anniversary present to him. It was engraved: "With undying love, your Evie." That was how much he had taken her character away from her.

Gerard said, "You're up early."

He was a very lean man, with thick black wiry hair that was just beginning to turn gray. His face was long and angular, with a thin, sharp nose and sharply defined lips. His eyes were deep-set and dark, and yet she had always felt they were oddly lacking in expression. You couldn't look at him for very long without having to glance away in search of something more sympathetic.

Francesca stood up. Eva was conscious of the receptionists's breasts, shifting under the thin silk of her blouse. Thirty-six C cup, she guessed, but definitely braless today. There were cheap silver puzzle rings on the girl's fingers, and Eva could almost picture those fingers clutching Gerard's stiffened penis. The same way any prizewinner holds a trophy.

"I, er—Evie, it's good to see you," said Gerard. He stood up, and came around his desk to greet her. He was far taller than she was, nearly six two, but somehow he seemed shorter today, diminished.

Francesca said uneasily, "I think I'll go make that coffee now."

"Sure," said Gerard, with pretended ease. "Would you

like some coffee, Evie?''

Eva shook her head. "I don't think so, thank you."

There was a moment of tension. Gerard rubbed his hand across his mouth, as if he was unconsciously making sure that there were no traces of strange kisses. "Well," he said, "I kind of guessed that you wouldn't."

Francesca was still standing by the door, and Gerard glanced across at her and closed his eyes briefly in a catlike expression which meant, *You go make coffee, I'll handle this.* Francesca paused, then left, leaving the office door fractionally ajar.

"Sit down, why don't you?" Gerard asked Eva, indicating a white revolving armchair.

Eva said: "No, thank you. I don't think it's going to take me long to ask you where you've been these past three nights."

He was walking back around his desk. He looked up at her, his dark head outlined against a bright golden painting of drying tobacco leaves. "Where I've *been*?" he asked her. "You know damn well where I've been."

"You've been working three days and three nights without sleep?"

"Almost. I had paperwork up to here." He raised his hand up to the level of his eyes.

"The Turkish consignment?"

He narrowed his eyes. "Mostly."

"So David Orlando's lying?"

"David Orlando? David's in Dallas."

Eva lowered her eyes. "I know he is," she said softly. "I called him there yesterday. He told me he handled the Turkish consignment all by himself, and finished up two days ago. He also told me you had almost no work in the office this week, and that you wouldn't be pushed until early next month."

Gerard stared at her for almost half a minute, without speaking. Then he opened his silver cigar box, hesitated, and finally chose a small Havana. He reached for his cutters, snipped the end off the cigar, and placed it with

exaggerated precision between his lips. Eva found his
silence, his meticulous actions, distinctly unnerving. His
eyes seemed less penetrable than ever.

If only she didn't want him so much, and need to know
that he still loved her. If only she was weak enough to stay
at home and be satisfied with what she had.

Outside, a fire siren warbled and whooped along the
Avenue of the Stars. Gerard waited until the echoes had
died away, and then he said: "You were that suspicious,
huh? Suspicious enough to call up David?"

"What would *you* have done, Gerard, if *I'd* stayed away
for three nights?"

He opened a box of kitchen matches. "You forget that
you don't have any reason for staying away nights. I do."

She tried to smile, but her mouth couldn't manage it.
"That's obvious enough," she said. "But the reason isn't
work, is it? It's *her*."

"Her?"

Eva nodded toward the half-open office door. "She's
the one, isn't she? Francesca?"

Gerard let out an abrupt, uncertain laugh that was
almost a cough. "Evie—" he said, "I don't really think
you're being very fair to me here—"

"You don't think I'm *fair*?" Eva interrupted, in an
intense whisper. "What the hell do you call *fair*?"

"I mean understanding," protested Gerard. "I mean
you don't seem like you're trying to understand what's
going down here."

"What's to understand? You're going to bed with your
receptionist!"

"Evie," Gerard said, raising his hand, as if he were
fending off a flapping bird. "Evie, every human situation
has its two sides. You don't seem to understand that."

Eva turned away. "You're just the same, aren't you?"
she said. "Always trying to make *me* feel guilty for the
things that *you've* done. Well, it won't work this time,
Gerard, because I do understand. I understand that you've
been leaving me at home to run your house and look after

your daughters while you go off fornicating with your
twenty-five-year-old receptionist."

Gerard let out a breath.

"Can you understand that I still love you?" he asked
her. "Can you understand that what I feel for Francesca
hasn't made the slightest difference to my appreciation of
what you are?"

She turned back toward him. She was frowning. "Are
you *serious*?" she asked.

"Never more serious in my whole life."

"My God," she said. "I don't believe you sometimes.
You treat love and appreciation as if they were brands of
tobacco."

He struck a match. It flared up, and there was a sharp
smell of burned phosphorus. He kept his eyes on her while
he lit his cigar. Then he waved the match to extinguish it,
and puffed smoke. Eva hated the smell of cigars.

"I love you, Evie. That's all I can say. If you don't
believe me, then I'm really sorry. But it's true."

"Do you love Francesca, too?"

He nodded. "Yes. In a different sort of way."

"What different sort of way? You mean, more sexually?
Is she better in bed than me? She's younger, I suppose?
Her breasts are more—I mean, her breasts are firmer? And
does she do things I won't do?"

Gerard continued to puff at his cigar. "She's different,
that's all. She's a different person."

"I see. Different. That tells me precisely zilch."

Gerard held out his hand toward her. She didn't take it.
She wished she could. Her anger had almost burned itself
out now, and a numb depression was gradually filling her
up, as if she were lowering herself into an unpleasantly
tepid tub of water. She could feel the tears on her
eyelashes, and she knew that if Gerard gave her any
sympathy now, any warmth, she was going to be lost.

"Evie," Gerard told her, in a gentle voice, "I'm the
kind of man who can never stay still. It's in my nature.
You've known that from the start. That was one of the

reasons you married me. You knew I wanted to go places, make money, widen my horizons."

"I didn't think your horizons included other women," said Eva sharply.

"It was inevitable. It's not a disaster. It won't do anything to break us up. I needed a different kind of relationship with a different kind of woman, and I found it with Francesca. That's all. There's no reason why we should have to make a big production out of it. It's happening all the time."

Eva opened her pocketbook and took out a crumpled piece of tissue. She dabbed at her eyes, and said, "You needn't think I'm crying. I'm angry, that's all."

"You don't have to be angry."

"I don't have to be angry? I've found out my husband's unfaithful and all I have to do is congratulate him?"

"You can *accept*, can't you? Take it for what it is?"

Eva looked at him, and slowly nodded. "I can accept, Gerard, but I can't forgive."

"What does that mean? You want a divorce?"

"I don't know. Yes. I mean, no, I don't."

He came nearer and held her arms. He gave her a wry, comforting smile, almost sad, and she could hardly believe that he was the same Gerard she'd married, the same earnest, ambitious, courteous young man who had given up his seat on a crosstown bus on a wet day in New York, and then sheltered her under his umbrella all the way back to her apartment door. The same young man who had taken her out to Mexican restaurants, and told her over the enchiladas, by the swiveling light of a tabletop candle, that he was going to be rich and famous, and that he wanted her to marry him and come to live in L.A., so that she could share his wealth and his fame, and his love too.

Here he was—rich, well known in his own business, but distant now, a remote and incomprehensible man who seemed to have sold himself somewhere along the line of their married life to some other idea of what life should really be. He looked the same, and she still adored him the same, but his attention appeared to be focused someplace else.

She saw herself in the amber-tinted mirror on the other side of the office. She looked pale and odd, but far less distraught than she'd imagined: In fact, she was surprised at her calmness. Gerard's back, dark and tall, looked like the back of a complete stranger.

"Well," said Gerard. "What are you going to do? If you're not going to divorce me—what?"

Eva bit her lip.

"You're trying to tell me you won't—"

Francesca came to the door. She wasn't carrying any coffee. Gerard held Eva's arms tightly, and warmly, but he said in his softest voice, "No. I won't give up Francesca."

CHAPTER THREE

A few minutes after ten o'clock that morning, the telephone started ringing in a shady, secluded apartment on the fourth floor of a yellow house on Alta Loma Road, off Sunset Boulevard. It rang and rang for almost five minutes before a sliding door opened somewhere in the apartment, and silk-slippered feet came padding along the polished wood floor of the corridor.

Nancy Shiranuka picked up the telephone with long red-lacquered fingernails. She said, *"Moshi moshi,"* in a flat, expressionless voice. Then she said, "Oh, it's you."

She stood silent, listening. She was a small, delicately boned girl, even for a Japanese. Her face had that startling wide-eyed Hokkaido prettiness that Japanese men find devastating, and even Americans consider magnetic, especially if they've served out East. It was an acquired taste, Nancy's prettiness, like *chazuke*, rice and tuna fish with green tea poured over them. She wore nothing but a loose silk robe of glistening black, open at the front. Her long black hair hung tangled and damp over her shoulders.

All around her, the apartment was lined with polished oak paneling, and split-bamboo blinds where drawn over the windows. There were two or three black and-white silk cushions on the floor, and a low table of carved black wood, but apart from these the room was bare. On the walls were three erotic woodblocks by Settei from the *Onna-shimekawa oshie-fumi*, the book of sexual instruction for women. The sun shone across the room in narrow stripes.

Nancy asked, "Are you sure this is true? Did Torii tell you? And what happened afterward?"

She paused, listening, and then said, "I see."

While she was listening, the sliding door opened again, and there was the sound of bare feet along the corridor. A very tall American came into the living room, his midriff wrapped in a towel, and he stood quite close to her, watching her with hooded eyes. He was gray-haired, at least sixty-five, and his body was gnarled and muscular and scarred. His face was composed entirely of angles, like Abraham Lincoln's image on the side of Mount Rushmore, and even before you knew who he was you would have guessed he was a military man.

His name was Ernest Perry Ouvarov, ex-U.S. Naval Commander. He had distinguished himself at Midway and Okinawa, and after the signing of the Japanese surrender on the deck of USS *Missouri*, he had been largely responsible for the brilliant reorganization of the American naval administration in the Pacific. Truman had once called him "the knight of the high seas."

Beneath the glittering armor, however, the knight had some fatal weaknesses. In 1951, at the peak of his influence within the Navy, a newspaper investigation had implicated him in a bottomless scandal involving opium, surplus war materials, and worst of all, the procuring of young Japanese girls, some of them no more than seven years old, for the pleasure of himself and other key naval personnel and politicians.

The corruption had been so deep-laid that Ouvarov had been permitted to resign his command without any formal proceedings against him. As one Pentagon official was heard to remark, "If they court-martial Ouvarov, they'll have to court-martial the whole damned Navy."

Ernest Ouvarov had changed his name, and worked for years in San Francisco for a transshipment company. Most people in San Francisco still called him "Fred Milward," and thought of him as nothing more than the moderately prosperous vice president of Bay Shipping, Inc. Two months ago, though, a young Japanese lady called Nancy Shiranuka had called at his office, and his life had never been the same.

He watched Nancy for a minute or two, and then crossed the bare room to the black table. He opened a lacquered box and took out a cigarette. He came back toward her, tapping the cigarette on his thumbnail.

Nancy said, "Okay, if that's the best you can do. Call me again when you have more news. Yes, I'm sorry, too. Yes. But tell them to keep a real low profile. That's right."

Ernest left the room and went into the kitchen in search of a light. He came back again, smoking with affected indifference. Nancy said, "Call me later," and put down the phone.

"Well," asked Ernest, "what was all that about?"

"I'm not sure yet."

"You're not sure? That was Yoshikazu, wasn't it?"

"Yes," she said. "But he thinks something's gone wrong. The police are everywhere, and he can't get close enough to find out."

"Wrong?" queried Ernest, wrinkling his nose, just the way he used to on the bridge of the USS *Ferndale*. "What the hell could have gone wrong?"

"I don't know. But Yoshikazu's worried."

Ernest sucked fiercely at his cigarette, and then blew out smoke. "The whole operation was perfectly planned. I can't believe that anything's gone wrong. Even Yoshikazu isn't that dumb."

Nancy absentmindedly tied the cord of her silk robe. The sun shone on her hair. "Perfect planning doesn't always mean perfect execution. You should know that. Even when you're dealing with ordinary people, things can go wrong."

"You don't have to give me a lesson in personnel management," snapped Ernest. "This whole thing was set up so tight that nobody had any room to move. Not even the brightest member of the team had room to think. There was no improvisation, no contingency plan, nothing but a sequence of precisely controlled and coordinated events. It can't have gone wrong."

"Yoshikazu seems to think it has."

"Well, in that case, he's probably talking his usual gibberish."

"What are you going to do?" smiled Nancy, slyly. "Clap him in irons? Send him off on the next clipper to Shanghai?"

Ernest scratched the iron-gray stubble on his angular chin. He still felt unsettled, working with civilians. His father had been a naval commander before him, and his grandfather had been a friend of Teddy Roosevelt, back in his Rough Rider days. Ernest could only think of life as a battle plan, and he mentally graded the people he had to deal with as admirals, fellow officers, or idiots. Each day presented its difficulties like a fleet of hostile ships, and each difficulty could only be overcome by classic naval tactics. He even walked his three retrievers, John, Paul, and Jones, in line formation.

Only Nancy Shiranuka knew all about those moments when he disembarked (inside his mind) from his self-imposed regime of naval discipline. Those moments when he sought, perversely and desperately, the consolation of girl-children, and extraordinary sexual techniques. He called those moments his "shore leave."

"We need some up-to-date intelligence," he said. "Can't Yoshikazu find out what's happening?"

"He's going to try, Commander. But right now the whole area is crawling with police."

Ernest crushed out his cigarette. "Dammit, I should have entrusted this one to somebody with experience." He added, with expressive contempt: "Yoshikazu. The nearest Yoshikazu's been to Tokyo is the Japanese take-out on Sunset and Fairfax."

"I trust him," said Nancy, pointedly. "I believe it's better if we simply wait."

Ernest looked at her with a testy expression, and then nodded. "All right. We'll give him an hour. If he doesn't report in by then, we'll go take a look for ourselves. Meanwhile, let's keep the television going. They might have a news bulletin."

Nancy gave a sarcastic salute. "Aye, aye, Commander. Anything you say."

The old commander ignored her. "Why don't you have Kimo fix some breakfast? I'm getting damned hungry. Have him fix some of that *dashimaki tamago*."

Nancy paused for a moment, a slight smile on her face. Then she picked up a small square silver bell from the telephone table and tinkled it. After a while, a young Japanese in a white shirt, white jeans, and a white headband came into the room and stood, waiting.

"The commander has a taste for your eggs this morning, Kemo," said Nancy.

Kemo looked across at the commander, and gave a brief, correct nod of his head. If anyone had nodded to him like that in the Navy, the commander would have had him up on a charge of dumb insolence. But Ernest turned irritably away, parted the slatted bamboo blinds with two fingers, and glared out at the trees of Alta Loma Road until Kemo had gone back to his kitchen.

Nancy asked, "What are you thinking about?"

He cleared his throat. "I was just wondering, for the six

hundredth time, whether this whole damned carnival is ever going to work.''

"You're not paid to wonder. You're paid to *make* it work.''

"Correction,'' said Ernest. "I'm paid to make *my* part of it work. I can't be responsible for the rest of this ragbag collection of Oriental hoodlums.''

Nancy gave a high, tittering laugh. "Sometimes you're so fierce. You're just like Cary Grant in *Destination Tokyo*.''

"You like that movie?'' asked Ernest, surprised.

"It's one of my favorites. I like especially the scene where the Japanese pilot parachutes into the water and stabs to death the American seaman who is trying to pull him out.''

"You would,'' growled Ernest. "But I never saw anyone, Jap or American, anything but eternally grateful to be hauled out of the drink. Maybe it just appealed to your cruel sense of humor.''

"I thought you enjoyed my cruel sense of humor.''

"Hmh? Well, there's a time and a place for everything.''

Nancy came toward him, raising her arms. The silk sash of her robe slipped apart, revealing her naked body. She was slim and pale, the color of Japanese provincial pottery, and her breasts were tiny and round with dark nipples that always reminded Ernest of those cups that conjurors use to hide dice. Between the thighs of her slim, short legs, her black pubic hair had been trimmed into the shape of a heart.

Ernest raised his skinny, sinewy arm. "Now, you get away, Nancy. It's too early. We've got this whole operation going snafu, we don't know what in hell's going on, and you know as well as I do that we're going to have Gerard Crowley coming down on top of us by the end of the day like fifteen tons of hot shit. The Huck Finn of Beverly Hills.''

Still smiling, Nancy pressed her bare body up against

him, and reached up to ruffle his silver hair. "You
shouldn't call him that," she cooed. "You know he
doesn't like it."

"What else should I call him? He's a good old country
boy, isn't he, if you want it put politely? Now, let go of
me, will you?"

"I wonder what you call *me* behind my back," Nancy
whispered. "The Dragon Lady?"

Ernest gripped her waist, and twisted her away from
him. But then his towel slipped, and he had to release her
to save his decency. She tittered again, that high birdlike
laugh, and Ernest's neck went red with irritation.

"I should have slammed the door in your face that very
first day I saw you," he growled.

"Oh, no, Mr. Milward," Nancy mocked. "That would
never have done. Think of what you would have missed."

Kemo appeared in the doorway with a tray of tea. Nancy
drew her robe around herself as he sulkily crossed the room
and set the delicate cups and teapot down on the low
table.

"*Dashimaki tamago* five minutes," he said, and slip-
slopped out again.

Ernest sighed and sat creakily down on the floor. Nancy
poured out two cups of tea, and then sat down beside him,
cross-legged. Her robe was wide open again, and he
couldn't help noticing how the heel of her right foot,
drawn up under her, parted the bright pink lips of her silk-
haired sex. He closed his eyes and inhaled the strange,
smoky smell of the Japanese tea.

"You have no need to fear anything," said Nancy, in a
quiet, monotonous voice. "Even if things have gone
wrong this morning, nobody can possibly trace the Tengu
back to us. You know that as well as I. And it had to be
done. It is all part of the preparations."

"There could have been some other way. I told Crowley
that." Ernest spoke without opening his eyes.

"Crowley wanted to make sure it really worked. And
you can scarcely blame him for that, can you, when you

think how much money he's spent?''

"I don't know. In my book, the best tactics are those which are mounted in secrecy. Then—when you can't keep the secrecy up any longer—you keep your enemy guessing by laying smoke, and taking up unexpected and confusing positions.''

"Ernest,'' said Nancy, in the same quiet voice, "we are not fighting frigates. This is not Midway anymore. And what in the world could be more confusing to everybody than what the Tengu was sent out to do this morning?''

Ernest opened his eyes. He peered into his steaming teacup, and watched the dark leaves floating around and around.

"My God,'' he said, under his breath. "What a strange assortment of lost individuals we are. What a cause we're fighting for.''

"Is money such a terrible cause?'' asked Nancy.

Ernest thought, and then grimaced, and shook his head.

Nancy leaned over toward him and kissed the roughness of his cheek. He kept his eyes open, watching her, so that when she came close he was almost squinting. She sat up straight again, and said, "I have a woodblock print somewhere by Eisen, in the style of *Ukiyo-e shunga* prints. It shows a Yoshiwara courtesan anointing her lover's organ with saké before they make love.''

Ernest stared at her suspiciously. But he made no attempt to ward her off when she reached across and loosened his towel. With one tug, she bared his already-stiffened penis and his salt-and-pepper hair.

She uncrossed her legs and knelt beside him. She kissed him again, on the forehead. She smelled slightly of sweat, but mostly of some musky, deep-noted perfume.

"We have no saké,'' she said. "But we have something that will please you even more.''

With one small hand, she stroked his penis up and down, so slowly and leisurely that he felt like gripping his hand over hers and forcing her to rub him faster. But this was one of those times when she was completely in control.

He had to wait. He had to obey. If he didn't, the spell, and the experience she had in store for him, would be forfeit at once.

He said hoarsely, "Nancy—"

She raised one immaculately lacquered fingertip to her lips. Then, still slowly stroking him, she reached across to the tea tray and picked up one of the small white towels that were laid beside a dish of salted plums.

Ernest felt his heart slow up, then quicken, like a man struggling to keep himself afloat in a heavy sea.

Nancy took the lid off the teapot and lowered the towel into the boiling-hot tea. She swirled it around for a moment, and then lifted it out. Hot tea ran onto the tray and across the table.

Ernest said, "You're not—"

She smiled. She said nothing. With a deft flick of her wrist, she wound the scalding towel around the hard shaft and swollen head of Ernest's penis, and gave him a brief, vicious squeeze.

He burst out with a short, sharp shout of pain. He felt as if his whole erection was exploding. But then the pain seemed to detonate into something else altogether. More than pain. More than pleasure. A brief dark instant of that terrible feeling which he craved and feared like a drug. It seemed as if his insides were boiling, as if his brain were going to burst into thousands of pieces. But then he ejaculated, and his semen fell across the back of Nancy's wrist.

The world and the room gradually refocused, as if he were adjusting a pair of binoculars. Everything returned, almost absurdly, to normal. Nancy wiped her hands and arms with the towel, and pulled her robe around herself with stylized modesty. Ernest, feeling stunned and sore, reached down and slowly gathered up his towel.

"Now you know the meaning of Ukiyo," said Nancy. "The floating world of pleasure."

"I also know the meaning of burned balls," Ernest told her in a coarse whisper. "You're a devil, you know that?

Much more of a devil than any of those damned Tengus.''

"Perhaps," said Nancy. "But even devils are sometimes obliged to live a symbiotic life. I need you, and you need me, and perhaps we should offer a prayer that we found each other in the prime of life."

Ernest, wincing, bent forward and took a salted plum from the tray. He chewed it thoughtfully.

"My prime," he said, "was when I was standing on the fantail of the USS *Ferndale*, watching the whole Japanese fleet blazing like the Fourth of July."

Nancy touched his hand consolingly. "I'm sorry I can't give you an action replay here in my living room. But it won't be long, will it, before I can offer you something very much like it?"

Ernest didn't answer. Kemo came in with the Japanese omelets.

CHAPTER FOUR

Sergeant Skrolnik of the Hollywood police department watched with deep moroseness as two medics from the coroner's office lifted the white-sheeted stretcher from the living room floor and took it unsteadily outside through the broken French doors.

The yellow drapes were stirred by the morning breeze as the medics made their way down the path between the fan palms and the poinsettia, and out to the waiting car. The sloping sidewalk was crowded with blank-faced, shuffling spectators.

The day was glaring and hot, and getting hotter. Skrolnik took off his crumpled linen coat and laid it over the back of a chair.

Detective Pullet came through from the bathroom with a pair of small blue satin panties in a self-sealing plastic bag. He stood beside Skrolnik without saying a word, chewing his lip and looking at the wide brown splatter of blood on the rug. There were even splashes of blood up the walls, in the shape of commas and question marks and exclamation points, as if Sherry Cantor's dying struggle had been punctuated like a comic book. Skrolnik offered Pullet a stick of Wrigley's, but Pullet shook his head.

"More hygienic than chewing your damned mouth," said Skrolnik, without any particular rancor.

Pullet nodded.

Skrolnik said, "There are more damned bacteria in the human mouth than down the damned sewer. If you kiss somebody's ass, instead of their mouth, it seems like you're doing yourself a favor."

Pullet nodded again.

The two detectives were noticeably ill matched. Skrolnik was short and heavily built, with fraying hair like fuse wire, and a bulbous Slavic face. When they were younger, his two sons had taken delight in squeezing his nose as if it were the horn on a Model T, and there were still one or two fellow officers who were sorely tempted to give it a quick *parp* when they passed him in the corridor.

But Skrolnik was known as a hard man. He played by the rules, straight down the line, and he made sure that everybody else did too, whether they were prostitutes or politicians, winos or brother lawmen. The bunco squad still talked about the day he had caught his partner taking money from a drug racketeer, and had taken him into an alley and beaten him so hard that the man had taken three weeks' sick leave with broken ribs.

Skrolnik was 41, a career policeman with twenty years of service behind him. His father, a barber, had always wanted him to be a judge. But Skrolnik had known his own limitations, and he was satisfied for the most part with what he was. He could be oddly romantic at times, and he doted on his plump wife Sarah and their two plump children. He liked beer and television and taking his family out to the International House of Pancakes.

Out on the streets, though, Skrolnik was caustic and unforgiving. He was even readier than most to shoot first and discuss the Dodgers afterward. Three of his partners had died in five years, and Skrolnik was quite certain that he didn't want to end up with his face on the road, watching his lifeblood draining away down the gutter.

Pullet, on the other hand, was nervous and erratic. He was tall and skinny, with a great wave of brown hair, loose wrists, and a way of grimacing so violently that people often thought they might have offended him without knowing how. At college in Philadelphia, Pullet's lecturers had marked him for a better-than-average research chemist. But one silent snowy night, Pullet's kindly parents had died in the wreckage of their 1961 Plymouth on the Burlington Pike, and Pullet had given up science and wandered off like a stray dog.

Pullet had traveled west by bus, and stayed for several months in a boarding house in San Francisco, under an assumed name. He had played chess in cafés and thrown pebbles at the ocean. He had eaten more Chinese food than was good for him. He had developed a passion for girls in very short shorts.

Eventually, one foggy fall, he had driven south to Los Angeles in a rented Pinto and signed up as a policeman. He could never say why; he didn't even understand it himself. But his officers found him enthusiastic and occasionally inspired, and they could almost forgive his twitches and his unpolished shoes. Skrolnik tried not to think about him too much, but liked him in a big-brotherly, scruff-of-the-neck fashion, and frequently invited him back to his suburban house in Santa Monica for burned wieners, half-thawed apple pie, and a tumble around the crabgrass with his two children.

Today, however, neither Skrolnik nor Pullet was happy.

They had been urgently called off the Santini investigation—an intriguing high-society poisoning with two equally beautiful sisters as prime suspects—and sent up to this bungalow in Hollywood without any warning that they shouldn't have eaten breakfast first.

Sherry Cantor's body had been strewn all over the living room rug. Her right leg had been hanging, bloodied and awkward, over the back of an armchair. Her stomach had been torn open in a pale gleaming slide of intestines. Somebody had gripped her face in one hand, with fingers pushed deep into the sockets of her eyes, and then wrenched most of the skin and flesh away from her skull.

Worst of all, the whole bungalow had been humming with blowflies.

Pullet had gone out into the garden and vomited up two scrambled eggs, Canadian bacon, and a side order of home fries. Skrolnik had lit up a cheap cigar, and then wished he hadn't.

Pullet asked, "Did you ever see anything like this before? Anything so darned *fierce*?"

Skrolnik shook his head.

Pullet said, "You remember the Edgar Allan Poe story? *The Murders in the Rue Morgue*? The one where they found the girl had been strangled by a large fulvous orangutan of the East Indian Islands?"

Skrolnik stared at him. "An orangutan? You think an orangutan did this?"

Pullet looked embarrassed. "I didn't exactly mean that. But I guess we shouldn't discount the possibility. Orangutans are incredibly strong, and you can teach them to do almost anything."

"So," said Skrolnik, pacing around the perimeter of the dark stain on the rug, "we could be looking for an orangutan."

"I didn't exactly mean that."

Skrolnik pretended he hadn't heard. "How do you think the orangutan got here? I mean, nobody walks in L.A. Did he have his own car? Would a taxi driver remember picking him up? Did he have the right change? Did he come dressed, or did he come *au naturel*? You have to ask yourself these questions, Pullet.''

"I have already," said Pullet. "But if you'll let me get a word in edgewise, you'll see what I'm trying to say."

"You're trying to say it could have been an orangutan."

"I'm trying to say it's so darned unusual it could have been anything or anybody. Come on, sergeant, we've both seen ax murders, and kitchen-knife murders, and sex murders. But what kind of a murder is this? It looks like the victim was torn to pieces like a telephone directory."

"Yes, you're right," said Skrolnik, chewing gum.

Pullet took out his handkerchief and fastidiously wiped sweat from his narrow forehead. "Of course I'm right. We have to entertain every possibility that anybody ever thought of, and a few more besides. We have to think *lateral*."

"I prefer to think standing up," Skrolnik told him.

Pullet said, "You make fun of orangutans. Okay, maybe orangutans are funny. I admit they are. But we can't discount them."

"Them? You mean there was more than one?"

"I mean somebody could have brought on orangutan, or a gorilla, or some other kind of wild beast right up the road in a truck. They could have let it loose in the victim's house, and then zowie."

Skrolnik chewed patiently for almost half a minute. "That had entered my mind."

"It had?" asked Pullet, surprised.

"Listen," Skrolnik told him, "we're going to have to tackle this homicide a little different from usual. If we don't, I don't believe we're going to be able to solve it."

"That's just what I've been saying."

"I know, and as a matter of fact you're quite right. But this is the way we're going to play it. You're going to think of all the nuttiest possibilities you can. Gorillas, men from Mars, anything you like. You're going to think how they got in here, how they killed the victim, and why. You're going to let your mind run totally loose."

Pullet pulled a face. "Well, that's okay," he said, sounding reassured. "But what are *you* going to do?"

Skrolnik stared down at the blood. "I'm going to get into it systematically, conventionally, and right by the rulebook. I'm going to go through all the clues, and I'm going to interview all Ms. Cantor's friends and relations and whatever lovers she might have had, and I'm going to build up a solid file of established facts."

Skrolnik paused. "If we're lucky," he said, "and I'm talking about *damned* lucky, the time will come when one of your off-the-wall ideas fits my proven evidence, and the other way around. And that's when we'll find out who did this, and for what reason, and where the hell they are."

Pullet blinked. "There has to be some explanation. Even if it's crazy. Remember that guy they pulled apart between two cars?"

There was a polite knock on the open door. It was a young forensic detective called Starkey. He was wearing a sweat-stained T-shirt and very crumpled white slacks, and he sported a small, dark, wispy mustache, which he had obviously grown to make himself look older than 19.

"Sergeant?" he asked.

"What is it, Starkey? Don't tell me you've found an orangutan's toeprint on the path."

"Pardon, sir?"

"Just tell me what you've found, Starkey."

"Well, sir," said Starkey, "it's the wrought-iron gates."

"What about them?"

"You said they must have been opened up with a crowbar, sir, something like that?"

Skrolnik's eyes narrowed. "What are you telling me, Starkey?"

"Well, sir, there's no evidence of that. No paint missing, no place where the crowbar might have been lodged to give it leverage. And so far we haven't found any crowbar, either."

"So," said Skrolnik, "any opinions?"

"It's kind of hard to say, sir. But it looks like the lock was twisted out of place by hand."

"By *hand*?"

Starkey went pink. "I know it's impossible, sir, but that's the way it looks. I'm not saying that's the only explanation. We won't know until we examine the lock for traces of human skin oils and sweat."

Skrolnik looked at Pullet, and for the first time there was something in Skrolnik's expression that made Pullet feel alarmed. The sergeant licked his fingers, took the gum out of his mouth, and wrapped it up in a crumpled Disneyland ticket.

"By *hand*," he repeated. Both Pullet and Starkey watched as he let the thought sink into his mind. Then he raised his eyes and asked, "But what about the French doors here? How were they forced open?"

"That's harder to say, sergeant. All the glass was broken. But the aluminum frame was bent pretty bad, too, and that may give us some answers."

"You haven't checked it yet?"

"No, sir. I was waiting for you to finish in here."

"You were waiting? A young girl's been torn to pieces, and you were waiting? Starkey—there are thousands of other young girls out there, and I'd hate to think that one single one of them has been put at risk just because you were waiting. Wouldn't you?"

"Yes, sir. I'm sorry, sir. I'll get at it right away, sir."

When Starkey had gone, Pullet said, "You shouldn't ride him too rough, sergeant. He's pretty good, in his own way."

"So are you," said Skrolnik harshly. "But that doesn't mean you can treat a serious homicide like a picnic in the park."

"No, sir."

Skrolnik was silent for a moment. Then he said, "Come on—let's go take another look at those gates."

They pushed their way through the flapping drapes and out into the heat. The faces of the silent crowd rippled in the rising air like hot pink pebbles on a seashore. There were five police cars parked across the street, their red lights ceaselessly revolving. Skrolnik wiped his mouth with the back of his hand.

Sherry Cantor's bungalow was set on the side of a steeply angled hill, so the detectives had to lope down a series of winding concrete steps before they reached the street. A high fence of black-painted wrought iron was set in a low stone wall, ostensibly to keep out intruders. At the foot of the path, the double wrought-iron gates were wide open, and there was a cluster of forensic men around them, with their aluminum attaché cases of fingerprint powder and litmus lying open on the path.

"Okay," said Skrolnik, "let's see that lock."

The forensic men stood aside. They all wore dark sunglasses and short-sleeved tennis shirts, and one of them had a bronzed bald head that gave off a dazzling reflection.

Skrolnik and Pullet bent forward and peered at the gate. The lock was a hefty five-lever deadlock with steel plates bolted onto either side to prevent housebreakers from drilling into the mechanism. It was welded into the decorative wrought-iron frame of the gate on all four sides. In normal conditions, Skrolnik would have pronounced it pretty well unbustable.

But this morning, someone or something had bent it inward, so that its reinforced tongue had been pulled clear of the plate on the opposite gate. Not just an inch or two, which would have been quite sufficient to open the gates without any trouble at all, but almost nine inches.

Skrolnik stood straight and glanced toward the sloping street.

"Now, if this lock had been bent *outward*," he said, "I would have guessed that someone tied a rope around it, and fixed the other end to the back of a car. But *inward*—"

"Like it's been pushed," said Pullet. "Or maybe *punched*."

The forensic men looked at each other in their dark glasses. Skrolnik looked at Pullet. The crowd looked at all of them, like baffled spectators at a tennis tournament, and didn't understand for a moment the strange fear they were feeling.

CHAPTER FIVE

The coroner's report was part nightmare, part fact.

It said that Sherry Cantor had probably died from brain damage following irreparable damage to the central nervous system. Any one of her other injuries, however, could have killed her almost immediately. Her right leg had been severed by twisting, and there were bruise marks on the thigh and calf which indicated clearly that the twisting had been done by a man's hands.

Her abdomen had been torn open from her vagina upward, and again the indications were clear that the tearing had been done by hand. Her facial flesh had been pulled clear of the bone in the same manner. The coroner guessed that most of the disfigurement had been done after Sherry Cantor had died. He hadn't been able to resist adding, "Thank God."

That afternoon, the television stations began to carry reports that a "King Kong Killer" was loose in the Hollywood hills, and that single women should take extra care to lock and bolt their apartments at night. Sergeant Skrolnik spent twenty minutes on the telephone to Bloomington, Indiana, and afterward went across the street to Matty's Cocktail Lounge and swallowed two Old Crows, straight up, no ice.

Pullet said, "I can't help thinking about that darned orangutan."

CHAPTER SIX

He was driving back from his weekly hour with the analyst when he turned the corner and found the whole street jammed with police cars and ambulances and jostling crowds. He slowed down, and a policeman came across and told him: "You can't come up here, mister. Not a hope."

"I live here," he said. "What's going on?"

The policeman laid a hand on the windowsill of his car. "Hold it right here," he ordered uninformatively. He beckoned across the street to a young ginger-haired detective in a splashy red-and-yellow Hawaiian shirt. The detective came over and said: "Who's this?"

"I live here. Number Eleven. Would you mind telling me what's going on here?"

The detective took a notebook out of his hip pocket and thumbed through it. "Number Eleven," he repeated. "That's Jerry Sennett, right?"

"That's right," Jerry told him. "Is something wrong?"

The detective put away the notebook. "I have to ask you some questions. Would you care to pull your car into your driveway? The officer will help you through the crowd. Take it slow, please."

Jerry nudged his eleven-year-old Dodge around the cluster of police cars, with the policeman walking in front of him, one hand custodially resting on the front fender. Then Jerry slowly turned into his sloping driveway, which ran alongside the wrought-iron fence of Sherry Cantor's garden next door, nosed the car right up to the low wall at the top of the gradient, and put on the handbrake. He climbed out. His shirt was wrinkled and sweaty at the back.

The detective in the Hawaiian shirt came up the driveway after him, taking off his Ray-Bans. "Do you mind if we go inside?" he asked. "It would give us more privacy."

"Sure," said Jerry. He led the way up the crazy-paving

steps to the front door of his pale-green bungalow. He couldn't help glancing toward Sherry Cantor's house as he took out his key and opened the door. There were four or five men in short-sleeved shirts and sunglasses poking around in the garden like golfers who had lost their balls.

"Miss Cantor's okay, I hope?" he asked the detective.

The detective said: "Let's just get inside, please."

Jerry walked through to the living room. It was gloomy and stuffy because the patterned drapes were drawn, and the air conditioning had been off all morning to save energy. Saving energy was one of the things that Jerry believed in, mainly because it saved him money, too. His service pension didn't stretch too far these days.

Jerry Sennett was fifty-nine, and on the last day of November he would turn sixty. But he had one of those lean, gentle, Gary Cooper faces that had improved with middle age. His eyes had an experienced, slightly sorrowful look about them, which always impressed the younger women he met at neighborhood parties. His hair was peppery and cut short. He stooped a little, and sometimes his movements seemed hesitant, but that was only because he was tall and rangy, and prone to knocking highball glasses off tables if he didn't make a deliberate effort to coordinate his movements.

His living room reflected his character. There were two frayed armchairs, a sofa with a wine stain on one cushion, a big old television set. On the walls were three prints of Connecticut in the summer. A 1950's style liquor cabinet, all veneer and pink-tinted mirrors, stood in the far corner.

He asked, "Do you want a drink? I have 7-Up here if you're not allowed alcohol on duty."

"Thanks," said the detective.

Jerry opened the cabinet and poured himself a Chivas Regal, and a 7-Up for the detective. "By the way," he said, coming across with the drinks, "did I ask to see your badge?"

"Do you want to?"

"Why not?"

The detective took his badge out of his shirt pocket and held it out. Jerry peered at it nearsightedly, and then nodded. "They tell you to check out the freezer repairman, so I guess it's doubly important to check out detectives."

The detective gave a humorless smile. His name was Arthur, and he'd been working under Sergeant Skrolnik long enough to have lost his sense of fun. He said, "Do you mind if we sit down?"

"Go ahead," Jerry told him, and sat down himself, crossing his long legs. He was wearing sandals, and there was a large Band-Aid on the end of his big toe.

"I have to tell you that Ms. Cantor has been the victim of a homicide," said Detective Arthur. "It happened this morning, around eight o'clock."

Jerry stared at him. "Sherry Cantor's *dead*?"

Detective Arthur nodded. "I'm sorry." He didn't sound particularly sorry.

Jerry let out a long breath. "That's terrible. My God, that's absolutely terrible. What happened? It wasn't a shooting, was it? I didn't have any idea."

"Someone broke into her bungalow and attacked her. I guess you'll hear it on the news in any case. She was kind of mauled."

"*Mauled*? What does that mean?"

Detective Arthur doodled with his pencil on the corner of his notebook. "Whoever it was, they must have been pretty crazy. She was just about torn into bits."

Jerry took a drink. His hand was trembling. "Do you have any idea who might have done it? Jesus—how can anyone *do* something like that?"

"We don't know yet. There are plenty of clear prints, stuff like that."

"My God," whispered Jerry. "She was so goddamned pretty."

"Did you know her well?"

Jerry looked up. "Hardly at all. She left for work real early, and I never get out of the sack before nine. But we waved to each other over the fence sometimes, and I talked to her once at a neighborhood party.''

''What kind of a girl would you say she was?''

''Hard-working. Career-minded. Who knows—I didn't really think about it. I guess I saw her on television more often than I did in the flesh.''

Detective Arthur sniffed. Jerry had turned on the air conditioning, and the flying fluff was getting to his sinus condition. ''Did you see any men friends coming and going next door?''

Jerry thought about it, then shook his head. ''Nobody special. One or two friends, yes, but it seemed like they came in groups, mostly. I never saw her with one special man.''

''What about you? Did she ever invite you next door?''

''Once, to a party, but I couldn't go. My son was down here for his vacation, and I'd promised to take him to a movie. He's here now, as a matter of fact. I have to go pick him up at two-thirty. He's playing baseball with some friends. You know how sociable kids are these days.''

Detective Arthur said, ''Do you mind if I ask you one or two personal questions, Mr. Sennett?''

''I'm sure you're going to anyway, whether I mind or not.''

''You're a widower, right?''

''That's right. My wife died six years ago come September.''

''And you're an architect, retired?''

''I still design an occasional gazebo. How come you know so much about me?''

''Neighbors.''

''You mean my neighbors know that much about me? My God, even loggias have ears.''

Detective Arthur jotted down a couple of notes. Then he said, ''I understand you're undergoing analysis.''

''Isn't everybody?''

''Can you tell me why?''

Jerry sipped his drink and looked at Detective Arthur

over the rim of his glass.

"You're not trying to prove that I'm crazy, I hope?"

"I have to be thorough, Mr. Sennett."

"Yes," said Jerry, "I guess you do."

He stood up and walked across to the windows. He parted the drapes, so that a bright triangle of sunshine fell across the worn-out rug. "I had a bad experience during the war," he said quietly. "It didn't make me crazy, but it left a lasting impression that sometimes makes me wonder if it's really worth carrying on."

"Suicidal?"

"No, not exactly. Despairing, if you can call it anything."

"Can you give me the name of your analyst?"

"Doctor Grunwald. His office is on El Camino Drive."

"Expensive, huh?" asked Detective Arthur.

Jerry turned away from the window. "With analysis, like everything else, you get what you pay for."

"What sort of progress are you making? I'm going to have to check that out with Doctor Grunwald in any case."

"Progress? Some, I guess. I'm keeping happy. But I don't expect to get over it completely. When you've seen what men are really capable of doing to other men—well, that's an experience it's hard to live with."

Detective Arthur said, "If that's the way you feel, it's probably just as well you didn't see Sherry Cantor this morning."

Jerry finished his drink. "Yes. It probably is."

"You didn't hear anything? Any shouting? Any breaking glass?"

"Not a thing."

"You didn't hear any cars? Maybe an engine revving up?"

"I'm sorry. I woke up at nine, or maybe a few minutes after. I fixed breakfast for David and me, and then I took him straight down to the Whartons' house on Rosewood. You can check the time I got there. After that, I drove over to Beverly Hills."

Detective Arthur read back his notes to himself. Then he said, "I guess that's going to be all for the time being. Sergeant Skrolnik may want to come around and ask you a few more questions, so I'd appreciate it if you stayed around."

"I wasn't planning on going anyplace," said Jerry.

Jerry escorted Detective Arthur to the door. They walked down the driveway together to the sidewalk and stood for a moment by the gate. Most of the police cars had left now, and the crowd had dwindled down to a few teenagers sitting on the curb drinking Coke and a couple of elderly women with nothing better to do.

It was grillingly hot.

Detective Arthur said, "Well, thanks for your help," and walked off.

Jerry stayed where he was for a while, feeling emotionally empty and upset. The men in sunglasses were still in Sherry Cantor's garden, searching the flowering bushes, and occasionally calling out to one another when they thought that might have come across something interesting.

On the low stone wall that Jerry's house shared with Sherry's bungalow, a lizard basked between the two numerals that made up the number 11.

After a few minutes, Jerry climbed back up his driveway and into the house. He went into the living room and fixed himself another whiskey and he stood by the liquor cabinet drinking it and thinking. The air conditioning whirred and gurgled, and he thought, without much conviction, that he ought to have it serviced.

He remembered the day that Rhoda had died, of cancer. It had been as hot as this. He had taken a walk in Hancock Park, and then sat on a bench in the shade of a tree and wondered how everything could be so damned normal, how traffic could come and go, how people could laugh and talk as if nothing had happened. Today, at eight o'clock, Sherry Cantor had died, and yet the sun was still shining, and the supermarkets were still open, and you could still take a drive to the ocean and paddle your toes.

Even *Our Family Jones* would go on without her. The scriptwriters would simply think of some reasonable excuse for writing Lindsay Jones out. They were probably thinking about it right now. She had already vanished, as if she had never been.

Jerry checked his watch. It was almost time to go fetch David. Quite honestly, he would be glad of the company. He sometimes thought that he was spending too much time alone these days. He wondered if David would like to take a drive out to Griffith Park this afternoon, and practice his pitching.

Doctor Grunwald had told him this morning, just as he'd told him dozens of times before, that he ought to stop feeling so guilty about what had happened. It hadn't been *his* fault, after all. But when the sun was shining like this, and when a pretty girl had died, the same way all those others had died, for no apparent reason—well, it was difficult not to feel responsible. Even now, all these years later.

"You didn't *know* what they were going to do," Doctor Grunwald had insisted. "You didn't *know*."

"No," Jerry had told him. "But I didn't question it, either. My sin was that I didn't even question it."

He went into the kitchen. It was narrow, tiled in blue, and it bore all the hallmarks of a man living alone. The catsup bottles were still on the table after this morning's breakfast, the counter beneath the toaster was strewn with crumbs, and the pans that hung underneath the wall cupboards had only been scoured in the middle, where it was essential. He opened the huge refrigerator and took out a pack of bologna sausage. He didn't really feel hungry after hearing about Sherry Cantor, but he knew that he would need the energy if he was going to take David out this afternoon.

He started to build himself a sandwich, with bologna and sliced pickle. He tried not to think about that hot day, thirty-four years ago, when he had first realized the

enormity of what he had done. A radio was playing "You
Don't Bring Me Flowers" somewhere outside, and he
raised his eyes and looked out of the kitchen window
toward the street.

A man in a white wide-brimmed hat and a white suit
was standing not far away from Jerry's gate. Spanish,
maybe, or Mexican. Although the shadow of the midday
sun obscured his face, the man appeared to be looking up
toward the house. His hands were pushed deeply into the
pockets of his coat, and he was smoking a cigarette. There
was something about him that was oddly unsettling, as if
he were a leftover from some black-and-white private-eye
movie of the 1950's.

Jerry watched him for a minute or two. He couldn't
understand why the man's appearance disturbed him so
much. The man stood quite still, his cigarette between his
lips. Then he crossed the street and walked downhill
toward the corner of La Sonoma Avenue. In a moment, he
was gone.

Jerry looked down at his hands. His fists were clenched
so tightly that his knuckles showed white through the tan.

CHAPTER SEVEN

By four that afternoon, Eva Crowley was quite drunk.
She was lying on the white leather couch of her tenth-floor
apartment in the better part of West Los Angeles, wearing
nothing but her black silk underwear, her hair tousled into
a fright wig and her face flushed.

A bottle of Tanqueray gin stood on the glass-topped
Italian table beside her, and it was two fingers away from
empty.

Eva's black maid Matilda had put her head around the door at about two o'clock that afternoon, but Eva had sent her away. This particular pain she wanted to nurse on her own. She wanted no sympathy, no help. She was determined to fight for Gerard, and she was determined to win him back. But just for a few self-indulgent hours, she needed to wallow in her own sense of loss.

She sat up. Her head felt like a hot-air balloon. All around her, the stylish living room tilted and swayed. She picked up the gin bottle, frowned at it, and then emptied the last dregs into her lipstick-smeared highball glass. She wished she didn't feel so suffocated and sick.

After this morning's row, the opulent décor of their apartment seemed even colder than ever. She had always thought Gerard's taste was sterile. He chose tables made of chrome and gray smoked glass, tapestries woven in bland abstract patterns, and chairs upholstered in neutral-colored leather. There was no emotional commitment in Gerard's surroundings. No warmth. He was an empty man with an empty mind.

She wondered, as she swallowed the oily-smelling gin, why she loved him at all. She only knew that she did, and that she didn't want to lose him. To lose Gerard would mean the loss of her dignity, her femininity, and her pride.

To lose Gerard would mean that her mother had been right all along, that Eva was "born to be unlovable."

She climbed unsteadily to her feet and balanced her way across the polished parquet floor to the liquor cabinet. There didn't seem to be very much left. A bottle of tequila. A bottle of strega. Quarter of a bottle of Jack Daniel's. Maybe she ought to mix herself a combined cocktail out of all of them and drink herself into total unconsciousness.

She was just trying to focus her eyes and her brain when there was a soft chime at the door. She stood up straight, one hand on the cabinet for support. It must be the twins, back from school. She stared at her Cartier wristwatch.

They were at least twenty minutes early.

"Coming!" she said, in a husky, high-pitched voice. She made her way out into the cream-painted hall with its bonsai plants and Spanish rugs, and unlocked the safety chain on the door.

"You're early," she said, opening the door and turning back into the hall. "How did you—"

She paused. Something was wrong. It wasn't the twins at all. Standing in the cool darkness of the hall was a swarthy, smartly dressed man in a white suit and striped maroon tie. He took off his hat and inclined his head slightly. He didn't attempt to come in.

"You must be Mrs. Crowley," he said, in a cultured South American accent. He emphasized *Mrs.* as if he was already well acquainted with *Mr.* Crowley. "I'm sorry if I—"

Eva clutched her hands over her breasts. Until the man had apologized, she'd forgotten that she was wearing nothing but a black transparent bra, black panties, and a black garterbelt and stockings. Her face felt suddenly hot, and she said, flustered: "Please—please wait there—I'll just get my robe—"

"Of course," smiled the man. But he didn't avert his eyes.

She retreated into the bedroom, colliding with the doorframe in her drunkenness and bruising her upper arm. She found her robe on the floor where she had left it that morning and struggled into it. She tried to remember where she had taken off her gray suit, but she couldn't. She couldn't even remember driving back from Gerard's office.

There were only fragments. Pushing past Francesca. Slamming the office door. Standing in the crowded elevator trying not to sob out loud.

She belted her robe and went back to the front door. The man was still politely waiting there, his hat in his hand, a small enigmatic smile on his face. He was short and lightly built, and the shoes that peeped out from under his unfashionably wide-bottomed pants were made of white kid, and as small as a tightrope walker's. His hair was oiled back into curls over his ears, and he wore a thin clipped mustache.

"Your husband isn't here?" he asked her.

"Gerard? He doesn't usually get back until late. Sometimes he doesn't get back at all."

"He hasn't called you? We had an appointment, you see. I was supposed to meet him at the office, but when I went there, his secretary told me that he'd already left for the day. I thought he might have come home."

Eva shook her head. There was an awkward pause.

"Do you think there's any point in my waiting for him?" asked the man, raising his hat as if he wanted to hang it up somewhere.

"Well," said Eva, "I don't know. He may be coming back. He may not. He hasn't told me."

"I'm very impertinent," said the man. "Here I am pushing myself on you like this, and I haven't even introduced myself." He inclined his head once again, like a respectable parrot. "My name is Esmeralda. I am a business acquaintance of Mr. Crowley. We are almost friends."

"Almost?" asked Eva.

The man smiled. "Nobody in business can really afford to have friends. Friends are a luxury."

Eva swayed a little. "Well, Mr. Esmeralda, since you're *almost* a friend of Gerard's, I guess it wouldn't do any harm to invite you in."

"You don't have to. I may be a robber. Or a rapist."

Eva took a deep breath. "The way I feel right now, Mr. Esmeralda, that'll be your lookout. Please come in."

She led the way into the living room, and Mr. Esmeralda closed the front door behind him. He hesitated in the hall for a moment, and then hung his white hat on top of Gerard's golf clubs. He followed Eva into the pale Italian-styled room, shooting his startlingly white cuffs and adjusting his necktie. Eva clumsily collected her empty gin bottle and smeary glass, but Mr. Esmeralda seemed to take that in his stride.

"Would you care for a cocktail?" asked Eva, blurrily. "I'm afraid I only have tequila or strega. Or maybe some bourbon, if you feel like it."

"I don't drink, as a rule," smiled Mr. Esmeralda. He paced over to the window with mesmerically precise steps and stood for a while admiring the Crowleys' two-thousand-dollar-a-month view of the Rancho golf courses. "You have a pleasant apartment here."

"Thank you," said Eva, sitting on the far end of the couch and tugging her wrap around her knees. "Actually, it's all Gerard's taste, not mine." She paused. "If I'd had my way, we would have furnished it in elegant Colonial."

Mr. Esmeralda smiled briefly. His smiles came and went like shadows on a cloudy day.

"I feel that you're not happy with the world today," he told her.

She frowned at him. Then she ran her hand through her hair. "I don't know what makes you feel that. Happiness is only relative, after all. At least I have a roof over my head, and enough to eat. And nearly enough to drink."

"You mustn't think that I'm being inquisitive," said Mr. Esmeralda.

Eva gave a dismisive wave of her hand. "I don't mind. I don't even know why I went to all the trouble of getting drunk. It hasn't made anything better, and it hasn't made anything worse. Getting drunk, Mr. Esmeralda, is only a way of deferring the pain until tomorrow."

Mr. Esmeralda turned and faced her. "No pain can be deferred without paying interest, Mrs. Crowley. Tomorrow, you will pay for these hours of forgetfulness with your hangover. Life is a business, like any other."

Eva thought about that, and then nodded. "Some business," she said, not particularly to her unexpected guest. Not even to herself.

There was another pause. Mr. Esmeralda walked across the living room, his tiny shoes clicking on the floor. He picked up a nautilus shell from a side table, and turned it over and over in his hands.

"Did you know something?" he asked quietly. "The first sailors who found these shells said that if you put your ear against them, you would hear the cries of every sailor who had ever drowned."

He inclined his head toward the open shell and listened. Then he set it down on the table again.

"Did you hear anything?" asked Eva.

He shook his head. "Only the sound of a woman in distress."

Eva looked away. "It's really not very interesting, you know."

"Your husband?"

She gave a humorless laugh, which turned into a cough. "Of course. What other kind of problems do women of my age and background ever have? We're too trusting to take lovers. We're certainly too conventional to fall in love with other women. Or dogs. Or whatever."

Mr. Esmeralda nodded. "You wait patiently at home, hoping that your spouses will have sufficient loyalty to keep away from pretty young receptionists."

Eva stared at him. "You know about Francesca?"

"Of course. I have taken your husband and Francesca to dinner on several occasions."

"I don't believe it," Eva whispered.

"Oh, I'm afraid it's true," Mr. Esmeralda told her. "But you don't have very much to fear. At the end of the day, Francesca is far more interested in disco music and fashionable clothes than she is in your husband. In time, their relationship will collapse of its own accord."

Eva licked her lips nervously. Mr. Esmeralda paced around the couch, this way and that, around and around, and he kept appearing on one side or the other, and disappearing again, as if there were three of him, three dapper triplets, all with maroon ties.

"Are you in tobacco, Mr. Esmeralda?" asked Eva, in a much higher voice than she'd meant to.

"I was once," said Mr. Esmeralda. "But times change, you know how it is. These days, I'm in this and that."

"I see," said Eva faintly. "Mr. Esmeralda—"

"Yes?"

"Well, I hope you don't mind, but—would you care to sit down? You're making me rather confused. Rather giddy."

Mr. Esmeralda stopped pacing. Then he said: "My dear Mrs. Crowley, of course," and sat down on the opposite end of the couch with all the grace of a settling butterfly. He laced his fingers together and smiled at her. He wore no rings.

"Gerard has never mentioned you," said Eva.

"No," said Mr. Esmeralda, "I don't suppose he has."

"You're very—"

She stopped what she was saying. She wasn't at all sure what she had been going to say anyway. She wanted to tell Mr. Esmeralda that she thought he was very soigné, very together, and really very clean. She had never seen such clean cuffs and fingernails before. But you couldn't say that to a total stranger.

Mr. Esmeralda said, "Go on," coaxingly, but she shook her head.

"Well," he said, leaning back on the cushions of the couch, "whatever you were going to say, it couldn't possibly have affected the way I think about you."

"About me? You scarcely know me."

"I know you, my dear Mrs. Crowley, as well as any unhappy woman needs to be known. In fact, my own view is that unhappy women hardly need to be known at all. Only two things matter. Their unhappiness, and their beauty. You have both."

She looked toward the liquor cabinet. She bit her lip. Then she looked back at Mr. Esmeralda.

"Are you trying to make a pass?" she asked him.

He smiled silently for a moment, and then he let out a sharp little bark of laughter.

"I don't see what's so funny," she said. She could hear

how much her voice was slurring.

"Nothing is funny," said Mr. Esmeralda. "And then again, everything is funny. Yes, I am trying to make a pass."

She blinked at him. "Why?"

"*Why*? That is one question that no woman has ever asked me before. My dear Mrs. Crowley, don't you *know* why?"

"Perhaps. But I want to hear you say it."

"Then I shall. I am trying to make a pass at you because you are a delicate, beautiful woman. You are sad, and you are drunk. Your husband has temporarily deserted you for a receptionist with a noticeable bust but no IQ, and therefore you are prey to any man who makes you feel attractive and confident once again."

Eva pressed the heels of her hands against her forehead. Mr. Esmeralda sat with his legs neatly crossed, watching her.

Eva said, "You must think I'm a fool."

He shook his head. "Not at all. There are only two fools in this ménage. Your husband, for rejecting you; and me, for laying my heart so openly on the line. I risk frightening you away. I know that. But if I don't make love to you now—who knows, your husband may decide to come back tomorrow, and my chance will be gone."

"You want to make love to me *now*?"

"I'm rushing you?"

She threw her head back and tried to laugh, but all that came out was a strangled, high-pitched *hih-hih-hih*. She turned to him, her eyes watering and her hand pressed over her mouth.

"I amuse you?" Mr. Esmeralda asked.

"No," she said. "No, you don't amuse me."

"You laughed," he pointed out.

"Yes." Then, more softly, "Yes."

She stood up. "I laughed because you frighten me."

He watched her carefully. "I told you I might be a robber," he said. "Or a rapist."

She didn't answer. She couldn't understand the feelings
rising inside her stomach. What was she doing here?
Where was this place, with its intolerable afternoon light
and its pale furnishings?

She said, without looking at him, "The twins will be
home in a quarter of an hour."

He didn't move. His eyes were liquid and dark; the eyes
of a conjuror, or a fairground hypnotist.

"We can't," she whispered hoarsely. "There isn't
time."

Mr. Esmeralda thought about that for a while, and then
nodded. Eva crossed the room and sat down opposite him,
on a natural-colored canvas chair with X-shaped chrome
legs. She hated the chair, but somehow her discomfort in
it made her feel better. More real.

She said, "I need to know who you are."

He lifted an eyebrow.

"I don't mean that's a *prerequisite*," she added,
hurrying her words. "I mean—I'm not saying that if I
know who you are, if you tell me—that I'll—"

Mr. Esmeralda nodded again. "I understand."

She breathed out. She could smell the gin on her own
breath. "I'm afraid you've caught me at a bad time," she
said. She hated the sound of apology in her voice. After
all, this was her apartment. This was her marriage. Her
pain. But somehow Mr. Esmeralda was the kind of man
who invited apologies. He was so calm, so self-possessed,
that she couldn't imagine him ever having done anything
wrong. Not socially, anyway.

Even his seduction had been a model of politeness.

They waited in silence. The apartment began to fade as
the afternoon light faded. They could even hear the sound
of the elevators rising and falling through the building.

Eventually Mr. Esmeralda stood up. He said, "You will
allow me to call you, then? One evening, when your
husband is engaged with work."

"You can call, yes," she said, her mouth dry.

"Perhaps dinner, a few cocktails. Dancing."

"Perhaps."

He smiled. The same smile. He bowed his head.

"I shall look forward to it, my dear Mrs. Crowley, in the same way that the night sky looks forward to the lighting up of the stars."

She lowered her eyes. "That's the first sham sentiment you've uttered."

"Yes," he agreed. "But I am a Colombian, and all Colombians are permitted one sham sentiment per day."

She said nothing more. He waited a while longer, and then left. His shoes clicked on the floor. He closed the apartment door behind him.

She sat in the X-legged chair, staring unblinkingly at the opposite wall and wondering if this was the way all marriages ended.

CHAPTER EIGHT

Sergeant Skrolnik pressed the doorbell for the third time. Beside him, Detective Arthur took out a Kleenex that was crumpled into a tiny, tattered ball and wiped his nose. Skrolnik said, "If you could run like your nose, Irving, you'd catch every murderer in town."

Detective Arthur sniffed and didn't answer. There was flowering jasmine tangled around the doorway of this shabby three-story building on Franklin Avenue, and flowering jasmine always got to his sinus. He wished somebody would hurry up and open the door so that he could ask for a fresh Kleenex. With almost masochistic regularity, he forgot to bring along a pack of his own.

"It doesn't look like there's anyone here," said Skrolnik, stepping back onto the cracked concrete path and shading his eyes so that he could peer up at the second-floor windows. "Can you make it back here this afternoon on your own? I have a briefing with Captain Martin."

Detective Arthur shrugged okay and sniffed again, more conclusively this time.

Skrolnik was turning to leave when a downstairs window opened, and a withered old man looked out. "Did you want something?" he asked in a tremulous voice.

Skrolnik turned back and stared at him. "No, no. I was just testing your response to your doorbell. It's a new city ordinance, you mustn't respond to your doorbell for at least ten minutes. But I'm glad to say you've passed with flying colors."

"Doorbell?" queried the old man. "That doorbell hasn't worked in fifteen years. You want anybody, you have to throw stones at the winders."

Skrolnik looked at Detective Arthur, and then back at the old man. "How foolish of me. I didn't realize. Is Mack Holt home?"

"Sure. He's on nights this week. He's probably sleeping."

"Should I throw a stone at his window, or might you come and open this door for me?"

"Maybe he doesn't want to see you."

"Maybe he doesn't have any choice," said Skrolnik, and produced his badge. The old man screwed up his eyes so that he could make out what it was, and then said: "Oh."

It took another two or three minutes before he came shuffling to the door to let them in. Skrolnik said: "Thanks. If you ever need us cops for any reason, I hope we come just as quick."

"It's upstairs," said the old man, oblivious to Skrolnik's sarcasm.

The hallway was dim, and smelled of Lysol and cheap tile polish. The walls were roughly plastered and painted an unpleasant shade of orange. Someone had penciled by the lightswitch: "Sherry: L called, wants to know if you can call back." It was an epitaph to Sherry Cantor's past. It would probably still be there when they tore the building down.

Skrolnik led the way up the noisy stairs. He crossed the landing and knocked loudly on the door numbered 2. Almost immediately, he knocked again. The old man waited downstairs in the hallway. Detective Arthur said, "Beat it."

There was a sound of bolts being shot back. A thin face appeared at the door, with curly blond hair and a slightly twisted nose. Two blue-gray eyes. A lean, brown twenty-five-year-old torso. Bright-green underpants.

"What do you want?"

Skrolnik pushed the door wide open and stepped into the room. It was dark, with all the drapes drawn tight, and smelled of stale marijuana and *frijoles refritos*. Mack Holt said tensely, "What is this? What do you want?"

Skrolnik flipped open his wallet and showed his badge to Mack Holt without even looking at him. His eyes flicked around the room, taking in the sagging basketwork chairs, the stacks of paperback books and magazines, the cut-price Japanese stereo, the posters for rock concerts and bull-fights.

"Is there anybody else here?" asked Skrolnik, nodding toward the half-open bedroom door.

"A friend."

"Go take a look," Skrolnik told Detective Arthur.

Mack Holt said, "Hey, now, hold on there. She's not dressed yet."

"Keep your hands over yours eyes," Skrolnik instructed Detective Arthur. "And no peeking."

Mack asked, "Listen—what is this? Do you have a warrant?"

"A warrant for what?"

"A search warrant. You can't search this place without a warrant."

"Who's searching?"

Skrolnik crossed the room. He touched the corner of the

bandanna that had been hung around the lampshade. He drew it toward him and sniffed it, then let it swing back. "As a matter of scientific fact," he said, "you'll find that Aramis works better than Carven when it comes to masking the smell of grass."

Mack said, "What are you, an aftershave salesman?"

Detective Arthur rapped at the bedroom door. A girl's voice called out, "Mack?"

"It's the heat," Mack called back. Then he looked at Skrolnik's stony expression and added, almost inaudibly, "The police."

"You'll have to wait a moment," said the girl. Skrolnik didn't take his eyes off Mack. Detective Arthur hesitated at the bedroom door.

Mack said quietly, "I suppose you've come about Sherry."

"That's right," nodded Skrolnik. "You were a friend of hers, weren't you?"

"More than a friend. She lived here."

Skrolnik gave the room an exaggerated reappraisal. "She sure took a step up when she moved out."

"Maybe," said Mack defensively.

Skrolnik walked around the room. "When did she leave?"

"Right after they gave her that part in *Our Family Jones*. What was that? Eighteen months ago. Eighteen, nineteen months."

"You've seen her since?"

"Once or twice."

Skrolnik searched systematically through the pockets of his doubleknit coat until he found a stick of gum. He peeled off the wrapper, folded the stick into his mouth, and then said offhandedly, "they tell me you were jealous of her."

"Jealous? What's that supposed to mean?"

"You were two out-of-work actors. She got a plum part and you didn't. Don't tell me that didn't make you jealous."

"I was pleased for he...

"So pleased that she pac...

Mack ran his fingers throug...

"All right," he admitted, "I was)

prove?''   ...ut out?''

"You tell me."   ...nd curls.

Mack folded his arms across his bare ch... that raised a finger and said incredulously, "You're to say that *I* killed her?''

Skrolnik stared at him with contempt. "Whoever k... Sherry Cantor was pretty well superhuman. I don't thi... you're quite in his league. Let's say it's the differenc... between Arnold Schwarzenegger and Woody Allen.''

Mack lowered his head. "Yes," he said. "I heard about it on the news.''

"Can you tell me where you were yesterday morning, around eight o'clock?''

The bedroom door opened wider, and Detective Arthur said, "Come on, miss. You don't have to be shy.''

"I was here, in bed," said Mack. "Olive will tell you.''

Skrolnik raised an eyebrow. Olive was a glittering, glossy-looking black girl, and she stalked into the living room with her dreadlocks shaking and her head held defiantly erect. She was wrapped in a thin flowered-silk sarong which barely concealed her enormous bouncing breasts. She was pretty in a wide-eyed, 1960's Tamla-Motown kind of way, and there were jingling gold bells around her left ankle. She paused, with her hand on her hip, and said, "That's right. He was here, all right.''

Skrolnik said, "The poorer the nabes, the fancier the domestic help. What's your name, miss?''

"It's Mrs.," said the black girl. "Mrs. Robin T. Nesmith, Jr. But you can call me Mrs. Nesmith.''

"Where's Mr. Nesmith? Hiding under the comforter?''

"Mr. Nesmith is in Honolulu, with the U.S. Navy.''

"And this is the thanks he gets, for serving his country?''

"I don't see that it's any of your business,'' said Olive,

...s about it. He reckons it's better

...thoughtfully. "Even when the devil's a

"but ... ...smith is white, too."

th...

...e. Can anyone else substantiate your where-
...ts?"

Mack put his arm around Olive and drew her closer. He said, "A couple of friends called on the telephone just before eight. But that's all."

"Give Detective Arthur their names, will you?" asked Skrolnik.

Detective Arthur took out his notebook and his ball-point, while Skrolnik turned his back on them and went to investigate the bedroom. There was a wide, sagging bed covered by stained red satin sheets. The room smelled of perfume and sex, and a blue tin ashtray beside the bed exuded its own peculiar fragrance. The walls were papered with faded floribunda roses.

Skrolnik stood there for a while, chewing and thinking. In one corner of the room, on the floor, were a paperback edition of H. R. Haldeman's *The Ends of Power* and a tiny pair of transparent purple panties.

The incongruity of human life, he thought.

He came back into the living room. Olive was sitting on one of the basketwork chairs, and Mack was stepping into a pair of newish Levi's. The jeans were so tight that he had difficulty zipping them up over his cock. Skrolnik said, "Need a shoehorn?"

Mack picked up a T-shirt with *Snoqualmie National Forest* printed on it. "You must be the life and soul of the squadroom."

"Mr. Holt," Skrolnik retorted, "if you saw people torn apart the way that Sherry Cantor was torn apart, then you'd understand just what it is that makes me talk the way I do. After despair, there's nothing left but humor."

Without raising his eyes, Mack asked, "Was she hurt? I mean, do you think she felt anything?"

Olive reached up and held his hand. Skrolnik said, "We don't know."

"I guess you're going to ask me if I knew anyone who could have done something like that," Mack told him. "But I didn't before, and I still don't. She used to get to people sometimes. She used to get to me. But that was only because life seemed so easy for her. There she was, fresh out of Indiana and raw as an onion, and success fell straight in her lap. That was what finished us, in the end, Sherry and me. And what made it worst of all, she was so nice about it. She used to say that success wouldn't change her, and it damn well didn't. She was just so damn *nice*."

"That's what I thought," Skrolnik said, mostly to himself. "And that's what makes it look like this homicide wasn't premeditated. Not for any personal reason, anyhow."

Olive kept hold of Mack's hand and stroked the back of it with her long, dusky fingers. "Do you think you're going to catch the guy who did it?" she asked Skrolnik.

Skrolnik grimaced.

Detective Arthur said, "Where are you working now, Mr. Holt? I have you down as a car-parking jockey at the Old Sonora Restaurant."

"I'm still there," Mack nodded. "The food's better than most."

"Maybe we'll drop by," said Skrolnik. "Meanwhile, I don't want you to leave the city."

Mack looked up. "Okay," he said. Then, hesitantly: "Can you tell me what actually happened? The television news didn't go into a whole lot of detail. Was it really that awful?"

"Mr. Holt," said Skrolnik patiently, "did you love Sherry Cantor?"

"Yes, sir, I did."

Skrolnik put on his hat. "In that case, you'll prefer it if I don't tell you. As it says in the Good Book: 'In much wisdom is much grief: and he that increaseth knowledge increaseth sorrow.'"

Mack stared at him. "You surprise me."

"I surprise myself," said Skrolnik, and pushed Detective Arthur out of the living room ahead of him. At the door, he turned around and said, "I want you to think about Sherry for the next few days. Yes, I'm sorry, Mrs. Robin T. Nesmith, Jr., but it's going to be necessary. I want you to think about every possible angle of what she was, all the people she knew, and everything she said. I want you to sieve through your memory, Mr. Holt, because you're the the only person who can. And if you think of anything unusual, anything that jars, anything that seems out of place, then give me a call."

Skrolnik took a card out of his breast pocket and tucked it in the crevice behind the lightswitch.

"So long," he said. "Pleasant dreams."

He closed the door behind him, and Mack and Olive stayed quite still, like a tableau in a shabby small-town museum, as the detectives' footsteps clattered down the stairs. The front door slammed, and after a while they heard the whinny of a car starter. Mack coughed.

Olive stood up. "Do you want me to go?" she asked Mack in a gentle voice.

He shook his head. "Not if you can stand a little mourning."

She smiled sadly. "I lost my first man in Vietnam. There's nothing you can teach me about mourning."

"You didn't tell me about that."

"There wasn't no need. I don't know nothing about you, and you don't know nothing about me, and that was the way we were meant to be."

Mack laid his hand on her bare shoulder, and leaned forward and kissed her. "You're very good for me. You know that?"

"Yes," she smiled, her eyes glittering.

He was silent for a moment. Then he said, "I guess I'll go out. Maybe get some beer and some food. We could have Dick and Lois around later, if you like."

"Come to bed first," she said. Her beaded black hair

rattled as she shook her head.

"I just got up."

"This is therapy."

"What kind of therapy?"

"Forget-your-sadness therapy. Come on."

She took his wrist and led him back into the bedroom. He stood silent while she tugged his Snoqualmie T-shirt over his head and then unzippered his Levi's. She knelt on the bedroom floor and pulled the pants down his legs.

He felt as if he couldn't catch his breath; the way you feel in a high wind. Olive's perfume was strong and flowery, and there was something about the way her long fingernails grazed over his skin that he found intensely arousing. She guided him toward the bed and gently pushed him backward onto the red satin sheet. He looked up at her, and the muted flare of the sun that shone through the blind behind her made her appear darker and more mysterious than ever.

He wondered if her first lover had been black or white. He wondered how he had died.

She unwrapped her sarong. It fell to the floor, pure silk, silent as a shadow. The soft sunlight gleamed on the brown skin of her impossibly huge breasts, nippled with black. She climbed onto the bed, and her breasts swayed.

"You have to forget everything," she whispered. He wasn't sure if her voice was far or near. The room was dim and warm and funky from their night of love. He felt her tongue run along the sole of his foot, and her teeth nip at his heel. Then she began to lick and kiss him all the way up the inside of his left leg, pausing every now and then to trace with the tip of her tongue a more elaborate pattern, like the shape of a butterfly, or a star. He had thought that last night was enough, but now he could feel himself hardening again, and a deep pulse between his legs.

Olive's searching mouth at last reached his thigh, and then her wet tongue was burrowing between the cheeks of his ass and licking around his tightened balls. He let out a short, tight breath.

Thoughts of Sherry still crowded his mind. Sherry standing in that same bedroom doorway. Sherry lying asleep on that pillow beside him. The unhappiness in him began to overwhelm him, and he could feel himself soften.

But to Olive, achieving this moment of oblivion was vital. Mack had to know that he could turn to her for forgetfulness when his sadness for Sherry was too much to bear. He had to know that she could blot out his grief.

She held him in her hand, her long fingernails gently digging into the flesh of his penis, and she licked his shaft until it stiffened again. Then she kissed and nuzzled the head with her lips, and probed the salty, secret crevice. She felt his thigh muscles tense up, heard him groan.

Olive took him deep into her mouth. Dark lips enclosed white flesh. Her head moved up and down, faster and faster, until her dreadlocks sounded like maracas. Her mind was a jumble of thoughts. Her eyes were tight closed. All she knew was that she wanted to suck out of him all the love she could. She felt his strong, thin fingers clutching at her breast, pulling at her nipple.

There was a long minute of tension. The world had closed its doors to memory, to Sherry, to Hollywood, to everything but one rising and irresistible sensation.

Then Mack said, "Ah," quite softly, and flooded Olive's mouth.

Olive, after a short while, sat up. Her lips shone in the shaded bedroom sun. "How was it?" she asked him, and she wasn't surprised to see tears in his eyes.

CHAPTER NINE

If his wife Nora hadn't given him sliced onion in his liverwurst sandwiches that morning, patrolman Ed Russo wouldn't have died. But the onion had given him heartburn, and he asked his partner Phil Massey to pull the car into the curb at the intersection of Hollywood and Highland so that he could buy himself a pack of Rolaids.

It was four minutes after eleven. Sergeant Skrolnik was just leaving Mack Holt's apartment building on Franklin Avenue. Olive Nesmith was just saying: "Forget-your-sadness therapy. Come on." In West Los Angeles Mrs. Eva Crowley was staring at her face in the mirror and trying to keep herself from throwing up, and Sherry Cantor had been dead for slightly more than twenty-seven hours.

Ed Russo, a slim, soft-spoken man with a heavy brown mustache, walked through the cold air-conditioned drugstore until he found the shelves he wanted. He bought two packs of Rolaids, one to keep in his locker and one for the car. He wouldn't need either of them.

The strawberry-rinsed woman behind the pharmaceutical counter said, "How are you doing?"

Russo held up the Rolaids. "My wife gave me onions today. I love onions, but onions sure hate me."

"Doesn't anybody or anything like cops?" asked the woman. "Even onions?"

Russo smiled, although the gripes in his stomach had twisted up his sense of humor as well. He walked back toward the checkout, juggling the indigestion tablets in his hand.

Through the ad-plastered window of the drugstore, Russo had a view of the traffic signals at the intersection outside. He watched a souped-up Dodge Charger brake at the line as the lights on Hollywood changed to red. The Charger was a pretty slick job, in crimson metallic-flake paint with chromed exhausts. Ed Russo could have done with a car like that himself.

He was only twenty-four, and he still hankered after beach parties and custom cars and big waves at Malibu. But somehow, after he'd married Nora, he'd settled down to a routine of brown-bag lunches, garage auctions, drive-in movies, and washing the car on the weekend. In subtle, unnoticeable stages, in ways that Russo could never quite recall, Nora had altered in three years of married life from a skinny, suntanned, nineteen-year-old nymphet, pretty and shy, into a talkative, opinionated, intolerant young housewife in a lurex headscarf and rollers, organizer of the local church social club, the La Mirada PTA, and a never-ending ten-ring circus of coffee-and-cake mornings, baby showers, and lectures by white-haired evangelists who stank of tobacco.

When Russo looked at Nora over the battlements of Kellogg's Corn Flakes and Post Toasties in the morning, he sometimes wondered if God was punishing him for some sin he couldn't remember committing.

Russo's change clattered into the tray of the change-maker. But as he reached for it, a squittering sound of tires made him look back out of the drugstore window. A dark blue van was driving straight through the red light, swerving to avoid a white Lincoln, and then turning north up Highland Avenue in a cloud of burned rubber.

Russo grabbed his change, pocketed his Rolaids, and ran for the sidewalk. He wrenched open the police car door and yelled to Phil Massey, "Let's get going!"

Their siren whooped as they U-turned on Hollywood, bucking on their suspension. Then they squealed left on Highland, and the V-8 motor roared.

"Did you see that?" asked Massey. He was young and gingery, with a face splattered with freckles. "He could've killed somebody, coming round that corner like that."

"There he is," said Russo.

The van was speeding round the S-curve by the Hughes supermarket. It shot the lights and kept on north toward the Hollywood Freeway, swaying from one side to the other as it overtook cars, trucks, and a northbound bus.

The police siren warbled and howled as Russo and Massey chased after it. They flashed through light, shadow, flickering sunshine.

Weaving through the traffic, the van sped ahead of them onto the glaring concrete of the freeway. But Massey put his foot flat down, and as they sped through the Hollywood hills, they gradually began to overtake the van, coming up on its left side.

Russo wound down his window and unfastened his holster. Then he put his arm out the window and flagged the van down, pointing to the hard shoulder.

At first, the van driver hesitated. But then Russo pointed to the hard shoulder again, fiercely, and the van driver put on his right-hand indicator and began to slow down. Massey slowed the police car, too, and nosed in behind the van as it pulled off the freeway and gradually came to a stop. Through his loudspeaker, Russo ordered: *"Get out of the van slowly and put your hands on the side panels where we can see them."*

Then he said to Massey, "Run a check on his plate, will you?" It was a Florida license. "And see if the Highway Patrol has any backup around."

Russo climbed out of the car and walked toward the van, putting on his cap. It was hot and dusty on the freeway, and he unhooked his sunglasses from his uniform pocket and put them on. The van driver was Japanese. He was standing beside his vehicle with his hands pressed against the dark-blue paneling, and he was watching Russo guardedly.

Russo walked around him and glanced in the driving compartment. It looked empty, except for a tartan holdall with a vacuum flask sticking out of it. He turned back to the driver. Five foot five or six. Late thirties. Dressed in a black satin windbreaker and cheap gray slacks. Cropped black hair, and a slight white scar on the left eyebrow.

Russo said, "Take out your license with one hand. Slowly. And hand it over."

The Japanese reached cautiously into his windbreaker

pocket and took out his license. He held it out, six inches from Russo's outstretched hand. Russo snatched it and stared intently at the Japanese for a moment before he opened it.

"Eric Yoshikazu? Of Emelita Street, Van Nuys?" asked Russo.

The Japanese nodded.

Russo inspected the license closely, and then folded it. "I'm going to have to book you for a serious traffic offense. And for failing to stop when requested to do so by a police officer."

Yoshikazu shrugged.

"You have anything to say about that?" asked Russo.

"I see my lawyer," said Yoshikazu.

Russo took out his citation book. "You can see as many lawyers as you like. That's your right. But it doesn't alter the fact that you ran a red light on Hollywood Boulevard and made an illegal turn and endangered the lives of yourself and innocent people."

"I don't say nothing," said Yoshikazu.

"That's your right," said Russo. He paced round the van and stood at the back for a while, noting down the license number in his book. Yoshikazu watched him all the time. The freeway traffic swished past them, and the air was sparkling with sunlight and grit and fumes.

Russo lifted his pencil and pointed toward the back of the van. "What you got inside there, Mr. Yoshikazu?"

Yoshikazu looked at Russo for a long time. "I don't carry nothing," he said at last.

"Your rear end is well down," commented Russo.

"I get fixed."

"Supposing it doesn't need fixing, Mr. Yoshikazu? Supposing you're carrying something heavy in the back of this van?"

"I don't carry nothing."

"Well, why don't you open it up and let's take a look?"

Yoshikazu thought about that. He wiped sweat away from his upper lip with the back of his hand. "I don't think I want to open," he said.

Russo put away his pencil. "Mr. Yoshikazu, I have the legal right to demand that you open your van. If you fail to do so, then I'm going to arrest you, and your van will be impounded."

"That's not possible," said Yoshikazu. "This van is not mine. I have no entitlement to open."

Russo adjusted his cap. The headband was sweaty. "If you don't open up this van, Mr. Yoshikazu, then I'm going to open it up for you."

"No!" shouted Yoshikazu, with unexpected vehemence. "You not open! I don't carry nothing! *You not open*!"

At that moment, Massey came up with his notebook in his hand. "You having trouble here?" he asked.

"Guy refuses to open the van," said Russo. "What you got?"

Massey held up the notebook. "It's a legitimate vehicle, not reported as stolen or missing. It belongs to the Florida office of the Willis Candy Corporation. Their head office is in Century City."

"You have candy in there?" Russo asked Yoshikazu.

Yoshikazu nodded. "Just gum. That's all. Just five cases gum."

"Good," said Russo. "In that case, you won't mind us taking a look."

There was a tense silence. Yoshikazu looked at the police officers wide-eyed. Russo could almost see the word *desperation* hovering over his head like a bubble in a cartoon. Whatever Yoshikazu was carrying inside this van, he was scared shitless about letting the police take a look at it.

"It's better you don't open," said Yoshikazu breathlessly. "I think I appeal to better nature. Here—I pay you money. You not open. Here—I pay you fifty dollars."

"Keep your hands in sight," snapped Massey, as Yoshikazu reached inside his windbreaker for his billfold. Yoshikazu paused, and then lifted his hands again.

"It's an offense to attempt to bribe a police officer,"
said Russo. "If you carry on this way, Mr. Yoshikazu,
you're going to wind up doing three to five. Now, let's cut
the crap and open this van up."

At that instant, there was a loud, hollow, metallic
beating noise from inside the van. Yoshikazu went pale.
Russo frowned at Massey, and then demanded of Yoshikazu, "What was that? What the hell have you got in
there?"

"Waking up," babbled Yoshikazu. "That's why I
hurry. That's why I run light. Waking up."

"Waking up? What's waking up?"

In reply, there was another burst of ferocious knocking
from inside the van. Someone or something rattled and
kicked at the doors, and thundered at the panels. Massey
held Russo's arm and pointed to the side of the van.
Bulges were appearing in the sheet metal as if the van were
being slugged from the inside with a ten-pound hammer.
In moments, the whole side of the vehicle was pimpled
with them.

Russo took out his revolver.

"All right, Mr. Yoshikazu, I want that van open."

"I not do it!"

"I said open it—and *move*!"

Yoshikazu dropped to his knees on the concrete.

Russo ordered Massey, "Go get the pump shotgun."
Massey ran back toward the patrol car, one hand holding
his hat on, as if all the dogs of hell were snapping at his
heels.

Russo edged up to the back of the van, his pistol raised,
and cautiously put his ear to the panel.

"Is there anyone in there?" he shouted.

There was silence.

"I said, Is there anyone in there?"

There was an ear-splitting bang, and the door of the van
was punched out into a huge bulge. He jumped back and
stood with his gun in both hands ready to fire. But the lock
on the van doors held, and whatever it was inside the van

shuffled off toward the front end. Russo could see the vehicle swaying as it made its way forward.

Massey came panting back with the shotgun. Russo said, "Give me some cover. I'm going to see if I can get those doors open."

Massey asked, "What is it in there? Some kind of wild animal?"

"I'm not sure. And Emperor Hirohito here isn't about to tell us."

"Maybe I should call the zoo."

"Maybe we should just find out what the hell we're dealing with. Did you ask for backup?"

"Sure," said Massey. "A couple of minutes, they said. There's been a multiple pileup on the Ventura Freeway."

"Okay," said Russo, sweating. "Then let's do it."

Russo advanced toward the doors again, his revolver held out in front of him. The van was motionless, silent. Russo coughed. Behind him, Massey raised his gun and clicked off the safety.

Russo reached the van. He glanced sideways at Yoshikazu, but Yoshikazu was still on his knees on the concrete, his face white and rigid. Russo waited for a short while, and then tapped on the van doors with the butt of his gun.

Massey said tightly, "It could have gone back to sleep again."

Russo turned to Yoshikazu. "That possible?" he asked.

Yoshikazu shook his head.

"You have one last chance to tell me what it is," said Russo.

Yoshikazu whispered, "You not open. I appeal to better nature. Easy thing, you let me go, say nothing, forget."

The Japanese was shaking, and his face was jeweled with sweat.

Russo looked back at Massey. "Now I've heard everything."

Massey grinned. "You have to admire his—"

The rear doors of the van burst open with a devastating

crash, and Russo was hurtled backward across the concrete. Massey fired his shotgun out of nervous reaction, but his shot went wide.

A short, heavily built man in a glaring white mask swung from the back of the van and threw himself on Russo. Russo felt as if a whole bag of cement had been dropped on him from a second-floor window. He pressed the muzzle of his gun against the man's side and screamed, "Get off, or I'll blow your guts out!" But the man seized Russo by the neck with mad, unstoppable ferocity and began to twist.

Russo saw scarlet. Nothing but scarlet. He didn't know where he was or what was happening. He fired his gun and felt the shock of the recoil and the thump of the bullet entering his attacker's body. But the pain didn't stop, and the viselike grip on his neck didn't let up, and he dropped his pistol—a numbness as agonizing and overwhelming as an electric shock stunned his reflexes.

Massey fired again, hitting the masked man in the muscle of the right shoulder. The shot turfed up a bloody lump of flesh, but the man kept on wrenching wildly at Russo's prostrate body as if nothing had happened. Massey ran two or three paces nearer, knelt down, aimed, and fired at pointblank range. There was a deafening report, and he saw the yellow cotton of the man's clothes scorch black where the bullet entered his side.

The masked man lifted his head, turned, and hit out with a swing of his arm that sent Massey sprawling. Massey knocked his head hard on the concrete, and for a moment he was stunned.

The masked man climbed to his feet, his clothes bloody and burned from the gunshots. He picked up Russo as if he were a child, and carried him over to his patrol car.

The masked man gripped Russo by his ankles and swung him around. Russo was choked and only semiconscious, but he was still alive. He could feel the grip on his ankles, and he could feel the world tilting and rushing around him as the man spun him around like a flail.

Then, with all of his terrible strength, the man gave Russo a final swing and smashed him face first into the windshield of his police car. Razor-sharp fragments of glass sliced the flesh away from Russo's cheeks and forehead, and a long sliver stabbed up into the soft skin under his chin and penetrated his tongue.

Russo couldn't scream, or cry, or do anything. He was helpless in the grip of his maddened killer. He could only close his eyes and hope that the pain would end.

The masked man swung him back, out of the shattered windshield, and then around again. He beat him against the police car's hood, and against the headlights, and against the grille, until the car was splattered with blood and jellyish brains, and Russo was crushed and dead. Through the darkness of his concussion, Massey could hear Russo's death as a series of soft, hollow thumps.

The traffic on the freeway passed by and didn't stop. But this was one time when you couldn't blame anybody. There was too much blood. Too much horror. And the sight of a mangled policeman with a head that was nothing more than a smashed watermelon, sliding off the hood of his wrecked car, well, that was reason enough to step on the gas pedal and keep going, trembling, until you reached home in Pasadena.

The masked man turned toward Massey. His breath came in deep, distinct whines. Massey opened his eyes and saw the man standing over him, and he tried to think where his shotgun was, and whether it was even worth struggling. He felt a moment of utter helplessness and fear.

But then the masked man turned away. Unsteadily, uncertainly, as if the pistol bullet and the two shotgun bullets had hurt him at last. He stood by the side of the freeway, rocking on his heels, and then promptly sat down. After another few seconds, he collapsed.

Massey tried to stand up. He had managed to lift himself onto all fours when Yoshikazu came around the van; he had been hiding on its other side. Yoshikazu raised a warning finger, instructing Massey to stay where he was. Then, with great difficulty, he gripped the masked man under the arms and began to drag him across the concrete back toward the van.

Massey watched Yoshikazu for a while. Then he crawled toward his shotgun, picked it up, pumped another round into the chamber, and knelt on the ground, pointing the gun at Yoshikazu's back.

"Don't you make another move," he said.

Yoshikazu turned. "I have to put him back in van. He could revive."

"You heard me," said Massey.

A green Plymouth station wagon slowed down beside the police car, but when the driver saw the blood, and the gun, and Yoshikazu laying the short man down on the concrete, he took off with a shriek of tires.

Massey said, "Stand up slowly and put your hands on top of your head."

Yoshikazu began to raise his hands. But then, quite suddenly, he dropped to the ground and rolled behind the body of the masked man, using him for cover. Massy fired twice. His first bullet hit the short man in the leg, the second ricocheted off the concrete.

Yoshikazu tugged an automatic out of his windbreaker and fired back. The bullet hit Massey in the side of the head, in an extravagant spray of blood. He reeled on his knees and then toppled face first onto the ground.

Yoshikazu scrambled to his feet. His teeth were clenched with tension and fear. He humped the bleeding body of the masked man back up to the van and succeeded in dragging him inside. He wedged the doors together, even though they were twisted, and prayed to the gods of fortune that they would hold. Then he ran forward to the open door of the driving cab and climbed in. Within fifteen seconds, he was off.

In the distance, from the Ventura Freeway, came the howl of sirens as the California Highway Patrol came to answer Massey's backup call.

Phil Massey lay on his face on the concrete and watched his own dark blood trickling into the dust. A few feet away, Ed Russo lay on his back, his hands stiffly clenched in front of his chest, his face already beaded with flies.

CHAPTER TEN

It was almost sunset. In his suite at the Los Angeles Bonaventure Hotel, Gerard Crowley was sitting in a Chinese silk bathrobe smoking a long Havana cigar and watching the CBS News. The suite was suffused with dying golden sunlight; on the double bed, naked, Francesca was stretched out asleep, exactly as he had left her. There was a plum-colored love bite on the side of her neck.

Gerard kept the cigar clenched between his teeth and smoked steadily, as if the cigar were an aqualung, essential to his survival. He always smoked that way. Once he lit a cigar, he puffed it furiously down to a finish and then stubbed it out. He treated his friends and his lovers in the same way. The only exception, ever, had been Evie.

On the television, a frowning commentator was saying, ". . . *throughout the Tennessee Valley area, and caused widespread damage to homes, shopping centers, and factories.* . ."

Gerard testily blew out smoke. On the rear bumper of his car was a sticker which read *God Bless America . . . She Needs It.* That was more than slightly ironic, considering what he was getting into now. But Gerard's life had always been haunted by religion, and by irony.

He thought about the pain and the hard work that had finally brought him to this thick-carpeted suite. He thought about Evie. He turned his head and looked at

Francesca, at her unconsciously parted thighs, and he thought about her too.

He should be feeling aggressively confident now. Macho, fit, on top of the world. But for some reason he didn't fully understand, he felt afraid.

Maybe his terror of his father still pursued him. His father had been a grocery-store owner in Westville, Virginia—a tall, spare, uncompromising man who had believed in work for its own sake and the severity of the Lord. After school, young Gerard had stacked shelves and weighed out bags of sugar until nine or ten o'clock at night; and before school in the morning he had bicycled around town and delivered orders. The only free time his father had allowed him was Saturday afternoon, after a whole morning of serving behind the counter.

Those Saturday afternoons had been golden and precious. Gerard had walked almost every week to the tobacco plantation outside of town, meeting his friend Jay Leveret for hours of games and adventures. They had played the Green Hornet in and out of the long pungent sheds where the tobacco leaves were hanging to cure; and they had run for miles across the fields, under skies that Gerard always remembered as indelibly blue.

When Saturday afternoon was over, Jay Leveret would return to the big white plantation house, to warmly lit lamps and the bright sound of laughter, while Gerard would trudge home along the dusty twilit road for a silent supper of fatback and beans with his parents, always concluded by a doleful hour of reading from the Bible.

His first introduction to drink had been a mouthful of surgical spirits in the back of the store. His first sexual experience had been with Ada Grant, a cheerful big-breasted woman whose husband had left her to go pick oranges in California, and who gladly took young boys into her high brass bed for three dollars.

Until he was sixteen, Gerard had been a hick. Rural-minded easygoing, and innocent. But on his sixteenth birthday, his life had been turned upside down. Jay

Leveret's father had written to say that there was a place for him on his tobacco plantation, if he cared for it. But Gerard's father had sourly refused. Gerard was to work in the store. Never mind if it was hard and unprofitable. To labor without reward was a blessing of the Lord.

After three miserable weeks of sweeping up, unloading sacks, and scooping beans, Gerard had had enough. One chilly mid-September dawn had found him thumbing a ride on the highway south. He had been bound for Florida, and eventually for Cuba. He didn't think about those years of his life very often. Not these days. He talked about them even less. But it was during those years that he had begun to make his money, first by fixing boats on the Florida keys, and later, in the last days of President Batista, by dealing in drugs and girls in Havana.

In six years, he had grown from a hick to a hard and knowledgeable young wheelerdealer. He had been shot at, stabbed in the left thigh, and beaten up. He had contracted gonorrhea eight times. He had spent days dead drunk in shanty whorehouses on the outskirts of Havana, days which in later years would wake him up at night, sweating and shaking. He had put his life and his determination on the line, and at the end of it all he had built up Crowley Tobacco into what it was today—a tight-knit, highly profitable corporation with a reputation for tackling unusual and different orders. Not all of those orders were concerned with tobacco. Some of the most successful deals were those Gerard called "capers."

Gerard's father, embittered by his son but well prepared for the Lord, had died of emphysema in 1958. Gerard had attended the funeral, although his mother had refused to speak to him. Four years later, she had died, too. Gerard had become an orphan. A wealthy, experience-hardened orphan.

On the bed, Francesca stretched. Her sex parted like a pink flower. Gerard continued to listen to the news. A busload of old folks had dropped off the edge of Slumgullion Pass, Colorado.

Francesca sat up and pulled at her tangled hair. "What time is it?" she asked.

"Seven-thirty," said Gerard, without taking his cigar out of his mouth.

"I must have fallen asleep."

"Uh-huh."

She yawned. "Do you mind if I call room service and get some Perrier water? I have an unnatural craving for Perrier water these days."

"You're not pregnant, are you?" Gerard asked her.

She laughed. Her breasts bounced. "Don't you know the rhyme? There was a little goil, and she had a little coil, right where it mattered most."

"I don't know why you're laughing," said Gerard. "I wouldn't mind if you were pregnant."

"You don't want another child," she said, although it was more of a question than a statement.

"No, I don't. But I still wouldn't mind if you were pregnant."

Francesca stood up. "Are you more chauvinistic than flesh and blood can stand, or am I missing something?"

"You're missing something."

She leaned over and kissed him on the parting of his dark hair. He smelled of cigars and medicated shampoo. "I could be persuaded to love you," she said.

He smiled.

She walked across the bedroom and picked up a pack of cigarettes from the windowsill. She took one out, lit it, and stood looking out through the nylon net drapes at the sparkling dusky lights of downtown Los Angeles. Gerard watched her appreciatively. She was an unusual girl. Not clever, but strong-willed almost to the point of ruthlessness. And pretty, and unquenchably fierce in bed, and to Gerard that was all that mattered. She appeared so aloof and elegant. She always dressed in pure silk. And yet she would do anything, and take it anywhere. That turned Gerard on.

She said, as calmly as if she were asking him what he

,wanted to eat for supper, "Have you decided what you're going to do about Evie yet?"

Gerard took out his cigar. "Do?" he asked her. "What do you mean?"

"Well, she's not going to let you get away with it."

Gerard shrugged. "What can she do? She can only divorce me, and she won't do that. She's too insecure; too dependent."

"She seemed very upset."

"She'll cool down. She'll drink the house dry, and then have a damned good weep, and that'll be it."

"Do you *want* her to cool down?"

Gerard looked at Francesca closely. She had wide green eyes. Green as glass.

"Yes," he said in a measured voice. "Of course I want her to cool down."

"So you want to stay with her?"

"Does it make any difference if I do?"

"Of course it does. Your home is still with her, instead of with me."

Gerard watched her for a while. Then he said: "As far as I'm concerned home is where I spend the most time. You and I see each other all day, we spend two or three nights a week together. We go to the theater. We have dinner."

"But you belong to her."

"That's where you're wrong," replied Gerard. "Evie belongs to me."

Francesca drew on her cigarette. "I don't really see the distinction. A slaveowner has just as many responsibilities to his slave as his slave has to him. And besides, you still sleep with her."

Gerard set his cigar down in the ashtray and stood up. Francesca came nearer, and he rested his hands on her bare shoulders. He was smiling at her, and yet his eyes were so remote and expressionless that she was unable to smile back.

"You're jealous," he said. She wasn't at all sure if he was joking or not.

"No," she whispered. "I'm just demanding."

"Demanding?"

"I want you. I want your time."

He ran his fingers down the length of her naked back. He cupped one cheek of her bottom in his hand, so that his fingertips just touched her in a sensitive place. He kissed her, so lightly that their lips scarcely grazed.

"Right at the moment, my time is preempted," he said.

"I know. By Esmeralda."

He nodded. "Esmeralda is just as demanding as you. *More* demanding, if anything. He seems cute, and old-fashioned, but underneath that bandleader's clothing he's a goddamned man-eating alligator."

She turned her face away. "He frightens me."

"He frightens me, too. But his money's good."

Gerard thought of Esmeralda, the very first day that Esmeralda had come into his office, and the arrogant way in which the Colombian had carefully tugged up one trouser leg so that he could perch himself on the edge of Gerard's desk. "I have a proposal for you, Mr. Crowley," Esmeralda had said. "Very unusual, but very profitable."

Gerard had eyed Esmeralda coldly. "I'm too busy for any new contracts. I'm sorry."

Esmeralda had smiled warmly. "You weren't too busy last October 24th to run twenty cases of AK-47 Russian machine guns into San Salvador, were you?"

Gerard had remained hard-faced; but he had been deeply disturbed. He was relying heavily these days on a confidential government contract to supply the rebels in Afghanistan with ammunition for their M-60 machine guns, smuggling them over the Pakistani border in convoys of jeeps, and the very last thing he needed was a public revelation that he had also armed Marxist-Leninist guerrillas in El Salvador.

"What do you want?" he had asked Esmeralda pointedly. "No screwing around. What do you want?"

"It's very simple," Esmeralda had smiled. "I have a

Japanese client who is looking for research facilities in California . . . somewhere private where he can undertake a little medical work.''

"What kind of medical work? What are you talking about?''

"Well, it's not much more than a health farm, really. Perhaps a *little* bit more than a health farm. You see, my client is a physiologist; and he discovered during the Tokyo Olympics that a certain combination of chemicals and anabolic steroids could develop an *ordinary* athlete into a *super* athlete . . . tireless, aggressive, and unstoppable.''

"I thought anabolic steroids were banned by most athletics associations,'' Gerard had interrupted.

"They are,'' Esmeralda had agreed. "Yes, they are. But my client has been clever enough to apply his knowledge to another field, a field of prime concern in the United States, and in many parts of the Middle East, and that is *personal security*. Using the techniques he developed at the Tokyo Olympics, my client now wishes to develop a stable of bodyguards, superbodyguards, who will be rented out to anybody who needs them. They will be available to protect industrialists, politicians, even senior *mafiosi*. They will be bodyguards of invincible strength, crushing capabilities. If Reagan had only had one when John Hinckley shot at him, Hinckley would have been torn to tiny shreds! You can call them killer bodyguards, if you like. They will terrify anyone who comes near them.''

Gerard had said, "I stopped believing in fairy stories when I was seven years old, Mr. Esmeralda.''

"You think I'm telling you a fairy story? You want some kind of proof?''

"I don't want anything from you. I just want you to leave.''

"Look at this,'' Esmeralda had said, and produced from the inside pocket of his coat a manila envelope. He had opened it, and taken out a 5 x 4 glossy black-and-white print, which he had passed over to Gerard in a hand that trembled ever so slightly.

Gerard had not looked down at the picture at first: but then he had slowly lowered his eyes and taken in a blurred, overexposed scene of a short, stocky man holding something up over his head. The picture must have been taken in the mountains somewhere: the ground was sloping, and there were conifer trees and rocks. It was only when Gerard had peered closer, though, that he had begun to understand what it was that the stocky man was holding up. It was a deer, or the remains of a deer, which looked as if it had been torn apart like a gory telephone directory. Its guts hung between the man's outstretched arms, and its head was falling back at a grotesque angle.

"This could have been staged," Gerard had said cautiously.

"Of course it could." Esmeralda had smiled. "But it was not. That man tore that deer to pieces with his bare hands."

Gerard had handed the photograph back and looked at Esmeralda with great suspicion. He had not yet wholly believed. But he had been prepared to listen.

Esmeralda had admired his well-polished fingernails, and then added, "My client needs somebody who can manage his interests in California. Someone to help him with organization and transportation; someone to fetch and carry. Someone sophisticated and unscrupulous. And that someone will be you."

Gerard had stood up and thrust his hands into his trouser pockets. "Mr. Esmeralda," he said fiercely, "I want you to get out of my office."

"Of course you do." Esmeralda had smiled, and his voice had been as oily and soothing as warm coconut milk. "But you've been running risks for years now, selling arms and drugs to whichever client will pay you the most money, and there always comes a time in lives like yours when chickens come home to roost. This is it, Mr. Crowley. This is when your chickens come home."

Gerard had slowly closed the door of his office, and then

he and Esmeralda had talked in private for three hours. At the end of that time, Gerard had agreed, grudgingly but curiously, to supervise the day-to-day fetching and carrying that was going to be needed by the men who were running the program, and to liaise with whomever else Esmeralda might appoint to assist him. "I have already chosen an interpreter, a Japanese woman," Esmeralda had informed him. "Also, a traffic-control expert, a retired naval commander. You will be in excellent company."

As he had adjusted his hat in front of the mirror in preparation for leaving, Esmeralda had added, "The super bodyguards will be called Tengus, after the Japanese word for powerful devils. You like that word, Tengus? They will be volunteers, each one of them . . . young Japanese men who are already physically fit and extremely strong. They know the risks of the drugs they will be taking, the steroids and so forth, and you will have to get used to the idea that some of them may become temporarily . . . well, unstable. My client's experiments are still in their early days."

He had opened the door, so that Francesca could hear what he was saying. "I want you to know, Mr. Crowley that this program is worth millions of dollars—millions. You understand me? You will get your share when the time comes, but only if you do exactly what you are told to do, and behave yourself. And there is one more thing."

"What's that?" Gerard had asked him flatly, annoyed that he had opened the door.

"You must know that the program has some enemies . . . people who look down on this kind of thing. Health officials, bleeding hearts. You know who I mean. After all, some of the drugs that my client will be using won't exactly be . . . *approved*, if you understand me. So, there may be people who have to be warned off, decisively."

Gerard had opened his cigar box and taken out a fresh cigar. He knew exactly what "warned off, decisively," meant. He was quite fluent in the euphemisms of smuggling and arms running. He took out a match, struck it, and looked at Esmeralda through the smoke and the flame. "All right," he had said. "We'll talk about that when the time comes."

Now, the time had come, and their attempt to "warn off" one of the program's enemies had ended in chaos and complications. Francesca could sense the unease and tension in Gerard's body, and she touched his forehead, stroked the backs of his hands, kissed him.

"Money isn't everything, Gerard," she said.

"I don't think I'm involved with Esmeralda for the money," Gerard told her. "In fact, I don't know why I'm involved with Esmeralda at all."

Francesca said, with unexpected softness, "I don't want you to get hurt."

"I've been hurt plenty of times," he said, kissing her quickly. "Once more wouldn't make any difference. Not that I *intend* to get hurt. I don't intend to get anything but very much richer."

The telephone warbled. Gerard picked it up. He listened, but didn't speak. Then he put the receiver down again.

"Put something on," he told Francesca. "Nancy Shiranuka's coming up."

Francesca took a pair of tight white corduroy jeans from the back of the bedroom chair and stepped into them. Then she buttoned a blood-red silk blouse over her bare breasts and ran her hands through her hair. She looked like a woman who had been making love for most of the afternoon. She smelled of sex and Chanel.

Gerard went into the living room and switched on the lamps. He called, "When you get through to room service, have them send up a couple of bottles of California chablis and some potato chips. Maybe some beer."

"When you entertain, you really go to town, don't you?" she said sarcastically, tucking her blouse into her jeans.

Gerard didn't answer. He had opened the drawer in the writing desk, and he was looking inside as intently as if he had found the dead body of a poisonous spider in there. Lying among the Hotel Bonaventure writing paper and postcards was a .357 Python revolver.

He didn't touch the gun. He knew it was loaded. He just wanted to make sure it was still there. Quietly, he closed the drawer.

"Is the commander coming up, too?" asked Francesca.

The door chimes rang. Gerard said: "He's staying out at the ranch for tonight. He's arranging to get Yoshikazu over the border."

He put his eye to the peephole in the door. Then he loosened the chain and opened it. Nancy Shiranuka stalked in, dressed in an olive-green safari shirt and slacks, and wearing a wide-brimmed straw hat. She took off her hat, tossed her long black hair, and looked around the suite disdainfully.

"For two hundred a night, you think they'd give you some decent prints on the walls," she said.

"I don't usually come here to look at the pictures," Gerard told her. He said it without humor.

"I know what you come here for," said Nancy blandly. "But sex is art, and art is sex. If they put up one or two Sugimura prints of ten-year-old courtesans, don't you think the room would look much better? And don't you think it would be a more stimulating place to take your lady-love?"

"Unfortunately, I don't think Westin Hotels have any leeway in their decorating budget for rare Japanese pornography," said Gerard.

Nancy sat down on the mock-antique sofa and elegantly crossed her legs. "Of course not. It's the great Caucasian failing. Budgets before art, budgets before sex, budgets before anything."

Gerard said, "And what about the great Oriental failing?"

His voice was quiet, but acidly sharp. Nancy sensed the change in tone.

"Have you heard from Ernest?" she asked him.

"I talked to Ernest an hour ago."

"Then he probably told you they've already disposed of the van."

"Yes."

"Well," said Nancy edgily, "I don't have much more to tell you."

"What did Doctor Gempaku say?" asked Gerard. "He was too busy when I called."

"He's not very hopeful. The Tengu was shot by the police several times, and he's still in a coma."

"What will Gempaku do if he can't be revived?"

Nancy opened her pocketbook and took out a green lacquered cigarette case. "The same as our noble employers do to *anyone* who doesn't fit in happily with their business schemes, I suppose" she said.

Gerard pursed his lips. He was angry, but controlled. He knew that most of what had happened had been ridiculous bad luck, and that Nancy wasn't really to blame. But now there had been two foulups in two days, two serious and disabling setbacks, and even if the caper hadn't been completely written off, it had certainly been delayed.

Worse, it had shaken Gerard's credibility, and with Esmeralda breathing so closely down his neck, Gerard needed all the credibility he could muster. Working for Esmeralda was all bluff and double bluff, and living on your nerves.

Gerard said, "I suppose Yoshikazu knows how much this has cost us."

"Of course he does. But it wasn't his fault."

"He ran a red light right in front of a police car, and it wasn't his fault?"

"What else was he supposed to do?" Nancy demanded. "The Tengu was going mad. He couldn't sit in traffic while the whole van was torn to pieces around him." She lit her cigarette. Then she added, "Yoshikazu did very well. This has cost us, but it hasn't cost us everything."

"Not unless the police trace the van. Not unless the

customs people pick him up at the border. Not unless
some smartass with a long memory puts six and seven
together and comes up with unlucky thirteen.

"I think you're fretting too much about what your
precious Mr. Esmeralda thinks of you," said Nancy.
"Don't worry about him. You know the police won't trace
the van. You also know that Ernest will get Yoshikazu
safely into Mexico."

"That's two problems out of three," put in Gerard.
"But what about our friend Sennett? The one for whom
that sad young starlet died in vain?"

"That's up to Esmeralda, not to me."

"He made it *our* responsibility," Gerard insisted.

"It's not a responsibililty I want to accept."

"You'll have to. If you don't, this entire scheme is
going to collapse like a half-cooked soufflé."

"I didn't accept this job to murder people," snapped
Nancy.

"It's too late for that, my dear. You're an accessory
already. And what did you think you were letting yourself
in for, really, when Esmeralda told you he was building up
a crack stable of killer bodyguards?"

Nancy said, "I'm beginning to wonder if *any* of us is
safe. If Esmeralda can order one man killed, why not
another? Why not us? Why did he chose any of us in the
first place? Because we are all magnificently unprincipled,
and because we all have connections in the grubbiest
places? Or because, if any of this business goes wrong, we
can all be dropped quietly into the ocean without anybody
making too much noise about it?"

Gerard nodded. The cold smile was back on his lips.
"My thoughts exactly," he said.

Francesca came into the room, her hair brushed and
shining. "That wine's taking its time," she remarked.

Gerard said, "They're probably waiting for it to become
a respectable vintage."

"Are you going out to the ranch yourself?" Francesca
asked him.

"In a couple of days. Once, I get all this administrative mess sorted out. And replace Yoshikazu."

"You could try Kemo," suggested Nancy.

"Kemo? Your houseboy?"

"That's right. He's quick, he's eager, and he's got a good head on his shoulders."

"As long as he doesn't object to having it knocked off."

"He knows the risks."

Gerard pinched the bridge of his nose tiredly. He was beginning to feel that maybe he wasn't as energetic as he had been two or three years ago. A whole afternoon of drinking and lovemaking was more than he could comfortably manage, especially if he wanted to stay alert during the evening. "Okay," he said, "I'll have a talk with him. Now, what other problems do you have for me?"

"Only details. They spotted a couple of prowlers around the ranch yesterday afternoon, but they turned out to be hippies looking for a place to crash. Doctor Gempaku says he needs more power, perhaps another generator, and maybe you can arrange for a temporary stopgap. A mobile generator maybe."

"What's he running out there?" Gerard demanded. "A sound-and-light show?"

"He's hoping to open the new center in six weeks. He has to do it, Gerard, or he'll never meet the deadline."

"All right," said Gerard. "I'll get on it. Francesca?"

Francesca made a scribbled note on the hotel pad, and pulled a tight, unhelpful expression which Gerard recognized as trouble.

CHAPTER ELEVEN

Jerry and David ate breakfast together in silence; a cup of black coffee for Jerry and a bowl of Lucky Charms for David. On the radio, they were still talking about the white-masked copkiller, but by now the story had been chewed over by so many expert opinions and so much tough talk from the Hollywood police that it bore little resemblance to the violent event it had actually been.

David was as rangy as his father; a long-legged, untidy boy of fourteen; but he had inherited, unmistakably, his mother's forehead and eyes. Jerry could stare at him sometimes, when he was watching television or doing his math homework, and see Rhoda, exactly as she had been before the cancer had dulled and wasted her and at last taken her away.

"That's some weird murder,' huh?" asked David. "Do you hear what they said? Some guy in a white mask swinging this cop around by the ankles."

"Sure," said Jerry unenthusiastically. "Real weird."

David said, "You're okay, aren't you, Dad?"

"What makes you ask that?"

"I don't know. You seem like you're down."

Jerry shrugged. "I don't know. I don't know what it is. I just get the feeling there's something strange going on. You know that feeling you get just before an electric storm? Kind of a *tension*. Like two magnets when you try to push them together and they resist each other."

David finished his cereal, drained his glass of orange juice, and then went to the sink to wash his dishes. "Are you seeing Doctor Grunwald today?" he asked matter-of-factly. Dad's continuing analysis was a part of daily life which he had grown to accept as quite normal; besides, half the kids in his class had parents undergoing psychiatric treatment. Kim Pepper's mother had taken an overdose last month and nearly died. It was nearly as fashionable to attempt suicide as it was to Sierra-Stone your poolside.

Jerry said, "Maybe. I mean, yes, I probably will."

David stood by the sink, in his T-shirt and faded Levi's, and looked at his father with a mixture of sorrow and exasperation. "You don't really need him, you know. You could manage on your own, if you tried."

Jerry gave his son a quick and vinegary smile. "Day-to-day living I can manage on my own. *You* I can manage on my own. The only thing I can't manage on my own is Japan."

David was quiet for a long time, but then he said, "That all happened thirty-eight years ago, Dad. You know? Thirty-eight years."

"I know, David. But memories aren't necessarily erased by passing years. Sometimes, they grow more relevant, sharper, more disturbing. And now there's something in the air . . . this tension. . . . It kind of reminds me of Japan. I don't know why. But it has the same feeling of complete doom."

"*Doom?*" repeated David, with exaggerated wide-eyed emphasis. "Jesus, Dad, only comic strip characters say 'doom'!"

Jerry glanced up at David wryly. "Maybe that's my real problem. Maybe, in reality, I'm a comic strip character. Jerry and the Pirates."

David said, "Never," and gave his father a friendly cuff on the arm.

Jerry drove David to school, dropping him outside the gates. Then he cruised slowly back home to Orchid Place, listening to Hilly Rose on KMPC 710 and thinking about Japan.

Japan . . . and those hot still days in the Chugoku Sanchi, under a sky the color of melted lead, hidden deeply in a camouflaged crevice of the forest, with no sound but the chirruping of insects and the endless warbling of the radio. He pulled up at an intersection, and for a split second he didn't know where he was. A garbage truck pulled up behind him and gave him a noisy blast on its horn to remind him that he was back in the present day.

On the radio, Hilly Rose was talking to Sergeant Skrolnik. "Is there anything apart from the white mask which connects these two murders? Any other clue whatsoever? I mean, are we dealing with a *single* murderer here, or a look alike?"

Sergeant Skrolnik was on his best media behavior, and his voice sounded strangled. "The connections are many and varied. You understand what I mean. It's not just the mask. The *modus operandi* is strikingly similar, in that both victims were wrenched apart by bare hands. No sign of any kind of blunt instrument, or weapon of any description. This is a job committed by somebody of almost superhuman strength."

"Somebody crazy, perhaps?" asked Hilly Rose. "Somebody with lunatic strength?"

"Lunatic strength is a myth," said Skrolnik. "What we're dealing with here is somebody who naturally and normally possesses unusual physical power; and that's who we're looking for. Somebody who trains day and night in karate, something like that. Maybe a bodybuilder."

"What about this white mask?"

"We don't have any clues about the mask so far . . . but a police artist has been reconstructing the mask based on the evidence supplied to us by witnesses who passed the homicide location on the Hollywood Freeway, and we hope to be able to show that mask on television tonight, in the hope that it's going to jog somebody's memory. All I can say about it so far is that it's dead white, kind of expressionless . . . and probably varnished. One eyewitness said that it had some kind of pattern on it, on the forehead, but for tonight's reconstruction we're omitting that detail because nobody else saw it, and the witness admits that it might have been a fleck on his own windshield. . . ."

Jerry thought, *White, expressionless*. . . . There was something about the way in which Sergeant Skrolnik was trying to describe the murderer that made his stomach turn over, something which disturbed old memories. . . .

We've located it, sir. No question about it. We've taken sixteen radio bearings and we have it right on the button.

In that case, withdraw immediately. I repeat, immediately. You will be picked up at 2125 hours on the 15th on the beach at Kokubu.

"Yes, sir," Jerry whispered to himself, aloud, as he turned into the driveway of his home.

He climbed out of the car. A young man in a sleeveless T-shirt and shorts was sitting on the wall, smoking and obviously waiting for him. The young man was blond and curly, and looked as if he spent most of his day down at the beach or sunning himself on a flat roof somewhere. Jerry said flatly, "Good morning. You looking for me?"

"You're Mr. Jerry Sennett?"

"That's right. Who wants to know?"

"Mack Holt's my name. I used to be Sherry's boyfriend. Sherry Cantor? That was in the days before *Our Family Jones*. But we broke up when she got into that."

Jerry slung his jacket over his shoulder and climbed up to his front door. "You broke up, huh?" he asked, as he took out his key. "What happened? Was she spoiled by success?"

"She wasn't, but I was. I was a would-be actor in those days, too. And I can tell you, it wasn't easy, parking cars for a living while she was the toast of the town. And it isn't easy to accept her death. That's why I came to see you, I guess. You're her neighbor, after all."

"Do you want a drink?"

"If it's not imposing on you."

Jerry gave him a wry smile. "*Nothing* imposes on me these days, young man. I have gradually crystallized into a kind of emotional rock formation, upon which nothing can make the slightest impression, let alone impose."

Mack, following Jerry into the living room, gave an uncomfortable laugh.

"Quiet kind of place you've got here," he said.

"Quiet, well, that's the word for it," nodded Jerry. "What'll you have? There's Chivas Regal or Chivas Regal."

"I'll have a Chivas Regal," said Mack, sitting down on the sofa.

"What happened to Sherry, that was a great shock to us here," said Jerry. "She was a nice girl. Friendly, pretty. Always bouncing and full of life. I wish now that I could have gotten to know her better."

"She was somebody special," said Mack. "Maybe too special."

Jerry gave Mack a drink and then walked across to the window. "I don't think we're talking about the usual kind of Hollywood nut murder here," he said. "Not a Charles Manson, or anything like that."

Mack said, "She was torn apart, you know. Literally torn apart."

"Yes," agreed Jerry. "But who uses a Sherman tank to crush a peanut?"

"You're a military man?" asked Mack guardedly.

Jerry came away from the window. "Used to be, in the days when it meant anything. Naval intelligence group."

"Now you're . . . ?" asked Mack, indicating the living room with his glass in his hand.

"Now I'm semiretired," Jerry told him. "Living off my investments and a little part-time architectural work. Oh, yes, I used to be an architect, too. But it was the intelligence group that made the big impression on me, made me what I was. You don't get hardened designing duplexes in Westwood. Not hardened the way I am."

In that case, withdraw immediately. I repeat, immediately.

Mack said, "You think they'll ever catch him? Not that it matters."

Jerry stared at him, unfocused. "Catch him? Well, they might. I don't know. I always get the feeling that the police are satisfied with anybody who's prepared to confess, whether he happens to be the real criminal or not."

Mack sipped his whiskey, shuddered, and then said, "You've got some kind of feeling about this, right? I mean, about what happened to Sherry?"

Jerry nodded. "I don't know why. But I noticed it this morning. There's something in the air. Something tense. I don't know what it is. I don't have a clue. But I think it's tied up with what happened to Sherry. And there's something else, too."

Mack sat and waited for Jerry to say what this "something else" was. A minute, two minutes passed, and in the end, Mack said, "What? What else?"

"Well . . . let me try an experiment," said Jerry. "I don't know whether you were listening to the radio this morning or not, but the detective who's handling Sherry's murder said that a police artist is busy reconstructing the same kind of mask that the killer wore, based on descriptions from witnesses, and that tonight it would be shown on television."

"I didn't know that," said Mack. He didn't. This morning, he'd been too busy with Olive. Not making love, but arguing about Sherry, arguing about his unwillingness to give himself to Olive while he mourned.

"I'll tell you what," Jerry said quietly, raising one finger. "I'll show you a mask I brought back from Tokyo after the war; and then you watch television tonight, and if you think the mask they show is similar—maybe not the same, but similar—then you call me. I'll be watching too."

Mack said uneasily, "You're not pulling my leg about this? I mean, you're not. . . ."

"I have a mask that happens to sound like the police description on the radio," said Jerry. "White, expressionless. But that doesn't mean that I had anything to do with Sherry being murdered. I can promise you, I wasn't even here at the time. And besides . . ." He looked down at his hands. "I'm too weak these days to lift a box of groceries. I'm getting old. And I think I did enough killing in the war to satisfy the most bloodthirsty killer's most bloodthirsty dreams."

Mack was quiet for a long time, watching Jerry suspiciously at first, then more sympathetically. The man was old, and deeply upset by what had happened to Sherry, he could see that. He could also see that there were shadows crossing his mind, shadows he would probably prefer to forget.

We've located it, sir. No question about it. No question about it. No question about it.

Mack said, "Sherry once said to me, before she got famous, 'I think that I'll love you forever.' And I said, 'What makes you think that?' and she said, 'Because everything you feel, you feel forever.' "

Jerry said, "What are you trying to tell me, Mack? Can I call you Mack?"

Mack said, "I'm trying to tell you that she still loved me when she was dying. You know that? When she was dying, she still loved me. And that makes me part of what happened. That makes me responsible."

Jerry swilled the whiskey around in his glass, without taking his eyes off this young curly-haired L.A. bum with the raggedy shorts and the tears in his eyes. "You're crying," he said baldly.

"Yes," said Mack miserably.

"Well," said Jerry, "that's a start."

After a while, Jerry left Mack to finish his drink and went down into the cellar. It was dusty and untidy, stacked with tea chests and packing cases and crumpled-up copies of the *Los Angeles Examiner* for the day he had moved in eight years ago. But once he had shifted two stacks of cordwood and a broken bicycle, he found the varnished trunk with the rusted iron bands which had followed him from apartment to bungalow to hillside house for nearly thirty-five years. He tugged out the six-inch nail which kept the hasp closed, and opened the lid. Inside, like the multi-colored body of a vampire waiting to be revived, lay his remnants of Japan. Kites, fans, *Wajima-nuri* lacquerware, masks, *Arita-yaki* ware, paper flowers.

Mack Holt was sitting on Jerry Sennett's sagging sofa, thinking about Sherry, and about the day they had hurtled on his motorcycle all the way down to Baja California, laughing, ridiculous, loving, and high on the best Mexican grass, when he was abruptly confronted by a ghastly eyeless face, as white as death. He spilled his whiskey and said, "Shit! You scared me!"

Jerry laid the mask carefully on the table. "It's only a mask. I picked it up in Japan after the war."

Mack breathed out unsteadily. "Some mask. But what makes you think it's the same kind of mask that Sherry's killer was wearing?"

"I have a feeling about it, that's all."

"A feeling?"

Jerry stared down at the mask. Its features were blank, apart from a V-shaped black mark which defined the forehead. To anybody who was uninitiated in Japanese demonology, the V looked like a fierce frown. But Jerry knew that it was a representation of the bird's beak which would usually have protruded from such a demon's head. The demon was called a Tengu; and it was supposed to be the supernatural reincarnation of a Shinto monk whose ways had become proud and corrupt. It was the most terrible of all Japanese demons: because it knew heaven as well as hell.

Jerry said, "The Japanese have a phrase: 'The crow kills by day and by night.' These days, they usually use it when they're warning one another to watch out for a particularly aggressive business colleague. In fact, most Japanese have forgotten what it meant originally. But in the old days, the very old days, back in the eighth century, it referred exclusively to the Tengus, the devils of Buddha. They had beaks like crows, which gradually developed into fierce jaws; and they weren't above tearing people to pieces when they felt the urge."

Mack eyed the mask suspiciously. "You're not suggesting that . . ."

"No," said Jerry. "I'm not suggesting anything. It's just that I have a feeling. The Japanese call it 'a cold wind.' "

Mack said nothing for a long time. He looked at Jerry,

and then back at the mask. "This is some kind of a puton, right?" he asked at last, but his voice betrayed his lack of conviction.

"It might sound like it," said Jerry. "I can't find any way to persuade you that it isn't. I'm not even sure about it myself. But the police said that a man in a white mask tore Sherry to pieces, and then assaulted and killed a cop on the Hollywood Freeway."

He swallowed a mouthful of whiskey, and then said, "I'm probably wrong. When they show the mask on television tonight, we'll probably find it's a Casper the Ghost mask from some joke store on Hollywood Boulevard."

"But you can feel 'a cold wind,' " said Mack.

Jerry nodded.

Mack finished his drink, hesitated for a moment, and then stood up. "I'll watch the news, and then I'll call you."

"Even if it turns out to be Casper the Ghost?" asked Jerry dryly.

Mack shook his head. "If it's Casper the Ghost, then I'll simply put you down as a stray fruitcake. And that, believe me, will be the most charitable thing I can do."

Jerry stood in his doorway watching Mack cross the street in the hazy mid-morning sunshine and climb into a dented green Volkswagen Beetle. The engine started up with a clattering roar and a cloud of blue smoke. Jerry closed the door and went back into the living room. The Tengu mask lay on the table where he had left it, staring eyelessly up at the ceiling.

"A stray fruitcake, huh?" Jerry repeated.

No question about it, sir. No question about it.

CHAPTER TWELVE

Mr. Esmeralda had learned very early in life that few
people are as deeply despised as those who provide a
service for a fee, no matter how exclusive their service, or
how rarefied their personal *hauteur*. As a thirteen-year-old
boy in Barranquilla, in Colombia, in a crumbling white-
stucco mansion enclosed within courtyards and wrought-
iron gates, and overshadowed by musty palm trees, he had
seen businessmen and entrepreneurs of all persuasions and
all nationalities come and go, their suits stained with
sweat, seeking assistance and paid favors from his father.

His father had held court on one of the upper balconies—Jesus Esmeralda, one-time Caribbean pirate,
famous gunrunner, narcotics smuggler, and spiriter-away
of hunted men. If you wanted anything to find its way in
or out of Colombia—a packing case crawling with poisonous spiders, a selection of priceless emeralds, a Browning
machine gun, a professor of social science who had spoken
out once too often against the régime—then Jesus
Esmeralda was your man.

But no matter how wealthy he was; in spite of his white
Hispano-Suiza and his twenty-two servants; regardless of
his talent for procuring faultless cocaine for fashionable
parties and tireless young men for Barranquilla's bored
middle-aged ladies, he was never accepted into respectable
society. Businessmen who had handed Jesus Esmeralda
thousands of dollars in used U.S. currency were unlikely to
invite him to dinner. Women who knew that he was living
off the fear of their husbands and lovers were scarcely
inclined to ask him into their beds. He was a lonely,
sardonic man, spasmodically wealthy, occasionally hysterical, troubled by coughing fits that he could control only
with desperate difficulty, and by extraordinary sexual
compulsions that he couldn't control at all. It is sufficient
to say that as he grew older and more jaded, he became
increasingly obsessed with watching women with animals,

and that his son's first glimpse of adult perversion was through the wrought-iron screen of his bedroom window, into the courtyard below, from which the clatter of hoofs and the cries of girls had been disturbing him since ten o'clock. He had seen through the palm trees a small, frisky pony with a long beribboned mane, a gray; and beneath it, naked, on all fours, a young blonde girl of no more than sixteen or seventeen, between whose parted buttocks the pony was thrusting something that looked, to young Esmeralda's, like a rolled-up red umbrella.

Mr. Esmeralda had been nine then. What he had seen had appeared to be magical and mysterious, a peculiar myth brought to life in front of his eyes. He had never forgotten it. It had been early evidence of the enchanted degradation of those who perform for money, their utter enslavement to the will of others. It had both repelled and mesmerized him.

During his schooldays in Colombia, and all through business college in Houston, Texas, Mr. Esmeralda had been friendly, helpful, and sociable. But no matter how many favors he did for his pals, he never accepted anything in return, not even a candy bar, nor a sixpack of root beer, nor the loan of a roommate's T-Bird. The other kids thought him unfailingly trustworthy; and it was on trust that Mr. Esmeralda eventually built his career as a used-car salesman, import-export agent, international entrepreneur, and helper of all those who needed help. He moved from Houston to Cleveland, from Cleveland to Seattle, from Seattle to L.A.

He never made the mistake of asking any of his clients for money, or even of mentioning money. He and his clients remained friends—golfing together, dining together, dating together. The financial side of his business was handled entirely by a pleasant and courteous man called Norris, who had a wonderfully pained and breathy way of pleading with defaulters not to upset Mr. Esmeralda, *please*, he respects and admires you *so much*.

Mr. Esmeralda had never married, although two or three

American ladies had been seen entering and leaving his elegant condominium at The Promenade on Hope and First streets. They were the kind of strawberry-blonde pneumatic 1960's Amazons that Vargas used to airbrush for *Playboy*—girls whom Gerard Crowley had unkindly described as "a greaser's idea of Miss Sexy America."

On the same morning that Mack Holt visited Jerry Sennett, Mr. Esmeralda was being driven in his blue air-conditioned Lincoln Town Car to a house set back among the trees in Laurel Canyon. His chauffeur was a young Chinese girl he had met in Peking two years ago. He had gone there to arrange for the import of forty-five tons of ballbearings and certain unidentified machine spares, many of which had borne an uncanny resemblance to the disassembled components of M-60 general-purpose machine guns. The girl's name was Kuan-yin, and although she looked no more than twenty-one or twenty-two, she claimed that she had once chauffeured Chiang Ching, the widow of Chairman Mao, before the downfall of the Gang of Four. She was calm, pretty, and remote, and Mr. Esmeralda particularly liked her in her severe gray jacket and jodhpurs.

Few of Mr. Esmeralda's colleagues clearly understood his relationship with Kuan-yin. There were stories that he had helped her to escape from Hangzhou during the Cultural Revolution; but why, or how, Mr. Esmeralda would never explain. There was another, less convincing story that he had found her in a Nevada cathouse called the Bucking Horse Ranch, and that she had nursed him through a coronary. But whatever the turth was (and truth, in Mr. Esmeralda's life, was rarely relevant, except on bills of lading), there was a bond between them which, for want of an exact word to describe the magnetism of two isolated and complex and in many ways unpleasant souls, could almost be called affection.

The Lincoln curved up the tree-lined driveway to the front door. A remote-control television camera watched the car suspiciously from its perch in an overhanging spruce. The house was an expensive split-level affair, all triangular rooftops and cedarwood decks, the kind of house that Los Angeles realtors usually describe as "a high-tech home built with old-world craftsmanship," and then price $125,000 over its value. Mr. Esmeralda said to Kuan-yin, "Turn around, and then wait for me. Don't get out of the car. I'll telephone you if they keep me waiting for very long."

In the rearview mirror, Kuan-yin's eyes nodded a passive acknowledgement.

Mr. Esmeralda walked up to the house. Another remote-control television camera, suspended from the eaves, observed his climb up the steps to the front door. He ignored it, and used the large brass knocker.

The door was opened almost instantly. From inside the "tasteful hardwood entryway" came the waft of incense and that other curious smell which always lingered here, and which Mr. Esmeralda had never been able to identify. A Japanese stood before him in black silk robes and a black silk facemask decorated with scarlet and gold thread, and beckoned him inside. The door was quietly and quickly closed behind him.

Mr. Esmeralda had been here three times before, but the strange atmosphere in the house disturbed him just as much today as it had on his previous visits. No electric lights were lit: the only illumination came from small candles placed in flat ceramic dishes of water all the way around the edges of the rooms and corridors. And there was always a faint and distant moaning, almost a keening noise, as if the summer winds were blowing through an abandoned *Koto*, the Japanese harp, or as if a woman were mourning her long-dead husband.

What was even more unsettling, the occupants of the house, of whom Mr. Esmeralda had so far counted eight, were always dressed in black and always masked. He had never even seen the face of the man who called himself *Kappa*, the man he had come to see. But then, Kappa was scarcely a man.

The Japanese who had opened the door for him said, "You will wait now."

"Mr. Esmeralda involuntarily checked his watch. "Is he going to be long? I have a heavy day."

"Kappa pays for your day. If Kappa says wait, then you wait."

"Very well," said Mr. Esmeralda. "Since you put it so persuasively."

"You would care for something to drink?"

"A glass of water would be admirable."

"So it shall be. Now please wait."

While the Japanese went to bring his water, Mr. Esmeralda wandered impatiently into the large empty area which, before this house had been taken over by Kappa and his entourage, must have been the "generous, over-sized family room." Now there was nothing here but bare floor boards and scores of flickering candles. The walls were white and bare, except for three or four sheets of handmade paper on which were written thousands of intricate Japanese characters. Mr. Esmeralda went over and peered at them, as he had peered at them before, and wished he could read Japanese. For all he knew, they were nothing more threatening than Tokyo-Kobe bullet-train timetables.

Upstairs, or next door, or wherever it came from, he could hear that distant moaning sound, and for a moment he held his breath and frowned and listened as hard as he could, trying to make out once and for all what it actually was.

At last, the Japanese came padding back with his glass of water. Mr. Esmeralda drank a little of it and then handed the glass back. "Tepid," he said. The Japanese didn't answer. Then Mr. Esmeralda asked, "Is Kappa going to be very much longer? I am not particularly good at waiting. It doesn't suit my temperament." Still the Japanese didn't answer. "You know, temperament?" repeated Mr. Esmeralda. "I am what they call a man of little patience. I have a short fuse."

A gong rang; a sound more felt than heard. The Japanese said, "Kappa will see you now. Please follow me."

Mr. Esmeralda took out his handkerchief and dabbed at the back of his neck. "Thank God for that." He glanced up at the ceiling and crossed himself quickly. "Thank you," he muttered.

Perhaps the house in Laurel Canyon disturbed him so much because he knew that he was going to have to confront Kappa again. Kappa still gave him occasional nightmares, even though he had seen beggars all over the Middle East, and lepers in Africa, and the deformed victims of mercury pollution at Minamata. Mr. Esmeralda liked to think of himself as a cosmopolitan, a man who could slip comfortably onto a stool at the Oak Bar of the Plaza one week and be greeted by the barman by name; and then be welcomed the next week at a small brothel in Marseilles with the same affability. He couldn't think, offhand, of a country he hadn't visited. He couldn't think of a major international gangster whose hand he hadn't shaken, and whose assistance he couldn't rely on.

But he had never met anything like Kappa; and he nightly prayed to the Virgin Mary that he would never meet anything like Kappa again.

Mr. Esmeralda had become involved with Kappa by accident, on board a ferry that was taking passengers from Tokushima to Wakayama, across the Kii-Suido. The ferry had been elegant, white-painted, and old, with two large paddles which left curling patterns of foam on the silver-gray water. It had been a strange misty afternoon, with the sun as red behind the mist as a Japanese flag, a supernatural scarlet orb. Mr. Esmeralda had been talking to his people in Kochi about heroin. They had left him unsatisfied: there had been a great deal of ceremonial tea-drinking, chanoyu, but very little in the way of firm delivery dates. Mr. Esmeralda was leaning on the rail of the ferry feeling irritated and tired. He often found that the so-called superefficiency of the Japanese was nothing more than an impressive display of Oriental ritual. He enjoyed subtlety in his dealings, but the Kochi people were so suble that they practically disappeared up their own inscrutability.

A voice had said close beside him, "You are Mr. Esmerarda?"

Mr. Esmeralda had shifted sideways to see who was talking to him. Anybody who knew his name was probably police or customs, and he didn't particularly want to speak to either. But, in fact, it had been a young Japanese in a khaki windbreaker and thin beige slacks, unexceptional-looking, the kind of Toyko student type you could have lost in a crowd in Nihonbashi just by blinking.

"Mr. Esmerarda?" the student had repeated.

"What do you want? You had better know that I am very selective when it comes to shipboard romances."

The Japanese student had stared at him unblinkingly. "You must prease accompany me."

"I am here. I am listening. What more do you want?"

"You must accompany me downstairs. Kappa wishes to speak with you."

"Kappa? Who's Kappa?"

The Japanese student had said, "You may have seen him carried on board."

Mr. Esmeralda had said quietly, "You mean the—" and the Japanese student had nodded. Nobody could have failed to notice the long black Toyota limousine that had drawn up to the dock just before the ferry was due to leave, and the extraordinary ensemble which had alighted from it and hurried to the gangway. Four men, hooded and gowned in black, bearing between them a kind of elaborate wickerwork palanquin, in which a diminutive figure nodded and swayed, completely swathed in a white sheet.

When Mr. Esmeralda had seen them come on board, he had crossed himself. Another passenger, an elderly Japanese, had actually disembarked, in spite of the arguments of his relatives, and refused to travel on the ferry in the company of demons. The palanquin had quickly been taken below and the lacquered cabin doors shut behind it, and the ferry had set off on its spectral journey through the mist of the Kii-Suido. But many of the passengers had appeared to be unsettled, and there had been a lot of forced laughter and whiskey-drinking.

Mr. Esmeralda had followed the Japanese student down the companionway to the cabin doors, on which were painted a fleet of fantastic ships and a grisly collection of sea monsters, in the style of the Shijó school. The Japanese student had knocked at the doors and then waited, watching Mr. Esmeralda blandly.

"I don't suppose you're going to tell me what this is all about?" Mr. Esmeralda had asked the student. The student had said nothing, but waited and watched as before, impassive and utterly calm.

The doors to the cabin had been opened. "You may go in now," the student told Mr. Esmeralda.

"You are sure that this is going to be worth my while?" Mr. Esmeralda had asked him.

"Go in," the student had repeated.

A small hand had taken hold of Mr. Esmeralda's wrist as he stepped into the cabin, to guide him down a flight of darkened stairs, and then along the length of an unlit corridor, to a door. It had been immediately opened, and Mr. Esmeralda had found himself in a private stateroom, hot and smoky with dozens and dozens of candles. Behind the swaying flames of the candles, only half-visible through the dazzle and the smoke, Mr. Esmeralda had seen that the basketwork palanquin had been converted into a throne—its bamboo carrying poles having been fixed vertically to the sides of the basket, instead of horizontally. He had shaded his eyes against the candles, but it had been impossible to see clearly who or what it was that was perched in the basket.

Apart from Mr. Esmeralda himself, there were several other people in the stateroom—two or three young Japanese men standing in the shadows, all of them with masked faces—and a very young Japanese girl, wearing

only a red-and-gold silk shirt and an extraordinary lacquered headdress of stylized flowers, similar to the flowers
worn by the Yoshiwara courtesans of the eighteenth
century. From her face, and from her half-developed
breasts, Mr. Esmeralda had guessed that she was only
twelve or thirteen years old.

"I seem to have been sent for," Mr. Esmeralda had said
loudly, in the general direction of the basketwork throne.

"Indeed you have," a voice had replied, slurred and
Japanese, but with a peculiar inflection all its own, as if it
were emerging from the black-haired throat of a tropical
insect. "I know who you are, Mr. Esmeralda, and why you
spent so much time at Kochi, in the company of Katsukawa Shunsho."

"I have many acquaintances in Japan," Mr. Esmeralda
had answered cautiously, screwing up his eyes to see what
this "Kappa" really looked like. "Katsukawa Shunsho is a
trading associate, nothing more."

"You are based in Los Angeles, in America?" the
peculiar voice had asked him.

Mr. Esmeralda felt the first slide of perspiration down
the middle of his back. Suddenly he felt less like the
conjuror than the conjuree, the perplexed victim whose
socks and cufflinks have been removed without his
knowledge. He gave what he hoped was an assured nod,
but he had never felt less assured in his life. "I return there
on Friday," he said. "Air Argentina, flight AX 109.
Perhaps you knew that, too."

"I need a certain task performed for me in Los
Angeles," the voice told him.

Mr. Esmeralda licked his lips. "Certain tasks" usually
turned out to be extremely complicated, costly, and
dangerous. If somebody in Japan wanted a straightforward
favor, they generally asked you for it outright. It was only
when it was unpleasant that they called it "a certain task"
and approached you so obliquely.

"I, er, I regret that *time* will not permit me to accept
any more commissions at present," Mr. Esmeralda had

replied. "I have an art shipment to take care of; a whole freighter loaded with *netsuke*. And I have a meeting in Detroit on Monday morning. And next Wednesday, I must speak to some of my new associates in Cairo. I would have liked to be able to accommodate you, but—" He shrugged, tried to smile.

There had been a second's silence. But then the voice had said, "Mr. Esmeralda, you will not turn me down. I will pay you $1.6 million in U.S. currency, and in return you will give me your absolute obedience. Is that understood?"

"I am not in the habit of performing favors for money," Mr. Esmeralda had replied, although some hint of caution made him add, "Not as a rule, anyway. Well, not often."

Kappa, from behind the swaying candle flames, had said something else hurriedly and authoritatively. Two more Japanese had come forward, both masked, as their colleagues were, dragging a large hardwood block, painted shiny red. Then the young Japanese girl in the headdress had stepped forward, knelt down, and pulled open the zipper of Mr. Esmeralda's white tropical trousers. She had reached inside, wrestled out his penis from his shorts, and tugged it out until it was stretched across the top of the red block.

Mr. Esmeralda had tried to thrash his legs and wriggle from side to side; but the two young Japanese boys had a firm grip on his arms, and the young Japanese girl had an unyielding grip on his penis.

A third Japanese youth had stepped forward, this one clutching a curvy-bladed samurai sword. He had lowered the sword until the sharp edge was just touching the skin of Mr. Esmeralda's penis, not breaking the skin, but resting it there so that Mr. Esmeralda could feel just how keen the blade was.

Then, without warning, the Japanese youth had let out a sharp cry, whipped back the samurai sword, and flashed it down toward the red hardwood block. Mr. Esmeralda had screamed, in spite of himself; in spite of the fact that he was a man of the world.

He had looked down to see that the Japanese youth had somehow managed to stop the blade's descent exactly an inch above the hardwood block. He had cut a thin line across the tip of Mr. Esmeralda's penis, but that was all. Only a scratch, nothing serious. Mr. Esmeralda had closed his eyes, and whispered, "*Madre mia.*"

There had been a lengthy silence. The girl had not released his penis the boy with the sword had not moved away. But the insectlike voice of Kappa had said, "you wish to assist me now."

Mr. Esmeralda had cleared his throat. "I see no reason why not."

"Well, that's excellent," Kappa had told him. "Welcome to the the Circle of the Burned Doves."

"The Burned Doves?" Mr. Esmeralda had asked.

There had been a short hesitation; then Kappa had whispered, "Come forward. Come nearer. Then you will see what I mean."

Mr. Esmeralda had glanced down at the girl, and then sideways at the boy.

"Let him go," Kappa had ordered, and the girl had stood up and shuffled quickly back into the shadows.

Mr. Esmeralda, zipping up his pants, had made a suspicious circuit of the rows of flickering candles. As he had approached the basketwork throne, a curious smell had reached his nostrils, a sweetish smell that would almost have been alluring if he hadn't been so sure that it was the odor of something curious and frightening. If it had put him in mind of anything at all, it was Japanese seaweed, cloying and slightly briny.

"Come nearer," Kappa had told him, his voice so hoarse and quiet now that Mr. Esmeralda could hardly hear what he was saying. Mr. Esmeralda, sweating in the candlelight, had finally come face to face with the creature that called itself Kappa.

Lying in the basketwork throne on a soiled cushion of

blue Japanese silk was a yellowish thing that looked, at first sight, like a hugely enlarged human embryo. Its head was more than man-sized, but Mr. Esmeralda could see nothing of its features because they were concealed behind a bland yellow-painted mask, a faintly smiling warrior of the reign of the Emperor Kameyama, an uncanny and disturbing masterpiece of Japanese decorative art.

The body, however, was naked, and completely exposed, and it was this grisly collection of distorted flesh and bone that subsequently gave Mr. Esmeralda so many nightmares. There was a narrow chest, which rose and fell as rapidly as that of a suffocating puppy; two tiny arms with budlike nodes instead of fingers; and a bulging stomach. The genitals were even more malformed, a gray and wrinkled array of folds and dewlaps, neither male nor female, which glistened in the candlelight with slippery mucus. The creature had legs of a kind, hunched beneath its genitals, but they were sticklike and obviously powerless.

"You wonder why I hide my face and leave my body exposed?" Kappa had asked Mr. Esmeralda hoarsely, as Mr. Esmeralda stared at him in horror.

Mr. Esmeralda had been unable to answer. His mouth hadn't been able to move itself into any kind of shape at all.

Kappa had watched him for a while through the expressionless eyeholes in his mask. Then he had said, "I hide my face because my face is normal; the face of a normal man. The rest of my body you are welcome to see. I am not ashamed of it. What happened to me was not my fault; nor the fault of my mother. Look at me, and see what the Americans were responsible for, with their atomic bomb. My mother was one month pregnant on August 6, 1945, when the first bomb was dropped on Hiroshima. She was staying with her uncle and aunt in Itsukaichi, but she had traveled to the city the day before to see an old friend of my father, who had been wounded in the Army. She was exposed both to the flash, which burned her, and the gamma rays, which eventually killed her, after eight years. But she was just outside the two-kilometer radius from ground zero within which all pregnant women had miscarriages and even though I was grotesquely premature I was born alive."

"The doctors didn't—" Mr. Esmeralda had begun, his voice thick and choked.

"Think of killing me at birth? No, they didn't do that. My mother was back at Itsukaichi for her confinement. After a while, in a strange way, she became attached to me, and she refused to contemplate euthanasia. She took me every day to water therapy, in the hope that my limbs would grow strong and my body develop. That is why they call me Kappa. It is Japanese for 'water devil'—a nasty little beast that lives in the water and refuses to compromise with anyone."

Mr. Esmeralda had deliberately turned his back on the revolting spectacle in the basketwork throne, and had made his way unsteadily back through the lines of candles to the far side of the room. During this time, Kappa had said nothing, but had watched him intently through his yellow warrior's mask. Mr. Esmeralda had felt closed-in and nauseous, and the slight roll of the ancient ferry as it had turned on the Pacific swell to dock at Wakayama had unsettled his breakfast, pork leg with mushrooms and too much hot tea.

"What is it you want me to do?" Mr. Esmeralda had asked Kappa at last, clearing his throat.

"A friend of mine, a doctor, must establish himself in America. You will arrange a work permit, and for somewhere private for his research. You can do this kind of thing: Katsukawa Shunsho told me. You have friends who can forge papers, friends who can arrange for green cards. This is so?"

Mr. Esmeralda had nodded queasily.

"You will also bring together four or five people who can help you with the further stages of my scheme. They should be experienced people, people like yourself, preferably with good knowledge of Japan and an understanding of the Japanese way of life. But you must understand that they might have to be dispensed with, especially if anything goes wrong. So I would advise you not to select friends or lovers, or anyone close to you.''

Mr. Esmeralda had said, ''When you say *dispensed with*, you mean murdered? Or do we speak a different language?''

''Was Hiroshima murder?''

''I am an entrepreneur, not a historical moralist. Hiroshima was war.''

There was a long, breathy pause. Then Kappa said, ''Pearl Harbor was war; Wake Island was war; Midway was war; Guadalcanal was war. War—men fighting each other like warriors. But Hiroshima was murder. And, for me personally, and all of my brothers and sisters who make up the Circle of the Burned Doves—that is to say, all those innocent children reared in secrecy, who have been born with terrible deformities because of the American atrocity—it has been worse than murder. If there is such a thing as living murder, then we have suffered it.''

Mr. Esmeralda had brushed the sleeves of his coat with mock fastidiousness. He didn't intend to argue with Kappa about the morality of revenge. Revenge, as far as he was concerned, was both petulant and boring. Revenge was for cuckolded husbands, rejected wives, and lunatics.

''This doctor friend of yours?'' he had said, ''What exactly does he want to do in the United States?''

Kappa had been silent for almost a minute. Then he had said, ''His name is Sugita Gempaku. He is a doctor of anthropology, not of medicine, a graduate of Keio University in Tokyo. I suppose you could call him something of a revolutionary. I first read about his work in a French science magazine. He was trying to recreate, as a historical experiment, some of the more specialized and arcane defense programs that Emperor Hirohito ordered toward the close of the war.

''One of these programs was an attempt to rediscover a derivative of the Heaven Drug, a kind of sleeping powder which the ancient samurai were said to have burned in censers around their battlegrounds, and which gave their enemies such strange and compelling hallucinations that they simply laid down their weapons and allowed themselves to be beheaded without a fight.

"Another was the Water Flute, a magical wind instrument about which there are many curious legends in Shikoku. Its music was said to induce self-destructive madness; and I can tell you that it was actually tried, during the American landings on Eniwetok atoll. There is no record, however, of its success or failure. Presumably, it failed."

Kappa had paused for a while to regain his breath. He had begun to pant very hard; the young girl had quickly and quietly approached the basketwork throne with a porcelain dish of saké. Mr. Esmeralda had tried to see if he would lift his mask to drink, but the girl had carefully placed herself between him and her master, so that the ritual of his refreshment was completely obscured.

The ferry had docked now at Wakayama, and Mr. Esmeralda glanced up at the ceiling of the cabin as the shuffling footsteps of disembarking passengers crossed the deck. He had been supposed to meet one of his agents on the pier, but he made no attempt to leave the cabin.

At last, Kappa had said, "The most secret and most effective of all the programs, however, was that of the Tengu. It was carried out in Hiroshima in 1945 by Toshiro Mitoma, an extraordinary religious ascetic who believed implicitly in all the magic and demonology of ancient Japan, and who was often consulted during the course of the war by Japanese officers of field and flag rank. Admiral Nagumo trusted him as implicitly as Hitler trusted Dr. Morrell."

"What, exactly, *was* the Tengu?" Mr. Esmeralda had asked.

"The Tengu was—*is*—the most terrible of all Japanese demons. There are stories of Tengus going back to the eighth century, and even earlier. They are related to the evil which manifests itself in all black birds, like crows and ravens and rooks. But they are capable of possessing a man's body, taking him over like a fit of madness, and giving him extraordinary strength and resistance to attack. A man possessed by a Tengu could be hacked into tiny pieces with a sword before he would give up. And even when they have been destroyed, Tengu-men have remarkable regenerative powers. If you are looking for a Western comparison, I suppose you could say that the Tengu is like a zombie, except that a zombie is already dead and a Tengu can hardly ever be killed.''

Mr. Esmeralda had said, "You'll excuse me for smiling.''

"You find this difficult to believe?''

"I have my own superstitions. My own little foibles,'' Mr. Esmeralda had said. "I try not to catch sight of the back of my head in a mirror. I do my best not to spill salt. But, Mr. Kappa, I really cannot invest any belief in ancient demons.''

Kappa had said to one of his aides, "Give him the papers.'' One of the young Japanese had come forward and silently handed Mr. Esmeralda a plastic envelope containing what looked like a military report sheet.

"What is this?'' Mr. Esmeralda had asked.

"Read it,'' Kappa had insisted.

It was a Xerox copy of a top-secret memorandum from USMC Intelligence Guam, dated October 17, 1944:

The failure of the attack on Cape Matatula on Tutuila Island on August 25 was due entirely to the presence on the Japanese side of no fewer than 10 but more than 12 individual troops wearing white masks and carrying no weapons but swords and knives. Reliable reports from five reputable career officers have indicated that these individual troops were able to walk through heavy enfilading rifle fire unharmed, and that they were responsible for the deaths of at least 80 of our own men. Some of our

men were killed by the Japanese soldiers' bare
hands, extremely brutally, although not in the style
generally known as *karate* or *kung fu*. One of the
Japanese troops was set afire by a Marine Corps
sergeant operating a flame-thrower, and yet he continued to attack our positions and succeeded in
strangling and killing two Marines while actually
ablaze. Comprehensive accounts of what occurred
were obtained from 15 officers and men during de-
briefing on USS *Oxford*, and these are attached.
Meanwhile it is suggested that priority be given to
intelligence investigation of these special Japanese
troops, whom we have codenamed "Hogs."

Mr. Esmeralda had handed the plastic envelope back
without a word.

"Well?" Kappa had asked him breathily.

"Well, what? All that happened a very long time ago.
Men make some very strange mistakes when they are
fighting battles. Perhaps all this talk of special Japanese
soldiers was nothing more than an excuse to cover up the
fact that the American Marines lost their nerve under fire,
and had to retreat."

Kappa had laughed. "You are being deliberately stubborn."

"Perhaps," Mr. Esmeralda had replied. "But why not?
I have nothing to gain by associating myself with you.
And, frankly, I find the idea of it extremely unpleasant."

"You forget that I will mutilate you if you refuse,"
Kappa had whispered.

Mr. Esmeralda had looked around him. The young
Japanese in their impenetrable black masks were tense and
poised, and he had been in no doubt at all that if he tried
to escape they would catch him in a flash, and treat him
without hesitation to whatever tortures Kappa might
direct. Mr. Esmeralda disliked the idea of working for a
shriveled quadriplegic in a basketwork chair; but on the
other hand he disliked the idea of being parted from his
penis even more.

He had said quietly, "You want me to smuggle your Doctor Gempaku into the United States, and provide him with research facilities? You want me to help him create more of these Tengus, is that it?"

Kappa had said, "I admire your quickness."

"But what is this all in aid of?" Mr. Esmeralda had insisted. "What exactly do you expect these Tengus to do?"

"Just one thing," Kappa had said. "Exact revenge on the American people for what they did in Hiroshima."

Now, at the house in Laurel Canyon, Mr. Esmeralda was once more entering the presence of the malformed Kappa. Here, Kappa had been laid out in a chromium-and-canvas cot, his body mercifully covered by a sheet and his heavy masked head propped up on pillows. There were two televisions suspended from the ceiling on amateurishly homemade gimbals and tape recorders and telephones within easy reach, all adapted for use by someone with the severest of handicaps. The room itself was hung with white cotton drapes and lit only by candles, a nest of them on a small white table. There were no pictures on the walls, no flowers, no miniature trees, none of the decorative art that Mr. Esmeralda expected to see in a Japanese room. And there was that pervasive smell of human flesh that wasn't quite dead but wasn't quite alive, either.

"I hear that things have been going dangerously awry," Kappa said, his eyes glittering through the holes in his mask.

"You could say that things haven't been going as they were planned to go," Mr. Esmeralda replied with great caution. "But, when one is asked to hire dispensable people, one sometimes has to make do with second best. The best people are indispensable."

"Nobody is indispensable," said Kappa.

"Good wheelers and dealers are indispensable," Mr. Esmeralda argued, "Especially when one is obliged to import dozens of illegal Japanese immigrants, along with whole crates of ancient artifacts and God knows how many live Japanese animals and birds. One can't expect miracles, Kapp."

"Do not fail me," whispered Kappa.

Mr. Esmeralda took out a pale lavender handkerchief and patted his sweating neck. "The last time I spoke to Doctor Gempaku, he said that everything was progressing quite well. We had difficulty with the first Tengu, I know, but by definition they aren't easily controllable."

"The man Sennett remains alive."

"It was an understandable mistake. Yoshikazu was given a house number, and it turned out that the number was posted on a concrete pillar between Sennett's house and the girl's house. The Tengu was directed to the wrong house, and there's nothing we can do about it. It's too late."

Kappa was silent for a while. Then he said, "You are sure that Sennett is the last remaining member of the naval intelligence team?"

"Quite sure. The only other person who might conceivably understand what is happening is Admiral Knut Thorson, formerly of the Naval Intelligence Command; and poor Admiral Thorson is currently in an acute-care hospital at Rancho Encino. Everyone else who might have known what happened, and why, is long dead."

"You didn't speak of this Admiral Thorson before."

"There was no need to. He suffered a stroke. His doctors say that he will probably never speak again."

"*Probably*?"

"You don't want me to send a Tengu to a *hospital*, to—"

"Do it," Kappa commanded.

"But—"

"*Do it*! And ensure that you deal with Sennett as well."

Mr. Esmeralda looked around him, unhappy. "All right," he agreed at last. "If you say so. But if your plan works out the way you want it to, it doesn't seem to me that there's going to be very much need to worry about Sennett, or Thorson, or about anybody else."

Kappa rolled his masked head away from Mr. Esmeralda and said in a muffled voice, "What is going to happen to the United States within the next few weeks must be a devastating mystery. They must never know why it happened, or how. It must seem like the revenge of God. If they were to discover that it was I who had initiated it, it would all seem explicable. They would be able to comprehend it; and in comprehending it, they would gradually be able to repair their morale and their spirit. That is what I specifically do not wish to happen. I wish this to be a blow of divine rage, from which the Americans will take years and years to recover. I want them to feel that they have been condemned to hell.''

Mr. Esmeralda thoughtfully tugged at his mouth with his hand. Quite illogically, he found himself thinking about Eva Crowley. There was something helpless and bruised about her; something which gave him the urge to punish her and degrade her even more. But, he knew that he would have to treat her very carefully. He had other plans for Eva Crowley, apart from bed and his own particular brand of Colombian seduction. Eva Crowley was Mr. Esmeralda's life-insurance policy.

CHAPTER THIRTEEN

Sergeant Skrolnik was dozing over his typewriter that afternoon when Detective Pullet came into his office, tripped over the wastebasket, tipped over his styrofoam cup of cold coffee, and knocked a stack of law books off the filing cabinet onto the floor.

"What the *hell*?" Skrolnik demanded grumpily. His eyes were puffy, and he felt as if an armadillo had been sleeping in his mouth. Then he said, "Oh. It's you."

Pullet dabbed ineffectually at the spilled coffee with a

crumpled-up piece of yellow legal paper. "I'm sorry. I'm sorry. I didn't realize you were resting."

Skrolnik gave Pullet a distinctly old-fashioned look, and sniffed. "I never rest. You should know that by now. I was simply seeking inspiration behind tactically closed eyelids."

"Did you find any?" asked Pullet. He was obviously pleased with himself about something. He picked up the law books, stacked them back on top of the filing cabinet, and frowned in irritation as they all clattered back to the floor again.

"Inspiration? No, not really," said Skrolnik. "But I did mentally marshal a number of interesting facts."

"Tell me," said Pullet. "*Sir*," he added when Skrolnik glanced across at him in disapproval."

"Well," said Skrolnik, "one of the most interesting facts is that when Officer Russo first caught sight of the van on Hollywood Boulevard, it was *already* speeding. That we know from the girl behind the counter at the drugstore where the officer stopped for antacid tablets. Now, why was it speeding, when there was no apparent pursuit, and when it contained a man who obviously wanted to do as little as possible to attract attention—since he had already torn Sherry Cantor into small pieces?"

Pullet nodded, and kept up his "yes, I'm interested" face as brightly as he could, although Skrolnik could sense that he was absolutely bursting to make a startling announcement of his own.

"The point is," Skrolnik went on, "the point is that something must have been *wrong*. So wrong that the driver of the van was prepared to risk almost anything to get our suspect out of town as fast as possible, and off to wherever he was going. That could fit in with your orangutan theory. Maybe the murderer was actually a wild ape, and his tranquilizers were wearing off. But if the orangutan was tranquilized, how did it kill Sherry Cantor? So what we have to look at is this—"

Detective Pullet couldn't contain his excitement any

longer. He reached into his frayed tweed sportscoat and produced, with a flourish, a folded-up poster.

"You told me to think laterally," he said. "Well, this is where lateral thinking got me."

The poster showed a hideous white masklike face, with a grinning red gash of a mouth. Underneath, it said, BRIGHT BROS. GRAND CIRCUS, ONE WEEK ONLY, ANAHEIM.

"A *circus*?" asked Skrolnik, wrinkling up his nose.

"Listen," Pullet enthused, "I thought of every situation in which a man wears or *appears to wear* a white mask. The white mask is crucial. It was seen by three independent witnesses, and all their descriptions are very similiar. Well . . . people don't wear white masks very often. Not full-face masks. A firefighter maybe. A skier. Maybe a ski mask would account for the pattern one of the witnesses said he saw on the suspect's forehead. But then I thought, supposing the mask wasn't a mask at all, but simply makeup, greasepaint? Who wears the white face? The clown in the circus. Where's the nearest circus? Bright Brothers at Anaheim, here this week. Now, you look at the clown's face, and you realize what that pattern probably was—the painted black eyebrows on the clown's forehead."

Skrolnik examined the poster for a long time, chewing his lips. Then he said, "Okay. . . . But you're talking about a clown who can tear a woman to pieces, limb from limb, and then smash a fully grown, fully trained police officer's head in?"

"You don't buy it?"

"I'm not saying I don't *buy* it. I'm just asking a sensible question."

Pullet reached across and tapped some lettering at the foot of the poster. "There's *one* possible answer."

Skrolnik reached into his breast pocket and took out a pair of hornrimmed spectacles. He perched them self-consciously on the end of his snubby nose, and then peered closely at the poster again. It said: EL KRUSHO, THE

STRONGEST MAN IN AMERICA, SEE HIM BEND IINCH-THICK
STEEL BARS, AS FEATURED IN THE MOVIE *Kung Fu Revenge*.

"El Krusho?" Skrolnik asked, taking off his spectacles.
"I have to go look for a homicide suspect called El Krusho?
How am I going to live it down?"

Pullet shrugged, a little embarrassed. "I know it seems
kind of stupid. But I did some checking with the Screen
Actors' Guild, and a nice lady there told me that El
Krusho is registered with them, and that his real name is
Maurice Needs, and that he comes from Fridley,
Minnesota."

Skrolnik repeated dully, "Fridley, Minnesota? El
Krusho, from Fridley Minnesota? I must be dreaming.
Look, I'm closing my eyes again. Come back into the room
quietly and wake me up, and tell me that I've been
dreaming."

"I'm sorry," said Pullet nasally, a little peeved. "I
know it all sounds peculiar, but you have to admit that it's
a pretty peculiar case. A peculiar case, begging for a
peculiar solution."

Skrolnik sniffed again, stood up, and said, "Why don't
you get some coffee? And bring me a couple of aspirin,
too, while you're at it. I feel like I'm going to have a
terrible headache."

"I think we ought to go down to Anaheim, interview
this guy El Krusho," said Pullet.

Skrolnik stared at him without any expression whatsoever.

"I mean," blustered Pullet, "it does say here that he
can bend inch-thick steel bars, and you remember the
gates at Sherry Cantor's house, the way they were—"

He trailed off. Skrolnik was still staring at him.

"You don't think . . . ?" Pullet began again.

Skrolnik said, "I don't want to belittle your in-
vestigative talents, Detective Pullet. You have true genius
at times. But you mustn't start leaping to conclusions
without sufficient evidence. You've come up with an excellent idea. White greasepaint, clowns, circuses, all that

stuff. It's an idea we're going to have to look into exhaustively. But before we leap into a car and howl down to Anaheim in pursuit of this . . . Maurice Needs . . . well, we're going to have ask *ourselves* a couple of questions, right? Like, how come the strong man is wearing the clown's greasepaint? Like, why would he want to break into Sherry Cantor's house and tear her to pieces? It certainly wasn't for money, nothing was taken. It wasn't a sexual attack, either. It was just *rrrippp*, killing for the sake of it. Dismemberment for the sake of it. So why? Because even if there isn't a reason, there has to be a reason why there isn't a reason. You get me?''

Detective Pullet reached into his coat pocket. ''This is the *pièce de résistance*,'' he said, and laid down on Skrolnik's desk a glossy black-and-white publicity photograph. Skrolnik irritably reached for his glasses again and held the picture up to the light of his desklamp. It showed a young, curly-haired man arm in arm with a hugely built wrestler type. Both of them were grinning at the camera inanely, as if they were slightly high on ganja.

''This curly-headed guy on the left is Mack Holt—Sherry Cantor's ex-boyfriend,'' said Skrolnik slowly.

''And the big muscle bound guy on the right is Maurice Needs, a/k/a El Krusho,'' said Detective Pullet. ''This picture was taken on the set of a movie called *Kung Fu Heroes*, which was the picture that El Krusho made just before *Kung Fu Revenge*. Mack Holt played a young Hell's Angel who appears on the screen just long enough to be smashed to pieces by three crazed exponents of the martial arts.''

Skrolnik sat down again. He stared at the photograph for a little while longer, and then tossed it away across his desk. ''I don't know whether to sing 'God Bless America' or go for a shit,'' he said. ''Forget the coffee. We're going down to Anaheim.''

They spoke very little as they drove through the dusty sunshine toward Anaheim. It was a very hot afternoon, and the Buick's air conditioning was gurgling and spluttering with every bump in the Santa Ana Freeway. Skrolnik said from time to time, as if it were the first time he had ever said it, "El Krusho. Jesus."

Bright Brother Grand Circus had erected its big top just two blocks south of Lincoln Avenue, on Euclid. Detective Pullet parked the Buick next to a filthy truck that had DANGER MAN-EATING LIONS stenciled on the side. "Your middle name isn't Daniel, by any chance?" asked Skrolnik, as he stepped out of the car ankle-deep into a dry sea of popcorn cartons.

It took them nearly a quarter of an hour to find the chief clown. He was a morose, aging man, with a face like a canvas bag full of plumbing tools. He was sitting on the fold-down sofa in his silver Airflow trailer drinking Coor's and watching baseball on a snowy-screened portable TV. His lean body was wrapped up in an aquamarine bathrobe.

"Mr. Cherichetti?" asked Skrolnik, tapping on the open door.

"Who's asking?" demanded the clown.

"Sergeant Skrolnik. Homicide. You got a minute?"

"For what?"

"For questions. Nothing personal. Just a few questions."

Cherichetti sniffed loudly and kept his eyes on the baseball. "I didn't murder anybody, if that's what you're asking."

"Did I say you murdered anybody?"

"You're from Homicide, right? Detectives from Homicide want to find out who murdered whom. Did you get that good grammar? Whom, right?"

Sergeant Skrolnik walked along the aisle in the middle of the trailer and made a show of admiring the Canvas-Tex reproductions of Olde Masters, including the "Monarch of the Glen" by Landseer and Boy'a "Maja Nude." He delicately touched the rim of a blue-and-yellow cut-glass vase with his fingertips. "Nice place you got here, Mr. Cherichetti. Tasteful. Can you tell me where you were at half past seven on the morning of August ninth?"

Cherichetti raised his hooded eyes and looked at Skrolnik with a noticeable lack of clownish humor. "I have to answer that? By law?"

"You don't have to answer anything. It depends whether you want to help me find the guy who tore an innocent young woman into pieces, that's all."

"Sherry Cantor?"

Skrolnik nodded.

"Well, I seen her once or twice, in the flesh," said Cherichetti. "That was before the TV show, you know? Two, three years ago. She used to come to see the circus with Maurice and some other guy."

"Maurice Needs? El Krusho?"

"El Krusho," said Cherichetti with disdain.

Skrolnik raised an eyebrow at Pullet. "Well," he said. "Tell me, Mr. Cherichetti, was there ever any evidence in your eyes that Maurice Needs and Sherry Cantor were more than just friends of the same mutual friend? What I mean is, do you think there was any kind of romance between Maurice Needs and Sherry Cantor? Anything like that?"

"Depends what you call romance," sniffed Cherichetti. "I don't call it romance, everybody getting into the same bed together."

Skrolnik gripped Pullet's wrist. For Christ's sake, he thought to himself, this kid Pullet has a nose for homicide like a hunting dog. Needs and Holt and Sherry Cantor all shared the same bed? What a motive for Needs and Holt to tear the poor girl to pieces. What an incredible 100 percent solid brass *motive. Both* of them were jealous, loverboy and strongman, and when she left *both* of them to rub shoulders with the glittering and the good-looking, both of them plotted to kill her. And how? With the ready-made weapon of El Krusho's invincible and irresistible hands. What a case! What a fucking gold-plated 100 percent amazing *case!*

"Is El Krusho here today?" asked Skrolnik. "I'd really like to talk to him."

Cherichetti shook his head. "He's gone up to Venice to see some girl. He won't be back until tonight's performance, seven o'clock."

"You know *where* in Venice? What kind of car he's driving? Anything like that?"

"He drives a '69 Pontiac, you know, the one with the long pointy hood. Turquoise blue, except for one door, that's beige. The girl lives on Rialto Avenue, pretty girl, he took me around there once to meet her. Her name's Bitzi or Titzi or something like that. Pretty girl."

Detective Pullet said, "Mr. Cherichetti, there's one more thing. Do you happen to have noticed if any of your greasepaint has been missing lately? Any of it been dipped into by somebody else, or maybe stolen?"

Mr. Cherichetti frowned at them. "My slap? Why would anyone want to steal my slap?"

"Well, it could be relevant," said Pullet.

"I don't know," said Cherichetti, slowly shaking his head. "I use so much of the stuff I wouldn't notice."

At that moment, a hefty black-haired woman in a spangled corset and fishnet tights came up the steps of the trailer, patting sweat from her face with a multicolored towel.

"What goes on here?" she asked.

"The police," explained Cherichetti. "They came to see me because they felt like a laugh."

The woman stalked aggressively into the trailer and planted her fists on her spangled hips. "They wasted their time, huh? Nobody gets a laugh from you."

Mr. Cherichetti raised his beercan and said, "This is Josephina, my girlfriend. The most beautiful woman in California, if not the universe."

Skrolnik looked from Josephina to Cherichetti and then back to Josephina again. He gave Cherichetti's shoulder a comforting squeeze. "Good luck," he said. "It looks like you need it. Come on, Pullet, let's go see what the score is in Venice."

CHAPTER FOURTEEN

Jerry Sennett was putting the finishing touches to a homemade pepperoni pizza when the doorbell rang. He dusted the flour off his hands, took a quick swallow of whiskey from the glass beside the pastry board, and then walked through his living room to answer it. It was Mack Holt, in jeans this time, and a T-shirt. He looked hot and agitated.

"Mr. Sennett? Jerry? I'm sorry. I should have called first."

"You saw the news bulletin?"

Mack nodded. "You're right. It's the same mask. The damned same mask! What was that you said about 'a cold wind'? That's like something psychic. Intuition, or something."

"Well, you can call it a hunch, if you want to," said Jerry. "Listen, I've just made a pizza. Do you want to stay and have some? It'll take a little while to bake."

"Pizza? Well, sure. I mean, I don't want to impose on you."

Jerry smiled. "I told you before. I am impervious to imposition. Anyway, my son David's staying with friends this evening out at the beach. He's reached the age when he has a social life of his own, which apparently doesn't include dear old Dad."

No Mom?" asked Mack. It was an innocent question, not prying.

"Mom—my wife, Rhoda—well, she died a few years ago," said Jerry. "Since then I've been trying to bring David up on my own. With varied success, I might tell you. He's cheerful. Ebullient, even. But I sometimes think he lacks the security that a mother could have given him. Do you understand what I mean?"

"I sure do," said Mack. "My parents broke up when I was ten, and I missed my dad like hell. He married some waitress from Albuquerque. Not that I *blame* him, she was half his age and real pretty. I mean, *real* pretty. But, you know, I didn't get any of that friendly cuffing around the head, none of that talk about football and airplanes and cowboys. I used to look at other kids who had two parents, two normal parents, you know, and I used to be so damned *jealous*."

"You're not jealous now, though?" asked Jerry, pouring Mack a drink.

"I don't know. Maybe. Maybe I still envy them their memories."

Jerry sat down on the sofa and crossed his legs, watching Mack with sympathy but also with the perceptiveness of a trained intelligence officer. It was a habit that thirty-eight years had done nothing to erase. Jerry wanted to know things because he had been trained to want to know things. His old instructor had rasped at him, "The intelligence officer who isn't incurably curious isn't worth doodly-squat. Dis-miss!"

Jerry said, "What about Sherry? Did Sherry represent any kind of security for you? Did you ever talk about getting married?"

"We lived together for quite a while," said Mack. "I guess I always assumed that we were going to stay together forever. She was very *warm*, you know. One of these girls you can sit with all evening, and you don't have to say a single word, and you know that you're getting through."

"I think that came over on the TV screen," said Jerry.

Mack swallowed Chivas Regal and shrugged in acknowledgment. "Sure. The trouble was, when everybody else started loving her, I started to feel crowded out."

"You argued?"

"*I* argued. She didn't say anything, just took it, hoping I'd learn to understand. I don't think she really wanted to leave me, but you know what insecure people are like. Forever saying, 'Get out of here, I don't need you,' in the hope that she'll say, 'You may not need me, but I need you.' Classic. She packed and left, and I didn't do anything to stop her. Five minutes later I was banging my head against the wall and wondering why the hell I was so damned stupid.''

Jerry looked across at him carefully. "Did the police question you?"

"Oh, sure. I'm not supposed to leave the city, and I have to rack my brains to think of anyone who might have killed her.''

"Any ideas?"

Mack tugged his fingers through his blond curls and shook his head. "Why did Manson's creepie-crawlies kill Sharon Tate? Why does anybody kill anybody? I don't know. This whole town is nutty. I thought *you* were nutty, until I saw that mask on television.''

Jerry stood up again. He needed to stand up to say what he had to say next. "I *am* nutty," he said. "Well, slightly. I had some bad experiences in Japan during the war, things to do with conscience, and guilt. Things you don't easily forget. You remember Colonel Paul Tibbets, who piloted the *Enola Gay*, the plane that dropped the first atomic bomb on Hiroshima? You remember what happened to him, how he turned into a kelptomaniac, that kind of thing?''

"The same thing happened to you?" asked Mack.

"I used to steal clocks and turn the hands back to 8 A.M. the minute before they dropped the atom bomb, in the hope that it might never have happened. I don't steal clocks anymore, but I still have dreams about it. That morning, we killed 78,150 people at one stroke, in one instant and burned or injured 37,425. Hundreds of people are still suffering for what we did, even today.''

Mack didn't say anything for a while, but then he suggested gently, "We were fighting a war, right? A whole lot more people would have died if we hadn't dropped it."

"You think so? Well, who can say? Yes, you're probably right. My doctor says the same thing. 'You helped to save the lives of countless American troops,' he tells me. 'It was either us, or them.' But that doesn't take away the enormity of what I had to do. That doesn't take away the fact that at one moment in history I was solely responsible for America's decision whether to drop that atomic bomb or not. I've never even told David about it, my own son, I'm so damned *ashamed*.

There was a garlicky smell of baking pizza coming from the kitchen. Mack swallowed a mouthful of whiskey and said, "You picked that mask up in Japan?" It was an obvious attempt to change the subject.

Jerry lifted the mask up from the table. The late-afternoon sun shone brilliantly through its empty eyeholes, giving it a disturbingly triumphant appearance. "You don't believe me?" he asked.

Mack shrugged. "It was Truman who decided to drop the bomb, right?"

Jerry hesitated for a moment, then looked down at his half-empty glass. "Yes, it was Truman who decided to drop the bomb."

Mack looked distinctly uneasy. "Maybe I shouldn't have come."

"Sure, it was Truman who decided to drop the bomb. It was Truman who said go. But Truman wasn't sitting beside me in those mountains by Yuki and Namata, with a high-power receiving set, listening to Japanese intelligence reports from Hiroshima. Truman didn't know whether I was fabricating everything I heard on that radio or not. When I said 'That's it,' Truman said go; but if I *hadn't* said 'That's it,' then Truman would have said forget it. You really believe he was eager to drop that thing? Maybe he was. Who knows?"

Mack finished his drink and put down the glass. "I don't know," he said. "I wasn't even born then."

"Sure," nodded Jerry. "You weren't even born. Well, that lets you out. You can think about Hiroshima with an easy mind."

"Listen," said Mack, "I don't even pretend to understand it. I came here because of the mask; and because of Sherry. I didn't come here for a lecture in moral philosophy, or some kind of psycho confession about World War Two.''

Jerry looked at Mack for a moment, and then nodded. "You're right. I'm sorry. I'm acting my age. I'm out of date. And I'm even more sorry that I'm having to say sorry.''

Mack said, "Okay. Listen, I wasn't very understanding. I never had to serve in the Army, you know? I don't even know what I'm talking about. I'm just as sorry as you are.''

Jerry thought for a while, then emptied his glass and set it down on the table beside him. "You want to talk about the mask?'' he asked Mack.

"Sure. I couldn't believe it when I turned on the television and there it was. The same goddamned mask. I don't think I've ever felt so creepy in my whole goddamned life.''

"You're happy it was the same mask?''

"If happy's the word for it.''

Jerry said, "Come on into the kitchen. That pizza's going to be ready before you know it.''

Mack perched on a stool while Jerry took the pizza out of the oven and fumbled it onto a wire rack to cool. Jerry said, "That white mask is similar to those they use in Nō theater, in Japan. There are two main kinds of traditional theater in Japan—Kabuki, which was the dance theater introduced for commoners at the end of the sixteenth century—and Nō, which was reserved for the aristocracy. There was also, of course, the Bugaku theater, which was performed exclusively for the Japanese royal family, and which wasn't seen by the public from the time it began in the seventh century until the end of World War Two. Can you imagine that? A whole art form which was kept secret for 1,300 years. When you start to think about that, you can start to think about what you're really up against when you're competing with the Japanese. I know, I know, you're thinking about Toyotas and Panasonic televisions and Suntory whiskey. But you're missing the point. Everybody's missing the point.

"Japan is a mystical, rigid, highly formalized society; a society in which magic and occult forces have considerably more strength because they're so widely accepted and believed. Japan is the last great magical society of the modern world; and that magic was only slightly diminished by losing the war to the United States. Oh—they were prepared to accept certain superficial changes, after Hiroshima and Nagasaki. There are times when even the dragon is prepared to surrender to the atomic bomb. But Japan remains, and always will. That extraordinary group of islands has a social and religious history more ancient than Americans can imagine. You know something? The city of Nara, that's about 26 miles south of Kyoto, that used to be the capital of Japan, from the year 710 to 784. Can you imagine that? One thousand years before the Declaration of Independence. And that's where the culture that created this mask, the culture that was responsible for Sherry Cantor's murder—that's where this culture began."

Mack said, "I'm not sure that I understand what you're saying."

Jerry began to slice up the pizza. "I'm not sure what I'm saying, either. No masks may make some kind of sense to *me*, but why should they have anything to do with Sherry? Did Sherry ever visit Japan?"

Mack shook his head. "She never traveled farther than Bloomington, Indiana. That's where her mother lived."

"Did she know any Japanese people? Work in a Japanese restaurant?"

"Not that she told me."

Jerry slid a plate out of the cupboard and handed Mack a steaming slice of pizza. "You want a beer?" he asked.

Mack said, "Sure. A light, if you've got it."

They sat side by side at the kitchen counter, devouring the pizza. Every now and then, Mack would stop to fan his mouth with his hand. "This is terrific pizza. I'm going to have a thousand blisters on the roof of my mouth tomorrow."

Jerry said, "We could be making a really bad mistake. I mean, *I* could. When the witnesses said that the murderer was wearing a white mask, they could have been confused. They were all in passing cars, remember. What they saw was probably nothing more than a glimpse. And the guy could have been wearing anything. A white stocking over his face. White makeup. Maybe he was just naturally pale, like an albino."

"But the police drawings," Mack put in. "They look just like that mask."

"Well, sure they do," agreed Jerry. "But what do we have here? Two eyes, a nose, a mouth; and a white, blank face. Not much to go on."

Mack looked up at Jerry narrowly. "That cold wind that you talked about. You don't feel it anymore? That intuition?"

Jerry toyed with his last triangle of pizza. "I'm not sure. Once you start analyzing it, once you start thinking about it, you lose it. It was in Kyoto once, after the war, walking along Shijo Street on my way to the Fujii Daimaru department store. I stepped off the curb just opposite the Shiro Karasuma station, and I felt that cold wind like ice. I stepped right back onto the curb again, and an Army truck grazed my hip. Just missed me."

Mack said, "You're sure, aren't you?"

"Sure of what?"

"You're sure that the guy who killed Sherry was wearing a Nō mask."

Jerry thought for a moment. "Yes," he nodded, "I'm sure."

Mack picked up his beer, and then put it down again. "Maybe this isn't relevant," he said.

"Maybe what isn't relevant?"

"Well . . . come with me for a second. I just want to show you something."

Jerry hesitated at first, but then he followed Mack out of the house, leaving the door open behind them, and down the sloping concrete driveway to the street. The day was humid and smoggy, and Jerry wiped his face with his hand to clear away the sweat.

Mack stood on the sidewalk and said, "Take a look at this."

Jerry said, "My house number. What of it?"

"No, but you're *used* to it," said Mack. "When *I* first came up here, I didn't know whether number 11 was your house or Sherry's bungalow next door. The party wall, the angle of the driveway. To someone who isn't familiar with the street, and the way the houses are arranged, it looks like *Sherry's* bungalow is number 11."

Jerry narrowed his eyes, and took a pace or two backward. After a while he said, "You know something? You're right."

Mack stared at Jerry through the sweltering heat of the afternoon. "You know what that could mean, don't you? What with the Japanese mask and everything? It would make more sense."

Jerry felt that cold wind again, blowing around the skirts of his soul. "You're trying to tell me that it would make more sense if the killer had made a mistake, mixed up the houses?"

"Sherry didn't know *anything* about Japanese people. Nothing. I don't think she'd even been to Benihana's. All she was interested in was *Our Family Jones*, and being a terrific television star, and that was it. I'm not sure—and I'm not trying to sound like a jealous ex-boyfriend or anything—but I don't think she was even dating anybody. Not seriously."

Jerry looked back at the low stone wall with 11 on it, and then nodded. "You're saying that the killer was after me, and not Sherry? You're saying that *I'm* the one who should've been torn to pieces?"

"It's only a theory."

"Oh, sure. Some theory."

"Listen," said Mack, "I know there are all kinds of holes in it. Like, how did the killer manage to mistake a young woman for a middle-aged man, and why did he kill her even when he knew that he was attacking the wrong person? But . . . you heard what the police said. The guy was crazy. Only a crazy person could rip the legs right off a girl's body, just for the hell of it. And if he was crazy, then maybe he didn't care too much *who* he killed.''

Jerry said, "Let's go back in the house. It's too damned hot out here. And besides, half the blinds in the whole damned street are twitching. They're a nosy bunch up here in Orchid Place. I've been thinking of rechristening it Rubberneck Mountain.''

Back in the kitchen, they finished their pizza and drank their beer in silence. Then Mack took out a packet of papers and rolled himself a cigarette.

"The most important clue to this thing is that Nō mask, isn't it?" he asked Jerry, blowing out smoke.

Jerry wiped beerfoam away from his upper lip. "It could be. I'm not sure. But as far as I know, I'm the only person in this whole street who has ever had anything to do with Japan; and boy, did I have something to do with Japan. It was practically up to me that the whole country got wiped out.''

"You think you ought to tell the police?"

"I don't know. I suppose so. It's just that I haven't worked it out in my own head yet, and I think I need to. If I tell the police about it now, that'll kind of take the onus off my own brain, and maybe I'll miss something important, simply because I don't feel I'm responsible for it anymore. I have to admit it, I've got a lazy mind. Old age, I guess.''

"Do you think somebody found out what you did in the war? One of these Japanese terrorist groups? Maybe that's it. You remember that trouble they had last year at the Japanese Film Festival, all those fanatical rightwing Japanese students threatening to disembowel themselves all over the place?"

Jerry didn't reply, but swilled the last of his beer around in his glass as if he couldn't decide whether he ought to drink it or not.

Mack said, "It wasn't your fault, you know, what

happened to Sherry. Even if it was all a mistake, and the killer was really looking for you. You can't blame yourself.''

Jerry gave Mack a forced smile. "You're just saying that to make me feel better."

"You think so?" said Mack. "I was Sherry's lover. I still am."

Jerry finished his beer, and then said slowly, "That Nō mask, that particular Nō mask, represents the absolute epitome of cruelty. It appears in only one or two traditional plays, and even then it seems to be treated with great ambiguity . . . do you understand? As if the actors themselves can't decide how they ought to react toward it. It's very powerful, very strange . . . as if it's the worst thing the actors could possibly imagine, something they ought to hate and reject, and yet they can't, because it's part of the human condition itself . . . Like, you may detest yourself for being unreasonably angry with somebody at work, or for swearing at somebody who pushes in front of you when you're standing in line, but anger and viciousness are part of what you are, and you can't completely reject them because that means you'd be rejecting part of yourself.''

Mack said, "What do they call it? This Nō character?"

Jerry put down his glass. "It has several names. The most common name comes from the Shinto monks who originally staged the Nō drama-dances; and that name is simply used to describe any monk who has sold his soul to total evil. The Tengu, they call him. The carrion monster. The tearer of hearts and souls."

Mack stood up and went across to the table where the mask lay, empty and emotionless, smiling but unsmiling, death without rhyme or reason. "Whatever the police do," he said hoarsely, "you and me, we've got to find this character, the guy who wore this mask; and we've got to take our own revenge."

Jerry said, "Revenge?"

"What would you call it?" asked Mack.

Jerry shrugged. "Justice? I don't know. No, you're right. Not justice. Revenge."

CHAPTER FIFTEEN

Gerard Crowley was sitting in the sauna on the twenty-third floor of Century Park East reading "It Pays to Increase Your Word Power" in the *Reader's Digest* when the telephone rang. He picked it up, sweating, and said, "Yes?"

"Mr. Crowley? This is Mr. Esmeralda."

"Well, good evening to you, Mr. Esmeralda."

"Not so good *yet*, Mr. Crowley. But, if everything goes well . . ."

Gerard took a breath of lung-scorching air. "You want something done, right? I detect that note of lip-licking anticipation."

"You're a good judge of latent emotion, Mr. Crowley. Yes, I want something done. Can we meet?"

Gerard lifted himself up slightly so that he could see the clock on the gymnasium wall through the sauna window. It was 6:47 P.M., and he was due to take Francesca to The Tower at 7:30 for dinner. He said, "Can't we make it tomorrow? I'm really tied up this evening."

"It's urgent, Mr. Crowley. More urgent than dining out with Francesca Allis."

Gerard wiped sweat away from his mouth with the back of his hand. "All right. I'll manage to cancel. Where do you want to meet?"

Mr. Esmeralda cleared this throat. "Meet me at Inca's, 301 North Berendo Street, at eight."

"Inca's?"

"It's a restaurant. South American."

"Listen, Mr. Esmeralda—"

"What is it?" Mr. Esmeralda's voice was calm and cold.

Gerard let out a short, testy sigh. "I'll see you at Inca's, at eight. That's all."

"Goodbye."

Gerard hung up, reached for his towel, and angrily punched open the door of the sauna. Joseph, the coach, was buffing up the chrome on the barbell when Gerard came stalking through to the changing room and banged open the door of his locker.

"You're getting dressed already, Mr. Crowley? Didn't you take a shower? Your pores are going to be way open, Mr. Crowley, like a Swiss cheese."

"Fuck my pores," snapped Gerard, tugging his shirt on to his damp back. Joseph glanced up at Mr. Corrit, from Corrit Film Productions, who was panting into his eighteenth mile on the Puch exercise cycle, and pulled an utterly perplexed face. How could *anybody* who cared *anything* for modern body-toning say anything like "fuck my pores"? It was a total denial of the fitness ethic.

Back at his desk on the twenty-seventh floor, Gerard tucked his shirt untidily into his belt, and called Francis Canu at The Tower. "Francis, I'm sorry. Your restaurant is beautiful. The best. I'm going to remember the Sunset Room when I'm in heaven. Well, wherever. But some other time, you know? Yes. Yes, I know. Well, me too." Then he called Francesca at her studio apartment at Culver and Elenda. "Francesca? Hi. It's Gerard. Yes. Listen, baby—yes, I know—but I have to tell you that tonight's off. No. No, listen, its not Evie. It's nothing to do with Evie. It's business, you got me? Genuine, legitimate business. Well, look. Will you please listen to what I'm telling you? Yes. I'll come by at eleven o'clock if I'm through by then. I should be, sure. And, listen—" He closed his eyes and listened for almost three minutes to a staccato rattle of complaint. Now and then he nodded and began to say something, but it was only when her anger was completely spent that he was able to say, "I'm sorry. You got that? You want me to spell it for you? And I love you, too, regardless. Yes. Well, you can think what you like. But I'm sorry. And I love you. And if I don't see you later tonight I'll see you tomorrow. Yes. Yes. Goodbye. Yes. Goodbye."

He was sweating afresh by the time he put down the phone. He wished—almost, but not really—that he had told Francesca just what to do with her fancy culinary tastes and her wretched language. But the truth was, he did, in his peculiarly self-destructive way, love her. They were right together, she and he, Gerard and Francesca. Suicidal, maybe, like the lovers in "Life in the Fast Lane," by the Eagles, which Gerard played at top volume on his Delco 8-track as he drove to work every morning. *He was brutally handsome . . . and she was terminally pretty. . . .* But wasn't that where he had always needed to be; wasn't that where he had been *born* to be; speeding along in the fast lane, reckless, crazy, high as a kite? He looked at the color photograph of Evie and the twins next to his telephone, and suddenly he knew that he could never go back; security and marriage and Evie's endless attentiveness were like suffocation and slow death. If he was going to die, then he wanted to die fast. So fast that he would never know what hit him.

On his way out of the office, he caught sight of himself in the screen of tinted glass which surrounded his receptionist's desk. He looked not chiseled, but tired; not brutally handsome, but middle-aged. It had never occurred to him before, not with such uncompromising clarity, that he might simply be growing too old for the kind of life he was trying to lead. He started to light up a cigar in the elevator, but a dignified black cleaning woman pointed wordlessly to the notice: NO SMOKING UNDER PENALTY OF LAW.

He had to wait in line for nearly ten minutes before they brought his car up from the underground parking lot, and he drove out of Century City with a shriek of tires and a bad-tempered blast on his horn. He had a stop to make before meeting Mr. Esmeralda.

Outside Nancy Shiranuka's apartment on Alta Loma, he parked his Buick aggressively between two other cars, colliding bumper-to-bumper with both of them, and then he got out and slammed the door. Kemo was waiting for him when he stepped out of the elevator on the fourth floor, impassively holding the door open. "Welcome, Mr. Crowley, he said. "Miss Shiranuka was not expecting you."

"Hi, Kemo," said Gerard, and gripped the boy's arm as he entered the hallway, so that he could balance himself while he slipped off his Bijan loafers. Nancy was sitting cross-legged on one of the black-and-white silk cushions on the living room floor, her eyes closed, listening to a tape of *koto* music. There was sandlewood smoke in the room, and the fragrance of tea. Kemo said to Gerard, "You wish for a drink, Mr. Crowley?"

"Scotch," Gerard told him. "And none of that Japanese stuff you gave me the last time. McKamikaze, or whatever it was called."

"Yes, Mr. Crowley."

Nancy opened her eyes and looked toward Gerard without turning her head. "This is an unexpected delight," she said blandly.

"I've had another call from Esmeralda," Gerard said, dragging over two or three cushions and sitting down closer to Nancy than Nancy obviously thought was comfortable. "I'm supposed to be meeting him at eight at a restaurant downtown called Inca's."

"Do you know what he wants?" asked Nancy. Her eyes were as dark and as reflective as pools of oil. You could have drowned in her eyes—you could have been swallowed up in their Oriental tranquility, but your feathers would have been slicked forever.

Gerard said, "It sounds like something important. Maybe we're going to have to go out to the ranch again.

Personally, I don't know what the hell's going on, and I don't particularly care. As long as Esmeralda keeps the bank deposits coming, that's all that matters.''

"A man of principle," said Nancy, quietly but acidly.

"That's right," Gerard agreed. "And the principle is that I make as much money as I can and stay alive for as long as possible."

Kemo came in with Gerard's whiskey on a square black-lacquered tray. Gerard took the drink, knocked back half of it, and then said, "one thing, though. It's time we found out who's pulling the strings around here. I mean *really* pulling the strings. If Esmeralda has something particularly important to tell me tonight, and it sounds as if he does, then he's probably going to go straight back to his employers to report that everything's okay, or whatever."

Nancy nodded almost imperceptibly. "You mean to follow him?" she asked.

"Not me, of course. But Kemo could. If he really wants to take Yoshikazu's place, it's time he statrted getting actively involved."

"You don't think that it might be excessively dangerous, trying to check up on our employers?" asked Nancy. "Esmeralda did insist from the very beginning, did he not, that we should do nothing except what he told us to do; and that we should refrain from being too inquisitive? And—let us make no bones about it, Gerard, anyone who can create a Tengu, as these people can . . . well, they are not to be played with."

Gerard said, "Of course it's dangerous. But which is going to be *more* dangerous? That's what we have to ask ourselves. Should we make an attempt to find out who's behind all this—who's giving the orders, who's paying the money? Or should we blindly go on doing all of Esmeralda's dirty work for him, never quite knowing when the police or the FBI or the very people we're working for are going to wipe us out? Just as you said yesterday, my dear, we were all chosen not so much for our individual

talents, however sparkling those might be, but because
we're all of us *dispensable*. Easy to get rid of. Each one of
us has been involved in enough shady little sidelines for
the police not to ask too many embarrassing questions if
we happened to meet with a nasty and unexpected
accident. I used to run guns in Cuba; the commander used
to traffic in children; and God only knows what *you* used
to be mixed up with, but I can guarantee that it was something less respectable than Sunday-school outings.''

Nancy thought carefully for a while, and then stood up,
gracefully slipslopping in silk slippers to the other side of
the room, where she switched off her *koto* music and slid a
bamboo panel across the stereo equipment.

''I have had a feeling for some time now that we do not
know the whole story of what we are doing and why we
have been employed,'' she said.

. ''I've had that feeling from the very beginning,'' said
Gerard. ''But when ten thousand dollars is credited to
your account every single month, on the first, without fail,
then who's arguing?''

''They pay you ten?'' asked Nancy. Her voice was
emotionless. The way she said it, Gerard didn't know
whether she was getting more than him, or less. Nancy
added, ''I wonder where the money is all coming from. I
know they are paying the commander seven thousand a
month, and Esmeralda has promised him a bonus if he
arranges everything to Esmeralda's satisfaction.''

Gerard said, ''Whoever they are, they're obviously
loaded.''

''Don't you think, more loaded than this Tengu project
warrants? Such an investment, such salaries, all for the
sake of bodyguards?''

''Very special bodyguards, so Mr. Esmeralda said. Completely invincible. The kind that a Mafia leader or an Arab
oil millionaire would pay up to a couple of million to have
beside him.''

''Do you think that really rings true?'' asked Nancy.

''Security is big business these days. There are condominium owners on Wilshire who would pay anything you asked for a bodyguard like one of Esmeralda's Tengus.''

''I don't know... . . . I find it difficult to be satisfied by what Esmeralda keeps telling us,'' said Nancy.

''Does it matter?''

''It didn't matter until they sent the Tengu to kill that Sennett man. Now we have two murders on our conscience. That poor actress, and that policeman.''

''On *your* conscience, maybe, but not on mine,'' said Gerard. He finished his whiskey in one throat-burning swallow, and then held up the glass for Kemo to bring him another one. ''Esmeralda said that Sennett used to work in Japan during the war, and that he will guess what the Tengus are all about the minute he hears about them. Gempaku's using some kind of process that isn't strictly in accordance with FDA regulations, you know? Some brand of anabolic steroids to build them up physically, give them muscle. It was either Sennett or us, and that's the hard old story of everyday life and survival. Besides, it gave us a chance to try out the Tengu, didn't it, to see how controllable he was?''

''Not very,'' said Nancy coolly.

''There was a pharmaceutical problem, that's all. Gempaku used too much stimulant, or so he said. The Tengu woke up in the van and blew his mind. It shouldn't happen again.''

''I don't know,'' said Nancy. ''Esmeralda is always full of explanations, but the *motivations* don't seem right. If you want to develop a team of extra-special bodyguards, why use such clandestine methods? And why use the name of an ancient Japanese demon?''

''You're spooking yourself, that's all,'' said Gerard. He watched her as she took out her green-lacquered case and lit a cigarette. ''As long as we appear to do what we're told, and make sure that Esmeralda never catches us napping, we'll come out of this several hundred thousand dollars richer, and still in one piece.''

Nancy blew two streams of smoke out of her nostrils, and then said quietly, "Let me tell you something, Gerard. I don't know whether Mr. Esmeralda is aware of this or not. It may be the whole reason he approached me and asked me to work for him. But when I was much younger, I belonged for several years to a Shinto shrine in Japan known as the Shrine of the Seven Black *Kami*."

Kemo brought Gerard his Scotch, and Gerard took a large mouthful before he said anything. "The Seven Black *Kami*?" he asked. "What are they?"

"In Shinto, every material object—every mountain, tree, lake, every person, every animal—is seen as a symbol of spiritual power. Everything and everyone has its *kami*, its spiritual essense, which is not so much its 'being' as its 'beingness.' There are evil *kami* as well as good *kami*, and the particular oddity of the Shrine of the Seven Black *Kami* was that its priests revered the seven most terrible of all Japan's ancient spirits, the most evil, in the hope that they would suffer in mind and body, and thereby achieve greater spiritual cleansing."

"I see," lied Gerard.

"Of course you don't see," said Nancy. "There is no way that I can explain the Shinto shrines to a Westerner. Shinto priests believe that the body and the mind are manifestations of spiritual power, and that if they starve themselves for weeks on end, or walk hundreds of miles barefoot, or immerse themselves for hours in freezing water, they will bring themselves closer to a state of purity."

"Not much chance of achieving a state of purity at Inca's," said Gerard, checking his watch.

Nancy sucked at her cigarette and then said, "Shrine Shinto came into being at the end of World War Two, after the abolition of State Shinto. There is also Imperial Shinto, which is forbidden to the public, and centered around the ancient rites performed by the Emperor of Japan; Sect Shinto, based on the thirteen sects which worship a high trinity of great and good *kami*—Amaterasu,

Izanagi, and Izanami; and Folk Shinto, the superstitious customs of the people who live in Japan's remotest rural regions. Shrine Shinto, however, is the most ritualistic and the most mystical."

Nancy went on, "It was my uncle who introduced me to the Shrine of the Seven Black *Kami*. Before that, I had always gone to the shrine of Fushimi Inari. But he told me that in conjuring up the demons and devils of old Japan, I would experience my inner self in a way that I had never been able to do before. He said, 'You cannot know total spirituality until you have known utter darkness and despair.' "

"Go on," said Gerard, watching her narrowly.

"I became obsessively involved with the Seven Black *Kami*," said Nancy. Her voice seemed softer and more Japanese-accented than ever. "I went through mental and physical pain such as I had never suffered before and I hope I never suffer again. Whether everything I saw and heard was happening in my mind alone, I shall never know. But I saw demons walking through the streets of Kyoto; real demons such as I can scarcely describe to you. And for night after night I felt myself on the very brink of something I would have to describe to you as hell itself.

"I walked for five miles on shoes that were filled with broken glass. I sat naked in a *karesansui* garden for a day and a night, impaled on a bronze phallus. I learned to talk the language of devils. I have photographs of myself taken when I was seventeen and eighteen years old, and to look at me you would not have thought that I was the same person. You remember the Manson girls? I looked like that."

Gerard said huskily, "What made you give it up?"

Nancy half-smiled at him. "I underwent the greatest of all the mortifications of the spirit and the flesh that a member of the shrine could attempt. I took into my-self—that is, I allowed myself to become possessed—one of the Seven Black *Kami*. Actually *possessed*. The idea was to experience complete evil from the inside; and thereby to conquer it forever."

She was quiet for a moment. Her long, immaculately painted fingernails traced a pattern on the polished wooden floor. Then she said, "It took me six years finally to shrug off that demon, and in the end I only managed it because I was taken in by a wise and knowledgeable old Shinto priest called Shizuota-Tani. He had seen me many times in Kyoto during the six years of my possession, and he had gradually come to understand that what I appeared to be was not my true self. I appeared to be a drug addict, a prostitute, and, indirectly, a murderess."

"A murderess?" asked Gerard. He felt the skin prickling at the back of his back.

"I procured girls for films which, in Japan, we call sacrifice dramas. In Los Angeles they are commonly known as 'snuff movies.' Films in which girls are involved in sexual orgies, and then, at the height of intercourse, are stabbed or strangled right in front of the camera."

Gerard said nothing. The room was as silent as a Japanese rock garden.

Nancy said, "I went through another year in the company of this priest, fighting to find out where, inside myself, my own *kami* had been imprisoned. Then, one night in February, the old priest took me to Nara, the ancient capital, on the evening of the lantern festival at the Kasuga Grand Shrine. I stood in the grounds of the shrine on that evening and saw thousands and thousands of lighted lanterns hanging from the walls and the eaves of the building, bobbing in the wind like the captive souls of happy people. At that moment, without my knowing it, the old priest passed over my head the purification wand, which drives out demons and devils. I fell to the ground as if I had been hit by a truck. They took me to the Kyoto University Hospital, and for three weeks they did not know if I could live. But I survived, and with the help of friends I managed to leave Japan and come here."

"Why are you telling me this?" asked Gerard in a harsh, soft voice. "What does it have to do with Esmeralda?"

"It has everything to do with Esmeralda. The demon which I accepted into myself was Kama Itachi, a kind of weaselike demon which thrives on pain inflicted by knives and blades. There were six other Black *Kami* to which I could have opened myself up: Raiden, the storm demon, for instance, who enters human bodies through the navel, and for fear of whom many Japanese people still sleep on their stomachs during thunderstorms. Kappa, the water demon. Pheng, the bird creature who can eclipse the sun Kami Amaterasu with his wings. Rinjin, the dragon beast, who rejoices in death by fire."

Gerard raised both his hands, a gesture of friendly impatience. "I'm sorry, Nancy, but I'm really not a superstitious guy. I mean, I'm not saying that you didn't experience any of this. I'm not saying that it wasn't as real to you when it happened as anything else you might have experienced. I know how people get when they're on drugs, that kind of thing. But I have to be getting along to see Esmeralda, and I really don't see how this is helping."

Nancy said, very quietly, "The most evil of all the seven Black *Kami* was called the Tengu. Even the most experienced adepts at the shrine were warned opening themselves up to the Tengu. It was said that the leader of the shrine had once done so, and had almost been driven mad. The Tengu had even caused him to bite off his own tongue to prevent him from exorcising the demon, and to curtail his prayers to Amaterasu."

"Nancy, please—" Gerard interrupted.

"*No*," said Nancy. "You must listen to me. The characteristics which the Tengu gave to all the men and women he possessed included invincible physical strength, the mad strength of the berserk; and the ability to stand up to ferocious attack from any kind of weapon. He had another characteristic: if the person he was possessing was chopped into the tiniest pieces, the pieces would regenerate themselves, and grow again into misshapen demons even more hideous than the original. What was more—"

"*Nancy!*" Gerard shouted. "For Christ's sake!"

"*No!*" Nancy hissed back at him. "You have to listen

because it's true! *They've done it*! Don't you understand what I'm saying to you? They're not building up men into bodyguards. They're not using steroids or chemicals or vitamins! They've brought it here, the Tengu, the real Tengu demon!''

She was shaking, and she paced from one side of the room to the other as if she were a madwoman who had been locked up for her own safety. "I didn't believe it at first. I didn't want to believe it. I couldn't! I thought, they are using the name of the Tengu simply because it also means a terrible and powerful being. When Esmeralda said we had to send it out to kill, I had fears enough then. But what happened to that girl, and the way that policeman was smashed to death . . . . That Tengu was no superathlete, no killer bodyguard. Perhaps Esmeralda doesn't even know it himself, but we're helping him to create a race of men who are possessed by the cruelest devil ever known. The Tengu is the devil of remorseless destruction; a god without a conscience and without pity. Those men have him in their souls, and they can *never* get rid of him.''

CHAPTER SIXTEEN

At nine o'clock that evening, Skrolnik and Pullet drew up outside a pink house on Rialto Avenue in Venice, and doused the lights of their car. Across the street, two or three young boys were smoking and playing a guitar and drinking beer. "I could do with a beer myself," growled Skrolnik. "That chili-dog is just about burning me up, from the inside out.''

"I could get you a Pepsi," suggested Pullet.

Skrolnik gave Pullet such a withering look in reply that Pullet found himself coughing, looking through his notebook, folding his arms, and finally saying, "Well, I *offered*."

Skrolnik said, "Okay, you offered. Next time, don't offer. Now, how are we going to tackle this El Krusho character? I have a feeling that if we invite him to accompany us back to headquarters, he's going to decline. You know what I mean? Guys with a fifty-pound advantage usually do. So, we're going to have to catch him by surprise. You go round the back of the house. I'll take the front. At nine-fifteen on the button we'll kick open our respective doors and shout '*Freeze, police*'! You got me?"

"Freeze, police?" asked Pullet.

"For Christ's sake," said Skrolnik.

They climbed out of their car and walked side by side across the sidewalk until they reached the low stone wall which surrounded Casita Rosa. Skrolnik hiked his police .38 out of his belt and cocked it. "Just remember," he said. "This guy is totally dangerous. If it looks like he's going for you, armed or not, open fire. Shoot to kill."

"What should I do if it looks like he's going for *you*?"

"Stand by idly and watch him grind me into a Wendy's hamburger," said Skrolnik sarcastically. "What the hell do you think?"

Pullet went around to the back, climbing uncertainly over a wrought-iron fence, while Skrolnik went to the front door, his revolver raised in his right hand, and tentatively rang the bell. There was a long silence, punctuated only by the lonely nighttime sound of a patrol car as it howled its way along Mildred Avenue, answering a call to a supermarket robbery. Skrolnik glanced up at the building and thought for a moment that he could see someone looking down into the street from the third floor, a girl's face. He leaned forward and pressed the bell again.

It was 9:11. If Skrolnik didn't get into the building now, right away, Detective Pullet would inevitably go leaping into the suspect's room, legs bent, revolver held in both hands in the approved Los Angeles Police Academy style, and get the holy shit beaten out of him. Skrolnik yelled, "Somebody open this goddamned door!" but after a whole minute of waiting, nobody did.

Skrolnik propped his back against one of the wooden pillars of the porch, lifted his left leg, and kicked against the lock. There was a loud bang, Kinney town shoe against solid oak, but the door didn't give one fraction of an inch. Skrolnik took a deep breath and kicked again. Nothing. The door was so damned thick that it wouldn't budge.

At that moment, however, there was a clicking noise, like a catch being released, and the door suddenly swung open. An elderly lady in a blue nylon scarf and a blue bathrobe stood there, blinking at Sergeant Skrolnik through bifocals.

"You don't have to *knock*, you know," she told him. She reached across and pointed to the bell. "You can always . . . you know . . . ding-a-ling-a-ling!"

Skrolnik flipped open his badge wallet. "Madam," he said. "I have reason to believe that there may be a dangerous criminal in this building."

"I'm eighty-three years old," the woman said, with a note of triumph.

"That's terrific," Sergeant Skrolnik told her. "Eighty-three! You don't look a day over sixty!"

"Well, you're very flattering," the old lady smiled. Skrolnik checked his watch; it was 9:14.

"Lady," he said, "in one minute flat my partner's going to come busting into the house from the rear, and I've got to be up there to give him some backup. So, will you please . . . ?"

The old lady clutched Skrolnik's sleeve. "Do you know something?" she said. "You remind me so much of my grandson—a fine, well-built fellow, just like you."

"Lady—" said Skrolnik, gently but firmly clutching her wrist and prising her away from him. But it was too late. There was the flat sound of a handgun shot from upstairs, then a scream, a girl's scream, and a door banging open so hard that plaster showered down the stairwell. Skrolnik threw himself against the wall, his .38 raised toward the stairs, his eyes wide.

"Pullet!" he shouted. "Pullet, what the fuck's going on?"

The next instant, a huge man came thundering down the stairs with a noise like an approaching avalanche. Skrolnik shrieked, "Freeze! Police!" but the huge man collided with him as he fired his first shot, and the bullet zonked harmlessly into the plaster.

Skrolnik, however, was a streetfighter, and not so easily put off by one simple dead-end football block. He made a grab for the big man's arm as he galloped for the front door, missed, but ran two steps, jumped, and clung onto the big man's shoulders.

There was a grunting struggle. The big man's hand pushed straight into Skrolnik's face, squashing his nose. Skrolnik punched him in the kidneys, once, twice, three times, and then in the side of the ear. They both toppled and fell over, while the old lady in the blue bathrobe had gone off to fetch a spiky-haired toilet brush, and now was hitting them both violently on the back and the legs.

Skrolnik jerked up the huge man's head and succeeded to getting a wristlock onto his throat, as well as a good firm handful of hair. He banged the head on the green linoleum floor to stun him, and followed that up with another punch in the ear. Then he painfully climbed off, and scrabbled around for his hat, and his glasses, and his .38. He found his gun on the other side of the hallway, wedged behind a cheap Chinese vase with a chipped rim. He picked the gun up, cocked it again, and walked over to the huge man lying half-conscious.

"You have the right to remain silent," he panted. "But you are advised that anything you say can and will be used against you in a court of law."

The huge man lifted his head and saw the muzzle of Skrolnik's revolver pointing at his nose. "All right," he said. "All right."

Skrolnik tugged his handcuffs out and locked the huge man's ankle to the bottom of the newel post. Then he quickly climbed the stairs, calling, "Pullet? Pullet, are you okay?"

The old lady shrilled out, "You can't leave this monster here! Not in my hallway!" and she slapped at the huge man with her toilet brush.

"For Christ's sake," the man complained. "I've surrendered!"

At that moment, one of the doors across the landing opened. Detective Pullet appeared, blushing. Behind him, inside the bedroom, Sktolnik glimpsed somebody bending over, and he pushed past Pullet's foolish grin and threw the door wide. "All right," he demanded. "What goes on here?"

The room was decorated with rose-covered wallpaper, and over the wide bed was a 3-D picture of Jesus the Savior, sad but forgiving, his hand raised, surrounded by a glittering gold chorus of 3-D cherubs. A young girl with very short-cropped blonde hair was sitting on the end of the bed, rolling on a pair of sheer black stockings. Apart from her stockings and a black garter belt, she was naked, small-breasted, suntanned, and Teutonically pretty. A Rhine maiden in shiny nylon.

"Is that your boyfriend, that man-mountain we've got downstairs?" asked Skrolnik. He watched impassively as the girl fastened her stockings and then reached for a sheer black bra. It is a good thing I'm a reliable family man, Skrolnik thought. Because, by God, if I weren't a reliable family man. . . .

"He hasn't *done* anything, has he?" the girl asked, in a snappy East coast accent. "He hasn't broken the *law* or anything?"

"What do you think?" asked Skrolnik. "You probably know him better than we do."

"He's a *real* gentle guy," the girl said. "Most of my girlfriends call him the Gentle Giant."

"Ever known him aggressive? Mad, for any reason? Drunk, maybe?"

The girl reached for a short black dress with a white Peter Pan collar. "Sometimes he gets sore about the whales."

"The whales?"

"You know, the whale-killing, Save the Whale. He hates the Japanese for what they're doing to the whales. And the Russians, he *hates* the Russians. I swear, if he ever saw a Russian, he'd tear him to *pieces*."

Skrolnik nodded. "I see. Is that what he does to people when he's mad at them, tears them to pieces?"

"Oh, sure. I mean, he'd tear *anybody* to pieces."

Detective Pullet was standing by the door with his notebook. Skrolnik turned around and gave him a jaundiced look. "What are you doing, detective? Taking down evidence, or sketching? You heard what the girl said. When he gets mad, he tears people to pieces."

Detective Pullet said, "Oh, sure," and jotted a few notes.

Sergeant Skrolnik looked around the bedroom. "This your room, miss?"

"It's my friend's room. But she lets me use it when I meet Maurice."

"Can you tell me your name please?"

"Oh, sure. Beverly Krauss, Bitzi for short. I live at 1803 Taft Avenue, with my parents. Walter C. Krauss, Consultant Pediatrician."

"Sure. I see. Have you known Maurice long?"

Beverly Krauss shrugged. "I guess a year, almost. Ten months. Maybe longer. I met him at the circus last spring. His circus name is El Krusho the Great."

"Sure. El Krusho."

"You've been lovers all that time?"

Beverly nodded. "Could you do me up, please? This catch is kind of fiddly."

Detective Pullet stepped smartly forward, but Sergeant Skrolnik gave him a sharp stare which sent him smartly back again. Skrolnik fumbled at the back of Beverly Krauss's dress with his fat, insensitive fingers, and at last managed to nudge the hook through the eye.

"Did you ever hear Maurice talk about any of his previous girlfriends?" asked Skrolnik.

Beverly frowned at him. "Sure. I talked about *my* old flames, he talked about *his*. What's he supposed to have done wrong?"

"Just bear with me for one moment," said Skrolnik, as reassuringly as he could. "Did Maurice ever mention a girl named Sherry Cantor?"

"Well, sure. I knew Sherry Cantor. I mean, I met her once or twice. Maurice said that he'd always had a kind of a crush on her. That was, until he met me."

Skrolnik sniffed dryly. "Did Maurice ever mention to you that Sherry Cantor and he and another man had all gone to bed together, a threesome?"

Beverly shook her head. "He never told me anything like that."

"Did Maurice ever say that he was sorry because he wasn't seeing Sherry Cantor any longer?"

"Un-unh."

"Did Maurice ever say that he disliked Sherry Cantor for any reason? Did he ever say anything about her? Anything at all?"

"Once," she said.

Skrolnik glanced at Pullet. "Can you remember what he said? This could be very important."

"Well," Beverly hesitated, "I don't really know if it's *relevant* or anything. We were sitting watching *Our Family Jones* because nothing else was on . . . and she came on the screen, Sherry I mean, and he said it. He was pretty drunk at the time."

"What did he say?" insisted Skrolnik.

"He said, 'I don't know why *she's* acting so pure and innocent, I gave it to her up her ass once.' "

Sergeant Skrolnik lowered his head and took a deep breath. "Miss Krauss," he said, "how old are you?"

"Seventeen, and a week."

"Seventeen and a week," Skrolnik repeated sadly. He wiped his forehead with the back of his hand. It was a warm night, warm and close, and there was no air conditioning in the room. "Well," he said, "I'll call a patrol car and have you taken back to . . . Taft Avenue. Meanwhile, I'm afraid we're going to have to take your boyfriend in."

"Take him in? You mean, arrest him?"

Skrolnik nodded.

"But for *what*—I mean, *why*?"

"Homicide, Miss Krauss. The first-degree murder of Sherry Cantor."

"Are you joking? Maurice could never even—"

"Swat a fly?" said Skrolnik. "Is that what you were going to say? The man who tears people to pieces when he's angry? He could never even swat a fly?"

"But that was only a figure of *speech*," protested Beverly. "I didn't mean he actually *does* it!"

"No, sure," said Skrolnik. "Pullet, will you call up the local cavalry and ask them, nicely, if they could take Miss Seventeen-and-a-Week here home to her folks?"

"But you *can't* arrest Maurice!" cried Beverly. "He hasn't done anything! He never killed anybody!"

Pullet said, "Just watch us."

Skrolnik made a quick check of the bedroom, opening drawers, opening the wardrobe, checking the lipstick and the makeup on the cheap varnished dressing table. He opened one drawer and produced, between two fingers, a white satin G-string.

"Well, what do *you* do to prevent embarrassing panty lines?" Beverly demanded.

Skrolnik grunted. "Seventeen and a week, huh?" he said. He took one last look at the room, and then he went downstairs to the hallway, where Maurice Needs was still lying on the floor, his ankle handcuffed to the newel post. The elderly lady in the blue scarf was standing nearby, sucking nervously at her dentures.

"All right, El Krusho," said Skrolnik. "I'm going to release you now, and I want you to come peacefully with me to the police precinct, where you will have the opportunity to call your lawyer. You understand me?"

Maurice Needs nodded. He was very big—bigger than Skrolnik had imagined he would be, from his photograph. Six foot six, at least, and built like Arnold Schwarzenegger's older brother, all trapezoids and deltoids and overdeveloped triceps. He had dark curly hair, and he was dressed in jeans and a slim-fitting black shirt that probably would have flapped around Skrolnik like a bedouin tent.

Maurice Needs painfully stood up. There was a large red bruise on his forehead, and he had the beginnings of a black eye; but he was a good-looking boy, a mixture of Clark Kent and a young Elvis Presley, with a hint of Clint Walker around the eyes. He hopped a little, and then bent over to massage his ankle.

"Sorry I hurt you," said Skrolnik. "Had to keep you tied down somehow."

El Krusho shrugged. "You needn't have bothered, you know? If I'd wanted to, I'd have torn that newel post out by the roots."

Pullet, coming down the stairs, gave Skrolnik a sick little smile. "Seems we've got our man, sergeant."

Skrolnik said, "Let's go. We can talk about this down at the precinct."

Pullet frowned, and began to say, "You don't think that—?"

"I've charged him now, fuckhead," snarled Skrolnik. "But, no, I don't."

CHAPTER SEVENTEEN

Over Inca's *aji de gallina* and *anticuchos*, Mr. Esmeralda carefully explained to Gerard Crowley about Admiral Thorson.

"He was in Japan during the war, and became very friendly with some of the doctors who later worked on the Tengu program for the Tokyo Olympics. He found out about the research simply by accident. He may suspect nothing, but we cannot risk him blowing the whistle on us."

"What I really want to know is this," Gerard said. "When do we stop killing people, and when do we start getting on with building up this team of bodyguards?"

"We have to take everything by orderly steps," said Mr. Esmeralda. He forked up some of his barbecued beef and chewed it assiduously.

"Nancy Shiranuka is getting distinctly restless," Gerard remarked. "She doesn't like this killing any more than I do. If you were intending to create a hit squad of homicidal maniacs, you should have told us. At least we would have known what we were letting ourselves in for. I'm no angel, Esmeralda, and neither is Nancy Shiranuka; and we all know about the good Commander Ouvarov. But the only reason any of us agreed to submit to your rotten blackmail was because we thought we were in on a shady but highly profitable bit of merchandising. Hired thugs for the protection of the wealthy. *Now* what's happened? We've taken an innocent young actress to pieces, as well as a cop, for no reason at all; and two days later you're asking me to take a Tengu out to Rancho Encino Hospital and rip some poor old retired admiral to shreds."

Mr. Esmeralda pushed his plate away, then changed his mind and drew it back again, so that he could fork up a last piece of beef. He kept his eyes on his food and spoke to Gerard lightly, almost absent-mindedly.

"The very first day I approached you, Mr. Crowley, I warned you that you had very little option but to do as you were told. I also warned you not to question my instructions."

"Maybe you did. But now I'm questioning."

"My clients will not be happy about that," smiled Mr. Esmeralda. "They're very particular people when it comes to secrecy and security."

Gerard snapped his fingers at the waiter and said, "Scotch." Then he folded his arms and leaned forward across the table. "Death comes at a pretty high price in California, Mr. Esmeralda, and I'm beginning to think that perhaps you're not paying enough for it."

"You know what your reward will be when the Tengu program is completed."

"A million six? I'm beginning to wonder whether it's worth it. I'm also beginning to wonder if you've really been giving me the whole picture about these so-called bodyguards."

Mr. Esmeralda watched Gerard carefully. "It does not pay, in your business, Mr. Crowley, to be too curious."

"Is that a statement or a warning?"

"What do you think?"

"I think it sounds like a warning, Mr. Esmeralda, and I also think that I'm beginning to get a hook into you the same way you've got a hook into me. There's such a thing as plea bargaining, you know; and if I were to make a clean breast of everything I happen to know about Sherry Cantor's death to the police . . . well, there's a good chance that I wouldn't get more than one-to-three."

"You are not deceiving me for one instant, Mr. Crowley." Mr. Esmeralda smiled. "Go out to the ranch tomorrow with Kemo and pick up the Tengu. Doctor Gempaku will be waiting for you. Oh—and by the way, we are expecting a new consignment of volunteers on Monday from Kyoto. I will let you know the details tomorrow morning. Fifteen of them. So you can see that the bodyguard program *is* actually getting under way."

"I think I'm dreaming this," said Gerard.

"No," said Mr. Esmeralda, and nodded to the waiter as his dessert—*plátanos fritos*—was set in front of him. "It's not a dream. It's simply a manifestation of the peculiar violence inherent in modern living. The world is in imbalance, Mr. Crowley, between those who have and those who want; and the greater the imbalance, the more violent the confrontation between the two. The people who have the most will always be the prime targets for the people who have the least; and that is why they will pay anything for one of our Tengus. The ultimate weapon is personal security—that is how we are going to advertise them."

Gerard swilled his Scotch around in his glass. "I don't believe you, Mr. Esmeralda. Something's happening here. Some really big caper that you're not telling me about. And, you take notice, sooner or later I'm going to find out what it is."

"I have already taken that into account," said Mr. Esmeralda, thinking of Evie—drunk, in her underwear.

"Well, you take notice," Gerard repeated. "I'm on to you, and if you start pushing me too hard, you're going to regret it. I suspected you from the start. This Tengu thing—if it's such a big secret, why did you tell me so much about it, right from the beginning? This killer-bodyguard story—it's just that, a story. If that was all there was to it, you wouldn't have told me anything about it. But you've told me everything. You've answered every question I might have had about it, even before I've asked them. And that smells to me like a decoy."

"You are drunk," said Mr. Esmeralda. "Why don't you go away now, nurse your hangover, and think about it again in the morning?"

"Oh, don't worry," said Gerard. "I'll do what you want me to do. I'll take out this Thorson character. I'll take him out like a dream. That's always provided the Tengu behaves himself, and goes to the correct address. But take notice that I'm on to you, Mr. Esmeralda. Too much pushing from you, and it's plea-bargain time."

Mr. Esmeralda glanced around the restaurant to make sure that nobody was listening. "You've talked to Nancy?"

Gerard nodded. "Nancy is an interesting lady. More interesting than I first understood."

"Beware of Nancy Shiranuka," said Mr. Esmeralda. "Nancy Shiranuka is by no means everything she appears to be." Mr. Esmeralda ate some of his fried bananas in silence. Then he said, "Mr. Crowley, have you ever heard of a Japanese demon called Kappa?"

"You're the second person who's talked to me about Japanese demons tonight."

"Nancy Shiranuka mentioned them?"

"Nancy Shiranuka's an expert, as far as I can gather. And, yes, she did mention a demon called Kappa. Some kind of water demon, isn't it?"

Mr. Esmeralda nodded. "A small, hideous creature with the limbs of a variety of different creatures, like lobsters and rabbits, all mixed up. A huge, saucer-shaped head. I looked it up in the Huntington Library."

"Why did you do that, Mr. Esmeralda?"

Mr. Esmeralda put down his spoon and laced his fingers together. The band in the restaurant was playing "Samba Pa Ti." "No particular reason. The Tengu, as you know, is named after a Japanese devil. I suppose I was just curious."

"I thought you said that curiosity didn't pay in this business, Mr. Esmeralda."

"Maybe. It depends on the circumstances. But the Kappa is a particularly interesting demon because it has one fundamental weakness."

"What's that, Mr. Esmeralda?" Gerard took out a cigar and clipped the end off it, watching Mr. Esmeralda all the time.

"In its saucer-shaped head, the Kappa keeps a quantity of water, magical water which gives it its strength. The way to defeat the Kappa is to approach it without fear, bow to it, and say, 'Good morning.' In accordance with Japanese custom, it will bow in return, and it will spill the water out of the top of its head, thereby weakening itself so much that you can pass by unscathed."

Gerard's expression was concealed for a moment behind curls of blue cigar smoke. Then he spat out a fragment of leaf and said, "What are you trying to tell me, Mr. Esmeralda?"

"I am giving you a chance to save yourself," said Mr. Esmeralda. "I am telling you that the way in which you can survive in this particular adventure is to remain calm and polite, and to observe all the necessary courtesies."

"In other words?"

Mr. Esmeralda raised a single warning finger. "In other words, Mr. Crowley, you are in danger of your life, and you ought to be aware of it."

Gerard thought about that, and then crossed his legs and sniffed. "What are those bananas like?" he asked Mr. Esmeralda.

CHAPTER EIGHTEEN

When Mr. Esmeralda left Inca's restaurant at 11:17 P.M., a little over a half-hour after Gerard Crowley's departure, he was watched intently from the shadows of Inca's parking lot by Nancy Shiranuka's houseboy, Kemo. Kemo had been sitting patiently in his red-striped Toyota for almost three hours, smoking menthol cigarettes and listening to a tape of Stomo Yamashta. As soon as Mr. Esmeralda appeared, white-suited, his hair shining in the neon light of a Los Angeles night, Kemo started up his engine and crushed out his latest cigarette.

Mr. Esmeralda's metallic-blue Lincoln appeared from

the darkness on the other side of the parking lot, with Kuan-yin at the wheel, and Mr. Esmeralda climbed quickly in. The Lincoln then swerved north on Berendo, with a squeal of tires, and ran two red lights on its way to Beverly Boulevard. Kemo, alert and sweating, took a fast right at 3rd Street, then a left at White House Place, and managed to end up only two cars behind the Lincoln as it turned west on Beverly Boulevard and cruised through the Wilshire Country Club toward Highland Avenue.

Only one car apart, the Lincoln and the Toyota sped north to Laurel Canyon. Kemo was tense and sweating as he drove, although the Toyota's air conditioning was set to cold, and whenever he was forced to slow down, his fingers drummed impatiently on the wheel.

Follow him closely, Nancy Shiranuka had ordered Kemo. *Follow him and don't let him go.*

At last, unexpectedly, just past Lookout Mountain Avenue, the Lincoln screeched off to the right without making a signal. Kemo, who was being tailgated by an impatient procession of home-going valley-dwellers, was forced to drive on for another few hundred yards and make a right at Willow Glen. He parked his Toyota close to the side of the road and climbed out, looking nervously from right to left to make sure nobody had seen him. But why should anyone have seen him? he asked himself. He was nothing more than one more pair of headlights in a night bustling with headlights. He wished he could suppress the fear which kept rising inside him; the feeling that death was very close at hand.

Running silently on rope-soled slippers, Kemo went back down Laurel as far as the driveway where the Lincoln had turned off. There were no signs there, no house numbers; only a mailbox with its flap hanging down and an overgrown hedge of bougainvillea. Kemo squinted up through the trees and saw a large wooden house in which two or three lights were shining. He also glimpsed, for an instant, the Lincoln's taillights, before Kuan-yin switched them off. He glanced back up the road to make sure that nobody had been following him; and then, momentarily concealed by the darkness between two passing cars, he rolled over sideways into the shrubbery.

It took him nearly a quarter of an hour to get close to the side of the house. He crept through roots and foilage as silently and unobtrusively as a lizard. He noted each of the television cameras as they emotionlessly inspected the driveway and the surrounding bushes; and he also noted Mr. Esmeralda's Chinese driver, waiting in his Lincoln limousine. She was listening to Barry Manilow on the radio.

At last, he reached the concrete pilings on the south side of the house, well hidden in darkness, and he lay there panting quietly for a minute or two before he went on. Then he skirted around the house to the back, where a wide patio had been cantilevered out of the side of the canyon, with huge terra-cotta pots on either side, and where a silent fountain collected leaves and lichen. He ran and tumbled from one side of the patio to the other, until he reached the corner of the house. Kemo was an adept in judo and in the specialized art of *Noma-oi*, the "wild horses," in which an opponent was overwhelmed by a barrage of blows so fast and violent that he looked afterward as if he had been run down by a herd of horses. Kemo was silent and quick and strong. He had killed a sailor once, in a bar on Fisherman's Wharf in San Francisco, with a flurry of blows that nobody else in the bar had even seen. But Nancy Shiranuka had chosen him more because he was quiet and self-controlled, and because he could cook exquisitely, and because he had disciplined himself to make love for hours and hours on end without reaching a climax. With Kemo, Nancy had reached what she described as "the state of the angels."

Kemo waited at the back of the house on Laurel Canyon for almost ten minutes. Then, silently, he shinned up the drainpipe to the guttering that surrounded the first-floor balcony, and swung himself over the cedar railings. The wide sliding doors to the back bedroom were open a quarter of an inch, and Kemo slipped his fingers into the crevice and slid them back just enough to allow him to slip inside. The bedroom was bare, no drapes and no furnishings, only a *futon* on the floor for someone to sleep on. There was a smell of candles and incense—a smell that reminded Kemo of Japanese shrines—and something else. A bitter aroma of death. Kemo waited, motionless. His hearing was so acute that he could detect the suppressed sound of someone holding his breath. He decided that it was safe for him to move quickly forward to the bedroom door.

With infinite care and in utter silence, he opened the door and stepped out onto the landing. From here, he could see down into the hallway where Mr. Esmeralda had waited only the day before. Mr. Esmeralda was there again now, his hands in his pockets, sweating in the light of the candles which flickered along the side of every wall. Kemo stared down at Mr. Esmeralda, then slipped silently along the landing to the stairs, keeping himself well back against the wall.

It took Kemo nearly five minutes to descend the staircase in total silence. He tested every one of the cedar treads before he put his weight on it, and then he stepped down so gradually and with such care that not even the molecules in the wood were disturbed. Mr. Esmeralda was still waiting impatiently in the hall, but Kemo passed him by, only eight or nine feet away, treading as silently and swiftly as a draft. Mr. Esmeralda was not even conscious of his passage. It was a *Noma-oi* technique known as "unseen shadows."

Kemo found himself in a long corridor. To his left was the kitchen: he could detect the smell of *Butaniku to Harusame no Sunomono*, chilled pork with noodles. He could also hear the sound of knives slicing through fish and vegetables; and that meant to him that a Japanese of importance was staying here, a Japanese who could afford two or three personal cooks. He paused for a moment, and then padded silently to the end of the corridor, where there was a door marked with Japanese characters. They were in the old language, but he read them quickly: A SANCTUARY FORBIDDEN TO NONBELIEVERS.

Carefully, Kemo pressed his head against the door, to pick up the vocal vibrations of whoever might be talking in the room beyond. He closed his eyes in concentration, but there was utter silence. Either the room beyond was empty, or those who were in it were silent. Nancy Shiranuka had said, *Find out where he goes, who it is that he sees*. The decision to enter the room or not was not his. He had been told that he must.

Using the *Noma-oi* movement called "the September breeze," Kemo swiftly turned the door handle and opened the door. He paused in the doorway, in a combative stance, but the room was deserted. Three or four cushions, a bird painting on the wall, rows of candles, but nothing else. He crossed the room to the next doorway, his feet as light as a butterfly landing on a leaf, his body as well coordinated as *ikebana*, the arranging of flowers, each muscle tense and disciplined, each nerve sensitive to the dangers of the house.

On the second door was a plaque of iron, engraved with characters which Kemo had never seen before. As far as he could tell, the characters meant "drowning" or "beware of overwhelming water." He touched the plaque with his fingertips, as if to reassure himself. Then he pressed his forehead to the door and closed his eyes, trying to gather voices or breathing, trying to detect the rustle of robes or slippers.

There was somebody in there. Somebody breathing, deeply and noisily. It sounded to Kemo like an invalid, somebody suffering from asthma or a chest infection. He listened again, picking up every single sound and vibration that he could, and after two or three minutes he was sure. There was a sick man in there, but the sick man was probably alone.

Soundlessly, Kemo opened the second door and stepped inside. The inner room was illuminated by hundreds of candles, so many that it was almost impossible to breathe. Kemo dodged to the left and kept close to the wall, touching the door closed behind him with his fingertips, *touch*, silently and gently.

Then he froze, listening, watching, his body rigid as *kokeshi*, the Japanese folk dolls made without arms or legs. All he could hear was the sizzle of the candles as the wicks burned into the wax, and the regular pounding of his own heart.

A voice said, "Who are you? Who let you in?"

Kemo shielded his eyes against the dancing brilliance of the candles. He took one step forward, then another; and gradually he was able to focus on the creature that had spoken to him.

He had been ready to speak: ready to give some spurious explanation about working for Mr. Esmeralda and losing his way. But when he saw the monster in the basketwork throne, the words tangled in his mouth and he was unable to speak at all. And there was that *face*: that yellow-masked face. Unemotional, half-smiling, cruel as death.

There was a moment for Kemo when he felt as if the whole world had tipped off its axis, as if everything were coming to and end. He turned away from the creature in the basketwork throne and stared at the candles as if they could at least offer him sanity. But then the door swung open again, and there was three of them there, black-masked, cloaked in yellow, each of them posed in the martial discipline known as *Oni*, the art of the devils. *Oni* had been forbidden in Japan since the fourteenth century, but Kemo knew it from drawings and paintings. He also knew that its one purpose was to dismember and kill. In *Oni*, death was the only possible outcome.

Kemo wasted no time. He jumped at his three opponents with his hands whirling in the *Noma-oi* "windmill of oblivion." He struck one of his opponents on the neck, his hands blizzarding at 70 or 80 miles per hour, and the man spun away as violently as if he had been hit by an automobile. Then Kemo leaped aside and changed the rhythm of his attack to "the corn-beater," a slower, irregular pattern of hand-fighting which was impossible for any opponent to predict.

The second man went down, whirling to one side as if he had been caught by an exploding grenade. But Kemo was not fast enough for three. The third man, his eyes glittering behind his black silk mask, lashed out with his heel and sent Kemo reeling back against the wall with three ribs broken and two badly cracked.

Kemo heard a high-pitched shriek, almost a cackling sound, from the basketwork throne. Then the third man was on him, in a style of attack for which Kemo could find no defense. A swift lunge with two outstretched fingers rammed into Kemo's eyeballs and burst them both. A fist speeding upward penetrated his abdominal muscles, parted his lungs while they were still breathing, and wrenched his heart away from its moorings in a blast of blood. By the time the third blow hit him, a knuckle-punch which was designed to pulverize the frontal lobes of his brain, Kemo was already dead and collapsing on his feet. The *Oni* adept had killed him in less than three seconds: the same kind of death that Gerard had thought about only a few hours before. So fast that he never knew what hit him.

Mr. Esmeralda came into the room, staring, aghast. He looked down at Kemo's mutilated body, then at Kappa, then at the last remaining *Oni* guard. He started to say something, but then he simply shook his head and stood there in silence.

"You were followed," said Kappa in a hoarse whisper.

"I didn't know," said Mr. Esmeralda. "Believe me, I didn't know."

"You were followed," repeated Kappa. He made the words a chilling indictment.

"Yes," said Mr. Esmeralda. Then, almost inaudibly, "Yes."

CHAPTER NINETEEN

Eva was very drunk when Gerard let himself into their apartment at three o'clock the following morning, turned on all the lights, and began packing a suitcase. She was crouched on the white leather sofa, a bottle of Polish vodka three-quarters empty by her feet. She was wrapped up in one of Gerard's bathrobes, and she looked like the rescued victim of a hotel fire.

"Where are the girls?" Gerard asked her as he walked through the living room to find his cigar case. "Or are you so damned sloshed that you never even noticed they aren't here?"

"They called," said Eva in a blurry voice. "Melanie Radnick invited them to spend the weekend riding."

"Do we know anyone called Melanie Radnick?"

Eva lifted her head and tried to focus on him, but the glaring lights hurt her eyes. "Melanie Radnick is Kelly's best friend. They've been friends for—I don't know, ever since Kelly started going to Seven Hills. The Radnicks have a ranch at La Crescenta."

"That's nice for the Radnicks."

Eva tensely rubbed the side of her face, as if she wanted to reassure herself that she was still real. "George Radnick works in gas, or something like that. Don't you remember him? We met him at the Devoes' anniversary party."

Gerard counted the cigars in his case, and then closed it. "Evie," he said, "go take a shower and sober up. You're a fucking mess."

He walked through to the bedroom again, opening drawers and taking out underwear and handkerchiefs and socks. He finished packing his suitcase neatly and quickly, and then clicked it shut.

Eva was leaning in the doorway now, a smeary vodka glass dangling from one hand, her mascara blotting her eyes like ink on a sentimental letter. She watched him open the glass jar on top of the dressing table, the Steuben

duck that had been given to them by the California
Republicans for the work and the money they had put into
the election of President Reagan, and with conscientious
pain she watched him take out his cufflinks. She said,
"You're leaving me, is that it? You're going off with
her?"

"I should be so lucky," said Gerard sourly.

"Then what? What are you doing? What are you
packing for?"

Gerard said, "I have to go away for the weekend.
Business, that's all. Nothing important. Nothing exciting.
Just business."

"You're taking Francesca?"

"Does it matter if I am? Look at the condition you're
in."

"I don't want you to come back," said Eva. "Just stay
away. The girls and I can survive very well without you."

"You think so?" asked Gerard, absent-mindedly.
"Now, where the hell did I leave my keys?"

"Gerard," insisted Eva.

Gerard pecked her on the cheek as he walked through
the door. "You're a wonderful woman, Evie."

She lost her balance, and snatched at the door frame to
straighten herself up. "I'm in love," she said loudly. "Do
you know that? I'm in love with another man. Not you.
Somebody else. And he loves me too."

"Well, that's good news," said Gerard, taking his coat
out of the hall closet. "Good news for *you*, I mean. Not
for him."

"Gerard—"

Gerard put down his coat and his suitcase, and came
over to Eva and held her shoulders in his hands. She
noticed for the first time that a muscle in his cheek kept
wincing, as if there was an unbearable tension inside him.

"Evie," he said, and for a moment his voice sounded
gentle and almost caring, the way it used to before they
were married. A wave of memory from the days when they
had been lovers came spilling onto the empty beach of

tonight's argument, tonight's drunkenness, and Eva remembered a day at Malibu, swimming, eating lobster, laughing, running.

The wave ebbed away. "You're a bastard," she said quietly. "However sweetly you put it, you're a 110 percent bastard."

"I'm not trying to put it sweetly," he told her. "But just don't forget that it takes two people to make a marriage, and it takes two people to wreck a marriage."

"Three," put in Eva, slurrily but with great vehemence. "You forgot Francesca."

She swayed again, and he held her tighter. "The lovely Francesca," she repeated.

Gerard waited for a moment and then released her. "I'll be back the day after tomorrow," he said, watching her with cold disgust. "Make sure you've sobered up."

"I will," said Eva. "But not for you. By the time you come back the day after tomorrow I shall make love to my lover ten times at least, and probably more." She focused on him sharply, and then said in a voice of pure jealousy and hatred, "If and when you ever want me again, Mr. Gerard Crowley, then you shall have to anoint that precious and unfaithful organ of yours deep in another man's."

Gerard, his eyes telegraphing nothing at all, slapped her fiercely across the face. His wedding ring split her lip, and one side of her face was instantly spotted with blood.

She didn't collapse, though, or even cry. She remained standing where she was, disheveled and bloody, and stared at him with an expression of defiance and contempt that could have turned orange juice to acid. Gerard looked back at her sharply, questioningly, and then picked up his coat and his suitcase, looked again, and made a *hmph* kind of noise, as if he weren't sure that he had really hurt her enough. He opened the door.

"Go," said Eva, through swollen lips. "Don't let me stand in your way."

Gerard hesitated.

"Go," said Eva, and Gerard went, frowning to himself as he closed the door behind him. He whistled an uncomfortable tune as he descended in the elevator to the garage, although the tune died away as he crossed the empty concrete to his car. He opened up the trunk, stowed away his suitcase, and then climbed into the Buick like a man who has a very long distance to travel but doesn't quite know where.

"Shit," he said to himself, thinking about Eva. Then he started up the engine.

It took him less than an hour to drive out to Pacoima Ranch. Although the false dawn was already lightening the eastern sky behind the San Gabriel mountains, the highway was deserted, and the only signs of human life he saw were at San Fernando Airport, where an executive plane was plaintively winking its lights on the runway. He drove past Pacoima Reservoir and then out onto the Little Tujunga Road.

Pacoima Ranch was a ramshackle collection of huts at the end of a twisting, dusty driveway, with corrugated iron rooftops and sagging verandas. The kind of place where unspeakable helter-skelter rituals might have been performed, or where Nancy Drew might have gone in search of ghosts or kidnapers or fugitives from justice.

Gerard turned the car around in front of the main ranch house, and killed the engine. Even before he had fished out his suitcase, two Japanese appeared on the veranda, one of them carrying a Uzi machine gun, both of them masked in black. They watched him, motionless, as he slammed the lid of his trunk and walked toward them. Four or five yards away, he paused.

"Good morning." He smiled at them.

The two Japanese didn't answer, but moved aside to let Gerard cross the veranda and enter the ranch house through the screen door. Gerard asked. "Did the commander get here yet?" and one of the Japanese nodded each pointed upstairs. "Ah," said Gerard. "Sleeping it off, no doubt."

Inside, the ranch house was empty of furniture except for three or four neatly tied-up *futons* in the large living room, but it was scrupulously clean. On the walls were rice-paper scrolls and symbols, and a collection of black silk flags. Gerard had once asked Doctor Gempaku what the flags signified, but Doctor Gempaku had simply told him, "It would take only a minute for me to explain, but twenty years for you to understand."

Gerard left his suitcase in the bare living room, and then walked through to the kitchen. There, sitting on a *zabuton*, a large flat cushion, was Doctor Gempaku himself, eating his breakfast. In the far corner, over the old-fashioned black-iron range, another of the masked Japanese was stirring vegetables in a *donabe*. It was only just past five o'clock in the morning, but Doctor Gempaku always rose early to say his prayers.

"Would you care to eat?" he asked Gerard as Gerard sat down next to him on another *zabuton*. Doctor Gempaku was tall and lean for a Japanese, with a closeshaven head and small, oval-framed spectacles. There was always a certain grace and mystery about him, as if he were living partly in California and partly in some tranquil Japanese garden, a garden of chrysanthemums and golden carp and esoteric riddles.

Gerard peered into Doctor Gempaku's blue-lacquered bowl. "What's on the menu?" he asked.

"*Kitsune udon*," smiled Doctor Gempaku. "In English, that means 'fox noodles.' It is a particularly compelling mystery why a dish of bean curd and noodles should have become historically associated with the fox, which is one of the most evil of Japanese spirits. Some say that the fox was always fond of bean curd. Others say that *kitsune udon* is the last meal you are given before you are sent to everlasting hellfire."

"Do you have any cornflakes?" asked Gerard.

Doctor Gempaku spoke quickly in Japanese, and the black-masked boy came over and set a bowl for Gerard, as well as a paper packet of chopsticks and one of the white china spoons usually used for eating soup.

Before the noodles were served, Gerard observed the small ritual of *oshibori*, wiping his hands with a hot, lightly scented towel. Even at Pacoima Ranch, Doctor Gempaku insisted on the civilized niceties. The black-masked boy filled Gerard's bowl with *kitsune odon*, bowed, and returned to his cooking.

Gerard ate in silence for a while, and then asked, without looking at Doctor Gempaku, "Esmeralda's told you what we're supposed to be doing next?"

"Yes."

"What do you think?"

"I think it is possible. I can have the next Tengu ready by tomorrow night."

"I'm not asking you if it's *possible*. I know it's *possible*. What I'm asking you is, what do you *think*?"

Doctor Gempaku watched Gerard carefully for a moment or two, and then said, "What do you want me to think?"

"I just want your reaction, that's all."

"My moral reaction? Or my philosophical reaction?"

Gerard chased a piece of bean curd around the inside of his bowl. In the end, he gave up and set the half-emptied bowl down on the table.

"We're sending a Tengu out to kill a man. I want to know how you respond to that. Whether you think it's the right thing to do, not just as far as the law is concerned, but as far as the whole project is concerned."

Doctor Gempaku picked up his chopsticks, tested them with his hands, and then snapped them in two. "Japanese esthetics," he said, "are preoccupied with the idea of the perfect moment, the 'accident' that is spontaneous, and yet carefully controlled—so that it takes on an artistic and spiritual deliciousness beyond any experience that occurs either *wholly* accidentally or *wholly* deliberately. To me, this is one of the satisfactions of the Tengu. We have created the strongest and fiercest of human beings, a creature that can terrify and overwhelm anybody and everybody. He obeys our directions, and yet he is also unpredictable. We cannot tell what he might take it into his mind to do, what grisly horrors he might suddenly decide to perpetrate. The death of the girl Sherry Cantor was a perfect example. To the Western mind it seemed like random and brutal murder, purposeless and bloody. To us, however, it was an event of terrible beauty. The Tengu did as he was bidden; and yet the error he made in killing Sherry Cantor added an indefinable ecstasy to the whole event. We are asked to send out a Tengu to deal with Admiral Thorson. Perhaps a smiliar mistake may occur. The only criteria can be destiny and the demands of perfection. So when you ask me, is it *right*? I can only say that it can only be *right* when it actually takes place. Will it be an esthetic event or not? We cannot tell."

Gerard sat back on his *zabuton* and took out his cigar case. "Are you serious?" he asked Doctor Gempaku.

"Perhaps," said Doctor Gempaku, and smiled.

Gerard clipped the end off a cigar and pasted down a stray piece of broken leaf with saliva. "The Tengu we sent out to deal with Sennett . . . how's he doing? He was shot up pretty bad, wasn't he?"

"He's still in a coma. But most of the body injuries are beginning to heal satisfactorily. You know that a Tengu is so unnaturally strong partly because his metabolism is so drastically accelerated. It gives him a shorter life, of course; but it also means that any wounds or injuries heal themselves with remarkable speed. It's his mental state that concerns me more. Something happened after he killed Sherry Cantor that seriously and dangerously unbalanced him. It seems to me that it was a similar reaction to that of a child whose body temperature rises suddenly and dramatically. A kind of convulsion, or fit."

"Do you think it might happen again?" asked Gerard. He struck a match and leaned forward slightly to light his cigar.

"I would prefer it if you smoked outside," said Doctor Gempaku. "Tobacco smoke will upset the delicate balance of aromas in this kitchen. It is already bad enough that I can smell it on your clothes and hair.''

Gerard stared at Doctor Gempaku for a moment, and then slowly waved out the match. "I'll leave the cigar until later," he said. "Let's go take a look at the Tengus."

Doctor Gempaku clapped his hands, and the black-masked cook removed their bowls. Then the doctor rose from the table, and Gerard followed him through to the front of the house again, where the two black-robed guards were still keeping watch. "We've had one or two unwelcome intruders lately," said Doctor Gempaku as he slipped on his shoes. "Nobody dangerous, no police or anything like that."

"Has anybody come up to the house?" asked Gerard.

Doctor Gempaku shook his head. "They don't get the chance. Usually I send Frank out with his shotgun to turn them around before they get the idea that anything unusual is happening here. My young *bushi* stay well out of sight."

The sun was already up and warm as they crossed the yard to what appeared at first sight to be a rundown barn. It was only from close up that it was possible for anyone to see the modern prefabricated building which had been constructed inside the gappy, collapsing timbers, and to hear the deep humming of portable electric generators. Doctor Gempaku led the way through the sagging barn doorway, and then up a short flight of stainless-steel steps that took them to the interior door of the Tengu building. He unlocked the door, using two keys, and when it swung open he rapped on it with his knuckles to show Gerard how solid it was.

"Four-inch carbonized steel," he said. "We fitted it last week."

"I know," Gerard responded coldly. "I had to pay $7,500 for it. I just hope that it proves to be worth the price."

Doctor Gempaku smiled. "If any one of our Tengus goes berserk again, then believe me, it will be worth the price. Not even a Tengu can break his way through four inches of carbonized steel. Well, we hope not.''

Inside the building, which ran nearly 90 feet in length, the only illumination came from tiny, beadlike red safety lights. The temperature was well below 55 degrees, dry and constantly controlled. Doctor Gempaku held Gerard's sleeve while both of them stood in the entrance, waiting for their eyes to become accustomed to the darkness and their skin accustomed to the cold. Gerard felt the sweat in the middle of his back freezing like a cape of ice.

At last, Doctor Gempaku's face began to emerge from the crimson twilight, and Gerard could look around him and see a long, narrow corridor, with doors going off on either side. He had been here before, when the building was just erected, but there were more partitions now, more rooms where Tengus could be concealed. There was also a different resonance, a deep, almost inaudible drumming sound, both irritating and strangely threatening, like the first tremors of an earthquake. A smell, too: of incense and stale flowers and one thing more—sickly and overwhelming, the smell of dried blood.

Gerard said, ''If hell could ever be created in a cabin, then this would be it.''

Doctor Gempaku steered him toward the first door on the right. ''Come see the Tengu we're trying to save. If we have not lost him overnight. A young student of ancient Japanese religion, before he joined us. A very dedicated young man. The sort of personality that refuses to be diverted from the essence of spiritual truth.''

''This is the guy who killed Sherry Cantor?''

Doctor Gempaku nodded. ''He was always our most promising Tengu. But the most promising are usually the most unbalanced. It requires a high level of emotional susceptibility for a man to be suitable for the role of a Tengu, and extreme physical strength and emotional susceptibility are also a volatile mixture. Like nitroglycerin, the Tengu is both powerful and touchy.''

He unlocked the plain metal door and slid it back. It was no lighter on the other side than it had been in the corridor, but Doctor Gempaku guided Gerard into a small antechamber and then swiftly locked the door behind them. "This is always the moment of no return," he said. "If anything should go wrong, it is better for just one or two of us to be slaughtered by the Tengu than to try to give ourselves an escape route and risk letting it out."

"Well," said Gerard, "I would call that a matter of opinion."

"Nothing about the Tengu is a matter of opinion," Doctor Gempaku corrected him, politely but adamantly. "The Tengu represents the ultimate physical power which any human being can achieve, coupled with a spiritual compulsion which is the greatest that any human brain can stand. When we tried out our earliest Tengu program at the Yoyogi Olympic stadium in Tokyo, during the weight-lifting events, a Tengu was able to lift over 430 kilograms. Unfortunately, because our methods were not recognized by the Olympic committee, we were forced to withdraw under conditions of great secrecy."

"Mr. Esmeralda told me about that."

Doctor Gempaku was silent for a second or two. Then he said, "Follow me. But remember to stay quiet. The Tengu is still sensitive to disturbances."

"I'll be quiet," Gerard assured him.

Doctor Gempaku drew aside a curtain of fine jet beads which, in the darkness, Gerard hadn't seen before. Stepping silently on slippered feet, he led the way into a room draped with black silk curtains, a room in which scores of black silk ribbons hung from the ceiling, tied with silver temple bells, birds' feathers, pomanders of cloves and cherry blossoms, bamboo tokens, and *haniwa*, the clay figures usually found in ancient Japanese graves. Gerard, who had been expecting something more like a surgical theater, with cardiopulmonary resuscitators and electronic monitors and oxygen equipment, was considerably taken aback.

"What is that?" he hissed. "Where's the Tengu?"

Doctor Gempaku raised a finger to his lips to indicate

total silence. Then, very gradually, he raised the lighting in the room with a dimmer switch located behind the drapes, until Gerard could see the Tengu who had torn Sherry Cantor to pieces.

The Tengu was suspended from the ceiling, like all the icons and bells which hung around him; except that he wasn't tied up by ribbons. He was naked, and he was held up by fifteen or twenty silver claws, shaped like the hands of a demon or an old woman, whose long silver nails actually pierced deep into his flesh. Each of these claws was tied to a black silk braided cord, and in turn these were all gathered and knotted close to the ceiling, and attached to a strange kind of metal frame.

Gerard slowly approached the Tengu, with chilly sweat sliding down the insides of his armpits and a taste in his mouth like congealed grease. He had seen many horrors in Cuba. But for human butchery, he had never seen anything like this, and he could scarcely believe that the mutilated creature hanging in front of him was real.

The Tengu was still masked with his white varnished mask. He was breathing, in shallow, interrupted gasps, but Gerard wouldn't have laid money on his survival, especially not hung up like this from the ceiling. The silver claws had dug so far into his chest muscles that they had lifted them up in bruised and dead-looking peaks, and the claws in his buttocks had almost disappeared into the flesh altogether. There were claws in his leg muscles, in his shoulders, in his arms. The claws in his feet had gone so deep that one of them had actually broken right through, from the sole to the instep. There was even a claw in his genitals, dragging up his scrotum and piercing his foreskin so that his penis looked like a hooked eel.

"This is crazy," said Gerard. "What the hell are you doing here? You're supposed to be making the guy better and you're injuring him even worse than he was before!"

Doctor Gempaku dimmed the lights again. "What you are witnessing here is not a traditional Western form of healing."

"What you're doing here has just about as much to do with the traditional Western form of healing, or *any* form of healing, as Belsen had to do with summer camp," Gerard retorted. "You're going to kill him, doctor; and if you kill him, then more than a few hundred of thousands of dollars are going to be lost with him. Money for which *I* am supposed to be responsible."

Doctor Gempaku took Gerard's arm and guided him back toward the antechamber. "You have nothing to fear, Mr. Crowley. The responsibility for getting the Tengu into the country may have been yours; the responsibility for the building of this center may have been yours; and the day-to-day administration of this plan may be yours. But, don't you see? Everything we are doing here is planned, with great precision; every step I take, whether it is scientific or whether it is spiritual, is taken according to a very careful premeditated scheme."

He unlocked the door, and they emerged into the corridor again. "Do you want to see the Tengu we are preparing for Admiral Thorson?"

Gerard asked, "Is he . . . hung up like the other one?"

"He is undergoing a similar ordeal."

"In that case, no."

Doctor Gempaku said, "They told me you weren't squeamish. They told me you were a man of the world."

Gerard said, "It depends which world you're talking about."

They left the barn and walked back across the yard to the house. Gerard lit up his cigar and took two or three deep puffs. Doctor Gempaku glanced at him from time to time and smiled.

"I don't know what you think is so damned amusing," Gerard snapped as they took off their shoes on the veranda.

"You are like all Occidentals. You are so concerned by the sight of other people undergoing mutilation or pain. It disturbs you, but it also fascinates you. To us, pain is as much a part of existence as happiness. The moment of exquisite, controlled agony can bring on as much heaven as the moment of sexual climax.''

Gerard said, "You think I don't know about De Sade, that stuff? I've spanked a girl or two, had my back scratched. But what you've got back there, doctor—that's something else.''

"Something else?''

The guards watched them through the thin slits in their silk masks as they went upstairs to Doctor Gempaku's study. Gerard glanced back at them quickly, but by then they had turned to the window again, in their silent watch for unwelcome intruders.

Doctor Gempaku's study was simple and silent, *tatami* mats on the floor, a low table spread with papers, two scrolls hung on the wall, a framed photograph of *tancho-zuru*, the Japanese red-crested crane. No family pictures, no mementoes of the Tokyo Olympics, nothing to show that Doctor Gempaku had friends or family or even a past.

Gerard picked up the picture of the cranes. "You're a bird watcher?'' he asked.

Doctor Gempaku sat down on a cushion. "I keep that picture there to remind me of the proverb: 'The crane lives for a thousand years.' ''

"What does that mean?''

"Many things. It could be a reminder that there are forces in the universe which live forever, and yet which can be conjured up in ordinary mortals.''

"You're talking about the Tengu?''

Doctor Gempaku said, "It does not pay to be too inquisitive about what we are doing here, Mr. Crowley, or how we do it.''

"Doctor Gempaku,'' said Gerard, taking his cigar out of his mouth. "I was shocked back there, I'll admit. Who wouldn't have been? But believe me, I'm not inquisitive. I'm just here to do what I've been paid to do. You just go ahead and do whatever you want, don't mind me.'' Now Gerard was laying on his down-South good-ole-boy accent really thickly. "You can hang fellas up, doctor. You can prick 'em and pat 'em and mark 'em with T. You do whatever you want. You just go right ahead. Why," he said, and now his smile was cold, and he looked at Doctor Gempaku with an expression which anybody from Batista's Havana would immediately have recognized as his 'I've-got-you-sized-up' look, "why, you can even raise the *devil* if the mind takes you. You won't catch me sticking *my* nose in."

Doctor Gempaku slowly closed the small book which was lying on the table in front of him. He took off his spectacles. Gerard watched him and puffed at his cigar, watched and puffed, while the sun suddenly filled the room with dazzling morning light.

CHAPTER TWENTY

Jerry Sennett was falling asleep in front of the television when the telephone rang. He had been dreaming about Japan, and as he crossed the room to the telephone he was still crossing the Rikugien gardens in Tokyo, under a sky that threatened rain.

"Mr. Sennett? Sergeant Skrolnik, Homicide." The harsh voice brought Jerry back to Orchid Place, and Dan Rather, and a sort of reality.

"Hallo, sergeant."

"Are you okay?" asked Skrolnik. "You sound like you've got yourself a cold."

"I was sleeping. Well, nearly."

"I'm sorry. But we've got ourselves a suspect in custody, and I'd appreciate your coming down to headquarters to take a look at him. You know—see if you recognize him or not."

"Sergeant, I was out when Ms. Cantor was murdered. I didn't see anybody."

"Sure, I know that," said Skrolnik. "But there's a chance that seeing this guy could jog your memory. You know, maybe you glimpsed him in the locality one day, something like that."

"Can I bring Mr. Holt along with me?"

"Mr. Holt?" asked Skrolnik sharply. "You mean Mack Holt, the victim's last known romantic association?"

Jerry was drinking from a stale glass of whiskey with a sticky rim. He coughed, and almost choked. "If you want to put it so poetically, yes. That's him."

"You're an acquaintance of his?"

"Only since the murder."

"Well . . . okay then, bring him down. Why not? We can kill two birds with one stone."

Jerry went to the kitchen, stuffed a couple of cheese crackers into his mouth, and then, puffing crumbs, switched off all the lights and locked the back door. He pulled on an old plaid jacket, switched off the television, and then went out to his car. He was fumbling for his keys when he became aware of something on the windshield, something white, flapping in the evening breeze.

He approached the car slowly, then picked the sheet of paper out from the windshield wiper. It was thin paper, the kind that Japanese calligraphers used for scrollwork. On it were written, with a brush, the English words "The hawks will return to their roost."

Jerry held the paper up to the streetlight. There was the Japanese character *gwa* watermarked into it, but that was the only identifying mark. He stood silent and alone on the driveway for almost five minutes, holding the paper in his hand, thinking, searching his memory and imagination for what this could mean, and where it could have come from.

It convinced him of one thing: Sherry Cantor's death had really been a mistake, after all. Whoever had smashed his way into her house that morning had been looking for him.

There was nothing about that thought that consoled him. It meant simply that Sherry had died for no reason at all, and that whoever had killed her was still on the loose. Whoever Sergeant Skrolnik was holding down at headquarters, it was unquestionably the wrong man.

The message itself was more subtle. "The hawks will return to their roost." It reminded him of something he had read years and years ago, when he was in Japan. It had an important meaning—he was sure of that. And somebody had taken a considerable risk to tuck it under his windshield wiper. It was a warning of some kind, that was obvious. But against what, and by whom, he was completely at a loss to imagine.

He drove slowly and thoughtfully to Mack Holt's house on Franklin Avenue. Mack was standing in the doorway outside, talking to a shaven-skulled Krishna disciple in saffron robes. When he saw Jerry drawing into the curb, he raised his cigarette hand in salute, and Jerry could see him saying something to the young man in the robes, something which made the young man nod as if he were impressed.

"How are you doing?" asked Jerry as he slammed the car door behind him and walked up the cracked concrete path. It was a warm, dusky evening, and moths were weaving around the naked bulb over the porch.

Mack said, "Okay, how are you?"

"You busy?" asked Jerry.

"Kind of. Depends. Olive's upstairs, and we're expecting some people over later. They've got a pirate videotape of the new *Star Wars* picture, and two gallons of Christian Brothers Pinot Chardonnay."

Jerry glanced up toward the lighted window of Mack's apartment. "I wouldn't keep you long," he said. "It's just that the police have found a suspect, and they'd like us to go to headquarters and take a look at him."

"They've *found* somebody?" asked Mack, as if he had expected that the criminal would disappear int the Xth Dimension, like Dr. Strange.

"They're not sure if it's the right guy," said Jerry. "But

I guess we owe it to Sherry to take a look. Sergeant What's-his-name, Skrolnik, said we might recognize him just from some casual encounter in the street.''

"Do you think I could bring Olive?" asked Mack.

Jerry gave him a lopsided shrug.

Mack disappeared upstairs for a minute or two, while Jerry remained on the stoop, smiling vaguely from time to time at the shaven-haired Krishna convert and whistling "The Way We Were." Across the street, a fat strawberry-blonde woman was trying unsuccessfully to persuade her pet poodle to do what he had been dragged out of the house to do.

At last Mack reappeared, closely followed by Olive. They both looked slightly high. Olive was wearing a shocking-pink satin jogging vest that did little to conceal her improbably large breasts, and the tightest of white satin shorts. Mack said to Jerry, "This is Mrs. Robin T. Nesmith, Jr. Her husband's in Honolulu, with the Navy."

"Delighted," said Jerry, and shook Olive's hand. "I was a Navy man once, myself."

"Don't knock them," grinned Olive.

"I hope I'm not spoiling your evening," said Jerry.

"Not at *all*," Olive told him, climbing into the Dodge beside him and wriggling her hips enthusiastically to make room for Mack. "I've had enough of videotapes and cheap wine to last me till Doomsday. It's a change to do something *unpredictable*."

It was dark by the time they reached the police headquarters. A jaded sergeant sat at the desk in the lobby and regarded them with eyes that had long ago faded into disinterest at the sight of oddballs, hookers, pimps, and general fruitcakes, the flotsam of Hollywood Boulevard and all parts east. He told them to wait, and they sat side by side on a patched vinyl bench, tapping their feet and staring at a poster which reminded them that 10,728 people died in the United States last year as the victims of handguns. Officers came and went, tired and sweaty from hours of duty, one or two of them whistling and fooling around, most of them silent. Mack said to Olive, "This is unpredictable?"

At last, his shoes squeaking on the plastic-tiled floor, Sergeant Skrolnik appeared, with Detective Pullet and Arthur following close behind him. "I'm sorry I kept you good people waiting," said Skrolnik, directing his attention with some humility to Olive's breasts. "Sherry Cantor's case is just one of three similar homicides. I have on my books right now, and I'm afraid that my time is kind of limited."

"You said you've caught somebody," said Jerry. "I didn't hear any announcement on the news."

Skrolnik thrust his hands into his sagging pockets. "That's because I haven't yet announced it to the media. I've detained somebody, yes, and I've charged him with the first-degree homicide of Ms. Sherry Cantor, and the reason I've done that is because I'm not at all sure who *else* apart from this guy could have physically torn a twenty-one-year-old girl to pieces. But I have to tell you that there are doubts in my mind, serious doubts, and that's why I'm looking for all the corroborative evidence I can find. The guy plainly has the capability to inflict serious injuries on people with his bare hands. He had some personal involvement with the victim. But two or three important details still don't seen to add up."

"Does that really bother you, as long as you've made a bust?" asked Mack.

Skrolnik gave him a look of tired disgust. "I want more than an arrest, Mr. Holt. I want to catch the guy who ripped a pretty and innocent young woman into so much raw meat."

Without saying anything else, he squeaked off again along the corridor, and Pullet and Arthur followed. Arthur was busy blowing his nose, but Pullet indicated with a cursory nod of his head that Jerry and Mack and Olive should come along, too.

They were ushered into a small interview room that smelled of stale cigars and Brut 33. On the far wall was a two-way mirror; behind it, disconsolate and edgy, sat Maurice Needs, a/k/a El Krusho, on a cell chair that seemed to be three sizes too small for him. Every now and then he punched his fist into the open palm of his hand, impatiently blew out his cheeks, and looked toward the cell door.

"I don't believe it," said Mack. "That's *Maurice*!"

"That's right," nodded Skrolnik. "Maurice Charles Needs, from Fridley, Minnesota; also known as El Krusho."

"*El Krusho?*" asked Jerry in disbelief.

"My reaction entirely," said Skrolnik. "But in spite of that somewhat fanciful name, he was a close acquaintance and possible lover of Ms. Sherry Cantor. According to two different witnesses, he was involved in a *ménage à trois* with Sherry Cantor and with you, Mr. Holt. Three in a bed, so I'm told."

Olive took Mack's arm, as if to reassure him that whatever had happened in the past wasn't going to affect the strength of their friendship now. Mack said disjointedly, "There was something like that, yes. But not serious, and only one time. It started as a party, and then I guess we all had a little too much wine. There was no bad feeling afterward, no problems."

"You don't think that, having slept with her once, Maurice Needs may have thought that Sherry Cantor was a lover of his? That he might have gotten overpossessive about her? Jealous, even?"

"Look," said Mack, "this is all completely off the wall. Maurice never hurt anyone, never would. We had a scene with Sherry, all right, I admit it, but it was one time only and that was it. We all stayed good friends. Sherry and me used to go down to the circus to see him, and he was always totally friendly. He wouldn't do anything like that, not to anybody, and especially not to Sherry."

"Mr. Sennett?" Skrolnik asked Jerry. "Did you ever see that man before? Lurking around your street maybe?"

Olive said, "That guy couldn't *lurk* if he tried. Look at

the size of him. But don't you think he's *cute*?''

"Don't get ideas," said Mack. "He isn't very big where it really counts. These Muscle Beach types never are."

Sergeant Skrolnik impatiently put in, "Will you take a look at the suspect, please, Mr. Sennett? A real good look?"

Jerry shook his head. "I'm sorry, sergeant. I never saw him before."

"Can we talk to him?" asked Mack. "I mean, you're not going to hold him, are you? Not really?"

Detective Pullet said, "You can talk to him if you want to. But until we have some pretty good evidence that he *didn't* murder Sherry Cantor, he stays right here."

Mack said, "Jerry—Olive—can you wait for me? I'd really like to give the poor guy some encouragement."

"Don't *over*encourage him," said Skrolnik, glancing at Pullet in a way which showed that he didn't really think that allowing Maurice Needs to speak to Mack was a very good idea. But Pullet said, "It could help, right? Anything which gets us nearer to the nub of what actually happened."

"All right," said Skrolnik. "But not longer than five minutes. Then I'm going to have to tell the commissioner we've hauled someone in."

Detective Arthur sneezed loudly.

Outside again, on the vinyl bench, Jerry and Olive waited and smoked while Mack was given time to talk to El Krusho. Olive said, "What were you in the Navy, Jerry? Afloat or ashore?"

"Mostly ashore. Naval Intelligence Department. Nothing very much like the Navy and not very intelligent, either."

"My husband's in Records. Right now he's working on some kind of official history of Midway, something like that."

"Do you miss him?" asked Jerry, looking at her carefully through the winding cigarette smoke.

She nodded. Her eyes gave away just how much she

missed him.

"I can't believe this guy is called El Krusho," Jerry said, to change the subject. "Did Mack ever talk about him before?"

"He did mention he used to know a circus strongman. But that was all."

Jerry said, "He didn't really look the *type* to commit murder, did he? You see the way he kept looking at the door? Sort of soft and hopeless, like he's waiting for his gray-haired momma to come bail him out."

"He looked *strong* enough," remarked Olive.

"Well, sure, and that's obviously one of the reasons they're holding him. But unless he had an accomplice, I don't really believe he did it." He reached into his plaid jacket and took out the sheet of soft scrollwork paper he had found under his windshield wiper. "If anything convinces me that it wasn't him, this does. I found it on my car tonight, just after Sergeant Skrolnik called me."

Olive took the paper and read it carefully, "The hawks will return to their roost?" She frowned. "What the hell does that mean?"

"I don't know. It sounds like an old Japanese proverb. But like all Japanese proverbs, it could have several meanings. Maybe something like 'that which has been troubling you before is going to come back and trouble you again.' On the other hand, it could mean something altogether different."

"Do you know who might have put it on your car?"

Jerry took back the paper, folded it up, and shook his head. "Not a clue. But I think whoever did it knows who killed Sherry Cantor; and whoever did it knows exactly what's going to come down next."

Olive stared at him. "You mean—the murderer's still out there? He could do it again?"

"I hope not," said Jerry dryly. "And the *reason* I hope not is because the next murder could well be mine."

Mack was almost a half-hour. Jerry took a stroll around the hallway, smiling at the impossible desk officer; trying to pat a police dog on the head, going over to talk to a young blonde woman police officer who was typing up reports at a desk to one side.

"Hi," he said. "It looks like you're pretty tied up tonight."

The policewoman looked up at him, sharply. "I'm sorry," she said, "but visitors are requested to wait over there."

"Okay," said Jerry. "I was only trying to support my local police department."

At that moment, however, just as Jerry was turning away, a lieutenant came up, sweating and paunchy, and handed the policewoman a sheaf of documents.

"Janice, can you do me a favor and get these sorted out for me? I mean, real quick. I need them two hours ago."

"Which one's this?" the policewoman asked him, leafing through the notes.

"The Japanese one. The young guy they found in that culvert out by West Covina."

"Okay, lieutenant," the policewoman said, and laid the papers on the edge of her desk.

Jerry didn't ever quite know what led him to do it. But as the lieutenant headed for the squad room, he turned around and deliberately knocked against the police-woman's desk, so that all the papers were scattered on the floor, swooping and tumbling.

"I *asked* you to wait over there!" the policewoman snapped, getting up from her seat. But Jerry was quicker. He knelt down and gathered the papers up, and as he did so he snatched a quick read at every page. A name: *Kemo Toyama.* Part of a report by the officer who first arrived at West Covina: *Seriously mutilated, heart dislocated, brain damaged.* Names of witnesses, no time to read any of those. And then, like a newsflash, a name and address: *c/o Nancy Shiranuka, 1114 Alta Loma Road.*

Jerry handed the papers back to the policewoman with a sheepish smile. "I'm truly sorry. I guess I've always been clumsy. Can I buy you dinner to make up for my boobery?"

The policewoman sat down again and zipped a fresh

sheet of paper into her typewriter.

"Just sit down and behave yourself, and I'll resist the temptation to arrest you for interfering with police business," she said.

Jerry saluted. "Yes, ma'am."

CHAPTER TWENTY-ONE

On the way back to Franklin Avenue, Mack said, "The poor guy's completely innocent. I don't even know how they can hold him."

"Does he have an alibi?" asked Jerry.

"He was in bed asleep."

"Alone? Or accompanied?"

"Alone as it happens."

Jerry made a face. "Lying alone in your own bed, no matter how peacefully, is not really much of an alibi. What about the police killing?"

"He doesn't have an alibi then, either. But he couldn't have done either of them. It just isn't in him."

Jerry produced the Japanese paper and handed it across the car. "This is what really convinces me it wasn't him."

"This piece of paper? What does it mean?"

"It's a warning of some sort. It's Japanese. And it must have been attached to my car long after Sergeant Skrolnik locked your friend Maurice Krusho up in the cells."

"Why didn't you show this to Skrolnik?"

"I don't know. I suppose I'm still not sure that what *I* think about Sherry Cantor's death isn't just another manifestation of my neurosis about Japan."

"But if it could have sprung Maurice from jail . . ."

"It's not evidence," said Jerry, taking it back. "Not the

kind of evidence that Skrolnik is looking for."

"For you, though?"

Jerry tapped his forehead with his finger. "For me, it sets off that cold wind."

They had reached Mack's apartment, and Jerry drew over to the curb. Mack said, "Are you sure you don't want to stay with us tonight? If there's a killer on the loose and he's looking for you . . . ?"

"I'll be okay," said Jerry. "I've got a Colt automatic in the bedroom and I can still remember some of my judo."

"You're welcome to wine and *Revenge of the Jedi*," smiled Olive.

Jerry shook his head. "Thanks, but I've got to get back for my son. He was supposed to be home a half-hour ago. But let me think this all over tonight, and maybe I'll call you in the morning. There's something real complicated going on here, you know. Something that makes some kind of sense if only we could fit all the pieces together. I just need to get it all assembled in my brain."

It was almost nine o'clock by the time Jerry swung his car into Orchid Place. Considering that David was supposed to have gotten back from the Lechner's by eight o'clock at the latest, he was surprised and concerned to find that the house was still in darkness. He parked his car, locked it, and went to open the front door. It was already two or three inches ajar. He stood and looked at it for a moment, unsure of what to do. Then he reached out with his fingertips and nudged it open.

In the hall, he paused and held his breath. The killer could be waiting for him anywhere, in any shadow. He took two or three steps forward, trying to remember what his old judo instructor had told him. *You are the wind, nothing more. You are the air. When your enemy attacks you, you will become the air, invisible yet strong. You will give way; but in your giving way you will vanquish your enemy instantly.*

Something else came into his mind. An unbidden thought that made him feel cold and alarmed. A single word. *Tengu*.

He called, "David? Are you there, David?" but there was no reply. Either David had come back early and then gone out again when he found that his father wasn't home, leaving the door unlocked by accident, or else—

Jerry reached for the living room light and flicked it on. Everything was in chaos—cushions, chairs, vases, books were scattered all over the rug. Even the liquor cabinet had been wrenched open and its pink-tinted glass smashed. One of the drapes had been pulled down, and there was a smear of blood on the wallpaper.

With stiff, chilled movements, too shocked now to think about judo, Jerry crossed the room. Sprawled on the sofa was a Japanese *Hotei* doll, a puppet of one of the seven gods of fortune. White-faced, cloaked in black, with massive earlobes and the joking, malevolent smile of a trickster. Jerry gently lifted it up, and its head and arms flopped back. Where it had been lying, there was another sheet of scrollwork paper, neatly rolled and tied with string. He opened it up and read, in growing fright, the message: "We have your son. Wait patiently for instructions. Tell nobody."

Beneath the writing was a brushwork picture of a dove with its wings aflame.

Jerry went immediately to the telephone, picked it up, and dialed Sergeant Skrolnik's number. Then, before the police switchboard had answered, he set the phone down again.

He felt at last as if his nightmares had broken through from the past into the present day, like devils crawling and scrambling out of one of those huge pandemonic eggs in a painting by Hieronymus Bosch. He felt as if everything had turned to fire, as if hell had come to life, as if Hiroshima and Nagasaki were again incandescent.

He said, "Oh, God," but the words sounded empty and pitiful.

BOOK TWO
BLAZING EAGLES

CHAPTER ONE

They had expected Admiral Knut S. Thorson to die within hours of his last and most paralyzing stroke. He was 78, after all, and his last ten years of life had been dogged by serious heart disease and delibitating collapses. But "Inch-Thick Thorsen," as the Navy had always nicknamed him, was made of tough, durable stuff, and his hours of life had lengthened into days, then months.

He had lain for nearly a year now inside his oxygen tent at Rancho Encino Hospital, one of the most luxurious acute-care facilities in the whole of southern California, a stumpy little gray-haired man with ferocious eyebrows and a ruddiness in his weathered face which even twelve months of hospitalization had been unable to fade.

Every two days his wife visited and sat watching him breathe inside his plastic cocoon; a plain woman who always wore flowers in her hat. On holidays and anniversaries, his entire family came to Rancho Encino, and stared at him with respect, regret, and boredom. "Inch-Thick" remained with his eyes closed, his heartbeats monitored by the latest and most sensitive of cardio-pulmonary equipment, his brainwaves monitored by electroencephalograph.

His wife was still with him at 9:06 the evening after Jerry Sennett had been asked by Sergeant Skrolnik to come down to police headquarters and look at Maurice Needs. She had said nothing to him for most of the afternoon; but toward nightfall she had recited to him, without any hope

201

that he could hear or understand her, one of the love
poems he had written to her during the war.

> How can a love so gentle be so fierce?
> How can a soft caress grip with such strength?
> How can your tenderest glance so quickly pierce
> My heart its very depth, my life its length?

Admiral Thorson had never written any poetry before
the war; and he never wrote any more afterward. But Mary
Thorson kept in an old ribboned candy box in her
dressing-table drawer a collection of nearly 40 poems that
had expressed his feelings for her in those days when it was
quite possible he would never see her again.

They were the only words of his that she now possessed.

At 9:08, Nurse Abramski, a brusque but charming
woman with a striking resemblance to Mary Tyler Moore,
looked in to check the admiral's heartbeat and drip, and to
ensure that his waste-disposal bags did not need emptying.
She smiled the whole time, but said little; she knew that
Mary Thorson preferred not to chatter. Mary Thorson had
enough to cope with, paying this long drawn-out homage
to her comatose husband and lover.

Nurse Abramski finished in Admiral Thorson's suite at
9:11. At the very moment she closed the door behind her,
a Chevrolet van drew up outside the hospital grounds on
Balboa Boulevard and doused its headlights. Out of the
driver's seat climbed a young Japanese called Masahiro
Yoshino, a *kendo* adept who had arrived in Los Angeles
only four days ago from Kobe. Out of the passenger seat,
puffing slightly, climbed Commander Ernest Perry
Ouvarov, wearing a belted raincoat and chewing an unlit
corncob pipe, an unconscious impersonation of Mac-
Arthur.

The commander took off his tinted glasses and looked
around the hushed hospital grounds. The spreading
California oaks rustled in the warm evening wind, and the
lights from the hospital facility sparkled through their

leaves. "Okay," he said at last, in a hoarse voice. "Let's get it over with."

He and Yoshino went around to the back of the van. Yoshino unlocked it and opened both doors wide. Inside, the van was almost dark, except for a row of beady red safety lights. The walls, floor, and ceiling were padded with black silk quilting. Among these flags, suspended on silver claws, swung the second Tengu, dressed this time in nothing more than a black headband and the tightly bound loincloth of the sumo wrestler. The motion of the van on its way to Encino had caused the silver claws to work their way even more deeply than usual into the Tengu's flesh, and one of them had pierced his thigh muscle completely. The Tengu was not alone: sitting next to him in the darkness were two of Kappa's black-masked disciples. After Yoshino had opened the doors, they quickly and quietly took over, lowering the Tengu to the floor of the van and speaking to him in long, magical murmurings as they raised him up to a sitting position.

Commander Ouvarov said, "We don't have too long, you guys. This place has one of the hottest security patrols going."

The black devil-people didn't turn to look at him. Their concentration was reserved entirely for the Tengu, who was now rhythmically raising and lowering his white-masked face and uttering a high, keening sound that made Commander Ouvarov shiver. It reminded him of a 4.7-inch naval shell screaming high and deadly overhead.

Yoshino glanced at the commander nervously. He was a serious young man, devoted to the samurai ways, a fanatical believer in Japan's ancestral honor. He was close to his gods. But dealing with a Tengu was something different. A Tengu was the fiercest martial horror that ancient Japan and her magical traditions were capable of creating; and until today, Yoshino had never seen one in the flesh.

In Japanese, the black disciples of Kappa incanted, "O great and terrible Tengu, master of all that is evil and frightful, stalker of the night, deathless one, wrencher and devourer of flesh and spirit, use this servant of human clay to revenge our dishonor.''

At last, the Tengu rose jerkily to his feet, the claws still hanging from his body. One by one, the disciples unhooked them, until the Tengu stood free, his muscles still distorted, his body still pierced with ghastly wounds, but breathing strongly now behind his bland white mask, breathing powerfully and harshly like a wolf that rushes up behind you in the night.

"He is ready," said the black-masked Japanese, bowing to Commander Ouvarov.

"Yoshino," said Commander Ouvarov. "Wait here with the van. Any trouble, any questions from security guards, tell them you're having a problem with the electrical system, you've called for a tow truck. And, for Christ's sake, *smile* a lot. What's the time?"

Yoshino checked his large stainless-steel wristwatch. "Nine nineteen, sir."

"Right, we shouldn't be longer than six or seven minutes. If we're very much longer, or if you hear a disturbance, wait five more minutes and then go straight back to Nancy Shiranuka's. You got me?"

"Yes, sir."

Quickly now, with Commander Ouvarov leading the way, the four of them crossed the lawns surrounding Rancho Encino Hospital, keeping to the shadows of the trees. Behind him, Commander Ouvarov could hear the Tengu's panting, foul and suppressed. For the first time since he had started working for Nancy Shiranuka and Gerard Crowley, he really understood that he was involved in something far more hair-raising than murdering two or three innocent people for the sake of some rich client's revenge. The discreet disposal of business opponents or political enemies or smart young men who had overplayed their romantic overtures to rich men's daughters—that was all a question of day-to-day American business which Commander Ouvarov could accept.

But this Tengu was something different. Behind that expressionless white mask was the face of a man who was actually *possessed*, body and soul, by something from what Commander Ouvarov could only conceive as hell itself. The Tengu's eyes glowed like blue coals in a midnight furnace, his breath rushed and thundered inside his mask, his nearly naked body was hideous with weals and deep holes that actually bared the fibers of the muscles and the bones themselves.

The Tengu was a demon-creature, a man who had voluntarily given himself to a fate which other men would have happily committed suicide to avoid. Yet, according to Doctor Gempaku, to become a Tengu was a far greater honor than to commit *seppuku*. The *bushi* who committed *seppuku* were simply opening the way for themselves to heaven, those who gave themselves to the Tengu were condemning themselves to eternal life and endless purifying pain. It was the Shinto principle of mortification of the flesh to the nth degree.

That was why the first Tengu mission had been less than a complete success. The Tengu had not had sufficient pain inflicted on him to reach a state of total possession by the ancient demon; he had been halfway between euphoria and utter agony, and when Yoshikazu had tried to drive him back to the ranch, his demon had gradually slipped away from him, leaving him in terrible pain but without the spiritual possession that would have enabled him to endure it. Lying in the van, he had gone partly mad.

This time, with the second Tengu, Doctor Gempaku had taken no such chances. He had suspended the Tengu on hooks until the last possible moment, to maximize his suffering. Beneath the Tengu's loincloth, which was already spotted with fresh blood, a ten-inch-long steel spring, an eighth of an inch in diameter, had been pushed inside his urethra, the length of his penis, into his bladder. The pain from this device alone, Doctor Gempaku had told Commander Ouvarov, would make a god out of anyone.

They reached the corner of the hospital's main administration building. From there, they would skirt around the gardens where the patients sat during the day to the intensive care building. According to the drawings of the hospital Commander Ouvarov had secured yesterday from the Encino planning department, they could gain access to the room where Admiral Thorson lay in his oxygen tent by forcing a pair of double doors, walking the length of a 32-foot corridor, and then turning left.

Close by Commander Ouvarov's shoulder, the Tengu breathed beneath his mask with all the roughness of a creature that knows it is about to kill. Commander Ouvarov took a deep breath himself, to steady his nerves, and then said, "Let's go."

They walked quickly between the rows of flowering bushes; past the ornamental pool and the deck furniture. Their feet were silent on the grass and the patio paving. Only that lascivious breathing betrayed their presence.

Suddenly, with no warning at all, a dazzling security light picked all four of them out in blinding relief. The Tengu stopped, twisting this way and that. But Commander Ouvarov hissed, "Keep going! We've taken them by surprise, so keep going!" A door slammed. A voice shouted, "Mr. Davison—there's someone out there!" Then another door slammed, and there was the sound of running feet.

The four of them had almost crossed the gardens now, and were only twenty feet away from the double doors which would take them into the intensive-care unit. But from both sides of the building, hurrying to intercept them, came two security guards with drawn guns.

"Okay, *freeze!*" one of the guards ordered. "Put your hands *up*," and don't move!"

The black-masked Japanese hardly broke stride. One of them uttered a terrifying screech and rushed forward at the security guard with his arms whirling as fast as helicopter blades. The guard fired one wild shot before the Japanese struck him on the bridge of his nose with a *Oni* move known as "the splinter." The broken cartilage of the guard's nose was rammed upward into his brain, killing him instantly.

The other guard, a heavily built man with a gingery mustache, backed away down the side of the intensive-care block, holding his revolver in both hands.

"Keep back there, or I'm going to blow your head off!" he shouted, his voice high-pitched and frightened. "Keep well back there!"

The second *Oni* adept zigzagged toward him, running in such a fast and complicated dance that the guard could hardly keep his gun trained on him. *Oni* students were taught this evasive running by having to dodge a constant shower of crossbow bolts. But even "the dance of the dragonfly" was not enough to protect the Japanese from an erratic and nervous security guard with a .38 revolver. As he flickered toward the guard like a hovering shadow, the guard fired one shot which hit the Japanese straight in the face. A spray of blood pattered on the paving stones, and the Japanese rolled backward.

The first adept took up where his dead comrade had left off: dodging toward the security guard with his hands flailing. The security guard should have fired a second time, but his nerve and his eye failed him. The Japanese screamed out, "Kappa!" and dropkicked the guard on the side of the head. The guard went down with his neck broken, and lay on the ground twitching like a dead chicken.

Now all the floodlights in the hospital grounds had been switched on, and Commander Ouvarov knew that it would be only minutes before the police arrived. He could cope with a few security guards and frightened nurses, but the police would be altogether different. He rapped out to the one remaining Japanese, "Set him loose! Set the Tengu loose!"

The Japanese uttered a strange, chanting cry. The Tengu, who had been standing a little way behind them, now moved purposefully forward to the double doors of

the intensive-care unit and stood in front of them, his
mutilated chest rising and falling as he gathered his
strength. Each door was glazed with a small circular
window, out of which light illuminated the Tengu's white
mask. The Japanese called out again, and this time the
Tengu lifted both his fists, hesitated, and then plunged
them with a slushy crash through the wire-reinforced glass.

Hooking both arms through the broken windows, the
Tengu tore the double doors off their hinges and hurled
them away across the grass.

Commander Ouvarov waited as long as he dared; but he
could already see three more guards making their way,
crouched and furtive, across the hospital gardens. He said
to the Japanese, "Let's get out of here. I'll give you a hand
with your friend." In the distance, police sirens were
warbling, and it was becoming more than clear to Commander Ouvarov that the highly sophisticated security
which protected most of southern California's wealthier
citizens was going to prove a severe obstacle if Gerard
Crowley wanted anyone else done away with. He helped
the Japanese lift the dead *Oni* adept from the lawn, and
between them they dragged him away through the bushes
and into the shadows, and began to make their way back
to the van.

"We go back for the Tengu?" asked the Japanese.

Commander Ouvarov shook his head. "This has all
gotten out of hand. We're going to leave the Tengu
behind. If he doesn't, then it's tough luck. But you won't
catch me scampering back into the arms of the law, just for
the sake of some masochistic Oriental."

The Japanese looked at Commander Ouvarov through
the eye-slits of his mask. It was clear that he was uncertain
and suspicious.

"We cannot leave the Tengu," he argued. "It is our
holy order that we must stay with him, and bring him
back."

"I'm in charge of this particular sortie," said Commander Ouvarov, as they dragged the dead Japanese

through a low cypress hedge. "If I say we leave the Tengu, then we leave him."

"We must go back," insisted the Japanese. The howling of police sirens was already very close.

Commander Ouvarov let the body of the dead Japanese drop to the grass. "C'mere," he said to the *Oni* adept. "I'll tell you what we'll do."

Commander Ouvarov had learned, more years ago than he could remember, that cunning must always be countered with cunning. He had sent countless irate letters to the Pentagon during the Vietnam War, protesting the way in which American forces had blundered with their bombing and defoliants and armored vehicles into a country of philosophical ruthlessness and extraordinary tactical subtlety. You cannot frighten a man who is not frightened of death, he had told them again and again. You cannot overwhelm an enemy whose dedication to fighting and winning grows fiercer, rather than weaker, the nearer he is to defeat. If you live on steak and French fries, if you drive even a moderately comfortable car, if you sleep in a bed and like beer and television, you cannot possibly confront face to face—and beat—a man who knows and wants nothing more than rice, shoes made out of Goodyear tires, and political independence. Not face to face.

That was why, when the *Oni* adept approached him, a trained killer who could have plunged his fist right into the commander's body and wrenched out his living heart, the commander smiled, and put his arm casually and amicably around the boy's shoulders. The boy didn't even realize that he had walked straight into the five-inch shaft of the commander's open switchblade until the arm around his shoulders abruptly tightened around his neck, and the commander gave a loud grunt of exertion and ripped him upward from his groin to his ribcage.

The Japanese stared at Commander Ouvarov, startled. Then his insides slid out like a bloody fertilized egg yolk sliding off a spoon, and he collapsed on top of them.

Commander Ouvarov snapped his knife shut and began to hobble and run for the van, hoping that the Tengu would be causing enough commotion to divert attention from the front of the hospital. It wasn't the first time he had killed a man. He had probably killed hundreds, with sixteen-inch naval shells, from distances of twenty miles away; and once in Okinawa he had cut the throat of a Indonesian pimp who had been trying to hustle him over the price of an eight-year-old girl.

Inside the intensive-care block, the Tengu had reached the door of Admiral Thorson's suite. It was 9:28, and inside the suite Mary Thorson had only just become aware of all the shouting and commotion outside. She put down the faded poems she had been reading, and stood up to see what was going on.

With two powerful kicks, the Tengu smashed down the outside door of the suite and stepped into the chintz-decorated anteroom. He stood there in his white *Nō* mask, both hands raised, turning his head slowly from side to side as he sensed where to go next. His hearing and eyesight were as sharp as samurai sword edges; he was alert to every shuffle and scrape of everything and everybody around him. The pain which burned in his body, gave his senses a demonic acuteness, and he could feel, like a roaring white fire, the presence within him of the Tengu itself, the relentless devil of evil and destruction.

As the Tengu stepped forward to Admiral Thorson's door, he was accompanied by tiny flames that danced in the air: the foxfire *Kitsune-bi*, the visible evidence of evil. Foxfire had pursued Yayegaki Hime, one of the characters in an ancient and still-forbidden Nō play, and it was the mask of Hime that the Tengu wore tonight. It was Kappa's idea.

Mary Thorson, terrified by the sound of the anteroom door being smashed, stood in the middle of the room, her eyes wide, one hand across her breasts, the other half raised as if to protect her husband's oxygen tent. "Who's there?" she demanded. But all she could hear was a dragging sound, and then a clatter as the Tengu threw aside one of the chairs.

The Tengu kicked at the door once, and splintered it. But just as he was about to kick again, Nurse Abramski came unexpectedly through the shattered doorway into the anteroom. The security guards and the police had seen Commander Ouvarov and the second Japanese *bushi* escape across the gardens, and hadn't realized that the Tengu had actually forced his way into the intensive-care unit.

Nurse Abramski shrieked, "Stop! You mustn't!" and ran forward to seize the Tengu's arm, thinking only that he was small and nearly naked, and that he mustn't disturb Admiral Thorson at any cost.

It was only when she gripped the Tengu's wrist that she understood her mistake. He turned, and his face was blank and white, with eyes that seemed to Nurse Abramski to glow with a fluorescent life of their own. His body was deeply muscular, although it was marked all over with terrible scars and weals, and the loincloth he wore was soaked in crimson blood. It was the sheer *evil* he exuded that terrified Nurse Abramski the most, though. It overwhelmed her like a tide of freezing vomit. She tried to step back, tried to release her grasp, but the evil was so intense that she didn't seem to be able to make her legs move properly, didn't seem to be able to open her mouth and scream for help.

With the bursting, flaring sound of a gas ring lighting, a crown of flames ignited around the Tengu's head. His eyes pulsed a mesmerizing blue. With one hideously powerful movement, he seized the lapels of Nurse Abramski's uniform, and the skin of her collarbone with them, and tore the flesh off her shoulders and ribs. Sternomastoid or cleidomastoid muscles, deltoid muscles, pectoral muscles—all, including her breasts, ripped raw from the bone, all the way down to her abdominal muscles.

Beneath her exposed ribs, her lungs expanded in one last powerful shriek of horror. The realization of death.

Then she dropped to the floor and lay dying of shock in her own blood. The Tengu stared down at her, the foxfire still hovering around him. Then he turned back toward the half-splintered door of Admiral Thorson's suite.

Inside, Mary Thorson knew now that she was in terrible danger. She backed away from the door until she reached the edge of her husband's bed. She glanced behind her. There was a window, and although it was closed she knew that it wasn't locked. But what about Knut? How could she leave Knut, comatose and defenseless, to whatever it was that was rampaging in the next room?

She heard more police sirens warble down Balboa Boulevard; she heard the wail of an ambulance, then another. Then there was another shattering kick at the door, and the top hinge burst free.

Panicking, she stared down at "Inch-Thick" lying with his eyes peacefully closed inside his oxygen tent. The door was kicked again. This time the paneling cracked wide apart, and she saw for the first time her assailant's bare and bloody foot. The cardiopulmonary unit beside her husband's bed bleeped on, unconcerned, and the endless electronic ribbon on the electroencephalograph showed normal, ten alpha waves per second.

She could still have made it to the window. But she was already sure that she wasn't going to try. As fearful as she was, she had stayed with Knut through war and peace, through career struggles and great triumphs, through all of his children and all of his hopes; and through almost a year of unconsciousness. How can a love so gentle be so fierce? she thought. How can a soft caress grip with such strength?

There was one final wrenching noise as the shattered door was hurled across the room; and there in front of her stood the Tengu, his hands gloved in drying blood, his masked face surrounded by floating fires as hot and noisy as blowtorches.

"Oh, my dear Lord," she whispered. "Oh, my dear Lord, save me."

The Tengu stalked forward and tried to thrust her away

from the oxygen tent. The magical instructions he had been given by Kappa's servants were explicit: slay the one in the tent of air. It was the man whose blood he was smelling, the man whose body he wanted to rip to pieces. But the woman clawed and struck and screamed at him, and even when he threw her aside across the room, she climbed painfully to her feet and shrieked at him to stop.

Inside the oxygen tent, miraculously, Admiral Thorson opened his eyes. Mary's screaming had penetrated deep into his comatose sleep, and already the alpha waves on his electroencephalograph were hesitating and jumping. He heard her scream again. He actually *heard* her. He tried to turn his head to see what was happening, but he couldn't. He willed himself, *Turn, turn, turn your head*, but his nervous system wouldn't respond.

The Tengu tore at the plastic tent, and it opened with a soft exhalation, a dying beast. But when Mary Thorson threw herself at him again, screaming and screaming, trying to tear off his mask, scratching and clawing at skin that had already been tortured past human endurance.

Pushing her roughly away from him, the Tengu picked up the chromium stand on which Admiral Thorson's nutritive drip was hanging, and gripped it in both hands like a spear. The foxfire around his head burned even brighter as he took up the *Oni* stance called *Shishi-mai*, the lion dance. Then with a howl that was old as Japan and her demons, a cry that came straight from the mouth of a triumphant devil, he thrust the stand deep into Mary Thorson's stomach and lifted her up on it, struggling and kicking and silent with shock. He rammed the stand straight into the wall, so that she was impaled, alive, with her feet more than two feet from the floor.

Panting harshly, the Tengu turned to Admiral Thorson. But his time had already run out. Three policemen appeared in the doorway, two of them armed with revolvers and the third with a pump shotgun; while a fourth policeman smashed the window with the butt of a rifle and thrust the muzzle through the shattered frame.

"Freeze! Lie flat on the floor with your arms and your legs spread!" one of the officers ordered.

The officer with the pump shotgun, however, wasn't going to wait. He fired one deafening shot and hit the Tengu in the chest. The Tengu pitched around, staggered, but remained upright, his chest smoking, swaying on his feet. The officer reloaded and fired again, and this time blew the Tengu's head apart, so that nothing rose from between his shoulders but the bloody pipe of his neck. As if in nervous reaction, the other officers fired at the headless body too, six or seven times, until it sagged at the knees and dropped heavily to the floor.

Slowly, walking knee-deep through their own glutinous fear, the officers stepped into the room. One of them said, "Jesus H. Christ."

They lifted Mary Thorson down from the wall as carefully as disciples in a religious painting. They looked down at the Tengu, and then looked away again and holstered their guns. They couldn't think of anything to say.

"Will you look at this guy?" one of them said at last. "These goddamned marks all over his body."

After five minutes they declared the room safe for paramedics, medical examiners, forensic staff, TV, press, and anybody else who wanted to mill around and stare at all the blood. A newspaper woman came in, took one look, and hurried outside again to be sick. The medical examiner kept asking for body bags, but nobody seemed to have remembered to bring them. One of the paramedics kept saying, "What is he, Japanese or something? What do you think, Japanese?"

"No head, could be anything," replied a local detective, in a voice as crackly as an old-time radio. "I don't know what kind of *charge* the uniformed guys are putting in their shotguns these days, but you can bet your ass that somebody's going to start an inquiry about it. Look at that, no head. Could have been hit by a fucking cannon."

"Did you bring those bags or didn't you?"

"Speared her, right to the fucking wall."

"Will you move back, please?"

At last, arguing and pushing as he came, Admiral Thorson's personal physician was able to force his way into the room. Dr. Isaac Walach, was a tall, thin, balding man, one of the country's wealthiest and most expert specialists in apoplexy and brain seizures. He ignored the police and the blood and the medical examiners crouched over the corpse of the Tengu, and went straight to Admiral Thorson's bedside. All the monitoring equipment had been torn loose and the oxygen pump disconnected, although one of the policemen had been quickwitted enough to turn off the oxygen supply in case of fire. Doctor Walach made a quick check of the Admiral's pulse rate and vital signs, lifting back his eyelids to check his response to light, listening to his heart. Then he quietly tugged one of the paramedic's sleeves and said, "Help me get this patient out of here, please. He's still alive."

CHAPTER TWO

She came to the door in a black silk robe, painted by hand with modern graphic designs by Shigeo Fukuda, yellow-and-green faces interlinked to form the falling figure of a bird. She said, "Yes, what is it?" in a mystified tone that was strangely attractive.

He recognized her for what she was: Hokkaido Japanese, probably from Sapporo. He said, "My name's Sennett."

"Yes?" she asked.

Jerry hesitated. He had come to Nancy Shiranuka's apartment on Alta Loma Road on nothing more than a hunch: another cold wind that had blown through his mind. He didn't know what he had been expecting to find: David bound and gagged and tied to a chair maybe? He didn't even understand what it was that haunted him so persistently about Japan. Now, here he was, facing a pretty Japanese girl who had asked him what he wanted, and he didn't have the first idea what to say.

"I, er, I heard about Kemo," he told her in a hoarse voice.

She raised one eyebrow. A perfect arch, finely drawn.

"I was down at police headquarters," he said. "They told me there."

"Are you a police officer?"

He shook his head.

There was a lengthy silence. Nancy at last said, "You've come about your son, I suppose?"

"You know where he is? Is he safe?"

Nancy reached out and gently held the sleeve of his jacket. "He's safe for the time being. Come in. There's nobody here at the moment."

Jerry felt as if his head were exploding with questions and anxiety, but he knew Japanese etiquette well enough to hold his tongue, and to follow Nancy into her silent, austere apartment.

"Sit down," said Nancy, indicating a cushion. Jerry eased himself into the cross-legged position which he had once accepted as the only way to sit, but which now required some painful tugging at his shins.

"You're certain he's safe?" he asked.

"Certain," said Nancy. "They have taken him for the express purpose of flushing you out of your home, to entice you to a place where they can easily dispose of you. They will take great care of him until you are dead."

"Who's *they*?" demanded Jerry.

Nancy went across to the liquor cabinet, slid it open, and took out a bottle of Gekkeikan export saké. She poured it carefully into a flask and left it to warm. She said, "I do not know their identity any more than you do. But they are hawks."

"It was you who left that scroll under my windshield?"

"It was a friend who put it there. But the message came from me."

"I should have understood it," said Jerry, with bitter realization. 'The hawks will return to their roost.' To catch the lamb, of course. It's from something by Tanizaki Jun'ichiro. *Chijin no Ai*?"

Nancy said, "You impress me."

"A Westerner shouldn't be conversant with sadistic Japanese literature of the 1920's? Why did you leave me the message if you didn't think that I'd understand it?"

"I hoped you would grasp it intuitively."

Jerry tugged again at his awkwardly folded leg. "As it turned out, I was in too much of a hurry. The police wanted me to look at a suspect they've charged with murdering Sherry Cantor and that police officer out on the Hollywood Freeway."

Nancy poured out a little saké and handed it to Jerry in a fragile porcelain cup. She took some herself, and then sat down close to him. "You are an unusual man," she said. "I sense that there is something hanging over your head."

"A mushroom cloud," he told her wryly, and raised his glass. "*Kampai*!"

"*Kampai*!" she echoed.

They drank, and sat in silence for a while. Then Jerry said, "These people who have taken David—they're the same people who sent that man to murder me?"

Nancy said, "You understand, then, that Sherry Cantor's murder was a mistake?"

"I understood the minute the police described the assailant as wearing a white Nō mask. And—I had a feeling, I guess—something to do with the fact that I've been undergoing psychiatric treatment for years after what happened to me in Japan—and, I don't know. I just guessed."

Nancy reached forward and picked up the saké flask again. Her black robe opened a little, and Jerry was conscious in a way that made him feel curiously old, but also curiously aroused, that he had glimpsed the dark areola of her nipple. Underneath that thin silk robe, she must be naked.

How can I be so anxious about David, he thought of himself, and still think something like that? But then she passed him a fresh cup of saké and he remembered that he was sitting with a Japanese woman. His mind, after all these years, had slipped back into the timeless traditional way of observing every ritual scrupulously, whatever its importance. There was a time for everything, for anxiety, for passion, for pursuit, and revenge. There was also time for saké, and quiet intensive conversation, and the studied but accidental glimpse of a beautiful woman's breast. It was quite possible she had allowed the accident to happen, to reassure him.

"Are you one of them?" Jerry asked her.

Nancy stared at him for a moment, as if she were unsure. Then she said, "No, it is impossible to be 'one of them.' They are not a gang, in the conventional sense of the word, nor a sect. I am unsure what they are; but I do now realize that they are evil and powerful. I am employed by one of their hired running dogs as a translator, organizer, general drag lady."

She sipped at her drink, and then said, "A few days ago I became curious about them: why they wanted to kill you, who they really are. I sent my houseboy Kemo to follow one of them after a meeting. If you saw my address at the police headquarters, then you will know what happened to him."

"I only glimpsed the report," said Jerry, with a dry mouth. "It seems they tore his heart out."

"It is a technique used in a particular martial art known as *Oni*, the art of the demons," Nancy explained, almost as if she were talking to a party of tourists. Then she looked up at Jerry, and her eyes were hard and dark and unforgiving. "The adept's arm is swung around to gain velocity, in the same way that a baseball pitcher winds up. By the time it reaches his intended victim, his hand is formed in the shape of a chisel, fingers straight, and it is traveling as fast as a bullet train. The technique is to drive the hand right through the muscular wall of the stomach, upward and slightly to the right, and to seize the victim's heart.''

Jerry said quietly, "I've heard of *Oni*. But it's forbidden, isn't it? I mean, it's actually illegal."

"Illegality, danger, death, they are all part of what makes the Japanese personality what it is," said Nancy. "You are speaking of the people who invented *seppuku* and *kamikaze* and the rituals of Shrine Shinto. You are speaking of people who eat *fugu* fish not because it tastes better than any other, but because it can kill within minutes. Can you imagine sitting down to a dinner, not knowing if you will ever arise from it alive?"

"Is there any particular reason why I should believe you?" asked Jerry. "Can you give me any *guarantee* that David is unhurt and still alive?"

Nancy Shiranuka watched him for a while, and then said, "No. But if you have only half an understanding of what is happening here, you will know that I am risking my life telling you any of this. If I fail, the next Tengu they send out will be for me."

Jerry lifted one finger, his mouth half open, in sudden and complete understanding. "The Tengu," he whispered. "So I was right."

"You guessed it was the Tengu? That was what they were afraid of. That was why they sent him to kill you. There can be only two or three people in the United States who know what a Tengu is, what a Tengu can do. They wanted to launch their program without anybody knowing what they were doing."

"What program?" Jerry asked her. "What are you talking about?"

"They are creating a corps of killer bodyguards," Nancy told him. "A band of fanatical and superbly fit Japanese who will do whatever they're told to protect their masters. Well, that is what they *claim* they are doing. Whether they are speaking the truth or not, I don't know. That's all they ever tell us. But they may have underestimated what I knew about the Tengu from the days in which I was a disciple of the Seven Black *Kami*. And they may have underestimated my intuition."

"Your cold wind?" asked Jerry gently.

"My cold wind," nodded Nancy. "The cold wind which tells me that if they are creating Tengus, they have more in mind than a mildly profitable scheme to sell killer bodyguards to rich Arabs and Arizona *mafiosi*. If they are creating Tengus, they have only one thing in mind. And that is, apocalypse."

Jerry thought for a long while. Then he said, "Where is my son?"

"They have a ranch out at Pacoima, in the San Gabriel Mountains near San Fernando Airport. That is where they have been keeping the Tengus. I expect they took your son there as well."

Jerry said, "You're not tricking me, are you? This isn't part of a setup, just to get me out to some place where they can kill me quietly and get it over with? Or is it naive to ask?"

She said softly, in her Japanese accent, "I have been through varying degrees of hell in my life, Mr. Sennett. I have committed crimes of greed and crimes of passion and the greatest crime of not taking care of my soul or my body. I can be many things to many different men. I can experience pleasure, and call it pain. I can experience pain, and call it pleasure. I was blackmailed into helping these people. They threatened to turn over to the FBI a file of photographs and documents which would have implicated me in child pornography, abduction, pimping, illegal sexual activities, and manslaughter. At the same time, they offered me a very great deal of money. They told me they required absolute secrecy and absolute devotion. I was to translate technical data for them; arrange house leases and car rentals and hotel facilities; and act as hostess and translator for their employees and guests."

"And they told you they were creating this special team of bodyguards?"

"That's correct. They said that one of their doctors had discovered a new technique during the Tokyo Olympics for making men stronger and more tolerant to pain. They called the men Tengus—which at first I thought was simply a nickname like calling a baseball team the Red Devils. It was only after they killed that girl, Sherry Cantor, that I began to doubt them. Now, I am quite sure that they have been misleading me."

Jerry asked, "Have you told anybody what you think?" His voice was dull and expressionless.

Nancy said, "One of them, a man called Gerard Crowley. He is the go-between, the man who arranges for all the Japanese to come into the United States without being stopped by immigration officers; the man who takes care of the finance."

"What did he say?"

"He didn't know whether to believe me or not. They told him nothing more than they told me. But, he may be sympathetic. I'm not sure. He is a very cold person, very difficult to reach."

Jerry held out his cup for more saké. He wasn't at all drunk. It usually took more than half a bottle to get him anything near tipsy. He felt highly suspicious of Nancy Shiranuka, and yet he couldn't really see any reason why he should. She had tried to warn him, after all, as subtly as she knew how, and if he hadn't understood her message about the hawks, then it had been his own fault. She certainly hadn't advertised her address, so she couldn't have been prepared for him to come around. The Japanese were always so meticulous: even their accidents didn't happen by accident. But Jerry couldn't believe that he had been afforded a glimpse of Nancy's address by design.

He said, "You know why they wanted to kill me, don't you?"

Nancy replied. "It was something to do with the war. Something to do with the fact that, if any of the Tengus had been mentioned in the press or on television, you would have known at once what they were. It was a question of security, they told me."

"Well, you're partly right," said Jerry. "In fact, they needn't have worried. A Tengu attacked Sherry Cantor next door, quite horribly and spectacularly, and even when I heard what had happened to her, I didn't put two and two together, not at first. It was all too long ago, too far away. The thing still haunts me, still gives me nightmares, but who would have imagined that it would return for real? Not me. I would have been the last one to think of a Tengu, no matter how grotesquely anyone was butchered. It was only the Nō mask that reminded me. The face of the greatest *Oni* of all, the demon of a hundred identities and a million cruel ways."

Nancy said, "You know about the Tengu, don't you?" Jerry nodded.

"Tell me everything," she said. "I promise we will do whatever we can to find your son. But tell me everything. It could help me to understand what is happening, and who is creating these monsters, and why."

Jerry stood up, and walked across to the window. "I'm not supposed to tell you this," he said. He felt very tired and empty, and somehow his disloyalty to his country's secrets tasted like ashes, as if all the confidential dispatches which had comprised the Appomattox Papers had been burned, as a punishment, on his tongue. "But, during the latter part of the Pacific war, when I was a lieutenant in the Naval Intelligence Command, bright, intelligent, just out of college, I was told that I had volunteered to be parachuted at night into Japan, into the Chugoku Sanchi, not far from Hiroshima, to monitor at close quarters the military radio messages that were being sent to and from Hiroshima to Tokyo."

Nancy said nothing, but lit a cigarette.

Jerry said, "I was the ideal candidate for the job, they told me. I was young and fit. I spoke fluent Japanese. I had worked for nearly two years on Japanese naval codes, and I could put on a headset and understand what the commander of the *Akagi* was saying to the commander of the *Soryu* without even bothering to jot it all down."

He paused for a moment or two, and then he said, "They called the mission 'Appomattox.' They warned me that the chances of my returning to the United States alive were not particularly high; but that what I was going to do was going to be crucial to the entire course of the war. In fact, more than that, to the entire course of twentieth-century history.

"They said that, all across the Pacific theater, U.S. Marines had been suddenly met by fierce opposition from special Japanese troops they had codenamed 'Hogs.' The exact casualty ratio was top secret, they told me, and as far as I'm aware, it still is today. But to give you some idea, five amphibious landings on small Pacific islands yielded a U.S. casualty list of more than twenty-three thousand men dead, and eighteen million dollars of equipment lost, and these were on nothing more than atolls and reefs of minor strategic importance. The island of Pulau Thuap only fell to the Marines after three separate attempts at storming its beaches, and seventeen saturation-bombing missions by B-25's."

"The Tengus," whispered Nancy.

Jerry tiredly rubbed his eyes. "The Japanese were sending Tengus out to every possible location in the Pacific, in a last hopeless attempt to turn the tide of the war. There must have been hundreds of them, even thousands. At that time, it couldn't have been difficult to find enough fanatical young Japanese who were prepared to submit themselves to the pain which was necessary for them to become . . . well, what they became."

"Possessed," Nancy prompted him.

"I don't know," said Jerry. "I wasn't sure then, and I'm still not. After the war was over, and I was sent back to Tokyo, I spent days reading everything I could on ancient Shinto rituals and Japanese demonology. But who knows? The human mind and the human physique are capable of extraordinary things under stress, and in conditions of trance or religious ecstasy. The members of the Pentecostal Holiness Church in Kentucky drink strychnine and burn their feet with blazing torches, just to show that the Lord will protect them against harm. I saw a fire-walk myself in Polynesia, when a man walked twenty yards over white-hot coals with bare feet and appeared to be unscathed. You think to yourself, are these people really possessed by angels, or devils, or are they simply using their ordinary human capabilities to the utmost—something which most of us rarely do?''

Nancy said nothing, but waited for Jerry to continue. It was growing dark outside, and somewhere in that darkness David was being held captive, for a ransom which amounted to nothing less than Jerry's own life. The thought was clinging around his mind like a tangle of barbed wire, and already his emotions and his desperate love for David were scratched and bleeding and raw.

"They parachuted six of us into the Chugoku Sanchi at night, with a high-power Stromberg wireless receiver and enough food to last us for a week. We set up three base camps in the mountains and trekked from one to the other, listening at each one to the military and code messages that the Japanese were putting out from Hiroshima. Most of the wireless traffic was routine—which ships were docking, how many troops were being embarked for where, how much ammunition was available, what their civil-defense plans were in case of an American assault. But after three days we picked up a different batch of signals from the center of the city, from a building which we pinpointed on our street plans, by simple triangulation, near a bridge across the Ota River. All the signals were related to what they called the Tengus, the devil-people. We listened for four days and four nights, and by the end of that time we were absolutely certain that it was right there, in that building in Hiroshima, that the Hogs were being trained.''

Jerry came away from the window and sat down again. Nancy poured him another drink, and watched him with caution and sympathy. It was clear from the look in his eyes that he had relived those wartime days in Japan over and over again, dreaming and awake, and that he would carry the responsibility for what he had done forever.

"They had briefed me, before I was dropped into Japan, that if I found the place where the Hogs were being created, I was going to be giving the President the go-ahead to use a completely new type of bomb, an incredibly devastating firebomb, they told me, which would instantly incinerate the Hogs and give them no chance of survival whatever. They had Japanese experts helping the U.S. Intelligence Commands—experts in Japanese demonology, as I later found out—and it was the opinion of these advisers that the only way in which the Tengus could be eradicated without any fear of their revival would be to vaporize them with an atomic bomb. You know the legends, I expect. If a Tengu is chopped to pieces, even *one* piece, on its own, remains capable of independent life. And so nothing could remain. Not even a fingernail.

"Well, I was sure that I had found the place. Every signal confirmed it. I radioed a message to the USS *Value*, which was waiting off Mi-Shima in the Sea of Japan, and the *Value*, in turn, relayed the message to the U.S. Pacific Fleet. President Truman was at Yalta at the time, with Stalin and Churchill. They gave him the message, and he said go. The official justification was that, if America had the means to bring the war to a swift conclusion, she ought to do so, which as far as it went was quite true. But what they omitted to tell the public and the press was that two or three thousand Tengus could have held up the American advance for five or six years, even longer; and that General MacArthur had already expressed the opinion in a confidential memorandum to President Truman that an invasion of the Japanese mainland would cost an unacceptably high number of American casualties. That is, unless the Tengus were eliminated, totally."

"Which is what you justifiably did," said Nancy.

"Yes," Jerry agreed. "But when I confirmed the position of the Tengu training center, right in the middle of Hiroshima, among ten square kilometers of wooden houses, I didn't understand that our 'incredibly devastating firebomb' was going to be an atomic bomb. I didn't understand that, for the sake of killing three or four hundred fanatical young Japanese soldiers, we were going to wipe out eighty thousand men, women, and children in the space of a split second, and that another sixty thousand were going to die of radioactivity within a year.''

He was silent for a very long while. Then he said, "I didn't *know*.''

"And if you *had* known?'' asked Nancy.

Again he was silent. "I'm not sure,'' he replied at last. "When you're in a war, everything looks different. I lost all five of the men who were with me. We got caught in crossfire on the beach at Kokubu, when the landing craft tried to pick us up. Japanese Coast Guardsmen, most of them not much more than sixteen and seventeen years old. They caught us like ducks on a pond. I only got away because I could swim. Five men lost out of six, and I thought it was a massacre.

"Then I heard that they'd dropped the atomic bomb. Compared to that, my massacre was a school picnic.''

Nancy allowed Jerry to settle into repose. Then she said, "Nagasaki?''

"I don't know,'' said Jerry. "They might have suspected another Tengu center there, but I doubt it. They probably realized that the atomic bomb was so damned effective that they could end the war almost immediately. Jesus—once you've killed a hundred and forty thousand people, what does it matter if you kill seventy thousand more?''

Nancy said, "You still blame yourself after all this time?''

"Wouldn't you? I could have sent back a radio message saying that I hadn't found anything.''

"Then you would have had to take the responsibility for all of the American soldiers who would have been killed by the Tengus.''

Jerry gave her a wry, lopsided smile, the first smile he

had managed since he had heard that David had been kidnapped. "You see my problem," he told her.

Nancy went to her tape deck and switched on a soft recording of *koto* music. There was something about her stillness, something about the peace of her apartment, that made Jerry feel as if whole centuries might have passed by since he had first rung her doorbell.

He said, "I don't know why I've told you all of this. Apart from my shrink, you're the first person I've ever discussed it with. They could put me into jail for twenty years for what I've said to you tonight."

Nancy said, "You want your son back."

"Yes."

"And your son is more important than twenty years in jail?"

"Yes."

"Then you have been justified in telling me about the Tengus, and about the bomb. You and I have more in common than you think."

Jerry reached across and took out one of Nancy's cigarettes. "How's that?" he asked her.

"The Tengus have affected both of our lives. You, because of what you did in the war. Me, because I am now being blackmailed into helping them come back to life. And also because I was once a member of the shrine that worships the Seven Black *Kami*, of whom the Tengu is the greatest and the most terrible."

Jerry said, "I want my son, Miss Shiranuka. What can I do?"

"You can stay here and wait for a while," said Nancy. "Gerard Crowley is due here in just about an hour's time, and you can talk to him."

"It must have been Gerard Crowley who arranged for the Tengu to kill me in the first place. The Tengu who murdered Sherry Cantor."

"It was," said Nancy blandly.

"Then how can I talk to him about David? I mean, how can I—"

"Gerard Crowley has changed a little in the past few days, the same as I have," said Nancy. "Like me, he is beginning to realize that he is extremely dispensible; and that unless he hedges his bets, he may find himself a very bad loser. We are all in fear of our lives."

Jerry said, "Forget it. I'm going straight out to that Pacoima Ranch right now."

"You want to bring your son back alive?"

"Of course I do."

"Then control your anger. Hold back your impatience. Wait and speak with Mr. Crowley. You are up against an enemy which only Presidents and atomic bombs have been able to defeat in the past. You are up against the accumulation of centuries of Japanese history, and a devil that speaks with many voices. Gerard may help. Gerard may tell you how to get your son back. But you must beware, for even Gerard himself may be the devil, or the devil's disciple."

CHAPTER THREE

Mr. Esmeralda heard the news from Rancho Encino at a few minutes after eleven o'clock, on ABC television's evening roundup. He was standing in front of the mirror in his rented house on Camden Drive, fastening his red-and-white silk necktie, in preparation for Commander Ouvarov's imminently expected return from Encino and for the visit he would have to make subsequently to the split-level house in Laurel Canyon, to give Kappa his report that Admiral Thorson had been successfully slain.

Through the half-open bedroom door, he could see Kuan-yin sitting in the parlor in her chauffeur's uniform, her tunic unbuttoned as far as her heavy bronze belt buckle, her brown-booted legs crossed, reading *TV Guide*. His Spanish maid, Luisa, was clearing the table from the evening meal. Then he heard, "From Encino tonight, we've just heard that a maniac killer—"

"Turn it up!" Mr. Esmeralda demanded. "Quickly, turn the sound up!"

Kuan-yin reached for the remote control and casually increased the volume. Mr. Esmeralda walked slowly into the parlor, his hands still holding his half-fastened necktie, listening with dreadful attention to the news which he had feared from the very beginning.

"—examiner says that she died instantly from her injuries, although he would not yet detail what these actually were. His only comment was that it was a 'terrible multiple murder, the work of a madman.' The bodies of two other Japanese were discovered in bushes in the hospital grounds, one of them shot by security guards, the other apparently the victim of a knife attack by his Caucasian associate. Detectives from Hollywood who have been working on the barehanded killings earlier this week of *Our Family Jones* star Sherry Cantor and a uniformed police patrolman by the side of the Hollywood Freeway have been in close contact with Encino detectives as—"

Mr. Esmeralda scarcely heard the rest of the report. He sat down on the arm of the sofa and gradually tugged his necktie loose, twisting it around his hands like a garotte. So, Commander Ouvarov had failed, and the Tengu had not only been seen and caught, but killed. He supposed it wasn't really the commander's fault. Breaking into the hospital and attempting to silence Admiral Thorson had been a fanatical idea at best. But Mr. Esmeralda knew that Kappa would never take the blame for what had happened, and he also knew that Kappa would lay much of the blame on *him*.

Worse still, the police would now be in possession of a wealth of circumstantial and forensic clues which could lead them, eventually, to an arrest. They were likely to be questioning the Japanese community already about

unusual comings and goings among Japanese; and if
Gerard Crowley had been even slightly careless in his
dealings with the immigration authorities, they could pick
him up within hours.

He listened to the end of the bulletin, to see if there was
any news about Admiral Thorson himself, but the
announcer didn't even mention him. That meant the old
man was probably still alive; and if that was the case,
Kappa's fury would be devastating. Twice the Tengus had
been sent out to kill, and twice they have failed. Mr.
Esmeralda had warned Kappa again and again about
employing unstable people like Gerard Crowley and
Ernest Ouvarov, but Kappa had been adamant that their
hirelings should not only be dispensable, but "tainted
with the breath of evil." Only men and women without
any social or sexual morals would be able to undertake the
greatest task of all, the task for which the Tengus had been
created from the beginning.

Kuan-yin asked Mr. Esmeralda, "It has gone wrong?"

Mr. Esmeralda glanced toward Luisa, to indicate to
Kuan-yin that she shouldn't discuss Tengu business in
front of the maid. But he nodded and said, "Badly wrong.
There will be serious trouble now."

"What will you do?" asked Kuan-yin, when Luisa had
gone back down the short flight of stairs that led to the
dining room and the kitchen.

"I will have to face them, whatever," said Mr.
Esmeralda. "You cannot run away from people like the
Circle of Burned Doves. Especially if you want to continue
working in Japan."

"They will kill you," said Kuan-yin.

"No," said Mr. Esmeralda. "Not yet. They have gone
this far, but they have not yet completed whatever it is
they want to do. I think I am comparatively safe until they
have accomplished their purpose."

"You have never told me their purpose."

Mr. Esmeralda lifted the points of his collar and began
tying his necktie again. "I have not wished to burden you.

What they want to do is utterly catastrophic. If I told you, you would not understand. But, I have committed myself to helping them."

"Why?" asked Kuan-yin. In the evening lamplight, her face looked very pretty and serene. "I always thought you were a man of great independence. The son of the great pirate Jesus Esmeralda."

Mr. Esmeralda tugged the knot of his necktie straight and examined himself carefully in the gilt-framed mirror that hung on the parlor wall. The shiny hair was perfectly combed back, and the mustache was immaculately scissored. He thought he looked handsome, but also out of date, like a character out of a 1950's movie. If he hadn't been able to play the part of "Mr. Esmeralda" as if he were acting, he probably wouldn't have the nerve to survive. The world in which he lived was dangerous and bizarre, where sudden death was considered to be the least of a man's worries.

Kuan-yin stood up and walked across to him, laying her hand on his arm. She said, "It is years since we were lovers."

"You cannot measure what I feel for you in years," he told her, his dark eyes looking down at her with compelling steadiness. There was a moment of silence, and then Kuan-yin let him go. It was no use. He was the kind of man whose soul lived somewhere else, away from his body. What you saw was suntan and greased-back hair and clipped mustache; a papier-mâché mask with nothing behind it but cocktails, sentimental chatter, and emptiness. The real Mr. Esmeralda was unreachable.

"Do you think you are in very great danger?" she asked him.

He looked at her unblinkingly, and said, "It is no time for losing my head. There is too much money at stake. And too many lives. The Japanese are not deterred by such concepts as fairness or justice; and they are certainly not deterred by American law. If they wish to murder me, they will. But they will have to outwit me first."

When he had finished, he asked Kuan-yin to drive him across to West Los Angeles, to Eva Crowley's apartment. Kuan-yin said nothing, but went to fetch her cap. In the car, while Mr. Esmeralda listened to the radio news in the hope of finding out more about what had happened at Rancho Encino, Kuan-yin remained silent and aloof, although Mr. Esmeralda could see her eyes watching him in the rearview mirror.

"What if Commander Ouvarov comes back and finds that you've gone out?" she asked him at last.

"Commander Ouvarov will never come back. Didn't you hear what they said on the television? One of the Japanese was probably killed by his associate. That means that Commander Ouvarov panicked and ran, but not before he had disposed of anyone who could identify him. In my opinion, he probably killed Yoshikazu in the same way. So much less trouble than taking him all the way down to Mexico and smuggling him over the border. Commander Ouvarov is a profiteer, an opportunist, a murderer, a pimp, and a sexual deviant. He had a reputation for efficient organization, and that is why I asked Nancy Shiranuka to hire him. Maybe I was wrong. Maybe he was too old for the job. It is too late to be concerned about that now, and too late to be concerned about him. He is probably halfway to Mexico already."

"Supposing he goes to the police?"

"Commander Ouvarov has been involved in too many rackets and too many unsavory deals to risk going to the police. He is still wanted in five states, including Washington and Nevada. He is wanted in New York for jumping bail. Commander Ouvarov will never go to the police."

"Not even for a little plea-bargaining?"

Mr. Esmeralda didn't answer. He knew from experience how little honor there was among thieves. And among the motley hirelings he had been obliged to collect for the Tengu project, there was no honor whatsoever. All they had in common was fear and greed, and if someone else could frighten them more, or offer them more money, then their allegiance to Mr. Esmeralda would evaporate like Pacific fog. He had no illusions about them.

Kuan-yin pulled the limousine into the curb outside Eva Crowley's apartment. Mr. Esmeralda said, "Come back for me at six A.M. Bring some hot towels with you, and a change of clothes."

Kuan-yin said, "You're not taking the lady any flowers?"

Mr. Esmeralda smiled at her wryly. "I can do better than that," he said, and took out of his pocket a gold-and-diamond bracelet.

Eva Crowley came to the door in a smart, schoolmarmish blouse with a pleated bib and a severe black pencil skirt. She said breathlessly, "I didn't expect to see you again."

"But, I'm here," said Mr. Esmeralda, with a self-satisfied grin. "Aren't you going to invite me in?"

"The twins are home. We were just about to have a snack. Then we were going to watch a little television and go to bed."

"You don't want me to meet your daughters?"

"Well, it's not that I don't *want* you to . . ."

"Then invite me in." Mr. Esmeralda beamed. He reached through the half-open door and held her wrist. "You can tell them that I am an old friend of your husband's. A cigar exporter from Dominica."

"Well . . ." Eva hesitated.

Mr. Esmeralda reached into his pocket and took out the bracelet, dangling it in front of Eva's eyes. "You won't even let me in if I *bribe* you?" he asked her.

Eva relaxed and smiled. "All right. But only for an hour or so. The girls have to go on a field trip tomorrow for school, and I want them to have a moderately early night."

"Your wish is law," said Mr. Esmeralda, and bowed.

Inside the Crowley's apartment, the mathematical sterility of Gerard's modern Italian décor had already been overwhelmed by dozens of rock records and magazines and scruffy-looking schoolbooks, as well as two girls' college sweaters, three fluorescent-yellow sneakers, a pink Fiorucci bag crammed with hairbrushes and makeup, and a disassembled hair-dryer which looked as if it could never assembled again. On the Giulini sofa, in tight matador pants and T-shirts, sat Kathryn and Kelly Crowley, both 17, identical twins, painting their toenails, Kathryn plum and Kelly green. They were very pretty girls, an inch taller than their mother, with dark wavy hair and wide slate-and-lavender-colored eyes.

"We-e-ell," said Kelly saucily, looking up from her toenail painting. "Who's this, Moth-*err*?"

"Don't you be so fresh," Eva Crowley snapped back. "This is a business colleague of your father's, Mr. Esmeralda. Mr. Esmeralda, this is Kelly, and this is Kathryn. Girls, clean up all this mess, will you? Mr. Esmeralda came by to see your father, but the least we can do is offer him a drink. Isn't that right, Mr. Esmeralda?"

"It is a great pleasure," replied Mr. Esmeralda, exaggerating his South American accent. "It isn't often that one sees *one* young girl as beautiful as you, let alone two."

"Do you have a Christian name, Mr. Esmeralda?" asked Kathryn boldly.

Mr. Esmeralda nodded. "I was baptized Jesus, after my father. But, for understandable reasons, most of my close friends call me by second name, Carlos."

"I think I prefer Jesus," said Kathryn.

"Would you like a drink?" Eva interrupted. "I've restocked the cabinet since you were last here."

"Mother's *always* restocking the cabinet." Kelly winked at Mr. Esmeralda. "She *does* like her little celebration now and again."

"Thank you, Kelly," said Eva sharply.

Mr. Esmeralda said, "I'll have a negroni, if you don't mind. Shall I mix my own?"

"Oh, please."

"Can we call you Carlos?" asked Kathryn. "Carlos Esmeralda, it sounds very romantic. Do you come from

South America, Carlos?''

Mr. Esmeralda took out gin and Campari. "I didn't think for one moment that your daughters would be so grown up," he told Eva. "when you said 'twin daughters,' I imagined two little moppets in ribbons and frills."

"Moppets?" Kathryn exclaimed. "I haven't heard anyone say 'moppets' since I was a moppet. Oh, you're wonderful, Carlos. You're just like Desi Arnaz. Or Ricardo Montalban."

"Kathryn, will you stop being so *personal*," demanded her mother.

"I don't mind," said Mr. Esmeralda, shaking his cocktail in Gerard's most elegant Italian silver shaker. "When you are swarthy, like me, and when you have a South American accent, as I do, you deliberately cultivate a social personality that is halfway between Edmundo Ros and Rudolph Valentino. Perhaps it's outdated, but people like it."

"You're so outdated you make me *dizzy*," said Kelly.

Eva laughed. "I hope you can take all this ribbing," she told Mr. Esmeralda. Mr. Esmeralda poured out his cocktail with all the deftness of a bartender, turned around, raised his glass, and grinned. "From three such beautiful ladies, a man can accept anything."

"*Anything?*" asked Kelly in a deep, melodramatic voice.

Mr. Esmeralda put down his glass. "In actual fact, I came here to invite your mother out.

"We had planned an early evening," said Eva.

"I'm sure your lovely daughters will not miss you," smiled Mr. Esmeralda. "Now please, you cannot refuse me."

Eva smiled and blushed. "I don't know. I shouldn't really."

"Oh, go *on*, Mother," insisted Kelly. "God knows you deserve to have a night out. Especially a really *old-fashioned* night out. What could be better?"

"All right," said Eva, after a moment. "But you'll have

to give me a minute to change."

"Bravo!" said Kathryn, and clapped her hands over her head.

While Eva dressed, Mr. Esmeralda mixed himself another negroni, and told the twins fanciful anecdotes about his life in the Caribbean and the Far East, and a far-fetched story about the time he had agreed to stand up against a wooden fence in Nightmute, Alaska, as the human target for a Canadian bowie-knife thrower. "The sweat froze on my forehead like seed pearls," he said, and the girls giggled in disbelief and delight.

"I can't think why Mother hasn't talked about you *before*," said Kelly.

Mr. Esmeralda gave her a noncommittal shrug. "Sometimes a lady likes to keep certain things to herself. Don't you have secret thoughts, secret ideas, of your own?" He raised one dark, well-combed eyebrow. "Don't you have your own secret desires?"

Kathryn giggled. Mr. Esmeralda was so much of a Latin smoothie that she couldn't decide whether to be amused, amazed, flattered, impressed, or simply skeptical. Yet because he was so stereotypical, because he seemed to have stepped down from the conductor's podium of some cheap rumba band in Rio de Janeiro, she found herself responding to him in a stereotypical way, flirting with him, flashing her eyes at him, metaphorically clutching a rose between bared teeth.

"You won't keep Moth-*err* out too late, will you?" she asked him. "Or maybe you will."

Mr. Esmeralda laughed. It was a laugh as flat and humorless as castanets.

"We'll see," he said. "Life is more exciting when it is uncertain, don't you think? Certainties dull the palate."

Kelly was about to answer when the door opened and her mother reappeared, in the cream-colored Bill Blass cocktail dress she had bought when she first found out about Gerard and Francesca. Her hair was brushed, diamonds sparkled in her ears, she looked prettier and more confident than she had for months. She came across and took Mr. Esmeralda's arm. He, in turn, laid his hand over hers and smiled as possessively as a bridegroom.

"You have beautiful daughters," he told her. "And it is very easy to see how they inherited their looks."

"You're teasing me," said Eva.

"No," said Mr. Esmeralda. "It is one of the firmest rules of my life, never to tease."

They were driven by taxi to the Occidental Center on South Olive. It would have been easier for Kuan-yin to drive them, but Mr. Esmeralda did not want to risk being seen too obviously in public with Eva. It was a question of discretion, rather than absolute secrecy. In the back of the taxi, Eva said, "I haven't been taken out by a strange man for years."

"I am so strange?" asked Mr. Esmeralda.

She looked at him. "No," she said. "Not so strange. Not really."

They knew Mr. Esmeralda well at The Tower; he was ushered at once to a table by the window, overlooking the twinkling lights of Greater L.A. He ordered drinks for both of them and talked fluently and endlessly, about money, about trading, about the Far East, about the beauty and perversity of life in Bangkok, Rangoon, Shanghai and Ho Chi Minh City, once called Saigon.

"You must have known a great many women," Eva told him gently.

Mr. Esmeralda shook his head. "I am a selective man; not promiscuous. Of course one could have women, thousands of them. But that kind of life means nothing to me. What I have always sought is the woman who can give me a deep, romantic affair; an affair with roses and wine and dancing, and expressions of true love. Perhaps not an affair that lasts forever, but one which ends with no regret, no bitter feelings, and no promises."

Eva set down her glass, then reached across the table and took Mr. Esmeralda's hand. She stared into his eyes for a long time, as if she were searching for reassurance. She said, "I have to tell you the truth, Carlos. I've never felt this way about anyone else, apart from Gerard. This is the first time in all of my years of marriage that I've actually dared to believe I could be happy."

"Gerard makes you so miserable?"

She looked away. "Gerard still attracts me. Perhaps I'm a masochist. Perhaps I get some painful pleasure out of being cheated. Perhaps I deserve everything I get."

"Would you like to think that you are a martyr? St. Eva the Sanctimonious, broken on the wheel of her husband's inconstancy?"

"That's unfair."

"No," said Mr. Esmeralda. "It is quite true. If you were really angry at Gerard, you would have left him years ago. But you enjoy being degraded. You enjoy catching Gerard with Francesca, and hearing about his passion for her. It excites you. It gives your life some spice, some variety. It makes you believe that Gerard is more exciting then he really is. He must be, if some other girl wants him, too. A pretty young girl like Francesca. The fact is, however, that Gerard is an uninteresting petty criminal; a man whose little struggles with authority have done nothing to mature a personality that is essentially boorish and self-centered and vulgar. Some men, if they had been schooled in the same way that Gerard has, would have become swash-buckling heroes. Gerard has achieved nothing but a condition of abject meanness, both of spirit and of flesh. It is time you recognized it, if you haven't already. And it is time you said to yourself, 'Is this what I really want for the rest of my life? A man like Gerard?"

Eva said in a hushed voice, "Mr. Esmeralda, you're wooing me."

"Wooing?" he asked in surprise. Then, "Yes, if you want to use such a word. Yes, I suppose I am. Wooing."

She stared across the restaurant unashamedly admiring her own reflection in the glass of a picture frame for a long time, while Mr. Esmeralda admired her profile. It was her better profile thank God; and the flickering candlelight gave her looks magic which made her appear younger, more serene, mysterious. She *felt* mysterious, too, which helped. Calm and erotic and mysterious. And drunk.

"I suppose you want to go to bed with me," she said. The words didn't quite come out the way she had meant them to. They sounded squeaky and unbalanced, instead of alluring and Garboesque; but once she'd spoken them it was too late. She turned and stared at him, and he stared back.

"Yes," he said. "Of course."

They were silent in the taxi on the way back to Eva's apartment. They didn't even hold hands. When Eva let them in, they found that the twins had gone to bed. The sitting room was tidied up and in darkness. Mr. Esmeralda loosened his necktie and said, "How much would you like a cocktail?"

Eva came back across the soft white carpet and put her arms around his neck, kissing the tip of his nose. "Not as much as I'd like you."

"Then let's take two cocktails into the bedroom. Do you have any peach brandy? I mix a formidable Fish House Punch."

"A dry martini will do."

Mr. Esmeralda looked down at this woman clinging to his neck, and for one moment he had an almost uncontrollable urge to tug her arms away and slap her into sensibility. But he needed her, and he had learned years and years ago that you never upset anybody you need, no matter how much contempt you might feel for them.

"It will be as quick as my trembling hands will allow," he whispered.

The bedroom, too, was Italian. Mirrors, chrome, and smoked glass. The only touches of human life were a slender vase of lilies, a framed photograph of Gerard after he had won the visitor's golf tournament at San Pedro, and a single white stocking draped over the side of the stainless-steel dressing-table stool.

Mr. Esmeralda took off his jacket and hung it over the

back of a chair. "Gerard is a man who lives inside of himself," he remarked, looking around him. "How can you reach the soul of such a man? I am surprised he loves anybody; although if it has to be anybody, Francesca is the least surprising of all. A chilly, stupid girl. If you knew her better you would like her worse."

Mr. Esmeralda stripped off his tie. Then he approached Eva, and held her in his arms, his eyes liquid and brown and delightfully quizzical. He kissed her, and then began to unzip her dress. She said, "Carlos . . ." but he hushed her and said, "You must call me 'my dear,' and that is all. Names have unhappy memories."

He gently tugged the dress from her shoulders, kissing her face and neck. She felt as if she were afloat, like a balloon. Eva, the Inflatable Woman—so light and heady that the slightest warm breeze could carry her upward into the early-morning smog of West Los Angeles and away across the San Gabriel Mountains.

Mr. Esmeralda unhooked her beige lace bra. Her breasts were firm and full for a woman of her age, and he held them in his hands with obvious pleasure. Her nipples stiffened between his fingers, and he played with them until her wide pink areolas crinkled and she began to feel that tingling which she hadn't felt for so long.

She murmured, "My dear . . ." as if she were quoting from a play. Mr. Esmeralda said, "*Sshh*." He pushed her gently back onto the bed, onto the white-on-white bedspread, and removed her stockings and sheer panties.

She watched him as he deftly undid his shirt buttons, unbuckled his alligator belt, peeled off his socks. Soon he was kneeling over her naked, his chest shaggy with black hair, his penis rearing from the curly forest between his thighs as purple as an overripe plum."

He gripped her legs and opened them up wide, so that the crimson lips of her vulva parted as stickily as a mouth that has been feeding on cranberry syrup. He lowered his mustachioed face and licked at her clitoris with the tip of his tongue, then probed her urethra so deeply that she

shivered. She moaned and twisted her hips, but Mr.
Esmeralda clasped her tight, and plunged his tongue into
her again and again.

She closed her eyes. She shuddered, deep within herself.
She thought, this is mad, and bad. This isn't the way to
solve anything. This isn't the way to save my marriage or to
salvage my self-esteem. But, God, it feels beautiful.

He rose up at last, and mounted her, his chin shiny and
his eyes bright with lust. She reached both her hands down
between her legs and opened herself up for him, as wide as
she could, so that the very first time he thrust into her, he
thrust extravagantly deep, the head of his penis touching
the neck of her womb and making her jump in erotic
shock.

He thrust again and again, grunting with each thrust;
and Eva tugged herself wider and wider, as if she wanted
to take all of him inside her, as if she wanted to take so
much that he killed her. He was right: she wanted to be
martyred. But only to the cause of her own excitement.

She felt herself gradually ascending the foothills of an
orgasm. She knew it would come this time, that if she concentrated all her mental and muscular energy, she would
climax. She very rarely climaxed with Gerard, only when
she was so drunk that she didn't care about his remoteness,
or when she knew that he had been with Francesca only
hours before. Mr. Esmeralda panted and lowered himself
onto her, his hairy chest thick and wiry against her bare
breasts, and for a split second she felt an extra-ordinary
sense of unreality and alienation, as if she were dreaming
that she was making love to some dark-pelted beast.

At eight, Mr. Esmeralda swung himself out of bed and
quickly began to dress. Kuan-yin would still be waiting for
him outside, and while he had abused her unmercifully as
a lover, he didn't like to treat her inconsiderately as an
employer. You could only expect so much, even from
people who were uncritical and devoted.

As he tied up his necktie, he leaned over the bed and
kissed Eva on the ear. "You don't have to open your

eyes," he whispered. "If you are awake, I will call you. If you are asleep, I will call you, too. You have been ecstasy beyond belief."

He tiptoed to the hallway, and released the chain on the door. He was just about to close it behind him when he heard a soft voice say, "Mr. Esmeralda?"

He peered back into the apartment through an inch-wide opening in the door. "Who's that?"

"It's me, Kelly." She came up to the door with tangled hair, dressed in a striped nightshirt. "I wanted to say goodbye, and thank you."

"Thank you?"

"I've never seen Mother looking as pleased as when you invited her out last night."

Mr. Esmeralda opened the door a little wider. "Well," he said, "thank you for saying thank you."

"She's our mother," said Kelly. "I know she drinks a lot, and I know she's silly sometimes, but we love her. You will take care of her, won't you?"

"Of course," replied Mr. Esmeralda. He took her hand and kissed it. "She will be marvelously taken care of, I promise."

He left, clicking the apartment door behind him. As he went down in the elevator, he hummed to himself that sentimental old Latin tune, "The Rose of Rio."

Across the street, in a morning that was still chilly, Kuan-yin was sitting behind the wheel of Mr. Esmeralda's limousine, listening to KMPC 710 and eating a cold break-fast of take-out *odamaki mushi*, steamed egg and noodles. Mr. Esmeralda simply said, "Good morning," as he climbed into the back of the car. There were hot-towels waiting for him in an electric steamer, and his shirt and suit were neatly laid out on the seat.

"You looked tired," said Kuan-yin.

"I need some breakfast, that's all," said Mr. Esmeralda, stripping off his jacket, and then gratefully burying his face into the cologne-scented towels. "It's been one of those nights."

"You want to go straight home?"

"No. Take me to Laurel Canyon."

"You're sure?"

"*Now* I'm sure, yes."

Kuan-yin didn't ask what Mr. Esmeralda meant. It wasn't her place to ask, and in any case she wasn't interested. She wasn't a jealous person, but she did expect something more from Mr. Esmeralda than the functional employer-chauffeur relationship they were going through now. Perhaps he would grow softer toward her when he found someone else who could excite him as much as she used to. Perhaps he would always hate her for having summoned up his greatest strengths and for having simulataneously exposed his greatest weaknesses. She knew there was very little left in her life, apart from Mr. Esmeralda and the few Chinese friends she knew in downtown Los Angeles. And the Chinese proverb did say, "When you have only two pennies left, spend one on a loaf of bread, and the other on a lily." She would have to start taking care of herself, both financially and spiritually. She had a feeling that her time with Mr. Esmeralda was coming to an end.

Mr. Esmeralda, buttoning up his clean blue shirt in the back of the limousine, was already sure that the weather was changing, and that a storm was going to break before too long. At least he was prepared for it, as much as anyone who had to deal with a creature like Kappa could ever be prepared. Doctor Gempaku, very early on, when they were first converting the ranch at Pacoima into a center for developing Tengus, had told him, "Once you have instructed a Tengu to kill somebody, then the Tengu *must* kill, whether it is the person you *want* to see killed or not. I suppose the only way to protect yourself against a Tengu is to elect a substitute to be killed in your place. It is written in the old scrolls that if you offer the Tengu the blood of somebody you have lain with—a woman or a man with whom you have had sexual congress—or somebody who owes you a lasting favor, then the Tengu is obliged to accept your offer. Such an offer, after all, heightens the evil of what is about to happen; and no devil as iniquitous as the Tengu could refuse *that*."

Doctor Gempaku's words had crossed Mr. Esmeralda's mind the very first time he had walked into the Crowleys' apartment and found Eva deserted, half naked, and drunk. Here is a woman who is crying out for consolation, he had thought to himself. Here is a woman who will take me as her lover just to spite her husband. And, quite apart from the fact that taking Eva Crowley to bed will enable me to score a particularly ironic point against that cold and arrogant Gerard Crowley, it will also provide me with a living, loving sacrifice to throw to the Tengus if Kappa ever sends them after me.

This morning, however, Mr. Esmeralda was more than satisfied. This morning, he felt unusually safe. Not only could he offer Eva Crowley to any Tengu which Kappa might direct to kill him; he could also offer Kelly and Kathryn, bound to him by their gratitude. His life-insurance policy had trebled in value in the space of a single night.

CHAPTER FOUR

At the same moment that Mr. Esmeralda closed the door of Eva Crowley's apartment, Sergeant Skrolnik opened the door of El Krusho's cell, folded his arms, took a deep breath, and said, "It's all right. We've dropped the charges. You can go."

Maurice had been working out by lifting and lowering his stool with one hand. He blinked at Sergeant Skrolnik and said, "What?"

Sergeant Skrolnik said, "You deaf or something?"

"I don't know. What? You said I could go?"

"You think I'd leave the fucking cell door wide open if you couldn't? Go. Collect your belongings at the desk."

Maurice looked almost disappointed. "You found out who really did it?" he asked, as he tugged on his T-shirt and tried to straighten his hair in the two-way mirror. Skrolnik watched this impromptu primping with disgust. "We didn't find out who did it," he said. "We just happen to know that it wasn't you. Although, believe it or not, I said from the *beginning* that it wasn't you. I only had to take one look at that sheep's behind of a face of yours, and I knew it wasn't you."

"You really thought I was innocent?"

"You're about as homicidal as a pet llama. Physically, could have taken us both to pieces when we arrested you, but you weren't even angry. You didn't know what you were being arrested for, and you weren't even angry."

Maurice said, "Can I claim compensation?"

"Compensation for what?"

"Well, for spending a couple of nights in the cells. It was pretty uncomfortable. And my mother's totally convinced that I'm a mass murderer."

Sergeant Skrolnik took El Krusho's beefy arm and led him down to the desk to collect his belongings. He said confidentially, "If I were you, I would get the hell out of this place, and not worry about compensation or defamation or any of that shit, because the best place that anyone can ever be is miles and miles away from the law. You got me?"

Maurice counted his $27.76, thrust it into the back pocket of his jeans, and nodded. "I still think there ought to be some kind of compensation. You know, a month's exemption from parking tickets, something like that?"

Just then, the swinging doors of the police headquarters opened and Mack Holt strode in, with Olive close behind him. "Hey, Maurice!" said Mack. "They told me you were sprung."

"You know *why* he was sprung," said Sergeant Skrolnik, poker-faced.

"Well, yes, I'm sorry about that," said Mack. "I guess I'm just pleased that Maurice is out, that's all. Are you coming back to my place, Maurice? How about it? A couple of beers, a steak or two? Fifteen eggs? Maurice has to keep up his strength," he explained to Sergeant Skrolnik.

"*Why* was I sprung?" asked Maurice, his eyes on Skrolnik. "You didn't tell me that. You just said I was free to go."

Mack glanced at Sergeant Skrolnik, then at El Krusho, and then back again to Sergeant Skrolnik. "Ah," he said uncomfortably.

But Sergeant Skrolnik said, "You were sprung because I didn't believe you were guilty, that's all; and because twelve hours' intensive police work has so far failed to tease out the slightest evidence that you were the man responsible for Sherry Cantor's murder, or that you were anywhere near the Hollywood Freeway when Patrolman Ed Russo was killed."

Skrolnik hesitated. Olive started to say something, but Mack nudged her to keep quiet. This was, after all, Skrolnik's show; and Mack considered that Skrolnik was reasonably human. Whatever Mayor Tom Bradley had said about "the dimensions of violent crime," whatever Sheriff Peter J. Pitchess had said about everybody in Los Angeles suffering from a "siege mentality," whatever Governor Jerry Brown had said about prisoners taking karate lessons in California's prisons "so that when they get out, they're more dangerous than ever," it was Sergeant Skrolnik who had to go out on the streets and track down the killers and the weirdos and the homicidal freaks, and Mack respected him for that. If Maurice had actually committed those murders, Mack wouldn't have gone near Maurice with a loaded .45 and half a division of the California National Guard. Yet Skrolnik had arrested Maurice, albeit mistakenly, with nobody to help him but Detective Pullet.

Sergeant Skrolnik laid his hand on El Krusho's shoulder and said, "The main reason you were sprung is because last night someone broke into the Rancho Encino Hospital, and tore several people wide apart in the same way that Sherry Cantor was torn apart. The similarities of the killings are overwhelming; and besides that, we have the body of the man who did it. So, what happened at Orchid Place quite obviously wasn't down to you."

"You *caught* the guy?" asked Maurice.

"If you want to know the confidential truth, we caught the guy and blew his fucking head off," said Skrolnik.

"Instant justice," said Olive.

Skrolnik looked at her balefully. This morning she was wearing a thin cheesecloth blouse that dimly revealed the darkness of her nipples and an extremely tight pair of canary-yellow pants. The effect of the pants, as Detective Pullet was to remark afterward in a moment of intense lateral thinking, was to remind him of two bananas side by side.

Mack said, "It's over, then? You've caught him and killed him?"

"*You* think it's over. The *governor* thinks it's over. The *mayor* thinks it's over. Even the police commissioner thinks it's over. But, of course, *we* now have several weeks of intensive and incredibly tedious investigation to carry out to discover who this fruitcake was, and why he committed those killings."

"Isn't that what we pay you for?" asked Olive sharply.

Skrolnik grinned tightly. "You also pay me to keep the *next* murderer away from your door, Mrs. Nesmith. And the next. Hillside Stranglers, Manson gangs, Lawrence Bittakers. Hell's Angels, muggers, intruders, rapists, perverts, sadists, lone headcases. You're not safe now. I'll never pretend that you are. But you're a whole lot safer than if I wasn't here, taking care of you."

El Krusho said, "I could use a beer."

Skrolnik said, "Sign here for your belongings and you can go sink as many beers as you like."

Olive asked, "Where's the body now?"

"What body?" said Sergeant Skrolnik, watching El Krusho sign "M. Needs" in a large, rounded scrawl.

"You said you killed him. The murderer. Where's his body now?"

"They're keeping it on ice for me, in the morgue at Rancho Encino. I'm going up there to collect it later today. The medical examiners can't wait to slice it up and see what made it tick."

Olive said, "I'm sorry."

"Sorry for what?" asked Skrolnik.

"I'm sorry I bugged you. I don't know. Don't press me. Just accept that I'm sorry."

Sergeant Skrolnik put his meaty, red-freckled hands on Olive's bare black shoulders and smiled at her. "Listen," he said, "if only one-tenth of the population said what you just did, *sorry*, then Los Angeles would be a happier city. We make mistakes in the police department. Everybody does. If it costs you, as a taxpayer, then I personally apologize. But it's nice to hear someone say sorry in return. After all, we're all in this thing together."

"This is all getting unnecessarily emotional," said Mack. "Do you think we might leave now?"

"Go ahead," said Skrolnik, and gave Olive a comfortable squeeze on the behind.

"As the criminals get weirder, the cops get weirder," Maurice remarked as they climbed into Mack's battered Volkswagen.

"At least you're out of there," said Mack. He gave Maurice a friendly punch on his muscular arm. "You know, it's fantastic to see you. You're looking great."

"What happened up at Encino?" asked Maurice as Mack started up the Volkswagen's blaring engine, stuck his hand out of the window, and pulled out right in front of a lumbering Hostess Cupcakes truck.

"You shithead!" roared the truck driver.

"I see your driving hasn't improved," Maurice remarked. "Do you remember the time you drove off the edge of that cliff at Santa Barbara?"

"I didn't drive off any cliff," Mack protested. "It was just a *gully*, that's all. Don't give me cliff."

Olive said, "We heard about it on the radio this morning. Some mad guy broke into the hospital at Rancho Encino and ripped a nurse to pieces. Some other people were shot. The police went in there and killed him."

"Was that all?" asked Maurice.

"So far. The cops are being really cagey about giving out information to the media. I guess they don't want to make the same mistake they made with the Hillside Strangler, catching people every two or three days and then having to let them go again."

"If they blew this guy's head off and it's the wrong guy, at least they won't have the problem of letting him go again," said Olive.

Mack said, "Despite her sensitive apologies to Sergeant What's-his-name just now, Olive is still very deeply into citizen's rights vis-à-vis the police and the civil authorities. Olive believes that arrest and trial should be a sociobiological process activated by mutual concern and respect for the general well-being of the human village, rather like eaeting health foods and wearing shoes that are higher at the front than they are at the back."

"We should *absorb* crime, rather than attempt to excise it from our systems," added Olive. "Law and order is a digestive process, not a surgical one."

"Is this lady for real?" Maurice asked Mack. "Digestive? You mean the cops are supposed to eat you, instead of bust you?"

"El Krusho is not known for his sociological perception," Mack said to Olive.

They turned on the radio and tuned it to KABC. There were a few minutes of chatter about sophisticated city dwellers moving out to Santa Ynez to take up farming, then a news bulletin.

"Listen to this," said Olive, turning up the volume.

"Police at Encino have released more details this

morning of the grisly murder at Rancho Encino hospital of Mrs. Mary Thorson, wife of Admiral Knut Thorson. Also the violent slaying of a hospital nurse and two armed security guards. Apparently, the crimes were committed by a multiracial hit team, including at least three Japanese and a Caucasian. The bodies of two of the Japanese were found in the hospital shrubbery after the attack; one obviously slain by a security guard's bullet, the other the apparent victim of his Caucasian colleague. The principle assailant, who was shot and killed by police after his homicidal attack on Mrs. Thorson and on Nurse Ruth Abramski, was also said to be Japanese.

"Admiral Thorson, who survived the attack, has already spoken with the police, although no details have yet been released.

"Chief of Detectives Harry Calsbeek said that the crime was similar in most respects to the recent homicide of television star Sherry Cantor, who played the part of Lindsay in *Our Family Jones*. He is cooperating closely with Hollywood detectives in an attempt to discover why such an attack should have been launched against this luxury private hospital, and by whom. So far, said Calbeek, the butchery remains a mystery."

Mack switched the radio off. "We were right. Did you hear that? We were right from the very beginning."

"*Who* was right?" asked Maurice.

"Me! *I* was right! And Jerry Sennett, the guy who lives in the house next door to Sherry's place, he was right too. He said he was sure that the killer was Japanese, something to do with Japan. You remember that face they showed on television? Well, maybe you didn't see it. But Jerry said it was an ancient Japanese Nō mask. And when I pointed out that it was easy to mistake *his* house number for Sherry's, he agreed that the killer could have been after *him*. And the clincher was that he fought against the Japanese during World War Two, something to do with Naval Intelligence, and as far as I can work out, he was personally responsible for some really important Japanese defeat."

Maurice pulled a face. "This is all beginning to sound extremely complicated. I think I need a beer first."

"It's not complicated at all," said Mack. "I believe that the Japs are getting their revenge on us, that's what. Anybody who did anything really heroic or important during World War Two—the Japs are wiping them out with a hit squad. Don't you think that's *amazing*?"

"I also think it's unbelievable," said Maurice. "Is it very much further? My goddamn neck's aching in the back of this mobile peanut."

They drew up outside Mack's apartment on Franklin Avenue. It was beginning to grow warm. Mack helped El Krusho out of the car and then led the way along the path. Olive said, "It looks like you've got yourself a visitor, Mack."

In the shadow of the porch, unshaven, smoking a cigarette, stood Jerry Sennett, with the look of a man who has had a hard and unsuccessful night.

"Did you hear the news?" Mack asked him as he came up to the door. "Did you hear what happened at Rancho Encino?"

Jerry nodded. "I heard. And that's presumably why they released your friend here?"

"That's right. El Krusho is loose. Maurice, this is Jerry Sennett. Jerry, this is the strongest man south of Visalia."

"Visalia?" asked Jerry, shaking El Krusho's hefty hand.

"We had an interesting evening in Visalia once," explained Mack. "It was something to do with three women and four bottles of Wild Turkey. The rest I forgot."

Olive looked at Jerry and pulled an expression which very clearly meant, "Who are *they* trying to kid?" Jerry smiled back at her, impressed by her wild Rastafarian beauty, and by the tightness of her canary-yellow pants. But there was a frightened ache deep down inside him which wouldn't go away, an ache that made pleasantries impossible.

He said, as steadily as he could manage, "I'm sorry I came around so early. I don't want to break up any parties

or anything. But I think I've found out who's behind all
these killings, and why they're committing them."

"You have?" asked Mack. "Well, who is it? Have you
told the cops?"

Jerry shook his head. "I can't tell the cops. I'm not
supposed to tell anyone at all, and I'm only telling you
because I can trust you to keep quiet. They've kidnapped
my son, David. They're holding him hostage somewhere,
so that I'll give myself up to them. They want *me*, because
of what I know. That was why they tried to kill me in the
first place. And that's why they tried to kill Admiral Thorson out at Rancho Encino. Admiral Thorson directed the
same operation during the war that I was involved in,
Operation Appomattox."

Olive said, "You'd better come inside. This isn't any
kind of a problem to be talking about on the porch."

Jerry was exhausted. After he had spoken to Nancy Shiranuka, he had waited for hours for Gerard Crowley to
come around to her apartment. But by four o'clock in the
morning, Gerard still hadn't showed, and Nancy, bringing Jerry tea and *anago mushi* she had prepared for him
herself had told him softly that it was useless for him to
wait any longer. It was the first time that Jerry had eaten
steamed egg custard and eel in the small hours of the
morning; and the way his stomach felt now, he hoped it
would be the last. But he had been afraid to refuse
Nancy's hospitality. If he was ever going to have to cultivate Nancy and strengthen her confidence in him. Nancy
was as terrified of the Tengus as he was; what she urgently
needed was a friend she could trust.

Olive made coffee while Jerry sat on Mack's broken-
down sofa and explained what had happened. Mack and
Maurice listened intently, and then sat back and sipped
their hot coffee and tried to look as if they were thinking
extraordinarily hard about some way of rescuing David and
destroying the Tengus.

"You really *believe* in these things, these Tengus?"
asked Mack.

"President Truman believed in them; enough to drop the first atomic bomb the world had ever seen."

Maurice said, "Let's face it, Mack, I'm strong. But the way those murder victims were torn to pieces, I couldn't do that. That takes somebody superhuman. I couldn't rip your leg off with my bare hands. I couldn't even start. I might *feel* like it but I actually couldn't do it."

"Maurice, those are very comforting words," said Mack. "But what do we do now? What *can* we do? Should we do anything at all? I really think that Jerry should go see Sergeant Skrolnik. I mean it. He's a cop, but he's all there, and and he's only as mean as he needs to be."

"Supposing the kidnappers found out I went to the police?" asked Jerry. "If they can tear a heavily guarded hospital apart, for the sake of trying to kill one poor old retired naval officer in a coma, what the hell do you think they'd do to David? A young, live, alert witness to everything they've been doing?"

"What if you do give yourself up to them?" asked Olive. "What guarantee do you have that they won't kill you both?"

Jerry put down his coffee mug and rubbed his eyes. "No guarantee at all. I don't know whether I'm dealing with criminals or mystics or madmen. Nancy Shiranuka may be double-dealing me, although I can't for the life of me guess why, or what she could conceivably get out of it. I just don't know what to do. It might have been easier to understand if I'd been able to talk to Gerard Crowley."

"Why not talk to him now?" Maurice suggested. "If he's involved in any kind of business, he's probably in the phone book."

Olive clapped her hands. "You see, he's not all muscle. Good thinking, El Krusho!"

Mack picked up his tattered telephone book and thumbed through it. "Here you are," he said at last. "Gerard F. Crowley, Crowley Tobacco Imports, Inc. 2029 Century Park East."

Jerry said, "You really think it's worth a shot?"

"Why not?" said Mack. "You don't have anything to lose. You might get your son back. Look, I'll dial it for you."

It was just nine o'clock, still early for a Los Angeles businessman to be at his desk, but Mack got through to Francesca right away, and Francesca said guardedly, "Yes, Mr. Crowley's here. who is this?"

"Tell him it's Mr. Sennett. Mr. Sennett of 11 Orchid Place."

There was a silence, then Francesca said, "Hold on for just a moment, please," and switched Mack to a holding tape of "Raindrops Keep Fallin' on My Head." Jerry looked quizzical, but Mack held his hand over the receiver and said, "I'm holding."

At last, a tired voice said, "Mr. Sennett?" and Mack passed the phone across to Jerry.

"Mr. Crowley?" said Jerry testily. "I was waiting at Nancy Skiranuka's apartment for you last night. Apparently you were supposed to show up there, but you didn't."

"Well, I was busy," replied Gerard, obviously cautious. "I'm sorry if you had a wasted evening."

"Not evening. *Night*. I waited all goddamned night. I'm still waiting, to hear what you've done with my son."

"Mr. Sennett," said Gerard, "we've got ourselves a critical difficulty here."

"You bet your ass we've got ourselves a critical difficulty," snapped Jerry. "We've got more than that. We've got kidnapping, extortion, blackmail, and murder. That's what we've got. And for some reason this is all connected with what I did in the war, in Japan. I want to know *what*, and *why*, and what the hell I'm supposed to do to get my son back safely."

"Mr. Sennett, I don't really want to talk about this on the telephone," said Gerard. "Apart from the fact that you might be tape-recording this conversation, other people could well be listening in."

"What other people?"

"Believe me, people you wouldn't care to meet."

Jerry said, "All right. Let's meet. Do you know Zucky's, Fifth and Wilshire?"

"I've heard of it. I can find it."

"Meet me there at twelve, for lunch. I'll be sitting in the far corner. I'll leave my name at the counter."

Gerard hesitated for a moment, and then said, "Okay, I'll be there," and put down the phone.

"What did he sound like?" asked Olive. "Suspicious?"

"A little," said Jerry thoughtfully. "But he was much more cooperative than I would have expected. If you ask me, what happened last night at Rancho Encino was a foul-up. They were trying to murder Admiral Thorson, right? And they failed. He's still alive. Better than that, he's out of his coma. What's more, the police have killed the Tengu and recovered the bodies of two Japanese, which means that they could now have a pretty straightforward lead to whoever it is who may be organizing this thing—whatever "this thing" may be. Nancy Shiranuka is convinced that her employers have been trying to do a whole lot more than create a corps of expensive killer bodyguards. Mack here may have come up with a good idea when he suggested that some cranky Japanese outfit is trying to take revenge on American war heroes. Maybe he's right. But, whatever—*something's* happening, something dangerous and volatile and much bigger than it looks. In fact, I think it's so dangerous that Gerard Crowley actually *wants* to talk to me about it. All I can do is wait and see."

"If you're meeting him at Zucky's, try the blintzes," said Maurice.

CHAPTER FIVE

The van drew up by the side of the hot and dusty highway, its right rear tire flapping with a sudden blowout.
The young Japanese switched off the engine and sat back
in his vinyl seat, blowing out his cheeks in exhaustion.
Commander Ouvarov, sitting beside him with his corncob
pipe gritted between his teeth and his .45-caliber Colt
automatic resting loosely on his lap, turned his head and
stared at him with an exaggerated lack of sympathy.

"Well?" he said. "There's a spare in the back."

Yoshino said, "I'm very tired, Commander. Can't we
rest now? Driving for eight hours."

"You were hired as a driver, what do you expect?"

Yoshino wiped his forehead with the back of his hand.
"Please, Commander."

Commander Ouvarov checked his watch. They hadn't
made bad time, considering they had been driving at
night. They had left Encino at high speed; but instead of
making a conventional getaway they had driven just four
or five miles to a nearby Howard Johnson's, where they
had eaten, cleaned themselves up, and gassed up their van
for a long, hard journey. Even as they sat here now, eight
hours later, by the side of the highway which runs just
south of the Superstition Mountains, a few miles east of
Phoenix, Arizona, two police officers were questioning the
manager and the waitresses at Howard Johnson's, trying to
determine which way the fugitives had been heading, and
how much of a head start they had managed to get.

Commander Ouvarov squinted northward through the
August heat haze, towards the broken, uncompromising
outline of the mountains. It was only ten o'clock in the
morning, but the temperature was already into the low
90s. "We can't waste too much time here, Yoshino," he
said. "If we don't make El Paso by evening, we're going to
be in big trouble. That customs officer at El Paso is a close
personal friend of mine; I did him a favor a few years back.

He's the only man who's going to let us through that border without any questions, no matter what.''

Yoshino resignedly opened the driver's door and stepped down onto the dusty roadside. There was no traffic in sight for two or three miles in either direction. He walked around to the back of the van and loosened the spare. Commander Ouvarov stayed where he was, his automatic on his lap, listening to the radio. "And now it's 91 degrees at Sky Harbor, with a prospect of 111 to 113 degrees by noon." He knocked the dottle of his pipe out, and meticulously refilled it with Old Geronimo tobacco. He had smoked the same pipe tobacco since 1942.

He felt the van being jacked up beneath him; but he remained where he was, his arms folded, calmly smoking. He felt no guilt about having made a run for it. He'd had his doubts about Mr. Esmeralda and Gerard Crowley right from the very start. Too many sharks in the same pool for Commander Ouvarov's liking, too many people with difficult pasts and uncertain futures. And as for those peculiar Japanese, with their black silk masks, and those tortured Tengus . . . well, the only good Japanese as far as Commander Ouvarov was concerned was a disemboweled Japanese. He hadn't asked too many questions; he'd done whatever they'd asked of him; but the whole plan was ill conceived, badly managed, amateurish, and too damned strange.

He took off his hat and mopped his sweating forehead with his handkerchief. It was a pity about Nancy Shiranuka, he thought. The sensations that Nancy could give to a man, selflessly, purely for the erotic artistry of it, were disturbing enough to haunt him forever. When he was lying on his deathbed, he would remember what she had done to him with a Mexican bead necklace. His last words before he was carried upward by the angels would be, "Nancy, the beads . . ." At least, he fondly imagined they would.

After a quarter of an hour, he felt the van being jacked down onto the road again. He called out, "Yoshino? You through now?'' but he couldn't be sure if Yoshino had heard him.

He opened his door and swung himself heavily out onto the roadside. "Yoshino?" he called.

Yoshino had been packing away the flat. He came around the van, wiping his hands on a rag, his face and chest glossy with sweat. "All done now, Commander. We can go. Make El Paso by dark."

"Good man," said the commander. He turned his back on Yoshino. And that was fatal. The next thing he knew, there was a blinding crunch in his back, as Yoshino drove the sharp end of the van's tire iron between his ribs into his guts.

The commander let out a sharp, barking shout. His hand scrabbled around behind him to tug the tire iron out. But suddenly his nerves went, his coordination froze, and he pitched sideways into the dust.

His brain still worked, but the tire iron had severed vital nerves and left him paralyzed. He watched in glassy, jack-rabbit helplessness as Yoshino bent down and picked up his .45, hesitated for a moment, and then disappeared from view.

Japanese, he thought to himself. Never trust a Japanese. All these years I've preached nothing else. All these years I've been warning them. They never listened. They went their own sweet unconscious way while Datsun and Toyota and Sony and Toshiba took the dollars from under their noses, the bread from their family tables. They're wily by nature, the Japanese. Treacherous by birth. All these years I've said so, and today I forgot my own damned warning; today I neglected my own damned advice. And here I am; helpless and dying on a hot highway in Arizona.

Yoshino climbed into the van and started the engine. Lying on his side by the road, Commander Ouvarov shouted, "No! Don't leave me!" But Yoshino had no intention of leaving him. Instead, carefully watching Commander Ouvarov in his side mirror, he shifted the van into reverse and began to creep back toward him, until

Commander Ouvarov could feel the hot gasoline breath of the exhaust on his neck, and smell the oil and rubber and hydraulic fluid.

With all the precision of an expert driver, Yoshino backed the van up until its rear tire was resting against the side of Commander Ouvarov's head. Commander Ouvarov could feel the wheel pinching his hair, and he wildly tried to heave himself out of its way. But his paralysis was complete. His brain thought *heave*, and nothing happened. His arms remained tangled side by side on the road; his legs seemed to have disappeared altogether. The only feeling he had left was in his face and his head, resting against the gritty pavement.

Yoshino said an ancient Shinto prayer; a prayer for long life, for guidance. Then, with great care, he backed the van over Commander Ouvarov's head.

There was a moment when Commander Ouvarov felt as if his skull could actually withstand the vehicle's two-ton weight. But the pressure built up until it was utterly intolerable, and then his skull collapsed with a snap like a breaking terra-cotta bowl, and his eyes bulged out of their sockets and tumbled bloodily onto the road, promptly followed by a long squirt of brains. He died thinking of nothing but pain. The words "Nancy, the beads . . ." never even occurred to him.

Yoshino shifted the van back into drive, and sped off, leaving behind him a high trail of drifting desert dust and the body of a man who had betrayed himself more than his country. For twenty or thirty yards, the van left a repeated smudge of blood on the road, a telltale tireprint that would have inevitably brought Yoshino to Death Row if his intentions hadn't been different.

After six or seven minutes of driving, he reached a small Exxon station next to a use-car lot, and parked a half-mile out of Apache Junction. He pulled across the road and parked in front of a pump. An old-timer with grizzled white hair and a sport cap was washing the windshield of a Chrysler pickup on the other side of the island. He called out, "Be with you in two shakes there, son."

Yoshino climbed calmly out of the van, unhooked the handle from the nearest pump, started the pump's motor, and dragged the hose across to the van. Then, while the old-timer was busy making change for the driver of the Chrysler, Yoshino sat in the driver's seat, pointed the nozzle of the gas pump toward his chest, and began to splash gasoline over himself, gallons of it. It gushed out all over his clothes, over the seats, over the floor.

It took a moment or two before the old-timer realized what was happening. Then he shouted, "Hey! Goddamn it! What you doing there, son? Hey, stop that!"

Yoshino scarcely heard him. He was already entering the first gate to another world. In his mind he was gliding weightless through one of the *torii* that stand by the shores of the Inland Sea. He lifted the .45, muzzle upward, and tightened his grip on the trigger. This would be an ecstatic way to die.

The old-timer was only five or six feet away when Yoshino fired the automatic, and the interior of the van exploded in a soft, superheated furnace. Yoshino felt nothing but a wave of heat; the old-timer shrieked as he was hurled, blazing, onto the roof of his own gas station.

There was another explosion, louder, as the van's tank blew up. Chunks of burning metal were tossed into the air. A fiery tire careered across the forecourt, bounced across a stretch of grass, and lay there flaring and smoking. Then the station's 500-gallon underground storage tank went up, a blast that demolished the building in a ball of glaring orange fire and set fifteen parked trucks alight in the used-car lot.

The fire burned for hours, sending up a rolling black column of smoke. The police who attended the scene of the explosion were unable to determine the cause, since there were no recognizable survivors. They couldn't even tell that Yoshino was Japanese—not at first, or they might have grasped the irony that all the burning trucks in the lot were Toyotas.

CHAPTER SIX

When Mr. Esmeralda arrived at the house in Laurel
Canyon, a few minutes after nine o'clock, he was admitted
immediately to Kappa's inner sanctum. Kappa was suspended from a ceiling beam in a basket lined with scarlet
silk and padded with cushions. His tiny deformed body
was still shining with the scented oils with which his young
female attendants had been massaging him, in an attempt
to ease his scores and to conceal the odor of his oozing
wounds and purulent, convoluted genitalia. He was
wearing a different disguise today, a burnished ivory-
colored mask that was almost smiling; a face that looked as
if it were about to react to a happy surprise.

Mr. Esmeralda was not fooled. The more cheerful the
mask Kappa wore, the fouler his temper was likely to be.
He had only once seen Kappa wearing a mask that actually
laughed, and on that day Mr. Esmeralda had been lucky to
escape from the inner sanctum with his life.

He noticed that there were six or seven *Oni* guards in the
room today, two or three more than usual, as well as
Kappa's half-naked girl assistant. There were scores more
candles, too; burning bright and hot in row after row of
wrought-iron holders. It was like High Mass in hell.

"Good morning," said Mr. Esmeralda.

Kappa watched him, without blinking, through the
eyeholes in his mask. "You have failed me," he said. His
voice was more chirrupy and insectlike than ever. "You
have failed me *disastrously*."

"Kappa, I said right from the very start that I didn't
think it was a good idea to go for Admiral Thorson."

"Thorson knows about the Tengu. Thorson must die."

"You've heard that all the violence in Thorson's room
woke him up from his coma?" asked Mr. Esmeralda, perspiring from the heat of the candles. "We're worse off
now than we were before."

Kappa was silent, although Mr. Esmeralda was sure that

he could hear a grating sound inside the mask, as if the creature were grinding his teeth.

"We could try to get in to Thorson with just a regular hit man," Mr. Esmeralda suggested, "although I expect that he's pretty heavily guarded at the moment. Or we could just ignore him."

"We cannot ignore him," Kappa whispered. "Fortunately, the Tengu's body is still at the hospital. I have already spoken to Doctor Gempaku, and Doctor Gempaku is sure that he can work the necessary rituals."

"The necessary rituals? The necessary rituals for what?"

"Leave Admiral Thorson to Doctor Gempaku," said Kappa. "I have had enough of your incompetence."

"To be fair, Kappa—"

"To be *fair*, you and our meddling assistants have almost destroyed my dream! Where is Commander Ouvarov now? Where is Gerard Crowley? Who is keeping a watch on Nancy Shiranuka? Your assistants are all as bungling and treacherous as you are. The only reason I am not going to direct my *Oni* to kill you now is because I have no time to find anybody else to replace you. Commander Ouvarov has vanished, nobody knows where, but there is no doubt that he was responsible for murdering Kenji. Yoshino has apparently fled with him."

"They'll be back, I'm sure," said Mr. Esmeralda, trying to sound confident.

Kappa let out a harsh, high-pitched noise that could have been a snarl or a mocking laugh. "If you believe that, Mr. Esmeralda, then you are a bigger fool than I have always thought you to be. They'll never be back. They'll run and hide, in fear of their lives, as very well they might. The influence of the Circle of Burned Doves reaches everywhere, financed and supported by some of the greatest of Japanese businesses. Many of Japan's most eminent financiers and politicians have relations who were deformed or killed by the bombs at Hiroshima and Nagasaki. Twelve thousand people a year are still dying in Japan as a direct effect of America's brutality. The Circle of

Burned Doves is the richest secret society in the world after the American order of Freemasons. We can never forgive, and we can never forget. Usually, our energies are devoted to bringing the United States to her knees economically. All the research that went into microJapanese shipbuilders and electrical manufacturers receive funding from our central bank. Our influence reaches to Canada, Europe, and the Middle East. So wherever your precious Commander Ouvarov tries to hide himself, he will be found and summarily executed for what he did.''

Mr. Esmeralda said, ''I am impressed. I also regret what occurred. But I did respectfully try to warn you that using the Tengu to assassinate Admiral Thorson was not a good idea. It would have been just as easy to send somebody in to finish him off with a knife. Quiet, no mess, effective.''

''What is easy and what is just do not always coincide,'' whispered Kappa. ''Admiral Thorson was in charge of the mission called Appomattox, to discover the training center for the Tengus in 1945 and direct the first atomic bomb onto it, in order that the Tengus might be utterly destroyed. It was simple justice that Admiral Thorson should be killed by the very being which he tried to wipe out forever, especially when you consider how many innocent lives he considered it necessary to extinguish or maim at the same time.''

Kappa paused, and then said throatily, ''If Japan had possessed the atomic bomb and had dropped it on San Francisco—if that bomb had been exploded in the sky over Telegraph Hill, the most powerful bomb ever used, two thousand times more powerful than anything that had ever been dropped before, the explosive force of 20,320 tons of TNT, coupled with heat and fire and gamma rays that could penetrate the thickest concrete wall as if it didn't exist—what would Americans think today? Even today, thirty-eight years later, they would spit at Japanese in the street. I doubt if the United States, even now, would have resumed diplomatic relations with Japan. Well, many of us Japanese feel the same way, but our nature is less demonstrative than yours. Our emotions and our memories tend to be suppressed, although never forgotten. We borne your occupation of our country with dignity, we accepted the infiltration into our traditional ways of your trashy culture—''

"Please, I am a native of Colombia," said Mr. Esmeralda, embarrassed but firm. "What the Americans did has nothing to do with me."

Kappa watched him in silence. Then, quietly, he said, "We will have our revenge, Mr. Esmeralda."

"What do you propose to do now, if I might ask?" said Mr. Esmeralda, glancing uncertainly at the black-masked *Oni* guards.

Kappa said something in Japanese to the girl who was standing close by. She came forward with a jar of jade-colored ointment, and began to massage it into the grayish folds between his legs. Mr. Esmeralda felt distinctly nauseated as he watched her slender, well-manicured fingers disappearing into the crevices and dewlaps of Kappa's deformed genitalia, but he swallowed hard and tried to think of Colombia in the summer, the jasmine and the bougainvillea. He tried to think of cigars and good wine, and his father laughing loudly on the balcony.

Kappa said, "Because of your carelessness and your incompetence, I have brought forward the Day of Fate to the day after tomorrow, fifty-eight hours from now. I have talked to Doctor Gempaku, and he assures me that he can have another Tengu ready by then. I would have liked to have had more than one. I wanted to make absolutely sure that my plan was a success. But we will have to take the risk. The Day of Fate must come."

"If you say so," said Mr. Esmeralda.

"Don't try to mock me," snapped Kappa. "You have angered me enough already to warrant death. And you can be well assured, your incompetent and untrustworthy colleagues will die on the same day."

Kappa spoke quickly to one of his guards, and the man came forward with a roll of blueprints. Mr. Esmeralda

knew what they were: he had obtained them himself, for
$2,500, from a disgruntled secretary at the California
Center for Nuclear Fusion. They were the detailed plans of
the new fusion reactor and power station on the shoreline
at Three Arch Bay, just north of Salt Creek and Capistrano
Beach, where the southbound Santa Ana Freeway sweeps
in a southward curve from San Juan Capistrano toward the
Pacific Ocean.

Three Arch Bay Fusion Reactor, one of the world's most
advanced nuclear-energy centers, was fueled by deuterium
and tritium, processed from the waters of the Pacific itself.
Unlike light-water reactors, or their advanced cousins the
fast-breeder and thermal reactors, the fusion reactor did
not require uranium or other fissionable materials.
Deuterium and tritium are both forms of hydrogen, and
are present in the world's oceans in an inexhaustible
supply, free. All that was required of the Three Arch Bay
reactor to tap that was that it should fulfill the two major
conditions necessary for a fusion reaction: produce intense
confined heat as high as 100 million degrees Celsius, and
sustain that temperature for one second.

Kappa had chosen this particular reactor as his target
because any intererence in its fusion process would
produce an explosion far greater than anything that had
ever been witnessed in the world before. He had cal-
culated, with the help of Japanese physicists sympathetic
to the cause of the Circle of Burned Doves, that to
destabilize the fusion process during the one critical
second of 100-million-degree heat would lead to a nuclear
detonation with a force equivalent to 150 million tons of
TNT—50 million tons greater than the largest hydrogen
bomb that the United States or the Soviet Union had ever
produced.

Southern California would be devastated. Los Angeles
would die instantly. And the winds from the Pacific would
carry the radioactivity far across the Midwest, polluting the
crops, poisoning the air, and destroying countless millions
of Americans for not only months but years to come.

Three Arch Bay, however, was only intended to be the start. Kappa planned to attack one nuclear-power station after another, year by year, until America's spirit was broken and her lands were glowing with radioactivity. She would never rise again. What Kappa wanted to do was to release so much nuclear energy into her atmosphere that her children would be born dead or deformed for centuries to come. It was the least he could do to avenge his mother. It was the least he could do to avenge himself.

Mr. Esmeralda asked, "You have worked out a way for the Tengu to break in?"

Kappa's mask nodded on his shrunken shoulders. "The Tengu will walk straight through the perimeter fence, across the main yard, and break down the doors that lead into the observation room. It is possible that he may be seen by security guards, and it is possible that he may be shot several times. But Doctor Gempaku has promised me that the Tengu he is creating now is his most powerful so far. Nothing short of utter destruction will be able to stop him; a few bullets won't even make him flinch."

Mr. Esmeralda said nothing, but lowered his eyes.

Kappa went on, "The Tengu will start the fusion process. He has been trained how to do it. At the critical moment, he will short-circuit the power supply by ripping out the main control cables—here, and here—and joining them together with his bare hands. The fusion reactor will go into wild imbalance, and within thirty seconds it will explode."

Mr. Esmeralda took out his handkerchief and dabbed at his forehead. It was infernally hot and rancid inside this room; and his equilibrium wasn't helped by the fact that he was so hungry and that Kappa was so repulsive to look at. Neither was he consoled by the thought that Kappa's wild and malevolent scheme to blow up a nuclear-power station was only two days away, and very real. When he had first met Kappa in Japan, all that time ago, it had seemed like a joke; at the very worst, a nuclear scare like Three Mile Island, with hardly any real damage to be done to anyone. But here, today, Kappa was talking about blowing up Three Arch Bay the day after tomorrow, in a 150-megaton nuclear blast, seven thousand times more powerful than Hiroshima. It was absurd, and unimaginable. He couldn't even think what a 150-megaton blast could possibly look like, or sound like, or do. Yet Kappa fully intended to set one off: not just once, but over and over again.

"I gather you're leaving Los Angeles, then," said Mr. Esmeralda. "You were afflicted by one nuclear blast; I'm sure you wouldn't want to go through another."

"I want you to rent me a private boat," said Kappa. "It should be comfortable, well appointed. I will take the minimum of crew with me and sail northward to San Francisco, in order that I may witness the devastation from a safe distance."

"What time are you planning on letting the Tengu loose?"

"At nine o'clock in the evening, the day after tomorrow. It will hinder rescue services even more if it is dark."

"When will you pay me the money that you promised me?"

Kappa was silent for a moment. Then he asked, "Do you think I should pay you at all?"

"You should, unless you want me to call a SWAT squad the moment I walk out of the door."

"You are trying to say that I must either pay you or kill you?"

Mr. Esmeralda took a deep breath. "You could put it like that, if you so wish. But, if nothing else, I have always taken you to be a man of your word."

"Very well," said Kappa. "You will be paid. All the remaining money that I agree to pay you will be credited to your bank account by tomorrow morning. But I expect you to remain in Los Angeles until the Day of Fate to make sure that the Tengu goes and that all possible arrangements for the destruction of the reactor have been com-

pleted. If I were you, I would arrange for a private plane to
fly you out of Los Angeles as soon as the mission begins.
You can fly far enough and fast enough in a single hour to
avoid the main effects of the blast."

"I suppose there is some comfort in that."

Kappa said, "You have no word of Sennett yet?"

"The boy is still being held at Pacoima Ranch. But, no,
his fahter hasn't responded yet."

"Gerard Crowley is supposed to be in charge of
capturing Sennett, is he not?"

Mr. Esmeralda nodded. "He would have succeeded
immediately if Sennett had been at home. He sent in
Yoshino and Toshiro, and they took the boy without
anybody noticing. Crowley was supposed to contact
Sennett with instructions for the boy's release this
morning, but so far I haven't heard of any developments.
Crowley will catch him, I am sure of that. Sennett isn't the
kind of man who would risk his son's life, not for anything."

"Is that what you think?" asked Kappa. "Then what if
I were to tell you that Sennett has been to see Nancy
Shiranuka?"

Mr. Esmeralda stared at him, at that hideous, nearly
smiling mask. "Sennett has been to see Nancy Shiranuka?
But how? He doesn't even *know* her."

"I do not understand how, I can only surmise," said
Kappa. "Either Sennett knows more about us than we
think; or else somebody in this little group of ours has
betrayed us. According to the *Oni* who watched Nancy
Shiranuka's apartment last night, Sennett arrived there
late yesterday evening and stayed until the early hours of
the morning."

"Was Gerard Crowley there?"

"No, although I *do* know who spent the night with
Gerard Crowley's wife."

Mr. Esmeralda asked, "You've been watching *me*,
too?"

"Of course. You don't think that you're exempt from

my suspicion, do you? Nobody is."

"But Gerard Crowley was supposed to go to Nancy Shiranuka's to brief her about the attack on Rancho Encino Hospital, and work out new plans for Doctor Gempaku."

"Crowley didn't arrive," said Kappa. "One of my men went to check Crowley's apartment, where he was fortunate enough to see *you* arriving; then he checked the Bonaventure Hotel, where Crowley has been keeping a room; and the house on Packard Street, where Crowley's mistress lives. No Crowley. No mistress, either."

"I'll check on it myself," said Mr. Esmeralda. All the time he was thinking: My God, not Crowley, too. Crowley had already threatened to go to the police and try to plea-bargain his way out of trouble. Why hadn't he gone to Nancy Shiranuka's, as he was supposed to? And what had Jerry Sennett been doing there? The treacherous group that Mr. Esmeralda had assembled to carry out Kappa's "bodyguard" project was proving even more treacherous than he had ever imagined. Kappa was right to bring the Day of Fate forward to the soonest date he could manage. And even so, Mr. Esmeralda was beginning to wonder if they could pull it off before the police discovered what they were up to. There was no honor among entrepreneurs.

Kappa said harshly, "I want you personally to drive Doctor Gempaku to Rancho Encino so that he can perform the necessary rituals. Then, I want you personally to make sure that Sennett is snared, and that both he and his son are killed. You can leave Crowley and Nancy Shiranuka to me—and Commander Ouvarov, too, when we find him. They have all been useful in their way. They have enabled us to bring into America all the people and all the equipment we needed. But now, they are growing restless; and restless servants are dangerous ones."

Mr. Esmeralda asked, "I can go now?"

"Yes," whispered Kappa. "But don't think that I have forgiven *your* mismanagement and *your* carelessness. You will only be able to purge your errors by making sure that the rest of my program is fulfilled without a single mistake. And, to make certain that you have the necessary incentive, I have already taken your Chinese chauffeur as a hostage. You will have to drive yourself from now on, until this mission is successfully accomplished. We will take the girl on the boat with us when we sail to San Francisco, and we will release her only when the atomic sun rises in the southern sky. Otherwise, she will die. My *Oni* have many diverting ways of killing women, some of which take several days.''

Mr. Esmeralda felt as if cold leeches were sliding down his back. There were a dozen angry things he could have said. If he had been younger, fitter, and more reckless, he might have tried to seize Kappa and throttle him. But he had been surviving for too many years, staying alive in cities and situations where more impulsive men had died violent deaths, and he had lost the instinct to do anything rash.

"Promise me that you will release her when the power station blows," was all he said. "Promise me on your honor."

"I promise," said Kappa, and his eyes glistened behind his mask like the eyes of a hermit crab peering through the shell of a long-dead host.

CHAPTER SEVEN

David was dreaming about sunbathing on the beach at San Luis Obispo when the screen door slid back and Doctor Gempaku stepped in. Just behind him stood one of the black-masked *Oni* with an oblong lacquered tray, on which there was a bowl of *oshi-zushi*, pressed rice with

ham and prawns and cucumber. Doctor Gempaku bent
over David, shook his shoulder, and said, "Breakfast,
young sir."

David blinked, rubbed at his eyes, and then sat up awkwardly. He was naked, covered only with a thin gray
blanket, and there was no sign of his clothes. He said,
"Has my father called yet?"

"You must have patience," said Doctor Gempaku.
"Your father does not yet know where you are, or what we
are expecting of him."

"You're out of luck if it's money you want," said
David. "Dad's practically bankrupt."

"Oh, no, we're not after money," smiled Doctor
Gempaku. "We're looking instead for *silence*."

"Silence? What's that supposed to mean?" David
watched out of the corner of his eye as the *Oni* adept set
down the breakfast tray, and then retreated to the doorway. The Japanese went no further, though, and it was
obvious that he intended to keep a sharp watch on David
until Doctor Gempaku's visit was over and the door could
be locked again.

Doctor Gempaku said, "Your father knows about
things that ordinary men like him should never really have
had the misfortune to discover."

"This is something to do with Japan?" queried David.
"Something to do with the war?"

"You're a bright young fellow," said Doctor
Gempaku. "If you had been born Japanese, you would
have gone far. But, well, things must be different. A very
great pity."

"You're not going to harm my father?" asked David.

Doctor Gempaku reached across to David's breakfast
tray, crumbled off a piece of oshi-zushi, and began to
nibble at it. "Do you know what your father did in the
war? Do you know why he still has to have psychiatric
treatment?"

"Sure," frowned David. "He was on a mission for
Naval Intelligence, and all his friends got killed by the

Japanese, right in front of his eyes."

"Do you know what the mission was?"

David shook his head. "Something to do with—I don't know—spying out landing sites for American aircraft to invade the Japanese mainland. That's what he told me once."

Doctor Gempaku took out a clean handkerchief and industriously wiped his hands, and then his mouth. "Your father has been lying to you; or, at least, not telling you the whole truth. Under the direction of a special Naval Intelligence task force, a task force of only fifteen men and yet a task force which was considered so important by the U.S. Joint Chiefs of Staff that it was put under the direction of an Admiral—Admiral Knut Thorson—your father was parachuted into Japan to detect, with a high-powered radio, the exact location of a very special Japanese military training center."

"What's so special about that?" asked David.

Doctor Gempaku ruffled David's hair. "You do not understand at all, do you? That military training center was devoted to the creation of a special kind of Japanese soldier; a soldier who would be religiously as well as patriotically inspired, to the point where he would no longer feel pain, no longer feel fear. It was one of several attempts to protect the Japanese homeland. As futile as all the rest, perhaps; as futile as arming women and children with sharp bamboo sticks. But you cannot blame any nation, when it is isolated and afraid, for seeking to survive."

"What happened?" asked David. He was hungry, but he still hadn't touched his *oshi-zushi*.

Doctor Gempaku shrugged. "The usual American over reaction. A fierce and unreasoning desire to avenge Pearl Harbor, perhaps. Something like that: who can understand the American psychology? The American mind is a mixture of cloying sentimentality and hideous brutality. Who can possibly reconcile the contradictions of Los Angeles, a city in which nearly eight hundred people are murdered every year, a city in which there are nearly two hundred rapes every month, and yet a city which can gleefully produce *The Great Muppet Caper* and *On Golden Pond*. You smile? Perhaps you find it amusing that a nation can publicly exalt the human spirit while at the same time wallowing in the deepest slough of moral degradation in civilized history.''

David said, ''I don't really understand what you're saying.''

''Let me tell you what your father did in Japan. Then you may grasp what I am trying to get into your head. Your father located the training center at Hiroshima, and sent back to the American high command a signal which he *knew* was the go-ahead for the dropping of the first atomic bomb. Although he was quite aware that his signal would lead to the instant and horrible deaths of thousands of civilians, he said, ''Do it''; and they did it. You know that your father goes to a psychiatrist, of course. Well, now you know why.''

David stared at Doctor Gempaku in disbelief. ''That's crazy,'' he said. ''They wouldn't have dropped the atomic bomb just to wipe out one training center.''

''They considered it necessary,'' said Doctor Gempaku. ''By their own lights, they considered it worthwhile.''

''But they dropped the atomic bomb to shorten the war. Japan was never going to surrender. They were going to fight until the very last man. I mean, the war could have gone on for *years*.''

Doctor Gempaku helped himself to some more of David's breakfast. ''How readily the young absorb the lies of their parents,'' he said. ''By May of 1945, Japan was already defeated, and even the most fanatical of her leaders knew it. The Japanese merchant navy, on which the whole country depended for food and supplies, had been reduced from ten million tons to one million. Over forty percent of all of Japan's sixty major cities had been destroyed by bombing. Her navy and her air force were shattered; what remained of her fleet was immobilized for lack of fuel. In May, we attempted to discuss peace with the Americans, using the Russians as mediators. But the Americans relentlessly insisted on unconditional surrender, *unconditional*, and failed to make it clear to the Japanese people that our Emperor, who is divine, would not be treated as a war criminal, and would be allowed to remain as Emperor under any Allied occupation force. This failure by the Americans to understand even the simplest fact of Japanese life and religion was what prolonged the war beyond the early summer of 1945. And through the hand of your father and his military henchmen, it was this failure that eventually led to the dropping of the first atomic bomb.''

David was silent. Doctor Gempaku stood up straight, then walked across to the window. "I am sorry if I have been lecturing you. But you should know why you are here.''

"Do you want to kill my father?'' whispered David.

Doctor Gempaku made a face. "I do not *want* to kill him,'' he said.

"But you're going to?''

"Almost certainly. And you, too.''

David stared at Doctor Gempaku, shocked. He felt as if all the blood had drained out of his body; he was ice-cold and empty.

"They'll catch you,'' he said unsteadily.

"Who will?''

"The police. The Los Angeles police.''

Doctor Gempaku turned around. "By tomorrow night, there will be no Los Angeles police. More than that, there will be no Los Angeles.''

David couldn't think of anything else to say. He chewed nervously at his lip, and looked at Doctor Gempaku against the diffuse light of the window.

Doctor Gempaku said, "It will be interesting to see how brave this man who killed so many thousands of Japanese during the war can actually be.''

CHAPTER EIGHT

Gerard Crowley looked unshaven and tired as he pushed his way between the crowded tables of Zucky's deli-restaurant a little before noon. His tie was loosened, and his shirt was crumpled and dirty. He was halfway through his second cigar of the day.

Jerry, in spite of his anxiety and his nervousness, had felt hungry when he had arrived at Zucky's, and had ordered himself a turkey sandwich and a cold beer.

Gerard Crowley, when he arrived, stood a foot or two away from Jerry's table with his hands in his pockets, his cigar between his lips, an expression on his face that was half cautious and half apologetic, like a man who has cornered a wounded Doberman and doesn't quite know whether he ought to try to bind the dog's foot or run for his life.

"Listen," he said, "I'm sorry about what happened. I'm sorry about all of it."

Jerry couldn't think what to say to that. The last thing he had expected from Gerard Crowley was an apology. The waitress came back with Jerry's sandwich and asked Gerard, "You're eating, sir?"

"Just give me a Scotch for now," said Gerard. He took the cigar out of his mouth and sat down next to Jerry, tugging the sleeves of his jacket down to cover his grubby cuffs. All around them, the deli was noisy with talking and laughter and music. Gerard said, "I don't suppose you want to shake hands."

"I just want to know how to get my son back," Jerry told him.

Gerard said, "The last I heard, an hour ago, your son's safe. You know why they're holding him, don't you? It's *you* they want. It's you they wanted right from the very beginning. Sherry Cantor died because they wanted you."

"The Tengus?" asked Jerry.

Gerard nodded. "They were afraid you'd guess. It looks like you did."

Jerry said tightly, "What's this all about? What the
hell's going on? Nancy Shiranuka said something about
bodyguards."

"That's a blind," said Gerard. He crushed his cigar out
in the ashtray and wiped his mouth with the back of his
hand. "I don't know what they're really into, but I can't
believe it's anything to do with bodyguards. When they
first approached me, they said it was nothing more than a
moneymaking scheme for protecting rich Arabs and
nervous *mafiosi*. Killer bodyguards, each one worth a
million dollars of anybody's money. That's what they *told*
me. They offered me the kind of money that nobody in his
right mind would possibly turn down; and they backed up
the carrot with a big stick. They knew about some contraband business I'd been involved in, and they said that if I
didn't help them, they'd fix me up."

"Because of that, you agreed to murder?" asked Jerry.
He tried to keep his voice as level as possible, but he was
seething with frustration and anger at David's kidnapping, and at Gerard Crowley's impossible weakness.
He was weak himself, he knew it. He still hadn't been able
to find a way to face up to his own past. But Gerard's
weakness was of an even more insidious variety: Gerard's
weakness was a steady and unstoppable corrosion of the
spirit. In Gerard's life, there was no hope of redemption,
only meaningless apology.

Jerry thought it was ironic that their names were so
similar: Jerry and Gerard. They were like the two faces of
Dorian Gray, the unspeakably corrupt and the falsely
innocent. They were different victims of the same human
problem: an inability to cope with the utter immorality
which was the prerequisite of success or even survival.

Gerard said, "The hits didn't seem like anything very
special at first. They were a way of trying out the Tengus,
proving that, as a market commodity, they worked the way
they were supposed to. I know you find that difficult to
swallow, but you haven't been working for twenty years in
the import-export business like I have. You can believe

me—anything that turns a buck gets sold. Drugs, fertilizers, chemicals, guns, surface-to-air missiles, tanks, mines, spirits, tobacco, pornography, girls, animals, boys. If you have enough money, you can buy anything, from anywhere. Let me tell you something, my wife thinks I'm a cold fish, unreachable. But if you're going to keep yourself alive and moderately wealthy, you have to keep your soul under lock and key, and that's what I've been doing. They told me to hit you, and that's what I arranged to do. They told me to kidnap you, take you out to the mountains, and dispose of you; so, I found that you weren't at home, I took your son instead.''

"It was *you*?''

Gerard nodded. "I arranged it. I was told to flush you out, and that seemed like the best way.''

Jerry was dumbfounded. "So now what?'' he said. "I'm supposed to forgive you, or something? *Now* what? I want my son back, and that's all there is to it.''

"Would you give up your life for your son? If I said you can have him back, but only if you allow me to kill you, what would you say then?''

Jerry stared at him. "Are you serious? Are you asking that as a serious question?''

Gerard didn't even blink.

Jerry put down his turkey sandwich. His throat was drier than ever. "If that's the way it has to be . . . then yes. If that's the only possible condition for David's release.''

Gerard smirked, and then let out a grunt of a laugh. "You're even more innocent than I imagined,'' he said. "Do you really think that anybody who wanted to kill you would actually honor this agreement, and release your boy? Your boy's being kept alive for one reason only: you're still alive. Once you're dead, why should anyone bother? Your boy will be knocked off, too. You're not likely to come back from the grave and argue about it, are you? And your boy will be far too damning a witness for us to let him go.''

Jerry was silent for a long time, staring at Gerard in

hopeless anxiety. Then he said, "You've come to meet me for a reason, right? Either to have me killed, or to put up some kind of a suggestion."

"That's right," said Gerard. The waitress brought his whiskey, and he paid for it with a $20 bill. "You see, everything was fine until yesterday night. Then, they sent out a Tengu to kill Admiral Thorson, who is the only other man apart from your good self who might have jeopardized the Tengu project by recognizing what the Tengu actually are and by helping the police to trace them back to where they came from."

"Admiral Thorson was in a coma. He had been for months. Why should they bother to send out a Tengu to kill him?"

"They're *crazy*, that's why," said Gerard. "And, besides, they're Japanese. Although they won't admit it, a whole lot of what they're doing has got something to do with the ancient Japanese principles of revenge and honor. You and Thorson knew about the Tengus: you had to die. Don't ask me why. The whole thing's like some kind of nightmare."

Jerry said, "I get the feeling you're trying to tell me that you're changing sides. You're not trying to threaten me, are you? Or are you? You're trying to find out if I'll forgive you enough for what you've done to help you."

Gerard took out another cigar and clipped off the end. "This Tengu project isn't what it seems, believe me. There's something really heavy going down; and when I say heavy, I mean *heavy*."

Jerry picked up his sandwich, looked at it, and then put it down again. He said, "You took my son, right? All I want to hear from you is that you're prepared to help me get him back again."

Gerard briefly closed his eyes, to indicate his assent.

"I don't *trust* you," said Jerry. "For Christ's sake, how can I trust you? It was you who took him in the first place."

"I'm not asking for anything," Gerard said. "Not

sympathy, not forgiveness, nothing. I'm just asking you to believe that in the past twenty-four hours, I've changed my mind about the people I work for, and I've begun to change my mind about myself. The motivation has been completely selfish. I'm scared, if you want to know the truth. I've never been scared of anyone or anything in my life, but I'm scared now. And the reason I'm scared is because I'm in love. I've been dating my secretary, Francesca. I was supposed to go back to Nancy Shiranuka's place last night and talk about the Tengus, report on what we'd been doing out at Rancho Encino. But I didn't go. Instead, I took Francesca to L'Ermitage, where nobody was going to find us, and I spent the whole night talking myself out. My past, my present, and my future. The whole Rancho Encino thing went wrong, it all turned into a massacre. I can't live with that. When you're really in love for the first time, you realize you can't accept half the things you accepted before. You've got a responsibility to yourself, and to the person you love.''

He smoked, and rubbed at his forehead, and then he said, ''I can't erase what's happened, you know? I can't bring Sherry Cantor back to life. But I would if I could. And I'll do whatever I can to help you get your son back. I thought I was a frigid, emotionless tough guy before any of this started, and the fact is that I'm not. I don't think anybody is, when you really take it down to the bottom line. You can't be a lover and a killer at the same time. And that's why I said I was sorry when I first came in.''

Jerry said, ''Nancy Shiranuka told me they were holding David at some ranch near Pacoima.''

''That's right.''

''What goes on there? When you say 'they,' who do you mean? How many people do they have there?''

''The ranch at Pacoima is where they're creating the Tengus,'' said Gerard. ''The head guy there is Doctor Gempaku, he's the guy who actually develops the Tengus, brings them into being. Then there's ten or eleven guards; they all wear black masks on their faces, so you can never tell which is which. But they're all armed, and they're all skilled in *Oni*, which is some kind of ancient martial art.''

"I know about *Oni*," said Jerry.

"In that case, you'll be quite aware that these guys are totally deadly," said Gerard.

"Yes," said Jerry. He felt awkward with Gerard, suspicious of him. And yet at the same time he could recognize that Gerard was going through an inner turmoil that, if he only allowed it to, could bring him out of a life that had been shallow and cynical and exploitative, and into an existence that would be honest even if not particularly profitable.

Jerry hadn't been at L'Ermitage, during those hours in which Gerard had drunk whiskey after whiskey, and talked, and argued, and made love to Francesca in ways that had been both tender and fierce. Jerry hadn't seen that the news from Rancho Encino had shocked Gerard more than Gerard was prepared to admit, even to himself. Wheeling and dealing was one thing. Hearing secondhand stories about hits on treacherous Chinese dope dealers was chilling, but not personally alarming. But the slaughter at Rancho Encino and the kidnapping of David Sennett had made Gerard Crowley realize at last that he was out of his league. In spite of his apparent remoteness, in spite of his cynicism, he was a man who needed to feel that he was loved; and with loving and being loved came morality, and with morality came hesitation.

"The only way you can rescue your son alive is by hitting Doctor Gempaku when he's least expecting it," said Gerard. "Do you own a gun?"

Jerry shook his head.

"You'll need something heavyweight," said Gerard. "These *Oni* guards have Israeli Uzis, and they won't hesitate to use them if they think that something's wrong. I can get you an M-60E1 and a couple of Ingrams. You have some friends who could help you?"

"I have some friends, for sure," said Jerry. "But whether they'd help me or not . . . Are you suggesting I *storm* this place?"

"What else are you going to do?" asked Gerard. "The minute those people see anything that looks like a police car, they're going to kill your boy stone dead. My suggestion is that I take you in there, like you've given yourself up, and then two or three of your friends bust into the place and go through it with machine guns until there's nobody left."

Jerry said, "You're out of your *mind*! First of all you tell me, quite calmly, that it was *you* who kidnapped my son. Now you're telling me that you're prepared to help me rescue him by blowing all your fellow kidnappers away. I'm asking you, Crowley, are *you* nuts or am *I*?"

Gerard looked away. Then he said quietly, "This has all come too late—my conversion, if you want to call it that. Too late for any kind of sensible action. I'm just making a suggestion, that's all. If you don't like it, if you can think of something better, then do it. I won't stand in your way. But I'm going to have to ask you one thing."

"What's that?" asked Jerry.

"I'm going to have to ask you to plead on my behalf, if this ever comes to the law. I'm in love with a beautiful girl, Sennett, and I don't particularly feel like spending the next ten to twenty years in the penitentiary. That's why I agreed to meet you today; that's why I'm trying to help. It's got to be a deal or else it's no deal. You speak on my behalf; I'll help you get your son back."

Jerry finished his beer, taking as long as he could, watching Gerard Crowley all the time.

"You'll get me the guns?" he asked at last.

"An M-60E1, easy," said Gerard. "Do you think you'll know how to use it?"

"I was trained on a Browning during the war."

"You'll manage. I'm not so sure whether I can get the Ingrams, but I'll do my best."

Jerry said, "Surely the police can manage this better. Maybe the SWAT team. I'm an old man, Crowley. Well, not *old* exactly, but getting on. I'm not even sure that my friends will want to help me."

"If you call the police in, I'm finished," said Gerard.

"Not only that, but your son will be too. You know how ham-fisted the cops can be, when it comes to a confrontation like this. It'll be blood and dead bodies, and that's it."

"You can show me where this place is, at Pacoima?"

"Sure," said Gerard. "Only I have to have your promise that you'll back me up in court."

Jerry pressed his hands together in a mimickry of prayer. Then he said, "In principle, okay. In practice, I don't know. I'll have to go talk to my friends first. You're asking me to risk *my* life so that you don't have to risk *yours*."

"I'm supposed to tell you that your son has thirty-six hours to live," said Gerard. "Either you come out to Pacoima Ranch by midnight, or David dies."

Jerry said, "You're a bastard, you know that?"

"Sure I'm a bastard," Gerard replied. "But every bastard has his moment of glory."

Jerry pushed his away his half-eaten sandwich. The world seemed suddenly strange, and cold, and threatening beyond belief. "Glory," he said, mostly to himself. "Some glory."

CHAPTER NINE

Francesca was still at L'Ermitage, pinning up her hair, when Gerard and Jerry said goodbye to each other on the sidewalk outside of Zucky's and walked off in opposite directions. She looked at herself in the mirror and thought: Francesca, you'd better not fall in love. Whatever else you want to do with your life, don't fall in love. Not with Gerard Crowley.

Last night, she had seen a side of Gerard which she

hadn't even realized existed. Gerard afraid. Gerard sensitive. Gerard thinking about nothing but her, and pleasing her; with champagne, and gardenias, and breast of duckling with Bordeaux sauce.

She brushed out her long auburn hair in front of the mirror. She was naked except for a white lace G-string from Janet Reger of London. She had developed expensive tastes in the three years she had worked for the CIA, first as an undercover agent, and then as a kind of highly paid, high-class callgirl-cum-entrapment-operative.

Gerard Crowley was not a particularly big fish. But Crowley Tobacco Imports was the central clearinghouse for five or six heavy smuggling operations, particularly the heroin business operated by the Jonas brothers, and the Metaxas weapons-smuggling ring which supplied machine guns and missiles to the terrorist groups of the Middle East. It had been Francesca's job to gather sufficient evidence against Gerard Crowley to persuade him to testify against Billy and Nathan Jonas, Salvatore Mazzarino, and Giorgio Scarantino.

She hadn't reckoned with the surprise bonus of Mr. Esmeralda; but although she had reported back to her local CIA chief of operations everything she could find out about Gerard's dealing with him, she hadn't yet been able to decide exactly what it was that Mr. Esmeralda was up to. Gerard was obviously frightened of him; and did whatever he told him to. But whenever she tried to question Gerard about him, Gerard said nothing at all, or very little of any interest, and quickly changed the subject.

Last night, she had known that Gerard was frantically worried. Instead of meeting her at the Bonaventure or her apartment, he had insisted on taking her to L'Ermitage, where he had booked a room for two and ordered up the most lavish meal on the menu. Then, he had talked for hours about his childhood, and about his days in Cuba, and how life had tricked him and trapped him into being a stooge. "How can you have any scruples when society expects you to be rich instead of poor, and yet makes it impossible for you to be rich by honest and honorable means?''

He had made love to her four or five times, urgently and violently. She liked him because, over a period of several months, she had made an effort to like him. This was her third "secretary-mistress" operation, and she had learned that she had to do everything she could to see the best in her "marks," no matter how brutal and coarse they were. There were some nights when she had lain in the dark with a man's semen leaking out of her, as tackily as drying blood, and heard him snoring on the pillow next to her, and known that in two weeks' time she would be standing in court testifying against him. And still she liked him.

She didn't know whether she was actually capable of love.

She knew that Gerard had invested all of his affections in their relationship: that his marriage had fallen to pieces, and he was looking to her to provide him with his future. But she didn't feel sorry for him, or guilty. One way or another, one day or another, with or without her, he would be caught for smuggling or milk extortion or drug-running or arms dealing or pimping. He was one of those men who had been born without a future, no matter how hard they tried. Next month, Francesca would be smiling seductively at a new employer, and Gerard Crowley would be forgotten altogether.

She finished brushing her hair, then walked across to the closet where her dress was hanging up.

"Poor Gerard," she thought. "My God, poor, lonely Gerard."

CHAPTER TEN

After the killings, the staff of Rancho Encino Hospital had moved Admiral Thorson to the next wing, to a lemon-yellow room with a reproduction of "Some Steps in the Hospital Garden" by Van Gogh on the wall above his bed. Admiral Thorson was still shocked by what had happened, and by the realization that his wife was dead, but he was conscious and coherent. During the day he spoke three or four times to hospital staff, and to Harry Calsbeek, the Chief of Detectives from Encino police headquarters.

There was little he could say: his wife had screamed, he had woken up to see a dark, flailing shape through the plastic of his oxygen tent. Then he had heard a salvo of gunfire, and blood had splattered in front of his eyes like an action painting. "I can tell you this, though," the admiral had said hoarsely, "I shall never forget my Mary screaming until I leave this earth. I shall never forget it, ever."

Sergeant Skrolnik and Detective Pullet arrived at Rancho Encino during the evening, tired, vexed, and arguing with each other. Detective Pullet had been attempting some more bursts of lateral thinking, and had come up with the idea that the killer might be a failed Japanese restaurateur with a grudge against American naval officers. Maybe they had patronized his original restaurant in Tokyo, but hadn't taken the trouble to patronize his new restaurant in Los Angeles? Skrolnik had had enough of lateral thinking, and had told Pullet to keep his mouth shut and his mind on the facts.

Calsbeek was waiting for Skrolnik outside Admiral Thorson's room.

Calsbeek was heavily built, red-haired, with a face that looked scraped, like a raw rutabaga. His tweed suit hung around him in fold after fold, each pocket crammed with pieces of paper, rolled-up magazines, clips of .38 bullets, chewing gum, Life Savers, Swiss Army knives, loose

buttons, and string. But while his appearance may have
been gentle, sloppy, and shuffling, his mind and his
tongue were as abrasive as sandpaper.

"You should have been here three hours ago," he told
Skrolnik. "I've talked to the man all I can, there's nothing
more to be done."

"You took notes?" asked Skrolnik.

"Of course I took fucking notes."

"By the way, this is Detective Pullet," said Skrolnik.
"Detective Pullet is our number one deductive thinker."

"I see," said Calsbeek. "Well, maybe he can deduce
why three loony Japs and a white man decided to burst
into Rancho Encino Hospital and slaughter everybody in
sight, because sure as hell *I* can't."

Pullet said, "You have to go back to the fundamental
reasons why anybody kills anybody else. Believe it or not,
there are only *eight* reasons why people kill other people:
robbery, rape, jealousy, self-defense, violent disagreement, pity, revenge, and to keep them quiet.
Well . . . nobody wanted to *rob* Admiral Thorson, because he didn't have any money on him. Nor did they
want to *rape* him. I doubt if *jealousy* was the motive,
because he didn't have a particularly distinguished career,
and he certainly wasn't fooling with anybody's wife."

Skrolnik said, "Will you get to the point, Pullet?"

"Sure," said Pullet. "Nobody killed him after a violent
disagreement, because he was in a coma, and unable to
argue with anybody. It's unlikely that anybody attacked
him so violently out of *pity*. That leaves us with
revenge—which, considering his record in the Pacific
theater of war against the Japanese, could well be likely.
Or, the motive of keeping him quiet."

"He was in a coma, what could he say to anybody about
anything?" asked Skrolnik. "Why should anybody want
to keep him quiet?"

"You're right," said Pullet. "So what are we left with?
Revenge. A Japanese attacks a World War Two admiral,
presumably with the intention of revenging Midway, or

Leyte Gulf, or whatever. It's my guess that when you manage to identify this turkey, you'll find that his father or his older brother went down with the *Hirvu*, something like that."

"Takes your breath away, doesn't it?" said Skrolnik, turning to Calsbeek.

Calsbeek said, "You can question the admiral at midnight, when they wake him up to give him his medication. Don't press him too hard, you know? Give an old, sick man an even break. He's just lost his wife and it hasn't sunk in yet."

"We understand," said Skrolnik. "Now, can we see the bodies?"

Pullet said, "I'll wait here, you know, stand guard."

Skrolnik said wearily, "Come on, Pullet. You've got all the theories, you've got to see the bodies, too."

Calsbeek led the way to the hospital morgue. A pale-faced young man unlocked the door for them, and they trooped reluctantly into the chilled, fluorescent-lit room where the hospital kept the remains of loved ones who had passed away during their stay.

"Drawers eight, nine, and six," the young man told them.

Skrolnik, without hesitation, rolled out No. 8. It was Kenji, the Japanese who had been stabbed by Commander Ouvarov. His face was still locked in a ridiculous grimace of pain.

"You can't say that *he* died a serene death," remarked Skrolnik.

They opened the next drawer, No. 9. It was the Japanese who had been hit pointblank by one of the hospital security guards. The bridge of his nose was blown away, and his eyeballs were collapsing toward the middle of his face, giving him a ludicrous but horrifying squint.

"You didn't tell me this hospital had been attacked by Ben Turpin," said Skrolnik laconically. Neither Pullet nor Calsbeek could find it in them to laugh. "Number six," instructed Skrolnik, unperturbed.

The body of the Tengu lay on the slab with his arms tucked neatly beside him, his bloodstained loincloth already black and fetid, his chest and thighs gaping with anemic wounds. There was no head: only the protruding trachea, and a tangle of muscles and tendons and nerves.

"Well, your boys certainly put paid to him," said Skrolnik. "What do you arm them with, howitzers?"

"We killed him before he could kill Admiral Thorson," said Calsbeek acidly. "That's all you need to know."

"Has the coroner been over this body yet?"

"He's taking it tomorrow. There was a mass poisoning two nights ago at Strawberry Drive, up by the reservoir. His slabs are kind of crowded right now."

"Well, life's busy in Encino right now," remarked Skrolnik. "What are you trying to do, beat out the Los Angeles homicide statistics?"

"Believe me, this is the last thing I want," grated Calsbeek. "Encino's supposed to be quiet and neighborly. Neat yards and law-abiding suburbanites. Up until now, the worst crime we've had all year has been inconsiderate roller-skating on the sidewalk."

Skrolnik rolled back the drawer, and the Tengu's mutilated body disappeared from sight. "Do you want some coffee?" he asked Calsbeek. "Stiffs always make me thirsty."

Calsbeek gulped a few mouthfuls of scalding machine-made coffee with them, and then left. Skrolnik and Pullet sat for the next two hours in the reception area, listening to the splash of the illuminated fountain and the syrupy warbling of Muzak, and leafing through copies of *Reader's Digest* and *Encino*.

"I never realized that Encino was such a goddamned dull place," said Skrolnik, tossing one of the magazines back onto the table.

Just after midnight, a short, bespectacled doctor with a shock of black wavy hair came scuttling into the reception area to tell them, blinking, that Admiral Thorson would now be available for a short period of police questioning.

"As long as you understand that he's a very sick man, you got me?"

"Yes, sir," grunted Skrolnik. "Aren't we all?"

Considering the trauma that he had been through, Admiral Thorson looked remarkably fit. He was no longer the old "Inch-Thick" of Navy days. His eyes were sunken and shadowed. But when Skrolnik and Pullet were shown into his room, he nodded to them alertly and said, "What's this? More damn fool questions?"

Skrolnik smiled uncomfortably and perched his rump on the edge of an uncomfortable stacking chair. Pullet went across to the other side of the bed and peered with almost morbid interest at the admiral's cardiopulmonary monitors and electroencephalograph. Skrolnik said, "We won't keep you very long, sir. We know that you've been through a lot. But what happened here at Rancho Encino bears a close resemblance to a homicide we're investigating in Hollywood."

"I'm sorry to hear it," said Admiral Thorson. "Would you mind passing me that glass of lemonade? A man gets damn thirsty all wired up like this, tucked up in bed like a damned invalid."

Skrolnik passed him the lemonade, and the old man took four or five sips and then handed it back. "Used to be bourbon and branch, in the old days," he grunted.

Skrolnik said, "What particularly interests us, sir, is that your assailant was Japanese. Detective Pullet here has been theorizing that maybe the attack has something to do with your war record. We've had one or two cases of white people attacking Japanese because they lost somebody they loved during the war; usually when they're drunk or depressed or suffering from some kind of nervous collapse. But on the face of it, your assailant was psychotic, to say the least, and Detective Pullet thinks that maybe . . ."

Admiral Thorson looked from Skrolnik to Pullet, and then back again. "Anything that I did during the Second War is faithfully and fully recorded in my memoirs, sergeant. *From Saipan to Kyushu with Admiral Knut*

Thorson, published by the Institute for Naval Studies. Rather than interview me, and wear out what little there is left of me, I suggest you go buy yourself a copy.''

Skrolnik wedged his fingers together and raised his eyebrows toward Detective Pullet in an expression of testy patience. ''What I was trying to get at, Admiral, if you'll forgive me for pressing you, is whether you were involved in anything personal or private that may have excited some Japanese fruitcake to try to get even with you. I understand that the Japanese have very severe codes of honor and duty; maybe you inadvertently trod on someone's face during the war, upset them more than you'd meant to. Something to do with a woman, maybe? I'm not trying to pry.''

Admiral Thorson was silent for a moment. Then he gestured toward his bedside cabinet and said to Skrolnik, ''Open the top drawer. Take out the letter you'll find in there.''

Skrolnik did as he was told. He lifted out the faded V-mail envelope and opened it.

''Read it,'' said Admiral Thorson.

> *How can a love so gentle be so fierce?*
> *How can a soft caress grip with such strength?*
> *How can your tenderest glance so quickly pierce*
> *My heart its very depth, my life its length?*

Sergeant Skrolnik said cautiously, ''It's poetry.''

''Yes,'' said Admiral Thorson. ''I wrote it to my wife in October 1944, just before the battle of Leyte Gulf. It was one of many. Let me ask you if a man who writes poetry like that to his wife is likely to get involved with a Japanese woman?''

''I'm sorry,'' said Skrolnik. ''But you understand that I have to chase after every possible idea.''

''Admiral,'' put in Detective Pullet, running his hand through his tangled hair, ''was there any other operation you were in charge of, during the war, anything that maybe didn't get into your memoirs?''

"Anything that didn't get into my memoirs was excluded for reasons of national security," Admiral Thorson answered. "There were one or two operations I was able to write about in the revised edition of my book, in 1968, but since then nothing else, as far as I know, has come off the top-secret list."

"Was there anything that might have motivated an attack of revenge—the kind of attack that happened here last night?"

Admiral Thorson said, "I can't discuss anything that isn't in my memoirs without a specific security clearance from the Secretary of the Navy. I'm sorry."

Pullet sensed something, he wasn't at all sure what it was. But the way in which Admiral Thorson had abruptly invoked the rulebook aroused his nose for the obscure and the unusual. Admiral Thorson had an inkling of what had happened to his wife, and why. Pullet was sure of it. And if Pullet knew anything at all about the psychology of retired military commanders, Admiral Thorson wasn't refusing to discuss it because it was secret. He was refusing to discuss it because he was afraid of being ridiculed. The attack on Rancho Encino Hospital had been pretty wacky, as homicides went, and Pullet was convinced that Admiral Thorson had an equally wacky theory about it.

He said, "This guy who assaulted your wife and the rest of the hospital staff. Did you ever see anyone who looked like him before? All those wounds on his body? Would you have any idea what they were?"

"I'm afraid I can't answer that," said Admiral Thorson.

"Then you *do* know something about it?" demanded Pullet.

"I didn't say that. I simply said that I can't answer your question."

"You can't answer the question because it's a matter of national security?"

"That's correct. Now, please—"

Pullet dragged over a chair and sat astride it, frowning at Admiral Thorson with scruffy concern. "Admiral," he said, "there was a multiple homicide here last night.

Your own wife was among the victims. Now, if you refuse
to discuss what happened here because you believe that it's
going to be an infringement of national security, then you
must have some kind of notion what it was all about. I
mean, otherwise, how do you know that it's likely to be an
infringement of national security?''

"I'm tired," said Admiral Thorson. "I'm tired and
you're playing with words. I don't have anything to say to
you."

"Admiral—"

"The man is *dead*, isn't he?" Admiral Thorson demanded. "He's been caught, and executed on the spot.
What's the purpose of investigating any further?"

"Admiral," said Skrolnik as gently as he could, "It's
conceivable that there might have been a conspiracy to
attack you, involving a considerable number of people. So
far, we don't have a single clue *why*. But we believe there
are men still at liberty who were concerned in the killing of
your wife. We want to catch those men."

Admiral Thorson shook his head. His voice was hoarse
now, and desperate. "You'll have to leave me alone for
now. I'm too tired. Please—will you call the doctor?"

Skrolnik took a deep breath and stood up. "Okay,
Admiral. If you don't want to help, then I guess I can't
force you. Pullet, will you push that bell, please? We're
going to leave the admiral to think things over, see if he
can't come up with some kind of surprise recollection.
Something meaningful to add to his memoirs."

The doctor came in and asked, "All finished now?"

"I hope not," said Skrolnik.

"You haven't upset him?" asked the doctor.

"He's okay, *I'm* the one who's upset," Skrolnik
complained.

Skrolnik and Pullet left the hospital and walked out into
the warm night air. Skrolnik's car was being repaired in
the police workshop, and he had borrowed a dented black
Lincoln Continental from his next-door neighbor. He had
parked it on the far side of the hospital parking lot, and so

he and Pullet had to cross almost to the perimeter of the hospital to reach it. They were almost there, walking side by side in irritated silence, when Pullet said, "What's that? Do you see something?"

"Where?" asked Skrolnik.

"Out on the road there, beside those bushes. No—you see that low stone wall. That's it. There."

Skrolnik strained his eyes in the darkness, and made out the shape of what appeared to be a man, kneeling in the road. As Skrolnik took two or three steps nearer, he saw that in front of the man there were two smoking bowls, and he also glimpsed what looked like two shiny crossed swords.

Skrolnik immediately hiked out his .38 revolver and released the safety. Pullet did the same. Without a word, Skrolnik ducked down behind the nearest parked car, ran the length of it with his head bent low, and then crossed the hospital lawn at a quick canter, making obliquely for the bushes beside the road, but keeping a screen of shrubs and trees in between himself and the man with the smoking bowls and the swords.

As he neared the road, Skrolnik waved his arm behind him to indicate to Pullet that he should circle around on the other side. Then, without any hesitation, he hurled himself straight through the bushes, with a crash of leaves and broken branches, and struck a knees-bent stance on the road, his gun held in front of him in both hands, and yelled, "Police! Freeze!"

There was a shot from the other side of the road, and Skrolnik felt the wind of a bullet flash past his cheek. He dropped to the ground and rolled himself back into the bushes again, firing off a quick diversionary shot that hit something on the other side of the road with a sharp *spang*! of metal.

The man who had been kneeling on the roadway had already scurried crabwise to the protection of the low stone wall. Skrolnik gingerly raised his head and shouted, "Pullet? Where the fuck are you?" but before Pullet

could answer there was a roar of an engine starting up, and
a large limousine backed out of the trees on the other side
of the road, reversed wildly up to the stone wall, its tires
smoking and its suspension bucking, and Skrolnik knew
that their mysterious suspect was about to make a fast
getaway.

He knelt among the dust and the leaves, steadied his
hand, and fired off four shots, in what he hoped was a
tight cluster, toward the limousine's front window. There
was a crackling of broken glass, but the limousine gunned
its engine, and took off down the road with its tail snaking
from side to side and its tires screaming like slaughtered
pigs.

"Get on the radio!" Skrolnik bellowed at Pullet. "Get
an alert out on those jokers! Go on, *move*!"

Pullet pushed his way out of the bushes and went
running back across the lawn to the parking lot, trying to
stuff his gun back into his trousers as he went. Skrolnik
meanwhile walked along to the place where the man had
been kneeling and hunkered down to examine the
evidence that he had left there.

One of the bowls had been tipped over, and its contents
were strewn across the blacktop. It was still smoldering,
though, a grayish powdery substance that looked like
incense or charcoal. There was a light, sweetish smell
around, which reminded Skrolnik of something he
couldn't immediately put a name to. Something unusual
and exotic and, for some reason, very disturbing. He licked
his finger, touched the powder, and tasted it. It could have
been dried flowers or the burned gum from some species
of tree.

He recognized at once what the two crossed swords were.
Samurai swords, curved and sharp and decorated with
lacquer and silk bindings. He didn't touch them; he
wanted them photographed and fingerprinted first. But
they confirmed what he and Pullet had just been saying to
Admiral Thorson. The attack on Rancho Encino had been
connected with Thorson's war record, and his assailants

almost certainly wanted revenge. What for, Skrolnik couldn't even begin to guess. He reloaded and holstered his gun, and planted his fists on his hips in a gesture of thoughtful determination. It was a pose that everybody in Skrolnik's department recognized as a sure sign that Skrolnik was now going to get tough.

Pullet came running back, breathless.

"You're out of condition," said Skrolnik. "Why don't you take up jogging? Listen, run back to the car and get my accident signs, will you? I don't want any of this stuff moved until Rabinowitz's boys have had a go at it."

Pullet said, "What the hell do you think he was doing? Are those swords?"

"Samurai swords," Skrolnik nodded. "Whatever he was up to, it was something to do with that attack on Admiral Thorson. Just, for Christ's sake, don't ask me what."

"I'll get the signs," said Pullet; but the moment he turned around, every floodlight in the hospital grounds was suddenly switched on, and the alarm began to bellow through the trees. Skrolnik said, "*Thorson*," and took out his gun again.

CHAPTER ELEVEN

They arrived at the doors of the hospital puffing and blowing. But Skrolnik forced his way in, past a screaming nurse and a dazed security officer who was waving his gun around at nobody and nothing, and jogged heavily down the corridor toward Admiral Thorson's room.

Another security officer came cantering toward them, shouting, "Get back! Get back!" but Skrolnik and Pullet simply dodged aside to let him run past, and he didn't even attempt to clear them out of the corridor.

"That guy's frightened," remarked Skrolnik.

"Aren't you?" asked Pullet.

They turned the corner and collided with Admiral Thorson's doctor. His hair seemed to be standing on end, and his eyes were as wild as Harpo Marx's.

"What the hell's going on here?" Skrolnik shouted at him, with all the coarseness he could muster. "What the hell is everybody running for?"

"It's that *thing*," garbled the doctor. Then he tore himself free from Skrolnik and ran off toward the hospital lobby.

"That *thing*, huh?" asked Skrolnik, wiping his nose with the back of his gun hand. "This is beginning to sound like some kind of monster movie. The Thing from Rancho Encino."

Pullet said, "We'd better go take a look in any case."

"I was afraid you'd suggest that," Skrolnik retorted. "You're becoming far too conscientious for a rookie."

They turned the last corner, into the corridor that took them directly to Admiral Thorson's room, and Skrolnik froze. At the end of the corridor was a wired-glass door, and through the distorting, refracting glass he could see a short, bulky shape, like a man with his head bent forward in contemplation. Skrolnik said, "The Thing?" and Pullet shrugged. "How do I know? I never met a Thing before. Challenge it."

Skrolnik raised his .38. "You!" he shouted harshly. "You, behind that door! Come out of there with your hands on your head!"

For a long moment, the bulky silhouette remained motionless. Skrolnik said, "Cover me," and took one or two apprehensive steps forward, his gun still raised.

"Do you hear me?" he shouted. "Come on out from behind that door with your hands on your head! You don't have a chance!"

The silhouette raised its arms, slowly and deliberately. "He's giving up," said Pullet, with relief, half-lowering his revolver. But then, with a terrifying, rending smash, the silhouette thrashed its fists into the glass door, tearing it apart in a wreckage of tangled wire, broken glass, and splintered wood.

"Oh, Jesus," said Pullet.

The creature that forced its way through the broken door may have been human once, but it was human no longer. It was the Tengu from the morgue, revived, and walking, mutilated not only with the scars of Doctor Gempaku's hooks, but with the gaping bloodless bullet wounds it had sustained from the Encino police. The worst thing of all, though, was that it had no head, only that raw pipe that rose from between its shoulders and the gristly remnants of its neck.

Skrolnik said, "It can't be. Pullet, that damned thing can't *be*."

The headless Tengu took one heavy step after another, dragging itself clear from the glass and the wire, heading toward Admiral Thorson's door. It may have been an optical illusion, but Skrolnik could have sworn that he saw tiny blue flames dancing in the air around the Tengu's shoulders.

He fired into the Tengu's chest, twice. Dead, white flesh flapped up as the Tengu's body absorbed the bullets, and the Tengu appeared momentarily to hesitate. But then it continued to shuffle toward Admiral Thorson's door, and at last it bumped against the oak veneer, its mutilated but muscular shoulder cracking the wood, its hands clawing toward the handle.

Skrolnik, white-faced, sweating, fired two more shots, only an inch apart, into the area of the monster's heart. The Tengu jolted with the impact and swayed, but then continued to beat dully against the admiral's door. Smoke from the bullets that had entered its chest cavity rose from the open pipe of its severed neck.

Pullet shrieked, "You can't kill it! For God's sake, it won't die!"

Hesitantly, Skrolnik approached the creature, his gun

held out in front of him. He fired two more shots, from pointblank range. One of the bullets went right through the Tengu's stomach and exited from its back. The other hit it in the chest. Neither bullet seemed to make any impression at all, except that the fires which flared around the Tengu's shoulders seemed to roar and grow fiercer.

Skrolnik, sickened and scared, but high on the adrenalin of sheer danger, tried to reach out and seize the monster's arm. But with a sideways chop, the Tengu knocked him aside, so that he collided heavily with the opposite wall of the corridor and twisted his ankle.

With six or seven splintering blows, the Tengu tore down Admiral Thorson's door and stepped into the dimly lit room. Skrolnik, wincing with agony in the corridor, knew now that there was absolutely nothing he could do. He also recognized that for the first time in his life he was up against something completely unstoppable; something which refused to obey any of the laws of nature, or at least the laws by which Sergeant Skrolnik organized his life and his police work. This thing, whatever it was, was supernatural, a ghost or a ghoul or a zombie, a thing that was undead and couldn't be killed by any conventional weapons, or defeated by any conventional prayers. Skrolnik knew that for certain: his brain had been spinning with frenzied appeals to the Lord his God ever since the Tengu had burst through the glass door.

"Pullet!" shouted Skrolnik. "Break open that fire cabinet down there! Get me that fire ax!"

Through the doorway, Skrolnik could see the Tengu approaching Admiral Thorson's bed; standing there, headless, swaying slightly as if it were recovering from a great and painful effort of will. The blue flames still jumped and blazed around it, but now it appeared to have a dark glow of its own, a frightening and almost visible aura, like a torturing iron that has just lost its red-hot radiance but is still capable of searing a man's flesh.

"Admiral!" bellowed Skrolnik. "Admiral, if you can manage it, get the hell out of there!"

Skrolnik limped on his one good ankle to the torn-apart doorframe. Now he could see Admiral Thorson sitting up in bed, his face papery and wrinkled, his sunken eyes bright with fear.

"Admiral!" shouted Skrolnik.

But the admiral's eyes were on the Tengu alone. The Tengu took one shuffling step nearer after another, until it was standing right up against the admiral's bed. Knut Thorson stared at it in horror and recognition.

"I never believed it could be real," he whispered. "Not even then."

Skrolnik said, in a determined hiss, "Admiral, I want you to roll off that bed, roll away from the monster onto the floor. Then dive right under the bed and leave the rest to me. Pullet, where the fuck's that fire ax? For Christ's sake, move your ass."

Whether he had heard Skrolnik or not, the admiral stayed where he was, propped up on his pillows, his monitoring equipment betraying every overstimulated beat of his heart, every jump of fear in his brain. He gave no indication that he had understood a single word, nor that he was going to try to save himself. But just then, Pullet came jostling up with the fire ax and handed it clumsily to Skrolnik, as if it were the baton in an amateur relay race.

"Stand back," grunted Skrolnik, and took one limping step forward into Admiral Thorson's room, swinging the long-handled ax in both hands.

Admiral Thorson shouted, "*Mary!*" at the top of his quavery voice, and then Skrolnik whirled the ax around and chopped it deep into the Tengu's severed neck, splitting its breastbone with an audible crack. Skrolnik stumbled backward on his twisted ankle, toppling Pullet over as well, but there was nothing they could do to save Admiral Thorson now. With the ax handle still sticking out from its back, the Tengu seized Admiral Thorson by the neck and wrenched him out of his bed, half lifting him in the air. Admiral Thorson hung in the headless creature's powerful hands, awkward and powerless; his cardiopulmonary monitor giving one last screech as the monster wrenched the wires loose.

With one flailing tear, the Tengu ripped off the admiral's hospital nightgown, baring his scrawny, ribby body; then, without hesitation, it plunged its fist through the flesh of the admiral's stomach, in a spattering welter of blood and fluid, and seized the admiral's backbone as if it were grasping the skeleton of a snake. Soundlessly, wordlessly, because it could never speak, or hear, or see—because whatever it could do, it could do only through the possession of the ancient demon Tengu—it pulled the admiral's spine right out through his torn-open belly, virtually turning his body inside out.

Skrolnik was utterly unable to speak, or even to think. All he knew was that the headless Tengu with the ax still stuck between its shoulders was throwing the admiral's gory corpse aside, so that nerves and intestines and tendons slid in bloodstained strings onto the floor, and that now it was turning toward him.

"Pullet," he said. "I do not want to be here."

Together, they scrambled to their feet, and with Skrolnik leaning his weight on Pullet's shoulders, they hopped and hobbled and half ran down the corridor to the hospital lobby, closing and locking the last door behind them. A crowd was already gathering there—nurses and medics and police, including a furiously disgruntled-looking Harry Calsbeek.

"Why do you foreigners always bring trouble?" he snarled. "What's going on here?"

Skrolnik caught Calsbeek's sleeve and pulled him aside, shoving away an inquisitive reporter from the *Encino Star*. "What I'm going to say I'm only going to say once," he told Calsbeek, scarcely opening his mouth as he spoke. "That creature you shot last night is still alive, and still walking around. It's just burst into Admiral Thorson's room and tore the poor old guy to very messy shreds. I don't know how it can still be alive. I don't know why. Maybe it's all just a nightmare. But if it is, then you're in it too, and you're going to have to act accordingly. My best suggestion is that you go get a couple of cans of gasoline, and as soon as the creature appears, we set fire to it."

"We can shoot it, can't we?" asked Calsbeek. Then, "What am I talking about? I don't even *believe* you. Are you off your head or something? What's going on here?"

He was answered almost immediately. There was a screech of tearing wood and ripped-off hinges. Then a massive smash, and a low moan of fright among the hospital staff and patients gathered in the lobby. One of the nurses screamed, and then another, and then everybody was rushing for the main doors, jostling and pushing and knocking over potted plants.

"*Don't panic!*" yelled Skrolnik, the veins standing out on his neck. "*Don't panic, or somebody's going to get crushed!*"

Calsbeek said, "Oh, my God."

The door to the lobby came sailing over their heads, tumbling and turning, to crash noisily into the ornamental pool. Dark, and yet still radiating that awesome aura, the headless Tengu stood in the open doorway, the ax protruding from its neck, its scarred and mutilated chest rising and falling with the breath of one of man's oldest and most terrible enemies, a devil even more vicious than Lucifer.

Skrolnik said, "*Now* will you get the gasoline?"

"Evans!" bellowed Calsbeek. "Guttierez! Get out to the wagon and bring in those spare cans of gas, and do it so damn fast I don't know you've gone!"

Calsbeek's two officers elbowed their way as quickly as they could through the last stragglers pushing each other to get out of the hospital, while Skrolnik and Calsbeek and Pullet retreated toward the reception counter, drawing their revolvers and watching the Tengu warily. For a while, the Tengu stayed where it was, in the doorway, no flames dancing around its shoulders at the moment, no movement to suggest what it might be considering next. But as Evans and Guttierez came clanging back with their heavy

cans of gasoline, the Tengu took one clumsy step forward
and raised both arms as if it were feeling its way across the
lobby, sensing the presence of vulnerable humans through
the nerves in the palms of its hands.

To Skrolnik, the Tengu looked like a bloody carcass of
beef, headless and gutted; or the hideous human corpse in
Goya's painting of Saturn devouring his children. The
body was human, but the missing head had taken away all
its identity, all its humanity.

"Get your men to splash as much gas on that thing as
they can," said Skrolnik. "Just tell them to keep out of its
way. Once it gets hold of you, you're dead beef."

Calsbeek gave the order, and Evans and Guttierez
opened up two of the gasoline cans and began circling the
Tengu cautiously, swinging the cans back so that they
could slosh as much fuel over the creature as possible. The
Tengu didn't even flinch, but kept walking slowly and
deliberately across the lobby toward the reception counter.
Skrolnik and Calsbeek retreated from the counter, and
climbed clumsily around the edge of the ornamental pool
to keep as much distance between themselves and the
Tengu as they possibly could.

The Tengu hesitated for a second or two, confused by
their movement. Then Skrolnik saw the tiny foxfires
glittering around its severed neck again, and it swung
toward them, its hands still extended, a grisly caricature of
Frankenstein's monster. Skrolnik thought, *I'm going to
wake up in a minute. I'm going to wake up and find that
I'm late for breakfast. Oh, holy Jesus, please let me wake
up in a minute. Or preferably sooner.*

Pullet reached across to the low coffee table in the
middle of the waiting area and picked up a copy of *Los
Angeles* magazine. He attempted to rip it in half, but because this was August, it was the 404-page restaurant-
guide special, and he couldn't do it. "For Christ's sake,"
said Skrolnik. "Tear out individual pages, roll them up,
make a torch."

Step by step, they backed off toward the open hospital

door. Evans and Guttierez splashed the last of the third can of gasoline over the Tengu, until the creature was so drenched that it gave off rippling fumes. Pullet had made his torch now, and was lighting it with a book of matches.

The paper flared up. The Tengu suddenly made a volent and unnervingy accurate rush toward them. The ghostly blue fires around its shoulders roared up like a locomotive roaring through a tunnel. Calsbeek said, "Oh, *shit*," and collided with the doorframe as he tried to scramble his way out. Skrolnik yelled, "*Throw the goddamned torch, Pullet*!"

Pullet threw it. It fell immediately to pieces and fluttered into separate blazing pages. Skrolnik thought for one dreadful second that Pullet had missed altogether, but then a wayward draft from the open door blew one of the burning pages up against the Tengu's chest.

The Tengu stumbled toward them, arms outstretched, groping for them, but then the burning paper ignited the gasoline on its chest and fanned a pattern of orange flames across its ribcage. There was a dull, breathy, thumping noise, and the gasoline that Calsbeek's two officers had splashed into the Tengu's lungs and stomach through its wide-open neck exploded, and blew chunks of flaming flesh across the hospital patio.

The Tengu staggered, burning fiercely from thighs to shoulders. It took one slow step forward, then another, even though Skrolnik could see right through its charred ribs to where the fire was blazing inside its chest, and its bones were crackling and popping with heat.

Unnerved, Calsbeek fired off two shots, but they made no impression on the Tengu at all. It stood where it was, fiery and defiant, a walking corpse that refused to bow down, even to immolation. It was only when the flesh of its thighs had actually burned through to the femur that it spun around and collapsed onto the paving stones with a noise of flaring fat.

Skrolnik limped closer, and stood over the guttering body with horror and relief. As the flesh burned away from the neck and upper cheset, the ax blade suddenly dropped onto the patio with a clunk, and he jerked back in involuntary shock.

Calsbeek was calling harshly on his radio for reinforcements, so that the hospital could be screened off. The hospital administrator, with a great deal of shouting and bustling about, had already arranged for the patients to be moved to different rooms, away from the intensive-care unit where Admiral Thorson had been murdered. The night was echoing with whooping choruses of sirens, and the trees around the hospital were alight with the flashing of red-and-white police beacons.

At last Calsbeek came over and stood beside Skrolnik with an expression that put Pullet in mind of a cartoon bulldog who has discovered that bones can fly. "I don't know how the hell I'm going to report this," he said. "I've already filed a memorandum saying the guy's dead. Now I've got to file another one saying he came to life again, and we killed him for a second time."

Skrolnik watched the Tengu's corpse sputter and glow, and the ashes blow away in the evening wind.

"Shit," he said, and limped back to his car, followed by a silent Pullet.

CHAPTER TWELVE

The *Los Angeles Times* carried the headline ADMIRAL SLAIN BY 'DEAD' KILLER—ASSASSIN, 'FATALLY' SHOT BY POLICE, REVIVES TO FINISH OFF THWARTED MURDER MISSION.

Mack Holt read the story carefully, sniffing from time to time, and then passed the newspaper back to Jerry Sennett

with a shrug. "I agree with you. It sounds like this Tengu
stuff is all true, and it's happening here. But what am *I*
supposed to do about it? I cared for Sherry, you know that.
I really cared about her a lot. But it's not my responsibility, any of it. I mean, what moral justification can
there possibly be for me to attack some farm somewhere,
out at Pacoima, and start shooting up a whole lot of
Japanese I've never even met?"

Jerry pointed to the penultimate paragraph in the news
story. "Sgt. Skrolnik revealed that certain Japanese artifacts, including two samurai swords, had been discovered
close to the scene of the crime. He expressed the opinion
that they were directly linked to the murder of Admiral
Thorson, although he was not yet prepared to say how or
why."

Mack settled back on his saggy sofa and crossed his
ankles. Olive was sitting beside him in a yellow UCLA
T-shirt and nothing else, idly scratching and stroking at
the blond curls at the back of his neck with her clawlike
fingernails.

Jerry said empthatically, "The only two people the
Tengus have tried to kill so far are Admiral Thorson—
who's dead, at the second attempt—and me. As far as I
know, Admiral Thorson and I were the only two surviving
servicemen left in the entire United States who knew right
from the very beginning, what the whole Appomattox
mission was all about. And even *I* didn't know everything
that was going on until the A-bomb had actually been
dropped. There must be plenty of senior officers in the
Naval Intelligence Command today who have access to the
files on Appomattox; and I'm sure that successive Presidents have been alerted to what went on. But, as of last
week, only two people in the whole damned country could
have known *immediately* what was happening if they
heard on the news about Japanese killers who were impervious to bullets, and had the strength of five men put together. Me, and Admiral Thorson. And that must be why
they went for us."

"I still don't understand," said Olive, running a nail around Mack's earlobe. "Why should they want to kill you or something which happened such a long time ago? Supposing you *did* find out that someone had been making these Tengu-people? So what?"

"I don't know," said Jerry. "All I can guess is that they're intending to use the Tengus for something really spectacular. A bank robbery, maybe. Or maybe they want to assassinate the President. The President's supposed to be taking a vacation at Rancho Cielo next month, isn' he? Maybe it's some kind of weird retaliation against American trade restrictions on Japanese cars. I just don't have any idea. All I knnow is that they wanted both me and Admiral Thorson dead, presumably so that we couldn't tell any tales."

"Didn't Crowley know what was going on?" asked Mack.

Jerry shook his head. "He suspected there was more to the Tengu program than building up a team of body-guards, but he didn't have any coherent ideas about what it might be."

"You believe him?"

"I don't think I have much choice."

Mack said, "You really want us to help you break into that place, and rescue your son?"

Jerry pulled a noncommittal face. "I can't *force* you to help me."

"But that's really *dangerous*, man," said Olive. "Any one of you could get killed."

Jerry said, "It's a risk I've got to take. My son's in there and I've got to get him out. I can't see that I have any choice."

"You won't be much good to your son if you're dead," said Olive.

"No, I won't," Jerry agreed. "But the way Crowley sees it, they're intending to kill me anyway, and David, too, no matter what I do."

"You trust Crowley? The same guy that actually kidnapped your son?"

Jerry raised both hands in a gesture of mute acceptance.

Mack, with his arm around Olive, shook his head in disbelief—more at the fact that he was sitting here listening to what Jerry had to say, than at the absurdity of Japanese samurai possessed by ancient devils. "This whole thing's insane, you know. What can you possibly do about it, as a defenseless, untrained, private citizen? Your best choice is to call the police, and you know it. I mean, that's my advice, and you know what *I* feel about the police."

"Crowley said that David wouldn't stand a chance if I called the police."

"Kidnappers always say that," said Mack dismissively.

"How many kidnappings have *you* been involved in?" Jerry demanded.

"Well, none."

"Let's take this particular kidnapping on its own particular merits, then, shall we?" asked Jerry. "Crowley is my only contact; and whether he's lying to me or not, he's the only person who's suggested a way in which I might conceivably get David back unharmed."

Mack and Olive were silent for a while, uncertain of what to say. They saw before them a tired middle-aged man who had already lived through thirty-eight years of guilt for annihilating thousands of innocent men, women, and children; a man who secretly felt that he was solely responsible for turning nuclear theory into nuclear practice. Until he had said *go*, the idea of dropping an atomic bomb over a populated city had been no more than that: an idea. In the Chugoku Sanchi, alone, under a summer sky more than a third of a century ago, he had singlehandedly initiated the age of nuclear confrontation, an age which Mack and Olive took for granted because they had never known anything else, but which Jerry regarded as a Dark Age of his own making.

Now he was faced with an equally bitter choice over just one life: that of his only son, the only child he and Rhoda had conceived together. If Jerry himself were to die, David would never know from Jerry about all those times when his mother was young. He would never hear the explanations behind the photographs in Jerry's albums—this is the moment when your mother saw a goose chasing a woman across a barnyard in Massachusetts, that time just before you were born when we decided to take one last second honeymoon; this is the time a young black man offered to take our picture overlooking Niagara Falls, and took the best damned picture of two ordinary people in love that there ever was.

Mack said, "You really think Crowley's going to get you a machine gun?"

"He said he'd try. An M-60 and a couple of Ingrams."

Mack slowly shook his head. "This whole business is crazy."

At that moment, Maurice Needs appeared in the bedroom doorway, naked to the waist, scratching his head and yawning. "Boy, did I sleep good," he said, flexing muscle after muscle in turn. "Is there anything for breakfast? Eggs, maybe?"

"Eggs, he says," remarked Olive sarcastically. She climbed off the sofa, and stalked bare-bottomed to the kitchenette, watched with a mixture of pride and jealous annoyance by Mack. Jerry glanced after her, too, and then turned back to Mack and smiled.

"She's some woman, isn't she?" asked Maurice. "Dynamite. Doesn't care a two-bit shit for anybody."

"She loves her husband," Mack corrected him.

Maurice shrugged, with a big bunching of muscles. "Well, that's good. I always did believe in fidelity."

Jerry stood up and picked up his coat from the floor. The sleeves of his wrinkled gray shirt were rolled up, and the brown leather belt around his pants was cracked and worn. There was something defeated about him, which made Maurice look quickly over to Mack and frown, as if he were asking a question: Something's wrong here, what's happening?

Jerry said, "You know that if you don't help me I'll try to do this myself."

Mack said, "You're putting me in a position, aren't

you? You know, deliberately, you're putting me in a position."

"What position? What? What are you talking about?" asked Maurice.

Mack briefly, with expletives, explained about the Tengus, Gerard Crowley; and how David had been kidnapped. He also told about Gerard's offer of an M-60E1 and two or three Ingrams.

Maurice made a face. "An M-60? Jesus, that's a brute. My older brother used one in 'Nam. Six hundred rounds a minute. You could cut a guy in half with one of those."

"He's offered one," said Jerry. "He's agreed to call me at eleven o'clock this morning to talk about delivery."

"*I'll* come with you," said Maurice. "Jesus, what the hell. It's better than bending iron bars in a goddamned circus."

Olive came into the room, holding a plate of scrambled eggs with bacon strips. "Do I pamper you or do I pamper you?" she asked Maurice, setting the plate down on the table. Jerry couldn't help noticing the plump black lips of her vulva, shaved smooth and glossy as a King's Country plum. He thought: I'm in another age, another morality, another existence. He felt as if the atom bomb had obliterated for ever the world of zoot suits and Plymouth Road Kings and "Mairzy Doats," and beached him like the hero of some 1940's radio comedy on an unknown planet. He thought, my God, that's what Hiroshima did to me. It suspended me in 1945, a man in amber, and I don't think I've grown a day older since.

He said to Maurice, "Do you know something, there used to be a show called *Duffy's Tavern,* and every program started with this guy on the phone saying, 'Duffy's Tavern . . . Archie the manager speaking. Duffy ain't here. Oh, hello Duffy.' "

Maurice stared at him, and nodded. "When was that?" he asked, just to be polite. "I don't think I ever saw it."

"Radio," said Jerry. "Sometime before you were born."

"Oh," said Maurice.

The telephone rang. Mack said, "Answer it, will you, Olive?" but Olive was in the bedroom now, dressing. Mack picked the receiver up and said, "Duffy's Tavern . . . Archie the manager speaking."

There was a pause. Then Mack held the receiver out to Jerry, his face serious. "Did you give my number to Crowley?" he asked.

Jerry said, "I'm sorry. You know how urgent it is. I left a message on his recorder."

"Well, feel free," said Mack. "I just hope the guy isn't a psychopathic killer, like the rest of his friends."

Jerry took the phone and said, "Mr. Crowley?"

"That's right. I'm at the office right now. Did you hear the news?"

"Yes," said Jerry. "I'm not sure what it means."

"It means that this whole thing's falling apart, that's what. If there's something big in hand, they're going to try to do it quick, or else they're not going to try to do it at all. They're going to be pulling out of Pacoima within the week, believe me, and that means you've got to get your boy out of there just as soon as you can."

Jerry asked, "Have you told them you've been in touch with me?"

"I told them we've arranged a meet for later on today. I've told them you're willing to do any kind of a deal to get your son back, and that I should be able to cajole you back to the ranch."

"You've got the guns?"

"I've got the M-60 and six belts of ammunition, as well as two spare barrels, although you probably won't need them. I couldn't get any Ingrams, but I've got you a Canadian SMG and a couple of Browning high-power automatics."

"Sounds like enough for World War Three," said Jerry. Across the room, Mack raised his eyebrows and lit up a handrolled cigarette. Maurice was already mopping up the last of his egg.

"Just listen," said Gerard. "All the guns are in the trunk of a white Grand Prix, parked at the Chateau Marmont, on Sunset. All you have to do is go to the desk and ask for Mr. Wisby's keys. You got that? Mr. Wisby's keys. They'll give you the keys and you can go straight down to the parking lot and drive the car away. Then I'll meet up with you at the intersection of Van Nuys Boulevard and San Fernando Road, by the Whiteman Air Park, at three o'clock on the button. You with me? I'll be driving a Riviera, but I'll see you before you see me."

Jerry was silent. Then he said, "How do I really know that I can trust you?"

"You *don't* know," Gerard retorted. "But if someone gives you a heavy-duty machine gun and a heap of ammunition, and offers to help you get your son back, free of charge and with no strings attached except a good reference, well, that could be a sign that he isn't entirely antagonistic, wouldn't you say?"

Jerry said, "Okay. I'll meet you at three."

He handed the phone back to Mack, who hung it up and stared at him, with smoke blowing evenly out of his nostrils. "Well?" Mack asked him. "That sounded like all systems go."

"He's got the machine gun," said Jerry. "We're going out to Pacoima at three o'clock this afternoon."

Olive came in, wearing lemon-yellow jeans and a loose crocheted top. "Don't ask Mack to go with you," she said. "Please, I'm scared."

Maurice said, "*I'll* go. No problem. Just so long as I get to use the M-60. Can you imagine my brother's face when I tell him about it?"

"You probably won't *live* to tell him about it," said Olive.

"Aw, come on, Olive," grinned Maurice. "Where's your good old American sense of humor?"

"That's right, sweetheart," put in Mack. "Haven't you learned that it's *fun* to kill people, especially when they're of different racial origin? These are Japanese. We killed millions of them in World War Two. What's half a dozen more?''

Olive looked at him warily. "Don't tell me you're going, too?"

Mack puffed at his cigarette and nodded. "You think I'm going to let Maurice use an M-60, and I'm not even there?"

"But you said just a minute ago that—"

Mack stood up, and reached for his wornout cotton-twill jacket. "Forget what I said a minute ago. These guys killed Sherry, right? The least I can do is help to wipe them out."

"Oh, *John Wayne*," said Olive sarcastically. "When I started going out with you, I thought I was getting into a free-and-easy laid-back Hollywood hanger-on situation, bed and avocado-burgers and a little late-night music. I didn't realize I was joining the Green Berets."

"It's pronounced *berays*, not *barettes*," said Mack, kissing her on the forehead. "And, believe me, I'll stay way out of trouble."

"Do you have to go *now*?" Olive wanted to know. "It's only eleven-thirty."

Jerry said, "I think it would be a good idea if we all went around to my place and picked up some maps. I'd like to go get my own gun, too, in case of problems."

Olive lowered her eyes. "All right. If that's the way you want it. But I can't guarantee that I'm going to be here when you get back. *If* you get back."

"*Sweetheart*," Mack appealed.

"Sweetheart my fanny," retorted Olive.

"You see what being married to a sailor does to a girl?" asked Mack.

CHAPTER THIRTEEN

Outside, in the sunshine, Detective Arthur was standing beside Jerry's car, his notebook tucked under his arm, inhaling violently from a Dristan nasal spray.

"Good morning, officer," said Jerry. "How's the allergy?"

"Worse," said Arthur. "Some other damned plant has started pollinating now. It's killing me. And yesterday they gave me a case near a eucalyptus grove."

"What can I do for you today?" asked Jerry.

"Sergeant Skrolnik wanted you to know that Lieutenant Edward Smith is assuming overall direction of the Sherry Cantor case, after that thing out at Rancho Encino last night. Sergeant Skrolnik was out there himself, twisted his ankle or something. Now he's hobbling around like an alligator with a jalapeño pepper up its ass. Having to report to Lieutenant Smith isn't helping his temper much, either."

Jerry asked, "Is there anything else? I was just about to go home."

"Well," said Detective Arthur, wiping his nose again and then opening up his notebook, "Sergeant Skrolnik did want to ask you if knew anything about some sort of Japanese ritual where you have two blue-and-white porcelain bowls . . . that's what he's written down here in my notebook . . . and two crossed samurai swords. The bowls are supposed to contain some sort of stuff like ash or incense."

Jerry frowned. "It isn't like anything that *I've* ever heard of. But I'm not an expert on Japan. I was just there during the war and the occupation."

"He wanted you to think about it, that's all. He also asked me to advise you not to leave town, not for a day or two."

"So Sergeant Skrolnik thinks there's some kind of connection between Sherry Cantor's murder and Admiral

Thorson's murder?'' asked Jerry. "Some kind of Japanese connection?''

Detective Arthur put away his notebook, and spent a long time trying to push the clip of his ballpen into the torn lining of his inside pocket. "The guys who tried to knock off Admiral Thorson were all Japanese except one, who was an unidentified Caucasian. Three of them were killed: one by security guards at the hospital, one by police, and one by this unknown Caucasian.''

Jerry asked, "The killer who was supposed to have come to life again and killed Admiral Thorson last night—he was Japanese, too?''

"That's what I said. They were all Japanese except one unidentified Caucasian.''

"It doesn't say in the *Times* that he was Japanese.''

Arthur sniffed, and shook his head. "If you want to know the truth, Skrolnik's playing the whole thing so tight to the chest that *nobody* knows what's going on. I can tell you something, though, a few heads are going to roll for what happened out at Rancho Encino last night. A killer was supposed to be dead and he wasn't? He actually got out of the morgue and attacked his victim for the second time? I'm glad *I* wasn't in charge, believe me. Poor old Harry Calsbeek's been put on suspension—he was the officer responsible. They'll probably bust him without a pension; and Skrolnik's not much safer, either. They'd probably suspend him, too, if they had the manpower.''

"What's Skrolnik doing now?'' asked Mack.

"Putting the shit up the whole Japanese ethnic community, that's what,'' said Detective Arthur. "He's got foot patrols going around to every *sushi* bar, every teriyaki joint, every tempura restaurant, you name it. There isn't a *tatami* mat in town that's going to go un-turned. He's already had complaints from the Japanese community-relations people. They still remember what we did to the Issei and the Nisei during the war. But the guy's desperate. Two spectacular buchery cases and nothing to show for it. He's even been around to the Japanese Culture

Department at UCLA, asking about those porcelain bowls
and those swords. If it's got anything to do with Japan,
Skrolnik's going to shake it down. Karate clubs, flower-
arranging classes—he's hitting them all.''

Jerry turned back to Mack and raised his eyebrows. Mack
shrugged noncommittally. They'd just have to hope that
Skrolnik didn't locate the ranch out at Pacoima before this
afternoon.

Jerry said to Detective Arthur, ''I'll keep in touch,
okay? Right now I'm going home. If I can think what
those bowls and swords were all about, I'll call you.''

Detective Arthur went back to his car. Maurice said to
Jerry, ''Do you actually know what those bowls and swords
could have been?''

''I don't have any idea,'' said Jerry. ''But Nancy
Shiranuka may know. Perhaps if you guys could go pick up
the car with the guns on it, and drive it back to my house,
you could drop me off at Alta Loma Road on the way, so
that I can talk to her.''

They climbed into Jerry's Dodge, with Maurice taking
up most of the rear seat. Jerry heard the suspension groan
as El Krusho made himself comfortable.

Jerry drove to Alta Loma Road and parked outside
Nancy Shiranuka's apartment house. ''If I'm not back out
again in two or three minutes, just drive off and get the
Grand Prix,'' he told Mack. ''And for Christ's sake, be
careful. I don't want Olive's worst fears to come true.''

''Me neither,'' said Mack, sliding across behind the
wheel.

Jerry went up to Nancy's apartment and pressed the
bell. After a little while, he heard the slap of her slippers
on the polished wood floor, and she opened the door
herself. ''Jerry,'' she said, with mild surprise. ''Why don't
you come in? I'm on the telephone.''

Jerry took off his shoes and followed her into her serene
living room. He sat down on a *zabuton* and waited while
Nancy spoke in Japanese to someone who was obviously a
girlfriend of hers.

"Well," she said when she had finished. "I didn't expect you back so soon."

"I saw Gerard Crowley yesterday."

"He told me. He also told me what he plans to do."

"What do you think about it?" asked Jerry.

"About attacking the Tengus? I think it is very dangerous. But there are ways of protecting yourself."

"You think it's better not to call the police?"

Nancy nodded. "The *Oni* at the ranch would kill your son and everyone else if they even so much as glimpsed a police car or a uniform."

"You say there are ways of protecting ourselves?"

"Of course. The world is populated by good *kami* as well as black *kami*. It is possible to invoke their help against any of the demons, including Tengu."

"How?" asked Jerry.

Nancy said, "The greatest protection of all is the bond between two people who have been physically and mentally unified. The apotropaic spirit of that bond can be contained in any token or artifact that belongs to the person with whom you have joined. Do you have a lover?"

Jerry blew out a little tight breath of anxiety. "No," he said. "Not exactly. There was only Rhoda, my wife, and as you know she's—well, you know what happened."

Nancy looked at Jerry with those dark, liquid eyes and said nothing. Jerry tugged at his leg, in an attempt to tuck it under himself Japanese-style, but his knee was too stiff. He said, "Out of practice. Out of practice in lots of things, I guess."

Nancy said, "The bond must necessarily be with a living person. Once the person is dead, his *kami* has left for another plane of life altogether, beyond the gates of heaven."

"Then I guess I'll just have to do without it. I haven't been with anyone since Rhoda."

Nancy thought for a moment or two, and then stood up. "Come," she said, and held out her hand for him. He stared at her, uncertain of what it was that she expected of

him. But then he took her hand, climbed up off the
zabuton, and followed her along the corridor to a plain,
wood-floored anteroom. Its walls were hung with a
collection of five erotic woodblocks in the style of
Kiyomitsu, beautifully dressed Japanese women in flowing
silk robes, their clothes only slightly lifted or parted to
vreveal the huge gnarled penises that were penetrating
their vaginas.

Without a word, Nancy loosened Jerry's necktie, and
began deftly to unbutton his shirt. Jerry stayed still, his
hands by his sides, watching her with a feeling of unreality
but also, for the first time since he had heard that David
had been kidnapped, a feeling of peace. As he had noticed
the last time he had visited her, Nancy had an extraordinary quality of inner tranquility, a calm that reminded
him of the still lake around the Gold Pavilion in Nara, of
walking along the little alley called the Path of Philosophy
by the Old Canal in Nanzenji, when the rows of cherry
trees silently blizzarded their blossoms into the water.

In a matter of moments, with humility but also with
dignity, Nancy had stripped him naked. His penis rose
higher with every heartbeat. She ran her hands down his
bare chest, making him shiver, and down his thighs. Then
she loosened her own pale-pink silk robe and let it slide on
to the polished floor. She was slim and small-breasted,
naked except for an embroidered ribbon of white silk that
was fastened around her waist and between her legs, tied
so tight that it disappeared into the cleft of her sex.

She untied the ribbon, and drew it off herself, to reveal
that it had been keeping in place, inside her, a miniature
jade figure of a baldheaded deity carrying a peach, the
symbol of the female vulva. Without comment, she set the
figurine aside, and then took Jerry's hand and led him into
the bathroom.

Under a sharp, needling shower, Nancy soaped his
shoulders, his back, and his buttocks. She cupped his balls
in her hand for a moment, while she soaped up and down
the shaft of his erection; but not for too long. The true

stimulation would come later. Then she stood with her
eyes closed, her long dark hair spreading wet across her
shoulders, as Jerry slowly and firmly lathered her back, her
breasts, and her slender thighs. The water dribbling
between her legs turned her dark heart-shaped pubic hair
into a tail.

Afterward, fresh and dried, they closed themselves in
the bedroom, where a large soft *futon* lay on the floor.
Nancy insisted that Jerry close his eyes and lie on his back.
She massaged him with lightly scented oil, and spoke to
him monotonously and matter-of-factly about the mystical
power of yin and yang, the sexual union; and of the
nutritive powers which wise men could gain from drinking
"the medicine of the three mountain peaks" from the
women they couple with. The first juice was the juice of
the Red Lotus Peak, saliva from the tongue; the second
juice was from the Double Lotus Peak, milk from the
breasts; the third was the most nourishing juice of all, and
should be imbibed by men in the greatest quantities
possible, the precious juice of the Mysterious Geteway.

Jerry lay back on the *futon*, feeling Nancy's fingers
working at his muscles, feeling her naked skin against his,
and although his anxiety for David never left him, it became tempered with a new determination, more resolute
and more balanced. He began to feel that if he had gone
to Nancy Shiranuka for help, instead of his shrink, he
might have forgotten Hiroshima years ago.

At last, with exceptional elegance, as beautifully curved
as a bamboo-brush painting, Nancy lifted herself over
him, and took his penis in her hand, so that she could
couch it in the slippery curves of her vulva, and, with a
musical sigh, sink down on him, so deeply that she
trembled with a sensation that was part pleasure and part
shock.

She was like no other woman, Caucasian or Oriental,
that Jerry had ever slept with. She seemed to give herself to
him totally, surrender her pride and her personality without any reservation whatsoever. She rose up and down on

him as if she were conjuring the very soul out of him, through his penis; and at the instant of his first climax she withdrew herself, only by a fraction of an inch, so that they could both witness the jets of semen anointing her open lips.

They were locked together in the bedroom for an hour and a half, and during that time she brought him to three climaxes, opening her body up to him in every possible way. Yet, when it was finished and she lay next to him on the *futon* smoking a cigarette, he felt as if he had been through a mystical rather than a physical experience. He understood now what she had meant about the bond between two living people, the knot tied between their spirits, as if every movement had twisted one silken cord around another, as if each act of intimacy had tightened the ties.

When they were quiet again, when their breathing was gentle and even, Jerry said, "There's something else I have to ask you."

Nancy lay beside him, her face so close that he could scarcely focus on it. He'd been growing increasingly far-sighted with age, and he found that he was reading news-papers at arm's length these days. Eyeglasses, bridgework, baldness—how the human body decayed. Nancy didn't know how much of a gift of youthfulness she had given him by making love to him this afternoon.

"The police say they found two bowls and two samurai swords out at Rancho Encino Hospital. Blue porcelain bowls, containing incense or ash. And the swords were crossed. They've drawn the obvious inference that they were part of some sort of Japanese ritual, but they don't know what, and neither do I."

Nancy was silent, stroking Jerry's shoulder. Then she said, "The police shot and mortally wounded the Tengu who was sent to kill Admiral Thorson the night before last. It would have required a magical ceremony close to the Tengu's body to draw back the demon and revive the Tengu. The ceremony with the bowls and swords is called the Hour of Fire. It directs the Tengu back toward the dead meat of his previous host, and encourages him to bring it back to life again. A Tengu can be revived even if he has been burned to ashes. The Hour of Fire is specifically forbidden, not only by the priests of Shrine Shinto themselves, but, by secret agreement, by the Japanese police. Anyone who is thought to be trying to perform the ritual of the Hour of Fire is arrested and imprisoned, and usually meets with a fatal accident while in police custody."

"They take it *that* seriously?"

"They take the Tengu seriously," Nancy corrected him. "The Tengu is the darkest of all Japanese demons because he thrives on the weakness and corruption of the human soul. The purer the soul that the Tengu can corrupt, the greater the social and ethical damage to Japanese society, and the greater the Tengu's increasing strength. The company boss who takes a bribe after twenty years with a spotless record; the hardworking man who decides to steal; the woman who murders her husband—they are all victims of the Tengu. Has it never occurred to you why Japanese society is structured like it is? Why large companies act so paternally and protectively to their workers? They are shielding the people for whom they are responsible from the madness and violence that the Tengu always brings with him; the madness of war, the madness of murder, the madness of cruelty. The Tengu has affected Japanese thinking for hundreds of years. *I* believe it, no matter how much you smile at me. Some Japanese learned to control his influence: the samurai warriors, for instance were always balancing between strict morality and utter violent insanity. They courted possession by the Tengu, and hoped that they could control him. But the Tengu eventually brought Japan to war with the United States, which was the ultimate madness, politically and historically and socially. Japan recovered, but the Tengu lives on, and always will, to haunt and taint the Japanese spirit. You must forgive us for many things, Jerry. We are a people possessed."

It was nearly a quarter to two when Jerry dressed again, and called a cab to take him back to Orchid Place. Nancy had warmed him a little deluxe saké, the saké with the gold leaf floating in it, and they sat facing each other in the living room, drinking and enjoying each other's satisfaction and warmth.

At last, she opened her sleeve, and gave him a small porcelain box, decorated with erotic paintings and perforated with elaborate holes.

"What's this?" he asked her, turning it over and over.

"That is your keepsake for what we did today. That is your talisman. It will help to protect you. All you have to do is have faith in it, and have faith in the joining-together we achieved this afternoon."

He said, "If I thought that it was possible for a man to fall in love with a woman after meeting her only twice, I'd say that it has just happened to me."

Nancy smiled. "I have loved too many men, and been used by too many men. I have become because of my many experiences the *symbol* of a woman, rather than an individual woman whom you could love as a mistress or a wife. Would you really like to kiss every morning as you leave for work the lips of a woman who has fellated a whole forest of penises, white, black, and yellow? Would you really like to make love to a body that has been used and abused so many thousands of times? Sex to me has become something spiritual, something close to the very heart of the meaning of my existence. It is no longer a way of forming an attachment with one man. I don't care if I have one man or many men. All that I care about now is understanding my life, and reaching the peaks of sensory excitement that help me to do so."

Jerry looked at her without speaking for almost a minute. Then he looked down at the porcelain box she had given him and asked, "Can you tell me what this is?"

"It's a cricket cage," she said. "Chinese ladies used to catch singing crickets and put them inside, and then store the cages inside their sleeves, so that wherever they went walking in their gardens, they were accompanied by the singing of crickets."

"There's no cricket in it now," said Jerry.

"No," said Nancy. "But instead I have put inside it something even more attractive, and protective. A *koban*-sized *shunga* print, a *kachi-e*, a victory picture for you to carry into your conflict. It shows a highborn lady having intercourse with her lover in front of a mirror. It is by Shunchō, and it was printed in the mid-1780's, as one of a series called *Koshukū-zue jūni-kō*. It represents the acts which you and I have performed this afternoon, and it will guard your life against the Tengu."

Jerry held up the cricket cage in his hand. "I wish I could believe that."

"You *must* believe it. If you doubt it, think to yourself: Why did this woman who is almost a total stranger make love to me today, if it were not to form a bond of strength against the demon?"

Jerry looked at his wristwatch, the same gold wristwatch they had given him when he left the Navy. His prize for bombing Hiroshima. He said, "I have to go now."

Nancy held his wrist and placed his hand inside her silken robe, against her breast, so that he could feel her nipple rising against the palm of her hand. "I come from the *ukiyo-machi*," she said. "You must never think of me as a lover, but only as a bond. Someone with whom you formed a sexual and a mystical union."

Jerry leaned forward to kiss her, but she turned her head to one side. "When you have defeated the Tengu," she said, "come back here at once and drink your fill of the juice of the Mysterious Gateway, to restore your strength. Until then, you should thirst."

Jerry went to the door and opened it. "You're a very strange and beautiful person," he told her. He felt moved by what had happened to him in the past two hours. Nancy remained where she was, striped by the brilliant sunshine through her venetian blinds, her black hair shining, one breast still bare.

The cab was waiting for him. Jerry said, "Eleven Orchid Place, please."

CHAPTER FOURTEEN

Gerard was shrugging on his coat, and reaching for his keys and his pen, when Francesca came back into the office from lunch. "Gerard," she said, "you didn't tell me you were going out."

Gerard gave her an evasive grin. "Listen, I won't be long, okay? I have to see Chatfield about those Dutch cigars."

"Henry Chatfield called yesterday. It's all cleared up. He's probably back in New York by now."

Gerard stared at her coldly. "Listen," he said, "if I have to see Chatfield about those cigars, then I have to see Chatfield about those cigars. You understand me? Jesus Christ, you're not my wife."

Francesca raised her head a little and looked at Gerard through long, mascaraed lashes. "Gerard," she said, "I have to know where you're going."

"I'm going out, okay? Out of the door and along the corridor and down to the parking lot, and out."

Francesca said, as gently as she could manage, "That's not enough."

"What do you mean, 'That's not enough?' What are you talking about?"

Francesca sat down, crossing her long artificially sun-tanned legs. She looked Gerard directly in the eye, with a look he hadn't seen before. Almost *official*. She said, "This morning you went to the Avis desk at the airport and rented a white Pontiac Grand Prix in the name of Hudson Foss. Afterward, you drove to a lock-up garage in Westwood, which is rented from Westwood Star Properties by someone who calls himself P. B. Sexton. That garage contains a number of contraband items, including video equipment, pornographic viedeotapes and magazines, cocaine, whiskey, vodka, men's apparel, and weapons, one of which was an M-60E1 machinegun complete with ammunition and spare barrels."

Gerard was silent as Francesca continued. "You were

seen to load the M-60 machine gun and other weapons
into the trunk of the Grand Prix, and then drive it to the
Chateau Marmont hotel on Sunset Boulevard, where you
checked into one of the bungalows in the name of Wisby.
Then you immediately caught a cab and came back here.''

Gerard looked down at the polished surface of his
leather-topped desk, and then back up at Francesca. All of
a sudden, he saw what she was. Hard, certainly: but with
that implacable well-trained hardness of a law-enforce-
ment officer. Aquisitive, yes, but only for facts and figures
and damning information. A gold digger who was digging
for convictions, not diamond bracelets. She had gone to
bed with him not for himself but for evidence. Everything
he had boasted about, every extravagant gift he had
bought her—it had all gone down in a notebook somewhere, to be given as meticulous information for the pro-
secution when he was eventually brought to court.

"Well," he said, "it seems like I've made quite a fool
of myself."

Francesca said, "You can still save yourself a lot of
trouble if you tell me what's going on. You're involved in
something, aren't you, with Mr. Esmeralda? Something
more than forming a team of karate bodyguards."

Gerard struck a match and slowly began to feed a cigar.
"What are you?" he asked her. "U.S. Customs? What?"

Francesca didn't answer. All she said was, "There's only
one way you can save yourself, Gerard. You have to tell me
what's going on."

Gerard asked, "You've reported any of this? The guns?
Do your bosses know what's going on?"

"They will."

"They *will*, huh?"

"I have a certain amount of discretionary power when
I'm operating undercover in the field."

Gerard slowly shook his head, like a man who has
watched his favorite hockey team let in eleven goals in a
row. "So, going to bed with me was 'operating in the
field,' was it? I'm glad to know that romance is not yet
dead."

"You've been running guns and you've been smuggling narcotics," said Francesca. "You've also been dealing in industrial and military information. You didn't really expect the CIA not to show *some* interest in you, did you? You're not that modest?"

"I don't think modesty has much to do it," said Gerard frostily. There was a feeling inside of him like boiling oxygen, the kind of freezing steam that surrounds a rocket just beore its launch. "I was actually stupid enough to believe that you were my lover. I run a few deals, sure. You know that. You've helped me to organize some of them. A caper here and a caper there. Something to keep the cashflow flowing. But is it really worth *this*? Is it really worth your sleeping with me, pretending to love me, taking me away from my wife? Wouldn't you call than entrapment? Well, maybe you wouldn't. It seems like your morality is a whole lot different from mine."

"Gerard, I have to know what the guns are for."

Gerard shook his head. "No, Francesca, you don't have to know what the guns are for. You're going to get the hell out of this office, and get the hell out of my life, and if I ever set eyes on you anywhere near me again, I'm going to bang you one right in the nose. You understand me?"

"Do you want me to have you arrested?" asked Francesca. "I can do that just by picking up the phone."

"Go on, then," said Gerard. "Pick up the phone."

Francesca stayed where she was. "Gerard," she said, "you're making this too difficult."

"It's easy," Gerard told her. He lifted up the receiver and held it out to her. "Here it is. Dial. Have me arrested."

"Gerard—"

Gerard slammed the phone down again. He was furious, shaking with temper. "You dumb bitch! Either bust me or leave me alone! If you've got the goddamned nerve to go to bed with me, at least have the goddamned nerve to finish the job and pull me in!"

"Gerard, I need to know about Esmeralda. I need to know about the guns."

"Well, fuck you," shouted Gerard, "because I'm not going to tell you anything about either of them without a formal arrest and without a lawyer. And if you're not going to arrest me, or question me formally, then you can get the hell out of here because you're *fired*, as my secretary, and right now you're trespassing."

Francesca stood up. "All right," she said. "Don't say that I didn't give you a fair chance."

"If your name never passes my lips again, baby, that'll be far too often for me. Now, out."

Francesca hesitated for a moment, looking at him, trying to appeal to him. But he rammed his hands into his trouser pockets and stalked to the window, staring out over the Avenue of the Stars and smoking his cigar in steady, furious puffs.

She said, "It wasn't all business, Gerard. I can't turn around now and say that I wasn't fond of you, or that you weren't any good in bed. You're selfish, and you're distant, but you know how to give a woman what she wants."

Gerard said nothing, but continued to puff at his cigar.

"So long, then" said Francesca.

She opened the office door, and it was then that the Tengu burst in, half tearing the door off its hinges, knocking Francesca right back against Gerard's desk, sprawling over the top of it in a shower of calendars, pens, photographs, paper clips, and letters. She didn't even have time to scream.

Gerard shouted, "*Who the f—!*" but then he saw the white Nō mask, the brutally scarred, half-naked body, the wealth of snake and dragon tattoos, and a sensation of utter cold dread soaked through him like ice water soaked up by blotting paper. He knew what it was all about. He knew why the Tengu was here. Esmeralda had sent it around to silence him, and to punish him for his failure in arranging the death of Jerry Sennett and Admiral Thorson. The deal was up, the game was over. He had been right from the very start. Esmeralda had particularly selected him and Nancy Shiranuka and all the rest of the team be-

cause they were dispensable, murderable, easily disposed
of at the end of the day's work.

Panting heavily behind his mask, the Tengu circled the
office and stalked toward him. Gerard backed off,
reaching for the wall behind him, his cold eyes darting
from side to side, calculating, checking distances, looking
for any way to get out. Francesca was climbing slowly to
her feet, dazed, her skirt torn open to the waist.

Gerard moved round behind his desk, keeping his eyes
on the Tengu all the time. He coaxed open the top right-
hand drawer, and there was his .357 Python revolver. He
curled his finger into the drawer and hooked the gun out
by the trigger guard.

Francesca screamed, "Gerard!" as the Tengu made a
sudden and inexorable rush toward him. Gerard cocked
his revolver, held it high with both hands, and fired. The
bullet went right through the Tengu's chest in a splatter of
blood, and the impact of it made the Tengu stagger. But it
raised its masked face, with a question mark of its own
blood splashed onto one cheek, and kept coming toward
him, more slowly, more cautiously, but just as threaten-
ingly.

Gerard raised his revolver once again and carefully
squeezed off a shot at close range, into the Tengu's face.
The bullet was fired so near that the varnish on the
Tengu's Nō mask was burned black on one cheek by flaring gunpowder. From the neat hole in the papier-mâché,
the slug must have drilled straight into his left cheekbone.
But still the Tengu kept coming, grunting with pain and
effort, and it was clear to Gerard that nothing would stop
it. Hadn't Mr. Esmeralda told him, with a warm smile,
that the Tengu were unstoppable?

Tense, sweating, Gerard reached for the arm of his high-
backed leather swivel chair and drew it cautiously between
himself and the Tengu. The Tengu raised his hands, ready
to seize Gerard and tear him to pieces. Francesca said, in a
high, almost hysterical voice, "Gerard, what shall I do?
Gerard, *tell me what to do*!"

Gerard didn't listen to her. Instead, he pulled back his chair as far as he could against his legs and gripped it as tightly as possible, until white spots showed on his knuckles. He licked his lips, his mouth dry, judging his moment, judging his distance.

"Francesca," warned Gerard, "move away from the window. Get over toward the door."

Francesca, panicking, said, "What?"

"Just do what I tell you, get away from the window."

But then it was too late. The Tengu rushed forward, and Gerard couldn't think about anything but shoving his chair toward it as fast and as powerfully as he could, catching the Tengu right in the knees, sweeping it into the rolling castored chair with the sheer momentum of his desperate forward run; half wheeling, half forcing the Tengu clear across the room and driving him straight into the floor-to-ceiling window at a careering, uncontrolled pace, right into the net curtains, until there was an awesome creaking of glass, and then an explosive shatter. The Tengu hurtled straight out into the afternoon sky, followed by the black leather chair, and both dropped 27 floors, 332 feet, the Tengu spread-eagled, surrounded by glittering tumbling glass, and taking slightly less than four seconds to hit the ground. They heard the bang of flesh against concrete, even from so far up, and the clatter of the chair.

Francesca held Gerard very tight, clinging, almost clawing. Her face was so tense that it was ugly. Time passed, thirty seconds, a minute.

"Gerard," she said.

Gerard covered his mouth with his hand. Then he said, "Listen. I know what you think you've got to do. I know you're supposed to arrest me, and all of that. But just give me twelve hours. Can you do that? You've given me plenty of rope until now. Give me twelve hours more."

Francesca said, in a jumbled voice, "I don't love you, you know. I don't love you enough to want to stay with you."

"Francesca, I just want the *time*."

She released her grip. The sound of police and ambulance sirens was already echoing across the plaza below them. The wind billowed the nets and sent letters headed CROWLEY TOBACCO IMPORTS snowstorming across the room. "All right," she said. "But call me tomorrow morning, when you've done whatever it is you have to do. Don't fail me, Gerard, because if you do, I'll have to send them out looking for you, and you know they'll find you. They may even kill you."

Gerard said nothing, but went to his desk and took out a handful of cigars, which he pushed into his inside pocket. He gave Francesca one last look, and then he walked out the torn-open door, and through the reception area. In the corridor, he met two breathless policemen.

"Hey, did you see which office that guy fell out of?" one of the cops asked him.

Gerard pointed two doors down, along the corridor, HERMAN & GUBLENIK, ATTORNEYS AT LAW. "I think it was that one," he said. "Those two are always fighting, Herman and Gublenik. It wouldn't surprise me if one of them pushed the other out of the window. Either Gublenik or Herman, who knows?"

"Okay, friend," said the cop, and went hurrying on.

Gerard walked along to the elevator, stepped in, and pressed the button for the lobby. When the doors closed, his eyes closed, too. Only his cold self-control prevented him from trembling like a newborn foal.

CHAPTER FIFTEEN

The ambulance had been quick, but Mr. Esmeralda,
who had been parked in his limousine by the curb on the
Avenue of the Stars, had been quicker. With one of
Kappa's nameless Japanese to help him, he had shoulder-
ed his way through the crowds which had surrounded the
Tengu's fallen body and dragged the Tengu off to his car.
A man had protested, "I'm a doctor. You can't take that
man off like that. The police are going to want to see
him."

Mr. Esmeralda had smiled at the doctor, all teeth and
Latin charm. "You must understand that *I* am this man's
personal physician," he had lied. "If he had fallen from a
window, it is necessary that I examine him before the
police. Ethics, you know."

The doctor had started to protest again; but with a kick
to the kidneys that was so fast that it was practically invisible, the *Oni* paralyzed the doctor where he stood, so
that the doctor could do nothing but grasp in agony at his
back and gasp for breath.

Sweating, Mr. Esmeralda had humped the Tengu's
body into the back of his limousine, slammed the door,
and driven off in a howling U-turn toward Santa Monica
Boulevard. Just as he had reached the traffic signals, a
Doheny Medical Services ambulance had come howling
around the corner, its red lights flashing. Mr. Esmeralda
had put his foot down and barged his way into the east-
west traffic, provoking a chorus of very non-California
hornblowing. Then he had roared off westward, as fast as
he could, toward Eva Crowley's apartment.

Now Mr. Esmeralda glanced in his rearview mirror at the
dead Tengu, propped up in the back seat, where Mr. Esmeralda himself used to sit, before Kappa had detained
Kuan-yin as a hostage. Mr. Esmeralda had imagined when
he was younger than when people fell from tall buildings,
they were smashed into pieces; it was only when he had

seen *Life* magazine's celebrated picture of a 23-year-old
girl who had thrown herself 86 floors from the observation
deck of the Empire State Building, to lie peacefully and
apparently undamaged on the dented roof of a limousine,
that he had realized how peculiarly calm a death it was.
You fall, you stop falling. That was all.

It had been essential, however, for him to rescue the
Tengu's body before the police and ambulance arrived.
This was the last Tengu who was anything near to
readiness, and, as it was, Doctor Gempaku was going to
have to perform the Hour of Fire again to revive him. Considering they were supposed to attack the nuclear-power
station at Three Arch Bay at eight o'clock tomorrow night,
that didn't leave Doctor Gempaku very much time. Mr.
Esmeralda silently cursed Kappa and his penchant for
hiring the weak and corrupt and dispensable. But then he
thought: Kappa hired me for the same virtues, or lack of
them. Perhaps there is some method in his madness, after
all. It was doubtful whether anyone who wasn't weak and
corrupt and constantly live in fear of his life would ever
contemplate helping Kappa to destabilize a nuclear-power
station and extinguish half of California. To perform such
actions needed a particular kind of personality deficiency;
and while Gerard Crowley and Nancy Shiranuka and
Commander Ouvarov might all be dangerously inefficient
and unreliable, at least when the moment came to set off
the final explosion, they would none of them have serious
moral qualms. Nor did Mr. Esmeralda have any qualms
about killing them.

He was unsure what had happened to Gerard Crowley.
Perhaps the Tengu had killed Crowley before he fell from
the twenty-seventh floor, perhaps he hadn't. In any event,
there was no time to find out. It had been difficult enough
taking the Tengu into the building and up in the elevator,
draped in a long Mexican blanket to conceal his Nō mask
and his scarred body, an insane pantomime. Now all Mr.
Esmeralda wanted to do was get the Tengu back to
Pacoima Ranch.

There was only one stop he had to make, now that things were heating up so much, and that was to Eva Crowley's, to collect his living insurance policy. He pulled into the front driveway of the Crowleys' apartment building and said to the *Oni*, "Keep your head down. I won't be longer than five minutes."

Eva was still wrapped in a towel, fresh out of the shower, when Mr. Esmeralda rang the doorbell. Kelly and Kathryn were home, too, playing backgammon.

"Carlos," said Eva, surprised. "I didn't think I was going to see you until tomorrow."

"Well," said Mr. Esmeralda with an elasticated little smile, "you see me now. How soon can you get dressed?"

"Carlos, I'm sorry I can't go out—I have to meet some friends of mine for a bridal shower this afternoon, and the girls are coming with me."

Mr. Esmeralda glanced down at his gold wristwatch. "You have three minutes to put something on. Anything, a dress, a pair of slacks."

"Carlos, I've told you. I'm going out. Now, it's very good to see you. I'm delighted you came. Girls, Carlos is here, if you want to say hello. But really, Carlos—"

Mr. Esmeralda raised both his hands to silence her. "Please, Eva, listen to me. You have no choice. You have to come with me, right away; and the girls too."

Eva blinked in astonishment. She said, "How many times do I have to—"

Mr. Esmeralda reached to the waistband of his white tropical pants and brought out a small .32-caliber automatic. It was like a gesture out of a 1940's gangster movie.

"Put that away," Eva told him, shocked. "Carlos, how can you—?"

Mr. Esmeralda said, "Eva, my dear lady, you have two minutes to put on some clothes. If you are not dressed and ready to come with me by then, I will shoot you and kill you. Now, move."

Behind Eva, Kelly and Kathryn had now stood up, and were staring at Mr. Esmeralda and his gun with undisguised alarm. Mr. Esmeralda said, "If you do what I tell you, there is no personal danger. But, please, for your own sakes, be quick."

Kelly reached for the telephone, but Mr. Esmeralda swung his pistol around so that it was pointing directly at her. She froze.

"This is going to be my first and only warning," said Mr. Esmeralda. "I have killed people before, for being far less troublesome, and if you cause me any problems, I will not hesitate to kill *you*. Believe me. I also have to tell you that I am not going to explain why I am taking you with me, or for how long. So do not trouble to ask me; I will not answer you. All that I require from you is silence and obedience and calmness. Those three things are all that will protect you in some trying times."

Eva said, "I suppose it's no good appealing to your better nature."

"You are right," said Mr. Esmeralda. "I do not have a better nature."

CHAPTER SIXTEEN

They reached the perimeter fence of Pacoima Ranch shortly before four o'clock in the afternoon. It was warm and breezy in the hills, one of those golden California afternoons when the sun turns the grass to sparkling fire, and the mountains lie wrinkled and dry and orange as terra cotta under a dense blue sky. They had left the Little Tujunga Road, and driven out over rough country to the southeast side of the ranch, down a narrow and stony *arroyo secco*, and then up through a sloping grove of white firs. At last they halted beside a split-rail fence, and

Gerard stopped his Buick and climbed out. His first move was to light a fresh cigar.

"Well," he said, as Jerry and Mack and El Krusho got out of the white Grand Prix, and walked up the slope to join him, "this is the boundary. From here, it's going to be all on foot."

"How far are the ranch buildings from here?" asked Jerry.

"A mile, no more," said Gerard. "But they don't have any defenses at all on this side. It's steep, and it's difficult going, and in any case they're not looking for anybody to hit them. They may be nervous about the police, but the police have a way of storming right up to the front door. They certainly won't be expecting anybody to come creeping in from the side."

"If you say so," said Mack, who had taken a sharp dislike to Gerard Crowley from the moment he had first met him. Mack was not at all enthralled by men who smoked large cigars and dressed like loan sharks.

Gerard ignored him and turned to Maurice. "Do you think you can carry that M-60?" he asked. "It doesn't weigh more than twenty-five pounds. Mr. Holt, if you don't mind carrying the belt box."

Maurice, his muscles bulging under his tight white T-shirt, lifted the long-barreled M-60E1 machine gun out of the trunk of the Grand Prix and hoisted it over one shoulder, complete with its bipod. Mack reluctantly took the box of 7.62-mm. ammunition, while Jerry carried the Canadian SMG, a very light submachine gun rather like the old British Sterling, and three magazines of 9-mm. Parabellum bullets. Gerard stuffed the two Browning high-power automatics into the pockets of his suit.

They climbed over the split-rail fence and began to scale the hillside at an angle of 45 degrees. The mountain air, as they walked, became gradually cooler. Gerard at last drew up close to Jerry and said, "They tried to finish me off this afternoon. They sent a Tengu around to my office."

"What does that mean?" asked Jerry, wiping the sweat

from his face with his hand. "You've outgrown your use-fulness to them?"

"I guess. I didn't stop to find out."

"You got away from the Tengu?"

"I shoved him out a twenty-seven-story window."

Jerry raised his eyebrows, but said, "That doesn't necessarily mean you've seen the last of him."

Gerard looked at Jerry without any expression on his face. "A couple of weeks ago, I would have said you were pulling my leg. Now I know you're telling me the truth. Those damned Tengus are indestructible."

"Not *totally* indestructible," said Jerry. "That was why we dropped an A-bomb on them in the war."

Gerard took his cigar out of his mouth, and spat. "That's all we need, then? An A-bomb? You should have told me. I would have stocked up."

It was nearly five o'clock by the time they crested the ridge which overlooked Pacoima Ranch from the south-east. They sat among the scrub, sharing the water bottle Jerry had brought along, the same one he had used in the mountains of Japan, while Gerard briefly outlined the ranch buildings to them and pointed out the dilapidated barn where the Tengus were concealed.

"In my judgment," Gerard said, "someone has to go in there and lock all those reinforced doors, so that the Tengus can't be released. That will give us *half* a chance of storming the place successfully, at least. Now, Doctor Gempaku's quarters are over there, in the main farm-house; while your son, Jerry, is being held at the back of that outbuilding. My feeling is that you should take the SMG and go straight in there on your own, with the sole purpose of getting your son out. Leave the rest to us."

"How many Japanese guards are there?" asked Mack.

"It varies. Never fewer than five, often as many as seven. Then there's a cook and a housemaid. It would make life more pleasant if we didn't wipe *them* out as well, but for God's sake don't risk anything on their be-half. He who cooks for the devil should use a damn long ladle.''

They discussed the attack for nearly a quarter of an hour. Then Maurice and Mack carried the M-60 down toward the southern side of the ranch, keeping as close as they could to the scrubline, and positioned themselves behind an outcropping of rock about a hundred yards away from the main ranch buildings, well within the range of their machine gun, which could fire effectively for over three-quarters of a mile. Once they had settled, they waved back up the hill to Jerry and Gerard to show they were ready.

"I'll go down and see if I can lock the Tengus in," said Gerard. "You skirt around the back and see what you can do to get your son out of there. The signal for the attack to start will be three quick pistol shots, one after the other. Then we just go in there, giving them everything we've got.''

Jerry said, "You didn't have to do this, did you?''

"What do you mean?'' asked Gerard.

"You didn't have to help me rescue my son.''

Gerard took out one of his automatics and checked the clip. "I'm doing this for myself,'' he said. "If I don't waste these people now, they're going to be after me for the rest of my life. I don't know who they are, or what they're into, but they're the kind of people who never let go.''

Jerry said, "Are you really such a self-centered shit?''

Gerard got to his feet and smiled. "Yes,'' he said. "When it comes down to it, we're all busy looking after number one, aren't we? And don't tell me that sons and wives and lovers don't count as number one, too. You look after your own. That's what *you're* doing here, and that's what *I'm* doing here.''

It was 5:18. Without saying anything else, Gerard tossed away his cigar and made his way down the eastern side of the slope that led toward the ranch. Jerry watched him for a while, with extraordinarily mixed feelings—part anxiety, part confusion—and then cocked his machine gun and slid and skated down the stony slope himself, circling even farther to the east.

There was no sign of life in the ranch, no clue that it was being used to develop the most brutal warriors that the world had ever known; nor that it was being guarded by armed and fanatical men. It could have been a quiet, normal, Tujunga horse ranch late on a summer afternoon; the kind of place where Roy Rogers might have tethered Trigger, or Rin-Tin-Tin might have returned home for his Gravy Train. Jerry ducked low as he ran through the thorn-bushes toward the outbuilding where David was being held, feeling surprisingly self-conscious with his machine gun. He wondered fleetingly what he would do if someone stopped him and challenged him: how he would explain the fact that he was running around on private property with a very lethal weapon. But then he looked quickly down toward the barn, and saw Gerard Crowley dodging toward the open door with an automatic raised in his right hand, and he knew that what they were doing was not only deadly serious but deadly. Nobody was going to stop him and ask him what he was doing. They would probably shoot first.

Down in the barn, Gerard stepped quickly and nervously toward the prefabricated building where the Tengus were kept, his pistol held high, his eyes wide, his whole body wired with tension. He ran up the steps to the door-way of the prefabricated building and tried the handle. It was locked, which meant that Doctor Gempaku was not inside. He swung back the two lock covers, and then went back down the steps to scoop up a handful of dirt and gravel from the barn floor. Spitting on the dirt to make it more pliable, he pressed it into the locks, liberally mixed with gravel and grit, so that Doctor Gempaku would never be able to get his key inside—at least, not in a hurry. The Tengus would never be able to get out, either. That door was four solid inches of carbonized steel.

Once he had jammed up the locks, Gerard ran the length of the prefabricated building until he reached the far end, where the electric cables ran inside to power the air-conditioning and lights. The ideal conditions for imbuing a man's soul with the evil *kami* of the Tengu were 55 degrees of cold and an atmosphere low on oxygen. In the ancient magical days of the samurai, warriors had opened up their souls and their minds to the Tengu by sitting on the upper slopes of Shirane-san, overlooking Chuzenji-ko, sometimes nailing one of their hands to a board inscribed with occult characters, to hasten their possession by the most terrible devil known to man. The samurai never climbed Fuji-san, though—despite the fact that it is nearly 1,000 feet higher, and much nearer to the gods. The climb up Fuji-san was, and remains, a recreation for ordinary people, and the upper-class samurai would never deign to go any farther than the Sengen Shrine at the mountain's base.

Gerard located the power cables, and didn't hesitate. With three or four grunting tugs, he pulled them free of the generator, in a shortcircuiting fritz of crackling electricity. From inside the prefabricated building, he heard the air conditioning whir to a stop; and from the generator he heard a cough, and a stutter, and finally silence.

The Tengus were locked inside, without air or light. Most of them were in a painful and suspensory trance, so they wouldn't notice. But the few who *did* notice, and discovered that they were gradually suffocating from lack of oxygen and stiffling with heat, could beat on the door all they wanted. They would never get out alive.

Gerard ducked out of the barn, raised his automatic high, and fired off three shots. They cracked loudly in the still mountain air and echoed from the distant ridges.

It took only seconds for five *Oni* guards to come running from the main ranch building. They caught sight of Gerard as he ran around the back of the barn,. They paused, aimed, and opened up a quick burst of fire with their Uzi submachine guns. Suddenly the afternoon was applauding with echoes.

One of the *Oni* called to the others that they should circle the barn and prevent Gerard from running away. But just as he said that, Maurice and Mack, who had been crouching patiently behind their rocks with the M-60E1, opened fire on them from what—to a general-purpose machine gun with a muzzle velocity of 2,800 feet per second and a cyclic rate of 600 rounds per minute— amounted to point—blank rage.

All five *Oni* jumped and danced like marionettes. The ground around them pattered with bullets, and dust rose up in scores of tiny spurts, until they spun and collapsed, awkward, disjointed, and lay dead.

Gerard appeared from the other side of the barn and shouted, "Okay! There can't be more than one or two of them left! Let's get in there!"

El Krusho hoisted up the machine gun, followed by Mack with his ammunition box, and together they loped down the lower part of the slope and across the ranch compound.

Meanwhile, Jerry had reached the window of the outbuilding. He flattened himself against the wall and took a quick, darting look inside, the way the Marines had taught him before he had been dropped into Japan. He could see David lying on a cot in there, mercifully and miraculously alive; but he also glimpsed a Japanese guard in a black silk mask standing by the door. Jerry had two distinct advantages, however: surprise, and the fact that he was holding a submachine gun, while the guard appeared to be armed with nothing more than a holstered revolver.

Jerry thought, *I'm too old for this. Too slow, too tired.* But all the same, he curled himself backward, like Kent Tekulve winding up for one of his odd submarine pitches, and then he rolled himself, shoulder first, through the window of the outbuilding, with a smash of glass and rotten wood framing, and across the floor.

The Japanese guard snatched for his revolver, but he was split seconds too late. Jerry slammed off a deafening burst of 9-mm. bullets, almost a whole magazine, and the guard's chest and legs and belly turned into pulped tomatoes.

There was an odd silence. The room was filled with sharp, gunpowdery smoke. The guard turned, uttered a very Japanese-sounding sigh, and fell to the floor. David said, "*Dad*—"

Jerry raised a hand, indicating that David should stay where he was, keep quiet. "Are there any more of them?" he whispered.

"Five," said David, wide-eyed. "Six altogether."

It was then that they heard the deep, bronchial rattle of the M-60E1. Jerry stood up, and changed the magazine of his SMG, recocking it, ready for more killing. David had never seen his father like this before. Not cold and ruthless and efficient, handling a machine gun as if he handled one every day. He began to understand at that moment that war was something you never forgot. There are bespectacled insurance assessors in Cleveland who can still strip an M-3A1 without hesitation.

Jerry said, "Are you okay, David? They haven't hurt you?"

David, frightened, shook his head.

"All right," said Jerry. "Let's get out of here. Out the window. Then turn sharp right, and run like hell, up the slope, toward the treeline. If you hear any firing at all, dive for the ground and stay there. I'll be right behind you, but just remember that you can run faster than me."

David climbed cautiously out the window. "It's okay, Dad," he said. "There's nobody out here."

Jerry climbed after him, stiffly, wondering how the hell he had ever managed to roll through the whole window-frame. Then the two of them ran side by side toward the trees, keeping their heads well down. Within a minute, they were safe in the bushes, behind the rocks. Jerry panted, "It's okay, we can stop here. Stop, we're all right."

From the hillside, Jerry saw what happened next from a bird's-eye view. Mack and El Krusho were still jogging across the ranch compound—Maurice with his machine gun angled across his shoulders—when a silvery-blue Lincoln limousine appeared, speeding toward the ranch with an ocher-colored plume of dust rising up behind it. Almost simultaneously, Gerard came into view from behind the barn, shouting something to Mack and Maurice, and waving his arm toward the Lincoln.

David said, "What's happening? What are those guys doing?"

"Those guys helped me to save you," said Jerry tersely.

The Lincoln swerved around in the front yard of the ranch, scoring a wide semicircle in the dirt with its tires. As far as Jerry could see, there were at least four or five people in it, two or three of them women. He faintly heard Gerard Crowley shouting, "Mack—for Christ's sake, don't shoot—that's my wife! Those are my daughters!"

Then, from the ranch house, a man came running, sprinting toward the Lincoln with his head down. Gerard raised his automatic and fired two sharp shots at him, missing both times. But the man dodged and weaved and stumbled, and only just made it to the limousine as it gunned its engine and began to speed back the way it had come. A door flapped open, and a hand reached out to drag the man inside the car. He almost missed, desperately clawing for the door handle to give himself leverage. But then the Lincoln slowed momentarily, and he managed to scramble in.

Gerard raised his pistol once more, but as the Lincoln roared away down the drive, he realized that he probably wouldn't hit it anyway, and pushed his gun back into his pocket.

Jerry and David stayed where they were for five or ten more minutes, while Maurice and Mack and Gerard searched the ranch. At last, Gerard called, "It's clear! You can come down now!"

Stiffly, slowly, Jerry and David came down the slope to the ranch house. Maurice and Mack were already on the veranda, their machine gun propped against the rail, both

of them looking scared, a little shocked, but satisfied.
Gerard was puffing noisily at a cigar, and pacing up and
down with his hands thrust into his pockets.

"You didn't see that, man," said Mack to Jerry. "Five
of them, in five seconds. I couldn't believe it."

"My brother's going to eat shit," said Maurice.

Gerard asked, "How's your boy, Jerry? Okay?"

"I'm fine, sir, thank you," said David. He paused, and
then he said, "And thank you, for everything you did."

"I'm afraid my motives weren't entirely philan-
thropic," said Gerard, his cigar glowing in the twilight. "Apart from which, it looks like the one who
actually rescued you was your dear old papa. I saw that
guard, Jerry. Squashed canteloupe isn't in it."

"Who was in that limousine?" asked Jerry. "I thought I
heard you say your wife and daughters."

Gerard puffed, blew out smoke, and nodded. "That
limousine belongs to Mr. Esmeralda, the guy who
originally employed me to work out all the finances and
building work that this program was going to take. I was
also responsible for bringing Japanese workers and recruits
in from Kobe. They're not all here now, although I always
had to make sure that they were delivered here.

"As far as my own personal experience with him goes,
Esmeralda is a snake. The kind of guy you'd pay quite a lot
of money to have nothing to do with. I don't know what
the hell he's doing with my wife and daughters. Maybe
he's holding them as hostages. But you may as well know
that I've been living apart from my wife—well, most of
the time—and I don't get on very well with Kelly or
Kathryn. I guess when they're older, I might. But not
right now."

"Who was the man who ran from the ranch and jumped
into the limo?" asked Jerry. "He looked Japanese to me."

"*That*," replied Gerard, "that was the one man we
should have captured or wasted. That was the man who's
been running all of this Tengu business, Doctor
Gempaku. Gempaku claimed that he'd once discovered a

way to make Japanese athletes into the best in the
world—faster and stronger and totally tireless. Well, they
banned him from the Toyko Olympics because he was
using weird and unethical training methods. But you can
understand what kind of a guy he is: dedicated, peculiar,
unethical, very old-style Japanese. He would have gotten
on well with Yamamoto, all those guys."

Jerry said, "What's going to happen to the Tengus?
How many was he trying to prepare?"

Gerard smiled. "Six altogether, I believe. But they're
all contained in that prefabricated building now, without
air and without cooling. They're probably feeling pretty
damned uncomfortable right about now, and if you ask
me, I think they deserve it."

"What are you going to do?" asked Jerry.

"Do?" said Gerard. "I'm going to leave them there.
They're shut in behind four inches of reinforced steel, and
there's no way at all that they can get themselves out."

Jerry said, and his voice was unsteady, "They're men.
They're people. You're just going to let them die?"

Gerard snapped, "They killed Sherry Cantor, didn't
they? They killed Admiral Thorson. They damned well
nearly killed me."

"So you're going to be their judge and executioner?"

"For fuck's sake," said Gerard, "you've been watching
too many episodes of *Kaz*."

There was an explosion from the direction of the barn.
Glass was knocked out of the ranch-house windows like
afternoon sleet, and the ground itself, hard-baked as it
was, felt as if it were recoiling from a seismic shock. They
rushed to the windows in time to see the huge rolling
column of fire that was all that was left of the prefabricated
Tengu building, and the flaming chunks of timber and
aluminum which turned over and over in the sky.

"What the hell happened?" said Mack.

Gerard watched the sparks showering down. His face
was blank, far away, the face of a man who has almost
managed to achieve what he always wanted. Revenge?

Satisfaction? It was impossible to tell.

He said, "I don't know for sure. There was an oxygen pump there, designed to take some of the oxygen out of the air in the building, make it thinner, you know? That's what they asked me for when I arranged to have it built. I disconnected the generator wire; maybe the sparks from the wire ignited the oxygen."

Maurice Needs watched him with a frown, as he said, "Anyway, we did what we set out to do, didn't we? Huh? Those Tengus are broiled burgermeat by now."

Gerard said, "That's not enough. We've still got to get Gempaku, and Esmeralda, too, if we can."

"I think it's time we left this to Sergeant Skrolnik," said Jerry.

"Are you kidding?" snapped Gerard. "Do you think the police could have pulled off an attack like this one, and still brought your boy out safe? That's my wife and daughters that man has there, and even if I don't particularly get on with them, I don't want to see them hurt, either. What's more, if we let even *one* of those Japanese bastards live, they're going to keep after us until they kill us. How would you feel if Gempaku or Esmeralda were caught by the police, and then released on bail? I know how I'd feel. I'd feel like leaving the goddamned country, and fast."

David held Jerry's hand. "Do you think we could go home now?" he asked.

Jerry ruffled his hair. "Sure. I think we're finished up here for now. Gerard? Can you guide us back?"

Gerard nodded and ran his hand through his hair. "Okay," he said. "I think we did the best we could. Let's go."

They were just about to leave when they heard a telephone ringing. Jerry said, "Leave it. Don't answer it." But Gerard opened the front door of the house, listened, and then ran quickly upstairs to Doctor Gempaku's office. He snatched up the phone and said, "Yuh?"

A man's voice said, "Mr. Esmeralda?"

Gerard hesitated, and then answered, "Yes. That's right. Who is this?"

"You don't *sound* like Mr. Esmeralda."

Gerard said, in what he hoped was a strong Colombian accent, "Of course this is Mr. Esmeralda. Who else do you think is going to be sitting out here in this godforsaken ranch at this time of day?"

"I'm sorry," the man said. "This is John O'Toole, from the Tahiti Way pier at Marina del Rey. I've fixed up the yacht you wanted. I was lucky, the guy who was renting her this week suffered a heart attack, and had to bring her in early. She's really neat, you'll like her. The *Paloma*. Real luxury through and through. Television, air conditioning, waterbeds."

"Is she going to cost extra?" asked Gerard, taking a blind stab at a businesslike question.

"Thirty bucks a day, that's all. And that includes all the paraplegic facilities we're putting in, the ramps, and the special toilet."

"Paraplegic facilities?"

There was an awkward pause. Then O'Toole said, "You did ask for paraplegic facilities, didn't you? Don't tell me I've gotten hold of this goddamned special toilet for nothing."

"Oh, sure," said Gerard. "I was distracted. Somebody just came in. Sure, the paraplegic facilities are great. Well done. Terrific."

"I got all the Japanese food, too," said O'Toole, a little uncertainly. "I'm up to my ears in bean curd and *haru-same* noodles. You're going to want that? My secretary spent the whole afternoon shopping for it."

"Yes, we'll want all that," said Gerard. "Now tell me, what time did I say we'd want to sail?"

There was another pause, longer. "This *is* Mr. Esmeralda, isn't it?" O'Toole asked again.

"You think I'd be asking you all these questions if I wasn't?" Gerard demanded.

"*You're* not Mr. Esmeralda," insisted O'Toole, and

banged the phone down.

Gerard sat for a moment in silence. Then he came downstairs to find Jerry Sennett waiting for him inside the house.

"What was it?" asked Jerry.

"A call from Marina del Rey, of all places. The guy thought I was Esmeralda. Apparently, Esmeralda's renting a yacht called the *Paloma* from the Tahiti Way pier—when and why, he didn't say. But he did confirm that the yacht was stocked with Japanese food, and he also said that it was specially fitted out for a paraplegic."

"A *paraplegic*?" Jerry frowned.

"Don't ask me," said Gerard. "I never knew there were any paraplegics involved in this."

"But Esmeralda obviously does," said Jerry. "And when Nancy Shiranuka sent Kemo to find out who it was that Esmeralda was seeing—you remember, after he'd met you at Inca's restaurant—Kemo was killed by one of these *Onis*."

"I don't see what you're trying to say," said Gerard.

"Somebody powerful is running this Tengu business, that's what I'm trying to say. Somebody who has kept his or her identity secret the whole time, using Esmeralda as a go-between. Esmeralda's not the top guy, is he? I mean, he's made it clear to you that he's only passing on instructions, rather than initiating them. Kemo was killed because he tried to find out who the top banana was, and it's my guess that the top banana is this paraplegic."

"Well, well," said Gerard sarcastically. "Sherlock Holmes."

"Nothing of the kind," Jerry retorted. "We have an organization here that consists mainly of *Oni* adepts, and that means young, physically fit men, the fastest and the most deadly exponents of any Japanese martial art ever devised. Those guys can make kung-fu adepts look like idiots, as you well know. They have to go through six years of shadow-training before they're even allowed to fight each other. So what is a paraplegic doing among people like this? He obviously can't compete with them on a physical level, so he can't be one of the regular gang. The only way in which he can possibly compete is on a mental level, and that means to me that he's probably the boss."

"Jerry," said Gerard, unexpectedly putting his arm around his shoulders, "you are a genius. The only problem is, what is this dictatorial paraplegic up to, and why, and where the hell is he?"

Jerry said, "He must be here in Los Angeles, otherwise Kemo wouldn't have been killed so quickly when he tried to locate him. Second point: if he's going to do anything soon, like assassinate the President or the Governor, then he's going to have to do it pretty damned quick, because he knows that we're on to him, and the police are, too. Why do you think Esmeralda was renting a yacht for him? To make his getaway, I suspect, when his assassination or robbery or whatever it is starts going down."

"A getaway, by *yacht*?"

"It makes sense. The first place that the cops cordon off is the airport, followed by the highways, followed, as a distinct afterthought, by the seaways. You're probably fifty times more likely to get away with a crime if you escape by water than by any other means."

"You've carried out a survey?" asked Gerard sharply. "Maybe I should rob a couple of million from Wells Fargo and flush myself down the toilet. I'll be floating off to Hawaii in the company of ten tons of soggy toilet tissue before the police even know that I'm gone."

Jerry let out a short, testy breath. "You don't buy this, do you?"

"I don't see why I should," said Gerard. "There could be a thousand reasons why Esmeralda wanted equipment for paraplegics on a cruise to Panama. Maybe his sister has polio. Who knows? You can't read anything into it until you know the truth."

"By that time," said Jerry, "it all may be far too late"

Gerard said, "This is ridiculous. Let's start heading back to the cars."

"Just a minute, listen," insisted Jerry. "We've got ourselves a paraplegic, right? And the odds seem to be that
he's Japanese. For some reason, he's involved in a series of
unusually violent killings, either against Americans in
particular, or Americans in general. Who does he hit? First
me, unsuccessfully, killing Sherry instead; then an
innocent policeman who's only trying to do his duty by
busting a couple of Nipponese lunatics for running a red
light. Then, *en masse*, the security and intensive-care staff
of Rancho Encino Hospital and Admiral Thorson. What's
he trying to do? He's one of the most eclectic killers I've
ever come across."

"We were supposed to be trying to keep you quiet,"
said Gerard. "Esmeralda said that if you'd heard about
Tengus on the media, you'd have immediately warned the
authorities."

"Yes, but why *should* I have heard about Tengus in the
media?"

"I don't know. They were supposed to have been killer
bodyguards for very wealthy people. Don't tell me *that*
isn't a story. 'Richard Burton buys Liz Taylor a million-
dollar Japanese martial-arts expert, just to keep would-be
admirers out of her hair.' "

"If it was all going to be *that* innocuous," said Jerry,
"why bother to keep us quiet at all? Or maybe there's
something heavier going down?"

"Search me," said Gerard uncomfortably.

Jerry held his arm. "Wait a moment," he said. "If this
Japanese is a paraplegic, and he's been trying to take his
revenge on American people, then he must have been
doing it for a reason. Maybe it's *our* fault, maybe it's *my*
fault, that he was born a paraplegic."

From the veranda Mack called impatiently, "Come on,
you guys, it's a long haul back to the cars."

"Just a minute, Mack," Jerry called back. Then to
Gerard, "Listen, there have been nearly ten deaths in the
past few days, but all of them have been connected with
your attempts to kill just two people: me and Admiral
Thorson."

"That's right," agreed Gerard suspiciously.

"Admiral Thorson and I have one thing in common: we are the only two surviving members, as far as I know, of a Naval Intelligence team that gave President Truman the go-ahead to bomb Hiroshima."

Gerard stared at Jerry. Then he said slowly, "You've been talking about revenge, right? A Japanese paraplegic taking revenge, because of Hiroshima? Could that be it? Maybe he was crippled by the A-bomb. Maybe he was radiated with gamma rays when he was still in the womb and born deformed. "That happened to thousands of babies—thousands."

Jerry beckoned to Mack. "Mack," he said, "Gerard and I are beginning to think that this whole Tengu business has something to do with what I did at Hiroshima."

Mack glanced at Jerry suspiciously. He knew that Jerry had been to a psychiatrist, and the last thing he wanted to do was set off in hot pursuit of another man's neurosis. But Gerard gave him a quick, quiet nod of the head, which meant to Mack that Jerry was probably still quite sane.

"Olive's husband works for the naval records department, doesn't he?" asked Jerry.

"Sure. He's a whiz on Pacific war history. He can tell you the whole of the battle of Midway, in detail, like it's some kind of drama. The *Kaga* sunk at 7:25 P.M., the *Akagi* was scuttled at five o'clock the next morning. He's amazing. He's also amazing to trust me with Olive."

Jerry said, "Is there any way that Olive can get in touch with him?"

"Sure, he's on the phone. The area code for Honolulu is 808. She calls him once or twice a week. At the Navy's expense, I hasten to tell you, not mine."

"Right," said Jerry, "call her now, from the phone upstairs, and ask her if she wouldn't mind contacting him as soon as she can, and asking him to check if there were any clubs or organizations formed after the war to help Japanese people injured or deformed by the atomic bomb. Can you do that?"

"You think this guy is going to belong to the Happy Disabled Club of Tokyo?" asked Gerard.

"No," said Jerry. "But anyone who has been severely handicapped has to come into contact at some time or another with official organizations, even if he's only seeking advice or equipment. It's likely, anyway, even if it isn't a dead certainty."

Gerard said to Mack, "You want to give it a try?"

"Okay," breathed Mack. "But I think you're wasting your time."

Gerard dry-washed his face with his hands. "Just do it," he said. "Then we can all go back to the city and get ourselves a drink."

CHAPTER SEVENTEEN

It was a bad break, the worst of an operation that had been nothing but a whole series of bad breaks. He should never have listened to that voice on the Kii-Suido ferry; he should never have been tempted by Kappa's money or Kappa's beguiling voice. But everything that he was doing now had a terrible flawed inevitability about it; as if the foundation stone of an ancient Mayan ruin had cracked, and the balance of tons and tons of decorative stone could do nothing but crack and crack and eventually collapse.

He had driven Doctor Gempaku and the dead Tengu to Laurel Canyon, and left them there. Doctor Gempaku had been unsympathetic and ungrateful for being rescued. He blamed Mr. Esmeralda for all the inadequacies of the security arrangements, and was furious that six *Oni* adepts had been shot dead so easily. He didn't yet know that the Tengu building had blown up, and that half a dozen prospective Tengus had been blown into lumps of meat and bone. None of them was yet fully possessed by Tengu, and so their remains would never rise, not even for the Hour of Fire.

When he left Doctor Gempaku and the Tengu at Laurel Canyon, Mr. Esmeralda was told that Kappa himself was sleeping, in preparation for tomorrow's big day, and was not to be disturbed. If ever Mr. Esmeralda had felt like storming into Kappa's inner sanctum, shaking the little toad awake, and twisting his head off his neck, it was then; but he knew that the *Onis* who guarded Kappa were faster than the human eye, and that he wouldn't even have laid hands on Kappa before he was dead.

As a Catholic, the kind of death that the *Onis* gave out to their victims appealed to Mr. Esmeralda very little. He did at least want to go to his grave intact. He mumbled, "Everything is completely under control," and drove off before they could argue with him.

He was alone now. He had left Eva Crowley and her twin daughters locked in the bedroom of his house on Camden Drive—all of them naked in case they felt like trying to escape—and an *Oni* guard at their door. Kappa didn't realize that one of his own men was helping to protect Mr. Esmeralda's own insurance policy, his ultimate protection against the wrath of the Tengu. Mr. Esmeralda whistled "La Cumparsita" as he drove. Then, at the intersection of Laurel Canyon Boulevard and Sunset, at a red light, his foot accidentally slipped from the brake pedal and he noisily rearended a large Mercury station wagon.

The driver of the station wagon climbed out, a ginger-haired woman in upswept eyeglasses.

Mr. Esmeralda let down his window. "Madam," he said, "I take full responsibility. I apologize. I am a clumsy idiot."

"You could have *killed* me, you know that?" the woman demanded. "As it is, you've whiplashed my neck. Do you have any idea how much it's going to cost in doctor's bills to straighten my neck out? Can you *imagine?*"

Just then, a young motorcycle cop came over. "Is anything the matter here?"

"It was all my fault," said Mr. Esmeralda. "Usually, my chauffeur drives this car. I slipped on the pedal. My foot. I will pay for any damage to this lady's automobile."

"This is your car, sir?" asked the cop.

"Mine, in a sense," said Mr. Esmeralda. "It belongs to my company."

"May I see your driver's license, sir? And your registration?"

Mr. Esmeralda opened his black alligator wallet and produced his license. The young cop said, "Will you wait here a moment, please?"

"I'm in a hurry," said Mr. Esmeralda. "I have an appointment."

"I won't keep you longer than I have to, sir."

Mr. Esmeralda sat sweating in his seat as the cop walked back to his motorcycle, and began to read his license-plate and driver's-license numbers over his radio. The woman whose car he had hit remained beside him, saying, "It's going to cost a *fortune* to straighten my neck out. I know it is. A *fortune*."

The cop came back, his eyes invisible beneath the peak of his helmet. Esmeralda tried to smile, but the cop unbuttoned his holster and said, "I want you to get out of the car, sir, please, keeping your hands in sight."

"I don't understand, it was an accident," protested Mr. Esmeralda.

"This has nothing to do with the accident, sir," the cop told him in that same even voice. "You're under arrest for attempting to murder a man named Gerard Arthur Crowley."

CHAPTER EIGHTEEN

It was nearly seven o'clock the following morning before Olive's husband called back from Honolulu and told them what they wanted to know. He sounded tired, and more than a little slurred. "I've been drinking all night with this Japanese guy, Hachiro Nakamata. Suntory whiskey on the rocks. Hachiro used to work for the memorial museum in Hiroshima, indexing and filing the names of survivors. He knows more about the people who escaped from that blast than anybody. What happened to them, how they tried to live their lives afterward."

Olive said, "Did he know anything about societies for crippled people?"

Robin Nesmith burped into his first, a burp that carried 2,000 miles, and said, "Sorry. Yes, he did. He knows all of them. The Society for the A-Bomb Handicapped, the Hiroshima Benevolent Group, dozens of them. But he particularly mentioned something that I'd never heard about before, the Circle of Burned Doves."

"The Circle of Burned Doves? What's that?"

"It's a group of people who were born deformed because of the effects of gamma radiation when the bomb dropped. All of them, in one way or another, have become wealthy and influential, and they apparently have wealthy contacts in several of the largest and best-known Japanese industries. When you consider that many of the chairmen and managers of the big Japanese industrial combines were officers in the Japanese forces during the war, it's not surprising that they've been diverting some of their money and energy into getting revenge. The Japanese are not as fatalistic as many Western people seem to think; they're fiery and emotional, and they *never* forget. The general feeling in Japan is still, even today, that the dropping of the atomic bombs was unnecessary and unjustified, apart from all the moral questions involved. And the Circle of Burned Doves is dedicated to making America pay for what she did—through economic attack and through any other means at their disposal. According to Hachiro—although I can't say how true this is—our car industry was sunk almost entirely through the economic planning of the Circle of Burned Doves.''

Jerry, who had his ear pressed to the phone so that he could hear what Nesmith was saying, asked Olive, "Find out what 'any other means at their disposal' might mean.''

Nesmith said, "I asked Hachiro that myself, but he was incredibly vague. All he said was, 'It could mean an eye for an eye.' ''

"You mean dropping an atomic bomb on America?''

"He wouldn't say.''

Olive gave Robin her love, and then put down the phone.

"Well,'' said Mack, "where does this get us?''

"Nowhere at all, much,'' said Jerry. "Have you heard of the Circle of Burned Doves, Gerard?''

Gerard hadn't slept very well on Jerry's sofa. His eyes were ringed with dark circles, and he was breakfasting off crackers, cheese, and Chivas Regal. He shook his head. "It doesn't ring any bells.''

Maurice said, "I'm going out for some muffins and stuff. Anybody want anything? Olive?''

"No, thanks, Maurice.''

Jerry, rolling up his shirtsleeve and nervously scratching at his elbow, walked across the window and stared out at the sunshine. "It looks as if we've been guessing right up until now, but I still don't see why they've brought back the Tengus. They didn't spend all that money and set up that center just to kill off me and Admiral Thorson. They've got to have something really catastrophic in mind.''

At that moment, the phone rang again. It was Sergeant Skrolnik, sounding as tired as Robin Nesmith. "Mr. Sennett? I thought you might like to know that we've arrested a man in connection with the murder of Sherry

Cantor, and with several other murders.''

"You've arrested someone? Who is it?''

"I'd like you come down to headquarters, if you don't mind, and take a look at him. His name's Jesus Carlos Esmeralda, he's a Colombian. We picked him up after a tipoff from the CIA.''

Jerry said, "I'll be right down,'' and hung up the phone.

"What's going on?'' asked Gerard.

"That was Sergeant Skrolnik. He's arrested your man Esmeralda. Apparently he was tipped off by the CIA.''

"*Francesca*,'' snapped Gerard angrily. "She agreed to give me some goddamned time.''

Jerry said seriously, "Come on, Gerard, I think this is the time for us to throw in our hand with the police. We've come so far, but there isn't very much else we can do, not on our own. If they've picked up Esmeralda, the police must be quite close to clearing this up themselves. Maybe we could help them.''

"They didn't say anything about my wife and daughters?'' asked Gerard.

Jerry said, "No. They just said Esmeralda.''

"Fucking Esmeralda,'' said Gerard.

Mack put in, "Jerry could be right, you know? Maybe there's some clue that we have that the cops don't know about. And maybe they've got a whole of information that *we* don't know.''

Gerard opened his cigar case and found that it was empty. He tossed it onto the table, and stuck his hands into his pockets with undisguised glumness. "All right,'' he said. "But you realize that I'm heavily implicated in all of this? If I go down to police headquarters with you, they're going to bust me, too.''

"You stay here, then,'' said Jerry. "Maybe you can do me a favor and keep an eye on David; although why I'm entrusting you with the same boy you just kidnapped, I don't know.''

"You can trust me,'' Gerard told him. "Just give me a

call if you hear anything about Eva and the girls."

"Sure," Jerry told him. "Mack? Maurice? Olive? You want to go?"

Down at police headquarters, accompanied by a sweaty and pasty-faced Skrolnik, who was exhausted after a long and futile night of questioning, arguing, and delicatessen coffee, they stared at Mr. Esmeralda through the two-way mirror in the side of his cell. Jerry said with certainty, "That's the man I saw at Orchid Place, the day Sherry Cantor was murdered."

"You're sure of that?" asked Skrolnik.

"Positive. He was standing in the street, watching my house. I remember thinking that he looked like somebody out of an old Humphrey Bogart movie."

"We think he's the ringleader," said Skrolnik.

Detective Pullet came into the room just then and gave Maurice a funny, half-apologetic smile. "We're still getting in data from the CIA on Esmeralda's activities abroad. Apparently he's been dealing with arms and drugs and stolen antique furniture like he's Ralph's or something. Hello, Mr. Needs. Glad you could be here."

"The pleasure's mutual," said Maurice. "How's the lateral thinking?"

"Still going strong," said Pullet. "We'll crack this business before you know it."

"Not if you think that Esmeralda is the ringleader," Jerry told him.

"What's that supposed to mean?" Skrolnik demanded.

Jerry said, "Is there some place where we can talk? In private?"

"Sure," grunted Skrolnik. "Come across to Welch's and watch me eat breakfast. You like corned-beef hash? They do the best."

CHAPTER NINETEEN

Mr. Esmeralda was released on $50,000 bail at two o'clock that afternoon, and told that he was not to leave the city of Los Angeles. His attorney told Judge T. N. Slattery that his client was "a pillar of international goodwill." The prosecution raised no objection to the granting of bail, especially since Mr. Esmeralda had no previous criminal record in the United States, and had once been decorated by President Sukarno of Indonesia for "services to the people of Djokjakarta and Surakarta."

Immediately after he left the courthouse in the company of his lawyer, Mr. Esmeralda caught a taxi to his address on Camden Drive, where he stayed for two hours, until just after 4:20 P.M., talking on the telephone. All of his conversations during this period were tapped by the police, under the jurisdiction of a special warrant.

His first call was to Mercury Custom Air Services, at Torrance Municipal Airport, confirming his booking of a Gulfstream III for 7:45 that evening. Destination: Liberal, Kansas.

"Liberal, Kansas?" asked Skrolnik, wrinkling up his nose.

Pullet said, "I'll check with the private air services at Liberal. He's bound to be using it as nothing more than a stopover."

The next call that Mr. Esmeralda made was to Twentieth-Century Bandbox, a dry-cleaning company, asking them to send over his two white suits and six shirts.

The third call was more mysterious. It was traced to the number of a house in Laurel Canyon. Mr. Esmeralda said, "Tell Kappa I was picked up by the police for a traffic offense. A rearender, nothing serious. I'm out now, and everything's fine for tonight. Everything's arranged. Kappa can leave immediately away for Marina del Rey. Yes, I know. But tell him everything's fine. I'll come to the house at seven precisely and make sure that everything's going smoothly. How's the Tengu? You did the Hour of Fire? He's fine? Okay, doctor. Okay. That's good. Tonight's the night, then. I'll see you when I see you. Just one thing—Kuan-yin's all right? What? You're sure about that? Very well. All right. Take care of that Tengu."

The fourth call was to a man called John O'Toole, of O'Toole's Luxury Yachts, at Tahiti Way, Marina del Rey.

"The yacht is ready, Mr. O'Toole? That's excellent. My clients will be ready to leave in less than an hour. Very well. No, you have no need to do that. Good. And, listen, you don't have to worry about yesterday. I know who that man was, the one who answered the phone at the ranch. You have nothing to worry about. Yes. That's right. Thank you."

Skrolnik listened to the last conversation and sat back in his swivel chair. "Tonight's the night, then? And they're going to do something with that Tengu of theirs?"

"That's right," Jerry nodded.

"He didn't give any indication, did he? No indication at all."

"I'd bust him now, if I were you," said Mack.

Skrolnik shook his head. "I've learned my lesson often enough, Mr. Holt. You don't jump on anybody until they're actually involved in the commission of a crime, *in flagrante*. The times I've gone to court with wiretaps that would make your curly hair stand on end, and had them thrown out because *conspiracy* to commit a crime, without the crime having actually been committed, is one of the hardest imaginable offenses to prove. All Esmeralda has to do is say, 'I was joking, Your Honor. I was fooling around with a friend.' And anyway, you take a look at a transcript of those conversations, and you won't see *nothing*, nothing indictable. He spent most of his time saying 'yes' and 'no' and 'okay,' and unless you can establish exactly what it was he was talking about, you won't get anywhere."

Jerry said, "What are you going to do?"

Skrolnik grimaced. "I'm going to do my duty, Mr. Sennett. Ordinary, functional police work. I'm going to have Esmeralda tailed, and arrested if he attempts to leave Los Angeles in contravention of the terms of his bail. I'm going to assign a team to track down that house in Laurel Canyon and follow the Tengu wherever he goes. Any attempt by the Tengu or any of his assistants to commit any kind of violent crime, and *shazam*! I'm going to throw his tail in jail."

There was a silence. Then Mack said, "How?"

"How what?" asked Skrolnik crossly.

"How are you going to throw the Tengu's tail in jail? I thought the Tengus were pretty well unstoppable. Look what you had to do at Rancho Encino. The thing was dead, supposedly, and it still came after you."

"You weren't there at Rancho Encino," said Skrolnik.

"No, I wasn't. But from what Jerry's told me, it sounds like these Tengus are pretty invincible characters."

Skrolnik stood up, wrapping his beefy arms around his chest. "Let me tell you something, junior," he said. "When that Tengu came for me at Rancho Encino, it had no head."

"No *head*?" asked Jerry.

"That's right. Calsbeek's men had blown its head clean off its shoulders. But that didn't stop it. It came right on in there, headless. We burned it, but if we hadn't, it would probably have torn us to pieces. So I know what I'm talking about, and when I say that I'm going to throw that Tengu's tail in jail, that's exactly what I'm going to do."

"What did you do with the ashes?" asked Jerry.

"What?" frowned Skrolnik.

"Even a Tengu's ashes are capable of being revived by the appropriate ceremony," said Jerry.

Skrolnik made a dozen faces, each one more grotesque than the last. "Just leave this fucking thing to me, will you? That's all I ask. If I make a mistake, let it be *my* mistake, not yours. You got me?"

"You'll keep us in touch?" asked Jerry.

"Sure, I'll keep you in touch. Now, why don't you get back home and watch the whole thing on television. You'll be warmer and safer, and you won't be getting under my feet."

Mack said, "Wait a minute—" but Jerry took his arm and raised a finger to tell him that he should keep quiet.

They went across the street to Welch's, and ordered hamburgers and beer. Jerry went to the pay phone and called David. Gerard was being the prefect babysitter, David told him. They had been playing checkers together, and so far David was ahead by nine games to six. "He told me what he did in Cuba, and all about the time when he was a boy on a tobacco farm."

Jerry said, "Underneath that frozen exterior, I think a nice guy may be thawing out. Take care, David. I love you, and I'll see you later."

When he got back to the table, Maurice said, "I've been thinking, you know?"

"You've been *thinking*?" Mack teased him. "Do you mind if I call the networks?"

"No, seriously," said Maurice. "They've got one Tengu left, okay? But even if there's only one, the cops don't have much chance of stopping him, do they? They don't have much chance of knocking him off before he does anything really serious."

"It took an atomic bomb to wipe out the first community of Tengus," agreed Jerry.

"Right," said Maurice. "But supposing the Tengu met up with another Tengu—an even stronger Tengu?"

"Maurice,' you're talking through your ass," said Mack. "If there's only one Tengu left, where's this other Tengu, this even stronger Tengu?"

Mack knew what Maurice was trying to suggest even before he'd finished speaking, but the idea of it was so stunning that there was nothing he could do but sit there with his half-eaten cheeseburger in one hand and his mouth open and wait for Maurice to point to his own

T-shirted chest and say, "Right here. *Me*. I could be a Tengu, couldn't I?"

Jerry said intently, "Maurice, you don't even know what you're suggesting. The only way in which anybody can open themselves up to being possessed by the Tengu is through excruciating agony. That, and all the necessary invocations and rituals."

"You've got that Japanese woman, don't you?" asked Maurice. "That Nancy Shiranuka. She'd know all the rituals."

"Well, I guess she would, but—"

"But nothing. Let's go over there and ask her to do it."

"Are you *crazy*?" Jerry hissed at him. "To turn yourself into a Tengu would mean pain so great that you wouldn't even know where you were. Besides, once you've been possessed, it isn't that easy to become *un*possessed, to be exorcized. Nancy Shiranuka almost died when she was purified of one of her Japanese demons. And that demon was nothing compared to the Tengu. The Tengu is absolutely the worst demon ever."

Maurice put down his avocado-and-bacon burger, his second. "Listen," he said quietly, "what you guys don't seem to understand is that I'm just a strongman in the circus. El Krusho, nothing else. Can you imagine what it's like, being El Krusho? Even my fucking name's a joke. I bend steel bars in my teeth, and pick up fat ladies, one in each hand, and if I accidentally slip a finger up their snatch when I'm lifting them, they love me forever. I'm *nothing*, man. A pile of muscles, a freak show. If I'm lucky, I'll get a different pretty girl every Saturday night, and a $20 bonus to buy myself a steak dinner at Charlie's. I run a creaking '69 Corvette, and all I own in the world is three pairs of sneakers and about 108 T-shirts."

"So?" Mack challenged him.

"So, I want to do something *exciting*, *weird*, *different*. What we did yesterday, attacking that ranch—that was a blast. I haven't done anything like that in my whole life.

Listen, you think I'm afraid of some *pain*? Have you tried lifting weights, working out in a gym? You want to talk about pain, when you're lifting 350 kilos of solid iron?''

"Maurice," said Jerry, "this is something different. This is *spiritual* pain, too."

"So what are you going to do?" Maurice demanded. "You're going to let this Tengu character run around killing people? Or what?"

Jerry looked across the table at Mack, and suddenly he didn't feel hungry anymore. Mack shrugged. Maurice was one of those plain people who were impossible to convince of anything, if they didn't want to be convinced.

"We don't have too much time," said Jerry. "A couple of hours, at the most. That may not be long enough. You may go through a whole lot of pain for nothing."

"The sooner we get started, the better, huh?" said Maurice.

Mack said, "For Christ's sake, Maurice. You want to be a martyr or something?"

"I don't know," said El Krusho. "Maybe. Anything's better than being El Krusho."

CHAPTER TWENTY

In Nancy Shiranuka's apartment on Alta Loma Road, Maurice Needs went through the pain and the ritual required to make him a Tengu.

Gerard Crowley and Jerry Sennett tied his wrists and ankles, and then left him in the bedroom with Nancy. Mack Holt had already started on the Gekkeikan saké, and they silently joined him, sitting on *zabutons* with their legs uncomfortably crossed, trying not to think of the agonies

Maurice was voluntarily suffering in the next room.

Nancy had reduced the light in the bedroom to a single crimson candle. She was naked, except for the tight silk ribbon which she wore around her waist to keep her carved jade *harikata* in place. Her skin was shiny with perfumed oil, and her hair was tied tightly back from her forehead.

She sang to him "The Song of the Lost Warrior" and then "The Night Forest." As she sang, she began to scratch his chest with steel skewers, gently at first, more irritating than painful; but then deeper, until his chest and his stomach were scored with their points, and the blood began to break through the skin in rows of crimson beads. For the first time, he closed his eyes and gritted his teeth.

There was one advantage that Nancy Skiranuka had over Doctor Gempaku: she had been possessed by a demon herself, and she had been a member of the Shrine of the Seven Black *Kami*. She knew what the world of the demons *felt* like. She could sense when she was getting close to that dark, fluttering, cloud-world of evil beings. She could summon them by name. She knew what each of them sounded and smelled like: O Goncho, the wolf-howling bird of Yamahiro; Jinshin Uwo, the beast of earthquakes; Kappa; and Raiden, the thunder devil. They were stylized and fanciful beings in Japanese literature and art. Millennia of educated priests had changed their faces and distorted their legends. But Nancy knew they were real. She had experienced the ghostly shadows of their malevolence inside her head. Their ill will had twisted her body, and their corruption had almost destroyed her.

She chanted the longest of the devil-summoning rituals of the Shrine of the Seven Black *Kami:* the Calling Down. In the next room, Jerry and Gerard and Mack looked at each other in subdued silence, and poured out another round of Gekkeikan. Whether this was right or wrong, it was more than they could bear.

Mack unexpectedly began to recite the 23rd Psalm. Gerard didn't join in, but he closed his eyes and lowered

his head, and when Mack had finished, he said, "Amen."
Only Jerry remained stiff and quiet, with his eyes wide
open.

Nancy slowly twisted and dug the skewers into the
muscles of El Krusho's arms and chest. There was a
crackling, tearing sound as she lifted the pectorals away
from his chest. She didn't have the ritual silver claws that
Doctor Gempaku had used, but she was capable of inflicting sufficient pain to rouse up the Tengu.

"Tengu, come into your slave," she chanted. "Tengu,
possess your slave. Tengu, O emperor of all that is violent
and corrupt, come into him." As she chanted, she lifted
herself slightly up and down, so that her heel pushed the
jade dildo in and out of her. She closed her eyes in a
mixture of ecstasy and agony.

Outside, Gerard said, "I don't know why the hell
Esmeralda kidnapped my wife and daughters. I don't
know why the hell he did that."

Mack said, "You'll find out soon enough."

"Well, I don't know whether I will," said Gerard,
patting his pockets in search of cigars which he knew very
well he didn't have.

In the bedroom, Nancy leaned over El Krusho's
bleeding chest and slowly sliced the point of a Japanese
cooking knife deep into his upper arm. She had seven
knives in all, representing the Seven Black *Kami*, and with
these she pinned El Krusho's flesh to the wooden floor of
her apartment. El Krusho twitched and groaned out loud,
but his eyes were closed now, and he was already approaching the first levels of a deep trance.

Now, with El Krusho crucified to the floor, Nancy lit
incense. The sacred smoke trailed over him, and perfumed
the air with rare and expensive spices, in a way which
would entice a demon. Her voice became so high-pitched
and strange that Mack, in the next room, raised his head in
bewilderment. "What the hell's that woman *doing* in
there?"

Another hour passed. It was well past seven. Outside the

apartment, the sun was sinking into the evening smog of the Pacific shoreline like an angry and sullen god. Jerry leaned against the window and watched the skyline over downtown Los Angeles slowly turn purple, the color of grape jelly stirred into cream of wheat. He had telephoned David a half-hour ago, and David was fine.

Gerard checked his watch. "If this takes any longer, we'll be too late," he said. He turned the saké flask upside down, but it was empty. "Mack," he said, "go take a look in that liquor cabinet. See if Tokyo Lil's got any more saké."

Jerry shot Gerard a sharp, critical look. Gerard shrugged and said, "I'm sorry. I'm just edgy, is all."

CHAPTER TWENTY-ONE

Eva Crowley had never felt so humiliated. Nor had she ever felt so frightened. Not just for herself, but for her children. After a day's naked captivity in Mr. Esmeralda's apartment, without food or water or sanitary facilities, hours in which they had alternately wept and talked and argued with each other, sometimes hysterical, sometimes calm, sometimes vengeful, they had at last been let out and told to dress themselves under the unblinking supervision of their black-masked *Oni* guard. They hadn't argued. The guard had kept his Uzi machine gun raised at them the whole time they were dressing, and had then hurried them out of Mr. Esmeralda's house into his waiting Lincoln limousine.

"I hope you have not had too uncomfortable a day," Mr. Esmeralda had asked Eva smoothly, as he drove out into the evening traffic.

Eva had said nothing. She had been shaking with rage
and fear and embarrassment. Now, as they cruised softly
southward on the San Diego Freeway, past Culver City and
Inglewood, she sat with her face close to the limousine's
tinted window, watching the sun set beyond the airport,
and the red-and-amber lights of the cars overtaking them
on either side. Kathryn silently cried, she hadn't stopped
crying since this afternoon. Kelly tried to comfort her, but
she too was stony-faced with shock.

"Have you ever been to Kansas?" Mr. Esmeralda asked,
turning off the freeway onto Hawthorne Boulevard,
heading directly south through Torrance toward the airport.

"Kansas?" asked Eva, confused.

Mr. Esmeralda glanced at her in his rearview mirror and
his eyes smiled. "We're about to take a little flight."

He drove up to the wire airport gate which led onto the
tarmac. There was a high-pitched whistling of executive
jets, Learjets and Canadairs, and an oily smell of aviation
fuel on the wind. The security guard came out of his hut,
and Mr. Esmeralda showed him his pass.

"Mercury Custom Air Services down there to your left,"
he said.

A black van had drawn up behind Mr. Esmeralda's
limousine. "This is my baggage," Mr. Esmeralda smiled.

"You got a pass for your baggage? I'm not supposed to
allow baggage vehicles on the field without a pass."

"Of course," said Mr. Esmeralda. "Just go ask the
driver."

Mr. Esmeralda waited, his eyes fixed on his rearview
mirror, while the security guard walked back to the van.
Eva said, "Carlos, what's happening? We can't go to
Kansas! For God's sake, what's happening?"

Mr. Esmeralda smiled. In his mirror, he had seen the
flying fist of one of Kappa's *Oni* adepts drop the security
guard to the ground. He tugged the Lincoln's gearshift
into drive and turned left along the perimeter fence.

The Gulfstream III was waiting for them on its apron, a

large executive jet with its lights flashing and its engines already warming up. As they drew up to the side of the tarmac, Mr. Esmeralda said to Eva and her girls, "We are going to alight from the car now, and we are all going to be smiling. You understand me? This is going to be a happy family flight to Kansas. I have my gun in my pocket, and if any one of you attempts to make a fool of herself, like shouting or signaling or trying to run away, then I shall instantly shoot to kill. Believe me, this is not a jest."

A steward from Mercury Custom Air Services opened the limousine doors for them, and they stepped out into the warm and breezy evening. "Mr. Esmeralda? Right this way, please. This way, ladies. Fine evening for a flight, isn't it? You should have a wonderful view of the city as you take off."

"I shall be just one moment," said Mr. Esmeralda. The van had now parked behind his Lincoln, and flashed its lights just once. "I have to speak to my employees before I leave."

He took two steps toward the van, and he knew that it was all going to go wrong. The arrangements had been for the Tengu, in the company of Kappa's last three *Oni* escorts, to follow Mr. Esmeralda down to the airport for a final briefing, before driving farther south to Three Arch Bay, and their ultimate destination—the nuclear-power station. But Mr. Esmeralda had felt in his bones, right from the very beginning, that the Tengu needed no further instructions, any more than Kappa's vicious *Onis*. And when he heard the rear doors of the van banging open, and one of the *Onis* screeching "*Tora! Tora! Tora! Tora!*" he hesitated for only a split second before he turned around and began running toward the jet, shouting at the Mercury Air representative, "Get this plane off the ground! Now!"

Kathryn and Kelly screamed. For as Mr. Esmeralda ran past them, the Tengu appeared in the lights which flooded the Mercury Air apron, both arms raised in a ritual greeting to the devils which swarmed in the night air. He was even more grotesque than the previous Tengu: his body was not only gaping with the wounds from Doctor Gempaku's silver claws, but smashed and misshapen from his 27-story fall from Gerard Crowley's office window. His eyeballs were totally white: he did not need to see, not in the ordinary sense of the word. He was already dead, although not yet dead, and he strode toward Mr. Esmeralda with all the purpose of a creature that is possessed by a hideously powerful devil.

Mr. Esmeralda was halfway up the steps to the jet's cabin, leaving Eva and the girls on the tarmac, when the Tengu reached the foot of the steps, grasped them in his hands, and shook them violently, until they rattled and thundered.

"*Take them*!" shrieked Mr. Esmeralda, pointing to Eva and her twins. "Take them instead! They are yours, as a substitute!"

The Tengu raised his face blindly toward Mr. Esmeralda, then hesitated, turned, and groped the air. Eva and the girls stood where they were, mesmerized by fright.

"Take them!" screamed Mr. Esmeralda. "Take them!"

Still the Tengu hesitated, but then he took one or two uncertain steps toward Eva, his hands raised, his wounds glistening blue in the airport lights. Although Mr. Esmeralda couldn't hear her above the whistling of the Gulfstream's engines, she stepped forward to meet the Tengu and whispered, "You can have me. But not my daughters."

With one sweeping blow, the Tengu knocked Eva's head sideways and snapped her neck. She stood where she was for a second or two, her head at a sickening angle, and while she did so, the Tengu wrapped his arms around her, dug his hands into her lower back until he had seized her ribcage, and then, with one grisly and explosive wrench, opened her chest out like the ribs of an opening umbrella. Stomach and guts splashed onto the concrete apron, and even Mr. Esmeralda stood on the steps of the jet and stared in horror.

Without even looking at Kathryn or Kelly, the Tengu stalked back toward the black van. Two of the three *Onis* were waiting, arms folded, to receive him and help him back into the van. The third *Oni* was hidden in the shadows, although what he was doing, Mr. Esmeralda couldn't tell.

"I want to get out of here," he said to the stewardess who was standing behind him, white-faced, in the cabin doorway.

The stewardess couldn't speak. "We have to leave *now*!" snapped Mr. Esmeralda. "We have to!"

The stewardess shook her head, speechless, too shocked by the murder she had witnessed to move.

"Where is the captain?" Mr. Esmeralda demanded. "We have to go!"

There was a sharp swishing sound, and a flash, and Mr. Esmeralda halfturned to look back down toward the van. That was the last conscious movement he made. The third *Oni*, resting against the hood of the van, had fired a single antitank round from an 84-mm. Carl Gustaf rocket-launcher, a 5.7-pound high-explosive projectile which penetrated the fuselage of the Gulfstream close to the wing and instantly exploded.

Fully loaded with fuel, the plane blew up in a huge, rumbling burst of orange fire. Pieces of incandescent aluminum were hurtled into the air like a fireworks display.

The black van was already speeding away, without lights. But as it reached the perimeter of the airport and turned south again on the Pacific Coast Highway, it was picked up for the second time that evening by a beige Cutlass, driven by Detective Pullet. Beside him sat Sergeant Skrolnik, and in the back seat were Detective Arthur and a police marksman named Woschinski, who had blotchy red acne and a habit of sucking peppermints, but who could hit a moth at 250 yards and clip only its legs off.

Skrolnik rapped into his radio, as Pullet followed the van. "Something's happened at Torrance Airport. A damned great explosion. As soon as you get any word on it, let me know. Meanwhile, what about that call to Sennett? Did you get through? Did you tell him to get down here? I want him *down* here! He knows what the hell's going on, all this Japanese crap, which is more than I do. Tell him to take the Long Beach Freeway as far as the Pacific Coast Highway, and then head south. Tell him to get his ass in gear. Does he have CB? Well, that's one goddamned relief. Tell him to get down here fast. This is it. The balloon's going up.''

CHAPTER TWENTY-TWO

Four miles out of Marina del Rey, a U.S. Coast Guard cutter intercepted the yacht *Paloma* and hailed her to heave to. The yacht immediately cut her engines and wallowed for almost ten minutes in the water, without navigation lights, without putting down her anchor. After hailing the yacht four more times and raking her from stem to stern with floodlights, the Coast Guard captain finally decided to send aboard three armed enlisted men.

They discovered, on the foredeck, still alive—but only just—a tall Japanese who was later identified as Doctor Gempaku. He had knelt by the rail, and in the ritual manner of *seppuku*, and sliced open his own stomach with a razor-sharp samurai sword. Down below, in the galley, they found a Chinese girl who had been killed by being garrotted with a redhot wire. There were signs of her breasts and buttocks of severe sexual assault.

In an inner cabin, dead, were three young Japanese men

wearing black silk masks. They had all committed suicide by thrusting sharp knives, one in each hand, into their own eyes and deep into their brains.

It was in the very last cabin, though, that they found the greatest horror of all. Sitting in a cushioned basket, surrounded by hundreds of burning candles, a small deformed figure, naked, like a glistening fledgling that had fallen featherless from its nest before it could learn to fly. The heat and the stench inside the cabin were overpowering, but the tiny figure smiled at them as they stepped in, their eyes wide with caution and fright, their carbines held high.

"Holy shit," said one. "Holy shit, this isn't even *real*."

The tiny figure continued to smile at them. The most unnerving thing about it was that, on top of that deformed and twisted body, it had a perfectly normal head, the head of a handsome 37-year-old man.

"Good evening, gentlemen," it whispered. "It seems that you have caught me at a disadvantage."

One of the Coast Guardsmen nodded; and, ritually, in return, the tiny figure nodded too. It's heavy head dropped forward onto its chest, and for a moment it whined, and whined again, and then fell silent.

"What's the matter with it?" asked one of the Coast Guardsmen. "Do you think it's okay?"

"Would you think *you* were okay, if you looked like that?"

"Jesus, I don't know. Why don't you go take a look."

"I'm not taking no fucking look."

The other man glanced behind him, to make sure that no other Coast Guardsmen had boarded the yacht. Then, with the barrel of his carbine, he knocked five or six lighted candles onto the blankets and cushions that lay on the floor. He watched them for a second or two, to make sure they were well alight. Then he closed the cabin door and struck at the lock with the butt of his gun to jam it.

"We didn't even go in there, right?" he asked his companions.

"We didn't even go in where?"

The man checked his watch. "Let's give it ten seconds," he said. "Then we'll shout fire."

The *Paloma* burned for less than twenty minutes before listing over to port and quickly sinking. Kappa, the water devil, had returned at last to the water. There was a smell of steam and oil and charred varnish on the wind.

CHAPTER TWENTY-THREE

They reached the power station at Three Arch Bay only five minutes after Sergeant Skrolnik. Jerry parked the Dodge beside Skrolnik's Cutlass, and turned immediately around to look at El Krusho. Wrapped in a blanket on the back seat, alternately nursed and tortured by Nancy Shiranuka, Maurice was in a state of feverish trance, twitching and mumbling and murmuring. Mack and Gerard, both in the front seat with Jerry, glanced at him uncertainly, as if they weren't at all sure they should continue.

"This isn't going to kill him or anything?" asked Mack. "I've known that poor sucker for years."

"He is completely possessed now," said Nancy. "Nothing will hurt him, not even bullets."

"Nothing?" asked Gerard. "Not even another Tengu?"

Skrolnik came over to their car and slapped on the roof. "Esmeralda's dead," he told them. Jerry lowered the window to hear what he was saying. "He was trying to escape in an executive jet at Torrance Airport, and it seems like these Japanese bastards fired some kind of rocket at him. The whole plane went up. Six, maybe seven people killed altogether. Most of the corpses haven't even been identified yet.''

"My wife—my daughters," said Gerard. "Any news of them?"

"You're Gerard Crowley?" asked Skrolnik.

"Yes, sir."

Skrolnik raised his head, so that his face couldn't be seen from the interior of the car. Then he said, "I'm sorry, Mr. Crowley."

Gerard said, "Jesus. Did they suffer?"

"Not as far as I know."

Gerard was silent after that. Jerry said to Skrolnik, "If they're attacking this power station, then presumably they're going to try to set off some kind of nuclear explosion."

"That's what I thought," agreed Skrolnik. "They've parked their van around the side there, not far from the beach. We're keeping them under close observation, and I've already called for reinforcements. They won't even get close, I promise you."

"Don't count on it," said Jerry.

Skrolnik peered in through the open window. "Is that Needs you've got in the back?"

"Yes, sergeant."

"What's the matter with him? He looks sick."

"He's okay. He needs some air, is all."

Detective Arthur came over and said hastily, "Sergeant, they want you around at the fence."

"Okay," said Skrolnik, and then to Jerry, "Don't wander away too far. I may need you."

"Okay," said Jerry.

Once Skrolnik had gone, Jerry and Mack and Gerard climbed out of the car, opened the rear door, and helped El Krusho onto the grass. He coughed and swayed, 325 pounds of entranced muscle, a human machine possessed by a violent spirit. Jerry could have sworn that he saw tiny blue fires twinkling around El Krusho's head, but he guessed it was fatigue or reflections from the power station.

The power station was floodlit now: a compact collection of white concrete buildings with a tall red-and-white striped chimney, a battery of shiny aluminum ventilator shafts, and a cylindrical roof over the fusion reactor itself like a huge sailor's cap. Plumes of steam rose from the slender chimneys that exhausted the power station's cooling plant, and the deep reverberating thrum of generators was carried toward them by the evening wind.

"Tell Maurice to go in there and kill the Tengu," Jerry instructed Nancy.

Nancy said, "You are sure this is what you want?"

"It's what Maurice wants."

"Very well, then," said Nancy, and spoke rapidly to Maurice in Japanese.

"He's going to understand that?" asked Mack. "He doesn't even understand English."

"I am speaking to the Tengu, not to Maurice," said Nancy.

She had to pause for a moment while a police helicopter flackered overhead, its searchlights running across the ground like a frightened ghost. Then she finished her incantation and bowed to Maurice with the respect of one who recognizes extreme power when she confronts it.

There was shouting from the far side of the fence around the power station, and a sharp crackling of gunfire. Nancy said to Maurice, "It's started. You must go. Kill the Tengu. Kill it swiftly."

Without hesitation, Maurice seized the wire of the perimeter fence and ripped it apart like unraveled knitting. He stepped straight through it, followed closely and anxiously by Jerry and Mack. Gerard stayed behind with Nancy.

As they came around the corner of the cooling plant, they saw a double cordon of police and security guards, all armed, facing the Tengu across the parking lot. Every

floodlight was lit, giving the scene the brilliant unreality of
a movie set.

But there was no question that the Tengu was real. He
came slowly forward, toward the main doors of the power
station, his head bound tightly with a scared sweatband
painted with magical characters, his eyeballs white as
boiled eggs, his body damaged and scarred and torn so
viciously that the naked sinews showed through his
wounds. *God,* thought Jerry, *you can see the blood puls-
ing through his arteries.*

Nobody challenged the Tengu. The police had bull-
horns, but they didn't use them. Instead, an officer simply
said, *"Fire,"* and there was an ear-spitting fusillade of
carbine and pistol shots.

The Tengu was hit again and again. Bullets blew lumps
of raw flesh from his shoulders and his chest. One bullet
turfed the skin and muscle away from the left side of his
face, so that his jawbone and teeth were bared. But he
didn't waver. He kept advancing on the ranks of police
and security guards, his arms raised above his head, even
when a sharpshooter hit his forearm and elbow, smashing
the bone and digging up the muscle.

The police cordon began to waver and break, unnerved.
"Fire!" demanded the officer, but none of them did.
They watched in horrified fascination as the Tengu,
bloody and maimed, walked right through their ranks, up
the concrete steps of the power-station entrance, and then
burst open the doors with a single blow of his fists. Before
anybody could react, he had disappeared inside.

Skrolnik ran forward, screaming, "Stop him! For God's
sake!" but the confusion and panic were too much. Most
of the officers stayed where they were, unable to admit to
themselves that they had seen a man hit by seventy or
eighty large-caliber bullets and still walk. Jerry and Mack
guided El Krusho up the concrete steps to the broken
doors of the power station, and although one policeman
challenged them and asked, "What are you doing?"
nobody else stood in their way.

In a moment they were inside, following the spatters of blood which the Tengu had left behind him on the floor. Inside the power station, it was coolly air-conditioned, and lit with dim, greenish fluorescent lamps. The floor was polished vinyl, as reflective as water, and the walls were as white and sterile as a hospital.

Skrolnik, at the smashed door, yelled, "Sennett! What the hell do you think you're doing?"

But Jerry and Mack kept pushing El Krusho onward, up a flight of steel stairs, along a steel latticework catwalk, and around at last to the main hall where the fusion reactor was housed. Mack pointed down to the reactor itself and said, "There he is. For God's sake, he's playing around with all those switches!"

The fusion reactor was quite small, the first of America's experiments in nuclear fusion. It was no more than 20 feet high, shaped like a giant metal donut in a frame of pipework and valves and electrical wiring. The control console was a white upright cabinet, no bigger than a Space Invaders game, with five power-indicator dials, and a circular screen to indicate the build-up of nuclear energy. The Tengu had already flicked down a whole row of switches, and the fusion reactor was beginning to hum as it built up the extraordinary charge of power necessary to raise its internal temperature to 100 million degrees Celsius.

Skrolnik came banging along the catwalk, followed by six armed policemen and the scientific director of the Three Arch Bay complex, a young but balding man with hornrimmed glasses as heavy as Clark Kent's.

"He's *tampering* with it, for God's sake," shouted the scientific director. "He's started it up!"

"Cut the power, then!" snarled Skrolnik.

"I *can't*! If I shut off the power now, the whole damned thing will go unstable!"

"Shoot him!" Skrolnik directed his officers. "Blow his goddamned head off!"

"No!" insisted the scientific director. "One stray

bullet, and the whole reactor could blow up!"

"Well, *what* then?" screamed Skrolnik in utter frustration.

"Go, Maurice," said Jerry in a gentle voice. "Go kill him."

Everybody watched in morbid fascination as Maurice strode purposefully along the catwalk and down the steps which led to the main floor of the reactor room. The Tengu, at the reactor's console, neither saw nor acknowledged him, but he must have sensed that he was there, since both of them were possessed by the same evil spirit. Different manifestations of the same spirit, invoked for different reasons—after all, like the demons of Christendom, the devils of Japan were legion—but the same fundamental spirit. The atmosphere within the nuclear-reactor hall crackled with evil and with the huge power of the fusion reactor, as it steadily amassed incredible power.

"Kill him!" shouted Jerry, and Mack leaned over the rail of the catwalk and yelled, "Sic him, Maurice!"

El Krusho stepped forward and seized the Japanese Tengu by the neck. His bruised and lacerated muscles bulged with power as he wrenched the Tengu's head this way and that, and then twisted the Tengu's arms around behind his back. But the Tengu, for all that he was lighter and less muscular then El Krusho, had been an *Oni* adept when he was alive; and as El Krusho tried to claw back his head and break his neck, he twisted powerfully around, and threw El Krusho against the metal staircase.

El Krusho lurched to his feet again and tore into the Tengu with the madness of a wild animal. He dug his fingers into the Tengu's wounds, and ripped yards of red muscle away from the Tengu's bones. He butted the Tengu repeatedly with his skull, and at last the two of them became locked together in the clinch which, in *Oni*, is known as the Fatal Embrace. It is one of the few slow moves in *Oni*, a twisting together of arms and backs which can be fatal to either antagonist, or both.

There were three or four minutes of grunting strain, as the Tengu pulled against El Krusho and El Krusho pulled back. Then, with enormous effort, El Krusho staggered to his feet, carrying the Tengu on his back like the carcass of a slaughtered bull, and walked with him, step by agonized step, out of the reactor hall and out toward the huge pool where spent nuclear fuel was kept submerged, prior to re-processing.

The pool hall was as cold and echoing as a swimming pool. Beneath the deep-turquoise water, lit by underwater floodlights, stood rack after rack of tubular steel where the fuel rods were stored.

At the very edge of the pool, El Krusho and the Tengu wrestled and chopped and grappled with each other. The Tengu at last seized Maurice by the neck and flailed him from one side to the other, howling with a weird echoing howl that sounded as if it had come from hell itself.

There was a moment of physical ballet, a moment of strain and tension and ultimate pain. Then both of them, Tengu and El Krusho, toppled and fell into the radioactive pool.

Mack and Jerry stood by the edge, watching the two figures claw at each other beneath the surface, their bodies distorted by the water, a huge burst of bubbles rushed to the surface from El Krusho's lungs, but still neither of them came up.

It was then that Skrolnik came through and urgently touched Jerry's arm. "Listen," he said, "the reactor's gone out of control. It's like a runaway train. The director doesn't think he's going to be able to control it."

Jerry looked down into the depths of the pool, where El Krusho and the Tengu were struggling their last among the racks of plutonium and U-235. He could already feel the deep hum of the fusion reactor reverberating throughout the building. He glanced at Mack, and then at Skrolnik again.

"Hiroshima," he said. "That's what this is all about.

Goddamned Hiroshima." He felt a crunching of broken porcelain in his pocket, and realized it was the cricket cage.

CHAPTER TWENTY-FOUR

At 8:27 P.M., the sun rose over San Juan Capistrano, just south of Los Angeles. The explosion of the reactor at Three Arch Bay was exactly similar to the detonation of a hydrogen bomb, since the release of neutrons caused by the fusion of the reactor led to fission of the plutonium and uranium waste in the used-fuel pool, and the discharge of violent radioactivity.

The evening turned to daylight as an immense white fireball ascended thunderously into the sky, and then hung there, rumbling, glowing with malevolent heat and power. A young starlet who was prancing out of her car on Santa Monica Boulevard was immortalized in the glass of the Palm Restaurant window. A famous producer who was drinking his tenth collins of the day looked southward from his Bel Air balcony when he first saw something flashing, and was evaporated where he stood.

Within seconds, a roaring wind blew through Garden Grove and Anaheim and Lakewood, turning Disneyland to fiery wreckage, melting the dummies in the Hollywood Wax Museum, melting human beings, too. Dreams and reality both died that day. Reels of movies waiting to be edited at Twentieth-Century Fox and Universal Studios flared up in seconds.

David Sennett was watching television when he heard the first crack and rumble. Then a terrifying flash filled the

room, and the drapes billowed out as if a hurricane had
caught them.

"Oh, Dad," he thought. He knew what had happened.
"Oh, Dad, Oh, God."

The Devils of D-Day

'The worst sort of devils are those who rejoice in wars and effusion of blood, and afflict men with most cruel stripes.'
   – Francis Barrett

AUTHOR'S NOTE

All of the devils and demons that appear in this
book are legendary creatures of hell, and there is
substantial recorded evidence of their existence. For
that reason, it is probably inadvisable to attempt to
conjure up any of them by repeating out loud the
incantations used in the text, which are also
genuine.
I would like to point out that the Pentagon and the
British Ministry of Defence strenuously deny the
events described here, but I leave you to draw your
own conclusions.

– Graham Masterton,
London, 1979

CHAPTER ONE

I could see them coming from almost a mile away: two small muffled figures on bicycles, their scarves wound tightly around their faces, pedalling between the white winter trees. As they came nearer, I could hear them talking, too, and make out the clouds of chilly vapour that clung around their mouths. It was Normandy in December – misty and grey as a photograph – and a sullen red sun was already sinking behind the forested hills. Apart from the two French labourers cycling slowly towards me, I was alone on the road, standing with my surveyor's tripod in the crisp frosted grass, my rented yellow Citroën 2CV parked at an ungainly angle on the nearby verge. It was so damned cold that I could hardly feel my hands or my nose, and I was almost afraid to stamp my feet in case my toes broke off.

The men came nearer. They were old, with donkey-jackets and berets, and one of them was carrying a battered army rucksack on his back with a long French loaf sticking out of it. Their bicycle tyres left white furry tracks on the hoar frost that covered the road. There wasn't much traffic along here, in the rural depths of the Suisse Normande, except for occasional tractors and even more occasional Citroën-Maseratis zipping past at ninety miles an hour in blizzards of ice.

I called, '*Bonjour, messieurs,*' and one of the old men slowed his bicycle and dismounted. He wheeled his machine right up to my tripod and said, '*Bonjour, monsieur, Qu'est-ce que vous faîtes?*'

I said, 'My French isn't too good. You speak English?' The man nodded.

'Well,' I said, pointing across the valley towards the cold silvery hills, 'I'm making a map. *Une carte.*'

I

'*Ah, oui,*' said the old man. '*Une carte.*'

The other old man, who was still sitting astride his bicycle, pulled down his scarf from his face to blow his nose.

'It's for the new route?' he asked me. 'The new highway?'

'No, no. This is for someone's history book. It's a map of the whole of this area for a book about World War II.'

'*Ah, la guerre,*' nodded the first old man. '*Une carte de la guerre, hunh?*'

One of the men took out a blue packet of Gitanes, and offered me one. I didn't usually smoke French cigarettes, partly because of their high tar content and partly because they smelled like burning horsehair, but I didn't want to appear discourteous – not after only two days in northern France. In any case, I was glad of the spot of warmth that a glowing cigarette tip gave out.

We smoked for a while, and smiled at each other dumbly, the way people do when they can't speak each other's language too well. Then the old man with the loaf said, 'They fought all across this valley; and down by the river, too. The Orne. I remember it very clear.'

The other old man said: 'Tanks, you know? Here, and here. The Americans coming across the road from Clècy, and the Germans retreating back up the Orne valley. A very hard battle just there, you see, by the Pont D'Ouilly. But that day the Germans stood no chance. Those American tanks came across the bridge at Le Vey and cut them off. At night, from just here, you could see German tanks burning all the way up to the turn in the river.'

I blew out smoke and vapour. It was so gloomy now that I could hardly make out the heavy granite shoulders of the rocks at Ouilly, where the Orne river widened and turned before sliding over the dam at Le Vey and foaming northwards in the spectral December evening. The only sound was the faint rush of water, and the doleful tolling of the church bell from the distant village, and out here in the frost and the cold we might just as well have been alone in the whole continent of Europe.

The old man with the loaf said, 'It was fierce, that fighting. I never saw it so fierce. We caught three Germans but it was no difficulty. They were happy to surrender. I remember one of them said: "Today, I fought the devil." '

The other old man nodded. '*Der Teufel*. That's what he said. I was there. This one and me, we're cousins.'

I smiled at them both. I didn't really know what to say.

'Well,' said the one with the loaf, 'we must get back for nourishment.'

'Thanks for stopping,' I told him. 'It gets pretty lonely standing out here on your own.'

'You're interested in the war?' asked the other old man.

I shrugged. 'Not specifically. I'm a cartographer. A map-maker.'

'There are many stories about the war. Some of them are just pipe-dreams. But round here there are many stories. Just down there, about a kilometre from the Pont D'Ouilly, there's an old American tank in the hedge. People don't go near it at night. They say you can hear the dead crew talking to each other inside it, on dark nights.'

'That's pretty spooky.'

The old man pulled up his scarf so that only his old wrinkled eyes peered out. He looked like a strange Arab soothsayer, or a man with terrible wounds. He tugged on his knitted gloves, and said, in a muffled voice, 'These are only stories. All battlefields have ghosts, I suppose. Anyway, *le potage s'attend*.'

The two old cousins waved once, and then pedalled slowly away down the road. It wasn't long before they turned a corner and disappeared behind the misty trees,

3

and I was left on my own again, numb with cold and just about ready to pack everything away and grab some dinner. The sun was mouldering away behind a white wedge of descending fog now, anyway, and I could hardly see my hands in front of my face, let alone the peaks of distant rocks.

I stowed my equipment in the back of the 2CV, climbed into the driver's seat, and spent five minutes trying to get the car started. The damned thing whinnied like a horse, and I was just about to get out and kick it like a horse deserved, when it coughed and burst into life. I switched on the headlights, U-turned in the middle of the road, and drove back towards Falaise and my dingy hotel.

I was only about a half mile down the road, though, when I saw the sign that said *Pont D'Ouilly, 4 km.* I looked at my watch. It was only half past four, and I wondered if a quick detour to look at the old cousins' haunted tank might be worth while. If it was any good, I could take a photograph of it tomorrow, in daylight, and Roger might like it for his book. Roger Kellman was the guy who had written the history for which I was drawing all these maps, *The Days After D-Day,* and anything to do with military memorabilia would have him licking his lips like Sylvester the cat.

I turned off left, and almost immediately wished I hadn't. The road went sharply downhill, twisting and turning between trees and rocks, and it was slithery with ice, mud and half-frozen cowshit. The little Citroën bucked and swayed from side to side, and the windshield steamed up so much from my panicky breathing that I had to slide open the side window and lean out; and that wasn't much fun, with the outside temperature well down below freezing.

I passed silent, dilapidated farms, with sagging barns and closed windows. I passed grey fields in which cows stood like grubby brown-and-white jigsaws, frozen saliva

4

hanging from their hairy lips. I passed shuttered houses, and slanting fields that went down to the dark winter river. The only sign of life that I saw was a tractor, its wheels so caked with ochre clay that they were twice their normal size, standing by the side of the road with its motor running. There was nobody in it.

Eventually, the winding road took me down between rough stone walls, under a tangled arcade of leafless trees, and over the bridge at Ouilly. I kept a lookout for the tank the old cousins had talked about, but the first time I missed it altogether; and I spent five minutes wrestling the stupid car back around the way it had come, stalling twice and almost getting jammed in a farm gateway. In the greasy farmyard, I saw a stable door open, and an old woman with a grey face and a white lace cap stare out at me with suspicion, but then the door closed again, and I banged the 2CV into something resembling second gear and roared back down the road.

You could have missed the tank in broad daylight, let alone at dusk in the middle of a freezing Norman winter. Just as I came around the curve of the road, I saw it, and I managed to pull up a few yards away, with the Citroën's suspension complaining and groaning. I stepped out of the car into a cold pile of cow dung, but at least when it's chilled like that it doesn't smell. I scraped my shoe on a rock by the side of the road and then walked back to look at the tank.

It was dark and bulky, but surprisingly small. I guess we're so used to enormous Army tanks these days that we forget how tiny the tanks of World War II actually were. Its surface was black and scaly with rust, and it was so interwoven with the hedge that it looked like something out of Sleeping Beauty, with thorns and brambles twisted around its turret, laced in and out of its tracks, and wound around its stumpy cannon. I didn't know what kind of a tank it was, but I guessed it was maybe a Sherman or something like that. It was obviously American: there was a faded and rusted white star on its side, and a painting of some kind that time and the weather had just about obliterated. I kicked the tank, and it responded with a dull, empty booming sound.

A woman came walking slowly along the road with an aluminium milk pail. She eyed me cautiously as she approached, but as she drew near she stopped and laid down her pail. She was quite young, maybe twenty-three or twenty-four, and she wore a red spotted headscarf. She was obviously the farmer's daughter. Her hands were rough from pulling cows' udders in cold dawn barns, and her cheeks were bright crimson, like a painted peasant doll's. I said: '*Bonjour, mademoiselle*,' and she nodded in careful reply.

She said, 'You are American?'

'That's right.'

'I thought so. Only Americans stop and look.'

'You speak good English.'

She didn't smile. 'I was au-pair in England, in Pinner, for three years.'

'But then you came back to the farm?'

'My mother died. My father was all alone.'

I said, 'He has a loyal daughter.'

'Yes,' she said, lowering her eyes. 'But I expect I will go away again one day. It's very *solitaire* out here. Very lonesome.'

I turned back to the grim brooding bulk of the abandoned tank. 'I was told this was haunted,' I said. 'At night, you can hear the crew talking.'

The girl said nothing.

I waited for a while, and then turned again and looked across the road at her. 'Is that true, do you think?' I asked her. 'That it's haunted?'

'You mustn't speak about it,' she said. 'If you speak about it, it turns the milk.'

I glanced down at her aluminium pail. 'You're serious?

6

If you speak about the ghosts in the tank, the milk goes off?'

She whispered, 'Yes.'

I thought I'd heard everything, but this was amazing. Here, in modern France, an intelligent young lady was whispering in the presence of a beaten-up old Sherman tank, in case her fresh milk curdled. I rested my hand on the tank's cold rusted mudguard, and I felt as though I'd found something quite special. Roger would have adored it.

'Have you heard the ghosts yourself?' I asked her.

She quickly shook her head.

'Do you know anybody who has? Anybody I could speak to?'

She picked up her pail, and started to walk off down the road. But I crossed over and kept pace with her, even though she wouldn't look at me, and wouldn't answer.

'I don't want to be nosey, mam'selle. But we're getting a book together, all about D-Day and what happened afterwards. And this seems like the kind of story I could really use. I mean it. Surely someone's heard the voices, if they're real?'

She stopped walking, and stared at me hard. She was quite pretty for a Norman peasant. She had that straight nose you see on 11th-century women in the Bayeux tapestry, and opalescent green eyes. Underneath her mud-spattered jerkin and her sensible skirt and her rubber boots, she had quite a noticeable figure, too.

I said, 'I don't know what you've got to be so sensitive about. It's only a story, right? I mean, ghosts don't exist, right?'

She kept staring. Then she said, 'It's not a ghost, it's different from that.'

'What do you mean, different?'

'I can't tell you.'

She started walking again, and this time she walked so quickly I had difficulty keeping up. I guess if you walk

7

three miles to the cowsheds and back twice a day, your leg muscles get themselves built up pretty tough. By the time we'd reached the mossy stone gate where I'd turned my car round, I was wheezing for breath, and my throat was sore from the chill foggy air.

'This is my farm,' she said. 'I have to go in now.'

'You won't tell me any more?'

'There's nothing to tell. The tank has been there since the war. That's more than thirty years, isn't it? How could you hear voices in a tank after thirty years?'

'That's what I'm asking you,' I told her.

She turned her face away in profile. She had sad, curved lips; and with that straight aristocratic nose, she was almost beautiful. I said, 'Will you tell me your name?'

She gave a small, fleeting smile. 'Madeleine Passerelle. *Et vous?*'

'Dan, short for Daniel, McCook.'

The girl extended her hand, and we shook. 'I am pleased to have made your acquaintance,' she said. 'Now I must go.'

'Can I see you again? I'm up here again tomorrow. I have a map to finish.'

She shook her head.

'I'm not trying to pick you up,' I assured her. 'Maybe we could just go for a drink. Do you have a bar around here?'

I looked around at the cold soggy countryside, and the mournful cows gathering at the fence across the road.

'Well, maybe a small hotel?' I corrected myself.

Madeleine swung her pail of milk. 'I think I am too busy,' she said. 'And besides, my father needs a lot of care.'

'Who's the old woman?'

'Which old woman?'

'The old woman I saw at the stable door when I turned my car round. She had a white lace cap.'

8

'Oh . . . that's Eloise. She's lived at the farm all her life. She nursed my mother when she was sick. Now, *there's* someone to speak to if you're interested in stories about the tank. She believes in every superstition.'

I coughed in the cold twilight. 'Could I speak to her now?'

Madeleine said, 'Not tonight. Perhaps another day.'

She turned, and started to walk across the farmyard, but I caught up with her and grabbed the handle of her milking pail. 'Listen, how about tomorrow?' I asked her. 'I could come around noon. Could you spare a few minutes then?'

I was determined not to let her get away without making some kind of firm commitment. The tank and its ghosts were pretty interesting, but Madeleine Passerelle herself was even more so. You don't usually get much action when you're drawing up a military map of northern France, and a few glasses of wine and a tumble in the cowshed with the farmer's daughter, even in the deep midwinter, was a lot more appealing than silent and solitary meals in the brown garlic-smelling mausoleum that my hotel jocularly called its dining room.

Madeleine smiled. 'Very well. Come and eat with us. But make it at eleven-thirty. We lunch early in France.'

'You've made my week. Thanks a lot.'

I reached forward to kiss her, but my foot slid on the churned-up mud of the farmyard, and I almost lost my balance. I saved most of my dignity by turning my slide into three rapid steps, but the kiss was lost to the freezing air, a puff of vapour that vanished in the dusk. Amused, Madeleine said, '*Au revoir*, M. McCook. Until tomorrow.'

I watched her walk across the yard and disappear through the stable door. A cold wet drizzle was beginning to sift down from the evening sky, and it would probably turn into snow in an hour or two. I left the farm and began to trudge back down the road towards the Pont D'Ouilly, where I'd left my car.

Along the road, it was silent and soaking and dark. I kept my hands shoved deep in my overcoat pockets and my scarf pulled up over my mouth. Way over to my right, I could hear the Orne rushing over the brownish granite rocks of its shallow bed, and on my left, just beyond the hedge, reared the slabby blocks of the cliffs that gave this part of Normandy its name – Swiss Normandy. The rocks were jacketed in slime and moss, and laced up with hanging tree-roots, and you could just imagine strange and malignant creatures lurking in their crevices and cracks.

I hadn't realised how far I'd walked along the road with Madeleine. It took me almost five minutes before I saw my yellow car by the verge, and the huddled black bulk of the abandoned tank. The drizzle was turning into large wet flakes of half-melted snow now, and I pulled my coat collar up and walked more quickly.

Who knows what odd tricks your eyes can play in the snow and the dark? When your eyes are tired, you can see dark shadows like cats slipping away at the corner of your field of vision. Shadows can seem to stand on their own, and trees can seem to move. But that evening, on the road to Pont D'Ouilly, I was sure that my eyes weren't playing up, and that I did see something. There's a French road sign which warns that the night can deceive you, and possibly it did, but I still think that what I glimpsed wasn't an optical illusion. It was enough to make me stop in the road, and feel a tight chill that was even colder than the evening air.

Through the tumbling snow, a few yards away from the derelict tank, I saw a small bony figure, white in the darkness, not much taller than a child of five, and it seemed to be hopping or running. The sight of it was so sudden and strange that I was momentarily terrified; but then I ran forward through the snow and shouted, 'Hey! You!'

My shout echoed flatly back from the nearby rocks. I

peered into the dark but there was nobody there. Only the rusting bulk of the Sherman tank, woven into the brambles of the hedge. Only the wet road, and the noise of the river. There was no sign of any figure; no sign of any child. I walked back across to my car and checked it for damage, in case the figure had been a vandal or a thief, but the Citroën was unmarked. I climbed thoughtfully inside and sat there for a minute or two drying my face and hair with my handkerchief, wondering what the hell was going on around here.

I started the Citroën's engine, but just before I drove off I took one last look at the tank. It gave me a really peculiar feeling, thinking that it had been decaying by this roadside since 1944, unmoved, and that here at this very place the American Army had fought to liberate Normandy. For the first time in my map-making career, I felt history was alive; I felt history move under my feet. I wondered if the skeletons of the crew were still inside the tank, but I decided that they'd probably been taken out years ago and given a decent burial. The French were beautifully and gravely respectful to the remains of the men who had died trying to liberate them.

I released the Citroën's brake and drove down the gloomy road, across the bridge, and back up the winding hill to the main highway. The snow was crowding my windshield, and the car's tacky little windshield wipers were having about as much success in clearing it away as two geriatrics sweeping up the ticker-tape after Lindy's parade through Wall Street. When I joined the main stream of traffic, I almost collided with a Renault which was bombing through the snow at eighty-five. *Vive la vélocité*, I thought to myself, as I crawled back towards Falaise at twenty.

Next day, in the high-ceilinged hotel dining room, I ate a solemn breakfast of croissants and coffee and confitures, watching myself in the mottled mirrors and trying to

11

decipher what the hell was happening in the world today from a copy of *Le Figaro* on a long stick. Across the room, a rotund Frenchman with waxed whiskers and a huge white napkin tucked in his shirt collar was wolfing down breadrolls as though he was trying to put up the price of shares in the bakery industry. A waitress in black with a pinched face rapped around the black-and-white tiled floor in court shoes and made sure you felt you were lonely and unwanted, and that you only wanted breakfast because you were an unpardonable pest. I thought of changing hotels, but then I thought of Madeleine, and things didn't seem too bad.

I spent most of the morning on the new curve of road that comes into Clécy from the south-east. A dry wind had lifted away most of the snow during the night, but it was still intensely cold, and the village lay frosted in its valley, with the broad hump of the hills far behind it, and tiny villagers came and went from its doors, tending their gardens or their washing, or fetching in logs, and the hours rang from the tall church spire, and New York seemed a very long way away.

Maybe my mind was distracted, but I only managed to finish half the readings that I'd hoped to take, and by eleven o'clock, as the church tolled its hour, I was wrapped up and ready to drive across to Pont D'Ouilly I'd taken the trouble to stop at a store in the village and buy a very reasonable bottle of Bordeaux, just in case Madeleine's father needed a little appeasing. I also bought, for Madeleine herself, a box of crystallised fruit. They're very big on crystallised fruit in Normandy.

The rented Citroën coughed and choked, but finally found its way down the twisting road to the bridge. The countryside didn't look very much more hospitable by daylight than it had by night. There was a cold silvery haze over the fields, and mist was hanging under the elms like soiled net curtains. The cows were still there, standing patiently in the chill, chewing the colourless grass and breathing out so much steam they looked like roomfuls of heavy smokers. I drove over the stone bridge, with the Orne gargling beneath me, and then I slowed down so that I could take a look at the tank.

There it was – silent and broken – wound in brambles and leafless creeper. I stopped the car for a moment and slid open my window so that I could see the corroded wheels, the collapsed tracks, and the small dark turret with its scaly sides. There was something deeply sinister and sorrowful about it. It reminded me of the abandoned Mulberry harbour that still lies off the shore of Arromanches, on Normandy's channel coast, a grim memorial to June 6, 1944, that no stone monument or statue could ever adequately replace.

I looked around at the dank hedgerow for a while, and then I started the car up again and drove along to Madeleine's farm. I turned into the gate and splashed across the muddy yard, with chickens flapping and skittering all around me, and a flock of grubby geese rushing away like athletes on a cross-country run.

I stepped out of the car, being careful where I put my feet, and reached in for my presents. A door opened behind me, and I heard someone walking my way. A voice said, '*Bonjour, monsieur. Qu'est-ce que vous voulez?*'

A short Frenchman in muddy pants, muddy boots and a muddy brown jacket was standing in the yard with his hands in his pockets. He had a long Norman face, and he was smoking a Gauloise that appeared to be permanently stuck to his lip. His beret was pulled well down to his ears, which made him look pretty rural, but his eyes were bright and he looked like the kind of farmer who didn't miss a trick.

'My name's Dan McCook,' I told him. 'Your daughter Madeleine invited me for lunch. Er – *pour déjeuner?*'

The farmer nodded. 'Yes, monsieur. She tells me this. I am Jacques Passerelle.'

We shook hands. I offered him the bottle of wine, and

said, 'I brought you this. I hope you like it. It's a bordeaux.'

Jacques Passerelle paused for a moment, and reached in his breast pocket for a pair of wire-rimmed spectacles. He hooked them around his ears, and scrutinised the bottle closely. I felt as if I'd had the down-right effrontery to give a vacuum pack of A&P bacon to a Kentucky hog farmer. But the Frenchman nodded again, put away his spectacles, and said, '*Merci bien, monsieur*. I save this for *dimanche*.'

He ushered me through the stable door into the kitchen. The old woman Eloise was there, in her dark grey dress and her white lace cap, boiling a huge copper pan full of apples. Jacques introduced me, and we shook hands. Her fingers were soft and dry, and she was wearing a silver ring with a miniature Bible on it. She had one of those flat, pale, wrinkled faces that you sometimes see staring out of the windows of old people's homes, or from the windows of buses on old people's outings. But she seemed to be independent and strong around the Passerelle home, and she walked with a stright back.

She said, 'Madeleine told me you were interested in the tank.'

I glanced at Jacques, but he didn't seem to be listening. I coughed, and said, 'Sure. I'm making a map of these parts for a book about D-Day.'

'The tank has been here since July, 1944. Mid-July. It died on a very hot day.'

I looked at her. Her eyes were washed-out blue, like the sky after a spring shower, and you didn't quite know whether she was looking inwards or outwards. I said, 'Maybe we can talk after lunch.'

Out of the steamy, apple-aromatic kitchen, we walkeo along a narrow dark hallway with a bare boarded floor Jacques opened a door in the side of the hall, and said 'You would care for an aperitif?'

This was obviously his front parlour, the room he kept only for visitors. It was gloomy, heavily-curtained, and it smelled of dust and stale air and furniture polish. There were three chintz armchairs in the style you can see in any large French *meubles* store, a copper warming-pan hanging on the wall, a plastic madonna with a small container of holy water, and a dark-varnished sideboard with photographs of weddings and grandchildren, each on its own lace doily. A tall clock ticked away the winter morning, weary and slow.

'I'd like a calvados, please,' I told Jacques. 'I don't know anything better for warming yourself up on a cold day. Not even Jack Daniels.'

Jacques took two small glasses from the sideboard, uncorked the calvados, and poured it out. He handed one over, and lifted his own glass solemnly.

'*Santé*,' he said quietly, and downed his drink in one gulp.

I sipped mine more circumspectly. Calvados, the apple-brandy of Normany, is potent stuff, and I did want to do some sensible work this afternoon.

'You have been here in summer?' asked Jacques.

'No, never. This is only my third trip to Europe.'

'It's not so pleasant in winter. The mud, and the frost. But in summer, this is very beautiful. We have visitors from all over France, and Europe. You can hire boats and row along the river.'

'It sounds terrific. Do you have many Americans?'

Jacques shrugged. 'One or two. Some Germans some-times, too. But not many come here. Pont D'Ouilly is still a painful memory. The Germans ran away from here as if the devil himself were after them.'

I swallowed some more calvados, and it glowed down my throat like a shovelful of hot coke. 'You're the second person who's said that,' I told him. '*Der Teufel*.'

Jacques gave a small smile, which reminded me of the way that Madeleine smiled.

'I must change my clothes,' he said. 'I don't like to sit down for lunch looking like a mud man.'

'Go ahead,' I told him. 'Will Madeleine be down?'

'In a moment. She wanted to put on cosmetics. Well . . . we don't have many visitors.'

Jacques went off to clean himself up, and I went over to the window and looked out across the orchard. The fruit trees were all bare now, and pruned, and the grass was white with cold. A bird perched for a moment on the rough fence of silver-birch at the far end of the garden, and then fluttered off. I turned back into the room.

On the sideboard, one of the photographs showed a young girl with a wavy 1940s hairstyle, and I guessed that must have been Madeleine's mother. There was a colour picture of Madeleine as a baby, with a smiling priest in the background, and a formal portrait of Jacques in a high white collar. Besides all these was a bronze model of a medieval cathedral, with a ring of twisted hair around its spire. I couldn't really work out what that was supposed to mean, but then I wasn't a Roman Catholic, and I wasn't really into religious relics.

I was just about to pick up the model to take a better look when the parlour door opened. It was Madeleine, in a pale cream cotton dress, her dark-blonde hair brushed back and held with tortoiseshell combs, her lips bright red with lipstick.

'Please—' she said. 'Don't touch that.'

I raised my hands away from the tiny cathedral. 'I'm sorry. I was only going to take a look.'

'It's something of my mother's.'

'I'm sorry.'

'That's all right. Don't think about it. Did father give you a drink?'

'Sure. A calvados. It's making my ears ring already. Are you going to join me?'

She shook her head. 'I can't drink it. They gave it to

me once when I was twelve and I was sick. Now, I only drink wine.'

She sat down, and I sat opposite. 'You shouldn't have dressed up specially for me,' I told her. 'But all the same, you look beautiful.'

She blushed. Not much, just a small tinge on the cheeks, but it was a blush all right. I hadn't come across that kind of modesty for years.

I said, 'I had a real weird experience last night. I was walking back to my car, and I could have sworn I saw something on the road.'

She looked up. 'What was it?'

'Well, I'm not too sure. It was like a small child, but it was too thin and bony for a small child.'

She looked at me for several silent seconds. Then she said, 'I don't know. It must have been the snow.'

'It scared the hell out of me, whatever it was.'

She picked absentmindedly at the braiding on the arm of her chair. 'It's the atmosphere, the *ambience*, around the tank. It makes people feel things, see things, that aren't there. Eloise will tell you some of the stories if you want.'

'You don't believe them yourself?'

She shrugged. 'What's the use? All you do is frighten yourself. I'd rather think of real things, not of ghosts and spirits.'

I put down my glass on the small side-table. 'I get the feeling you don't like it here.'

'Here, in my father's house?'

'No – in Pont D'Ouilly. It's not exactly the entertainment centre of northern France, is it?'

Madeleine stood up and walked across to the window. Against the grey winter light, she was a soft dark silhouette. She said, 'I don't think so much of entertainment. If you've lived here, in Pont D'Ouilly, then you know what sadness is, and anything at all is better than sadness.'

'Don't tell me you loved and lost.'

She smiled. 'I suppose you could say that. I loved life and I lost my love of life.'

I said, 'I'm not sure I understand.' But at that moment, a gong rang from across the hall, and Madeleine turned and said, 'Lunch is ready. We'd better go in.'

Today, we had lunch in the dining room, although I suspected that they usually ate in the kitchen, especially when they had three inches of mud on their boots and appetites like horses. Eloise had set out a huge tureen of hot brown onion soup on the oval table, with crisp garlic bread, and I suddenly realised that I was starved of home cooking. Jacques was already standing at the head of the table in a neatly-pressed brown suit, and when we had all taken our seats, he bowed his thinning scalp towards us, and said grace.

'Oh Lord, who provides all that we eat, thank you for this nourishment. And protect us from the conversations of evil, in the name of the Father, and of the Son, and of the Holy Spirit, amen.'

I looked across the table at Madeleine, and tried to put the question in my eyes. *The conversations of evil?* What was that all about? The voices in the tank? Or what? But Madeleine's attention was fastened on the large tureen, as Eloise dished up piping-hot platefuls of transparent brown soup, and whether she intended to avoid my gaze of not, she didn't look up again until her father had started to talk.

'The upper field is frozen,' he said, dabbing his lips with his napkin. 'I ploughed a hectare this morning, and there was ice coming up with the soil. It hasn't been so cold here for ten years.'

Eloise said, 'There are worse winters to come. The dogs know it.'

'The dogs?' I asked her.

'That's right, monsieur. When a dog stays close to

home, and when he calls in the night, that's when the nights will grow cold for three years, one after another.'

'You believe that? Or is that just a French country saying?'

Eloise frowned at me. 'It is nothing to do with belief. It is true. I have seen it happen for myself.'

Jacques put in: 'Eloise has a way with nature, Mr McCook. She can heal you with dandelion broth, or send you to sleep with burdock and thyme.'

'Can she exorcise ghosts?'

Madeleine breathed, 'Dan—' but Eloise was not put out. She examined me with those watery old eyes of hers, and almost smiled.

'I hope you don't think I'm impertinent,' I said. 'But it seems to me that everybody around here is kind of anxious about that tank, and if you could exorcise it . . .'

Eloise slowly shook her head. 'Only a priest can exorcise,' she said gently, 'and the only priest who will believe us is too old and too weak for such things.'

'You really believe it's haunted?'

'It depends on what you mean by "haunted", monsieur.'

'Well, as far as I can make out, the dead crew are supposed to be heard talking to each other at night. Is that it?'

'Some say that,' said Jacques.

I glanced at him. 'And what do others say?'

'Others will not talk about it at all.'

Eloise spooned up her soup carefully. 'Nobody knows much about the tanks. But they were not like the usual American tanks. They were different, very different, and Father Anton, our priest, said they were visitations from *l'enfer*, from hell itself.'

Madeleine said, 'Eloise – do we have to talk about it? We don't want to spoil the lunch.'

But Eloise raised her hand. 'It doesn't matter. This

young man wants to know about the tank, then why shouldn't he?'

I said: 'How were they different? It looks like a regular tank to me.'

'Well,' explained Eloise, 'they were painted black all over, although you cannot see that now, because the rust and the weather have taken away the paint. There were thirteen of them. I know, because I counted them as they came along the road from Le Vey. Thirteen, on the thirteenth day of July. But what was most strange, they never opened their turrets. Most American tanks came with their tops open, and the soldiers would throw us candy and cigarettes and nylon stockings. But these tanks came and we never saw who drove them. They were always closed.'

Madeleine had finished her soup and was sitting upright in her chair. She looked very pale, and it was clear that all this talk about the strange tanks disconcerted her. I said, 'Did you talk to any Americans about them? Did they ever tell you what they were?'

Jacques, with his mouth full of garlic bread, said, 'They didn't know, or they wouldn't speak. They just said "special division", and that was all.'

'Only one was left behind,' put in Eloise. 'That was the tank which is still there, down the road. It broke a track and stopped. But the Americans did nothing to take it away. Instead, they came along next day and welded down the turret. Yes, they welded it, and then an English priest came and said words over it, and it was left to rot.'

'You mean the crew was left inside?'

Jacques tore off some more bread. 'Who can say? They wouldn't let anyone near. I have talked many times to the police and to the mayor, and all they say is that the tank is not to be moved. And there it stays.'

Madeleine said, 'And ever since it's been there, the village has been dead and depressed.'

'Because of the voices?'

Madeleine shrugged. 'There have been voices. At least, that's what some people say. But more than anything else, it's the tank itself. It's a terrible reminder of something that most of us now would prefer to forget.'

Eloise said, 'Those tanks could not be stopped. They set fire to German tanks all along the river, and then they set fire to the Germans themselves who tried to escape from them. You could hear the screams all night of men burning. In the morning, the tanks were gone. Who knows where, or how? But they came through in one day and one night, and nothing on earth could have held them back. I know they saved us, *monsieur*, but I still shudder when I think of them.'

'Who's heard these voices? Do they know what they say?'

Eloise said, 'Not many people walk along that road at night any more. But Madame Verrier said she heard whispering and laughter, one night in February; and old Henriques told of voices that boomed and shouted. I myself have carried milk and eggs past that tank, and the milk has soured and the eggs have gone rotten. Gaston from the next farm had a terrier which sniffed around the tank, and the dog developed tremors and shakes. Its hair fell out, and after three days it died. Everybody has one story about the evil that befalls you if you go too near the tank; and so these days nobody does.'

I said, 'Isn't it just superstition? I mean, there's no real evidence.'

'You should ask Father Anton,' said Eloise. 'If you are really foolhardy enough to want to know more, Father Anton will probably tell you. The English priest who said words over the tank stayed at his house for a month, and I know they spoke of the tank often. Father Anton was never happy that it was left by the road, but there was nothing he could do, short of carrying it away on his own back.'

Madeleine said, 'Please let's talk about other things. The war is so depressing.'

'Okay,' I said, lifting my hands in mock surrender. 'But thank you for what you've told me. It's going to make a real good story. Now, I'd love some more of that onion soup.'

Eloise smiled. 'You have a big appetite, monsieur. I remember the American appetites.'

She ladled out more of that scalding brown soup, while Madeleine and her father watched me with friendly caution, and a little bit of suspicion, and maybe the hope that I wasn't really going to bother to do anything unsettling, like talk to Father Anton about what happened on July 13, 1944, on the road from Le Vey.

After lunch of hare casserole, with good red wine and fruit, we sat around the table and smoked Gauloises and Jacques told me stories of his boyhood at Pont D'Ouilly. Madeleine came and sat beside me, and it was plain that she was getting to like me. Eloise retreated to the kitchen, and clattered pans, but returned fifteen minutes later with tiny cups of the richest coffee I'd ever tasted.

At last, at well past three o'clock, I said: 'I've had a marvellous time, but I have to get back to work. I have a whole mess of readings to take before it gets dark.'

'It's been good to talk with you,' said Jacques, standing up and giving a small bow. 'It isn't often we have people to eat with us. I suppose we are too close to the tank, and people don't like to come this way.'

'It's that bad?'

'Well, it isn't comfortable.'

While Madeleine helped to take out the last dishes, and Jacques went to open the farm gate for me, I stood in the kitchen buttoning my coat and watching Eloise's bent back as she washed up over the steamy sink.

I said, 'Au revoir, Eloise.'

She didn't turn round, but she said, 'Au revoir, monsieur.'

I took a step towards the back door, but then I paused, and looked at her again. 'Eloise?' I asked.

'*Oui, monsieur?*'

'What is it really, inside that tank?'

I saw the almost imperceptible stiffening of her back. The mop stopped slapping against the plates, and the knives and forks stopped clattering.

She said, 'I do not know, *monsieur*. Truly.'

'Have a guess.'

She was silent for a moment. Then she said, 'Perhaps it is nothing at all. But perhaps it is something that neither heaven nor earth knows anything about.'

'That only leaves hell.'

Again, she was silent. Then she turned from the sink and looked at me with those pale, wise eyes.

'*Oui, monsieur. Et le roi de l'enfer, c'est le diable.*'

The priest was very old. He must have been almost ninety, and he sat at his dusty leather-topped desk like a sagging sack of soft potatoes. But he had an intelligent, kindly face; and even though he spoke slowly and softly, as his lungs filled and emptied with the laboured aspiration of ancient bellows, he was lucid in his words, and precise. He had fraying white hair and a bony nose you could have hung your hat on, and as he talked he had a habit of steepling his long fingers and lifting his neck so that he could see down into the grey cobbled courtyard that fronted his house.

He said, 'The English cleric's name was the Reverend Taylor,' and he peered out of the window as if expecting the Reverend Taylor to appear around the corner at any moment.

'The Reverend Taylor? There must be five thousand Reverend Taylors in England.'

Father Anton smiled, and did something complicated inside his mouth with his dentures. 'That is probably so.

23

But I am quite certain that there is only one Reverend Woodfall Taylor.'

It was four-thirty now, almost dark, but I had got so caught up in the mystery of this decaying Sherman that I had skipped my cartographic readings for the day, and taken a trip up to the opposite end of the village to talk to Father Anton. He lived in a huge, sombre, forbidding French house in the severest style, with a hall of dark polished wood that you could have landed a 747 on, and staircase after staircase of chilled marble, flanked by gloomy oil paintings of cardinals and Popes and other miserable doyens of the church. Everywhere you looked, there was a mournful face. It was as bad as spending the evening at a Paul Robeson record night in Peoria, Illinois.

Father Anton said, 'When he came here, Mr Taylor was a very enthusiastic young vicar. He was full of the energy of religion. But I don't think he truly understood the importance of what he had to do. I don't think he understood how terrible it was, either. Without being unkind, I think he was the kind of young cleric who is easily seduced into thinking that mysticism is the firework display that celebrates true faith. Mind you, the Americans paid him a great deal of money. It was enough to build himself a new steeple, and a church hall. You can't blame him.'

I coughed. It was wickedly cold in Father Anton's house, and apart from saving on heating he also seemed to have a penchant for penny-pinching on electricity. The room was so shadowy and dark that I could barely make him out, and all I could see distinctly was the shine of the silver crucifix around his neck.

I said, 'What I don't understand is why we needed him. What was he doing for us, anyway?'

'He never clearly explained, monsieur. He was gagged by your oaths of secrecy. Apart from that, I don't think he truly understood himself what it was he was required to do.'

24

'But the tanks – the black tanks—'

The old priest turned towards me, and I could just make out the rheumy gleam of his eye.

'The black tanks were something about which I cannot speak, *monsieur*. I have done all that I can for thirty long years, to have the tank taken away from Pont D'Ouilly but each time I have been told that it is too heavy, and that it is not economical to tow it away. But I think the truth is that they are too frightened to disturb it.'

'Why should they be frightened?'

Father Anton opened his desk drawer and took out a small rosewood and silver snuffbox. He asked, 'You take snuff?'

'No, thanks. But I wouldn't mind a cigarette.'

He passed me the cigarette box, and then snorted two generous pinches of snuff up his cavernous nostrils. I always thought people sneezed after they took snuff, but all Father Anton did was snort like a mule, and relax further into his creaky revolving chair.

I lit my cigarette and said, 'Is there something still *inside* that tank?'

Father Anton thought about this, and then answered. 'Perhaps. I don't know what. The Reverend Taylor would never speak about it, and when they sealed down the turret, nobody from the whole village was allowed within half a kilometre.'

'Did they give any kind of explanation?'

'Yes,' said Father Anton. 'They said there was high explosive inside it, and that there was some danger of a blast. But of course none of us believed it. Why should they need a vicar to sanctify the sealing of a few pounds of TNT?'

'So you believe that tank has something unholy about it?'

'It's not what *I* believe, *monsieur*. It's what your Army obviously believed, and I have yet to meet anyone more sceptical than a soldier. Why should an Army call in a cleric to deal with its weapons? I can only assume that there was something about the tank that was not in accordance with the laws of God.'

I wasn't entirely sure what he meant by that, but the slow and lisping way in which he said it, the way the words came out in that freezing and sepulchral room like dead flowers, that was enough to make me feel chilled and strangely frightened.

I said, 'Do you believe in the voices?'

Father Anton nodded. 'I have heard them myself. Anyone brave enough to go near the tank after dark can hear them.'

'You heard them yourself?'

'Not officially.'

'How about unofficially?'

The old priest wiped at his nose with his handkerchief. 'Unofficially, of course, I *made* it my business. I last visited the tank three or four years ago, and spent several hours there in prayer. It didn't do my rheumatism a great deal of good, but I am sure now that the tank is an instrument of evil works.'

'Did you hear anything distinct? I mean, what kind of voices were they?'

Father Anton chose his next sentence with care. 'They were not, in my opinion, the voices of men.'

I frowned at him. 'I don't understand.'

'*Monsieur*, what can I tell you? They were not the voices of human spirits or of human ghosts.'

I didn't know what to say after that. We sat in silence for a few minutes, and outside the day grew grainier and darker, tinged with that corroded green that always threatened snow. Father Anton seemed to be deeply buried in thought, but after a time he raised his head and said, 'Is that all, *monsieur*? I have studies to continue.'

'Well, I guess so. The whole thing seems like a real mystery.'

'The ways of war are always a mystery, *monsieur*. I

have heard many stories of strange and inexplicable events on battlefields, or in the concentration camps. Sometimes, holy miracles occur, visitations by saints. I have a parishioner who fought at the Somme, and he swears he was visited every night by Saint Thérèse. Then again, monsters and agents of hell have been seen, seeking out the cowardly and the vicious. It was said that Heinrich Reutemann, the SS commandant, kept at Dachau a dog that was possessed by the devil.'

'And this tank?'

The pale withered hands formed their reverent steeple. 'Who knows, *monsieur*? It is beyond my comprehension.'

I thanked him, and got up to leave. His room was like a dark musty cave. I said, 'Do you think it's dangerous?'

He didn't turn his head. 'The manifestations of evil are always dangerous, my friend. But the greatest protection from evil is a steadfast belief in Our Lord.'

I stood by the door for a moment, straining my eyes to see him through the gloom. 'Yes,' I said and then went down the cold and silent marble staircases to the front door, and out into the wintry street.

I didn't drive straight there, partly because I was waiting for the late afternoon to grow darker, and partly because the whole thing made me unusually nervous. By seven o'clock, though, after a roundabout tour through the muddy shuttered villages of the *Route Scenique* of the Orne Valley; past farmyards and peeling houses and roadside shrines where pale effigies of Christ crucified leaned mournfully into the evening frost; past inkblot trees and cold whispering fields; I arrived at the Passerelle's farm, and drove into the yard.

The evening was bitter and still when I climbed out of the Citroën and walked across to the farmhouse door. A dog was yapping at some other farm, way across the valley; but here everything was quiet. I knocked on the door and waited.

Madeleine came to the door. She was wearing a blue check cowboy shirt and jeans, and she looked as if she'd just finished changing a wheel on a tractor.

'Dan,' she said, but she didn't sound surprised. 'You left something here?'

'No, no. I came back for you.'

'For me? *Je ne comprends pas.*'

I said, 'Can I come in? It's like the North Pole out here. I only wanted to ask you something.'

'Of course,' she told me, and opened the door wider.

The kitchen was warm and empty. I sat down at the broad pine table, scarred from a hundred years of knives and hot saucepans, and she went across to the corner cupboard and poured me a small glass of brandy. Then she sat down opposite, and said, 'Are you still thinking about the tank?'

'I went to see Father Anton.'

She smiled faintly. 'I thought you would.'

'Am I that easy to read?'

'I don't think so,' she smiled. 'But you seem like the kind of man who doesn't like to leave puzzles unsolved. You make maps, so your whole life is spent unravelling mysteries. And this one, of course, is a very special enigma indeed.'

I sipped my brandy. 'Father Anton says he's heard the voices himself.'

She stared down at the table. Her finger traced the pattern of a flower that had been scorched into the wood by a hot fish-kettle. She commented, 'Father Anton is very old.'

'You mean he's senile?'

'I don't know. But his sermons ramble these days. Perhaps he could have imagined these things.'

'Maybe he could. But I'd still like to find out for myself.'

She glanced up. 'You want to hear them for yourself?'

'Certainly. I'd like to make a tape-recording, too. Has anyone ever thought of doing that?'

'Dan – not many people have ever gone to listen to the voices on purpose.'

'No, I know that. But that's what I want to do tonight. And I was hoping you'd come along with me.'

She didn't answer straight away, but stared across the kitchen as if she was thinking of something quite different. Her hair was tied back in a knot, which didn't suit her too much, but then I guess a girl doesn't worry too much about the charisma of her coiffure when she's mucking out cows. Almost unconsciously, she crossed herself, and then she looked back at me. 'You really want to go?'

'Well, sure. There has to be some kind of explanation.'

'Americans always need explanations?'

I finished my brandy, and shrugged. 'I guess it's a national characteristic. In any case, I was born and bred in Mississippi.'

Madeleine bit her lip. She said, 'Supposing I asked you not to go?'

'Well, you can ask me. But I'd have to say that I'm going anyway. Listen, Madeleine, there's a fascinating story in this. There's some kind of weird thing going on in that old tank and I want to know what it is.'

'*C'est malin*,' she said. 'It is wicked.'

I reached across the old table and laid my hand over hers. 'That's what everybody says, but so far I haven't seen anything that proves it. All I want to do is find out what the voices are saying, if there are any voices, and then we can go from there. I mean, I can't say that I'm not scared. I think it's very scarey. But a whole lot of scarey things turn out to be real interesting once you take the trouble to check them out.'

'Dan, please. It's more than simply scarey.'

'How can you say that unless you investigate it?' I asked her. 'I don't knock superstition, but here's a superstition we can actually test for ourselves.'

She took back her hand, and crossed her arms across her breasts as if to protect herself from the consequences of what she was about to say. 'Dan,' she whispered. 'The tank killed my mother.'

I raised an eyebrow. 'The tank did *what*?'

'It killed my mother. Well, it was responsible. Father isn't sure, but Eloise knows it, and I know it. I have never told anyone else, but then nobody else has shown such interest in the tank as you. I have to warn you, Dan. Please.'

'How could the tank have killed your mother? It doesn't move, does it? The guns don't fire?'

She turned her elegant Norman profile away from me, and spoke in a steady, modulated whisper. 'It was last year, late in summer. Five of our herd died from disease. Mother said it was the tank that had done it. She always blamed the tank for everything that went wrong. If it rained and our hay rotted she would blame the tank. Even if one of her cakes wouldn't rise. But last year she said she was going to fix the tank for ever. Eloise tried to persuade her to leave it alone, but she wouldn't listen. She went down the road with holy water, sprinkled it across the tank, and spoke the dismissal of demons.'

'The dismissal of demons? What the hell's that?'

Madeleine touched her forehead. 'The words of exorcism. Mother always believed in devils and demons, and she has the words in one of her holy books.'

'Well, what happened?'

Madeleine slowly shook her head. 'She was only a simple woman. She was kind and she was loving and she believed deeply in God and the Virgin Mary. Yet her religion couldn't save her. Thirteen days after she sprinkled the holy water on the tank, she started to cough blood, and she died in hospital in Caen after a week. The doctors said she had some form of tuberculosis, but they could never say precisely what form it was, or why she had died so quickly.'

I felt embarrassed now, as well as afraid. 'I'm sorry.'
Madeleine looked up, and there was that wry smile again.
'You have no need to be. But you can see why I'd rather
you didn't go near the tank.'

I thought for a while. It would be easy enough to forget
the tank altogether, or simply add a footnote to Roger's
book that the last remaining Sherman tank of a secret
special division was still decaying in the Norman countryside, and that local yokels believed it was possessed by
evil. But how can you dismiss something like that as a
footnote? I didn't particularly believe in demons and
devils, but here was a whole French village that was
scared half to death, and a girl seriously claiming that
malevolent spirits had deliberately killed her mother.

I pushed back my chair and stood up. 'I'm sorry,' I
said, 'but I'm still going to take a look. If it's true, what
you said about your mother, then we've got the biggest
supernatural story here since Uri Geller.'

'Uri Geller?' she frowned.

I coughed. 'He, er, bends spoons.'

She sat at the table looking a little sad. Then she said:
'Well, if you *insist* on going, I'll have to come with you.
I don't want you to go on your own.'

'Madeleine, if it's really that dangerous—'

'I'll come with you, Dan,' she repeated firmly, and all
I could do was lift my hands in acceptance. I was glad of
the company anyway.

While I turned the 2CV around in the yard, Madeleine
went to get her overcoat. The clouds were beginning to
clear a little, and there was a washed-out moon up above
us like a white-faced boy peering through a dirty window.
Madeleine crossed the yard, climbed into the car, and we
bounced off across the ruts and the puddles until we
reached the road. Just before we turned, Madeleine
reached over and squeezed my hand. 'I would like to say,
"good luck," ' she whispered.

'Thanks,' I told her. 'And the same to you.'

31

It took us two or three minutes to reach the hedge where the tank lay entangled. As soon as I saw the shape of it, I pulled the Citroën over on to the opposite verge, and killed the motor. I lifted my battery-operated tape recorder out of the back seat, and opened the car door.

Madeleine said: 'I'll wait here. Just for the moment, anyway. Call me if you need me.'

'Okay.'

Down here by the river, under the brow of the cliffs, the pallid moonlight barely reached. I crossed the road and stepped right up to the tank, touching its cold corroded mudguard. It seemed so dead and desolate and rusted that, now I saw it again for real, it was hard to believe that there was anything supernatural about it. It was nothing more than the abandoned junk of war.

There was a rustling sound in the grass around the tracks, and I froze. But then a rabbit jumped out from underneath the tank, and scampered off into the hedge. It was kind of late in the year for rabbits, but I guess they could have made their nest inside the tank itself, or underneath it somewhere. Maybe that was the real answer to Pont D'Ouilly's haunted relic – squeaking and rustling wildlife.

I walked round the tank as far as I could, but its right side was completely tangled in brambles, and it would have taken a sharp machete and three native bearers to go round and take a good look at that. I satisfied myself with the left side and the back. I was interested to see that even the air vents for the engine had been welded up tight, and so had the grille over the driver's porthole.

Slinging my tape recorder over my shoulder, I heaved myself up on to the tank's mudguard. I made a lot of noise doing it, but I didn't suppose that thirty-year-old ghosts really objected that much to being disturbed in the night. Carefully, I walked across the blackened hull, and my footsteps sounded booming and metallic. I reached the turret, and hammered on it with my fist. It sounded very empty in there. I hoped it was.

As Jacques Passerelle had said, the tank's hatch was welded shut. It was a hasty-looking weld, but whoever had done it had known his job. As I strained forward to look at it more closely, however, I saw that the hatch was sealed by other means as well – means that, in their own way, were just as powerful.

Riveted over the top of the tank was a crucifix. It looked as if it had been taken from the altar of a church and crudely fastened to the turret in such a way that nobody could ever remove it. Looking even nearer, I saw that there was some kind of holy adjuration, too, engraved in the rough metal. Most of the words were corroded beyond legibility, but I could distinctly make out the phrase *'Thou art commanded to go out.'*

Up there on the hull of that silent ruined tank, in the dead of winter in Normandy, I felt frightened of the unknown for the first time in my life. I mean, really frightened. Even though I didn't want it to, my scalp kept chilling and prickling, and I found I was licking my lips again and again like a man in an icy desert. I could see the Citroën across the road, but the moon was reflecting from the flat windshield, so I couldn't make out Madeleine at all. For all I knew, she might have vanished. For all I knew, the whole of the rest of the world might have vanished. I coughed in the bitter cold.

I walked along to the front of the tank, pushing aside wild brambles and leafless creeper. There wasn't much to see there, so I walked back again to the turret, to see if I could distinguish more of the words.

It was then, as my fingers touched the top of the turret, that I heard someone laughing. I stayed stock still, holding my breath. The laughter stopped. I lifted my head, and tried to work out where the sound might have come from. It had been a short, ironic laugh, but with a peculiarly metallic quality, as if someone had been laughing over a microphone.

I said: 'Who's there?' but there was silence. The night was so quiet that I could still hear that distant dog barking. I laid my tape-recorder on top of the turret and clicked it on.

For several minutes, there was nothing but the hiss of the tape coursing past the recording head, and that damned dog. But then I heard a whispering sound, as if someone was talking to himself under his breath. It was close, and yet it seemed far away at the same time. *It was coming from the turret.*

Shaking and sweating, I knelt down beside the turret and tapped on it, twice. I sounded as choked up as a grade school kid after his first dry martini. I said: 'Who's there? Is there anybody inside there?'

There was a pause, and then I heard a whispery voice say: '*You can help me, you know.*'

It was a strange voice, which seemed to come from everywhere at once. It seemed to have a smile in it as well; the kind of voice that someone has when they're secretly grinning. It could have been a man or a woman or even a child, but I wasn't sure.

I said, 'Are you in there? Are you inside the tank?'

The voice whispered, '*You sound like a good man. A good man and true.*'

Almost screaming, I said: 'What are you doing in there? How did you get in?'

The voice didn't answer my question. It simply said, '*You can help me, you know. You can open this prison. You can take me to join my brethren. You sound like a good man and true.*'

'Listen!' I shouted. 'If you're really inside there, tap on the turret! Let me hear that you're in there!'

The voice laughed. '*I can do better than that. Believe me, I can do far better than that.*'

'I don't understand.'

34

The voice laughed softly. *'Do you feel sick?'* it asked me. *'Do you feel as if you're seized with cramps and pain?'*

I frowned. I did, as a matter of fact, feel nauseous. There was something in my stomach that was turning over and over; something foul and indigestible. I thought for a moment that it was something I ate for lunch; but then I was seized by a stomach spasm that made me realise I was going to be violently ill. It all happened in an instant. The next thing I knew, my gut was racked by the most terrible heaving, and my mouth had to stretch open wide as a torrent of revolting slush gushed out of me and splattered the hull of the tank. The vomiting went on and on until I was clutching my stomach and weeping from the sheer exhaustion of it.

Only then did I look at what had made me puke. Out of my stomach, out of my actual mouth, had poured thousands of pale twitching maggots, in a tide of bile. They squirmed and writhed all over the top of the tank, pink and half-transparent, and all I could do was clamber desperately off that hideous ruined Sherman and drop to the frozen grass, panting with pain and revulsion, and scared out of my mind.

Behind me, the voice whispered: *'You can help me, you know. You sound like a good man and true.'*

CHAPTER TWO

Father Anton carefully poured me a glass of Malmsey and brought it across his study at arm's length, as if it was a medical specimen. I took it unsteadily, and said, 'Thank you, father. That's very kind.'

He waved his hand as if to say not at all, not at all; and then sat his baggy ancient body in an armchair opposite, and opened up his snuff box.

'So you went to hear the voices,' he said, taking a pinch of ground tobacco.

I nodded.

'You look, forgive me for saying so, as if they alarmed you.'

'Not them. It.'

Father Anton snorted, sneezed, and blew his nose like the Trump of Doom. Then he said: 'Demons can be either. One demon can be *them*, or *it*, or whatever they please. A demon is a host of evils.'

I reached across to the small cherrywood sidetable and picked up my tape-recorder. 'Whatever it is, father, it's here, on tape, and it's an *it*. One infernal *it*.'

'You recorded it? You mean, you did actually hear it?'

The old priest's expression, which had been one of patient but not altogether unkind indulgence, subtly darkened and changed. He knew the voice or voices were real, because he had been to the tank himself and heard them. But for me to come along and tell him that I'd heard them, too – a perfect stranger without any kind of religious knowledge at all – well, that obviously disturbed him. Priests, I guess, are used to demons. They work, after all, in the spiritual front line, and they expect to be tempted and harassed by demonic manifes-

36

tations. But when those manifestations are so evil and so powerful that they make themselves felt in the world of ordinary men, when the bad vibes are picked up by farmers and cartographers, then I reckon that most priests get to panic.

'I didn't come around last night because I was too sick,' I told Father Anton. 'I wanted to, but I couldn't.'

'The tank brought on your sickness? Is that it?'

I nodded, and my throat still tightened at the thought of what had poured out of my mouth.

'Whatever it is inside that tank, it made me vomit worms and bile. It took me half a dozen whiskys and a handful of paracetamol to get me over it.'

Father Anton touched the ecclesiastical ring on his finger. 'You were alone?' he asked me quietly.

'I went with Madeleine Passerelle. The daughter of Jacques Passerelle.'

Father Anton said gravely: 'Yes. I know that the Passerelles have been troubled by the tank for a long time.'

'Unfortunately, Madeleine didn't hear the voice first-hand. She stayed in the car because it was cold. But she's heard the recording, and she saw for herself how sick I was. The Passerelles let me stay the night at the farm.'

Father Anton indicated the tape-recorder. 'You're going to play it for me?'

'If you want to listen.'

Father Anton regarded me with a soft, almost sad look on his face. 'It has been a long time, *monsieur*, since anyone has come to me for help and guidance as you have. In my day, I was an exorcist and something of a specialist in demons and fallen angels. I will do every-thing I can to assist you. If what you have heard is a true demon, then we are facing great danger, because it is evidently powerful and vicious; but beguiling as well.'

He looked towards the empty fireplace. Outside, it

was snowing again, but Father Anton obviously believed it was more spiritual to sit in the freezing cold than to light a fire. I must say that I personally preferred to toast my feet and worry about the spirituality of it later.

Father Anton began. 'One thing I learned as an exorcist was that it is essential correctly to identify the demon with whom you are dealing. Some demons are easy to dispose of. You can say "The Father, the Son and the Holy Ghost, *boo!*" and they vanish back to hell. But others are more difficult. Adramelech, for instance, who is mentioned in the *Pseudomonarchia Daemonum*, which I have on the shelves right here. Or Belial. Then there is Beelzebub, Satan's successor, who was always notoriously difficult to banish. I never faced him myself, and it is probably best for me that I didn't. But I have an interesting account of how he possessed a nun at the Ursuline Convent at Aix-le-Provence in the seventeenth century, and how it took seven weeks of determined exorcism to dismiss him back to the netherworld.'

'Father Anton,' I said, as kindly as I could. 'This is all kind of medieval. I mean, what I'm trying to say is, we have something here that's evil, but it's modern.'

Father Anton smiled sadly. 'Evil is never modern, *monsieur*. It is only persistent.'

'But what happens if we have an ancient demon right here?'

'Well,' said the priest. 'Let us first hear the tape. Then perhaps we can judge who or what this voice might be. Perhaps it is Beelzebub himself, come to make a match of it.'

I wound back the cassette, pushed the 'play' button, and laid the tape-recorder on the table. There was a crackling sound; then the clank of metal as the tape-recorder was set down on the turret of the tank; then a short silence, interspersed with the barking of that distant dog. Father Anton leaned forward so that he could hear better, and cupped his hand around one ear.

38

'You realise that what you have here is very rare,' he told me. 'I have seen daguerrotypes and photographs of manifestations before, but never tape-recordings.'

The tape fizzed and whispered, and then that chilling, whispery voice said: *'You can help me, you know.'*

Father Anton stiffened, and stared across at me in undisguised shock.

The voice said: *'You sound like a good man. A good man and true. You can open this prison. You can take me to join my brethren. You sound like a good man and true.'*

Father Anton was about to say something, but I put my finger against my lips, warning him that there was more.

The voice went on: *'You can help me, you know. You and that priest. Look at him! Doesn't that priest have something to hide? Doesn't that priest have some secret lust, concealed under that holy cassock?'*

I stared at the tape-recorder in amazement. 'It didn't say that. There was no way it ever said that.'

Father Anton was white. He asked, in a trembling tone: 'What does this mean? What is it saying?'

'Father, father,' whispered the tape-recorder. *'Surely you recall the warm summer of 1928. So long ago, father, but so vivid. The day you took young Mathilde on the river, in your boat. Surely you remember that.'*

Father Anton rose jerkily to his feet, like a Victorian clockwork toy. His snuff tipped all over the rug. He stared at the tape-recorder as if it was the devil himself. His chest heaved with the effort of breathing, and he could scarcely speak.

'That day was innocent!' he breathed. 'Innocence itself! How dare you! How dare you suggest it was anything else! You! Demon! *Cochon! Vos mains sont sales avec le sang des innocents!'*

I reached out and seized Father Anton's sleeve. He tried to brush me away, but I gripped him more firmly, and said: 'Father, it's only a trick. For Christ's sake.'

Father Anton looked at me with watering eyes. 'A trick? I don't understand.'

'Father, it has to be. It's only a tape-recording. It's just some kind of trick.'

He looked nervously down at the cassette recorder, its tape still silently spinning. 'It can't be a trick,' he said huskily. 'How can a tape-recorder answer one back? It's not possible.'

'You heard it yourself,' I told him. 'It must be.'

I was as puzzled and scared as he was, but I didn't want to show it. I had the feeling that the moment I started giving in to all this weirdness, the moment I started believing it for real, I was going to get tangled up in something strange and uncontrollable. It was like standing at the entrance of a hall of mirrors, trying to resist the temptation to walk inside and find out what those distorted figures in the darkness were.

I pressed the tape-recorder's 'stop' button. The gloomy room was silent.

'Sit down, Father Anton,' I asked him. 'Now, let's play that tape back again, and we'll see how much of a trick it is.'

The old priest said: 'It's Satan's work. I have no doubt. It's the work of the devil himself.'

I gently helped him back to his armchair, and picked up his snuffbox for him. He sat there pale-faced and tense as I rewound the tape back to the beginning, and then pushed the 'play' button once again.

We waited tensely as the tape began to crackle and hiss. We heard it laid down on the turret again, and the dog barking. Then that voice began once more, and it seemed colder and even more evil than ever. It sounded as if it came from the throat of a hoarse hermaphrodite, some lewd creature who delighted in pain and pleasure and unspeakable acts.

'*You can help me, you know,*' it repeated. '*You sound like a good man. A good man and true. You can open this prison. You can take me to join my brethren. You sound like a good man and true.'*

Father Anton was sitting rigid in his seat, his knuckles spotted with white where he was clutching the frayed upholstery.

The voice said: *'Father Anton can take away the cross that binds me down, and cast away the spell. You can do that, can't you, Father Anton? You'd do anything for an old friend, and I'm an old friend of yours. You can take me to join my brethren across the waters, can't you? Beelzebub, Lucifer, Madilon, Solymo, Saroy, Theu, Ameclo, Sagrael, Praredun—'*

'Stop it!' shouted Father Anton. '*Stop it!*'

With unbelievable agility for a man as old as ninety, he reached out for the tape-recorder, held it in both hands, and smashed it against the steel fireguard around the grate. Then he sat back, his eyes staring and wild, snapping the broken pieces of plastic in his hands. He dragged out the thin brown tape, and crumpled it up into a confused tangle of knots and twists.

I sat watching all this in total amazement. First, I seemed to have a tape-recorder that said whatever it felt like. Now, I had a priest who broke up other people's property. I said: 'What's wrong? Why the hell did you do that?'

The priest took a deep breath. 'It was the conjuration,' he said. 'The words that can summon Beelzebub, the Lord of the Flies. There were only three more words to be said, and that demon could have been with us.'

'You're not serious.'

Father Anton held up the smashed fragments of Sony tape-recorder. 'Do you think I would break your machine for nothing? Those words can bring out of the under-world the most terrible of devils. I will buy you another, never fear.'

'Father Anton, it's not the tape-recorder I'm worried about. What concerns me is what goes *on* here. If there's

41

a creature inside that tank, can't we do something about it? Exorcise it? Burn it out. Blow it up?'

Father Anton shook the smashed-up tape-recorder out of the skirts of his cassock and into the waste-paper basket. 'Exorcisms, my friend, are woefully misunderstood. They are hardly ever performed these days, and only in very serious cases of possession. As for burning the tank, or blowing it up, that would do no good. The demon would still haunt Pont D'Ouilly, although he would be more like a fierce dog on a long leash instead of a fierce dog inside a locked kennel. He cannot finally get away until the holy cross is lifted from the turret, and the words of dismissal erased.'

I opened the cigarette box on the table and took out a Gauloise. I lit it up and took a long drag. I was getting used to this pungent French tobacco, and if it didn't have as much tar in it as a three-mile stretch of the Allegheny Valley Expressway, I think I could have smoked it all the time. I said: 'Whatever it is, it obviously wants out.'

'Of course,' agreed Father Anton. 'And it appears to have a strong desire to rejoin its fellows. Its brethren. Perhaps it means that there were demons or devils possessing the other twelve tanks.'

'You mean *all* of them were possessed?'

'It seems likely. Why were they all painted black? Why were they all sealed down? You have said yourself that the Germans felt as if the devil was on their heels. I don't know whether you have yet had time to read your friend's history of the war, but the Orne Valley was taken at record speed – far more quickly than any of the surrounding countryside. Caen was shelled flat. But here – the tanks came through at top speed, and nobody short of Our Lord Himself could have stopped them.'

I blew out smoke. 'What you're suggesting is that this special division was made up of demons? I don't see

42

now that's possible. Demons are – well, dammit, they're *demons*. They're medieval. They're imaginary. They 1on't fight wars.

'On the contrary,' said Father Anton. 'That's precisely what they *do* do.'

'But how come nobody ever heard of this special division before? How come the Army even allowed it to happen? That's supposing it *did* happen, and all this isn't some kind of hoax.'

'Much that happened in the war is still secret. And, anyway, what were thirteen tanks among hundreds? Perhaps your government decided on a little experiment with black magic.'

'Father Anton, this doesn't seem real. If there's one thing that the Pentagon is not involved in, it's black magic!'

Father Anton went across to the tall window and looked down on his courtyard. Although it was mid-morning, it was as dark as late afternoon, and a few flakes of snow were tumbling idly across the village. The church clock struck eleven.

'What people forget,' he said, 'was that the war was mystic and magical in the extreme. Hitler set great store by magic, and made a particular point of confiscating the Spear of Longinus, the very spear that pierced Christ's side on the cross, from the Hofburg Museum in Vienna, because he believed that whoever possessed it could control the destiny of the world. On the side of the Allies, many experiments were made in sending messages by telepathy, and in levitation, and there was a Dutch priest who claimed he could invoke the wrath of the ten divine Sephiroth to bring down German planes with bolts of fire.'

I listened to this patiently, but I felt weary and sick. I said: 'Father, this is all very well, but what are we going to do about the tank?'

Father Anton turned towards me. 'There is nothing

43

we can do, *monsieur*. Wiser men than us have sealed that evil entity away, and it would be foolish to disturb it. If the authorities will not remove the tank, then it will have to stay there.'

'And the Passerelles will have to suffer the consequences for the rest of their lives? You know that Madeleine believes the tank killed her mother?'

The old priest nodded. 'She didn't tell me, but I guessèd as much. I wish there was more that I could do. All I can say is that I am very thankful we were left with only one tank, instead of many.'

I took a last hot drag of my Gauloise, and stubbed it out. 'Well, I think you're being too cautious,' I told him. 'Maybe it's time that someone gave the Passerelles a break, and maybe it's time the Pentagon got their dirty washing back.'

Father Anton looked at me and crossed himself. 'I can only warn you, *monsieur*, that to open the tank would be more than foolish. It would be tantamount to suicide.'

I stood up, and brushed ash off my pants. 'The tape-recorder was 189 francs,' I said. 'But I'd be more than happy with half of that. It *was* kind of a joint venture, after all.'

Father Anton slowly shook his head. 'Perhaps one day I will understand Americans,' he said. 'And perhaps one day they will understand themselves.'

I met Madeleine for a glass of wine at lunchtime, in a small smokey café unappealingly called the Bar Touristique. A grossly fat woman in a floral housecoat served behind the bar, and occasionally forayed out to slap at the red formica-topped tables with a wet rag, as if they were disobedient dogs who kept playing up. The house wine was robust enough to clean your family silver with, but I'd managed to find a stale pack of Luckies in the local tobacconist's, so my palate wasn't complaining quite so vigorously as it had this morning.

44

Madeleine came in through the plastic-strip curtain looking very pale and waif-like, and when she saw me she came across the bar and put her arms tight around my neck.

'Dan, you're all right.'

'Of course I'm all right. I've only been talking to Father Anton.'

I took her speckled tweed coat and hung it up next to a sign that warned *Defense de Cracher*. She was wearing a plain turquoise-blue dress that was probably very fashionable in Pont D'Ouilly, but in Paris was about eight years out of style. Still, she looked good; and it was a lift to meet someone who really cared about my welfare. Ten-ton Tessie behind the bar brought us our wine, and we clinked glasses like one-time lovers meeting in a seedy bar at the back of Grand Central Station.

'Did you play Father Anton the tape?'

'Well, kind of.'

She touched my hand. 'There's something you don't want to tell me?'

'I don't know. I guess we're at a crossroads right now. We can either open the tank up, and find out what's in there, or we can forget it for ever, just like everyone else has.'

She reached up and stroked my cheek. Her pale eyes were full of concern and affection. If I hadn't been feeling so goddamned sick last night, lying doubled-up in the Passerelle's draughty spare bedroom, I think I might have tiptoed along the corridor and tapped on Madeleine's door, but I can tell you from first-hand experience that making love is the last thing you feel like after puking a mouthful of maggots; and I guess that even those who love you dearly find it kind of hard to give you a wholehearted kiss.

She sipped her wine. 'How can we leave it there?' she asked me. 'How can we just leave it there?'

'I don't know. But the mayor and the civic authorities

45

and even Father Anton himself seem to have managed to leave it there for thirty years.'

Madeleine said: 'You must think that I have a bee in my bonnet.'

'Where did they teach you to say that? The school of colloquial English?'

She looked up, and she wasn't smiling. 'The war was over years and years ago. Didn't we lose enough? Enough fathers and brothers and friends? They still sell postcards of Churchill and Eisenhower at the seaside resorts, and that makes me angry. They saved us, yes, but there is nothing glorious to celebrate. To fight wars is not glorious, not for anyone. It is better to forget. But, of course, they have left us their tank, and we can never forget.'

I sat back in my cheap varnished chair. 'So you want to open it up?'

Her eyes were cold. 'The thing itself said that it wanted to join its brethren. What can it want with us? If we let it out, it will go to meet its friends, and that will be the end of it.'

'Father Anton said that opening the tank would be as good as committing suicide.'

'Father Anton is old. And anyway, he believes that demons and devils have power over everything. He told me that once, in catechism class. "Madeleine," he said, "if it weren't for Jesus Christ, the whole world would be overrun with demons." '

I coughed. 'Supposing we open it up and there is a demon?'

She leaned forward intensely. 'There must be *something*, Dan. Otherwise we wouldn't have heard that voice. But demons don't have horns and forks. There's probably nothing inside there at all that the human eye can see.'

'Supposing there is?'

'That's what we have to find out.'

46

I drank some more wine, and I could almost feel it put hairs on my chest as I sat there. I said: 'What do they put in this stuff? Rust remover?'

Madeleine answered: 'Ssh. Madame Saurice used to entertain an American sergeant in the war, and she knows English well. All the slang English, like shucks.'

'*Shucks*? You sure it wasn't the war of 1812?'

Madeleine said, 'I never wanted to open the tank before, Dan. I never met anyone who gave me the strength to do it. My father wouldn't have touched it; nor would Eloise. But Eloise will tell us how to ward off demons and evil spirits while we do it, and I'm sure Father Anton will give you help if you ask him.'

I lit another cigarette. 'I don't see why it's so important to you. If you dislike the tank that much, why don't you move away? There isn't anything to keep you in Pont D'Ouilly, after all.'

'Dan, it's important because it lies on my father's farm, and my father's farm has always been home. Even if I go away for ever, that farm will still be the place where I was brought up, and that tank will still be there.'

She drank a little wine, and looked at me intently. 'And, anyway,' she said, 'I have dreamed about that tank ever since I was a little girl. That tank has given me terrible dreams.'

'Dreams? What kind of dreams?'

She lowered her eyes. 'They were cruel dreams. Nightmares. But they were exciting as well.'

'Sexually exciting?'

'Sometimes. I dreamed of being forced to have sex with bristly beasts and strange creatures. But sometimes the dreams were different, and I imagined that I was being mutilated or killed. That was frightening, but it was exciting, too. Pieces were being sliced off me, and there was lots of blood.'

I reached across the table and held her thin wrist.

47

'Madeleine . . . you know this tank isn't a joke. What's in there, whatever it is, is something really malign.'

She nodded. 'I have always known it. But I have also known, all my life, that one day I would have to face up to it. Of course, I tried to evade my responsibility. I tried to persuade you not to go down there to make your recording. But I am led to the conclusion that the time has probably come.'

'Well,' I said, 'it looks as though we've talked ourselves into it.'

She gave a fleeting, humourless smile.

Later that afternoon, I telephoned Father Anton and told him what we were planning to do. He was silent for a long time on the other end of the line, and then he said: 'I cannot persuade you otherwise?'

'Madeleine's set on it, and I guess I am, too.'

'You're not doing this out of a mistaken sense of affection for Madeleine? Because it can only do her harm, you know. You must realise that.'

I looked across the polished floor of Pont D'Ouilly's post office, marked with muddy footprints where the local farmers had come in to draw their savings or to post their letters. There was a tattered poster on the wall beside me warning of the dangers of rabies. Outside, a thin wet snow was falling, and the sky was unremittingly grey.

'It has to be done sometime, Father Anton. One day that tank's going to corrode right through, and that demon's going to get out anyway, and maybe someone completely unsuspecting is going to be passing by. At least *we* have some idea of what we're in for.'

Father Anton was silent for even longer. Then he said hoarsely: 'I'll have to come with you, you know. I'll have to be there. What time are you planning to do it?'

I glanced up at the post office clock. 'About three. Before it gets too dark.'

'Very well. Can you collect me in your car?'

48

'You bet. And thank you.'

Father Anton sounded solemn. 'Don't thank me, my friend. I am only coming because I feel it is my duty to protect you from whatever lies inside that tank. I would far rather that you left it alone.'

'I know that, father. But I don't think we can.'

He was waiting for me at the front door of his house, dressed in his wide black hat and black button-up boots, his cape as severe and dark as a raven. His housekeeper stood behind him and frowned at me disapprovingly, as if I was particularly selfish to take an old man out on an afternoon so cold and bleak; probably forgetting that it was colder inside his house than it was out. I helped him to climb into the front passenger seat, and smiled at the housekeeper as I walked around the car, but all she did was scowl at me from under her grubby lace cap, and slam the door.

As we drove off across the slushy grey cobbles of the priest's front courtyard, Father Anton said: 'Antoinette is what you probably call a fusspot. She believes she has divine instructions to make me wear my woollen underwear.'

'Well, I'm sure God cares about your underwear as much as He cares about anything else,' I told him, turning on the windshield wipers.

'My friend,' replied Father Anton, regarding me solemnly with his watery eyes, 'God will take care of the spirit and leave the underwear to look after itself.'

It took us about ten minutes to drive the back way around the village to the Passerelle's farm. The trees all around us were bare, and clotted with rooks' nests; and the fields were already hazy and white with snow. I beeped the Citroën's horn as we circled around the farmyard, and Madeleine came out of the door in a camel-hair duffel-coat, carrying an electric torch and an oily canvas bag full of tools.

I climbed out and helped her stow the kit away in the back of the car. She said: 'I got everything. The crowbars, the hammers. Everything you told me.'

'That's good. What did your father say?'

'He isn't so happy. But he says if we must do it, then we must. He's like everyone else. They would like to see the tank opened, but they are too frightened to do it themselves.'

I glanced at Father Anton, sitting patiently in his seat. 'I think that's how the good father feels about it. He's been dying to tackle this demon for years. It's a priest's job, after all. It just took a little coaxing.'

As I opened the door to let Madeleine into the back of the car, I heard Eloise calling from the kitchen. She came out into the dull afternoon, holding her black skirts up above the mud, and she was waving something in her hand.

'*Monsieur*! You must take this!'

She came nearer, and saw Father Anton sitting in the car, and nodded her head respectfully. 'Good day, father.'

Father Anton raised a hand in courteous greeting.

Eloise came up close to me and whispered: '*Monsieur*, you must take this. Father Anton may not approve, so don't let him see it. But it will help you against the creatures from hell.'

Into my hand, she pressed the same ring of hair that had been tied around the model cathedral in Jacques Passerelle's parlour. I held it up, and said, 'What is it? I don't understand.'

Eloise glanced at Father Anton apprehensively, but the old priest wasn't looking our way. 'It is the hair of a firstborn child who was sacrificed to Moloch centuries ago, when devils plagued the people of Rouen. It will show the monsters that you have already paid your respects to them.'

I said, 'I really don't think—'

Eloise clutched my hands in her own bony fingers. 'It doesn't matter what you think, *monsieur*. Just take it.'

I slipped the ring of hair into my coat pocket, and climbed into the car without saying anything else. Eloise watched me through the snow-streaked window as I started up the motor, and turned the car around. She was still standing on her own in the wintry farmyard as we drove out of the gates and splashed our way through the melting slush en route to Pont D'Ouilly itself, and the tank.

Twisted into the hedgerow, the tank was lightly dusted with snow, and it looked more abandoned than ever. But we all knew what was waiting inside it, and as we got out of the Citroën and collected together the torch and the tools, none of us could keep our eyes off it.

Father Anton walked across the road, and took a large silver crucifix from inside his coat. In his other hand, he held a Bible, and he began to say prayers in Latin and French as he stood in the sifting snowflakes, his wide hat already white, with the low cold wind blowing the tails of his cape.

He then recited the dismissal of demons, holding the crucifix aloft as he did so, and making endless invisible crosses in the air.

'I adjure thee, O vile spirit, to go out. God the Father, in His name, leave my presence. God the Son, in His name, make thy departure. God the Holy Ghost, in His name, quit this place. Tremble and flee, O impious one, for it is God who commands thee, for it is I who command thee. Yield to me, to my desire by Jesus of Nazareth who gave His soul. To my desire by sacred Virgin Mary who gave Her womb, by the blessed Angels from whom thou fell. I demand thee be on thy way. Adieu O spirit, Amen.'

We waited for a while, shivering in the cold, while

Father Anton stood with his head bowed. Then he turned to us, and said, 'You may begin.'

Hefting the canvas bag of tools, I climbed up on to the tank's hull. I reached back and helped Madeleine to scramble after me. Father Anton waited where he was, with the crucifix raised in one hand, and the Bible pressed to his breast.

I stepped carefully across to the turret. The maggots that I'd vomited yesterday had completely disappeared, as if they'd been nothing more than a rancid illusion. I knelt down and opened the canvas bag, and took out a long steel chisel and a mallet. Madeleine, kneeling beside me, said, 'We can still turn back.'

I looked at her for a moment, and then I reached forward and kissed her. 'If you have to face this demon, you have to face it. Even if we turn back today, we'll have to do it sometime.'

I turned to the tank's turret, and with five or six ringing blows, drove the edge of the chisel under the crucifix that was riveted on to the hatch. Thirty years of corrosion had weakened the bolts, and after five minutes of sweaty, noisy work, the cross was off. Then, just to make sure, I hammered the last few legible words of the holy adjuration into obscurity.

Breathing hard, I stood still for a while and listened. There was no sound except for my own panting, and the soft whispery fall of the snow. In the distance, it was almost impossible to see the trees and the farm rooftops any more, because the snow was thickening and closing in; but Father Anton stood alert with his white hat and white shoulders, still holding the silver crucifix up in his mittened hand.

I tapped on the turret, and said, 'Is anyone there? Is anyone inside?'

There was no answer. Just the dull echo of my cautious knock.

I wiped my chilled, perspiring forehead. Madeleine,

her hair crowned in snowflakes, tried to give me a confident smile.

'Well,' I said, 'this is the big one.'

With a wide steel chisel, I banged all the way round the hatch of the turret, breaking the rough welding wherever I could, but mostly knocking dents in the rusted armour plating. I was making my seventh circle of the hatch when the blade of the chisel went right through a deeply corroded part of the metal, and made a hole the size of a dime.

Even in the freezing cold, even in the blanketing snow, we heard the sour whistle of fetid air escaping from the inside of the tank, and a smell came out of that Sherman like I'd never smelled anywhere before. It had the stomach-turning sickliness of rotten food, mingled with an odour that reminded me of the reptile houses at zoos. I couldn't help retching, and Madame Saurice's rough red wine came swilling back up into my mouth. Madeleine turned away and said: '*Mon Dieu!*'

I tried to hold myself steady, and then I turned back to Father Anton and said, 'I've broken a hole through, father. It smells really disgusting in there.'

Father Anton crossed himself. 'It is the odour of Baal,' he said, his face grey in the afternoon cold. Then he raised the crucifix higher and said: 'I conjure bind and charge thee by Lucifer, Beelzebub, Sathanas, Jauconill and by their power, and by the homage thou owest unto them, that you do torment and punish this disobedient demon until you make him come corporally to my sight and obey my will and commandments in whatsoever I shall charge or command thee to do. Fiat, fiat, fiat. Amen.'

Madeleine whispered: 'Dan – we could seal it up again. There's still time.'

I looked at the tiny hole, out of which the polluted air still sang. 'And then how long before it gets out of here, and comes after us? This thing killed your mother,

Madeleine. If you really believe that, we have to get rid of it for good.'

'Do *you* believe it?' she asked me, her eyes wide.

'I don't know. I just want to find out what's inside here. I want to find out what it is that can make a man puke maggots.'

I licked my lips, and raised the hammer once again. Then I struck the turret again and again until the hole grew from a dime to a quarter, and eventually the armour plating began to break off in leaves of black rust. Within twenty minutes, I'd broken all the metal away around the hinges of the hatch, and the hole was the size of a large frying-pan.

Father Anton, still waiting patiently in the snow, said: 'Can you see anything, *monsieur*?'

I peered into the blackness of the tank's interior. 'Nothing so far.'

Taking a crowbar from the canvas bag, I climbed up on top of the Sherman's turret, and inserted one end of the crowbar into the hole. Then I leaned back, and slowly began to raise the hatch itself, like opening a stubborn can of tomatoes with a skewer. Eventually, the welding broke, and the hatch came free. I stood there breathless and hot, even in the sub-zero temperature of that gloomy afternoon, but at least the job was done. I said to Madeleine: 'Hand me the flashlight.'

Her face pale, she passed it over. I switched it on, and pointed the beam downwards into the Sherman's innards. I could see the tank commander's jumpseat, the breech of the cannon, and the gunlayer's seat. I flicked the beam sideways, and then I saw it. A black sack, dusty and mildewed, and sewn up like a mailbag, or a shroud. It wasn't very large – maybe the size of a child, or a bag of fertiliser. It was lying next to the side of the tank as if it had fallen there.

Madeleine touched my shoulder. 'What is it?' she whispered in a frightened voice. 'What can you see?'

I stood straight. 'I don't know. It's a kind of black bag. I think I'll have to go down there and lift it out.'

Father Anton called: '*Monsieur*! Don't go in there!'

I took another look at the bag. 'It's the only way. We'll never get it out of there otherwise.'

The last thing in the whole world I wanted to do was get down inside that tank and touch that bag, but I knew that if we tried to hook it out with the crowbar we'd probably tear the fabric. It looked pretty old and rotten – more than thirty years old, maybe more than a hundred. One rip and whatever was inside it was going o come spilling out.

While Madeleine held back the jagged hatch for me, ı carefully climbed up on to the turret and lowered my legs inside. Even though my feet were freezing cold, I had a strange tingling feeling, as if something inside the tank was going to bite them. I said hoarsely, 'I always wanted to see what a tank looked like inside,' and then I lowered myself into the chilled, musty interior.

Tanks are claustrophobic enough when they're heated and lighted and they're not possessed by aemonic sacks. But when I clambered down into that cramped and awkward space, with wheels and instruments hitting my head and shoulders, and only a flashlight for company, I felt a surge of fear and suffocation, and all I wanted to do was get out of there.

I took a deep breath. It still smelled pretty foul in there, but most of the odour had dispersed. I looked up and saw Madeleine's face at the open hatch. She said nervously, 'Have you touched it yet?'

I shone my torch on the sack. There was something or somebody inside it, whatever it was. As close as this, the fabric looked even older than I'd imagined. It could almost have been a piece of the Bayeux tapestry, or a medieval shroud.

I reached my hand out and touched it. The cloth was soft with age. I ran my fingers gently along the length

55

of it, and I could feel various protrusions and sharp knobs. It felt like a sack of bones; an old and decaying sack of bones.

I coughed. I told Madeleine: 'I'm going to try and lift it up to you. Do you think you can take it?'

She nodded. 'Don't be long. Father Anton's looking very cold.'

'I'll try not to be.'

I wedged the flashlight against a hydraulic pipe so that it shone across the inside of the turret, and then I knelt down beside the sack. It took a lot of summoning-up of nerve, but in the end I put my arms around the black fusty cloth, and lifted it a foot or so upwards. It was saggy, and whatever was inside it, the bones or whatever they were, tumbled to one end of the sack with a soft rattling sound. But the fabric didn't tear, and I was able to gather the whole thing up in my arms and lift it towards Madeleine. She reached down and gripped the top of it, and I said: 'Okay, heave.'

For one moment, for one terrifying moment, just as Madeleine took the weight of the sack and hoisted it upwards, I was sure that I felt it wriggle, as if there was something alive inside it. It could have been a bone shifting, or my own keyed-up imagination, but I took my hands away from that sack as fast as if it was burning.

Madeleine gasped. 'What is it? What's happened?'

'Just get that sack out of here quick!' I yelled. '*Quick!*'

She tugged it upwards, and for a few seconds it snared on the rough metal around the broken-open hatch. But then she swung it clear, and I heard it drop on the hull outside. Taking the flashlight, I climbed out of the tank on to the turret, and I haven't ever been so glad to see snow and miserable gloomy skies as I was then.

Father Anton was approaching the side of the tank where the black sack lay. He was holding the crucifix and the Bible in front of him, and his eyes were fixed on our strange discovery like the eyes of a man who comes across the evidence, at last, that his wife has really been cuckolding him.

He said: '*Enfin, le diable.*'

I touched the sack tentatively with my foot. 'That was all there was. It feels like it's full of bones.'

Father Anton didn't take his eyes away from the sack for a second.

'Yes,' he said, 'the bones of a demon.'

I swung myself down from the hull of the tank, and helped Madeleine to jump down after me. 'I didn't know demons *had* bones,' I remarked. 'I thought they were all in the mind.'

'No, no,' said Father Anton. 'There was a time, in the Middle Ages, when demons and gargoyles walked the earth as living creatures. There is too much evidence to refute it. Paul Lucas, the medieval traveller, tells how he actually met the demon Asmodeus in Egypt, and the demon Sammael was said to have walked through the streets of Rouen as late as the twelfth century.'

Madeleine said: 'We don't yet know that it's really bones. It could be anything.'

Father Anton returned his Bible to his pocket. 'Of course, of course. We can take it back to my house. I have a cellar where we can lock it up safely. It seems to be acquiescent enough now.'

I looked at Madeleine, but she simply shrugged. If the priest wanted to take the sack back home with him, then there wasn't much we could do to stop him. I just hoped that the thing wouldn't decide to wake up and take its revenge on any of us for being disturbed so unceremoniously on a cold December afternoon.

I opened the back of the Citroën, and between us we carried the sagging, musty sack across the road and laid it gently in the car. Then I collected up the tools that Madeleine's father had lent us, and climbed into the car myself. Father Anton, taking off his hat and shaking the snow off it, said: 'I feel strangely elated. Can you understand that?'

I started the motor. 'This is what you've wanted to do for thirty years, isn't it? Open the tank and find out what the hell's happening.'

'Mr McCook,' he said, 'you should have come here years ago. It takes unusual simplicity, unusual directness, to do something like this.'

'I'm not sure whether that's a compliment or not.'

'I didn't mean naïveté.'

We drove through the gathering dusk, and the thick snowflakes whirled and tumbled all around us. But the time we reached Father Anton's house in the middle of the village, the church clock was striking five, and we could hardly see through the pouring snow. The housekeeper opened the door as we arrived, and stood there with a sour face and her hands clasped across her apron as I helped Father Anton into the porch.

'*Il a quatre-vingt-dix ans,*' she snapped, taking the old man's arm and leading him inside. '*Et il faut sortir dans la neige pour jouer comme un petit garçon?*'

'Antoinette,' said Father Anton reassuringly, patting her hand. 'I have never felt so healthy.'

Madeleine and I went round to the back of the Citroën, and lifted out the sack. From the dark hall, Father Anton called: 'That's right, bring it inside. Antoinette – will you bring me the keys to the cellar?'

Antoinette stared suspiciously at the black bundle we were carrying through the snow.

'*Qu'est-ce que c'est?*' she demanded.

'*C'est un sac de charbon,*' smiled Father Anton.

With one last backward look of ultimate distrust, Antoinette went off to fetch the cellar keys, while Madeleine and I laid our unholy bundle down in the hall.

Father Anton said: 'If these *are* bones, then I have a ceremony for disposing of them. The bones of a demon are just as potent as the live demon itself, so the books

58

say; but they can be scattered in such a way that the demon cannot live again. The skull has to be interred in one cathedral, and the hands and the feet in three others. Then the remaining bones are laid to rest in churches all around the intervening countryside, in ritual sequence.'

I took out my handkerchief and blew my nose. It was so cold that I could hardly feel it. 'Supposing we ask the Pentagon how to get rid of it?' I asked. 'After all, they put it there in the first place.'

Father Anton looked down at the black sack and shook his head. 'I don't know. I think the most important thing is to exorcise this beast as quickly as possible.'

Antoinette came bustling back with the cellar keys, and handed them to Father Anton. She pursed her lips in disapproval, but then Father Anton said gently, 'I would love some of your barley broth, Antoinette,' and she softened a little, and went off to the kitchen to prepare it.

Madeleine and I lifted the soft, yielding sack once more, and Father Anton said; 'Follow me.' But as we shuffled off down the long polished hallway, I glanced back at the place where the sack had been lying, and a feeling went down my shoulders like ice sliding down the inside of my shirt.

The wooden floor had been burned, as if by a poker. Where the black sack had been laid, there was the distinct, unmistakable outline of a small, hunched skeleton.

'Father Anton,' I whispered.

The old priest turned and saw the burns. He said: 'Lay down the sack, gently.' Then while we settled the decaying black fabric on the floor again, he walked back on creaking boots and knelt stiffly and painfully down His fingers traced the pattern that was scorched into the woodblock flooring, touching it as respectfully and gently as a fine medieval brass. I stood behind him and said 'Do you know what it is?'

He didn't look up. 'Oh, yes,' he said quietly. 'I know what it is. It is the mark of the demon. This house is holy, you see. It has been the vessel of years of prayer and blessings. And a demon's bones cannot touch it without making a mark.'

'It looks very small. Not much more than a child.'

'It is no smaller than the devils and gargoyles that are carved on medieval churches, my friend. We forget that many of those were carved, secretly, from the actual bodies of such fiends. I have the memoirs upstairs of a stonemason who worked at Chartres, and he tells of how the monks would bring him skulls and bones of creatures that he could never identify.'

Madeleine came up and took my arm. 'What are we going to do?' she asked softly. 'What if it tries to break free?'

'We must take it to the cellar at once,' said Father Anton. 'I can confine it there by the power of the crucifix and the power invested in me by Our Lord Jesus Christ. Then, at the first opportunity, we must take the skeleton to pieces and scatter those pieces according to the *Sepher Ha Zohar*, which is the most important book of the Kabbalah.'

We returned to the black sack, and this time all three of us took hold of it, and we walked with it as quickly as we could to the carved oak door of the cellar, way down at the end of the hall. Once we were there, Father Anton took out the largest of his keys, and put it into the lock.

Inside the door, it smelled of limestone and must. Father Anton switched on the light, and said, 'Be careful of the stairs. They're very old and uneven.'

Like the cellars of most French houses of any size, Father Anton's was enormous, and divided into several rooms. I could see wine racks through one half-open door, and inside another, garden tools and pieces of medieval masonry. But Father Anton directed us down to the very farthest recesses of the cellar, to a heavy door studded with black iron nails, and opened it up with another elaborate key.

This room was totally dark inside, and airless. There were no windows, and the room was empty but for a few broken flowerpots and a rusted mangle. It was floored with dusty clay tiles, and whitewashed with lime. Father Anton switched on the single bare bulb and said: 'Lay the sack down here. This room was originally used for storing valuables and furniture. The lock is very strong.'

We set the black bag down in the centre of the room, and stood back from it with considerable relief. Father Anton reached inside his coat and took out his worn brown spectacle case.

'First of all, we have to find out what kind of a demon this is,' he said. 'Then we can do our best to dismiss it. Mr McCook – you'll find a garden sickle in the next room. Perhaps you'd be kind enough to bring it in.'

I went to fetch the sickle while Father Anton stalked impatiently around the flaccid, lumpy bag, staring at it closely through his gold-rimmed spectacles, and coughing from time to time in the cold air of the cellar.

There were five sickles of varying sizes, so being a native of Mississippi I chose the largest. I took it back to Father Anton, and he smiled, and said, 'Will *you* cut it open? Or shall I?'

I looked across at Madeleine. She was tired and tense, but she obviously wanted to know what horrors were contained inside this sack just as much as I did. She nodded, and I said, 'Okay – I'll do it.'

I leaned over the sack and pushed the point of the sickle into the ancient fabric. It went in easily, and when I tugged, the bag ripped softly open with a dusty, purring sound, as fibre parted from fibre after centuries of waiting for unimaginable reasons in places that could only be guessed at.

61

The bag was full of dust and bones. I stood back, and stared at the bones with a kind of horrified curiosity, because they weren't the bones of any human or beast that you'd recognise. There were narrow ribs, curved thighbones, long claw-like metatarsals. They were dull brown and porous, and they looked as if they were six or seven hundred years old, or even more. I'd once dug up the skeleton of a Red Indian at my father's place at Louin, in Jasper County, and that had the same dry look about it.

It wasn't the bones of the body that frightened me so much; though they were grotesque enough in themselves. It was the skull. It had its jawbone missing, but it was a curious beaklike skull, with slanting eye-sockets, and a row of small nib-like teeth. There were rudimentary horns at the back of the head, and if it hadn't have been for the reptilian upper jaw, I would have said it was the skull of a goat.

Madeleine took my hand, and squeezed it hard. 'What is it?' she said, in a voice unsteady with fear. 'Dan – *what is it?*'

Father Anton took off his spectacles, and closed them with a quiet click. He looked at us, and his eyes were red from tiredness and cold, but his face was alive with human compassion and religious fortitude. He had been a priest for seventy years, twice as long as either of us had been alive, and even though he was elderly, he had seen in those seventy years enough miracles and enough demonic fears to give him strength where we had very little.

He said, 'It is just as I suspected.

I raised an eyebrow. 'You suspected something? You mean, you *guessed* what this was beforehand?'

He nodded. 'It was after we spoke, after we talked about the thirteen tanks. I spent an hour or so looking through the *Pseudomonarchia Daemonum*, and I came across a small reference to *les treize diables de Rouen*. There is very little there, very little information. But it appears from what Jean Wier says that in 1045 the city of Rouen was terrorised by thirteen devils which brought fire, pestilence, sorrow, and disaster. They were the thirteen acolytes of Adramelech, who was the eighth demon in the hierarchy of the evil Sephiroth, and the grand Chancellor of Hell.'

I reached inside my coat for my stale Lucky Strikes. I said, 'Is it that unusual to find devils in teams of thirteen?'

'Well, quite.'

'But what were thirteen eleventh-century devils doing in thirteen American tanks in the Second World War? It doesn't make any sense.'

Father Anton shrugged. 'I don't know, Mr McCook. Perhaps if we knew the answer to that, we would know the answer to everything.'

Madeleine asked: 'What happened to the devils of Rouen? Does the book say?'

'Oh, yes. They were imprisoned in a dungeon by a powerful spell imposed on them by the medieval exorcist Cornelius Prelati. The book is in medieval French, so it's a little difficult to decipher exactly how, or for how long. But it mentioned the word *coud^e*, which I thought at first meant that the devils were imprisoned very close together, rubbing shoulders. However, when I saw this sack I realised that there could be some connection. The French word *coudre*, as you may know, *monsieur*, means "to sew up."'

Madeleine whispered, 'The devils were sewn in bags. Just like this one.'

Father Anton said nothing, but raised his hands as if to say, *c'est possible*.

We stood around the bones for a long time in silence. Then Madeleine said: 'Well, what's to be done?'

Father Anton sucked at his ill-fitting dentures. 'We must spread the bones across the countryside, as the

Kabbalah recommends. But of course we cannot do it tonight. In any event, I shall have to call every one of the church authorities involved, and ask for permission to bury the bones in such a way.'

'That's going to take forever,' I told him.

Father Anton nodded. 'I know. But I'm afraid that it's necessary. I cannot simply bury the bones of a creature like this on sacred ground without the knowledge of the church.'

Madeleine took my hand. Very naturally, very easily, and very affectionately. She said, 'Dan, perhaps you ought to stay with Father Anton tonight. I don't like to leave him alone with this thing.'

Father Anton smiled. 'It is kind of you to feel such concern. But you really needn't worry.'

'No, no,' I told him. 'I'd like to. That's if you don't mind.'

'Of course not. We can have a game of chess together after dinner.'

I said to Madeleine, 'I'll run you home.'

Father Anton switched off the light in the room where the demon's remains lay scattered. For a moment we paused at the door, looking back into the pitch darkness. I could have sworn I felt a light breeze, sour with the same odour that had pervaded the tank, coursing out of the room. Of course, it was impossible. The room had no windows. But all the same, there was this strange, unsettling sensation, as if you were awakened in the night by the breath from some creature's nostrils on your cheek.

Father Anton closed the heavy door and locked it. Then he stood before it, and crossed himself, and spoke a prayer I'd never heard in my whole life.

'O devil,' he whispered, 'thou who hast touched no food, drunk no water, tasted not the sprinkled flour nor known the sacred wine, remain within I command thee. O gate, do not open that the demon within may pass; O

64

lock hold thyself firm; O threshold stay untrod. For the day of the Lord is at hand, when the dead shall rise and outnumber the living, in His name's sake, amen.'

The old priest crossed himself again, and so did Madeleine. I wished right then that I'd had that kind of religion, too – the kind of religion that gave me words and actions to guard me against the devils of the night.

'Come,' said Father Anton. 'Perhaps you'd like a calvados before you take Mademoiselle Passerelle home.'

'I think I could use it,' I told him, and we went upstairs, with only one backward glance at the door that held back the bones of the demon.

After drinks and cakes, I drove Madeleine home through the streets of Pont D'Ouilly to her father's farm. The snow had eased up, and now the Orne Valley was silent and cold and the hills surrounding the river were as white as furniture covered in dust-sheets. There was a pale moon rising, weaker than last night, and the snow-grey fields were patterned with the footprints of birds and stoats.

I stopped the car at the gate. Madeleine buttoned up her coat and said, 'You won't come in?'

'Maybe tomorrow. I promised Father Anton a game of chess. I think he's deserved it.'

She nodded, and reached out for my hand. 'I don't know how to thank either of you. It's like a great weight that's been taken off my family's shoulders.'

I rubbed my eyes. I was feeling the strain of what we had done this afternoon, both mentally and physically. My arms were aching from all that chiselling and hammering, and my mind was still a little tender from those claustrophobic moments inside the tank. I said, 'Thank me tomorrow, when I can work out why the hell I wanted to do it in the first place.'

She smiled. 'I thought Americans were just naturally helpful.'

65

'More like naturally nosey!'

She leaned across the car, which wasn't difficult, because the 2CV's so tiny that you're sitting pressed together like canned frankfurters in any case. Her lips touched my cheek, and then we kissed, and I suddenly discovered that Norman farm girls have a really good flavour that almost makes demon-hunting worthwhile.

I said quietly, 'I thought French people kissed each other on the cheeks.'

She looked at me closely, and said: 'That's only when they're handing out medals.'

'Isn't that what you're doing now?'

She didn't answer for a long time, but then she said: '*Peut-être, monsieur. Qui sait?*'

She opened her door and climbed out into the snow. She stayed where she was for a while, looking up and down the white and silent road, and then she leaned into the car and said, 'Will I see you tomorrow?'

'Sure. Why don't you come up to Father Anton's sometime during the morning? I guess we have a lot of phoning to do. Calling up all those priests and getting rid of all those bones.'

Her breath smoked in the reflected light from the Citroën's headlights. She said, 'Sleep well, Dan. And, again – thank you.'

Then she shut the car door, and walked through the snow-topped gate-posts into her father's farmyard. I watched her for a while, but she didn't turn round, so I backed up the car and drove off towards Pont D'Ouilly, with only a quick sideways glance at the hulk of the Sherman tank which now rested in the hedge like the black discarded chrysalis of some monstrous insect.

The library, with its rows of leather books and its dismal portraits, was chillingly cold; so while we played chess after dinner, Father Anton allowed us the extravagance of two large elm logs on the fire, and we sat with glasses of Napoleon brandy beside the flickering flames, talking and playing slow, elaborate games until almost midnight.

'You play quite well,' observed Father Anton, after checkmating my king for the third straight time. 'You're out of practice, though, and you're too impatient. Before you move, think – and then think again.'

'I'm trying to. I guess I have other things on my mind.'

'Like our demon? You mustn't.'

'It's kind of hard to forget.'

Father Anton took a pinch of snuff and poked it ceremoniously up his left nostril. 'The devil thrives on fear, my friend. The more you fear him, the fiercer he becomes. You must think of what we have downstairs in the cellar as nothing more than a heap of stray bones, such as any hound might have buried in the cabbage-patch.'

'Well, I'll try.'

Father Anton moved his pawn to rook six, and then sat back in his studded leather armchair. While I frowned at the chessboard and tried to work my way out of a situation that, on the face of it, looked like a fourth checkmate in three moves, he sipped his brandy ruminatively, and said, 'Does it surprise you that demons actually lived? That they had flesh, and bones?'

I looked up. He was staring at the fire, and the flames reflected from his spectacles.

I said, 'I don't know. I suppose it does. I wouldn't have believed it unless I'd seen it for myself.'

Father Anton shrugged. 'It seems strange to me, you know, that in an age as pragmatic as ours, an age so bent on seeking evidence and demonstration, that the tangible manifestations of religion, like demons and devils, should be scoffed at.'

'Come on! Not many people have ever seen a demon.'

Father Anton turned his head and looked at me

67

seriously. 'Haven't they? They'd be surprised. Demons and devils have evolved like the rest of us, and it's remarkable how many of them still hide on the face of the earth.'

'Does the same go for angels?' I asked him. 'I mean – do we have anyone on our side?'

Father Anton shook his head. 'Angels never existed as actual creatures. The name "angel" describes a state of divine energy that is terrible in the classic sense of the word. I know that angels are the messengers of God; and that they often protect us from harm and from the temptations of Satan. But I know enough about them to say that, in this life, I would prefer not to meet one. They are fearsome to say the least.'

'Can they be summoned, like demons?'

'Not in the same way. But if you're interested, I have a book on my shelves on the invocation of angels. It was a great favourite of the Reverend Taylor when he was here during the war, surprisingly. Perhaps his involvement with your country's demons alarmed him sufficiently to seek some assistance from the cohorts of God.'

We fell silent for a few minutes while I made my next move on the board. Outside the tall windows, the snow began to fall again, thick and silent, piling softly on to northern France until it looked like the moon. An easterly wind was blowing across Poland and Germany and Belgium, bringing low clouds and an endless winter of grey cold.

Father Anton inspected the chessboard. '*Ce n'est pas mal, ça,*' he said, nodding his head in approval. But then his bony, liver-spotted hand moved his queen across towards my king, and he said: '*Malheureusement, c'est éche et mat.*'

With one move, he had stymied my king; and all I could do was lift my hands in surrender. 'I guess I had to learn the hard way. Never play chess with nonagenarians.'

68

He smiled. 'We must play some more, if you're staying in the Suisse Normande. You're a worthy opponent.'

'Thanks,' I said, lighting a cigarette. 'But I'm afraid that baseball's more my style.'

We finished our brandy as the carved mahogany clock on the mantelpiece struck twelve. The logs in the grate sparked and dropped, and all around us was the silence of a dark clerical mansion in the heart of a small wintry village in the shouldering hills of Normandy. Father Anton spoke. 'This is a brave thing you have done today. You must realise that. I know that Madeleine is appreciative, but I am, too. I'm very sad that, for all these years, there hasn't been a man among us with sufficient courage to do what you did, and open the tank up.'

'You know what they say,' I told him. 'Ignorance is bliss. If I'd known as much as you do about devils and demons, I probably wouldn't have gone near it.'

'Nonetheless, *monsieur*, I am grateful. And I want you to wear this tonight, my crucifix, as a protection.'

He lifted the large silver cross from around his neck and passed it over. It was weighty, and embossed with the figure of Christ. I held it in my hand for a moment, and then I offered it back to him. 'I can't wear this. This is yours. You need protection as much as I do.'

Father Anton smiled. 'No, *monsieur*. I have my wits and my training to protect me, and above all I have my God.'

'You don't think that it – well, might attack us?'

The old priest shrugged. 'You can never tell with devils. I don't yet know which devil this is, although we've guessed it might be one of the thirteen demons of Rouen. It might be powerful, it might be weak. It might be treacherous or wrathful. Until we have done the seven tests on it, we shall not be able to find out.'

'The seven tests?'

'Seven ancient tests which identify whether a devil is

69

of hell or of earth; whether it spreads its evil by pestilence or by fire; whether it is high in the ranks of the evil Sephiroth, or whether it is nothing more than a servile thing that creeps upon the face of the earth.'

I rose from my chair and walked across the room. Outside, the snow tumbled and twisted through the night, and the front of Father Anton's house was like a pale execution yard, untrod, unmarked with blood.

'Are you frightened?' Father Anton said, in a husky voice.

I paused for a moment to think. Then I said: 'Yes, I think so.'

'Then kneel here, *monsieur*, if you will; and I shall say a prayer for you.'

I turned round. He was sitting by the dying fire with a look of real concern on his face. I said gently: 'No thank you, father. Tonight I think I'll trust to luck.'

CHAPTER THREE

I was to sleep in a high green-painted iron bed in a small room on the uppermost floor. Father Anton lent me a voluminous white nightshirt, white bed-socks, and a copy of *L'Invocation des Anges*, leather-bound and smelling of dust, to read by the light of my shaky bedside lamp.

We said goodnight on the second floor, where Father Anton himself slept, and then I creaked up through the gloomy house to the long narrow corridor where my own room was. Antoinette had left the light on upstairs, despite Father Anton's usual frugality, and I was grateful for it. I beetled along that corridor as if the ten evil Sephiroth were panting down my neck, closed my door and locked it.

The room was plain, but it wasn't bad. Apart from the bed, there was a cheap pine dresser with a mirror, and one of those vast French wardrobes in which to hang my crumpled coat and shirt. There was a washbasin in one corner, and a circular window with a view over the snowy rooftops of Pont D'Ouilly. I washed with hard kitchen soap, rinsed my mouth out with water, and then pulled on Father Anton's nightshirt. I looked like Stan Laurel in one of those movies where Laurel and Hardy have to spend the night in a haunted house.

The springs complained noisily when I climbed into bed. I sat upright for a while, listening to the sounds of the house and the night outside; and then I opened the book that Father Anton had lent me, and started to read.

My French was so halting that it took me half an hour to read the first page, and that was a lengthy apology from the author, Henri St Ermin, for his platitudinous style and his lack of talent with a pen. I couldn't have

71

agreed with him more. I skipped the text and looked at the engravings instead.

I began to understand what Father Anton had meant when he said that angels were terrible. There were drawings of angels that were nothing but intense sources of light with spreading wings. There were angels like fierce, proud beasts. And there were angels who were unseen, but who came at night like violent storms, and laid waste to the houses of the wicked. It was plain from the captions under each of the pictures that you had to invoke the right angel for the right temporal task, otherwise you might find yourself, metaphorically speaking, plugging a flashlight bulb into a nuclear power station. One caption warned of 'the angel which comes in a cloak of clouds, in which are the faces of those who have sinned and repented their sins'.

Outside in the snow, the church clock struck two, and I closed my less-than-reassuring midnight reader, switched off my light, and settled down to get some sleep. In the dark, the house seemed even noisier than it had with the lights on. Something scurried and flurried up in the attic above me, and the joists and timbers creaked and groaned and complained to each other like arthritic old women in a doctor's waiting-room.

I slept for maybe ten minutes; and woke to hear my watch ticking on the bedside table. The house was quieter now, and I fell asleep again, although this time I began to dream. I dreamed I was opening doors in a gloomy building, and behind each door there was something fearful. I could hardly bear to place my hand on the doorknobs and turn them, but I had a terrible compulsion to find out what was there. Through the tenth or the eleventh door, there was a narrow corridor, and at the end of the corridor someone was standing. Someone small, like a child, with its back to me. I began to work my way slowly and glutinously down the corridor to see who it was, and all the time I knew that it was someone frightening, but all the time I was compelled to find out, compelled to go on.

As I came close, the small figure turned towards me, and for one moment I saw a face that grinned like a goat, with hideous yellow eyes. I was so scared that I woke up, and I was sitting upright in bed with my nightshirt tangled around my legs, sweating and chilled, and this time the church clock was just pealing three.

I switched on my bedside light and swung out of bed. I listened, but the house seemed reasonably quiet. Maybe the day's events were just making me edgy. I tiptoed across to the door, and pressed my ear against the wood panelling; but all I could hear was the faint sad moan of the draught that perpetually blew around the house, rattling window sashes and setting chandeliers tinkling, and the usual creaks of floorboards and hinges.

The house was like an old ship at sea, rolling and heaving through a black silent ocean where no fish swam.

A voice whispered: '*Monsieur.*'

I stood slowly away from the door, my mouth salt with shock. I was sure that the voice had come from outside – right outside. It was a dry, sexless voice, the voice of an old woman, or a strange eunuch. I backed off, reaching behind me for the reassurance of my bed, when the voice again said: '*Monsieur.*'

I called hoarsely, 'Who's there? Is that you, father?'

'*Of course,*' answered the voice. '*Who else?*'

'What do you want? It's late.'

'*This is my house. I shall walk where I please.*'

I bit my lip uncertainly. 'Listen,' I said, 'I don't think that you *are* Father Anton.'

'*Who else could I be?*'

'I don't know. Beelzebub?'

The voice cackled. '*Perhaps you ought to open the door and find out.*'

I waited, with my heart taking great irregular gallops under my ribs, and my pulse banging away in sympathy.

73

I heard a shuffling noise outside and then the voice said: *'Monsieur?'*

'What is it?'

'Open up, monsieur. I have something to show you.'

'I don't really want to, thanks. Listen, I'm in bed. I'll talk in the morning.'

'Are you afraid, monsieur?'

I didn't answer that one. Whatever or whoever it was outside, I didn't want them to know just how frightened I was. I looked around the room for some kind of a weapon, and in the end I picked up a cheap alloy candlestick from the washstand. It wasn't very heavy, but it made me feel better.

The voice said: *'The girl is beautiful, isn't she?'*

'Which girl?'

'Madeleine.'

'Can't we talk about it tomorrow? I'm tired. And anyway, I'd like to know who you are.'

The voice laughed. *'I told you. I am Father Anton.'*

'I don't believe you.'

'You don't believe that priests enjoy sex as much as anyone else? You don't believe that I can look at Madeleine and think of her body? She gets me boiling, monsieur! Oh, yes, she gets me rampant as a goat in the rutting season! Now, don't you feel that way, too?'

I was shaking with nerves. I took one awkward step towards the door, deliberately stamping my bare foot as loudly as I could on the floorboards, and I shouted: 'Go away! Just get out of here! I don't want to listen!'

There was a pause. A breezy silence. I thought for a moment that the thing might have gone. But then it said, in a treacly, self-satisfied tone, *'I've scared you, haven't I? I've really scared you!'*

'You haven't scared me at all. You're just disturbing my night's rest.'

I felt a vague wind blowing across my room from the direction of the door, and I was certain that I could detect that sour, sickening odour of the demon. Perhaps

74

it was just my imagination. Perhaps I was having a dream. But there I was, defenceless in my nightshirt and my goddamned ridiculous bedsocks, clutching a light-weight candlestick and hoping that whatever whispered behind that door was going to stay behind it, or better still, leave me alone.

'*We must talk, monsieur,*' said the voice.

'I don't think we have anything to talk about.'

'*But of course we do. We must talk about the girl. Don't you want to talk about the girl? Wouldn't you like to sit down for an hour or two, like men of the world, and talk about her bubs, perhaps, or the inner folds of her sex?*'

'Get out of here! I don't want to listen!'

'*But of course you do. You're fascinated. You're fearful, but fascinated. We could talk about the many ways in which girls can have intercourse with animals and reptiles. The pain of it, and the sheer delight! After all, we must have her for the grand gathering, mustn't we? We couldn't do without her.*'

I retreated, trembling, back towards the bed. Whatever stood outside my door, its lewd words seemed to crawl all over me like lice. I groped for, and found, the book of angels which lay on my bedside table; and I also picked up, out of plain old-fashioned superstitious terror, the ring of hair which Eloise had given me for protection against devils and demons.

I raised the book of angels and said tightly: 'I command you to go away. If you don't go away, I'll invoke an angel to drive you away. No matter how dangerous it is, I'll do it.'

The voice chuckled. '*You don't know what you're talking about. Invoke an angel! How can you possibly believe in angels?*'

'The same way I'm beginning to believe in devils.'

'*You think I'm a devil? Well, I'll prove you wrong! Just open the door and I'll show you.*'

I kept the book held high. 'I'm not going to. If you want to talk, talk in the morning. But right now I want you to go. I don't care if you're Father Anton or not. Just go.'

There was a long, dull silence. Then I heard a clicking noise. I couldn't think what it was to begin with, but then I looked again at the door and saw, to my utmost dread, that the key was slowly revolving in the lock. One by one, the lock levers opened; and then the brass bolt at the top of the door slid back as if it was being tugged by a magnet.

My throat constricted. I hefted the candlestick and raised it behind me to hit whatever was out there as hard as I possibly could.

The doorknob turned. The door opened, and that soft sour draught began to course through my bedroom again. Then, untouched, the door swung wide by itself.

Outside, in the corridor, it was totally dark. The house stirred and shifted. I waited and waited, my candlestick raised over my head, but nothing happened. Nobody appeared. Nobody spoke.

I said, 'Are you there?'

There was no reply. I swallowed, and my swallow seemed like the loudest sound in the world.

I took one step forward towards the doorway. Maybe it was waiting for me to come after it. Well, perhaps I shouldn't disappoint it. After all, a demon was only a demon, wasn't it? It was only some croaky voice in the night. Only some whisper in a derelict tank. Nothing more than a scattered heap of bones that Father Anton had sealed in his cellar.

I reached the doorway. The best thing to do would be to jump right out across the corridor. Then, if anything was hiding beside the door, ready to claw out at me, I could turn round and hit it first.

I said, loudly and unsteadily, 'Are you there? Answer me! If you're so damned smart, answer!'

There was nothing. It was so quiet in that moment

that I could hear my watch ticking on the bedside table. I cleared my throat.

I tensed the candlestick in my hand, crouched down a little, and then I threw myself out of the open doorway, across the painted boards of the corridor, and scrambled around so that I was ready with my arm raised and my muscles tightened for action.

There was nothing. The corridor was empty. I felt a shiver that was both fear and relief, intermingled.

Perhaps the best thing to do now would be to go down and check that Father Anton was all right. After all, that whispery voice had claimed to be him, and if it was opening doors all over the house, it could have opened his, too. I pulled up my bedsocks, which were falling down round my ankles, and walked back along the dark corridor as far as the head of the stairs. On the landing below, an old French wallclock was tiredly counting away the small cold hours of the night, and a cardinal with a face about as happy as a hundred-year-old horse was looking gloomily out of an ancient oil painting.

I started to go down the stairs. My nightshirt made a soft sweeping sound on the boards, and I paused once to listen for any unusual noises. The wallclock suddenly whirred and struck the half hour, and I froze. But when the chimes had died away, there was silence again. I walked across the landing, and headed down the corridor where Father Anton's bedroom was.

It was very dark along that corridor. Somehow the atmosphere was different, as if someone else had recently walked down here, disturbing the chilly air. I went as softly as I could, but my own breathing seemed almost deafening, and every floorboard had a creak or a squeak of its own.

I was halfway down the corridor when I saw something down at the far end. I stopped, and strained my eyes. It was difficult to make out what it was in the shadows, but it looked like a child. It was standing with its back to me,

77

apparently gazing out of the small leaded window at the snow-covered yard. I didn't move. The child could have been an illusion – nothing more than an odd composition of light and dark. But from thirty feet away it appeared remarkably real, and I could almost imagine it turning around *and for one moment in my nightmare I had seen a face that grinned like a goat with hideous yellow eyes.*

I took one very cautious step forward. I said: *'You!'* but my voice only came out as a whisper.

The small figure remained still. It was solitary and sad, in a way, like a ghost over whose earthly body no prayers had ever been spoken. It continued to look out over the yard, not moving, not turning, not speaking.

I took one more step nearer, then another. I said: 'Is that you?'

One moment the figure seemed real and tangible, but then as I came even closer, the hooded head became a shadow from the top of the casement, and the small body melted into a triangle of dim light from the snow outside, and I stepped quickly up to the window and saw that there was nobody and nothing there at all.

I looked round, but I knew it was useless. I was so crowded with fears and superstitions that I was seeing things that weren't even there. I walked back to Father Anton's bedroom door, waited for a moment, and then softly knocked.

'Father Anton? It's Dan McCook.'

There was no answer, so I waited for a while and then rapped again.

'Father Anton? Are you awake?'

There was still no answer. I gently tried the door. It wasn't locked, and so I pushed it open and peered into the darkness of his bedroom. It smelled of mothballs and some mentholated rub that he obviously put on his chest at night. On one side was a tall mahogany wardrobe, and on the other was a chest-of-drawers, above which hung a large ebony crucifix with an ivory figure of Christ

78

hanging on it. Father Anton's oak bed was set against the far wall, and I could just make out his pale hand lying on the coverlet, and his white hair on the pillow.

I crept across the worn rug on the floor, and stood a few feet away from him. He had his back turned to me, but he looked all right. I was beginning to think that I was suffering from nightmares and delusions and not enough sleep. I whispered: 'Father Anton?'

He didn't stir, didn't turn around, but a voice said: '*Yes?*'

My grip tightened on my candlestick. It *sounded* like Father Anton, but on the other hand it didn't. It had some of that dry, sardonic quality that I had heard in the voice upstairs. I came a little nearer the bed, and tried to lean over so that I could see Father Anton's face.

'Father Anton? Is that you?'

There was a second's pause. Then Father Anton rose up in his bed as if he was being pulled upright on strings, and he turned to face me with his eyes glassy and his white hair dishevelled. He said, in that same unnatural voice: 'What is it? Why did you wake me?'

I felt there was something curiously and frighteningly wrong. It was the way he was sitting there in his white nightshirt, as if he was unsupported by gravity or anything at all. And it was his peculiar manner, partly calm and partly hostile. There was nothing of the rambling old priest about him. He seemed strangely self-possessed, and his eyes seemed to be observing me as if there was someone else behind them, staring through.

I took a few steps back. 'I think I must have made a mistake,' I said. 'Just a nightmare, that's all.'

'You're frightened,' he said. 'I can tell that you're frightened. Now, why?'

'It's okay,' I told him. 'I guess I just didn't get enough sleep. I'll go right back upstairs now, and I'll—'

'You needn't go. Don't you want to talk? It's very lonesome at this time of night, don't you agree?'

Father Anton's face was rigidly white, and his jaw seemed to move up and down when he spoke with the same mechanical movements of a ventriloquist's dummy. Talking to him right then was like listening to a badly dubbed movie.

'Well, yes,' I said. 'But I'd really rather go. Thanks all the same.'

Father Anton raised a hand. 'You mustn't go.' He turned his head stiffly and looked towards the door. It swung on its hinges, and silently closed, all by itself.

I lifted my candlestick.

'Now then,' admonished Father Anton. 'There's no need to be belligerent. We can be friends, you know. We can help each other.'

I said, quietly: 'You're not Father Anton at all.'

Father Anton abruptly laughed, throwing his head back in a way that terrified me. 'Of course I'm Father Anton. Who do I look like?'

'I don't know. But you're not Father Anton. Now just stay there because I'm getting right out of here and you're not going to stop me.'

Father Anton said: 'Why should I want to stop you? You're a good man and true. You helped me out, so now I'm going to help you.'

I was shivering like a man with pneumonia. I kept the candlestick raised over my head, and I stepped back towards the door. 'Just stay away,' I warned him.

Father Anton gave an awkward, empty shrug. 'You mustn't misunderstand me, *monsieur*.'

'I understand you all right. I don't know what you are, or what you're trying to do, but keep away.'

The old priest's eyes glittered. 'If we don't find the other twelve, you know, we could be in terrible trouble.'

'The other twelve what?'

'The other twelve *brethren*. There are thirteen of us, you know. I told you that. Thirteen of us. We have been separated for such a long time, and now we must get together again.'

I kept on shuffling my way backwards. 'You don't know where they are?' I asked him.

Father Anton swayed. Then he looked up oddly and said, 'They've been hidden. They've been sewn up and sealed, just like before. I was the only one who wasn't taken with them. Now you must help me find them. You and the girl together. We need the girl.'

I shook my head tautly. 'I'm not going to help you find or do anything. I'm getting right out of here and I'm going to get some help.'

Father Anton lifted one jerky leg out from under the bedclothes, then the other. He stood up unsteadily, his arms hanging by his sides, and he grinned at me. For a split second, I thought I saw a thin dark tongue flick from his mouth – a tongue as forked as a reptile's – but then it flicked back again and I wasn't sure if it was just an illusion or not.

'We will have to find the Reverend Taylor in England,' said Father Anton, in a soft, rustling voice. 'Then we will have to discover where the Americans hid the rest of us. My lord Adramelech will be deeply pleased, I can assure you. He will reward you, *monsieur*, in a way that no man on earth has ever been rewarded before. You can be rich beyond any comprehension. You can be powerful as a thousand men. You can spend years indulging your tastes for the finest foods and the greatest wines. And you can have sex with any woman, any man, any animal, you choose, and your virility will be limitless.'

I didn't know what to say or do. It seemed as though Father Anton had been completely taken over. But was he really possessed, or was he just suffering from nightmarish nerves? Maybe he'd taken too many heart pills, or drunk too much before he went to bed. I just couldn't look at this elderly shambling priest in his long white nightshirt and believe that I was talking to a devil.

81

Father Anton took one staggering step towards me. I retreated even further.

'Father Anton,' I said, 'you're sick. Now, why don't you lie down for a moment, and I'll go and get a doctor.'

'Sick?' he hissed, 'I'm not sick. I'm free.'

'Will you stay back, please?' I asked him. 'I'n going to have to hit you if you come any nearer, and I don't want to do that.'

'You amuse me,' whispered the priest. 'But I am never amused for long. Father Anton was not amusing. Fortunately, he was weak. A man who believes in us is so much more susceptible than a man who doesn't.'

'You took over Father Anton? You possessed him?'

'You could say so, yes.'

'What does that mean?'

Father Anton took another step nearer. 'Possession is more physical than mental. I possess Father Anton now, because I am inside Father Anton.'

I went cold with foreboding. I said: 'I don't understand you. What do you mean – you're *inside* Father Anton?'

The white-dressed priest came clumsily towards me. His expression was grey and blank, and apart from those dark, penetrating eyes, I might have been looking at a corpse.

'A man, like a demon, is a mechanical device,' he said, in a voice that was even less like Father Anton's than before, and so much like the voice that I had heard in the tank that I *knew* – despite everything I was trying to do to persuade myself otherwise – that this was the devil we had tried to seal in the cellar, the disciple of Adramelech who had once brought plague and misery to Rouen.

I said nothing. I guessed I was five or six paces away from the door now. The old priest kept stepping woodenly towards me.

'From inside, I can manipulate his legs and his arms like a marionette,' said the devil. 'I can look through the sockets of his eyes, and breathe through the cavities of his nostrils. It's a secure home inside here, *monsieur*. Warm and bloody, and sweet with decay already. I could even seduce that shrivelled old housekeeper of his through his own dangling penis!'

I stared at the priest with mounting fright.

'Are you lying?' I taxed him, knowing he wasn't. 'My God, if you're lying—'

'Your God won't help you. He didn't help Father Anton.'

'Well, where *is* Father Anton?' I demanded. 'What have you done with him?'

The stiff figure marched so close that I could have reached out and touched him.

He said, in that coarse, throaty voice, 'You're almost standing in him.'

At first. I didn't want to take my eyes off the devil. But then I glanced quickly down behind me, and I saw something that made my stomach tighten and turn over. On the floor beside the chest-of-drawers, spread out in pale mucus-coloured strings, clotted with dark-red kidneys and blueish cakes of liver, were Father Anton's entrails. The devil had disembowelled him, and climbed into his empty body like some hideous kind of parasite.

The devil hadn't moved. I looked back at it in fear and nausea, and said: 'You've killed him.'

The devil grunted in evil amusement. 'On the contrary, I think I've given the old fool some new life. He was almost dead anyway. His heart wouldn't have lasted much longer, particularly after you dragged him out in all that snow.'

I paused, anxiously biting my lip. If the devil could rip Father Anton open, it could certainly do something equally disgusting to me. I looked quickly up at the ebony crucifix on the wall, and wondered if everything I'd seen in vampire movies was true. Was it really possible to ward off demons and ghosts with the Holy Cross?

83

Sidestepping Father Anton's glutinous remains, I reached over the chest-of-drawers and wrenched down the crucifix. Then I brandished it right in the devil's face, and shouted as heroically as I could: '*I dismiss you! In the name of the Lord, I dismiss you!*'

With one powerful blow, the old priest knocked the crucifix out of my hand. He gave a hissing snarl, and moved towards me again, his eyes as dark and cruel as an alligator's.

I swung my arm back, and belted him across the side of the face with my candlestick. His head jerked to one side, and the base of the candlestick raised a weal; but no blood flowed because Father Anton's heart wasn't pumping any longer, and his occupied cadaver simply shuddered and stepped forward again.

'Your violence amuses me,' it whispered. 'Now let's see if *mine* amuses *you*.'

I edged back. I knew that I'd never make the door in time. I kept my eyes on Father Anton's grey, bruised face, and I began to wish that I'd never seen that damned tank, and never dreamed of opening it.

'It's such a pity, you know,' said Father Anton. 'You could have assisted me so much. But I have only survived the centuries by protecting myself against the moral and the conscientious, and I'm afraid that I shall have to deal with you as I have dealt with so many others.'

I only had one gambit left. I reached into the pocket of my nightshirt and produced the small ring of hair which Eloise had given me, the hair which was supposed to prove that I had already paid my dues to the hierarchy of hell.

There was an electric silence. Father Anton raised his eyes and stared at the hair with undisguised malevolence. I thought for a moment that he was going to tear the hair aside, just like the crucifix. But then that forked tongue flickered again, and the demon moved warily aside, watching me with a hard, poisonous look that made me so nervous I could hardly speak.

'Well,' said Father Anton, keeping his eyes on the ring of hair. 'I see that you're less *naïf* than I thought. You're not a witch, or a necromancer, and yet you keep the first-born's locks with you. Now, I wonder how you got hold of them?'

'That's none of your business. Just keep back.'

Father Anton jerkily raised his hands in a gesture of conciliation. 'There is no need for us to quarrel, *monsieur*. There is no need for us to fight. After all, you must remember that you can protect yourself only *once* with this ring of hair; and for each protection thereafter you will need to sacrifice some other first-born to Moloch. It will only take the rising of tomorrow's sun, and its setting at evening, and all the power you have in that ring will have died with the day.'

'I'm not interested. I'll have you behind bars by then.'

Father Anton threw back his head again, and laughed. Then, without warning, the door banged wide open and slammed shut again, and the windows exploded in a hailstorm of shattered glass. The sheets were whipped off the bed in a screaming indoor hurricane, and the furniture was thrown violently around the room, clattering and bumping.

Most hideous of all, Father Anton's body was hurled this way and that, its arms flailing wildly in all directions, until there was a shrieking blast of wind, and it was thrown face-first into his dressing-table mirror, the sharp slices of glass opening up his face like a skinned chicken.

The noise died away. I lowered my arm away from my eyes. The room was very dark now, although the curtains were flapping open, and a grey strained light was reflected from the snow outside. With the windows broken, it was intensely cold.

Something small and shadowy was sitting in the far corner of the room, on the oaken post of Father Anton's bed. I couldn't make it out very well, but I could see stubs of horns and eyes that slanted like a goat's. It made a dry, leathery sound as it shifted on its perch.

'*Monsieur*,' it whispered.

'What is it?' I asked, chilled.

'I must warn you, *monsieur*, not to interfere again. Next time, you will have no protection.'

'There isn't going to *be* any next time,' I asserted.

'*Monsieur*,' said the devil, 'I am going to find my brethren with or without your assistance. Although, if you have any taste for what is best for you, you will do what you can to help me.'

'What about Madeleine?'

'She must come too.'

'That's out of the question.'

The devil rustled, papery and ancient as Hell itself.

'I will strike a bargain with you,' it whispered. 'If you help me to find my brethren, you and Madeleine, then I will restore this fool to life.'

'That's insane.'

The devil laughed. 'Insanity is a human word which almost always describes the activities of devils. Yes, in that sense, it is insane. But Adramelech can do it.'

'How about you? Can you do it?'

'It is not within my powers.'

I hefted my candlestick again. I wondered what the devil was capable of doing in the time it would take me to cross the room and smash him off his perch.

I said: 'I thought only God could give the gift of life.'

The devil shifted its unseen claws. 'Life is not a gift, my friend. It is a curse. Adramelech is quite capable of giving such a curse.'

My mouth felt very dry. I said: 'How can I believe you? How can I trust you?'

There was a moment's pause. The winter wind raised and lowered the drapes, and flakes of snow came tumbling over the window-ledge. The devil stirred, and said in that throaty, sexless voice: 'You don't doubt what I can do, surely?'

I moved cautiously across the rumpled rug, trying to get as near to the devil as I could.

'I doubt your existence,' I said. 'I doubt if you're anything more than a nightmare.'

The devil cackled. 'Then watch,' it said. 'Just watch.'

There was a silence. The shadows of the drapes rose and fell, like the wings of dreadful creatures. Then the house was pierced by a high, hideous shriek, and I heard furniture falling, glass breaking; and someone keening and moaning like an animal in agony. I turned. The door banged open again. From out of the corridor came a low, howling wind, and then the sound of someone staggering towards us, mumbling in pain as it came.

There was a crackle of electricity, and the whole room was dazzlingly lit by a blueish light. Then there was darkness again, and a rumble of thunder that compressed my eardrums and almost threw me over. Then there was another fierce blitz of electricity, even brighter than the first, and in the wide-open doorway, her arms raised in desperation, her face blotted white by the demonic lightning, I saw Antoinette, the elderly maid, in a nightdress soaked by torrents of blood, her whole body, her arms, her legs, her stomach, her face, porcupined with knives and forks and scissors and skewers. It was as if every sharp instrument in the whole house had flown from its drawer and stabbed itself into her.

Her voice almost swallowed by another burst of thunder, she moaned: '*Father Anton, save me* . . .' and collapsed to her knees with a clatter of knife and scissor handles.

I turned back to the devil, and I was stunned and furious. 'Is *that* your damned power? Slaughtering old women? You damned maniac!'

The voice came from somewhere else now – on top of

the dark mahogany wardrobe, in a corner where I couldn't see.

'You would consider it powerful if it happened to you, *monsieur*. Or if it happened to Madeleine. I could make it happen to Madeleine right now. Every pitchfork and castrating knife in the whole of her farm could stick itself into her right now, right this minute. You only have to say the word.'

I said, quaking: 'What are you? What kind of a devil are you?'

The devil laughed. 'I am Elmek, sometimes known as Asmorod, the devil of knives and sharp edges. I am the devil of swords and daggers and razors. Do you like my work, you with your blunt cudgel and your blunt anger?'

I hurled my candlestick towards the shadows where the devil's voice came from, but it clattered uselessly against the wardrobe door, and dropped to the floor.

'You have a choice, *monsieur*,' the devil said. 'You can either help me or try to hinder me. If you help me, Adramelech will reward you. If you hinder me, these dead will remain dead, and I will make sure that your precious Madeleine is sliced up like so much meat.'

I pressed my hands to my forehead. I could hear Antoinette gurgling and choking in her own blood, but there was nothing I could do. If I tried to fight this devil any longer, it was going to cut everyone to pieces, including Madeleine and Eloise and Jacques Passerelle, and once the sun had risen and set, it would probably cut me to pieces, too. I knew then that I was going to have to pacify this demon, and play for as much time as I could get. If we searched for its brethren, it's twelve brother devils, it could take us months, and by that time I might have found some way to exorcise it for good.

I lowered my eyes, trying to look resigned and obedient. I said: 'All right. It's a bargain. What do you want me to do?'

The devil rustled in pleasure. 'I thought you might see sense. You *are* a good man and true, aren't you?'

'I'm just trying to save people's lives,' I told him.

'Of course. Very commendable. Life is full of commendable deeds, and it's such a pity that they usually cause so much pain. I am the devil of suicide by throat-cutting or slashing of wrists, did you know that? I am always honoured when someone slices himself up nicely.'

'Just tell me what to do.'

'Of course,' said the devil. 'All in good time.'

'What am I going to do with these bodies? What if the police ask me about them?'

'That's very simple. When we have left, the house will burn. Not a severe blaze, but enough to gut this room, and the room along the corridor where this lady slept. It will be a great tragedy. Everybody will be sorry that their old priest is dead, but he was senile, wasn't he, and perhaps he let the candle fall on his bedspread, or a stray log drop on to his rug. Nobody will think to question you. You will have had no motive for arson, and so nobody will suspect your involvement.'

'For Christ's sake, I didn't kill them anyway!'

The devil laughed. 'How many murderers have said that! How many witches have protested their innocence! How many Nazis claimed they were only obeying their orders!'

I shut my mouth tight, and told myself, silently and firmly, to keep my fear and my anger bottled up tight. If this devil ever suspected that I was trying to play it along, it would probably cut me up like shish-kebabs in a split-second. I still couldn't get that sickening apparition of Antoinette out of my mind, and I knew that I was going to have nightmares about those forests of knives and scissors for the rest of my life. There was no sound, now, from the doorway. I guessed she was probably dead.

'How are we going to get you to England?' I asked the devil

Elmek was silent for a moment. Then it said: 'There is a copper-and-lead-bound trunk in the cellar. It was first used for carrying sacramental robes and chalices in the days when the king travelled around the countryside, staying at the chateaux of French barons. I will enjoy the irony of travelling in it myself. You will arrange for transportation across the Channel this afternoon, and all you will have to do is collect the trunk from the cellar and take it with you.'

'Supposing I deliberately forget? Supposing I leave you behind?'

'Then these two people will remain as dead as they are now, and your precious Madeleine will have the nastiest death I can devise. And so will you.'

Outside the shattered window, the sky was growing greyer as dawn approached. I said: 'All right. If that's what you want.'

'That's precisely what I want. I am looking forward to meeting the Reverend Taylor again.'

I stood in the ruined room, wondering what I ought to do next. I kept the ring of hair curled around my finger, and I couldn't even bear to look at the carnage around me. I felt a sourish, bilious taste in my mouth.

The devil said: 'You can go now. Get dressed. The sooner you arrange our journey, the better.'

I looked up at the gloomy corner where it was hidden. I said: 'If I disbelieved in you – if I refuted your very existence – would you disappear?'

Elmek laughed once again. 'If I disbelieved in *you*,' it said, 'if I refuted *your* very existence, would *you* disappear?'

I wiped my soiled and sweaty face with my hand, and I felt about as desperate and depressed as I ever had in my whole life.

I reached the Passerelle's farm just after seven, in a chill, thick fog. I parked the Citroën in the muddy yard, walked across to the stable door, and knocked. A black-and-white dog with matted fur came and sniffed at my knees, and then loped off round the side of the farm buildings.

Jacques Passerelle appeared at the door, wiping his hands on a towel. His braces were hanging from his belt, and he still had a blob of white shaving cream clinging to his left ear. He was smoking one of his Gauloises and coughing.

'Mr McCook, *qu'est-ce que c'est qui se passe?*'

'Is Madeleine here? It's rather urgent.'

'She's milking. Round the side there, third door. You look bad. A night on the tiles?'

I grimaced. 'Would you believe I spent a night with Father Anton?'

Jacques laughed. 'These priests! They're worse than the rest of us!'

I stepped around the thickest ruts of mud until I reached the cowshed door. It was warm and musky in there, scented with the breath of cows. Madeleine was perched on a stool, wearing a blue scarf around her head, jeans, and muddy rubber boots. Her hands worked expertly at the cow's teats, and the thin jets of milk rang against the sides of the zinc pail. I leaned against the door for a while, and then I said: 'Madeleine.'

She looked up, surprised. In her work clothes, she had a casual, *gamine* attractiveness that, in normal circumstances, I couldn't have resisted. She said: 'Dan! *Quelle heure est-il?*'

'Ten past seven.'

'Why have you come so early? Is anything wrong?'

I nodded, trying to keep my shock and nausea under control. I said: 'I don't know how to tell you.'

She let go of the cow's udder, and set the pail down on the cobbled floor. Her face was pale and strained, and it looked as if she hadn't slept a lot more than I had

She said: 'Is it Father Anton? Is he all right?'

I shook my head.

'He's not—?'

I was so exhausted that I leaned my head against the frame of the cowshed door, and when I spoke I could only manage a dull, tired monotone. I felt as if I'd been gutted, like a herring, and left to drain on somebody's sink.

'The devil broke out somehow. I heard it in the night. I went downstairs and it had killed Father Anton. Then it killed Antoinette in front of my eyes, to prove its power.'

Madeleine came across the shed and touched my shoulder. 'Dan – you're not serious. Please.'

I lifted my head and looked at her. 'How serious do I have to be? I was there. I saw the devil cut Father Anton open, and I saw him kill Antoinette. It says its name is Elmek, the devil of sharp knives. It said that if we didn't help it find its brethren, it would cut us to pieces as well.'

'I can't believe what you're saying.'

'Well, you'd better damn well believe it, because it's true! If you don't want to wind up like Antoinette, you'd better find some way of making your excuses to your father and getting yourself an indefinite vacation.'

She frowned. 'What do you mean?'

'I mean that all the time we have is the time that devil decides to grant us. It insists we help it find its brethren, and we're only going to stay alive as long as we appear to be co-operating. It wants to leave for England this afternoon. If we leave at eight, we can just catch the ferry at Dieppe.'

Madeleine looked completely confused. 'Dan, I can't just walk out of here! What can I say to papa? I'm supposed to be here to help!'

I was so tired and upset that I was near to tears. 'Madeleine,' I insisted, 'I wouldn't ask you if it wasn't deadly serious. If *you* won't make your excuses to your father, then *I'll* have to go and tell him the truth.'

'But Dan, it seems so *unreal*.'

'Don't you think I feel the same way?' I asked her.

92

'Don't you think I'd rather get on with my damned work and forget this thing ever happened? But I've seen it for myself, Madeleine. It's real, and we're both in danger of death.'

Those pale Norman eyes regarded me seriously. Then Madeleine slowly pulled the scarf from her hair, and said: 'You mean it.'

'Yes, I damned well mean it.'

She looked out of the cowshed across the foggy yard. Over the hills, behind the dim tracery of leafless elms, the sun glowered through the grey haze of another winter day in the Suisse Normande.

'Very well,' she said. 'I'll go and tell my father. I can pack in half an hour.'

I followed her through a flock of grubby geese and into the farmhouse. Jacques Passerelle was in the red-tiled hallway, combing his short hair into a neat parting. Madeleine came up behind him and held him round the waist. He glanced up at her face in the mirror and smiled.

'You've finished the milking already?' he asked her.

She shook her head. 'I'm afraid that Dan came with an urgent message. I have to spend a little time in England.'

He frowned. '*Angleterre? Pourquoi?*'

Madeleine lowered her eyes. 'I can't lie. It's something to do with the tank. We have to go and find some information for Father Anton.'

Jacques turned around and held his daughter's arms. 'The tank? Why do you have to go to England because of the tank?'

'Because of the English priest, father. The Reverend Taylor, who was here in the war. He is the only man who really knows about the tank, and what was inside it.'

I put in: 'We won't be away long, *Monsieur* Passerelle. Maybe a week at the outside. Then I promise I'll bring her straight back.'

Jacques rubbed his shiny shaven chin. 'I don't know

93

what to say. All this tank seems to bring is trouble and more trouble.'

I said, 'Believe me, *monsieur*, this is going to be the last of it. Once we're back from England, you won't ever hear about that tank again. Not ever.'

Jacques Passerelle sniffed. He didn't seem to be particularly impressed by that. He turned to Madeleine and asked: 'Why does it have to be you? Can't Mr McCook go by himself? It always seems that you have to do the work that others should do. And what about Father Anton?'

Madeleine looked across at me appealingly. I knew she didn't want to leave her father to cope by himself in the middle of winter. But I shook my head. The last thing I was going to do was cross that devil again. My ring of hair was going to protect me only until the sun set, and then I would be as vulnerable as Madeleine.

'*Monsieur*,' I told him, 'we really have to go, both of us. I'm sorry.'

The farmer sighed. 'Very well, if that's what you have to do. I will call Gaston Jumet and ask him if Henriette can come up and help me. You said a week, no more?'

'About a week,' I told him, although I had no idea how long it was going to take us to dig up Elmek's twelve infamous brethren.

'Very well,' he said, and kissed his daughter, and shook my hand. 'If this is something really important. Now, would you like some calvados and coffee?'

While Madeleine packed, I sat at the kitchen table with Jacques and Eloise. Outside, it began to snow again – thin, wet snow that dribbled slowly down the window panes. We talked about farming and cows and what to do when turnips started to mildew in the ground.

After a while, Jacques Passerelle knocked back his calvados, wiped his mouth with his spotted handkerchief, and said: 'I must get to work. We have two fields to plough by the end of the week. I wish you *bon voyage*.'

We shook hands and then he went off into the hallway to pull on his wellingtons and his thick jacket. I stirred my coffee carefully, waiting until he was out of earshot, and then I said, 'Eloise?'

The old woman nodded. 'I know.'

'You know? How do you know?'

She said nothing, but reached in the pocket of her apron, and produced a worn sepia photograph of a young cleric. He was holding a boater in his hands, and squinting into the sun.

I looked at the picture for a long while, and then I said: 'This is Father Anton.'

'Yes, *monsieur*. I have known him for many years. When we were young, we were close friends. We were so close, in fact, that we hardly had to speak to know what each other was thinking. Well, Father Anton reached me last night, after a fashion. I woke in the night and felt that I had lost him; and when I saw you this morning, I knew that he was dead.'

'You didn't tell Jacques?'

'I told nobody. I wasn't really sure it was true. I hoped that it wasn't. But then I saw you, and I knew.'

I took out the ring of hair which she had given me. 'Listen, Eloise,' I asked her, 'is this all the hair you have?'

She lifted her grey head and looked at me closely through her flour-dusted spectacles. 'You want more? Why?'

'The devil is loose, Eloise. It was the devil who killed Father Anton. That's why we're going to England. The devil insists.'

'Insists?'

'If we don't do what it says, it's going to stab us to death. Madeleine and me. Its name is Elmek, the devil of knives.'

Eloise took the photograph of Father Anton from me with shaking hands. She was so agitated that she couldn't speak at first, and I poured her a small glass of calvados.

She drank half of it, and coughed, and then looked back at me with a face so ghastly with strain that I felt frightened myself.

'Did he suffer?' she whispered. 'Did poor Father Anton suffer?'

'I don't know. I don't think so. But I saw Antoinette die too, his housekeeper, and she was in terrible pain.'

'What's going to happen? What are we going to do?'

'There's not much we can do except what we're told. The devil is going to burn the bodies so that nobody knows what happened – and Eloise, it's desperately important that you don't tell them.'

Eloise was weeping. 'What about Madeleine?' she said, wiping her eyes with her apron. 'It won't hurt Madeleine, will it?'

I took her hand. 'It won't if we do what it tells us to do. I have to find out how to destroy it first, how to exorcise it. Meanwhile, we're going to have to go along with it, and help it find its twelve brethren.'

Eloise said: 'There is only one thing I can do to help you. Wait for one moment.'

She rose stiffly from her chair and walked across the tiled floor to the kitchen dresser. She opened a drawer, fumbled around for a while with tins and jars and boxes, and eventually took out a small tin with the name of a popular brand of French throat pastilles printed on it. She brought it over to the table and carefully lifted the lid.

I peered inside. There was nothing there but a small heap of what looked like grey powder.

'What's this?' I asked her.

She closed the lid again, and handed the tin to me. 'It is said to be the ashes of the seamless cloak which Christ wore when he was crucified. It is the most powerful relic I have.'

'What will it do? Will it protect us?'

'I don't know. Some relics have real magical properties

96

and some are simply frauds. It is all I can do. It is all I can give you.'

She turned away then, her eyes filled with tears. I didn't know what to do to comfort her. I slipped the tin of ashes in my pocket and finished my coffee. The clock on the kitchen wall struck eight; I knew that if we were going to make the lunchtime ferry to Newhaven, we were going to have to hurry.

Madeleine came downstairs with her suitcase. I got up from the table and took it from her, and gave Eloise a last affectionate pat on the shoulder.

Madeleine said: 'What's the matter? Why is Eloise crying?'

'She knows about Father Anton. And she's worried that the same thing's going to happen to you.'

Madeleine leaned over the old woman and kissed her. 'Don't worry,' she said. 'We won't be gone long. Mr McCook will look after me.'

Eloise nodded miserably.

'Come on,' I said, 'we're going to be late.'

We went out into the yard, and I stowed Madeleine's suitcase in the back of the 2CV. The thin snow fell on us like a wet veil. We only had one more piece of luggage to collect – the medieval trunk from the cellar of Father Anton's house. We climbed into the car and I started the engine. Then we bounced off along the narrow, icy roads, the car's heater blaring, and the windshield wipers squeaking backwards and forwards.

Although the French rise early, the village was still deserted by the time we reached Father Anton's house and pulled up in the front yard. I got out of the car, walked round, and opened Madeleine's door for her.

'What do we need here?' she asked me, stepping out.

'The devil,' I said gravely. 'We're taking it with us.'

'Taking it with us? I don't understand.'

'Just come and help me. I'll tell you what it's all about later.'

97

Madeleine looked up at the house. She could see the broken window of Father Anton's bedroom, with the curtains flapping and twisting in the cold wind. She said: 'Is Father Anton up there? And Antoinette?'

I nodded. 'We have to be quick. As soon as we leave, the devil's going to set the house alight.'

Madeleine crossed herself. 'We should call the police, Dan. We can't just let this happen.'

I took her wrist, and pulled her towards the house.

'Dan, we ought to! I can't bear to leave Father Anton this way!'

'Listen,' I told her bluntly, 'we don't have any choice. If we don't do what Elmek tells us, we're going to die like them. Can you understand that? And besides, it's Father Anton's only chance of survival, too.'

I unlocked the heavy front door and pushed it open.

'What do you mean?' she said. 'He's dead. How can he have a chance of survival?'

I looked at her straight. 'Because I made a bargain. If we help Elmek to find his twelve brethren, and the thirteen brethren between them raise the demon Adramelech, then it will ask Adramelech to bring Father Anton and Antoinette back to life.'

Madeleine stared at me. 'You don't believe that – surely?'

'What else can I believe? I saw the devil, Madeleine. I saw it with my own eyes. I saw Antoinette covered in knives. I saw Father Anton cut open like a beef carcass.'

'Oh, God,' she said, in a low, haunted voice. 'I can't go through with it.'

'You have to. Now, come on.'

Together, we walked down the echoing length of the polished hallway. I took the cellar key down from its hook, unlocked the cellar door, and led Madeleine down into the musty darkness. At the foot of the stairs I found a lightswitch, and turned it on.

The copper-and-lead trunk was waiting for us. It was

an ancient, dull-coloured rectangular chest, locked with three copper hasps. It must have been six or seven hundred years old, and it was decorated with copper inlays of horses and helmeted riders, and fleurs-de-lys.

Madeleine whispered: 'Is that it? Is the devil in there?'

I nodded. 'You're going to have to help me lift it. Do you think you can manage?'

'I've been milking cows and mucking-out stables for weeks. I think I'm strong enough.'

Full of foreboding, we approached the trunk and stood beside it. Then we took its curved handles in both hands, and slowly lifted it off the cellar floor. It was staggeringly heavy. It must have weighed all of two hundred and twenty pounds, dead weight, and we had to drag it and slide it across to the stairs. Then we hefted it up, step by step, until we reached the hallway.

It was a matter of three or four minutes to get the trunk out of the house and into the yard. I opened up the Citroën's rear door, ready to receive it but I was just rearranging my own cases, when Madeleine said: 'Look! Just look at that!'

Where the trunk rested, the snow was melting. No snow settled on top of it, either. It was almost as if the snow was shrinking away from our evil and malevolent burden in fear.

'One last heave,' I said dryly, and we lifted the trunk into the back of the Citroën. Then I checked my watch. If we took the Route Nationale from Caen, we could be in Dieppe in about three hours. I shut and locked the back of the car, and we climbed in and settled ourselves down.

I said to Madeleine, softly: 'You don't have to go through with this if you don't want to. I mean, if you don't really believe this devil's going to hurt you, you could take a risk and stay at home.'

'What do you mean?'

I shrugged. 'I'm not sure. But I've always felt that any

kind of devil only has as much power as you're prepared to concede it. If we weren't afraid of Elmek, then maybe it couldn't hurt us.'

Madeleine shook her head. I believe in this devil, Dan. I've believed in it longer than you have. And I started all this terrible killing, too, so I think I have a duty to see it through.'

'It's your choice,' I told her, and switched on the engine. Then I pulled out of the snowbound yard, and drove through the cold, empty streets of Pont D'Ouilly. I kept glancing in my mirror at the dull shape of the medieval trunk – and also to see if any smoke was rising yet out of Father Anton's house But the trunk remained silent and closed, and it only took a few minutes of driving down those winding roads before the village disappeared behind the trees and the hills, and I never saw Elmek's strange powers at work.

Madeleine said: 'I'm sorry, Dan. If I'd only known.'

'We'll beat them yet,' I told her. 'Elmek and Adramelech and the whole damned team.'

But when I looked again at the sinister bulk of that ancient trunk, I felt far from confident; and I couldn't even guess at what hideous atrocities its nightmarish inhabitant was already scheming.

A French onion-seller wavered across the road in front of me on his bicycle, and I blew my horn at him angrily.

'*Cochon!*' he shouted, and shook his fist as he dwindled out of sight in the snow.

Dieppe was as grey and tatty as any Channel port, and we only stopped in the cobbled square in the centre of town for a few minutes, just to change some French francs into British pounds. It was almost lunchtime, and we were lucky to make the bank before it closed. In France, they take their lunch seriously. Then we drove out to the SNCF ferry, past the cluttered little cafés and tourist arcades and bars called 'Le Bar Anglais' or 'Le

Bar Churchill', where day-tripping British tourists spent their last few francs on very ordinary *vin ordinaire*; past the cranes and the docks and the clutter of crates and trucks; until we turned the corner and saw the black-and-white ship with its red-painted funnel, and the English Channel the colour of pale green soup.

I bought tickets, and we waited nervously in line for twenty minutes before our Citroën was waved down the metal ramp into the bowels of the ship. We parked the car in a jampack of Mercedes and Audis and Renaults, and then climbed to the upper decks to wait out the three-and-a-half hour journey.

The trip across the Channel to Newhaven is one of the dullest sea voyages there is. We went into the ferry's restaurant, and ate leek soup and veal with congealed gravy, while the ship's engines drummed and the sea rose and tipped outside the salt-stained windows.

Madeleine said: 'You're very quiet.'

I mopped up soup with a piece of stale French bread. 'I was thinking about last night.'

'Was it really terrible?'

'I was scared stiff, if that's what you mean.'

She looked out of the window. 'Do you think we can exorcise it? Do you think there's any way?'

'Well, maybe the Reverend Woodfall Taylor will know the answer to that – if the Reverend Woodfall Taylor's still alive.'

'Oh, God, I hope so.'

They brought the meat and a selection of overcooked vegetables. At least they had a decent wine – a bottle of rich, heady Margaux that almost sent me to sleep with its fumes. I ate because I was hungry, but every mouthful was like balsa wood.

Madeleine said: 'Couldn't we simply throw the trunk over the side?'

I sipped my wine. 'I suppose we could do. But I don't think devils drown, do you? And what if he killed us before we could throw him over? Or after? And apart from any of those problems, the ship's crew would probably stop us. I shouldn't think they're very keen on people tossing strange boxes into the Channel.'

She put down her fork, although she had hardly touched her veal.

'Dan,' she said, 'I'm frightened.'

'You have every right to be.'

'No, Dan, I mean *really* frightened. Like something awful is going to happen.'

I looked at her over the rim of my wine glass, and there was nothing I could say. I couldn't pretend that things were going to get better, because it looked as if they were going to get worse. I couldn't even pretend I had a plan to get us out of trouble. All I was doing was playing for time, with the terrible knowledge that Elmek was probably going to sacrifice both of us to Adramelech in any case. Why should he keep his bargain, if he could cut us to shreds by magic at any time he chose, and we were powerless? The ship rolled steadily, and the cutlery and cruets and glasses and ashtrays all rattled and jingled and vibrated in a ceaseless cantata.

Later, we stood by the rail and watched the whitish smudge of England appear on the port side – the seven chalk cliffs they call the Seven Sisters, sloping gradually down on the westward side towards Seaford beach and Newhaven harbour. The ferry turned herself round to back stern-first into the narrow harbour entrance, and a barely intelligible French voice told us over the intercom to return to our cars.

We were both depressed and fearful as we went down the stairs to the car decks and unwillingly rejoined our hellish charge. Neither of us spoke as we sat waiting for the stern doors of the ship to open up, and neither of us looked around at that dark medieval trunk in which the devil nestled. I felt unbearably claustrophobic inside that ship, as if tons of metal were pressing down on me from up above.

At last, the crew waved us out of the ferry and up the ramp to the dockside. It was one of those bright, grey afternoons, with a damp sea-breeze blowing. A cheerful-looking customs official beckoned us towards a vacant inspection bay, and we drove in and stopped.

Madeleine opened her window, and the customs official leaned in. He had that relentless urbanity that always disturbs me in British excise officers – a little different from the laconic gum-chewing lady in the fur coat who always insists you open up all your bags at JFK. He said: 'How long do you plan to stay in Britain, sir?'

'I don't know. About a week. Maybe two.'

'Holiday?'

'Yes, that's right.'

He shaded his eyes against the reflection from our window glass, and peered into the back of the car. Then he walked all the way around, and came up to my window. I opened it, and sat there with what I hoped was a calm, obliging smile. I probably looked like Sylvester the cat when Tweety-Pie's bulldog pal suddenly appears in the garden – all clenched teeth and sick grin.

The customs official said: 'Do you know that it is a serious offence to try to smuggle live animals into the United Kingdom, sir?'

I nodded like an idiot. 'Yes, I knew that. Something to do with rabies, right?'

'That's right, sir. Now, would you care to tell me what you have in that box?'

'Box? Oh, you mean that trunk.'

'Yes, sir.'

'Well, that's just a few odd bits and pieces. I collect antiques. I have a few books in there, a couple of statuettes. Bits and pieces.'

The customs official made a note on his clipboard. Then he pointed with his ballpen to a side bay where a couple of Germans were already having their Mercedes thoroughly searched. He was just about to say something when he frowned, and looked back at me, and then looked around as if he'd lost something.

I said, 'Is everything all right?'

He shook his head, as if it was foggy. 'Yes, sir. I just had the feeling I was going to say something. I can't remember what it was.'

I licked my lips tensely, and glanced over at Madeleine. Neither of us said a word.

The customs official said: 'Very good, sir. Have a pleasant time,' and stuck a label on the Citroën's windshield. I started the engine up, and we drove out of the docks and into the town. It was only when we were out of sight of the cranes and the ships that I let out a long whistle of relief.

Madeleine whispered: 'The devil must have *known* what was going to happen! Did you see what it did to that man's mind? It wiped him *clean*.'

I took a quick look round at the dull lead-coloured trunk. I was beginning to feel so nervous about it now that I kept imagining itches on my skin, and my right eye flickered with a tic that I couldn't control. I didn't dare try to imagine what that thing inside it really looked like. I had seen enough in the darkness of Father Anton's bedroom, and heard enough of its rustling body and scratching claws and its husky, evil voice.

We drove aimlessly around the town of Newhaven, which wasn't much more salubrious than Dieppe. Mean, red-roofed houses with primrose-painted gates. Warehouses and shops. Madeleine said, 'What are we going to do now?'

'I don't know. Find a place to stay, I guess.'

She checked her watch. 'I think we ought to try to find where the Reverend Taylor lives before we do that. The pubs are open now. Let's have a drink and something to eat, and then we can go to the local library. They have a clerical directory called Crockford's in England, and if he's still alive, we'll find his name in there.'

We parked the Citroën in a municipal car park, and crossed the road to a big, dingy Victorian pub called The Prince of Wales, which smelled of spilled beer and cooking fat. We sat by the engraved-glass window drinking some tepid Skol lager, and eating cold sausage rolls with no sausage in them. Gastronomically speaking, England is always a miserable experience after France. Mine host behind the bar was a fat fellow with a check shirt and walrus moustache, who kept pulling pints of beer for himself and discussing the relative merits of the A23 and the A24, which turned out to be roads. One of the Englishman's greatest obsessions, after cricket scores, is route-planning; and when you see the roads you know why.

After our drink, we went in search of the library. It turned out to be a small brick building not far from the car park, where a spinster in a pale-blue cardigan and upswept glasses was almost ready to close for the night. She found a copy of Crockford's Clerical Directory for us, and brought it over to the checking-out table with a face as long-suffering as a Rhesus monkey with a mouthful of vinegar. We flicked through the pages as quickly as we could, while she pulled on her coat, and huffed, and tugged on her gloves, and huffed again, and switched off all the lights at the far end of the room.

But after a quick search through the directory, we found what we were looking for. Taylor, Percy Woodfall. The vicar of St Katherine's, in the village of Strudhoe, near Lewes.

Madeleine breathed: 'That's it! That's him! He's still alive!'

I looked up, and called to the lady librarian: 'Excuse me, ma'am. Can you tell me where Lewes is? Is it near to here?'

She huffed and sniffed and looked at me as if I was

mentally defective. 'It's eight miles up the road. You can't miss it. It has a ruined castle.'

And Strudhoe.'

'Well, oh dear, that's even closer. Three miles along the Lewes road, on the right. Between the main road and the river.'

I turned to Madeleine and I guess I was as pale as she was. If the Reverend Taylor lived that close, and if he knew where the twelve brother devils of Elmek were, then we could have this whole grotesque business finished by tonight.

CHAPTER FOUR

In winter, the valley of the Sussex Ouse is grey with mist, and you can hardly see the long backs of the Downs that surround it on both sides. At the head of the valley, you can make out the cluttered rooftops of Lewes, with its dark tumble-down castle, and from there the river Ouse flows indifferent and colourless between raised banks, sliding towards the sea. As we drove out of Newhaven and headed north along the west bank of the river, it was almost too dusky to see anything, but we could make out blotted clumps of trees, and patches of half-melted snow on the fields.

I kept the window of the car open. The English countryside in winter has a distinctive flat smell to it, mingled with the sharp aroma of woodsmoke from log fires; whereas French fields always smell of dung and frost. Madeleine strained her eyes to catch the road-sign for Strudhoe, and kept reminding me nervously to drive on the left. In the back, the copper-and-lead chest rattled softly and ominously against the side of the car as we bounced over the twisting roads.

'There!' said Madeleine. 'That's it! Next on the right!'

· saw the sign flash past in the light of my yellow French headlamps, and I put on the brakes. The turning was almost hidden by overhanging branches and narrow flint walls, and when I negotiated the Citroën across the main road and down towards the village, I felt as if we were disappearing down a rabbit-hole.

We drove slowly past whitewashed houses with ancient clay-tile roofs; tiny walled gardens and narrow brick pavements. The village was only twenty or thirty houses, all of them hundreds of years old, and I almost drove right through it and down to the fields before I realised that we'd arrived. I stopped the car, and pulled on the handbrake.

Madeleine said, 'I wonder where the vicarage is.'

'I don't know. I guess it's going to be easier to get out and look for it on foot.'

She reached over and held my hand tightly. 'Oh, God, Dan, I'm scared.'

I switched off the engine. It was only then that we heard the soft, subtle noises from the trunk at the back. We sat tense and silent in our seats, staring at each other in horror, and then we heard Elmek's dreadful whispering voice again.

'*We are near, aren't we?*'

I said nothing.

Elmek insisted: '*We are near, aren't we?*'

Madeleine nodded at me, encouraging me to answer, and I said in a taut, strained voice: 'Yes. Yes, we're near.'

'*You have done well. You have found the Reverend Taylor quickly. I will reward you, you know. I will give you the power to snap a man's neck, if that is what you want. Or to thrust knives and razors into a girl's sex. You'd enjoy that, wouldn't you?*'

I closed my eyes in desperation, but Madeleine squeezed my hand and whispered, 'Agree, Dan. All you have to do is agree.'

I said loudly: 'Yes, Elmek. I'd enjoy that.'

Elmek laughed. Then it said: '*Are you going to find the Reverend Taylor now? I can feel him! He's close by!*'

'Yes, we're going to find him.'

'*And you won't do anything foolish, will you? I am sure that the Reverend Taylor's house contains as many knives as Father Anton's. Just remember Antoinette. Didn't she scream! Didn't those knives and skewers hurt her!*'

I swallowed, painfully. 'Yes,' I said. 'They did. They hurt her very much.'

The devil laughed with a soft, creaking noise that made me shudder. I said: 'Come on, Madeleine. Let's go and find the Reverend Taylor,' and I opened the door of the car.

As I stepped out, Elmek whispered from out of its locked trunk: '*Remember – the sun has set. Your ring of hair no longer protects you. So tread wisely!*'

I climbed out of the car into the cold night air. There was a single street lamp by the corner of an old weatherboard house, shining dimly through a halo of fog. You could tell we were close to a river by the bone-chilling cold, and an almost imperceptible movement in the air, as if ghosts were brushing past us, unseen and unheeded. I coughed.

Together, we walked up the sloping street. We looked right and left, but the village was deserted. Far away, across the other side of the river, we heard a train clattering towards Newhaven, and for a moment we saw the lights of its windows through the trees.

Madeleine said, 'Dan – there's a sign here.'

I peered through the fog. On one of the old flint walls, there was a white-painted notice reading 'St Katherine's Church & Vicarage'. It pointed uphill into the gloom. I turned back for a moment and looked at our Citroën, parked at an angle beside a low hedge, and then I said: 'All right, then. We'd better see if the Reverend Taylor's at home.'

My mouth felt as if I was chewing furry caterpillars. I reached out for Madeleine's hand, and we walked as slowly as we could, but it only took a few steps before St Katherine's came into view around the houses – an ancient steepled church with a moss-covered lych-gate and a graveyard of leaning headstones. Close beside it, its windows warmly lit, was a Queen Anne vicarage, fronted with shiny blue-black bricks. There was a white porch trailed with leafless creeper, and an imposing black front door, as glossy as a coffin.

We walked across the street and approached the porch as quietly as we could. It somehow seemed sacrilegious to march around this silent fog-bound English village talking in strident voices. Madeleine leaned forward to read the engraved brass plaque on the door, and whispered: 'There it is, Dan. The Reverend P. Woodfall Taylor.'

I pulled her closer, and kissed her cheek. She smelled of French perfume and soap. She said: 'Your nose is cold.' Then I lifted the weighty brass knocker and struck it twice. Across the road, someone switched on a bedroom light.

Inside the vicarage, I heard doors opening and closing. Then the sound of someone walking towards the door. A key was turned in the lock, and then a slice of light fell across the path, and an elderly face appeared at the crack in the doorway.

'Yes?'

I said, uncertainly: 'Are you the Reverend Taylor, sir?'

'That's correct. Did you want to see me?'

I coughed. 'I'm sorry to disturb you, sir. But there's something I have to discuss.'

The old man looked at me suspiciously. He had a crest of wiry white hair, and that ruddy, well-polished face that always makes me think of English clergy as a boxful of Carolina apples. He was wearing a clerical collar and carpet slippers, and a pair of shiny grey pants that looked as if he'd pressed them under the mattress. There were deep indentations at the side of his nose where he usually wore spectacles, and that was probably why his pale, bulging eyes were regarding me so fixedly.

'You're American, aren't you?' the vicar asked, in precise tones. He even pronounced 'aren't' as 'ah-runt'. He said: 'You're not from the Mormons? Because I'm afraid I have nothing to say to the Mormons.'

'I'm not a Mormon, sir.'

'They're a terrible pest, you know. And all this ridiculous nonsense about Moroni and Boroni.'

Madeleine said, 'We've come about the tank.'

The vicar swivelled his jowly head in his stiff clerical collar and blinked at her. 'The *tank*? How very odd.'

'Why is it odd?' I asked him. I wondered if he, like Eloise, had felt some kind of premonition or psychic wave.

'Well,' said the Reverend Woodfall Taylor, 'they only came around to empty it on Tuesday.'

I stared at him uncomprehendingly and he stared back at me.

'The septic tank,' he explained. 'Isn't that what you meant?'

If I hadn't felt so sick and serious about Elmek, I think I could have laughed. But all I could say was: 'Not *that* tank, sir. The tank you once said prayers over in Normandy, during the war.'

His mouth slowly opened, as if some strong invisible hand was pulling his jaw down. He said, perplexed: '*Normandy*? The tank in *Normandy*?'

I nodded. 'It's been opened, Mr Taylor. The devil's got out.'

He stared at me in absolute slow-motion horror. Then he opened the door wide, and almost dragged us both into his cluttered little hall, among the crowded umbrella-stand and grandfather clock and coat-rack hung with ecclesiastical raincoats and hats. He slammed the door behind us, and locked it.

'You'd better come through,' he said worriedly, and ushered us into his sitting-room. 'My wife is out tonight, organising a beetle-drive for the women's institute, and that's probably just as well.'

The sitting-room smelled of pipe-smoke and logs. There was a wide open hearth, in front of which toasted a marmalade cat and three shabby armchairs. One wall of the room was lined with books like *With Net And Specimen Jar In Lahore* and *The Way Of Christ Vol. IX*, and on the chimney-breast was a muddy oil painting of the Sussex Downs at Fulking. The Reverend Taylor said: 'Sit down, please, sit down. Perhaps I can get my woman to make you a cup of coffee. Or there's whisky, if you prefer.'

'A whisky would be wonderful,' I told him. 'We came all the way over from France this morning.'

The vicar went to an antique sideboard and took out three ill-matched glasses. He filled each with neat Vat 69, and brought them over to the fireside with trembling hands. He swallowed his where he stood, wiped his mouth with a crumpled handkerchief, and said. 'Cheers.'

Madeleine said: 'We're looking for your help, Mr Taylor. We know something about the devil, but not much. Ever since the war, it's had a terrible effect on our village.'

'Oh, dear,' said the Reverend Taylor. 'I told them this business would come to a bad end I told them a hundred times. But oh no, they never listened. You do *your* part, they said, and we'll take care of *ours*.'

'Who were *they*?' I asked him.

The Reverend Taylor looked at me in surprise. 'My dear fellow, I couldn't possibly tell you that. Quite out of the question. I was bound by the Official Secrets Act, and unless I hear to the contrary, I still am.'

'Mr Taylor,' I told him, 'I don't like to sound offensive, but this young lady and I are both in serious danger because of that tank, and I'm afraid the Official Secrets Act is going to have to go where the monkey put his nuts.'

There was a silence. A log in the crackling fire shifted and dropped, and a shower of sparks flew up the chimney.

The Reverend Taylor said: 'I'm afraid I've never really understood that expression.'

Madeleine leaned forward intently. 'Mr Taylor, she said, 'you have to help us. The devil is threatening to kill us both, unless we help it to find its brethren

'It's name is Elmek,' I said quietly. 'The devil of sharp knives and cuts. If we don't bring all thirteen devils

112

together again, it has promised us the worst death that anyone could think of.'

The vicar sat back in his chair. His eyes went from Madeleine to me and back again. Then he said: 'You know about it, don't you? You know about it already.'

'Only some of it. Just a few fragments of information we managed to get together in France, and some good guesswork by Father Anton.'

'Father Anton!' said the Reverend Taylor, brightening. 'I had no idea that he was still alive! I'm amazed! How is he? He was so kind to me during the war, you know. A real gentleman of the cloth.'

'Father Anton died last night, Mr Taylor. He was killed when Elmek got loose.'

The Reverend Taylor dropped his gaze. 'Oh,' he said quietly. 'I'm very sorry.'

I said: 'Mr Taylor, more people are going to get hurt unless you can tell us about these devils. Father Anton said they were probably the thirteen devils that terrorised Rouen in 1045. They were exorcised by Cornelius Prelati, and sewn into sacks, but that was all he could discover.'

The Reverend Taylor sadly blew his nose. 'He was a clever man, Father Anton. Yes, he was absolutely right. They were the thirteen devils of Rouen. *Les treize diables de Rouen.*'

'But how did they get into American tanks?' asked Madeleine. 'I don't understand it at all.'

The vicar shrugged. 'I understood very little of it myself. It all happened a long time ago, when I was a very enthusiastic young vicar, and I had just been appointed to my first church in Sussex.'

'Can you tell us about it?' I asked. 'We'll keep it to ourselves, you know, if you're really worried about the Official Secrets Act.'

The Reverend Taylor looked up at me. 'Well,' he said, 'I suppose there's no harm, since you already know so much about it. Would you care for some more whisky? No? Well, I'll have one.'

We waited in silence while the vicar poured himself another drink. Then he came over and sat by the fire, and stared into the red-hot caverns of logs and branches, a man remembering hell.

'What you have to know about this part of Sussex,' he said, 'was that it bore the brunt of the Norman invasion by William the Conqueror in 1066. All this valley was occupied, and Lewes became the seat of William de Warrenne, who was one of William the Conqueror's most trusted officers. The castle at Lewes was built by de Warrenne, and on the southern slopes of the town an immense Priory was constructed, one of the largest ecclesiastical buildings ever erected in England. In its time, it was even greater than Canterbury Cathedral.'

The Reverend Taylor swallowed half a glass of whisky, and patted his lips with the back of his sleeve.

'Of course, when Henry VIII broke with Rome, the Priory was dissolved, and most of its stones were pilfered by local people to build houses. But the Priory kept some of its secrets for many centuries afterwards. It was only when Victorian railway engineers came to excavate the site where the Priory had stood, to build a line to Brighton, that they came across several remarkable things.'

I looked up at the clock on the Reverend Taylor's mantelpiece. Eight o'clock. I wondered how long Elmek would stay patient in his medieval trunk. Madeleine touched my hand, and I knew she was thinking the same thing.

The Reverend Taylor said: 'First of all, they found the tomb of William de Warrenne's wife, Gundrada, whose burial place was unknown until then. This discovery was well-publicised. But there was another find, which wasn't publicised at all. As they dug deeper, they found a sealed vault, chiselled deep into the chalk, and this contained thirteen ancient sacks of bones.'

Madeleine whispered: 'The thirteen devils.'

'Precisely,' the vicar nodded. 'The thirteen devils, the disciples of Adramelech. And according to words engraved on the lid of the vault, they had been brought across the Channel from Rouen by William de Warrenne as devils of war, concealed in strange suits of armour. He had unleashed them at Senlac, the field on which the Battle of Hastings was fought, and they had flown on Harold and his English soldiers with such ferocity that the battle was won in a matter of hours.'

The Reverend Taylor turned to me, his ruddy face made redder by the heat from the fire.

'I expect you know the story that William's archers fired their arrows into the air, so that they landed amongst the English. Well, they were not arrows, but devils; and the thing that tore out Harold's eyes was a beast from hell.'

I took out a cigarette, my first for a whole day, and lit it. I asked the Reverend Taylor: 'That was nine hundred years ago, wasn't it? How did *you* get involved?'

He looked up. 'My oldest church records showed that William de Warrenne had somehow struck a bargain with the devils. If the devils helped the Normans conquer England, he would give them his wife Gundrada as a sacrifice to Adramelech. That's why the devils came to Lewes, and that's why Gundrada died when she did. But there were powerful French exorcists at the Priory, and they managed to quell the evil spirits, and sew them up again in sacks. It was only when the railway engineers opened up the vault that they saw the light of day once more.'

'What happened to them then?'

The Reverend Taylor finished his whisky. 'They were taken to what are now the vaults of St Thaddeus, by night, and sealed away by seven Roman Catholic priests.

This, apparently, was what it took to keep them from breaking out.'

I whispered: 'Father Anton tried to seal the devil away on his own. My God, if only we'd found this out earlier.'

'A single priest would not have sufficient power,' said the Reverend Taylor. 'It had to be seven, and they had to invoke seraphim to help them. The thirteen devils of Adramelech were not to be played with.'

'And then what?' asked Madeleine. 'How did the Americans find out about them?'

'I was never really sure, my dear,' answered the vicar. 'I found out the story myself, and I wrote a short article about it in my parish magazine, in 1938. I can't imagine that my little publication ever reached as far as Washington, but some very mysterious American gentlemen got in touch with me in 1943, and asked me a great many questions about the devils and the vaults and what could be done to control them.'

'And you told them?' I asked.

'I told them all I knew, which wasn't very much. I didn't think about it for a while, but in January, 1944, I received a letter from Bishop Angmering, saying that Allied forces had a patriotic interest in the devils of Rouen, and that I was to give them every co-operation possible.'

The Reverend Taylor was obviously disturbed by his memories. He got up from his chair, and began to walk up and down the worn carpet of his sitting-room, his hands clasped firmly behind his back.

'They came one day with Roman Catholic priests, and they took the thirteen sacks away. I didn't know where they were taking them, but I begged them to be careful. I said the devils were not to be meddled with, but they said that they were quite aware of that, and that was why they wanted them.'

He sat down again, and rubbed his eyes with his knuckles.

'The next I knew, I was ordered to go to Southampton, and report to an American colonel called Sparks. He was a very brusque man, I remember. Very crisp. He said that my devils were to be used by the American forces for a secret mission. A special division. They had been brought back to life by the conjurations of the Kabbalah, and they had been promised great rewards if they fought on the side of the Allies against the Hun. I never found out what these great rewards were, but I suspect now that they may have involved . . . well, human sacrifices. I asked one of the American officers, but all he ever did was smile, and tell me that what they were doing was for western liberty and freedom.'

'So you went across to France with this division?' I asked the Reverend Taylor.

'I did, although I was kept in the rear most of the time. Since it was impracticable to take seven Roman Catholic priests along with us, it was my duty to make sure the devils stayed in their tanks, and I did this with silver crosses that had been blessed by seven priests, and with incantations from the holy exorcism. I was only required once, as you know, when one of the tanks broke a track, and they found it impossible to move.'

Madeleine slowly shook her head. 'Didn't it ever occur to you, Mr Taylor, that the devil you left in that tank would bring misery to all who lived near it?'

The Reverend Taylor frowned. 'I sealed it away . . . and they told me the tank would last for ever.'

'But, out of all the thirteen devils, this was the only devil who hadn't been rewarded, right?' I asked him.

'I suppose so.'

'So it was bound to be troublesome, and dissatisfied?'

'Well, yes.'

I sat back, and wearily ran my fingers through my hair. 'What you did, Mr Taylor, left a thirty-year plague on that community. Milk went sour, eggs went rotten, and

117

now the devil's got out, and two people have died. Three, if you count this young lady's mother.'

The vicar licked his lips in embarrassment. He said, in a low voice: 'Is there anything I can do to help? Anything to protect you, or assist you?'

'You can tell us where the other twelve devils are.'

The Reverend Taylor blinked at me. 'The other twelve? But I haven't the faintest idea. They took them away after the war, and I never found out what happened to them. I suppose they sealed them away, once they had had their rewards, and took them off to America.'

'America? You have to be kidding! We have a devil out there who's—'

The Reverend Taylor's eyes bulged. 'You have it *out there*? You have Elmek outside my house?'

I took a deep breath. I hadn't really meant to tell him straight away. But I said, in the most controlled voice I could muster: 'I have him locked in a lead trunk, in the back of my car. He forced us to bring him to England, on pain of death by cutting or slicing or whatever it is he does. He wants to join his brethren.'

The vicar was so flustered that he got out of his chair, and then sat down again straight away. 'My dear man,' he said, breathlessly, 'do you have any notion how dangerous that creature is?'

'I saw it kill Father Anton's housekeeper, and I saw what it did to Father Anton.'

'My God,' said the Reverend Taylor, 'that was why the Americans wanted them. They're devils of war – devils of violence. Thirteen devils in army tanks were as vicious and terrible as three divisions of ordinary troops. They swept through the hills of the Suisse Normande in a matter of days. The Germans just couldn't stop them. I wasn't right up at the front line, so I never saw what they did first hand, but I heard dreadful stories from some of the German prisoners-of-war. Some of the Hun were dying of leprosy and beriberi. Tropical diseases, in northern France! Some were blazing like torches. And others were drowning in their own blood, without any apparent signs of external injury. It was a terrible business, and I was glad when Patton stopped it.'

'Why *did* he stop it?' asked Madeleine.

The Reverend Taylor pulled a face. 'Once he'd broken through Normandy, I think he felt it would be more discreet, with regard to future war trials, if his tanks didn't leave behind them the bodies of men who had died in unnatural and unholy ways.'

I took a deep drag on my cigarette. 'What I can't understand is why the church was so ready to go along with it. These devils are *enemies* of the church, aren't they?'

'People's standards are different in time of war,' said the vicar. 'I believe that the Bishop felt he was doing the right thing. And after all, the Americans did agree to take the devils away after it was all over, and dispose of them. We were all glad of that.'

I sighed, tiredly. 'But you've no idea *where* they were taken, or who took them?'

The vicar said: 'I know that Colonel Sparks took care of them once they were shipped back to England. But where he took them, or how, I was never told. It was an extremely hush-hush operation. If any inkling had leaked out – well, there would have been a terrible flap.'

Madeleine asked: 'They were brought back to England? They weren't shipped direct to America from France?'

'No, they weren't. The last time I saw them myself was at Southampton, when they were unloading them from ships. The usual dockers were told to keep well away.'

'So what makes you think they took them off to America? Couldn't they still be here?'

The Reverend Taylor scratched his head. 'I suppose so. There's only one way to find out.'

'What's that?'

'Well, you'd have to talk to Colonel Sparks himself. He always sends me a Christmas card, every year, although we never met after the war. I have his address somewhere.'

Madeleine and I exchanged anxious glances as the Reverend Taylor went across to his desk and started sorting through stacks of untidy papers in search of the American colonel's greetings cards. It was now eight-twenty, and I began to have a fearful, restless feeling that Elmek wasn't going to give us much more time. The Reverend Taylor said: 'I was sure they were here, you know. I never throw anything away.'

I took out another cigarette, and I was just about to lift it to my lips when Madeleine said: 'Dan – look. Your hand.'

I couldn't think what she was talking about at first, but then I looked down at the cigarette I was holding and saw that it was soaked pink with blood. I had a small deep cut on the end of my finger.

'It's Elmek,' said Madeleine, in a tight, desperate voice. 'Oh God, Dan, he's warning us.'

Tugging out my handkerchief, I bound up the end of my finger as best I could, but it didn't take long before the thin cotton was drenched. I said: 'Mr Taylor – I'd really appreciate it if you hurried.'

'Sorry – did you say something?' asked the vicar, looking up from his papers.

'Please hurry. I think Elmek's getting impatient.'

The Reverend Taylor shuffled through some more papers, and then he said: 'Ah – here we are! This is last year's card, so I expect he's still living there.'

He passed over the Christmas card, and Madeleine opened it up. Almost immediately, uncannily, my finger stopped bleeding, and the wound closed up. I was left with a crimson handkerchief and no visible scar at all.

The Reverend Taylor said: 'My dear chap, have you cut yourself?'

*

The transatlantic line to Silver Spring, Maryland, was crackling and faint. It was just after lunch in the States, and Mr Sparks, onetime colonel, was out mowing his lawn. His cleaning lady dithered and fussed, but eventually agreed to get him on the line. I was glad I wasn't paying the Reverend Taylor's telephone bill that quarter.

At last, a sharp voice said: 'Hello? Who is this?'

Madeleine watched me as I answered: 'I'm sorry to trouble you, sir. My name's Dan McCook, and I'm standing right now in the home of the Reverend Woodfall Taylor.'

'Oh, really? Well, that's a surprise! I haven't seen Mr Taylor since 1945. Is he well? You're not calling to tell me he's passed away, are you?'

'No, no, nothing like that. Mr Taylor's in fine shape. But I am ringing about that little business you and he were involved in on D-Day.'

There was a crackly silence.

'Can you hear me okay?' I asked him.

'Sure, I hear you. What do you know about that?'

'Well, sir, I guess I know almost everything.'

'I see. It's a Pentagon secret, I hope you realise.'

'Yes, sir, I do. But right now we need some help.'

'Help? What kind of help?'

My hand suddenly began to feel sticky on the telephone receiver. I was bleeding again, from cuts all over my hands, and the blood was running down my sleeve. Madeleine said: 'Oh Dan, tell him to *hurry*. Elmek will kill you!'

I whispered, 'Okay, okay – the cuts aren't bad. He's just trying to needle me.'

Mr Sparks said: 'Are you there? Are you still there?'

'Yes, Mr Sparks, sorry. Listen, I need to know where the twelve remaining sacks were taken. You left one behind in Normandy. Where are the rest? Were they shipped to the States? Or were they left in England?'

There was another silence. Then Mr Sparks said: 'Well . . . I'm not sure I'm allowed to tell you that.'

'Mr Sparks, please. It's a matter of life or death. That devil you left behind in Normandy has got out of its tank. We have to find the rest of them.'

'Well, Mr McCook, we called them ANPs, which was short for Assisting Non-Military Personnel. We certainly never knew them as, well, devils. They were ANPs.'

'All right, Mr Sparks. ANPs. But where were they taken? Are they hidden in the States?'

'No, they aren't,' said Mr Sparks, reluctantly. 'They were shipped back to England, and put into cold storage, militarily speaking. I believe that General Eisenhower wanted them taken back to the States, but the problems of carrying them over and keeping them under lock and key were too tricky right then. We knew very little about them, and so we left them where they were.'

'And where was that?'

'Well, we wanted to take them back to St Thaddeus, where they originally came from. But we'd made a deal with the Bishop that we would take them off his hands. So we transported them to London, and they were sealed up in a house that belonged to the British War Office.'

'You mean they're still there? Now?'

'As far as I know. I've never heard any news to the contrary.'

The blood was beginning to dry on the back of my hand. Madeleine was staring at me anxiously, and through the door I could see the Reverend Taylor, pouring himself another Scotch. I can't say that I blamed him.

I said hoarsely: 'Mr Sparks, do you know where the house is? Even roughly?'

'Why sure. Eighteen Huntington Place, just off the Cromwell Road.'

'Are you sure?'

'Sure I'm sure. I had to go there four or five times.'

I leaned back against the brown flowers of the Reverend Taylor's wallpaper, and closed my eyes.

'Mr Sparks,' I said, 'I don't know how to thank you.'

'Don't bother. I shouldn't be telling you anyway.'

'If we get out of this alive,' I told him, 'I'll pay you a personal visit and bring you a bottle of brandy.'

There was a long pause. I could hear another faint voice on a crossed line. Then ex-Colonel Sparks said: 'What do you mean – if you come out of this alive?'

I didn't know what to answer. I just set down the telephone receiver and said to Madeleine: 'He knew where they were. We're going to have to drive to London.'

The Reverend Taylor came out to the hall and his face was even more flushed than ever. 'Are you sure you won't have another drink?' he asked us. 'Or how about some sandwiches? My woman's going home in a moment, but she could rustle up some tongue sandwiches.'

'Really,' I said, 'that's very kind of you, but we have to go right away.'

The vicar looked at me nervously. 'Did Colonel Sparks know where they were? Did he tell you?'

I nodded. 'He knew where they were sealed away after the war. Whether they're still there or not is another matter. But we're going to have to go to find out.'

'Oh, dear,' said the Reverend Taylor, 'this is all very distressing. I told them it would come to a bad end.'

Madeleine said: 'It wasn't your fault, Mr Taylor. You weren't to know.'

'But I feel dreadfully responsible,' he told us worriedly. 'I feel as if it was my negligence that killed poor Father Anton.'

'Well, maybe you can make up for it, I suggested. 'Maybe you can give us some idea of how to protect ourselves against these thirteen devils and against Adramelech.'

The Reverend Taylor's face fell. 'My dear fellow, I hardly know what to say. It was only because we had such a great number of priests during the war that we were able to keep the devils under control. But as for Andramelech himself – well, I'm afraid I don't know what to tell you. Adramalech is one of the greatest and most terrible of the evil Sephiroth. Perhaps only one of the *divine* Sephiroth would be able to help you, and according to what is written about them, the divine Sephiroth are almost as unmanageable as the evil ones. Adramelech's counterpart among God's ranks is Hod, the seraph of majesty and glory; but whether Hod could possibly be summoned to help you – well, I really couldn't say. It's all so infernally mythical.'

I lit a fresh cigarette. This time, my fingers stayed intact. Perhaps Elmek had realised that we had the information that we'd come for, and that he'd soon be rejoining his malevolent brethren.

I said: 'Do you really believe in all this? In Adramelech and Hod? And all these devils. I never knew the Protestant church held with devils.'

The Reverend Taylor stuck his hands in his pockets and looked a little abashed.

'You will rarely find a Protestant cleric who admits to the actual physical existence of devils,' he said. 'But every Anglican priest is told in strict confidence of the evidence that exists to support them. I couldn't possibly divulge what the books say, but I assure you that the evidence I have personally seen for the existence of the divine and the evil Sephiroth is more than overwhelming. There are demons and devils, Mr McCook, just as there are angels.'

Just then, I felt a low-frequency vibration tremble through the house. It was like a sinister train passing, a train that blew a deep dark whistle. I looked up at the ceiling, and I saw a hairline crack that ran all the way from one plaster moulding to the other.

The Reverend Taylor looked up, too. 'What on earth's that?' he blinked. 'Did you feel it?'

'Yes, I felt it,' said Madeleine. 'Maybe it was a supersonic plane passing.'

The Reverend Taylor frowned. 'I don't think Concorde flies this way, my dear. But I suppose it could—'

There was another rumble, louder this time. The floors shook and a fiery log dropped out of the grate and into the hearth. The Reverend Taylor hurriedly unhooked the tongs from the firedog, and stacked the log back on the fire.

I said: 'It's Elmek. I'm sure of it. He's restless. Come on, Madeleine, I think we ought to get out of here before anything worse happens.'

The Reverend Taylor raised his hand. 'You mustn't leave on my account. I was just as responsible for what happened as anybody. And perhaps I can help.'

He went across to his bookshelves, and spent three or four minutes searching for what he wanted. He tugged it out at last – a small book as thin as a New Testament, with black leather covers and a frayed silk bookmark. Holding the book longsightedly at arm's length, he licked his thumb and leafed through six or seven pages. Madeleine and I waited impatiently, while the clock struck nine.

'Ah, here it is. The invocation of angels.'

'I have a French book about that in my luggage,' I told him. '*L'Invocation des Anges* by Henri St Ermin. The trouble is, I can hardly understand a word of it.'

Again, the house trembled. A china donkey with a dried-up cactus in its pannier was shaken off its shelf, and shattered on the floor. Two or three books dropped out, and the windows vibrated in their frames with a sound that set my teeth on edge.

'*L'Invocation des Anges* is just what you need,' said the Reverend Taylor, a little breathless. 'But this book will help you identify each of the twelve other devils in turn and call an appropriate angel to dismiss it. Did Father Anton mention the seven tests to you?'

'You mean the seven tests of a devil's identity? Yes, he did.'

The Reverend Taylor nodded gravely. 'A brilliant man, Father Anton. I can't tell you how sorry I am that he's gone. Well, he was absolutely right. When you find the devils you must identify each in turn, and use your book *L'Invocation des Anges* to send them away. They are French devils, you see, and French dismissals will have a greater effect on them.'

Madeleine said: 'If we dismiss them, will that prevent them from summoning Adramelech?'

The Reverend Taylor looked at her seriously. 'One hopes so, my dear. But of course devils are devils, and one can never quite predict how they are going to behave, or what tricks they are going to use. Take this terrible beast Elmek, for example—'

The curtains covering the windows suddenly flapped, as if they were being blown by a wind that we couldn't even feel. I turned towards the window in fright, and I was sure that for one second I glimpsed, in the darkness outside, the evil slanting eyes of the demon of knives. Above us, the lights went dim and sickly, until we could hardly see each other, and a sour smell of decay flowed through the room.

The Reverend Taylor shivered. Then he raised his hand and drew the sign of the cross in the air, and called: 'Devil, begone! I adjure thee, O vile spirit, to go out! God the Father, in His name, leave our presence! God the Son, in His name, make thy departure! God the Holy Ghost, in His name, quit this place! Tremble and flee, O impious one, for it is—'

There was a howl so loud that I jumped in terror. It sounded as if a fearsome beast was actually devouring the whole room. The curtains lifted and flapped again, and a whole row of books toppled like dominoes and splayed across the carpet. Madeleine clutched my arm in fear, and the Reverend Taylor raised both his hands to protect himself from the rushing sound of demonic hate.

'It is God who commands thee!' shouted the Reverend Taylor. 'It is I who command thee!'

The windows burst in a cloud of tumbling, spraying, razor-sharp glass. Fragments flew across the room and hit the Reverend Taylor in a glittering explosion that sliced into his upraised hands, ripped the ecclesiastical cloth from his arms and chest, and slashed his face and hands right down to the raw nerves. Before he collapsed, I saw the whiteness of his forearm bones, laid bare amidst the chopped meat of his flesh.

Miraculously, or devilishly, the glass passed Madeleine and me and left us almost unscratched. We watched in horror as the Reverend Taylor sank to the floor, ripped into bloody pieces, and Madeleine pressed her face into my shoulder, gagging with horror.

The last fragments of glass tinkled on to the floor, and a freezing wind blew in through the window. Holding Madeleine close, I said: 'Elmek.'

There was no answer.

'*Elmek!*' I said, louder.

Outside, in the darkness, there was a dry, laughing sound. It could have been laughing or it could have been the swish of the trees as the wind moaned through their leafless branches.

The door of the sitting-room opened and I froze in fright. But then a red-faced woman in a turquoise overcoat and a turban hat peered around the door and said: 'What a commotion! Is everything all right? I thought I heard glass.'

The Sussex Constabulary kept us at Lewes Police Station for almost three hours. Most of the time, we sat on hard wooden seats in a green-painted corridor and read the same crime-prevention posters over and over. An unsmiling superintendent with a clipped black moustache and shoes that were polished beyond human reason asked us questions and examined our passports, but we knew from the start that the Reverend Taylor's hideous death could only look like an accident. A freak accident, of course. But an accident all the same.

Elmek, in his lead-and-copper trunk, was not going to be delayed or thwarted, especially by the procedures of the British police.

At five minutes to midnight, the superintendent came out of his office and handed us our passports.

'Does this mean we can go?' I asked him.

'For the moment, sir. But we'd like a forwarding address. You may have to give evidence at the inquest.'

'Well, okay. The Hilton Hotel.'

The superintendent took out a silver propelling-pencil and wrote that down. 'All right, sir. Thanks for your help. We're advising your embassy of what's happened, just as a matter of courtesy.'

'That's all right by me.'

The superintendent tucked away his pencil and regarded us for a moment with eyes that looked as if they'd been pickled in bleach. I knew that he didn't really understand how the Reverend Taylor's window had blown in with such devastating force, or how Madeleine and I had escaped with nothing but superficial cuts. But there was no sign of explosives, no sign of weapons, no motive, and no possibility that we could have cut him to shreds ourselves with thousands of fragments of glass. I had already heard one constable muttering to his sergeant about 'peculiar vacuums' and 'thousand-to-one chances', and I guessed that they were going to put the Reverend Taylor's death down to some wild peculiarity of the English weather.

'You won't be leaving the country, sir?' asked the superintendent. 'Not for a few days, anyway?'

'No, no. We'll stick around.'

'Very well, sir. That'll be all for now, sir. I'll bid you goodnight.'

We left the police station and walked across the road to the sloping car park. The Citroën, silent and dark, was the only car there. We climbed into it warily, and sat back in the rigid little seats. Madeleine yawned, and pulled her fingers through her dark blonde hair. I glanced back at the devil's chest, and said: 'If Elmek's going to let us, I think it's time we had some rest. I didn't sleep last night, and I don't suppose we're going to get ourselves a lot of relaxation tomorrow.'

There was no answer from the dull medieval box. Either the devil was sleeping itself (although I didn't know if devils slept or not) or else it was silently granting me permission to rest. I started up the car, and we went in search of somewhere to stay.

We spent half an hour driving around the streets of Lewes in the dark before Madeleine spotted a bed-and-breakfast sign on the outskirts of town, on a gateway just opposite the forbidding flint walls of Lewes prison. Set back from the road in a driveway of laurel bushes was a red-brick Victorian mansion, and someone was watching a black-and-white television in the front downstairs room. I turned the Citroën into the driveway, parked it, and went to the front door to knock.

I was answered, after a long and frosty wait, by a small hunched old woman in a pink candlewick dressing-gown and paper curlers. She said: 'It's very late, you know. Did you want a room?'

I tried my best not to look like a dishevelled madman or an escaped convict from across the road. 'If that's possible. We've come from France today and we're pretty well bushed.'

'Well, I can't charge you the full rate. You've missed three hours' sleep already.'

I looked at her in disbelief for a moment, and all I

could say was: 'That's okay. That's wonderful. But I'll pay the full rate if you want me to.'

I called Madeleine, and the old woman let us into the house. She took us up a cold flight of stairs to a landing laid with green-and-cream linoleum, where a painting of ducks by Peter Scott hung under a frayed and dusty lampshade. She unlocked a door for us, and showed us into a typically freezing British bedroom, with a high double bed of cream-painted iron, a cheap varnished wardrobe, a cracked sink and a gas fire with half of its fireclay missing.

'We'll take it,' I said wearily, and I sat down on the bed and took off my shoes before she could even answer. The mattress felt as if it was crowded with unravelled fencing wire, but right then it was heaven. The old lady left us alone together, and we undressed, washed in Arctic water, and fell into bed. I don't remember falling asleep, but it must have been pretty quick, because I didn't even have time to put my arm around Madeleine's naked back.

I was wakened by a scuffling noise. For a second, I wasn't sure if I was dreaming or not, but then I heard it again, and I lifted my head from the pillow and looked around. I held my breath, and tried to suppress the *pump-pump-pump* of my heart. The room was very dark, suffocatingly dark, and even though I strained my eyes, I couldn't see if there was anything there. I lifted myself up on one elbow, and the bedsprings creaked and complained like a tired orchestra.

There was silence. I whispered, though I didn't want to: 'Elmek?'

No reply. Madeleine stirred in her sleep, and turned over.

I whispered again: 'Elmek?'

There was another scuffle, then a rustling sound. They seemed to come from down behind the foot of the bed. I sat up, my skin electric with fear, and I tried to see what was hiding there in the darkness.

Again, there was silence. But I was sure I heard a faint scratching and rustling on the worn linoleum, and I was sure that a darker shadow shifted and moved in the gloom.

I kept absolutely still. I could feel that Madeleine was awake now. She reached across the bed and squeezed my hand, too frightened to speak. But I bent my head towards her and said softly: 'Don't panic. It's in here somewhere, but don't panic.'

She nodded, and swallowed. In the hush of the night, we waited for the devil to stir again, our hands tightly clenched together, our breath held back into shallow gasps.

Suddenly, Madeleine said: 'Dan. The window. *Dan!*'

I turned towards the window. I flinched in shock. There was someone silhouetted against the curtains, a tall figure of clotted shadows, unmoving and quiet. I took one look, and then my hand went scrambling in search of my bedside lamp, but I tangled my fingers in the flex by mistake, and the lamp tipped over and crashed on to the floor.

In the terrible silence that followed, a woman's voice said: '*Are you rested?*'

It was a strange, throaty voice; too deep for a woman, really, but too vibrantly female for a man. The dim figure stirred, and moved silently across the room. I could just make out a pale face – a smudge of grey in the grainy blackness.

'Who are you?' I demanded. 'Who are you?'

The figure didn't reply for a while. It seemed to be grating its teeth together, with an edgy, squeaking sound. Then it said: '*We take many forms, you know. Many substances. Aren't you afraid?*'

I said: 'Are you Elmek?'

'*Elmek or Asmorod or Kaphis. We have more names than nights that have passed since the crucifixion. Don't think that your book can identify us, because it won't.'*

'What do you know about that?'

The thing gave a hoarse, blowzy laugh. *'I know that you are wasting your time in religious folly. Angels! You must be demented. You have struck yourself a bargain with me, my friend, and with my master Adramelech, the Grand Chancellor of Hell, the peacock and the serpent. Don't talk to me of angels!'*

Madeleine said: 'What are you going to do with us? You're not going to keep your bargain, are you?'

There was a sound of crackling, as if the beast were tugging its knuckles, or biting into bones. Then it said, in a much deeper, more slurred and masculine voice: *'Bargains are struck for good and evil. Bargains have always been struck for good and evil. The priests and the bishops have struck bargains before, and not been disappointed. We didn't only fight at Senlac, you know. We were there with Charlemagne, and we were there with Jeanne d'Arc. No wonder the English burned her! The stories told of monstrous devils whirling around her head in battle, and they were true, mon ami. It is only now that the church has seen fit to rewrite its history, and deny the existence of all the unholy allies it used for its so-called holy wars!'*

Madeleine was shivering in fright. I put my arm around her and held her close, but the devil wasn't disturbed.

'Think of the Spanish Inquisition,' it whispered. *'Think of the torture chambers of England and France. Each had its devil! In times gone by, devils walked the earth freely, and they still walk the earth! They made bargains with men, for mutual advantage, because man is an evil creature, thank the stars, as well as a good one.'*

Over in the corner of the room, near the door, I saw a faint blueish light, like the phosphorescence in the ocean at night. Then, to my horror, something began to appear out of the darkness. I stared and stared, and, half-distinguishable in the shadows, its mouth stretched back in a wolfish grin, was a beast that could have been a devil, could have been a whoreish woman, could have been some hideous slimy subaqueous squid. There was a sour smell in the room, and the blue light crawled and flickered like the foul illumination from decaying fish.

I saw everything in that moment that disgusted and horrified me. I saw what looked like a woman's hands seductively drawn back up a curving shining thigh, only to realise that the thigh wasn't a thigh at all, but a desperately wriggling trunk of tentacles. I saw pouting lips that suddenly turned out to be festering cuts. I saw rats crowding into the mouth of a sleeping woman. I saw living flesh cut away from living bones, first in ribbons of skin and muscle, and then in a stomach-turning tangle of sodden flesh.

Madeleine, beside me, shrieked.

'*Elmek!*' I yelled, and rolled out of the bed towards the ghastly apparition.

There was a paralysing burst of white light, and I felt as if someone had cracked me over the head with a pickaxe handle. Dazed and dazzled, I fell sideways on the cold lino, bruising my shoulder against the leg of the bed. I tried to get up, but something hit me again, something heavy and soft.

Madeleine screamed: 'Dan! It's in the bed! *It's in the bed!*'

Stunned, wiping blood away from a split lip, I gripped hold of the edge of the mattress and pulled myself upright. Madeleine was beating in terror at the blankets, as if something had scurried its way under them, and was crawling around her legs. For a half-second, in the eerie blue light of that failing phosphorescence, I saw something reach out from under the covers and touch her naked leg. It was black and claw-like and hairy, like a grossly overgrown spider. I hit at it, yelling in fear and anger, and then I seized Madeleine's wrist and yanked her off the bed and halfway across the floor.

There was a moment of sheer panic when I thought

that whatever was under those blankets was going to come crawling after us. I heard something heavy drop off the bed, and the scratch of claws on the floor; but then the blue light suddenly began to flicker again, and go dim, like a torch with used-up batteries, and the sour odour of devil began to fade away. I heard a soft soughing noise, a wind where no wind could blow, and then there was silence. Both of us crouched on the floor, panting from fright. We listened and listened, but there was no sound in the room at all, and after a while we cautiously raised our heads.

'I think it must have gone,' I said quietly.

Madeleine whispered: 'Oh God, that was terrible. Oh my God, I was so scared.'

I switched on the overhead light. Then I went over to the bed and prodded at the covers with the broken bedside lamp. In the end, I gathered up enough courage to lift the blankets and turn them over. There was nothing there. If it hadn't been a terrifying illusion, then it had left us.

Madeleine came up behind me and touched my back. 'I don't think I could sleep any more,' she told me. 'Not in that bed. Why don't we start out for London?'

I found my wristwatch where it had been knocked on the floor. It was five-thirty in the morning. It would soon be dawn.

'All right,' I said, feeling very little better than I had when we first went to bed. 'It looks like Elmek's pushing us on, in any case. Remind me to remember that devils rarely sleep.'

Madeleine put on her blue jeans without panties, and combed out her hair in front of the dingy mirror. I said: 'I can't take much more of this. I don't even know why it does these things.'

'Maybe it's boasting,' suggested Madeleine. 'They're supposed to be vain creatures, aren't they, devils?'

'It could be that. If you ask me, it's just relishing how

134

frightened we are. It intends to squeeze the last ounce of fear and agony out of us two and get its goddamned money's worth.'

Madeleine tugged a grey ribbed sweater over her head. It was so cold in that bedroom I could see the outline of her nipples through the thick Shetland wool. 'I don't know,' she said. 'I have the feeling it's *excited*, as if it's getting itself all worked up to join its brethren. All that boasting about what devils had done in the past. And that figure, whatever it was, with all those squids and snakes and things. That was like some horrible kind of showing-off.'

I brushed my hair, and did my best to shave with a blunt razor and no soap. There were dark smudges of tiredness under my eyes, and I looked about as healthy as a can of week-old tuna. In fact, I was so exhausted that I could hardly feel frightened any more. When we were ready, we tiptoed out on to the landing, and went downstairs through the dark, creaking house. There was no-one around, so I left three pounds on the hall table and we let ourselves out into the freezing early morning

The sun came up over the Sussex Downs just as we were driving out of Brighton. On each side of us, the long frosted hills stretched into the haze; to Chanctonbury Ring in the west, and to Ditchling Beacon in the east. At that time of the morning, in winter, Sussex has a strangely prehistoric feel to it, and you become uncannily sensitive to the memory that Ancient Britons trod these downs, and Roman legions, and suspect that across the smokey plain of the Sussex Weald, the fires of Anglo-Saxon ironfounders could be seen glimmering in the depths of the forests. Beside me, Madeleine sat huddled in her coat trying to doze as we turned northwards towards London

We drove along roads white with ice, past old cottages and pubs and filling stations and roadside shops advertising home-made fudge and large red potatoes. Behind us, in the back of the car, the copper-and-lead box was silent as a tomb. The sun rose on my right, and flickered behind the spare trees as I sped on to the motorway. In another hour, we would reach the suburbs of London. By noon, we would probably discover whether Elmek was going to keep his bargain or not. I thought of the saying that 'he who sups with devils must needs use a long spoon', and it didn't encourage me very much.

As we left the fields and the countryside behind, and came into the crowded grey streets of Croydon and Streatham, the sky grew ominously dark, and I had to drive with my headlamps on. On the wet sidewalks, shoppers and passers-by hurried with coat-collars turned up against the cold, and a few first flakes of snow settled on my windshield. The traffic was crowded and confused, and it took another hour of edging my way between red double-decker buses and black shiny taxis before I crossed the Thames over Chelsea Bridge, and made my way towards the Cromwell Road. The snow was falling heavily now, but it melted as soon as it touched the busy streets and pavements. I passed Sloane Square, with its fountains and bedraggled pigeons; turned left at Knightsbridge, and then juddered along in solid traffic past Harrods and the Victoria & Albert Museum. Today, London looked grimly Dickensian; and as we drove by the Natural History Museum, with its twisted Gothic pillars and its gardens arranged with petrified trees, I felt as if bringing this medieval devil into the city was part of some dark and sinister Victorian plot. Only my tiredness and my fear reminded me that what was inside that locked trunk was hideously real, and that this morning in December in London was overshadowed with the vicious horror of mankind's most ancient enemies. I lit up a cigarette, and coughed.

At last, we arrived outside 18, Huntingdon Place. It was a late-Victorian house of grimy yellow-and-grey bricks, in that gloomy hinterland between Cromwell

Road and High Street Kensington, all shared flats and registry offices and unfashionable mews. I pulled the car into the kerb, and nudged Madeleine awake. She blinked, and stretched, and said: 'Are we here already? That was the best sleep I've had in days.'

There was no sign on the black spiked railings outside the house to show that it still belonged to the Ministry of Defence. But I climbed stiffly out of the car, and walked up to the front door to see if there was any kind of identification by the two rows of doorbells. There was nothing at all, not even the name of a tenant. The door itself was firmly locked, and by the condition of its cracked grey paint, looked as if it hadn't been decorated for twenty years. I tried to peer through a dirty pane of spiderweb glass beside it, but inside the house it was completely dark.

Madeleine came across the sidewalk. 'Any luck?' she asked me.

'I don't know. It looks as if it's empty. Maybe they just shut the devils up here and left it.'

'But that was thirty years ago.'

I shrugged. 'We could always ring the bell and see.'

I looked back towards the Citroën, parked against the kerb in the softly-falling snow. 'We have to get in here somehow,' I told her. 'Otherwise it's going to be cold cuts for lunch.'

'Maybe the next-door neighbours know something,' she suggested. 'Even if the house is empty, it must belong to somebody. If we could only get ourselves a key, and take a look round. We could always pretend we wanted to buy it.'

I stepped back and looked up at the second and third floors of the house, blinking against the snow that fell in my upturned face. 'I can't see any lights. I guess it must be empty.'

I went back up to the porch and pushed all the bells. I could hear some of them ringing in different parts of the

137

house. Then I waited for a while, shuffling my feet to bring the circulation back to my toes. Madeleine looked at me tiredly, and I knew that both of us were pretty close to the end of our tether. A taxi drove by, blowing its horn.

We were just about to turn away when we heard a noise inside the house. I raised my eyes in surprise. Then there were sharp footsteps coming along the corridor, the rattle of security chains, and the door opened. A lean young man in a black jacket and grey business pants stood there, with a haughty and enquiring expression on his face.

'Did you want something?' he asked, in that clipped voice that immediately told you he'd been given a superior education and probably read *Horse & Hound*.

I gave him an uneasy kind of a smile. 'I'm not sure,' I told him. 'Does this building still belong to the War Office?'

'You mean the Ministry of Defence.'

'That's right. I mean the Ministry of Defence.'

The young man looked sour. 'Well, that depends who you are and why you wish to know.'

'Then it does?'

The young man looked even sourer.

I said: 'The reason I want to know is because I have some property that belongs to the Ministry of Defence. Part of a set of wartime equipment. And what I'm doing is bringing it back.'

'I see,' said the young man. 'And would you mind telling me what this piece of equipment might be?'

'Do you have a superior officer here?' I asked him.

He gave a patronising grimace. 'I haven't even said this is Ministry property yet.'

'Okay,' I told him. 'If it *is* Ministry property, and you *do* have a superior officer, tell him we have Adramelech's thirteenth friend. Right out here, in the back of the car.'

'I *beg* your pardon?'

138

'Just tell him. Adramelech's thirteenth friend. We'll wait here for five minutes.'

The young man pulled a very disconcerted face, and then he said: 'I suppose you'd better wait inside. I won't be a moment.'

He opened the door wider, and we stepped into a musty-smelling hall with an olive-green dado that was worn shiny with age. I lit another cigarette and passed one to Madeleine. She wasn't an experienced smoker, and she puffed at it like a thirteen-year-old with her first Camel, but right now we needed anything that could steady our nerves. On the peeling wall just behind us was a mildew-spotted photograph of Earl Haig, and if that wasn't an out-and-out admission that 18, Huntingdon Place belonged to the Ministry of Defence, I don't know what could have been, apart from a tank parked outside.

I took out my handkerchief and blew my nose. What with losing two nights of sleep, and chasing around in the bitter winter weather, I was beginning to show all the symptoms of a headcold. Madeleine leaned tiredly against the wall beside me, and looked too drained to say anything.

After a few minutes, I heard voices on the upstairs landing, and then an immaculately-creased pair of khaki trousers came into view down the stairs, followed by a crisp khaki jacket with a Sam Browne belt and medal ribbons, and then a fit, square face with a bristling white moustache and the kind of eyes that were crowsfooted from peering across the horizons of the British Empire.

The officer came forward with a brisk, humourless smile. He said: 'They didn't give me your names, unfortunately. Remiss of them.'

I flipped my cigarette out into the snow. 'I'm Dan McCook, this is Madeleine Passerelle.'

The officer gave a sharp, brief nod of his head, as if he were trying to shake his eyebrows loose. 'I'm Lieutenant-Colonel Thanet, Special Operations Branch.'

There was a silence. He was obviously expecting us to explain why we were here. I looked at Madeleine and Madeleine looked back at me.

Lieutenant-Colonel Thanet said: 'They tell me you have something interesting. Something that belongs to us.'

'I guess it does in a way,' I told him.

He gave a tight, puckered smiled. The kind of smile that my grandfather, who came from Madison, Wisconsin, used to describe as 'a close view of a mule's ass.' He said: 'Something to do with D-Day, if I understand correctly.'

I nodded. 'You can threaten us with the Official Secrets Act if you want to, but we know what happened anyway, so I don't think there's much point. We know about the thirteen ANPs that you British loaned to Patton, and we know what happened to them afterwards. Twelve of them came here, and were sealed up, and the thirteenth one was left in a tank in Normandy, and conveniently forgotten. What we have out here, in the back of our car, is your thirteenth ANP.'

The colonel looked at me with those clear, penetrating eyes. I could see that he was trying to work out what kind of a johnny I was, and what official category this particular problem fitted into, and what the correct follow-up procedure was going to be.

But what he said wasn't army jargon, and he didn't say it like a man whose decisions are usually taken by the letter of the military rulebook. He said: 'Are you telling me the truth, Mr McCook? Because if you are, then I'm very seriously worried.'

I pushed the door wider so that he could see the Citroën parked at the kerb. 'It's in the trunk,' I told him. 'And it's the real thing. Its name is Elmek, or Asmorod. The devil of knives and sharpness.'

He bit his lip. He was silent for a while, and then he

said: 'Is it safe? I mean, is it sealed up, in any religious way?'

I shook my head.

The colonel asked: 'Do you know anything about it? Anything about it at all?'

'Yes. It told us it was a disciple of Adramelech, the Grand Chancellor of Hell. We took it out of the tank in France because it was disturbing the people who lived near it, and because Mlle Passerelle believed it was responsible for killing her mother. But since then, it's killed three other people, and it's threatened to do the same to us.'

Madeleine said to the colonel: '*Monsieur le colonel*, you don't seem at all incredulous. I would even say that you believed us.'

The colonel managed a twisted little grin. 'It's hardly surprising, *mademoiselle*. It has been my particular brief for the last six years to look into that ANP business after D-Day. I probably know more about that special division of tanks than anybody alive.'

'Then it's true?' I asked him. 'The other devils are really here?'

'Who told you that?'

'An American gentleman named Sparks. He was one of the people involved in the special division during the war.'

Lieutenant-Colonel Thanet sighed, as if he expected that kind of behaviour from Americans.

'Is it true?' I questioned him. 'Are they really here?'

Thanet said: 'Yes. They're sealed in the cellars. All twelve of them. It's been part of my job to work out a way of using them again.'

'Using them again? Wasn't once enough?'

'Probably. But you know what departments of defence are like. Anything cheap and unusual and lethal always appeals to their sense of humour. And these days, they particularly like nasty alternatives to nuclear weaponry.

141

So they dug out the file on the ANPs, and sent me here to see what I could do.'

'And have you done anything?' asked Madeleine.

'Not much so far. We've had a couple of beggars out of their sacks and had a look at their bones and their general physiology, and we know that as long as their seal is broken, they can take on flesh again, and live. That was how it was done in World War Two, and that's why we haven't broken any of the seals. But we're planning on greater things, once we're sure we can keep them under control.'

'Greater things?' I queried. 'What does that mean?'

'Well,' said the colonel, with a furrowed frown, 'we were going to try to conjure up their master, because he's supposed to be several thousand times more powerful.'

'*Adramelech?*' breathed Madeleine, her eyes wide.

'That's right. The great and terrible Samarian deity. Well, I wouldn't have believed it back when I was at Sandhurst, but once they showed me what that special division had done under Patton . . .'

He looked at me with a meaningful inclination of his cropped and white-haired head.

'There were photographs taken after D-Day, you know,' he told us. 'Photographs and even colour films. They were quite extraordinary. I should think that, apart from the H-Bomb, they're unquestionably the most spectacular and most secret things that NATO have got.'

I said: 'How can we control something like Adramelech, when we can hardly control these thirteen devils of his?'

Lieutenant-Colonel Thanet rubbed the back of his neck. 'Well, that's a tricky one, and that's why I'm rather worried that you've brought our friend Elmek over. We *don't* know how to control these devils for certain, and we certainly have no idea what to do with Adramelech. We don't even know what Adramelech could possibly look like, and that's always supposing one could actually see

142

such a thing with the human eye. One way we've kept the situation under control is by leaving the thirteenth devil where it was, in France. Oh yes, we knew it was there. But we wanted to leave it there, at least until we worked out a foolproof way to prevent these other twelve beggars from setting fire to us, or giving us leprosy, or strangling us with our own guts.'

I reached out for Madeleine's hand. Her fingers were very cold when I touched them.

'Now they're all back together, of course, there's a definite risk that they'll summon up their master,' said Thanet. 'Patton's men prevented such a thing from happening during the war because they promised Adramelech some human sacrifices, and plenty of blood. One could do such a thing in wartime. But now, well . . . the only blood that's immediately available is ours.'

I took out another cigarette, and lit it. Outside the door, the snow had stopped falling, but the sky was still a grim metallic green. The Citroën stood silently by the kerb, and through the reflecting glass of the rear window, we could just make out the side of the copper-and-lead trunk.

'I was afraid of that, too,' I said hoarsely, and Madeleine looked away with an expression of such sadness that even Lieutenant-Colonel Thanet noticed it, and half-raised his hand to comfort her.

CHAPTER FIVE

They gave us a in Lieutenant-Colonel Thanet's upstairs office, and we sat on uncomfortable folding chairs while he took out his files on the special division of tanks – codename *Stripes*. He leafed through them with the quick, concentrated frown of a speed-reader, pausing now and then to study a chart or a graph, and to glance up at Madeleine and me and give a swift apologetic *moue* for the time he was taking.

The office was cold, and the pale-blue walls with their defence maps of Britain and Western Europe made it seem even colder. A radiator the size of a small pig rattled and steamed in one corner, but it was all noise and no heat. There were three khaki tin filing cabinets on the opposite wall, and these, apart from Lieutenant-Colonel Thanet's desk and three collapsible chairs, were the only furniture.

I stood up and took my cup of scalding tea across to the window. In the dull, glistening street below, three British Army sergeants were lifting Elmek's box from the back of the Citroën. The devil hadn't spoken a word since our arrival, but we knew the risks of ignoring it. It expected to be reunited with its twelve brethren, and if it wasn't, then God help any of us who were close to a window, or a knife, or anything that could cut into human flesh.

Lieutenant-Colonel Thanet cleared his throat, and neatly collated his files in front of him.

'Did you find anything?' I asked him.

He pulled a face. 'Not very much, I'm afraid. Not much more than I was aware of already. The whole history of this particular operation was kept under wraps, and there really isn't a great deal of documentary evidence to go on. It appears from the early approaches made by the Pentagon to the British War Office that General Patton was largely responsible for thinking it up and carrying it through, although Eisenhower certainly knew about it six or seven months before D-Day. There are several references here to Operation Stripes, and this paper here is the requisition order for preparing the tanks. Each tank cost eighteen thousand dollars to refit, mainly because of the steering mechanisms, which were partly remote-controlled.'

Madeleine said: 'Does it mention Adramelech? Does it say how they kept him under control?'

Thanet slowly shook his head. 'There's only one reference here that might be relevant. It refers to the transportation of German prisoners-of-war to England, including one French woman, a Nazi collaborator. They were taken to the army camp at Aldershot under the direct authority of Colonel Sparks – that's your American friend – and Colonel T. K. Allingham, who was his British counterpart, and that means their movement order must have had something to do with Operation Stripes. It's possible that these prisoners may have been used to appease Adramelech. Sacrifices, for want of a better word.'

'A man for each of the thirteen devils, and a woman for Adramelech himself,' Madeleine suggested quietly.

'Quite possible,' said Lieutenant-Colonel Thanet, smiling an uneasy smile. 'Your theory is as valid as anybody's. That movement order is the only written evidence of those prisoners that survives.'

I came away from the window and laid my thick-rimmed government teacup back in its saucer. 'Colonel Thanet,' I told him, 'we may have only a few hours, even a few minutes, before those thirteen devils get together and call up their master. Then what are we going to do?'

'We're not going to panic, and that's for certain,' said the colonel. 'First of all, we're going to make quite sure that the devils' religious seals are quite intact, because there isn't much they can do while they're nothing more than exorcised bags of bones.'

'Supposing Elmek can free them – bring them back to life?'

'It would have to be a pretty powerful kind of devil to do that. Each one of those seals has been blessed by seven Roman Catholic priests and kissed by a Roman Catholic cardinal. You may be cynical about religion, but I can tell you from my own experience, that's strong medicine.'

Madeleine lowered her eyes. 'We have seen Elmek cutting up clerics like so much cheese,' she said softly.

'Well, the best thing we can do is go downstairs and have a look for ourselves,' said Lieutenant-Colonel Thanet. 'They should have brought your box in by now, so our ANPs are all together again for the first time since the war.'

He stood up, and tugged his tunic straight. 'You haven't finished your tea,' he remarked, in obvious surprise.

I shrugged, embarrassed. 'I guess army refreshments are pretty much the same all over the world,' I told him.

He peered into my cup. 'Funny. I thought our chaps made pretty good tea.'

At that moment, the door opened, and one of the sergeants came in and saluted.

'The box is down in the quarantine area now, sir,' he reported. His beret was glistening with snow. 'Very weighty it was, too.'

'Very good, sergeant,' said Lieutenant-Colonel Thanet. 'We're on our way now. Mlle Passerelle? Mr McCook? Would you care to follow me?'

We clattered down the uncarpeted stairs, past the hall where we had first walked in, and along a corridor to the back of the house, where there was a wide cellar door, built of solid oak and hinged with steel hinges. To my right, out of the glass panes of the back door, I could see

146

a sodden, tangled garden, and the dingy houses in the next street. Somewhere deep beneath our feet, a Tube train rattled on its way to Earl's Court.

The sergeant unlocked the cellar door, and swung it open. When I saw the back of it, I gave Madeleine a nudge, and pointed. Nailed on to the wood was a cross identical to that silver crucifix welded over the hatch of the tank at Pont D'Ouilly. Lieutenant-Colonel Thanet said: 'That's what you'd call our longstop, if you played cricket. We have it re-blessed every year by Father Mullaney, just to make sure.'

With his head bowed to avoid the low whitewashed ceiling, Lieutenant-Colonel Thanet stepped through the cellar door and down the wooden staircase. I followed, and Madeleine came behind.

At the bottom of the stairs, we found ourselves in a wide white basement, lit by naked bulbs in wire cage holders. Along the walls of the basement were twelve plain trestle tables, six each side, and on each table was a black, dusty sack. The twelve acolytes of Adramelech, nothing but bones right now, but each capable of hideous and warlike life. In the centre of the floor, silent and still, lay the copper-and-lead trunk that we had brought over from France. Elmek, or Asmorod, the devil of sharp knives.

We walked slowly up and down the room, looking at each of the sacks in turn. Then Lieutenant-Colonel Thanet said: 'Well? What do you propose we do?'

'We have to identify them first, devil by devil,' I told him, looking around the basement. 'Then we might be able to exorcise them. I have the books upstairs.'

'You can exorcise them? How?' asked Thanet. He looked sceptical.

Madeleine said: 'By the invocation of angels. It's the only way.'

The Lieutenant-Colonel's face went tight. '*Angels?*' he said, incredulous. 'Did you say *angels?*'

Madeleine nodded. 'You can believe in devils, colonel. Why can't you believe in angels?'

'Because they're – well, because they don't exist, do they? Or *do* they?'

I rubbed my eyes tiredly. 'We don't actually know, colonel. But it seems to me that it's the only alternative we have left. Father Anton gave me a book about invoking angels, and so did the Reverend Taylor, and they were both well versed in the techniques of exorcism. I guess it's the only way.'

There was another deep, rumbling noise; only this time I wasn't so sure it was the Tube. I looked quickly at Madeleine, and she said: 'Please, Colonel. I think Dan is right. We don't have much time.'

Lieutenant-Colonel Thanet cast his eyes around the basement, and then at our box, and sighed. 'Very well. If you think you can do some good. But I warn you – if anything looks as if it's going to go wrong – or if you attempt to damage any of these ANPs – then I shall have you out of here straight away. These things are government property, and it's worth my whole damned career if you break 'em.'

Slowly, ominously, the lights in the basement began to dim; as if some other enormous power source was feeding off the electricity. I snapped to Madeleine: 'Get those books – quick! They're up on Colonel Thanet's desk!' and then I pulled the Lieutenant-Colonel away from Elmek's copper-and-lead trunk.

The lights dimmed and dimmed until all we could see was their orange filaments, barely glowing in the darkness. Lieutenant-Colonel Thanet called: 'Sergeant Boone! Bring three men down here with Sterlings!'

The darker it grew, the quieter it became. We could hear shouting and footsteps upstairs in the house; but down here in the cellar the silence seemed to fall in on us like soft tufted cotton. Lieutenant-Colonel Thanet touched my arm in the strange twilight and whispered: 'What is it? Do you know what it is? What's happening?'

'It's Elmek,' I whispered back. 'Ten-to-one it's Elmek.'

We hadn't seen or heard the lid of the trunk open, but when I looked down at it, the lid had been thrown right back, and even in the faint light of the glowing electric filaments, I could see the stained, centuries-old silk that lined the trunk's insides, and I could also see that it was empty. I gripped Lieutenant-Colonel Thanet's shoulder in warning, and I slowly scanned the basement with straining eyes for any sign of our thirteenth devil.

Lieutenant-Colonel Thanet said: 'This is all most odd. I don't know what the damned things are trying to achieve.'

'I guess they want their freedom,' I told him. 'They've been sewn up in these goddamned sacks since the eleventh century, apart from that brief excursion during the war. And they also want to bring their master back into the world.'

'You really think they're going to raise Adramelech?'

'That's what Elmek said. And Elmek should know.'

In the depths of that basement, we heard a long, slow breathing noise, like the breathing of a man under heavy anaesthetic. I looked down towards the far end, between the trestles, where it was darkest. For a moment, I couldn't see anything at all, but when I screwed up my eyes I thought I could make out a darker shape. A shape that I dreaded more than any other. The dwarf-like form of the devil Elmek, with his nightmarish eyes and his hideous rustling body.

'Elmek,' I said softly. 'I command you.'

Lieutenant-Colonel Thanet turned to me in incredulity. 'What are you doing?' he asked me, impatient and fretful. 'Who are you talking to?'

I ignored him. There wasn't time for explanations. The basement was beginning to shake like the engine-room of a ship at sea, and I could hear the wooden trestles rattling against the walls and the floor.

'Elmek, listen. We have fulfilled our bargain. What about yours? Here are your twelve brethren. Give us back our priest, Father Anton, and give us back Antoinette.'

The devil stirred, and chuckled. Lieutenant-Colonel Thanet took a step backwards, and tried to tug me back as well.

'Elmek,' I said again.

There was a moment's silence, and then the devil said: 'I have told you before. Only Adramelech can breathe back life into your departed friends. We must first summon Adramelech.'

Thanet shouted: '*Sergeant!*'

A rush of heavy boots began to come down the cellar steps. Sergeant Boone came first, a solid-looking soldier in light khaki fatigues and a maroon beret, carrying a light machine-gun under his arm. Behind him clattered three others, all with those bullet-like heads and young implacable faces that British soldiers seem to have developed through unnatural selection.

'Down the end there, sergeant,' said Lieutenant-Colonel Thanet crisply. 'Hold your fire for now.'

I pointed out, rather morbidly: 'Do you really think that guns are going to do us any good, sir?'

Lieutenant-Colonel Thanet gave me a sour glance. 'I'm sure they won't, Mr McCook. But we have to be prepared for every eventuality.'

We waited for a few minutes in the dark and silence of that London basement, and I could see the soldiers looking apprehensively at the way the lightbulb filaments glowed and pulsed like electric worms. At the far end of the basement, completely concealed in shadows, Elmek watched us and waited.

'Elmek,' I said at last, 'what do you want us to do?'

The devil shifted in the dark.

'We can't help you summon Adramelech unless you tell us what to do,' I prompted it.

Elmek said, in the voice of an old woman: 'Bring down the girl. We must have the girl here.'

Lieutenant-Colonel Thanet said: 'First of all, we have to know what you intend to do with her.'

Sergeant Boone and his men looked at their colonel in bewilderment. To them, he was their superior officer, and nobody hiding in the shadows down at the end of a basement would normally dare to speak to their superior officer with such blatant disrespect.

Sergeant Boone said: 'We could always go down there, sir, and snatch him. Corporal Perry and me were both in Ulster, sir. It's our specialty.'

Lieutenant-Colonel Thanet didn't turn to look at his sergeant. He simply ordered: 'Don't move, sergeant. Not until I tell you,' and kept staring into the darkness.

'The girl's coming,' I told the devil. 'She went upstairs, but she's coming.'

Among the shadows, I could perceive how Elmek constantly stirred and altered shape. Madeleine had been right about it. It was probably elated at joining its brethren, and it was churning through an endless physical metamorphosis in sheer excitement. I saw suggestions of diseased and slithering shapes in the darkness that made me feel nauseous, and when Sergeant Boone's men grew accustomed to the dim light, and could make out for themselves some of the sickening and repulsive forms that glistened and slithered at the end of the basement, they exchanged looks of mounting mystification and horror.

Through the muffling, suffocating silence, I heard Madeleine coming downstairs and opening the cellar door. Then she appeared, with my two books under her arm. I nodded towards the dark end of the cellar, and told her: 'Elmek. It's appeared.'

Madeleine handed me the books. She whispered: 'What is it doing? Has it said what it wants?'

I shook my head. 'It wants *you*, but I don't know why.'

Elmek cackled: 'You don't know why? You can't even guess? Don't you know what that poor girl Jeanne d'Arc did for the benefit of our help in battle? Can't you imagine what befell poor Gundrada, the wife of William de Warrenne?'

Sergeant Boone lifted his Sterling machine-gun. But Lieutenant-Colonel Thanet raised a hand and warned: 'Steady, sergeant. We're not dealing with the IRA now.'

I called, 'What do you want us to do, Elmek? The girl is here now. What do you want us to do?'

The basement trembled and shook again, and there was a low, irritating sound like thousands of blowflies swarming over a dead horse. It was so dark now that we could hardly see at all. One of the soldiers said: 'Christ, it's like a bleeding grave down 'ere.'

'Quiet that man,' snapped the sergeant.

Elmek whispered, in a hoarse, mocking voice: 'The girl must open each sack in turn. Only the girl will do. Only the girl has any religious faith. She must open each sack in turn, and say over it the words of the conjuration.'

While Elmek was talking, I was straining my eyes in the dim light to read the pages which the Reverend Taylor had marked in his thin black book. The section was headed *The Seven Accurate Tests of An Evil Spirit's Identity*, and it told you what you had to do to discover the true name of a demon or devil. But as I read more and more, my confidence sank. The first test was to ask the devil its name by the power of Sammael, the arch-demon whom they called 'the venom of God'. The second test was to burn the devil's hair or scales and see whether the smoke sank downwards or rose upwards. The third test was to sprinkle various herbs on its skin – borage, fennel, parsley, and dozens of others, because different devils were marked or repelled by different plants. The fourth was to spray a silver spoonful of devil's blood across twenty-six cards with letters of the alphabet on them, and the blood would fall on every card except those with the letters of its own name. The fifth and the sixth and the seventh were equally impossible, and all of them were obviously devised for a full-scale ritual exorcism. What we had here, in this cellar in Huntingdon Place, was an occult emergency.

'Madeleine,' I hissed. 'Madeleine, I can't do these tests. They're too complicated.'

She lifted a finger. 'Wait,' she whispered back. 'There may be some other way.'

'What other way? What are you talking about?'

'You will have to trust me,' she said.

'Well, what do you want me to do. You can't go around opening up those sacks!'

'I must.'

'Madeleine, I—'

She reached out in the darkness and held my arm. 'Trust me,' she said. 'As I open up each sack, I will try and discover the name of the devil within it, and I will try to pass that name on to you. These are only lesser devils. They're fierce and warlike and loathsome, but they're not wise.'

'And what do I do when you've told me their names?' I asked her. 'Always supposing that we live that long.'

She pressed her hand against *L'Invocation des Anges*. She said: 'Look up each name in the book, and beside it you will see another name, the name of the devil's corresponding angel. Invoke that angel by repeating the words of the conjuration.'

I frowned at her. 'How do you know all this? I thought that—'

Elmek wheezed: 'Come on, girl, open up these sacks for me! Tear open these sacks and release my beloved brethren! Hurry, girl, there is little time left!'

The basement lights pulsed brighter, and then dimmed

dark again. I could feel a deep, systematic throbbing throughout the whole room, like the gristly beating of some gruesome heart. Between me and Elmek, Sergeant Boone and his men now stood with their machine-guns raised, and Lieutenant-Colonel Thanet was turning towards us with an expression of responsible concern. I suppose they teach them responsible concern at officer school.

He said: 'I can't advise you to do what the devil says, Mlle Passerelle. In fact, I'll have to order you to stay back.'

Madeleine gave my hand a last, gentle squeeze. 'I'm sorry, Lieutenant-Colonel. But I cannot do what you ask.'

Elmek, in what sounded like eight vibrant voices speaking at once, called: 'Open the sacks, girl! Asmorod is impatient!'

Madeleine took one step forward. As she did so, a hideous shape emerged from the shadows at the far end of the basement – a shape like the black glossy skull of a beetle. There was a shivering, rustling, grasshopper sound, the chirring noise of insects. But it wasn't an insect, because I could make out tentacles as well, and some grotesque shape attached to its abdomen like a deformed Siamese twin of itself.

Lieutenant-Colonel Thanet shouted: '*Fire!*'

What happened next seemed to happen so slowly that I remember every detail of it, like some repulsive action replay that goes over and over inside your mind. I saw the sergeant and his three soldiers raise their machine-guns. I saw Lieutenant-Colonel Thanet taking one pace backwards. Then, out of one soldier's mouth, in a dreadful torrent, came gallons and gallons of bloody chopped-up slush, splattering all over the concrete floor. It looked as if he was puking a hundredweight of raw hamburger meat, and Madeleine turned her face away with a mewl of anguish. Transfixed, I watched as the soldier's whole body seemed to collapse like an empty cushion-cover, and he twisted over and lay flat on his face on the gory floor. Beside him, Sergeant Boone collapsed in the same way, his fatigues black with bile and blood, and then the other two soldiers. The sweetish smell was overwhelming, and I had two dry heaves before I could control my stomach.

The darkness, almost thankfully, closed in again. I wiped cold perspiration away from my forehead, and pulled Madeleine back, away from the four dead soldiers. It was silent for a minute or two; but then I heard Elmek's creaky laughing, the voice of an old crone, but a harshly inhuman voice as well, as if its breath were piping through a throat lined with black hairs.

'They dared to threaten me,' the devil mocked us. 'They dared to raise their weapons against me. It's almost a pity that you couldn't see, from the outside, the artistry of what I did to them. But then that's the elegance of such a death. Their bowels and their stomachs and their lungs and their kidneys were sliced up and vomited out, leaving their bodies as empty as their stupid heads.'

Lieutenant-Colonel Thanet, his voice shaking, said: 'I think we'd better try to make a run for it, Mr McCook.'

I said: 'I don't think there's much point, Colonel. We could be minced up like that before we even got up the first step. Damn it, that's why we were forced to come here in the first place!'

Madeleine interrupted: 'It won't harm us, *monsieur le colonel*, if we do what it tells us to do. Now, I must open those sacks. We don't have any more time to waste.'

Lieutenant-Colonel Thanet snapped: 'I forbid it! I forbid you to take a single step!'

'Then I shall take several,' said Madeleine, defiantly, and pushed past him into the gloom.

Elmek's husky rustle of approval made me feel as if my shirt had been suddenly soaked in iced water. I tried to follow Madeleine, but she turned round and instructed me quietly: 'Stay there, Dan. Please. Stay back. Just listen to the names when I tell you, and invoke their angels.'

Elmek hissed: 'What are you saying? What are you talking about?'

Madeleine turned and looked straight into the convoluted shadows where the devil lurked. 'I am doing what I have to do,' she said simply, and went up to the first trestle table.

She stood over the table for what seemed like minutes on end, but was only a few seconds. Then she said: 'I summon thee, O being of darkness, O spirit of the pit. I command thee to make thy most evil appearance. I order thee to come forth, and I nullify all seals upon thee, all ties that bind thee. *Venite* O spirit.'

Then she gripped the musty fabric of the sack, and ripped it open.

From where I was standing, it was difficult for me to see. But I could glimpse strange bones, and smell arcane dusts, and hear the rattle of fiendish vertebrae. Madeleine reached into the sack, and lifted out the devil's skull, holding it up for Elmek to see.

'The devil Umbakrail,' she said. 'The devil of darkness and evil events after nightfall.'

I was so fascinated by what she was doing that I almost forgot to look up the name Umbakrail in *L'Invocation des Anges*. But as she moved to the next trestle, I hurriedly turned through the pages until I found it. Umbakrail, also Umbaqurahal, also S'aamed. The devil of dark. There was even an etching of it – a grotesque beast with staring eyes and razor-sharp claws. On the facing page, in Henri St Ermin's laborious French, was a description of its seraphic counterpart, the angel Seron, and below that were the words which would call down Seron to banish the evil presence of its hellish adversary.

'O angel,' I muttered, fearful that Elmek might hear what I was doing, 'I adjure thee in the name of the blessed Virgin Mary, by her holy milk, by her sanctified body, by her sanctified soul, to come forth. I ask thee by all the holy names: Eloy, Jehova, El Oristan, Sechiel, Laaval . . .'

Lieutenant-Colonel Thanet said: 'What the hell are you doing?'

I glanced up at him. 'You mean what the *heaven* am I doing. I'm calling down the angels to get us out of this.'

'For God's sake, man, that girl's in deadly danger! We've got to—'

I hissed: 'Shut up! There's nothing else we can do! You saw what Elmek did to your men! Now, just give us a chance to do it our way!'

Lieutenant-Colonel Thanet was about to protest, but a low, unpleasant rumbling went through the cellar, and he turned towards the writhing shapes of the demon Elmek in alarm. Madeleine had spoken the words of the conjuration over the second sack, and was pulling apart the soft medieval fabric to reveal the terrifying skeleton within.

Again, she raised the skull. It was long and narrow, with slanted eye-sockets, and the nubs of two horns. I felt a chilly ripple flow out from it, as if someone had opened the door of a cold-store. The lights in the cellar sank and flickered, and I sensed the mounting presence of unspeakable malevolence and cruelty.

'Cholok,' said Madeleine, identifying the devil for me. 'The devil of suffocation. The devil who smothers children and asphyxiates victims of fires.'

Lieutenant-Colonel Thanet glared at me in helpless desperation, but I was too busy leafing through my book. There it was. Cholok, sometimes known as Nar-speth. A devil with a face of absolute dispassion, and the leathery wings of a reptile. On the page opposite, I saw that its heavenly opposite was Melés, the angel of purity and happiness. I spoke the words to summon Melés, and then watched Madeleine as she went to the third sack.

Skeleton by skeleton, from the third sack to the fourth, and then to the fifth and the sixth and the seventh, the skeletons of each devil were taken from the ancient material in which they had been sewn up for so long. As yet, they took on no life, but I guessed that when all of them were free from their religious captivity, they would clothe themselves in flesh the way that Elmek must have done in Father Anton's cellar.

The noise in the cellar was hideous and unnerving. As each devil was freed, the chorus of hellish voices grew louder; until the whole place sounded like an insane asylum, with scratching insect sounds and grotesque shrieks, and voices that whispered incessantly of death and plague and aberrations beyond human understanding. I was sweating so much that my fingers made damp dimples on the pages of *L'Invocation des Anges*, and Lieutenant-Colonel Thanet was holding his hands to his ears in stunned disbelief.

At last, Madeleine spoke the words to free the last devil from his sack – the demon Themgoroth, the hawk-like devil of blindness. In my turn, I mumbled the invocation that would bring down Themgoroth's angelic opponent Asrul.

I didn't forget to call Elmek's angel, either. Jespahad, the angel of healing.

Madeleine stepped back towards us. All the bones were revealed now, and the ghastly skulls faced each other across the cellar, with the distorted form of Elmek twisting and shifting between them. The stench was disgusting – a fetid mixing of thirteen nauseous odours that made my eyes water and my stomach tense in physical rebellion. Beside me, Lieutenant-Colonel Thanet gagged, and had to wipe his mouth with his handkerchief.

The cacophony of voices and sounds was growing, too. As I leaned towards Madeleine and whispered: 'I did it.

I think I did it,' she could hardly hear me over the shrieks and cries and gibbering noises. She said: 'What?'

'I did it. I called all the angels. What happens now?'

'Yes,' said Thanet, his face pale. 'Where are they? If they're supposed to come and help us, where are they?'

Madeleine looked at us for a moment. Her pale green eyes were very bright and very intense. She seemed to have taken on some indefinite charisma of pure strength and determination, as if she knew now exactly what had to be done, and how, and that she was going to carry it out whatever the cost.

She said: 'It is not yet time. But the angels will come. First, we must let these devils call up Adramelech.'

'Adramelech?' asked Lieutenant-Colonel Thanet, aghast. 'But we don't stand any kind of a chance against Adramelech!'

Elmek's voice boomed and grumbled over the screams and whispers of his fellow devils. 'I am pleased,' it said, in a frighteningly amplified tone. 'I am well pleased. At last, my brethren and I are reunited! You will have your reward, mortals. You will have your reward!'

Madeleine turned to the devil, and called back: 'We are pleased to serve you, my lord.'

I said: 'Madeleine—' and reached for her arm, but she brushed me away.

'We are true disciples of Adramelech and all his works,' she cried out, her voice high and thin over the bellowing and groaning of the thirteen devils. 'We will follow Adramelech wherever his chancellorship should lead us, and we will gladly bow before him in the courts of the nether kingdom!'

'For Christ's sake, Madeleine,' I snapped. But she ignored me, and lifted her arms high.

'Summon Adramelech when you will,' she shrilled. 'Let us abase ourselves before his evil glory and his malevolent majesty!'

There was a thunderous roar, like a locomotive at full

159

speed. The lights went out altogether, and we were plunged into a darkness that was loud with horrifying sounds and whispers, and sickening stenches of putrefaction. I said: 'Madeleine—' again, but she called back: 'Don't move! Just stay where you are! The devils are taking on flesh!'

Lieutenant-Colonel Thanet put in sharply: 'We're going to have to move. We can't stay here. We're sitting targets. I vote we go for the steps while it's still dark.'

'Colonel, these things are creatures of darkness. They can see you standing there as easily as if it were daylight.'

'But, dammit, we can't just stay here! One of us has to go for help!'

Madeleine begged: 'Please, Colonel! Just stay calm and keep still! We do have a chance, if you'll just stay calm!'

It was a little like asking someone to stay calm in a pitch-black cage of mentally-disturbed leopards. What made it more difficult was that Lieutenant-Colonel Thanet was trained for action. His whole philosophy of life was – if in doubt, *do* something. He said: 'I'm going to make a run for it, that's all!'

Madeleine shouted: 'No!' and I tried to grab the colonel's arm in the darkness, but I guess he was practised at rugby or something, because he ducked deftly out of my way, and was gone.

We couldn't see them, but we *heard* them. As Lieutenant-Colonel Thanet dodged across the basement floor, the devils abruptly turned on him, their bodies rustling and clattering in a hideous excited rush. He reached the foot of the stairs, and I think he managed to stumble up the first two or three steps. But then he said: '*Ah!*' in an odd, choked voice, and I heard him trip and fall heavily on to the floor.

Madeleine said: '*Oh, mon Dieu . . .* ' but both of us knew that it would be suicidal to go to help him The darkness was total, and we would have been snapped up like baby mice tossed to a rat.

Suddenly, though, the ghastly hustle and flurry of devils died away; and out of the dark I saw a dim phosphorescent outline, which I recognised as Elmek. It shuddered and twisted, changing through images of bizarre and vicious reptiles to formless squids and threatening clouds of ectoplasm. Then, in a voice so grating that it was hardly recognisable, it spoke to its twelve brethren.

'Leave . . . the man . . . unharmed . . . He is a morsel . . . for our master . . . Adramelech . . .'

Gradually, the lights in the cellar began to glow again. They didn't shine brightly, and all we could see of the devils was a grotesque huddle of shadowy shapes around the foot of the steps. But they showed that Lieutenant-Colonel Thanet was still alive, crouched on the floor with his hands held over his head to protect himself from claws and teeth and leathery wings that had only just spared him.

'These mortals . . . will all be offered . . .' continued Elmek harshly. 'That is their reward . . . for helping us . . .'

Madeleine took a step forward, and the cluster of devils whispered and rustled.

'Is that your idea of a bargain?' she said, in a clear tone. 'Is that your idea of keeping your promises?'

Elmek laughed, and its laugh came out like shattered splinters of glass.

'You said . . . you wished . . . to serve Adramelech . . .'

'And we will! We will be the two most devoted mortals that his malevolence has ever known! But we cannot serve him if you use us as sacrifices!'

I stayed well back while Madeleine argued with Elmek. For one thing – although I couldn't guess how – she seemed to have the situation under some kind of control. Either she hadn't been levelling with me when we first met by the tank in Normandy, or else she was showing a side of her character I just hadn't guessed at. But whichever it was, she was making a skilfull play at keeping us alive, and that was all that mattered.

Apart from that, I stayed well back because those devils, those terrifying gargoyles who lived and breathed and ground their teeth in almost overwhelming blood-lust, were the shadowy stuff of nightmares, and I knew that if I came any closer, I would find out that the nightmares were real.

The devil Umbakrail raised its bony head from the crawling mass of demons, and I saw the dim basement lights blotted out by the narrow goatish shadow of its skull.

'*The highest act of devotion which a mortal can pay to Adramelech is to offer life, breath and blood. How can you say you are Adramelech's loyal servant if you are reluctant to offer your greatest gifts?*'

Madeleine said: 'I have a greater and more mysterious gift for your master Adramelech than my life, breath and blood.'

The devils whispered and murmured. They were exuding a stench now that made me feel as if I was trapped in a zoo. A sour, dry fetid odour like the urine of bears or apes.

Umbakrail said harshly: '*You will soon have the chance to prove what you have, mortal woman. We shall now call up Adramelech from his sleep of many years, and you shall have the honour of offering your gift directly.*'

Madeleine was silent for a moment, and then she said: 'Very well,' and turned her back on the thirteen devilish acolytes of Adramelech as if they were no more vicious than thirteen chained dogs.

On the floor by the steps, Lieutenant-Colonel Thanet coughed, and moaned. I called: '*Colonel! How do you feel?*'

He coughed again. 'I don't know . . . pretty rough. I think I broke a rib on the stairs. And something's dug its claws into my back. I can feel the blood.'

Yet another thunderous rumble shook the basement, and the devils' groans and whispers rose in a wave of discordant lust. Cholok said: '*It is time. It is time for the summoning.*'

While Madeleine and I kept ourselves back against the wall, the devils moved themselves into a semi-circle around the centre of the floor. I tried to look at them as they stood there in the dense, clotted shadows; tried to see what they really were. But they seemed to have shadows of their own making, actual cloaks of darkness, and all I could make out were scaly wings and curved horns and eyes that glistened and glowed with hellish lights. They were medieval devils of the most legendary kind – the devils that have plagued men and women from Europe's earliest times. It was almost no surprise at all to find that they were not figments of some frustrated nun's imagination, but that they walked the earth with real claws and real teeth, and that we have as much to fear from devils when the nights are dark as we have from muggers or murderers.

Madeleine bent towards me and whispered: 'What you are going to see now will be frightening. You will be in danger of your life. But whatever happens, don t panic or try to get away. You saw what happened to Lieutenant-Colonel Thanet.'

I nodded, dumbly. The stench and the darkness were beginning to close in on me now, and I felt as if I was faced with some horrible but inevitable moment of fear, like sitting in a 747 with faulty landing-gear and knowing that you have to come down sometime. I think I would have done anything for a cigarette. I *know* I would have done anything to be somewhere else.

The devils began to chant some long litany in a language I couldn't recognise. It had a curiously compulsive rhythm to it, a repetitive harshness that made me feel unexpectedly nauseous. The basement grew stuffier and stuffier, and it was impossible to take a breath that wasn't ripe with the stench of demons. I wiped sweat from my forehead with the back of my sleeve, and tried to keep my stomach muscles tense so that I wouldn't heave.

'*Adramelech chastu remlishthu narek. Adramelech hismarad yonluth. Adramelech chastu remlisthu narek.*'

At first, there was nothing but this unsettling chanting. But then I felt an odd sensation, a kind of singing metallic emptiness, as if I was under novacain at the dentist. The next thing I knew, the temperature dropped lower and lower and lower, and I had the feeling that the far wall of the basement had vanished, and that there was nothing there at all but a void of freezing darkness.

'*Adramelech chastu remlisthu narek. Adramelech hismarad yonluth. Adramelech chastu remlisthu narek.*'

Now, the walls of the basement seemed to dwindle away, and a chill astral wind blew across us. We appeared to be poised somewhere timeless and airless, and I couldn't work out which was up and which was down, or how far away anything was, or how close.

The devils were still there, though. They were chanting their conjuration over and over again, in their harsh insect voices, and I could feel whatever it was that they were summoning draw nearer, the way you can feel someone approaching you in the pitch blackness of a darkened room. Something indescribably frightening was coming, called up by this evil and arcane chant that hadn't been heard on earth since the Middle Ages. I thought I heard Lieutenant-Colonel Thanet shrieking, but the piercing sound of it was overwhelmed by the devils' litany, and by the endless emptiness all around us.

Madeleine turned slowly towards me, slowly, slowly, like a woman in a dream. I tried to say: 'Madeleine . . .' but my voice came out as nothing but an endless blur of whispered sounds. She shook her head, and half-smiled, and turned away again.

'*Adramelech usthul! Adramelech hismarad! Adramelech ghu-thil!*' called the devils.

And then their dark membrane-like wings lifted wide and stiff, and their eyes glared through the darkness, and I saw with my own eyes the first manifestation of Adramelech, the Grand Chancellor of Hell, since Patton and Montgomery had raised him during the war.

The vision was so terrifying that I went cold with wave after wave of shock. In the middle of the reptilian circle of devils, huge and hideous, stood a dark thing that looked like a giant deformed donkey, rearing up on its hind legs. It had a monstrous head, and a chest covered with shaggy hair, but its stomach and its hind quarters were afflicted with some kind of crusty excrescences, like tumours. As it appeared through the darkness, there was a screaming sound all around it, a thousand decibels of feedback, and the air itself was distorted like heat rippling from a road. For endless minutes, the eighth demon of the evil sephiroth stood there, turning its head to gaze with stately malevolence at his thirteen acolytes, and the noise was so overwhelming that I thought it was going to deafen me for ever.

Madeleine went down on her knees, and I followed her. She shouted, unheard by the devils in the howling noise: 'This is Adramelech! He takes on the form of a donkey to mock Our Lord's ride into Jerusalem!'

'What the hell are we going to do?' I yelled back. 'Even more to the point – what's Adramelech going to do to *us*?'

'Wait!' she told me. 'When the moment comes – we'll act!'

There was a deep rumble, and then the feedback noise dropped off to a low howl. The basement walls began to rematerialise, and within a few moments the awesome Adramelech was standing amongst us in the cellar, slowly taking in his surroundings, and waiting for the subservient rustling of his devils to subside.

I was aware of such evil in the air that my pulse refused

to calm down. It was more terrible than I could have imagined possible. It was a hundred times more scaring than being jostled by hoodlums on your way home, or waking up in the night to hear someone breaking the window of your back door. It was absolute high-pitched fear that went on and on and on and never subsided.

Adramelech turned towards Madeleine and me. I heard a clear, cultivated whisper say: 'Who are these?'

'They are mortal disciples, converted to the ways of hell by Elmek,' responded Umbakrail.

There was a pause, but I didn't dare to look up. Beside me, Madeleine stayed on her knees, her hands clasped together as if she were praying. I didn't blame her. In the face of the demon Adramelech, there didn't seem to be much else you could do.

Adramelech said: 'I am pleased, Elmek. You have brought us together again at last, as the Nine Books of Hell have always predicted. Does it not say in the Third Book that we shall help in a mortal war which shall divide us, but that we shall come together in time for yet another mortal war?'

'Those are the words, master,' said Umbakrail, in a subservient tone.

Adramelech turned his attention to Lieutenant-Colonel Thanet, who had been forced to kneel in front of him by two of the devils.

'And which is this?' he asked.

Cholok said: 'This is one of the mortal warmakers, who has been attempting for years to discover the words which could summon you up, O master, but also those words which could send you back.'

Adramelech laughed. 'Only a blood-bargain can send me back, little warmaker,' he said. 'And each time I am summoned, the blood demanded must be more. You are even more ignorant than those warmakers of times gone by.'

Lieutenant-Colonel Thane   aised his bruised face and

looked up at the demon Adramelech. 'Would you really help us?' he said, unsteadily. 'If we struck a blood-bargain, would you really help us, like you did during the war?'

'Which war?' demanded Adramelech. 'We have fought in many wars! We fought at Agincourt, and we turned the Romans back at Minden! We fought in South Africa, with the Boers; and we fought best of all on the Somme, and at Passchendaele, and Ypres, where we did what you wanted us to do, and exterminated a whole generation of your young men.'

'I know that,' said Lieutenant-Colonel Thanet. 'But will you help us now?'

'You want to exterminate *more*?' asked Adramelech. 'Then you have a lust for destruction and violence which pleases me. There is a close bond between the hierarchy of hell and mortals like you, and it pleases me. One day, perhaps, when mortals finally understand the purpose for which they were created, they will destroy themselves no more, and despair no more; but I trust that we can stay that day as long as we can.'

Lieutenant-Colonel Thanet, for one rare moment, looked up at Adramelech like a man, instead of a soldier. 'You *know*?' he asked the demon. 'You *know* why we're here? Why there are humans on earth?'

Adramelech's sardonic laugh sounded like a thousand tons of rock dropping down a thousand empty mineshafts. '*Know?* But of course I know! But why should that trouble you? Your purpose is infinitely tinier, yet infinitely more exciting! To destroy, and to have in your hands the power of destruction! To inflict pain on yourselves! To pull down everything that the works of man and God between them have created! Why should you concern yourself with philosophy when you have such pleasure at your disposal?'

Clustered around Adramelech like fawning courtiers, the devils hissed and whispered. There was a pause, and then Lieutenant-Colonel Thanet said: 'We need your power for NATO. Do you know what NATO is?'

'Of course, little warmaker. Adramelech is omniscient.'

'Well, it's been my brief to summon you up, and ask for your help.'

Adramelech looked down on Lieutenant-Colonel Thanet with indulgence. 'You do not have to *ask* for my help. But you do have to *bargain* for it. Tell me what destruction you desire to be wreaked, and I will tell you what price you will have to pay. The price, I warn you, is always blood.'

Lieutenant-Colonel Thanet looked disconcerted. 'I don't want any destruction,' he said. 'I simply want to have you on hand as a defence unit.'

Adramelech laughed. 'Defence is nothing more than latent destruction! Why pretend that what you are arming yourselves for is defence, when all you wish to do is destroy those who you believe to be your enemies? Show me the difference between a weapon of attack and a weapon of defence! Do they kill differently? Is one less dangerous than the other? You are even more of a fool than I thought!'

Lieutenant-Colonel Thanet tried to get to his feet. 'Now look here!' he snapped. 'It was my work that brought you here, and it's about time you appreciated it!'

Adramelech, for a moment, was quiet. Then he said: 'I appreciated the work of Patton and Eisenhower, little warmaker. Patton had me summoned through the circle of my thirteen acolytes, and he came to me as a man bent on destruction. He wanted the Germans killed, and killed quickly. I admit that he was frightened of us, and that he kept us in check with his priests. But he desired death for his enemies, and he paid us in blood, and we were satisfied. Patton and Eisenhower were both men that I could be proud of. But *you*? What are *you* saying? That you don't want to kill after all?'

Lieutenant-Colonel Thanet was flustered. He was also

terrified, although he was trying desperately not to show it. He said shakily: 'We can't ask you to go out on a rampage of death and destruction right now. There isn't a war. Not like there was with Patton.'

'Why should that matter?' asked Adramelech drily. 'If you unleash us on your enemies, we will make a war for you. A war that you will win.'

'I don't want you to!' shouted Thanet, wincing in pain from his broken rib.

'You have no choice,' said Adramelech. 'Now we are summoned, you cannot send us back without fulfilling a bargain. You have absolutely no choice at all.'

Lieutenant-Colonel Thanet said: 'What kind of a bargain would you settle for? You've already killed four of my men.'

Adramelech turned his monstrous head. 'I would settle for you,' he suggested, in that sinister whisper. 'I would definitely settle for you.'

'Me?' asked Thanet, horrified. 'What do you mean, me?'

'I would find it enjoyable to bite off your head,' said Adramelech.

Lieutenant-Colonel Thanet was very white. He knelt there for a long while, swaying with shock and stress. Even then, I don't think that he could truly believe that Adramelech was real. His mind had retreated into itself, and his subconscious was probably busy reassuring him that he'd drunk too much bitter and eaten too many pickled onions, and that he was going to wake up soon.

'What's the alternative?' he said queasily. 'War? Is that it?'

Adramelech said nothing.

Lieutenant-Colonel Thanet twisted his head around painfully and looked at Madeleine and me. Madeleine hissed: 'Don't offer him anything! Sit tight and don't offer him anything!'

Lieutenant-Colonel Thanet looked back at the Chancellor of Hell. He said, in an almost inaudible voice: 'You have to give me some time.'

Adramelech said: 'There is no time.'

'But I don't know what to do! I can't let you—'

Adramelech bellowed, in a surge of ear-splitting feedback: '*There is no time!*'

There was a frozen moment when the demon was glowering at Thanet and Thanet was staring back at him in terror. Then the Colonel heaved himself up from the floor and made a dive for the cellar steps, screaming at the top of his voice at the pain from his broken rib.

It was Askalon, the devil of fire, who stopped him. As Thanet reached the fifth or sixth step, he was suddenly engulfed in fierce, roaring flames. The spectacle was horrifying. Thanet screamed again, and tried to beat out the fire that shrivelled his hair and his skin and burned up his body fats, but his hands were alight, too, and all he did was fan the flames even more ferociously.

He stood for a moment, a man of blackened flesh and fire, and then he dropped sideways off the steps and collapsed on the floor.

Adramelech watched him in grotesque silence. Then the demon whispered: 'A coward and a fool. Not a warmaker at all. At least Patton gave me blood.'

Madeleine touched my hand. She whispered: 'Don't move. Don't say a word,' and then she stood up and faced Adramelech and his devils with a calmness and a straight-backed self-confidence that I think I would have found impossible.

She said: 'Adramelech.'

At first, the demon didn't hear her, although some of his lesser devils did, and turned their slanted goat-like eyes towards her.

Madeleine said, louder: '*Adramelech!*'

The demon lifted his strange mulish head. He said nothing for a while, until Madeleine had walked right up to his deformed feet.

'I *know* you,' he whispered, suspiciously. 'I recognise you from times gone by.'

Madeleine stayed where she was – erect and unafraid.

'I have seen you before,' said Adramelech. 'Speak your name, mortal!'

'My name is Madeleine Passerelle,' answered Madeleine. 'But you know me first as Charlotte Latour; and you shall know me by another name, too.'

'What do you mean?' growled Adramelech. There was something about Madeleine that unsettled and disturbed him.

Madeleine placed her hands together in the gesture of prayer. She said quietly: 'I was the girl given to you by General Patton in payment for Operation Stripes. They said I was a collaborator, and that I had betrayed the French resistance movement. Only God knows that this was not true, and that jealous friends had given the story around. But I had to suffer for it, all the same, and I was taken to England and put before you, to appease your destructive wrath. I shall never forget what you did to me, how you gave me agony beyond any endurance, and how you abused my womanhood to the ends of natural or supernatural imagination.'

Adramelech didn't answer, but his devils were disturbed, and I could hear their claws scratching impatiently on the floor.

'I died,' said Madeleine simply. 'I died and I ascended into the realms of Our Lord, and into the care of Our Lady Queen of Heaven. I know now what heaven is; and because I know what heaven is, I can understand hell. Heaven is the state in which the faith and steadfastness of the heart are rewarded in the very way in which your mind imagines Heaven to be. Hell is the working of ignorance and self-indulgence against the real purpose of humanity.'

Adramelech said: 'If you died, Charlotte Latour, how are you here?'

Madeleine lifted her head. 'I was reborn on the day of my martyrdom as the daughter of Jacques and Edith Passerelle. I did not know that I was a reincarnation, not until the time came to take Elmek from the tank, and to reunite your acolytes in this cellar. It is only today that my mind has fully realised the wholeness of my destiny, and that, as a reincarnation, I have a heavenly duty to perform.'

Adramelech laughed a torrent of ugly laughter. 'Heavenly duty? You're crazed! You're as crazed as Jeanne d'Arc! She summoned us up, supposing that to be her duty, and now you've done the same! The girls of France are as simple today as they ever were!'

But Madeleine held her ground. She raised her arms, so that she stood like a human crucifix, and when she spoke, her voice sounded so clear and penetrating that I could hardly believe it was her.

'I am more than a human reincarnation, Adramelech. I am a human reincarnation born to be possessed!'

'Possessed?' retorted Adramelech. 'Possessed?'

'Possessed by what?' asked Elmek. 'By man or by mule?'

The devils rustled in bloodthirsty glee. For my part, I kept as far back in the shadows as I could.

It was then that Madeleine underwent a transformation that had only just been beginning when she had first spoken of angels and had taken the crisis in hand. The air all around her began to darken, and she herself became harder to see, until there was scarcely anything visible at all. Where she had been standing was what you could only call an intense black glow – a darkness so dark that I could hardly bear to look at it.

I didn't have much in the way of scientific training. After all, I was only a cartographer. But I knew what I was looking at. Whatever Madeleine really was, or whatever was possessing her, she was now so physically dense that no reflected light could leave her body and enable us to see her. She was like a black hole in space, only she was standing right amongst us.

Her voice rang through the basement. A high, clear, beautiful voice. She said: 'You recognise me now, Adramelech! You recognise me now for what I am!'

Adramelech ferociously tossed his great donkey-like head, and bared his teeth. His devils scrambled all around him, but he hurled them aside with a brutal sweep of his arm.

'*Hod!*' he shrieked. '*The angel Hod!*'

The devils groaned and howled, and retreated away from the glowing blackness. Adramelech himself drew back, but he was changing now, looking less like a monstrously diseased donkey, and more like a black Satanic beast with reddened eyes and a mouth that was thick with fangs.

Madeleine's voice said: 'I have waited centuries for this moment, Adramelech. Now I have you all together, all in one time, all in one place, all in one earthly dimension. You and your thirteen leprous disciples!'

Adramelech roared in fury, and the basement shook. Bricks were dislodged from the walls, and loose cement sifted down from the ceiling.

'I have my devils!' he screamed. 'You are nothing against me and my devils!'

He swept his black, scaly arm towards his acolytes, and the air of the cellar became thick with fire and smoke and the rank smell of disease. He swept his arm again, and we were enveloped in swarms of flies and mosquitoes. He raised both arms, and brought them down in a powerful sweep of destruction, and there was a tremor that must have shaken the whole building by its foundations.

'*Begone, Hod! Out, deceitful angel! Get out of this place and never return!*'

There was another tremor, and part of the cellar steps collapsed, half-burying the burned body of Lieutenant-

Colonel Thanet. Slowly, cautiously, their reptilian wings lifted, the devils encircled the shimmering darkness of the angel Hod, their claws lifted and their teeth bared in an ecstasy of murderousness. I could see their slanted eyes through the dust and the smoke and the swarming blowflies, and I could smell that stench they exuded whenever they were aroused.

Hod said clearly: 'You have no chance, Adramelech! My angels are already invoked! I call you down, my messengers! I call you down, my legions! I call you down to destroy these vile devils, and dismiss their remains to everlasting hellfire!'

I saw, for one moment, the horns of the devils silhouetted against the ultimate blackness of the divine angel Hod. I saw Adramelech rearing in the background, more hideous and bestial than ever before, his rows of teeth glistening with saliva. I saw the whole cellar lit with the phosphorescence of diseased flesh, and clouded with flies.

Then, my vision was blinded by white intense light. Everything was blotted out in brilliance – the brilliance of angels who had not yet attained the ultimate brilliance of total darkness. I clapped my hands to my face, and turned towards the wall, but the after-image still exploded over my retina. Every one of those thirteen angels we had summoned down had *arrived*, in a burst of holy energy that wiped out human sight, and dazzled human understanding.

The basement trembled. I heard shrieks of agony, and screams of intolerable fear. I half-opened my eyes, squinting against the light, and I saw tall, impossibly attenuated outlines of flickering fire; things that radiated energy in all directions, and cut their way through the devils in swathes of light. I saw Umbakrail fall, its strange ribcage cloven open by light, its insides exploding in ancient dust. I saw Cholok's flesh torn from its bones in papery flakes, and scattered in a hurricane of light. I saw

Themgoroth try blindly to flee, only to be sliced apart by an angel's dazzling arm. And I saw Elmek, too, a wriggling mass of tentacles that shrunk in on itself in pain, seared beyond endurance by the heat and the light of the angels.

In a few minutes, it was almost over. The devils lay as they had before, as bones. The angels faded, until they left nothing but shapeless memories of what they were on the sensitised rods and cones at the back of my eyes. A cool wind blew across the cellar floor, and seemed to blow the dust away, and the stench of Adramelech's devils.

Only Adramelech and Hod remained. Adramelech's encrusted feet were set squarely on the basement floor, his gigantic black bulk overshadowing everything, and the grand Chancellor of Hell itself glared viciously around him. Hod, the shimmering black angel, stood before him like an hallucination.

'Hod,' whispered Adramelech. 'You cannot dismiss me. It is not within your power.'

'I am conscious of that,' replied Hod, in the voice of Madeleine. 'But you shall go, all the same.'

'You cannot dismiss me! I shall stay! Only a mortal can dismiss Adramelech, and only a mortal with proof that your precious God once lived! You know that as well as I!'

Hod glowed darkly, and remained silent.

Adramelech growled: 'For what you have done today, Hod, I shall encourage a war on this earth such as has never been seen before. You have destroyed my servants. Well, I shall destroy millions of your mortal charges. Tonight, such weapons will be used that the earth will seem to burn from pole to pole, and the generations of man will be cursed with sickness and disease and deformation for ever after.'

'The Lord God will—'

'The Lord God will do nothing! The Lord God has never done anything, never intervened, and he will not intervene now! I will see this earth burn, Hod. I will see it burn! And then your precious Lord's precious plan will be seen for what it really always was.'

With my back against the basement wall, I heard this booming, echoing exchange of hostilities like the voices that you hear in dreams. I was uncertain at first, and desperately scared, but then I took one step forwards into the light, and the warring beings fell silent, and were obviously observing me with curiosity and surprise.

I said, hoarsely: 'I dismiss you, Adramelech.'

The grand Chancellor of Hell, looming over me in glistening coils of black snake-like flesh, paused for a while to think about what I had said. Then his yellowish mouth opened, and he laughed such a cruel, evil laugh that I knew that I had probably made a mistake. I took another step, but this time it was backwards.

'So,' said Adramelech, 'you dismiss me, you pathetic mortal? You dismiss me, do you?'

Terrified, I nodded yes. I remembered as much as I could of the dismissals that Father Anton and the Reverend Taylor had spoken, and I said: Adramelech, I adjure thee to go out! In the name of God the Father leave my presence! In the name of God the Son make thy departure! In the name of the Holy Ghost leave this place! For it is God who commands thee, and it is I who command thee! By Jesus of Nazareth who gave his soul, by the blessed angels from whom thou fell, be on thy way I demand thee! Amen!'

Adramelech remained where he was. His teeth gnashed together, and he glared down at me with such fury and hatred that I was ready to do what Lieutenant-Colonel Thanet had done, and make a run for it. Maybe the angel could protect me while I got away. On the other hand, maybe it couldn't. I felt lukewarm sweat running down my back, inside my shirt.

The angel Hod said quietly: 'Do you not go, Adramelech?'

Adramelech laughed. 'Not until this mortal produces his proof that Jesus of Nazareth actually lived. If he can.'

There was a long, tense silence. I turned towards the angel Hod, but its black brilliance was so intense that I couldn't see whether it was encouraging me or warning me. I turned back to Adramelech.

'Without proof of Jesus, you are doomed,' grinned Adramelech. 'I shall devour you, mortal, and Hod will be powerless to prevent me. The choice of the human race was self-destruction, and not even the greatest of angels can prevent it.'

I coughed. Then I reached into my pocket and took out the pastille tin that Eloise had given me. I carefully prised off the lid, and held it up towards Adramelech.

'What is that?' asked the demon, turning its grotesque head away.

I held the tin higher. 'It is irrefutable proof of the life of Our Lord Jesus Christ. It is the ashes of his seamless robe, which was taken from him on Calvary.'

Adramelech twisted and shuddered uneasily. 'It's a fake,' he said, in a harsh voice. 'All relics are fakes.'

I felt frozen with fear. But I kept the tin held aloft, and I repeated, as steadily as I could: 'It is the ashes of Christ's robe, and it is not a fake. Christ lived, and these are the remnants of his robe to prove it.'

'*You lie!*' shrieked Adramelech. '*Take that thing away!*'

'It's the truth!' I yelled back. 'Christ must have lived because nobody in the whole goddamned universe could have tolerated a world where you and your devils ruled alone! Christ's life was logical, as well as divine, and that's all there is to it!'

'*You lie!*' fumed the demon. '*You lie!*'

'Do I?' I shouted back. 'Then take this!'

I raised my arm, and hurled the tin of ashes over the serpentine body of the grand Chancellor of Hell in a powdery spray.

There was a second in which I thought that nothing

was going to happen, and that the demon was going to attack me with those rows and rows of vicious teeth. But then Adramelech bellowed, so loudly that bricks and dust collapsed from the basement ceiling in thunderous showers, and bellowed again, and again, until I had to cover my ears.

His black snake-like skin sloughed off him in heavy, wrinkled folds. Beneath that, he was all raw glistening flesh – greys and yellows and purple veins. Then his flesh began to slither away from his bones, and evaporate into sickening, stomach-turning steam. Finally, his bones dropped to the floor, and out from his ribs crawled a twitching iridescent slug creature that subsided on to the concrete and shrivelled into nothing.

For a long time, I stood there staring at Adramelech's remains, and couldn't speak. It was hardly possible to believe what had happened. Then I turned back towards the dark glow of the angel Hod, and I said: 'Is that it? Is Adramelech really dead?'

Madeleine's voice said: 'In this life, yes. We have much to thank you for, mortal. You have acted wisely.'

I wiped dust and dirt from my face. 'What about Madeleine?' I asked the angel. 'Is she going to come back? Or do you have her for ever?'

The blackness gleamed. 'Madeleine is gone now, mortal, just as Charlotte Latour did before her. She is not dead, but will live in another form. Perhaps one day you will meet her again.'

I coughed. The air in the basement was dusty and stifling. I said: 'What does that mean? She's going to be reborn?'

'In a way.'

'Can you tell her something for me?'

'I'm afraid not. She will know nothing of what went before. But she will be happy. I hope that is some consolation for you. She has served us well, and deserves happiness.'

I wiped my face with my handkerchief. 'And what about Father Anton, and Antoinette? Elmek promised that Adramelech would revive them.'

If such a thing was possible, the blackness smiled. Or at least, it radiated affection. It said: 'The promises of devils are rarely kept. Only the Lord thy God has the final power of life or resurrection. But you may know that Father Anton is in his heaven, where he deserves to be, and that his Antoinette is with him. Those who struggle against evil are rewarded in the life hereafter.'

I was beginning to feel very tired. It was a long, long time ago since those two old men had come down the road on bicycles and interrupted my map-making to tell me about the tank at Pont D'Ouilly.

I said: 'What about the devils? Are we ever going to see them again?'

'As long as man makes wars, Adramelech and his thirteen acolytes will survive, in one form or another. A demon of the evil sephiroth cannot be totally destroyed, except by disbelief. The same is true for angels of the divine sephiroth. If no man believed in glory, which is my realm, then I should vanish for all eternity.'

'I see,' I told the angel, although I wasn't sure that I did. I looked round at the ruined basement, and said: 'What do I do now? Is there anything else you want me to do?'

There was no answer. I turned around, and the black glow had disappeared. I was alone again in the world of mortals.

Very wearily, very slowly, I climbed the cellar steps, and opened the door that led out into the hallway. There was nobody around. Up here, the building looked as ordinary and normal as when we had first pushed the doorbell. The front door was open, too, and I could see my rented Citroën parked outside, with a parking ticket tucked under the windshield wiper.

I went down the steps into the wintry street. It was

almost dark now, and it was beginning to snow. I lifted up my wiper and took out the ticket, and as I stood there on that wet, cold London pavement, I was glad of the icy drizzle, because nobody could see that my eyes were filled with tears.

Mirror

À François Truchaud
Merci, mon ami!

CHAPTER ONE

Morris Nathan lifted his folded sunglasses up in front of his eyes like a lorgnette and watched in satisfaction as his fourth wife circled idly around the pool on her inflatable sunbed. 'Martin,' he replied, 'you should save your energy. Nobody, but nobody, is going to want to make a picture about Boofuls. Why do you think that nobody's done it already?'

'Maybe nobody thought of it,' Martin suggested. 'Maybe somebody thought of it, but felt that it was too obvious. But it seems like a natural to me. The small golden-haired boy from Idaho state orphanage who became a worldwide star in less than three years.'

'Oh, sure,' Morris agreed. 'And then got himself chopped up into more pieces than a Colonel Sanders Party Bucket.'

Martin put down his drink. 'Well, yes. But everybody knows that, I mean that's part of the basic legend, so I haven't actually shown his death in any kind of graphic detail. You just see him being driven out of the studio that last evening, then fade-out. It's a bit like *Butch Cassidy and the Sundance Kid*. You remember the way that ended.'

Morris lowered his sunglasses and squinted at Martin thoughtfully. 'You know something, Martin? I used to deceive myself that I married for intellect, can you believe that? Conversation, wit, perception – that's what I wanted in a woman. Or at least, that's what I *kidded* myself I wanted in a woman. My first three wives were all college graduates. Well, you remember Sherri, don't you – my third? Who could forget her, I ask? But then one day just after Sherri and I were divorced, I was looking through my photo albums, and I realized that each of my wives had one thing in common that wasn't anything to do with intellect.'

He turned and looked fondly out at the twenty-nine-year-old titian-haired woman in the tiny crochet bikini circling around and around on the breeze-ruffled surface of the pool.

'Jugs,' he said, 'that's what I married them for. And I was being a fool to myself for not admitting it. I was like the guy who buys *Playboy* and tells himself he's buying it for the articles.' He wiped his mouth with his open hand. 'It's infantile, sure. But that's what I like. Jugs.'

Martin shielded his eyes with his hand and peered out at the woman in the pool. 'You made a good choice this time, then?'

'Well, sure. Because Alison has the figure without the brains. If you subtract her IQ from her bra size, you get a factor of eleven. And, believe me, next time I meet a woman I take a shine to, that's going to be the only statistic I'll ever want to know.'

Martin paused for a moment before getting back to the subject of Boofuls. He didn't want Morris to think that he wasn't interested in Alison, or how small her mind was, or how enormous her breasts. He picked up his vodka-and-orange-juice, and sipped a little, and then set it down on the white cast-iron table.

'I have the treatment here if you want to read it,' he said, clearing his throat.

Morris slowly shook his head. 'It's poison, Martin. I can't think of a single producer who isn't going to hate the idea. It has the mark of Cain. All the sickness of Fatty Arbuckle and Lupe Velez and Sharon Tate. Forget it. Everybody else has.'

'They still show *Whistlin' Dixie* on late-night television,' Martin persisted. 'Almost anybody you meet can remember at least two lines of "Heartstrings", even if they don't know who originally sang it.'

Morris was silent for a long time. A pair of California quail fluttered onto the roof of his Tudor-style poolhouse and began to warble and look around for dry-roasted peanuts. Eventually, Morris said, 'You're a good writer, Martin. One day you're going to be a *rich* writer, that's if you're lucky. But if you try to tout this particular property around Hollywood, you're not going to be any kind of writer at all, because nobody

2

is going to want to know you. Just do yourself a favor and forget that Boofuls ever existed.'

'Come on, Morris, that's ridiculous. That's like trying to say that Shirley Temple never existed.'

'No, it's not. Shirley Temple wasn't brutally hacked to death by her grandmother, now, was she?'

Martin rolled up his screenplay into a tight tube and smacked it into the palm of his hand. 'I don't know, Morris. It's something I really want to do. It has absolutely everything. Songs, dancing, a sentimental story line.'

Alison had paddled herself to the side of the pool and was climbing out. Morris watched her with benign possessiveness, his sun-reddened hands clasped over his belly like Buddha. 'Isn't she something?' he asked the world.

Martin nodded to Alison and said, 'How're you doing?'

Alison reached out and shook his hand and sprinkled water all over his shirt and his screenplay. 'I'm fine, thanks. But I think my nose is going to peel. What do you think?'

'You should use sunscreen, my petal,' said Morris.

Alison was quite pretty in a vacant sort of way. Snub nose, with freckles. Pale green eyes. Wide, orthodontically immaculate smile. And really enormous breasts, each one as big as her head, barely contained in her crochet bikini top. By quick reckoning Martin worked out that her IQ was 29, give or take an inch.

'Are you staying for lunch?' Alison asked him. 'We only have fruit and yogurt. You know – my figure and Morry's tum-tum.'

Martin shook his head. 'I only came over to show Morris my new screenplay.'

Alison giggled and leaned forward to kiss Morris on his furrowed scarlet forehead. 'I hope he liked it, he's been *so-o-o* grouchy today.'

'Well, no,' said Martin, 'as a matter of fact he hated it.'

'Oh, *Morry*,' Alison pouted.

Morris let out a leaky, exasperated sigh. 'Martin has written a screenplay about Boofuls.'

Alison made a face of childish disgust. 'Boofuls? No wonder Morry hated it. That's so *icky*. You mean a horror picture?'

'Not a horror picture,' Martin replied, trying to be patient.

3

'A musical, based on his life. I was going to leave out what happened to him in the end.'

'But how can you do that?' asked Alison innocently. 'I mean, when you say "Boofuls", that's all that anybody ever remembers. You know – what happened to him in the end.'

Morris shrugged at Martin as if that conclusively proved his point. If a girl as dumb as Alison thought that it was icky to write a screenplay about Boofuls, then what was Paramount going to think about it? Or M-G-M, where Boofuls had been shooting his last, unfinished picture on the day he was murdered?

Martin finished his drink and stood up. 'I guess I'd better go. I still have that *A-Team* rewrite to finish.'

Morris eased himself back on his sunbed, and Alison perched herself on his big hairy thigh.

'Listen,' said Morris, 'I can't stop you trying to sell that idea. But my advice is, don't. It won't do you any good and it'll probably do you a whole lot of harm. If you do try, though, you don't bring my name into it. You understand?'

'Sure, Morris,' said Martin, deliberately keeping his voice flat. 'I understand. Thanks for your valuable time.'

He left the poolside and walked across the freshly watered lawn to the rear gate. His sun-faded bronze Mustang was parked under a eucalyptus just outside. He tossed the screenplay onto the passenger seat, climbed in, and started the engine.

'Morris Nathan, arbiter of taste,' he said out loud as he backed noisily into Mulholland Drive. 'God save us from agents, and all their works.'

On the way back to his apartment on Franklin Avenue he played the sound track from Boofuls' last musical, *Sunshine Serenade*, on his car stereo, with the volume turned all the way up. He stopped at the traffic signals at the end of Mulholland, and two sun-freckled teenage girls on bicycles stared at him curiously and giggled. The sweeping strings of the M-G-M Studio Orchestra and the piping voice of Boofuls singing 'Sweep up Your Broken Sunbeams' were hardly the kind of in-car entertainment that anybody would have expected from a thin, bespectacled thirty-four-year-old in a faded checkered shirt and stone-washed jeans.

'Shall we dance?' one of them teased him. He gave her a tight smile and shook his head. He was still sore at Morris for having squashed his Boofuls concept so completely. When he thought of some of the dumb, tasteless ideas that Morris had come up with, Martin couldn't even begin to understand why he had regarded Boofuls as such a hoodoo. They'd made movies about James Dean, for God's sake; and Patricia Neal's stroke; and Helter Skelter; and Teddy Kennedy's bone cancer. I mean, that was *taste*? What was so off-putting about Boofuls?

He turned off Sunset with a squeal of balding tires. He parked in the street because his landlord, Mr Capelli, always liked to garage his ten-year-old Lincoln every night, in case somebody scratched it, or lime pollen fell on it, or a passing bird had the temerity to spatter it with half-digested seeds. Martin called the Lincoln 'the Mafiamobile', but not to Mr Capelli's face.

Upstairs, in his single-bedroom apartment, his coffee cup and his breakfast plate and last night's supper plate were stacked in the kitchen sink, exactly where he had left them. That was one feature of living alone that he still couldn't quite get used to. Through the open door of the bedroom, he could see the rumpled futon on which he now slept alone, and the large framed poster for Boofuls' first musical *Whistlin' Dixie*. He walked through to the bare white-painted sitting room, with its single antique sofa upholstered in carpetbag fabric and its gray steel desk overlooking the window. Jane had taken everything else. She and her new boyfriend had simply marched in and carried it all away, while Martin had carried on typing.

The boyfriend had even the nerve to tap the desk and ask Jane, 'You want this, too?'

Without looking up from the tenth draft of his *A-Team* episode, Martin had said, in his B A Baracas accent, 'Touch this desk and you die, suckah!'

Jane's departure had brought with it immediate relief from their regular shouting contests, and all the tension and discomfort that had characterized their marriage. It had also

5

given Martin the opportunity to work all day and half of the night without being disturbed. That was how he had been able to finish his screenplay for *Boofuls!* in four days flat. But after three weeks he was beginning to realize that work was very much less than everything. Jane might have been demanding and awkward and self-opinionated, but at least she had been somebody intelligent to talk to, somebody to share things with, somebody to hold on to. What was the point of sitting in front of the television on your own, drinking wine on your own, and laughing out loud at *E.R.* with nothing but a lunatic echo to keep you company?

Martin dropped his rejected screenplay onto his desk. The top of the desk was bare except for his Olivetti typewriter, a stack of paper, and a black-and-white publicity still of Boofuls in a brass frame. It was signed, 'To Moira, with xxx's from Boofuls'. Martin had found the photograph in The Reel Thing, a movie memorabilia store on Hollywood Boulevard: he had no idea who Moira might have been.

The wall at the side of his desk was covered from floor to ceiling with photographs and cuttings and posters and letters all of Boofuls. Here was Boofuls dancing with Jenny Farr in *Sunshine Serenade*. Boofuls in a sailor suit. Boofuls in a pretend biplane in a scene from *Dancing on the Clouds*. An original letter from President Roosevelt, thanking Boofuls for boosting public morale with his song 'March, March, March, America!' Then the yellowed front page from the *Los Angeles Times*, Saturday, August 19, 1939: 'Boofuls Murdered. Doting Grandma Dismembers Child Star, Hangs Self'.

Martin stood for a long time staring at the headlines. Then, petulantly, he tore the newspaper off the wall and rolled it up into a ball. But his anger quickly faded, and he carefully opened the page out again and smoothed it on the desk with the edge of his hand.

He had always been entranced by 1930s Hollywood musicals, ever since he was a small boy, and the idea for *Boofuls!* had germinated in the back of his mind from the first week he had taken up screenwriting (that wonderful long-gone week when he had sold a *Fall Guy* script to Glen A Larson). *Boofuls!* had glimmered in the distance for four years now, a golden mirage, his one great chance of fame and glory. *Boofuls!*, a musical by Martin Williams. He couldn't write music, of course, but he didn't need to. Boofuls had recorded over forty original songs, most of them written by Glazer and Hanson, all of them scintillating, all of them catchy, and most of them deleted, so they wouldn't be too expensive for any studio to acquire. *Boofuls!* was a ready-made smash, as far as Martin could see, and nobody had ever done it before.

Morris Nathan was full of shit. He was only jealous because *he* hadn't thought of it and because Martin had shown his first signs of creative independence. Morris preferred his writers tame. That's why people like Stephen J Cannell and Mort Lachman always came to him for rewrites. Morris' writers would rewrite a teleplay four hundred times if it was required of them, and never complain. Not out loud, anyway. They were the galley slaves of Hollywood.

Although he never worked well when he was drinking, Martin went across to the windowsill and uncorked the two-liter bottle of chardonnay red which he had been keeping to celebrate Morris Nathan's enthusiastic acclaim for the *Boofuls!* idea. He poured himself a large glassful and drank half of it straight off. Morris Nathan. What a *mamzer*.

He went across to the portable Sony cassette recorder which was all the hi-fi that Jane had left him, and rewound it to the beginning of 'Whistlin' Dixie'. Those gliding strings began again, that familiar introduction, and then the voice of that long-dead child started to sing.

> *All those times you ran and hid*
> *Never did those things you should have did*
> *All those times you shook in your shoes*
> *Never had the nerve to face your blues*
> *You were – Whistlin' Dixie!*

Martin leaned against the side of the window and looked down into the next-door yard. It was mostly swimming pool, surrounded by bright green synthetic-grass carpeting. Maria was there again, on her sunbed, her eyes closed, her nose and her nipples protected from the morning sun by paper

7

Sno-Cones. Maria worked as a cocktail waitress at the Sunset Hyatt. Her surname was Bocanegra, and she had thighs like Carmen Miranda. Martin had asked her for a date one day, about fifteen seconds before a huge Latin bodybuilder with pockmarked cheeks had appeared around the corner of her apartment building and scooped his arm around her and grinned at Martin and said, '*Cómo la va, hombre?*'

Martin had blurted out a quick '*Hasta luego*', and that had been the beginning and end of a beautiful relationship.

He sipped wine and thought about getting back to the *A-Team* rewrite, but it was pretty hard to get into Murdock's latest outbreak of nuttiness when he was feeling so down about *Boofuls!* He whispered the words along with the tape. '*You were – Whistlin' Dixie!*'

Just then the telephone rang. He let it ring for a while. He guessed it was Morris, more than likely, wanting to know when the rewrite was going to be completed. The way he felt at the moment, January 2010. At last, however, Martin turned away from the window and picked up the receiver.

'Hello? Martin Williams.'

'Hey, Martin!' said an enthusiastic voice. 'I'm real glad I got in touch with you! This is Ramone!'

'Oh, Ramone, hi.' Ramone worked behind the counter at The Reel Thing, selling everything from souvenir programs for the opening night of *Gone With the Wind* to Ida Lupino's earrings. It was Ramone more than anybody else who had helped him to build up his unique collection of Boofuls souvenirs.

'Listen, Martin, something real interesting came up. A lady came into the store this morning and said she had a whole lot of furniture for sale.'

Martin cleared his throat. 'I could use some furniture, sure. But actually I was thinking of taking a trip out to the Z-Mart furnishing warehouse in Burbank. I can't afford anything antique.'

'No, no, no, you're not getting my drift,' said Ramone. 'This lady bought some of the furniture from Boofuls' old house. There was an auction, you get it, after the kid was killed, and everything was sold. Drapes, tables, knives and forks. They even sold the food out of the refrigerator. Can you imagine what kind of a ghoul would want to eat a murdered kid's ice cream?'

'But what happened? This woman bought some of the furniture?'

'Maybe not her personally, but her husband or her father or somebody. Anyway, she has, what, lemme see, I made a list here – she has two armchairs, a liquor cabinet, a sofa, four barstools, and a mirror.'

'Are you going to sell it for her?'

'No, not my scene, furniture. And – you know – apart from you, nobody's too keen on Boofuls stuff. I told her to advertise in the paper. Maybe some sicko will want it.'

'What are you trying to say? That I'm a sicko, too?'

'Aw, come on, man, I know you're legitimate. You should see some of the guys who come in to look through Carole Landis' underwear, stuff like that.'

Martin said, 'I'd like to see the furniture, sure, but I really don't have too much spare cash right now.'

'Well, that's up to you,' Ramone told him. 'But if you're interested, the lady's name is Mrs Harper, and she lives at 1334 Hillrise. There's no harm in taking a look, is there?'

'All right, I guess not, thanks for thinking of me.'

'No sweat, man. Whenever I hear the name Boofuls, I think of you.'

'I hope that's a compliment.'

'*De nada*,' said Ramone, and hung up.

Martin finished his wine. He knew what he ought to do: and that was to sit down dutifully at his typewriter and zip another sheet of paper into the platen and carry on writing the *A-Team*. However much he disagreed with Morris; however chagrined he felt for Morris' reaction to *Boofuls!* Morris was an industrious agent with matchless contacts, and he made his writers money. If Martin didn't finish this rewrite by tomorrow morning, it was quite conceivable that Morris would never be able to sell him to Stephen J Cannell Productions ever again.

But, damn it, he was so dispirited, and so damn sick of writing slick and silly dialogue. An expedition to Hillrise Avenue to look over some of Boofuls' original furniture might

9

be just what he needed to lift his spirits. Just to *touch* it would be something – to touch the actual furniture that little Boofuls had sat on himself. It would make him seem more real, and Morris Nathan more imaginary, and just at the moment Martin couldn't think of a better tonic than that.

Hillrise Avenue was a steeply sloping street up by the Hollywood Reservoir. The houses had been avant-garde in 1952; today they were beginning to show signs of shabbiness and wear. Hillrise was one of those areas that had never quite made it, and was resignedly deteriorating for the eventual benefit of some smart real-estate developer.

Martin parked his Mustang with the rear wheels cramped against the curb and climbed out. From here, there was a wide, distant view of Los Angeles, smoggy today, with the twin tombstones of Century City rising above the haze. He mounted the steep concrete steps to 1334, sending a lizard scurrying into the undergrowth.

The house was square, strawberry pink, with Spanish balconies all the way around. The garden around it was dried up and scraggly. The paths were overgrown with weeds, and most of the yuccas looked sick. The roof over the front porch was heaped with dead, desiccated vines, and there was a strong smell of broken drains.

He rang the doorbell. It was shrill, demanding, and distant, like a woman shrieking in the next street. Martin shuffled his Nike trainers and waited for somebody to answer. '*All those times you shook in your shoes,*' he sang softly. '*You were – Whistlin' Dixie!*'

The front door opened. Out onto the porch came a small sixtyish woman with a huge white bouffant hairstyle and a yellow cotton mini-dress. She wore two sets of false eyelashes, one of them coming wildly adrift at the corner of her eye, and pale tangerine lipstick. She looked as though she hadn't changed her clothes or her makeup since the day *Sergeant Pepper* had been released.

Martin was so startled that he didn't quite know what to say. The woman stared at him, her left eye wincing, and eventually said, 'Ye-e-es? Are you selling something?'

'I, uh –'

'I don't see anything,' the woman remarked, peering around the porch. 'No brushes, no encyclopaedias, no Bibles. Do you want to clean my car, is that it?'

'Actually, I came about the furniture,' said Martin. 'You're Mrs Harper, right? Ramone Perez called me from The Reel Thing. He's kind of a friend of mine. He knows that I'm interested in Boofuls.'

Mrs Harper stared at Martin and then sniffed, pinching in one nostril. 'Is tha-a-at right? Well, if you're interested in Boofuls, you seem to be just about the only person in the whole of Hollywood who *is*. I've taken my furniture to every auction house and movie memorabilia store that I can *find*, and the story's always the same.'

'Yes?' said Martin, wanting to know what it was – this story that was always the same.

'Well,' pouted Mrs Harper, 'it's *macabre*, that's what they say. I mean, there's a market in motion picture properties. The very coffin that Bela Lugosi lay in when he first played Count Dracula. The very bolt that went through Boris Karloff's neck. But nobody will *touch* poor little Boofuls' furniture.'

Martin waited for a moment, but Mrs Harper obviously wasn't going to volunteer anything more. 'I was wondering – maybe I could come in and take a look at it.'

'With a view to purchase?' Mrs Harper asked him sharply; then fluttered her left eye; then squeezed it shut and said, 'Darn these lashes! They're a new brand. I don't know what you're supposed to keep them on with. Krazy Glue, if you ask me. They will . . . *curl up*. I've seen centipedes behave themselves better, and live ones at that.'

She led Martin into the hallway. The interior of the house was sour-smelling and gloomy, but it had once been decorated in the very latest fab 1960s style. The floor was covered with white shag carpet throughout, matted like the pelt of an aging Yeti. The drapes were patterned in psychedelic striations of orange and lime and purple, and white leather chairs with black legs and gold feet were arranged around the room at diagonal angles. There was even a white stereo autochange record player, which reminded Martin so strongly of the

11

Beatles and the Beach Boys and his high school dances that he felt for one unnerving moment as if he were sixteen years old.

'I'm a widow,' said Mrs Harper, as if she felt a need to explain why the interior of her house was a living museum of twenty-year-old contemporary design. 'Arnold died in 1971, and, well – it all just *reminds* me.'

Martin nodded, to show that he understood. Mrs Harper said, '*He* didn't like the Boofuls furniture, either. I mean he actually hated it. But his father had bought it, just before the war. His father was setting up house, you see, and he went to an auction and bought it – well, because it was so *cheap*. It was only afterward that somebody told him who it used to belong to. And what's more . . . it used to stand in the very *room* where poor little Boofuls was – you know – done away with. Quite the most awful thing ever. I mean even worse than Charles Manson, because she *chopped* that dear little child into – well, I don't even like to think about it. And nor does anybody else, more's the pity.'

'Can we – er – look at it?' asked Martin.

'Well, of course. It's down in the cellar. I mean it hasn't seen the light of day since Arnold's father gave it to us. Arnold didn't even want it but his father insisted. Arnold never had the nerve to stand up against his father. Well, not many people did. He was an absolute tyrant.'

Mrs Harper led the way through to the kitchen. She stood up on tiptoe, revealing so much skinny leg that Martin had to look away, and groped around on the top shelf of the kitchen cupboard to find the key to the cellar.

'I should sell up, you know, and move to San Diego. My sister lives there. This big old house is such a nuisance.'

She unlocked the cellar and switched on the light. Martin hesitated for a moment and then followed her down the steep wooden steps. The smell of drains was even stronger down here, and it was mingled with a smell of dried-out lumber and cats.

'You watch your step, now,' said Mrs Harper. 'Those last two steps are pretty rotten. We had termites, you know. Arnold thought they were going to eat the whole house right around our ears.'

'They didn't touch the furniture?'

'Don't ask me why,' said Mrs Harper, her pink-fingernailed claw illuminated for a moment as she clutched the stair rail. 'They ate just about everything else. They even ate the handle of Arnold's shovel, I'll always remember that. The whole darned handle. But they never touched the furniture. Not a nibble. Perhaps even termites have respect for the dead.'

'Yes, maybe they do,' said Martin, peering into the gloom of the cellar.

Mrs Harper beckoned him forward. 'It's all over here, behind the boiler.'

Martin caught his sleeve on an old horse collar which was hooked on a nail at the side of the stairs. It took him a moment to disentangle himself, but when he had, Mrs Harper had disappeared into the darkness behind the boiler. 'Mrs Harper?'

There was no reply. Martin groped forward a little farther. The boiler was heavy cast iron, one of those old-fashioned types, and almost looked as if it had a grinning face on it, with mica eyes. 'Mrs Harper?'

He came cautiously around the corner of the boiler and there she was. But the back of his scalp shrank in alarm, because she was suspended three feet above the floor, at a frightening diagonal angle, her white bouffant hair gleaming like the huge chrysalis of some gigantic moth.

'Ah!' Martin shouted; but almost at the same time Mrs Harper turned her head and he realized that he was looking at a reflection of her; and that the real Mrs Harper was standing beside him quite normally.

'I'm sorry,' she said without much sympathy. 'Did I startle you?'

'No, I uh –' Martin gestured toward the mirror that was hanging from the ceiling.

'Well,' Mrs Harper smiled. She rubbed her hands together. 'That was Boofuls' mirror. That was the very mirror that watched him die.'

'Very nice,' said Martin. He was beginning to wonder whether it had been such a good idea coming down here to look at Boofuls' old furniture. Maybe the tedium of retyping his *A-Team* script had something to recommend it. Maybe some memories are better left alone.

'The chairs and the sofa are back here,' said Mrs Harper. She dragged at the corner of a dustcover and revealed the shadowy outlines of an elegant reproduction sofa and two matching chairs. They were gilded, French château style, with pale green watered-satin seats – grubby and damp-stained from so many years in Mrs Harper's cellar. Martin peered at them through the gloom.

'Do you have any more lights down here?' he asked.

'Well, there's a flashlight someplace . . .' Mrs Harper fussed, making it quite obvious that she didn't want to go looking for it.

'Don't worry,' Martin told her. 'I can see them pretty good. Is that the liquor cabinet back there?' He pointed toward a huge rococo piece of bowfront furniture with engraved windows, partially concealed by a sheet.

'That's right; and it still has *all* the original decanters, with solid-silver labels. Gin, whiskey, brandy. Not that Boofuls ever *drank*, of course, at his age.'

She thought this was quite amusing and let out a high, whinnying snort.

Martin approached the furniture with a mixture of dread and fascination. He ran his hand along the back of the sofa, and thought, *Boofuls actually sat here*. The experience was more disturbing than he had expected. News clippings and photographs were one thing – but they were flat and two-dimensional. Boofuls had never actually touched them. But here was his furniture. Here were his chairs. Here was the mirror that must have hung over his fireplace. Real, touchable objects. To Martin, they were as potent as Hitler's shirts, or Judy Garland's ruby slippers, or Jackie Kennedy's pink pillbox hats. They were proof that a legend had once been real; that Boofuls had actually lived.

He said nothing for a long time, his hands on his hips, breathing the musty sawdust atmosphere of Mrs Harper's cellar.

'You said that nobody was interested in buying them,' he remarked to Mrs Harper at last.

'I didn't say that nobody was interested in *buying* them,' Mrs Harper retaliated. 'I simply said that nobody seemed interested in selling them for me. It's the profit margin, I suppose.'

Martin nodded and looked around him. It was the two chairs he coveted the most – those and the mirror. The mirror would look absolutely stunning on his sitting room wall, instead of all those cuttings and photographs and letters – and it would have a far greater emotional effect. Instead of saying, 'Oh, yes, here's my collection of publicity pictures of Boofuls,' he would be able to announce, 'And this – this is the actual mirror which was hanging in Boofuls' sitting room when he was murdered.'

Shock! Shudder! Envy!

'Erm . . . how much do you want for this stuff?' Martin asked Mrs Harper casually. 'Chairs, mirror, sofa, liquor cabinet, stools. Supposing I took them all off your hands?'

'Well . . . I wouldn't mind that at all,' said Mrs Harper. She rubbed the back of the gilded sofa and sucked in her false teeth, and her eyelashes fluttered like chloroformed moths.

'How much?' asked Martin, thinking of the $578 sitting in his savings account at Security Pacific. Surely she wouldn't ask more than five hundred bucks for a few worn-out pieces of 1930s furniture. She might even pay him to cart them away.

Mrs Harper thought for a moment, her hand pressed to her forehead. 'I don't know,' she said. 'I've had so many different valuations. Some very high, some very low. But you're a real Boofuls fan, aren't you? A genuine devotee. And, you know, it seems kind of *mean* to make you pay an extortionate price – especially since you're trying to keep his memory alive.'

Martin shrugged, and shuffled his feet. 'That's really generous of you. But I wouldn't like you to take a loss.'

'Don't you worry about that. As far as I'm concerned, the most important thing is for Boofuls' belongings to have a loving home.'

Martin looked up at the mirror. Now that his eyes were becoming more accustomed to the shadows, he could distinguish the details of the gilded frame. It was quite a large mirror – six feet wide and nearly five feet high – which had obviously hung over a fireplace. The sides of the frame were carved as luxuriant tangles of grapevines. At the top, there was a grinning gilded face which looked like Bacchus or Pan. The glass itself was discolored and measled at one corner, but most of it reflected back Martin's face with a clarity that was almost hallucinatory, as if he were actually looking at himself in the flesh, instead of a reflection. No wonder he had been so alarmed to see Mrs Harper floating in the air.

He reached out to touch the mirror and felt the chilly glass of its surface, untouched by sunlight for nearly twenty years. How does a mirror feel when it has nothing to reflect – nobody to smile at it, nobody to preen their hair in it, no rooms for it to look at, no evanescent pictures for it to paint of passing lives? *'Mirrors are lonely,'* Tennyson once wrote.

'Seven thousand,' said Mrs Harper. 'How about that?'

'I beg your pardon?' asked Martin, caught off balance.

'Seven thousand for everything,' Mrs Harper repeated. 'It's the lowest I can go.'

Martin rubbed the back of his neck. Seven thousand was out of the question. Even his car wasn't worth seven thousand. 'I'm sorry,' he said. 'That's more than I can afford. I'm not Aaron Spelling, I'm afraid.'

'I couldn't go any lower,' said Mrs Harper. 'It would be worth a whole lot more, even if it *hadn't* belonged to Boofuls.'

'Well, that's that, I guess,' said Martin in resignation. 'Thank you for letting me look at it, anyway. At least it gives me some idea of how Boofuls' room was furnished. That could be quite a help with my screenplay.'

'How much *can* you afford?' asked Mrs Harper.

Martin smiled and shook his head. 'Nothing like seven thousand. Nothing like *one* thousand. Five hundred, and that's tops.'

Mrs Harper looked around. 'I guess I could let you have the barstools for five hundred.'

'You'd be willing to sell pieces separately?'

'Well, I wasn't planning to. But since you're such a devotee.'

'Do you think you could sell me the mirror for five hundred? I really covet the mirror.'

Mrs Harper puckered her lips. 'I'm not at all sure about

that. That's very special, that mirror. French, originally – that's what Arnold's father told me.'

'It's very handsome,' Martin agreed. 'I can just imagine it in my apartment.'

'Maybe seven-fifty?' Mrs Harper suggested. 'Could you go to seven-fifty?'

Martin took a deep breath. 'I could pay you five hundred now and the rest of it next month.' That wouldn't leave him very much for living on, he thought to himself, but if he finished his *A-Team* rewrite tonight and maybe asked Morris to find him a couple of extra scripts to work on – anything, even *Stir Crazy* or *Silver Spoons*.

Mrs Harper stood in silence for a long while, and then she said, 'Very well. Five hundred now and two-fifty by the end of next month. But you make sure you pay. I don't want any trouble. I've got lawyers, you know.'

Martin found an old wooden fruit box and dragged it across the cellar floor so that he could stand on it to reach the mirror. The late Arnold Harper had hung it up on two large brass hooks, screwed firmly into the joists of the sitting room floor above them. Martin lifted the mirror gently down, making sure that he didn't knock the gilded frame on the floor. It was desperately heavy, and he was sweating by the time he had managed to ease it down onto the floor. Mrs Harper watched him, making no attempt to assist him, smiling benignly.

'It's a wonderful thing, isn't it?' she said, peering into it and teasing her bouffant hair. 'They sure don't make mirrors like this one anymore.'

Martin found that he didn't have the strength to lift the mirror and carry it up the stairs, so he bundled a dustcover underneath one corner of it and dragged it across the floor. Then, panting, step by step, he pulled it up the wooden stair-case until he reached the hallway. It took him almost five minutes to maneuver it through the cellar door into the kitchen. Mrs Harper stood halfway up the stairs watching, still offering no help. Martin almost wished that he hadn't bought the goddamn thing. His arms were trembling from the weight of it. His cheek was smeared with grime and he was out of breath.

'You can bring your car up to the side of the house if you want to,' said Mrs Harper – and that was the only contribution she made. Martin nodded, leaning against one of the kitchen cupboards.

'You'll take a personal check?' he asked her.

'Oh, sure. Just so long as you're good for it. It's all money isn't it? That's what Arnold used to say.'

After another ten minutes, Martin managed to drag the mirror out of the kitchen door and tilt it into the back seat of his Mustang. Mrs Harper allowed him to borrow the dustcover to protect it, provided he promised that he would bring it straight back. 'I promise,' he told her. 'I'll bring it straight back.'

He drove off slowly down Hillside, and Mrs Harper stood on her steps and waved his check. Glancing at her in his rearview mirror, he thought that for somebody who had just let him have a valuable antique at a knock-down price, she looked a little too pleased with herself. She had probably asked him for double what the mirror was actually worth.

Still, he was now the owner of the actual mirror that had graced Boofuls' fireplace, and maybe that would bring him luck. He hummed 'Flowers From Tuscaloosa' as he slowly drove his huge angular purchase back to Franklin Avenue.

Mr Capelli was home early, and he helped Martin to carry the mirror upstairs. Mr Capelli was small and rotund, with a bald head and spectacles that looked as if they had been ground out of two glass bottle-stoppers. 'I shouldn't even lift a basket of groceries,' he grumbled. 'My doctor's going to kill me alive.'

'Mr Capelli, you don't know how much I appreciate this,' Martin told him. 'This mirror used to belong to Boofuls. True. It used to hang over his fireplace, in his sitting room in Bel Air.'

Mr Capelli examined the mirror with his mouth turned down at the corners. 'This used to belong to Boofuls? This actual mirror?'

'This actual mirror. In fact, when his grandmother chopped him up, this actual mirror was probably reflecting the whole scene.'

Mr Capelli shuddered. 'That's bad, you shouldn't keep something like this.'

'It's a mirror, Mr Capelli, that's all.'

'Well, that's what you say. But in Sicily, you know what my grandmother always used to do? Whenever somebody died, she went around and smashed every mirror in the house, and this was because every time a person looks in a mirror, the mirror takes a little tiny teentsy bit of their soul. So the only way that their whole soul can go to heaven when they die is for somebody to smash all of their mirrors, and let out that little bit that the mirror took away from them when they were alive.'

Martin shoved his hands into the back pockets of his jeans and smiled. 'What's the famous Italian sausage?' he asked.

'Mortadella,' said Mr Capelli.

'No, no, the other one. The big, smooth one.'

'Baloney.'

'That's it!' said Martin. 'And I couldn't agree with you more.'

'Hey! You don't talk to me that way,' snapped Mr Capelli. 'You want me to make you take this mirror back out again?'

'All right, I'm sorry,' said Martin, and laid his hand on Mr Capelli's shoulder. 'It's really going to look great. It's going to make this apartment look twice the size.'

'Hmh,' Mr Capelli retorted. 'Maybe I should charge you twice the rent.'

Just then, Mr Capelli's young grandson, Emilio, came out of Mr Capelli's apartment to see what all the noise was about. He was five years old, with straight black hair and olive skin and huge eyes like a sentimental painting of a sad puppy. As soon as he saw they were carrying a mirror, he made faces at himself in it.

'That's a great improvement,' said Martin as Emilio crossed his eyes and squashed his nose flat with his finger.

'Hey, that's my grandson you're talking about,' Mr Capelli protested. 'He's a good-looking boy.'

'That's because he doesn't take after his grandfather,' Martin said, grinning.

'Treble the rent!' retorted Mr Capelli.

'Watch yourself, Emilio,' Martin warned. 'This mirror's real heavy. You don't want to get squished.'

'I do too want to get squished,' Emilio told him cheekily.

'That can be arranged,' said Martin under his breath.

When Mr Capelli had gone, Martin carefully took down all his Boofuls photographs and cuttings. Then he dragged the mirror noisily up against the wall beside his desk. There were four brass plates at the side of the mirror, two on each side, which had obviously been used to screw the mirror firmly into the chimney breast over Boofuls' fireplace. Martin rooted around in his desk drawer until he found four two-inch screws and half a dozen wall plugs. Jane had taken his electric drill, but the wall was quite soft, and he was able to gouge out four holes in the plaster with his screwdriver.

It took him nearly an hour to fix up the mirror. But when it was screwed firmly into place, he stood back and admired it and didn't regret for one moment that he had spent all of his savings on it, even if Mrs Harper had probably screwed him for two or three hundred dollars more than it was actually worth. With its gilded frame and its brilliant glass, it gave his apartment a whole new dimension, adding light and space and airiness.

He poured himself a glass of wine. Then he sat down at his desk. Portrait of a successful young screenwriter feeding a sheet of paper into his typewriter. Portrait of a successful young screenwriter knocking next season's *A-Team* into shape.

He worked all afternoon. The sun began to steal away, sliding out of the room inch by inch, lighting the building next door, then shining on nothing but the tallest yuccas in the street outside.

BA: I swear – if this fruitcake don't stop – I'm going to take him apart.
Hannibal: Come on now, BA, we're talking comradeship here. Shoulder to shoulder.

It was well past seven when Martin switched off his typewriter and sat back in his chair. He knew that he was going to have to rewrite the scene in which Hannibal disguises himself as a monk, but apart from that he was just about finished. He was particularly pleased with the moment when Murdock starts juggling pool balls and B.A. joins in the juggling act in spite of himself. He jotted on his notepad, '*Can Mr. T juggle? If not, can he be taught? Are there any brilliant black jugglers? There must be! But what if there aren't? Can some white juggler black his hands up and stand right behind him while he dummies it?*'

He poured himself another glass of wine. Maybe his luck was going to change, after all. Maybe some of Boofuls' success would radiate out of his mirror and bless Martin's work. Martin raised his glass to himself and said, '*Prost!*'

It was then, in the mirror, that he saw a child's blue and white ball come bouncing through the open door behind him, and then roll to a stop in the middle of the varnished wood floor.

He stared at it in shock, with that same shrinking-scalp sensation that he had felt this afternoon when he had seen Mrs Harper floating in midair. 'Emilio?' he called. 'Is that you?'

There was no reply. Martin turned around and called, 'Emilio?' again.

He got up out of his chair, intending to pick the ball up, but he was only halfway standing when he realized that it wasn't there anymore.

He frowned, and walked across to the door, and opened it wider. The passageway was empty; the front door was locked. 'Emilio, what the hell are you playing at?'

He looked in the bedroom. Nobody. He even opened up the closet doors. Just dirty shirts and shorts, waiting to be washed, and a squash racket that needed restringing. He checked the bathroom, then the kitchen. Apart from himself, the apartment was deserted.

'Hallucination,' he told himself. 'Maybe I'm falling apart.'

He returned to the sitting room and picked up his glass of wine. He froze with the glass almost touching his lips. *In the mirror, the blue and white ball was still there, lying on the floor where it had first bounced.*

Martin stared at it and then quickly looked back into the

real sitting room. No ball. Yet there it was in the mirror, perfectly clear, as plain as milk.

Martin walked carefully across the room. Watching himself in the mirror, he reached down and tried to pick the ball up, but in the real room there was nothing there, and in the mirror room his hand appeared simply to pass right through the ball, as if it had no substance at all.

He scooped at it two or three times and waved his hand from side to side exactly where the ball should have been. Still nothing. But the really odd part about it was that as he watched his hand intently, it seemed as if it were not the ball that was insubstantial, but his own fingers – as if the ball were real and that reflection of himself in the mirror were a ghost.

He went right up close to the mirror and touched its surface. There was nothing unusual about it. It was simply cold glass. But the ball remained there, whether it was a hallucination or a trick of the light, or whatever. He sat in his chair and watched it and it refused to disappear.

After half an hour, he got up and went to the bathroom to shower. The ball was still there when he returned. He finished the wine, watching it all the time. He was going to have a hangover in the morning, but right now he didn't much care.

'What the hell *are* you?' he asked the ball.

He pressed his cheek against the left side of the mirror and tried to peer into his own reflected hallway, to see if it was somehow different. *Looking-Glass House*, he thought to himself, and all those unsettling childhood feelings came back to him. If you could walk through the door in the mirror, would the hallway be the same? Was there another different world in there, not just back to front but disturbingly different?

In his bookshelf, he had a dog-eared copy of *Alice Through the Looking-Glass* which Jane had bought him when they were first dating. He took it out and opened it up and quickly located the half-remembered words.

Alice was looking into the mirror over her sitting room fireplace, wondering about the room she could see on the other side of the glass.

It's just the same as our drawing-room, only the things go the other way. I can see all of it when I get upon a chair – all but the

bit just behind the fire-place. Oh! I do so wish I could see that bit!
I want so much to know whether they've a fire in the winter:
you never can tell, you know, unless our fire smokes, and then
smoke comes up in that room, too – but that may only be pretence,
just to make it look as if they had a fire. Well then, the books are
something like our books, only the words go the wrong way: I
know that, because I've held up one of our books to the glass, and
then they hold one up in the other room. But now we come to the
passage. You can see just a little peep of the passage in Looking-
Glass House, if you leave the door of our drawing-room wide
open: and it's very like our passage as far as you can see, only you
know it may be quite different on beyond.

Martin closed the book. The ball was still there. He stood
looking at it for a long time, not moving. Then he went across
to his desk and switched off the light, so that the sitting room
was completely dark. He paused, and then he switched it back
on again. The ball in the mirror hadn't moved.

'Shit,' he said; and for the very first time in his life he felt
that something was happening to him which he couldn't
control.

He could have gotten Jane back if he had really wanted
to – at least, he believed that he could. He could have been
wealthier if he had written all the dumb teleplays that Morris
had wanted him to write. But he had been able to make his
own decisions about things like that. This ball was something
else altogether. A ball that existed only as a reflection in a
mirror, and not in reality?

'Shit,' he repeated, and switched off the light again and
shuffled off to the bedroom. He dropped his red flannel bathrobe and climbed naked onto his futon. He was about to switch
off his bedside light when a thought occurred to him. He
padded back to the sitting room and closed the door. If there
was anything funny about that mirror, he didn't want it coming
out and jumping on him in the middle of the night.

Irrational, yes, but he was tired and a little drunk and it was
well past midnight.

He dragged the covers well up to his neck, even though he
was too hot, and closed his eyes, and tried to sleep.

*

23

He was awakened by what sounded like a child laughing. He lifted his head from the pillow and thought, *Goddamned Emilio, why do kids always have to wake up at the crack of dawn?* But then he heard the laughter again, and it didn't sound as if it were coming from downstairs at all. It sounded as if it were coming from his own sitting room.

He sat up straight, holding his breath, listening. There it was again. A small boy, laughing out loud; but with a curious echo to his voice, as if he were laughing in a large empty room. Martin checked his clock radio. It wasn't the crack of dawn at all: it was only 3:17 in the morning.

He switched on his light, wincing at the brightness of it. He found his bathrobe and tugged it on, inside out, so that he had to hold it together instead of tying it. Then he went to the sitting room door and listened.

He listened for almost a minute. Then he asked himself: *What are you afraid of, wimp? It's your own apartment, your own sitting room, and all you can hear is a child.*

He licked his lips, and then he opened the sitting room door. Immediately, he reached out for the light switch and turned on the main light. Immediately, he looked toward the mirror.

There was nobody there, no boy laughing. Only himself, frowsy and pale, in his inside-out bathrobe. Only the desk and the typewriter and the bookshelf and the pictures of Boofuls.

He approached the mirror slowly. One thing was different. One thing that he could never *prove* was different, not even to himself. The blue and white ball had gone.

He looked toward the reflected door, half open, and the peep of the passageway outside. *It's very like our own passage as far as you can see, only you know it may be quite different on beyond.*

How different? thought Martin with a dry mouth. How different? Because if a ball had come bouncing into the reflected room, there must have been *somebody there to throw it;* and if it had disappeared, then somebody must have walked into that reflected room when he was asleep and picked it up.

'Oh God.' He swallowed. 'Oh, God, don't let it be Boofuls.'

CHAPTER TWO

Henry Polowski, the gatekeeper at Metro-Goldwyn-Mayer, swore that when Boofuls was driven out of the studio that night in August 1939, he pressed his face to the rear window of his limousine and just for one terrible second he looked like a skull. Bone-white, with hollow eye sockets and naked teeth. Henry had shouted out loud.

'You can laugh all you want, but it was a genuine premonition,' Henry told the reporters who had been crowded all night around the Hollywood police headquarters. 'I saw it, and if you don't believe it, then that's your problem, not mine.'

'Didn't you tell anybody what you saw?' Henry was asked by Lydia Haskins of the *Los Angeles Times*. 'If you really saw it, and you really believed it to be a genuine premonition, why didn't you make any attempt to warn somebody?'

'What would *you* have done?' Henry retaliated. 'My partner heard me shout and asked me what was wrong, and I said Boofuls just went by and – I don't know – he was looking funny. So my partner said, what kind of funny? Making faces, that kind of funny? I said no, but I was sure something bad was going to happen to that boy.'

'And that was the only attempt you made to tell anybody what you thought you saw?' Lydia Haskins persisted.

'Lady,' said Henry, 'I didn't *think* I saw it. I saw it.'

'How does that make you feel now?' called out Jim Keller, from the *Hollywood Reporter*. 'Does that make you feel guilty in any way, now that Boofuls is dead?'

'How would *you* feel?' Henry retorted. 'I saw that little boy looking like a skull at 5:27 that evening, and by 6:30 he was hacked into pieces. I loved that little boy. We all did. How the hell would *you* feel?'

Jim Keller shrugged. 'Pretty damn bad, I guess.'

'Well,' said Henry, 'that's the way I feel. Pretty damn bad.'

Martin pressed his remote control, and the video-recorded newsreel shrank from his television screen. He had watched that recording over and over during his research for *Boofuls!* For some perverse reason, he had always wanted to believe that Henry Polowski was telling the truth – even though the gatekeeper had been fired two weeks later after the *Hollywood Reporter* revealed that he was an alcoholic and had twice been hospitalized for D Ts.

Martin had the discolored press cutting lying on his desk. ' "I Saw Skull" Gatekeeper Saw Giant Roaches, Martians.' Martin had some sympathy for him. Anybody would, if they had seen in their sitting room mirror the reflection of a blue and white ball for which there was no corresponding blue and white ball in the material world.

But the ball had vanished, just as Boofuls had vanished. Not just the boy, but his glory, too. Martin thought it was remarkable that so few people could recall the hysterical adulation that used to be showered on the small golden-haired boy called Boofuls. His limousine was often mobbed to a standstill in the middle of the street. Women were caught almost every night trying to break into his mansion in Bel Air to kidnap him. 'He *needs* me,' they used to plead as they were dragged away across the lawns. 'He needs a mother!'

It was true, of course, that Boofuls was an orphan. He had been born Walter Lemuel Crossley in Boise, Idaho, in March 1931, the illegitimate son of Mary Louise Crossley, a nineteen-year-old stenog at Ressequie State Insurance on Fort Street, Boise.

Mary Crossley brought Boofuls up alone for two years, apparently relying on welfare and home typing and occasional *ex gratia* payments from Boofuls' unknown father.

The day before Boofuls' second birthday, however, Mary Crossley took an overdose of aspirin after an argument with one of her boyfriends (not, apparently, Boofuls' father). As far as Martin had been able to make out, it seemed unlikely that she seriously intended to kill herself. She had taken overdoses before. But this time she developed pneumonia after being stomach-pumped, and died four days later. Boofuls was taken

26

into state care for six months, then fostered for a further three months, and eventually sent to live with his recently widowed grandmother, Mrs Alicia Crossley, ninety miles away in Twin Falls.

In February 1935 – for reasons that Martin had never been able to discover – Mrs Alicia Crossley took Boofuls to Los Angeles, California. They lived for a while at the Palms Boarding House in Venice. Mrs Crossley appears to have supported them both by taking a waitressing job and then housecleaning. But in May of the following year – again for no clear reason – Boofuls was taken by his grandmother to audition for Jacob Levitz' new musical, *Whistlin' Dixie*. Almost miraculously, he was selected out of more than six hundred juvenile hopefuls for the part of Tiny Joe. He had no drama experience, he couldn't tap, his voice was untrained. His only assets were his golden curls and his heart-shaped face and his sweet, endearing lisp.

Jacob Levitz, however, was thrilled with his discovery. He called him 'the Boy Shirley Temple'. His only stipulation was that the boy would have to change his name. 'Walter Lemuel Crossley' didn't sound like a five-year-old child movie star; it sounded more like a middle-aged insurance agent from Boise.

Metro held a 'Name the Child Star' contest in the newspapers, and the short list of names was sent to Louis B Mayer. Mr Mayer read them, hated them all, and scribbled in the margin, 'B. Awful'. This half-illegible comment was taken by a wholly illiterate secretary to be Mr Mayer's own suggestion for little Walter's new name, and she typed it and sent it to the publicity office. At least, that was the way that Mr Mayer told the story, and Boofuls himself never contradicted him.

Whistlin' Dixie, of course, became one of the most successful musicals of all time. Booful's show-stopping song 'Heartstrings' sold more copies that year than 'All My Eggs in One Basket'; and when he accepted his Oscar in 1937 for *Captains Courageous*, Spencer Tracy joked that he had only beaten Boofuls for the award 'because they thought it was too heavy for him, and he might drop it'.

Boofuls never won an Oscar, although one hit musical

followed another – *Dancing on the Clouds, Suwanee Song, Sunshine Serenade*, and *Flowers From Tuscaloosa*. Boofuls appeared on the cover of every major magazine, golden-haired, shining-eyed, from *Screenland* to *McCall's*. It was reported in *Variety* in the spring of 1938 that he was a millionaire six times over. Just before Christmas, 1938, he and his grandmother moved into a huge white mock-Gothic house on Stone Canyon Drive in Bel Air. They engaged sixteen servants, including a butler and a cook; two private tutors; a dance teacher; and a drama coach. They owned seven automobiles, including two white Lincoln limousines, one for each of them. They named the mansion 'Espejo'.

In June 1939, Boofuls was cast for the leading role of Billy Bright in Jacob Levitz' most ambitious musical to date – a nine-million-dollar production called *Sweet Chariot*. Billy Bright was supposed to be a dead-end kid accidentally shot dead while trying to prevent his father robbing a bank – to become (almost inevitably) a do-gooding angel.

On Friday, August 18, three days after the start of principal photography, Boofuls was driven home in his limousine from M-G-M at 5:27 P.M., according to the log kept by doorman Henry Polowski. He was seen by a group of fans turning into the east gate of Bel Air, and he waved to them and smiled.

His head gardener, Manuel Estovez, saw Boofuls come out onto the loggia at the back of the mansion at approximately 6:12 P.M. He was wearing a yellow short-sleeved shirt and white shorts and white ankle socks. He waved to Mr Estovez, and Mr Estovez waved back.

Shortly after 6:21 P.M., the Bel Air police received a garbled telephone call from the Crossley mansion, a woman's voice saying, 'He's dead now. I've got him at last. He's dead.' A police patrol arrived at the house just before 6:35 P.M. and gained entry to the house through the French windows which over-looked the swimming pool. It appeared that – unusually – all of the indoor servants had been given the day or the afternoon off.

Inside the white-carpeted sitting room, they found what was left of Boofuls – 'chopped into spareribs', as one officer put it. Another officer said that he had never seen so much blood in his life. A quick search of the twelve-bedroom house also revealed the body of Mrs Crossley, hanging by a noose from the wrought-iron chandelier in the main stairwell, half strangulated but still alive. She died twenty minutes later without saying anything at all.

The coroner's verdict three weeks later was that Mrs Alicia Crossley had murdered her grandson, Walter Lemuel Crossley, while suffering from temporary mental disorder and had then taken her own life. Boofuls was buried with unusual quietness at Forest Lawn. The horror of what had happened kept many people away – the thought that they were burying nothing more than a box of bits. A plain white Carrera marble headstone was erected, with the simple gold inscription 'BOOFULS, 1931–1939'. You can still see it now.

Over the years, nine books had been written about the Boofuls murder, probably the best of which was *Boofuls: The Truth*, by Kenneth Mellon. Martin had read them all; and to put it kindly, some of them were more sensational than others. All of them agreed, however, that Mrs Crossley's irrational attack on her celebrated young charge could probably be traced back to earlier bouts of depression that she had suffered when she was younger. She had lost a little boy of her own in 1911, and after she had given birth to Mary, Boofuls' mother, she had been warned by her doctor not to get pregnant again.

Three of the books suggested that Mrs Crossley was taking revenge on Boofuls for her daughter's suicide attempt and subsequent death. Punishing him, as it were, for living a life of wealth and fame when her dear dead daugher had died in poverty, and known none of it.

The author of *Hollywood Hack!* claimed that she had killed Boofuls to get her revenge on his unknown father, but there was no serious evidence to support this theory, and in any case nobody had ever been able to find out who his unknown father was. Some reporters had pointed their finger at Howard Q. Forbes, the vice-president of Ressequie State Insurance, but Howard Q. Forbes had been balding and bespectacled, with a cardiac history, and even if it was not impossible that he was Boofuls' father, it seemed at least unlikely.

There was an unconfirmed report that Mary Crossley had

been seen one night on Kootenal Street in Boise in the passenger seat of a large black Cadillac limousine, but the supposed witness had later admitted that he might have been 'overtired'.

Martin had collected scores of magazine articles, too – even the ridiculous 'true life' dramatizations from *Thrilling Detective* and *Sensational Police Stories*. 'The tiny body desperately twisted and turned beneath her as she hacked into his snow-white sailor suit with her blood-spattered cleaver.' Boofuls hadn't been wearing a sailor suit, of course; and oddly enough, the murder weapon had never been found.

In spite of Boofuls' gruesome and infamous death, however, Martin had always felt that the child had been possessed of some kind of special magic. Some incandescence that was almost unreal. His friend Gerry at the M-G-M library had videotaped all of Boofuls' musicals for him, and he watched them again and again. Every time he saw that curly-headed little boy dancing and singing, he found it harder to believe that a seven-year-old could have such brightness and energy and wit, such absolute perfection of timing.

Every time he looked at Boofuls' movements, listened to his breathing, watched his choreography – and in particular when he looked at his eyes – he felt as if he were watching a grown man masquerading in a child's body.

'He passed me by as close as this, and I wasn't mistook. I saw it clear like daylight. He was white, white like bone, and his eyes were empty, no eyeballs, just like a skull, and naked teeth.'

Martin had played the fifty-year-old newsreel over and over. The same blurting sound track, the same flickering of flashbulbs, the same evasive ducking of the head, as if Henry Polowski had been damned by his inattention to play the same scene over and over and over again.

'And what did you do, Mr Polowski?'

'What would *you* do? You wouldn't believe your eyes. You can laugh all you want, but it was a genuine premonition. I saw it, and if you don't believe it, then that's your problem, not mine.'

Martin switched off the video recorder with his remote control. It was almost ten o'clock; and in twenty minutes he had an appointment with June Lassiter at 20th Century-Fox. He knew June well enough to wave at her across the crowded bar of the Cock 'n' Bull, and to be assured of a wave back; but he didn't know how sympathetic she was going to be to the idea of a big-budget musical. Especially a big-budget musical about Boofuls.

Still, he thought, gathering up his screenplay and sliding it carefully into his Reel Thing tote bag, nobody ever got anywhere in Hollywood by sitting at home and wishing.

He took one last look at the mirror before he left. It reflected nothing but the sitting room and himself and the morning sunlight. He was beginning to think that he must have hallucinated that ball. Maybe he would go talk to his friend Marion Gidley about it. She was into self-hypnosis and self-induced hallucinations and all that kind of stuff.

As he closed the door of his apartment behind him, he came across Emilio playing on the landing with a Transformer robot. 'How're you doing, Emilio?' he asked him.

Emilio looked up with big Hershey-colored eyes. 'Hi, Martin. Doing good.'

'What's that you've got there?'

'Datson 280 sports car, turns into an evil robot, look.'

With a complicated fury of clicking and elbow twisting, Emilio turned the sports car into a robot with a pin head and spindly legs. Martin hunkered down and inspected it. 'Pretty radical, hunh? I wish my car would turn into a robot.'

'Your car's junk.'

'Who said that?'

'My grandpa, he said your car's junk, and he wishes you wouldn't park it right outside the house, people are gonna think it belongs to him.'

'My car's better than that hearse that *he* drives.'

'My grandpa's car turns into a robot.'

'Oh, yeah?'

'It does, too, turn into a robot. He told me.'

Martin affectionately scruffed Emilio's hair, which Emilio hated, and got up to leave. He was halfway down the next flight of stairs, however, when he thought of something. 'You don't happen to own a ball, do you?' he asked Emilio through the banister rails.

'Grandpa gave me a baseball.'

'No, no – I mean one of those bouncing plastic balls, blue and white.'

Emilio wrinkled up his nose and shook his head, as if the idea that he would own a bouncing blue and white ball was utterly contemptible. 'No way, José.'

Martin reached through the banister and tried to scruff his hair again, but Emilio ducked away. 'Don't keep *doing* that!' he protested. 'What do you think I am, some kind of gerbil?'

Martin laughed, and went off to keep his appointment at Fox.

June Lassiter was very calm and together and California-friendly; a woman's woman with frizzed-up black hair and pale, immaculate, hypo-allergenic makeup that had been created without causing any pain to animals. She wore a flowing white suit and a scarf around her neck that had been hand-printed on raw silk by Hopi Indians. She took Martin to the Fox commissary and bought him a huge spinach salad and a carafe of domestic Chablis that was almost too cold to drink.

'You're raising ghosts, that's the trouble,' she drawled. Martin had a large mouthful of spinach, and all he could do was look at her thin wrist lying on the table with its faded tan and its huge loose gold bangle, and munch, and nod.

June said, 'Boofuls is one of those code words in Hollywood that immediately make people's brains go blank; you know, like Charles Manson.'

'People have tackled difficult Hollywood topics before. Look at *Mommie Dearest*.'

'Oh, sure,' June agreed. 'But in *Mommie Dearest*, Joan Crawford eventually redeemed herself, and all the terrible things that she was supposed to have done to her children were rationalized and forgiven. She was a drunken carping bitch but she was a star, and in Hollywood that excuses everything. How can you do that with Boofuls? The boy was chopped up by his crazed grandmother and that was the end of the story. No redemption, no explanation, just an abrupt and brutal ending – even if you *don't* depict it on the screen.'

Martin wiped his mouth with his napkin. 'So what's the verdict?'

'Well, Martin, I haven't read your screenplay yet and it may be brilliant. I mean I've heard Morris talking about you and he's *very* complimentary about your work. But I have to tell you that Boofuls is the kiss of death. The only person who might conceivably touch it is Ken Russell; and you know what kind of a reputation *he's* got; *enfant terrible*, even at his age. Even if he'd agree to do it, you'd still have the devil's own job raising the money for it.'

Martin sat back. 'I don't know. It seems like such a natural. The music, the dancing, and if you could find the right kid to play Boofuls . . .'

June shook her head. 'My advice to you is to file it and forget it. Maybe one day you'll be wealthy enough and influential enough to develop it yourself.'

They spent the rest of their lunch talking gossip: who was making which picture, and who was making whom. When they were leaving, June stood in the empty parking space marked G. Wilder and said, 'Get your name painted here first, Martin. Then make your musical.'

Martin gave her what he hoped was a laconic wave and walked back to his car, with his screenplay under his arm. As he went, he whistled 'Heartstrings'.

> *You play . . . such sweet music*
> *How can . . . I resist*
> *Every song . . . from your heartstrings*
> *Makes me feel I've . . . just been kissed*

But he drove back along Santa Monica Boulevard with the wind whirring in the pages of the screenplay as it lay on the seat beside him, and he felt like tossing it out of the car. He was beginning to believe that Morris was right, that he was carrying this screenplay around like a sackful of stinking meat.

Hollywood's golden boy of the 1930s had died more than one kind of death.

*

33

He returned to his apartment shortly before three o'clock. Emilio was playing in the sunshine on the front steps. Emilio had obviously finished his lunch, because his T-shirt was stained with catsup. The steps were proving an almost insurmountable obstacle to a deadpan plastic Rambo; and the afternoon was thick with the sound of machine-gun fire.

'Full-scale war, hey?' asked Martin. Emilio didn't look up. Martin sat down on the steps and watched him for a while. 'It beats me, you know, how *Rambo* can gross seventy-five million dollars, with all its shooting and killing and phony philosophy . . . and here, *here*' – slapping his screenplay in the palm of his hand – 'is the most entertaining and enchanting musical ever made, and everybody sniffs at me as if I've trodden in something.'

Emilio continued his war; this time with heavy shelling, which involved extra saliva.

'You should come up and watch some of my Boofuls movies,' Martin told him. 'Then you'd believe, you little Philistine.'

Emilio shaded his eyes with his grubby hand and looked at him. 'Who's Boofuls? Is he a cartoon?'

'Is he a cartoon? My God, doesn't that grandfather of yours teach you anything? Boofuls was a boy, just like you, except that he could sing and dance and make people happy. In other words he didn't sit in the dirt all day with some grotesque reproduction of Sylvester Stallone, pretending to zap Asiatics. Who's Boofuls, for God's sake.'

Emilio picked up a green plastic helicopter and waved it around for a while. 'That boy in your room can dance,' he remarked.

'Well, that's Boofuls,' said Martin. 'The boy in the poster, just above my bed.'

'No,' Emilio contradicted, shaking his head. 'The boy in your other room. The real boy.'

Martin frowned; and then reached out and took hold of Emilio's wrist, so that the helicopter was stopped in midattack. 'What real boy? What are you talking about?'

Emilio pouted and wouldn't answer.

'You went into my room?' Martin asked him. 'Today, when I was out, you went into my room?'

Emilio refused to do anything but pout.

'Listen, Emilio, if you went into my room I won't be mad at you. Come on, it's your grandfather's house, you can go where you want.'

Emilio slowly and sulkily twisted his wrist away.

Martin glanced up toward his sitting room window. It was blank, as usual, with the sky reflecting off the glass.

'You won't talk?' he said to Emilio. 'In that case, I'd better go see for myself.'

He got up from the steps and bounded quickly upstairs, three steps at a time, until he reached the landing just outside his front door. There was a small plastic name tag on it saying *M. Williams*. Underneath, *J. Berrywell* had been scratched out. Even when they were living together, Jane had insisted on keeping her maiden name.

He hesitated. *A real boy.* For some irrational reason, he felt a prickle of genuine alarm. There were no boys in his apartment, of course, real or unreal. Emilio had simply invented an imaginary playmate. He was just the age for it, after all, and he had no friends of his own age, not on this block. But all the same, Martin found the idea of it unexpectedly unsettling, as if his apartment had been intruded upon by something he didn't understand.

He opened the front door. He hardly ever locked it, because there was nothing worth stealing, except for his typewriter, and he had been hoping for years that somebody would take that, so that he could buy a new one with the insurance money.

The apartment was silent. The midafternoon sunlight fell across the wood-block floor in a dazzling diagonal. From the bedroom, the pale face of Boofuls watched him as he trod softly along the corridor to the sitting room door.

He paused. He called, 'Hello?' But there was no reply.

What did you expect? he asked himself. *A whole chorus of Walt Disney ghosts to come charging out of the closets chorusing 'Fooled you, Martin!'?*

He eased the sitting room door wide open. Then he peered

around it. In the mirror, his own face peered back. There was nobody else in the room. No boy; not even a *sign* of a boy, like an abandoned blue and white ball.

'Kids,' he said under his breath, meaning Emilio in particular.

It took him only a couple of moments to look around the rest of the apartment. There were no boys hiding in the closets among his clothes; there were no boys crouching under the bed. But as he went through to the kitchen to find himself a fresh bottle of wine, he was sure for an instant he could hear somebody giggling.

He hesitated and listened, but there was nothing. He stepped out of the kitchen into the hallway, holding the bottle of wine in his hand, and there was Emilio with his hands in the pockets of his shorts. Martin looked at him without saying anything.

'Can I play with him?' asked Emilio.

'Can you play with whom, Emilio?' Martin replied, deliberately pedantic.

Emilio swung one shoulder toward the sitting room. 'The boy, of course.'

Martin said, 'Emilio, my little lunatic, there is no boy.'

'There is, too, a boy.'

'Well, that's right, and your grandfather's car turns into a robot.'

'I've seen it! He showed me!'

'All right,' cooed Martin. 'All right, don't lose your cool. Let's just say that I'm one of these real skeptical adults you see on children's television – you know the kind of adult I mean. The kind of adult who can't understand what the hell Flipper is trying to say to him, and takes a swipe at Lassie when she's trying to drag him off to the abandoned mine by the trouser leg.'

Emilio didn't understand a word of what Martin was saying; but it made Martin feel better, and it stopped Emilio's fretting.

'If there really is a boy,' said Martin gently, 'all you have to do is introduce him to me. Let me shake the boy by the hand, and say good afternoon, boy. Then I'll believe you.'

36

'You can't shake his hand,' Emilio retorted.

'I know I can't, Emilio, because he's imaginary.' He tapped Emilio's forehead with his fingertip quite hard. 'He exists only in there.'

'No,' Emilio protested. 'He's real. But you can't shake his hand because he's in the mirror.'

Martin straightened himself up. Emilio was looking up at him, his grubby little face serious, his eyes wide, his fists clenched.

'Emilio,' he said, 'has it occurred to that one-byte brain of yours that the real boy in the mirror might be you? A reflection of you? Or was your face so filthy that you didn't recognize yourself? Maybe you thought it was Paul Robeson.'

Emilio was getting cross again. 'He's real! He's real! But he's only in the mirror! I'm in the mirror, and he's in the mirror. But I'm in the room, and he's not in the room!'

Martin thought of the blue and white ball, and how it had come bouncing into the mirror. He thought of how he had gone back to look at it again and found that it had vanished. *It's very like our passage as far as you can see, only you know it may be quite different on beyond.*

A slow cold feeling crawled down his back, like a snail making its way down a frozen drainpipe.

'This boy ... did he look anything like you?' he asked Emilio.

Emilio wiped his hand over his face as if he were attempting to erase his own features and come up with some other face: placid, blank, with eyes like Little Orphan Annie.

'He looked like ...' and he tried to explain, but he couldn't, even with mime. 'He looked like ...' and then he suddenly rushed through to the bedroom and pointed to the poster of Boofuls pinned to the wall.

'He looked like that?' Martin asked him, with a deeper feeling of dread.

'He's a real boy,' Emilio repeated. 'He's a *real* boy!'

Martin laid his hands on Emilio's shoulders and looked him straight in the eye. 'Emilio, he *was* a real boy, but he's been dead for nearly fifty years.'

Emilio frowned.

'I don't know what you saw in that mirror,' Martin told him, 'but it wasn't a real boy. It was just your imagination. Do you understand what I mean? It was just like ... I don't know, your mind was playing a trick on you.'

'I saw him,' Emilio whispered. 'I *talked* to him.'

Martin couldn't think what else to say. He stood up and rubbed his hands on the legs of his pants, the way pitchers do. 'I don't know, Emilio, man. It sounds pretty screwy to me.'

At that moment there was a cautious knock at the apartment door, and Emilio's grandmother came in. She was carrying a glass oven dish with a checkered cloth draped over the top of it.

Martin had always liked Mrs Capelli. She was the grandmother that everybody should have had: cheerful, philosophical, always baking. She had white hair braided into elaborate plaits and a face as plain and honest as a breadboard. She wore black; she always wore black. She was mourning for her dead sister. Before that, she had been mourning for her dead brother. When she and Mr Capelli went out shopping in their long black Lincoln together, they looked as if they were going to a funeral.

'I brought you lasagne,' she said.

Martin accepted the dish with a nod of his head. 'I'm trying to diet. But thanks.'

'Well, you can share it with the boy.' Mrs Capelli glanced around the apartment as if she expected to see someone else.

'The boy?' asked Martin.

'Emilio told me you had a boy staying here. He was playing with him all morning. He's your nephew you spoke to me about?'

Martin exchanged an uncomfortable look with Emilio. If he said that there was no boy, then Emilio would get a hard time for lying. On the other hand —

But, no. He needed Emilio's confidence right now. If there *was* something odd in the mirror, if there *was* some kind of manifestation, then so far young Emilio was the only person who had seen it. Emilio might be the only contact with it, like a medium. After all, he was a boy and Boofuls had been a boy.

38

Maybe there was some kind of left-over vibe in the mirror that Emilio was tuning in to. Or something.

He lifted up the cloth that covered the lasagne and inhaled the aroma of fresh tomatoes and thyme and fresh-grated Parmesan cheese. 'Petey will probably eat all of this on his own,' he remarked as casually as he could. 'Petey's a real pasta maven.'

He saw Emilio's eyes widen; as if the Hershey chocolate of his irises had melted into larger pools. But he winked at Emilio behind the upraised cloth, and he could see that Emilio understood.

'He's here now?' asked Mrs Capelli, beaming. 'I love boys! Always rough-and-tumble.'

'Well, he – er – he's running an errand for me – down at the supermarket.'

'You send a little boy all on his own to the supermarket? Ralph's, you mean?'

'Oh, no, no, just to Hughes, on the corner.'

'Still,' said Mrs Capelli disapprovingly. 'That's a bad road to cross, Highland Avenue.'

'Oh, he's okay, he walks to school in New York City, crosses Fifty-seventh Street every morning, hasn't been squished yet.'

Mrs Capelli's forehead furrowed. 'I thought you said he lived in Indianapolis.'

'Sure, yes, Indianapolis! But that was a couple of years ago. Now he lives in New York.'

Slowly, Mrs Capelli turned to leave, her eyes still restlessly looking around the apartment as if she expected 'Petey' to come popping out from behind a chair. Martin knew that she kept a constant watch on the landing from her chair in the parlor downstairs, and since she hadn't seen Petey go out, she was obviously suspicious that Martin was keeping him hidden. Maybe he had measles, this Petey, and Martin didn't want her to know, because Emilio may catch them.

'You do me a favor,' she said at last as she went out through the door. 'You bring your Petey down to see me when he gets back. I give him chocolate cake.'

'Sure thing, Mrs Capelli,' Martin told her, and opened the door for her. She eased herself down the stairs, one stair at a time, holding on to the banister. When she reached the door of her apartment, Martin gave her a little finger-wave, and said, 'Don't you worry, I'll bring him down. He'll feed your canary for you. If there's anything he likes better than pasta, it's chocolate cake.'

Mrs Capelli paused, and then nodded, and then disappeared into her apartment, leaving the door slightly ajar.

Martin came back to Emilio and stood in front of him with his arms folded.

'You believe me,' said Emilio. 'You believe there's a boy.'

'Did I say that?'

'But you said "Petey".'

'Emilio, there is no boy. I said that just to get you out of trouble. What do you think your grandmother would have said if I had totally denied it? She would have thought you were some kind of juvenile fruitcake. She would have had you locked up, or worse.'

Emilio looked bewildered. 'There *is* a boy,' he insisted. 'Come and see him.'

'All right,' said Martin, 'let's take a look at him; even if we can't shake him by the hand.'

Emilio ran into the sitting room and stood right in front of the mirror, impatient to prove that he was right. Martin followed him more slowly, checking the details of the real room against the reflected room. Two realities, side by side, but which one was real?

He checked everything carefully, but there were no obvious discrepancies. The screenplay of *Boofuls!* lay on his desk at corresponding angles in each room; one of his shoes lay tilted over, under the chair. The venetian blinds shivered in the sunlight.

Emilio pressed the palms of his hands against the glass. 'Boy!' he called loudly. 'Boy, are you there? Come out and play, boy! Come say hello to Martin!'

Martin, in spite of himself, found his attention fixed on the doorway in the mirror. It didn't move; not even a fraction; and no boy appeared.

'Boy!' Emilio demanded. 'Come out and play!'

They watched and waited. Nothing happened. No blue and white ball, no laughter, no boy. Martin was seriously beginning to believe that this was all a hallucination.

'Maybe he doesn't feel like playing anymore,' Martin suggested.

'He does, too!' Emilio protested. 'He said he *always* wants to play. The trouble is, they make him work, even when he's tired, and they always make him wear clothes he doesn't like, and he has to sing when he doesn't want to and dance when he doesn't want to.'

'Did he tell you what his name was?' asked Martin.

Emilio said nothing.

'Emilio, listen to me, this is important, did he tell you what his name was? He didn't call himself Boofuls, did he? Or Walter maybe? Or just Walt?'

Emilio shook his head.

'Well, what did he do? Did he play ball? Did he dance? Did he sing?'

Emilio stared at Martin but remained silent.

'Listen,' said Martin, turning back toward the mirror, 'maybe he doesn't want to play right now. Maybe it's – I don't know, bathtime or something. Even boys who live in mirrors have to take baths, right? Why don't you come back tomorrow and we'll try again?'

Emilio banged both hands on the mirror. 'Boy!' he shouted, his voice more high-pitched and panicky. 'Boy! Come out and play!'

Martin hunkered down beside him. 'I really don't think he wants to come out, Emilio. Come back tomorrow morning, okay, and we'll call him again.'

Emilio suddenly turned on him. His voice was a sharp little bark. 'You don't *want* me to see him, do you? You don't want me to play with him! You think he belongs to you! It's not your mirror! It's not your mirror! It's *his* mirror! He lives in it! And you can't tell him what to do, so there!'

Martin had never heard Emilio screaming like this before, and he was mildly shocked. He took hold of Emilio's shoulder and said, 'Listen . . . this may be a story that you've made up to impress me, and on the other hand it may not. But either way, I'm on your side. If there is a boy in that mirror, I want to find him.'

'And let him out?' asked Emilio.

Martin made a face. 'I don't know. Maybe there just isn't any way of *getting* him out.'

'There's a way,' Emilio told him quite firmly.

'Well, how do you know?'

'Because the boy told me, there's a way.'

'All right, as long as it doesn't involve breaking the mirror – I just paid seven hundred fifty dollars for that thing.'

'We won't break the mirror,' Emilio assured him with unsettling maturity.

Martin leaned back against the peach-painted landing wall and looked down at this self-confident little child with his chocolate-brown eyes and his tousled hair and the catsup stains on his T-shirt, and he didn't know whether to feel amused or frightened.

After all, the likelihood was that this was the biggest leg-pull ever. Either that, or Emilio was simply making it all up. After all, there were pictures of Boofuls all over Martin's apartment. If he was going to pretend that he had played with an imaginary boy there, what could be more natural than pretending he looked like him?

He closed the apartment door and walked back into his bedroom. The soulful eyes of little Boofuls stared at him from the *Whistlin' Dixie* poster. He reached up and touched with his fingertips the golden curls, the pale, heart-shaped face.

'You don't scare me, little boy,' he said out loud. 'You don't scare me at all.'

But he gave the poster a quick backward look as he left the room, and went back to work on the *A-Team*.

He awoke abruptly at three o'clock in the morning, his eyes wide, his ears singing with alertness. He hesitated for a moment, then he sat up in his futon so that he could hear better. He was quite sure that he could hear somebody crying, a child.

The sound was muffled by the rattling of the yuccas in the

street outside, and by the steady warbling of the wind through the crack at the side of his bedroom window. But it was a child, all right, a boy, keening and crying as if his heart were going to break.

Shivering with apprehension, and with the chill of the night, Martin reached across the floor and dragged his red flannel bathrobe toward him. He wrapped himself up in it and tied the belt tight, and then he climbed out of his futon and tiptoed across the bedroom and opened the door.

The sobbing kept on, high and despairing and strangely echoing. There was no doubt about where it was coming from, though. The sitting room door was half open, and the moonlight was shining hard and detailed on the wood-block floor, and that was where the crying was coming from.

The real boy, thought Martin. *Oh, Jesus, it's the real boy.*

But the real boy, whoever he was – *whatever* he was – would have to be confronted. *Come on, Martin, he's only a kid, right? And if he turns out to be Boofuls, then he's not only a kid but a ghost, too. I mean – how can you possibly be frightened by the prospect of coming face-to-face with a ghost kid?*

He reached out his hand as stiffly as if it were attached to the end of an artificial arm, and pushed the sitting room door open wide. The door gave a low groan as it strained on its hinges. The boy's crying went on, a hair-raising *oh-oh-oh-oh-oh* that aroused in Martin both urgency and terror. Urgency to save the child from whatever it was that was causing him to cry so pitifully. Terror that it might be something so unexpected and so dreadful that he wouldn't be able to do anything at all but freeze.

Shortly after Jane had left him, Martin had dreamed again and again of being rooted to the spot, unable to move while people laughed at him, while bristle-haired monkeys ran away with his furniture, while Jane was gruesomely raped in front of him by grinning clowns.

The greatest fear of all was the fear of walking into this sitting room and finding that he couldn't do anything but stand paralyzed and helpless.

He took a steadying breath, then another, and adrenaline surged around his veins like nighttime traffic on the interstate.

Then he took three decisive steps into the room, and immediately ducked and turned to face the mirror, with a heavy off-balance interpretation of the football block that his high school coach had always been trying to teach him, *duck, Williams, weave, for Christ's sake, you're a quarterback, not a fucking cheerleader*, and he couldn't help shouting out *ah!* because he came face-to-face in the mirror with his own terrified wildness – white cheeks, staring eyes, sticking-up hair, and his bright red bathrobe wrapped around him like bloodstained bandages.

He paused for a moment while his heaving chest subsided and his pulse gradually slowed, and he caught his breath.

'Shit,' he whispered; because his own appearance still unnerved him. But cautiously, he took two or three steps toward the mirror, and then hesitated and listened. The boy's sobbing continued, although it had become quieter and more miserable now, an endless low-key *oh-oh-oh*, that was even more heartrending than the loud sobs and cries that Martin had heard before.

He reached out and touched the mirror. The glass was cold and flawless and impenetrable. There was no question of it melting into a silver mist like Alice's mirror in *Through the Looking-Glass*. He pressed his forehead against it. His gray eyes stared expressionlessly back at him from only an inch away. *God*, he thought, *what can I do?* But the boy continued to weep.

Martin moved to the extreme left side of the mirror, in an effort to see into the corridor. He could make out two or three feet of it, but that was all. He went back to the sitting room door and wedged a folded-up copy of *Variety* underneath it to keep it wide open, but when he returned to the mirror he found that he couldn't see very much more.

Yet it sounded as if the child was crying in his bedroom. Not his real bedroom, but the bedroom in the mirror.

He shivered. The sitting room felt unnaturally cold. And the strained, high pitiable voice of that crying child was enough to make anyone shiver. He thought, *What the hell am I going to do? How the hell can I stop this sobbing?*

He remembered what Mr Capelli had told him about his

grandmother, how she smashed every mirror in the house when somebody died, because mirrors took a little piece of your soul every time you looked into them. Maybe if he broke this mirror, the real boy's soul would be released, and he wouldn't have to suffer anymore. On the other hand, supposing this mirror was his only contact with the real world, and with anybody who could help him? Supposing he was crying out to be saved? Yet from what, or from whom? And if life in the mirror was that desperate, why hadn't he cried out before, during all those years when the mirror had been hanging up in Mrs Harper's cellar?

Or maybe he had, and Mrs Harper had chosen to ignore him.

The weeping went on, *oh-oh-oh-oh-oh!*

Martin slapped the flat of his hand against the mirror. 'Listen!' he shouted. 'Can you hear me? Whoever's in there – can you hear me?'

He waited, but there was no reply. He felt an extraordinary mixture of rage and helplessness, pinned against this mirror, and because he was hyperventilating, he felt that he was floating, too, like a fly pressed against a window, and for one moment he didn't know whether he was up or down. It was a split-second insight into life without gravity, life without an understanding of glass. A fly can beat against a window until it dies, and never realize that the world outside can easily be reached by flying round a different way.

'Can you hear me?' Martin shouted. 'I'm here! I'm right here! I can help you!'

Then suddenly he thought: *What the hell am I doing? If the boy's in my bedroom, I can take the mirror down from the wall and drag it into the bedroom and then I can see for myself.*

He went to his desk, opened up two or three drawers, and at last found his ratchet screwdriver. Fumbling, overexcited, he took out the screws that held the mirror to the wall, one by one; and then hefted the mirror as gently as he could manage onto the floor. When he had done so, the mocking carving of Pan or Bacchus was grinning directly into his face: ancient carnality staring with gilded eyeballs at modern fright.

Martin lifted his jacket off the back of his chair, folded it up, and wedged it under the bottom of the frame so that it wouldn't be damaged when he dragged it across the floor. Then, a little at a time, he pulled it toward the open door, pausing every now and then to wipe his forehead with the back of his arm and to catch his breath.

'Jesus, why am I doing this?' he asked himself. But the child's weeping went on; and that was why.

He dragged the mirror across the room until it faced the open door which led to the hallway. Then he leaned over the glass and peered inside. The real hallway was empty, and so was the hallway in the mirror. Everything was identical. Identical door, identical carpet, identical wallpaper, brightly illuminated by the light that fell across the corridor from Martin's bedroom.

But the light appeared only in the mirror. When Martin glanced back toward the real corridor, his bedroom was in darkness, just the way he had left it. He had gone looking for the real boy without switching on his bedside lamp. Quite apart from which, the light that shone out of his mirror-bedroom was bright and clinical, like the lights in a hospital or an institution, while his real bedside lamp was muted by an orangey shade.

The boy's whimpering suddenly turned to high-pitched, terrified gasps. Martin rested the huge mirror against the corner of his desk and hurried clumsily toward his bedroom.

He hadn't yet reached the door, however, when the light in the mirror-bedroom was hurriedly switched off, and the child's gasps died away. Martin stood in the doorway for nearly a minute, straining his eyes, straining his ears, but the manifestation had gone. The apartment was silent, the mirror reflected nothing more than the sitting room door and part of the wall and a 1937 poster for *Sunshine Serenade*.

'You're . . . *Whistlin' Dixie* . . .' whispered the faintest of echoes; and it might have been nothing more than a truck horn blaring, far across the valley, or the early morning wind blowing under the door.

Martin looked around his bedroom, although he knew that he wouldn't find anything. The spirit of the mirror had gradu-

46

ally evaporated with the false dawn. He went back into the sitting room and looked at it, gilded and baroque and full of its own secrets.

He could take it back to Mrs Harper, he supposed; but she would probably insist that a contract of sale was a contract of sale, and refuse to return his money. He could try to sell it to Ramone Perez at The Reel Thing, but he doubted if Ramone would give him more than a couple of hundred bucks for it. Or he could take it down to the city dump and heave it onto the smoldering piles of trash and forget that he had ever seen it.

But, cautiously laying his hand on it, he began to feel that this mirror and all its mysteries were a burden which he had been chosen by destiny to accept. Not great historical destiny; not the kind of destiny which had steered the lives of Julius Caesar or Alexander the Great or George Washington; but that quirky, accidental, walked-through-door-A-instead-of-door-B destiny that affects the lives of almost all of us. The mirror had been hanging in Mrs Harper's cellar waiting for him, ever since he was small. He had gone to school, played ball, grown up, started writing teleplays, argued with Morris Nathan, and all the time the mirror had been there, waiting for that phone call, waiting for those last few steps up Mrs Harper's cracked concrete path.

Grunting with effort, he dragged the mirror back to the wall where it had been hung before, propped it up on his typewriter case, just as he had before, and screwed it back into place. Then he tossed his screwdriver back into his desk drawer and went through to the kitchen. He opened up the refrigerator, took out a carton of deeply chilled orange juice, and drank almost half of it straight from the carton. His palate ached with the cold, and he stood in the middle of the kitchen for a while with his hand clamped over his mouth, his eyes watering.

'You're a martyr,' he told himself. 'You know that?'

He went back to the bedroom, loosened the sash of his bathrobe, and straightened his futon. Above him, Boofuls smiled up at heaven, with his golden curls and his wide eyes and his white, heart-shaped face.

'Could be that you've scared me just a *little*,' Martin admitted.

Then he frowned at the poster more closely. He stood on his futon, and raised his hand, and gently touched the paper with his fingertips. Beneath Boofuls' eyes it was dimpled, as if it had been moistened and then left to dry.

He stared at Boofuls for a very long time. 'Could be that you've scared me a hell of a lot.'

Later that morning he drove over to Morris's house with the rewritten *A-Team* script. It was roastingly hot, and he walked up Morris's pathway between the red-flowering bougainvillea, feeling exhausted and irritable. Alison was lying on her inflatable sunbed, slowly rotating on the pool, her nose gleaming with sunscreen like a white beacon. A stereo tape player on the diving board played music from *Cats*.

He found Morris in the white Mexican-tile solarium reclining on a huge white ottoman surrounded by white telephones and stacks of multicolored screenplays. Morris was swathed in white toweling, and he was feeding himself with small green grapes.

'Good morning, Morris,' he said, dropping the rewrite onto the floor beside him.

'Ah, just the man I was looking for,' Morris replied. 'Pull up a seat. Pour yourself a glass of Perrier. Do you want a grape?'

Martin noisily dragged over a white-painted cast-iron chair, startling a white crested cockatoo that hung from the solarium ceiling in a white cage that Morris had brought back from Tangiers. The cockatoo screeched while Morris gave Martin one of his long old-fashioned looks and fed his mouth with grapes as if he were loading the chamber of a .38 with bullets.

'Listen, Martin,' he said at last, and then paused while the cockatoo let out one more screech. 'This Boofuls thing, it's going to do you some damage if you're not careful. Yesterday evening I was having dinner at the Bel Air Hotel and June Lassiter came over and gave me a *very* difficult time about that dreck you tried to sell her. She said she doesn't like to deal with writers direct, and more than that she doesn't like to deal with projects like that. It's a hoodoo, I told you. You're going to embarrass everybody. You've already embarrassed me. What could I say, that I washed my hands of it? But in any case I apologized on your behalf.'

Martin snapped, 'You had absolutely no right to do that.'

'Well, somebody had to.' Morris smirked, shifting his weight on the ottoman. 'You drag that idea around to one more major studio, my friend, and you will find that the drawbridge of opportunity has lifted and you are standing like a *shlemiel* on the outside. And let me tell you this: I'm not going to be the *nebach* who throws you a rope to get back across the moat.'

Martin stood up, noisily scraping his chair back and setting off the crested cockatoo into a frenzy of whooping and screaming. 'You've been watching too many old Burt Lancaster movies,' he retorted. 'And do you think I'd take hold of the rope even if you threw it to me?'

'Calm down, will you?' Morris told him; and then turned around to the cockatoo and bellowed, 'Stop that *krechsing*, you dumb bird!'

'Morris,' said Martin, 'this sounds crazy, but I think I've found him.'

'Who? What are you talking about? Shut up, bird! You know what Alison calls that bird? Dreyfuss. She thinks it looks like Richard Dreyfuss.'

'Boofuls,' Martin told him, his voice unsteady.

'Whunh?' Morris frowned. 'Martin will you make yourself clear? I have sixty screenplays to go through here, sixty. Look at this one, *Scarlett O'Hara, the Early Years*. What's the matter with these people? And you've turned into some kind of *nar* over Boofuls. All I hear from you is Boofuls, Boofuls, Boofuls. I would wish him dead, if he weren't already.'

'Well, that's it,' Martin interrupted. 'I don't think he is. I mean, not properly.'

Morris picked another grape and ate it very slowly. 'You don't think that Boofuls is properly dead?'

Martin nodded.

Morris heaved himself up into a sitting position. 'Martin, if I thought you could afford it, I'd send you along to Dr

Eisenbaum. What is it, the heat? I'm giving you too many *A-Team* rewrites, what?'

Martin took a deep breath. 'I bought a mirror that used to hang in Boofuls' house. In fact, it was supposed to be hanging over the fireplace the day that his grandmother killed him.'

'Go on,' said Morris, his voice low with apprehension. Whatever Martin was going to say, Morris definitely wasn't going to like it.

'Well – I've only had it a couple of days – I bought it Wednesday – just after I came out to see you – some woman on Hillside Avenue had it stored in her cellar.'

'And?'

'It's pretty difficult to explain, Morris, but I think he's in it.'

'In what?' Morris frowned.

'In the mirror,' Martin explained. 'I think that, somehow, Boofuls is kind of – well, it's real hard to describe it, but he's kind of *stuck*, you know, stuck inside the mirror. Maybe not him, but his spirit, or part of his spirit. Jesus, Morris, he was crying last night, he was crying for almost a half hour! I heard him!'

Morris thought about this for a long time, his hand poised just in front of his open lips. 'Boofuls is stuck inside your mirror?'

'I knew it!' said Martin. 'I knew you'd think I was crazy! But it's true, Morris. I don't know how it's happened and it's scaring me shitless; but he's there!'

'You've seen him?'

'No, I haven't, but I heard him crying.'

'How do you know it's Boofuls if you haven't seen him? How do you know it wasn't some kid crying in the next apartment?'

'Because there are no kids in the next apartment, and because I've watched every single movie that Boofuls ever made, over and over and over. If I don't know Boofuls' voice when I hear it, then nobody does!'

Morris pressed his grape into his mouth, burst it between his bright gold teeth, and flapped his chubby little hand at Martin dismissively, almost effeminately. 'Martin, you're letting this whole thing get to you, that's all. It's got to your brain! It happens, I've seen it happen before. Some writer called Jack Posnik wanted to make an epic war picture about the Philippine War, that's another one of those hoodoo subjects. He ended up wearing an army uniform and calling himself Lieutenant Roosevelt.'

'Morris,' said Martin, 'I went back to my room and my poster was wet. My poster of Boofuls had tear stains on it. I swear it!'

Morris looked at him narrowly. 'Are you a Catholic?' he asked him, and his tone was unusually fierce. 'You know, I've heard of weeping madonnas, stuff like that –'

'Morris, listen to me, for God's sake. Think what kind of a story we've got here! Think what kind of a picture this could make!'

At that moment, Alison came padding into the room on wet bare feet. Today she was wearing a bright yellow bikini that scarcely covered her at all. She was a darker shade of brown than she had been before, apart from that white blob of sunscreen on her nose.

'Martin!' she exclaimed. 'I thought it was you!'

'Well, I think I was just leaving,' said Martin.

'I guess you were,' Morris told him. 'But listen – *please* – for your own sake and for mine, too, let this Boofuls business rest for a while. I'll tell you what I'll do. Next week, you and I will fly down to San Diego together, and we'll spend a lazy weekend on my boat, yes? Fishing and eating and drinking wine, and we'll talk this whole thing through, unh? See if we can't come up with something a little more acceptable, yes? Something with a little more taste? And, you know, something you can *sell*, already, without raising everybody's hackles.'

Martin looked at Alison, and Alison laid her hand possessively on Morris' shoulder and gave Martin an encouraging smile. Nice girl, he thought, not so much of a *tsatskeh* as he had first thought. She deserved better than Morris and his chauvinistic garbage about jugs.

'My mother used to adore Boofuls,' she said by way of being conciliatory.

51

'Sure,' said Martin. Then, to Morris, 'Enjoy the rewrite. I may be a *shlemiel* but I can still write first-rate dialogue.'

He walked back out into the hot sunshine. This was one of those times when he felt like buying himself a very large bottle of chardonnay and sitting in his room listening to ZZ Top records and getting drunk.

On his way home, he felt so hot that he stopped at a 7-Eleven and bought two frozen juice bars, one for himself and one for Emilio. When he arrived home, however, carrying one empty stick and one leaking juice bar, he found Emilio's toy cars lying in the dust beside the front steps, but no sign of Emilio.

'Emilio!' he called around the side of the house. The sticky orange juice was already running down his wrist.

A small boy in a rainbow-striped T-Shirt was walking a scruffy ginger mongrel along the sidewalk. 'Hey, kid!' Martin called. 'How would you like a juice bar? It's a little runny but it won't kill you.'

The boy stuck out his tongue and ran away, sneakers pit-patting on the sidewalk, all the way to the corner of Yucca. Martin shrugged. He guessed it was better that children didn't talk to strange sweating screenwriters with melting juice bars. He dropped the bar into the gutter, and across the street an elderly woman in a cotton hat stared at him as if she had discovered at last the man responsible for polluting the whole of the Southern California environment.

Martin went into the house and climbed the stairs. It smelled of disinfectant and Parmesan cheese, but at least it was cool.

Morris had depressed him this morning. He didn't mind so much that Morris disliked the idea of a Boofuls musical; he was professional enough to accept that some people were going to regurgitate their breakfast at nothing more than the mention of motion pictures that other people swooned over. But he was deeply upset that June Lassiter could have called up Morris behind his back and complained about him. It made him feel like a clumsy amateur, an outsider; as if he hadn't yet been accepted by Hollywood Proper.

He had almost reached the top landing when he heard

Emilio laughing. Too bad, he thought philosophically – the juice bar wouldn't have survived the climb from the street in any case. But as he turned the corner of the stairs he saw that his own apartment door was ajar and that the upper landing was illuminated by a triangular section of sunlight.

He approached the apartment door as quietly as he could. He heard Emilio giggling again.

'You can't throw it! You can't throw it!' And then more laughter. Then, 'You can't throw it, it won't come through.'

Martin eased open the door and tiptoed as quickly as he could along the hallway toward the sitting room. Emilio was scuffling around, his sneakers squeaking on the wood-block floor, and he was giggling so much that Martin was worried for a moment that he was choking.

Martin tried to see through the crack in the doorjamb. He glimpsed Emilio's faded red sneakers, flashing for a moment, and then Emilio's black tousled hair. But the door wasn't open wide enough for him to be able to see the mirror on the end wall; and if he had opened it any farther, he suspected that he would scare away *who*ever or *what*ever Emilio was playing with.

Emilio laughed. 'Stop throwing it!'

But then Martin heard another voice – a voice that didn't sound like Emilio's at all. A young, clear voice, echoing slightly as if he were talking in a tunnel or a high-ceilinged bathroom. '*Get another ball! Get another ball!*' And then a strange ringing giggle.

Martin felt as if somebody had lifted up his shirt collar at the back and gradually emptied a jug of ice water down his back.

What had he said to Morris? *If I don't know Boofuls' voice when I hear it, then nobody does.*

Emilio said, 'What? What? Another ball?'

'*We have to have two! If you throw a ball to me, I can throw a ball back to you!*'

A moment's hesitation. Then Emilio saying, 'Okay, then, wait up', and dodging toward the door on those squeaking sneakers.

At once, Martin swung the door open wide. It banged and

53

shuddered against the wall. He lifted Emilio bodily out of his way and jumped right into the middle of the room.

He thought he saw a blur that could have been an arm or could have been a leg. But then again, it could have been nothing at all.

The mirror was empty, except for himself and the room and the late morning sunlight; and just behind him, a bewildered-looking Emilio.

Martin swung around. 'Where is he?' he demanded, his voice cracking.

Emilio shook his head. 'I don't know what you mean.'

'The boy, the real boy. Where is he?'

'He's –'

'Listen, Emilio, I was standing right behind the door. I *heard* him. I heard him with my own ears.'

Two clear tears unexpectedly dropped onto Emilio's cheeks, and rolled down on either side of his mouth, and fell on the floor.

'He said I mustn't tell anybody. He said they punish him if anybody finds out.'

Martin got down on one knee and hugged Emilio close. 'You listen to me, old buddy, I'm not going to hurt him. I'm his friend, the same way that you are.'

'He says he's frightened.'

'Well, what does he have to be frightened about? He doesn't have to be frightened of me. I can help him. At least, I *think* I can help him.'

Emilio shook his head. 'He says he's frightened.'

'All right,' said Martin, and stood up. He looked toward the mirror and wondered if the real boy was listening to them. 'But if that boy really is who I think he is – and if he's gotten himself trapped inside that mirror or something – for whatever reason – and he's frightened – well, I'm sure that I can find some way to help him – because I know more about him than he knows about himself.'

Emilio glanced quickly at the mirror, almost furtively, and then asked, 'Can I go now?'

Martin grinned and shrugged. 'Sure you can go. This isn't the third degree.'

Emilio didn't know what he meant but he went, anyway. He was passing the kitchen door, however, when he said, 'Are you going to have him through for dinner?'

'*Through?*'

'Well, you know, like through the mirror.'

Martin came along the hallway and gave Emilio a pretend Rocky punch. 'You're way ahead of yourself Emilio.'

'But he likes lasagne.'

'He told you that?'

'He likes Swedish meatballs and he likes lasagne and he likes pecan pie.'

'So your grandmother's lasagne won't go to waste?'

'No, sir.'

Martin watched Emilio climb back down the stairs. It was extraordinary how easily children accept the strange and the supernatural, he thought. But maybe this mirror wasn't as strange and as supernatural as it appeared to be. He had read in *Popular Radio* that mirrors could sometimes pick up radio signals from powerful transmitters, because of their silver backing, and that their glass could vibrate sufficiently to make people hear disembodied voices. Late one night in 1961, in Pasadena, the wife of a grocery-store manager was lying in bed waiting for her husband to come home when her dressing-table mirror began to pick up a live Frank Sinatra interview from Palm Springs. Her husband, coming home late, heard a man's voice in his wife's bedroom, and shot to kill. He wounded his wife and then turned the gun on himself.

He returned to the sitting room and leaned against the mirror with his arms upraised and listened and waited for a long time. No boy. Nothing.

'Walter!' he shouted. 'Boofuls! Come here, Boofuls, let me take a look at you! I'm your biggest fan, Boofuls! Why'n't you step out and give me that sailor's hornpipe, hunh? Come on, Boofuls, I've devoted three years of my life to writing and rewriting about you. Three years – and three complete transfusions of blood and sweat. The least you can give me is a couple of minutes of hornpipe.'

He waited five minutes, ten. Nothing happened. No Boofuls

55

appeared. After a while, Martin turned away from the mirror and looked across at his typewriter. He had some work to do on a *Knight Rider* teleplay. He might just as well sit down and get to it. Trying to get in touch with boys who lived in mirrors wasn't going to pay the rent.

He switched on his tape player and inserted the sound track of *Suwannee Song*. Immediately the flutes thrilled and the drums rattled, and the sitting room was filled with the opening march, when Boofuls was strutting like a drum major in front of a regiment of two hundred black minstrels, as they paraded along the levee.

> *Surrr . . . wannee Song! Suwannee Song!*
> *You can blow your flute and you can bang your drum*
> *and you can march along!*

Martin sat down at his desk, zipped a fresh sheet of paper into his typewriter, and started work on the latest adventures of Michael Knight. He wondered mischievously if Kit the talking car could turn out to be gay: if he could come out of the garage, so to speak.

> *Surr . . . wannee Song! Suwannee Song!*
> *It's the song, it's the song, it's the song of the South!*

He didn't know what it was that caught his eye; what it was that stopped him typing '*What is it, David? Bad guys?*' and turn around in his chair and stare intently at the mirror. But the blue and white ball came rolling out from under the table, halfway across the room, to settle there, rocking slightly from side to side before it came completely to rest.

He turned to look at the real room. The ball wasn't there. He switched off his typewriter and walked up to the mirror and stared at the blue and white ball for two or three thoughtful minutes. Then he went back to his desk and opened up the bottom drawer and took out a tennis ball that he had used for practice last summer.

'*We have to have two!*' the boy had called out. '*If you throw a ball to me, I can throw a ball back to you.*'

Martin hesitated for a while, tossing the old gray tennis ball up and down in his hand. Then, without warning, he threw it at the mirror, quite hard, half expecting to break it, half *hoping* to break it.

There was a sharp smacking sound, and the ball ricocheted off the glass and rolled across the floor. It came to rest only five or six inches away from the toe of his Nike sneakers.

But it wasn't a dingy gray tennis ball. It was a bright new blue and white bouncing ball. And when he turned in shock and looked toward the mirror, he saw his own tennis ball there, in exactly the corresponding place, five or six inches away from his toe.

He picked up the blue and white ball. It was quite hard and smelled strongly of rubber and paint. His mirror image picked up the tennis ball and sniffed that, too.

'My God,' he whispered; and approached the mirror, holding up the blue and white ball until it was touching the mirror's surface. His reflection did the same with the tennis ball, until the two balls apparently touched.

Martin could scarcely believe what he was seeing. He turned the ball this way and that, but it remained, without argument, a blue and white ball, while the ball in the mirror remained the same balding gray tennis ball that he had been punting around last year.

He tried one more experiment. He stepped back, and wound back his arm, and pitched the blue and white ball straight toward the glass. Again, there was a smacking sound; but this time the blue and white ball came bouncing back into the real room.

Martin picked up the blue and white ball, turned it around in his hand, and then set it down on his desk, next to his bronze paperweight of a *fin de siècle* plume dancer. He sat there and watched it, and then poured himself some wine, and watched it some more.

The sun rotated around the room. Next door, beside the pool, Maria Bocanegra came and went, sunning herself with Sno-Cones to protect her nipples; but Martin didn't bother to get up and look. He couldn't keep his eyes off the blue and white ball.

The day died. He didn't understand it. It was a clear night, the lights were sparkling all the way to Watts.

He slept in his chair. The blue and white ball stayed where it was, unmoving.

CHAPTER THREE

He dreamed that night that he was the smallest of sea creatures, crouched in the tiniest of shells, on a broad moonlit beach.

He could feel the grit. He could taste the salt. He could hear the slow, restless convulsions of the ocean; rocks into stones, stones into pebbles, pebbles into sand, year in and year out, even when there was nobody to listen to it.

He felt the terrible fear of being small and defenseless.

He opened his eyes. He was sweating. It should have been hot, but it was stunningly cold. He shivered. He sat up in bed and his breath smoked. He couldn't decide if he was awake or still asleep – if he was Martin Williams or if he was still a mollusk. He called, 'Hello?' even before he was properly awake.

From the sitting room, he could hear whispered voices: two children sharing secrets. He could see lights flickering, too: cold clinical lights, as if somebody were silently welding.

'Emilio?' he called. Then, louder, 'Emilio?'

He drew back his futon and reached for his robe. Quickly he stepped out into the hallway and approached the sitting room door. The light inside the sitting room was spasmodic but intense, and he had to lift his hand to shield his eyes.

He paused outside the door. This time, he didn't feel so much frightened as deeply curious. If he was right, and it *was* Boofuls, or Boofuls' spirit, then what an encounter this was going to be. If he had lived, Boofuls would be coming up to his sixtieth birthday; Martin was only thirty-four.

He pushed open the door. The room was glaring with static and crackling with cold. He turned and saw Emilio in his Care Bears nightshirt, kneeling in front of the mirror, one hand lifted, and facing him – instead of a true reflection – a small white-faced boy with golden curls, dressed in pale-yellow pajamas.

Martin's heart hesitated, bumped, hesitated, the same way it did on Montezuma's Revenge at Knott's Berry Farm. And the same hyped-up, almost hysterical reasoning: *I don't want to do this more than anything else I can think of, but I have to, because it scares me so much I can scarely think how much it scares me.*

There was no doubt about it at all. The boy in the mirror was Boofuls. Martin stared at him in horrified fascination. He was there, smiling, his eyes much smaller and paler than Martin would have imagined, but then the studio makeup artists had probably darkened his lashes before he appeared in front of the lights. His hair was thinner, too. Gold, yes, bright gold; and very curly; but thin, the way that little children's hair goes when they're anxious or allergic, or suffering from sibling rivalry.

Emilio bowed his dark head toward the mirror and Boofuls bowed his head toward Emilio. Their movements were exactly reflected, although it was impossible to tell which of them was initiating the action and which was following; or if somehow they were empathizing so intensely that they could both move at once, identical movements.

The scene oddly reminded Martin of one of those Marx Brothers movies in which Harpo appeared behind an empty mirror frame, mimicking the movements of the poor sucker who was trying to adjust his necktie in it.

Emilio whispered, 'We could do it now.'

And Boofuls nodded, and Emilio nodded.

Emilio stood up, his arms by his sides. The white-faced Boofuls stood up, too and smiled at him, his arms by his sides.

'One! Two! Th*ree!*' said Boofuls.

And it was then that Martin understood what they were going to do – the old gray tennis ball flying into the mirror-world and the bright blue and white ball flying out of it – except that he had found it impossible to throw the blue and white ball back.

'*Emilio!*' he bellowed. '*Emilio, no!*'

Emilio turned, startled. Boofuls turned too – but here his mirror-mimicking failed him, because he looked straight toward Martin the same way that Emilio did. His tiny eyes flared bright sapphire blue for a moment, welding-torch eyes, and he snatched for Emilio with both arms.

But in that instant Williams, who couldn't duck or weave, did his high school coach proud – with a sliding tackle that caught little Emilio around the waist and sent him sprawling across the floor.

For one second, Martin felt an extraordinary pull on Emilio, as forceful and demanding as if he were being sucked out of a depressurized airplane; but he grabbed hold of his desk with one hand, slipped, grabbed again, and clung on to Emilio with the other. After a split second of ferocious suction, the force subsided, the flickering lights died away, and the two of them were left lying on the floor, in cold and darkness and silence.

Martin ruffled Emilio's hair. 'You okay, old buddy?'

To his surprise, there were tears glistening on Emilio's cheeks.

'Hey, come on now,' he said, sitting up. 'What's wrong?'

'I wanted to go,' Emilio sobbed.

'You wanted to *go*? Go where?'

'Through the mirror, I wanted to go.'

Martin looked at the mirror. Boofuls had vanished. All the glass reflected was themselves and the moonlit room. Somewhere outside, heading south on La Brea, a police siren was whooping. Lonely echoes of urgency and danger.

'Come on,' said Martin, taking hold of Emilio's hand and helping him up. 'Let's go find ourselves a Coke.'

Emilio stood up and looked sadly toward the mirror. 'He only wanted to play.'

'Is that what he said?'

Emilio nodded. 'He said we could play all day, I wouldn't have to go to school. He wants me to meet his friends. He wants me to meet his old man.'

'His old man? You mean his father?'

'That's right. He says we could go for rides; swim in the sea; anything.'

Martin leaned across his desk and picked up the blue and white ball. 'Emilio,' he said, 'do you know where this came from?'

'Unh-hunh.'

'Emilio – it came from in there. It came from the mirror.

Take a look in the mirror right now. What am I holding up? A worn-out old tennis ball right? Yet look at this one. It doesn't make any sense. Like seeing that boy doesn't make any sense. You're not supposed to look into mirrors and see somebody else instead of yourself.'

Emilio wiped his tears with his sleeve.

Martin said, 'The trouble is, Emilio, I can't get my tennis ball back.'

'But this ball's okay,' Emilio told him. 'Why do you want the other one back?'

Martin tossed the ball up into the air and caught it again. 'Emilio, that's not the point. I can't get it back whether I want it or not. Now, supposing *you* went through that mirror. The way I see it, for anything to get through, one *real* thing has to be traded for one *mirror* thing. Can you understand that? It's the same as the boy was telling you yesterday. You can't play ball with just a reflection, it won't go through. You need two balls – one to go in and the other to come out. Just like you need two boys. One to step into the mirror, one to step out.'

Emilio scratched his head like one of the Little Rascals. 'But if that boy has to come out when I go in, how do we play with each other? He said he was going to show me his lead soldiers.'

Martin said, 'Listen to me, planet brain. If this blue and white ball came through the mirror and I can't get my old ball back, do you have any reason to suppose that when that boy comes through the mirror, I'm going to be able to get *you* back?'

Emilio was silent for a moment, pouting. Then he said, 'I don't want to come back. I don't care. Anything's better than Grannie and Gramps. They always smell like garlic, and there are dust balls under the bed.'

'The same dust balls exist in that mirror,' Martin assured him. 'So do the beds they're under. They've got the same garlic, the same people, the same world. The only difference is that everything's back to front.'

Emilio said wistfully, 'I wish I could see it.'

'It is not so hot, believe me.'

'But it is! Look at that writing!' And he pointed to the

letters *Sunshine Serenade* 'I' wonder how you speak it. It's cool.'

'Cool.' Martin smiled, shaking his head, and laid an arm around Emilio's shoulder. 'You should've been a printer, that's what printers have to do, read type back to front. Come, let's get that Coke.'

They went through to the kitchen. Emilio perched on the stool while Martin opened up two cans of Coke.

Emilio said, 'That boy, his name's not really Petey, is it?'

'No,' Martin told him. 'That boy's name is Boofuls.'

'You mean like the same kid in the picture in your bedroom?'

'The very same kid.'

Emilio made a loud sucking noise with his drinking straw. 'But that picture comes from the olden days.'

'That's right. Nineteen thirty-six, to be precise. And that's more than fifty years ago.'

Emilio continued to suck Coke while he thought about that. His face was pale because it was the middle of the night and he should have been asleep, and there were plummy little circles under his eyes.

'How come he's still a kid?' Emilio suddenly wanted to know.

'I don't know,' Martin admitted. 'He's supposed to be dead. I mean I don't think he's actually a real kid. That kid you can see in the mirror is more like a ghost.'

Emilio thought about that and then said, 'Wow. I never met a ghost before.'

'Me neither.' Martin tugged open a bag of Fritos. 'That's why I don't think it's such a good idea your playing with him,' said Martin. '*You* don't want to wind up a ghost, too, do you?'

'Would I be invisible? I mean if I was a ghost? Could I walk through walls?'

'I don't know. But from everything I've heard about ghosts, ghosts are not too happy. I mean, Boofuls isn't too happy, is he? Listen – do you want anything to eat? Fritos or something? I've got some what–do–you–call–'ems someplace Twinkies.'

Emilio shook his head. He was too tired, and too fascinated by the otherworldly nature of the friend he had met in Martin's sitting room. Martin could almost see it all churning around in his mind, like five different colors of Play-Doh, *'I've been playing ball with a ghost, I've been talking to a ghost. A ghost! A real live ghost! Not like Casper; not like* Poltergeist, *like me! A ghost kid just like me!'*

Martin said, 'It's possible, Emilio – it's just possible – that playing with Boofuls might not be safe. Do you understand that? I mean, Boofuls doesn't mean you any harm. Leastways, I don't think he does. But this is all pretty weird stuff, right? And until we can find out what's happening, why he's here, what he wants – well, I think it's better if you don't come up here.'

Emilio looked completely put out. 'Doesn't Boofuls like me?'

'Sure he likes you, Emilio. He probably thinks you're his best pal ever. But just at this moment you two guys have got something to work out between you. Like, he lives on one side of a mirror and you live on the other. And the way I see it, either you're here and he's there, or he's here and you're there. And that's a little too weird for anybody to handle.'

Emilio yawned. 'All right,' he surrendered.

Just then, Mr Capelli came stomping into the kitchen, wrapped up in a gleaming striped satin bathrobe in chrome yellow and royal purple. Underneath it, Martin glimpsed gray woolen ankle socks.

'Emilio!' he exclaimed. 'I've been searching for you everywhere! I walked all the way down to Highland!'

'You've been walking the streets in *that* robe and they didn't arrest you?' asked Martin with pretended astonishment.

Mr Capelli tugged his bathrobe tighter. 'Mrs Capelli gave me this robe for Christmas.'

'Don't tell me, tell the judge. Thank your lucky stars they don't send people to death row for premeditated bad taste.'

'And what do *you* call taste, anh? Your wreck of a car, parked outside my house?'

Martin lifted Emilio off his stool and gave him a good-night kiss on the top of the head. Funny how kids' hair always smells the same: fresh, alive, pungent with youth, chestnuts and hot pajamas and summer days.

64

'Here,' he said, 'you'd better take this young somnambulist back to his bed.'

Mr Capelli took hold of Emilio and clasped him in his arms. 'You're a crazy person, you know that, just like your mamma.'

Martin said quietly, as Mr Capelli carried Emilio toward the door, 'Listen, Mr Capelli . . .' but he realized when Mr Capelli turned around that there were tears in his eyes, one of those sudden unexpected pangs of grief for his dead daughter; one of those moments of weakness that hit the bereaved when they're least expecting it.

Emilio's mother, Mr Capelli's daughter, had died three years ago. Her husband, Stanley had walked out on her. (Mrs Capelli had told Martin all about this, like a soap opera, complete with actions: you should have seen the fights, you should have heard the cursing, how two people could *hate* each other so much, you'd've never believed it.)

Sad, disoriented, feeling that she had somehow fallen from grace, Emilio's mother had overdosed one Sunday morning on Italian wine and Valium. She had been found dead in her apartment white as Ophelia, her arms outspread, her hair outspread, almost beautiful, but smelling like hell itself, and the whole apartment thunderous with blowflies.

Stanley had gone to Saskatchewan to chop timber. Mr and Mrs Capelli had been given custody of Emilio. Garlic, dust balls, and all.

Mr Capelli said, 'It's all right, Martin, he has to get back to bed.'

'Mr Capelli, I have to talk to you,' Martin insisted. 'Could you come right back?'

'Talk?' Mr Capelli demanded.

'About Emilio, please. Can you spare me five minutes?'

'It's gone three o'clock.'

'Sure, yes, I know, but please. I don't know whether it's going to keep until tomorrow.'

He tore off a piece of kitchen towel and handed it to Mr Capelli, and Mr Capelli wiped his eyes. It was an act of acceptance, an act of reconciliation.

'Okay,' Mr Capelli promised. 'But five minutes, no more.'

Martin looked at Emilio resting against his grandfather's shoulder and Emilio was already asleep.

Mr Capelli came up ten minutes later and rapped at the door.

'Hey, come on in,' Martin told him.

Mr Capelli stood in the hallway in his yellow and purple bathrobe, looking tired and embarrassed. 'I'm sorry,' he said, 'I shouldn't've sounded off. It just gets to me sometimes, you know what I mean, Andrea and all.'

Martin slapped his arm. 'I know. I'm sorry, too. You know what scriptwriters are. Smart-asses, all of us. It's the way we make our living.'

Mr Capelli nodded, oblivious to Martin's irony. 'She was so beautiful, Andrea; and Emilio looks just the same way; nothing of Stanley; that jerk; Stanley had eyes that were too close together, you know? But Emilio is Andrea. Beautiful, Italian, what can I say?'

Martin suggested, 'How about some coffee?'

Mr Capelli said, 'No – no thank you. I don't sleep good already. Just talk.'

'Okay,' said Martin, taking a deep breath. 'This isn't easy okay? Try to bear with me. But even if it doesn't sound logical, try to accept that I wouldn't be telling you if I weren't worried about Emilio.'

'Why are you worried about Emilio?' Mr Capelli demanded. 'Why should *you* worry about Emilio?'

'Listen, Mr Capelli, Emilio is your grandson, but Emilio is also my friend. Well, I hope he is. I don't think it matters very much how *old* anybody is, do you? I mean the difference between your age and my age is a lot more than the difference between my age and Emilio's age. So you can't say that he and I don't have any right to be buddies, can you?'

'No, I didn't say that,' replied Mr Capelli stiffly, his hands resting on his knees.

'All right, then,' said Martin. 'What I'm saying is in Emilio's best interest, believe me. If Emilio comes up to my apartment anymore – well I don't want him here anymore.'

Mr Capelli leaned forward, his hands still clutching his knees. 'You're not saying . . . what, you're gay?'

'Oh shit, Mr Capelli!' Martin shouted at him, slapping at the hallway wall. 'I'm not talking about me! Gay! What the hell is the matter with you? It's that mirror you helped me to carry upstairs.'

'The mirror, hah? Boofuls' mirror? What did I tell you, you shouldn't give it houseroom.'

'Maybe you were right,' Martin admitted. 'I don't know what it is, but there's something wrong with it,' Martin told him. 'It's hard to say what. But it's not your usual kind of everyday mirror.'

'It's a trick mirror,' said Mr Capelli, trying to lighten up this dire and ominous conversation before Martin started talking about death and hackings and all the other gory topics of conversation that (along with *saraghine alla brace*) invariably gave him nightmares and agonies of indigestion. 'You look in the mirror and what do you see? You don't got clothes on.'

'No, Mr Capelli, it's nothing like that. I mean, it's a kind of a trick mirror, but it doesn't make your clothes disappear or anything like that. It's – well when you look at it, you don't always see what's really there.'

Mr Capelli said nothing; but waited on Martin to explain; his eyes blinking from time to time like a pelican at San Diego Zoo.

'The thing is,' said Martin, 'if Emilio plays with it, he might start to see things – *people*, maybe, who don't really exist. And – well – if he sees things – people – stuff that doesn't exist – it could be kind of –'

He paused. Mr Capelli was staring at him in that same pelicanlike way, as if he believed that he had completely flipped.

Martin added, 'Dangerous,' and then gave Mr Capelli an idiotic grin.

Mr Capelli tugged at the bulb of his fleshy nose and thought for a while. Then he said, 'Martin, I like you. You've got a choice. Either that mirror goes, or you go, whichever.'

'You're throwing me *out*?' asked Martin in surprise.

'Of course not. Just the mirror.'

'Mr Capelli, I'm not at all sure I can do that.'

'Why not? Are you crazy? One minute you're saying it's dangerous; you see things in it that aren't there; you're worried about Emilio; the next minute you're saying you can't do that; well, you *can* do that, it's easy, just do it. Am I asking too much?'

Martin laid his hand on Mr Capelli's shoulder. Mr Capelli peered at it from very close up. 'There's nothing fundamentally wrong with the mirror, Mr Capelli,' said Martin, and Mr Capelli echoed, 'Fundamentally.'

'All I'm saying is, it has this vibe. I don't know, you can call it what you like. It's like a visual echo. An echo you can see.'

'An echo you can see?' Mr Capelli repeated and Martin could see that he was vexed and tired, and that he didn't even *want* to understand. Mr Capelli's answer to everything that he didn't like, or wasn't sure of, was to turn his back on it.

'All right,' said Martin. 'Boofuls has come alive. Don't ask me how. He's in the mirror, and Emilio has been playing with him, and Emilio has come within an inch of getting inside the mirror, too.'

Mr Capelli stood up. He glanced quickly at Martin, almost casually then nodded. 'Mumh-humh,' he said, and nodded again. Martin watched him with increasing tension.

'Good night, Martin,' said Mr Capelli at length, and turned to leave.

'That's it? Good night?'

'All right, a *very* good night. What more do you want?'

'I just want you to promise me that you won't let Emilio come up here for a while. I mean, tell him he mustn't. This whole apartment is strictly no go.'

Mr Capelli said, 'In the morning, Martin, you make up your mind. That mirror goes, or you go. The first thing I told you when you brought that mirror back here, what did I say? No good is going to come out of it. That was the first thing I said. And now what's happened? No good has come out of it.'

'Mr Capelli, it could very well be that there's a real boy trapped in that mirror.'

'That's right and it could very well be that some clever

people can train a pig to fly straight into a bacon slicer, and another pig to drive the bacon down to Safeway.'

'Mr Capelli –'

'*No!*' replied Mr Capelli. 'That mirror goes by tomorrow night, otherwise you go. Now, it's late, I don't want to talk about it no more.'

He left, closing the apartment door sharply behind him.

Martin remained in the kitchen, feeling drained and somehow diminished, as if his dream of being a mollusk had shrunk his consciousness down to a microscopic speck. Tired, probably, and anxious, and unsettled by what had happened in the mirror.

He went back to bed and fell asleep almost straightaway. He had no dreams that he could remember, although he was aware of blundering through darkness and wondering if it would ever be light, ever again.

It was nearly eight o'clock, however, when he thought he heard a child's voice, close to his ear, whisper, '*Pickle-nearest-the-wind*'.

He sat up. He looked around the room, which was quite bright now. Everything looked normal, although he had the oddest feeling that the drapes and the furniture had jumped back into place when he opened his eyes, as if the whole room had been misbehaving itself, right up until the moment when he had woken up.

The drapes stirred a little as if a child were hiding behind them, but then Martin realized that it was only the morning breeze.

Pickle-nearest-the-wind. What the hell did that mean?

But all the same, he went through to the sitting room, and found a scrap of typing paper on his desk and wrote it down in green felt-tip pen. The phrase had a peculiar quality about it that reminded him of something, although he couldn't think what. Some childhood storybook with drawings of clouds and chimney pots and faraway hills.

He glanced toward the mirror. The grinning gold face of Pan presided over a scene that appeared to be a scrupulous representation of the real room. Only the blue and white ball on his desk remained uncompromisingly different from the gray tennis ball on his reflected desk.

Still holding the scrap of paper in his hand, he walked right up to the mirror and stared at his own face. He looked quite well and quite calm, although he didn't feel it. He wondered if there really was a world beyond the door, a different world, a world where Boofuls had survived after death, a Lewis Carroll world where clocks smiled and chess pieces talked and flowers quarreled, and you had to walk backward to go forward.

> *Twas brillig, and the slithy toves*
> *Did gyre and gimble in the wabe . . .*

He remembered with a smile the words of 'Jabberwocky', the mirror-writing nonsense poem in *Alice Through the Looking-Glass;* and how it had always amused him as a small boy to hold the book up to the mirror and read the words the right way around.

It had always seemed so magical that the lettering obediently reversed itself and gave up its secret, every time.

He held up the piece of paper on which he had written 'Pickle-nearest-the-wind'. Perhaps the words meant something if they were reversed: after all, everything *else* that had been happening to him seemed to have some connection with this damned mirror.

But to his slowly growing astonishment, the words weren't reversed at all. In the mirror, in his own handwriting, the words clearly said, 'Pickle-nearest-the-wind', the right way around.

He stared at the real piece of paper, his hand trembling. 'Pickle-nearest-the-wind', the right way around.

The words refused to be reversed by the mirror. He crumpled the paper up and then uncrumpled it and held it up again. No difference. For some reason beyond all imagination, those words that had been whispered to him in the early hours of the morning completely denied the laws of optical physics.

He stood still for a while, looking at himself in the mirror, wondering what to do. *My God*, he thought, *what kind of a game is going on here?*

He left the sitting room, step by step backward, keeping his eyes on the mirror all the time. He shut the door behind him, and locked it, and took out the key. Then he went back to his bedroom, stripped off his bathrobe and dressed.

Ramone was having breakfast when Martin arrived at The Reel Thing; his custom-made sneakers, purple and white and natural suede, perched on the counter like exhibits unto themselves. He was dark, shock-headed, with multiple-jointed arms and legs, and one of those ugly spread-nosed Latino faces that you couldn't help liking. His breakfast was a giant chili dog, with everything on it, and a bottle of lime-flavored Perrier.

'Hey, Martin!' he cried, waving one of his spidery arms.

Martin came over and leaned tightly against the counter, close to the cash register.

'Allure, Ramone,' he greeted him. Saying 'allure' instead of 'hello' had been kind of a private joke between them ever since they had gone downtown together one evening to watch a Brazilian art movie, in which everybody had said 'allure'.

'*Allure, Juanita.*'

'*Allure, Gaspar.*'

Ramone said, 'That ginger-headed girl was in here, yessday afternoon, asking about you.'

'Yeah?' said Martin. 'That ginger-headed girl' was a student from his Monday evening tele-writing class, Norma, who had considered his *A-Team* rewrites 'miraculous'; and had wanted to take him to bed to 'you know, transfuse the talent'.

The Reel Thing was more than a store: it was a shrine. Anything and everything that was important to movie buffs was assembled here. Shirley Temple dolls in sailor suits and cowboy outfits and Scottish plaids. Buck Rogers disintegrator guns and rocket ships. Tom Mix pocket knives and six-shooters. And box after box after box of signed studio glossies – Joan Crawford and Adolphe Menjou and Robert Redford and Dorothy Dell.

The whole store smelled of forty-year-old movie programs and dust and old clothes and stale cigarette smoke from a thousand long-forgotten parties. But anybody who cared for movies could spend hours in here, touching with reverence the gowns of Garbo; or the white Stetsons of William Boyd; or the short-sleeved shirts of Mickey Rooney. The artifacts

71

were nothing at all. It was what they conjured up that made them valuable.

Martin picked up a yellowed copy of *Silver Screen* with the enticing headline 'What It Takes to Be a 1939 Girl'.

'Did you look at the stuff?' Ramone asked him scooping up chili and pickle with his fingers.

Martin dropped the magazine back into its rack. 'Oh yes, I looked at the stuff, all right.'

'No good?' asked Ramone.

'Depends what you mean by no good.'

Ramone's tabby cat, Lugosi, was resting on a stack of *Screenlands*, his paws tucked in, his eyes slitted against the sunlight that came in through the window.

Martin stroked him under his chin, but Lugosi opened his eyes and stared back at him in irritation, his vexation emphasized by the way one pointed tooth was caught on his lip. Lugosi was definitely a one-man cat.

Ramone said, with his mouth full, 'It was genuine Boofuls stuff, I saw the paperwork. It was auctioned by M-G-M along with a whole lot of Shirley Temple properties.'

'I bought the mirror,' said Martin. Then, 'Listen Ramone, can you get some time off? I have to talk this over with *somebody*.'

Ramone wiped his hands on a paper napkin, rolled it up, and tossed it with perfect accuracy into a basket. 'I was going out to Westwood, anyway. Kelly can take care of the store. Kelly! *Dónde está usted?*'

A small girl with owlish designer spectacles and a long blond braid down the middle of her back came into the store from the back. She wore a loose white T-shirt with the slogan 'Of All the T-shirts in All the World I Had to Pick This One'.

'*Hasta luego*, Kelly,' said Ramone, picking up his car keys. 'I'm going down to Westwood with Fartin' Martin here to look at that stuff in Westwood.'

'Kay,' said Kelly in a nasal Valley accent, and began to shuffle movie programs. Ramone whistled to his cat Lugosi and Lugosi jumped down straightaway and followed them out of the store.

*

The 'stuff in Westwood' proved to be disappointing. Two crushed and faded cocktail gowns that were supposed to have belonged to Marilyn Monroe. The nervy middle-aged woman who was selling them chain-smoked and paced up and down. 'They have stains on them,' she said at last, as if this were the selling point that was going to make all the difference.

'Stains?' asked Ramone, holding one of the gowns up.

'For goodness' sake, you know, *stains*,' the woman snapped back. 'Robert Kennedy.'

Martin, who was sitting back on the lounger watching Ramone at work, shook his head in disbelief. He couldn't conceive of anything more tasteless than trying to sell Marilyn Monroe's cocktail gowns with Robert Kennedy's stains on them.

Ramone dropped the gowns back on the chair. 'I'm sorry, I can't offer you anything for these. There's no authentication, nothing. They're different sizes, too. They could have belonged to two different people, neither one of whom was Marilyn.'

'You're doubting my word?' the woman said stiffly.

'That's not what I'm saying. All I'm saying is, thanks – but no thanks.'

They took a walk along the beach. There was a strong ocean breeze blowing and it ruffled their clothes. Lugosi followed them at a haughty distance, occasionally lifting his head to sniff the wind.

'I never knew cats liked the seashore,' Martin remarked.

'Oh, Lugosi loves it. All that fish, all those birds. He'd go swimming if he could find a costume the right size.'

Ramone took out a cheroot and lit it with a Zippo emblazoned with the name *Indiana Jones*, his hands cupped over the flame.

'How about that woman with the Marilyn Monroe dresses,' said Martin. 'Wasn't she something?'

'If they were genuine, I would have given her a hundred fifty apiece,' Ramone told him.

'How do you know they weren't?'

Ramone shook his head. 'You get an eye for it; a touch for

73

it. Marilyn never would've worn anything that looked like that. A *shmatteh*, that's what the Jewish people call dresses like that. And besides, there are no pictures of Marilyn wearing them, either of them, and if she *ever* wore two tight low-cut gowns, like that, don't you think that somebody would've taken pictures? She was a chubby broad, to say the least.'

When he saw Martin looking at him in surprise, he grinned and said, 'It's true! I can remember every Marilyn Monroe picture ever, in my head. And James Dean. And Jayne Mansfield. *And* what they were wearing.'

Martin said, 'I want you to come take a look at this boy in the mirror. I want you to tell me that it's Boofuls.'

Ramone blew out smoke. 'Pretty far-out shit, hunh?'

'You don't have to believe me until you see it for yourself.'

'I believe you!' Ramone replied, spreading his arms. 'Why shouldn't I believe you? I come from a very superstitious family.'

'I just don't know what to do,' said Martin. 'I mean, supposing it really is him? Supposing there's some way of getting him out of there?'

'Like the tennis ball, you mean? Well, I don't know. It's pretty far-out shit. But whatever happened, if you did it, if you got him out, you'd be sitting on some kind of a gold mine, hunh? You're the guy who wants to make a Boofuls musical, and what do you got? You got the actual Boofuls. And all this stuff about him being chopped up, well, they're going to have to forget that, aren't they, if he's all in one piece?'

'I guess so,' Martin agreed, a little unhappily. 'It was just the way that he tried to grab Emilio and pull him into the mirror – well, that scared me. It's possible that nothing would have happened . . . I mean, maybe this particular mirror has some kind of weird scientific property which allows objects to pass right through it. Maybe Emilio could have gone to play in mirrorland and come back whenever he felt like it.'

'Do you *really* think that's possible?' asked Ramone.

Martin shook his head. 'If the same thing happens to Emilio that happened to that ball . . . well, maybe he could get inside the mirror, but I'm not at all sure we'd ever get him out again.'

Ramone tossed away his cheroot and stood for a moment with his hands tucked into the pockets of his jeans, staring out at the ocean. 'You know I come down here every time I feel that life is terrible, that people are mean and small and bitter, that human ambition is just a crock of shit.'

He paused, watching the gray water glittering in the sunshine. 'And you know something?' he said. 'Looking out at all that infinity, looking out at all that water, all that distance, that does nothing for me, whatsoever. So the sea is big, so what, that doesn't make life any better.'

They drove back along Sunset in Ramone's patched-up Camaro, with Lugosi sitting primly in the back seat. Together, they sang two or three verses of 'Whistlin' Dixie'; and then fell silent.

'That's it, then,' said Martin, unlocking the sitting room door and ushering Ramone inside.

Ramone gave a soft whistle and padded toward the mirror on squeaking sneakers, holding Lugosi in his arms so that the cat's body hung down. 'That's some piece of glass. Nice frame, too. Who's the dude in the middle?'

'Pan, I think. Or Bacchus. One of those woodsy Roman gods.'

'He's a dead ringer for Charlton Heston, if you ask me. Do you think Charlton Heston ever posed for mirrors? You know, before he became famous?'

Ramone tentatively touched the mirror's surface, then stepped back. 'It's something, isn't it? What did she ask you for it?'

'Five hundred,' Martin lied.

'Well,' said Ramone, 'I think she took you. I wouldn't have paid more than two-fifty, two seventy-five. But it's a piece of glass, isn't it?'

'There's the ball,' said Martin, and pointed out the blue and white ball on the desk. Ramone glanced at it, then glanced at the tennis ball in the mirror.

'Now, that is what I call *extraño*,' said Ramone. He peered at the blue and white ball carefully, and then he said, 'Is it okay if I pick it up?'

'Sure. I've picked it up. It doesn't feel any different from any other kind of ball.'

Ramone threw the ball in the air and caught it, watching himself in the mirror with delight. 'How *about* that!' he said, laughing. 'In here I'm throwing a blue ball; in there I'm throwing a totally different ball.'

'Try throwing it at the mirror,' Martin suggested, walking across to the windowsill to get the bottle of wine. 'That's it, directly at the mirror.'

'Heyy . . .' said Ramone. 'I just thought of something. If this ball here isn't the same as the ball in the mirror, maybe that guy in the mirror who looks like me – well, maybe he isn't me. Maybe he's somebody who *looks* like me, okay, but isn't.'

Martin poured them each a glass of chardonnay. 'Why don't you ask him?' he suggested.

'Hee! Hee!' Ramone laughed; and then called to his reflection in the mirror. 'Hey, buddy, are you me, or are you just somebody pretending to be me? Because, let's be truthful here, you've got your right arm on your left side and your left arm on your right side, and I sure don't. Why don't you take down your pants and let's see that skull-and-crossbones tattoo, which side of your ass it's on?'

'You didn't tell me you had a skull-and-crossbones tattoo on your ass,' said Martin.

Ramone looked embarrassed. 'I don't either. I was joking, all right. But you say one word!'

'Anyway,' said Martin, 'try throwing the ball at the mirror. Not too hard. You don't want to break it.'

Winding his arm back, Ramone said, 'This is it! This is Rip Collins, just about to make the pitch of his whole career!'

'Just not too hard, okay?' Martin told him.

Ramone threw, and the ball smacked against the mirror. Lugosi the cat immediately jumped for it, dancing toward his own reflection. The blue and white ball bounced off the glass and rolled back into the room, but to Martin's horror, *Lugosi dived halfway into the mirror's surface right up to his middle, as if he had dived into water.*

It looked as if Lugosi had turned into an extraordinary headless beast with a tail at each end, and two pairs of hind legs that clawed and scratched and struggled against each other to get free.

'Get him out!' yelled Ramone, his voice white with terror. 'Martin – for God's sake – get him out!'

Martin scrambled down onto the floor and caught hold of Lugosi's narrow body. He could feel the cat's rib cage through his fur, feel his heart racing. Lugosi's hind legs lashed out wildly, and his claws scratched Martin all the way down the inside of his arm.

Ramone did what he could to keep Lugosi's legs from pedaling, while Martin tried to drag him out. But Martin could feel that same irresistible force that he had felt when he tackled Emilio: that same relentless sucking.

'Martin! Help him!' Ramone shouted. 'Holy shit, Martin – he's being pulled in!'

The force was too strong, too demanding. The cat's body was dragged through Martin's hands, inch by inch, even though he clung on so tightly that he was pulling out clumps of tabby fur. His body, his hind legs, his shuddering outstretched paws, all of them vanished one by one. His reflection shrank too – until at the very end there was nothing but a single dark furry caterpillar that appeared to be waving in midair, and that was the tip of his tail.

Then there was nothing at all, he was gone, and the surface of the mirror was flawless and bright.

Ramone was sweating, 'If I hadn't seen that – if I hadn't seen that, right there in front of me, with my own eyes! *Madre mia!*'

Martin stood up. His face in the mirror was gray, the color of newspaper. 'Ramone . . . I don't know what to say. I had no idea it was going to do that.'

'But it *pulled* him! It pulled him in!'

Ramone touched the surface of the mirror quickly as if he were touching a hotplate to make sure that it was switched on.

'Ramone –,' warned Martin, 'Christalmighty man, be careful. Supposing *you* got sucked in?'

Ramone's fright was fragmenting into grief and anger. 'Man – that's my *cat*! That's my fucking cat! Six years I've had that cat! I didn't love and feed and take care of that cat just to have some stupid mirror take him away! Some stupid *mirror*!'

Martin came over and gently gripped Ramone by the shoulders. 'Ramone – I'm sorry! If I'd have guessed what was going to happen –'

'Martin, am I blaming you?' Ramone fumed. 'I'm not blaming you, okay? It wasn't your fault! But I want my cat back! He went in the mirror, where is he?'

'Ramone, I really don't know. He's gone, I don't know how and I don't know where.'

Ramone stood up, his eyes staring. 'Well, there's got to be one way to find out, and that's to break this god-damned stupid mirror to pieces!'

'No!' shouted Martin. 'Ramone – listen – there's a boy in that mirror. For all we know, he's managed to stay alive some way – you know, by hiding in the mirror, or something. Listen, I don't understand any of it. But until I do – please, Ramone, don't touch that mirror. You don't know what the hell might happen – how many people might die.'

Ramone bit his lip for a moment and took three angry paces away from the mirror, and then three angry paces back again. 'Thass bullshit! Thass bullshit, Martin, and you know it! What do you care, how many people might die! What the hell just happened to Lugosi? Thass my *cat*!'

Martin didn't know what to say. Both of them were still shocked by Lugosi's hair-raising disappearance – into where? into what? It didn't make any sense. It wasn't even as if a mirrorland cat had jumped out to replace him, the way that Boofuls' blue and white ball had come bouncing out to replace Martin's tennis ball.

Martin had thought that he had discovered the mirror's logic; that an object could only pass through to the mirror-world if another object was sent back in return. But Lugosi had been sucked into the surface of the mirror and vanished utterly. And – judging from the way in which his hindquarters had struggled and his heart had been beating – it had been an agonizing and terrifying experience.

Ramone touched the surface of the mirror again; quickly, nervously, jerking his hand back.

'It can suck in a ball, it can suck in a cat. Do you really think it can suck in a man?'

'Ramone,' said Martin, 'that's an experiment I don't even want to think about trying.'

'We-e-ell, maybe; maybe not. But that's my cat in there. I mean he's *in* there some way. And all I want to do is get him out.'

'Wait,' Martin told him. 'I have an idea. Maybe I can get Boofuls to tell us.'

'Oh, man, Boofuls? You're cracked. Boofuls is dead, Boofuls is hamburger.'

'Yes, well, perhaps he is,' Martin replied trying not to sound too frosty about it. 'But his soul or his spirit or something of what he was is still here – still inside this mirror.'

'Oh, yeah? Where? I don't see any Boofuls. All I see is me and you and some stupid ball that's blue here and gray there, and that doesn't prove anything, and most of all it doesn't get Lugosi back.'

'Will you be patient?' Martin shouted at him.

'I don't want to be patient!' Ramone retorted. 'I didn't even want to come here in the first place!'

'Then go!' yelled Martin.

Ramone tugged open the door. He hesitated for a moment, but then he lowered his head, and turned away and said, 'Shit, man', and left. Martin stood in the sitting room, still breathless, still trembling, and heard Ramone take the stairs three and four at a time.

Then he went to the bathroom and stood over the basin for a long time, listening to his stomach growling. He didn't actually vomit, but he felt as though the inside of his mouth and throat were lined with grease.

Mr Capelli came up to his apartment at half past six that evening. Martin was typing away furiously at an episode of *As the World Turns*. Mr Capelli knocked on the sitting room door and then stepped in. He was wearing a dark three-piece suit, very formal, and some strong lavender-smelling cologne. He tugged at his cuffs, and cleared his throat, and nodded toward the mirror.

'You don't get rid of it?' he asked.

Martin stopped typing and turned around in his revolving chair. 'I'm sorry. Somebody's coming to pick it up first thing tomorrow morning. That was the earliest I could manage.'

Mr Capelli approached the mirror and straightened his black spotted necktie. Then, with the flat of his hand, he smoothed the hair on the back of his head.

'Going out tonight?' asked Martin, watching him, hoping he wouldn't step too close to the mirror.

Mr Capelli leaned forward and bared his teeth at his reflection. 'Twenty-one thousand dollars' worth of dental work,' he declared. 'Twenty-one thousand dollars! And what do you get? Teeth is all you get.'

Martin said, 'Thanks for keeping Emilio away.'

Mr Capelli turned around. 'Well, it wasn't easy. He said he wanted to play with your nephew.'

'Mr Capelli –'

'Don't say nothing,' said Mr Capelli, raising one hand. 'Whatever it is, I don't want to hear it.'

'Mr Capelli, I tried to explain to you yesterday – my nephew isn't here at all. The boy that Emilio was playing with was Boofuls.'

'Sure,' said Mr Capelli.

'Boofuls appeared in the mirror and Emilio saw him. He was as clear as you are. I saw him myself, with my own eyes.'

'Sure,' said Mr Capelli.

'You don't believe me,' said Martin. 'You don't believe me for one moment.'

'Sure I believe you,' Mr Capelli told him, his mouth taut. 'When I was a boy, my mother and father told me all kinds of stories about ghosts and monsters and things that stared at you out of mirrors. My father used to tell me one story, how he went past his parlor one night, and take a quick look at the mirror, and sitting at the dining table was six people dressed in black, with black veils over their heads, sitting silent, but only in the mirror.'

Martin looked back at Mr Capelli but didn't know what to say.

'I believe you,' said Mr Capelli. 'I believe you, but I don't want to hear nothing about it. I don't want to hear nothing about no other worlds, no mirror-people. Life is hard enough in this world, praise God.'

He turned vehemently back to the mirror. 'Every mirror is evil. Mirror's are for nothing but vanity, for look at your own face, and not the face of other people. This mirror has special evil. Tomorrow morning, you get rid of it. Otherwise, I'm sorry, you have to go.'

Martin nodded. 'All right, Mr Capelli. The guy's coming around at eleven.'

Actually, Martin had made no arrangements yet for getting rid of the mirror. He was simply stalling for time. If Boofuls was really inside it; and if Ramone's cat was inside it, too, he wanted to keep hold of it and make sure that it was safe. He had called Ramone to ask him if he would store the mirror at the Reel Thing for a while, but Ramone had still been out, and Kelly had told him that she didn't have the 'athaw'ty' to say yes.

Mr Capelli laid his hand on Martin's shoulder. 'You get rid of that mirror, understand but you make sure you don't break it, not in this house, anyway. Breaking a mirror like that, who knows what you're going to let out.'

'Sure thing, Mr Capelli,' said Martin. 'And – you know – have a good time.'

Mr Capelli looked down at his suit. Then he stared at Martin as if he had said something utterly insane. 'A good time? We're going to have dinner with my wife's sister.'

CHAPTER FOUR

An old college pal from Wisconsin called him just before seven: Dick Rasmussen, who used to date Jane's younger sister, Rita.

Dick had come to Los Angeles on business, selling luggage, and he insisted they meet for a drink and maybe dinner?

'Dick, I'm real busy. I'm working on *As the World Turns*.'

'You mean somebody actually sits down and *writes* that shit? I thought the actors made it up as they went along.'

Reluctantly, Martin agreed to meet Dick at eight o'clock at the Polo Lounge. 'I have to tell you, though, Dick, the only people who go to the Polo Lounge these days are tourists.'

'Martin, I'm under orders from the commandant. If I get back home and Nancy finds out I didn't go to the Polo Lounge, believe me, she's going to have my balls.'

'You married *Nancy?*'

'Not Nancy Untermeyer. Oh, no, no such luck. Nancy Brogan. You remember Nancy Brogan? Little blond girl, used to go around with that pig-faced fat girl, Phyllis whatever-her-name-was. Yeah, we got spliced! Two kids, now, boy and a girl. No – not Nancy Untermeyer, very regretfully. Do you remember the way Nancy Untermeyer used to play the cello in the school orchestra? Whee-oo. She used to look like she was screwing it.'

Reluctantly, Martin dressed in a clean blue shirt and put on his best and only white suit, and rubbed a scuff off his white Gucci sneakers with spit and a Kleenex. He made sure he locked the sitting room door before he left. He didn't want Emilio wandering up here while he was out. On the way out he passed a pink ten-speed bicycle parked against the hall stand: it belonged to Emilio's baby-sitter, Wanda.

His evening with Dick was just as bad as he had imagined it was going to be. Dick was energetic and loud and endlessly excited about Hollywood. He wore a small brown toupee to conceal his thinning crown and a red-and-green-plaid sports coat that might just as well have had 'Hayseed' embroidered on the back. Whenever anybody came into the Polo Lounge, he nudged Martin conspicuously and asked, 'Is that somebody? That isn't Katharine Ross, is it?'

Dick drank piñā coladas with paper parasols in them and ate the orange slices with noisy relish. 'This is the land of the orange, right? That isn't Warren Beatty, is it? I mean, you must know all of these people personally, right?'

'Well, I get to know one or two of them.'

Dick slapped him on the thigh. 'George Peppard! I'll bet you know George Peppard!'

An elegantly dressed woman at the next table turned around and gave them a cold, patronizing look. Martin flashed her his Quick Boyish Smile, but she didn't smile back. He felt more like an outsider than ever. He finished up his white-wine spritzer and listened to Dick jabbering and wondered glumly if Rubishness was contagious.

Dick insisted they go for dinner at the Brown Derby. The restaurant was almost empty, apart from a couple from Oregon who had come to Hollywood for a second honeymoon. '*We're* not on our second honeymoon, as you might have guessed,' Dick told the wine waiter, and slapped the table and laughed until he was red in the face.

It was midnight before Martin dropped Dick back at the Hyatt on Sunset. Dick wanted to have another drink, but Martin stayed in the car with the engine running. 'Dick – I have to work. This may be magic land to you, but to me it's the salt mines. So do me a favor, will you, have a safe journey home, and give Nancy a kiss for me, and good night.'

'I loved you, you know,' Dick told him, leaning over the side of the Mustang with his eyes boiled and his toupee crooked. He breathed wine and rum straight into Martin's face. 'I loved you like a fucking brother.'

'Good night, Dick,' Martin told him, and clasped his hand for the tenth time, and at last managed to drive away.

'Fartin' Martin!' Dick shouted out as he teetered on the

sidewalk outside the hotel. 'That's what they always called you! Heeyoo! Far-Tin Mar-Tin!'

'Dick the Prick,' Martin replied under his breath as the traffic signals at Sierra Bonita intersection turned green, and he turned left on squealing tires toward Franklin Avenue.

When he let himself back into the house, Wanda's bicycle was still parked in the hallway, and he tripped over it in the darkness, catching his shin on the pedal. 'Goddamn it!' he hissed at it, and would have kicked it if the landing light hadn't been suddenly switched on, and Wanda hadn't appeared.

'Martin?' she called. 'Is that you?'

Martin climbed the stairs. 'It is I, fair Wanda, and the pedal of your bicycle has just added injury to the most insulting evening of my entire adult life.'

Wanda was a short blond girl of seventeen. She was still plump with puppy fat, but her face was pretty, like a little painted *matrioshka* doll, with rosy cheeks and China-blue eyes. She was wearing a pink jogging suit with a printed picture of Bruce Springsteen on the front, and pink sneakers. Oddly, she was carrying a saucer half filled with milk.

'Where are you going with that?' Martin asked her.

'Your cat was crying; I thought it might be hungry.'

Martin glanced up toward the door of his apartment. 'My cat?' he said in a hollow voice.

'It's been crying for hours; ever since you left, almost.'

Martin took a breath. Thank God for that, Lugosi must have reappeared. At least Ramone and he could be friends again. 'Come on,' he told Wanda, and took the saucer from her, and led the way upstairs. 'You couldn't have gotten in, anyway, the door's locked.'

'I don't mind cat-sitting as well as baby-sitting,' Wanda told him. 'I love cats.'

Martin unlocked the apartment door. 'This cat doesn't belong to me. It just decided to pay me a visit this afternoon, and not to leave.' He switched on the light in the hallway. 'It's called Lugosi – you know, after Bela Lugosi, who played Dracula. Believe me, it's well named.'

84

He opened the sitting room door. 'Lugosi! Your uncle Martin's home!'

He reached around to switch on the light, but the bulb popped instantly, and the room remained dark. 'Damn it,' said Martin. 'That's about the fifth bulb in five weeks. They don't make anything the way they used to. Hold on, I'll switch on the desk lamp.'

He crossed the room; and his dark reflection crossed the room toward him. 'Mr and Mrs Capelli are late,' he remarked to Wanda as he reached over to find the desk-lamp switch.

'It's an anniversary or something,' Wanda told him. 'They said they wouldn't get back until one o'clock.'

'You're not going to cycle home at one o'clock?' Martin asked her.

He tried the desk lamp, but that didn't work, either. 'Would you believe it? This one's gone, too. Wanda –'

He was about to ask her to go to the kitchen and bring him two new light bulbs when he heard a low, guttural, hissing sound. He froze, still holding the saucer of milk.

'Lugosi?' he called.

'Was that him?' asked Wanda, peering into the shadowy room. 'He sure sounded weird.'

Martin paused for a moment, listening. Then he heard the scratching of claws on the wood-block floor, and that same hissing sound.

'Lugosi, it's only me. It's your uncle Martin. Come on, chum. Wanda's brought you some milk; some luvvy-wuvvy nonradioactive low-fat enriched-calcium milk.'

There was a very long silence. Wanda said, 'What's his name? Lugosi?'

'That's right. Why don't you try calling him?'

'Okay,' said Wanda. 'Lugosi! Lugosi! Here, pussy-pussy-pussy! Come on, Lugosi!'

Martin set the saucer of milk down on the desk. There was something about Lugosi's utter silence that he didn't like. He strained his eyes to see through the shadows – looking for anything, a paw, a tail, a reflection of yellow feline eye. Maybe the cat's experience in the mirror had traumatized it; maybe it was hurt. He looked and he listened but for one suspended heart-beat after another the room was silent, except for the muffled growling and grinding of greater Los Angeles, outside the window in the California night.

'Here, Lugosi!' called Wanda. 'Here, pussy-pussy!'

It was then that Martin heard the faint *thump-thump-thump* of a furry tail on the floor, and the low death-rattle sound of a cat purring.

'Sounds like he's under the desk someplace,' he told Wanda, and hunkered down to take a look.

Thump, thump, thump. Prrrrrr-prrrrrr-prrrrrr.

'Lugosi?' he asked, and his voice was clogged with phlegm.

Two eyes opened in the darkness. Two eyes that burned incandescent blue, like the flames of welding torches.

'Lugosi?' asked Martin, although this time it was scarcely a question at all.

Something hard and vicious came flying out from under the desk and landed directly in his face, knocking him backwards onto the floor. He was so surprised that he didn't even shout out, but Wanda did – a startled wail, and then a piercing scream.

He felt claws tearing at his neck; claws tearing at his cheeks. His mouth was gagged with soft, fetid fur.

Panicking, he seized the cat's body in both hands and tried to drag it away from his face, but its claws were hooked into his ears and his scalp, and he couldn't get it free.

'Aaahh!' he heard himself shouting. 'Wanda, help me! Wanda!'

Wanda came blustering into the room and slapped at the cat, but didn't know what else to do. Martin rolled over and over on the floor, tipping over his chair with his pedaling legs, colliding against his desk; but the cat clung viciously to his head, lacerating his face with claws that felt like whips made out of razor wire.

My eyes! thought Martin in terror. *It's trying to claw out my eyes!*

He managed to force his left hand underneath the cat's scrabbling body and cover his face. He could taste blood and choking fur. With his right hand, he groped for his desk, missed it, then found it, and dragged open the bottom drawer

with a crash. His hand plunged into it, searching for anything –
a knife, a hammer, a pair of pliers.

His fingers closed around the handle of a large screwdriver –
the same one he had used to fix the mirror to the sitting room
wall. Grunting, struggling, he raised the screwdriver and
jabbed it into the cat's body: once, twice, three times – blunt-
edged metal into soft thrashing fur. The third time, the cat
spat like a serpent and tore at him wildly, and so he stabbed it
again. It uttered a long, harsh scream that was like nothing
that Martin had ever heard in his life before.

The cat sprang off him, careened sideways against the wall,
then flew at Wanda, tearing at her legs. Wanda screamed and
fell. The cat instantly leaped onto her face and ripped at one
side of it with an audible crackle of skin and muscle.

But Martin was up on his feet now. Coughing, stumbling,
he seized hold of the cat by the scruff of its neck, and lifted it
up and held it high, even though it was flailing and writhing
like a maggot on a fishhook, and scrabbling furiously at his
hand with its hind legs.

Martin rammed the cat's head against the wall, burying his
thumb into its neck so that it cackled for air. Its eyes bulged –
those flaring blue eyes – and it stretched its mouth open so
wide in strangulated hatred that it dislocated its jaw.

Wanda cried out, '*No!*' but Martin drew back his arm and
then crunched the screwdriver straight through the cat's chest
and pinned it to the wall.

He stepped back, staggered back. The cat didn't scream. It
twisted and struggled and swung from side to side, staring at
him, staring at him, as if it didn't mind dying, impaled on this
screwdriver, provided it was sure that Martin would soon die,
too.

Wanda began to sob hysterically. Martin said, 'Come on,
come on, it's all over now. The cat went crazy, that's all. It just
went crazy.'

He led her toward the door, back to the Capellis' apartment. He shielded her face as they passed the cat. It was still
alive, bubbling blood from its stretched-open mouth, still staring, still trying to swing itself free.

They opened the door. Wanda leaned against the wall, white

and shivering, her forehead and her upper lip beaded with perspiration, her hand pressed against her lacerated cheek. 'I'm sorry,' she said, 'I have to be sick,' and she went off to the bathroom. Martin stood light-headed in the hallway, swaying from side to side, and heard her regurgitate the chicken-and-stuffing frozen dinner that the Capellis had left her.

Emilio had heard the screaming and the banging around upstairs, and he was sitting up in his bed wide awake. 'Boy,' he said, impressed, when Martin came into his bedroom and switched on the light. 'What happened to *you*?'

'I had a fight,' Martin told him. 'Listen – you'd better get back to sleep. Your grandparents will be home soon.'

'Who did you fight with?' Emilio wanted to know. 'Was it a ninja? Boy, I'll bet you got those cuts from a ninja throwing-star.'

'It was a cat, as a matter of fact,' Martin told him. He sat down on the end of Emilio's bed and dabbed at his face with his handkerchief. He was amazed by the amount of deep red blood that spattered all over it. 'Am I hurt that bad?' he asked Emilio, and stood up to look in his He-Man mirror.

His face was appalling; like a newsreel photograph of somebody who had just been blown up by a terrorist bomb. His eyes were puffy, his cheeks were swollen, his whole face was crisscrossed with deep scratches. His ears were torn, and his left earlobe was almost hanging off, and dangled when he moved his head.

'You'd better get to the hospital,' said Emilio sensibly.

Martin saw this grotesque, bloodied face nod back at him. 'Yes,' he said. 'A-one idea.' He couldn't understand why it didn't hurt more than it did, or why he was able to walk around and talk so sensibly when he looked so terrible.

Wanda came into the room, still white, pressing a blood-stained pad of toilet tissue to her lacerated cheek. 'Oh, my God,' she said, and her eyes were filled with tears. 'I never knew a cat to do anything like that.'

Martin dabbed at his face with his handkerchief. 'I'm going down to the hospital, okay? I don't want to wind up like Van Gogh, with only one ear. Wanda – will you be all right?'

'I guess so,' she said. 'I'll call up my pop and tell him what's happened.'

Martin lifted the tissue away from her face and examined her scratches. They were deep, but quite clean, and he hoped for everyone's sake that they wouldn't scar. He didn't relish the idea of being sued by Wanda's parents.

'Come on, you'll be okay,' he told her, although he could feel her trembling through her jogging suit; that unstoppable shaking of the shocked, and the truly afraid.

He left the Capellis' apartment and went upstairs to get his car keys. When he reached the landing, he hesitated. Supposing the cat had worked itself free? Supposing he opened the front door and it came flying out at him, just as ferociously as it had before? He wiped his lips with the back of his hand, smearing his knuckles with blood and saliva. Then he cautiously reached out his hand and eased the door open.

The cat was hanging exactly where he had impaled it, its tail and its hind legs dangling, its front paws cocked, its flat anvil-shaped head lolling to one side. Dark rivulets of blood ran down the wall beneath it.

Martin tiptoed along the hallway until he was almost opposite it. Its eyes were closed, its mouth was silently snarling open. It didn't look at all like Lugosi. It was a big brindled tom, with a heavy shaggy body and vicious claws. It stank of cat's urine and some other unutterable sourness that Martin couldn't even begin to recognize.

'You miserable sonofabitch,' he told it between puffed-up lips. The cat had even managed to scratch his tongue.

He went into the sitting room. He tried the light switch again, and this time, unaccountably, it worked. He found his car keys gleaming under the desk. He made a point of not looking in the mirror. If everything in the mirror was the same as it was in here, then that was fine. If it wasn't, then he didn't want to know. Not now, not just yet. His ear was beginning to throb and his face felt as if it was already swollen up to three times its normal size.

He went back into the hallway. He wondered what he ought to do with the cat's body. He couldn't just leave it hanging there, but now that the adrenaline had all drained out of him, he found the thought of touching it almost too repulsive to think about.

But supposing Mr Capelli came looking for him, when he was down at the hospital, and found it? There wouldn't be any question about it then. Immediate eviction – futon, desk and typewriter straight out onto the street, no argument, so sue me.

In the kitchen drawer, Martin found a large green trash bag. He went back out to the hallway, rolled up the trash bag like a giant condom, and arranged it under the place where the cat was hanging. His idea was to yank out the screwdriver, whereupon the cat's body would drop neatly into the trash bag. He could then unroll the trash bag, twist-tie the top, and heave it out of his car in some dark and lonely stretch of the freeway.

He stood in front of the cat's body for a long time before he could summon up the courage to take hold of the screwdriver handle. *What's the matter with you, wimp? It's only a cat, and a dead cat at that.*

What's the matter? I'm scared shitless, that's what's the matter. I mean – where did it come from, this cat? The windows were locked, the door was locked, nobody else had a key. Where the hell did it come from, except out of the mirror?

Mr Capelli's right. That mirror's driving you bananas. Get rid of it, before something comes shimmering out of it that gets rid of you.

He grasped the screwdriver handle tightly and tugged. Nothing happened. The blade was jammed too tight. *God almighty*, he thought, *I must have had the strength of ten men to dig this into the wall. But look at me now. Hundred-and-sixty-pound weakling.*

He placed the flat of his left hand firmly against the plaster, readjusted his grip on the screwdriver handle with his right hand, and tugged again.

The result was instantaneous. The cat's eyes flared open, and it screamed at him. He screamed, too, just as loudly.

The cat dropped. Martin fell backward, jarring his back against the handle of his bedroom door. But as quickly as he could, he bundled the green plastic around the writhing animal and twisted the top of the bag tight.

'Oh God, please make it die,' he gibbered. 'Oh God, oh God, please make it die.'

But the cat twisted and turned and ripped furiously and noisily at the plastic with its claws, screaming with a cry like a tortured baby.

Martin picked up the screwdriver, but dropped it again. It rolled across the floor, out of his reach. The cat savaged a long rent in the plastic. He saw its hate-filled face, with its mouth still stretched wide. He saw its eyes burning.

Crying out with effort, he lifted up the bag and twisted it tighter to keep the cat imprisoned inside it. Then he swung it around his head, once, twice, like a hammer thrower, and smashed it as hard as he could against the wall – and then smashed it again, and again, and again.

When the animal seemed to have stopped struggling, he dropped the bag onto the floor, scooped up his screwdriver, and crunched the blade into the cat's body over and over again, so many times that he completely lost count. Then he knelt back on his heels, gasping for breath. 'Oh, shit,' he panted. 'Oh, shit.'

He dragged the bag to the front door. It seemed impossibly heavy, just for a cat. But just as he was about to open up the door and heave the bag out, he heard voices. Italian voices, amplified with wine and indignation. The Capellis had arrived home.

'What's that? A cat? He doesn't have no cat! He's not allowed no cat! Terms of the lease! You need a doctor, you know that? Look, you're bleeding! What's your father going to say? Where's Martin? What do you mean, he's worse? What could be worse?'

Martin hesitated: then, with a rustling plasticky noise, he dragged the bag through to the kitchen, leaving calligraphic tracks of blood across the tiles. He took the lid off the big gray plastic trash bin and dropped the cat's body inside. He mopped up the floor with his squeegee mop. He felt like a murderer as he squeezed blood-streaked water into the sink. God, he thought, what was it like when you hacked up a human being?

How did you ever get rid of the blood? The blood swirled around the sink like the shower stall in *Psycho*.

Mr Capelli appeared at the door, flushed, sweating, smelling of brandy. 'Martin?' he shouted; then, when Martin turned around, 'My God! Look at you? What are you doing? My God!'

Martin leaned against the wall and gave Mr Capelli a twist of his mouth that was intended to be a smile. 'I'm okay, Mr Capelli, I'm fine. I was just looking for my car keys – you know, to drive myself down to the hospital.'

Mr Capelli frowned at him and then held out his hands. Martin reached out to take hold of them, but somehow they weren't really there, and everything was black, and none of this really mattered, anyway.

He fell flat on his face on the kitchen floor, and he was lucky not to break his nose. Mr Capelli dithered for a moment and then called down the stairs, 'Wanda! Call for an ambulance! Tell them *pronto!*'

He woke up and the first thing that he could hear was clicking. *Clickety-click; clickety-clack*; pause *clickety-click; clickety-clack*. He lifted his head, and there was Ramone, sitting cross-legged on one of those uncomfortable hospital chairs, furiously working at a Rubik's Magic. The blinds were closed, so that the room was very dim, although he could hear traffic and noise and all the sounds of a busy day. There were flowers everywhere, roses and orchids and huge apricot-colored daisies; and a blowfly was tapping against the window. He tried to speak, but his mouth felt as though it were fifty times the normal size, and he couldn't remember what you had to do to form words.

'Mamown . . .' he blurred. 'Mamown . . .'

Ramone turned his head and peered at him. 'Hey, man! You're still alive and kicking!' He put down his Rubik's Magic and came across to the bed. His black face loomed over Martin like a bulging-eyed fish looking out of an aquarium. 'We all thought you was definitely ready for the coma room – you know, where you don't wake up, so they cut your legs off and donate them to some rich South American rumba dancer with leg cancer.'

'Can you see my legs dancing the rumba?' croaked Martin.

Ramone took hold of his hand and squeezed it. 'Guess not, brother, but good to see you're alive. How do you feel?'

Martin tried to lift his head, but his scalp felt as if it had been sewn to the pillow. 'Sore,' he said. Then, 'Jesus.'

'Hey – Mr Caparooparelli told me all about that *cat*,' said Ramone. 'That was weird, man, that was definitely far out.'

Martin asked, 'Could you pour me some water? I can hardly swallow.'

Ramone noisily poured him a large glass of Perrier. 'It's not surprising you feel like that. It's the anesthetic, always makes you feel like shit. Remember when I totaled that Thunderbird? I was under for four hours, came out feeling like shit.'

Martin drank, and then said, 'How long was I . . .?'

'Two and a half hours, man. They gave you thirty-eight stitches.'

'Jesus,' said Martin. He felt sore and swollen and inflated. He knew that he ought to be worried, too, and working on something or other – some TV script – but he was too drowsy to remember what it was.

'Mr Caparoopadoopa got rid of the cat,' said Ramone. 'Dropped it in the trash outside the supermarket. Let's just hope the good old Humane Society doesn't hunt him down.'

'The cat . . . came through the mirror . . .' said Martin in a blurred voice. 'Must have. *Must* have. No other way. Doors locked, windows locked.'

'You truly think it came out of the *mirror*?' Ramone asked him. He added, in the Mr T accent that both he and Martin could mimic, 'Now, you listen here, suckah, I've had enough of this jibbah-jabbuh.'

'But it's just like I said before,' Martin insisted. 'One for one. Tit for tat, cat for cat. Balance. Lugosi went into the mirror, and sooner or later some other poor cat had to come out.'

'But that kitty cat wasn't anything *like* Lugosi.'

'Doesn't matter,' Martin told him. 'The tennis ball and the rubber ball – they were just as – what do you call it? They were just as dissimilar.'

'Dissimilar, right,' agreed Ramone, 'dis-simil-ah,' and

nodded; but then said, 'What happens now? I mean you killed that cat, right? Does that mean Lugosi was killed in the mirrorland, or what? Is he still alive, or dead, or what?'

'That's just the question I've been asking,' said Martin. 'Not just about Lugosi, but Boofuls, too.'

Ramone picked up his Rubik's Magic and flicked it a few times. 'Oh, well, Boofuls, yeah. I haven't had the pleasure yet. If it *is* a pleasure.'

Martin drank a little more water. Then he managed to lift himself up onto his elbows. 'What time is it?'

'Three o'clock in the afternoon.'

'I have to get out of here.'

Ramone pushed him back onto the pillow. 'You sure as hell don't. You have to stay here one more night, *compadre*, for observation. That's what they said. It's a good thing you got medical insurance.'

'But the mirror.'

'What about the jive mirror?'

'Mr Capelli said he wanted it out. And not only that, he wanted it out by tonight. Supposing he does something lunatic, like smash it up or throw it on the dump? What's going to happen to Lugosi then? Or Boofuls, come to that?'

Ramone said, 'You don't have to worry yourself about that, man. I already took care of that. I told Mr Capacloopi that I was going to take the mirror off of your hands. I'm supposed to collect it later this afternoon and store it down at The Reel Thing.'

'Will you do that?' asked Martin with relief.

'Sure I'll do it. That's unless some cat-out-of-hell comes jumping out of it and tries the same kind of number on *me* that it did on *you*.'

Martin reached out his hand. 'You're a pal, Perez.'

'Well, you're all heart, Mart.'

Martin lay back and thought for a while, and then he said, 'Do you know something? What we need is a medium.'

'A medium what?' asked Ramone.

'I mean a medium medium. A clairvoyant. Somebody who can get in contact with the spirits.'

'Are you pulling my leg?'

'No,' Martin told him, 'I'm serious. It seems to me that this mirror is acting like some kind of *gateway*, do you know what I mean, between the real world and the spirit world. You can't tell me that Boofuls isn't a spirit, can you? And these mediums – they should be used to handling this kind of thing, shouldn't they? Like when they talk to the spirits, they create their own way through to the other side, right? I would have thought that any medium worth his money would jump at the chance of talking to the spirits the same way that Emilio talks to Boofuls. I mean to see the spirit as clearly as your hand in front of your face, that's something else.'

'Seeing your favourite cat being swallowed up is something else, too,' Ramone complained. '*And* seeing your main man looking like he's just come out of the ring with Ivan Drago. "*You will lose*,"' he said, imitating the Russian boxer in *Rocky IV*.

'Do you know anybody who's into that kind of thing?' said Martin.

Ramone shook his head. 'Not me. But I know somebody who might know. One of my customers is Elmore Sweet – you know, the pianist. Liberace without the restraint. His mother died about two or three years ago, but every time he comes in he tells me that he's been rapping with Momsy about this or that. I used to think he'd lost his marbles at first, but then Dorothy Dunkley told me that he *gets in touch*, you know, with séances and everything.'

'Good,' said Martin. 'So why don't you call him and ask him the name of his medium.'

'I'll try.'

There was a longer pause. Ramone checked his Spiro Agnew wristwatch. 'Guess it's time I went back to the store. Kelly's okay, but she can be kind of remote. Also, she doesn't believe in responsibility. It's something to do with this sect she's gotten into. The Maharishi Nerdbrain or something.'

'Take care,' said Martin. 'And thanks for looking after the mirror for me.'

'It's not for you, my friend. It's for Lugosi. Wherever the poor bastard may be.'

*

Martin spent a bad night at the hospital. The nurse had given him a sedative to help him sleep, and for three or four hours he slept as heavily as a lumberjack: but all the time his mind was alive with the most vivid and terrifying nightmares. He saw Boofuls – or something he thought was Boofuls – right at the very end of a long tunnel of mirrors. Just an arm, just a leg, just a fleeting glimpse; and then an echo of laughter that sounded melodious at first, and then rang as harshly as a butcher's knife on a butcher's steel.

'*Pickle-nearest-the-wind,*' somebody whispered, so close and so distinct that he opened his eyes and looked around the room. '*Pickle-nearest-the-wind.*'

Then he was running across a wide, well-mowed lawn, trying to catch up with a scampering boy dressed in lemon yellow. The day was bright. The boy was laughing. But then the boy disappeared behind a long row of cypress bushes; and a cloud dragged its gray skirts over the sun; and the laughter stopped.

Martin walked along the row of cypress bushes, slowly at first. 'Boofuls?' he called. 'Boofuls?'

He started to jog, and then to run. 'Boofuls, where are you? Boofuls!'

'*Pickle-nearest-the-wind,*' somebody whispered, and then again, faster, like a train gathering momentum. '*Pickle-nearest-the-wind.*'

He ran even harder. He was terrified now. Something burst out of the cypress bushes right behind him and came running after him, just as fast, faster. He turned wild-eyed to see what it was, and it was a small boy, dressed in lemon yellow, but his face was the gilded face of Pan, snarling at him.

He stumbled, fell, rolled over; and then he woke up in bed sweating and clutching the bed rails. The nightmare garden faded; the cypresses were folded up like dark green tents and hurried away; the gilded face gleamed with momentary wickedness and then vanished.

He switched on his bedside light. Outside his door, two nurses and an orderly were loudly discussing next week's Hospital Hootenanny. Sirens wailed down by the casualty department as the victims of the night's violence were hurried in. Tragedy didn't sleep; anger didn't sleep; junkies and hookers didn't sleep; and neither did knives.

He called for the nurse. Nurse Newton opened his door; a huge black woman with an irrepressible smile who reassured him more than all the other nurses put together. 'What is it now, Mr Willy-ams?'

'Do you think you could bring me a bottle of red wine? It's the only thing that gets me to sleep.'

'Red wine, Mr Willy-ams? That's against regulations. And besides, you're up to your ears in sedatives.'

'Nurse, I need some sleep.'

Nurse Newton came over, took his temperature, and felt his pulse. 'You're cold,' she remarked, frowning. 'How come you're so cold?'

'Nightmares,' he said.

'Nightmares? Now, why should a big grown-up man like you have nightmares?'

Martin said, 'God knows. I don't.'

'Well, what are they about, these nightmares?'

'You're going to think I'm bananas.'

Nurse Newton leaned over him and examined the dressings on his ear. 'I'm a nurse, Mr Willy-ams. I'm paid to take care of people, not to make judgments about their mental health. Mind you, I might think differently about you in my spare time.'

Martin winced as she turned his head to one side. 'Did you ever hear about a little boy called Boofuls?' he asked her. 'He was a child star, back in the thirties.'

Nurse Newton stared at him in surprise. 'Why, what makes you ask that?'

'I just wanted to know, that's all.'

'Well, of *course* I heard about Boofuls. Everybody knows about Boofuls here at the Sisters of Mercy.'

Martin tried to sit up, but Nurse Newton pushed him back down again. 'You stay put. You're not well enough to start hopping around.'

'But what's so special about the Sisters of Mercy? How come everybody *here* knows about Boofuls?'

Nurse Newton took out his thermometer and frowned at it.

'There's a kind of spooky story about him, that's why. They brought his grandmother here, the evening she killed him.'

'That's right. I mean – *I* know that, because I've been making a special study of Boofuls. But how come *you* know that, too?'

Nurse Newton smiled. 'It's because of the spooky story, that's why. They tell it to all the nurses and the interns. Usually at the Christmas party, you know, at midnight, when it's all dark and there's just candles.'

Martin said, 'I thought I knew everything about Boofuls that it was possible to know. But I never heard any stories connected with the Sisters of Mercy.'

Nurse Newton lifted her head and half closed her eyes, and said, 'What was that song? "*Surrr . . . wannee Song! Suwannee Song! You can* blow *your flute and you can* bang *your drum and you can* march *along!*" That always used to make me cry when I was a child.'

Martin nodded. 'He was amazing, that little boy.'

'But spooky,' Nurse Newton added, lifting one finger.

'Can you tell me about it?' Martin asked her.

She winked. 'You've been having nightmares about him. Do you think I should?'

'Nurse – listen – I'm the world's expert on Boofuls. If there's something about Boofuls that I don't know –!'

Nurse Newton shook the mercury back down her thermometer with three decisive flicks of her wrist. 'Well . . .' she confessed, 'don't tell any of the hospital administrators that I told you this. I might get myself into big trouble. The board don't want the paying patients getting hysterical; and, believe me, if you told this story to some of the banana trucks on this floor, they would. Get hysterical, I mean.'

She jotted a note on Martin's chart and then sniffed and shook her head. 'Besides,' she said, 'you shouldn't speak ill of the dead, that's what my mamma always used to tell me. Someone who's dead can't defend themselves.'

'Supposing I take you to dinner,' Martin coaxed her.

Nurse Newton whacked the side of her thigh in hilarity. '*You* – take *me* for dinner! With all those bandages on your face? Talk about the Invisible Man meets Winifred Atwell! Besides, I'd *eat* you for dinner!'

'Supposing I arrange for you to meet Mr T, in person,' said Martin much more subtly. 'I write for the *A-Team*. You could meet him in person. I don't know – lunch, dinner. Maybe a little dancing later.'

Nurse Newton stared at him narrowly. 'You could do that?'

'Of course I could do that! I've known him for years. Mr T and I, we're like this!' and he held up two intertwined fingers.

'You're not fooling?'

'Cross my heart and hope to die.'

'You shouldn't say that. Nobody should hope to die. But could you do that? Me and Mr T?'

Martin nodded. 'You and Mr T. Just say the word.'

Nurse Newton glanced over her shoulder, almost as though she expected the hospital governors to be standing right behind her. 'Well,' she said quietly, 'I wasn't even born when this happened, don't you forget, so no smart remarks.'

'It was 1939,' said Martin. 'August 1939.'

Nurse Newton nodded. 'Some of the older staff can still remember it. Dr Rice remembers it, he was an intern in those days; and Sister Boniface remembers it, too. Like I say, they used to tell us all about it at the Christmas party. I guess it was just a ghost story. But they used to sound so serious, you couldn't help believing it, you know? And they made us all promise not to say nothing to nobody, never. Maybe they were worried about libel or something.'

Martin said, 'I don't think you have to worry about libel. You can't libel the dead, and Boofuls has been dead for a very long time.'

The nurse shrugged. 'Hmh, that didn't seem to make too much difference. His being dead, I mean.'

'What do you mean by that?' asked Martin.

'Oh, come on, now,' said Nurse Newton. 'It's nothing but a story, really. Every hospital has its spooky stories. There's a lot of stress in hospitals. Lot of *death*, too.'

'Story or not, I'd like to hear it.'

Nurse Newton went over to the door, listened for a moment, and then closed it tight. She came tippy-toeing back over to the bed. 'It was just after Boofuls was found dead,' she whispered. 'The police had cut his grandmother down – you know she tried to hang herself? – and brought her here. They thought she was dead, and Dr Rice said they should have let her die, because her neck was broken, and her throat was so bruised and swollen that she could barely speak. But she was still alive; and I guess they thought they might have a million-in-one chance of saving her.'

She hesitated and smiled. 'Boofuls, of course – they took him straight to the mortuary. There was nothing else that anyone could do. Can you imagine trying to sew him all back together? Dr Rice said he was chopped up into two hundred and eleven separate pieces. The coroner had to count them all; and there were still bits of him they couldn't even find. Dr Rice said that it was a joke for months in the hospital commissary – anytime somebody found a bone in their pork chop, they'd pick it up on the end of their fork and say, "Hello, piece number two hundred and twelve!" Well, you know what doctors are. Doctors have the sickest sense of humor of anybody.'

'Boofuls' grandmother didn't say anything before she died?' asked Martin. 'I mean – the police say that she didn't, but maybe one of the nurses heard her.'

Nurse Newton shook her head. 'She died pretty soon after they brought her into the hospital; that's what Sister Boniface said, and she was sitting beside her when she died. I don't think she said anything at all, except she called out a couple of times for Boofuls.'

'So what's this spooky story?' asked Martin.

'Listen, mister – three nurses and two doctors all saw Boofuls walking around the hospital that night calling for his grandma. "*Grandma! Grandma! Where are you?*"'

'What do you mean – *after* he was supposed to be dead? After he was chopped up into two hundred eleven pieces?'

Nurse Newton nodded. 'That's what's so spooky. Isn't that spooky?'

Martin considered it. 'Yes,' he said. 'That's spooky. But didn't any of them report it? Didn't they tell the newspapers, or the police, or the hospital authorities?'

'Would you?' asked Nurse Newton.

Martin patted his bandages. 'No,' he admitted. 'I guess not.'

Nurse Newton leaned forward and plumped up Martin's pillows. 'Of course, what was spookiest of all was that every time one of the nurses or the doctors caught sight of him, they'd go after him – you know, imagining that he was a real boy – but every time they got to where he was at, they realized that he wasn't there at all. What they could see was just a reflection in one of the mirrors at the end of the corridors.'

This time, Martin sat bolt upright. 'They saw Boofuls in the *mirrors?*'

'Hey, now, calm down,' Nurse Newton urged him. 'You don't want to go getting yourself so waxed up. You'll split your stitches.'

'They saw Boofuls in the mirrors – nowhere else?'

'Well, that's right, that's what Dr Rice says; and he was one of the doctors who saw it. But you're not supposed to know about this. It's just one of those little bits of hospital history, you know? Like, Ripley's Believe It or Not.'

Martin swung his legs out of bed. 'I have to talk to this Dr Rice. Can you find him for me?'

'Come on, honky, this is the middle of the night. Dr Rice is at home, getting his ugly-sleep. And you need yours, too. Now, you just get yourself back in that bed before I do you a physical injury they'll *never* be able to stitch together.'

Martin's heart was racing. 'Listen,' he said, 'I'll get back into bed on one condition – that as soon as Dr Rice gets here in the morning, he comes in to see me. Now, is that a promise?'

'Mr Willy-ams, I can't promise anything like that.'

'Then so help me God, I'll scream. I'll scream so loud that the whole goddamned hospital will wake up.'

'My goodness, Felicity-Ann!' said Nurse Newton. 'Aren't you the fierce person? But all right, I'll go right down to Dr Rice's office now, and I'll leave him a message. He doesn't come in till eleven o'clock, he only does consultancy these days. But I'll do my best to get him up here right away.'

'Nurse Newton, you're an angel.'

Nurse Newton forced him back onto the pillow. 'I am not an angel, Mr Willy-ams. I am a *nurse*.'

Martin dozed for the rest of the night. His nightmares rushed through his head like a carousel that had broken away from its moorings; dark and urgent, wild and clamorous, the carnival rides of the mind.

He dreamed that he was running down a long sliding corridor; and at the very end of the corridor stood Boofuls, smiling and innocent. As he approached, however, Boofuls' head began to revolve on his neck, slowly at first, with a low grating noise, then faster and faster, until it began to spray out blood. A fine drizzle of gore.

Martin shouted out, and woke up; or thought he had woken up. He sat up in bed, listening. He could hear someone whispering outside the door of his hospital room. '*Pickle-di-pickle-di-pickle-di-pickle.*'

He stayed where he was, listening, sweating. Then he climbed out of bed and glided toward the door with his hand outstretched. '*Pickle-nearest-the-wind,*' giggled the voice outside in the corridor.

Slowly fearfully, he turned the handle and opened the door. There was nobody there; only the black, echoing corridor, only the distant whooping of sirens. Tragedy never sleeps, knives never sleep. '*Martin,*' whispered the tiny wee voice. '*Come on, Martin, don't be afraid. Why are you afraid, Martin?*'

He stepped out into the corridor. At the very far end, he saw Boofuls. Small and smiling, sweet as candy, sugar-dandy, but in some peculiar way more dwarflike and crunched up than he had appeared in the mirror in Martin's sitting room. Boofuls looked white; so white that his face could have been poured out of alabaster.

'*Are you afraid, Martin?*' he whispered. His voice and his lips didn't seem to synchronize, like a badly dubbed film. He stretched out his arms, a young messiah. '*You don't have to be afraid of anything.*'

It was then that Martin realized that Boofuls wasn't standing on the floor at all, but was suspended halfway between the floor and the ceiling. Martin's hair prickled in fear, but something compelled him to start running toward Boofuls, to catch him, to prove at last that he was nothing more than a memory.

Boofuls laughed as Martin waded toward him through the treacle of his nightmare. A sweet, high laugh that echoed and reechoed until it sounded like thousands of pairs of clashing scissors. Martin reached the end of the corridor at last, and reached out to Boofuls to snatch him down from his invisible crucifix. But – with a cold and bruising collision – he came up against a sheet of frigid plate glass. Boofuls laughed at him. He was nothing more than an image in a mirror – a reflection of a boy who was long dead.

Martin struck out wildly, shouting and kicking and thrashing his arms. 'Boofuls! Boofuls! For God's sake, Boofuls!'

Dr Ewart Rice poured himself another cup of lemon tea. The late morning sunshine played softly through the rising steam and across the olive-green leather of his desk. There was such quiet in his office, and such tranquillity in his manner, that Martin felt almost as if he had found a sanctuary, and this was its priest.

'You're sure you won't have another cup?' Dr Rice asked him. He was a thin, drawn man, with a beak of a nose and furiously tangled white eyebrows. He wore a brown tweed suit, and a very clean soft shirt in tattersall check. There was the faintest lilt of Scottishness in his accent; a great precision in the way he pronounced his words.

'We tell the story for amusement, of course,' he explained, tapping his spoon on the side of his teacup. 'But I suppose, in a way, we also tell it as a ritual of faith. Because, it *did* happen, you know. We *did* see Boofuls, all five of us. We all decided that it would be worse than useless to tell the newspapers or the police. At the very least, we would have been laughed at. At the very worst, we might have ruined our careers. But it was real enough, don't you know, the first and last time that any of us had seen what you might describe as a ghost, and that was why we embroidered it into a hospital legend.'

He smiled. 'I suppose you could say that by keeping the story alive, we were exorcising the ghost. An annual ritual of bell, book and candle. Or, at the very least, a way of reassuring ourselves that we hadn't all gone mad.'

'You're not mad,' Martin told him.

Dr Rice sipped his tea and then set his cup down. 'You seem very certain about that.'

Martin nodded. 'I am. Because *I'm* not mad, and I've seen Boofuls, too.'

'*You've* seen him?' Dr Rice asked with care. 'I suppose by that you mean recently?'

Martin said, 'I've been a Boofuls fan ever since I was young. I'm a screenwriter now; I write for movies and television. I've written a musical based on his life – not that I've managed to sell it yet. In Hollywood, the name of Boofuls seems to carry a built-in smell of its own. The smell of failure, if you know what I mean.'

Dr Rice said, 'Aye,' and sipped more tea.

'This week, I bought the mirror that used to hang over Boofuls' fireplace,' Martin explained. 'Ever since then, I've had nothing but trouble.'

'And you say you've *seen* him?'

'In the mirror, yes. And that's why I wanted to talk to you.'

Dr Rice said, 'Yes, I can see why. It's all very disturbing. As a rule, I am not a believer in mysterious occurrences. I am a gynecologist; and once you have seen the mystery of human creation repeated over and over again in front of your eyes, then I am afraid that, by comparison, other mysteries tend to dwindle into insignificance.'

'I don't think there's anything insignificant about this mystery,' Martin told him, and explained about the two mismatched balls; and how Emilio had tried to step into the mirror; and what happened to Lugosi.

'I'm in the hospital because of that mirror,' said Martin. 'I've had thirty-eight stitches, and I could have been killed. That's not insignificant to me.'

Dr Rice was silent for a long time, his soft, withered hands lying in his lap like fallen chestnut leaves. When he spoke, his voice was quiet and controlled, but that made his account of what had happened on the night that Mrs Alicia Crossley was brought to the Sisters of Mercy sound even more frightening.

'There was, of course, enormous excitement. The press were everywhere. The lobby was filled with reporters and photographers and cameramen from movie newsreels. I arrived at seven o'clock for my night duty, and I had to struggle to get into the building.'

He paused, and then he said, 'Mrs Crossley died around eight o'clock, I think. After that, there were a few hours of comparative quiet, because the press had all rushed off to file their stories for the morning editions. I was on the gynecological floor, that's floor five. There were two babies being delivered that night, so I was constantly to-ing and fro-ing between the two delivery rooms.'

'Is that when you saw Boofuls?' asked Martin.

Dr Rice said, 'Yes. It was a quarter of ten. I was walking along the corridor between what they used to call Delivery Room B and the main stairs when I saw a small boy standing at the end of the corridor, looking lost. I called out to him, but he didn't seem to hear me. He was crying, and saying "Grandma, where's grandma?" over and over.

'I went right up to him. I was as close to him as you and I are sitting now. Closer, maybe. I put my hand out, I could see what was right in front of my eyes, but somehow my brain wouldn't believe it. I put my hand out to touch him even though he was standing not outside but *inside* the mirror. The mirror was like a glass door, no more; or a window. It was completely impossible; it couldn't happen. It flew right in the face of everything I'd ever understood about science, about the world, about what can exist and what can't exist. And, believe me, this couldn't exist, but there it was, right in front of my eyes.

'The boy had stopped crying, and he had covered his face with his hands, and was playing peek-a-boo through his fingers. I shouted at him, "Can you hear me?" two or three times, and then at last he took his hands away from his face. I wish he hadn't.'

Martin sat back, waiting for Dr Rice to finish, knowing that it took extra courage for him to explain what he had seen.

'His face looked normal at first. A little pale, maybe, but in those days a lot of children used to suffer from anemia. But then suddenly something red and thin started to dangle from his nostril, then another, then another, until they were dropping out onto the floor. He opened his mouth and stuck out his tongue, and his whole tongue was wriggling with them. Meat worms, the kind that eat corpses. They were pouring out of him everywhere. I expect you can understand that I dropped my clipboard and my smart new stethoscope and ran outside. I was in a terrible state.'

'Do you think it was some kind of hallucination?' asked Martin. 'After all, everybody knew that Boofuls was dead; there was mass hysteria; and you were right there in the thick of it.'

Dr Rice smiled ruefully. 'Don't you think I've asked myself that same question a thousand times? Was it a hallucination? Was it a dream? Was it tiredness? But no, my friend, I'm afraid not. I saw Boofuls quite clearly. I was in perfectly sound health, well rested, no hangovers. I couldn't afford to drink in those days! The only conceivable explanation as far as I'm concerned was that he was really there. Or, at least, that his *spirit* was really there.'

'Do you believe in spirits?' asked Martin.

'Do you?' Dr Rice retaliated.

'I don't *dis*believe in them, let's put it that way. Especially now that I've seen Boofuls.'

Dr Rice said, 'Altogether, five of us saw him. Well – I believe six, but one of the nurses refused to admit that she'd seen anything out of the ordinary. All five of us had similar experiences – that is, we all saw Boofuls weeping in a mirror – all at approximately the same time, about quarter of ten, but what makes the whole affair so fascinating is that we were all on different floors, and two out of the five who saw him I didn't even know.'

Martin cautiously touched his bandaged chin. 'So there could have been no – what would you call it? – group hysteria, something like that? I mean you didn't get together and discuss the Boofuls murder to the point where you all temporarily flipped?'

Dr Rice shook his head. 'There was no "flipping" that night, I can assure you. I had to drink three large Scotches one after the other, just to reassure myself that I wasn't completely losing my reason.'

'The other doctors and nurses – are they still here?'

'Only Sister Boniface. The rest, I regret, have passed on. Cirrhosis, cancer, auto accident; a fair cross section of modern fatalities.'

'Can I speak to Sister Boniface?'

'You may, if you wish; but her sighting was extremely brief. She had been sitting with Mrs Crossley before she died; and after her death she stayed to do the usual tidying up. She was covering Mrs Crossley's face with a sheet when she thought she heard a noise, just above her head. She looked up, and there was Boofuls – well, *lying*, as it were, on the ceiling. She screamed, and the police guard came in, and Boofuls vanished.'

Dr Rice picked up a gold mechanical pencil from his desk and began to turn it end over end. 'It disturbed her deeply, seeing Boofuls like that. Who would ever believe that she had seen a dead boy smiling at her from the ceiling? She went quite to pieces. Well – it was only our annual storytelling rituals that helped her to keep her feelings in perspective. She's a poor soul, Sister Boniface, and no mistake.'

Martin looked at Dr Rice narrowly. 'What do *you* think of all this?' he asked him bluntly. 'I mean, is it bullshit, or are we all going crazy, or what?'

Dr Rice gave him a tight smile. 'I saw what I saw, Mr Williams. You saw what you saw. To each, his own experience. Let us simply say that no one can take that experience away from us, no matter how unhinged they think we might be.'

He raised his head and looked at Martin benignly. 'Either we were all witnesses to an extraordinary manifestation – the power of love, perhaps, to extend beyond the moment of death – or else we are all quite mad.'

Martin sniffed, and found it painful. 'Welcome to the nuthouse, in other words.'

Sister Boniface was taking her lunch in the hospital gardens when they found her. She was sitting in the shade of an Engelmann oak, eating a vege-burger out of a polystyrene box.

She was so thin that she was almost transparent; with rimless spectacles; and a face that looked like Woody Allen if he had been seventy years old, and a nun. She blinked as Martin and Dr Rice approached, and closed her lunch box, as if she had been caught doing something indiscreet.

'Hello, Sister,' said Dr Rice. 'This is Martin Williams. Martin, this is Sister Boniface. Martin writes for television, Sister.'

'Yes?' Sister Boniface smiled. 'How do you do, Mr Williams? You're not writing one of those hospital series, are you? *St Elsewhere*? Something like that?'

Martin shook his head. 'You watch all of those things? Do you know something, I can never imagine nuns watching television.'

'We tend not to *collectively*,' said Sister Boniface. 'The wimples get in the way.'

'Humorist, too,' Dr Rice muttered out of the side of his mouth. 'You know what I mean?'

Sister Boniface said, with some precision, 'You came about Boofuls.'

Martin glanced at Dr Rice. 'How did you know about that?'

'Well, Mr Williams, all hospitals have their grapevines. I understand you had nightmares last night; Nurse Newton told me. Naturally, I asked her whether you were suffering from any particular anxieties – and, well, Nurse Newton is an excellent nurse, but not discreet.'

Martin was sweating. The midday sun was hot; and the salt from his perspiration irritated his stitches.

'I understand that you saw Boofuls in his grandmother's room, the night she died.'

Sister Boniface nodded, her starched wimple waving up and down like a snow-white sea gull. 'That is correct.'

'He was floating on the ceiling, right?'

'That is quite correct. He was floating on the ceiling.'

Her voice was so equable that when she looked up at Martin and her eyes were filled with tears, he was taken by surprise. She put aside her vege-burger and reached out her hand and clutched the sleeve of his shirt. 'Oh, Mr Williams, that poor child! It still haunts me now!'

Dr Rice said, 'Mr Williams has seen Boofuls, too, Sister Boniface, just this week.'

'Then you *believe*?' asked Sister Boniface, her eyes widening.

'Well, of course I believe,' said Martin. 'I saw –'

Sister Boniface awkwardly climbed onto her knees on the pebble paving. 'Mr Williams, all these years, it's been such a trial! Whether to believe in it or not! A miracle, a vision, right in front of my eyes!'

Martin knelt down beside her and gently helped her up onto her feet again. Underneath her voluminous white robes, she felt as skeletal as a bird. 'Sister Boniface, I'm not sure that it's a miracle. I don't know what it is. I'm trying to find out. But I'm not at all sure that it's – well, I'm not at all sure that it comes from God.'

Sister Boniface reached out her long-fingered hand and gently touched Martin's cheek. 'You are a good man,' she said. 'I can feel it in you. But it had to be a miracle. What else? He was floating on the ceiling, smiling at me. As clear as daylight.'

'He didn't speak?' asked Martin.

'No, nothing,' said Sister Boniface. 'He was there for a second, then he was gone.'

'You screamed?'

'Of course I screamed! I was very frightened.'

'Well, sure, of course you were. What with Mrs Crossley's body and everything.'

Sister Boniface sat up straight. 'I am not frightened by death, Mr Williams. I am frightened only by the face of pure goodness; and by the face of pure evil.'

'How long did you stay with Mrs Crossley that evening?' Martin wanted to know.

Sister Boniface shrugged. 'They asked me to come into the room to help with the last rites. Mrs Crossley was a Catholic, you know. Afterward . . . well, I just stayed where I was, helping, until it was time for them to take her away.'

Martin slowly massaged the back of his neck. This was getting him nowhere at all. He had learned that Boofuls had appeared as a mirror-ghost on the night he was murdered; but he had learned nothing at all about why he had been killed; and how he had gotten into the mirror-world, or why he should have decided to reappear now.

'You've been very helpful,' he told Sister Boniface. 'I'm sorry if I brought it all back to you.'

Sister Boniface smiled distantly. 'You haven't brought it back to me, Mr Williams. I never forget it. I never stop thinking about it. Was I visited by God, do you think, or by the devil? I fear that I shall never know. Not in this life, anyway.'

Martin hesitated for a moment, and then bent his head forward and kissed her hand. Her skin was dry and soft, like very fine tissue paper.

'There is one thing,' she said.

Martin looked up. Sister Boniface's eyes were unfocused, as if she were trying to distance herself from what she was going to say next.

'What is it?' he asked her.

'I was the only member of the hospital staff who stayed with Mrs Crossley from the moment she was brought into the hospital to the moment she died.'

'And?'

'She didn't speak,' said Sister Boniface. 'But she did regain consciousness for a very short time. She lay there, staring at the ceiling, gasping for breath. Then, when she and I were alone together for a short while, she beckoned me closer. She pointed toward her bracelet, which they had taken off when they first tried to resuscitate her, but which was still lying on the table beside the bed. It was a charm bracelet, with little gold figures of cats and moons and stars on it. But there was a key attached to it, too; quite an ordinary key. She gestured that I should take the key off the bracelet, and when I had done so, she pressed it into my hand, and closed my fingers over it.'

Sister Boniface reached under the folds of her habit and took out a small leather change purse. She opened it up, and reached inside, and produced a small steel key. 'This is the very key, Mr Williams.'

'I see . . . what does it unlock?'

'I have absolutely no idea. Mrs Crossley did nothing more than press it on me, insisting that I keep it. Her throat was almost completely closed, poor thing, and she could scarcely catch her breath, let alone speak. But it seemed as if the key were terribly important, because she kept staring at me and trying to nod, and catching at my sleeve.'

Martin said, 'May I?' and took the key out of Sister Boniface's hand. It was small and plain, with the number 531 punched on it. He turned it over. The manufacturer's name, Woods Key, was embossed on it, but that was all. There was no clue where it might have come from, or what door it might have fitted.

'Whatever secret this key was guarding, it probably vanished years ago,' said Dr Rice.

Martin said, 'It looks like a suitcase key. No – maybe it's a little too big for that. A locker room key, what do you think? Or the key to a cash box?'

'Could be anything,' said Dr Rice. 'Sister Boniface showed it to us before, and we tried it on every locker and cupboard we could find. We thought we might discover a hidden fortune, I suppose. Pretty fruitless exercise. All it proved was that it didn't fit any of the lockers in the hospital. I think Dr Weddell took it down to the bus depot one afternoon and tried locker number 531 there, but that was no use. It didn't fit the lockers at any of the local airports, either.'

'Well, it's probably a bank key or a hotel safe-deposit key,' said Martin. 'In which case we have about as much chance of finding it as a –' He was about to say 'cat in hell' but suddenly thought of that stinking brindled tomcat snatching at his eyes, and left his sentence unfinished. Despite the midday heat, he shivered, and felt uncomfortably cold.

Sister Boniface said, 'Mr Williams, why don't you keep that key? Perhaps you can find the lock it fits. You are the one who is closest to Boofuls now. Perhaps Boofuls will himself tell you.'

Dr Rice laid a hand on Martin's shoulder. 'Go on, take it,' he said. 'It'll make her feel happy.'

'Sure,' Martin agreed, and slipped the key into his pocket.

They walked back across the hospital courtyard. Martin turned around, shielding his eyes against the sunlight. Sister

Boniface had returned to her vege-burger and was placidly munching it.

'She's tormented, you see,' said Dr Rice. 'She can't decide if she's been blessed with a vision of heaven or cursed with a glimpse of hell.'

Martin took out the key. He felt, oddly, that he had always been meant to have it; in the same way that he had been meant to buy the mirror. He also felt that – one day soon – he was going to discover what lock it fitted, what secret it hid. The trouble was, he wasn't at all sure that he wanted to know.

CHAPTER FIVE

He drove back to his apartment late that afternoon to find a rusty blue and white pickup parked outside and Ramone arguing with Mr Capelli in the front yard.

'Hey, what's going on?' he asked, slamming his car door and crossing the sidewalk.

Mr Capelli immediately looked around. 'They let you out of hospital? Look at you! You look like the curse of the mummy's tomb!'

'Thanks, Mr Capelli, I feel better already. What's wrong here? Didn't Ramone pick up the mirror?'

'He says he can't,' Mr Capelli interjected before Ramone could open his mouth. 'He says it's too heavy, he can't lift it, and *I* can't help him, my doctor will do worse to me than that cat did to you.'

Ramone lit a cheroot and inhaled the smoke up his nostrils. 'This guy thinks I'm Arnold Schwarzeneggs-benedict or something.'

'Oh, come on, Ramone,' said Martin. 'The mirror's heavy but it's not *that* heavy. I moved it myself the other evening.'

'Well, maybe you did, but you must have been taking some kind of evening classes in You Too Can Have a Body Like Mine. *I* can't shift it, and that's all there is to it, and if you want to call me Mr Weak 'n' weedy, well, there's nothing I can do about it, because, man, that mirror will not *move*.'

Mr Capelli tugged and twisted at the crocodile on his Lacoste T-shirt. It was a nervous habit, that was all. When he wasn't wearing a Lacoste T-shirt, he twisted his back hair around his finger. 'This fellow, he doesn't even try! You and me, Martin, didn't we carry that mirror inside the house, just you and me, and God knows what kind of a physical shape *I'm* in! I surprise myself I'm not dead!'

'Plenty of people your age are,' Ramone retorted. 'And some of them *ain't*, and should be.'

'Come on, let's take a look,' said Martin. 'Ramone and I can probably manage it between us.'

'Thinks I'm Arnold Schwarzenfriedeggs,' Ramone grumbled as he followed Martin and Mr Capelli upstairs.

They reached Martin's apartment. The door was open, and they could hear singing. High, piping singing – Emilio. Martin stopped and listened, and felt a sudden surge of fear. 'I thought I told you not to let Emilio up here, for Christ's sake!' he barked at Mr Capelli, and he bounded up the last flight of steps three and four at a time.

'*Sur . . . wannee Song! Suwannee Song!*' Emilio was singing.

Martin burst into the room. The door shuddered. Emilio was marching up and down in front of the mirror, his head held high, his elbows swinging, his knees prancing like a young circus horse.

'*You can* blow *your flute and you can* bang *your drum and you can* march *along!*'

Martin turned toward the mirror. For one fraction of a fraction of an instant, he thought he glimpsed Boofuls, prancing up and down the mirrored sitting room. But then all he could see was Emilio's own reflection, brown eyes bright, dark hair shining.

'*Sur . . . wannee Song! Suwannee Song!*'

'Emilio?' said Martin.

Emilio stopped marching and turned around. 'Hey, look at you!' he gasped. 'You look just like the mummy!'

'Thank you,' said Martin. 'But didn't I tell you not to come up here anymore?'

'He wanted to play, that's all,' Emilio protested.

'Hey, now – *who* wanted to play?' Mr Capelli demanded. 'There's nobody here, just you and us.'

'Well, Mickey Mouse, of course,' Emilio replied, wrinkling up his nose in sarcasm. Without hesitation, Mr Capelli pushed his way past Martin and slapped Emilio hard across the side of the head.

'You don't talk like that to your elder-better! You dare! You want to grow up to be a deadbeat?'

'The way he's going, I think he's probably going to grow up to be President,' remarked Ramone laconically.

'That's what I mean!' Mr Capelli retorted.

Emilio's eyes were wet with tears. He rubbed his head and said, 'I'm sorry Grandpa. But he was here. That boy, Boofuls. He learned me that song.'

Mr Capelli clutched Emilio close and affectionately scruffed his hair. 'Eh ... I'm sorry, too. It's my fault. Martin told me not to let you come up here. Eh, no crying, unh? I'm just your silly old grandpa.'

But Emilio struggled free from his grandpa's embrace and turned toward the mirror. 'He's gone,' he said sadly. 'You frightened him away.'

Mr Capelli chuckled and shook his head. 'Some imagination, hunh?' But he looked toward Martin, and Martin could see the anxiety in his eyes. Mr Capelli believed in things that lived in mirrors; and Mr Capelli was afraid of them.

'Now, then, let's get this mirror out of here, hey?' Mr Capelli suggested. 'You can take one end, Ramone; and you can take the other end, Martin; and lift; and then I can direct you down the stairs.'

Ramone said, 'I've got a better idea. You carry it downstairs on your own and we'll just sit here and watch you.'

Nonetheless, Ramone and Martin bent down on each side of the mirror and prepared to lift it up. Ramone had already taken out the screws and laid a blanket on the floor to protect the gilt frame, and so all they had to do was pick up the mirror and carry it down to the street.

'When I say three!' announced Mr Capelli.

He counted three, and they lifted. Or they tried to lift. But they couldn't budge the mirror even half an inch off the floor. It felt as if it had been nailed down.

'Come on, Ramone, let's try it again,' said Martin; and they grunted and heaved; but still the mirror refused to move.

Martin propped his elbow against the mirror and puffed out his cheeks in exhaustion. 'I don't understand this. I mean, this is ridiculous. If Mr Capelli and I could carry it up three flights of stairs and screw it up on the wall, then you'd think that you and I could lift it between us – I mean, easily.'

'You're out of shape, that's all,' said Mr Capelli.

'Who's out of shape?' Ramone demanded. 'I play two hours of squash every afternoon, and I don't even get out of breath!'

'Sure, but what do you have to lift in squash? Just that little racket. That doesn't weigh nothing at all.'

Ramone lifted up his arms in resignation, then dropped them again, like one of the crows in *Dumbo* flapping its wings. '*Me duele!* What can you do with a man who thinks like this?'

'Come on, Ramone, let's give it another try,' Martin suggested.

'You don't get that mirror out of here, I'm going to call professional removers, and charge you what it costs, *and* throw you out, too!' Mr Capelli yelled at him.

'Come on, Ramone,' Martin urged him. 'He's getting into one of his Don Corleone moods.'

'Schwarzeneggburger,' Ramone growled under his breath.

They took hold of the mirror. Mr Capelli chanted, 'One-a, two-a, three-a –'

Without a word, both Martin and Ramone released their grip, and stood up, and stepped away. They looked into each other's eyes; and each of them knew that the other had shared his experience.

When they had tried to lift the mirror, a strong dark wave had gone through each of their minds, black and inhuman but undeniably alive, like centipede legs rippling, or the cilia of some soulless sea creature, cold, pressurized, an intelligence without emotion and without remorse and with no interest in anything at all but its own supremacy and its own survival.

For the first time, Martin felt that he had touched the very core of the mirror's existence, and it was more pitiless than anything he could have imagined.

Martin and Ramone stood facing each other, as stunned and subdued as if they had experienced an unexpected electric shock. But there was no question in either of their minds what that wave of feeling had been intended to tell them. They had been categorically ordered by whatever lived in the mirror to leave it where it was.

Mr Capelli was not so insensitive that he couldn't appreciate that something had gone badly wrong – that some feeling of hostility had suddenly caused them to back away.

'What is it?' he demanded. 'Martin – what is it?'

'I don't know,' Martin told him. 'I'm sorry, Mr Capelli, I don't know. But I'm not touching that mirror again, not just now.'

'Well, what?' Mr Capelli shouted. 'What do you mean, you're not touching it again? Why? What's the reason? Why don't you touch it again?'

Ramone said plainly, 'This mirror, Mr Caparooparelli – this mirror wants to stay right here. This mirror does not plan to be moved. Not that we *can* move it. I mean, we're too weak, right? We can only lift squash rackets, and suchlike. We can only lift stuff that is seriously deficient in avoirdupois.'

Mr Capelli stood rigid, his hands by his sides, the blood draining from his face so that he looked quite waxy, and his head too big for his body.

'All right,' he said. 'You brought this mirror here, what are you going to do?'

'I don't know,' Martin confessed. 'If I *could* get rid of it, right now I believe that I would. Boofuls or not.'

'Boofuls,' said Mr Capelli, keeping his false teeth clenched close together. 'That's the problem, right? Boofuls. That woman, she killed that little boy, she chopped him into millions of pieces –'

'Two hundred eleven, I'm reliably informed,' put in Martin, but he wasn't joking.

Mr Capelli spat out of the side of his mouth. 'How many exactly, who cares? But his spirit is here! His ghost! You found him a home, and now he doesn't want to go! And so what do I have? I have a house that's haunted, that's what! A haunted house with a ghost!'

'Maybe we should go get ourselves a priest,' Ramone suggested.

'I thought you were looking for a medium,' Martin reminded him.

'A priest, yes!' Mr Capelli enthused. 'A priest!'

'We could get both,' said Ramone. 'A priest *and* a medium.'

'Oh, God, this is ridiculous,' Martin told him. 'I don't

know what to do. Maybe the best thing we can do is do nothing. Just wait it out, see what the mirror wants.'

It was then that – without warning – the blue and white ball dropped off Martin's desk and bounced onto the wood-block floor – once, twice, three times. Then it rolled toward the mirror, almost as if the floor were tilting, like the deck of a ship. At the same time, the dirty gray tennis ball dropped off the desk in the mirror and came rolling to meet it.

'Something's happening, man,' warned Ramone. 'Something's happening. I can feel it.'

None of them knew what to do. But they could all feel the air in the sitting room *warping* almost; like ripples of heat rising from a hot blacktop; or the distortion of a highly polished sheet of thin steel. Their voices sounded strange, too – muffled and indistinct.

'It's *pulling*,' said Martin. 'Can you feel that? It's pulling things toward it.'

They didn't notice Emilio at first. He had been standing two or three feet behind his grandfather, staring at the mirror wide-eyed. Gradually, however, he began to move forward, his arms by his sides; and as he passed them by he started to laugh, an extraordinary high pitched laugh just like Boofuls.

At once, Martin turned around. 'Emilio?' he said. Then, '*Emilio!*'

'Holy God!' Mr Capelli cried out.

Emilio was sliding toward the mirror without even moving his feet. He was being drawn toward it as if it were an irresistible magnet.

'Emilio!' Mr Capelli shouted, and tried to snatch him.

Emilio threw both his arms wide and tossed back his head, and his laugh was loud and metallic like garden shears. In the mirror, his reflection slid toward him just as irresistibly, but there was something in his reflected face that didn't match his real face. Something different, something whiter, something smaller-eyed, piggy, untrustworthy, something that jumped and smirked like a face from a long-forgotten movie.

'*Ramone!*' Martin yelled; and Ramone dodged, and feinted, and caught hold of Emilio's arm at the very moment that Emilio collided with the surface of the mirror. Emilio screamed:

a hideous piercing scream that went through Martin's head like a chisel. He thrashed and clawed and kicked at Ramone, and it took all of Ramone's strength to hold him.

'*Bastard!*' Emilio screamed. '*Bastard!*'

'Emilio, what are you doing! Emilio!' Mr Capelli quivered and tried to snatch Emilio's flailing arm. But Emilio screamed '*Bastard!*' at him, too, and kicked him first in the stomach and then between the legs. Mr Capelli coughed, gasped, and dropped to the floor.

'*Bastard! Bastard! Bastard!*' Emilio screeched. He threw himself from side to side like a wild animal, hair flying, spit spraying.

Ramone shouted hoarsely, 'Martin! I can't hold him! Martin!'

For one desperate moment it looked as if the mirror was going to drag both Emilio and Ramone into its brilliant shining surface. But then Martin grabbed hold of Ramone's collar and deliberately fell backward, using his whole weight to pull them over. The three of them collapsed against the desk and tumbled onto the floor next to Mr Capelli. Emilio knocked his head against the corner of the desk: Martin heard it crack. Then Emilio lay still with his face against the floorboards, suddenly white, his eyes still open but flickering with concussion, and just as suddenly as it had begun, the magnetism from the mirror died away.

'*Madre mia,*' said Ramone, heaving himself up onto his feet, his sneakers squeaking on the boards.

Martin grasped Emilio's T-shirt and dragged him toward him. '*Out,* Ramone. We have to get him out.'

Mr Capelli was up on his knees now, coughing and coughing as if he were going to choke. Martin laid a hand on his shoulder and said, 'Mr Capelli? You all right, Mr Capelli? I have to get Emilio out of here.'

Mr Capelli coughed and nodded and coughed some more.

Ramone helped Martin to pick Emilio up and carry him through the hallway and down to the Capellis' apartment. Emilio wasn't badly hurt. There was a swelling red bruise on the left side of his forehead, and his eyes wandered sightlessly, but he was beginning to regain consciousness.

'Boofuls,' he murmured. 'Where's Boofuls?'

'No more Boofuls,' Martin told him. 'Boofuls is gone for good.'

'Or just about to, if I have anything to do with it,' growled Ramone.

Mrs Capelli came flapping out of her parlor. 'What now? All this noise! Did somebody fall over? Where is Constantine? Emilio! What's happened? Look at his head! Nothing but noise and trouble this past week! Oh, what a bruise! You men, you're like children! Nothing but thumping! Can't you do anything quietly? Now he's hurt! My poor Emilio! Come on now, bring him in here!'

'He'll be okay,' Martin told her. 'Just knocked his head on the side of the desk, that's all.'

'My poor boy! You men are all the same!'

Once they had left Emilio with his grandmother, Martin and Ramone went back upstairs to see what they could do to help Mr Capelli. He had managed to pull himself upright, but he looked gray in the face, and he had to lean against the wall to help himself along.

'Come on, Mr Capelli, let's get you downstairs,' Martin told him.

Mr Capelli coughed and sniffed. 'That mirror – that mirror has the devil in it! What did I say, no good would come out of it! You get rid of that mirror, you get rid of it right now! Right now! No argument!'

'You may want that mirror out of your house, but I'm not at all sure that mirror wants to *go*,' said Ramone.

Mr Capelli clung heavily on Martin's arm. 'That mirror goes, right now! I don't care how! You get rid of it! You smash it into small pieces, if that's what it takes!'

'Breaking a mirror, that's serious bad luck,' Ramone cautioned him as they helped him to shuffle down the stairs, one stair at a time.

'A kick in the nuts from my five-year-old grandson, that's *good* luck?' hissed Mr Capelli.

'All right, Mr Capelli, we'll do what we can,' Martin soothed him. 'Let's just get you downstairs.'

Ramone peered at Martin and said pessimistically, 'Your bandages are all bloody. Looks like you burst some stitches.'

'That's all I need,' said Martin, wincing with effort as the taut bulk of Mr Capelli's belly forced him against the banister.

Mrs Capelli came out again and fussed over her husband just as much as she had fussed over Emilio. 'This house is a madhouse! Never again! Tenants, always the same!'

'It's all right, Mrs Capelli,' said Martin, 'everything's under control.'

'Under control!' Mr Capelli burst out. 'My grandson goes crazy! That's under control? Look at you! Blood, bandages! Everybody's hurt!'

Martin tried to give Mrs Capelli a reassuring smile and backed off onto the landing. Ramone followed him.

'The old man's right,' said Ramone as they climbed back up again to Martin's apartment. 'That mirror has to go. Somebody's going to get hurt, or worse, and I sure don't like to imagine what that "worse" might be. Come on, Martin, we almost lost that boy, same way we lost Lugosi.'

'But if we break the mirror, you're going to lose any chance you ever had of getting Lugosi back,' said Martin. He was frightened by the mirror; but he was still reluctant to get rid of it until he knew more about Boofuls, and why he was trapped, and why Boofuls' dying grandmother had given Sister Boniface that key.

But Ramone shook his head. 'Lugosi is probably dead, anyway. Think about it, man. I've accepted it already. I was hoping he had a chance, you know, but the more I think about it . . . Man, he disappeared into *glass*, didn't he? Solid glass. You don't think he lived through that? I sure as hell don't. I'm going to light a candle for him, that's all, and say a little prayer. I don't think there's very much else I can do.'

Martin said, 'I'm sorry, Ramone.'

'Ah, forget it,' said Ramone dismissively.

They walked back into the sitting room; and their mirror reflections walked back into the sitting room, too. They stood staring at themselves for a very long time.

'He was right, you know,' Ramone remarked.

'Who was?'

'Mr Caparooparelli. You heard what he said. That mirror's bad news.'

Martin said, 'Boofuls is still inside it.'

'And that's your reason for not getting rid of it? Some kid who's been dead for fifty years is lurking around – where? Behind it? Inside it? Mirrors are flat. Mirrors don't have no insides.'

'But your cat's inside it.'

Ramone was angry. '*My* cat is *my* business, okay? And nothing lives *inside* a mirror, right? A mirror is glass, and silver, and that's it. Reflections, nothing else. Optical illusions; no depth; nothing you can walk into. I mean – what's behind that mirror? Nothing! A solid wall, nothing! There's no Boofuls living there, man. There's nothing at all!'

Martin said, 'Look.'

His voice was so cold, so prickly with alarm, that Ramone looked around without saying a word. There, in the mirror, sitting on Martin's reflected desk, was the blue and white ball. And there, on the floor, in both the mirror-room and the real room, was the dingy gray tennis ball.

But on Martin's desk in the real room, what looked like a new ball had appeared. A furry, bristling, gray and black ball. A living ball, with eyes that blinked. A ball which soundlessly opened and closed its mouth. A ball which wasn't a ball at all, but Lugosi's detached head – still panting for breath, but without a body, without ears, a grotesque living plaything.

Ramone approached the head in terror and disgust. Its yellow eyes were dimmed with a film of mucus, but they managed to follow him as he came nearer.

'What the hell is it?' whispered Ramone. The furry ball stretched open its mouth and silently cried.

'*What the hell is it?*' Ramone screamed out loud, almost hysterical.

Martin didn't know what to say. His stomach tightened, and he suddenly broke out into the cold sweat of rising nausea.

Ramone reached out for the ball-head with fingers that shook uncontrollably. The head opened its mouth, biting or crying, and Ramone instantly snatched his fingers away.

'Oh, God, I can't touch it,' he quaked. 'Oh, God, forgive me, Martin, I just can't touch it.'

Martin swallowed bile and approached the desk as near as he dared. The head opened its mouth yet again, and its eyes stared at him in agonized desperation.

'I don't know what to *do!*' shouted Ramone, hoarse with panic. 'He's hurting, Martin! I don't know what to do!'

Martin said, 'Go out of the room.'

'What?'

'You heard me – go out of the room.'

Ramone stared at him. 'What you going to do?'

'Just go!' Martin shouted.

Still shaking, Ramone retreated from the sitting room. Martin heard his sneakers squeaking along the hallway toward the kitchen, heard the kitchen door slide shut.

With a bitter-tasting mouth, Martin edged up to the desk and took hold of his typewriter. It was a heavy Olivetti electric. His father had given it to him when he sold his first teleplay: it was reconditioned, from the typing pool at the Security Pacific Bank. It hadn't ever worked too well: it kept skipping *j's* and *m's*. But all that Martin cared about right now was that it was the heaviest liftable object in the room.

He tugged out the electric cable, rolling out the page of screenplay he had been working on. The cat's head opened its mouth in another hideous yawn, its eyes trying to focus on him as he circled around the back of the desk and picked the typewriter up in both hands. He licked his lips. His heart was thumping like a skin drum. His blood rushed through his head and almost deafened him.

'Oh, God,' he whispered, and lifted the typewriter up above his head. If he caught Lugosi's head with one of the corners, he should be able to shatter his skull in one blow. It was crucial, however, that he didn't lose his nerve and pull the typewriter back at the very last moment.

Give yourself a count of three, he told himself. *Then do it.*

The typewriter was so heavy that his arms were beginning to tremble. *Do it!* he ordered himself. *One, two three, and do it!*

At that second, though, the cat's head seemed to rear up from the desk and swivel around. Martin almost dropped the typewriter, then cradled it in his arms staring at the head in paralyzed horror.

It rose higher and higher, on a furry neck that seemed to pour right out of the surface of the desk like a snake, yard after yard of it, until it looped and coiled down the side of the drawers and onto the floor. It was more like a python than a cat, and its sleek strange head remained lifted up in front of him on its endless ribboning neck, staring at him with agony and venomous hostility.

There was a moment when Martin believed he was really going mad – when he could hardly grasp that he was standing here at all, clutching his typewriter, with his cat-apparition swaying in front of him, and still pouring out of his desk.

He was breathing through his mouth in harsh, staccato gasps, as if he had been running. *Ha–ha–ha–ha!*

Then the cat started to lean toward him, its teeth bared, and he knew that it was no joke, no dream, no optical illusion. He heaved the typewriter – but it missed and bounded noisily across the floor. Then he threw his jelly jar of pencils and ballpoints, and that caught Lugosi on the side of the neck; but all the cat did was to sway back and hiss at him in fury.

'*Ramone!*' he yelled. But whatever Ramone was doing, he didn't hear. He was probably standing in the kitchen with his fingers jammed into his ears, so that he wouldn't have to listen to Martin crushing Lugosi's head.

Martin edged around his desk and the cat snake began to flow around it after him, its head still balanced five or six feet in the air, at eye level, fixing him with its unblinking yellow stare. He hesitated, and the cat-snake hesitated. There was no sound in the room but his own tightened breathing and the whispering of the cat-snake's fur across the boarded floor, like a woman trailing a long mink scarf.

'Ramone,' Martin repeated, but so quietly that Ramone couldn't possibly have heard him.

He cautiously reached forward, keeping his eyes on the cat-snake all the time, until his fingers touched the brass handle of his top drawer. The handle rattled, and the cat-snake flared its mouth open, its teeth dripping strings of glistening saliva, and its body began to slide toward him across the floor.

Now or never, he told himself. He yanked open the drawer, scattering the contents everywhere – pencils, erasers, rubber bands, paper clips, typewriter ribbons, book matches, correction fluid, and, most important of all, correction-fluid thinner.

The small plastic bottle of thinner rolled across the room and under his sofa. Martin glanced quickly at the cat-snake and then scrambled for it. The bottle had rolled almost out of reach, right under the back of the sofa next to the woven basket which contained his yucca pot.

He lay flat on his stomach and stretched his arm under the sofa. His fingertips touched the very edge of the bottle. It rolled a half inch farther away. Straining his arm even more, his shoulder pressing painfully against the underside of the sofa's frame, he just managed to reach the bottle and delicately take hold of the cap between two fingertips, so that he could tease it nearer.

'Come on, suckah,' he said under his breath.

He had just managed to flick it into the palm of his hand when he felt something indescribable slide around his right thigh. He screamed out loud and rolled over, and there was Lugosi, the cat who had metamorphosed into a snake, winding itself around his leg and forcing its sleek reptilian head under his left arm and around the back of his neck.

Martin scrabbled behind him and snatched at the cat-snake's fur. Underneath the softness, there was a hard muscular hosepipe of a body. Martin managed to get a grip on it, grunting with effort, and then he rolled over twice on the floor like a child turning somersaults at nursery school, so that the cat-snake unwound from his back.

'Ramone!' Martin shouted. *'Ramone, for God's sake!'*

He managed to catch the cat-snake just below the jaw and clench it tight. It spat and fumed at him and twisted its head from one side to the other. It was unbelievably strong; and the tighter he gripped it, the stronger it seemed to grow – until he was using every ounce of strength just to keep its spitting jaws away from his face.

He rolled over again, and again, and this time he managed to wedge up his knee and pin the cat-snake against the floor. It thrashed and whipped and it writhed, fifteen or sixteen feet of it. In seconds, it would thrash its way free, and then God only knew what it was going to do.

With his teeth, Martin unscrewed the cap of the thinner fluid, and then held Lugosi's head flat against the floor while he squirted almost the whole contents straight into the cat-snake's eyes and mouth and all over its head, until its furry scalp was furrowed with pungent liquid.

The cat-snake twisted and turned in agony, and for the first time uttered more than a hiss: a low, guttural *kkhakk-khhakk-khakkk* which prickled the hair at the back of Martin's neck. He dropped the bottle of thinner and grasped the cat-snake's neck in both hands, squeezing and squeezing as tightly as he could.

The sitting room door opened: Ramone walked in. He was obviously expecting to see Martin clearing up the remains of Lugosi's smashed head. Instead, he was confronted with a flailing snake out of a nightmare.

'*Lighter,*' Martin shouted. '*Lighter – before it dries!*'

Ramone was open-mouthed. 'Wha – *dries?* What dries? What are you talking about? What, man? What the hell is that? Oh, Christ!'

'*Your lighter!*' Martin repeated, practically shrieking at him now. '*Set light to its head! I've just sprayed it with thinner!*'

Ramone, stunned, fumbled in his shirt pocket for his Zippo. He thumbed it clumsily, but it flared up, and he held it out to Martin at arm's length.

'*Light it!*' Martin shouted. '*Light it, for pete's sake!*'

With jiggling, juggling hands, Ramone touched the flaming Zippo to the top of Lugosi's head. Immediately, the cat-snake's fur burst into flame, and its yellow eyes bulged with pain. A terrible convulsion went right through its body, a convulsion that Martin felt right down to his stomach: a shudder of fear and suffering and self-disgust. But all he could do was hold on tight, while the cat-snake wagged its fiery head from side to side. He knew for a certainty that if he released his grip, it would still go after him, and it would probably burn *him* to death, too.

The sitting room began to fill with the suffocating smell of burned fur and burned flesh. As Martin held the cat-snake up in front of him, like a torchbearer, the creature's head blazed and crackled, fur and skin and muscle. It was still staring at him as its yellow eyes milked over, its optic fluid cooked. Its mouth was still gasping that *khakkk-khakkk-khakkk!* as fire began to lick out of its throat and between its needle-sharp teeth, and the skin of its tongue frizzled and charred.

At last, it died, and Martin was left gripping a snake with a smoking head, its jawbones showing yellowish-brown through its incinerated cheeks, its mouth stretched wide in a hideous snarl.

Martin dropped it, and the head broke off and lay smoldering in a corner. The rest of the body shrank and dwindled and thickened, and even while Martin and Ramone watched it, it took on the shape of a normal tabby cat.

'Lugosi,' Ramone whispered. 'I just killed Lugosi. I wanted to save him, man, and I *killed* him.'

Martin walked stiffly to the window and opened it, so that some of the sour-smelling smoke could eddy out of the room. He retched once, then again, then pressed his fist against his mouth and managed to steady himself.

'That wasn't Lugosi,' he managed to say with a dry mouth.

'You think I don't know my own cat?' Ramone protested. 'Look at him!'

Martin took a deep breath. Below the window, next door, Maria Bocanegra was strutting out on a date with her body-builder boyfriend. Tight white skirt, dagger-sharp white stiletto heels that made her totter along with her hips swaying from side to side, tight white T-shirt through which her nubby Sno-Cone-protected nipples were startlingly obvious, even to those who didn't particularly want to see them.

God, thought Martin, *normality*.

They heard loud footsteps clattering up the stairs. An imperious banging on the apartment door. 'More noise!' shouted Mrs Capelli. 'What's that noise? And smoke? Is something burning? No fires allowed!'

'It's okay, Mrs Capelli, no problem. Just a cigarette butt, dropped on the couch.'

Martin sat unsteadily down at his desk, and dry-washed his face with his hands.

Ramone kept shaking his head and saying, 'I *killed* him,

man! You told me to do it, and I did! I can't believe it! I *killed* him!'

'No,' said Martin. 'You didn't kill him. It wasn't your fault. But we've learned something – or at least, I think we have.'

'What? What? What have we learned?' grieved Ramone, his face wet with tears.

'Well, for beginners, we learned that if something comes out of that mirror, something else has to go in. And vice versa, get it? Kind of a trade. I mean it may be weird but it has a certain kind of logic to it, like Isaac Newton saying that for every action there has to be an equal and opposite reaction.'

'All right,' said Ramone suspiciously, keeping his eyes averted from Lugosi's body.

'There's something else, too,' said Martin. 'The way it looks now – what happened to Lugosi – whatever happens inside that mirror, it *changes* things. Look – it changed Lugosi into God knows what. A snake? A cat? Some kind of mirage? I don't know what it was, but it damn near killed me. So – can you imagine what would have happened if Emilio had gotten sucked in? What would have happened to him? A boy-snake? It doesn't even bear thinking about.'

Ramone said nothing, but jammed his hands into the pockets of his jeans, and flared his nostrils, and paced up and down with his sneakers ferociously squeaking.

'I'd better get a trash bag,' said Martin.

'An eye for an eye,' Ramone remarked with vehemence. 'We kill the mirror-cat; the mirror kills my cat. But whatever it is, that's only some jive mirror, that's all. Nothing else. It's a piece of glass.'

Martin didn't say anything. He knew that Ramone had experienced just as acutely as he had the wave of darkness that had flowed out of the mirror. He knew that Ramone wouldn't attempt to move it or break it, no matter how bitter he felt about what had happened to Lugosi.

He also knew that, however much Ramone dismissed the mirror as 'a piece of glass', it was time for them to seek the help of people who knew about such things. A priest or a spiritualist. Someone who could tell them exactly what kind of souvenir Martin had bought for himself; and what influences were at work behind its shining surface; whether they were holy or whether they were evil; and what they could do to protect themselves against it.

He opened the door, and the smoke from Lugosi's charred head swirled and eddied in the draft.

Homer Theobald arrived that Sunday morning in a bright yellow Volkswagen Rabbit and parked it right in Mr Capelli's driveway. Mr and Mrs Capelli had taken Emilio to church – to pray for his immortal soul, and to keep him away from the mirror while Homer Theobald came to see it.

Martin let Homer in. Homer Theobald was plump and hairless like Uncle Fester in the *Addams Family*, with horn-rimmed spectacles and a splashy red and green Waikiki shirt. He smiled like a visiting doctor and held out his plump, damp hand.

'Mr Williams? I'm Homer Theobald. Your friend Ramone Perez called me?'

'That's right, come on in. Ramone isn't here yet, but you can take a look at the mirror if you want to.'

'Well, yes,' Homer Theobald beamed. 'He told me it was something to do with a mirror. That's not unusual, you know? Mirrors reflect the soul, don't they, as well as the face?'

Martin led the way upstairs. Homer Theobald sniffed and said, 'Italian?'

'I'm sorry?'

'I was just wondering if you were Italian.'

'Oh, no. But my landlord is. First-generation.'

Homer Theobald giggled. 'I didn't divine that by psychic means, I'm afraid. It's just that I have a keen nose for aromas. I can smell bolognese sauce simmering.'

'Mrs Capelli's a wonderful cook,' Martin told him. 'Maybe we can settle your fee in pizzas.'

'Well,' giggled Homer Theobald, 'I'm not so sure about that. Did Ramone tell you that I do for Elmore Sweet? Well, and lots of other stars besides. Jocelyn Grice, Nahum Ferris, the Polo Sisters. We all like to keep in touch with our loved ones, don't we, the rich and the poor, the famous and the faces in the crowd?'

Martin stopped on the landing and Homer Theobald almost collided with him.

'You can really do that?' Martin asked. 'I mean – you can *really* get in touch?'

Homer Theobald's smile lost something of its scoutmaster brightness. 'I hope you're not questioning my psychic credentials, Mr Williams. I'm known throughout Southern California as the Maestro of Mediums. I once talked to Will Rogers.'

Martin said, 'I'm sorry. I didn't mean to suggest –'

'No, no, not at all,' said Homer Theobald, patting Martin's arm and immediately regaining his cheerfulness. 'Most people are skeptical at first, even though they want to believe. It's only natural. But once they realize that they can speak to their lost loved ones as easily as making a long-distance telephone call – well, that skepticism just *melts* away!'

Martin opened the door of his apartment and let Homer Theobold in.

'You don't mind if I just stand here a moment and *take in* the atmosphere?' asked Homer Theobald.

Martin shrugged. 'Go ahead. This is all new to me. I never came across anything psychic in my life. Not until this, anyway.'

Homer Theobald suddenly looked at him more acutely. 'Those cuts –' he said, indicating the bandages around Martin's neck and the dressings on his cheeks and ears. 'If you don't mind my asking you a personal question – did you sustain those cuts in an auto accident, or are they anything to do with this mirror business?'

'I don't think you'd believe me if I told you.'

'Mr Williams,' said Homer Theobald, suddenly testy, 'you may think that I do nothing more for my considerable income than kid movie stars that I'm talking to their dead relatives. I told you, most people think that at first. But the fact remains that I have a gift of sensitivity that extends beyond the normal range of human faculties.'

He reached out and he gently drew his fingertip along the stitches in Martin's chin. 'These injuries have some connection with the mirror, am I right? I sense that you're frightened. I sense that you feel out of your depth. You don't know how to handle what's happening to you. You don't know whether to laugh or scream. Well, that's right. The beyond is always alarming. In the beyond, the same physical rules don't apply. Objects fly; people change shape. I don't often tell my clients that. They wouldn't understand, most of them, if I told them that their beloved parents are appearing to me in the shape of intelligent turtles, or that their heads have been stretched until they're nine feet high. But you know, it stands to reason, in a way. Why should the world beyond obey any of the laws of our own world? It would be more bizarre if it *did*.'

Martin nodded, and quoted, '*It may be quite different on beyond*.'

Homer Theobald frowned. 'I beg your pardon?'

'I was quoting. From *Alice Through the Looking Glass*.'

'Yes, well,' said Homer Theobald. 'There was always more to *that* book than meets the eye. The Victorians had a *very* finely developed sense of death and the world beyond.'

He lifted his head, and looked around the hallway, and listened. Then, without hesitation, he crossed to the wall where Martin had impaled the brindled tomcat, and touched it. At least, he was about to touch it, but he suddenly drew his hand back.

'Anything wrong?' asked Martin.

Homer Theobald turned to stare at him. 'Something *very* unpleasant has happened here.'

Martin nodded.

'Do you want to tell me about it?' asked Homer Theobald.

'Why don't we take a look at the mirror first?' Martin suggested. 'Then I can tell you the whole story from the beginning.'

'I just want to know one thing,' said Homer Theobald. 'Is there something in this mirror that isn't reflected in the outside world?'

'Yes,' said Martin.

'Is it a person? If it is, say yes, but don't tell me what his or her name is. I have to keep my mind clear, you see. Thinking of somebody's name is an immediate invitation for them to get inside my mind.'

'It's a person,' said Martin.

131

'Is it somebody you knew?'

'Somebody I know of; but not somebody I knew. He died a long time before I was born.'

'I see,' said Homer Theobald. He took out a clean handkerchief, unfolded it, and patted the perspiration from his bald head. 'So it's a man.'

'A boy, as matter of fact.'

'So he died an unnatural death?'

'Extremely unnatural, yes. He was murdered.'

Homer Theobald closed his eyes and thought for a while. Then he said, 'Cats.'

'Yes,' Martin agreed.

Without opening his eyes, Homer Theobald stretched out both arms and felt cautiously at the air all around him. 'There was a cat. There was more than one cat. But the first cat came to the back door and wouldn't go away. It sat there and sat there and the boy used to feed it. There was an argument. No, you can't feed the cat. That cat is unhealthy, you only have to smell it, it stinks. But I love it. Nobody can love a cat like that. I want it in the house. Certainly not, you can't have a filthy animal like that in this beautiful house, we'll all get fleas.'

Homer Theobald stopped talking as abruptly as he had started. He opened his eyes and he looked at Martin with the same kind of expression as an auto mechanic when he's about to tell you that your whole transmission's shot.

'I'm still in the hallway, right? I haven't even *seen* this mirror yet. It's in there, right, in that room, against the wall?'

'Yes,' said Martin.

Homer Theobald rubbed his forehead. 'I don't know what I'm going to be able to do for you here, Mr Williams. I truly don't. This isn't anything like I'm used to dealing with. It's spirits, yes. It's something trying to get in touch with us from beyond the moment of death. But if I can pick it up as clearly as this from the *hallway* . . .'

'What are you saying?' Martin asked him. 'You can't do anything about it, or what? All I want to do is get rid of it!'

'Mr Williams,' Homer Theobald appealed to him, 'what I'm trying to tell you is that I'm too frightened.'

Martin licked his scabby, split lips. 'You mean you won't even take a look at it?'

'No, sir.'

'Do you have any idea who it is? Whose spirit it is?'

'I have a pretty fair idea. Come on, Mr Williams, I've been living and working in Hollywood all my life. I know what goes on.'

'And what's *that* supposed to mean?'

Homer Theobald took a deep breath. 'Mr Williams, you bought yourself a whole load of trouble when you bought this mirror. You didn't do it on purpose, of course not. Most people could have bought it and hung it on their wall and never noticed a thing. But you yourself have latent psychic powers. Nothing amazing. Compared with mine, they're about as strong as a kid's flashlight compared with a klieg light. But you're intensely interested in the spirit which possesses this mirror – I say "possesses" for want of any better word. And your intense interest, coupled with your psychic powers, low-voltage as they are – well, they've obviously been enough to stir this spirit out of his stasis. It's not sleep, spirits don't sleep in the normal sense.'

Martin said, 'Why don't you take a look at it? I mean, just take a *look*!'

'No-o-o, sir,' said Homer Theobald. He was adamant.

'You're just going to turn around and walk out?' Martin demanded. 'You're going to leave me here, not just me, but the people downstairs, everybody who comes into contact with this thing – you're just going to leave us to be terrorized by this spirit for the rest of our lives? There's a kid threatened here, too. A boy of five. What do you want me to tell him?'

'Do you seriously think that I don't *want* to help?' Homer Theobald shouted back. 'Do you think I'd turn my back on you if there was anything else that I could do?'

'Well, that's what it looks like,' Martin challenged him.

'Listen, my friend,' said Homer Theobald, stubbing his finger against Martin's chest. 'I'm not a medium or a spiritualist or a psychic. I'm a sensitive. That means my *mind* is sensitive. What you have in this apartment is a raging beast, my friend. It's already tried to claw you to pieces, but only

133

your face. If *I* go in there, it's going to claw my *mind* to pieces. I'm sorry, I understand your problem, but I don't wish to spend the rest of my life with the I Q of a head of broccoli.'

'All right,' said Martin, 'if that's the way you feel.'

'I'm *sorry*,' Homer Theobald repeated. He took a menthol cough drop out of the pocket of his shirt, unwrapped it, and popped it into his mouth. 'Talking to somebody's dead husband is one thing. Raging beasts from beyond is quite another. I'm not putting you on, Mr Williams, it's a raging beast. So what you're asking me to consider here is the same as putting my head into the mouth of a hungry lion which has a special taste for heads.'

'Can't we just talk about it?' asked Martin. 'I mean, you keep telling me this is a raging beast — what kind of raging beast? And all this stuff about the cats?'

Homer Theobald hesitated, noisily sucking his candy. 'All right,' he agreed at last. 'But not here. There's just too much vibration here.' He lifted his fingers to his temples and winced. 'You can't believe it. The *voices*.'

'You can actually hear voices in here?'

Homer Theobald shrugged. 'Let's say that "hear" isn't quite the right way of describing it. But, essentially, yes. I can hear voices.'

'The boy's voice?'

'Sure. And a woman's voice, too. An elderly woman. And somebody else.'

'Somebody else? Who? Is it a man or a woman?'

Homer Theobald grimaced. 'I don't know. It's hard to tell. It's kind of harsh, and shrill, and metallic; but it sounds like it's closed up somewhere, do you understand what I'm saying? As if it's muffled. Somebody talking in another room, or maybe inside a box.'

'Can you make out what it's saying?'

'I'm not too sure that I want to.'

'Could you please try?' Martin begged him.

Homer Theobald reluctantly took off his spectacles and closed his eyes. 'I'm warning you, though, your little-boy spirit may get itself real worked up and excited by this.'

'Please,' said Martin.

'It's the way this kid keeps carrying on about the cat. The

cat is real important to him for some reason. But I've never had a pet before. You had those terrapins, what was wrong with those terrapins. You can't cuddle a terrapin, they're not the same and besides they all got away. Oh sure, they got away, they were crawling all over the kitchen, cook was standing on a stool. But I love Pickle, I love him.'

Martin grabbed hold of Homer Theobald's furry bare forearm. 'Mr Theobald!'

Homer Theobald blinked open his eyes. 'What's the matter? What's wrong?'

'*Pickle*, that's what you said.'

Homer Theobald nodded. 'That's right. The cat's name was Pickle.'

'None of the books ever mentioned him.'

'None of what books?'

'The books about –'

'Ah – ah!' Homer Theobald interrupted. 'Don't you mention his name! I've got a pretty good idea of who he is, but I don't want to start speaking any names in my mind, you understand? No mental pictures. The mind is a mirror, too, Mr Williams.'

'You'd better call me Martin if we're going to get *this* damned frightened together.'

'Well, I'm Homer, but most of my friends call me Theo. You know, on account of the hair loss. Theo Bald.'

Martin said, 'I'm sorry I interrupted you. It was just that the name Pickle came as a shock. Do you think you can pick up any more?'

'I don't know,' said Theo, but he was plainly not happy.

'Just the voice – you know, the shrill voice. The voice you said sounded like it was shut up in a box.'

'Well . . . okay. But I may get nothing. And I'm sure not staying around if it begins to wake up to the fact that I'm here, and that I'm listening in.'

'All right, I understand.'

Theo closed his eyes. 'The boy's still talking. He's a real chatterbox, that boy. When he was alive, he was real popular, real sweet. But there was something which he always kept hidden. Some important part of his personality which he never showed to anybody. He's still keeping it hidden, even now, and that's very strange indeed, because once people are dead they don't keep their personalities hidden anymore. They let themselves go. That's why they take on all kinds of weird shapes. They begin to *look* like they actually should. They drop the sheep's clothing, if you understand what I mean, and show you the wolf. Or vice versa, of course.'

He 'listened' harder. Clear buttons of perspiration popped up on his freckled scalp and on his upper lip. He began to mutter and mumble, a higgledy-piggledy rush of conversation, pleading, argument.

'I can't, Grannie, I told you I can't. You have to. You have to give thanks. I don't want to. I can't. Well, what do you think everybody's going to say about you if you don't go.'

Theo lifted one plump hand, his eyes still tightly shut. He was indicating to Martin that he was picking up the other voice, the shrill voice. 'Don't you go, she can't tell you what to do, don't you go, Pickle will fix her if she argues, don't you go, don't you go.

'I'm not going. You can't make me. Pickle will fix you if you make me. That cat, how dare you talk to me like that. That cat is going to go out and that's all there is to it. You're a hateful child. You're a disgrace to your poor mother. And you're *damned* for saying that, you're *damned*.'

While Theo was hurriedly muttering all of this argument between Boofuls and his grandmother, the latch of the sitting room door, without warning, released itself, and the door swung slowly open. Because his eyes were closed, and because he was concentrating on the voices in his head, Theo didn't realize that a sharp geometric pattern of light was gradually illuminating him brighter and brighter.

'Theo –' Martin warned him, his heart racing. 'The door.'

Theo opened his eyes and stared at the door in alarm. 'Did you open it?' he asked Martin.

Martin shook his head.

'Did you touch it at all?'

'I didn't go anywhere near it.'

Theo wiped his mouth with the back of his hand. 'I have to tell you, Martin, I don't know what's going on here, and I don't particularly *want* to know. I'll talk, yes, I'll tell you whatever I can. But I'm not staying here any longer, and I sure as hell am not going anywhere near that mirror of yours.'

'All right,' said Martin. 'Agreed. Let's go down to Butterfield's, I'll buy you a drink. You look like you could use it.'

Theo replaced his spectacles. As he did so, the sitting room door slammed so thunderously loudly that one of the panels was cracked.

'God, what was that?' Martin asked him.

Theo smiled grimly. 'That was your mirror, saying good riddance.'

Martin left a note on the door for Ramone, telling him that they had gone to Butterfield's. They drove there in Theo's Rabbit. Theo steered like a taxi driver, grinding the gears with every change, sweating, swearing under his breath, challenging every other car he encountered on the Strip, whether they were Porsches or Rolls Royces or Eldorados.

'I don't believe in being protean,' he remarked as he parked halfway up the curb outside Butterfield's. 'Sometimes it's refreshing to do something really badly.'

Butterfield's was on the south side of Sunset, with steps leading down through frondy palms and flowering shrubs to the table areas, where lean brown people in designer khaki sat under green and white umbrellas and talked about movies and other people's diets and themselves, but mostly themselves. There was plenty of fresh fruit and yogurt and Perrier water in evidence. Of all people, Morris Nathan was there, his wide backside bulging out on either side of a small white cast-iron chair. Alison was leaning against his shoulder, her face shaded by a dipping white hat, her eyes concealed by Mulberry sunglasses, her darkly suntanned breasts bulging out of a small white Fiorucci sun top. The Nabobs of Bulge, thought Martin.

'Martin!' called Morris, waving one fat arm. 'Join us!'

But Martin's need to talk to Theo was urgent: and, besides, Martin was sitting with Ahab Greene, an independent producer with wavy blond hair and protuberant eyes and white cowboy boots who always reeked of Armani after-shave, and

Martin couldn't sit next to Ahab Greene for more than six and a half minutes without starting a blistering argument.

'Thanks!' he called back. 'But – you know – business!'

Morris peered suspiciously at Theo, wondering if he was another agent, but Alison whispered something in his ear and he was obviously reassured. Alison wasn't particularly bright, but she was one of those well-connected Hollywood girls who knew every modish astrologer and every up-to-the minute masseuse and every fashionable beautician; she had once been a manicurist, and she had probably come across Homer Theobald more than once. After all, Hollywood husbands were always dying, and Hollywood wives were always feeling a need to get in touch, if only to reassure their loved ones that their money was being well spent.

A pretty, disinterested waitress found them a table, and Martin ordered champagne. 'Champagne?' queried Theo, although he was obviously used to champagne.

'I feel like it,' said Martin. 'What the hell.'

Theo leaned his elbow on the table. 'Let me tell you something, Martin. When people die their spirits move on. There's no question about that. Like I said, the place they move on to – the beyond, if you want to call it that – it's totally different from the world we know here. It doesn't abide by the same rules. Morally, physiologically, or scientifically. I don't know. It's very hard to describe. You can't think of it in normal terms – left, right, top, bottom. But it's there. It's where people go when they die.'

Martin looked away for a while. In spite of everything that had happened in the past few days, he still found it difficult to believe in Theo's beyond. He still found it difficult to believe in Theo.

When he spoke, it was almost a complaint – an aggrieved and baffled student asking his lecturer to explain some inconceivable theory about space and time. 'But how can this place – how can this world beyond – how can it appear in a mirror? And not just appear, but send things jumping out? I mean, I haven't told you the half of it. I saw a child's ball in that mirror that wasn't there at all. And Ramone's cat was sucked right into it – literally sucked into the glass. And then there was Pickle, the cat who came out of the mirror – at least I believe that was Pickle – he came out of that mirror and I can prove it, because the door was locked and the windows were locked and there was no way that cat could have gotten into my sitting room. And he almost killed me – well, look at me. And then Ramone's cat came back out of the mirror and he was like some kind of snake, like a python, you know, or a boa constrictor, and we had to burn him to death, I mean literally burn him. And that's why we called you. But of course you can't help. Or won't.'

The girl poured out their champagne. It wasn't very good quality, but it was cold and fizzy, and that was all Martin wanted. 'Okay,' he told her, and she went prancing off.

Theo sipped his champagne and then said heavily, 'That happened, all of that stuff?'

Martin said, 'You don't believe me, do you?'

'Oh, I believe you,' said Theo. 'Martin – let me tell you this – mirrors are no joke. Mirrors never *have* been a joke, particularly for us sensitives. A mirror is, what? People think of them like pictures on the wall; but they're into pictures, they're more like cameras. Think about it. You look at your mirror with more *intensity* than anything else you look at in your whole life. People don't even look at their husbands and wives with the same intensity they do their mirror.'

'I don't understand,' Martin admitted; and he really didn't.

'Listen,' said Theo, 'you've heard of rooms that somehow retain the feelings of stressful or tragic events that happened in them, long after those events are over? Sometimes it happens not just to rooms, but to whole houses, like Amityville. Oh, they turned that into a series of horror flicks, but the house was truly afflicted as many houses are. Some people can sense it the moment they walk into a place, some people can't. Some people have an ear for music, others don't. Being sensitive to the world beyond isn't something you can study in night class.'

'What are you trying to say?' asked Martin. 'You're trying to tell me this mirror has kind of *remembered* what happened to Boofuls?'

Theo winced. 'I did ask you not to mention his name.'

139

'I'm sorry. But you must have guessed.'

'Oh, certainly. Who else could it have been? So you bought a mirror that belonged to Boofuls, did you, and you hung it on your wall? In psychic terms, that's a little like buying Adolf Eichmann's toothbrush and using it. Do you know where the mirror used to hang? What I'm trying to say is – is there any chance that it might have been a witness to what happened to him – that the mirror might have seen Boofuls die?'

Martin said, 'It was hanging over the fireplace in the main living room. That was where Boofuls was killed.'

Theo took a deep breath and sharply drummed his fingers on the table. 'That accounts for it. That's why you're having all this trouble. The mirror *remembers* Boofuls being killed. Now all of those feelings, all of that fear, all of that pain, all of that hatred, it's all coming back to you. It's like a delayed reflection, that's all. But it can seem real. It can take on real shape, and it can do real damage. That cat Pickles – for some reason it was obviously important to Boofuls. Boofuls loved it but his grandmother didn't want him to keep it. So the situation about the cat was all part of the stress.'

Martin set down his glass. 'I don't know. It seems to me that there's more to this than just reflections. People must have murdered other people in front of mirrors before. I mean, almost every house has a mirror someplace. But you don't hear about cats and monsters and God knows what jumping out of mirrors all the time, do you?'

Theo said, 'You asked me for an explanation. I gave it to you.'

'But what about the third voice you heard? That voice that was supposed to sound like somebody in a box or something?'

Theo was beginning to sweat. 'Don't you think it's hot out here? Maybe we should go inside.'

Martin reached into his shirt pocket and produced the key that Sister Boniface had given him. 'When you said box, I thought about this key, because this key was given to one of the nurses at the Sisters of Mercy Hospital by Mrs Crossley, Boofuls' grandmother, the night she killed him. And what I was wondering was –'

Theo stared at the key with bulging eyes. The sun reflected from it and played a bright key pattern on his forehead.

'My God, put that away,' whispered Theo.

'But Theo – what I want to know is – since you're sensitive – maybe you could hold this key and tell me –'

'*Put it away!*' Theo ordered him, his voice so hoarse and penetrating that several people looked around.

'Theo . . . the nurse told me that Mrs Crossley couldn't speak, but the nurse was absolutely convinced that this key was very important. If you could just touch it, hold it, see if it gives off any kind of vibration. It could be the key to the whole darn thing.'

'Put – that– key –' Theo began; but then abruptly his nose fountained blood, all over his Waikiki shirt, all over his twill pants, spattering the tablecloth and turning his champagne cloudy pink. A girl at the next table screamed. Martin dropped the key and reached out for Theo at once.

'Theo! What's the matter? Theo!'

'*Lung!*' gasped Theo; and then vomited up a basinful of startling red blood that splashed all over Martin and all over the flagstones and dripped from the white-painted chair like glutinous paint.

'Ambulance!' Martin shouted. 'Somebody call an ambulance, for Christ's sake!'

Theo lurched sideways in his chair. Martin tried to keep him upright, but he was enormously heavy and off-balance and slimy with blood. At last, with the help of one of the waiters, Martin managed to lower him gently onto the ground.

'Is he dying, or what?' the waiter asked him, his eyes wide open with fright.

'Martin – are you okay?' shouted Morris. 'They've just called for the paramedics.'

Alison gave him an anxious little wave, too. Martin waved back to tell them they were doing all they could. Theo was lying with his face against the paving stones, a bubble of blood between his lips, his eyes filmy.

'*Key* . . .' he whispered. He lifted his right hand and took hold of Martin's wrist, drawing him closer.

'*Key* . . .'

'What about it?' asked Martin. 'Listen, just rest. They've sent for an ambulance.'

'Key . . . acts like . . . lightning conductor . . .'

'What? What do you mean?'

'Mirror . . . doesn't want me to pry . . . punctured my lung. Located us . . . you got it? . . . moment you said . . . Boofuls.'

Martin said, 'I'm sorry, Theo. I didn't have any idea.'

'Well . . . not your fault,' Theo grunted. 'I should have said no . . . right from the very beginning . . . moment I felt that coldness . . . moment I felt that *black*.'

'I felt that, too,' Martin told him.

Theo coughed a gout of blood. In the distance, they could hear the ambulance siren whooping. 'Come on, Theo,' said Martin. 'You're going to make it . . . the paramedics are almost here.'

'Where's that . . . key?' asked Theo.

'I don't know. I guess I dropped it.'

'Find it . . . give it to me. Come on, quickly.'

'Theo – if it's that dangerous –'

Theo lifted his head. His mouth was so bloodstained he looked as if he had been cramming raspberries into it all morning. Sticky, red, peculiarly childish.

'If you don't give me that key, I'm never going to speak to you again.'

The threat was so absurd that Martin realized Theo was serious. He dabbled around in the spreading lake of blood, and there by the leg of Theo's dark-stained pants was the key. Theo reached out for it, and Martin pressed it reluctantly into his hand.

The ambulance had parked on Sunset, outside the entrance to Butterfield's; and the paramedics were already hurrying down the steps. Theo closed his eyes and for a moment Martin, kneeling in his rapidly cooling blood, was sure that he was dead. The paramedics came up to him and lifted the table aside and said, 'Okay, sir, give us some space, will you?'

Theo lifted one bloody arm. 'Martin . . .' he mouthed. 'Martin . . .'

Martin tried to get close to him, but one of the paramedics

backhanded him away. 'Come on, friend, this man needs space.'

'Martin!' Theo choked. 'Martin!'

Martin pleaded with the paramedic, 'I have to get close. Listen, I have to hear what he's got to say.'

'You want to kill him, or what?' the paramedic demanded. 'This man has a punctured lung. Now, do us all a favor, and take a powder – and that's being polite.'

They were testing Theo's vital signs and unwrapping an oxygen mask. But before they could press the mask over Theo's face, he propped himself up on one elbow and bubbled, 'Martin! Martin, listen to me! The Hollywood Divine! The Hollywood Divine!'

'What?' asked Martin, baffled.

'Used to go there . . . when I was a boy . . . father took me . . . cocktail lounge . . . Here! take the key! The Hollywood Divine! Leopard-skin banquettes . . . gold-tinted mirrors . . . Here! Martin! The key!'

Theo waved the key; and impatiently, one of the paramedics passed it back to Martin. 'Guy's out of his tree,' the paramedic remarked, covering Theo's face with the oxygen mask.

Martin waited while the paramedics sent back Theo's vital signs to the hospital. Then he asked, 'Where are you going to take him?'

'Sisters of Mercy, that's the nearest.'

'All right,' said Martin, 'I'll follow you.'

'No tailgating, that's all,' the paramedic told him as he rolled Theo's bloody body onto a stretcher.

'In a Rabbit?' said Martin bitterly.

CHAPTER SIX

Theo died at 3:46 that afternoon. Martin was sitting in the reception area when Sister Michael came rustling up in her white habit and white wimple to tell him that all their efforts to save him had been to no avail.

'Was he a close friend of yours, Mr Williams?' Sister Michael asked him, with a face like the Angel of Solicitude carved in wax.

Martin said, 'No, I met him for the first time today.'

'We did everything possible. But his lungs collapsed. You can talk to the doctors later, if you wish.'

Ramone appeared, wearing a black T-shirt and black jeans and looking unhappy. 'I called his house. Some boy answered. His boyfriend, I guess. Said he thought there was a sister in Indiana, anyway he's going to check through his address book and call her.'

'At least he's at peace now, in the Kingdom of Heaven,' said Sister Michael.

'What?' asked Ramone. Then, 'Sure – oh, yes.' He glanced at Martin and made a face. Martin had already told him about Theo's description of the world beyond, with its talking turtles and its people with stretched-out heads.

Sister Michael laid a cool pale hand on Martin's shoulder. 'If there's anything else that I can do, please don't hesitate to call me. When somebody passes on, we do recognize the need to comfort those who are left behind.'

'Yes, thank you,' said Martin.

Ramone sat down on one of the gray fabric couches and tightly crossed his arms. Up above his head, a painting of a gentle-faced Madonna smiled down at him, with an expression that forgave all human weakness. 'What do we do now?' Ramone wanted to know. 'If Homer Theobald couldn't help us – if *he* wound up getting wasted – then what hope do the rest of us have?' He leaned forward and asked, 'You really think it was the *mirror* that wasted him? All that way away?'

Martin shrugged. 'He seemed to think so. I showed him that key and he went white. I mean he was *gibbering*. I wish to God I hadn't now. He might still be alive.'

Ramone took out a cheroot, but the nun at the nurses' station silently pointed to the sign which said *No fumadores*.

'How did she know I speak Spanish?' Ramone whispered, replacing the cheroot in its carton.

'She must've guessed. Or maybe she read ¡Viva Las Patillas! on the back of your T-shirt.'

Ramone said, 'Let's take a look at that key.'

Martin handed it to him. While he had been waiting to hear if Theo would survive, he had taken it to the hospital washroom and carefully rinsed Theo's blood off it. Ramone turned it over and over and then handed it back. 'It's just a plain ordinary key.'

'Well, maybe it is and maybe it isn't. I think we should go to the Hollywood Divine and find out, don't you? There's nothing to keep us here.'

'I don't even know if the Hollywood Divine is still standing,' said Ramone. 'They demolished most of that block last year.'

'All we can do is take a look.'

Sister Michael intercepted them again as they walked toward the elevators. 'Mr Williams! Mr Perez! Did you want to *view* Mr Theobald before you left?'

Martin looked at Ramone, and Ramone bulged his eyes in an expression which unequivocally meant 'no way'.

'Thanks,' said Martin. 'But I think I'd just like to remember him the way he was.'

'How was that?' asked Ramone as they went down in the elevator to the hospital lobby.

'Alive,' Martin replied.

The Hollywood Divine Hotel had been erected in 1927 by Daniel T. Rolls, the wealthy second son of the Rolls hotel family of Pasadena. It stood two blocks north of the celebrated intersection of Hollywood and Vine, a fanciful creation in the neoclassical picture-palace style that had been popularized by Eve Leo.

In its heyday, the Hollywood Divine had been celebrated for its eccentric and arty clientele – the West Coast equivalent of the Algonquin in New York. But with the squalid death of its founder in 1938 (cocaine, bourbon, inhalation of vomit), it had quickly lost its cachet. Now it stood shabby and seedy and ready for demolition, its pale pink stone corroded by vehicle fumes, its marquee half collapsed, its marble steps stained with urine and measled with chewing gum.

'I could have sworn they knocked this place down already,' Ramone remarked as they parked outside in Martin's Mustang.

They were immediately approached by a thin-faced kid with a crimson punk hairstyle. 'Hey, friend, take care of your car?'

Martin reached into his shirt pocket and gave the kid two dollars. 'There's another three where that came from if the stereo stays where it is.'

'You got it,' the kid told him.

Three young hookers were standing outside the hotel, two black and one white, in skintight satin miniskirts and halter tops. They were all pretty: one of them was almost beautiful. She winked at Martin as he went up the steps and he couldn't help smiling back.

'Made yourself a friend?' asked Ramone.

They pushed their way through the bronze and glass doors of the Hollywood Divine and into the gloomy lobby. The carpet was rancid; so filthy and stained that it was impossible to tell what color it had originally been. There was a suffocating smell of marijuana and body odour and disinfectant. Six or seven scarecrows were sitting on the ripped-open leopard-skin seats where John Barrymore and Bette Davis had once sat, sharing bottles of muscatel from brown paper bags and sniffing in chorus.

The great chandelier hung from the lobby ceiling like the desiccated corpse of a giant spider, still dangling in its web.

Martin and Ramone approached the desk. The desk clerk was surprisingly young and clean: a young man in a shocking-pink shirt with blond crew-cut hair. It was only when he laid his thin arms on the marble counter that Martin saw the needle tracks.

'You people checking in?' he asked them. His eyes were as pale and as expressionless as two stones you find on the beach.

Martin shook his head. 'I was wondering if you still had safe-deposit boxes here.'

'Safe-deposit boxes?' The young man blinked.

'Yes, you know. Somewhere your guests can keep their valuables.'

'What, are you kidding? If any of our guests happen to have any valuables, they keep them on their persons. Besides, they don't usually stay for longer than a half hour.'

'But are the original boxes still here – the boxes that were put in when the hotel was built?'

'I don't think so,' the young man told him. 'Pretty much everything has gone. Somebody walked out with a goddamned bathtub last week. Can you imagine that? Nobody knows how he got it through the door.'

Martin gave a tight grimace and looked around him. One of the scarecrows was waving his arms and singing. '*Sur . . . wannee song! Suwannee song! You c'n blow your flute 'n' you c'n bang y'r drum 'n' you c'n –*'

'Will you shut up?' one of his companions screeched at him. 'Will you shut up?'

Martin stared at the old scarecrow for a while. Then he turned back to the desk clerk and said, 'Who's that?'

'Who's what?' The young man may have looked quite presentable, but his brain was somewhere in another galaxy.

'That old bum singing. The one singing "Suwannee Song".'

The young man focused his eyes across the lobby. 'Oh, that's Fido. Well, everybody calls him Fido. He's been hanging out for just about a hundred years. I think he used to work here or something. He's always telling stories about how he walked in on Bill Haines, and Bill Haines was wearing nothing but a brassiere and a garter belt and a picture hat.'

Martin left the desk and walked across to the group of scarecrows. Fido was sitting right in the middle of them, on

147

one of the leopard-skin banquettes. His face was puffy and flowered with gin blossoms. He wore a fifties-style suit with wide flappy lapels. It had once been fawn, but now it was greasy gray. Martin couldn't approach too close. The collective stench of these down-and-outs was overwhelming.

'Fido?' he asked.

Fido looked up at him blearily. 'That's me, your honor.'

'They tell me you used to work here,' said Martin.

There was a chorus of groans and raspberries from Fido's companions. 'Don't ask him!' one of them begged in a voice reedy with phlegm. 'Do us a favor, will you, friend? Don't ask him!'

'Was the gemmun addressing *you*?' Fido demanded with all the indignation of an Oliver Hardy.

'He worked here, he worked here, now go!' the other scarecrow appealed.

Martin said to Fido. 'Maybe we can talk in private? I wouldn't like to antagonize your friends.'

'Friends? Call this riffraff friends? These just happen to be items of flotsam who have eddied their way into the same backwater.'

'Oh, can it, Fido,' groaned another scarecrow. 'You make my ears want to scream.'

Fido teetered his way out of the assembly of winos around the banquette and accompanied Martin and Ramone to the far side of the lobby, beside the gilded fountain that had long ago dried up, and whose shell-shaped bowl was now crammed with cigarette butts and empty bottles and used needles.

Ramone wrinkled up his nose as Fido lurched a little too close to him. 'You won't get arrested for taking a shower, did you know that?'

Martin said, 'Ssh,' and waved Ramone to keep quiet. He didn't want to upset Fido before he'd had the chance to talk to him.

'Is it true you worked here?' he asked.

'What's it worth?' Fido wanted to know.

Martin held up a ten-dollar bill. Fido sniffed, and took it, and snapped it between his fingers to make sure that it was genuine. 'All right, then,' he said. 'I worked here.'

'Were you here in 1939?'

Fido nodded, his white prickly chin making a crackling sound against the collar of his grubby shirt. 'Sure, 1939. I was promoted to bell captain that year. March 1939.'

'Did you ever see Boofuls here?'

'Boofuls?' asked Fido suspiciously. 'Why'd you ask that?'

'I'm just interested, that's all. I'm writing a book about his life.'

'Well,' sniffed Fido, 'he didn't have too much of a life, did he? But he sure had a memorable death.'

'Did you see him?'

'Of course I saw him. He was here all the time, him and that Redd woman. Every month; and all kinds of others, too. Famous actors, you'd know them all. Famous directors, too.'

Martin frowned. 'You mean Boofuls used to meet a whole lot of other actors and directors here, every month?'

'That's right. It was a joke. Nobody was supposed to know. Big secret, don't tell the press, that kind of thing. And to tell you the truth, I don't think the press ever did find out. But we knew, all of the staff. You couldn't help recognizing somebody like Clark Gable, now, could you? And there was George Cukor and Lionel Atwill and dozens of others. All the big names from 1939, they came here. Maybe not every month, but pretty well.'

Ramone warned, 'You'd better not be putting us on, Mr Fido.'

'Why should I put you on?' Fido challenged him. 'It's true, it happened. Every month, here at the Hollywood Divine, in the Leicester Suite.'

'And Boofuls was *always* here?' Martin asked him.

Fido nodded. 'They wouldn't start without Boofuls.'

'Wouldn't start what?' said Ramone.

Fido puffed out his blotchy cheeks. 'Don't ask me, how should I know? It was all supposed to be secret, right? We laid them on a spread before they started – chicken, lobster, stuff like that – and then we had to lock the doors and leave them to it – whatever it was they were doing. But believe me, they were all famous. You'd have known them all. Errol Flynn, he used to come. Joan Crawford. Wilfred Buckland, the art director. Fifty or sixty of them, every month, sometimes more.'

Martin said, 'You're *sure* about this?'

'Sure I'm sure. I was the bell captain.'

'Well, how long did these get-togethers go on for?'

'Two, three in the morning, sometimes longer.'

'And Boofuls stayed there all that time?'

'I used to see him leaving, four o'clock in the morning sometimes. That Redd woman used to cover him up with a cloak and a hood, but you couldn't mistake him.'

Martin said, 'He was only eight years old, what was he doing staying up all night?'

Fido coughed and then noisily cleared his throat. '*I* don't know what the hell he was doing, staying up all night. We used to listen at the door sometimes, but we could never hear nothing. Sometimes music. But they used to have girls in as well. Not exactly hookers but what you might call starlets.'

Martin looked at Ramone, but all Ramone could do was shake his head. 'Don't ask me, man, I never heard of anything like this. Either this guy's shooting us a line, or else his brain's gone, or else we just came across the biggest Hollywood mystery that ever was.'

'Listen,' Martin told Fido, 'when you were working here, where did they keep the safe-deposit boxes? Can you remember that?'

'Certainly I can remember,' said Fido. 'What's it worth?'

Reluctantly, Martin handed Fido another ten-dollar bill. He snapped it, the same way he had snapped the first one. Then he sniffed and said, 'They used to keep the safe-deposit boxes in back of the manager's office, through the archway behind the desk. But if you're looking for them, I can save you some trouble, because they ain't there now. Round about 1951, when the Hollywood Divine really started losing money, there was some kind of plan to refurbish it, you know, and they shifted a whole lot of stuff down to the basement. The only trouble was, the plan fell through, lack of money, zoning problems, something like that, and everything that was shifted down to the basement just stayed there.'

'So that's where the safe-deposit boxes are now?'

'You've got it, your honor. Not to mention two thousand square feet of moldy carpet, and enough velvet drapes to make Little Lord Fauntleroy pants for every down-and-out in Greater L A.'

Ramone gave a sharp, unamused laugh. Fido shrugged and gave a goofy grin, baring abscessed gums and brown, tartar-clogged teeth.

'One more thing . . .' put in Martin. 'Who's this Redd woman you keep talking about? I thought that Boofuls was looked after by his grandmother.'

Fido said, 'I never knew too much about her. But she was the one who booked the suite, that's how we got to know her name. R–E–D–D, Redd, that was it, but it could have been a what's-it's-name, you know, pursue-dough-name.'

'Do you have any idea what her relationship to Boofuls was?'

Fido shook his head. 'No idea. She just rushed him in before it began and rushed him out again when it was over.'

'Did you get to see her face? What she looked like?'

'Well . . . briefly. It's a long time ago now. But she was pale, you know what I mean, the sort of pale that looks like somebody's been ill, or shut up for a long time without going out in the sunshine. Pretty, in a way, but kind of *sharp* pretty. Sharp nose, sharp chin, sharp eyes. Classy, too. Definitely classy. But sharp.'

'What did she used to wear?'

'Always the same, black evening cloak, red dress under-neath. Never saw what style it was. She was in and out of here so darned quick.'

Martin was mystified by all this. He had never heard of any other woman escorting Boofuls besides his grandmother; and he had certainly never heard of monthly get-togethers of movie stars at the Hollywood Divine Hotel, with Boofuls apparently presiding.

'I hope for your sake this is on the level,' he told Fido.

Fido saluted with a hand that was gray with grease. 'You never came across a servant so true, your honor.'

For twenty more dollars, the vacant-eyed desk clerk took

Martin and Ramone up to what had once been the Leicester Suite. They climbed the wide marble stairs to the mezzanine floor and crossed an echoing landing that smelled of Sterno. The desk clerk led them up to two wide carved doors – some of their panels broken now and nailed up with sheets of ply – and unlocked them with keys from a huge jangling ring.

'We have to keep this place locked, every junkie in town was using it as a shooting gallery. We used to drag out two or three stiffs every single morning, OD'd on crack.'

Inside, by the light of half a dozen bare bulbs, they cautiously explored a hotel suite that must once have been magnificent. Because it was on the mezzanine floor, its rooms were half as high again as any other rooms in the hotel. Its walls gleamed with gold and silver wallpaper, and there were gilded Renaissance moldings on its murky ceilings and around the doors.

The desk clerk led them through an inner lobby, and then through more double doors to a cavernous room that must have been the lounge. There was a grand gilded fireplace and a gilded chandelier, but all the furniture and the carpets had been taken out. The floor was littered with old yellowed newspapers and rat droppings; and in the far corner there stood, unaccountably, a green and white garden swing-seat.

Their footsteps scuffed and echoed. Ramone, with his hands in his pockets, said, 'You can't believe that Clark Gable was ever here, can you?'

'What was he *doing* here, that's what I want to know,' said Martin. 'What was Boofuls doing here?'

'Orgies, maybe?' suggested Ramone. He walked around the swing-seat and then pushed it. It creaked backward and forward, backward and forward, *squueaakkk-squikkkk, squeeeaakk—squikkkk*.

Martin said, 'A small boy holding orgies? It doesn't make sense.'

'Well, don't ask me, man,' said Ramone. He sniffed. 'This place gives me the heebie-jeebies.'

The desk clerk asked, 'You done now? There's nothing else to see.'

'Yes,' said Martin, 'I guess we're done. Can you take us down to the cellars?'

They left the Leicester Suite and the double doors were locked behind them. The desk clerk took them downstairs to the lobby and then along a narrow corridor to the kitchens and the service areas. The kitchens were filthy: strewn with rubbish and deserted. The grease-encrusted oven doors hung open. It was difficult for Martin to believe that the Hollywood Divine's celebrated *homard orientale* had once been prepared here, as well as the famous fiery pudding of red cherries and Grand Marnier created especially for Gloria Swanson.

The desk clerk unlocked the cellar doors. 'There's a light switch down on the left. You can look all you want; I have to get back to the desk. Just tell me when you're through.'

Together, Martin and Ramone groped their way down the first flight of wide concrete steps. Martin found the light switch and flicked it; a row of fluorescent tubes illuminated a wide vaulted cellar stacked to the ceiling with chairs, tables, folding beds, mattresses, chalkboards, lampshades, statuettes, signs saying Exit and No Smoking, boxes, crates, and rolled-up carpets.

Martin began carefully to climb through this collected detritus of the Hollywood Divine's history, his arms stretched out to keep his balance. He trod on a cardboard box full of brass lamp sockets, and they showered onto the floor like Aladdin's treasure.

'Any sign of those safe-deposit boxes?' Ramone asked him.

'I don't know. There's a whole lot of stuff covered by sheets, right at the back. I'm going to take a look now.'

Martin clambered across stacks of rollaway beds to reach the far side of the cellar, where it was darker and the air was suffocatingly still. Something tall and angular was concealed by a stained gray sheet; something as tall as a man with one arm outstretched. Martin tugged at the sheet, but it was caught.

'What's that?' called Ramone, clambering after him across the beds. He pushed one foot through the springs of a rollaway bed, and there was a loud *gddoinngg* noise, followed by a sharp exclamation of 'Goddamn it!'

Martin pulled at the sheet again, and this time it tore wide open. He shouted out in fright, and trod backward, and almost lost his balance. Out of the ripped sheet a shining black face was staring at him, a face with white eyes and reddened lips.

Ramone came forward and tore off the rest of the sheet. 'Heyy . . .' He grinned. 'Not bad. She shouldn't've scared you.'

It was a 1930s statue of an African dancer, probably made out of plaster. She was wearing ostrich feathers in her hair and a grass skirt and carrying a zebra-skin shield. 'Very bodacious ta-tas,' Ramone remarked, peering inside the sheet.

They climbed farther along the length of the wall and, at last, jammed into one of the corners, they came across the safe-deposit boxes. There were four banks of them, lying on their backs on the floor, and almost completely buried under dozens of folding wooden chairs.

'At least nobody could stroll out with *these*,' said Ramone.

It took them more than ten minutes simply to move all the chairs off the top of the safe-deposit boxes. Martin rubbed dust and grime from the topmost bank of boxes 1–100. That meant that they would have to lift the entire bank of boxes out of the way in order to get to number 531 somewhere underneath.

They each took hold of one end of the boxes and tried to lift them up. They were impossibly heavy. 'We're going to rupture ourselves, shifting these,' said Martin. 'Maybe we'd better slide them instead.'

Grunting, cursing, they managed to slide the top bank of boxes off to one side; then tilt it so that it dropped upright onto the floor.

'What do you bet the numbers we want are right at the bottom of the stack?' said Ramone.

He peered at the labels of the next bank of safe-deposit boxes and then rubbed one or two of them with the heel of his hand. 'Numbers 500 through 600, thank the Lord.'

Martin climbed up onto the boxes and ran his fingers down the labels until he found 531.

'I'll give you a thousand to one the key don't fit,' said Ramone. 'Nobody with *your* luck is going to find the right box first time.'

'Theo said the Hollywood Divine,' Martin told him. 'And,

believe me, Theo was really psychic. Well, sensitive, that's what he said.'

'I guess anybody would be sensitive working for Elmore Sweet,' Ramone commented.

Martin took out the key that Sister Boniface had given him and fitted it into the lock of the safe-deposit box. As he did so, he was certain that he heard somebody whistling, somewhere upstairs in the derelict hotel. He hesitated, and listened, and then he heard it again. It was an odd little melody from *Sunshine Serenade*. Boofuls sang it at the very end of the movie, when he believed (mistakenly, of course) that he had lost his mother.

> *Apples are sweeter than lemons*
> *Lemons are sweeter than limes*
> *But there's nothing so sweet as the mem'ry of you*
> *And the sadness of happier times*

The song was unusual because it had been written by George Garratt rather than Boofuls' regular team of writers; and because – after Garratt had argued with L. B. Mayer over 'artistic differences' – the whole sequence had been cut out of the prints that had been sent out on general release. Martin knew the song because it was still included in the video of *Sunshine Serenade* that his friend Gerry had sent him from the M-G-M archives, but who else would have known it?

Fido, possibly, if he had ever heard Boofuls singing it. Or George Garratt, except that in 1958 George Garratt had washed down two bottles of chloral hydrate pills with a fifth of Polish vodka and been found to be DOA at Laurel Canyon Hospital. Or – if his image in Martin's mirror had been more than just an image, and if there was any truth at all in what Nurse Newton had said about him – Boofuls himself.

'*That didn't seem to make too much difference – him being dead.*'

Ramone said, 'What's wrong, man? You look like you seen a ghost.'

Martin strained his ears, but the whistling had died away,

faint and echoing, somewhere upstairs in the gloomy corridors of the Hollywood Divine Hotel.

'Did you hear something?' he asked Ramone.

Ramone shook his head.

'I don't know . . . I thought I heard somebody whistling.'

Ramone sniffed. 'Probably the wind, *mi amigo*. Or the plumbing.'

All the same, Martin was sure that he had heard that plaintive, unremembered song. 'The Sadness of Happier Times', words and music by George Garratt, vocal rendition by Walter Lemuel Crossley, known all over the world as Boofuls.

Martin tried to turn the key in the lock of the safe-deposit box. It was stiff and rusted, but he gradually managed to budge it. 'There! It's the right key, I'm sure of it! It's just so darn hard to turn it!'

'Just don't break it, that's all,' Ramone cautioned him, 'otherwise you're never going to get this suckah open.'

The levers grated together; and then quite suddenly the key turned all the way around, and Martin was able to lift open the door. The door of the safe-deposit box was quite small – only nine inches by four – but the inside was nearly two feet deep. Now that it was resting on its back, Martin would have to put his hand inside it like a lucky dip. He peered into it cautiously. Ever since that brindled cat Pickle had come flying out at him from the darkness underneath his desk, he had felt cautious about sticking his head in where it wasn't wanted, and also where it *was* wanted.

Ramone tried to look inside, too, and they bumped heads.

'Looks like it's empty,' said Ramone; not without relief.

'Well, I won't be able to tell until I put my hand in,' Martin replied.

'You're going to put your hand in? Supposing there's something *in* there?'

Martin lifted his head and looked at him. 'Something *in* there? Something like what?'

'Well, I don't know, man, supposing it's a trap. Supposing that nun that gave you the key wasn't a real nun, supposing she was just another one of these hallucinations – well, it *could* have happened, you can't deny it *could* have happened – and supposing she knows there's some kind of booby trap inside here, just waiting for somebody like you to stick his hot little hand right into it. I mean, supposing it's something as bad as that cat? I mean, do you *like* your hand, or what?'

'Ramone –' Martin interrupted him. 'The likelihood of there being *any*thing inside this box is pretty damn remote, wouldn't you say? Quite apart from the high probability that whatever was in here was probably collected by its rightful owner fifty years ago, the hotel management wouldn't have simply dragged these boxes down here and dumped them without going through them first. People used to keep money and diamonds and passports in these boxes, my friend. I can't believe that anything like *that* would have gotten left behind, can you?'

Ramone said, 'Money and diamonds and passports don't bite your fingers off. I'm talking about that supernatural stuff.'

Martin hesitated for a moment. He didn't like to admit it, but it had occurred to him, too, that something vicious from the world beyond might be nestling in the bottom of this safe-deposit box; or even something vicious from the here and now. Hadn't he read that scorpions can survive for fifty years without food or water?

At length, however, he carefully dipped his bare hand into the darkness of the open box, feeling all around the sides as he did so. Bare metal, nothing so far. He ventured further. All the time, Ramone was watching him intently, chewing at his lip. 'You feel anything, man? Is there anything there?'

Martin was about to take his hand out when his fingers skimmed something that felt like soft tissue paper. 'Hold on,' he said. 'There's something here.'

He patted the bottom of the safe-deposit box and felt a package of some sort, in very fine crinkled paper.

'It's not a booby trap, is it?' Ramone asked him.

'No, no. I don't think so. It's a package. I can't work out what's in it. Something hard, by the feel of it; no – more than one, maybe three or four. They're hard and they're curved. There's something *crunchy*, too. Maybe it's straw, or wood shavings. Hold on – if I can squeeze my other hand in, I can lift it out.'

With intense concentration, Martin pushed his other hand into the safe-deposit box until he could take hold of the package on both sides. It was very loosely wrapped together, and he was worried that if he lifted it up with one hand, the contents – whatever they were – would tumble out.

'Steady, man,' said Ramone as he slowly raised the package out of the safe-deposit box and laid it carefully down.

Martin reached back inside the box, but there was nothing else there. 'This is it,' he said. 'The sole contents.'

The package was a loose assembly of thin black tissue paper, tied with a thin greasy braid of something that could have been human hair. Where the hair was knotted, it was sealed with black wax, on which somebody had imprinted the crest from a signet ring or a brass seal. Martin gently shook the package, and inside he could feel a number of heavy curved objects, about four or five inches long, and a wad of crisp padding.

'Let's take it under the light and open it up,' Martin suggested.

Ramone's eyes widened. 'Supposing the mirror doesn't want us to? Supposing it tries to fix *us* the way it fixed Homer Theobald? You want to die with your lungs coming out of your mouth, because sure as hell I don't.'

'I always thought you were the great *Huevo Duro*,' Martin teased him.

'*Huevo Duro*,' Ramone repeated with contempt. It was Spanish for hard-boiled egg.

Martin gently carried the package over to one of the scores of tables that had been stored in the Hollywood Divine's cellar. He cleared off the dust and the rat droppings, and then he laid the package down. 'Do you have a knife?' he asked Ramone. Without saying a word, Ramone unenthusiastically produced a switchblade and flicked it open.

'*Huevo Duro*,' he muttered.

Handling the knife with extreme care, Martin sawed through the braided hair which seemed to be all that was keeping this messily tied package together. Then he folded back each leaf of the black tissue paper until he revealed what was inside. As soon as the package was open, Ramone crossed himself and whispered, '*Madre mia.*'

Lying on the black paper were four claws – thick and horny and black. They were like no other claws that Martin had seen before. They weren't lion claws, because lion claws are narrow and hooked at the end. They weren't eagle talons – they were far too large. Martin reached out and picked one up between finger and thumb, and asked, 'What in hell kind of a creature did these come from?'

'Believe me, I'm sure glad the rest of it ain't here,' Ramone told him. 'Come on, man, that stuff is bad news. I mean really bad news.'

Martin laid down the claw and picked up the wad of padding. It was black and shiny, not unlike horsehair. In fact it *was* hair of some kind, and it was attached to a small soft leathery patch that looked like a torn piece of dried-up scalp. It felt extremely old, almost mummified, and it felt extremely nasty.

'What do you think it could be?' Martin asked.

'Well, I don't know,' said Ramone, 'but I *hate* it.' He peered at it more closely, and then he said, 'You know what it reminds me of? It reminds me of voodoo. You know, witch doctors, that kind of thing. And those disgusting African statues all covered in skin and bits of fabric and you don't know for sure where any of it's *been*, you know?'

Martin juggled the heavy claws in the palm of his hand. 'I don't know. What on earth was Boofuls' grandmother doing with the key to *this* stuff?'

'Maybe she wasn't,' Ramone suggested. 'It's been fifty years, right? Maybe this stuff belongs to somebody else altogether.'

'You don't think that, do you?' Martin replied. 'Not after what's been happening with the mirror? This all ties up somehow.'

Ramone peeled back the tissue paper a little farther. 'Hey, look – you missed something.'

In one corner of the package, there was a small screwed-up piece of black tissue. Martin opened it up and found another key, identical to the key with which he had opened the safe-deposit box. He held it up and examined it closely.

'I wonder what *this* opens?' he asked.

He turned it over. There was the same manufacturer's name on it, Woods, and it looked as if it probably opened another of the boxes. But this time there was no number on it.

'If we had all night, we could try opening every box here,' Ramone suggested.

But at that moment, the desk clerk reappeared, wending his way through the furniture. 'I got to lock up now. Did you find what you were looking for?'

'More or less,' said Martin.

The desk clerk frowned at the black-tissue package. 'That's not dope or anything?'

Martin shook his head. 'Sorry to disappoint you. This is just relics; and not particularly valuable relics at that. You know what I mean, sentimental value only.'

The desk clerk sniffed dryly; the thumping sniff of the habitual cokehead. 'Sure, sentimental value only. Now I got to lock up.'

Dr Ewart Rice stood in his dressing room in his undershirt and his formal black pants, his suspenders hanging down like a recently released catapult. He was shaving, and humming to himself. The early evening sun shone warmly through the white percale blind that he had drawn down over the window, and reflected in the hot water in the washbasin, so that a spindly light fairy danced on the wall in front of him.

He and Mrs Rice had been invited to dinner that evening by one of his pleasantest friends, Bill Asscher, the movie producer. The Asschers' dinners could always be counted on for superb food, hilarious conversation, pretty girls, and generous martinis. Mrs Rice always said that he made a fool of himself when he went to the Asschers' dinners, but Dr Rice always replied that if a man couldn't make a fool of himself by the time he was sixty years old, then he was a fool.

He rinsed his razor in the washbasin and reached for his hand towel. From the bedroom next door, he heard Mrs Rice calling, 'Aren't you ready yet, Ewart? If we have to go, we might as well go on time. Then we can *leave* on time!'

'Won't be a moment!' Dr Rice called back.

He examined himself closely in the mirror. He never let it show, not to other people, but he was really quite vain. He liked to look absolutely immaculate: immaculately groomed, immaculately shaved. As far as he was concerned, the thought of going out in public with sleep in the corner of his eye or hair growing out of his nostrils was anathema.

He turned his face from one side to the other. Sixty, but still handsome in a Celtic way. Perhaps that left-hand sideburn could do with a trim. He couldn't stand the thought of a pretty girl sitting next to him at dinner covertly glancing at his left-hand sideburn and thinking, *What raggedy sideburns this old coot has.* Dr Rice's vanity was vanity of top Wesselton quality, in that he could imagine himself inside the minds of everybody he met, and of course in his imagination they were all thinking about *him* and nothing else.

Dr Rice opened the drawer next to the washbasin and took out his sharp hairdressing scissors – professional scissors, not on sale to the public. He leaned toward the mirror again, holding up the scissors in his right hand, tugging the skin of his cheek with the fingertips of the left hand, taking a last appraising look.

He blinked. His eyes seemed to blur. He blinked again, but his face in the mirror was still blurry. He wiped the glass with a dry facecloth, thinking it must have steamed up, but his face remained just as indistinct.

'Agnes!' he called, thinking that the maid had tried to clean his mirror with wax polish. 'Agnes, this mirror, I can't see a thing!'

'I'm just putting on my eyelashes,' Mrs Rice replied.

Dr Rice looked back at the mirror; and then he shivered, the way people do in a sudden icy draft. *Staring at him out of the reflected bathroom was not his own face, but the face of a child, a blond-haired, bland-faced child, with pinprick eyes and an expression of bright childish malice.*

Almost paralysed with fright, Dr Rice widened his eyes and tried to outstare the image in the mirror. If he stared at it hard enough, it would go away. Ghosts and spirits can never stand up to scrutiny in broad daylight.

But outside the window, the evening sun began to die, and the dressing room suddenly grew darker, as if it were a cage that had been draped in black baize. And the pale child's face remained, staring back at Dr Rice fierce and unabashed, almost gleeful.

'*Pickle-nearest-the-wind*,' the child mouthed. '*Pickle-nearest-the-wind*.'

'Go away,' said Dr Rice in a hoarse whisper. 'Go away, do you hear me? Go away!'

'Did you say something, dear?' his wife called out.

'Go away, go away, go away,' Dr Rice intoned.

'*You told tales*,' the child replied. '*Tell-tale-tit, your tongue shall be split, and every cat and dog in town shall have a little bit*.'

'Go away,' Dr Rice begged him.

But now the child's eyes opened wider, and his smile grew broader and merrier, and Dr Rice found himself raising his right hand up to the side of his face, his right hand in which he was holding his sharp professional scissors.

'*No*,' he pleaded.

The child smiled. '*Tell-tale-tit*.'

'I didn't mean to tell. He asked me. I didn't think I was doing anything wrong.'

'*You told, you told, you told*.'

'I didn't mean to!' Dr Rice wept. 'Please, my God, I didn't mean to. He *asked* me about you, that's all. I didn't think you were still –'

'You didn't think I was still alive? You didn't think I was still here? Then you are foolish, aren't you? Just as foolish as your wife says you are. Because I have been here since time began and I shall always be here, long after *you* are ashes!'

Mrs Rice said, 'Ewart? Is anything wrong? You really do sound most peculiar.'

But Dr Rice, when he opened his mouth, found that he was unable to speak. His throat felt as if it were being gripped in a steel claw; he couldn't do anything but gag for air. His left hand scrabbled against the counter beside the washbasin, knocking over his Gucci razor stand and his bottles of after-shave and his porcelain dish of Chanel soap. His right hand turned toward his face, his thumb and fingers slowly and inexorably prized apart by some uncontrollable tightening of his muscles, so that the pointed blades of the scissors opened, too.

As he gargled for air, his mouth stretched open and his tongue protruded, mauve from lack of oxygen, fat with effort, glistening and wagging.

'Tell-tale-tit, your tongue shall be split, and every cat and dog in town shall have a little bit!'

Dr Rice cut into his own tongue with the hairdressing scissors. There was a terrible crunch of flesh that he could feel right down to the roots of his tongue, right down to the pit of his stomach. His throat muscles contracted in an attempt to scream, but the grip on his neck remained, and there was nothing he could do but choke and struggle.

Blood gushed down the front of his undershirt as if he were pulling on a bright red sweater, and splattered into his shaving water. But the child in the mirror hadn't finished with him yet. His trembling hand opened up the blades of the scissors again, and enclosed his tongue from the side this time, so close to his lips that he cut his mouth as well. He could feel the sharpness of the scissors on the top and bottom of his tongue, and his eyes bulged in hysterical terror.

If I've split my tongue, that can be sewn up and healed. But oh, God, if I cut it right off –

The boy's face was sparkling with delight. 'You told, you told, you *told*!'

'Gggnnggghh,' pleaded Dr Rice.

'You told, and you shouldn't, and now you have to pay!'

Dr Rice's right hand went into a taut slow-motion convulsion and closed the grips of the scissors. He cut right through to the first split, and half of his tongue dropped into his washbasin. Then, shuddering all over, he raised his left hand and gripped the remaining half of his tongue by its tip and scissored that off, too.

Then he stood in front of the mirror, staring at it in shock, his lips closed, but a thin, dark, glutinous cascade of blood poured down his chin. Everything was bloody: his face and his hair and his clothes and his dressing room. He looked like a circus clown who had gone beserk with his pot of scarlet makeup.

Mrs Rice came into the dressing room, her hair stiffly lacquered, buttoning up the cuff of her shiny blue evening dress as she came. 'Ewart, what on *earth* are you playing at? We've only got fifteen minutes before we –'

Her husband stared at her pitifully out of a mask of blood. She stood with her hand over her mouth, staring back at him, and she didn't know what to do.

The man came flip-flapping on monkish leather sandals along the sidewalk, his spectacles reflecting the streetlights, his pipe clenched comfortably between his teeth. His Standard poodle trotted beside him on a long leash.

'Just as far as the bushes at the end of the development,' he informed his poodle. 'Then you can do your ah-ahs and we can turn around and head for home.'

He passed the front door of the Rice house. 'That poor Dr Rice. God alone knows what happened to *him*. Taken away like that, in an ambulance. God alone knows.'

It was then that the poodle stopped and stiffened and started to growl, way down deep in its throat.

'What's the matter, Redford? What is it, boy?'

The poodle continued to growl. The Rices' neighbor peered through the shadows at the side of the Rice residence; and there was a window open and a white blind flapping.

The neighbor hesitated. He wasn't too keen to go and investigate, since he knew that Dr Rice was still in the hospital and Mrs Rice was with him, and that the house was empty. There had been three armed burglaries already that month in the Hollywood Reservoir district; and in one of them, a friend of his had been shot in the shoulder. All the same, he waited, frowning, to see if there was any sign of a burglar in the house, and he slipped his poodle off the leash.

'Heel, Redford.'

There was a lengthy pause. All the man could hear were the endless orchestrations of the cicadas and the distant muttering of traffic on the freeways. The poodle whined and snuffled.

Suddenly, the white blind at the side of the house snapped

up, with a heart-stopping clatter, and a large dark shape bounded out of the window and ran across the lawn.

The poodle rushed silently after it and caught up with it just behind a large flowering shrub. The neighbor ran forward, then abruptly stopped and told himself 'Whoa!' when he heard the ferocity of the snarling in the shadows. He reached into his coat pocket and took out his flashlight, and cautiously probed the darkness with its thin beam.

He didn't understand what he saw; but it still made his stomach feel as if it were gradually filling up with ice water. A hefty brindled tomcat was crouched in the bush, savagely gnawing at a piece of blue-gray meat. His own poodle was standing beside the cat, and he was chewing something, too. A shredded piece of it was hanging from one side of his jaw.

'Redford!' the neighbor screamed at his dog. And then, to the cat, he screamed, 'Shoo! Get the hell out of it! Shoo!'

The cat stayed where it was, staring at him with eyes that gleamed frighteningly blue in the light of his flashlight. The poodle, too, refused to come to heel.

'Redford, you son of a bitch!' the neighbor screeched, and lifted the leash to smack his poodle across the nose.

But the cat spat at him so evilly, and Redford growled with such mutinous ferocity, that the man backed away, and shrugged, and said, 'Okay, forget it. Forget it. You want to squat in a bush and eat squirrels, see if I care. Just don't expect any Gravy Train tomorrow, that's all.'

Detective Ernest Oeste of the Hollywood police was sent back to the Rice residence at eleven-thirty that evening in order to retrieve two pieces of Dr Rice's tongue which had been overlooked by paramedics when they first answered his wife's emergency call.

There was no question of the pieces being sewn back into place. The damage to Dr Rice's tongue was far too extensive. But they were needed as evidence that Dr Rice had (almost unbelievably) inflicted his injuries upon himself.

'He loved to talk, why should he do such a thing?' Mrs Rice had wept.

Detective Oeste had to report after a lengthy search that Dr

Rice's tongue had apparently been taken and eaten by a rat or a cat.

Detective Oeste's immediate superior, Sergeant Frederick Quinn, sat for a very long time in front of his report sheet before typing, '*Cat got his tongue*'. Almost immediately, he deleted it, and typed, '*Evidence removed by predatory animals*'.

'Can you believe this case?' he asked the world.

CHAPTER SEVEN

Martin returned to Franklin Avenue that Sunday night exhausted; and a little drunk, too. Ramone had taken him to his favorite restaurant and bar, Una Porción, on Santa Monica, three blocks west of the Palm. They had drunk three bottles of López de Heredia and eaten countless *tapas* – cheese, squid, spicy sausage, sardines, meatballs.

Ramone had said, as they drove home along Santa Monica with the warm gasoline-fumy breeze blowing in their faces, 'Sometimes you have to make a deliberate effort to forget things, you know that? Otherwise you'd end up crazy. I forgot Lugosi already. He never happened. He was nothing but a figment of my imagination. When you forget, there's no pain. And who needs pain?'

'I'm trying to forget that my stomach is having a protest march,' Martin replied.

'What's the matter, you don't like Spanish food?'

'Each individual piece is okay, but somehow they don't seem to cohabit in my stomach very well. I can hear the sausages arguing with the squid. What are *you* doing here, eight-legs, this stomach isn't big enough for the two of us.'

Ramone had slapped him on the shoulder. 'Heyy, come on, you're going to be all right. What you need is a nice big glass of Fundador.'

'Ramone,' Martin had insisted. 'I'm going to take you home.'

He had dropped Ramone off; gripped his hand for a second as a thank-you; and then headed back toward his apartment. He parked awkwardly, his rear wheels well away from the curb, but he decided that whatever was good enough for Hunter was good enough for him. He switched off the car stereo, cutting off Simply Red in midfalsetto, and vaulted out of the car without opening the door.

He had only just pushed his key into the lock, however,

when the landing lights were switched on, and by the time he had stepped into the hall, Mr Capelli appeared at the head of the stairs, in his lurid gold bathrobe and his monogrammed slippers. 'Martin? Martin? Is that you? I've been calling all over!'

'Oh, hello, Mr Capelli. How are you doing? Did you have to wear that robe? I'm feeling a little nauseous.'

'Is Emilio with you?' Mr Capelli demanded, ignoring his gibe.

'Emilio? Of course not. I've been out with Ramone.'

Mr Capelli came halfway down the stairs, and then stopped, holding the railing, looking gray-faced and serious. 'Emilio is gone, Martin. Disappeared.

'What do you mean, gone?' asked Martin, trying to keep a steady eye on Mr Capelli in spite of three bottles of Spanish rosé. Then, '*Gone?* Gone where?'

'How should I know? One minute he was playing on the stairs with his toy cars; then his grandmother called him in for his bath; and he was gone.'

'He didn't go upstairs, did he? He didn't go up to my apartment?'

'How should I know? I don't know where he went!'

Martin clasped Mr Capelli's shoulder and gave him a reassuring squeeze. 'Don't worry, Mr Capelli, we'll find him. Everything's going to be fine.'

'But where is he? He never wandered off before.'

'Listen, really, he's going to be fine.'

'We called the police,' said Mr Capelli. 'We called the police straightaway.'

'And what did they say?'

'Well, they said they were going to put out a bulletin, what else could they do? But still no word.'

Martin said, 'Please – if you hear anything – don't forget to tell me, okay?'

'I tell you, I tell you.' Mr Capelli was deeply distressed. First to lose his daughter; then to lose his daughter's only child.

Martin climbed the stairs to his apartment. He had locked the door before he went out, but Mr Capelli had a drawerful of spare keys, and it was quite possible that Emilio had found one and let himself in. He prayed not. But he had a terrible feeling that the playmate in the mirror had proved irresistible and that Emilio had come upstairs to see him. He opened the door and went inside. He listened. No voices, no singing. Silence. He waited for a little while, and then he walked along the hallway and opened the sitting-room door.

The room was empty. Only the sofa, only the desk, only the mirror, with its chilly, uncompromising surface. Martin stepped slowly in, his shoes sounding loudly on the bare boards, his heart silently racing. *Pickle-di-pickle-di-pickle-di-pickle*.

He approached the mirror, reached out his hand, and touched it. It was cold, unyielding.

'Emilio?' he called quietly.

There was no reply. Only the sound of nighttime traffic on Highland; only the drone of an airplane headed toward Burbank. Only the wind, tapping at the venetian blinds like Blind Pew groping his way toward the Admiral Benbow.

'Emilio?'

Again, no answer. Martin stood for a long time in front of the mirror, quivering cold, wondering what the hell he was going to do. Because what *could* he do if Emilio had actually disappeared into the mirror, looking for Boofuls? How could he find him? How could he get him out? And what, finally, could he tell Mr and Mrs Capelli? That his obsession with Boofuls had lost them their only grandchild? How could he possibly compensate them for that?

He felt a chill in his body that was worse than the chill of death. It was the chill of total helplessness; of total loss.

Mr Capelli came into the room and stood staring at him.

'You called out Emilio,' he said.

'I, uh –'

'You called out Emilio. Why did you do that?'

'Mr Capelli, I have to be honest.'

'Honest, yes,' said Mr Capelli. 'Be honest. Be honest and tell me what you really think, that your mirror has taken Emilio. Your mirror has taken my grandson!'

Martin rubbed his aching head. 'Mr Capelli, I have no way of telling. You saw what happened before – you saw the way he was almost sucked into it. Well, I locked the door when I left the apartment this morning, but it's possible, isn't it, that Emilio might have found one of your spare keys? And if he did that . . .'

He paused. He didn't really know what to say.

Mr Capelli shuffled forward in his slippers and peered into the mirror. All he could see, however, was his own gray face and Martin's empty sitting room.

'If the mirror has taken him,' he said in a thick voice, without looking around, 'what can we do? How can we get him back?'

'I have no idea,' Martin admitted.

Mr Capelli kept on staring at his own reflection. 'There isn't anybody who knows about these things? You talked about finding a priest. Maybe a priest would know. My own priest, Father Lucas.'

Martin swallowed. 'I had somebody here this morning . . . a kind of a medium called Homer Theobald. I'm afraid he wouldn't go near it.'

'He wouldn't go near this mirror? Did he say why not?'

'Well, he said it was – powerful, dangerous, I don't know.'

'And he wouldn't help?'

Martin shook his head.

'Maybe I can talk to him,' said Mr Capelli. 'Maybe I can persuade him.'

'I don't think so, Mr Capelli. Homer Theobald died this afternoon. He had some kind of hemorrhage. I don't know whether it had anything to do with the mirror, but believe me, it seems like the mirror doesn't like to be crossed.'

Mr Capelli said, 'I'm going to call Father Lucas.'

'All right,' Martin agreed. 'I guess anything's better than sitting on our hands.'

Mr Capelli went downstairs. Martin waited for a while, watching the mirror in the hope that Emilio might reappear; then he went through to the bathroom and took a hot shower. By the time Mr Capelli came back he had sobered up, and coffee was perking in the kitchen.

'Did you talk to the priest?' Martin asked him.

'I talked to his housekeeper. She says he's at the hospital, somebody's dying, he has to give them the last rites. He's going to call me when he returns home.'

Martin poured out coffee. 'In that case, there isn't anything else we can do, is there? Just sit tight and hope that Emilio *hasn't* gone into the mirror; and that the cops find him.'

Mr Capelli went through to the sitting room, and Martin followed him.

'I never dreamed such a terrible thing could happen,' said Mr Capelli. He approached the mirror and touched its surface with both hands. 'I never dreamed.'

He turned around and there were tears streaming down his cheeks. 'You don't know what Emilio means to me, Martin. You just don't know. He's all I have left, all I have left. And now I can't find him, I feel like I've lost my own soul.'

Martin hugged Mr Capelli close and patted his back to soothe him. 'Come on, Mr Capelli, everything's going to work our. We'll find Emilio, I promise you.'

Mr Capelli looked up. 'How can you make such a promise?'

'Because I'm not going to rest until we get him back. I'm going to try everything. Police, priests, mediums, everything. And I'm going to find out all about this mirror, why it's got this power, what the hell it wants.'

'Well, you're a good boy, Martin,' said Mr Capelli with a sniff. 'I just wish you never bring this terrible mirror home with you. I could cut off my own hands for helping you to carry it.'

When Mr Capelli had gone back downstairs, Martin went into the kitchen and drank two strong cups of black coffee, one after the other. Then he returned to the sitting room and pushed the sofa around so that it faced the mirror. He was determined he was going to keep a vigil here, in case Emilio reappeared.

He switched out the lights and made himself comfortable on the sofa under an Indian blanket that Jane had bought when she went to Phoenix that time. The only reason she hadn't taken it with her was that Martin had kept it in the trunk of his car and she hadn't found it.

He took off his wristwatch and propped it on the arm of the sofa so that he could see it easily. It was a few minutes after midnight. Monday morning already. He yawned, stifled it, and then yawned again. He shouldn't find it difficult to stay awake all night. After all, his mind was racing and he was up to his ears in caffeine; and if he *did* start feeling at all sleepy, he had a few bennies in the bottom drawer of his desk.

He stared at himself in the mirror. A pale-faced man sitting on a sofa in a moonlit room. It looked rather like one of those surrealistic paintings by Magritte. He remembered seeing one Magritte painting in which a man is looking into a mirror, and all he can see is the back of his own head.

Mirrors, he thought, have always been mysterious. But he was going to unravel the particular mystery of *this* mirror even if it killed him.

He didn't realize that he was gradually falling asleep; that his head was drooping to one side, that his fingers were slowly opening like the petals of a water lily.

He jerked, and his eyes fluttered open for a moment, but then he dropped even more deeply into sleep than he had been before. His breathing became thick and harsh, the breathing of a man who has drunk too much wine. His wristwatch ticked softly beside him: one o'clock, one-thirty. Outside, the street was deserted, the night was silent.

He dreamed that he was traveling through the night on a bus, mile after mile, hour after hour, and that he was the sole passenger. He knew that the bus was traveling in the wrong direction, and that it would take him days to get back to where he really wanted to go. He tried to stand up, to talk to the driver, but the bus was swaying so much that he kept overbalancing back into his seat.

He shouted out. His voice sounded small and congested, but he was sure the driver could hear him. The driver, however, refused to turn around, refused to answer.

They drove farther and farther into the darkness. 'Where are we going?' he kept shouting. 'Where are we going?'

At last the driver turned around. To Martin's terror, his face was the gilded face of Pan. He grinned wolfishly and stared at Martin with gilded eyeballs.

'Pickle-nearest-the-wind,' somebody said, with cold breath close to Martin's ear.

He whispered and groaned and shifted in his sleep, but he didn't wake up. His wristwatch showed that it was two o'clock.

In the mirror, the sitting room door opened a little way, although the real sitting room door didn't move at all. A cold stripe of moonlight fell across the floor, and in that moonlight was a small shadow, the shadow of a boy.

The shadow remained still, unmoving, for almost a minute; but you could have told by the faintest trembling of the door that the boy was holding the handle, and listening, and waiting.

At last the boy came into the reflected room. He was about eight years old, with curly blond hair and a pale face with tiny pinpricked eyes. He was wearing a lemon-yellow shirt and a pair of lemon-yellow shorts, and white ankle socks and sandals.

The moonlight caught his curls so that they gleamed like white flames. His expression was extraordinary: elated, fierce, like a child who has become so overexcited that he begins to hyperventilate.

He stood motionless for a moment; and then he smiled even more widely and began to walk toward the mirror. He didn't hesitate for a second, but stepped straight through it, so that he was standing in the moonlight in the real room. Behind him, the surface of the mirror warped and rippled for a moment, as if it were a pool of mercury.

The boy approached the man sleeping on the sofa. He watched the man for a very long time. The man's watch softly chirruped away the minutes. The man snuffled and groaned and said something indistinct. The boy smiled to himself; and then reached out and took hold of the man's open hand.

Martin, in his sleep, felt the small cold hand slide into his.

'Emilio?' he asked. His mouth felt dry, and he opened and closed it two or three times to try to moisten his tongue. His eyes flickered, then opened.

The boy grinned. 'Hello, Martin.'

Martin opened his eyes wide and stared. The shock of waking up and finding that Boofuls was actually holding his hand was so violent and numbing that he couldn't do anything at all, he couldn't move, couldn't speak.

'Did I frighten you?' asked Boofuls. His voice was clear and reedy, with the precise enunciation of prewar years. 'I didn't mean to frighten you. You knew I was coming, didn't you? You did *know*.'

Martin's hand shrank out of Boofuls' grasp. He began to shudder and to draw his legs up on the sofa. For one instant, his mind was right on the very edge of complete madness; right on the brink of giving up any kind of responsibility whatsoever. But the boy was so calm and smiling, so utterly real, that the madness shrank away, like a shadow disappearing under a door, and Martin found himself sitting on his sofa face-to-face with a real boy who had been horribly and publicly killed nearly fifty years ago.

'I *have* frightened you, haven't I?' said Boofuls.

Martin gradually eased his feet back onto the floor. He didn't take his eyes off Boofuls even for a moment. He was frightened that, if he glanced away, Boofuls would disappear. He was just as frightened that he would still be here.

'You mustn't be frightened, really,' said Boofuls. 'I'm only a boy, after all.'

'You're a *dead* boy,' Martin whispered.

Boofuls laughed. 'Do I *look* dead? Do I *feel* dead? Here — take my hand and tell me that I'm dead.'

Martin hesitated, but Boofuls took his hand and pressed it against his chest. Martin could feel the steady beating of his heart; the rising and falling of his lungs.

'Well, okay, you're not dead,' he said. 'You ought to be dead, but you're not.'

'You don't *want* me to be dead, do you?' asked Boofuls. 'Not like *she* did. And she wasn't the only one, either. Lots of people wanted me dead. But I'm here, I'm me. That's enough, isn't it? And you *like* me, don't you? I know you do!'

'I like your pictures,' said Martin, although it seemed like a pretty vapid thing to say, under the circumstances. But then —

looking over Boofuls' shoulder, back toward the mirror – he said, 'Where's Emilio? Did Emilio go into the mirror?'

'Emilio?' Boofuls replied quite tartly. 'I don't know anybody called Emilio.'

'The boy you were playing with. The little Italian boy.'

'Oh, *him*,' said Boofuls. 'He's all right.'

'Is he *in* there?' Martin demanded, pointing toward the mirror. 'That's what I want to know.'

Boofuls said, 'You mustn't shout at me, you know. If anybody shouts at me, I have one of my fits.'

'I know about your fits. I know pretty well everything about you.' Martin stood up, circling around Boofuls and then approaching the mirror. 'But you listen to me, I know something about this mirror, too. It has its own particular properties. It tries to suck things in; it *can* suck things in if it's allowed to. But for everything that goes in, something else has to come out. A ball for a ball, a cat for a cat, and now what? *You're* here – and the only way you could have gotten out is if somebody similar went into the mirror to take your place. I think that somebody similar was Emilio.'

Boofuls listened to this, and then smirked, and then burst out laughing, a brassy little childish laugh.

'Did I say something funny?' Martin asked him savagely. And all the time he was thinking: *What am I doing? I'm actually talking to Boofuls, the real Boofuls, the real genuine murdered boy from all those years ago*. The shadow of madness still quivered behind the door.

'He *wanted* to play,' said Boofuls. 'I didn't *make* him. He came because he wanted to. I didn't make him, I promise.'

'So where is he now, exactly?'

'I don't know. He's probably playing somewhere. There are lots of children to play with. Well, some of them want to play, anyway.'

'It's nearly three o'clock in the morning.'

'Well,' said Boofuls, 'it's *different* in there.'

'Is he safe?' Martin demanded. 'If I were to go into that mirror, too, could I find him and bring him back?'

Boofuls frowned and looked away.

'I asked you a question,' Martin shouted at him.

Boofuls' lower lip stuck out, and his eyes suddenly filled up with tears. 'I didn't – I didn't mean to do anything wrong – I thought – it would be all right. He wanted to play – he said that he *wanted* to play – and it was all right – his grandfather said it was all right.'

Martin hunkered down beside this strange curly-headed boy in his lemon-yellow clothes and laid a hand on his shoulder. 'Emilio told you that? Emilio said that he had permission from his grandfather?'

Boofuls nodded tearfully and wiped his eyes with the back of his hand. 'I didn't mean to do anything wrong.'

Martin held Boofuls close. He felt cold under his thin summer clothing, but apart from that he felt just like any other child. His tears fell on Martin's shoulder.

At last, Martin sat down on the sofa and took hold of Boofuls' hands and looked him straight in the face. 'Walter,' he said, 'I have to ask you some serious questions.'

'You mustn't call me Walter. Nobody's allowed to call me Walter.'

'That's your name, though, isn't it?'

'That was *his* name.'

'Your father's name, you mean?'

Boofuls nodded. 'I'm not allowed to talk about my father.'

'Do you know who he was? Did you ever meet him?'

'I'm not allowed to talk about my father.'

'But, Boofuls, listen, those people who didn't allow you to talk about your father, they're all dead now; and they've been dead for a very long time. It doesn't matter anymore. What we have to do now is find out how *you* managed to stay alive in that mirror and how we're going to get Emilio back and what we're going to do about you.'

'You can't get Emilio back.'

Martin felt a small sick feeling in the bottom of his stomach; and it wasn't only caused by last night's Spanish wine. When he thought about Lugosi's grisly transmogrification into a cat-snake, the prospects of getting Emilio back from beyond the mirror seemed desperately remote. Or even if they *could* get him back, it seemed highly unlikely that he would be the same normal five-year-old boy that he had been before.

It seemed to Martin that the mirror changed the shapes of living creatures so that they took on the physical appearance of what they really were. Lugosi, like most cats, had been sinuous and coldhearted and carnivorously minded. That was why he had taken on the shape of a snake.

Maybe he was wrong, but Martin strongly suspected that the world beyond the mirror was just like the world of the dead, the way that Theo had described it to him. Maybe it was the very same world. Maybe the mirror was a window that looked into heaven; or purgatory; or straight into hell.

The strongest piece of evidence was Boofuls, the living, breathing, long-dead Boofuls.

Martin said, a little unsteadily, 'Okay . . . let's take this one step at a time. First of all, what's beyond that mirror?'

Boofuls turned to the mirror and frowned. 'Hollywood,' he said.

'But not *this* Hollywood?'

'No,' Boofuls agreed. 'Hollywood the other way around.'

'Let me ask you this: where do you live in Hollywood?'

'Sixteen sixty-five Stone Canyon Drive, Bel Air. The house is called Espejo.'

'Is your grandmother still alive?'

Boofuls shook his head. 'She hung herself.'

'But she didn't hang herself until she'd killed *you*. So how come you're still alive and she's not?'

'Because I didn't want her to be.'

'But that's not up to you, is it? Deciding whether people live or die?'

Boofuls said nothing in reply to that question, but stared at Martin intently with those piggy little eyes. Martin could see now just what the M-G-M makeup department had done to give him that wide, dreaming look. Boofuls was pretty, in a way, but if Martin had been Jacob Levitz, he certainly wouldn't have looked at him twice when he auditioned for *Whistlin' Dixie*.

Perhaps Boofuls had been fresher looking in 1935, thought Martin, with a sudden dash of black humor. After all, in those days, he hadn't been dead for fifty years.

Martin slowly rubbed the palms of his hands together.

'Okay,' he said, 'if your grandmother's dead, who takes care of you?'

'Miss Redd takes care of me. Miss Redd always took care of me.'

Martin sat back. 'I never heard of Miss Redd.'

Boofuls shrugged, as if to say that wasn't *his* fault. 'Would you like some orange juice?' Martin asked him. 'Anything to eat?'

Boofuls brightened up. 'Do you have Ralston's?'

Martin said, 'I'm sorry. How about Count Chokula?'

Boofuls looked disappointed. 'I'm collecting Ralston box tops, for the Tom Mix Straight-Shooters ring.'

'The Tom Mix Straight-Shooters ring? That's a radio premium, isn't it. Or *wasn't* it? They haven't given away stuff like that on the radio since –'

He stared at Boofuls in horrified fascination. He suddenly realized that he wasn't simply talking to a living ghost, he was talking to a ghost who still lived in 1939.

Boofuls sat at the kitchen table with a large bowl of Count Chokula and a glass of milk. Martin had made himself another cup of strong coffee. It was four o'clock in the morning, and his head felt as if it were slowly being closed in a car door. Outside the kitchen window, the sky was gradually beginning to lighten; false dawn, the hour of false promises.

Martin sat opposite Boofuls, straddling one of the kitchen chairs. He tried to discover what kind of life Boofuls lived in 'Hollywood the Other Way Around'. He found it almost impossible to imagine an entire city in complete reverse. Yet of course he glimpsed it every day of the week, every hour of the day. Hollywood the Other Way Around appeared in store windows, barbershop mirrors, polished automobiles, shiny cutlery – everywhere and anywhere he came across a reflecting surface.

It was the idea of walking around *inside* those reflecting surfaces that he found so difficult to grasp. But Boofuls, with his mouth full of chocolate cereal, said, 'Why? You do it all the time. You can see yourself there.'

'Well, sure,' said Martin, 'but that's not actually *me*, is it, that's Me the Other Way Around. A left-handed me, a me who parts his hair on the opposite side, a me with a mole on my right cheek instead of my left.'

Boofuls smiled at him. Martin wasn't too keen on his smiles. They had a sly coldness to them that he couldn't quite pin down. Boofuls said. 'That you in the mirror is more like you than you are.'

'And what's that supposed to mean?'

'Look in any mirror, Martin, and you'll see the truth.'

It wasn't only Boofuls' smile that Martin found disturbing. It was the way he talked. Sometimes he was quite childish, only using eight-year-old words, and eight-year-old ideas. But occasionally the mask of childhood would slip slightly, and he would say something that was too calculating and too philosophical for a boy of his supposed age. Although, what *was* his age? He was ageless; he was dead. He was nothing more than a glamorous memory that had stepped out of a mirror.

'Tell me something else,' said Martin after a while. 'If I lay a mirror flat on the ground and look down into it, the world looks upside down, as well as the other way around. Everybody's clinging onto the ground by the soles of their feet. How do you guys cope with that?'

Boofuls finished his milk and wiped his mouth with his hand. 'It's different, that's all.'

'I'll say,' Martin remarked.

Boofuls propped his chin on his hands and stared at Martin with supreme confidence. 'The thing is, Martin, she didn't kill the real me. That's why she hanged herself. When she was doing it, she suddenly realized that she wasn't killing the real me.'

Martin thought about that. Then he said, 'All right, if she didn't kill the real you, which one of you was the real you? The Boofuls in this Hollywood or the Boofuls in Hollywood the Other Way Around?'

Boofuls smiled. 'Which one of you is the real you, Martin? If I were to kill *this* you, who would be left? What would be left?'

'I really don't know, to tell you the truth,' Martin admitted.

'Well, you'd know if it happened. You'd *know*.'

'All right,' Martin agreed, 'she didn't murder the real you. But what happened then, after the you who *wasn't* you got himself chopped up into two hundred eleven pieces?'

'There was nothing I could do but go away,' said Boofuls. 'Everybody thought I was dead. They closed down *Sweet Chariot* and everybody was paid off. Have you seen any rushes from *Sweet Chariot*?'

Martin shook his head. 'I've seen everything else you've done. I've even seen your screen tests for *Flowers From Tuscaloosa*. They were pretty dire, weren't they?'

'I had the grippe. I still got the part.'

'Well, sure you did. There was nobody else. There was only one Boofuls. Well – *is* only one Boofuls.'

The hot coffee had steamed up Martin's glasses. He took them off and polished them with the pulled-out tail of his shirt. Boofuls watched him for a little while and then said, 'We could finish that picture, couldn't we?'

Martin peered at him. He was shortsighted, and without his glasses Boofuls' face appeared white and fuzzy, with dark circles around his eyes. Almost – for a moment – like a skull.

'What do you mean we could finish the picture?'

'Well, imagine it,' said Boofuls, licking his lips with the tip of his tongue. 'Screenwriter discovers boy who can sing and dance and act just like Boofuls, *just* like Boofuls, and plans to finish Boofuls' last unfinished picture.'

'But I *don't* plan to finish Boofuls' last unfinished picture. I plan to present a musical of my own called *Boofuls!*'

Boofuls was silent for a long time. He traced a pattern on the Formica tabletop with his finger. At last he said, 'I want to finish *Sweet Chariot*.'

'Well . . . it's a possibility, I suppose,' said Martin. 'But it's going to be pretty difficult finding backing. I had enough grief trying to sell my own musical. And the whole idea of *Sweet Chariot* is pretty much out of date these days. A boy turning into an angel? Everybody's done it – Warren Beatty, Michael Landon . . . all that *Heaven Can Wait* stuff. George Burns even played God.'

'George Burns is still alive?' asked Boofuls in surprise.

'Well,' said Martin, 'some people like to think so.'

'I want to finish *Sweet Chariot*,' Boofuls repeated. His eyes widened in sudden ferocity. 'It's *important!*'

'Come on, you're talking about a twenty-five-million-dollar production here. I don't think many producers are going to risk that kind of money on a remake of a 1939 musical.'

'But it's a Boofuls musical,' Boofuls insisted.

'Ho, ho, ho, don't tell me that,' replied Martin. 'In this town, there are half a dozen names that stink, and as far as I can make out, Boofuls is the Least Desirable Aroma of the Year.'

Boofuls slowly shook his head. His eyes had a tiny, faraway look, as if he were peering down the wrong end of a telescope. 'You're wrong, Martin. Things are going to change. Boofuls is going to be famous again. Boofuls is going to be loved!'

Martin stood up and collected Boofuls' bowl and glass. 'All I can say to that is, convince me.'

'I will. I promise.'

'Meanwhile,' said Martin, 'I have something a whole lot more serious to talk about. I want to get Emilio back.'

'I told you. You *can't* get him back.'

'Does that mean *ever?*'

Boofuls was silent. Martin leaned forward across the table and snapped. 'Does that mean *ever?* Or what?'

'There is a way,' said Boofuls.

'Oh, really? And what way is that?'

Boofuls glanced up and smiled, and looked away again. 'We could make a deal. If you help me to finish *Sweet Chariot,* if you take care of me, then when it's finished, you can get Emilio back.'

'Why not before?' Martin demanded.

'Because I won't,' said Boofuls.

'What the hell do you mean you won't?'

'I won't, that's all. I can, but I won't. That's the deal.'

Martin banged the kitchen table with his fist. 'Listen to me, you beady-eyed sprout! There's an old couple downstairs and Emilio is all they've got in the whole entire world! Either you get Emilio back or you don't get squat from me, *comprende?*'

'I won't,' Boofuls repeated.

'What do you want me to do?' Martin challenged him. 'Put you over my knee and spank you?'

'You mustn't shout at me,' Boofuls replied. 'If you shout at me, it brings on my fits.'

'I want Emilio back,' Martin told him in a soft, low, threatening voice.

'I want to finish *Sweet Chariot*.'

Martin tried to stare Boofuls out; but there was something about the little boy's eyes that made him feel unnerved; almost vertiginous; as if he were about to fall into a cold and echoing elevator shaft forever.

He backed away. Boofuls didn't take his eyes away from him once.

'I don't lift one finger until I get Emilio back,' Martin told him, but much less convincingly than before.

'But – if you *do* get Emilio back – how will I be sure that you will still help me to make *Sweet Chariot*?' Boofuls asked him.

'You don't know. You'll have to trust me.'

'I don't trust anybody.'

Martin finished his cup of coffee. 'Maybe it's time you started.'

At seven-thirty that morning, Martin tugged up the venetian blinds and greeted the bright California sunshine. Boofuls was sitting at the desk, solemnly doodling with Martin's black Conté pen: clouds and faces and disembodied smiles.

Martin turned around and looked at him. He was a real boy, right enough, flesh and blood, freckles and buck teeth. His legs were lightly tanned, and there was a grazing of white skin on his knee where he must have fallen. Martin crossed the sitting room and watched him drawing for a while, and Boofuls even *smelled* like a boy – biscuity and hot. Without even thinking about it, Martin ruffled his curls.

Boofuls immediately knocked his hand away. 'Don't do that. Nobody's allowed to do that.'

'All right, I'm sorry.' Martin smiled. 'I guess I wasn't treating you quite like a big movie star.'

'I am a big movie star,' Boofuls said petulantly.

'You *were* a big movie star,' Martin reminded him.

Boofuls didn't bother to reply to that; but by the look on his face Martin could tell just how contemptuous he felt about it. Martin knew plenty of grown-up movie stars, and their total egotism never came as any surprise. It was as much a part of the job they did as a steady hand is to a carpenter. But it was a shock to meet such consummate vanity in a child of eight – even a child of eight who had walked into his life in wildly unnatural circumstances. Somehow Martin had always liked to believe that prepubescent children had a natural cynicism, a gift for self-squelching, which made such vanity impossible.

Not this kid, however. As far as Martin could tell, Boofuls had no interest in anybody but himself. Martin could already begin to understand why he had won such rapid and rapturous success – what star quality it was that Jacob Levitz had seen in him that first day he had auditioned for *Whistlin' Dixie*. A good movie star is interested in nothing but what other people think about him; and a brilliant movie star is *obsessed* by what other people think about him.

Martin said, 'We're going to have to think about what we're going to do with you. You can't suddenly appear out of nowhere at all and expect to continue living your life as if nothing had happened. If you're going to stay this side of the mirror, you're going to need education, social security . . . And how are you going to get those? Your birth certificate shows you were born in 1931 and yet you're only eight years old.'

Boofuls stared at him. 'All I want is new clothes. Then we can start making the picture.'

'What's so important about this damned picture?'

But Boofuls wouldn't answer. He sat on Martin's chair swinging his legs and doodling: clouds as high as clifftops and strange seductive smiles.

Just then, there was a knock at Martin's apartment door. Boofuls glanced up, and there was a look of cold curiosity in his eyes, but Martin said, 'Stay here, okay? I don't want anybody finding out that you're here yet.' He went to answer the door. It was Mr Capelli, in a blue Jack Nicklaus T-shirt and blue-and-white-checkered seersucker golfing pants. He had dark damson-colored circles under his eyes, and he was a little out of breath from climbing the stairs.

'Hey, Martin, I didn't wake you?'

'No, I was up already. Come on in.'

'I called the police about ten minutes ago,' said Mr Capelli. 'They told me no news.'

Martin closed the door. 'How's Mrs Capelli taking it?'

'Terrible, how do you think? I had to give her Tranxene last night.'

'You want some coffee?' Martin asked him.

'Sure, why not?'

'Have you eaten anything? I've got a couple of raspberry Danishes in the freezer.'

Mr Capelli gave him an odd look. 'Is something wrong?'

'Wrong?' said Martin in feigned surprise. 'What do you mean wrong?'

'You're fussing,' said Mr Capelli. 'I don't know, you're all *flibberty*.'

Martin shrugged. 'I'm a little tired, that's all. I didn't sleep too good, worrying about Emilio.'

He ushered Mr Capelli into the kitchen, glancing quickly toward the sitting room to make sure that Boofuls hadn't decided to make an appearance. Mr Capelli said, 'I called Father Lucas, too. He's coming around at nine o'clock.'

Martin spooned Folger's Mountain Blend into the percolator. 'Oh, yes, Father Lucas. I'd forgotten about him.'

'I don't know how serious he took it,' Mr Capelli replied, dragging out one of Martin's kitchen stools and perching his wide backside on it. 'When I told him we were having trouble with a mirror, you know, the way it nearly sucked in Emilio and all that stuff – well, he sounded a little distracted. You know what I mean by distracted? Like he was thinking about his breakfast instead, or maybe what he was going to preach in church next week.'

'Sure,' said Martin. 'I know what you mean by distracted.'

'He's a good priest, though,' Mr Capelli remarked. 'Kind of old-fashioned, you know, traditional. But I like him. He baptized Emilio; he buried my daughter.'

The water in the percolator began to jump and pop. Martin

took down two ceramic mugs and set them on the table. As he did so, Boofuls appeared in the open doorway, behind Mr Capelli's back. The look on his face was unreadable. Martin couldn't tell if he was angry or bored or amused. His eyes flared in tiny pinpricks of blue light, as if they could cut through steel.

'Some of these young priests, they seem to take a pleasure in challenging the old ways. You know what I mean by challenging? They say, why shouldn't a priest marry? Why shouldn't people use a contraceptive? What's so special about the Latin mass?'

Mr Capelli looked up at Martin's face.

'Hey,' he said. 'What's wrong? You look like you just remembered it was your mother's birthday yesterday.'

Slowly, frowning, Mr Capelli twisted around on his stool so that he was facing the door. He saw Boofuls standing there, silent and small, with that eerie expression on his face that wasn't smiling and wasn't scowling and wasn't anything at all but *triumph*, sheer, cold *triumph*.

Mr Capelli was silent for one long second, and then he shouted out '*Yah!*' in terror, and jumped off from his stool, which toppled noisily over backward onto the kitchen floor. He stood with his back pressed against the cupboards, both hands raised, too shocked and frightened even to cross himself. When he managed to shout out a few desperate guttural words, his Italian accent was so dense that Martin could scarcely understand what he was saying.

'Whosa dis? Whosa dis boy? Donta tellmi. Martin donta tellmi!'

Boofuls remained silent: still triumphant, but placid. Mr Capelli edged away from him, right around to the far side of the kitchen, and stood staring at him in horror.

Martin said, 'It's Boofuls. He came out of the mirror.'

'He came out of the mirror, he tells me. Holy God and All His Angels. Ho Lee *God!*'

Martin laid a hand on Mr Capelli's shoulder. 'I was hoping he wouldn't come in. I didn't want to frighten you.'

'He didn't want to frighten me!' Mr Capelli repeated.

Boofuls came gliding forward into the kitchen. He held out

his hand. 'You mustn't be frightened,' he told Mr Capelli. 'There's nothing to be frightened of at all.'

Mr Capelli crossed himself five times in succession, his hand flurrying wildly. 'You're a dead person! You stay back!'

Boofuls smiled gently. 'Do I *look* dead?' he asked.

Mr Capelli was shaking. 'Don't you touch me, you stay back. You're a dead person.'

But Martin came forward and laid his hand on Mr Capelli's shoulder and said, 'Mr Capelli, he *should* be dead, by rights. But he isn't. You can see that he isn't. And I don't think that he's going to do anything to hurt us.'

'Nothing to hurt us, eh? So where's Emilio? Emilio went into the mirror, and this boy came out, is that it?'

Martin was about to explain that, yes, there was a chance that Emilio might have gone into the mirror, but that Boofuls was certainly going to help to get him back. But Boofuls forestalled him by saying in that piping voice of his, 'You're quite right, sir. Emilio is in the mirror. He went to play with some of my chums.'

This was more than Mr Capelli could take. His face turned ashy blue, and Martin had to drag over a chair for him so that he could sit down. He sat with his hand pressed over his heart, breathing deeply. Boofuls stood beside him, still smiling.

'Emilio's quite *safe*, sir,' he told Mr Capelli.

'Safe?' said Mr Capelli harshly, in between breaths. 'Who cares about safe? I want him back.'

'I'll get him back,' said Boofuls.

'Well, then, go on then, what are you waiting for?' Mr Capelli demanded.

But Boofuls shook his pretty little head. 'All in good time, sir. All in good time.'

Mr Capelli reared up; and Martin had to grab hold of his shoulders to make him sit down again. 'What's this, "all in good time"? You go in there, and you go get my grandson for me, and if he isn't here in five minutes, *five* minutes, I'm going to give you the hiding of your life whether you're a dead person or not, do you get me?'

Boofuls stared at Mr Capelli in surprise, and then lowered his head and covered his face with his hands.

Mr Capelli said with less confidence. 'What're you doing? You go get Emilio, do you hear me?'

Boofuls' face remained concealed. Martin stepped toward him, but he sidestepped away, without lowering his hands. For a moment, Martin had the disturbing feeling that if he tried to prize Boofuls' hands away, he would uncover not the pretty pale features of Boofuls, but the gilded sardonic face of Pan. He hesitated, glanced back at Mr Capelli, then shrugged. He didn't know what he ought to do.

It was then that Mr Capelli saw the tears that were squeezing out between Boofuls' fingers. The boy's shoulders were trembling; and it was clear that he was deeply upset. Mr Capelli frowned and reached one hand forward.

'Listen, young man . . .'

'It's Boofuls, Mr Capelli,' said Martin. 'It really is. And that's what he likes to be called.'

Mr Capelli cleared his throat. 'Well, here, listen, Boofuls. I'm sorry. I didn't mean to yell like that. But the truth is, I'm real worried about Emilio. I don't like that mirror at all, and I don't want him wandering around in there, it's not healthy, do you know what I mean by healthy?'

Boofuls hands remained closed over his face. Mr Capelli looked anxious now and shifted his chair a little closer. Boofuls, in response, stepped back another pace.

'Listen to me,' said Mr Capelli, 'I'm a grandfather. I love children. I don't know where you've come from, I don't know how you can be dead but still walking around and talking, but I'm willing to accept that maybe I don't understand absolutely everything in this universe. I don't understand accumulated earnings tax, does that make me a bad person? But I love Emilio. Emilio is all I've got. And even if he's safe wherever he is, I need to have him back.'

Boofuls at last lowered his hands. His face was stained with tears. He looked utterly bereft and miserable.

'Oh, Mr Capelli,' he said, 'I'm so unhappy.'

'Hey, come on,' said Mr Capelli, and held out his arms. Boofuls hesitated for a moment and then came up to Mr Capelli and hugged him as if he were his own grandfather.

'Do you know something, you're right,' said Mr Capelli,

beginning to smile. 'You don't look dead at all. You sure don't *feel* dead. I don't know how it happened, but you're a live boy!'

Martin watched all this with caution. There was no doubt at all that Boofuls was a most appealing child, yet he couldn't rid himself of that feeling he always had when he watched a Boofuls musical: that here was a grown-up man, a cunning grown-up man, masquerading as a small boy. Boofuls was just a little too clever; just a little too calculating. Seeing him win over Mr Capelli was almost like watching a skillfully written scene in a movie, specifically aimed at tugging at the audience's heartstrings.

'Oh, aunt,' Freddie Bartholomew had wept in *David Copperfield*, 'I'm so unhappy.' And Boofuls had used the same line in exactly the same way. A last desperate tug at a grandfather's heartstrings. *David Copperfield* had been released in 1935, so Boofuls could easily have seen it.

'Mr Capelli –' warned Martin.

But Mr Capelli said, 'Shush now, Martin. I'm a grandfather. Besides, what have we got here? A famous movie star.'

'Mr Capelli –' Martin repeated, but there was little that he could do. Boofuls shot him a quick hostile look that Mr Capelli didn't see: a look which meant *you stay out of this, or you'll never see Emilio again*.

'Emilio's safe, sir,' he told Mr Capelli, wiping his tears with the back of his hand. 'There are plenty of people who are going to take care of him. But the moment Emilio comes back, then I have to go back into the mirror, I *have* to.'

'But inside the mirror,' said Mr Capelli, 'that's where you really live, right? You don't truly *belong* in this world anymore.'

Boofuls swallowed miserably, and tears began to fill up his eyes again. 'I don't *live* there, sir, nobody *lives* there. It's a kind of a place where you go if you can't get to heaven.'

'Purgatory,' put in Martin.

'Well, some people call it that,' said Boofuls. 'But you *can* get to heaven if you fulfill your life's work, the work that God intended you to do.'

188

'And making *Sweet Chariot*, that was the work that God intended *you* to do?'

Boofuls nodded. 'If I can make that picture, then I can rest.'

'What's this *Sweet Chariot*?' Mr Capelli wanted to know.

Martin said nothing for a moment, watching Boofuls. Then he poured out coffee, and passed a cup to Mr Capelli, and explained, 'It was Boofuls' last picture, wasn't it, Boofuls, before his grandmother murdered him. Or *thought* she'd murdered him. It was about a street urchin who becomes an angel, and who flies around doing good deeds in order to meet with the Almighty's approval. A musical; something of a tearjerker, believe me.'

Boofuls clung to Mr Capelli's neck. 'I never finished the picture, I never managed to finish it, and if I don't finish the picture I'm going to have to stay in the mirror forever and ever, and never get out.'

Martin sipped his coffee. 'You see what he's asking, Mr Capelli? He's asking if you'll allow Emilio to stay in the mirror so that he can make his picture and fulfill his life's destiny and go to meet his Maker.'

Boofuls sobbed, 'I know it's an awful lot to ask you, sir. I know it is. And I know how much Emilio means to you. But please, I beg of you. Otherwise I can never sleep for all eternity. And I'm so tired, sir. So terribly, *terribly*, tired.'

Tears welled up in Mr Capelli's eyes, too, and he patted Boofuls' narrow back. 'I don't know what to say,' he replied thickly. 'I don't know what to say. How can a man and a grandfather turn away somebody like this, some little boy who needs his help?'

'Mr Capelli,' said Martin, 'doesn't Emilio have any kind of say in this?'

'Well, sure he does,' agreed Mr Capelli. 'But if Boofuls is telling us the truth, then Emilio *wanted* to go play in the mirror. He *wanted* to.'

'Couldn't we ask Emilio for ourselves?' Martin suggested.

'Can we do that?' Mr Capelli asked Boofuls.

Boofuls nodded. 'We can ask him, yes. But you mustn't try

to get him out of the mirror. Until I'm ready, it could be very dangerous. He could die.'

'Let's just go and see him, shall we?' said Martin.

They went through to the sitting room. The sunlight was very bright in here, and Mr Capelli shielded his eyes with his hand. The mirror seemed larger than it had before: larger and clearer. Anybody who hadn't known that there was a mirror there might have been forgiven for thinking that it was nothing more than a gilded archway through to another identical room.

As they approached the mirror, Martin saw with a prickle of surprise that he and Mr Capelli were accompanied not by a reflection of Boofuls, but by a reflection of Emilio. The two boys stood in perfectly matching positions, and if one of them nodded his head, then the other one nodded, too.

'Emilio . . .' whispered Mr Capelli. Then, rushing up to the mirror, '*Emilio!*'

But of course all that Mr Capelli managed to do was to press himself against his own reflection. Emilio stood *behind* Mr Capelli's reflection, just as Boofuls was standing behind him in the real room. Mr Capelli hesitated and then stepped back again, so that he could see Emilio more clearly.

'Emilio?' asked Martin. 'Are you okay?'

Emilio was wearing a *Star Trek* T-shirt and red shorts and scruffy red and white trainers. He looked a little pale and tired, but otherwise well. The lick of black hair which usually fell across the left side of his forehead fell across the right side instead, and his wristwatch was on his right wrist. His face had an oddly asymmetrical appearance, simply because Martin was used to seeing it the other way around.

Emilio called, 'I'm fine, I'm okay. I'm having fun.'

'Who's taking care of you?' Mr Capelli asked him. Emilio held hands with the reflected Mr Capelli, and Boofuls held hands with the real Mr Capelli. Both of them smiled.

'*You're* looking after me, of course,' said Emilio.

'Me?' asked Mr Capelli, mystified.

'You and Grandma. 'You're in here, too. So's Martin; so's everybody. It's just like home.'

Mr Capelli pressed the heel of his hand against his forehead. He couldn't understand this at all. 'All I want to know is, are you okay? Me and Grandma, we're taking care of you okay? Feeding you good? Nobody's hurting you, nothing like that? Nobody's telling you that you *have* to stay there?'

'Grandpa, I like it here. I'm happy.'

Mr Capelli looked toward Martin for support; but Martin was too busy examining their reflections in the mirror for something which gave him a clue to how this apparent hallucination actually worked. Yet there seemed to be nothing, no tricks at all. He was seeing a blond-haired motion-picture star of the late 1930s whose reflection in the mirror was a dark-haired Italian boy of the late 1980s, and that was all there was to it.

'Emilio,' Martin said, 'if I told you that you could come back over here, right now, right this second, what would you say to me?'

'I like it here,' Emilio repeated. 'I'm happy.'

But there was an edginess in Emilio's voice that made Martin feel that he wasn't telling the whole truth.

'Emilio,' he asked, 'what's it *like* in there? Is it really like home? Boofuls said it was different.'

'Well, sure, it's *different*,' said Emilio. He wasn't smiling at all.

'Listen, I have a suggestion,' said Martin to Boofuls. Boofuls wasn't smiling either. 'Why don't you get back into the mirror while I start putting your movie package together? It's going to take months before anybody's going to tell us yes or no; and months more to rewrite and cast the picture; and even more months before they can get around to set building and costumes. We'll be lucky to have this production finished in eighteen months, two years. And Emilio can't stay behind that mirror for two years.'

Boofuls' eyes tightened and darkened. 'I was trapped in the mirror for fifty years, Martin. Fifty! If I don't get out now, I'm never going to get out, ever.'

'But you can't possibly expect Emilio to stay in that mirror-world until he's seven!'

'The picture won't take two years to make,' said Boofuls.

'Oh, yes, and how can you be so sure about that?'

'I'm sure, that's all. Once it starts production, it'll be easy. None of the sets were destroyed; none of the costumes were spoiled.'

'How do you know that?'

'I *know*, that's all. They're all at a warehouse in Long Beach.'

'Well, well,' Martin replied, trying not to sound too bitter about it, 'we're all ready to roll, then. We've got the star, we've got the screenplay, we've got the costumes, we've got the sets. All we seem to have forgotten is that minor detail called finance. Twenty-five million dollars for a full-scale musical, and that's the bottom line.'

Boofuls didn't respond to Martin's sarcasm, but smiled and said, 'We'll see.'

Mr Capelli, confused, called out to Emilio. 'Emilio, hey, I love you?'

'I know, Grandpa,' said Emilio. 'But Boofuls can't rest if I come back now.'

'Emilio, listen –'

'You must help him,' little Emilio insisted in a tone far graver than any that Martin had heard him adopt before.

'Martin,' begged Mr Capelli, 'what can I do?'

'Quite seriously, Mr Capelli,' said Martin, 'if I were you I'd *demand* –'

But Mr Capelli's dilemma was settled for him; because at that moment a cat's tail swished black and gingery from behind the door in the reflected sitting room, and Emilio immediately darted after it, out of the door, and disappeared. Martin turned around. Boofuls had run out of the room too. They heard him giggling in the kitchen, as if he were playing with a pet.

'*What* can we believe?' asked Mr Capelli, stretching his arms out wide. Martin could see that he was very close to collapse; and the shock of this morning's events was beginning to make *him* feel swimmy and light-headed, too. Too much caffeine, not enough sleep, not enough to eat.

Martin said, 'I don't know, Mr Capelli. I really don't know. Maybe your Father Lucas will tell us what to believe.'

*

Sister Boniface was kneeling at early prayer in the chapel of Sisters of Mercy Hospital; her head bowed; her eyes tightly closed; her mind very close to God.

The chapel was modern and very simple. Plain oak pews, plain oak floor, an altar of polished gray marble.

Its richest feature was its stained-glass window, depicting the Madonna holding the naked Christ-child, with rays of multicolored light transporting her up to the clouds. Sister Boniface adored this window. The light strained through it differently at different times of the day. Sometimes it looked peaceful and slightly melancholy: at other times, when the sun shone fully, it blazed with holy glory.

Today Sister Boniface was praying in particular for the soul of Homer Theobald. She had learned through the hospital grapevine that he had died; and she had learned from Sister Michael that Martin and Ramone had been with him. However, she had been afraid to call Martin to confirm her deepest anxiety – that the key which she had given him had attracted the attention of a vengeful Satan. She was mortified that she believed in evil spirits; and she was wracked with guilt for having given Martin the key.

When she met him last week, it had seemed to Sister Boniface that Martin could well be the messenger for whom she had been waiting for fifty years: the man who would settle her torment once and for all, and give her peace. She had sensed an aura of honesty about him; an aura of blessed destiny. But now she was beginning to suspect that Satan might have been deceiving her, and that all he wanted to do was to relieve her of the key which she had guarded for so long.

She had no idea what the key unlocked, but she knew that it was more terrible than anybody could imagine.

She prayed for her fellow sisters, she prayed for the hospital, she prayed for a small boy in St. Francis of Assisi ward who was dying of AIDS from a contaminated blood transfusion. She prayed for peace and fulfillment, and that Homer Theobald had found his place in the Kingdom of Heaven.

She was finishing her prayers when a voice whispered, *'Sister Boniface'*.

She looked up; looked around. There was nobody there. The chapel was deserted.

'*Sister Boniface.*'

She listened. At last, she stood up, brushing down her white habit, and said in a quavering voice, 'Who's there? Is anybody there?'

'*Sister Boniface, you betrayed me,*' the voice said.

'I betrayed no one,' said Sister Boniface. 'I have always kept my word and my sacred trust.'

'*You gave away the key, Sister Boniface.*'

Sister Boniface stepped out into the aisle and walked toward the altar, looking from left to right for any sign of the whisperer hiding behind the pews or the pillars.

'*You betrayed me, Sister Boniface, now you will have to be punished.*'

Sister Boniface stopped in front of the altar. On her right, beside one of the smooth Italian-marble pillars, scores of votive candles burned brightly and were reflected in her eyes. The dear Madonna smiled down at her from the stained-glass window. She knew that nothing terrible could happen to her in the sight of the dear Madonna.

'*Nobody can betray me and go unpunished,*' the voice said, just as close to her ear as it had been before. '*Warm hands, warm, the men have gone to plough; if you want to warm your hands, warm your hands now.*'

Sister Boniface said, 'Who are you? *What* are you? What do you want?'

'*She gave you the key to keep,*' whispered the voice. '*She gave you the key to keep. Not to lose, not to give away. To keep forever, and to take with you to your grave.*'

Sister Boniface whirled around, but there was nobody behind her, nobody anywhere to be seen. Her mouth felt suddenly parched, and she started to tremble. 'O Holy Mother, protect me,' she prayed. But she was beginning to feel that prayer alone was not going to be enough. 'In the name of the Father, and of the Son, and of the Holy Spirit . . .'

'*Warm hands, warm,*' murmured the voice. '*The men have gone to plough. If you want to warm your hands, warm your hands now.*'

It was then that she caught sight of his face; and she screamed out loud. Her scream echoed in the chapel, but there was nobody there to hear her.

He was smiling at her from the small mirror just above the banks of votive candles – childish, white-faced. The same boy who had floated over his grandmother's bed all those years ago. The same boy whose unearthly appearance had tormented Sister Boniface for the rest of her life.

'*Ah,*' whispered Boofuls, '*you've seen me.*'

Sister Boniface walked towards the mirror, her left foot dragging slightly, her habit rustling on the marble floor. Boofuls watched her approach and his eyes were tiny piercing lights.

'I never betrayed you,' said Sister Boniface, her voice shaking.

'*You were supposed to take that key to your grave, you miserable old witch,*' Boofuls spat back at her. '*When you gave that key away, you gave away part of my secret. You should have known better than that, witch, even you.*'

Then, in a slow, measured rhythm, he sang, '*Warm hands, warm; the men have gone to plough; if you want to warm your hands, warm your hands now.*'

Sister Boniface shuddered. 'You are Satan,' she declared, 'I know you now! You are Satan!'

Boofuls laughed. He laughed and laughed. He laughed so much that – for one peculiar second – his face in the mirror almost seemed to turn itself inside out, and reveal something dark and gristly and insectlike. Sister Boniface cried out '*Satan!*' and reached up over the banks of votive candles to take the mirror down.

It was then that she felt every muscle in her body lock tight. She was paralyzed, with her arms held over the candles. She tried to move, tried to cry out, but her nervous system simply refused to obey her.

Satan, she thought wildly. Satan!

There were more than seventy candles burning just below her outstretched hands. What at first had felt like a wave of warmth now began to feel like a furnace. The boy's face in the mirror watched her in delight as Sister Boniface gradually began to realize what was going to happen to her.

O Mother of God, protect me, the pain! thought Sister Boniface. But she was completely powerless to move her hands away from the heat of the candles, or to scream out for help. She had never known anything so agonizing. Her hands began to redden, and she began to smell a strong aroma of scorched meat. Each finger-nail felt as if it were white-hot.

Please, she begged Boofuls inside her mind. *Please release me, please! I'll get back the key, I promise you! I'll take it to the grave with me, just as you ask!*

But all Boofuls did was to chant, '*Warm hands, warm, the men have gone to plough; if you want to warm your hands, warm your hands now!*'

Slowly, inch by inch, Sister Boniface found that she was lowering her hands toward the candle flames. The heat was so intense that she could scarcely feel it. The skin on the palms of her hands blackened and shriveled, and strips of it dropped off and fell onto the candleholders, where it hung, smoking. The sleeves of her habit began to smolder; and as her hands came lower and lower, they burst into flame, so that her bare wrists were licked by the fire as well.

Tears poured from Sister Boniface's eyes and down her wrinkled cheeks. The agony was thunderous. She wanted to do nothing but die, even though her paralysis made it impossible for her to turn and see the face of the dear Madonna.

The flesh of her hands was actually alight now, and it burned with a sputtering sizzle. Gradually the layers of skin were burned through, and the flesh charred, and the bones were exposed, her own fingerbones bared in front of her eyes.

'*Warm hands, warm, the men have gone to plough!*'

It was just when the agony reached its greatest that Boofuls released Sister Boniface from her paralysis. She didn't realize what had happened at first; but then she let out a scream of sheer tormented pain that pierced the chapel from end to end.

She lurched back, away from the candles, holding her blazing arms out in front of her like a sleepwalker. *The holy water,* she thought in desperation, *I can douse my hands in the holy water.*

She began to make her way step by step along the aisle. Her hands were nothing but blackened stumps now, and her sleeves were leaping with orange flame. Her wimple, incendiary with starch, suddenly flared up like a crown of fire and set light to her short-cropped hair underneath.

By the time she had managed to make her way half-way down the aisle, her habit was ablaze from hem to shoulder. She was a shuffling mass of fire, her head alight, her eyes wide with shock and terror, no longer able to scream or even to whimper.

She knew that she would never be able to reach the holy water. She twisted, collapsed, then fell onto her side. She could hear the fire roaring in her ears. She could see the flames dancing past her eyes.

In a last agonized effort, she managed to lift her head, just long enough to glimpse the stained-glass window behind the pews. The dear Madonna still smiled at her, as she had always done. Sister Boniface tried to say something, the smallest of prayers, but her habit had burned through to her under-clothing now, and the skin on her legs was alight, and she died before she could whisper even one word.

Although he was patrolling the second floor, one of the hospital security officers had heard Sister Boniface screaming, and had gone to investigate. He had thought at first that it was one of the cleaners laughing or larking about. He opened a dozen office doors before he eventually reached the chapel.

'Jesus,' he said when he opened the doors.

The chapel was dense with smoke. In the middle of the center aisle, a blackened figure was huddled on the floor, a few last flames still flickering on its chest. The security officer felt his throat tighten with nausea, and he didn't know whether he ought to go into the chapel or not. There was no chance at all that the figure on the floor was still alive.

Eventually, he took a deep breath, masked his nose and mouth with his padded-up handkerchief, and cautiously stepped inside. He made his way up the aisle until he reached Sister Boniface's body. Then he just stood and stared at it in horror.

Her head had been burned so fiercely that most of her skull had collapsed into ashes. Her ribs curved up from an indistinguishable heap of burned cloth and carbonized flesh; her pelvis lay like an unwanted wash-basin.

The only way in which the security officer could tell at once that it was Sister Boniface was her crucifix, a large bronze cross, mottled with heat, from which the figure of Christ had melted into small distorted blobs of silver.

He thought he heard a rustling noise in the chapel, like somebody moving about on tiptoe, but when he peered through the smoke he saw nobody at all.

He unhitched his walkie-talkie from his belt, switched it on, and said, 'Douglas? This is Andrej. Listen, you'd better get down to the chapel. Sister Boniface has had some kind of an accident. No, burned. I don't know, maybe she got too close to the candles. No, dead. No, *dead*. Are you kidding? She hasn't even got a mouth left to give the kiss of life to.'

He clipped the walkie-talkie back on his belt and then stood staring at the ashes of the woman who had made the mistake of giving away Boofuls' key.

CHAPTER EIGHT

Father Lucas had sprained his ankle that weekend playing baseball with the boys of St Ignatius' Little League team. He came heavily up the stairs to Martin's apartment, rocking himself between the banister rails, and grunting noisily. Mr Capelli came up behind him, trying to make himself useful, but proving to be more of an irritation than a help.

'It's all right, Mr Capelli,' Father Lucas insisted. 'I've worked out my own rhythm. Don't upset it, or you'll have me falling down the stairs backward.'

'Watch for this corner,' fussed Mr Capelli. 'Sometimes I trip here myself, and how long have I lived here?'

Upstairs in the sitting room Boofuls sat placidly watching *Sesame Street*. Martin stood by the window, watching Maria Bocanegra sunning herself before going off to work. She must have fallen asleep, because one of the Sno-Cones had been blown off by the morning breeze, and one nipple was bared. It looked like a soft, wrinkled prune, thought Martin. The kind you could gently sink your teeth into.

From time to time, he glanced at Boofuls. As soon as Father Lucas had visited, he was going to take Boofuls out to Sears and buy him some new clothes. T-shirts, sneakers, so that at least he *looked* like a kid from the 1980s. He thought it was extraordinary that he had come to accept Booful's presence so easily. Yet if somebody's actually *there*, he thought, talking and walking and living and breathing, what else can you do? It doesn't matter if they came out of a mirror or down from the moon.

Father Lucas knocked at Martin's front door. 'Hello there! Mr Williams!' Martin lowered the venetian blind and came away from the window. 'This'll be the priest,' he told Boofuls. He had already told him that Father Lucas was coming to visit, but Boofuls had appeared to be completely uninterested. He didn't seem to be any more interested now.

Without waiting to be shown in, Father Lucas appeared at the sitting room door. He was a barrel-chested man with a leonine head that seemed to be far too big for the rest of his body. His silver hair was combed straight back from his forehead. He wore heavy horn-rimmed glasses that reminded Martin of a pair of 1950s television sets, side by side, each showing a test transmission of a single gray eye.

Father Lucas swung himself into the room and grasped Martin's hand. 'Mr Capelli tells me you've been having some trouble, Mr Williams.' He looked around and then he said, 'You won't mind if I have a seat? I was trying to show my Little Leaguers how to throw a forkball, and I got rather carried away.'

He limped across to the sofa where Boofuls was sitting watching *Sesame Street*. 'Hello, young fellow!' he said, beaming and ruffling Boofuls's hair. 'You don't mind if I park myself next to you, do you?'

Without even looking at him, Boofuls said, 'Yes, I *do* mind. And don't scruff up my hair again. You're not allowed to.'

Father Lucas stared at Boofuls in bewilderment. He had always liked to think that he was 'pretty darn good' with children, especially young boys.

Mr Capelli snapped, 'Hey! You! Kid! You're talking to a priest here! You're talking to a holy father!'

Boofuls reluctantly took his eyes away from Kermit the Frog and looked Father Lucas up and down.

'I'm Father Lucas. And you are –'

For one moment – so quickly that it was like a rubber glove being rolled inside out and then the right way round again – an expression rippled through Boofuls' face which made Martin shiver. He had seen hostility in children's faces before; but nothing like the concentrated venom which disfigured Boofuls. He scarcely looked like a child at all: more like an evil-tempered dwarf.

But then the hostility vanished, and Boofuls was smiling and pretty once more – so angelic, in fact, that Father Lucas smiled back at him with pleasure, and said, 'Well, now, aren't *you* the uppity one?'

All the same, he backed off, and sat down at Martin's desk, and nodded and smiled at Boofuls almost as if he were afraid of him.

'It's the mirror,' said Mr Capelli, his eyes glancing from Boofuls to Father Lucas and back again.

'I'm sorry? The mirror?' asked Father Lucas. He turned around in his chair and looked at himself in the mirror on the far wall. 'Oh, yes. The mirror. Well, it's very handsome, isn't it?'

'It took my grandson,' said Mr Capelli.

'It –?' asked Father Lucas, lifting his spectacles, not at all sure what Mr Capelli meant.

'It took my grandson, took him away. He's in there now.'

Father Lucas looked at Martin for some reassurance that Mr Capelli was quite all right and not suffering from some temporary brainstorm. The heat, you know. Maybe the male menopause. Men of this particular age sometimes acted a little feverish. But Martin gave him a nod to assure him that it was true.

'We didn't expect for one minute that you were going to find this easy to believe,' he told Father Lucas. 'But this definitely isn't your ordinary common or garden mirror. It's like a way through to another world.'

'Another world?' said Father Lucas, looking even more unsettled.

'It's still Hollywood in there,' Martin told him. 'But it's Hollywood the other way round. And the reflections that appear in that mirror aren't always the same as the real people and objects that are standing in front of it. Did you ever read *Alice Through the Looking-Glass*?'

'Yes, of course,' said Father Lucas, still baffled.

'Then that'll give you some idea of what's happening here. You remember in *Alice* how the looking-glass world was completely different once Alice was out of sight of the mirror. I think this mirror's similar. Once you walk through that sitting room door in there, the whole world's turned on its head.'

Without looking at Boofuls, Martin said, 'I know for a fact that people can survive after death, inside that mirror.'

'You know that for a *fact*?' queried Father Lucas.

Martin nodded.

There was a lengthy and embarrassing silence. Boofuls continued to watch *Sesame Street* with no obvious concern at Father Lucas' presence. Father Lucas sat on his chair with his double chins squashed up by his dog collar, his eyes fixed on the floor, his forehead furrowed like a Shar-Pei, trying to think of an appropriate response. He had known Mr Capelli for years and years, and he had never known him to be anything but sincere. Pompous, occasionally irascible; but never foolish or dishonest.

Father Lucas had never met Martin before, but Martin certainly didn't *look* wild or eccentric; or like a malicious practical joker.

'You'll have to forgive me,' he said. 'I'm not at all sure that I understand what you're asking; and even if I *could* understand what you're asking, I'm not at all sure why you're asking *me*.'

He stood up and walked toward the mirror. 'You're trying to tell me that people can walk in and out of this mirror?'

Martin said, 'Sometimes. Not always.'

Father Lucas knocked on the glass with his knuckle.

'Seems pretty solid to me. What's behind it?'

'An outside wall. Back of the house.'

Father Lucas breathed on the mirror's surface and wiped it with his cuff. 'And you say that if you *can* get into the mirror . . . then beyond that sitting room door, things are very different from the real world?'

Mr Capelli put in, 'We saw a ball, yes? A child's ball. In here it was blue and white, in there it was a tennis ball.'

He swallowed hard, and then he added, 'I saw Emilio in there, my own flesh and blood; but here it was –' He lifted one arm towards Boofuls, then dropped it against his side. 'In here it was this boy.'

'*This* boy?' queried Father Lucas, inclining his head toward Boofuls.

Uneasy, Mr Capelli wiped his sweating palms on the sides

of his pants. Father Lucas walked back toward Boofuls and hunkered down beside him, inspecting him through his television-set spectacles as if he were a doctor and Boofuls had been brought to him with suspected mumps. Boofuls completely ignored him and carried on watching television.

Father Lucas held out his hand, but Boofuls, without looking at him, moved his own hand away.

'What's your name, son?' Father Lucas asked him in a gentle voice.

Boofuls' eyes remained fixed on Grover. 'My name is Lejeune,' he said.

'Lejeune? Is that French?'

Boofuls shook his head. Father Lucas waited for him to say something else, but when he didn't, he rose to his feet and said, 'He's a relative of yours?'

'He's my –' Martin began; but Mr Capelli immediately interrupted.

'He's a friend of Emilio's; a good, good friend. Best buddies. His parents had to go away for a week or two. So – well – he's staying with us. With me and Mrs Capelli.'

Boofuls didn't make any attempt to deny this fiction; but kept on smiling.

'Well . . .' said Father Lucas. 'I'm not too sure what it is you want me to do.'

Mr Capelli grasped his arm and spoke to him racetrack-confidential. 'I want you to tell me if that mirror is a good mirror or an evil mirror. I want you to tell me what you feel when you touch it. Also, I was hoping that maybe you could think of some way to get Emilio out. Some *holy* way, do you understand what I mean by holy? Just so that nobody gets hurt. You see Lejeune here, well, I wouldn't want *him* to get hurt, for instance.'

'Why should there be any danger of him getting hurt?' asked Father Lucas.

'Father,' Mr Capelli replied, 'I just don't know. But maybe prayer can help. You know – maybe you can ask God.'

Father Lucas tried to look benign. 'God isn't exactly an agony uncle on some local radio station, somebody you can call up just whenever you feel like it.'

'I know that. He's better. Look at His ratings. God has better ratings than anybody you can think of, on any station.'

'Mr Capelli,' said Father Lucas, 'let's just take this one step at a time. You're asking me to tell you whether the mirror is good or evil. Well, let's find out. There's a little test we can do. I suppose you could call it a litmus test for blasphemy.'

'Litmus?' frowned Mr Capelli, as Father Lucas took a small phial of silver and dark blue glass out of his coat pocket.

'Didn't you do any science at school?' Martin asked him. 'Litmus is a powder that turns red in acid and blue in alkali. They make it out of moss.'

'And this is litmus?' Mr Capelli asked, pointing to Father Lucas' phial.

Father Lucas smiled and shook his head. 'Not quite, Mr Capelli. But it has a similar effect. It is water from the Holy Shrine at Lourdes, mixed with salt from the Sea of Galilee. It is said that if it touches any evil or desecrated object or person, it will burn them, like acid.'

Boofuls looked across in interest when Father Lucas said this; but after a while he returned to the television. *Little House on the Prairie* seemed to entertain him more than foolish priests who sprained their ankles playing baseball.

Father Lucas unscrewed the cap of the phial and lifted it up in front of the mirror. 'In the name of the Father, the Son, and the Holy Ghost,' he intoned, and cast drops of holy water at the surface of the mirror in the sign of the cross.

To his astonishment, the holy water *flew right through the surface of the mirror and splattered onto the floor in the reflected sitting room.*

Father Lucas stared at the image in the mirror, then touched the glass of the mirror itself, then stepped back to stare at the real floor.

'My God,' he whispered. 'It's *there*, in the mirror, but it's not *here*.' He licked his lips anxiously. 'It went right through. How could that happen? It's solid glass.'

Martin said, 'Now you know why we called you.'

Father Lucas waited for a moment, plainly unsure what he was going to do next. 'There could be some scientific explanation,' he suggested. 'I always look for the scientific explanation before I start imagining that I'm face-to-face with something demonic. Well, it's only right. Science in itself is a wonder of the Lord; and if a phenomenon eventually turns out to *defy* science, well then, it's all the more wonderful for that.'

'So what are you going to do?' asked Mr Capelli. 'All you lost in there was some holy water. I lost my grandson.'

'Well,' said Father Lucas. 'This isn't really my bag, so to speak. I'm not an exorcist; and I'm not too sure that an exorcist is what you need. You may be better off with a physicist.'

Boofuls laughed out loud, but it wasn't at all clear whether he was laughing at the television or at Father Lucas. Mr Capelli gave him a stern look, and he said, 'I'm sorry.'

Stiffly, Father Lucas got down on his hands and knees and patted the floorboards where (in the mirror) they were wet. Martin had done the same thing when Boofuls' ball first bounced into the reflected room; and with an equal lack of success.

'I can see myself touching it,' he said, 'and yet my fingers aren't wet. It's quite astonishing.'

He held out his hand to Martin to help him back up again; but just as he did so, something came flying *out* of the mirror in exactly the same parabola as the holy water had flown *in*. It splattered onto Father Lucas' forehead and down the side of his cheek.

He cried out 'Ah!' in surprise, and lifted his fingers to his face. He had been hit by several white glutinous droplets, which dripped onto the floor, and hung from his fingers in thin sticky strings.

'Here,' said Mr Capelli, taking out a large clean handkerchief and unfolding it. 'Here, Father, wipe yourself with this.'

'What in God's name is it?' Father Lucas asked in disgust. He lifted his fingers to his nose and sniffed. Then he sniffed again. Then – his horror so strong that he almost panicked – he snatched the handkerchief from Mr Capelli's hand and wiped and wiped his face until it was bright scarlet all down one side.

'Semen!' He quivered. 'Semen!'

Mr Capelli crossed himself, and then crossed himself again. Martin helped Father Lucas to climb to his feet. Once he had steadied himself, Father Lucas stared at the mirror in anger and frustration. 'This is the work of the devil, you must have realized that from the very start.'

'But what can you do?' Mr Capelli begged him. 'The work of the devil is something that priests are trained to handle, eh? So you can do something for us?'

Father Lucas was about to say something when he turned unexpectedly and looked at Boofuls. Boofuls was staring at him with one of his triumphant, expressionless faces.

For a moment, their eyes engaged in a silent, careful game of question and answer. Then Father Lucas walked over to him and said, 'What do *you* know about this mirror?'

Mr Capelli caught hold of Father Lucas' arm. 'Listen, Father, he doesn't know nothing at all. He's only been in town since yesterday.'

Father Lucas continued to stare at Boofuls in the way that a confident man stares at a dog which has a reputation for being vicious and mad. 'Lejeune,' he said. 'That's your name, is it? Lejeune.'

Boofuls smiled fleetingly and said nothing, but he didn't take his eyes away from Father Lucas, not once. Martin didn't like the look of that smile at all. It made him shudder, as if somebody were stepping on his grave.

They went downstairs to Mr Capelli's apartment, leaving Boofuls on his own. 'Come in and have coffee,' Mrs Capelli begged Father Lucas. 'I have some beautiful polenta.'

Martin said, 'Go ahead, Father, please. There's something I want to show you.'

'All right, all right,' Father Lucas agreed. He took out his handkerchief and gave his reddened cheek yet another rub. 'But I can only stay for a quarter of an hour.'

'It won't take any longer,' Martin assured him.

While Mr and Mrs Capelli took Father Lucas through to the parlor, Martin ran downstairs and out into the street. He unlocked the trunk of his Mustang and carefully lifted out the black-tissue package that he and Ramone had discovered at the Hollywood Divine. Then he returned to the house with it and carried it upstairs.

Mrs Capelli was setting the table with plates and cups. She looked fretful and unsettled, and her braided hair was coming loose on one side. Father Lucas was talking to Mr Capelli about the mirror. They obviously hadn't told Mrs Capelli that it had ejaculated in Father Lucas' face. But Father Lucas looked extremely worried.

'You always associate this kind of demonic event with the Middle Ages,' he was saying, 'but the truth is that the devil never rests, any more than the Lord Almighty.'

'Amen, amen,' put in Mrs Capelli, clattering coffee spoons.

Martin came in and laid the black-tissue package on the lace tablecloth. Father Lucas shifted his chair around to examine it. 'What's this?' he wanted to know. 'Is it anything to do with the mirror?'

'I think so, but I don't know what. Let me tell you something, Father, before you open it. A man was killed yesterday, helping me to find this stuff. Whether it was an accident or not, I can't say. He might just have hemorrhaged. But I don't really think so.'

Mrs Capelli crossed herself. 'Holy Mother of God, what is it?'

Father Lucas untied the braided hair and teased open the tissue paper. He lifted one sheet up, and the black claws tumbled out onto the table with a rattling sound.

'God protect us,' Mr Capelli said hoarsely.

'Where did you get these?' Father Lucas asked, picking one of the claws up and turning it over.

Martin said, 'Just at the moment, I don't want to tell you. Well, I want to tell you, but I can't. It's all to do with protecting Emilio. But they *do* seem to have some connection with the mirror. A very strong connection.'

Father Lucas wrinkled up his nose as he took out the piece of dried scalp. Then he found the key.

'Do you have any idea what this opens?'

'A safe-deposit box, I think, in the same place where we found all this stuff. But there are dozens of them, and we don't know the number.'

'What was the number of the box you found these in?'

Martin dug into the pocket of his jeans and took out the key that Sister Boniface had given him. 'Here it is, 531.'

Father Lucas examined it carefully. 'Well . . .' he said. 'I know only a little about occult numerology, but I know enough to recognize the Number of the Beast when I see it.'

'The Number of the Beast?'

'Satan's number, 666. Don't you remember that film *The Omen*? They made great play of it in that.'

'Oh, yes . . .' said Martin. 'Wasn't it tattooed on Damien's scalp or something? I mean, is that real? Is that really the number of the devil?'

Father Lucas looked almost embarrassed. 'The story was fiction, of course, but the number was real. As far as I know it came from biblical times. But, you know, it used to be disguised by Satanists . . . split into quarters or tenths or halves or whatever. This is one of the things they taught us at Bible college. You see – what is the *reverse* of 531?'

Martin said without hesitation, '135.'

'Quite right . . . but if you add them together? 135 and 531?'

Martin said nothing. Mrs Capelli stood in the doorway with a dangerously tilting plate of polenta with pine nuts and stared at Father Lucas openmouthed, even though she didn't have the slightest idea what was going on.

Father Lucas gestured toward the claws. 'It would appear to me that what you have come across here is *half* of the artifacts used in the satanic Sabbat. It doesn't take a genius to guess that the other half can be found in locker number 135.'

Martin slowly sat down. He picked up one of the claws and held it up to the light. It was jet black, opaque, and extraordinarily heavy. 'So what are these things? What are they used for?'

Father Lucas said, 'I'm not an exorcist.'

'But?' asked Martin, catching the implication in his voice that he probably knew more.

'Well,' said Father Lucas, 'they used to tell us at St Patrick's that there were relics of Satan, just as there were relics of the True Cross, and the Holy Shroud, and the crown of thorns.'

'And that's what you think these are? Relics of Satan?'

'Well, now, who can tell? It could all be nonsense.'

'But it isn't nonsense, is it?' said Martin. 'You saw that

mirror for yourself. You threw the holy water and it went right through. You know that something evil is going down here, just as well as we do.'

Father Lucas sat and stared for a long time at the scattered claws. Then he said, 'They taught us at St Patrick's that the beast had been beaten, years ago, and that his body had been torn to pieces and scattered to the ends of the earth.'

'And?' asked Mr Capelli impatiently.

'And that's all,' said Father Lucas. 'Except that what you have here – these claws, this skin, this hair – they are all pieces of the beast. And whoever left them in that locker was obviously determined to bring them back together again – all the pieces, no matter where they were scattered – and re-create the creature that the Bible calls Satan. The *true* Satan, the very core of all evil – in the flesh.'

Martin rearranged the claws by nudging them with the tips of his fingers; but he didn't feel like holding them as tightly as he had before. Satan may be an oldfashioned concept, but it was still frightening.

Father Lucas asked, 'You really can't tell me where you found these, or where the remaining pieces might be?'

Martin thought about it for a while, but then he shook his head. He wanted to know more about Boofuls' monthly meetings at the Hollywood Divine before he let Father Lucas get involved. He wanted to know more about Boofuls himself. He had a feeling that if Father Lucas realized who Boofuls was, he would be back at the house within the hour with a busload of exorcists; and that their chances of getting Emilio back whole and undistorted would be put at serious risk.

What would be worse, the slightest hint of an exorcism would bring out the newspaper reporters and the television cameras, and Boofuls' appearance would be turned into a three-ring media circus.

Maybe there was another reason why Martin didn't want to divulge everything to Father Lucas just yet, a selfish reason. Maybe he wanted to see through this proposed remake of *Sweet Chariot*. If it could ever be filmed, it would be the sensation of all time – the only motion picture to star a reincarnated murder victim – and Martin would have his name on it.

There would be no stopping his career after that. He would become a movie legend. Notorious, perhaps, but never forgotten.

Father Lucas cut himself a slice of polenta and ate it thoughtfully. Martin found it rather dry, with too many pine nuts in it. At length, wiping his hands on one of Mrs Capelli's best white embroidered napkins, Father Lucas said, 'That boy upstairs; your grandson's friend, Lejeune. Does he have anything to do with this in any way?'

'What makes you say that?' asked Martin before Mr Capelli could answer.

'He has a *presence* about him, that's all. I can't quite put my finger on it. Perhaps it's nothing more than a freshness of youth.'

'He's a very bright young boy,' said Martin.

Father Lucas looked at him challengingly for a moment; and Martin looked back at him and steadily held his eye but gave nothing away.

'You're asking me to help you, yet you won't tell me the whole story,' Father Lucas told him. He turned around to Mr Capelli. 'Isn't that so, Mr Capelli?'

Mr Capelli looked embarrassed. But Martin said, 'Father – let's just say that we're hedging our bets a little. We're not quite sure what we're up against yet; and it could be dangerous if we go storming in with bells, books, and candles, trying to exorcise something that may not even *need* exorcising; or may not even *respond* to being exorcised.'

He paused for a moment, and then he said, 'We're not trying to be obstructive, Father. It's just that we're very worried about Emilio. One wrong step and we may never see him again; not whole, anyway; and not the way he was before. We need your help very badly. If there's anything you can find out about mirrors and worlds beyond mirrors – well, we're looking for anything, anything at all. But Emilio is at serious risk; and if we lose him forever simply because we weren't careful enough . . . well, I don't think *our* souls are going to rest, either.'

Father Lucas frowned. 'What do you mean by that? Your souls aren't going to rest, *either*? Who else has a soul that isn't at rest?'

Martin was almost tempted to tell him; but then he shook his head and said, 'Please, Father. Let's just take one step at a time.'

Father Lucas stood up and brushed crumbs from his coat. 'I really have to go now,' he said. 'But – all right – I'll accept your word that you can't tell me everything about the mirror. After all, Emilio's safety should be our first concern.'

He reached across the table and picked up the black-tissue package. 'Let me take these, however. I have a friend at St Patrick's who may be able to throw some light on these, and may even be able to tell us what the *other* safe-deposit box contains, before we risk opening it.'

Martin took hold of Father Lucas' hand and grasped it firmly. 'Thank you for having faith in all this,' he told him.

Father Lucas gave him a wry smile. 'I am regularly required to believe in the impossible, Mr Williams. It's not so hard for me to believe in the outrageous.'

Out on the landing, Father Lucas said good-bye to Mr and Mrs Capelli and thanked Mrs Capelli for her coffee and her cake. He was just about to go down the stairs when Boofuls appeared at the doorway of Martin's apartment. He stood there silently, staring down at Father Lucas with undisguised contempt.

'Good-bye, Lejeune,' Father Lucas called out, trying to be cheerful.

'Good-bye, Father,' Boofuls replied.

There was a moment of awkward silence. 'Well, then,' said Father Lucas, 'I must be off.'

'Father Lucas!' said Boofuls in a clear voice.

'What is it, my boy?'

Boofuls smiled at him. Then he said, 'Take care of your teeth, Father Lucas.'

Father Lucas laughed. 'Don't you worry, my boy. I brush them three times a day!'

Boofuls laughed, too; and then turned and disappeared back into Martin's apartment.

Martin looked serious. 'Take care of your teeth?' he said. 'What on earth did he mean by that?'

Father Lucas grasped Martin's arm. 'You just take care of yourself, Mr Williams. I'll call you if I find out anything about these relics. You work at home, don't you?'

Martin nodded. He stood at the head of the stairs watching Father Lucas go.

'I don't like this,' said Mr Capelli, rubbing his chin. 'I don't like this at all.'

Martin clapped him on the shoulder, and then slowly went back upstairs to see what Boofuls was doing.

CHAPTER NINE

The following morning was dull and humid; one of those overcast Hollywood days when all the buildings look tawdry and unreal, like a low-budget movie set. They drove up to Morris Nathan's house shortly after eleven o'clock. Morris had told Martin on the phone that he was too busy that morning to see anybody, but Martin had persisted. In the end, Morris had agreed to wedge him in between Joe Willmore and Henry Winkler. 'But four minutes only – *four* – no more.'

Because the day was so gray, there was nobody in the pool. Alison's inflatable sunbed circled around on its own, speckled with flies. Martin could see Alison herself in the sun-room, wearing a white silk caftan. Her manicurist was sitting at her feet like a religious supplicant, painting her toenails the color of 1956 Cadillacs. Alison waved as Martin and Boofuls walked across the patio to the front door.

Inside, Morris was saying good-bye to Joe Willmore. There was a strong smell of cigar smoke around. 'Come on in, Martin,' said Morris as Joe Willmore nodded to Martin, winked at Boofuls, and left. Martin followed Morris into his huge oak-paneled office with its sage-green shag-pile carpet and its framed photographs of Morris arm in arm with everybody who was anybody, from Frank Sinatra to Ronald Reagan.

'It's one of those days, you know?' said Morris. 'That *fonfer* David Santini has been arguing about the percentages on *Robot Killer III*; and don't ask me what Fox is trying to pull over *Headhunters*.'

'What *is* Fox trying to pull over *Headhunters*?' Martin inquired.

'I said don't ask,' said Morris. 'Believe me, if I told you, you wouldn't want to know.'

Martin laid a hand on Boofuls' shoulder. Boofuls had stayed quiet all this time, looking around. Today, he looked very much like any other small boy: Martin had taken him out yesterday afternoon and bought him shirts and T-shirts, shorts and jeans. He had stuck his hair down with gel, too, so that he didn't look quite so girly and ringleted.

Boofuls was still pale; and there was still something about him that wasn't quite ordinary; but at least he wasn't quite so obviously quaint.

'This is Lejeune,' said Martin. To avoid complications, they had decided to stick to the name that Boofuls had given to Father Lucas.

'Oh, yeah?' said Morris, leafing through a red-jacketed screenplay on his desk. 'Pleased to meet you, Lejeune. Don't tell me you're unlucky enough to have this *letz* for an uncle?'

'We're not related,' Martin explained. 'Lejeune here is my choice to play Boofuls.'

Morris slowly raised his eyes and stared first at Boofuls and then at Martin.

'Martin,' he said, 'I can spare you four minutes to talk about anything except Boofuls.'

'Will you listen for just *one* minute?' said Martin. 'I've decided to shelve my original idea. Instead, I want to put together a remake of Boofuls' last movie – the movie he never finished.'

Morris lowered his eyes toward the screenplay again. 'Martin,' he said with exaggerated patience, 'how long are you going to keep on *mutshing* me about Boofuls? Can't you take some advice? It's a loser. It's a dead duck. It's deader than a dead duck.'

But now Boofuls took one step forward and said in a high-pitched voice. 'No, sir. It's not dead at all.'

Morris looked at Martin in displeased surprise. 'Who's the *mazik*?' he wanted to know. *Mazik* was Yiddish for a mischievous little devil. It was less insulting than *mamzer*, the way Morris said it, but not very much less insulting.

Boofuls lisped, 'The picture was called *Sweet Chariot*. Maybe you don't remember it.'

'Remember it?' Morris protested. 'Of course I remember it. And if I hadn't remembered it, this uncle of yours would have reminded me, in any case, as if he wouldn't.'

'He's not my uncle,' Boofuls corrected him. 'He's my script editor, that's all.'

Morris couldn't believe this. '*He* is *your* script editor?'

Boofuls nodded. 'We're going to make this picture, Mr Nathan, and you're going to help us.'

'Martin, is this some kind of a practical joke?' Morris demanded. 'I'm a busy man, can you come to terms with that? I just can't stand here listening to all of this –'

He stopped in midsentence, with his mouth open. Because – without any further hesitation, and with stunning grace – Boofuls lifted both his arms, and began to dance slowly around Morris Nathan's office. His head was held high, his eyes were penetratingly bright, his arms and legs flowed through one complicated dance movement after another. Martin stepped back so that Boofuls could twirl past him, his toes scarcely touching the carpet as he went. He seemed to be unaffected by gravity – light and soundless, keeping perfectly in time with some unheard music. One-two-*three*-four, one-two-*three*-four, around and around and around.

Morris stared in fascination as Boofuls completed his dance, and bowed, and paused; and then clasped his hands together and stared up at the ceiling with an expression of pathos.

'I never saw *anybody* –' he began, but Martin shushed him, because Boofuls had started to sing. Martin had never heard this song before, although he had read the score. It came about halfway through *Sweet Chariot*, when the dead-end kid rises from his body as an angel.

Boofuls' voice was clear and sweet and penetrating. It sounded inhuman, as if it had come from the silvery throat of some long-forgotten musical instrument, rather than a child's larynx. It was so moving that Martin couldn't believe what he was hearing – and nor could Morris, from the expression on his face. There were tears in his eyes, and Martin had never ever seen tears in Morris Nathan's eyes before, and (except for his mother, when he was a tiny baby) neither had anybody else.

Like the dew, rising
To kiss the morning sun
I'm rising, I'm rising
To kiss the ones I love

Like the light, dancing
Where the river waters run
I'm dancing, I'm dancing
To that joyful place above

Boofuls finished the song and then stood with his head bowed and his eyes closed. There had been no music; no accompaniment; and yet Martin was almost sure that he had heard a sweeping orchestra; and that when Boofuls had finished singing, a single melancholy violin had laid his last note to rest. As for Morris, he dragged out a handkerchief and blew his nose loudly and looked toward Martin and lifted one hand as if to say, *Amazing, I take it all back, whatever I said about Boofuls, whatever I said about anything.*

Boofuls opened his eyes and smiled a sly little smile that only Martin saw.

'Well?' said Martin. 'What do you think?'

'I think I should shoot myself,' Morris told him, shaking his head in admiration. 'Then I should talk to June Lassiter.'

'You really like it?'

Morris came around his desk beaming. He laid his arm around Martin's shoulders and gave him an affectionate squeeze. 'Let me tell you something, Martin, there's a world of difference between concept and product. If you're talking *concept*, the idea of reviving Boofuls totally stunk. I told you it stunk, didn't I, how many times?'

He stretched over to ruffle Boofuls' hair, although Boofuls stepped back so that he was out of reach.

'What you have here, Martin, this is different, this is *product*. This is something that a studio can understand in terms of box office. What did you say your name was, kid?'

'My name is Lejeune,' said Boofuls.

'Well, we're going to have to think about *that*.' Morris grinned. 'Don't want you sounding too Frenchified, do we? Perhaps we can call you Boofuls II. Martin – you fix yourself a drink. How about you, Lejeune? What about a Seven-Up? Let me call Alison; she can take care of Lejeune for a while so that you and I can talk a little business.'

'I'd rather stay here and listen,' said Boofuls.

'Well, you don't want to do that,' Morris told him. 'This is grown-up talk; very boring. Alison will show you the peacocks. We have five now, did you know that, Martin? They make incredible watchdogs. Anyone come within five hundred feet of the house, they scream out like somebody strangling your grandmother.'

Boofuls suddenly looked white. 'I want to go,' he said.

'We won't be long,' said Morris, parking half of his enormous bottom on the side of his desk and punching out the sun-room telephone number. 'We just have to talk about how we're going to lick this whole thing into some kind of shape.'

'*I want to go,*' Boofuls insisted.

'Sure,' said Morris, 'sure. Just as soon as we've sorted things out. Oh – Alison? How are you doing, sweetie-pie? Would you mind coming into the den for a moment? Well, I've got a cute young friend here I'd like you to meet. All right, then, okay. Bysie-bye.'

The phone rang again. Morris picked it up. 'Hello? Oh Henry, how are you? Where are you calling from? You're kidding! Well – if it's unavoidable. What time can you get here? Okay, all right, that's fine. I can see you at two-thirty. Fine.'

'That was Henry Winkler,' he told Martin as he put down the phone. 'He's been held up at ABC. Now, how about that drink? I could use one myself. Lejeune, my friend, the lovely Mrs Nathan is going to show you around the yard while Martin and I have a little pow-wow, all right?'

'*I'm going,*' said Boofuls, his lips blue with rage; and he turned around and stalked out of Morris' study and slammed the door behind him.

'Morris,' Martin appealed, 'just give me a moment, will you?'

He went after Boofuls and saw him marching past the swimming pool, his chin lowered, his arms swinging angrily.

'Boofuls!' he called out. 'Just hold up a minute, will you?'

At that moment, however, Alison came out of the sun-room and began to walk toward the swimming pool in the opposite direction. When she saw Boofuls she waved and smiled and quickened her pace. Her white silk caftan floated in the gray daylight like a Pacific roller photographed in slow motion. She had almost reached Boofuls, however, when she covered her face with both hands, so that only her eyes were visible; and for no apparent reason at all she let him pass straight by, and disappear down the steps toward the front gate.

Martin hurried across the flagstones and took hold of Alison's hand. 'Alison? Are you okay?'

Alison nodded. She was shuddering. 'I think I'm going to have to sit down,' she said. Martin brought over a cast-iron garden chair, and she sat on it unsteadily and hung her head between her knees, breathing deeply.

'Who was *that*?' she managed to ask Martin at last.

'You mean that boy? He's a child actor I discovered. You know, singer and dancer. I brought him along to meet Morris because he's really got something special.'

Alison was still quaking. 'Is he sick?' she wanted to know.

Martin couldn't help letting out a grunt of amusement. 'Not so far as I know.'

Alison sat up straight, and clung on to Martin's sleeve. 'If he's not sick – why does he look so white? He looks so sick, like he's dead already.'

Martin said, 'What do you mean by that?' He glanced up. Morris was walking toward them now, his white sandals flapping loudly on the flagstones. 'What do you mean, he looks like he's dead already?'

'His face . . . oh, God, Martin – it was just like a *skull*.'

Martin found Boofuls sitting in the passenger seat of his Mustang, throwing stones at lizards, and usually missing. Martin climbed in behind the steering wheel and sat there saying nothing for two or three minutes, drumming his fingers on top of the dash.

At last, Boofuls said, 'I'm sorry, Martin. I didn't mean to spoil things. I haven't lost my temper like that in a long time.'

'You could have screwed things up permanently,' said

Martin. He took off his glasses and breathed on the lenses, buffing them up with his handkerchief. 'If Morris Nathan can't or won't fix anything for you, then you might just as well pack your suitcase and go back to wherever you came from.'

'Back through the mirror, you mean?' asked Boofuls. He hesitated for a while, and then he said, 'No, never. I'm never going back through there.'

'I'm talking in terms of making this movie,' Martin told him.

'The movie has to be made,' Boofuls insisted, not for the first time that day.

'The movie *will* be made,' Martin assured him. 'And when you've done that, you can do whatever the hell you like, just so long as we get Emilio back. But right now, be nice to Morris, because if Morris starts to think that you're unreliable or flaky, then this picture will take us *years* to get together – even if we can manage to get it together at all.'

Just then, Alison appeared at the gate. Boofuls moved his head to one side so that he could look at her. Alison said, 'Morris says he's sorry and do you want to came back in and talk turkey?'

Martin couldn't take his eyes off Boofuls' expression. It was both adult and lecherous. It was more like the gilded face of Pan than ever – hairy, wily, foxy-eyed. Alison was standing in the gateway with one hand raised against the gate. The faintest wash of late morning sunlight shone through the sheer white fabric of her caftan, and she was obviously nude underneath. She peered at Boofuls a little shortsightedly, and brushed the breeze-blown hair away from her face.

Boofuls climbed out of the car and walked ahead of them back to the house. Alison stayed close to Martin; and when Boofuls turned around from time to time to make sure that they were following, she hesitated, as if she were frightened of him.

'Was it *that* scary, what you saw?' asked Martin.

Alison nodded. 'He looked like a Halloween mask, you know? Just for a second. Then he looked normal.'

'Well, I don't know,' said Martin, trying to be reassuring. 'He's a pretty funny sort of kid.'

'Is he your nephew or something? You don't have children, do you?'

Martin shook his head. 'He's what you might call my protégé.'

Alison stopped and took hold of Martin's forearm. 'I don't want you to think I'm stupid or anything, I'm not exactly Miss I Q of America but I'm not stupid. All my life I've been able to see things that other people can't see. Even when I was little. I mean nothing important but kind of *auras*. Like when somebody's happy they shine; or when somebody's sad or sick or something bad's going to happen to them, there's this kind of dark smudge over their face, so that I can hardly see what they look like.'

Boofuls had reached the doorway. He turned around and waited for them. Martin lifted a hand and waved to him, to show him that they were coming.

Martin asked Alison, 'Seeing Lejeune's face like a skull . . . do you think that was the same kind of thing?'

Alison nodded. 'My aunt always said that I was – what do you call it? – *psychic*. She used to say that *every*body's psychic, just a little bit. You know when you get feelings that something's going to go wrong, you shouldn't get on that particular airplane, or you shouldn't cross the street. She said that was all part of being psychic. But some people can see much more than others. Some people can see things that haven't even happened yet: like when other people are going to die.'

She paused and glanced toward Boofuls. 'I don't mean to be rude or anything, but Lejeune gives me the *weirdest* sensations. I look at him, and I feel like I'm going down in an express elevator.'

Martin took hold of her arm and led her toward the house. 'Can you do me a favor?' he asked her. 'Can you keep these feelings to yourself, just for now?'

'Is there something *wrong*?' Alison asked him.

'I don't know. Right now, it's too difficult to explain; and even if I *did* explain it, I don't really think that it would help. But trust me.'

Alison hesitated for a moment, looking at Martin carefully as if she wanted to make quite sure that he wasn't lying. 'All right,' she said at last. 'But he's not sick, is he, Lejeune? He's not going to die? It wasn't just his face that upset me. There was a kind of *smell* about him, like something gone bad, and a *noise*, like hundreds of flies buzzing.'

'Are you coming, Martin?' called Boofuls impatiently.

'Sure, I'm coming. Let's go see what we can do to get this motion picture on the road.'

Martin led the way into the house. Alison stayed where she was, on the patio, her caftan ruffled in the breeze. Just as he stepped into the house, Boofuls turned around and stuck out his tongue at her in a lascivious licking gesture.

Alison stayed where she was, shocked and frightened. Boofuls had licked at her so quickly that it was impossible for her to tell for sure, but she could have sworn that his tongue was long and narrow and gray, the color of a snail's foot, and cloven at the end, like a snake's.

In spite of his disturbing precociousness, Boofuls ate and drank and slept like a normal boy. Martin gave him supper at eight o'clock, ravioli out of a can, and tucked him up on the sofa in the sitting room. He insisted on sleeping in the sitting room so that he could lie awake and watch the surface of the mirror. Martin didn't even like to look at the mirror now: all he could think about was Emilio, trapped in some unimaginable world where everything was back to front.

'You see,' said Boofuls as Martin went to turn off the light. 'I told you that it wouldn't be difficult, finding somebody to remake *Sweet Chariot*.'

'We're seeing June Lassiter tomorrow,' Martin told him. 'I think you're going to find her a whole lot tougher to win over than Morris Nathan.'

Boofuls smiled to himself. Martin switched off the light and stood in the doorway for a moment. He found it particularly disturbing the way Boofuls' eyes glittered blue in the darkness. It was the blue of decaying mackerel; the blue of cutting torches. He said, 'Good night, Boofuls,' and closed the door. He thought that he had probably never been so consistently frightened in the whole of his life, not just for himself, but for Emilio, too.

He went through to the kitchen, opened up the refrigerator, and helped himself to a red apple and a can of Coors Lite. Then he sat down at the kitchen table, where he had set up his typewriter, and began to peck out a few lines of corrected dialogue for *Sweet Chariot*. Boofuls had wanted him to update some of the story line, 'so that it isn't old-fashioned, and so that people really believe it'.

He had asked Boofuls yet again why he wanted so badly to make this film; but Boofuls had ignored his question and given him a brassy laugh.

He typed for almost an hour, gradually changing a bunch of 1930s kids from the Lower East Side into a gang of 1980s Hollywood Boulevard scuzzballs. The changes came surprisingly easily, and Martin began to feel quite proud of himself. 'Once a pro, always a pro,' he remarked, zipping out another piece of paper.

It was then that the phone rang. He scraped back his chair and picked up the receiver. A familiar voice said softly, 'Mr Williams? Is that you? I haven't caught you at an inconvenient moment?'

'Father Lucas? Is that you?'

'The very same, Mr Williams. Can I safely speak?'

'I'm not sure what you mean.'

'Is the boy there, that's what I mean.'

'No, no. He's asleep in the other room.'

'Very well, then, good enough. I have some news for you. I went to see my old friend Father Quinlan at St Patrick's this afternoon, and I took the relics with me. I also told him about the mirror.'

'And?'

'He wants to see you. He says it's desperately urgent. He says that something terrible is about to happen and that he must speak to you at once.'

Martin checked his watch. It was twenty after nine. 'Do you mean *now*? He wants to see me *now*?'

'He says there's no time to waste. Please, Mr Williams. It's very urgent indeed.'

Martin wearily rubbed his eyes. 'All right, tell me how to get there. Hang on – let me get my pencil. Okay, left off Alden Drive, just past Mt Sinai. All right . . . give me fifteen minutes at least. I have to make sure that Mrs Capelli can keep an eye on the boy.'

He folded the sheet of paper with Father Quinlan's address, tucked it into the pocket of his jeans, and then went through the hallway to the sitting room. The door was slightly ajar. Martin listened, and all he could hear was steady childish breathing. The little *mazik* was asleep.

Martin closed his apartment door quietly, then crept downstairs and knocked at Mrs Capelli's door. Mrs Capelli crossed herself when she saw who it was.

'Mrs Capelli, can you keep an eye on the boy for me . . . just for an hour or two?'

'Hmh! I should keep a watch on the devil's own? The one who stole my Emilio?'

'Mrs Capelli, please. The chances are that he's completely innocent.'

Mrs Capelli pointed fiercely upstairs. 'If that child is innocent, then God has abandoned this world altogether!'

Eventually, however, Mrs Capelli agreed to keep an ear open for Boofuls, no more. 'If he cries, he cries. I don't like that child. I don't trust him.' Martin gave her two quick kisses, one on each cheek, and galloped downstairs. He U-turned his Mustang on Franklin Avenue and headed westward. He didn't want to waste any more time. Father Lucas had sounded as if he expected the Apocalypse at any moment, or worse.

St Patrick's Theological College was one of those extraordinary 1930s structures that give Hollywood the appearance of being somewhere you remembered from a dream. It had been designed in the style of an English Tudor mansion, with latticed windows and red-brick battlements. It was easy to imagine Errol Flynn in doublet and pantaloons, rapier-fighting up and down the staircases.

Martin parked at the side, where Father Lucas had instructed him, and went up to the illuminated porch marked History Dept/Maintenance. He rang the doorbell and waited. A distant electrical storm flickered like snakes' tongues over the Hollywood Reservoir.

A young priest with a gray tweed sports coat and a shaven head answered the door. 'Yes?'

'I've come to see Father Quinlan. He said it was urgent.'

'Urgent?' the young priest asked. Nothing *urgent* ever happened at St Patrick's Theological College. The faculty had been discussing the implications of verses 20 and 21 of the first chapter of St Peter's second letter for the past seventeen years, 'no prophecy was ever made by an act of human will', and were still no nearer to an agreement on what they meant.

Martin followed the young priest along a narrow corridor with paneled walls and a highly waxed floor. At the very end of the corridor was a table with a flower arrangement on it; and above the flower arrangement, a painting of St Peter with a radiant gilded halo. Martin's shoes squeaked busily on the floor.

The young priest knocked at the second-to-last door. Martin didn't hear anybody inviting him to come in, but the young priest opened it and admitted Martin to a large untidy study, with leather sofas, side tables stacked with books, and a desk crowded with files and Bibles and framed photographs and dirty coffee cups.

Father Lucas was sitting next to the fireplace, although there was nothing in the hearth but an arrangement of dried flowers. Beside him stood a thin tall priest with a pinched face and long white hair and dark expressive eyes. He came forward to greet Martin with all the easy, stylized movements of a ballet dancer.

'I appreciate your promptness, Mr Williams,' he said, smiling. 'I am Father Quinlan, the head of historical studies here at St Patrick's.'

The young priest had been standing in the doorway, obviously hoping to pick up some gist of what they were going to discuss; but Father Quinlan, still smiling, waved him away. 'Do sit down,' he said to Martin. 'Perhaps you'd care for a glass of wine.'

'Don't mind if I do, thanks,' Martin told him, and sat down on one of the leather sofas. The seat cushion let out a loud exhalation of dusty air. Martin gave Father Lucas an embarrassed smirk. On the low coffee table between them, the black-tissue package had been opened out and the horny claws neatly laid out in a line. The fragment of hair had been laid to one side, along with the key.

Father Quinlan went to his bureau and stood with his back to Martin, carefully pouring out a glass of red wine from a Baccarat decanter.

'Mr Williams,' he said, 'it seems that you have managed to open up what you might call a Pandora's box.'

'You said it was urgent,' Martin commented.

Father Quinlan came over and handed him his glass. The wine smelled strong and aromatic. '"Urgent" was actually an understatement.' He smiled. 'Actually, it's critical.'

He watched as Martin sipped the wine and then beamed. 'Stag's Leap, 1976. I thought you'd enjoy it.'

'Tell me what's critical,' said Martin. He wasn't a wine connoisseur. As far as he was concerned, wine in itself was nothing important. It was the occasion on which you drank it, and whom you drank it with – that was what made an average wine into a memorable wine. Tonight he felt sour and edgy and any wine would have tasted the same.

Father Quinlan sat down at the opposite end of the sofa and elegantly crossed his legs. 'Father Lucas came to me yesterday and told me how worried he was. He described his experience with the mirror. Quite frightening, yes? to say the least. And he told me that both you and Mr Capelli appeared to be extremely anxious about what had happened to Mr Capelli's grandson.'

'If you want to talk about understatements,' Martin remarked, '"extremely anxious" is an understatement. Emilio disappeared into that mirror and we still haven't been able to get him out again.'

Father Quinlan nodded, to show that he understood, or – even if he didn't understand – that he was willing to help. 'Let's talk about mirrors first,' he suggested. 'Mirrors in general, and then *your* particular mirror.'

Martin glanced toward Father Lucas; but Father Lucas took off his magnifying spectacles and nodded reassuringly. 'All right,' said Martin, 'let's talk about mirrors in general.'

'There's an old Yiddish story about mirrors,' said Father Quinlan. 'A rich man tells his rabbi that he sees no point in giving charity to the poor. So the rabbi takes him to the window and tells him to look out over the marketplace, and then says, "What do you see?" The rich man says, "People, of course." So then the rabbi holds up a mirror in front of him and says, "What do you see now?" and he says "Myself." Well, the rabbi smiles and says, "Window and mirror, two pieces of glass, that's all. But it's extraordinary how a little silver makes it impossible for a man to see anything through that glass but himself."'

Father Quinlan sipped his wine, obviously conscious that he may have sounded too simplistic and patronizing; a fault with most priests, even when they mean it kindly. But then he said, 'Mirrors capture the soul, Mr Williams. Not metaphorically, but literally. They really do. They capture living pieces of our lives and our characters whenever we pass in front of them. Sometimes, in moments of terrible stress, they can take almost all of us.'

Martin deliberately said nothing but waited for Father Quinlan to continue.

Father Quinlan looked at Martin keenly, as if he were challenging him to not to believe in what he was saying. 'A mirror is like a living camera, Mr Williams. It's no coincidence that silver forms the backing for mirrors; and that silver salts are the light-sensitive medium which makes photography possible. Neither is it a coincidence that silver bullets kill those unfortunate afflicted people who are popularly known as werewolves. Like a mirror, like a photograph, a silver bullet instantaneously absorbs the wolf-image which has overwhelmed the human-image.'

'Werewolves?' asked Martin cautiously. He didn't want to hurt Father Quinlan's feelings, but really –

Father Quinlan said, 'I'm afraid I'm getting ahead of myself, Mr Williams. You can mock me if you like. But the historical records concerning the appearance of werewolves are quite clear. And so are the records concerning the extraordinary properties of mirrors.'

He paused, and sipped his wine, and watched Martin

closely. Then he said, 'Your mirror – do you know anything at all about it?'

Martin shrugged. 'I'm not sure that it's a good idea to tell you.'

'Where did you get it?'

'I bought it from a woman up on Hillrise Avenue, near the Reservoir.'

'And was she the original owner?'

Martin shook his head.

Father Quinlan waited for a moment in the hope that Martin was going to tell him who the original owner was, but when Martin stayed silent, he said, 'Let me give you some background, Martin. Then perhaps you and I can come to some arrangement and do what we can to deal with this situation.'

'I'm listening,' Martin told him.

'These claws,' said Father Quinlan, picking up one of the black hooked nails that was laid out on the table. 'These are the claws of Satan himself, do you understand what I'm saying? The *real* claws of Satan himself, in the dragon manifestation that was clearly predicted in the Book of Revelation.'

He went across to his desk and picked up one of his Bibles. 'Here it is. "*And I saw another beast coming up out of the earth; and he spoke as a dragon. And there was given to him to give breath to the image of the beast, that the image of the beast might even speak and cause as many who do not worship the image of the beast to be killed.*"'

Father Quinlan was silent for a moment, and then he read, '"*Let him who has understanding calculate the number of the beast; and his number is six hundred and sixty-six.*"'

He closed the Bible. 'The legend, Mr Williams, is that Satan was cast out of heaven by the angel Michael, and fell, and was shattered, so that the pieces of his body were strewn all over the earth. A claw here, a horn there, a hoof beyond the horizon.

'But the legend also says that – seconds before he struck the earth – his image was momentarily reflected in a river, and that the image in the river became the spirit of Satan, although he had no body in the real material world. His *real* body was spread around everywhere ... rather like the body of somebody who has died in an air disaster, except that Satan had fallen not from 23,000 feet, but from the vaults of heaven itself.

'For thousands of years, Satan was trapped inside the reflected world. Behind glass, behind mirrors, in rivers and lakes. He was able to *influence* the events of the real world. He was able to enter it, in a limited way, by possessing the souls of children and gullible people who were prepared to give him admission. But he was never able to escape. To escape, he required his material body to be reassembled. He needed somebody else to put back together again the jigsaw of his shattered body. Hence these claws, Mr Williams; hence this scalp. Whoever used to own these was undoubtedly the agent of Satan – trying to reincarnate the devil himself in the modern world. In the second deposit box, you will probably find more pieces; and you may even find another key, which will lead you on to yet more pieces.'

Martin said, 'Satan. I can't believe it. You mean the real genuine Satan?'

Father Quinlan nodded. 'The real genuine Satan, from the Bible.'

'But if he ever gets back together again, what will he do?'

Father Quinlan gave a tight smile. 'He has only one purpose in life, and that is to tear apart whatever God has created. That means us. He wants to bring the world to a spectacular and grisly end.'

Martin was silent for a moment. Then he said, 'Two weeks ago, I wouldn't have believed any of this stuff. I wouldn't have wasted my time.'

'But now?'

'Well – maybe it's a little different. I've seen enough to understand that what you're trying to say is true. Well, *partly* true; or *mostly* true. These bits of Satan, these claws and stuff – they were used by devil worshippers in Hollywood in the late 1930s. They used to meet once a month at the Hollywood Divine, and hold a what-d'you-call-it, don't tell me, Sabbath.'

Father Quinlan smiled in admiration. 'You know about the Hollywood Divine?'

Martin said, 'Yes. That's where we found these relics.'

'Well,' said Father Quinlan, 'I congratulate you. I've been

looking for them for years. It never occurred to me that they might still be there.'

'In the basement,' Martin told him, 'in the safe-deposit boxes.'

Father Quinlan was silent for a moment; then he said, 'As far as I can discover, it all started in the winter of 1935. There were so many stars in Hollywood who felt insecure. The studio system was tyrannical. One minute you were adored; the next minute you were sliding into oblivion. It was all alcohol and drugs and fast cars and promiscuity. You see those actors smiling and waving: my God, they lived on the very edge of their nerves. If there was any group of people who were ready for the promises of Satan, it was them.'

'What happened?' asked Martin.

Father Quinlan tapped the side of his nose with his finger. 'Father Lucas may have Coke-bottle eyeglasses, my friend, but he isn't blind and he isn't stupid. He saw all those pictures of Boofuls on your wall; and he found out that you've been trying to sell a musical of Boofuls for the past six months.'

'Oh he did, did he?' said Martin.

'You're offended?' asked Father Quinlan.

'I don't know, a little.'

'How can you be offended? Don't you realize how *serious* this is? Don't you realize how *dangerous* it is? Oh, we're talking about Satan, are we? What a laugh! But my God, my friend, we're talking about the very antithesis of peace and happiness; we're talking about plague and war and famine and destruction. My dear Mr Williams, we're talking about the world torn from pole to pole!'

He stopped for a moment, breathing deeply, and then he said, 'And *why* do we face such an appalling Apocalypse? Let me tell you why, Mr Williams. Because of the vanity of a handful of poor insecure actors who lived in Hollywood in the 1930s. Those glamorous people of the silver screen, Joan Crawford, Errol Flynn, John Barrymore, those people we used to idolize! They weren't glamorous at all, they were obsessed with the fear of failure. They were little and frightened, and terrified of the adoration that was showered on them. So they sought encouragement. They sought reassurance. And when one small boy came among them and said that they could be successful and happy forever, how do you think they reacted?'

Martin said nothing, but finished his wine and set down his empty glass next to the black-tissue package.

Father Quinlan said, 'I've been through St Patrick's files for the late 1930s. You wouldn't believe it, but we were given anonymous tip-offs year after year that somebody, somewhere in L A, was holding Black Sabbaths on a monumental scale. Phone calls, scrawled letters; one or two photographs. The Hollywood Divine was mentioned several times. But almost all of those tip-offs were ignored – even though one of the letters specifically warned that "*they have the relics*".'

'But what were these actors actually trying to do?' asked Martin.

Father Quinlan ran his hand through his wild white hair. 'They were trying to do nothing more than bring back Satan. The real, reincarnated Satan, in the flesh. It was a pretty straightforward arrangement. In return for bringing him back, Satan would give them youth and glamor and eternal popularity.'

Martin said nothing, but lowered his head in silent acknowledgement. He had seen too much in the past few days to be a disbeliever.

Father Quinlan said more quietly, 'It all started, somehow, with Boofuls. I had my suspicions, from the moment I started researching. I found a letter written by Bill Tilden ... well, you know what *he* was like, Stumpy Tilden. Tennis coaching for pretty young boys, that kind of thing. In 1936, he wrote a letter to a close friend, and said that he had met an exquisite child who had offered him hope and happiness, "unimaginable" hope and happiness. The boy's name was Walter Crossley, a.k.a Boofuls. But Bill Tilden wasn't the only one. Everybody in Hollywood, whether they were homosexual or not, was entranced by Boofuls: his sweetness, his apparent purity, and the feeling that, when they were around him, he made them feel confident and happy and capable of everlasting success.'

Father Quinlan said more seriously, 'He was nothing more and nothing less than a child possessed by Satan. That's my opinion, anyway, I was never able to confirm it. How can you confirm such a thing? I could never discover who his father was, and I could never discover the identity of the woman who always used to accompany him to the Hollywood Divine.'

'Miss Redd?' put in Martin.

Father Quinlan nodded. 'That's right, the mysterious Miss Redd. I've never been able to find any pictures of her or press references or anything at all. But several anonymous letters that were sent to the church in 1938 mention Miss Redd.' He reached over and poured Martin some more wine. 'However,' he said, 'let's get back to your mirror.'

'Boofuls' mirror,' Martin admitted.

Father Quinlan smiled. 'I thought so. Well – Father Lucas thought so.'

'He was quite right,' said Martin. He turned to Father Lucas and gave him a nod of admiration. Father Lucas, in return, lifted up his glass of wine.

Father Quinlan said, 'This isn't easy to piece together. Some of the faculty here think that I'm obsessive about it. But the Revelation contains some remarkably clear facts and figures, apart from scores of extraordinary implications. Miss Redd, for example. In the Revelation, Satan appears as a *red* dragon. Perhaps it means nothing at all. Perhaps I'm being paranoid. Oh, yes, priests can be paranoid. But we have one more important authority to turn to; and I'm rather proud of this.'

He walked across the room to a large oak cabinet, carved with bunches of grapes. He took a small key out of his vest pocket and opened it. Inside, there were rows of small shelves. Father Quinlan drew out a small package of papers, closed the door, locked it, and returned to the sofa.

'This,' he said, 'is an unpublished commentary on *Unusual Properties of Looking-Glasses*, by Charles Lutwidge Dodgson.'

Martin said, in astonishment, 'Charles Lutwidge Dodgson? You mean *Lewis Carroll*?'

Father Quinlan untied the faded silk ribbon which held the papers together. 'The very same; and we've had it authenticated, too, by the British Museum.'

'But it must be worth a million dollars. An unpublished book by Lewis Carroll?'

'Well ... another Alice adventure might be worth something. But not so many people know that Lewis Carroll was more of a mathematician than a storyteller. He wrote *A Syllabus of Plane Algebra* and an *Elementary Treatise on Determinants*, as well as *Euclid and His Modern Rivals*.'

Father Quinlan turned the musty leaves of the manuscript; and there was a smell of dust and burned cream. 'This is all very scrappy ... not what you'd call a book at all. Notes, really; and some of them very disjointed. But the most interesting part about it is what he has to say about mirrors. He always believed that there was some kind of wonderland on the other side of mirrors; but his first real revelation about mirrors came early in the winter of 1869 when he became extremely ill, pneumonia probably, and he lay in bed at his home in Oxford quite close to death.'

Father Quinlan looked Martin straight in the eye. 'Carroll may have been delirious; but he tells in this commentary how he walked through the mirror in his sickroom in just the way that Alice did. "*The glass melted away, just like a bright silvery mist.*" He found himself in looking-glass land, where everything was reversed.

'He writes here, "*Not just writing, and pictures, but Christian morality itself had been turned from left to right. Inside the mirror was the domain of demons, the ante-room of Hell itself.*"'

Father Quinlan said, 'He tried to tell his friends; he tried to tell the Bishop of Oxford. But after *Alice in Wonderland* they chose not to believe him. So he wrote *Through the Looking-Glass* as an Alice story ... mainly because he knew that it would find the widest audience. It was a warning, expressed in childish language, in the hope that – even if adults refused to believe the danger they were in – then perhaps children would. *Through the Looking-Glass* is the single most specific warning about the return of Satan since the Revelation itself.'

He handed Martin one of the pages. On it, in Lewis Carroll's own handwriting, was written 'Jabberwocky':

Beware the jabberwock, my son!
The jaws that bite, the claws that catch!

Father Quinlan brought over some more wine. 'Later in the book, Carroll explains away this gibberish-poem with all sorts of nonsensical definitions. But ask any *child* about the Jabberwock, and he or she will tell you about nothing except a dark wood, and a ferocious dragonlike creature, and a boy who slays it by chopping it into pieces. Alice herself says, "*Somehow it seems to fill my head with ideas − only I don't exactly know what they are! However* somebody *killed* something". See what it says here:

> "*The Jabberwock, with eyes of flame,*
> *Came whiffling through the tulgey wood,*
> *And burbled as it came!*"

'Then,

> "*One, two! One, two! And through and through*
> *The vorpal blade went snicker-snack!*
> *He left it dead, and with its head*
> *He went galumphing back.*"'

Father Quinlan smiled. 'Well, it's pretty amusing stuff. But these notes aren't amusing at all. Carroll says here, "*I believe that I came as close to death as a man may go and yet return to the real world. I saw darkness; and I saw unimaginable beings; human-beings with heads as huge as carnival-masks; creatures with hunchbacks; dogs that spoke. It seems to me now like a dream, or rather a nightmare, but I am convinced that I saw Purgatory, the realm in which each man takes on his true form. In the land beyond the looking-glass, in the world of reflections, is the life after death, and the life before death. I understand now the closeness of Christianity, which teaches each man that he will have his reward or his punishment in the world beyond, and the Hindu religion, which teaches that a man will be reincarnated according to the life he has led.*"'

'But the Jabberwock?' asked Martin. 'What does the Jabberwock have to do with Boofuls, and *my* mirror?'

'Absolutely everything,' said Father Quinlan. 'The Jabberwock is the mirror image of Satan. Carroll derived the name from Jabbok, a mountain stream of Gilead, one of the main tributaries of the River Jordan. It was in the waters of Jabbok that Satan's image was supposed to have been reflected when he fell from heaven. It may or may not be a coincidence that Carroll's doctor at the time was called Dr James Crowe, and that the letters *c-r-o-w-e* make up the remainder of the name Jabberwock.'

Martin put down his glass of wine and dry-washed his face with his hands. 'God, this seems so farfetched.'

'Any more farfetched than holy water flying straight through a mirror and landing only in the reflected room? Any more farfetched than your friend Emilio disappearing into a mirror and refusing to come back? No, Mr Williams, this isn't farfetched at all. What we are seeing here is Satan's plan for his own resurrection, as foretold in the Book of Revelation. Somehow, he possessed the boy Boofuls; and the boy Boofuls regularly held blasphemous Sabbaths at the Hollywood Divine; and he used his money and his influence to gather together the scattered remnants of Satan's physical body.'

Father Quinlan tugged out one of the sheets of Carroll's notepaper, and on it was Carroll's own sketch for the Jabberwock, on which the final drawing by Sir John Tenniel had been based. A snarling creature with dragon's wings and scaly claws and blazing eyes. 'You see,' he said, in quiet triumph, '*the jaws that bite, the claws that catch* – and here they are.' He picked up the black horny claws from the table. 'Almost exactly the same; and to the same scale.'

Martin said nothing. He was overwhelmed by tiredness and by the magnitude of what Father Quinlan was trying to tell him.

Father Quinlan said, 'When he had recovered from his pneumonia, Carroll spent a great deal of time at the Bodleian Library in Oxford, researching the legend of the fallen devil. He discovered that, according to Jacob and Esau, who met by the waters of the Jabbok, Satan and the children of Satan can be killed only by a sword blessed in the name of God and in the name of the angel Michael and engraved with the motto "Victory Over Ruin, Pestilence, and Lust". Hence the vorpal sword in the poem – V–O–R–P–A–L. And hence, I strongly suspect, the chopping up of Boofuls by his grand-mother.

'They never found the murder weapon, did they? But it must have been very sharp and very heavy. She was an elderly woman, remember. She could have dismembered him only with a weapon that had considerable weight of its own, like a Chinese cleaver, or a large two-handed machete – or a two-handed sword.'

Martin lifted his hand. 'All right – supposing this is all true – supposing Mrs Crossley killed Boofuls because she thought he was trying to bring back Satan – how do you think she found out about it? How do you think she found out what to do, to stop him? And where did she get hold of a sword blessed by God and the angel Michael?'

Father Quinlan smiled. 'Every mystery has its unanswered questions, Mr Williams. I'm a theological historian, not a police detective. Perhaps you ought to ask Boofuls himself.'

Martin didn't answer that. He wasn't yet prepared to admit to Father Quinlan or Father Lucas that the curly-headed boy at his apartment was actually Boofuls. Father Lucas may have suspected it, having seen the boy. But before Martin enlisted the help of men like Father Quinlan, he wanted to be quite sure that he could rescue Emilio unharmed from the world beyond the mirror.

'You told me this was urgent,' Martin told Father Quinlan, deliberately changing the subject. 'I'm afraid I don't quite see the urgency. If we have these claws here, and the key to the rest of the relics – well, there's not very much that anybody can do to bring the devil to life, is there?'

Father Quinlan nodded. 'You're quite right. But Satan is not to be underestimated. Neither is the prophecy that, to be given life, and to win back control over the world, Satan must be given as a sacrifice the lives of one hundred forty-four thousand innocent people.'

'Is that a special number?' asked Martin.

'In the Book of Revelation, it's the number of people who defied lies and wickedness and followed the Lamb. The first fruits of God. Satan cannot live and breathe until those one hundred forty-four thousand lie massacred.'

Martin raised his eyebrows. 'Pretty hard to massacre that many people in this day and age.'

'Hard, yes,' Father Quinlan agreed. 'But not impossible.'

Afterward, Father Lucas walked Martin out to his car. The night was warm. Martin couldn't help thinking of the Walrus and the Carpenter. *'The night is fine,'* the Walrus said. *'Do you admire the view?'*

Martin opened his car door. A police siren echoed high over Mulholland, where it twisted through the hills. Mulholland's hair-raising curves always attracted coked-up young drivers who believed they could fly.

'What do you think?' asked Father Lucas.

'I don't know,' said Martin. 'I'm pretty confused, to tell you the truth.'

'Father Quinlan is probably the country's greatest expert on theological legend. I know he rambles – but his research is quite extraordinary.'

Martin started up his engine. 'The question is, can anybody believe what he's saying?'

Father Lucas shrugged and smiled. 'That, of course, is a question of faith.'

'Let me think about this,' Martin told him. 'Call me tomorrow; maybe we can talk some more.'

'Before you go,' said Father Lucas, holding on to the car door, 'there's one question I have to ask you.'

Martin made a face. 'I think I know what it is.'

'Lejeune . . . that boy I met at your apartment. He does look awfully like Boofuls.'

'That's why I chose him.'

'It isn't remotely possible that when your young friend Emilio went *into* the mirror –?'

Martin cut him short. 'Father, anything's possible.'

'Well,' replied Father Lucas. He made the sign of the cross over Martin's head. 'If it *is* Boofuls, please take extraordinary care.'

'Lejeune is –' Martin began; and then he said, 'Lejeune is Lejeune, that's all. He's just a boy.'

'Perhaps you should study your Bible better,' smiled Father

Lucas. 'Mark 5, Chapter 5. "*And when He had come out of the boat, immediately a man from the tombs with an unclean spirit met Him. And Jesus was saying, 'Come out of the man, you unclean spirit!' and He was asking him, 'What is your name?' And the unclean spirit said to Him, 'My name is Legion; for we are many.'*"'

Although the night was so warm, Martin shivered. Through the oyster-shaped lenses of his spectacles, Father Lucas looked down at him with magnified, serious eyes. 'He is having a little joke with us, Mr Williams. I only wish it were funny.'

CHAPTER TEN

Boofuls was still asleep when Martin returned to Franklin Avenue. Mrs Capelli said she hadn't heard a sound. 'There was some scratching, that's all, but it was probably the squirrels, burrowing through the trash.'

Martin went quietly upstairs, let himself in, and then tiptoed along the hallway to the sitting room door. Boofuls was still huddled up on the sofa, breathing deeply, although there was an odd burning smell in the room, as if somebody had been trying to set fire to feathers or horsehair.

Boofuls was breathing deeply and regularly, and when Martin came up close to tuck him in, he remained pale-faced and still, sleeping a dreamless sleep; the sleep of those for whom reality is back to front, and who are ultimately damned.

'*My name is Legion; for we are many.*'

Martin looked at the mirror. He could see himself standing in the narrow band of light that crossed the room from the open door. He looked sweaty and exhausted. He wondered how the hell he had managed to get himself into all this.

He went up close to the mirror and leaned to one side, still trying to see through the sitting room door to the world where everything was different. He wondered how much of Father Quinlan's theories he ought to believe. A musty manuscript by Lewis Carroll proved nothing at all. Yet it was remarkable how closely Carroll's description of the life after death matched that of Homer Theobald, who had described 'talking turtles' and people with elongated heads.

At last, Martin closed the sitting room door and went to take a shower. As he soaped himself under the hot, prickling water he almost fell asleep. He was too tired to make coffee, so he drank three cold mouthfuls of milk straight out of the carton.

In his bedroom, on the wall, the poster of Boofuls stared at him and smiled. He stood looking at it for a long time; then he reached up and ripped it right off the wall, crumpling it up and tossing it across the room.

Breathing a little too quickly, he climbed into his crumpled futon, covered up his head, and made a determined effort to go to sleep.

He dreamed of claws, scratching on polished woodblock floors. He dreamed of cats, sliding between impossible railings. He dreamed of hot breath, and flaring blue eyes, and furry things that were as long as hosepipes. He sweated, and cried out, and clutched at his bedcover, but he didn't wake up.

'*Pickle-nearest-the-wind,*' somebody whispered. '*Pickle-nearest-the-wind.*'

Two things happened while he slept.

The first was that Boofuls suddenly sat up in bed, his small figure lit by the early moonlight. He stayed quite still for a long time, listening. On the far side of the room against the wall, the mirror was cold and clear.

After three or four minutes, Boofuls climbed out of bed and padded on bare feet across to the mirror and stood in front of it with his hands by his sides.

In the mirror, the sitting room door opened, and another boy appeared, wearing striped cotton pajamas. It was Emilio. He looked white and distressed, and he couldn't stop fidgeting.

'Where's Pickle?' whispered Boofuls. 'I told you to bring Pickle.'

'Pickle didn't want to come.'

'Pickle has *got* to come.'

'Well, I can bring her in the morning.'

Boofuls' eyes flared. 'You'd better, otherwise you can stay in that mirror forever and ever and ever!'

Emilio said, 'Please.'

'Please, what?'

'Please let me out. I want to get out.'

'What's the matter? You've got your grandpa and grandma, haven't you?'

Emilio's eyes filled with tears. 'Yes, but they're not the same. They're *different*.'

'Everything's different in the mirror.'

'Boofuls, please let me out. Please.'

Boofuls let out a little hissing laugh. 'You'll get out when the time comes. And *if* I feel like letting you out.'

'But I hate it here. It's frightening!'

Boofuls leaned close to the mirror, puckered his lips, and blew Emilio a kiss. 'You'll get used to it. You can get used to anything if you try hard enough!'

'Please,' begged Emilio.

'Bring Pickle in the morning,' Boofuls insisted. 'If you don't, you can stay there forever and ever, amen!'

Emilio covered his face with his hands and began to sob quietly. Boofuls watched him for a moment with a malicious look on his face and then went back to bed. When he looked around, Emilio had gone, and the sitting room in the mirror was empty. He smiled to himself and slept.

The second thing was that Father Lucas finished one last glass of wine with Father Quinlan and then prepared to leave.

'You have a safe at St Theresa's, don't you?' Father Quinlan asked him. 'Perhaps you'd better take these relics and lock them safely away. I don't altogether trust the cleaners here at St Patrick's. I lost a fine briar pipe once and a walking stick with a silver top.'

'That's not a very good advertisement, is it?' Father Lucas smiled. 'Theological College Is Den of Thieves, Claims Holy Father.'

Father Quinlan laughed, and wrapped up the claws and the hair, and carefully slid them into a padded envelope. 'Here's the key, too. We don't want to lose that.'

Father Lucas opened the study door. 'I'm not altogether sure that Mr Williams believes in the Book of Revelation,' he remarked.

Father Quinlan shrugged. 'It's rather lurid, I suppose, as prophesies go.'

'That boy at his apartment ... I'm ninety-nine percent certain that it's Boofuls.'

'Yes,' said Father Quinlan. 'It's a pity that Mr Williams doesn't yet feel able to take us into his confidence. Still – it's a lot to swallow, all in one go. The Revelation and Lewis Carroll all tied up together. I found it quite difficult to believe myself when I first looked into it.'

'But you have no doubts now?' asked Father Lucas.

Father Quinlan shook his head. 'None at all.'

Father Lucas said good night and left the college by the side door. He had left his dented red Datsun parked in the shadow of the chapel. He climbed in, and the suspension groaned like a dying pig. He started up the engine and was just about to back out of his parking space when he happened to glance at the padded envelope lying on the seat beside him.

Supposing he drove down to the Hollywood Divine and opened up the second safe-deposit box? The sooner he did it – the sooner he locked the relics in his safe at St Theresa – the less risk there would be of somebody else locating them first and trying to reassemble the scattered body of Satan.

He checked his watch. It was twenty after eleven, but he was pretty sure that there would be somebody on the desk at the Hollywood Divine. After all, most of its customers didn't know day from night.

He drove eastwards on Santa Monica. From time to time, he glanced at his eyes in the rearview mirror. They looked a little glassy and bloodshot, although he didn't know why. Too much of Father Quinlan's Pinot chardonnay, probably. He wasn't used to drinking. But, all the same, he was surprised how strange he felt; how detached; as if his body were taking him to the Hollywood Divine even though his mind wasn't too keen on coming along.

Father Lucas had always liked to think of himself as traditional and pragmatic. He believed in the forces of darkness; and he believed that people could be possessed by evil spirits. He even believed that Boofuls had somehow reappeared through the mirror in Martin's sitting room – like a sort of living hologram. But it hadn't been easy for him to accept Father Quinlan's theories about the second coming of Satan. To think that Satan the king of all chaos might actually appear

241

in Hollywood in the late 1980s *in the flesh* – well, that was one of those concepts that his well-disciplined mind was unable to encompass.

He drove along Hollywood Boulevard. At this time of night, it was at its sleaziest – the sidewalks crowded with punks and weirdos and junkies and strutting streetwalkers. One immaculately dressed black man drew up alongside Father Lucas in a white Eldorado convertible and raised his leopard-spotted fedora. 'Good evening to you, your reverence. What's going down in heaven these days?'

'Good evening, Perry,' Father Lucas replied. 'I'll tell you when I get there.'

'Don't you worry, your reverence, I'll be there first.'

Father Lucas smiled. 'I'm sure you will, Perry, I'm sure you will.'

He turned into Vine and parked outside the Hollywood Divine. A small Mexican boy no older than eight came up to him and offered to protect his car radio. 'Long gone, I'm afraid,' Father Lucas told him.

'Then what about your hubcaps?'

'Take them, if you think they're going to be more use to you than they are to me.'

'I don't want your hubcaps. If I was going to take anything, I'd take your whole crapping car.'

Father Lucas bent down over the boy, his hands on his knees, so that he could look him straight in the eye. 'If you so much as lay one greasy finger on my crapping car, I'll tear your crapping head off. And don't ever use language like that to a priest ever again; or to anyone; ever.'

The boy stared at him, wide-eyed. 'No, sir. Sorry, sir. I'll take care of your car, sir.'

Father Lucas made his way past the hookers and the hustlers to the steps of the Hollywood Divine. Somebody had vomited tides of something raspberry-colored all over the side of the steps, and hundreds of shoes had trampled it everywhere.

Father Lucas pushed his way through the shuddering revolving doors and crossed the dimly lit lobby. One of the Hollywood Divine scarecrows was shuffling around the perimeter of the lobby with a bottle in a brown paper bag, singing, '*You play . . . such shweet mushic . . . how can . . . I resish . . . every shong . . . from your heartshtrings . . . makes me feel I've . . . jush been kissh.*'

Boofuls, thought Father Lucas. *It seems like he's everywhere. Like a storm that's brewing, and everybody can feel it in the air.*

The desk clerk was sitting with his feet on the counter reading an *Elf Quest* comic and smoking a cigarette. A half-empty bottle of Gatorade and a half-chewed hot dog showed that he was halfway through dinner. He glanced up when Father Lucas approached the desk and sniffed loudly.

'How're you doing, Father?' he asked. 'Come to save our souls?'

'Would that I could,' said Father Lucas.

The young man flipped away his comic and swung his feet off the counter. 'Okay, then, what's it to be? Half an hour with Viva and Louise? For an extra ten bucks, they can dress up in nun costumes. Or how about a short time with Wladislaw? He's been doing great business dressing up like the Pope. The Catholic guys love it. He balls them, and then he forgives them, all included in the one price.'

'Careful, Gary,' Father Lucas warned him.

'All right, Father, forgive me, for I do not have the faintest idea what I do. Now, how can I help?'

Father Lucas held up his key. 'The safe-deposit boxes,' he said. 'I understand they're down in the basement.'

'That's right,' said Gary, narrowing his eyes. 'But it'll cost you. You're the second one in just a couple of days.'

Father Lucas reached into his pocket and counted out five bills. 'I'm sorry, I'm not exactly Aaron Spelling.'

'Well . . .' said Gary. 'Seeing as it's you.' He pocketed the money, unhooked the basement key from the board, and led Father Lucas across the lobby. One of the scarecrows called out, 'Bless you, Father! Bless you!' and dropped onto his knees on the filthy carpet, pressing his forehead to the floor. Father Lucas made the sign of the cross; and then followed Gary along the narrow corridor that led to the kitchens and the basement door.

Gary unlocked the door, reached inside, and switched on the light.

'Just watch your step, Father, okay? There's a whole lot of junk and trash down there. The safe-deposit boxes are way in back, by the wall. There's some kind of an African statcher back there, they're right behind it.'

'Thank you,' said Father Lucas.

'Hey, don't mention it,' Gary told him.

Gary went off; and Father Lucas climbed cautiously down the steps into the basement. He paused for a moment at the foot of the steps, looking around. The basement was utterly silent, a grotesque landscape of upturned chairs, hat stands, foldaway beds, and bureaux. Father Lucas caught sight of the 'African statcher' and began to make his way toward it, climbing over stacks of chairs and walking along rows of bedside tables.

Down here, he felt peculiarly shut off from the world; and a small familiar surge of claustrophobia rose in his chest. He didn't suffer from it very often or very severely; only in times of stress. But there were times when he had been forced to bite the inside of his cheek when he was traveling in a crowded elevator, to stop himself from shouting to be let out.

The worst thing was imagining the weight of the entire hotel bearing down on top of him, tons of concrete and steel, all those carpets and furnishings and staircases and people.

He gripped the back of a chair to balance himself, and hesitated for a moment, sweating. He wasn't *obliged* to open this safe-deposit box. He could turn around and go back and nobody would be any the wiser. Yet supposing he turned around, and somebody else got here first, somebody who was dedicated to resurrecting Satan? What would he think of himself then, as the world cracked from pole to pole?

Father Lucas mopped his face with his handkerchief, took a deep steadying breath, and then carried on, stumbling over the furniture like a lame goat. At last, however, he reached the safe-deposit boxes. He struggled his way around the African lady with the bodacious ta-tas; and then managed to climb up on top of the stacks of boxes. He was panting hard; and he had to take off his Coke-bottle spectacles and wipe steam off the lenses. God knows, he could never go down a mine.

He found box number 531, with its lid still open. What he needed now was 135. He slid down the side of the stack of boxes and pushed the top bank sideways – finally managing to lever them out of the way using a brass pole with a board on one end pointing the way to the Starlight Bar.

He was lucky. The next bank of boxes was 1–199. The numbers were quite clear, too. He found 135, and took out the key that Martin and Ramone had discovered in the first safe-deposit box.

He was about to fit it into the lock when he thought he heard a noise on the other side of the basement. He listened, sweating. There it was again. A faint scratching sound, like rats tearing the stuffed-cotton entrails out of a couch; or somebody stealthily making his way nearer across the furniture. He listened and listened, his key still poised, but the noise wasn't repeated.

'Overactive imagination,' he told himself, and inserted the key into the lock.

The lock was extremely stiff. He grunted and strained at it, and the key cut into his fingers. He wished he had thought of bringing a screwdriver and a pair of pliers, although he probably would have ended up breaking the lock that way. He twisted the key again, grunting with effort, and at last he felt it budge.

'One more try,' he gasped to himself. 'Come on, you bastard; open up!'

He was struggling so hard that he scarcely heard the singing. High, and clear, but oddly ghostlike, as if it could have been very close or very far away.

> Apples are sweeter than lemons
> Lemons are sweeter than limes
> But there's nothing so sweet as the mem'ry of you
> And the sadness of happier times.

He allowed himself to catch his breath; then with quivering fingers he turned the key all the way around and felt the levers in the lock slide rustily open.

The singing continued, but Father Lucas didn't hear it. He

lifted the lid of the safe-deposit box and peered inside. The lighting in this part of the basement was so poor, however, that he couldn't see anything at all.

'Well, now,' he told himself, 'it can't be anything to be frightened of. Only claws and tissue paper, and more of that hairy stuff.'

He cautiously inserted his left hand, groping around the sides of the box. It seemed to be empty. Perhaps somebody else had gotten here first and taken the contents away. Perhaps the claws and the hank of hair were all that was left.

He reached a little farther; and then his fingertips touched something wrinkled and supple and faintly oily; like a sack of soft and heavy leather. He didn't like the feel of it at all, but he ran his hand all the way around it, trying to make out what it was. He tried to lift it, so that he could see what it looked like in the light, but it was too heavy, and seemed to be fastened to the back of the safe-deposit box.

Father Lucas took his hand out. He found his handkerchief, wiped his fingers, and sniffed them. The thing in the safe-deposit box had a curious smell; rather like machine oil lightly mixed with fish.

He bent over and strained his eyes, trying to catch even the faintest reflection from the thing inside the box. 'Now, what the hell are you?' he whispered. 'If you're part of Satan, I'd darn well like to know *which* part.'

He was about to reach inside the box a second time when he heard a high, childish giggle. He looked up, alarmed, his heart pumping in huge, slow spasms. At first he couldn't make out where the laughter was coming from, but then right across the basement, on the far side, he caught sight of a face. Or rather, the *reflection* of a face in the tilted mirror of a discarded hotel dressing table.

Father Lucas shuddered. His eyesight wasn't very clear, but he had no doubt who it was. Those clear pale features, unnaturally white; those bright-burning eyes.

'Boofuls,' he whispered.

'*Hello, Father.*' Boofuls smiled. '*What are you doing here? Interfering? Poking your nose in where it's not wanted?*'

Father Lucas crossed himself. 'Almighty Lord, Word of

God the Father, Jesus Christ, God and Lord of every creature: Who didst give to Thy Holy Apostles power to tread upon serpents and scorpions – by Whose power Satan fell from heaven like lightning –'

'*Father Lucas!*' cried Boofuls. '*You meddled in matters which were nothing to do with you, and now you have to be punished! Look after your teeth, that's what I told you! Look after your teeth!*'

Father Lucas caught sight of a glint of glistening white down in the darkness of the safe-deposit box. He was so terrified that he was unable to move; literally unable to do anything but kneel where he was, open-mouthed. His mind told him to scramble down and run for his life, but his body refused to obey.

'*Meddler!*' screamed Boofuls. '*Meddler! Meddler!*'

His voice reached a pitch of unintelligible hysteria.

And then something reared out of the safe-deposit box that was all shiny gray gristle, a thick tangled column of unspeakable muscles and naked arteries. It was like nothing that Father Lucas had ever seen – blind, swollen, dangling with rags of slimy gray skin, reeking of oil and dead fish.

'Almighty Lord, Word of God the Father,' Father Lucas babbled. But then the thin skin around the top of the column peeled slowly back, revealing row after row of razor-sharp teeth, five, six – seven rows in all, glutinous with fluids. Father Lucas' voice disappeared, and all he could do was stare at this terrible apparition; trying not to believe in it, trying to tell himself that this was only a nightmare; and that any moment now he would fall off the safe-deposit boxes and find himself in bed.

His nervous system suddenly reconnected itself. He thought, *Jump!* But he was a fraction of a second too late. The glistening gray column swayed swiftly toward him and burst straight into his mouth, smashing all his teeth aside, dislocating his jaw, cracking his palate apart from front to back.

He couldn't scream: the thing filled his mouth. Blood sprayed wildly across the safe-deposit boxes and onto the basement ceiling.

Choking, he thought, *Out! Out! Got to get it out!* but it slithered through his hands, greasy, rubbery, unstoppable.

It forced its way down his throat, tearing away his larynx. The agony was all the more unbearable because his lungs were full and yet his windpipe was blocked and he *couldn't breathe, couldn't breathe!*

He struggled and thrashed and kicked his legs; and at last he lost his balance and toppled off the side of the safe-deposit boxes onto the floor, with the gray thing's tail still protruding from his stretched-open mouth. It had a tail like a soft, collapsed sphincter, a sphincter that contracted and expanded each time the thing forced itself farther down his throat.

Something had jarred in his back when he fell. He lay paralyzed on top of a folding chair, his eyes bulging, his face blue, his mouth bloody. And the gray creature pushed its way with tearing teeth down to his stomach, ripping soft membranes into shreds – inflicting on him the greatest pain that it was possible for a man to suffer. It was worse than *seppuku*, the most agonizing form of Japanese suicide, because it came from deep inside him, and it wouldn't stop, and it scissored and wrenched and ripped at every part of his vitals.

The thing's tail disappeared into his mouth. He felt its dry palpating sphincter slide down his throat. He choked, gagged, sicked up blood and pieces of flesh. He was conscious of every expansion and contraction as the thing bulged and heaved, bulged and heaved, caterpillaring its way into his abdomen. The most terrifying thing of all was that he knew that he was already dead. Nobody could survive this ruination inside the body and survive.

He felt his stomach straining. He looked down at himself, his eyes wide. There was a moment when he felt as if his pelvis were breaking apart; and that the whole world was collapsing on top of him. The Hollywood Divine, the night sky, everything. Ton upon ton of agony and humiliation.

'O God, help me,' he bubbled.

And then the gray column exploded out from between his thighs, its teeth bloody and decorated with viscera of all colors, his own torn manhood hardly recognizable among the shreds; and it stiffly swayed, nearly four feet long, the swollen member of the Lord of Darkness, mocking him, arrogant, obscene, Satan's penis between a priest's legs. Now he knew why the mirror had spat semen at him. Satan relished the sexual degradation of the clergy.

'O God . . .' Father Lucas whispered.

One by one, the rows of teeth were concealed by sliding skin. Then the gray thing dragged itself away from Father Lucas, its body rustling on the dusty floor, and burrowed itself deep beneath the stacks of folding chairs, into the darkest corners, where it shrank into dryness, like an abandoned sack, and waited for the day that was near now; nearer than ever. The day that was almost here.

And Father Lucas' blood slid stickily across the basement floor and in between the painted toes of the African statue. This little piggy went to market, this little piggy stayed at home.

That morning at eight o'clock sharp, Boofuls danced and sang for June Lassiter at 20th Century-Fox.

They used the set which had been built for the television mini-series *Ziegfeld Follies*, partly because nobody else was using it, and partly because it included a mock-up of a theater stage. June Lassiter sat right in front in her director's chair, dressed in an off-white suit by Giorgio Armani. Beside her sat her executive assistant and the bearer of her Filofax, Kathy Lupanek, all frizzy hair and huge spectacles and radical opinions.

Morris Nathan was also present, of course; with Alison. So was Chubby Bosanquet, the Fox finance director; John Drax, the choreographer; and Ahab Greene.

Martin sat at the very back, in darkness, feeling tired and withdrawn. He was praying in a way that 'Lejeune's' audition would prove to be a complete flop. If that happened – if it was obvious that nobody wanted to remake *Sweet Chariot* – maybe Boofuls would retreat back into his mirror and let Emilio go.

Some hope, thought Martin. *If Father Quinlan's theory about the reincarnation of Satan were even half true, Boofuls would make sure that, this time, he accomplished what he had been born to accomplish. No more interfering grandmothers this time. No more vorpal swords.*

At last, Boofuls appeared on the soundstage, and bowed.

He was wearing a royal-blue Little Lord Fauntleroy costume that he had borrowed from wardrobe, and Martin found it totally uncanny to watch him, fifty years after his death, strutting into the spotlights as if time had stood still, as if World War II and Korea and rock'n'roll and President Kennedy and going to the moon had never happened.

'Doesn't he look *adorable*?' June cried out, and clapped her hands.

Martin felt a sinking in his stomach. She was won over already: give him five minutes and Boofuls would have her eating out of his adorable hand.

Morris said, 'He's a natural; an absolute natural. Never seen a child star like him.'

'And what did you say his name was? Lejeune?'

Morris nodded. 'That's right. But don't worry about his name. You just listen to him sing.'

Boofuls knelt and sang 'The Sadness of Happier Times'. His voice was so pure and poignant that even Martin was moved. June Lassiter was unashamedly wiping her eyes with her handkerchief, and Morris blew his nose so loudly that Kathy Lupanek jumped.

When all of them were dewy-eyed, or very close to tears, Boofuls suddenly sprang up and danced the sunbeam dance from *Sunshine Serenade*. He kicked and flew and pirouetted as if gravity had no effect on him whatsoever; his blue-slippered toes scarcely touched the floor. Ahab Greene started applauding long before he had finished, and the rest of them joined him. Morris even stood up and shouted out, 'Incredible! That's incredible! Would you look at that, June? That's incredible!'

Boofuls finished his dance and bowed low. Still they clapped him. At last, his cheeks flushed, breathing hard, he came down the steps at the side of the mock-theater stage and walked directly up to Chubby Bosanquet, completely ignoring June Lassiter.

'Well?' he asked in his high-pitched voice. 'Will you do it?'

'Lejeune –' put in June. 'That really isn't Mr Bosanquet's decision.'

'He arranges the financing, doesn't he?'

'Well, certainly but –'

'Then that's okay. I know *you* like it, Ms Lassiter. All I have to know now is whether Mr Bosanquet is going to come up with twenty-five million dollars.'

Morris Nathan came forward and was about to lay his hand on Boofuls' shoulder, but Boofuls stepped away.

'Come on, now, Lejeune,' said Morris, smiling uncomfortably. 'Let's not go over the top about this. It's up to Ms Lassiter whether Fox makes this picture or not. And it's a little impertinent, don't you think, to assume that she likes it even before she's had a chance to read the screenplay or listen to any of the songs?'

Boofuls pouted. 'If I didn't think she was going to like it, I wouldn't have bothered to come down here.'

June Lassiter stood up and came closer. Boofuls beckoned to Martin to bring him the revised screenplay. Martin handed it over and said, '*Sweet Chariot*, a total rewrite. Updated, dialogue altered, motivations overhauled, characterizations sharpened up.'

'And what makes you think I'm going to approve it?' asked June. 'Remember, it was only last week when you tried to persuade me to do the Boofuls musical; and I turned you down very, very flat.'

'That was then,' said Martin. 'This is now.'

'So tell me the difference.'

Martin scruffed up Boofuls' hair. He was the only one whom Boofuls allowed to do it. 'This is the difference, and you know it. He sings and dances better than Boofuls. He's going to be the greatest child star there ever was.'

Kathy Lupanek pulled a so-what, child-stars-yuck kind of face. But June Lassiter gradually allowed herself to break into a smile.

'Do you know something, Martin, you're probably right. I'm going to recommend this project. Morris – you and I ought to talk some business.'

Boofuls said clearly, 'Mr Nathan is not my agent.'

Morris looked perplexed. 'Hey, come on, now! Didn't I set up this audition for you? You *have* to have an agent! You can't work without an agent! He's such a *mazik*, this kid!'

Boofuls approached Morris and stared at him with those welding-torch eyes. 'Not a *mazik*, Mr Nathan. A *dybbuk*.' Not a little devil, Mr Nathan, but a demon from hell.

June tried to break the tension by saying, 'Lejeune, honey – Mr Nathan's right. You do have to have an agent, just to protect your legal interests. I mean, if you don't want to use Mr Nathan, I can talk to your parents and recommend plenty more –'

'I don't have any parents,' said Lejeune. His voice was high but expressionless.

June looked uncomfortable. 'You must have *somebody* to take care of you. *Some* legal guardian.'

Boofuls paused for a moment, looking around. Martin could recognize that cunning strangeness in his face; the wolfish expression of an adult man. 'My grandmother,' he said. 'I live with my grandmother. She's my legal guardian.'

'Well, I'll call her myself and explain that you have to have an agent,' said June.

'I should work off my *toches* fixing this audition and then I don't even get ten percent of thankyouverymuch?' Morris demanded.

'I'm sorry, Morris, it's Lejeune's choice,' June told him.

Morris turned on Boofuls and stabbed a stubby finger at him. 'You're not a *mazik* and you're not a *dybbuk*. You're the *gilgul* of my old dead partner Chaim Selzer, that's what you are!'

Martin came forward and took hold of Morris' arm. 'Morris, forget it. I'm sorry. I just automatically assumed that Lejeune would want you to be his agent.'

Alison squeezed Morris close and said, 'Come on, Morry, forget it. It's better you don't represent him, believe me. If he can't be grateful for what you've done for him, Martin's right, you should forget it.'

Morris tugged his large white sports coat tightly around his stomach. 'Forget it, you bet I'll forget it. And *you*, Martin, you bet I'll forget you, too!'

'Oh, come on, Morry, don't be upset!' Alison cooed; but glanced across at Martin at the same time with an expression which meant don't worry, I'll cool him down.

'All right, all right already!' Morris snapped. 'I'm not upset,

I'm nice! Just don't let me have to look at that kid's face again, ever! And I don't want to hear his name, neither!'

Boofuls meanwhile had eerily circled around so that he was standing in Morris' way as Morris prepared to leave. Morris stopped and stared at him. Boofuls stared back, and then gradually smiled.

'Are you *sure* that's what you want?' Boofuls asked him. 'Never to see my face again, never to hear my name?'

'Got it in one, Goldilocks,' Morris told him. 'Now, if you'll kindly ex-*cuse* us!'

Taking Alison by the arm, Morris waddled out of the sound-stage and into the sunlight.

'I didn't mean to make him cross,' said Boofuls, watching him go.

June Lassiter laughed. 'Don't worry about Morris. He'll get over it. Now – let's go get some coffee and cake, shall we, and talk about this musical of yours? We must talk to your grandmother, you realize that, don't you, since she's your legal guardian.'

'I understand,' said Boofuls sweetly, taking hold of June's hand. Martin followed behind them, with a feeling of increasing dread. He wished to God that Morris hadn't yelled at Boofuls like that. If he had killed Homer Theobald just for touching the key to the safe-deposit box at the Hollywood Divine, there was no knowing what he might do to Morris.

Kathy Lupanek, walking beside him with her clipboard clutched to her flat chest, said, 'I really hate child actors, you know? Especially snootsy-cutesy ones like Lejeune.'

Martin said nothing. He didn't know how sharp Boofuls' ears were. He wasn't even sure that Boofuls couldn't penetrate right inside his mind, and hear him silently screaming, '*You hideous evil son of a bitch! I'd kill you if I had half the chance, and I'd chop you up into pieces, just the way your grandmother did!*'

They were back home in Franklin Avenue well before eleven o'clock. Martin wanted to go see Ramone, and so he told Boofuls to stay in the apartment and watch television.

'Can we go out later for hamburgers?' Boofuls asked him with a surprisingly childish whine.

'Sure. If you're hungry now, there's some baloney in the refrigerator, and some cake. Just don't drink the beer, that's all. You may be fifty-eight years old, but you're still under age.'

Martin left the house feeling shaky and scattered and fraught. He drove badly down to Hollywood Boulevard, bumping over curbs and arguing with a Ralph's delivery truck, and when he arrived at The Reel Thing he couldn't find anyplace to park, so in the end he left the car on Leland Way, which was almost as far away as Franklin Avenue.

Ramone was leaning on the counter with his shades pushed down right to the end of his nose so that he could read the small ads in *Variety*. He stood up when Martin came in and said, 'Hey, the wanderer returns! Where have you *been*, my man, I've been calling you for days! I even called round to your house this morning, around nine, and the Caparooparellis said you was away on biz-ness.'

Martin wiped sweat from his forehead with the back of his hand. 'When I tell you, you're not going to believe it.'

'Man – I saw that snake-cat. I'll believe anything.'

Martin said, 'Let's go get a beer. This is not one of those things that you can tell anybody about when you're stone-cold sober.'

'Okay, then. Kelly! Would you mind the store for a half hour?'

They left the store and walked out into the hot mid-morning sun. Ramone said, 'I asked Mrs Capelli about Emilio; but she said there wasn't no sign.'

'Was that all she said?'

Ramone nodded. 'She seemed pretty uptight, so I didn't like to bug her any more.'

'She didn't tell you about Boofuls?'

'No, she didn't. What about Boofuls?'

Martin hesitated. Then he said, 'I promised myself I was going to keep this a total secret. The only people who know the truth so far are Mr Capelli and myself; and Mr Capelli found out by accident, although I guess he was entitled to know, Emilio being his grandson and everything. But – damn it – I can't keep it in any longer. I can't go around with a secret this big, especially when I have a friend like you to share it with.'

Ramone stopped dead in the street, and a punk who had been walking close behind him collided into the back of him. 'Hey, man,' the punk complained, but Ramone silenced him with a grotesque glare, like Mick Belker in *Hill Street Blues*. 'What are you trying to tell me?' Ramone asked Martin fiercely. 'What the hell has happened?'

'Lugosi went into the mirror,' said Martin. 'That hellcat came out.'

'Go on,' Ramone urged him.

'Well . . . Emilio went into the mirror . . . and guess who came out in his place?'

Ramone stared at Martin in horror. 'Boofuls,' he whispered. 'Oh, Jesus, *Boofuls*.'

Shortly before eleven o'clock, Boofuls got up from the sofa, walked across to the television, and switched it off. Then he marched smartly to the mirror, his hands by his sides, and called out, 'Emilio! Emilio! Come on out, Emilio!'

There was a short pause, and then Emilio came into the reflected room. He was carrying a huge brindled cat, so heavy that he could only manage to carry it under its front legs. The rest of its body hung down, and swayed as Emilio walked, and its eyes were slitted in displeasure.

'You shouldn't carry Pickle like that,' Boofuls admonished him. 'She doesn't like it.'

Emilio put the cat down on the floor. There were crisscross scratches all over his small hands. 'She's so *heavy*.'

'She's well fed, that's why,' replied Boofuls. 'She eats the tongues of telltale tits; and she drinks the blood of people who meddle; and she doesn't like anybody who doesn't love her as much as I do.'

'I love her,' said Emilio. He looked exhausted and hungry. His T-shirt was grubby and there were crimson bruises on the side of his forehead, as if somebody had been cuffing him. *In mirrorland, everything is turned from left to right, even Christian morality*.

'She looks cross,' said Boofuls. 'Have you been taking care

of her properly?'

Emilio nodded. 'I play with her and I stroke her even when she scratches me.'

'All cats scratch,' Boofuls remarked scornfully.

He was just about to take another step toward the mirror when he heard footsteps on the stairs. 'Ssh!' he told Emilio, and listened. Somebody was coming up to the landing. Not Martin, the steps weren't heavy enough. Not Mrs Capelli, they were far too quick. He frowned and waited. Emilio waited, too, breathless, half hoping that somebody had come to rescue him at last.

There was a knock at the front door of the apartment; then another. Boofuls waited, not moving, not speaking. Then a girl's voice called, 'Coo-ee, Martin!'

'Go back,' Boofuls ordered Emilio.

'But you haven't –' Emilio began.

Boofuls snapped, 'Go back! Otherwise I'll *never* let you, ever!'

Reluctantly, Emilio left the reflected sitting room and disappeared through the door. The cat Pickle, however, remained, crouched on the sofa with its front paws tucked up. 'You stay there,' Boofuls told it, although it obviously had no intention of moving.

Boofuls went to the front door of the apartment and opened it. Standing outside in a sleeveless T-shirt and a pair of excruciatingly tight emerald-green satin shorts was Maria Bocanegra, from next door. Her glossy black hair was wildly back-combed, her purple lips gleamed, and her fingernails were all frosted purple. She wore emerald-green high heels and she had sprayed herself with enough Obsession to overpower any aroma that dared to be subtle within a radius of twenty feet.

Miss Loud Pedal, 1989.

'Yes?' asked Boofuls, his face white with innocence.

'Well, who are *you*?' Maria smiled. 'Aren't you just cute?'

'My name is Lejeune,' said Boofuls. 'Martin isn't here. But you can come in and wait if you wish.'

'Aren't you *po-lite*?' Maria giggled. 'If all men were as po-lite as you! But, listen, I can't stay! I just wanted to invite

256

Martin to my party on Saturday. We're having a wild, wild salsa party, can you imagine that? And since Martin loves South American rhythms, well I'm sure he'd love to be there! Can you tell him nine o'clock?'

'He'll be back in just a minute,' said Boofuls, straight-faced.

'Well, if you can't remember the message I'll call him,' said Maria. 'But I really have to fly!'

'I'm allowed to offer you a glass of wine, ma'am,' Boofuls told her.

Maria was captivated. 'Is that what Martin said? If a ravishing lady comes to the door, you're allowed to offer her a glass of wine?'

Boofuls nodded.

'Hm,' said Maria. 'How long did you say Martin was going to be?'

'Only a minute. Do come in, ma'am. I know that he'll be quite delighted to see you. He's always looking at you out of the window.'

'Ye-e-es, I know that, too,' said Maria. 'But all right, then, just one glass of wine. I don't want Rico thinking I've been fooling around with a strange man, do I?'

Boofuls opened the door and showed her through to the sitting room. She balanced her way around on her high heels, admiring it. Boofuls stood in the doorway watching her, his hands clasped together.

'Isn't this *neat*?' Maria commented. 'Very male, though. Nothing around like flowers or cushions or china ornaments. But, you know, *tasteful*. I always thought that Martin was tasteful. And that mirror's something, isn't it? Is that an antique?'

Boofuls smiled. That dreamy little smile. 'It's supposed to be lucky.'

'Is that right?' said Maria, peering at the mirror shortsightedly. She should have worn glasses but she was far too vain. Besides, she scarcely could have fitted them over her sweeping false eyelashes.

Boofuls said, 'There's a legend that comes with the mirror that if you kiss your own reflection, you'll get everything you always wanted.'

Maria laughed. 'All I ever wanted was a billionaire. Or maybe a millionaire, you know, at a pinch.'

'Go ahead, try it,' said Boofuls. His voice was oddly echoey.

'Aw, come on,' said Maria. 'If I kiss that mirror, all that's going to happen is that I'm going to leave a big fat pair of lipstick lips on it.'

Boofuls shrugged. 'Martin kissed it, and Fox is going to make that musical about Boofuls that he's been working on for years and years.'

'No kidding?' asked Maria. 'They're really going to do that?'

Boofuls nodded. 'Go ahead. You try it.'

Maria giggled. 'I feel like such a *fool*.' But she waggled her way over to the mirror, and bent forward so that she was face-to-face with her reflection. 'What do I do, wish first and then kiss – or kiss first and then wish?'

'It doesn't matter.'

'All right, then,' said Maria, closing her eyes. 'I wish that I could meet a man with a net worth of one billion dollars, and by the way could he please be good-looking, too, I don't want some rich old character with a face like a month-old cantaloupe.'

She placed her lips against the cold surface of the mirror, her eyes still closed. Up above her, the gilded face of Pan grinned with demonic blindness.

'*Mmmff*,' she said. Then – immediately – '*Mmm-mmfffffff!!!!*' because she couldn't pull her lips free from the glass.

She waved her arms frantically and slapped against the surface of the mirror with her hands. *But the mirror slowly and irresistibly dragged her in, so that she disappeared inch by inch into her own reflection.* First her face, so that her head looked like a narrow football completely covered with wildly tangled hair. Then – when her head had dwindled into a dark tuft and vanished – her real neck was joined to her reflected neck like an angled pipe.

All the time this gradual process of absorption into the mirror was going on, she kicked and struggled and hammered at the mirror, reaching behind her again and again in a desperate attempt to seek help from Boofuls.

But Boofuls stayed where he was, watching her with a placid smile. He hummed to himself as she disappeared into the mirror.

Apples are sweeter than lemons
Lemons are sweeter than limes

As she was drawn right up against the mirror, Maria pressed against its surface in a final effort to save herself. The heels of her hands skidded across the glass with a rubbery sound. But the mirror's suction was too demanding for her, and her hands were drawn in, too.

At last there was nothing left of Maria Bocanegra but her ankles and her feet – two separate triangles of human flesh with high-heeled shoes at the bases of them. One foot shuddered as it was sucked into the mirror's surface; the other remained still. A thin line of blood slid down one ankle and dripped off the metal tip of her stiletto heel just before she vanished completely. It fell onto the floor and remained there to mark Maria's passing.

Boofuls approached the mirror and stared at the reflection of the brindled cat Pickle sitting on the chair. 'Now, my beautiful darling,' he whispered, and held out his arms.

The cat's eyes, which had been squeezed shut, now opened a fraction. Then it lifted its head and stared at Boofuls haughtily.

'Come on, my beautiful darling,' Boofuls coaxed it.

At last the cat rose and stretched and yawned; and then dropped down from the chair onto the floor. It padded up to the mirror and sniffed at Boofuls. Then it sniffed at the single drop of blood that was all that remained of Maria.

'Come on, madam,' whispered Boofuls; and his whisper was cross and commanding.

The cat stepped back a little, hesitated, and then sprang. It jumped straight out of the mirror into Boofuls' arms. Boofuls staggered back two or three paces, because Pickle was so heavy, but he sank his little hands deep into her matted fur and held her up in front of him, and he tugged and tugged.

The cat spat and hissed at him, but he held it fast, and tugged even more forcefully. There was a tearing sound, like a Velcro fastener being torn apart, and he ripped the cat's stomach wide open, dividing the shaggy fur and revealing glistening flesh, mottled in red and purple. He paused, gasping for breath, but then he tore at the animal again, and now something extraordinary happened.

A woman's face emerged from the cat's stomach; a woman's head. She was completely bald, her eyes were closed, and she was covered in thin slime. But she was thin-faced, with high cheekbones, beautiful and severe; and as Boofuls tore more and more of the cat's stomach apart, her neck appeared and then her shoulders, and then Pickle's head was nothing more than an ugly flap hanging from her back, like the dried face of a fox on a fox-fur wrap.

The transformation was strange and prolonged. As Boofuls pulled the body of the cat wider and wider apart, the woman appeared with all the grace and dignity of a Chinese conjuring trick. When he dragged the last ripped-open remnants of cat away from her ankles, she stood naked and tall and silent, her eyes still closed, amniotic steam rising from her shoulders as if she had just been born.

Pickle was nothing more than an empty sack of brindled fur, like a diseased pajama bag.

Boofuls stepped back, a step at a time, and sat cross-legged on the sofa. 'Well, madam,' he said, and smiled, and rocked backward and forward.

The woman remained still for almost a half hour. Her eyes remained closed. Gradually, the slime on her body began to dry. She was very thin, very pale. Her skin was the color of ivory, with a tracery of blue veins branching through it. Her breasts were small and slanted, with nipples that were so pale pink that they scarcely showed. Her hip bones were high and prominent. She opened her eyes. The irises were pale amber; the pupils were wide and unfocused.

'Miss Redd,' smiled Boofuls.

Miss Redd smiled back; the taut smile of somebody who had just woken up.

'We're back,' said Boofuls. 'Aren't you happy, Miss Redd? After all those years, we're back.'

Miss Redd arched her head back and then circled it around to loosen her muscles. Then she worked her shoulders up and down. She looked around the room with eyes narrowed, trying to work out where she was; and what day it was; and what *year* it was. She was quite remarkable to look at. She could have been a *Vogue* model. There was something only half human about her; something feline and predatory; as if she had shrugged off a cat's body, but retained a cat's soul.

Boofuls came up to her and touched her thigh. 'Pickle-nearest-the-wind,' he said smiling.

Miss Redd ran her long thin fingers through Boofuls' blond curls. 'Never again,' she whispered.

'Why don't you wash?' Boofuls suggested. 'Then I can find you something to wear.'

'You always were the best of the boys,' Miss Redd told him.

'Martin will be back soon . . . we don't have long.'

'Martin?' asked Miss Redd.

'He was the one who bought the mirror . . . and brought it here. Our savior, if you like. He writes movies. He's going to help us finish *Sweet Chariot*. Miss Redd, it's happened at last. It's going to be wonderful. Fox wants to make the picture and everybody loves it and *at last* it's happened.'

Miss Redd got down on one knee and took hold of Boofuls' hand and kissed it. 'My Master,' she whispered.

Then she bowed her head forward so that her forehead touched the wood-block floor, and repeated, 'My Master . . . to whom I give my devotions.'

Boofuls leaned forward and touched the base of her knobby spine with a single fingertip. He ran it all the way up her back, in between her bare shoulder blades. She remained where she was, obeisant; as if she would have stayed there even if his fingertip had been a razor blade, and he had cut her open from top to bottom.

'You are the lowliest of slaves,' he told her. 'You are the most degraded of bitches.'

'Master,' she whispered, and opened her mouth wide and pressed it against the floor, licking the bare boards on which her master's feet had trodden.

*

Martin and Ramone came up the stairs about an hour later. Ramone was eager to see the real resurrected Boofuls for himself. Eager, but frightened, too. This all reminded him just a little too much of what used to happen at his grandmother's house. His grandmother used to call herself a witch and mix up potions of rum and gunpowder and licorice root, potions which were supposed to cure everything from plantar warts to pneumonia.

They reached Martin's door. Ramone laid a hesitant hand on Martin's arm and said, 'You'd better not be bullshitting me about this.'

'You said yourself you were ready to believe anything,' Martin replied.

'Well, I'm not sure about that. I mean if I died and I didn't realize and then somebody came up and told me I was dead, I wouldn't go much on believing *that*. I'd just as soon they hadn't told me in the first place.'

Martin was about to open the sitting room door when somebody opened it from the inside, swiftly and dramatically. A tall thin girl was standing there, dressed in nothing but one of Martin's checkered shirts, tied tightly around the waist with one of his two neckties, the red one, which he used for interviews with the IRS. The black one was for funerals. Around the girl's head was a turban, wound out of a red hand towel. Boofuls was sitting on the sofa, still cross-legged, like a little Buddha, still smiling.

'Look who came to see me!' Boofuls cried triumphantly.

'Oh, yes?' said Martin. 'Who's this?'

'It's Miss Redd!' Boofuls sang out. 'I told you she'd come!'

Martin stepped into the sitting room and looked Miss Redd up and down. She looked back at him, her eyes challenging him to speak. Ramone stayed where he was, in the doorway, still wide-eyed at the sight of Boofuls. *It was true, Boofuls was actually alive. He was alive – and he was sitting here talking and laughing just like a normal child.*

'How do you do?' Martin told Miss Redd. It seemed an absurdly formal thing to say, but he couldn't think of anything else. His mind was crowded with images of Boofuls in 1939, hurrying into the Hollywood Divine with Miss Redd close by his side, her black cape billowing like a thundercloud, her eyes, as sharp as razors.

Miss Redd said in a faintly middle-European accent, 'You rescued Walter from the mirror. We should be grateful.'

It was odd the way she said 'we *should* be grateful' instead of 'we *are* grateful'. There was a subtle implication that they should be grateful but they weren't; as if they didn't feel the need to be grateful to anyone.

Martin walked up to the mirror and stood staring at his reflection. 'You came out of the mirror, too?'

Miss Redd smiled. She was exceptionally beautiful; but Martin found her too thin to be really attractive. She was right on the edge of looking anorexic – like a starving gazelle or the liberated victim of a concentration camp.

'I emerged from one stage of my life into another,' she said. 'You'll have to forgive me for wearing your shirt. My clothes . . . well, my clothes became lost.'

Martin went over to the windowsill and poured two glasses of red wine without asking Miss Redd whether she wanted any. He glanced down into the yard, but Maria didn't seem to be around. Her sunbed was empty; her bent-back copy of Harold Robbins' *The Storyteller* was lying on the hammered-glass garden table. One of her Sno-Cones was floating in the pool. Martin handed one of the glasses of wine to Ramone and swallowed half of the other glassful himself, almost without breathing.

Miss Redd watched him without expression. Boofuls smiled and hummed 'The Sadness of Happier Times'.

'You're – what? Boofuls' nanny or something?' Martin asked Miss Redd.

'You could say that,' Miss Redd replied.

'To tell you the truth, I don't think he really needs a nanny. He seems to be doing all right for himself just the way he is.'

'There are some things which he is unable to do for himself,' Miss Redd answered.

'Like what?' Martin wanted to know. 'He seems to have gotten along okay so far.'

Ramone said, 'You came out of the mirror, too?'

Miss Redd smiled, but didn't reply.

263

'Well, if you came out of the mirror, you would know where Emilio is.'

'Yes,' agreed Miss Redd. 'I would. *If* I came out of the mirror.'

Martin finished his wine and set the empty glass down on the desk. 'If you *didn't* come out of the mirror, how did you get here? Stark naked, walking along Franklin Avenue?'

Miss Redd continued to smile. 'Emilio is quite safe,' she said. 'He's such a charming little boy, isn't he? Charming, but rather *grave*.'

Martin said, 'I've warned Boofuls about this, and now I'm going to warn you. If you so much as scratch that boy, I'm going to kill you.'

Miss Redd nodded. 'Well, I believe you might.' She sounded just like Greta Garbo. 'But it wouldn't do you any good at all. Because if you killed us, you would lose the ability to be able to bring Emilio back through the mirror. He would be trapped there forever; just as Boofuls and I were trapped.'

Ramone shook his head like a dog trying to shake a wasp out of its ear. 'Martin,' he said, 'we got to get a grip on this thing. I mean these people are walking all over you. And Jesus, Martin, they're not even *real* people!'

Miss Redd turned to Ramone and held out her hand. 'Here,' she said coldly. 'Take hold of my hand.'

Ramone hesitated, but then slowly put out his own hand. Miss Redd at once gripped him tightly and dug her fingernails into the inside of his wrist. Ramone shouted out, 'Heyy! Ow! That *hurts*!' But Miss Redd continued to dig her fingernails into him deeper and deeper.

'For Christ's sake, you're real! You're real!' Ramone protested. He twisted his hand free and then angrily nursed the scratches on his wrist. 'What the hell do you think you're trying to prove? You're worse than that cat!'

Boofuls laughed. Then he said, 'Miss Redd is going to take care of me now. Miss Redd will feed me and dress me and take me to the studios. You have served your purpose now, Martin, and I am grateful for what you have done. But there is nothing further for you to do.'

264

'What about *Sweet Chariot*?' asked Martin. 'Supposing they want some rewrites?'

'Miss Redd will supervise the rewrites. Your task is finished.'

'And Emilio?' demanded Ramone. 'When are you going to let him go?'

'When it suits me,' said Boofuls.

'Can you believe this runt?' appealed Ramone. 'He's eight years old and he's talking like he's my father or something. You listen here, runt —'

'Ramone,' warned Martin. 'Don't. Right now, Boofuls holds all the aces.'

Boofuls covered his face with both hands. They all watched him, saying nothing, holding their breath. When he eventually took them away again, he was smiling. Then he laughed, a high peal of laughter, bright as bells. 'You all look so *frightened!*' he crowed. 'You all look so terribly, terribly *scared!*'

For one unbalanced moment, Martin wondered whether Boofuls was playing them all for fools; whether he really did have power over Emilio; and whether the emaciated Miss Redd really had appeared through the mirror. But then Boofuls glanced at him quickly, and he saw the dead-certain coldness of those welding-torch eyes, and he knew that Boofuls was possessed by Satan just as surely as death sits on every man's shoulder.

Boofuls went across to Ramone and clung on to his sleeve. 'You shouldn't be frightened,' he told him. 'You have no cause to be frightened; no cause at all; just as long as you remember how long I have been gone and why I am here; and that no man speaks against me and lives to boast about it.'

Martin could see Ramone's anger rising up inside him. He could see his fists clenching and the veins in his neck swell. *Don't, Ramone, for God's sake*, he begged him in the silence of his mind.

Ramone looked across at him, and there was a look in his eyes which said, *Bullshit*, but he kept his mouth closed, and lifted his arm away from Boofuls' grasp, and gave the nearest thing to an agreeable smile that he could manage.

'Now,' said Boofuls, 'you promised me a hamburger,

Martin. And we must take Miss Redd to buy some clothes. Miss Redd likes black, don't you, Miss Redd? Black, black, black! Black cloaks! black skirts, black silk stockings!'

Ramone came up to Martin and laid a hand on his shoulder. 'I think I'll take a rain check on the hamburger, man. Are you going to be okay?'

'Oh, I'm going to be fine,' said Martin. He nodded and smiled at Boofuls. 'I'm going to be absolutely fine.'

Boofuls said, 'Big Mac, no pickle, giant-size fries, a strawberry milkshake, and an apple pie to finish!'

'Sure,' Martin agreed, but very quietly. He had just noticed the single spot of blood on the floor. It was thick, arterial blood, and it was still glistening. The most terrible part about it was not the fact that it was there, but that he didn't dare ask, in his own apartment, in daylight, what it was.

The police came to St Patrick's at two o'clock that afternoon to tell Father Quinlan that Father Lucas was dead.

'They found him in the basement about three hours ago. The desk clerk was so spaced out he didn't even remember that he'd let him go down there. He was pretty badly mutilated. Some crazy person, no doubt about it. But, you know, what's a fifty-five-year-old priest doing at the Hollywood Divine at that time of night? It's asking for trouble, asking.'

Father Quinlan stared at the swarthy face of the detective sitting opposite and wondered how it was that such a man could be the bearer of such tragic news. He looked more like a comedian than a detective. He had a baggy face and a bulbous nose and hair that stuck up at the back like a cockatoo's crest.

'Do you know how?' asked Father Quinlan.

The detective sniffed blatantly and shook his head. 'The ME's going over him now. But he was torn up pretty bad. That's why I say some crazy person. And of course the basement's teeming with rats. They tore him up, too, threw in their five cents' worth.'

Father Quinlan nodded. He felt curiously detached, as if none of this were really happening. He could see every detail of the detective's face with extraordinary clarity. He could see the dandruff on the collar of his tan-colored sports coat. Yet he felt as if he weren't here at all. Not dreaming, but *absent*.

'What we can't understand is this,' the detective said. 'What was he doing down in the basement of the sleaziest roach palace in town? A priest like him?'

'Perhaps,' Father Quinlan began, but when the detective quickly lifted an eyebrow, he snapped back to alertness and continued, 'perhaps he was looking for old furniture. We always need chairs and tables, you know, for our youth club activities, and our prayer meetings.'

'That time of night?' asked the detective, puckering up his nose.

'It's only a thought,' said Father Quinlan.

The detective frowned for a moment and then said, 'I have to remember to pick up a rib roast on my way home. My wife'll kill me.'

'If I think of anything,' said Father Quinlan.

'Oh, sure. Call me anytime you like, this number here. Ask for Hector. Just say Hector. Or ask for my partner, Fernandez.'

'There's one thing more,' said Father Quinlan. 'Did Father Lucas happen to have any kind of package on him? A package of black tissue paper?'

The detective took out his notebook, licked his thumb, and turned the pages. 'Wallet, keys, loose change, handkerchief, that was all. No package. No package in his automobile, either.'

'Oh, well,' said Father Quinlan, trying to sound as if it weren't important. 'Maybe he left it at home.'

'Yeah, maybe he did,' agreed the detective.

Father Quinlan saw the detective to the door. The detective said, 'I'm sorry I brought you such bad news. It's all I get to bring in this business, bad news.'

Father Quinlan nodded and said, 'Bless you all the same.'

'Thanks, Father.'

'And don't forget the rib roast.'

'You bet,' the detective said.

Father Quinlan closed the door of his study and stood for a long time without moving, stunned and saddened and frightened, too. He had not only misdirected an officer of the law, he had, indirectly, defended Satan. He had betrayed his holy trust as a priest and brought the day of Armageddon even closer.

Yet what else could he do? The police would never believe that Father Lucas had been searching for the scattered relics of the true Satan; and even if they did, there was nothing at all they could do about it. Father Quinlan would have to get in touch with Martin Williams urgently, and warn him that the claws and the hair had gone unfound – and presumably whatever was in the second safe-deposit box had been taken, too.

He picked up the phone and called Martin's number, but there was no reply. But Martin had left him his address on Franklin Avenue: perhaps he should drive up there and leave him a message. He had been thinking of calling Martin in any case. He wanted to see Boofuls' mirror for himself.

Father Quinlan scribbled Martin a letter, licked an envelope, sealed it, then raked a comb through his hair, shrugged on a crumpled linen jacket, locked up his study, and went outside to the college parking lot. It was a hot brilliant afternoon; his shadow followed him across the parking lot like an obedient black dog. He climbed into his elderly Grand Prix and started the engine.

He drove slowly and carefully. Half of the car's front bumper was hanging down and made a dull clatter as he went along. He had never been mechanically minded. Ever since he had been a young man he had been fascinated by the myths and legends of Good and Evil, the supposed reality of demons and angels. In 1954 he had been ordained to the office of exorcist, although he had only ever been called to one full-scale demonic possession – a young girl in San Juan Capistrano who had somehow managed to scorch the walls of every room in which she was locked up.

He could remember the words of the bishop's admonition even now: '*Learn through your office to govern all imperfections lest the enemy may claim a share in you and some dominion over you. For truly will ye rightly control those devils who attack others, when first ye have overcome their many crafts against yourself.*'

268

Over the years, Father Quinlan had grown to believe in the presence of demons. Not horned and cloven-hoofed; but evil nonetheless. He had seen their influence behind the actions of quite ordinary people; he had seen their eyes looking out from behind the eyes of politicians and financiers and movie stars and people in the street.

There was a *look* which Father Quinlan had grown to recognize. Only a demon looked at a priest in that particular way. Cold and sullen and viciously hostile. But you could see the look anywhere, when you least expected it. In the eyes of a bus driver. Behind a till at the Wells Fargo Bank. From a scrubwoman, sluicing the steps of a downtown office.

Through his belief in demons, Father Quinlan had evolved his belief in Satan himself. Actually, he had always *believed* in Satan, but now he knew for certain that the prophesies in the Revelation were based on verifiable fact. Satan had been defeated by the angel Michael; but he was due to return. Not in the shape of a man, but in his real demonic form, as the dragon of all destruction.

And the skies would remain perpetually dark; and the streets would run with the blood of the innocents.

Father Quinlan drove at a snail's pace along Santa Monica Boulevard, humming nervously to himself. He felt hot and uncomfortable because the Grand Prix's air-conditioning had packed up, and he couldn't afford to have it repaired. He found a crumpled Kleenex in his trouser pocket and dabbed his face with it.

He slowed down even more. He was caught between two trucks: an empty flatbed tractor-trailer in front of him and a huge grinding meat truck behind him. The noise of clashing gears and the stench of diesel added to his discomfort. He was more irritated when he reached a traffic signal and found that it was impossible to pull out from between the trucks because a shiny red Corvette boxed him in, its stereo blaring out Beastie Boys rock.

He glanced in his rearview mirror. All he could see was the dazzling chrome bumper of the massive Kenworth Trans-Orient behind him, and his own eyes. Then the traffic signals changed, and the truck in front of him pulled slowly away. But when Father Quinlan tried to shift into drive, he found that his gear lever was jammed.

The huge truck behind him blared its horn. Father Quinlan put down his window and tried to wave to the truck to move around him, but it was too close to the back of his car, and it couldn't. It blared its horn again; and this time it was joined by a chorus of horns from the traffic that was stuck behind it.

Sweating, Father Quinlan wrestled with his gearshift. *God forgive me for thinking uncharitable thoughts about truck drivers and auto mechanics.* But then the Kenworth driver leaned out of his cab and yelled, 'Get that heap of crap moving, you son of a bitch!' and Father Quinlan stuck his head out of his window and shouted back, 'I'm trying! I'm trying! the gearshift's stuck!'

The truck driver sounded his horn in one long continuous blast. Father Quinlan felt his temper rising. He looked at himself in the rearview mirror and his face was white and his eyes were blazing blue and it wasn't his face at all.

'*You connived against me, Father,*' whispered the face in the mirror.

Father Quinlan stared at the face in terror. He let out a low mewl and tugged even more furiously at his gearshift. It was the child of Satan: the one who comes before to prepare the way for Satan's resurrection. He knew it; and he knew how cruel and powerful it was; and that was why he grappled with his car so furiously. *Let me get away! For God's sake, let me get away!*

Again, the truck's horn bellowed like a dragon.

'*And he deceives those who dwell on the earth, telling those who dwell on earth to make an image of the beast who had the wound of the sword and has come to life.*'

Father Quinlan gripped his gearshift in both hands, wrestling it forward and sideways. His face was scarlet, and sweat was trickling down the sides of his face.

'*All your life you have wormed and connived against me, Father, and now is the time for you to pay. Those who use their minds to work against me must lose their minds.*'

There was a moment of maximum resistance. Then the gearshift clonked into drive. Father Quinlan's car lurched forward, its engine roaring, straight across the intersection, and straight toward the back of the flatbed truck that had been in front of him before, and which had now stopped for the next traffic signal.

Father Quinlan furiously pedaled the brake, but it went flat to the floor with no hydraulic pressure at all.

'*Conniver!*' screamed the white, white face in the mirror. '*Deceiver!*'

Father Quinlan saw the rear of the truck speeding toward him and the second truck was right behind him and he suddenly understood that he was going to die.

He didn't even have time to think of a prayer. With a crushing, grating, screeching sound, the Grand Prix burrowed its nose deep beneath the truck's bodywork, and the aluminium flatbed sheared off its roof at exactly four feet three inches above the roadway, straight through the front roof pillars, straight into Father Quinlan's face, wrenching his head right off his neck, straight through the windows in a sparkling shower of glass, straight through the rear roof supports.

The second truck shunted the Grand Prix's rear bumper and rammed it even farther beneath the first truck, so that it disappeared almost completely.

There was a prehistoric bellow, as one of the truck's tires burst; and then there was extraordinary silence.

It took the wrecking crew over two hours to winch Father Quinlan's car out from under the flatbed truck. A curious crowd stood on the sidewalk in the hot afternoon sunshine, watching and waiting. There was very little for them to see. The paramedics covered the Grand Prix with a sheet and backed the ambulance up close. Father Quinlan's body was lifted out and zipped into a bright blue body bag. It was only when one of the paramedics followed the gurney carrying another smaller plastic bag that somebody in the crowd said, 'Jesus, that's his head'.

Martin and Boofuls and Miss Redd drove past the accident on their way back from McDonald's. Martin said, 'Look at that, God, guy must've been killed instantly.'

Boofuls said nothing, but smiled at Miss Redd, and reached across to take hold of her hand.

That night, Martin went downstairs to play chess with Mr Capelli. He had been to the market with a shopping list that Miss Redd had given him. Veal, chicken, whole-meal bread, fresh fruit and vegetables. Miss Redd had announced that she was going to do the cooking: Boofuls needed his special diet. Martin was welcome to join them, she said; but Martin had no appetite for anything cooked by Miss Redd. It had been difficult enough, taking Boofuls and Miss Redd to McDonald's. To sit in his own apartment watching them eat would be like having dinner at the mortuary.

They were both dead creatures, as far as he was concerned; no matter how appealing Boofuls could be, no matter how courteously Miss Redd behaved.

Mr Capelli looked worn out, even though his doctor had given him Tranxene to help him sleep. Mrs Capelli had gone to spend the rest of the week with her sister in Pasadena. Her sister's husband ran a successful drain-cleaning business, Rothman's Roto-Rooter.

Martin and Mr Capelli shared a six-pack of beer and played chess for about an hour. The apartment seemed empty and depressing without Mrs Capelli. There was no singing from the kitchen, no chopping of garlic and onions, no aroma of bolognese sauce. Mr Capelli chain-smoked small cigars and wearily misplayed most of his moves.

'This woman, then,' he asked Martin, 'what is she? Is she real? Is she a ghost?'

'I don't know,' said Martin. 'I suppose she's pretty much the same as Boofuls. A kind of walking, talking image out of a mirror.'

'I got a very bad feeling about all of this,' Mr Capelli remarked, moving his queen. 'I got the feeling they're just using us, you know, for something worse, something bad.'

Martin hadn't told Mr Capelli what Father Quinlan had said about the second coming of Satan. He swallowed beer and moved his bishop to counteract Mr Capelli's queen. *Satan cannot live and breathe until those one hundred forty-four thousand lie massacred.*

Mr Capelli said, 'You know what I feel? I feel like this is my house, but it's not my house anymore. Not when Emilio's stuck in that mirror, and those people are living upstairs.'

Martin nodded. He knew exactly how Mr Capelli felt. He was glad that Stephen J. Cannell productions had just sent him a check for four months' worth of rewrites, because with Boofuls and Miss Redd in his apartment, smiling, talking, prowling, planning, he couldn't get near his typewriter; and even if he had been able to, he probably couldn't have written a single word worth squat. He was too worried about Emilio. He was too worried about what he had let loose on the world at large.

Satan? It seemed ridiculous. But Father Quinlan had believed it; and Father Lucas had believed it. Maybe one priest could be crazy; but two?

The decorated clock on Mr Capelli's bureau struck nine. Almost at the same moment, the door chimes sounded.

'Visitors?' asked Martin. 'You expecting anybody?'

Mr Capelli shook his head. 'My cousin Bernado's coming down next week, but that's all.'

'Let me get it,' said Martin, and went to the door. Outside, on the landing, stood Miss Redd, wearing the clinging black-satin dress she had bought this afternoon at Fiorucci, with black stockings and black stiletto shoes. With her high cheekbones and white skin, she looked like a page torn out of a 1940s fashion magazine.

'I'm not bothering you,' she said, so flatly that it was scarcely a question at all.

'What do you want?' asked Martin, closing the door behind him so that Mr Capelli wouldn't see her.

'I wanted to tell you that Lejeune and I will be moving out tomorrow.'

'Oh, yes?'

Miss Redd smiled. 'I just spoke to June Lassiter at 20th Century-Fox and she will provide a private bungalow for us on the Fox lot while *Sweet Chariot* is being filmed. So – you will be pleased to know that we will not be trespassing on your hospitality any further. We leave tomorrow morning.'

'What about the mirror?' asked Martin. 'Are you leaving that here?'

Miss Redd said, 'That's what I wanted to talk to you about. The mirror cannot be moved; not yet.'

'And Emilio?'

'Emilio will be safe just as long as you do not attempt to break the mirror or get him back out of it.'

'And when are you going to set him free?'

'Lejeune has made that quite clear.'

'Don't call him Lejeune to me, lady,' Martin retorted. 'That's a poisonous and ridiculous joke. His name is Walter Lemuel Crossley, also known as Boofuls.'

Miss Redd smiled provocatively. 'Anger makes you handsome, did you know that?'

'It also makes me determined,' Martin told her, although his voice was shaking. 'And if there's one thing I'm determined about, it's getting Emilio back in one piece. Now – how long is it going to take to finish this movie of yours?'

'Fifteen weeks,' said Miss Redd. 'Fox is going to put everything possible into it. All the best technicians, the best lighting cameramen, the best choreographers, the best musicians. They've already chosen Marcus Leopold to direct. It's going to be a marvel.'

'And you give me your solemn oath that when it's finished, you'll let Emilio go?'

'On the night of the premiere, we will let Emilio go.'

Just then, Mr Capelli came to the door. He stood and stared at Miss Redd in silent indignation.

Miss Redd said, 'I sincerely apologize for all the pain we have caused you, Mr Capelli. But sacrifices have to be made in all great causes.'

'They're moving out,' Martin told Mr Capelli. 'They're going to stay on the Fox lot until the picture's finished; then they promise they'll let Emilio go.'

'There is one more thing,' said Miss Redd. 'During the production of the picture, you will not attempt to come near us; nor speak to us; and neither will you speak to anybody else about us. You will remain silent and patient, and you will guard the mirror.'

Mr Capelli said, 'You, lady, are a harlot from hell.'

Miss Redd slowly and elegantly blew him a kiss. 'And you, sir, are more right than you will ever know.'

With that, she climbed the stairs back to Martin's apartment and closed the door.

Mr Capelli shook his head. 'We should call the cops, you know that?'

'Oh, yes? And what do you think the cops are going to say? "These people kidnapped your grandson, sir? Okay, where is he? In the *mirror*? Excuse me, sir, while I call for the men with the butterfly net."'

'Well, you're right,' said Mr Capelli tiredly. They went back into the apartment and closed the door behind them.

'There's just one other possibility,' said Martin. 'I could call Father Quinlan at St Patrick's Theological College. He's an exorcist – you know, a proper official exorcist. Once Boofuls and his lady friend have moved out – well, maybe, he could try to exorcise the mirror, I don't know – maybe he could get Emilio back for us that way.'

'Exorcist?' asked Mr Capelli, shaking his head.

Martin looked up St Patrick's in the telephone directory and then dialed the number. The phone rang for a long time before anybody answered. It was a solemn, young-sounding man.

'Can you put me through to Father Quinlan, please?' asked Martin.

'I'm sorry, I regret to tell you that Father Quinlan died this afternoon.'

Martin was shocked. 'He *died*? Oh, my God. How?'

'There was a car crash on Santa Monica Boulevard. He was killed instantly, I'm afraid.'

God, thought Martin, we actually drove past that crash. 'I'm sorry,' he said. 'I don't know what to say.'

'Did you know Father Quinlan well?' the young man asked him.

'I only just met him. My name's Martin Williams. I met him along with Father Lucas.'

'Oh, yes, I remember,' the young man replied. 'I was the one who let you in. Actually, Father Quinlan had an envelope for you in his car. He must have been on his way to

275

give it to you. The police found it in his car, down the side of the seat. I've got it here if you want to collect it in the morning.'

Martin frowned. 'No, no. Open it, read it to me over the phone.'

'Are you sure? It'll take a minute to go get it.'

The young priest was away for almost two minutes. When he returned, Martin heard him pick up the receiver and tear open the envelope.

'Here it is. "*To Mr Martin Williams. You may not have heard the distressing news that Father Lucas has been murdered.*"'

'Oh, God,' Martin interrupted. 'I didn't know that either. That's both of them.'

'Do you want me to go on?' the young priest asked.

'Yes, please,' Martin told him. Mr Capelli was frowning at him and whispering, 'What's wrong? What's happened?'

The young priest read, '"*He was found in the basement of the Hollywood Divine. The police think he was attacked by an addict. Somebody on angel dust perhaps. Father Lucas had the relics with him, but they are now missing. Whether you believe in the prophesies or not, it will do no harm to take all possible precautions. Remember the prediction of the innocents, the hundred and forty-four thousand lambs of God. Try to believe! Call me when you get back. Meanwhile make absolutely sure that no woman goes near the mirror, because Boofuls will have need of his witch-familiar, Miss Redd, and the only way he will be able to retrieve her from the mirror will be by—*"'

The young priest paused. Martin urged him, 'Go on, why have you stopped?'

'Well, are you really sure you want to —? I mean, it's kind of *odd*, isn't it, to say the least? Father Quinlan was always known as something of an eccentric.'

'Please,' Martin insisted, 'will you just finish reading the letter?'

'All right, sir, if that's what you want. Where was I? Oh, yes — "*the only way he will be able to retrieve her will be by trading one life for another — the way he did with the cat — and with your young friend Emilio. The witch-familiar will protect him and succor him until the day when he can revive his satanic*" *parent. Witch-familiars usually have ancient and ribald names like Blow-Kate and Able-and-Stout and Pickle-nearest-the-wind.*' The young priest coughed in embarrassment.

'Please,' Martin begged him. 'This may sound like nonsense to you but it makes a whole lot of sense to me.'

'Well, there's only one more paragraph,' the young priest told him. 'Father Quinlan says, "*Remember Alice, read it carefully; and remember, too, that only the child can destroy the child, and only the child can destroy the parent*":'

Martin asked, 'Is that all?'

'That's all,' the young priest told him. He sounded more officious now that he had done his duty to Father Quinlan.

'I'll come by and collect the letter in the morning,' said Martin. 'Perhaps you can keep it safe for me.'

The young priest hesitated, and then he ventured, 'I don't mean to speak ill of the dead, Mr Williams, but you do realize that most of the time Father Quinlan was out on a limb, so to speak? I mean theologically. The church these days doesn't recognize the old biblical legends as strict fact. The Revelation in particular. I mean movies like *The Omen* have set us back decades. We can't have people believing in Satan, not these days. There are so many other problems for them to deal with. Unemployment, debt, divorce, drug addiction, street crime, isn't that enough to worry about without worrying about the fiery dragon of the Revelation?'

Martin was silent for a moment. Then he said, 'With all due respect, hasn't it ever occurred to you that all of those contemporary evils you're talking about – divorce and debt and mugging and everything – hasn't it ever occurred to you that these evils are nothing more than the modern face of the same old fiery dragon?'

The young priest said stiffly, 'Well, sir, I don't really think that this is an appropriate time to get into a religious discussion. You can collect the letter at the secretary's office. And – sir – I do not believe in Satan, nor ever will.'

'Your choice,' said Martin, and put down the phone.

Mr Capelli looked up from their chess game. 'What's happening?' he wanted to know.

Martin came around and stood beside him. 'We're on our

own,' he told him. 'It's you and me and Ramone, because nobody else will believe us.'

Mr Capelli said, 'You've got something to tell me, don't you? Sit down, let's hear it. Tell me the worst. Come on, I'm an old man, I can take it. And aren't we friends? And by the way, I just took your bishop.'

CHAPTER ELEVEN

Principal photography started on *Sweet Chariot* in the second week of September. Fox took a full-page advertisement in *Variety*, trumpeting 'Pip Young, Geraldine Glosset, Lester Kroll, in Sweet Chariot, an angelic musical, words and music by Art Glazer and Michael Hanson'.

'Pip Young' was June Lassiter's inspired new name for Lejeune, the Fox board having decided that Lejeune was too foreign-sounding, especially for a boy with such a clipped foreign-sounding accent. Actually, Boofuls' accent wasn't foreign at all, it was simply fifty years out of date.

Martin kept in touch with *Sweet Chariot*'s progress through Morris; and through Kathy Lupanek, with whom he had made a special effort to be friends. He had even taken her out for lunch at Stratton's and brought her flowers. Kathy Lupanek had spent two hours telling Martin about her abused childhood. Martin had sympathized.

Back at Franklin Avenue, week after week, Martin and the Capellis lived a life of empty restlessness, waiting for *Sweet Chariot* to be shot and edited and scored and premiered. As far as Martin was concerned, time inside the house seemed to stand still, while the days rushed silently past outside his window, a speeded-up movie of clouds, sunsets, thunderstorms, smog.

He tried not to watch the mirror. He took his typewriter into the kitchen and kept up his income by pecking out rewrites for *Search for Tomorrow* and *The Guiding Light*. But every now and then he would find that he had dried up; and that he had been staring at his keyboard for almost a half hour without writing a word. Then he would walk into the sitting room and stare at his reflection in the mirror and whisper 'Emilio? Where the hell are you, Emilio? Are you alive? Are you dead?'

But there was nothing. No answers, no apparitions, nothing but a cold and clear reflection of the world as it was.

Sometimes Ramone came by, and they would sit on the sofa and look at themselves in the mirror and drink a couple of bottles of wine. To begin with – when Martin had told him all about Father Quinlan and his threats about the Revelation – Ramone had been all for smashing the mirror to pieces. 'Just break the bastard to bits, why don't we?' But the days went by, and he became calmer and more philosophical, and maybe Father Quinlan had been nothing but an oddball, after all.

One morning soon after Boofuls and Miss Redd had left the house they saw police next door. Maria Bocanegra had disappeared; nobody knew where. At first her landlady had assumed that she had gone home to her parents in San Diego, but then a month later her parents had arrived to visit her. Her clothes were still strewn around her room, her bed unmade, her lipstick still open and melted across her dressing table. Her father declared, 'It's a total mystery, like that ship with breakfass on it and no people, the whassname, the *Marry Sir Less*.'

They saw nothing at all of Boofuls and Miss Redd. Nobody was allowed anywhere near them, except at specially selected press calls, to which Martin was conspicuously not invited. Martin tried to call Boofuls on the telephone three or four times, but each time he was told that 'Mr Young is not accepting any calls, I'm sorry'. One Thursday afternoon, drunk on California Chablis, he had driven around to Boofuls' bungalow and yelled out, 'Boofuls! You bastard! You listen to me, you bastard! I want Emilio back!' He had been escorted off the Fox lot by two tetchy security guards, and June Lassiter had called Morris Nathan and told him to keep Martin Williams at least a mile away from Century City at all times; in fact, he wasn't even allowed to turn into Avenue of the Stars, on pain of never writing for 20th Century-Fox Television ever again, *ever*.

Martin bitterly wondered which was worse: Armageddon or never writing for 20th Century-Fox Television again.

Meanwhile, taking Father Quinlan's advice, he read and reread *Through the Looking-Glass*, and he studied the letter which Father Quinlan had been trying to deliver to him on the day he was killed.

'*Only the child can destroy the child, and only the child can destroy the parent.*' What the hell did that mean?

Ramone remarked, 'My old man, he was always saying that I was going to be the death of him. Maybe *that's* what it means.'

In the first week of November, Mr Capelli came stamping up the stairs and walked into Martin's kitchen without knocking. He was holding up a folded-back copy of *Variety*. He slapped it with the back of his hand and dropped it on the kitchen table. Martin had been typing out some new dialogue for *As the World Turns*, and he froze for a moment, trying to remember the end of the sentence he had been writing.

'It's there!' Mr Capelli declared. 'Premiere date! There it is! November 12! That's when I get my Emilio back!'

Martin picked up the paper. Another full-page advertisement. '20th Century-Fox announces the world premiere of *Sweet Chariot*, an angelic musical starring Pip Young, Geraldine Glosset, Lester Kroll ... unprecedented simultaneous premieres at Mann's Chinese Theater, Hollywood Boulevard, as well as Lux Theaters, Union City Theaters, Hyatt Theaters ... altogether four hundred movie theaters throughout the United States ... plus special international openings in London, Paris, Madrid, Rome ... Absolutely no previews.'

Martin slowly shook his head. 'Did you ever hear of anything like this? Simultaneous openings throughout the world? They're really going to send out four hundred prints before they have any idea whether anybody's going to *like* it or not?'

Mr Capelli didn't answer, but tapped the paper with his finger. 'That's the date, November twelfth. That's when I get my Emilio back.'

Martin pushed back his chair and went across to the telephone on the kitchen wall. He punched out Morris Nathan's number. 'Morris . . .?' he said at last. 'Yes, it's Martin. Listen, did you see how Fox is going to launch *Sweet Chariot*?'

'I saw it,' said Morris. 'And if you want my candid opinion, I think they're out of their tree. They've kept this whole picture secret. Nobody's seen any rushes; nobody knows whether it's good, or half good, or terrible. Still, they want to burn their fingers, who am I to tell them what to do? They're taking a hell of a chance. June told me the final production cost was $32.4 million. So I said, what's this, *Heaven's Gate* with music?'

'And what did she say?'

'She said, wait and see, that's what she said. And I said, just remember, I didn't have anything to do with this. If you lose $32.4 million because of some untrained juvey, don't come whining to me.'

'Do you know whose idea this was? This simultaneous premiere?'

'The kid's, or that nanny of his, who do you think?'

'And they gave in to him? June Lassiter gave in to an eight-year-old kid?'

'They had to. That's the way I heard it, anyway. They were three quarters of the way through shooting the picture and the kid appears in ninety percent of the scenes and sings every single song, and then he turns around and says they have to open worldwide in four hundred theaters and that's it, otherwise he walks. They could have sued him, but what for?'

'Okay, Morris, thanks,' said Martin.

'Did you finish that rewrite yet?' Morris demanded.

'Oh, sure, I'll run it up to you later this afternoon.'

Morris cleared his throat. 'You're a good writer, Martin. One of these days you're going to be a better than average writer.'

'Morris, you're an angel.'

'Don't talk to me about angels.'

The night before the premiere, Martin stood by his open window, looking out over the lights of the Hollywood Hills. Ramone turned the corner of the street and came walking toward the house, brandishing a large bottle of red wine. 'Hey, *muchacho*, fancy a little nerve suppressant?'

Ramone came upstairs and they stood side by side, drinking wine and feeling the cool night air blowing on their faces. Ramone lit a cheroot and blew smoke, and the smoke fled around the corner of the house as if it were trying to escape from something frightening.

'Sometimes I don't know why I stay in this town,' said Ramone. 'It's tatty and it's tawdry and where the hell are its *values*? Sometimes I feel like finding myself a small place in Wyoming and raising horses.'

'You'd hate that,' Martin remarked.

Ramone nodded. 'You're right, I would. Shit.'

They drank in silence for a long while, and then Ramone said, 'What are you going to do if he doesn't let Emilio go?'

Martin shrugged. 'I haven't thought about it. I don't think I've even *dared* to think about it. He promised after all.'

'I was thinking about it this afternoon, though,' Ramone went on 'and I couldn't quite get the whole deal to balance in my head.'

'What do you mean?'

'Well . . . what I'm trying to say is, as far as we know, Boofuls can't stay in the real world, can he, unless Emilio stays in the mirror-world? So the only way that Emilio is going to get free from that mirror is if Boofuls goes back into it?'

Martin nodded. 'I guess that's true.'

'Right,' said Ramone, 'but what I'm saying is – if this mirror-world is as disgusting as it appears to be from where *we're* standing, why should Boofuls agree to go back at all? I mean, *I* wouldn't, if I were him, would you? I'd say forget it, no matter what I promised. Unless – and this is what I was trying to get my brain around – unless he doesn't *need* to go back, once this movie's been premiered. Do you see what I'm trying to get at? Maybe there's something in the movie, maybe the movie changes things. Maybe Boofuls is going to become *real*, once people have seen his picture on the screen, and the reason he wants a worldwide premiere is that the more people who see it, the more real he gets. I don't know. This whole thing's got me baffled, I really hate to think, Martin. It's bad for my sinus. But this thing's making me think.'

Martin swallowed wine and nodded. 'I don't know, Ramone, maybe you're right. Boofuls was real anxious to start remaking *Sweet Chariot* – right from the moment he stepped out of the mirror.'

'So it was important to him, right?' said Ramone.

'That's right; it was crucial.'

'And if it was crucial, if it was life and death, maybe it was more than just a comeback, right?'

'Well, maybe it was and maybe it wasn't,' said Martin. 'It depends whose comeback you're talking about.'

'You mean —'

'Ramone, for Christ's sake, I don't know *what* I mean. But maybe this movie is like an up-to-date equivalent of the rituals in the Bible, the rituals that are supposed to resurrect Satan. I've been reading it and reading it and I *still* don't understand it, but the Bible talks about the great red dragon with seven heads and ten horns, and how his tail swept away a third of the stars from heaven and threw them to earth. But who the hell knows what it's all supposed to signify, because I don't?'

Ramone turned around and stared at the mirror. 'Maybe we ought not to wait. Maybe we ought to try getting Emilio out of there now.'

Martin shook his head. 'Too dangerous. Boofuls said we might kill him.'

'Well, he *would* say that, wouldn't he?'

'Supposing we did kill him?' Martin retorted. 'Would *you* tell Mr and Mrs Capelli?'

Ramone thought for a while, then chucked the last of his wine down his throat and wiped his mouth. 'Let's watch some television. I'm tired of thinking.'

Up at his house on Mulholland Drive, Morris Nathan was working late, reading over the boilerplate of a television contract with MTM. He sat in his study under a circle of light from his desk lamp, a cigar perched in the ashtray beside him. Alison didn't allow him to smoke anywhere else in the house.

He was almost finished when the doorbell rang. He took off his reading glasses, tightened the belt of his peacock-blue bathrobe, and walked through to the Mexican-tile hallway. Alison was just coming down the curved stairway, dressed in nothing but a loose pink T-shirt with *Andy Warhol 1928-87* printed in red over her breasts, and a red silk scarf knotted around her hair.

'It's okay,' said Morris. 'It's Benny Ito, he promised to call by this evening. And in any case, I wouldn't let you answer the door dressed like that.'

'Dressed like what?' Alison protested. 'I'm not dressed like anything.'

'Exactamundo,' Morris agreed.

The bell rang again. Morris pressed the intercom button and said, 'Who is it?'

'It's Benny, Mr Nathan. I brought the stuff you wanted.'

'Come on in, Benny.'

Morris opened the door and a young Japanese with a spiky black haircut and a black cotton jumpsuit came into the hallway, carrying a large padded envelope under his arm. 'Here you are, Mr Nathan. None of it's terrific; just outtakes. But you can't get near to the finished footage with a Sherman tank.'

'You promised me a complete print,' Morris protested.

'Believe me, I tried. But the Fox lot is up to its ass in security guards. And they won't deliver the prints to the movie theaters until one hour before they're due to start screening. That's what Walt Peskow told me, anyway, and he should know.'

Morris opened the envelope. Inside was a single can of movie film. He prized it open and looked inside disparagingly. There couldn't have been more than three hundred feet of stock in it, little bits and pieces spliced together to form one single reel.

'You expect five hundred dollars for this *chazzerei*?'

Benny shrugged and sniffed and shifted his weight from one foot to the other. 'Maybe two-fifty.'

'Two-fifty? Half? For what? For not even half of a movie?'

'Hey, come on, man, the risk was the same. I could have lost my job.'

'For this, you should have lost your balls.'

Nevertheless, Morris reached into the pocket of his bathrobe and took out a thick roll of twenty-dollar bills, neatly held together with a rubber band. He stripped off two hundred dollars and handed it to Benny Ito without a word.

Benny counted it and said, 'Two hundred? Is that it?'

Morris slapped him on the back and guided him toward the door. 'There's an old saying, Benny. Half the failures in life are caused by pulling in your horse, just when he's leaping. You know who said that? Well, neither do I. But you just did it. Good night.'

He closed the door, locked it, and then walked back across the hallway with the can of film. Alison had been watching him from the staircase. 'What's that, Morry?' she wanted to know.

'The one and only piece of *Sweet Chariot* that isn't in the vaults of 20th Century-Fox. It's not what I wanted. This is all *shtiklech und breklech*, and I wanted the whole damned movie. But at least we'll have some idea of what June Lassiter got for her $32.4 million, and if it looks like a real stinker we'll make absolutely sure the press get to see it first thing tomorrow morning.'

Alison came down the stairs, her breasts double-bouncing under her T-shirt. 'I wish you hadn't,' she told him.

'You wish I hadn't what? You wish I hadn't gotten hold of this footage? Did you think I was going to let that eight-year-old *faigeleh* treat me like a dumb stupid idiot, introducing him to June Lassiter, here you are, June, look at this hotshot kid, June, and what happens, all of a sudden I'm not his agent at all. Do you know what they *paid* that kid to appear in *Sweet Chariot*? Nine hundred eighty thousand dollars! And do you know what ten percent is of nine hundred eighty thousand dollars?'

Alison stared at Morris for a moment, dumbfounded. Then she whispered, 'No. I flunked math at school.'

Morris put his arm around her and led her through to the sitting room. 'Let's just say that "Pip Young" or "Lejeune" or whatever he calls himself has cut me out of enough profit to keep myself in new Ferraris for the rest of my natural days.'

'I thought you said you didn't like Ferraris.'

Morris went across the room and flicked two switches on the wall. With a low hum, a movie screen unrolled itself from the ceiling, and a 35-mm projector rose out of the middle of the coffee table. He pressed another switch, and the beige velvet drapes jerkily closed themselves, all the way around the room.

'Do you want to pour me a drink?' Morris asked Alison as he took the movie out of its can and began to thread it into the projector.

Alison went over to the liquor cabinet and fixed them both an old-fashioned. Then they settled down together on the beige velvet couch, and Morris pressed the switches to dim the lights and start the movie running.

On the screen, there was a brief flicker of numbers; then without warning the face of Boofuls appeared, slightly unsteady, slightly out of focus, but staring intently into the camera.

Morris watched this impatiently for a moment, sipping his drink, and then said, 'What the hell is this? Two hundred dollars I paid for this! A screen test!'

Alison patted his arm. 'Wait a minute, there's probably more.'

'There'd better be probably more,' Morris declared. 'Otherwise Benny Ito is going to suffer good, believe me!'

He was just about to switch the projector off when the voice of Boofuls came out of the stereo speakers, high and clear.

'*You said you never wanted to see my face again, didn't you, Morris? You said you never wanted to see my face and you never wanted to hear my name.*'

Morris stared at the screen in shock and then turned to Alison. 'Did you hear that? He's talking to me personally!'

Alison said, 'Morris, switch it off, please!'

'But he's talking to me, out of the screen, just like he's here! What the hell is that Benny trying to pull? A joke, already?'

'Morry, *please* –' Alison begged him. 'That boy Lejeune – he's *bad*, Morry, he's *evil*! There's something about him! Martin thinks so, too!'

'A *kaporeh* on Martin! Listen to this! Did you ever see such cheek? Benny must have gotten together with the kid and filmed this on purpose!'

'*You said you never wanted to see my face again, Morris, never ever! Well, now your wish has come true! And you said you*

287

never wanted to hear my name again, Morris, and you shall have that wish, too!'

Morris stood up and switched off the projector. 'Did you ever hear such garbage?' he asked Alison. 'Two hundred dollars I paid for that! I'll strangle that Benny Ito, with my bare hands!'

Alison finished her drink.

'How about another?' Morris suggested. 'Then we'll go to bed. I finished that contract for MTM.'

He went across to the liquor cabinet, turned his back to Alison, and poured out whiskey.

'Are we going to the premiere tomorrow?' Alison asked him. 'I bought this beautiful gold dress today at Alluci's.'

Morris reached out for two cocktail stirrers. 'Spending my profits again, hunh?'

'Oh, it's beautiful,' said Alison. 'I'll try it on for you when we go upstairs. It has a very low front, very daring, but a fantastic bow on one hip, and it's kind of split down the same side, all the way to the hem. It's very sexy but it's very chic.'

Morris turned around, a drink in each hand. 'Everybody's going to be looking at you, hunh?'

'Oh, Morry, you know it's all for you.'

'No point in doing it for me,' said Morris; and for the first time Alison caught the odd, tight tone in his voice. She turned and looked at him and at first she couldn't understand what he had done, but as he shuffled nearer with the two drinks, grimacing as he came, she suddenly realized in utter horror that Boofuls' mocking prediction had come true, and that Morris had fulfilled it.

A sharp cocktail stirrer protruded out of each of Morris' eyeballs. He had prodded one directly into the iris of each eye, as far as it would go, blinding himself instantly. Now he was groping his way toward Alison with thin glutinous runnels of optic fluid dripping down each cheek.

Alison screamed. A high-pitched genuine theatrical scream. '*Morry! Oh, God, Morry! What have you done! Morry, your eyes!*'

Morris hesitated, stumbled, and dropped both glasses of whiskey. One of them rolled on the carpet, the other caught the edge of the coffee table and smashed.

'It was the only thing I could do,' he said in bewilderment. 'It was the only thing I could do.'

Alison stood up, but she was so appalled that she couldn't go near him. 'Morry,' she wept, 'take them out, Morry. Please, Morry, take them out! I'll call for the ambulance, please, Morry, *Please!*'

Morris groped forward, trying to follow the sound of her voice. 'Alison, honey, I –' But then he stopped and turned his head around, as if he were listening to something. And at that moment, the projector clicked and whirred into life once again, all by itself, frightening Alison so much that she screamed and screamed and this time she couldn't stop.

Boofuls' face appeared on the screen yet again, that white, expressionless face, and his voice whispered from the speakers. '*You have one of your wishes, Morris. You will never see me again. What do you say, Morris? What do you say? Don't you ever say thank you when somebody gives you what you want?*'

Morris bent his head slightly forward and took hold of the sticks that protruded from his eyes. Shuddering, gasping, he drew them out, and when he did so a large clear glob of fluid swelled out of the punctured holes that he had made in each iris. Alison's screaming quietened to a high endless whimpering, but she couldn't take her eyes away from him, she couldn't move, she couldn't do anything to help him.

And all the time the high, childish teasing of Boofuls continued to pipe from the movie speakers, and Boofuls' bright face continued to stare at them out of the screen. '*You couldn't be nice, Morris, you couldn't be nice! You couldn't be sugar and spice. Now you'll get it, whatever you want, blind as a bat and deaf as a post!*'

'*Shut up! Shut up! For God's sake, shut up!*' Alison screamed, and rushed across to the movie screen and tugged at it and tore at it until it came rumbling down from the ceiling. Then she turned to the speakers, and lifted them up one after the other, and smashed them against the coffee table.

The projector, however, continued to run, and Boofuls' flattened-out face appeared on the back of the white-leather couch, silently mouthing the same words over and over. Alison hysterically threw herself at the couch and tried to drag the image of Boofuls off the leather with her fingernails.

Morris meanwhile had sunk slowly to his knees onto the white carpet. Between the finger and thumb of each hand, he held up the two cocktail stirrers.

'Alison, honey, I couldn't do anything else. There wasn't any choice, honey-pie.'

Alison threw back her head and sobbed, one harsh, strangulated sob after the other. 'Oh God, Morry, what are we going to do? What are we going to do?'

But Morris couldn't hear her. Morris' head was filled with the lisping monotonous voice of Boofuls, like an old silk dress being dragged across a floor, saying, *'You never wanted to see me, Morris; you never wanted to hear me. I can give you your wish, Morris! I can give you your wish!'*

Morris slowly raised the two cocktail stirrers and blindly prodded them against his cheeks until he found his ears. Then he inserted the points deep in each ear, so that he could feel them pricking painfully against his eardrums.

Alison had stopped sobbing and was messily wiping the tears from her face with her hands. 'Oh God, Morry,' she told him. 'I'm sorry. I couldn't stand to see you that way. I'd better go call for an ambulance.'

She turned, and there he was, kneeling on the floor with his hands up to his ears, and a cocktail stirrer in each hand. His injured eyes were closed, so that he looked almost normal, and there was an expression on his face of curious calm.

'*Morry?*' she questioned him. Then she saw the cocktail stirrers. '*Morry!*'

With a small suppressed gasp, Morris pushed the points of the sticks straight through his eardrums, puncturing both of them at once. He stayed quite still for a moment, holding his breath, and then gave each stick an extra twist, so that his tympanic membranes would be completely torn open.

Alison, trembling, picked up the cordless telephone and dialled 911. 'Mr Nathan's house,' she whispered. 'That's right, Mulholland Drive. Please, quickly.'

Then she put down the phone and went over to Morris and knelt down in front of him.

'Oh, Morry,' she said, and held him tightly in her arms, her deaf and blinded husband, and rocked him, and swore to herself that if she never did anything else in her life, ever again, she would have her revenge on Boofuls.

The morning of the premiere of *Sweet Chariot*, the Los Angeles basin was filled with thick sepia smog. Because of its elevation on the lower slopes of the Hollywood Hills, however, Franklin Avenue was clear of pollution, and when Martin looked out of his kitchen window he felt as if he were staring out over some strange and murky Sargasso Sea.

He drank two cups of hot black coffee, ate a little muesli sprinkled with wheat germ, and then dressed in a white T-shirt and khaki slacks and went downstairs to see if Mr Capelli would like to take a walk down to Hollywood Boulevard.

'A walk?' said Mr Capelli. 'You mean that thing when you put one foot in front of the other and don't stop till you get home again?'

They walked arm in arm, not saying much, but friends, brothers in crisis. They went downhill on La Brea; and then east on Hollywood Boulevard as far as Mann's Chinese Theater, where half a dozen workmen were dressing the marquee for tonight's opening. A huge 3-D billboard had been erected with a fifty-foot acrylic painting of Boofuls, flying through the clouds with a sweet smile of innocence. That scene came from the very end of the picture, when God decides that the young street Arab has done enough good deeds to redeem himself, and accepts His errant son into the Kingdom of Heaven.

Martin and Mr Capelli stood in front of the theater for a long while, watching the electricians connecting the klieg lights. Mr Capelli said, 'You know something, I saw the Kliegl brothers once, when I was a kid. They were arguing in the street about something really technical, like carbon arcs or something. And one of them said to the other – well, I don't know which one it was, John or Anton – but he said, "If it wasn't for me, movies wouldn't even *exist*." And the other one said, "Maybe that would have been a blessing."'

Martin smiled. 'You actually saw that?'

Mr Capelli nodded. 'That was a long time ago. Maybe things were more innocent then.'

Martin said, 'I don't think things have *ever* been innocent, Mr Capelli.'

Mr Capelli squeezed Martin's arm. 'I guess you're right, Martin. I wish you weren't.'

They went into Maxie's for a cup of coffee. They said very little; but then they didn't need to. They were both thinking about Emilio.

When they returned to Franklin Avenue (both perspiring, because the morning was growing hot now), they saw a pale blue Rolls-Royce Corniche convertible parked outside. The license plate was 10 P C.

'That's Morris Nathan's car,' said Martin in surprise. 'I thought Morris wasn't speaking to me – not after I went round to the Fox lot and tried to tell Boofuls what a bastard he was.'

'Just so long as he doesn't keep that heap of imported junk cluttering up my driveway,' Mr Capelli complained.

'Mr Capelli, that's a Rolls-Royce Corniche!'

'Listen, Martin, one day you'll learn. *All* automobiles are a heap of junk. What are they, plastic, chromium, foam rubber, bits and pieces. This one is a heap of *imported* junk, that's all.'

'But you love your Lincoln.'

'Sure I love my Lincoln. Do you know why? I always kid Emilio it turns itself into a robot, you know, like Transporters.'

'Transformers,' Martin corrected him; but kindly.

'Sure, that's right, Transformers. He loves it. He keeps telling me, Grandpa, I saw it happen, I saw it change. The wheels turned into hands and the hood turned into a hat and the trunk opened up and two legs came out, and who knows what?' There were tears in Mr Capelli's eyes. 'Martin, he's just a little boy. I love him so much. Can't we get him out of there?'

Martin said soberly, 'Boofuls did promise. So did Miss Redd.'

Mr Capelli shook his head. 'Those people,' he said. 'Those people.'

When they entered the house, however, they were surprised to find not Morris but Alison, sitting on the stairs in a tight white cotton suntop and a wide 1950s skirt and strappy high-heeled sandals, waiting for them.

As soon as she caught sight of Martin, she came up and flung her arms around him and burst into tears.

'Hey,' said Martin. 'Hey, what's happened? Alison? What's happened?'

'It's Morry,' she wept. 'Oh, Martin, it's Morry.'

Mr Capelli laid a hand on her shoulder. 'Hey, now, don't get upset. Look at you, you're all upset! And look at me, I'm all upset, too!'

Martin asked Alison, 'What's happened? Alison! Is Morry okay?'

Alison choked out, 'He's *blind*, Martin. He's blind! And he did it himself, with two cocktail stirrers, just like that! And then he stuck them in his ears and made himself deaf!'

'What?' said Martin. 'Are you kidding me, or what? Morris *blinded* himself? He *deafened* himself? Alison – he works in the movies!'

'Is that all you care about?' Alison screamed. 'He's my husband! I love him! He gives me everything! And now he's blind and he can't ever *see* me again, and he's deaf and he can't ever *hear* me again!'

Martin held Alison close. Mr Capelli, despondent, sat down on the stairs. 'I don't know, what the hell. You sometimes wonder if it's worth living.'

Martin said, 'Come on upstairs. There's another bottle of Chablis in the fridge. The very least we can do is get drunk.'

Alison drank two large glasses of cold Chablis one after the other and then told Martin and Mr Capelli everything that had happened last night, the way that Morris had pierced his eyes and ears. 'I couldn't do anything to help him,' she said; and the tears ran freely down her face. 'I broke the screen, I broke the speakers, but it didn't make any difference.'

Martin said, 'I'm sorry. I'm so sorry. Whatever arguments I ever had with Morris.'

Alison wiped her eyes with a crumpled tissue. 'Morry never

did anything worse than speak his mind. Nobody deserves to be blind and deaf, just because they spoke their mind. You know, Morry was always speaking his mind, and he was rude sometimes, but he never deserved that.'

'But you really believe that Lejeune did it?' Martin asked her.

Alison nodded. 'I wouldn't have come here otherwise. It was *his* face, it was *his* voice. And you remember what he said to Morry, when he was auditioning at Fox? When they had that argument? *You never want to see my face again, you never want to hear my name.* Well, that's just what he said on the movie. Exactly that – like he was talking to Morry face-to-face.'

Martin said, 'I'm sorry, Alison. I'm really sorry. But there's nothing I can do. I tried to get to Lejeune, but they wouldn't let me.'

Not long afterward, Ramone appeared. He stood in the doorway with his thumbs hooked through the belt loops of his jeans, looking like Carlos Santana on his weekend off. Martin told him, 'There's nothing. There's no news.'

'Maybe you should switch on the television,' Ramone suggested. 'They're showing an hour-long program, "The Making of *Sweet Chariot*", just about now, Channel Four.'

'I don't want to watch that,' said Mr Capelli. 'Maybe I'll get some pizza.'

'Pepperoni, deep-dish, with extra chilis, mushrooms, onions, and sweet corn,' said Ramone, easing himself onto the couch.

Mr Capelli stared at him in astonishment, but Martin gave him a nod to tell him that Ramone never took anybody for granted. 'I'll have whatever,' he told Mr Capelli.

Alison said, 'I'll pass. I'm sorry. I don't feel very hungry.'

For some reason, all four of them turned toward the mirror, where the gold-painted face of Pan grinned at them in silent triumph. They looked like a group portrait printed on sun-faded paper; an evanescent photograph of four people who had been brought together by pain and friendship and circumstance, and who would soon have to face the most harrowing experience of their entire lives.

As if to mock them, the mirror seemed to darken and dim, until they could hardly see their faces in it at all.

Mr Capelli watched the mirror for a moment, and then angrily and with great determination went off to buy some pizzas.

Just before six o'clock that evening, Martin said, 'Come on, I can't stand waiting around here any longer. Let's go down to Mann's and see the damn thing for ourselves.'

'You go,' said Mr Capelli. 'I'll wait here. Just in case – you know – Emilio gets to come out of the mirror.'

'I'll stay, too,' said Alison. 'You don't mind if I stay?'

'Sure, go ahead,' Martin told her.

At that moment, however, Ramone said, 'Look, on the television, there it is!'

It was a CBS report by Nancy Bergen, transmitted live from Hollywood Boulevard. In the background they could see the crowds of fans already assembling – even though the first stars weren't expected to start arriving for at least an hour – and the huge triumphant marquee picture of Boofuls.

Nancy Bergen was saying, '– motion-picture event of the decade – unknown child star discovered by June Lassiter at 20th Century-Fox – extraordinary natural talent for song-and-dance – won him the lead role in a thirty-five-million-dollar remake of a musical that was actually never made in the first place – or at least never completed – *Sweet Chariot* –'

Martin put in, 'Notice how she hasn't mentioned Boofuls, not once. He's still bad karma in Hollywood, always will be.'

Ramone said, 'Bad karma? He'll be catmeat if I ever get my hands on him.'

Nancy Bergen went on, '– such confidence in *Sweet Chariot*'s success that they are holding simultaneous premieres throughout the United States and Europe – which means that in London they're holding their first screening in time for an early breakfast, and in New York it's going to be a one-o'clock-in-the-morning affair – so sought after have the premiere tickets been, however, that –'

'You want some more wine?' Alison asked Ramone.

'Oh, sure, thanks, just a half glass,' Ramone told her.

'– thousand people will see *Sweet Chariot* simultaneously –'

'How many did she say?' Martin asked.

'What?' said Ramone.

'How many people did she say would be seeing *Sweet Chariot* tonight?'

Ramone shrugged. 'I don't know, man. I didn't hear. Must be quite a few thousand.'

Martin quickly pressed the remote and flicked the television from station to station, but none of the other channels were carrying reports about *Sweet Chariot*.

Martin told Mr Capelli, 'Give me the phone book.'

'Sure,' said Mr Capelli, 'but what's the problem?'

Flicking quickly through the pages, Martin found the number of CBS Television News. 'I thought I heard Nancy Bergen say a particular number, that's all. It rang a bell.'

He picked up the phone and dialed CBS. The switchboard took endless minutes to answer, and then endless more minutes to connect him with the news desk.

'Chuck Pressler,' announced a laconic voice.

'Oh, hi, sorry to bother you,' said Martin. 'I was watching Nancy Bergen's report on the *Sweet Chariot* premiere. She mentioned how many thousands of people were going to be watching the first screening simultaneously. Do you have that figure there? I missed it.'

There was some shuffling around, and then the laconic voice said, 'I don't have that information here, right now. Nancy's going to be back later tonight, around eleven o'clock. You could try calling her then. Or tomorrow morning maybe.'

Martin put down the phone and dialed 20th Century-Fox. This time there was no answer at all. 'Damn it,' he said. 'Come on, Ramone, let's get down there and ask Nancy Bergen for ourselves.'

They left Mr Capelli and Alison at the apartment and jogged down La Brea in the sweltering evening heat. When they reached the intersection with Hollywood Boulevard, they found that it was already crowded with thousands of fans and sightseers, and that there were police trestles all around the Chinese Theater. Inch by inch, sweating, alternately elbowing and apologizing, they forced their way through to the front of the lines, as close as they could to the CBS outside-broadcast truck. It took them almost ten minutes to get there, and when they did they found two cops standing right between them and the CBS crew.

Martin glimpsed Nancy Bergen, with her brushed blond hair and her shiny cerise evening dress, and shouted out, 'Ms Bergen! Ms Bergen!'

The girl standing next to him, scowled and said, 'That was right in my goddamned ear, you freak.'

Martin ignored her, and cupped his hands around his mouth, and yelled, 'Ms Bergen! Over here!'

At last, catching the sound of her name amid the bustle, Nancy Bergen turned around and frowned toward the crowd. Several of them waved, and she smiled and waved back. The noise around the theater was already tremendous: talking and laughing and shuffling of feet, and even when Martin bellowed, 'Ms Bergen!' one more time, she turned away because she obviously hadn't heard him.

Martin checked his watch. There were fewer than eleven minutes to go before the premiere. The first guests were already arriving, and there was a long line of shining limousines all the way up Hollywood Boulevard. With a cheer from the crowd, the klieg lights were switched on and stalked around the night sky on brilliant stilts.

Ramone said, 'Why is this so *important*, man? I'm getting my feet jumped on here.'

'Listen,' Martin told him, 'I want you to create a diversion so that I can get under the police trestle and across to the television truck.'

'Create a diversion? How the hell do I create a diversion?'

'Well, go farther down the line there and try to push your way through.'

'Oh, that's great, and get myself arrested?'

'Pretend you're sick, then. Pretend you're just about to have a heart attack.'

'That's right, and get myself carried off to the hospital.'

'Well, think of *something*, for God's sake. I have to talk to Nancy Bergen, and I have to talk to her now!'

Ramone rubbed sweat from the back of his neck and

nodded, 'Okay. But you'd better have a damned awesome reason for doing this, *amigo*.'

'Have faith, will you?' Martin told him.

Ramone jostled his way through the spectators who were crowding the police trestles until he was twenty or thirty feet away. He bobbed his head up and down a few times and then turned toward Martin and made a circle between finger and thumb, *Watch this, buddy*. Then he suddenly started flailing his arms and shouting out, '*Thief! Thief! You stole my wallet! Thief!*'

Everybody around him backed away. Either he was crazy and he was going to attack them, or else he wasn't crazy and somebody was going to be accused of taking his wallet, and either alternative was about as attractive as catching AIDS.

At first, the two police officers didn't see him, they were too busy standing in camera shot and trying to look groomed and tough, but then two or three girls stumbled and fell because of the commotion that Ramone was causing, and they hurried down the police line to see what was happening. Martin immediately ducked under the trestle, dodged around the back of the CBS truck, and approached Nancy Bergen from behind. She was listening to her producer talking to her over her earphone, and saying, 'Yes, Farley; okay, Farley; but they won't be arriving for at least five minutes.'

As soon as she had finished, Martin tapped her politely on the shoulder.

'Ms Bergen?'

She stared at him blankly. That hostile don't-bother-me stare that he had seen on so many faces of so many TV personalities when the grubby public came a little too close.

'Listen, you don't know me, Ms Bergen, my name's Martin Williams.'

'You're right,' she said, marching back toward the television truck. 'I don't know you.'

'Ms Bergen, I'm a screenwriter, I wrote most of the *Sweet Chariot* screenplay. Actually, I updated it from the original. They probably haven't given me credit on the screen, but –'

'– but now you're angry as all hell and you're going to sue. Well, believe me, Mr Wilson, it happens all the time, and if I were you I'd save your money. The only people who make money out of law are lawyers. I've been there, I know.'

'Ms Bergen, I'm not complaining about that. But there's a whole lot more to this production than meets the eye.'

Nancy Bergen's red-haired personal assistant came up with a glass of Perrier water, a clipboard, and a lit cigarette in an aluminum-foil ashtray. Nancy swallowed two mouthfuls of water, propped the cigarette in the corner of her mouth, and began to scribble notes on the clipboard. 'Do you have something to tell me, Mr Wilson? Otherwise I'm going to have to say *hasta luego*, you know?'

'Do you mind if I ask you a question first?'

Nancy Bergen continued to scribble, ignoring him.

Martin said, 'You mentioned that x-thousand people were going to be watching this premiere simultaneously all over the world.'

Nancy Bergen stopped scribbling, handed the clipboard back to her assistant, dropped her cigarette back in its ashtray, blew out smoke, and said, 'One hundred forty-four thousand, why?'

Martin took a deep breath. 'I'm going to sound like some kind of religious nut when I tell you this.'

'Then don't tell me. Hank, do you have that radio mike ready?'

'It's ready, Nance,' said a thin, shaven-headed man in a sweaty T-shirt.

But Martin said, 'One hundred forty-four thousand, that's the exact number in the Book of Revelation, the exact number of innocents who follow the Lamb – the exact number of people who have to be sacrificed so that Satan can come alive again.'

Nancy Bergen beckoned one of the CBS sound men. 'Harvey, will you escort Mr Wilson back to the barriers for me?'

Martin insisted, 'Ms Bergen, I don't think you understand what I'm saying here. That boy Pip Young isn't Pip Young at all.'

'Mr Wilson, I already know that. His real name is something Lejeune. Now, please, I'm going tonto here as it is.'

'Ms Bergen, Pip Young is Boofuls! The real Boofuls! The real murdered Boofuls, come back to life!'

A big blond man with biceps like Virginia hams and a sweatband around his forehead laid his hand on Martin's shoulder and whistled through ruined nasal cavities, 'Come on, man, let's be friendly here, hunh?'

'Boofuls was possessed!' Martin shouted. 'That was why his grandmother killed him! Boofuls was possessed by Satan! But he escaped! He went into the mirror! But now he's back and everyone who sees this movie is going to die! Ms Bergen! Listen! One hundred forty-four thousand innocent people are going to die!'

Nancy Bergen was already out of earshot, preparing her first star interview. A gleaming black Fleetwood had just pulled into the curb, and the door was opened so that Geraldine Grosset could step out onto the sidewalk in a clinging white dress splashed with diamanté. The crowds roared and whistled and screamed, and the klieg lights crisscrossed the evening sky as if it were wartime.

Martin struggled and kicked, but the big blond man twisted his arm around behind his back and hop-skip-jumped him back to the barrier. 'Ms Bergen!' Martin screamed at the top of his voice. 'He's bringing back Satan, Ms Bergen! He's bringing him back *tonight!*'

Several of the crowd turned to stare at Martin pityingly. The big blond man lifted him clear over the police trestle, said, 'Pardon me, lady,' to a woman who was pressed up against the barrier close by, and set Martin down onto the ground.

'Now, you listen, friend, you stay there, otherwise I swear to God you will never walk again.'

Martin was sweating and shaking and all fired up. All the same, he nodded and said, 'Okay, okay,' and rubbed his twisted wrist, and tried to look as if he had been effectively warned off. The big blond man returned to the CBS truck, glancing fiercely back at Martin from time to time, but all Martin did was smile and nod, okay, already, I'm behaving.

Ramone came pushing his way back through the crowd to

join him. 'Well?' he demanded. 'Did you get what you wanted?'

Martin took hold of his arm. 'It's true, it's one hundred forty-four thousand.'

'You've lost me, man.'

'That's why they're holding all of these premieres all at once, all over the world. That's why they've never showed the movie to anybody before. There's something in the movie – I don't know, something in the way it's made, something in the screenplay, some subliminal message, maybe. All of those people who see it tonight are going to be killed.'

'You're putting me on. One hundred forty-four thousand? What the hell for?'

'Because tonight is the night, trust me. Tonight is the night that is prophesied in the Revelation. The night that Satan comes back to life, the real dragon, for real, and if you and I don't do anything about it the sun isn't going to come up again tomorrow, nor ever.'

Ramone stared at him. For the first time, Martin could see that his friend didn't believe him. And for the first time he could hear the sound of his own voice and he sounded as if he were raving.

All around them, the screaming and the applauding of the crowd sounded like a thunderous landslide as a sapphire-white limousine appeared, bringing Pip Young, a.k.a. Lejeune, a.k.a. Boofuls.

'Ramone,' said Martin, 'you and I have been friends for a very long time.'

Ramone nodded. He looked exhausted, battered, almost sad.

'Believe me, Ramone, you've seen the mirror for yourself. These terrible things haven't been happening for nothing. They've been happening for a *reason*, Ramone, and the reason is it's *time*. It's time for Satan to come back to earth, it's time for the dragon. It's all in the Bible, in the Revelation, but what it says in the Revelation is that Satan's going to come back and then be defeated for good. That's why he's used Boofuls. Boofuls has made damn sure that he doesn't get defeated. He's going to come back if we let him and this time he intends to stay.'

Ramone lowered his head. 'I don't know, man. I used to believe in Satan when I was a little kid.'

Boofuls emerged from his limousine and stood alone for a moment on the crimson-carpeted sidewalk. He was wearing a white suit with silver-sequined lapels, and his hair was shining and curly. Close behind him came Miss Redd, pale-faced, with scarlet lips, in her sweeping black cape.

As Boofuls walked up toward the theater entrance, the crowd let out an extraordinary moan of delight, and two girls in glittery cocktail-waitress costumes came tottering up on stiletto heels to present him with cellophane-covered bouquets. Boofuls accepted the flowers gravely, then passed them back to Miss Redd, who in turn passed them back to the chauffeur.

Martin tugged at Ramone's sleeve. 'Right now, I don't care whether you believe in him or not. I want you to help me, that's all. *I* believe in it, and that'll be good enough for the two of us.'

'So what are you planning on doing?'

'I don't have any idea. But the first thing we have to do is get ourselves into this premiere, and see what Boofuls is planning to do.'

Ramone said, 'You and me, in sweaty old T-shirts, we're going to get into the most glamoroso premiere of the decade?'

Martin looked down at himself. 'I guess you're right. Damn it. Maybe we can sneak into the back.'

'Do you see those cops?' said Ramone. 'How the hell are we going to get past those cops?'

'Mandrake gestures hypnotically,' replied Martin bitterly. 'Instantly, our heroes are clad in immaculate tuxedos.'

'Hold up just one moment,' Ramone told him. He dug into his back pants pocket and produced his keys. 'I believe our problems are ov-ah.'

He grasped Martin's arm and together they struggled back out of the crowd. It took them almost five minutes to reach the opposite side of Hollywood Boulevard, but once they were clear of the police lines they were able to dodge and shuffle their way along quite quickly. They reached Ramone's store, The Reel Thing, and Ramone unlocked the front door, switched off the burglar alarm, and let them in.

'What's on your mind?' Martin wanted to know.

Ramone took him across to the side of the store, where there were rails of old movie costumes. Right in front, with a label on it, was the painter's smock that Spring Byington had worn in *You Can't Take It With You*. Ramone, however, was rummaging around at the far end of the rails, and after a few moments he triumphantly came out with two immaculate tuxedos.

'If you're the same size as William Powell, this'll fit,' he told Martin.

'You're as crazy as I am,' said Martin.

'I don't think so. Now, listen, I have shirts, too, and neckties, and evening pumps. Go into the back and wash up and I'll have it all laid out for you, better than a valet.'

Martin went through to the back of the store, splashed his face with cold water, and combed his hair. By the time he returned, Ramone was already half dressed. 'Believe me,' said Ramone, 'you and me are going to look like a couple of swells.'

Within ten minutes, they were leaving the store, dressed this time in tuxedos. Martin's vest was far too tight, and so he had ripped it up the back. Ramone's pants flapped around his ankles. But in the crowds and the excitement, they hoped that nobody would notice.

'God help us,' said Martin.

'He will,' Ramone reassured him. 'He will.'

Their timing was almost perfect. They managed to push their way through to the front of the crowds just as the last official limousine was pulling away, and the police were dragging a trestle to one side. Martin elbowed his way around the edge of the trestle, and slipped behind two policemen into the roped-off area reserved for celebrities and guests. Bud Zabetti from Columbia Pictures noticed him and waved, obviously unaware that he had no invitation, and that was enough of a credential for a beady-eyed security guard to turn away satisfied and let Martin and Ramone shoulder their way into the throng of people in the theater lobby.

The lobby was hot and crowded and smelled strongly of Giorgio. Martin gradually eased his way through the crowds, nodding and smiling to people he knew. At last he approached the magic circle: June Lassiter, in a striking but somewhat extraordinary directional evening dress, more like a turquoise kite than a dress; Lester Kroll, all wavy gray hair and protruding upper teeth, and heavy gold rings on his fingers that had been given to him by various boyfriends; Geraldine Grosset, always smaller than she looked on the screen, tiny in fact, in a black gown with a gold spray over one shoulder; some starlet who was showing her naked body through a gauzy white dress; Miss Redd; and in the epicenter of this small tornado of Hollywood influence, Boofuls himself, with noticeably staring eyes, gleeful, pale, sucking in every moment of adoration as if he needed it to stay alive.

Martin came right up to him and stood beside him and said nothing; but at last Boofuls turned and saw him. He registered a split second's surprise, then looked away.

'You're not actually supposed to be here,' he said. Martin was appalled at the way Boofuls looked. For the first time, he really looked *dead*, like a boy who had been killed and then resurrected. There was paint and powder on his face, as if he had been prepared by an unskilled mortician for viewing by his relatives.

'You could have sent me an invitation,' Martin told him. 'After all, I wrote sixty percent of the dialogue.'

Boofuls smiled to Esther Shapiro. 'It'll be out on VCR before you know it. Then you can watch it all you want.'

Miss Redd touched Martin's hand with her own hand, as cold as chilled chicken. 'I think Pip would prefer it if you left now, Mr Williams.'

Martin ignored her, and leaned toward Boofuls and said, 'It's tonight, Boofuls, isn't it? It's tonight.'

For the first time Boofuls looked up at him directly. His eyes were rimmed with red. 'I don't know what you're talking about, Martin. Go on, now. Go home. You'd be better off watching this on television.'

'Tonight's the big night, when you and Miss Redd plan to kill off one hundred and forty-four thousand innocent people, all at once, so that you-know-who can come back.'

'You're mad,' said Miss Redd in a low, harsh voice that was more like a man's than a woman's.

'We'll see,' Martin retorted. 'But let me tell you something,

Boofuls. Mad or not, I'm going to do to you what your grand-mother did; and that is to chop you up into more bits than anybody will ever be able to put together again. And this time there won't be any mirrors around to save your soul.'

'Martin,' said Boofuls. 'I'm trying to save you. I'm trying to do you a favor.'

'I don't want any favors from you. I just want this madness called off, that is all. One hundred forty-four thousand people, Boofuls. Think of the slaughter. Think of the grief. And what have they ever done to you?'

Boofuls took two or three deep breaths, feverish, unhealthy, like a child in a sickroom. 'I'll tell you what they did to me, Martin. They brought down my father; they brought him down; and my father has lived a life of exile and agony ever since.'

'Maybe he deserved it,' Martin replied.

'Oh no,' said Boofuls, vehemently shaking his head. 'Nobody deserves a punishment like that. Nobody deserves an exile that never ends. In the end, everybody deserves for-giveness, no matter how great their misdemeanor.'

'And this is the answer, to sacrifice all these people?'

'Martin,' June Lassiter interrupted, 'are you monopolizing our star? Come on, Pip, we have to get upstairs to our seats.'

But Boofuls beckoned Martin closer, and touched his shoul-der, and whispered, '*And I looked, and behold an ashen horse; and he who sat on it had the name Death; and Hades was following with him. And authority was given to them over the fourth of the earth. To kill with sword and famine and with pestilence and by the wild beasts of the earth.*'

Martin in spite of himself, shuddered. 'Boofuls,' he said, although he was quite aware how pathetically ineffectual he sounded. 'Boofuls, for Christ's sake, don't do it.'

Boofuls laughed. 'I liked you, Martin, from the moment I first saw you. I think I always will. But go home, now. There is nothing else that you can do. And don't ever ask me any-thing, for *Christ*'s sake.'

'I can bring the mirror down here and damn well force you back into it.'

'You'll never be able to lift it. You know that.'

305

'I'll try, God help me.'

For a fleeting moment, Martin thought he saw Boofuls flinch, as if the prospect of Martin trying to move the mirror somehow disturbed him.

'Leave the mirror where it is,' Boofuls told him. 'If anything happens to it, then Emilio will die. Do you want Emilio to die?'

Miss Redd now swept herself protectively in between them. 'Enough,' she said, staring at Martin with glittering eyes.

Martin tried to step around her, but she seized hold of his left hand and dug fingernails into it. The pain was sharp and intense; just like being scratched by a cat's claws. Martin whipped his hand away and it was bleeding.

'Is anything wrong here?' asked Lester Kroll, benevolently tilting his way over. He smelled strongly of whiskey. 'It's time we took our seats, isn't it? Come on, Pip, you young pip-squeak.'

June Lassiter came up to Martin and said, 'I don't know how you managed to inveigle yourself in here, Martin, and I don't think I want to find out. But since you're here, and since you wrote so much of the picture, and since poor Morris is in such a bad way . . . well, you can have a couple of seats at the back.'

'You're a princess, June,' said Martin, trying to tug his vest straight.

'Think nothing of it,' June told him. 'You're a good writer; and now you've gotten Boofuls out of your system, maybe you'll turn out to be a *great* writer. Tell me one thing, though.'

'Anything.'

'Where the hell did you get that tuxedo? It looks like it came off the city dump.'

Martin looked down at his drooping elephant's-ear lapels. 'You wouldn't believe me even if I told you.'

After a few minutes, Martin and Ramone were beckoned through the crowds by Kathy Lupanek and shown to two seats at the very back of the theater. The auditorium was already packed, and there was an endless cascade of excited conversation, as well as the usual coughing and shuffling and waving and women calling out, 'Aaron, *darling*! I didn't know you were here!'

306

'Long time since I sat in the back row,' Ramone remarked. 'And I never sat in the back row with a *guy* before!'

At last, the theater lights dimmed; and a single spotlight fell onto the stage in front of the drapes. There was a roll of recorded drums, and then Boofuls appeared, in the white suit that he would be wearing toward the end of the film, when he was pleading with God to let him be an angel. The audience roared and cheered, and one after another they got out of their seats to give Boofuls a standing ovation. 'And – Jesus – they haven't even seen the movie yet!' marveled Ramone.

'The power of publicity,' Martin remarked, standing up so that he could get a better look at Boofuls, but not clapping.

Boofuls raised his arms and eventually the clapping spattered away to nothing and everybody sat down. He paused for a short while, not smiling, but bright-eyed, and then he said, 'You don't know how happy you've made me. I hope only that I can make *you* just as happy in return.'

The audience applauded him some more. Again, he gently silenced them.

'Once upon a time,' he said, and his piping voice sounded weirdly echoing and distorted through the loudspeakers, as if he were talking down a storm drain. 'Once upon a time there was a boy; and that boy was a legend in his own short lifetime. Once upon a time there was a musical; and that musical was never finished.

'The story of that boy and that unfinished musical is too tragic for us to think about tonight. Instead, let us celebrate another boy, and a musical that has been finished. A boy, and a musical, which all of us who worked on *Sweet Chariot* have grown to believe will change the world.'

A large woman in a tight black dress who was sitting just in front of Martin leaned over to her red-faced companion and whispered, 'Cocky little so-and-so, isn't he? Just like Vernon was telling us. Do you know he wouldn't even let the *producer* see the whole picture. And they went through seven editors. Seven!'

'Ssh, Velma, he's magic,' her companion replied.

'Magic, my ass,' Velma retorted.

Boofuls left the stage and went to sit between June Lassiter and Miss Redd. The audience cheered him so vociferously that he had to stand on his seat and wave to them. At last the drapes swept back, and the audience fell silent, but there was a low murmuring of excitement all around.

Then the first chords of music sounded; and New York appeared on the screen; and the audience settled down.

Martin stared at the screen for over an hour without moving or saying a word. He was completely hypnotized. The music was so ravishing; the dances were so dazzling; the photography was unlike anything he had ever seen before. And right from the moment when he first appeared on the screen, Boofuls wrung his emotions in a way which Martin wouldn't have believed possible.

Martin hated this boy; he absolutely detested him. Yet when he was kneeling on the sidewalk trying to save the life of a dying friend, Martin found that his eyes filled up with tears and his throat choked up. He looked around the theater and saw everybody was weeping, *everybody*, including Ramone, and that some women were so upset that they were hiding their faces in their hands.

When the musical reached the moment when Boofuls has to choose between staying with his mother and becoming an angel, and sings a song while his mother goes about her daily chores, unable to see him, the grief in the audience became almost uncontrollable. Martin found himself smearing tears away from his eyes with his hand; and several people were sobbing in genuine grief.

> *Mother . . . how can I leave you*
> *Even when the angels are calling?*
> *Mother . . . how can I turn away*
> *Into the rain that will always and always be falling?'*

Martin turned from Ramone to wipe his eyes. But, as he did so, to his bewilderment, he caught sight of Boofuls and Miss Redd hurrying hand in hand toward the theater's side exit. And when he saw that, the melodramatic spell that *Sweet Chariot* had been casting over him was immediately and unexpectedly broken. He said, 'Ramone! *Ramone!*' and Ramone looked at him tearfully. 'Ramone, something's going down here, something bad.'

'Man, this movie makes me feel so goddamn *sad*,' Ramone said chokily.

'No,' said Martin. 'It's more than that. It's like mass hysteria.'

He looked around at the weeping, distraught audience. Their wet cheeks glistened in the half darkness. Some of them were covering their faces with their hands and sobbing as if they were totally distraught.

At last Martin began to understand why Boofuls had allowed hardly anybody to see the completed picture, and why he had insisted on its being premiered simultaneously throughout the world. It wasn't just a brilliant and captivating musical. It was a hymn to human tragedy. In a particularly subtle and convincing way, it dramatized not hope and faith and human optimism, like most musicals, but utter despair. It highlighted the inevitability of death and the uselessness of life. The only way to true fulfillment was never to be born at all.

Martin also began to understand why Mrs Alicia Crossley had felt it necessary to slaughter Boofuls before he had been able to finish the original version of *Sweet Chariot*. In some extraordinary mesmerizing way, *Sweet Chariot* was capable of drawing its audiences into a whirlpool of helpless emotion, like drowning moths being sucked down a drain, and Martin began to be desperately afraid of what was going to happen next.

'Come on,' he told Ramone. 'Let's get the hell out of here.'

'I want to see the end,' Ramone protested.

'Out!' Martin snapped at him, and grabbed hold of his sleeve.

Ramone struggled and argued, but then one of the ushers shone a torch at him and said, 'Out of there, please, sir. You're disturbing other folks' enjoyment.'

At last, still grumbling, Ramone allowed himself to be escorted out to the lobby.

'That movie is like some kind of drug, almost,' Martin

told him. 'Can't you feel what it's done to your emotions? It's washed you and spun you and hung you out to dry! God knows what's going to happen to the rest of that audience.'

Ramone took two or three deep breaths, then stared at Martin as if he had never seen him before. 'That was terrible,' he said, and he sounded genuinely shaken. 'I feel like I have a hangover. Man, I felt so *miserable*.'

'That, I think, is the whole idea,' said Martin. 'But Boofuls and that lady friend of his weren't going to stick around and get miserable with the rest of us.'

'They left?'

'A couple of minutes ago.'

'So where do you think they went?'

Martin said, 'I have a very good idea. But first I want to go home. I have a feeling that it's time we went looking for Emilio.'

They were only halfway across the lobby when they heard a high, agonized screaming sound: so high at first that it didn't sound human. They stopped and stared at each other; then they turned back toward the movie-theater doors. There was another scream; and then another; and then a terrifying howl and a noise like wooden buckets being knocked together.

One of the ushers, white-faced, said, 'Is that the sound track, or what?'

But then Martin went up to the swing doors and tried to push them open and there was a heavy collision of bodies on the other side, and more screaming, and he couldn't push them more than an inch or two.

'Man – what the hell's happening?' gasped Ramone.

A cop came running through the lobby, followed by two more. Martin said, 'I can't get the doors open, it seems like there's a whole lot of people pushing against them on the other side.'

The cops pushed with him, but there was a dead weight behind the doors which they couldn't budge. The screaming inside the theater grew louder, and there was more thumping and scrabbling and knocking.

'Upstairs!' shouted one of the cops. 'Jack – you take the side!'

The first cop bounded up the stairs to the theater balcony. Martin and Ramone followed him, panting with fear and effort. The noise inside the building was almost unbearable. It sounded like hell itself. There were no intelligible cries for help: only a muffled, brutish moaning, and endless screaming, and that terrible hollow knocking. The cop reached the doors to the balcony and instinctively drew his gun. Then he kicked the doors open and dodged to one side. Well – for Christ's sake, who knew *what* mayhem was going on in there. A fire, a riot, a sniper. It could be anything. Already Martin could hear police sirens warbling in the street outside.

There was a second's pause. Then the cop yelled out, '*Freeze! Police!*' But it was only fear that had made him shout. The woman who suddenly appeared in the open doorway was no threat to anybody.

Martin whispered, 'Oh, God. He's done it.'

Ramone crossed himself and shook his head, but couldn't speak.

The woman was blond, and might have been pretty when she first arrived at the premiere. But now it was impossible to tell. Her face was smashed as if it had been hit with a hammer. Her hair was stuck up with blood like a cockatoo's crest; one of her eyes was gone. Her white jawbone protruded through the raw flesh of her cheek, a mush of broken bone, and Martin could even see a gold tooth. She had been wearing a green silk evening dress and a white mink stole. The dress had been torn down to her waist at the front, baring her breasts, and the mink stole was nothing more than a bloodstained rope.

She swayed for a moment and made a crunching, bleating noise for somebody to help her; but as she staggered forward, Martin saw that her right arm had been torn off at the elbow, literally torn off, leaving a dangling loop of bloody muscle, and that the woman was bleeding to death right in front of them. She collapsed and slid down the side of the door, leaving a wide smear of blood.

'Ambulance!' the cop shouted out. 'For God's sake, get an ambulance!'

'Ramone,' said Martin tensely; and stepped past the fallen woman while the cop yanked off her bloodstained panty hose so he could improvise a tourniquet. The woman's smashed-up face was pressed close to the carpet. She didn't even murmur. Martin felt bile surge up inside his throat, but he had to swallow it down.

Ramone peered into the darkness of the theater. The screaming and the moaning had subsided a little now; but they could still hear tearing noises, and there was still an occasional drawn-out shriek of agony.

'You don't *have* to go in there,' Ramone told Martin, serious-faced.

'Yes, I do,' said Martin. 'I started all this. I let Boofuls loose.'

'Man, it wasn't your doing,' Ramone replied. 'There was Satan in that mirror and Satan would have found a way of getting out of there one day, no matter who bought it. If anybody let him out, Emilio did.'

Martin hesitated, and swallowed once more, and then said, 'I still have to go see what's happened.'

The cop shouted, 'Medics! Where the hell are those medics?' and then to Martin, 'You can't go in there, mister. I don't want any more casualties than we got already.'

Martin ignored him and stepped through the half-open doors into the semidarkness of the theater balcony. Followed closely by Ramone, he walked along the back row of seats and then stood looking down at the whole interior of the theater.

The movie had finished, the screen was silvery blank, and the theater was suddenly silent. A battlefield after a battle. Hundreds of people were strewn across the seats, and almost all of them were dead. The smell of flesh and blood and opened-up human bodies was so sweet and hot and pungent that Martin had to press his hand over his nose and mouth.

Gradually, the theater lights brightened, and police and paramedics appeared at the various entrances around the auditorium. They stood, like Martin and Ramone, in silence. There was nothing else they could do. Mann's Chinese Theater had been full to capacity this evening with nearly one thousand five hundred of Hollywood's glitterati, and now they were all torn to pieces.

'I wouldn't have believed it,' Ramone whispered. 'If I hadn't seen it with my own eyes, I wouldn't have believed it.'

Martin cast his eyes around the theater. A director from 20th Century-Fox Television with whom he had once had lunch at the Fine Affair lay sprawled just in front of him, his mouth wide open, his shirtfront crimson with blood. His head was a mass of blood and bruises. His wife lay beside him, almost naked, her hair torn from her scalp, one of her legs twisted underneath her.

A world-famous cinematographer, who two years ago had won an Oscar for his vivid scenes of death and destruction in Vietnam, stood half propped, armless, like a grisly Venus de Milo, against a tangle of bodies.

In every aisle, bodies in evening dress lay heaped, and blood soaked in dark tides into the carpet. The stench was intolerable – bile and blood and partially digested dinners. And everywhere, in every direction, there were heaps of jewelry, furs, silk, and glistening heaps of soft intestines. A massacre, in black-tie.

'What did they *do*?' Ramone asked hoarsely. 'What happened to them?'

'They clawed themselves to pieces, that's all,' said Martin. His voice in the huge auditorium sounded small and flat. 'They went mad with grief. Mad with despair. Mad with whatever, I don't know. You saw how upset they were, all that crying. They've been trampling on each other, strangling each other, tearing each other's arms off. And all that knocking, they were hitting their heads against the seats and the walls.'

Ramone said, 'I can't take any more of this, man. I never ever seen *one* dead person before, except for my grandmother. I can't take any more.'

It was then, however, that the movie screen flickered and came to life. A faint faded image of Boofuls, triumphant. Martin turned to face it and stared at it as if Boofuls were speaking to him personally.

And he said this: '*And He was asking him, "What is your name?" And he said to Him, "My name is Legion, for we are many." Now there was a big herd of swine feeding there on the mountainside. And they entreated Him, saying, "Send us into the swine that we may enter them." And coming out, the unclean*

*spirits entered the swine; and the herd rushed down the steep bank
into the sea, about two thousand of them; and they were drowned
in the sea.'*

Boofuls slowly smiled; and then laughed; that high-pitched
laugh that to Martin was now so familiar. Then his face faded
from the screen and he was gone.

They jogged all the way back to Franklin Avenue, stripping
off their tuxedos and their vests at the corner of La Brea, and
throwing them into the dust. They said nothing. They were
too shocked, too breathless, and they knew that if they didn't
hurry they could be too late. Lightning danced in the distance,
over the San Gabriel Mountains; and thunder bellowed all
across the Los Angeles basin, as if madmen were shouting at
each other from different rooms of an echoing old house.

When they reached Martin's house they found Mr Capelli
waiting for them at the front door. 'I heard on television,
some kind of disaster. Everybody killed. I thought maybe you
got killed, too, and then what was I going to do?'

Martin tugged the front of his shirt out of his waistband
and bent forward so that he could wipe the sweat from his face
on it. 'I guess we were lucky. But first, listen, we have to get
Emilio back.'

Mr Capelli clutched his arm. 'You can't! What are you
doing? You heard what Boofuls said. He could die if we try to
get him out.'

'Believe me,' said Martin, 'if we don't try to get him out,
he's going to have to stay there forever. I don't think that
Boofuls ever had the slightest intention of letting him out.'

'But he said, if we tried to get Emilio out, he could die!'

'Unh-hunh, suddenly, I don't think so,' said Martin. He
felt shocked and off-balance; but at the same time he felt a
strong certainty that he understood now what Boofuls was up
to; and how Boofuls had deceived them all. Boofuls was utterly
unscrupulous, because he was the son of evil incarnate, and
not a single word that Boofuls had ever told them had been
anything but self-serving trickery. He had prevented them
from rescuing Emilio partly by real occult power and partly
by bluff. At least, that was what Martin now believed.

And even if Boofuls had been telling the truth – even if Emilio really would be in mortal danger if they tried to rescue him out of the mirror – what in the end was the life of one small boy, when one hundred forty-four thousand had already been massacred?

They went upstairs to Martin's apartment. Through the open door on Mr Capelli's landing they could hear Tom Brokaw saying, '– a worldwide disaster – latest counts indicate that as many as one hundred thousand people may have died – not only here but in London, Paris, Stockholm, Bonn, and Madrid –'

Martin reached the top of the stairs and opened the door of his apartment. Mr Capelli lifted up one hand as if he were waving to him from a great distance. 'Martin – he's just a boy, think about that.'

Martin said, 'That's why we have to get him back, Mr Capelli. He's just a boy, yes. But he's an innocent boy. He's the boy that Boofuls traded places with so that he could organize all of this killing. Boofuls is the son of the devil, Mr Capelli; the actual son of Satan. But you remember what Father Quinlan said: *Only the child can destroy the parent.*' And do you know what that means to me? It means that Emilio is capable of wasting the devil. In fact, he could be the only person who can.'

'I just want him back,' said Mr Capelli with considerable dignity, his back as straight as if he were wearing a corset.

'Mr Capelli,' said Martin, 'we'll do our best.'

He opened his apartment door and went inside, with Ramone following. Alison was in the bathroom, and she called out, 'Martin? Is that you?'

'In here,' Martin called back.

Ramone breathed out and said, 'Man, those people . . . all those dead people . . . that had to be worse than Hiroshima or something.' He sat down on the sofa and held his head in his hands. 'Man, that was the worst thing I ever saw.'

'Are you okay?' Martin asked him.

'What do you think?' Ramone retorted. 'Okay? How can I be okay? I'm going to have nightmares about that for the rest of my life.'

Martin went across to the windowsill and opened the bottle

of red wine. He poured Ramone a generous glassful, and then one for himself. Then he sat on the edge of the desk staring at the mirror at the opposite end of the room.

'That's one son of a bitch,' Ramone remarked, staring at the mirror, too.

'But not unbeatable,' Martin told him.

'Oh, no?' said Ramone. 'We can't move it, we can't break it, we can't do nothing except sit here like the Two Stooges and wait for it to ruin our lives.'

'We can go into it,' said Martin with determination. 'We can go into it, and we can get Emilio back. And then, by God, we can use Emilio to get rid of Boofuls once and for all.'

'You're really going to try?' asked Ramone.

'Yes,' said Martin, although he was almost frightened to hear himself say the words out loud, 'I'm really going to try.'

He stood up, and at that moment Alison came into the room, white-faced. 'Martin? Ramone? Thank goodness you're all right! We were watching the premiere on television and when they said that everybody was getting killed –!'

Martin held her in his arms for a moment. 'It's okay; we're fine. Well, fine isn't the word for it, but we're still alive.'

'What *happened*? They were saying on the news that everybody just went crazy.'

Martin nodded. 'That's just about what happened, yes. But I have the feeling that something even worse is about to happen. It's pretty hard to explain, but Emilio is the key to it. We have to get Emilio back.'

Alison slowly turned and stared at the mirror. 'When you say something worse –?'

'I mean much worse. Like the sun never coming up, ever. Not in our lifetime, anyway.'

'And we have to get Emilio out?'

'That's right. We have to go into the mirror, if we can, and find out where he is, and bring him home.'

Alison hesitated for a moment, but then she said, 'Let me come with you.'

'Hey, come on, you're loco,' said Ramone.

'But I have *some* psychic sensitivity, don't I? I mean, not very much. But maybe it could help.'

Martin shook his head. 'I can't let you take the risk.'

'Then what are you going to do? Go on your own?'

'I don't know,' said Martin. 'I guess I am.' He reached out and touched the surface of the mirror. It was cold, hard, as impenetrable as real glass; but he had the feeling that if he closed his eyes and simply *walked right through it* that it would dissolve, just as the looking-glass in *Alice* had dissolved.

'Well, I think two heads are better than one,' Alison argued, 'especially when it comes to anything occult.'

'For instance?' asked Ramone.

'For instance, if you manage to get into the mirror, how are you going to get out again? Have you thought about that? Emilio can't get out. How will *you* be able to?'

Martin said, 'Trust to luck, I guess.'

'Oh, yes, and be trapped in the mirror forever, just the way that Boofuls was?'

'Well, do you have any bright suggestions?' asked Martin.

'I don't know. It may not be foolproof, but you could use a rope when you go into the mirror, just like they did when they went through the spirit-world in *Poltergeist*, because let's face it, that mirror is a spirit-world, right? And if you have a rope, somebody on this side can haul you back onto this side of the mirror if you get into any kind of trouble.'

'Well . . . that kind of *sounds* like some kind of sense,' Ramone admitted. 'Nutty, but sense.'

'Oh, sure,' said Martin, who was still uneasy about the idea of taking Alison with him into the mirror. 'And where do we find enough rope?'

'No problem,' said Ramone. 'I have about a thousand feet of nylon diving rope in the back of my store. I can go get it, easy.'

Martin thought for a while and then nodded. He couldn't think of any other way to guarantee their safe return to the real world. 'Okay, then. If you can go get the rope.'

'You'll be just like divers,' said Ramone. 'I'll stay here, holding on to the other end of the rope, and if you get into any kind of trouble, you can tug on it, and I can haul you in.'

Ramone went off to find his diving rope. Meanwhile Martin poured Alison a glass of wine. 'Maybe I should change into

317

something more practical,' she said. She was still wearing her tight white elasticated suntop and a wide 1950s-style skirt. 'Do you have a jogging suit I could borrow, something like that?'

Martin took her into the bedroom and rummaged through his closet until he found her a loose gray sweatshirt with a pull-cord neck and pair of white cotton shorts that had shrunk the last time he washed them.

She crossed her arms and tugged off her suntop, baring the largest breasts that Martin had ever seen. They bounced independently, as if they had a life of their own. Then she stepped out of her skirt; under which she wore a plain white thong. Martin watched her as she buttoned up his shorts and slipped on his sweatshirt, and knew exactly what it was that Morris had seen in her. The tragic part about it was, Morris would never see her again.

'Something's happening, isn't it?' asked Alison as she brushed her hair in front of the mirror. 'Something really serious?'

Martin swallowed wine. 'Yes. I guess you could call it Armageddon.'

'That's the end of the world, isn't it?'

'Just about. It could be worse than the end of the world.'

'Worse?' frowned Alison.

Martin shrugged. 'Somebody once defined Armageddon as all the most distressing things that you can imagine happening to you, all at once, forever. To me, that sounds worse than the end of the world.'

Outside, the sky crackled with fibers of lightning, and there was a smell of burned oxygen on the wind. Dogs began to bark, all over the neighborhood, and cats yowled and howled as if they were in heat. Down on Hollywood Boulevard, the klieg lights had been doused, but the ambulance lights still flashed and the sirens still wailed, and the desperate shouting of medics and firemen echoed from one side of the street to the other. Martin turned away from the window and tried not to think about the heaps of mutilated dead he had seen in Mann's Theater.

Martin switched on the television. There was a special report from London, showing fleets of ambulances outside the

Empire, Leicester Square, ferrying bodies to hospitals. Sandy Gall the newscaster was saying, '– already laying blame on the highly emotional content of the film. Dr Kenneth Palmer of the Institute of Social Studies drew parallels with the mass suicide in Jonestown of the followers of religious fanatic James Jones; and of incidents in Africa in the 1880s when whole tribes battered themselves to death in the belief that it was the only way for them to get to heaven. The Home Secretary, however –'

'Look at that,' said Martin. 'One hundred forty-four thousand people have killed themselves, all at the same time, all watching the same movie, and the news media are trying to rationalize it already. If you ask me, being rational is going to be the death of the human race. It's about time we started believing in the inexplicable. Or maybe it's already too late.'

It took Ramone almost twenty minutes to come back with the rope. He was sweating and out of breath. 'It's like a riot down there. Thousands of ambulances, thousands of police cars, TV trucks, you name it. And thousands of sightseers, too. People who get a kick out of seeing their fellow citizens lying dead.'

A police helicopter flew low overhead, followed by another, and then by a deep, reverberating grumble of thunder. 'I think we'd better hurry,' said Martin. 'We may not have too much time left. In fact, we may be too late already.'

They tied one end of the rope around the steel window frame opposite the mirror. 'I just hope this damn window holds,' Martin remarked. 'I don't want to yank on the rope when I'm in mirrorland and end up with a six-foot window in my lap.'

While Martin and Ramone prepared the rope, Alison stood in front of the mirror and called softly and coaxingly to Emilio. If she could persuade him actually to come into the sitting room, that would make their bizarre task a hundred times easier. But the door of the reflected room remained closed, and no Emilio peeped through it, and there was nobody in the mirror except themselves – Martin, Ramone and Alison.

At last, Ramone was satisfied that the rope would hold. 'Believe me, an elephant couldn't pull this free.'

'Thanks a lot,' Alison retorted with a nervous laugh. 'I've been trying to lose weight.'

Martin and Alison looped the rope around their waists, as if they were mountain climbers. 'Just remember,' Ramone reminded them, tugging at the knots to make sure they were firm, 'any trouble and I'll pull you back. All you have to do is yank on the rope.'

Martin took a deep breath and glanced toward the mirror. 'All this is supposing we can get into the mirror in the first place.'

'Faith, man,' said Ramone, laying a hand on his shoulder. 'Everything in this whole wide world requires faith.'

Martin nodded. He reached out and grasped Alison's hand. 'Let's do it,' he said, and together they stepped toward their own reflections in the mirror.

They waited. They felt none of the irresistible suction that had pulled Lugosi into the mirror, and which had almost taken Emilio and Martin and Ramone all at once. Martin looked at Alison and said, 'I hope to God we're not making fools of ourselves.'

'Faith,' Ramone exhorted them.

'What good will that do?' asked Alison.

'I don't know, but why don't you close your eyes and kind of *imagine* you can walk through the mirror. Then, when I count to three, take a step forward and just keep on walking.'

Martin gripped Alison's hand tight and closed his eyes. He tried to remember the words in *Through the Looking-Glass*: 'And certainly the glass was beginning to melt away, just like a bright silvery mist.'

'Are you okay?' he asked Alison without opening his eyes.

'I'm fine,' said Alison.

'I'm leaning forward,' said Martin. 'I'm going to press my forehead against the glass. You try doing the same.'

The glass felt flat and cold against his forehead and pressed his spectacles against the bridge of his nose. But he tried to use its coldness to imagine mist, instead of glass. *It's possible,* he told himself, you've seen it happen for yourself. A ball can bounce in and out of mirrorland. A cat can jump through.

Even a boy can walk into a reflected room and out again. If all that can happen, you can step through, too.

Lewis Carroll had done it — *'it seems to me now like a nightmare . . . the land beyond the looking-glass, in which each man takes on his true form.'* It's possible, it's been done, I've seen it done, and now I'm going to do it.

He thought he heard Ramone saying, 'One . . .' But then Ramone's voice slurred and twisted, and Martin was being wrenched forward, toward the mirror, headfirst, so violently and so suddenly that he lost his grip on Alison's hand.

He tried to reach her, he tried to cry out, but it was impossible. He was being pulled forward so strongly that he couldn't do anything at all but squeeze his eyes tight shut and contract his muscles and pray that he wasn't going to be pressed to death.

He knew, however, that he was being pulled through the mirror into the reflected room beyond.

It was the strangest experience. One moment he felt as if he were being stretched out, impossibly thin. Then he felt as if he were being compressed, impossibly squat. And all the time he could feel the mirror's surface drawing him in, as if it were mercury — a deep liquid chill that swallowed first his head and then his body and then gradually enveloped his legs.

He believed for one whole second that he was dead; that the mirror had killed him. But then he opened his eyes and he was standing in his own sitting room with Alison beside him. The only difference was that he was now facing the window, instead of the mirror. And when he turned round, to look at the mirror, there was no reflection either of him or of Alison. Only Ramone now existed both in reality and as a reflection.

'*Madre mia*, you did it,' Ramone exclaimed. 'You walked right through the mirror. You walked right through it, just like it was a door.'

Martin looked down at the rope that was attached to his waist. Instead of appearing through the mirror behind him, it was now fastened to the reflected window in front of him. 'Is the rope following us?' he asked, turning around to face the real Ramone.

'The rope's just fine. Why don't you try walking forward a little, let's see if it pays out from here.'

Martin took two or three steps across the unfamiliar, back-to-front sitting room, and Ramone called out, 'That's okay, that's terrific. The rope is following you into the glass.'

Alison took hold of Martin's hand. 'I can't believe this is happening, this is just too strange for words.'

Martin went across to his desk and picked up a copy of *Variety*. The headline read, *Sweet Chariot Rolls Tonite*, and underneath, the entire text was in reverse. He looked at Alison and saw that she was a mirror image of herself; that her hair was parted on the opposite side, and that her wristwatch had changed from her left wrist to her right. He checked his own watch. The second hand was sweeping around the dial counter-clockwise.

'We don't have too long, if this thunder and lightning is anything to go by,' Martin told Alison. It was thundering just as violently in the mirror-world as it was in the real world. 'Let's go see if Emilio's downstairs.'

He turned to Ramone and called, 'Ten minutes! Give us ten minutes! Then tug on the rope a little, just to remind us!'

'You got it!' Ramone shouted back.

Martin crossed the sitting room and opened the door, with Alison following closely behind him. It was odd to open the door the other way round, with the hinges on the right side instead of the left. The corridor that led to the front door of his apartment looked the same, however. Martin even noticed the small rectangular mark in the plaster where he had dug in his screwdriver to kill the cat. Exactly the same, except that it was on the opposite wall.

He glanced into the kitchen. Everything appeared to be identical to the real world, apart from the lettering on the spice jars – *Salt, Pepper, Thyme, Marjoram, Oregano* – and the newspaper lying on the table, *Los Angeles Times*. 'So far so good, as they say in the adventure stories,' he told Alison. More thunder shook the evening air; and somewhere they heard the rattle of shingles falling from a roof.

Still trailing the rope, Martin and Alison went to the front door of Martin's apartment and opened it up. The stairway was gloomy, but it didn't look any different from the stairway in the real world. Except – Martin lifted his head and sniffed. There was something different about it. There was no smell. No garlic, no herbs, no subtropical mustiness. In fact, no smell at all.

'What's the matter?' asked Alison, coming up close behind him and touching his shoulder.

Martin shook his head. 'Nothing, not yet. But there's no smell. Normally this place smells like La Barbera's.'

Alison sniffed, too. 'I guess it's because we're inside the mirror. Have you ever pressed your nose to a mirror? Cold, no smell.'

Cautiously, they made their way down the stairs. Their rope zizzed on the top stair as it paid out behind them; their only connection with the real world. They reached the landing and stood outside the Capellis' front door. The card next to the bell read illǝqɒↃ, in sloping handwriting.

'Okay, I'm going to ring the bell and see if Emilio's in here,' said Martin. 'But there's one thing you have to know. People in the mirror-world may sometimes look weird. You know, really grotesque. That's because they take on their real shape – their physical looks and their personalities combined. At least, that's what Father Quinlan said; and Lewis Carroll, too.'

Alison nodded mutely. Martin pressed the doorbell.

CHAPTER TWELVE

Ramone sat on the sofa, gripping the rope in one hand and a glass of wine in the other. He didn't feel at all happy, watching the rope disappear a little at a time over the gilded frame of the mirror and into nothing at all. He could see his reflection, holding the rope, and his reflection didn't look happy, either.

He jiggled his foot and whistled 'Samba Negra'. Outside the house, the thunder still collided, and spasmodic bursts of dazzling lightning pierced the venetian blinds. He heard more sirens, down toward Hollywood Boulevard. There was a smell of Apocalypse in the air, an end-of-the-world atmosphere, ozone and fear and freshly spilled blood.

Ramone stood up, still holding the rope, and went across to the windowsill to pour himself another glass of red wine. He parted the slats of the venetian blind, and down in the street he saw a woman running, not jogging, but really running, as if all the devils of hell were after her. A flash of lightning illuminated her face and it was grim and white, like one of those Japanese Noh masks.

Disturbed, Ramone closed the slats again and turned back toward the mirror.

To his surprise, Martin was standing in the room, right in front of the mirror, smiling at him.

'Martin! For Christ's sake! You trying to give me a heart attack or something?'

Martin said nothing, but approached him slowly, rubbing his hands together, still smiling.

'What happened?' asked Ramone. 'Where's Alison? Did something go wrong? You took your rope off.'

Martin said, 'Nothing's wrong. Everything's fine.'

'Did you find Emilio?'

'Emilio? Oh, no. No, not yet. But I guess we will, given time.'

Ramone peered at Martin closely. 'Man, are you all right? You sound really strange.'

Martin smiled. 'Strange?'

Ramone glanced over his shoulder toward the mirror. 'Are you sure everything's okay? What's Alison doing? Did you leave her in there, or what?'

Martin put his arm around Ramone's shoulders. 'The thing is, Ramone, we found out a couple of things while we were inside the mirror. We found out that you can live your life according to a whole lot of different values. You can live it meekly, you know, doing what you're told all the time, loving your neighbor, paying your taxes; or you can live it to the full.'

Ramone was completely bewildered. 'Man, I thought you were looking for Emilio.'

'Well, we were,' Martin admitted. 'But – what – he's only a boy, after all. And what's one boy, in the great glorious scheme of things?'

Ramone turned his head in an effort to free himself from Martin's embrace. It was then that he saw Martin's wrist-watch, on his *right* wrist, with a second hand that went around counterclockwise. He jerked around to stare into Martin's face, and he suddenly understood that Martin's hair was parted on the opposite side, and that the mole on his right cheek had somehow switched sides.

'Man, you're not –' he choked out.

But then Martin's eyes flared blue, incandescent blue, and his arm gripped Ramone tightly around the neck, so fiercely that Ramone heard something snap, a bone or a vein or a muscle.

'Get off me!' he screamed. 'Get off me!'

Martin hugged him closer and closer, still grinning, his eyes flaring so brightly that Ramone had to squeeze his own eyes shut.

He struggled blindly; and it was probably just as well that he didn't see Martin's mouth stretch wider and wider, and his jaw suddenly gape. Inch by inch, something protruded out of Martin's mouth. Not his tongue, but the slimy top of another head, pinky gray and wrinkled, which gradually forced its way out from between his teeth, rolling back his lips, compressing his nose and eyes and forehead into a grotesque little caricature of himself, like a Chinese monkey.

The head which emerged from Martin's mouth was another version of Martin, smaller and less well formed, but its pale eyes burned fiercely blue, and its mouth was filled with sharp savage teeth, dripping with glutinous saliva.

Ramone, fighting, kicking, opened his eyes. He stared for one terrified second, and then he let out a bellow of desperation.

Martin's second head stretched its mouth open with a sickening gagging noise and bit into Ramone's face. The lower teeth buried themselves in his open mouth; the upper teeth crunched into his eyebrows. The creature's jaws had a grip like a steel hunting trap; and when Ramone tried to force his hands into its mouth to prise it loose, its teeth were so sharp that his fingers were cut right down to the bare bone.

In a final convulsive effort to break free, Ramone twisted his body first one way and then the other. He couldn't see what effect this had – the creature's gaping mouth completely covered his eyes – but this twisting did nothing but drag the head further and further out of Martin's mouth, on a long slippery pinkish neck that seemed to disgorge forever.

Ramone dropped to the floor, rolling wildly from side to side, but the snakelike head refused to release its grip. Instead, it began to ripple all the way along the length of its neck as if its muscles were building up strength for one last terrible bite.

Ramone thumped on the wood-block floor, like a wrestler pleading for mercy. One thump – two, three – and then the creature's neck bulged once, in a hideous muscular spasm, and its teeth crunched through flesh and bone, right into Ramone's sinus cavities, biting his tongue through at the root, chopping his optic nerves; and then tugging backward, taking the whole of his face with it.

The creature began almost immediately to slither back into Martin's open mouth. Within six seconds, only the top of its head showed. Within seven, Martin's mouth had closed and returned to its normal size.

Within fifteen seconds – by the time Mr Capelli had puffed

his way up the stairs to find out what all the thumping and the thrashing was about – Martin had disappeared.

Mr Capelli knelt slowly down beside Ramone's savaged body. There was extraordinarily little blood; but the bite in his face was so terrible that Mr Capelli could do nothing at all but cross himself, and cross himself again, and then turn to stare at the mirror.

Martin rang the doorbell again. At last, they heard footsteps and a muffled voice called out, 'Who is it?'

'It's me, Martin, from upstairs. I was wondering if Emilio was home.'

There was a pause, and then bolts were slid back, and the door was opened. At first it was difficult to see who was standing inside. The hallway was very dark and there didn't seem to be any lights anywhere. Martin was aware of something huge and nodding and draped in black. It looked almost like a large parrot cage covered with a black cloth.

'Emilio went out,' the muffled voice told him.

It was then that the lightning flickered again, and Martin realized with a thrill of dread what he was looking at. It was Mrs Capelli, wearing a black mantilla on her head. But her head was huge, a cartoon head; like the drawings of the Duchess in *Alice in Wonderland*. Her face was enormous and waxy-colored; the face of a long-suffering Italian matriarch. Her mantilla was decorated with thousands of jet beads; and she was draped with jet necklaces and pinned with jet brooches; a mother in mourning for the old country, and for lost innocence, and for long-buried relatives.

This nodding huge-headed monster was Mrs Capelli amplified five-hundredfold. Her physical appearance exaggerated by her inner self.

Martin heard Alison gasp just behind him. But he was determined to find Emilio. He was determined to destroy Boofuls. And even though his voice was shaking, he managed to ask, 'Do you know – do you know where he went?'

Mrs Capelli shook her huge birdcage head. Her jet jewelry clattered.

327

'It's important,' Martin insisted. 'I really have to find him.'

Mrs Capelli stood silently for a moment and then turned back into her apartment. However, she left the door open, as if Martin should wait for a reply. Martin stepped gingerly into the apartment after her, following the huge swaying bulk of her mantilla.

She went into her parlor, across the patterned carpet. As she passed in front of the mirror on top of the chest of drawers, she changed, without warning – her huge swaying head dissolving like a conjuring trick back to its usual size, her mantilla swallowed up like smoke. It was only when she reached the far corner of the parlor, out of sight of the mirror, that her head expanded, and her black-bedecked mantilla returned.

Martin reached back and grasped Alison's hand. 'You see that? When she walks in front of a mirror, she's normal.'

Alison said. 'Yes, you're right. I get it now. Anybody looking into the mirror from the real world – they wouldn't see anything strange.'

They followed Mrs Capelli to the kitchen. It was there that they saw another apparition, even stranger. A bloated white-faced man – more like a huge jellyish egg than a human being – sitting at the kitchen table.

Martin was reminded of Humpty-Dumpty in *Through the Looking-Glass*: 'The egg got larger and larger, and more and more human. When she had come within a few yards of it, she saw that it had eyes and a nose and a mouth.'

There was no nursery-rhyme amusement in this creature, however. Illuminated only by intermittent flickers of lightning, he was soft and bulging, with black, glittering eyes, and he breathed harshly and softly, as if his lungs were clogged. He turned and stared at Martin with suspicion and contempt.

'Whaddya wan'?' he demanded in a thick stage-Italian accent.

'Mr Capelli?' said Martin. 'I'm looking for Emilio.'

'Why for?' Mr Capelli wanted to know. 'He's-a play someplace.'

'Mr Capelli, it's crucial. I have to find him.'

'Do I know you?' the egg-shaped creature wheezed. Something approaching recognition glittered in one of the eyes which swam on his featureless face.

'Martin, Mr Capelli. Martin Williams. Emilio and I have always been friends.'

'Martin Williams?'

'That's right, Mr Capelli, Martin Williams. I live upstairs.'

'Ah . . .' said Mr Capelli. He thought for a moment, his eyes opening and closing like mollusks. Then he coughed, cleared his throat, and flapped one pale flipperlike hand toward the door. 'He went to the market. Maybe with one of his friends. To buy coffee and candy. Now, leave me alone.'

Mrs Capelli stood silently in the corner, watching them with a face as huge as a white upholstered chair. Martin said nothing, but took hold of Alison's arm and piloted her back out of the apartment. He closed the door behind him and stood on the landing trembling, taking deep breaths, one hand against the wall to steady himself.

'Do we really have to go outside?' Alison asked him.

Martin said. 'There's no alternative.'

'But if the Capellis look like *that* –'

'There's no alternative, we have to find Emilio.'

Paying out their rope behind them, they went downstairs to the front of the building. The sky was inky black now; the wind was up; and the palms were rustling and rattling. 'The market's this way,' said Martin. 'I think we're going to have to get rid of this rope. Maybe I'll tug it a couple of times, just to let Ramone know that we're okay.'

He yanked at the rope twice and waited; but there was no answering pull from Ramone. Martin hesitated for a moment, wondering if he ought to go back and tell Ramone that they were venturing out without the rope, but then a deafening barrage of thunder changed his mind. This was the night that Satan was coming. There was no time to spare.

Quickly, they untied the knots around their belts, leaving the rope lying coiled on Mr Capelli's driveway. Then they hurried along Franklin Avenue toward the market, crossing La Brea and heading toward Highland. Martin found himself wildly disoriented, because the glittering lights of Los Angeles were on his left side now, instead of his right, and traffic was driving on the wrong side of the street. Neither of them looked too closely, but the drivers and passengers of some of the passing cars appeared to be peculiarly deformed, hunched figures in silently rolling vehicles.

The wind blew stronger. They felt rain on their faces. Across the street, a tall man with a head like a sheep hurried home with armfuls of groceries. His yellow eyes gleamed at them furtively, then turned away.

The market was right on the intersection of Franklin and Highland, its windows brightly lit. Martin began to jog as they approached, and Alison jogged to keep up with him. Even before Martin had crossed the street, he had glimpsed Emilio at one of the checkout counters, waiting to pay. That dark, tousled head; that small, pale face.

'There!' Martin exclaimed in relief. 'Look, there he is!'

Emilio wasn't difficult to pick out. He was the only person in the market who wasn't distorted. The cashier behind the register had a long rodentlike face with the skin texture of a withered carrot, and was tapping at the keys of the cash register with a long claw. Right behind Emilio waited a woman with a tiny head and a vastly swollen body, her small face nothing but a tight cluster of scarlet spots. As Martin and Alison reached the window and looked around the market, they saw nightmarish creatures moving up and down the aisles, some of them crawling like spiders, others with huge nodding heads like Mrs Capelli, others who were more like dogs. They were seeing firsthand the world that Lewis Carroll had written about in *Through the Looking-Glass* – the world which he had been able to describe only in a children's fantasy, because of its unbelievable horror. It was the world in which people appeared as they really are; and that was more than the Victorian imagination would have been able to accept.

As the creatures in the market passed the curved security mirrors at the far corners of the aisles, their appearance momentarily changed, and they took on a semblance of their everyday selves, except that their faces were swollen by the distortion of the mirrors, and their bodies and legs were shrunken like dwarves.

'Oh, my God,' murmured Alison. 'It's like some terrible kind of zoo.'

But Martin was set on getting hold of Emilio. He banged on the window; and banged again; and at last Emilio looked up and saw him. The little boy's face – at first despondent – broke into a wide smile. Martin beckoned him frantically to leave the market and come on outside.

Emilio dropped all of his groceries and came running out of the store and into the street. Martin opened his arms for him, and they hugged each other tight.

'You came!' sobbed Emilio. 'I didn't think you ever would! I thought I was stuck here forever and ever!'

Martin wiped Emilio's tears away, and affectionately ruffled his hair, and then stood up. 'It's time to go back,' he said. 'I don't think anything bad is going to happen to you if you step back through the mirror. But we have something important to do. Something dangerous.'

Emilio trotted along beside him as they made their way back toward the Capellis' house.

'Will you do it?' Martin asked him. 'You're the only one who can.'

'I'll try,' Emilio panted.

The wind was howling so strongly by the time they reached the house that they could scarcely walk against it. Sheets of newspaper tangled around their ankles and dry palm leaves whipped at their faces. The streets were almost deserted; but Martin could hear the howling of the fire sirens over the wind, and the distant shouting of a huge crowd, like a distant ocean lashing against the shore.

Martin picked up the loose end of the rope that they had left lying in Mr Capelli's driveway and wound it over his elbow as they went back into the house. Emilio tugged at Martin's sleeve and said, 'I don't have to go back to *them*, do I?' – meaning the mirror-Capellis. Alison put her arm around him and smiled. 'No way, José. You're staying with us.'

They climbed the stairs, with Martin still winding in the rope. The door marked illǝqɒꓶ was slightly ajar, and the sound of extraordinary garbled opera music was coming out of it, like a record being played backward. Alison ushered Emilio quickly past the door, although Emilio couldn't keep his eyes off it. God only knew what grotesque memories he would retain of what had happened there; of what distorted monstrosities he had seen; man in all his glory.

Martin had almost reached the head of the stairs when his own apartment door opened. He stopped, his heart bumping. Alison said fearfully, 'Who is it?'

The door hesitated, then opened a little wider.

'Who is that?' called Martin.

His question was answered almost at once. Out of the door came Martin himself, followed by Alison. Their own reflections, identical in every way, but somehow invested with an independent life of their own. They stood at the head of the stairs side by side and looked down at Martin and smiled benignly.

Martin felt a terror unequaled by almost anything he had experienced in the days since he had first opened his eyes and seen Boofuls standing over him. If he had encountered Boofuls at the head of the stairs, or Miss Redd, or that vicious cat Pickle, then he probably could have coped. But to come face-to-face with himself, smiling so blandly, that was more than his nervous system could cope with. 'Oh, God,' he whispered. 'Oh, God, that's the end of it.'

Alison stood white-faced, paralyzed with fear.

'What's wrong, Alison?' taunted her mirror image. 'Don't tell me that *you*, of all people, are afraid to look at yourself?'

Martin's mirror image smiled, and took the hand of Alison's mirror image as if they had been secret friends for years. 'What a daring fellow you are, Martin! Into the world of mirrors, just to save your five-year-old friend.'

Martin's mirror image came down two or three stairs, until he was standing directly in front of him. 'You always had big ideas, didn't you? Little man, big ideas. Well, I guess that we can forgive you. Every man's entitled to dream. And your best dream was Boofuls. *Boofuls!*, a musical by Martin Williams. Look what it led to! It changed the world, didn't it?'

Martin hoarsely said, 'Get out of my way.'

'Oh, come on, now, Martin, you're talking to yourself. The only person in your way is *you*.'

Martin felt the blood drain out of his head. His mouth was

dry, and he was close to collapse. But something told him that his mirror image was speaking the truth. The only person standing in his way was him. His vanity, his ambition, his carelessness, his bad tempers. Indirectly, *he* had caused the deaths of all those one hundred forty-four thousand innocent people.

In the Bible, James had said, '*For if any man is a hearer of the word and not a doer, he is like a man who looks at his natural face in a mirror; for once he has looked at himself and gone away, he has immediately forgotten what kind of person he was.*'

Now, however, Martin knew what kind of person he was; and he knew that it wasn't this smug, smiling character who was standing in front of him now.

'Get out of my way,' he repeated. He felt his strength returning. He felt his confidence surging back. '*Get out of my goddamned way!!*'

Instantly, as fast as a cobra, Martin's mirror image threw back its head and stretched open its mouth. Out from its lips poured the slippery pink head with snapping teeth, its eyes blazing bright blue. Martin dodged, ducked back, but the creature's neck swayed around and its teeth snagged at his shoulder, tearing his shirt and furrowing his skin.

Alison screamed; and Alison's mirror image screamed, too, not in fright but in shrill triumph. But Martin scrambled back down the stairs, missing his footing and tumbling down four or five of them at once. And as the snapping head came after him, he looped the rope around its neck and yanked it viciously tight.

The head choked and gargled, its eyes bulging. At the head of the stairs, Martin's mirror image gargled, too, and fell onto its knees. Whatever this vicious head was, it was deeply connected to the innards of Martin's mirror image, and if he could manage to strangle it, he could strangle his mirror image, too.

Martin pulled the rope tighter and tighter. The blazing blue eyes began to dim and to milk over. Saliva ran from the sides of the creature's lips; then bloody saliva; then blood. The head shrank and shriveled, almost like a collapsing penis, and then dropped against the stairs. Martin's mirror image came after it, head over heels; and the hideous body lay jammed against the side of the landing.

'Now,' said Martin to Alison's mirror image, looping the rope again and mounting the stairs, 'how about you?'

But Alison's mirror image drew back her lips and hissed at them and then ran down the stairs, pushing all three of them aside, and disappeared into the street.

Alison hugged Martin tight. 'You did it. You're beautiful! You did it.'

'Come on,' Martin urged her. 'I'm just hoping to God that we're not too late.'

They went into Martin's mirror-apartment, closing the door behind them. Then, with each of them holding one of Emilio's hands, they approached the mirror.

'Ramone's not there,' Martin frowned. 'Look – the rope's there. But no Ramone.'

'Let's just get ourselves back,' Alison begged him.

Hand in hand, they closed their eyes and pressed their foreheads against the cold glass of the mirror. *I can do it*, thought Martin. *I can step through glass. All I have to do is take one step forward, and I'll be there, back in the real world.*

He felt that sensation of being drawn out thin; and then compressed. His ears sang, and his heart thumped; and for one long, long moment he believed that he was dead. *I'm dead*, he told himself; and then he opened his eyes and he was standing with Emilio and Alison, back in his real sitting room.

'We made it,' he said. 'And, look, what did I tell you, Emilio's fine. Boofuls was bluffing us all along.'

Alison looked around, worried. 'No sign of Ramone. He didn't seem like the kind of guy who would get up and leave us, just like that.'

'Maybe Mr Capelli knows,' Martin suggested.

Emilio piped up, 'Where's Grandpa? Where's Grandpa? Is Grandpa here?'

Martin bent down and picked Emilio up in his arms, and together they went down to Mr Capelli's apartment. They rang the doorbell, and Martin could feel Emilio tense up. Without saying a word, he pointed to the name card on the door. *Capelli*, not illəqɒƆ.

Mr Capelli opened the door almost at once. He was about

to say something – but then he saw Martin and Alison, and best of all, Emilio.

He couldn't speak. He clutched Emilio close to him, and the tears ran down his cheeks. Martin and Alison waited, and all Martin could say was, 'He's fine, Mr Capelli. He'll have one or two nightmares, I guess. But he's fine.'

Mr Capelli finally put Emilio down, but still held him close. 'I have bad news,' he said. 'Your friend Ramone.'

Martin felt cold. 'What happened? Did he have to leave?'

Mr Capelli said, 'No, I'm sorry. It was very bad, very dreadful. I heard him banging the floor upstairs, I went up as quick as I could.'

'And?'

'Something from the mirror, I suppose,' said Mr Capelli. 'His face – all of his face. It was chopped away, like *bitten*, you know. I could hardly bear to look. I think he must have died straight away. The ambulance came to take him; the police will come later. They are so busy with all of those poor people who died at the Chinese Theater.'

'Bitten?' said Martin; and all he could think of was the chilling pink head which had poured out of the mouth of his own mirror image, with razor-sharp teeth.

'It was very dreadful,' said Mr Capelli. 'I'm sorry. It was very bad.'

Martin covered his eyes with his hand. For a moment, he felt close to crying. But no tears wanted to come. Not yet, anyway. First of all, he had to deal with Boofuls.

'Mr Capelli,' he said, 'I'm going to ask you a favor.'

'What favor?' asked Mr Capelli, with his arm tightly around Emilio.

'I want you to let Emilio come with us; just one last time.'

Mr Capelli slowly shook his head. 'I may be old, my friend, but I'm certainly not stupid. This boy has been through enough.'

High above the house, thunder cracked; so violently that plaster sifted down from the ceiling.

'Mr Capelli, if Emilio doesn't come with us now, believe me, the sun may never rise again.'

*

It took Martin almost ten minutes to change Mr Capelli's mind. Meanwhile, the storm outside rose even more violently. Two palms were uprooted, with a noise like tearing hair, and fell across the street; and the water in Maria Bocanegra's swimming pool frothed and splashed. The wind began to pick up so much speed that it screamed through the telephone wires: a high, tortured scream like desperate souls. Lightning branched everywhere, striking the twin towers of Century City and the Bonaventure Hotel downtown.

'Martin,' Mr Capelli argued, 'he's all I have. Suppose something should go wrong?'

'Mr Capelli,' Martin insisted, 'this world is all any of us have. I don't want to risk Emilio's life any more than you do. But the way I see it, we don't have any choice.'

'A curse on you for buying that mirror,' said Mr Capelli bitterly.

'Yes,' said Martin. 'A curse on me.'

Mr Capelli sat with his hands clasped together for a very long time, thinking. At last he said, 'You can take him. All right? I agree. You can take him. But you guard him with your own life. Your own life, remember. And one thing more. You break that mirror before you go. You smash it.'

Martin said cautiously, 'I'm not so sure that's a good idea.'

'Smash it,' said Mr Capelli. 'Otherwise, you can't take Emilio nowhere. Do you think I'm going to sit here, while you're gone, and any kind of monster could come jumping out? I saw what happened to your friend Ramone. You should count your lucky stars *you* didn't see it. Half his face, chomped!'

'Mr Capelli –' said Martin; but Mr Capelli was adamant.

'You smash that mirror. Otherwise, forget it. It's brought too much trouble already. And besides, I don't ever want Emilio going back there. Or even to *think* about going back there.'

Tired, shocked, still sick with grief for Ramone, Martin eventually nodded. 'I'll smash the mirror, okay? Will that make you happy?'

'Not happy; but better.'

Alison waited with Mr Capelli while Martin went back

upstairs to his apartment. Halfway up the stairs, he stopped, and leaned against the wall, and covered his eyes with his hand. *God, give me the strength to carry this through. God, help me.* He waited for a short while, to allow himself to recover, and then he climbed the last few stairs.

He opened the door of the sitting room and there was the mirror, with its gilded face of Pan, still there, still mocking him. The room felt very cold. It was like stepping into a meat market. It was so cold that the surface of the mirror was misted, almost opaque. But Martin ignored the mirror and closed the sitting room door behind him and walked across to his desk. He opened the drawer where he kept his tools and took out a hammer.

'This is it, you bastard,' he said out loud. 'And Mrs Harper had better forget about her second instalment.'

With one sweep of his hand, he wiped the clouded surface of the mirror and then swung back the hammer.

And stopped, frozen.

Because he wasn't there. There was no reflection of him swinging back the hammer. The room in the mirror was empty.

He stepped up to the mirror, his heart beating in long, slow bumps. He touched it. Then he understood what he had done. He had killed his own reflection. He could never appear in a mirror again.

He stood still. He felt an extraordinary sense of loss, like the boy Daniel who stole the sacred harp and lost his shadow.

Then he heard Alison calling, 'Martin?' and he swung back his arm and hit the mirror dead-center.

The glass smashed explosively. Huge shards dropped from the frame and clattered onto the floor. And the face of Pan on top of the frame roared out loud, scaring Martin so much that he jumped back two or three paces and almost fell over the sofa.

'God protect me,' he whispered, and stepped back up to the mirror again and hammered the face right off the frame, onto the floor. He beat it and beat it until it was nothing more than a smashed-up heap of gilt and plaster.

He stood up, breathing heavily. Now it was time to go for Boofuls. And now he needed a weapon with which to kill him.

A sword blessed by the angel Michael, Father Quinlan had told him. But where the hell was he going to find a sword? And even if he did, how was he going to get it blessed?

He was about to turn away when a flicker of lightning illuminated the room and flashed from a long shard of mirror glass. It was nearly four feet long, and slightly curved like the blade of a saber. Martin knelt down and carefully picked it up. He tested the edge with his finger and immediately cut himself, so that blood welled up and ran down his wrist. This would do. This would be his holy sword.

He rummaged in his drawer until he found a roll of insulating tape. Then he wound it around and around the end of the mirror-sword to make a safe handle. At last he lifted it up and swung it around. It made a thrilling whistle as it swept through the air. Boofuls was going to regret that he had ever stepped out of that mirror.

He held the sword by the blade, the way that he had seen knights hold their swords in storybooks, and he closed his eyes.

'God, bless this weapon, if You can. Or at least give me the strength and the intelligence to use it well. Thank You.'

Then, with the blood that ran from his cut finger, he smeared onto the mirror-sword's blade the letters V–O–R–P–A–L.

He walked downstairs. Alison and Emilio and Mr Capelli were waiting for him on the landing. 'It's broken,' he told Mr Capelli, and he lifted up the mirror sword.

'What in the name of God are you going to do with *that?*' Mr Capelli demanded.

'Make amends, I hope,' said Martin. Then, 'Come on, Emilio, let's go find that playmate of yours.'

> *He took his vorpal sword in hand:*
> *Long time the manxome foe he sought –*

They drove in Martin's Mustang across to Vine Street. Alison held the sword while Martin drove: Emilio sat in the back. The wind was still fuming across Los Angeles, and lightning was crackling from one side of the valley to the other, like the roots of giant electrified trees. There was hardly anybody else around. A few cars crept along the freeway, but it seemed as if most people had decided to stay home. A wild, dark night, thunderous with impending doom.

They reached the Hollywood Divine hotel. Martin parked on the opposite side of the street and they all climbed out of the car. Half a dozen hookers still strutted up and down outside, but otherwise the sidewalk was deserted.

'Hey, young boy,' one of the hookers called to Emilio, 'want me to pop your cherry?'

Martin pushed his way into the hotel lobby, with Emilio and Alison following. The usual collection of drunks and scarecrows were still there, but the young desk clerk was nowhere around. The lobby was gloomy and sour and smelled of urine and burned copper. Martin paused and listened, and he could hear a faint rumbling somewhere in the building, more of a deep vibration than a noise, and the sound of voices, chanting.

'Upstairs,' he said. 'The Leicester Suite.'

Alison said, 'Martin, I'm frightened. This is it, isn't it? I mean, this is really *it*?'

'Come on,' Martin reassured her. 'At least we've got God and all His angels on our side.'

'I wish I could believe that.'

'Martin –' she said.

He looked at her. He had a feeling that he knew what she was going to say.

'Not now,' he told her gently. 'Let's get this done first.'

They climbed the marble stairs until they reached the mezzanine. On the far side of the landing, the double doors of the Leicester Suite were wide open; and from inside a fitful flickering of pale light illuminated the paneling and the drapes. The vibration was even stronger now, even deeper. Martin hefted the mirror-sword from one hand to the other and then said, 'Here we go.'

They walked into the Leicester Suite. Three or four men in tuxedos was standing by the inner doors, but nobody made any attempt to stop them; or even to look at them. They were all staring in awe at the horrific spectacle which filled the high-ceilinged room.

When Martin stepped into the room and looked up at it, he almost felt like dropping to his knees. It was one thing to be told of Satan in storybooks. It was quite another to find himself standing in front of the Great Beast itself.

The room was dark, lit only by two wavering candelabra. Kneeling on the floor with their heads bowed were fifty or sixty of some of the most famous actors and actresses and directors and producers in Hollywood. Even in the darkness, Martin recognized Shany McKay and Derek Lorento and Harris Carlin and Petra Fell. Even Morris Nathan was here, at the very end of the front row, his head bandaged, leaning on the arm of his old friend Douglas Perry. It was like a Who's Who of Hollywood, all in one room.

At the very front of the kneeling celebrities, with his back to them, stood Boofuls, quite naked, his arms outstretched. His back was narrow and white-skinned, his blond curls flew upward as if he were standing in a fierce wind. Beside him, in her swooping black cape, stood Miss Redd, her hands pressed together in prayer.

In the shadows at the very far end of the cavernous room, Martin saw something stirring. Something huge, and leathery, and inhuman. He heard its claws shuffling on the marble floor, he heard its dry dragon wings rustling. It was the color of death: yellowy gray, its skin crazed with wrinkles. Its skull was wedge-shaped, with curled horns like an aging ram, and its eyes were narrow and dull and infinitely evil.

It stood three times as tall as a man, its head swaying slowly from one side to the other, surveying without emotion those who had been vain enough and proud enough and weak enough to raise it at last from its endless sleep.

'Is it real?' whispered Alison. 'It can't be real.'

Martin swallowed. 'It's real,' he said, and then swallowed again.

'*It's the devil,*' murmured Emilio.

'And there's Morry,' said Alison in disbelief. 'Right at the front – there's *Morry!*'

Martin tried to restrain her, but Alison hurried forward and took hold of Morris' arm and shook it. 'Douglas,' she said, 'why is Morry here? He should be back in the hospital!'

Martin came after her. 'Alison, for God's sake!' But Miss Redd had already turned round and seen them, and she touched

Boofuls with her long clawlike hand, and Boofuls turned around, too.

Deaf and blind, Morris turned his bandaged head. Douglas Perry said brusquely, 'I asked Lejeune, and he promised that Morry would be given his sight and his hearing back if I brought him here.'

'From *him*?' Alison almost shrieked. 'From the *devil*?'

It was then that Boofuls walked up to them – naked, smiling, beatific. 'Hello, Martin. So you came to pay homage?'

'I came to give you what you damn well deserve,' Martin told him.

'Too late.' Boofuls smiled. 'I have brought back my father from his exile, and he lives. You and Alison and young Emilio can provide him with his first feast.'

Behind him, the immense dragon-creature arched back its withered neck and let out a harsh gargling sound.

Boofuls said, 'He is back now, to rule his rightful domain. All praise. And all praise to those who found his scattered body, piece by piece, and brought it here, so that I could breathe life back into it. These actors and directors spent millions of dollars finding the last few pieces of my father's body . . . some were found in Europe, others were found in Arabia. And then all that was needed was the great sacrifice – one hundred forty-four thousand innocents, whose souls gave my father new life.'

Martin lifted the mirror-sword. 'I'm going to do now what your grandmother should have done, all those years ago. So if you've got some prayers to say, you'd better say them.'

Boofuls laughed. 'Do you think that *you*, of all people, can ward off the realm of endless night? The sun will refuse to rise tomorrow, my friend, and it will never rise again, and the world will die in chaos and darkness and storm and cold. The time was promised in the Bible, my friend, and the time is now!'

Behind Boofuls, the bulk of Satan suddenly and thunderously spread his wings and opened his jaws in a screech of triumphant fury. Dust and decayed fabric were stirred up into a whirlwind, and the devil clawed his way toward Martin with its eyes staring and his teeth bared. Boofuls lifted both arms, and stepped aside, and sang out, 'A feast for my father, that's what you'll be!'

Martin was so frightened that he could hardly think how to make his arms move. But he managed to lift the mirror-sword and swing it around and around so that it whistled cleanly through the dust and the murk, and gleamed like a helicopter blade above his head.

Satan lunged his head forward, and the tip of one of his horns caught Martin in the chest. Martin heard two ribs crack and felt a sharp, agonizing pain. Satan's head swayed around again and grazed against his shoulder. For a split second, he had a close-up of that watery, evil eye, and gingery fur that was thick with maggots; and when he breathed in he breathed the nauseating stench of excrement and dead meat.

Satan was playing with him, enjoying his fear, relishing his pain. Martin rolled aside and shouted out, '*Bastard!*' and took a swing with his mirror-sword at Satan's neck. But Satan rolled his head away, with fumes pouring from his nostrils, and Martin lost his balance, stumbled, and dropped the mirror-sword on the floor.

'A feast for my father!' screamed Boofuls, dancing up and down. 'A feast for my father!'

Martin felt one broken rib grate against the other. He tried to turn himself over and pick himself up, but Satan's wing was already flapping over him like a circus tent in a storm, and Satan's reptilian head was already diving toward him with its fangs agape.

'Oh, God, help me!' he yelled.

And it was then that Emilio ducked quickly under Satan's brushing wing and picked up the sword marked *VORPAL*. The glass blade was almost as tall as he was; but he grasped the insulating-tape handle in both hands and ran three or four paces forward, and just as Satan turned his head sideways to grip Martin with his teeth, Emilio jabbed it straight into the devil's eye.

It was so sharp that it slid all the way in, and its point came gleaming out of the back of the devil's withered neck.

Martin had his eyes shut. He didn't see the sword run in. But he heard Miss Redd scream; and he heard Boofuls shouting in dismay; and then he opened his eyes again and saw Satan rearing up, up, up, leathery trunk on leathery pelvis, wings stretched taut in agony, dust and maggots showering down from his shaken fur.

There was a moment of deafening silence. Everybody in the room rose from their knees and stepped backward in awe. The dragon that was Satan stood immensely high, his head arched back, the mirror-sword glittering out of that one eye. *Remember that only the child can destroy the parent.*

Then the dragon collapsed. He literally fell apart, limb from limb, claw from finger, bone from bone. His skull dropped from his neck and rolled across the floor with a hollow sound like an empty barrel. His wings folded and dropped. Within a few minutes, there was nothing left of his leathery eminence but all the fragments that had been so painstakingly and expensively collected over so many years by the vainglorious Satan worshippers of Hollywood. A pall of stinking dust hung over him for a while, but gradually sifted and settled.

Boofuls stood quite still, with his eyes wide open.

'*What have you done?*' he said. '*What have you done!!*'

Without a word, Martin limped over to the devil's skull, placed his foot against it, and tugged out the mirror-sword. Then he turned back to Boofuls and faced him, the sword lifted over his right shoulder, ready to strike.

'The son of Satan,' he whispered.

Boofuls said nothing, but continued to stare at him, wide-eyed. Miss Redd, a little farther away, weakly mouthed the word 'no'.

Martin swung the mirror-sword with all his strength. It flashed through the air and sliced Boofuls' head clean off his neck. The bloody blond head bounced across the floor. The small naked body stood in front of Martin for a moment, its neck pumping out squiggles of blood, and then it fell stiffly sideways, as if it were a tailor's dummy, and dropped to the floor.

Shaking, half berserk, Martin advanced on Miss Redd.

'You will never kill me with that,' she spat at him, backing away. 'I am quite different.'

'I know that,' said Martin. He tossed the mirror-sword aside, and it dropped to the floor and smashed into half a dozen pieces. 'But Father Quinlan told me to read my *Alice* carefully, and that's just what I did.'

Martin stepped forward and gripped hold of Miss Redd's cape. *She shook the Red Queen backwards and forwards with all her might.* He shook her violently, until she screamed. But he kept on shaking her and shaking her, so that her head was hurled from side to side, her whole body was jerked around. *The Red Queen made no resistance whatever: only her face grew very small, and her eyes got large and green: and still, as Alice went on shaking her, she kept on growing shorter – and softer – and rounder – and –*

Martin was holding nothing but an empty black cape. He dropped it, exhausted, just in time to see a brindled cat dodging off into the darkness of the Leicester Suite, and jumping up onto the drapes, and disappearing.

'That was Pickle!' said Emilio in astonishment. 'Martin – that was Pickle!'

Martin looked at his bloodstained hands; then at Alison; then at the decayed ruins of the angel whom God had banished from heaven forever. 'Yes, Emilio,' he said. 'That was Pickle.'

Together, Martin and Alison and Emilio turned away and walked through the silent assembly of actors and directors. Morris blindly called out, 'Alison!' but Alison ignored him and took hold of Martin's hand. Martin in turn took hold of Emilio's hand.

'*Alison!*' called Morris one last time; and that was the last word that echoed in the Hollywood Divine.

They buried Ramone next to his mother at Forest Lawn. Afterward, Martin took them to lunch at Butterfield's. Alison and Emilio, Mr and Mrs Capelli. They were all too hot, dressed as they were in black.

Alison looked at Martin for a long time. Then she said, 'I'm going away tomorrow.'

'Oh, yes?' Martin had been hoping they could spend the weekend together.

'Acapulco, just for a couple of weeks.'

'Hey, Acapulco, that's nice,' said Mr Capelli.

'By yourself?' asked Martin, trying to sound offhand.

'Well,' admitted Alison. 'There's this guy I met . . . he's an independent producer. He has this house in Laurel Canyon. I mean you wouldn't believe it! Nine bedrooms, *two* pools!'

Martin nodded. 'Quite a guy, by the sound of it.'

Alison reached over and squeezed his hand. 'You're not upset?'

'Upset? Why should I be upset?'

But then Emilio came around the table and laid his hand on Martin's shoulder and said, 'It's okay, Martin. You can play with me.'

They demolished the Hollywood Divine on the last day of November that year. As the wrecking crew brought down the great domed roof of the Leicester Suite, a brindled cat was watching from across the street, its eyes narrowed against the sunlight and the dust.

The cat was still watching as a passing derelict sifted through the rubble that had spilled into the street, attracted by something bright.

The derelict picked up a squarish fragment of mirror, turned it this way and that, and frowned into it. Then he buffed it up on his sleeve and dropped it into his pocket.

He shuffled southward on Vine Street, with the cat patiently following him.

Charnel House

'The rising sun finds me
The opening in the East sees me.
That can only mean
Coyote finds me,
With his bloodstained mouth!
Here comes mad Coyote,
He wears a necklace of eyeballs,
His mouth is red, his hands are red.
Mad Coyote
Sings a crazy song
And suddenly the West Wind blows!'
                              – Navaho song.

CHAPTER ONE

The old man came into my office and closed the door. He was wearing a creased linen jacket and a green bow-tie, and in his liver-spotted hands he held a Panama hat that had turned brown as a London steak from years of California sun. One side of his face was still prickly with white stubble, so I guessed he couldn't shave too well.

He said, almost apologetically, 'It's my house. It's breathing.'

I smiled, and said, 'Sit down.'

He sat on the edge of the chrome-and-plastic chair, and licked his lips. He had one of those soft, concerned old faces that make you wish you had a grandfather as nice as that. He was the kind of old guy it would've been satisfying to play chess with, idling away some fall afternoon on a balcony overlooking the beach.

He said, 'You don't have to believe me if you don't want to, young feller. But I called before, and I said the same thing.'

I turned over the appointments list on my desk.

'Sure. You telephoned last week, right?'

'And the week before.'

'And you told the girl your house was—'

I paused, and looked at him, and he looked back at me. He didn't finish my sentence for me, and I guess that was because he wanted to hear me say it, too. I gave him a tight, bureaucratic smile.

He said, in his gentle, crumbly voice, 'I moved into the house from my sister's old apartment up on the hill. I sold some stock, and bought it for cash. It was going pretty cheap, and I've always wanted to live around Mission Street. But now, well . . .'

He dropped his eyes, and fiddled with the brim of his hat.

I picked up my ballpen. I asked him quietly: 'Could you tell me your name please?'

'Seymour Wallis. I'm a retired engineer. Bridges, mainly.'

'And your address?'

'Fifteen-fifty-one Pilarcitos.'

'Okay. And your problem is noise?'

He looked up again. His eyes were the colour of faded cornflowers, pressed between the leaves of a book.

'Not noise,' he said softly. 'Breathing.'

I sat back in my black simulated-leather revolving armchair, and tapped my ballpen against my teeth. I was pretty used to cranky complaints in the sanitation department. We had a woman who came in regularly, saying that dozens of alligators that kids had flushed down the toilets in the 1960s had made their way to the sewers beneath her apartment on Howard and 4th, and were trying to make their way back up the S-bend to eat her. Then there was the young pothead who believed that his water heater was giving off dangerous rays.

But, cranks or not, I was paid to be nice to them, and listen patiently to whatever they had to say, and try to reassure them that San Francisco was not harbouring alligator swarms or hidden lumps of green Kryptonite.

So I said, 'Isn't it possible you made a mistake? Maybe it's your own breathing you can hear.'

The old man shrugged a little, as if to say that was possible, yes, but not really likely.

'Maybe you have a downdraught in your chimney,' I suggested. 'Sometimes the air comes down an old stack and finds its way through cracks in the bricks where the fireplaces are blocked up.'

He shook his head.

'Well,' I asked him, 'if it's not your own breathing, and it's not a draught in your chimney, could you tell me what *you* think it may be?'

He coughed, and took out a clean but frayed handkerchief to dab his mouth.

'I think it's breathing,' he said. 'I think there's some kind of animal trapped in the walls.'

'Do you hear scratching? Feet pattering? That kind of thing?'

He shook his head again.

'Just breathing?'

He nodded.

I waited to hear if he had anything else to say, but he obviously didn't. I stood up and walked across to my window, which overlooked the apartment block next door. On warm days, you'd occasionally see off-duty air hostesses sunning themselves on the roof-garden, in bikinis that made me consider that flying united had to be the best way. But all that was on show today was an aged Mexican gardener, repotting geraniums.

I said, 'If you *did* have an animal trapped between your walls, it could only survive for so long without food and water. And if it wasn't trapped, you'd hear it running around.'

Seymour Wallis, engineer, stared at his hat. I was beginning to realise that he wasn't a crank – in fact, he was rather a plain, practical man – and that coming down here to the sanitation department with stories of disembodied breathing must have taken quite a lot of careful consideration. He didn't want to look a fool. But then, who does?

He said, quietly but firmly: 'It sounds like an animal breathing. I know it's hard to credit, but I've heard it for three months now, almost the whole time I've lived there, and it's quite unmistakable.'

I turned back from the window. 'Are there any odours? Any unpleasant deposits? I mean, you're not

3

finding animal excrement in your larder or anything like that?'

'It *breathes*, that's all. Like a German shepherd on a hot day. Pant, pant, pant, all night long, and sometimes in the daytime as well.'

I returned to my desk and sat myself back in my chair. Seymour Wallis looked at me expectantly, as if I could pull some kind of magical solution out of my bottom left drawer, but the truth was that I was authorised to exterminate rats, cockroaches, termites, wasps, lice, fleas and bedbugs, but so far my authority didn't extend to breathing.

'Mr Wallis,' I said, as kindly as I could, 'are you sure you've come to the right department?'

He coughed. 'Do you have any *other* suggestions?'

As a matter of fact, I was beginning to wonder if a psychiatrist might be a good idea, but it's kind of hard to tell a nice old gentleman straight out that he might be going cuckoo. In any case, supposing there *was* breathing?

I looked across at the contemporary red-and-green print on the opposite side of the room. There was a time, before our offices were refurbished, when all I had on the wall was a tatty poster warning against handling food with unwashed hands, but these days the sanitation department was far more tasteful. There had even been talk about calling us 'environmental maintenance executives'.

I said carefully: 'If there's no dirt, and there are no visible signs of what's causing the breathing, then I don't quite see why you're worried. It's probably just some unusual phenomenon caused by the way your house is built.'

Seymour Wallis listened to this with a look on his face that meant, *you're a bureaucrat, you have to say all these reassuring things, but I don't believe a word of it.* When I'd finished, he sat back on the plastic chair and nodded for a while in reflective silence.

4

'If there's anything else you need,' I said. 'If you want your cockroaches wiped out or your rats rounded up . . . well, you're very welcome.'

He gave me a hard, unimpressed glance.

'I'll tell you the truth,' he said hoarsely. 'The truth is that I'm frightened. There's something about that breathing that scares the pants off me. I've only come here because I didn't know where else to turn. My doctor says my hearing is fine. My plumber says my drain-pipes are A-OK. My builder says my house is sound and my psychiatrist says there are no imminent signs of senility. All that reassurance, and I can still hear it and I'm still frightened.'

'Mr Wallis,' I told him, 'there's nothing I can do. Breathing just isn't my bag.'

'You could come and listen.'

'To breathing?'

'Well, you don't have to.'

I spread my hands sympathetically. 'It's not that I don't *want* to. It's just that I have more pressing matters of city sanitation to deal with. We have a blocked-up sewer on Folsom, and the folks around there are naturally more interested in their own breathing than anyone else's. I'm sorry, Mr Wallis, there's nothing I can do to help you.'

He rubbed his forehead wearily, and then he stood up. 'All right,' he said, in a defeated voice. 'I can understand your priorities.'

I walked round my desk and opened the door for him. He put on his old Panama hat, and stood there for a moment, as if he was trying to find the words to say something else.

'If you hear anything else, like pattering feet, or if you find excrement—' I told him.

He nodded. 'I know – I'll call you. The trouble with the way things are these days, everybody specialises. You can clean out sewers but you can't listen to something as strange as a house that breathes.'

'I'm sorry.'

He reached out and gripped my wrist. His bony old hand was surprisingly strong, and it felt as if I'd been suddenly seized by a bald eagle.

'Why not stop being sorry and do something positive?' he said. He came so close I could see the red tracery of veins in his cloudy eyes. 'Why not come around when you're finished up here, and just listen for five minutes? I have some Scotch whisky my nephew brought back from Europe. We could have a drink, and then you could hear it.'

'Mr Wallis—'

He let go of my wrist, and sighed, and adjusted his hat. 'You'll have to forgive me,' he said flatly. 'I guess it's been kind of a strain on the nerves.'

'That's okay,' I said. Then, 'Listen, if I find a few spare minutes after work, I'll call by. I can't promise, and if I don't make it, don't worry. I have a late meeting this evening, so it won't be early. But I'll try.'

'Very well,' he said, without looking at me. He didn't like losing control of his feelings and right now he was doing his best to gather them up, like a tumbled skein of loose wool.

Then he said: 'It could be the park, you know. It could be something to do with the park.'

'The park?' I asked blankly.

He frowned, as if I'd said something totally irrelevant, and then he said, 'Thanks for your time, young man,' and walked off down the long polished corridor. I stood at my open door watching him go. All of a sudden, in the air-conditioned chill, I began to shiver.

As usual, the evening's meeting was dominated by Ben Pultik, the executive in charge of garbage disposal. Pultik was a short, wide-shouldered man who looked like a small wardrobe in a plaid jacket. He had been in garbage ever since the general strike of 1934, and he considered its collection and eventual disposal to be one of the highest callings of mankind, which in some ways it was, but not in the sense of 'highest' that he meant it.

Today, we sat around the conference table and smoked too much and drank stale coffee out of plastic cups while outside the windows the sky was curtained with purple and faded gold, and the towers and pyramids of San Francisco settled into the glittering grainy Pacific night. Pultik was complaining that the owners of ethnic restaurants were failing to wrap kitchen refuse in black plastic garbage bags, and that his clean-up crews were having their coveralls soiled by exotic foods.

'Some of my men are Jewish,' he said, relighting his burned-down stogie. 'The last thing they want is to be soiled all over with food that ain't kosher-prepared.'

Morton Meredith, the head of the department, sat in his chair at the top of the table with a wan, twitchy smile on his face, and stifled a yawn behind his hand. The only reason we convened these meetings was because city hall insisted on inter-staff stimulation, but the idea of being stimulated by Ben Pultik was like the idea of ordering *moules farcies* at McDonald's. It just wasn't on the menu.

Eventually, at nine o'clock, after a tedious report from the extermination people on the use and misuse of Warfarin, we left the building and walked out into the warm night air. Dan Machin, a young beanpole of a guy from the health research laboratory, came pushing across the plaza towards me, and clapped me on the back.

'You fancy a drink?' he asked me. 'Those meetings are enough to turn your throat into a desert preservation zone.'

'Sure,' I told him. 'All I have to kill is time.'

'Time *and* fleas,' Dan reminded me.

I don't particularly know why I liked Dan Machin. He was three or four years younger than me, and yet

7

he had his hair crew-cut like a Kansas wheatfield, and he wore big unfashionable spectacles which always looked as if they were about to drop off the end of his snubbed-up nose. He wore loose-fitting jackets with patched leather elbows, and his shoes were always scuffed, yet he had a funny oblique sense of humour which tickled me, and even though his face was pallid from spending too many hours indoors, he played a good game of squash and he knew as many odd facts and figures as the editors of Ripley.

Maybe Dan Machin reminded me of my safe sub-urban upbringing in Westchester, where all the houses had coachlamps, and all the housewives had blonde lacquered hair and drove their children around in Buick station-wagons, and every fall the smell of burning leaves would signal the season of roller-skating and trick-or-treat. A lot of hard things had happened to me since then, not the least of which was a messy divorce and a fierce but absurd affair, and it was nice to know that such an America still existed.

We crossed the street and walked up the narrow sidewalk of Gold Street to Dan's favourite bar, the Assay Office. It was a high-ceilinged room with an old-style balcony, and the wood-and-brass furniture of a long-gone San Francisco. We found a table next to the wall, and Dan ordered us a couple of Coors.

'I meant to go up to Pilarcitos this evening,' I told him, lighting a cigarette.

'Fun or business?'

I shrugged. 'I'm not sure. Not much of either.'

'Sounds mysterious.'

'It is. An old guy came into the office today, and said he had a house that breathed.'

'*Breathed?*'

'That's right. In fact, it panted like Lassie. He wanted to know if I could do something about it.'

The beers arrived and Dan took a long swallow,

8

leaving himself with a white foamy moustache that quite suited him.

'It isn't a downdraught in the chimney,' I told him. 'Nor is it any kind of creature trapped inside the wall cavities. In fact, it's a genuine case of inexplicable respiration.'

That was meant to be a wisecrack, but Dan seemed to take it seriously. He said: 'Did he say anything more? Did he tell you when it happened? What time of day?'

I set down my glass. 'He said it was all the time. He's only lived in the place for a few months, and it's been happening ever since he moved in. He's real frightened. I guess the old coot thinks it's some kind of ghost.'

'Well, it could be,' said Dan.

'Oh, sure. And Ben Pultik's grown tired of garbage.'

'No, I mean it,' insisted Dan. 'I've heard of cases like that before, when people have heard voices and stuff like that. Under certain conditions, the sounds that were uttered in an old room can be heard again. Sometimes, people have claimed to hear conversations that could only have been spoken a century before.'

'Where did you find all this out?'

Dan tugged at his tiny nose as if he was trying to make it grow longer, and I could swear that he faintly blushed. 'As a matter of fact,' he said, embarrassed, 'I've always been pretty interested in spirit manifestations. It kind of runs in the family.'

'A hard-boiled scientist like you?'

'Now, come on,' said Dan. 'It's not as nutty as it seems, all this spirit-world stuff. There have been some pretty astounding cases. And anyway, my aunt used to say that the shade of Buffalo Bill Cody came and sat by her bedside every night to tell her stories of the Old West.'

'Buffalo Bill?'

9

Dan pulled a self-deprecating face. 'That's what she said. Maybe I shouldn't have believed her.'

I sat back in my chair. There was a friendly hubbub of chatter in the bar, and they were bringing out pieces of fried chicken and spare ribs, which reminded me that I hadn't eaten since breakfast.

'You think I should go up there?' I asked Dan, eyeing a girl in a tight white T-shirt with *Oldsmobile Rocket* printed across her breasts.

'Well, let's put it this way – *I'd* go. In fact, maybe we should go up there together. I'd love to hear a house that breathes.'

'You would, huh? Okay – if you want to split the taxi fare, we'll go. But don't think I can guarantee this guy. He's very old, and he may be just hallucinating.'

'An hallucination is a trick of the eyes.'

'I'm beginning to think that girl in the T-shirt is a trick of the eyes.'

Dan turned around, and the girl caught his eye, and he blushed a deep shade of red. 'You always do that,' he complained, irritably. 'They must think I'm some kind of sex maniac in here.'

We finished up our beers, and then we left the bar and caught a taxi up to Pilarcitos Street. It was one of those short sloping streets where you park your car when you're visiting a Japanese restaurant on the main drag, and which, queasy on too much tempura and sake, you can never find again afterwards. The houses were old and silent, with turrets and gables and shadowy porches, and considering that Mission Street was only a few yards away, they seemed to be strangely brooding and out of touch with time. Dan and I stood outside 1551 in the warm evening breeze, looking up at the Gothic tower and the carved balcony, and the greyish paint that flaked off it like the scales from a dead fish.

'You don't believe a house like this could breathe?' he asked me, sniffing.

'I don't believe *any* house can breathe. But it smells like he needs his drains checked.'

'For Christ's sake,' Dan complained. 'No shop talk after hours. You think I go round cocktail parties looking through my guests' hair for lice?'

'I wouldn't put it past you.'

There was a rusted wrought-iron gate, and then five angled steps which led up to the porch. I pushed the gate open, and it groaned like a dying dog. Then we went up the steps and searched around in the gloom of the porch for the front doorbell. All the downstairs windows overlooking the street were shuttered and locked, so there didn't seem much point in whistling or calling out. Down the hill, a police car sped past with its siren warbling, and a girl was laughing as she pranced along the street with two young boys. All this was happening within sight and earshot, and yet up here in the entrance of 1551, there was nothing but shadowy silence, and a feeling that lost years were eddying past us, leaking out of the letter-box and from under the elaborate front door like sand seeping out of a bucket.

Dan said, 'There's a knocker here. Maybe I should give it a couple of raps.'

I peered into the darkness. 'As long as you don't quoth "Nevermore" at the same time.'

'Jesus,' said Dan. 'Even the knocker's creepy.'

I stepped forward and took a look at it. It was a huge old knocker, black with age and weathering. It was fashioned like the head of a strange snarling creature, something between a wolf and a demon, and I didn't find it at all encouraging. Somebody who could happily hang something like that on their front door couldn't be altogether normal, unless they actually enjoyed having nightmares. Under the knocker there was engraved the single word *Return*.

While Dan was hesitating, I took hold of the knocker and banged it two or three times. The sound echoed flatly inside the house, and we waited patiently on the porch for Seymour Wallis to answer.

Dan said, 'What do you think that is? That thing on the knocker?'

'Don't ask me. Some kind of a gargoyle, I guess.'

'It looks more like a goddamned werewolf to me.'

I reached in my pocket for a cigarette. 'You've been watching too many old horror pictures.'

I was just about to bang the knocker again when I heard footsteps shuffling towards us from inside the house. Bolts were pulled back at the top of the door, and at the bottom, and then it shuddered open an inch or two, until it was stopped by a security chain. I saw the pale face of Seymour Wallis peering around it cautiously, as if he was expecting muggers, or Mormons.

'Mr Wallis?' I said. 'We came to hear the breathing.'

'Oh, it's you,' he said, with obvious relief. 'Just hold on a moment there, and I'll open the door.'

He slipped the chain, and the door shuddered wider still. Seymour Wallis was wearing a maroon bathrobe and slippers, and his thin bare hairy legs were showing. Dan said, 'I hope we haven't caught you at a bad moment.'

'No, no. Come in. I was only getting ready to take a bath.'

'I sure like your knocker,' I said. 'It's kind of scary, though, isn't it?'

Seymour Wallis gave me a flicker of a smile. 'I suppose so. It came with the house. I don't know what it's meant to be. My sister thinks it might be the devil, but I'm not so sure. And why it should say *Return* I shall never know.'

We found ourselves in a high, musty hallway, carpeted in threadbare brown, and with dozens of yellowing prints and engravings and framed letters all over the walls. Some of the frames were empty, and others were cracked, but most of them contained sepia views of Mount Taylor and Cabezon' Peak, or foxed and illegible maps, or lists of statistics written in a crabbed and faded handwriting.

Beside us, the newel post of the stairs was carved out of dark mahogany, and on top of it was a bronze bear, standing upright, with a woman's face instead of a snout. The stairs themselves, tall and narrow, rose towards the darkness of the second floor like an escalator into the gloomiest recesses of the night.

'You'd better come this way,' said Seymour Wallis, leading us down the hall towards a door at the end. There was a shabby stag's head hanging over it with dusty antlers and only one eye. Dan said, 'After *you*,' and I wasn't sure if he was joking about the house or not. It couldn't have been much creepier.

We entered a small, airless study. There were shelves all around that must have been lined with books at one time, but were now empty. The brownish figured wallpaper behind them was marked with the shadows of where they had once been. In the corner, under a doleful painting of early San Francisco, was a stained leather-topped desk and a wooden stockbroker's chair with two slats missing. Seymour Wallis had kept the shutters closed, and the room was suffocating and stale. It smelled of cats, lavender bags and cockroach powder.

'I hear the noise in here more than in any other room,' Seymour Wallis explained. 'It comes at night mostly, when I'm sitting here writing letters, or finishing my accounts. At first there's nothing, but then I start straining my ears, and I'm sure I can hear it. Soft breathing, just as if somebody's walked into the room, and is standing a little way away watching me. I try – well, I've *tried* – not to turn around. But I'm afraid that I always do. And of course there's nobody there.'

Dan Machin walked across the worn-out rug. The floorboards creaked under his feet. He picked up an astral calendar from Seymour Wallis's desk, and examined it for a moment or two. Then he said, 'Do you believe in the supernatural, Mr Wallis?'

'It depends what you mean by the supernatural.'

'Well, ghosts.'

Seymour Wallis glanced at me and then back to Dan Machin. I think he was afraid that we were putting him on. In his maroon bathrobe, he looked like one of those elderly men who insist on taking a dip in the ocean on Christmas Day.

Dan Machin said, 'I was telling my colleague here that some houses act as receivers for sounds and conversations from the past. If anything particularly stressful has happened inside them, they kind of store up the sound in the texture of their walls, and play it back like a tape-recorder, over and over again. There was a case in Massachusetts only last year when a young couple claimed to have heard a man and a woman arguing in their living-room at night, but whenever they went downstairs there was nobody there. They heard actual names being shouted, though, and when they went to their local church register and checked them up, they found that the people they could hear had lived in their house in 1860.'

Seymour Wallis rubbed his bristly chin. 'You're trying to say that when I hear breathing, it's a ghost?'

'Not exactly a ghost,' said Dan. 'It's just an echo from the past. It might be frightening, but it's no more dangerous than the sound you can hear from your television. It's just *sound*, that's all.'

Seymour Wallis sat slowly down on the old stock-broker's chair, and looked at us gravely. 'Can I get it to leave me alone?' he asked. 'I mean, can you exorcise it?'

'I don't think so,' said Dan. 'Not without knocking the house down. What you're hearing is within the fabric of the house itself.'

I coughed, and said politely, 'I'm afraid there's a

14

city ordinance against knocking down these old houses for meretricious reasons. Sub-section eight.'

Seymour Wallis looked very tired. 'You know something,' he said, 'I've wanted one of these houses for years. I used to walk by here, and admire their age and their character and their style. At last I've managed to get one. It means a great deal to me, this house. It represents everything I've done in my life to maintain the old true standards against the easy, false, beguiling modern world. Look at this place. There isn't a foot of Formica, an ounce of plastic, or a scrap of fibreglass. Those mouldings around the ceiling are real plaster, and these floorboards came from an old sailing-ship. Look how wide they are. Now look at those doors. They're solid, and they hang true. The hinges are brass.'

He raised his head, and when he spoke there was a great deal of emotion in his voice.

'This house is mine,' he said. 'And if there's a ghost in it, or a noise in it, I want it out. I'm the master of this place, and by God I'll fight any supernatural oddity for the right to say that.'

I said: 'I don't like to sound as if I don't believe you, Mr Wallis, because I'm sure you heard what you say you did. But don't you think you've been overworking? Maybe you're just tired.'

Seymour Wallis nodded. 'I'm tired all right. But I'm not so tired that I won't fight to keep what's mine.'

Dan Machin looked around the room, and said, 'Maybe you could come to some arrangement with this breathing. You know – strike some kind of compromise.'

'I don't understand.'

'Well, I'm not sure that I do, either. But lots of spiritualists seem to believe that you can do deals with the spirit world to have yourself left alone. I mean, the whole reason a place gets itself haunted is because the spirit isn't free to get itself off to wherever spirits hang

15

out. So maybe this breathing spirit is trying to get you to help it accomplish something. I don't know. It's just a thought. Maybe you ought to try and talk to it.'

I raised an eyebrow.

'What do you suggest I say?' asked Seymour Wallis cautiously.

'Be blunt. Ask it what it wants.'

'Oh, come on, Dan,' I butted in. 'This is ridiculous.'

'No, it isn't. If Mr Wallis here can hear the breathing, then maybe whatever's doing the breathing can hear him.'

'We don't yet know that there *is* any breathing.'

'But supposing there is.'

Seymour Wallis stood up. 'I guess the only way I'm going to convince you is if you hear it for yourself. Why not have a glass of Scotch? Then maybe we can sit down here for half an hour, if you can spare it, and we'll listen.'

'Sure, I'd love to,' said Dan.

Seymour Wallis shuffled out of the room and came back a few moments later with two bentwood chairs. We sat down, upright and uncomfortable while he shuffled off again to fetch his decanter.

I sniffed the musty air. It was really hot and stuffy in that tiny library, and I was beginning to wish I was back in the Assay Office drinking a cold Coors. Dan rubbed his hands together in a businesslike kind of way, and said, 'This is going to be wild.'

'You mean you think we're going to hear it?'

'Sure I think we're going to hear it. I told you. I believe in this stuff. I nearly saw a ghost once.'

'You *nearly* saw it? What does that mean?'

'I was staying at an old hotel in Denver, and I was going back to my room one night when I saw the chambermaid coming out of it. I put my key in the door, and she said "Are you sure you have the right room, sir? There's a gentleman taking a bath in there." Well, I checked my key number, and it was the right room, so I went inside. The chambermaid followed just to check, and when I looked in the bathroom there was nobody taking a bath, no water in the tub, no nothing. Hotels are great places for ghosts.'

'Sure, and the sanitation department is a great place for liars.'

Right then, old man Wallis came back with a tarnished silver tray bearing a decanter of whisky and three tumblers. He set them down on the table and poured us each a generous glassful. Then he sat in his chair, and sipped the Scotch as if he was testing it for hemlock.

Outside in the hallway, a clock that I hadn't seen when I walked in struck ten. Bong-chirr-bong-chirr-bong-chirr . . .

Dan Machin said, 'Do you have any ice, Mr Wallis?'

Seymour Wallis looked at him in confusion, and then shook his head. 'I'm sorry. The icebox is broken. I've been meaning to have it fixed. I eat out mostly, so I haven't felt the need.'

Dan lifted his glass. 'Well, here's to the breathing, whoever it is.'

I swallowed warm, neat Scotch, and grimaced.

We waited there in silence for almost ten minutes. It's surprising how much noise you make drinking whisky in total quiet. After a while, I could hear that invisible clock ticking out there in the hallway, and even the distant murmur of traffic on Mission. And there was that rushing sound of my own blood circulating in my ears. Seymour Wallis suppressed a cough, and then said: 'More whisky?'

Dan Machin held his glass out, but I said, 'If I have any more, I'll be hearing bells, not breathing.'

We settled back on our chairs again, with an awkward creaking of wood. Dan Machin said, 'Do you know anything about the history of this house, Mr Wallis? Anything that might help you identify who this mystery breather might be?'

Seymour Wallis nervously rearranged the things on his desk – pen, letter-opener, calendar – and then looked at Dan with that same defeated look he'd had on his face when he first came into my office.

'I looked at the deeds, and they go back to 1885, when the house was built. It was owned by a seed merchant, and then by a naval captain. But there wasn't anything unusual. Nothing to make you think there might have been stress here. No murders, or anything like that.'

Dan swallowed some more whisky. 'Maybe the breather sticks around because he was happy here. That sometimes happens. A ghost haunts a house trying to recapture its old joy.'

'The happy breather?' I asked, in disbelief.

'Sure,' retorted Dan defensively. 'It's been known.'

We lapsed into silence again. Both Dan and I sat there reasonably still, but Seymour Wallis seemed to twitch and scratch, as if he was really unsettled. The clock struck the half-hour, and still we waited, and still we heard nothing. All around us, the dark bulk of the old house remained hushed, with not even the sound of a roof-timber creaking or a window rattling. Over a hundred years, this building had done all the settling it was going to, and now it was dead, immobile, and quiet.

I laid down my whisky glass on the edge of Seymour Wallis's desk. He glanced up at me briefly and I smiled, but he simply turned away, biting his lip. Perhaps he was worried that there wouldn't be any breathing tonight, in which case he was either lying or going out of his mind.

Just then, Dan said, 'Ssshh.'

I froze, and listened. I said: 'I don't hear anything.'

Seymour Wallis lifted his hand. 'At first it's very soft,' he said, 'but it grows louder. Listen.'

I strained my ears. There was still the ticking of the clock outside, still the distant murmur of traffic. But there was something else too, something so faint that all of us were frowning in concentration as we tried to hear it.

It was like a sibilant whispering at first, like the wind tossing a piece of soft tissue across a room. But gradually it grew more distinct, and all I could do was turn to look at Dan to see if he was hearing what I was hearing, to make sure that it wasn't auto-suggestion or a trick of the wind.

It was breathing. Slow, deep breathing, like the breathing of someone asleep. It went in and out, in and out, with measured respiration, as if lungs were being endlessly filled and emptied with hopeless regularity, the breathing of someone who slept and slept and would never reach morning.

Now I knew why Seymour Wallis was frightened. This sound, this breathing, could make your skin prickle with cold. It was the breathing of someone who could never wake up. It was more to do with death than it was to do with life, and it went on and on and on, louder and louder, until we no longer had to strain our ears, but simply sat there, staring at each other in horror and fright.

Dan said, 'Christ.'

It was impossible to say where the breathing came from. It was all around. I even looked at the walls to make sure that they weren't sagging in and out with every breath. Seymour Wallis was right. The house was breathing. The house itself was not dead, as it had first appeared, but asleep.

I whispered, 'Dan – *Dan!*'

'What is it?'

'Challenge it, Dan, like you said. Ask it what it wants!'

Dan licked his lips. All around us, the breathing went on, slow and heavy. Sometimes I thought it was going to stop, but then another deep breath would come, and another, and if it had been breathing like this for more than a hundred years, it was probably going to go on for ever.

Dan coughed. 'I can't,' he said hoarsely. 'I don't know what to say.'

Seymour Wallis himself just sat there, tense and still for the first time this evening, his whisky untouched in his hand.

Slowly, cautiously, I stood up. The breathing didn't falter. It was as loud now as if I was sleeping next to someone in the same bed, and they had turned to face me in the darkness.

I said: 'Who's there?'

There was no response. The breathing went on.

'Who's there?' I said, louder. 'What do you want? Tell us what you want and we'll help you!'

The breathing continued, although for some reason I thought it sounded harsher. It was quicker, too.

Dan said: 'Don't – for God's sake!'

I ignored him. I walked into the centre of the room and called out: 'Whoever's breathing, listen! We want to help you! Tell us what to do and we'll help you! Give us a sign! Show us that you know we're here!'

Seymour Wallis said: 'Please – I think this is dangerous. Let's just listen and leave it alone.'

I shook my head. 'How can we? Dan here believes in ghosts, and you say it scares you. Well, I can hear it, too, and if I can hear it that means there's something there, because I don't believe in ghosts and I'm not particularly scared.'

The breathing grew quicker and quicker. It was still the breathing of a sleeper, but of a sleeper who dreams, or a sleeper who is going through nightmares. Seymour Wallis stood up, his face drawn and pale, and whispered, 'My God, it's never been as loud as this before. Please, don't say any more. Just leave it alone, and it'll go away.'

'Whoever's breathing!' I called crisply. 'Whoever's

20

there! Listen! We can help you! We can help you leave this house!'

The breathing was almost frantic now, panting, whining. Seymour Wallis, terrified, put his hands over his ears, and Dan was sitting rigid in his chair, his face white. As for me – I may not have been scared before, but this was insane. It was like a hideous fantasy. The breathing was mounting and mounting as if it was working up towards a climax, the peak of some grotesque effort.

Soon it was the screaming breath of a runner who runs too far and too fast, the breath of a terrified animal. And then suddenly, there was a roar of sound and energy that made me cover my eyes, and sent Dan Machin hurtling off his chair and halfway across the room. Seymour Wallis shrieked like a woman, and dropped to his knees. I heard a blizzard of splintering glass from somewhere in the house, and things clattering and falling. Then there was silence.

I opened my eyes. Seymour Wallis was crouched on the floor, shaken but unhurt. It was Dan I was worried about. He was lying on his back, unmoving, and his face was a ghastly white. I picked up his fallen chair, and then knelt beside him and patted his cheek.

'Dan? Are you okay? *Dan!*'

Seymour Wallis said: 'Maybe I'd better call an ambulance.'

I raised one of Dan's eyelids with my thumb. His twitching eyeball showed that he was still alive, but he must have been in a deep state of concussion or shock. They'd taught me that much in the Army, apart from how to blow up paddy-fields and defoliate twenty-five acres in just as many minutes.

While Seymour Wallis called the emergency service, I covered Dan with my jacket and switched on the beaten-up old electric fire to keep him warm. Dan didn't tremble or shake. He just lay there flat on his back, white and still, and when I listened close to his lips I could only just hear him breathing. I slapped him a couple of times, but it was just like slapping a lump of baker's dough.

'They'll be right around,' reported Seymour Wallis, setting down the phone.

I lifted my head. For a moment, I thought I heard that breathing again, that soft, rustling breath. But it was only Dan, struggling to keep himself alive. The house itself seemed to have gone back to its ancient secret sleep.

Seymour Wallis knelt slowly and arthritically, down beside me. 'Do you have any idea what that was?' he asked me. 'That noise? All that power? I couldn't believe it. It's never happened before.'

'I don't know. Maybe some kind of pressure release. Maybe you've got some kind of air pressure that sometimes needs to get free. I don't know what the hell it is.'

'Do you still think it's a ghost?'

I glanced at him. 'Do you?'

Seymour Wallis thought for a moment, and then shook his head. 'If it's a ghost, then it's a damned powerful ghost. I never heard of a ghost that could lay people flat.'

He looked down at Dan's pallid face and bit his lip. 'Do you think he's going to be all right?' he asked me.

I didn't know what to say. All I could do was shrug, and kneel in that dingy library and wait for the ambulance.

He was sitting propped up in bed when I went to visit him the following morning. He had a bright green-painted private room overlooking the Bay, and the nurses had filled the room with flowers. He was still pale, and the doctors were keeping him under observation, but he was cheerful enough. I gave him a copy of *Playboy* and that morning's *Examiner*, and I pulled up a tubular steel and canvas chair.

He opened the *Playboy* centre-spread and took a quick and critical look at a brunette with gigantic breasts.

'Just what I need,' he said dryly. 'A short burst of over-adrenalisation.'

'I thought it might work better than paracetamol,' I told him. 'How do you feel?'

He laid the magazine down. 'I'm not sure. I feel okay, in myself. No worse than if someone had knocked me on the head with a baseball bat.'

He paused, and looked at me. The pupils of his eyes, even behind his Clark Kent spectacles, seemed unusually tiny. Maybe it was just the drugs they'd given him. Maybe he was still in a mild state of concussion. But somehow he didn't look quite like the same Dan Machin that I had met for a drink the previous evening. There was something *starey* about him, as if his mouth was saying one thing but his mind was thinking another.

'You don't look yourself,' I told him. 'Is that what you mean?'

'I don't *feel* myself. I don't know what it is, but I feel definitely odd.'

'Did you feel anything strange when that explosion happened?' I asked him.

He shrugged. 'I don't even remember. I remember the breathing, and the way it built up, but after that — well, I just don't recall. I get the feeling I was attacked.'

'*Attacked*? By what?'

'I don't know,' said Dan. 'It's real hard to explain. If I knew how to tell you, I would. But I can't.'

'Do you still think it was a ghost, or a spirit?' I said.

He ran his hand through his crewcut. 'I'm not too sure. It could have been some kind of poltergeist — you know, the kind of spirit that hurls things around. Or it may even have been an earth tremor. Perhaps there's a fault directly under the house.'

'Suddenly you're looking for rational explanations

23

again,' I told him. 'I thought of that, and there's no tremor reported in the paper today. I asked around at the office, too, and nobody else felt one.'

Dan reached over and helped himself to a glass of water.

'In that case I haven't a clue. Maybe it was a ghost. But I always believed that ghosts were pretty harmless, on the whole. You know, they walk around with their heads under their arms, clanking their chains, but that's about it.'

I walked over to the window and looked down at the mid-morning traffic crossing the Golden Gate. The fog had lifted since early on, but a last haze still clung around the uprights of the bridge, smudging them like a watercolour painting.

'I've arranged to go back to the house this evening,' I said. 'I really want to take a good look all around, and see what's going on there. I'm taking Bryan Corder from the engineering department, too. I had a talk with him this morning, and he guessed it might be some kind of katabatic draught.'

Dan Machin, when I turned again, didn't appear to have heard. He was sitting up in bed, staring absent-mindedly across the room, and his lower jaw had dropped open slack.

'Dan?' I said. 'Did you hear that?'

He blinked at me.

'Dan?'

I walked quickly across to the bed, and took his arm. 'Dan, are you okay? You look real ill.'

He licked his lips as if they were very dry. 'Sure,' he said uncertainly. 'I'm okay. I guess I need some rest, that's all. Once I came out of the concussion, I didn't sleep too good. I kept having dreams.'

'Well, why don't you ask the nurse for a sleeping tablet?'

'I don't know. I just kept having these dreams, that was all.'

24

I sat down again and looked at him intently.

'What kind of dreams? Nightmares?'

Dan took off his glasses and rubbed his eyes. 'No, no, they weren't nightmares. I guess they were kind of scarey, but they didn't seem to frighten me. I dreamed about that doorknocker, you know, that one at old man Wallis's house. But it wasn't a doorknocker at all. I dreamed it was hanging on the door, but it was talking to me. Instead of metal, it was made of real hair and real flesh, and it was talking to me, trying to explain something to me, in this kind of quiet, whispery voice.'

'What was it saying? Don't light fires in the forest?'

Dan Machin didn't seem to see the joke. He shook his head seriously, and said: 'It was trying to tell me to go somewhere, to find something, but I couldn't make out what it was. It kept explaining and explaining, and I could never understand. It was something to do with that bear on Mr Wallis's stairs – you know, that little statue of the bear with a face like a woman. But I couldn't get the connection at all.'

I frowned at Dan's white, grave face for a while, but then I grinned and gripped his wrist in a friendly squeeze.

'You know what you're suffering from, Dan old buddy? Post-ghost delusion. It's an occult type of post-natal depression. Have a few days' rest and you won't even remember what you were worried about.'

Dan grimaced. He didn't seem to believe me at all.

'Listen,' I told him, 'we're going to go over that house tonight with a fine-tooth comb, and whatever it was that laid you out, we'll find it. We won't only find it, we'll bring it back alive, and you can keep it in a jar in your laboratory.'

Dan attempted a smile, but it wasn't much of one. 'Okay,' he said quietly. 'Do what you like.'

I sat there for a few more minutes, but Dan didn't seem to be in a conversational mood. So I gave him one more friendly squeeze of the hand, and said, 'I'll drop in tomorrow. Round about the same time.'

Dan nodded, without looking up.

I left him, and went out into the hospital corridor. A doctor was on his way to Dan's room, and he brushed past me as I came out. As he opened the door, I said: 'Doctor?'

The doctor looked at me impatiently. He was a short sandy-haired man with a pointed nose and purple bags under his eyes like the drapes of an old-fashioned theatre curtain. A badge on his lapel said *Doctor James T. Jarvis.*

I nodded towards Dan's room. 'I don't like to intrude. I'm only a friend of Mr Machin's, not a relative or anything. But I just wanted to know if he was okay. I mean, he seemed pretty strange today.'

'What do you mean by strange?'

'Well, you know. Not quite himself.'

Doctor Jarvis shook his head. 'That's not unusual after severe concussion. Give him a few days to get over it.'

'Was that really all it was? Concussion?'

The doctor lifted his clipboard and checked it out. 'That's all. Apart from the asthma.'

'Asthma? What asthma? He doesn't have asthma.'

The doctor stared at me baldly. 'You're trying to tell me my job?'

'Of course not. But I play squash with Dan Machin. He doesn't suffer from asthma. He never has, as far as I know.'

The doctor kept his hand on the handle of Dan's door. 'Well, that's your view, Mr —'

'What's *your* view?' I asked him.

The doctor smirked. 'I'm afraid that's confidential between me and my patient. But if he doesn't have asthma, he certainly does have a severe respiratory complaint. It was exacerbated by the concussion, and he spent three or four hours last night with a breathing-mask on. I don't think I've ever come across a case quite as severe.'

A pretty brunette nurse in a tight white uniform came along the corridor with a tray of hypodermic syringes and bottles of medicine. She said: 'I'm sorry I'm behind, Dr Jarvis. Mrs Walters needed changing again.'

'That's all right,' said Dr Jarvis. 'I've just been having a top-level medical conference with Mr Machin's learned friend here. I'm learning so much, I'm almost reluctant to drag myself away.'

He opened Dan Machin's door wider. But I said: 'Please – just one thing—' and held his arm. He paused and looked down at my hand as if something nasty had just dropped on his sleeve from a passing auk.

'Listen,' he said sourly, 'I don't know what kind of native expertise you have in the field of diagnostic medicine, but I have to continue with your friend's treatment programme right away. So please excuse me.'

'It's just the breathing,' I said. 'It could be important.'

'Of course it's important,' retorted Dr Jarvis sarcastically. 'If our patients don't breathe, we get seriously concerned.'

'Will you hear me out?' I snapped. 'Last night, Dan Machin and I got ourselves involved with something to do with breathing. I need to know what made you think he had an asthma attack.'

'What the hell are you talking about – something to do with breathing? You mean you were sniffing glue, something like that?'

'I can't explain. It wasn't drugs. But it could be real important.'

Dr Jarvis closed the door again, and sighed with exaggerated exasperation. 'All right. If you really need to know, Mr Machin was panting and gasping. Every ninety minutes or so, he began to breathe heavily, finally working up to a real climax of panting. That was all. It was severe, and it was unusual, but there was nothing to suggest that it wasn't a regular attack of asthma.'

'I've just told you. He doesn't have asthma.'

Dr Jarvis lowered his head. 'Will you get out of here?' he said quietly. 'Visiting time is over, and the last thing I need is homespun advice. Okay?'

I was about to say something else, but then I checked myself. I guess I would have been just as irked if somebody had strayed into my office and tried to tell me how to exterminate bugs. I raised my hands in a conciliatory gesture, and said: 'Okay. I get you. I'm sorry.'

The nurse opened the door and went in, while I turned to leave. Dr Jarvis said: 'I really didn't mean to be rude. But I do know what I'm doing. You can come back again at five if you want to. We should know some more by then.'

At that second, there was a shrill and horrified shriek from inside Dan Machin's room. Dr Jarvis looked at me, and I looked at Dr Jarvis, and we both banged the door wide open and pushed our way inside. What I saw right then I couldn't believe. It was there, in front of my eyes, but I couldn't believe it.

The nurse was standing, rigid with shock, by the side of Dan Machin's bed. Dan Machin himself was sitting upright in bed, in his blue-striped hospital pyjamas, as normal and ordinary as you could think of. But his eyes were terrifying. His glasses had fallen to the floor, and his eyes were total blazing red, the eyes of a vicious dog caught in a searchlight at night, or the eyes of a demon. What's more, he was breathing, in and out, in and out, with the deep groaning breaths that we had all heard in Seymour Wallis's house only last night, those heavy endless breaths of a sleeper who could never wake. He was breathing like the house itself, like everything that had chilled and frightened us in the gloomy and ancient rooms, and it seemed as if the hospital room itself went deathly cold with every breath.

Dr Jarvis said: 'My God. My God – *what is it?*'

CHAPTER TWO

One of the sourest things you can ever discover in life is that some of us have it and some of us don't. I guess it's just as well, in a way. If every young boy had the talent to fly airplanes, or drive racing cars, or make love to twenty women in one night, there wouldn't be many volunteers for clearing out backed-up sewers on Folsom. But it's still tough when you discover that it's *you* who doesn't have it, and that instead of living a luxurious life of fun and profit in Beverly Hills, you're going to have to take a nine-to-five job in public works, and cook on a gas ring.

I was born of reasonably well-shod parents in Westchester, New York, but when my father suffered a stroke, I left my mother with her house and her Sealyhams and her insurance money, and I headed west. I think I wanted to be a TV anchor-man, or something grandiose like that, but as it turned out I was lucky to eat. I married a woman who was seven years older than me, mainly because she reminded me of my mother, and I was fortunately broke when she discovered me in bed with a waitress from the Fox commissary, and sued me for divorce. My affair broke up, too, which left me high and dry and stranded, and having to look for the first time in my life at myself, at my own identity, and having to come to terms with what I could achieve and what I couldn't.

My name's John Hyatt, which is one of those names that people think they recall but in actuality don't. I'm thirty-one, and quite tall, with a taste for subdued well-cut sports coats and widish 1950s-style pants in grey. I live alone on the top floor of an apartment block on Townsend Street, with my Trio stereo and my houseplants and my collection of paperbacks with broken spines. I guess I'm happy and content in my work, but haven't you ever gone out at night, somewhere quiet maybe, and looked over the Bay at the lights twinkling all across America, and thought — well, surely there's more to life than *this*?

Don't think I'm lonely, though. I'm not. I date girls and I have quite a few friends, and I even get invited to pool parties and barbecues. Right at the time we went up to Seymour Wallis's house, though, I was going through a kind of stale period — not sure what I wanted out of life or what life wanted out of me. But I guess a lot of people felt like that when President Carter was elected. At least with Nixon you knew what side you were on.

Maybe what happened to Dan Machin helped me get myself together. It was something so weird and so frightening that you couldn't think about anything else. Even after he closed his eyes, just a few seconds after we burst into the room, and sank back against his pillow, I was still shivering with shock and fright, and I could feel a prickling sensation of fear across the palms of my hands.

The nurse said: 'He – He—'

Dr Jarvis stepped cautiously up to Dan Machin's bed, lifted his wrist, and checked his pulse. Then he took a deep breath, and raised his eyelid. I felt myself flinching away, in case the eye was still that fiery red colour, but it wasn't. It had returned to its normal pale grey, and it was plain that Dan was in another state of coma.

Dr Jarvis said: 'Nurse – I want full diagnostic equipment brought up here right away. And page Dr Foley.'

The nurse nodded, and left the room, obviously glad to have something distracting to do. I walked up to Dan Machin's bedside and looked at his pale, fevered face. He didn't look so much like the scientific hick from Kansas any more. The lines around his mouth were too deep, and his pallor was too white. But at least he was breathing normally.

I glanced up at Dr Jarvis. The doctor was jotting notes down on his clipboard, his expression intense and anxious.

I said, quietly, 'Do you know what it was?'

He didn't look up, didn't answer.

'Those red eyes,' I said. 'Do you know what could possibly cause that?'

He stopped writing, and stared at me.

'I want to know just what this breathing business you were involved in last night was all about. Are you absolutely sure it wasn't drugs?'

'Look – I'd tell you if it was. It was all to do with a house on Pilarcitos.'

'A house?'

'That's right. We both work for the sanitation department, and the houseowner invited us to come up to the house to listen to this – *breathing*. He said the house made a breathing noise, and he didn't know what it was.'

Dr Jarvis made another check of Dan Machin's pulse.

'Did you find out what caused it?' he asked. 'The breathing?'

I shook my head. 'All I know is that Dan's been breathing just like it. It's almost as if the breathing in the house has gone into him. As if he's possessed.'

Dr Jarvis set down his clipboard next to Dan Machin's bowl of grapes.

'Are you a fully-fledged member of the nuts' club, or just an associate member?' he asked.

This time, I didn't take offence. 'I know it's difficult to understand,' I said. 'I don't understand it myself. But possession is just what it seems like. I heard the house breathing, and I heard Dan breathing just now, when his eyes were all red. It sounded to me like one and the same.'

32

Dr Jarvis looked down at Dan and shook his head. 'It's obviously psychosomatic,' he said. 'He heard this breathing noise last night, and it frightened him so much that he's begun to identify with it, and breathe in sympathy.'

'Well, maybe. But what made his eyes go like that?'

Dr Jarvis took a deep breath. 'A trick of the light,' he said, evenly.

'A trick of the light? Now, wait a minute!'

Dr Jarvis stared at me, hard. 'You heard,' he snapped. 'A trick of the light.'

'I saw him myself! So did you!'

'I didn't see anything. At least, I didn't see anything that was medically possible. And I think we'd both better remember that before we go shooting our mouths off to anyone else.'

'But the nurse—'

Dr Jarvis waved his hand in deprecation. 'In this hospital, nurses are regarded as home helps in fancy uniforms.'

I leaned over Dan Machin and examined his waxy face, and the way his lips moved and whispered as he slept.

'Doctor, this guy is more than just sick,' I told him. 'This guy has something really, really wrong. Now, what are we going to do about it?'

'There's only one thing we can do. Diagnose his problem and give him recognised medical treatment. We don't undertake exorcisms here, I'm afraid. In any event, I don't believe this is any worse than an advanced case of hyper-suggestibility. Your friend here went up to the house and became hysterical when he thought he heard breathing. It was probably his own.'

'But I heard it, too,' I argued.

'Maybe you did,' said Dr Jarvis off-handedly.

'Doctor—' I said, angry. But Dr Jarvis turned on me before I could tell him how I felt.

'Before you start censuring me for lack of imagination, just remember that I work here,' he snapped. 'Everything I do has to be justified to the hospital board, and if I start raving about demonic possession and eyes that glow red in the dark, I'll suddenly find that my promotion has been shelved for a while and that I only get half the facilities and finance I need.'

He came round the bed and faced me directly. In a low, urgent voice, he said: 'I saw Mr Machin's eyes go red, and so did you. But if we want to do anything about it, anything effective, we'd better keep it quiet. Do you understand?'

I looked at him curiously. 'Are you trying to tell me that you believe he's really possessed?'

'I'm not trying to tell you anything. I don't believe in demons and I don't believe in possession. But I do believe that there's something wrong here that we need to work out for ourselves – without the knowledge of the hospital.'

At that moment, Dan Machin stirred, and groaned. I felt the hair on the back of my neck prickle upright in alarm, but when he spoke, he was obviously back to some kind of normal.

'*John* . . .' he murmured. '*John* . . .'

I leaned over him. His eyes were only open in slits, and his lips were cracked.

'I'm here, Dan. What's wrong? How do you feel?'

'*John* . . .' he whispered. '*Don't let me go* . . .'

I glanced across at Dr Jarvis. 'It's okay, Dan. Nobody's going to let you go.'

Dan Machin weakly raised one of his hands. 'Don't let me go, John. It's the heart, John. *Don't let me go.*'

Dr Jarvis came close, and said 'Your heart? Is your heart feeling bad? Do you have any constriction? Any pain?'

Dan shook his head, just a fraction of an inch each way. 'It's the heart,' he said, in a voice almost too faint to hear. 'It beats and it beats and it beats. It's still beating. It's the heart, John, it's still beating! *Still beating!*'

'Dan—' I whispered urgently. 'Dan, you mustn't work yourself up like this! Dan, for Christ's sake!'

But Dr Jarvis held me back. Dan was already settling back on to his pillow, and his eyes were closing. His breathing became slow and regular again, slow and painful and coarse, and even though it still reminded me of the breathing we'd heard at Seymour Wallis's house, he seemed at last to be catching some rest. I stood up straight, and I felt shaken and tired.

Dr Jarvis said quietly, 'He should be okay now. At least for an hour or two. These attacks seem to come at regular ninety-minute intervals.'

'Can you think of any reason for that?' I asked him.

He shrugged. 'There could be any number of reasons. But ninety minutes is the time-cycle of REM sleep – the kind of sleep in which people have their most vivid dreams.'

I looked down at Dan's drawn and haggard face. 'He mentioned dreams to me earlier on,' I said. 'He had dreams about doorknockers coming to life, and statues moving. That kind of thing. It was all to do with that house we visited last night.'

Dr Jarvis said quietly: 'Are you going back there? To the house?'

'I was planning a trip up there this evening. One of my engineering people thinks that what we heard could have been an unusual kind of downdraught. Why?'

Dr Jarvis kept his eyes fixed on Dan. 'I'd like to come with you, that's why. There's something happening here that I don't understand, and I want to understand it.'

I raised an eyebrow. 'All of a sudden you're not so sure of yourself?'

He grunted. 'Okay. I deserved that. But I'd still like to tag along.'

35

I took one last look at Dan Machin, young and pale as a corpse on his hospital bed, and I said, very softly, 'All right. It's 1551 Pilarcitos. Nine o'clock sharp.'

Dr Jarvis took out a ballpen and made a note of the address. Then, before I left, he said: 'Listen – I'm sorry about the way I spoke to you earlier on. You have to realise that we get a whole lot of friends and relatives who watch too much Hospital Story and think they know it all. I mean, I guess we're kind of defensive.'

I paused, and then nodded. 'Okay. I got you. See you at nine.'

That afternoon, a grey and gloomy line of ragged clouds blew in from the ocean, and threatened rain. I sat at my desk fidgeting and doodling until half past two, and then I took my golf umbrella and went for a walk. My immediate superior, retired naval lieutenant Douglas P. Sharp, would probably choose this very afternoon for a snap inspection, but right now I couldn't have cared less. I was too edgy, too nervous, and too concerned about what was happening to Dan Machin. As I crossed Bryant Street, a few spots of rain the size of dimes speckled the sidewalk, and there was a tense, magnetic feeling in the air.

I guess I knew where I was headed all the time. I turned into Brannan Street, and there it was, The Head Bookstore, a tiny purple-painted shop lit from within by a couple of bare bulbs, and crammed with second-hand paperbacks, Whole Earth Catalogues, posters and junk. I stepped in and jangled the bell, and the bearded young guy behind the counter looked up and said: 'Hi. Looking for anything special?'

'Jane Torresino?'

'Oh, sure. She's out back, unpacking some Castaneda.'

I shuffled past the shelves of Marx, Seale, and Indian incense, and ducked my head through the small

36

door that led to the stockroom. Sure enough, Jane was there, squatting on the floor and arranging Yaqui wisdom into neat stacks.

She didn't look up at first, and I leaned against the doorway and watched her. She was one of those girls who managed to look pretty and bright, no matter how scruffily she dressed. Today she was wearing tight white jeans and a blue T-shirt with a smiling Cheshire Cat printed on it. She was skinny, with very long mid-blonde hair that was crimped into those long crinkly waves that always remind me of Botticelli, and she had a sharp, well-boned face and eyes like that dog in the Tinder Box who had eyes like saucers.

I had first met her at a party out at Daly City to welcome the second coming of Christ, as predicted by an eighteenth-century philosopher. The principal guest of honour, not altogether surprisingly, didn't show. Either the predicted date was wrong, or Christ didn't choose to come again in Daly City. I wouldn't have blamed Him. But whatever went wrong with the second coming, a lot went right between me and Jane. We met, talked, drank too much tokay, and went back to my apartment for lovemaking. I remember sitting up in bed afterwards, drinking the intensely black coffee she had made me, and feeling pleased with what life had dropped so bountifully in my lap.

However, it didn't work out that way. That night, second-coming night, was the first and only time. After that, Jane insisted we were just good friends, and even though we went out for meals together, and took in movies together, the love-light that shone over the spaghetti bolognaise was mine alone, and eventually I accepted our friendship for what it was, and switched the love-light off.

What had developed, though, was a real easy-going relationship that was intimate but never demanding. Sometimes we saw each other three times in one week. Other times, we didn't touch bases for months. Today,

37

when I dropped by with my golf umbrella and my anxieties about Dan Machin, it was the first visit for six or seven weeks.

I said: 'The sanitation department sends you its greetings, and hopes that your plumbing is in full operational order.'

She looked up over her big pink-tinted reading glasses, and smiled. 'John! I haven't seen you in weeks!'

She stood up, and tiptoed carefully towards me through the piles of books. We kissed, a chaste kiss, and then she said: 'You look tired. I hope you're not sleeping with too many women.'

I grinned. 'That should be a problem? I'd rather stay tired.'

'Come outside,' she said. 'We just got a new shipment of books in this morning, and we're pretty cramped. Do you have time for coffee?'

'Sure. I've given myself the afternoon off, for good behaviour.'

We left the bookstore, and went across the street to Prokic's Deli, where I ordered us capuccino and alfalfa sandwiches. For some reason, I had a craze for alfalfa sandwiches. Dan Machin (God preserve him) had said that I was probably metamorphosing into a horse. I was trying to graduate from manure disposal (he said) to manure production.

Jane took a seat by the window, and we watched the rain spatter the street outside. I lit a cigarette, and stirred my coffee, and all the time she watched me without saying a word, as if she knew that I had something to tell her.

'You're looking good,' I told her. 'Time passes, and you grow tastier with each hour.'

She sipped her capuccino. 'You didn't come around to flatter me.'

'No, I didn't. But I don't like to miss an opportunity.'

'You look worried.'

38

'Does it show?'

'Blatantly.'

I sat back on my rush-seated chair, and blew out smoke. Up above Jane's head, on the wall, was a poster demanding the legalisation of pot, but judging from the underlying aroma in Prokic's Deli, nobody was that impressed by the laws anyway. You could have gone in there for nothing more than a glass of milk and a salami sandwich, and come out high.

I said: 'Did you ever in your whole life come across something so consistently weird that you didn't know how to understand it?'

'What do you mean – *consistently* weird?'

'Well, sometimes weird things happen, right? You see someone in the street you thought was dead, or something like that. Just an isolated incident. But when I say *consistently* weird, I mean a situation that starts off weird and keeps on getting weirder.'

She brushed back her hair with her hand. 'Is that what's bugging you?'

'Jane,' I said, in a husky voice, 'it's not bugging me. It's scaring me stupid.'

'Do you want to talk about it? Well – obviously, you do.'

'It sounds pretty ridiculous.'

She shook her head. 'Tell me, all the same. I like pretty ridiculous stories. On the surface, Castaneda is pretty ridiculous.'

Slowly, with a lot of interruptions and explanations, I told her what had happened round at Seymour Wallis's house. The breathing, the burst of energy, the way that Dan Machin had been knocked out. Then I described the incident at the hospital, and Dan's eerie luminous eyes. I also told her about his strange whispered words: *'It's the heart, John, it's still beating!'*

Jane listened to all this with a serious expression. Then she laid one of her long-fingered hands over

39

mine, and said: 'Can I ask you just one thing? You won't be offended?'

I could guess what she was going to say. I said: 'If you think I'm shooting a line, trying to get us involved again, you're wrong. Everything I just told you happened, and it didn't happen last month or last year. It happened here in San Francisco last night, and it happened here in San Francisco this morning. It's real, Jane, I swear it.'

She reached over and took one of my cigarettes. I held out my own and she lit it from the glowing tip. Then she said: 'It sounds like this thing – this ghost or whatever it is – it sounds like it's actually possessed him. It's like *The Exorcist* or something.'

'That's what I thought. But I felt so dumb trying to suggest it. I mean, for Christ's sake, these things just don't happen.'

'Maybe they do. Just because they never happened to anyone we know, that doesn't mean they don't happen.'

I crushed out my cigarette and sighed. 'I saw it with my own eyes, and I still don't believe it. He was sitting up there in bed, and I tell you, Jane, his eyes were *alight*. He's just an ordinary young guy who works for the city and still wears crewcuts, and he looked like a devil.'

Jane said: 'What can I do?'

I looked out of the deli window at the shoppers sheltering from the rain. The sky was a curious gun-metal green, and the clouds were moving fast across the rooftops of Brannan Street. Early that morning, before I went to see Dan Machin, I had telephoned Seymour Wallis to make an appointment to view the house again, and he had asked me that very same question. '*What can I do? For land's sakes, tell me, what can I do?*'

I said to Jane: 'I don't really know. But maybe you could come along tonight when we look over the house.

You know something about the occult, don't you? Spirits and ghosts and all that kind of thing. I'd like you to take a look at old man Wallis's front door-knocker, and some of the stuff inside. Maybe there's some kind of clue there. I don't know.'

'Why me?' she asked calmly. 'Surely there are better occult experts than me. I only sell books about it.'

'You read them as well as sell them, don't you?'

'Sure, but—'

I held her hand. 'Please, Jane, just do me a favour and come along. It's nine o'clock tonight, on Pilarcitos Street. I don't know why I need you along, but I feel that I do. I really feel it. Will you come?'

Jane touched her face with her fingertips as if gently reassuring herself that she existed, and that she was still twenty-six years old, and that she hadn't changed into anyone else overnight. Then she said: 'All right, John, if you really want me to. As long as it's not a line.'

I shook my head. 'Can you imagine a couple called John and Jane? It would never work out.'

She smiled. 'Just be thankful your name isn't Doe.'

I went around a little early to Pilarcitos Street that night. Because of the overcast weather, it had grown dark much sooner than usual, and the heavy-browed house was clotted with shadows and draped with rain. As I stood in the street outside, I heard its gutters gurgling with water, and I could see the scaley shine of its wet roof. In this kind of weather, in this kind of gloom, number 1551 seemed to draw in on itself, brooding and uncomfortable in the rainswept city.

I had called briefly at the hospital again, but the nurse had told me that Dan Machin was still sleeping, and that there was no change. Dr Jarvis had been away on a break, so I hadn't been able to discuss Dan's progress with him any further. Still, with any luck, he

41

would turn up tonight, and see what had happened for himself.

Across the Bay, lightning walked on awkward stilts, and I could hear the faraway mumbling of thunder. The way the wind was blowing, the storm would move across the city in half an hour, and pass right overhead.

I opened the gate and climbed the steps to the front door. In the dense shadows, I could just make out the shape of the doorknocker, with its grinning wolfish face. Maybe I was just nervous, and thinking too much about Dan Machin's dream, but that doorknocker almost seemed to open its eyes and watch me as I came nearer. I was half-expecting it to start talking and whispering, the way Dan Machin had imagined it.

Reluctantly, I put my hand out to touch the knocker and bang on the door. The moment I grasped it, I recoiled, because for one split-second, one irrational lurching instant, *it seemed as if I had touched bristles instead of bronze, fur instead of metal.* But I held it again, and I knew that I was imagining things. The doorknocker was grotesque, and its face was wild and malevolent, but it was nothing but cast metal, and when I banged on the door, it made a loud, heavy knock that echoed flatly inside the house.

I waited, listening to the soft rustle of the rain, and the swish of passing cars on Mission Street. Thunder grumbled again, and there was more lightning, closer this time. Inside the house, I heard a door open and shut, and footsteps coming up to the door.

The bolts and the chains rattled, and Seymour Wallis looked around the gap. He said: 'It's you. You're early.'

I said: 'I wanted to talk before the others arrived. Can I come in?'

'Very well,' he said, and opened the solid, groaning door. I stepped into the musty hall. It was just as ancient and suffocating as it had felt yesterday, and

42

even though their frames had been cracked and broken by last night's burst of power, the doleful pictures of Mount Taylor and Cabezon Peak still hung on the dingy wallpaper.

I went across to the strange figure of the bear that stood on the newel post of the banisters. I hadn't looked at it particularly closely last night, but now I could see that the woman's face on it was quite beautiful – serene and composed, with her eyes closed. I said to Seymour Wallis: 'This is a real odd piece of sculpture.'

Seymour Wallis was busy bolting the door. He looked older and stiffer tonight, in a loose grey cardigan with unravelled sleeves, and baggy grey pants. He smelled of whisky.

He watched me run my hand down the bear's bronze back.

'I found it,' he said. 'That was years ago, when I was working over at Fremont. We were building a traffic bridge for the park, and we dug it up. I've had it with me ever since. It didn't come with the house.'

'Dan Machin had a dream about it this morning,' I told him.

'Really? I can't think of any special reason why he should. It's just an old piece of sculpture. I don't even know how old. What would you think? A hundred, two hundred years?'

I peered closely at the bear-woman's passive face. I don't know why, but the whole idea of a bear with a woman's face made me feel uneasy and creepy. I guess it was just the whole atmosphere of Seymour Wallis's house. But who had sculpted such an odd figure? Did it mean anything? Was it symbolic? The only certainty was that it hadn't been modelled on life. At least, I damned well hoped not.

I shook my head. 'I'm not an expert. All I know is sanitation.'

43

'Is your friend coming? The engineer?' asked Seymour Wallis, leading me through to his study.

'He said so. And there's a doctor, too, if you don't mind, and a friend of mine who runs an occult bookstore on Brannan.'

'A doctor?'

'Yes, the one who's treating Dan Machin. We had a bit of an incident there today.'

Seymour Wallis went across to his desk and unsteadily poured two large glasses of Scotch. 'Incident?' he asked, with his back turned.

'It's hard to describe. But I get the feeling that whatever we heard in here last night has really got Dan upset. He's even been breathing in a similar kind of way. The doctors thought he had asthma at first.'

Seymour Wallis turned around, a glass of amber Scotch in each hand, and his face in the green-shaded light of his desklamp was strained and almost ghastly. 'Do you mean to tell me that your friend has been breathing the same way as *my* breathing – *my* breathing here?'

He was so intense that I almost felt embarrassed. 'Well, that's right. Dr Jarvis thought it might be psychosomatic. You know, self-induced. It sometimes happens after heavy concussion.'

Seymour Wallis gave me my whisky and then sat down. He looked so troubled and thoughtful that I couldn't help saying: 'What's wrong? You look like you lost a dollar and found a nickel.'

'It's the breathing,' he said. 'It's *gone*.'

'Gone? How do you know?'

'I don't know. Not exactly. Not for sure. But I didn't hear it at all last night, and I haven't heard it at all today. Apart from that – well, I *sense* it's gone.'

I sat on the edge of his desk and sipped my Scotch. The whisky was nine years old, and it tasted mature and mellow, but it didn't mix too well with half-digested alfalfa sandwich, and I began to think that I ought to have had something solid to eat before I went out ghost-hunting. I burped quietly into my fist, while Seymour Wallis fidgeted and twitched and looked even more unhappy.

'You think that the breathing might have somehow transferred itself out of the house and into Dan?' I asked him.

He didn't look up, but he shrugged, and twitched some more. 'It's the kind of thing that enters your mind, isn't it? I mean, if ghosts are really capable of haunting a *place*, why shouldn't they haunt a *person*? Who's to say what they can do, and what they can't do? I don't know, Mr Hyatt. The whole damned thing's a mystery to me, and I'm tired of it.'

For a while, we sat in silence. Seymour Wallis's study was as close and airless as ever, and I almost felt as if we were sitting in some small dingy cavern at the bottom of a mine, buried under countless tons of rock. The house on Pilarcitos gave you that kind of a sensation – as if it was bearing down on you with the weary weight of hundreds of years of suffering and patience. It wasn't a feeling I particularly cared for. In fact, it made me feel depressed and edgy.

'You said something about the park,' I reminded Seymour Wallis. 'When you first came to see me, you mentioned the park. I didn't know what you meant.'

'The park? Did I?'

'Well, it sounded like it.'

'I expect I did. Ever since I worked on that damned park I've had one lousy piece of luck after another.'

'That was the park at Fremont? Where you found the bear-lady?'

He nodded. 'It should have been the easiest piece of cantilever bridging ever. It was only a pedestrian walkover, nothing fancy. I must have built twenty or thirty of them for various city facilities all the way down the coast. But this one was a real bitch. The foundations collapsed six or seven times. Three wet-

45

backs got themselves seriously hurt. One was blinded. And nobody could ever agree on how to site the bridge or handle it. The arguments I had with city hall were insane. It took four months to put up a bridge that should have been up in four days, and of course it didn't do my reputation any good. I can tell you something, Mr Hyatt, ever since Fremont I've felt dogged.'

I lifted my whisky glass and circled it around to take in the study and the house. 'And this—' I said, 'all this breathing and everything – you thought it could have been part of your bad luck?'

Seymour Wallis sighed. 'I don't know. It was just a thought. Sometimes I wonder if I'm going crazy.'

Just then, the doorknocker banged twice. I said: 'I'll answer it,' and I went out into the shadowy hallway to open the front door. As I pulled back the bolts and the chains, I couldn't help glancing over at the bear-lady on the banisters. In the dark, she seemed larger than she had with the light on, and shaggier, as if the shadows that clung around her had grown into hair. And all around me, on every wall, were these dim and uninspiring views of Mount Taylor and Cabezon Peak, engravings and etchings and aquatints, but all apparently executed in the dullest weather. All I knew about either mountain was that they were in New Mexico someplace, which made it strange that every one of these dozens of views should have been drawn on overcast days.

The doorknocker banged again, and I snapped: 'All right! All right! I can hear you!'

I pulled the door open, and there was Dr Jarvis, standing in the porch with Jane Torresino. It was still raining and thundering out, but after being shut up in Seymour Wallis's study, the night air was cool and refreshing. Across the street, I could see Bryan Corder, his head bent against the sloping rain, his shoulders hunched as he walked quickly towards us.

46

'You two seem to have met,' I said to Jane and Dr Jarvis as I ushered them inside.

'It was just one of those chance encounters across a gloomy porch,' said Jane.

Bryan came running up the steps, shaking rain from his hair like a wet dog. He was a solid, bluff man of almost forty, with a broad, dependable face that always reminded me of a worldly Pat Boone, if such a thing could exist. He gripped my arm and said: 'Hi, John. Almost couldn't make it. How's things?'

'Spooky,' I said, and meant it. And before I closed the front door, I couldn't stop myself from taking a quick look at the doorknocker, just to see if it was still bronze, still inanimate, and still as fiercely ugly as ever. '

I led everyone through to Seymour Wallis's study, and introduced them. Seymour Wallis was polite but distracted, as if we were nothing more unusual than realtors who had come to value his property. He shook hands and offered whisky, and pulled up chairs, but then he sat back at his desk and stared at the threadbare carpet and said almost nothing.

Dr Jarvis looked less medical in a navy-blue sports coat and slacks. He was sharp, short and gingery, and I was beginning to like him. He took a swallow of whisky, coughed, and then said: 'Your friend hasn't made much improvement I'm afraid. He hasn't had any more of those attacks, but he still has respiration problems, and we can't wake him out of his coma. We're running some EKGs and EEGs later tonight to see if there's any sign of brain damage.'

'Brain damage? But all he did was fall off a chair.'

'I've known people die falling off chairs.'

Jane said: 'Do you still think it's concussion? What about his eyes?'

Dr Jarvis turned in his seat. 'If I thought it was concussion and nothing else, I wouldn't be here. But

47

it seems like there's something else involved, and right now I don't have a dog's idea what.'

Bryan Corder said: 'Was this the room where it happened? The breathing and everything?'

'Sure.'

Bryan stood up and walked around the perimeter of the study, touching the walls here and there and peering into the fireplace. Every now and then he tapped the plaster with his knuckles to feel how solid it was. After a while, he stood back in the centre of the room, and he looked puzzled.

'The door was closed?' he asked me.

'Doors and windows.'

He shook his head slowly. 'That's real strange.'

'What's strange?'

'Well, normally, when you get any kind of pressure build-up because of draughts or air currents, the fireplace is free and the chimney is unblocked. But you can put your hand here in the fireplace and feel for yourself. There's no downdraught here. The chimney is all blocked up.'

I went across and knelt on the faded Indian carpet in front of the fire. It was one of those narrow Victorian study fires, with a decorated steel hood and a fireclay grate. I craned my head around and stared up into the cold, sooty-smelling darkness, and Bryan Corder was right. There was no draught, no breath of wind. Usually, when you look up a chimney-stack, you can hear the sounds of the night echoing down the shaft, but this chimney was silent.

'Mr Wallis,' said Bryan, 'do you know for certain that this chimney is blocked? Did someone have it bricked up?'

Seymour Wallis was watching us with a frown on his face. 'That chimney isn't blocked. I had a fire in there just a few days ago. I was burning some old papers I wanted to get rid of.'

Bryan took another look up the chimney. 'Well, Mr

48

Wallis, even if it wasn't blocked then, it's sure blocked now. It's possible that the blockage may have had something to do with the noises you heard. Do you mind if I take a look upstairs?'

'Be my guest,' said Seymour Wallis. 'I'll stay here, if you don't mind. I've had enough of this for one day.'

The four of us trooped out into the hallway and switched on the dim light that illuminated the stairs. It was dim because of its olive-and-yellow glass shade, which was thick with dust and spider-webs. Everything in Seymour Wallis's house seemed to be musty and faded and covered with dust, but then I suppose that's what he called character. I was beginning to feel like a dedicated supporter of Formica and plastic and tacky modern building.

As Bryan mounted the first stair, Jane suddenly noticed the bronze statuette of the bear-lady.

'*That's* unusual,' she said. 'Did it come with the house?'

'No. Seymour Wallis dug it up in Fremont someplace when he was working on a bridge. He builds bridges, or at least he used to.'

Jane touched the serene face of the statuette as if she expected it to open its eyes at any moment.

'It reminds me of something,' she said softly. 'It gives me the strangest feeling. It's almost like I've seen it before, but I can't have done.'

She paused for a second or two, her hand touching the statuette's head, and then she looked up and said: 'I can't remember. Perhaps I'll think of it later. Shall we get on?'

With Bryan leading the way, we trod as quietly as we could up the old, squeaking staircase. There were two flights of about ten stairs each, and then we found ourselves on a long landing, illuminated by another dingy glass shade, and carpeted in dusty red. It didn't look as if the house had been decorated for twenty or

49

thirty years, and all around was that pervasive silence and that mouldering smell of damp.

'The study chimney must come up through this room,' said Bryan Corder, and led us across to a bedroom door that was set at an angle on the opposite side of the landing. He turned the brass handle, and opened it up.

The bedroom was small and cold. It had a mean sash window which overlooked the yard, where dark wet trees rose and fell in the wind and the rain. There was pale blue wallpaper on the walls, stained brown with damp, and the only furniture was a cheap varnished wardrobe and a shabby iron bed. The floor was covered with old-fashioned linoleum that must have been green many years ago.

Bryan went across to the fireplace, which was similar to the fireplace in Seymour Wallis's study, except that someone had painted it cream. He knelt down beside it, and listened, and the rest of us stood there and watched him.

'What can you hear?' I asked him. 'Is it still blocked?'

'I think so,' he said, straining his eyes to see up into the darkness. 'I just need to see round the ledge and I might be able to—'

He shifted himself nearer, leaned against the tiled surround, and cautiously poked his head up under the hood of the fire.

Dr Jarvis laughed, but it was a nervous kind of a laugh. 'Can you see anything?' he asked.

'I'm not sure,' answered Bryan Corder, in a muffled voice. 'There's a different kind of resonance here. Some sort of thudding noise. I'm not sure if it's echoing down the chimney or if it's vibrating through the whole house.'

'We can't hear anything out here,' I told him.

'Hang on,' he said, and shifted himself so that his whole head disappeared up the chimney.

'I hope you don't mind washing your hair before you come back to civilisation,' said Jane.

'Oh, I've done worse than this,' said Bryan. 'Sewers are worse than chimneys any day of the week.'

'Can you hear anything now?' I asked him, kneeling down on the floor next to the fireplace.

'Ssshh!' ordered Bryan. 'There's some kind of noise building up now. The same kind of thudding.'

'I still don't hear it,' I told him.

'It's quite clear inside here. There it goes. Thud – thud – thud – thud – thud. It's almost like a heart beating. *Thud – thud – thud* – why don't you time it? Do you have a second hand on your watch?'

'I'll time it,' put in Dr Jarvis. 'If it's a pulse, then it's my line of country.'

'Okay,' said Bryan, with a cough. 'I'm starting now.'

He kept his head right up inside the hood of the chimney, and groped his hand around until he could touch Dr Jarvis's knee. Then, as whatever he could hear began to thud in his ears, he beat out the time, and Dr Jarvis checked it on his watch.

'It's not a pulse,' commented Dr Jarvis, after a couple of minutes. 'Not a human pulse, anyway.'

'Do you have enough?' coughed Bryan. 'I'm getting kind of claustrophobic up here.'

'More like Santa Claustrophobic,' joked Jane. 'Will you bring a sack of toys out with you?'

'Ah, nuts,' said Bryan, and started to shift himself out.

Abruptly, horribly, he screamed. I'd never heard a man scream like that before, and for a second I couldn't think what it was. But then he shouted: '*Get me out! Get me out! For God's sake, get me out!*' and I knew something terrible was happening, and it was happening to him.

Dr Jarvis seized one of Bryan's legs, and yelled: 'Pull! Pull him out of there!'

Freezing with fear, I grabbed hold of the other leg, and together we tried to tug him out. But even though it was only his head that was up inside the chimney, he seemed to be stuck fast, and he was shrieking and crying and his whole body was jerking in agonised spasms.

'*Get me out! Get me out! Oh God, oh God, get me out!*' he gibbered.

Dr Jarvis let go of Bryan's leg and tried to see what was happening up inside the chimney hood. But Bryan was flailing around and shrieking so much that it was impossible to understand what was going on. Dr Jarvis snapped: 'Bryan! Bryan, listen! Don't panic! Keep still or you'll hurt yourself!'

He turned to me, and said: 'He must have gotten his head caught somehow. For Christ's sake try to hold him still.'

We both got a grip on the fireplace hood, and tried to wrench it away from the tiles, but it was cemented by years of dust and rust, and there was no getting it loose. Bryan was still screaming, but then suddenly he stopped, his body slumped in the fireplace.

'Oh God,' said Dr Jarvis. 'Look.'

From under the fireplace hood, soaking Bryan's collar and tie, came a slow stain of bright red blood. Jane, standing right behind us, retched. There was far too much blood for a minor cut or a graze. It dribbled down Bryan's shirt and over our hands, and then it began to creep along the cracks in between the tiles on the fireplace floor.

'Carefully now,' instructed Dr Jarvis. 'Pull him down carefully.'

Little by little, we shifted Bryan's body downwards. It seemed as if his head was still firmly caught at first, but then there was a sickening give of flesh, and he came completely out of the chimney, collapsing in the grate.

I stared at his head in rising horror. I could hardly

bear to look, but then I couldn't look away, either. His whole head had been stripped of flesh, and all that was left was his bare skull, with only a few raw shreds of meat and a few sparse tufts of hair remaining. Even his eyes had gone from their sockets, leaving nothing but glutinous bone.

Jane, her voice trembling with nausea, said: 'Oh, John. Oh my God, what's happened?'

Dr Jarvis carefully laid Bryan's body down. The skull made a sickening bone-like sound on the tiles. Dr Jarvis's face was as white and shocked as mine must have been.

'I've never seen anything like it,' he whispered. 'Never.'

I looked up towards the dark maw of the old Victorian fireplace. 'What I want to know is *what did it*. For Christ's sake, doctor – what's up there?'

Dr Jarvis shook his head mutely. Neither of us was prepared to take a look. Whatever it was that had ripped the flesh off Bryan Corder's head – whether it was a freak accident or some kind of malevolent animal – neither of us wanted to face it.

'Jane,' said Dr Jarvis, taking a card out of his breast pocket. 'This is the number of the Elmwood Foundation Hospital, where I work. Will you call Dr Speedwell and tell him what's happened. Tell him I'm here. And ask him to get an ambulance around here as fast as he can.'

'What about the police?' I said. 'We can't just—'

Dr Jarvis glanced cautiously across at the fireplace. 'I don't know. Do you think they'll believe us?'

'For Christ's sake, if there's anything up that chimney that rips people apart, I'm not going to go up there and look for myself. And neither are you.'

Dr Jarvis nodded. 'Okay,' he said to Jane. 'Dial the police as well.'

Jane was just about to leave the room when there was a soft knock at the door. Seymour Wallis's voice said: 'Are you all right in there? I thought I heard shouting.'

I went across to the door and opened it. Seymour Wallis stood there pale and anxious, and he must have seen from the look on my face that something had gone wrong.

'There's been an accident,' I told him. 'It's probably better if you don't come in.'

'Is someone hurt?' he asked, trying to look around my shoulder.

I said: 'Yes. Brian Corder is badly injured. But please – I suggest you don't look. It's pretty awful.'

Seymour Wallis pushed me aside. 'It's my house, Mr Hyatt. I want to know what goes on here.'

Well, I guess he was right. But when he walked into the bedroom and saw Bryan's body lying there, its skull grinning up at the ceiling, he froze, and he could neither speak nor move.

Dr Jarvis looked up. 'Get that ambulance,' he told Jane tersely. 'The sooner we find out what happened here the better.'

Seymour Wallis sat down heavily on the narrow bed, his hands in his lap, and stared at Bryan in unabating horror.

'I'm sorry, Mr Wallis,' said Dr Jarvis. 'He thought he heard some kind of noise in the chimney, and he poked his head up there to see what it was.'

Seymour Wallis opened his mouth, said nothing, and then closed it again.

'We had the feeling that something or someone attacked him,' I explained. 'When his head was up there, and we were trying to tug him out it was just like someone equally powerful was pulling him back.'

Almost furtively, Seymour Wallis turned his eyes towards the dark and empty fireplace. 'I don't understand,' he said hoarsely. 'What are you trying to say?'

Dr Jarvis stood up. There was nothing more he could do for Bryan Corder now, except try to discover what had killed him. He said seriously: 'Either he got his head caught in some kind of freak accident, Mr Wallis, or else there's a creature up there, or a man, who tore the flesh off Bryan Corder's head in some sort of psychopathic attack.'

'Up the chimney? Up the chimney of my house?'

'I'm afraid it looks that way.'

'But this is insane! What the hell lives up a chimney and tears people apart like that?'

Dr Jarvis glanced down at Bryan Corder's body, and then back at Seymour Wallis. 'That, Mr Wallis, is exactly what we have to find out.'

Seymour Wallis thought about this for a while, and then he rubbed his face in his hands. 'It makes no sense, any of this. First breathing and now this. You realise I'll have to sell this place.'

'You shouldn't lose your money,' I said, trying to be helpful. 'These old mansions are pretty much top-of-the-market these days.'

He shook his head tiredly. 'It's not the money I'm worried about. I just want someplace to live where things like this don't happen. I want some peace, for Christ's sake. That poor man.'

'Well, as long as the ghost doesn't follow you, I guess that moving away might turn out to be the best solution,' I told him.

Seymour Wallis stared at me in shock and annoyance. 'It's up the damned chimney!' he snapped. 'It just killed your colleague, and you're trying to talk about it like it isn't even important. It's up there, and it's hiding, and who are you to say that it won't come out at night and strangle me when I'm lying in bed?'

'Mr Wallis,' I said, 'I'm not Rod Serling.'

'I suppose you called the police,' retorted Mr Wallis, without even looking at me.

Dr Jarvis nodded. 'They should be here soon.'

At that moment, Jane came back upstairs, and said: 'Two or three minutes. They had a car in the neighbourhood. I called the sanitorium, too, and they're sending an ambulance right down.'

'Thanks, Jane,' I told her.

Seymour Wallis said: 'I have a gun, you know. It's only my old wartime Colt. We could fire it up the chimney, and then whatever it was wouldn't stand a chance.'

Dr Jarvis came over and said: 'Do you mind if I borrow a pillow-slip? I just want something to cover Mr Corder's head.'

'Sure. Take it off that pillow right there. It's a pretty gruesome sight. Can you think what the hell did it? Is there any kind of bird that does that? Maybe some kind of raven got trapped down the chimney, or maybe a chimpanzee.'

'A chimpanzee?' I queried.

Dr Jarvis said: 'It's not so far-fetched. There's an Edgar Allan Poe story about an ape who murders a girl and stuffs her up the chimney.'

'Sure — but whatever did this is real fierce. It looks more like a cat or a rat to me. Maybe it's starved from being trapped up the chimney-stack so long.'

Seymour Wallis got up off the bed. 'I'm getting my gun,' he said. 'If that thing comes out of here, I'm not standing here unprotected.'

Outside in the street, a siren wailed. Jane squeezed my arm, and said: 'They're here. Thank God for that.'

There was a heavy knocking at the front door, and Seymour Wallis went down to answer it. Then we heard feet clattering up the stairs, and two cops in rain-speckled shirts and caps came into the small bedroom, and knelt down by the body of Bryan Corder without looking at any of the rest of us, as if Bryan was their habitually-drunken brother they were coming to take home.

'What's this pillow-slip over his head?' asked one of the cops, a gum-chewing Italian with a drooping moustache. He didn't make any attempt to touch the pillow-slip, or move the body. Like most West Coast cops, he had a sense of suspicion that was highly-attuned, and one of the first rules he'd ever had to learn was *don't touch anything until you know what it is.*

I said: 'We were surveying the house. There were some noises here that Mr Wallis found a nuisance. My name's John Hyatt and I work for the sanitation department. This is Jane Torresino and this is Dr Jarvis from Elmwood.'

The cop glanced over at his buddy, a young Irishman with pale grey eyes and a freckly face that was almost more freckle than face. He said: 'How come the sanitation department is working so late?'

'Well,' I said, 'this came outside the usual type of sanitary investigation. This is what you might call personal.'

'How about you, doctor?'

Dr Jarvis gave a brief, twitchy smile. 'It's the same for me. I'm moonlighting, I guess.'

'So what happened?'

I coughed, and explained. 'This gentleman, Bryan Corder, he's an engineer from the same department as me. He's a specialist in house structure, and he usually works on slum clearance, that kind of thing. We brought him along because he knows about odd noises, and draughts, and everything to do with wood-boring beetle and dry-rot.'

The policeman continued to stare at me placidly, but still made no move to lift the pillow-slip from Bryan's head.

'He thought he heard a thudding noise in the chimney,' I said, almost whispering. 'He put his head up there to hear it better, and – well, that's the result. Something seemed to attack him. We didn't see what.'

The cop looked at his buddy, shrugged, and lifted off the pillow-slip.

A white-and-gold Cadillac ambulance whooped away

57

through the easing rain, bearing Bryan Corder's body off to the Elmwood Foundation Hospital. I stood on the front step of 1551 and watched it go, and beside me the police lieutenant who had arrived to deal with the case lit up a cigarette. He was a tall laconic man with a wet hat and a hawkish nose, and a manner of questioning that was courteous and quiet. He had introduced himself as Lieutenant Stroud, and produced his badge like a conjuror producing a paper flower out of thin air.

'Well,' he said gently, blowing out smoke. 'This hasn't been your evening, Mr Hyatt.'

I coughed. 'You can say that again.'

Lieutenant Stroud smoked for a while, and then he said: 'Did you know Mr Corder well?'

'We worked in the same department. I went round to his place for supper one night. Moira's a real dab hand at pecan cookies.'

'Pecan cookies, huh? Yes, they're a weakness of mine. I expect Mrs Corder will take this very hard.'

'I'm sure she will. She's a nice woman.'

An upstairs window rattled open, and one of the policemen leaned his head out and called: 'Lieutenant?'

Stroud stepped back a pace, looked upwards, and said: 'What is it, officer? Have you found anything?'

'We've had half of that goddamned chimney-breast out, sir, and there's no sign of nothing. Just dried blood.'

'No signs of rats or birds? No secret passages?'

'Not a thing, sir. Do you want us to keep on searching?'

'Just for a while, officer.'

The window rattled shut, and Lieutenant Stroud turned back to the street. The clouds had all passed overhead now, and stars were beginning to sparkle in the clear night sky. Down on Mission, the traffic booped and beeped, and out of an upper window

58

across the street came the sounds of the *Hallelujah Chorus*.

'You a religious man, Mr Hyatt?' asked Lieutenant Stroud.

'On and off,' I said cautiously. 'More off than on. I think I'm more superstitious than religious.'

'Then what you said about breathing and heartbeats in the house . . . you really believe it?'

I looked at him carefully across the porch. His eyes were glistening and perceptive. I said; 'Unh-hunh,' and shook my head.

Lieutenant Stroud said: 'What I have to consider is a number of alternatives. Either Mr Corder died in a particularly bizarre and unlikely accident; or else he was attacked by an animal or bird that was trapped in the chimney; or else he was attacked by an unknown man or woman who somehow hid him or herself in the chimney; or else he was attacked and killed by you and your friends.'

I stared down at the wet paving-stones, and nodded. 'I realise that.'

'Of course, there is the possibility that some supernatural event occurred, somehow connected with your occult investigations here.'

I glanced up. 'You consider that's a possibility?'

Lieutenant Stroud smiled. 'Just because I'm a detective, that doesn't mean I'm totally impervious to what goes on in this world. And *out* of this world, too. One of my hobbies is science-fiction.'

I didn't know what to say for a while. Maybe this tall, polite man was trying to win my confidence, trying to inveigle me into saying that Dr Jarvis and Jane and I had sacrificed Bryan Corder at some illicit black magic ceremony. His face, though, gave nothing away. It was intelligent but impassive. He was the first cultured-sounding policeman I'd ever met, and I wasn't sure I liked the experience.

I turned back to the door, and indicated the wolfish doorknocker with a nod of my head.

'What do you make of that?' I asked him.

He raised an eyebrow. 'I noticed it when I first came in. It does look a little sinister, doesn't it?'

'My friend thought it looked like a werewolf.'

Lieutenant Stroud stepped back. 'Well, I wouldn't know about that, Mr Hyatt. I might like science-fiction, but I'm not an expert on vampires and demons and all that kind of thing. And in any case, my superiors prefer flesh-and-blood killers they can lock in cages. I always look for the natural answer before I think of the supernatural one.'

'Well, you're a policeman.'

The front door opened a little wider, and Dr Jarvis stepped out. He was pale, and he looked as if he'd spent the evening giving blood. He said: 'John – can I just have a private word with you?'

Lieutenant Stroud nodded his assent, and I said: 'Excuse me.' Dr Jarvis led me into the hallway and, next to the statue of the bear-lady, he turned around and faced me with an expression that was even more shocked and grave than before.

I said, 'What's wrong? You look awful.'

He took out his handkerchief and patted the sweat from his forehead. 'I couldn't tell the lieutenant about this. He's going to find out sooner or later in any case. But I'd rather he heard it from someone else – someone who's actually there.'

Just then, Jane came down the stairs. She said: 'They've almost demolished the whole bedroom and they haven't found anything. John – can we leave now? I'd give my gold lamé tights for a gin-and-orange-juice.'

Dr Jarvis said: 'Jane – you might as well hear this, too. You were there when it happened. At least you'll believe it.'

Jane asked, frowning: 'What is it? Is anything wrong?'

I took the opportunity of putting my arm around her, and giving her a protective, masculine squeeze. It's strange how a man's sexual instincts go on working, even in moments of crisis and horror. But my ardour wasn't exactly firing on all eight. And when Dr Jarvis told us his news, my hand dropped to my side, and I stood there frightened and wooden and coldly convinced that what was happening in Seymour Wallis's house was growing darker and more powerful and more malevolent with every hour that passed.

Dr Jarvis said: 'I had a call from Elmwood. They took your friend Bryan Corder straight into the morgue, and began a post-mortem.'

'Did they find out how he died?' asked Jane.

Dr Jarvis swallowed uncomfortably. 'They didn't find out because they couldn't. In spite of what happened to his head, he's still clinically alive.'

My mouth fell open like a idiot. 'Still *alive*? He can't be!'

'I'm afraid that he is. At least, the surgeons believe he is. You see, his heart's still beating. They listened to his chest, and it's beating loud and clear at twenty-four beats to the minute.'

'Twenty-four?' asked Jane. 'That's not—'

'Not human,' put in Dr Jarvis. 'Not human at all. But the fact remains that his heart's beating and while it's beating they're going to try to *keep* it beating.'

It was then – right then – that I was sure I heard someone or something whispering. It may have been one of the policemen upstairs. It may have been an automobile's tyres on the wet street. But when I turned around instinctively to see who it was, I realised I was standing nearer to that damned hideous doorknocker than anything else, that doorknocker that said '*Return*.'

CHAPTER THREE

I tossed and turned on my sweaty, wrinkled bed for a couple of hours, and then at five in the morning I got up and made myself a mug of strong black coffee and topped it up with Calvados. It's what the old men of Normandy drink to brace themselves on cold December days. I stood by the window looking down over the wan early-morning street, and I felt as if the whole course of my life had subtly and strangely changed, like taking a wrong turning in a city you think you know, and finding yourself in an unfamiliar neighbourhood where the buildings are dark and tatty, and the people unfriendly and unsociable.

By six, I couldn't restrain my curiosity any longer, and I called Elmwood Foundation Hospital to see if Dr Jarvis was there. A bland receptionist told me that Dr Jarvis was taking no calls, but she made a note of my number and promised to have him call me back.

I sat back on my floral Chesterfield and sipped more coffee. I'd been thinking all night about everything that had happened at 1551 Pilarcitos, and yet I still couldn't understand what was going on. One thing was certain, though. Whatever force or influence was haunting that house, it wasn't anything friendly. I really hesitated to use the word 'ghost', even when I was thinking about it in the privacy of my own apartment, but what the hell else could it be?

There were so many odd sides to this situation, and none of them seemed to have anything to do with anything else. I had the feeling that Seymour Wallis was more important than he knew himself. After all, it was *his* house, and he'd been the first to hear all that breathing, and he'd said himself that bad luck had been dogging him around ever since he worked at that park on Fremont. He still had that odd souvenir of Fremont, too – the bear-lady on the banisters.

Above everything, though, I had the strongest feeling that whatever was going on wasn't erratic or accidental. It was like the opening of a chess game, when the moves appear casual and unrelated, but are all part of a deliberate stratagem. The question – *whose* stratagem? And why?

How Bryan Corder's terrible accident and Dan Machin's eerie concussion could possibly be connected, though, I couldn't understand. I didn't want to think about it too deeply, either, because I kept getting ghastly mental pictures of Bryan's fleshless head, and the thought that he might still be alive made the creeps twenty times creepier. I didn't have a strong stomach at the best of times. I was always the squeamish person who couldn't eat the squid in the seafood platter, and ordered his eggs well-boiled.

The telephone rang, and gave me a chill prickly feeling up the back of my scalp. I picked it up and said: 'John Hyatt here. Who is this?'

'John? It's Jane.'

I took a mouthful of coffee. 'You're up early,' I remarked. 'Couldn't you sleep?'

'Could you?'

'Well, not exactly. I kept thinking about Bryan. I called the hospital a little while ago, but they don't have any news yet. I almost hope he's dead.'

'I know what you mean.'

I carried the telephone over to the Chesterfield and stretched out. Right now I was beginning to feel tired. Maybe it was just the relief of having someone friendly to talk to. I finished my coffee and accidentally took a mouthful of grounds, and I spent the rest of the conversation trying to pick them off my tongue.

Jane said: 'The reason I called you was something I found out.'

'Something to do with Bryan?'

'Not exactly. But something to do with Seymour Wallis's house. You know all those pictures of Mount Taylor and Cabezon Peak?'

'Sure. I was wondering about those.'

'Well, I went and looked them up in some of my books back at the store. Mount Taylor's in the San Mateo Mountains, elevation 11,389 feet, and Cabezon Peak is way off to the north-east in San Doval County, elevation 8,300 feet.'

I spat grounds. 'That's in New Mexico, right?'

'That's right. Real Indian country. And there are dozens of legends connected with those two mountains, mostly Navaho stories about Big Monster.'

'Big Monster? Who the hell is Big Monster?'

'Big Monster was a giant who was supposed to terrorise the south-west centuries and centuries ago. He made his home on Mount Taylor. He had a blue and black-striped face, and a suit of armour made out of flints, woven together with the intestines of all the people and animals he'd slaughtered.'

'He doesn't sound like the John Weitz of the ancient world.'

'He wasn't,' said Jane. 'He was one of the fiercest giants in any legend in any culture. I have an eighteenth-century book right here that says he was in charge of all man-destroying demons, and that no mortal could destroy him. He was slain, though, by a pair of brave gods called the Twins, who deflected his arrows with a rainbow, and then knocked off his head with a bolt of lightning. They threw his head off to the north-east, and it became Cabezon Peak.'

I coughed. 'That's a very pretty story. But what does it have to do with Seymour Wallis's house? Apart from all the etchings of Mount Taylor and Cabezon Peak, of course.'

'Well, I'm not sure, exactly,' said Jane. 'But there's a reference here to the First One To Use Words For Force, which I don't really understand. Whatever or whoever the First One To Use Words For Force was, it was apparently powerful enough to have cut off Big Monster's golden hair, and make a mockery out of him, and there's something else, too. The First One To Use Words For Force was eternal and immortal, and his motto to all the gods and humans who tried to dispose of him was a Navaho word which I can't pronounce but which means "to come back by the path of many pieces." '

'Jane, honey, you're not making much sense.'

'John, darling, there's another word for "come back", in case you'd forgotten. "Return." '

I swung my legs off the Chesterfield and sat up straight. 'Jane,' I said, 'you're clutching at totally improbable straws. Now, I don't know why Seymour Wallis has all of those pictures of Mount Taylor and Cabezon Peak in his house. I guess they were there when he moved in. But you could take any mountain in the whole of the south-west and find some kind of Indian legend connected with it. It's no big deal, really. I mean, maybe we're dealing with some kind of supernatural power. Some latent force that has suddenly been released as a kinetic force. But we're not dealing with Navaho monsters. I mean, there's no way.'

Jane wasn't abashed. 'I still think we ought to look into it further,' she said. 'The trouble with you is you're too rational.'

'Rational? I work for the sanitation department and you think I'm rational?'

'Yes, I do. John Hyatt, the national rational. You're so rational they even named a hotel chain after you.'

I couldn't help laughing. Then I said: 'Listen, will you do me a favour? Will you call the office for me. Speak to Douglas P. Sharp, USN (Retd.), and tell him I'm sick. I want to get around to Elmwood Hospital this morning and see Dr Jarvis.'

'Shall I meet you for lunch?'

'Why not? I'll come by the bookstore and pick you up.'

'Will you call me when you find out how Bryan is? I'd appreciate it.'

'Sure.'

I laid down the phone. I thought about what Jane had said for a while and then I shook my head and smiled. She liked ghosts and magic and monsters. She had once dragged me off to see all the old original horror pictures, like Bela Lugosi's *Dracula*, and Boris Karloff's *Frankenstein*. Somehow, the idea that Jane believed in ghouls and monsters round at 1551 Pilarcitos was reassuring. It brought out the hearty patronising male chauvinist in me. Perhaps that's why I'd asked her along there in the first place. If Jane believed it, then it *couldn't* be true.

The telephone rang again just as I was shaving. With my chin liberally lathered with hot mint foam, I picked it up like Father Christmas taking an order for next winter's toys.

'John? This is James Jarvis. You left me a message to call.'

'Oh, hi. I was just wondering how Bryan Corder was.'

There was a pause, then Dr Jarvis said: 'He's okay. His heart's still beating.'

'You don't think he's going to live?'

'It's hard to say. I wouldn't like him to. In any case, he could never go out into the world again. He'd have to spend the rest of his life in a sanitised oxygen tent. The whole brain is exposed, and any infection would kill him straight away.'

I wiped foam away from my mouth with the back of my hand. 'Couldn't you pull the plug out and let him die anyway? I think I know Bryan well enough to say that he wouldn't want to go on living like *that*.'

'Well,' said Dr Jarvis, 'we have.'

'You have what?'

66

'We've taken him off life-support systems. He's getting no plasma, no blood, no intravenous nutrition or sedation, no adrenalin, no electronic heart pacing, no nothing. Medically, he should have died hours ago.'

He paused again, and I heard someone come into his office and say something indistinct. Then Dr Jarvis said: 'The trouble is, John, his heart's still beating and it won't stop. However serious his injuries, I can't certify that he's dead until it does.'

I said: 'What about euthanasia?'

'It's illegal, that's what. And no matter how bad Bryan's injuries are, I can't do it. I'm taking enough of a risk as it is, depriving him of life-support systems. I could lose my licence.'

'Has Moira seen him? His wife?'

'She knows he's had an accident, but that's all. We're obviously doing everything we can to keep her away.'

I said: 'How about Dan Machin? Any improvement?'

'He's still comatose. But why don't you come up to the hospital and see for yourself? I could do with some moral support. I haven't been able to talk about last night with anyone here. They're all so goddamned sane, they'll think I belong to a coven or something.'

'Okay. Give me half an hour.'

I shaved, dressed in my off-white denim suit and a red shirt, and splashed myself with Braggi. It's surprising what a change of clothes can do for your morale. Then I made my bed, rinsed up my coffee cups, blew a kiss to the picture of Dolly Parton that hung in my bijou hallway, and went downstairs to the street.

It was one of those bright mornings that make you screw your eyes up. The blue skies and the torn white clouds did a lot to reassure me that life was still capable of being ordinary, and that last night's accident could have been an isolated and unpleasant freak

67

of nature. I walked down to the corner and hailed a taxi. I used to own a car, but keeping the payments up on a sanitation officer's salary was like trying to clear a blocked-up sewer with a toothbrush. The hire purchase men had arrived one foggy morning and driven away my metallic blue Monte Carlo into the swirling pea-souper. It was only after they'd gone that I realised I'd left my Evel Knievel sunglasses in the glove box.

As we drove up Fulton Street towards the hospital, which was one of those multi-levelled teak-and-concrete structures overlooking the ocean, the taxi driver said: 'Look at them damn birds. You ever see anything like that before?'

I glanced up from my *San Francisco Examiner*. I'd been trying to find any mention of Bryan Corder's accident. We were turning between neatly clipped yew hedges into the hospital's wide forecourt now, and to my fascination and disquiet, the building's rooftops were thick with grey birds. It wasn't just a flock that had decided to settle. There were thousands of them — all along the skyline of the main building, and sitting on every outbuilding and clinic and garage.

'Now that's what *I* call weird,' said the taxi driver, circling the cab around the forecourt and pulling up by the main door. 'Weird with a capital "wuh".'

I climbed out of the car and stood there for a moment or two, looking along the fluttering ranks of grey. I didn't know what species of bird they were. They were big birds, like pigeons or partridges, but they were grey as a thundery sky, grey as the sea on a restless day. What's worse, they were silent. They didn't chirrup or sing. They sat on the hospital roof, their dark feathers ruffled in the warm Pacific breeze, patient and quiet as birds on a granite gravestone.

'You see that Hitchcock movie?' asked the taxi driver. 'The one where the birds go crazy?'

I coughed. 'I don't need reminding of *that*, thanks.'

68

'Well, maybe this is it,' said the taxi driver. 'Maybe this is where the birds take over. Mind you, I'd like to see a bird trying to drive this hack. The dynamo belt slipped off twice this morning. I'd like to see a bird put a dynamo belt back on.'

I paid the driver and walked through the automatic doors into the cool precincts of the hospital. It was all very tasteful in there. Italian tiles on the floor, paintings by David Hockney, palm trees and soft music. You didn't come to Elmwood Foundation Hospital unless your medical insurance was well paid up.

The receptionist was a buxom girl in a tight white dress who must have tipped the balance for many a touch-and-go coronary patient. She had bouffant black hair, in which her nurse's cap nestled like a neatly-laid egg, and enough teeth for herself and three others like her. Not that there could have been three others like her, or even one.

'Hi,' she said. 'I'm Karen.'

'Hi, Karen, I'm John. What are you doing tonight?'

She smiled. 'This is Wednesday. My hair-wash night.'

I looked up at her beehive. 'You mean you wash that thing? I thought you just had it revarnished.'

She went huffy after that, and prodded a button to page Dr Jarvis. 'Some of us still believe in the old values,' she said tartly.

'You mean like stiletto heels and cars with fins?'

'What's wrong with stiletto heels and cars with fins?'

'Don't ask me, ask Claes Oldenburg.'

The receptionist blinked sooty eyelashes. 'Claes Oldenburg? Is he an intern?'

Dr Jarvis mercifully appeared from the elevator, and came across with his hand out.

'John! Am I glad to see you!'

I nodded meaningfully towards the brunette receptionist. 'The feeling could be mutual,' I told him. 'I think your front-desk lady keeps her brains in her bottom drawer.'

Dr Jarvis ushered me over to the elevator, and we rose up to the fifth floor. Gentle muzak played *Moon River*, which (unless you had any taste in music) was supposed to be soothing.

We emerged in a shiny corridor that was lit by dim fluorescent tubes and hung with mediocre lithographs of Mill Valley, Sausalito. Dr Jarvis led the way down to a pair of wide mahogany doors, and pushed them open. I followed obediently and found myself in an observation room, with one glass wall that looked into the murky, blue-lit depths of an intensive-care unit. Dr Jarvis said: 'Go ahead,' and I walked across the tiled floor and peered through the glass.

The sight of Bryan Corder in that livid blue room, lying on a bed with his naked skull resting on a pillow, and his fully-dressed body in a green medical gown, was eerie and frightening. Even though I'd seen him before, and actually had the shock of trying to drag him out of the chimney, this grinning skeletal vision was almost too much for me. But what was worse was the electrical screen beside his bed, which showed his heartbeats coming slow but regular – tiny travelling blips of light that meant *I am still alive*.

'I don't believe it,' I whispered. 'I can see it with my own eyes, but I just don't believe it.'

Dr Jarvis came up and stood next to me. He was very white, and there were mauve smudges of tiredness under his eyes. 'Nor do I. But there it is. His heartbeat is very slow, but it's regular and strong. If we killed him now, there would be no doubt at all that we would technically be committing a homicide.'

A young intern standing next to us said: 'He can't hold out very much longer, sir. He's real sick.'

Dr Jarvis shrugged. 'He's not just sick, Perring. He's dead. Or at least he should be.'

I stared at Bryan Corder's white and glistening head

for almost four or five minutes. The vacant eye-sockets looked like dark, mocking eyes, and the jaws were bared in a bony grin. Beside me, Dr Jarvis said nothing, but I could see his hands out of the corner of my eye, twisting a ballpen around and around his fingers in nervous tension.

And in the depths of that blue-lit room, the heartbeat went on and on, the blips coursing ceaselessly across the screen, keeping Bryan Corder alive in a hideous aquamarine hell that he could never see or understand.

Dr Jarvis said hoarsely: 'I have some kind of a theory. Do you want to hear it?'

I was glad to turn away from that glass inspection panel, and keep my eyes and mind off that living skull. 'Sure. Go ahead. Jane's got herself some theories, too, although I have to tell you that they're pretty wild.'

'I don't suppose mine are any less wild than hers.'

I took his arm. 'Is there any way of getting a drink around here? I could sure use one.'

Dr Jarvis said: 'I have an icebox in my office.'

We left the observation room thankfully, and walked along the corridor a short way to Dr Jarvis's office. It was pretty pokey – there was just space enough for a desk and a tiny icebox and a narrow settee – and the view was only impressive if you liked staring at the backs of buildings. Apart from a cheap desklamp and a stack of medical journals, and a photograph of Dr Jarvis standing on a rustic bridge with a freckly young girl ('my daughter by my ex-wife, God bless her'), the room was undecorated and bare.

'I call this the broom-closet,' explained Dr Jarvis, with a wry grin. 'The best offices are all along the west wall, overlooking the ocean, but you have to work here for at least a century before you get one.'

He took a bottle of gin from his desk drawer, and produced tonic and ice from his diminutive fridge. He mixed us a couple of g-and-t's, and then sat back and

71

propped his feet on his desk. One of his shoes was worn through to the cardboard lining.

'Jane thinks that what's happening at Seymour Wallis's house is something to do with Red Indian legends,' I said. 'Apparently Mount Taylor used to be the home of some giant dude called Big Monster, and Cabezon Peak is his head. He had it knocked off by lightning.'

Dr Jarvis lit a cigarette and passed me one. I didn't smoke very much these days, but right then I felt like smoking the whole pack. There was a pool of nausea someplace down in my stomach, and every time I thought of Bryan Corder's sightless eyes, it stirred itself around and around.

'Well, I don't know about legends,' said Dr Jarvis, 'but there seems to be some kind of connection between what happened to Dan Machin and what happened to Bryan Corder. When you think about it, both of them were investigating some kind of noise at 1551 Pilarcitos, and both of them came away from that investigation actually producing the sound that they'd heard. Dan Machin is breathing like the breathing he heard in Seymour Wallis's study, and Bryan Corder's heart is beating just like the beat he heard up Seymour Wallis's chimney.'

I sipped my gin-and-tonic. I said: 'So what's the theory?'

Dr Jarvis pulled a face. 'That's it. That's the whole theory. The theory is that whatever influence or power is dominating that house, it's kind of smuggling itself out of there in bits and pieces.'

'Oh, sure,' I said laconically. 'What do we get next? Legs and arms? Noses and ears?'

But right at the very moment I was saying those words with my lips, my mind was saying something else. Reminding me of what Jane Torresino had said on the telephone only an hour or two ago. *A Navaho word which I can't pronounce which means 'to come back by the path of many pieces'.*

And on the doorknocker, it said '*Return.*'

'What's the matter?' asked Dr Jarvis. 'You look sick.'

'I don't know. Maybe I am. But something that Jane said about her Indian legend kind of ties up with something that you said. There was a demon or something that was capable of besting this Big Monster, even though Big Monster was almost indestructible by humans and demons and almost everyone else. This demon was called the First One To Use Words By Force, something like that.'

Dr Jarvis finished his gin-and-tonic and poured himself another. 'I don't see the connection,' he said.

'The connection is that this demon's motto was some Indian word which means "coming back by the path of many pieces".'

Dr Jarvis frowned. 'So?'

'So everything! So what *you* said was that whatever power was possessing Seymour Wallis's house, it's smuggling itself out of there in bits and *pieces*! First its breathing and now its heartbeat.'

Dr Jarvis looked at me long and level, and didn't even lift his drink from the table. I said, almost embarrassed: 'It's a thought, anyway. It just seemed liked too much of a coincidence.'

Dr Jarvis said: 'What you're trying to suggest is that these noises in Seymour Wallis's house are something to do with a demon who's gradually taking people over? Bit by bit?'

'Isn't that what *you're* suggesting?'

Dr Jarvis sighed, and rubbed his eyes. 'I don't exactly know *what* I'm suggesting. Maybe we ought to call round at the house again, and ask Mr Wallis if the heartbeat's vanished, too.'

'I'm game if you are. I haven't heard from him all day.'

'He left a message that he telephoned here,' said Dr Jarvis. 'He was probably asking about Bryan Corder.'

Dr Jarvis found the message on the pad and punched out Seymour Wallis's number. It rang and rang and rang, but in the end he put the receiver back and said: 'No reply. Guess he did the wise thing and went out.'

I finished my drink. 'Would *you* stay there? I wouldn't. But I'll call around there later this afternoon. I decided to take the day off work.'

Dr Jarvis said: 'Won't San Francisco miss its most talented sanitation officer?'

I crushed out my cigarette. 'I was thinking of a change anyway. Maybe I'll go into medicine. It seems like an idle kind of a life.'

Dr Jarvis laughed.

I drank some more, and said, 'Did you see the birds?'

'Birds? What birds? I've been shut up with Bryan Corder all night.'

'I'm surprised nobody mentioned it. Your whole damned hospital looks like a bird sanctuary.'

Dr Jarvis raised an eyebrow. 'What kind of birds?'

'I don't know. I'm not Audubon the Second. They're big, and kind of grey. You should go out and take a look. They're pretty sinister. If I didn't have better taste, I'd say they were buzzards, waiting for Elmwood's rich and unfortunate patients to pass away.'

'Are there many?'

'Thousands. Count 'em.'

Just then, Dr Jarvis's telephone bleeped. He picked it up and said: 'Jarvis.'

He listened for a moment, then said, 'Okay. I'm right there,' and clapped the phone down.

'Anything wrong?' I asked him.

'It's Bryan Corder. I don't know how the hell he's been doing it, but Dr Cane says he's been trying to sit up.'

'*Sit up?* You have to be kidding! They guy's almost a corpse!'

We left our drinks and went quickly back down the corridor to the observation room. Dr Cane was there, along with the bearded pathologist Dr Nightingale and a nicely-proportioned black lady who turned out to be Dr Weston, a specialist in brain damage. Nicely-proportioned though she was, she spoke and behaved like a specialist in brain damage, and so I left well enough alone. One day, she'd find herself a good-looking neurologist and settle down.

It was what was happening behind the window, in the blue depths of the intensive-care unit, that really stunned me. I had the same desperate breathless sensation you get when you step into a swimming-pool that's ten degrees too cold.

Bryan Corder had turned his head away from us, and all we could see was the back of his skull and the exposed muscles at the back of his neck, red and stringy and laced with veins. He was moving, though – actually moving. His arm kept reaching out, as if it was trying to grasp something or push something away, and his legs stirred under the covers.

Dr Jarvis said: 'My God – can't we stop him?'

Dr Cane, a bespectacled specialist with a head that seemed to be two sizes too large for his body, said, 'We've already tried sedation. It doesn't appear to have any effect.'

'Then we'll have to strap him down. We can't have him moving around. It's bizarre!'

Dr Weston, the black lady, interrupted him. 'It may be bizarre, Dr Jarvis, but it's quite unprecedented. Maybe we should just let him do what he wants. He's not going to survive, anyway.'

'For Christ's sake!' snapped Dr Jarvis. 'The whole thing's inhuman!'

Just how inhuman it really was, none of us really understood – not until Bryan Corder suddenly lifted himself on one elbow, and slowly swung himself out of his bed.

Dr Jarvis took one look at that stocky figure in its green robes, with its ghastly skull perched on its shoulders, standing alone and unaided in a blue light as blue as lightning, as blue as death, and he shouted to his intern: '*Get him back on that bed! Come on, help me!*'

The intern stayed where he was, white and terrified, but Dr Jarvis pushed open the door between the observation room and the intensive-care unit, and I went in behind him.

There was a strange, cold smell in there. It was like a mixture between ethyl alcohol and something sweet. Bryan Corder — what was left of Bryan Corder — stood only four or five feet away from us, silent and impassive, his skull fixed in the empty, ravenous look of death.

'John,' said Dr Jarvis quietly.

'Yes?'

'I want you to take his left arm and lead him back to the couch. Force him to walk backwards, so that when he reaches the couch, we can push against him and he'll have to sit back. Then all we have to do is swing his legs across, and we'll have him lying flat again. See those straps under the couch? As soon as we get him down, we buckle him up. You got me?'

'Right.'

'You frightened?'

'You bet your ass.'

Dr Jarvis licked his lips in nervous anticipation. 'Okay, John, let's do it.'

Bryan Corder's heartbeat, monitored in steady blips through the wires that still trailed from his chest, was real slow at twenty-four beats to the minute. But right then, my own heartbeat felt even slower. My mouth was dry with fear, and my legs were the bent wobbly legs of someone who wades into clear water.

Dr Jarvis and I both inched closer, our hands raised, our eyes fixed on Bryan's skull. For some reason I felt that Bryan could still see – even though his eye-sockets were empty. He took a shuffling step towards us, and the raw muscle that held his jaw in place started to twitch.

'My God,' whispered Dr Jarvis, *'he's trying to say something!'*

For one moment, I thought that I probably wasn't going to have the nerve to grab hold of Bryan's arm and force him back on the bed. Supposing he fought back? Supposing I had to touch that naked, living skull? But then Dr Jarvis snapped: *'Now!'* and I went forward, awkward and clumsy, with my courage as weak as a girl's. I think I even shrieked out loud. I'm not ashamed of it. At least I tried.

Bryan collapsed in our arms. Instead of forcing him back, we had to drag him, and we heaved him up on to the couch like a sack of meal. Dr Jarvis held the back of his skull to prevent any injury, and we laid him carefully down with his arms by his sides, and strapped him tight with restraining bands. Then we stood and looked at each other across his supine body, and all we could do was smirk with suppressed fear.

Dr Jarvis checked Bryan's heartbeat and vital signs, and they were still the same. Twenty-four beats a minute, and continuing strong. Respiration slow but steady. I took a deep breath, and wiped my forehead with the back of my hand. I was sweating and shaking, and I could hardly speak.

Dr Jarvis said: 'This beats everything. This guy is supposed to be dead. Every rule in the book says he's dead. But here he is living and breathing and even walking about.'

At that moment, Dr Weston came in. She looked down at Bryan Corder and said: 'Maybe it's a miracle.'

'Well, maybe it is,' said Dr Jarvis. 'But maybe it's a damned evil piece of black magic, too.'

'Black magic, Dr Jarvis?' said Dr Weston. 'I didn't think you white folks believed in that.'

'I don't know what to believe,' muttered Dr Jarvis. 'This whole thing is totally insane.'

'Insane or not, I have my tests to run,' said Dr Weston. 'Thank you for restraining him so well. And thank you, too, Mr Hyatt.'

I coughed. 'I won't say it's been a pleasure.'

We left Dr Weston and her interns to run through their brain-damage tests on Bryan Corder's exposed skull, and we went out into the corridor. Dr Jarvis stood for a long time by the window, staring out across the hospital car park. Then he reached into the pocket of his white medical coat and took out a packet of cigarettes.

I stood a little way away, watching him and keeping quiet. I guessed he wanted to be alone right then. He was suddenly faced with something that turned his most basic ideas about medicine upside-down, and he was trying to rationalise a bizarre horror that, so far, could only be explained by superstition.

He lit his cigarette and said: 'You were right about the birds.'

'They're still up there?'

'Thousands of them, all along the roof.'

I stepped up to the window and looked out. They were there all right, ragged and fluttering in the Pacific wind.

'They're like some kind of goddamned omen,' said Dr Jarvis. 'What's the matter with them? They don't even *sing*.'

'They look like they're waiting for something,' I said. 'I just hope that it's nothing more portentous than a packet of birdseed.'

Dr Jarvis suggested: 'Let's go take a look at Dan Machin. I could use some light relief.'

'You call what happened to Dan Machin light relief?'

Dr Jarvis took a last drag at his cigarette and nipped

it out between his finger and thumb. 'After what happened just now, a funeral would be light relief.'

We walked along the corridor until we came to Dan Machin's room. Dr Jarvis looked through the small circular window in the door, and then opened it.

Dan Machin was still in a coma. There was a nurse by his bedside, and his pulse and respiration and blood pressure were being closely observed. Dr Jarvis went across and examined him, lifting his eyelids to see if there was any response. Dan Machin's face was white and spectral, and he was still breathing in that same deep, dreamless rhythm that had characterised the breathing in Seymour Wallis's house.

Just as Dr Jarvis was checking Dan's body temperature, I said: 'Supposing—'

'Supposing what?' said Dr Jarvis, preoccupied.

I came closer to Dan Machin's bedside. The young boy from Middle America was so still and pallid he might have been dead, except for his hollow, regular breathing.

'Supposing Bryan Corder was trying to get *here*, to see Dan Machin.'

Dr Jarvis looked around. 'Why should he want to do that?'

'Well, each of them has one of the sounds that used to haunt Seymour Wallis's house. Maybe the two of them have enough in common that they want to get together. All that Indian stuff that Jane was talking about – you know, returning by the path of many pieces – well maybe that means some kind of reincarnation by numbers.'

'I don't follow.'

'It's pretty simple. If this power or influence or whatever it is that's haunting Seymour Wallis's house was all kind of split up – you know, breathing in one place and heartbeat in another – then maybe it might try to get itself back together again.'

'John, you're raving.'

79

'You've seen Bryan Corder walking around with no skin on his skull and you tell me I'm raving?'

Dr Jarvis made a note of Dan Machin's temperature on his chart, and then stood up straight. 'There's no point in trying to find far-fetched answers,' he said. 'Whatever's going on, there has to be a really simple explanation.'

'Like what? One man goes crazy and another man loses the skin off his head, and we have to look for a simple explanation? James, there's something planned and deliberate going on here. Somebody wants all this to happen like it's all been worked out.'

Dr Jarvis said: 'There's no evidence in favour of that theory. And I'd rather you called me Jim.'

I sighed. 'All right, if you want to take it the slow, logical, medical way, I don't suppose I blame you. But right now I feel like talking to Jane and Seymour Wallis. Jane has a theory that's worth listening to, and I'll bet you two Babe Ruths to six bottles of Chivas Regal that Seymour Wallis knows more than he's told us.'

Dr Jarvis said: 'I don't drink Chivas Regal.'

'Well, that's okay. I don't eat Babe Ruths.'

I took a taxi down to The Head Bookstore just after noon. As I was driven away from the hospital, I couldn't help looking back at the birds on the roof. From a distance, they looked like a grey and scaly encrustation, as if the building itself was suffering from some unhealthy skin condition. I asked the taxi driver if he knew what species of bird they were, but he was Filipino, and he didn't even know what 'species' meant.

Surprisingly, Jane wasn't there when I called at the purple-painted shop on Brannan. Her young bearded assistant said: 'I don't know, man. She just upped and went out, round about a half hour ago. She didn't even say *ciaio*.'

'You don't know where she went? I was supposed to meet her for lunch.'

'She didn't say a word, man. But she went that way.' He pointed towards The Embarcadero.

I went into the street. Slices of sunlight were falling across the sidewalk, and I was jostled and bumped by the lunchtime crowds. I looked around, but I couldn't see Jane anywhere. Even if I walked along to The Embarcadero, I'd probably miss her. I went back into the bookstore and told the boy to have Jane call me at home, and then I hailed another taxi and asked the driver to take me to Pilarcitos Street.

I was annoyed, but I was also worried. The way things had been going these past couple of days, with Dan Machin and Bryan Corder both in hospital, I didn't like to lose touch with anybody. In the back of my mind, I still had this unsettling notion that whatever was happening was part of some preconceived scheme – as if Dan Machin had been *meant* to go to 1551 Pilarcitos, and as if Bryan Corder had been deliberately manoeuvred into going there, too. And don't think I didn't wonder if something equally horrific was going to happen to me.

The taxi stopped on Pilarcitos, and I paid the driver off. The house looked shabby in the sunlight, and as grey as the birds on the hospital roof. I swung the wrought-iron gate open, and went up the steps. The doorknocker grinned at me wolfishly, but today, in the clear light of noon, it didn't play any tricks on me. It was heavy cast bronze and that was all.

I knocked three times, loudly. Then I waited in the porch, whistling *Moon River*. I hated that damn tune so much, and now it was stuck on my mind.

I knocked again, but there was still no answer. Maybe Seymour Wallis had taken himself off for a walk. I waited for another few moments, gave one final bang on the knocker, and then turned around to go home.

But just as I went back down the steps, I heard a creaking sound. I looked around, and the front door had opened a little way. My last knock must have pushed it ajar, and it obviously wasn't locked, or even closed on the catch.

Now considering how many bolts and chains and safety-locks Seymour Wallis had installed on that door, it was pretty much out of character for him to leave it completely unlocked. I stood by the gate staring at the door and thinking *what's wrong?* For some reason I couldn't even begin to describe, I felt chilled and frightened. Worst of all, I knew that I couldn't leave the door open like that and just walk away. I was going to have to go into the house — that ancient house of breathing and heartbeats — and see what was up.

Slowly, I remounted the front steps. I stood by the half-open door for almost a minute, trying to distinguish shapes and shadows in the few inches of darkness that I could see. The doorknocker was now looking away from me, up the street, but its smile was as smug and vicious as ever.

I looked at the doorknocker and said: 'Okay, smartass. What particular nasty traps have you set up this time?'

The doorknocker grinned and said nothing. I hadn't really expected it to, and I think I would have jumped out of my skin if it had, but it was one of those creepy situations where you just like to make sure that if the spooks *are* spooks, and not just doorknockers or shadows or hatstands, then they don't get the idea that they're fooling you.

I reached out like a man reaching across a bottomless pit, and I pushed the door open a way. It groaned a little more and shuddered. Inside, the hallway was swirling in dust and darkness, and that musty closed-up smell was still as strong as ever.

Swallowing hard, I stepped inside. I called: Mr Wallis? Seymour Wallis?'

There was no reply. Once I entered the hallway, all the sounds from the street outside were muffled and suppressed, and I stood there and heard nothing but my own taut breathing.

'*Mr Wallis?*' I called again.

I walked across to the foot of the stairs. The bear-lady, eyes closed, still reared on the banister post. I squinted up into the stale darkness of the second floor, but I couldn't make anything out at all. To tell you the God's honest truth, I didn't feel particularly inclined to go up there. I decided to take a quick look in Seymour Wallis's study, and if he wasn't at home, to get the hell out of there.

As quietly as I could, I tiptoed along the worn-out carpet of the corridor to the door under the stag's head. The study was closed, but the key was in the lock. I turned it slowly, and I heard the lock mechanism click in the impenetrable silence, disturbing that breathless air that seemed to have hung around the house for all the years that it had stood here.

I put my hand on the brass doorknob, and turned it. The study door opened. It was gloomy in there, and the drapes were still drawn, so I reached around the lintel to find the lightswitch. My fingers groped along the damp wallpaper, and I clicked the switch down, but nothing happened. The bulb must have burned out.

Nervously, I pushed the door wider and stepped inside. I took a quick, almost panicky look behind the door to make sure nothing and nobody was hiding, and I had a half-second of shock when I saw Seymour Wallis's bathrobe hanging there. Then I strained my eyes, and stared across at the dark shape of Seymour Wallis's desk and chair.

For a while, I couldn't see if there was anything there or not. But then my eyes grew gradually accustomed to the darkness, and something began to take

83

shape. I said: 'Oh, Christ,' and the words came out like strangled puppies.

Some enormous inflated man was sitting in Seymour Wallis's chair. His head was blackened and puffy, and his arms and legs were swollen twice their normal size. His face was so congested that his eyes were tiny slits, and his fingers came out of the sleeves of his shirt like fat purple slugs.

I could never have recognised him except by the clothes. It was Seymour Wallis. A distended, swelled-up, grotesque caricature of Seymour Wallis.

I could hardly get the words out. 'Mr W-Wallis?'

The creature didn't stir.

'Mr Wallis, are you alive?'

The telephone was on his desk. I had to call Dr Jarvis right away, and maybe Lieutenant Stroud, too, but that meant reaching across this inflated body. I circled the study cautiously, peering more and more closely at Seymour Wallis, trying to make up my mind if he was dead. I guessed he must be. He wasn't moving, and he looked as if every vein and artery in his whole body had haemorrhaged.

'Mr Wallis?'

I stepped up real close, and bent my knees a little so that I could look right into his purplish, blown-up face. He didn't seem to be breathing. I swallowed again, in an effort to get my heart back down in my chest where it belonged, and then I slowly and nervously leaned forward to pick up the telephone.

I dialled Elmwood Foundation Hospital. The phone seemed to ring for centuries before I heard the telephonist's voice say: 'Elmwood. Can I help you?'

'Can you get Dr Jarvis for me?' I whispered. 'It's an emergency.'

'Will you speak up, please? I can't hear you.'

'Dr Jarvis!' I said hoarsely. 'Tell him it's urgent!'

'Just a moment, please.'

The telephonist put me on 'hold', and I had to listen to some schmaltzy music while she paged Dr Jarvis. I kept glancing anxiously down at Seymour Wallis's bloated face, and I was hoping and praying that he wasn't going to jump up suddenly and catch me.

The music stopped, and the telephonist said: 'I'm afraid Dr Jarvis is out at lunch right now, and we don't know where he is. Would you like to speak to another doctor?'

'No thank you. I'll come right up there.'

'In that case please use the south entrance. We're having the city sanitation people around to clear away some birds.'

'The birds are still there?'

'You bet. The whole place is covered.'

I set down the telephone and backed respectfully away from Seymour Wallis. I was only two or three paces towards the door, though, when his revolving chair suddenly twisted around, and his huge body dropped sideways on to the carpet, face-first, and lay there prone. The shock was so great that I stood there paralysed, unable to run, unable to think. But then I realised he was either dead or helpless, and I went over and knelt down beside him.

'Mr Wallis?' I said, although I have to admit that I didn't hold out any hopes of an answer.

He stayed where he was, swollen up as badly as a man who has floated around in the sea for endless undiscovered weeks.

I stood up again. On his desk was a cheap shorthand notebook, on which he had obviously been writing. I picked it up, and flicked back some of the pages. It was written in a heavy, rounded hand, like the hand of a dogged, backward child. It looked as if Seymour Wallis had been struggling to complete his notes before the swelling made it impossible for him to write any further.

I angled the notebook sideways so that the dusky light from outside strained across the pages. The notebook read: 'I know now that all those disastrous events at Fremont were merely the catalyst for some far more terrible occurrence. What we discovered was not the thing itself, but the one talisman that could stir the thing into life. Perhaps there was always a predestined date for its return. Perhaps all these ill-starred happenings have been coincidental. But I realise one thing for sure. From the day I discovered the talisman at Fremont, I had no choice but to buy the house at 1551. The ancient influences were far too strong to resist for someone as weak and as unaware of their domineering power as me.'

That was how it ended. I couldn't figure it out at all. Maybe Seymour Wallis thought that his bad luck on the Fremont job had caught up with him at last, and, judging by his condition, I couldn't say that I blamed him. But right then, the first thing I wanted to do was get out of that house and contact Dr Jarvis. I definitely had the feeling that 1551 was harbouring some hostile, brooding malice, and if three people had already suffered so hideously while trying to discover what that malice really was, I was pretty sure that I could easily be the fourth.

I went out through the hallway, casting a quick backward glance up the stairs just in case something horrible was standing up there, and then I dodged past the doorknocker and out on to the porch. As I turned to close the door, though, I saw something that made me feel more unsettled and frightened than almost anything that had happened before.

The banister post was missing its statuette. The bear-lady had gone.

Outside the hospital, the vermin crew from the sanitation department were trying to scare the grey birds off with blank gunshots. I recognised one of them, Innocenti, and I went across to ask him how they were getting on.

Innocenti jerked a disgusted thumb at the serried

ranks of silent birds, still perched on the rooftops and undisturbed by the crackling racket of gunfire.

'I never seen birds like 'em. They just sits there. You shout and they sits. You yell and they sits. We sent Henriques up on the roof with a clapper, and what do they do, sits. Maybe they're hard of hearing. Maybe they don't give a damn. They sits, and they don't even shits.'

'Have you found out what they are?' I asked him.

Innocenti shrugged. 'Pigeons, ravens, ducks, who knows from birds? I ain't no ordinarythologist.'

'Maybe they have some special characteristic.'

'Sure. They're so fuckin' bone idle they won't even fly away.'

'No, but maybe they're a special type of bird.'

Innocenti was unimpressed. 'Listen, Mr Hyatt, they could be fuckin' ostriches for all I care. All I know is that I have to get 'em off of the roof, and *until* I get 'em off of the roof, I have to stay here and miss my dinner. Do you know what's for dinner?'

I gave him a friendly wave of my hand and walked across to the hospital entrance.

'Osso bucco!' he yelled after me. 'That's what's for dinner!'

I went into the hospital and walked straight across the Italian-tile foyer to the elevators. The elegant stainless-steel clock on the wall said seven o'clock. It was four hours now since I'd telephoned Dr Jarvis from the booth on the corner of Mission and Pilarcitos. Four hours since the ambulance crew had arrived to collect Seymour Wallis's distended body under a green blanket that any casual bystander could have seen was bulging grossly, bulging far too much for a natural corpse. Four hours since Dr Jarvis and Dr Cane had been carrying out a detailed post mortem.

I took the elevator to the fifth floor, and walked along the corridor to James Jarvis's office. I let myself in, and raided his desk for his gin bottle and his icebox for his tonic. Then I sat back and took a stiff, refreshing drink, and by Saint Anthony and Saint Theresa, I needed it.

I'd been trying all afternoon to locate Jane Torresino. I'd called every mutual friend and acquaintance I could think of, until I'd finally run out of dimes and energy. I'd revivified myself on a McDonald's cheeseburger and a cup of black coffee, and then made my way up to Elmwood. I felt helpless, lost, frustrated, and frightened.

I was just pouring my second gin-and-tonic when Dr Jarvis came in and flung his coat across his chair.

'Hi,' he said, a little tersely.

I lifted my glass. 'I made myself at home. I hope you don't mind.'

'Why should I? Fix me one while you're at it.'

I clunked ice into another glass. 'Did you finish the post mortem?' I asked him.

He sat down heavily, and rubbed his face with his hand. 'Oh, sure, we finished the post mortem.'

'And?'

He looked up through his fingers, and his eyes were red with fatigue and concentration. 'You really want to know? You really want to get involved in this thing? You don't have to, you know. You're only a sanitation officer.'

'Well, maybe I am. But I'm cool. And what's more, I'm involved already. Come on, Jim – Dan Machin and Bryan Corder were friends of mine. And now Seymour Wallis. I feel responsible.'

Dr Jarvis reached in his pocket for his cigarettes. He lit one unsteadily, and then tossed the pack across to me. I left it lying there. Before I sat back and relaxed, I wanted to know what was going on.

Dr Jarvis sighed, and looked up at the ceiling, as if there was a kind of teleprompt up there which might give him a clue what to say. He said: 'We tried every possibility. I mean, everything. But that bodily distension was caused by one factor, and one factor only, and no matter what we hypothesised, we always came back to the same conclusion.'

I sipped gin. I didn't interrupt. He was going to tell me, no matter what.

'I guess the cause of death will officially go down as blood disorder. That's a kind of a white lie, but it's also completely true. Seymour Wallis *was* suffering from a severe blood disorder. His blood wasn't lacking in red corpuscles, and it didn't show any signs of disease or anaemia. But the simple fact was that he had too much of it.'

'Too *much* of it?'

Dr Jarvis nodded. 'The normal human being has nine pints of blood circulating around the body. We emptied the blood from Seymour Wallis's body and we measured it. His arteries and veins and capillaries were swollen because he had twenty-two pints of blood in him.'

I could hardly believe it. I said: '*Twenty-two pints?*'

Dr Jarvis blew out smoke. 'I know it sounds crazy, but that's the way it is. Believe me, if I thought I could sweep this whole business under the rug, I'd empty that extra blood down the sink.'

He sat there for a while, staring at his untidy desk. I guessed that with all the weird ramifications of Seymour Wallis and his malevolent house, he hadn't had much time for his paperwork.

I said: 'Have the police been around?'

'They've been informed.'

'And what did they say?'

'They're waiting for the post mortem. The trouble is, I don't know what to tell them.'

I finished my drink. 'Why not? Just tell them he died of natural causes.'

Dr Jarvis grunted sardonically. 'Natural causes? With nearly three gallons of blood in him? And, anyway, it's worse than that.'

'Worse?'

Dr Jarvis didn't look my way, but I could tell how confused and anxious he was. He said: 'We analysed the blood, of course, and put it through the centrifuge. Dr Cane is one of the finest pathologists in the business. At least, he gets paid as if he is. He says that without a shadow of a doubt, the blood that we found inside Seymour Wallis was not human.'

There was a pause. Dr Jarvis lit another cigarette from the butt of the first.

'There isn't any question that all twenty-two gallons were the blood of some species of dog. Whatever happened to Seymour Wallis, the blood that he died with wasn't his own.'

CHAPTER FOUR

Jane Torresino called. She was sorry she hadn't been around at lunchtime, and she hoped I hadn't been anxious. I glanced across at Dr Jarvis and said: 'Anxious? Do you know what's happened?'

'I saw it on·television. Seymour Wallis died.'

'Well, it's worse than that. He died with more blood in his system than Sam Peckinpah gets through in a whole movie. Twenty-two pints. And what's more, Jim here says the blood wasn't even his own. They analysed it, and it turned out to be·some kind of dog's blood.'

'You're kidding.'

'Jane, if you think I'm in a mood for kidding—'

'I didn't mean that,' she said quickly. 'What I meant was, it all ties in.'

'Ties in? Ties in with what?'

'That's what I've been trying to tell you,' she said. 'I went out at lunchtime to Sausalito. You know all that Indian stuff I was telling you about? Well, I have friends out at Sausalito who know quite a few Indians, and they're all into Indian culture. They'd heard about this demon they call the First One To Use Words For Force, and they think I ought to go up to Round Valley and talk to one of the medicine men.'

I sighed, and said nothing. Jane said: 'John? Did you hear me?'

'Yes,' I said. 'I heard you.'

'But you don't think it's a good idea?'

'Just wait a moment.'

I put my hand over the receiver, and said to Jim Jarvis: 'Jane is convinced that everything that's been happening round at Seymour Wallis's house has been connected with some Red Indian legend. Now she wants to talk to some medicine man upstate. What do you think?'

Dr Jarvis shrugged. 'I don't know. Maybe it's a good idea. Any theory is better than no theory.'

I took my hand off the phone. 'Okay, Jane. Dr Jarvis says let's try it.'

'You couldn't have stopped me anyway,' she answered tartly.

'Jane,' I said, irritated, 'I spent the whole damned afternoon trying to find out where you were. We've had two people injured and one man dead. Right now, the least advisable thing for any of us to do is to go wandering off on our own.'

'I didn't know you cared,' retorted Jane.

'You know damned well I do.'

'Well, if you care that much, you'd better come to Round Valley with me. I'm borrowing Bill Thorogood's car.'

I put down the phone. At least it was Saturday tomorrow, and I wouldn't have to keep on inventing excuses for Douglas P. Sharp, USN (Retd.). I said to Dr Jarvis: 'It looks like I've roped myself in. I just hope it's worthwhile.'

He crushed out his second cigarette, and shrugged. 'There are times when you come up against things in medicine that make you feel excited. Real challenges, like difficult cases of poisoning, or unusual compound fractures. At times like that, you feel everything about being a doctor is worthwhile. The hospital politics, the squabbles over financial allocations, the whole bit.'

He looked up, and added: 'There are other times, though, like now, when you just don't understand what the hell is happening, and you're powerless. I can spend the rest of the day *schlepping* around from Dan Machin to Bryan Corder to Seymour Wallis, and I won't be able to do a damned thing to help any of them.'

He reached for the cigarettes. 'In other words, John,

92

go on up to Round Valley and consider yourself lucky that you're doing *something*. Because I can't.'

I looked at Dr Jarvis for a while, and then I said: 'I didn't know doctors got down in the dumps. I thought that only happened on television.'

Dr Jarvis coughed. 'And *I* thought that what's happening right now only happened in nightmares.'

Saturday morning was clean and clear, and we sped across the Golden Gate with the ocean sparkling beneath us, the sun flickering through the bridge's wires and uprights in a bright stroboscopic blur. Jane sat back in her seat, dressed in a red silk blouse and white Levis, with huge sunglasses perched on her nose and a red scarf around her hair. Bill Thorogood was lucky enough to own a white Jaguar XJ 12, and profligate enough to lend it out, so I sat behind the wheel and pretended I was some minor movie star on a day trip to someplace private and expensive, instead of a sanitation official on a one-hundred-and-sixty-mile flog up to Round Valley.

We burned up 101 through Marin and Sonoma Counties, through Cloverdale, Preston and Hopland, and we stopped at Ukiah for lunch, with the sun high and brassy up in the sky, and the wind blowing off Lake Mendocino. Sitting on a low breezeblock wall outside a roadside diner, we ate chiliburgers and watched as a father tried to cram his five kids into the back of his station wagon, along with fishing tackle, inflatable rafts, pup tents, and wellingtons. Every time he managed to get all of the gear inside, one of the kids would climb out, and then he'd have to get around to the back of the wagon again and rearrange everything.

'The futility of life,' remarked Jane. 'As fast as you do something, it gets itself undone again.'

'I don't think that life's futile.'

Jane swallowed Coca-Cola from the can. 'You don't

think that someone's using us as playthings? Like now?'

'I don't know. I think it's more serious than that. But I believe we have to try to fight it, whatever it is.'

, She reached over and touched my hand. 'That's what I like about you, John. You're always ready to fight.'

We climbed back in the car, and I drove it out of the carpark with a squeal of tyres. Then we headed north again, speeding on 101 until we reached Longvale, and then turning off into the hills to Dos Rios and the Eel River, and up into Round Valley Reservation.

The medicine man we had arranged to see was George Thousand Names. All that Jane knew about him was that he was one of the oldest and most respected of southwestern medicine men, and that he spent more time in San Francisco and Los Angeles than he did upstate, working for Indian investment corporations and protecting Indian rights. Right now, though he was back home at Round Valley with his family, and anybody that wanted to consult him had to make the trek.

The Jaguar bounced slowly across the grass and rutted tracks that led up the valley between tall pines and undulating hills to George Thousand Names' home. He kept himself apart from most of the trailers and houses where the Round Valley Indians lived, up on a wooded ridge overlooking the Eel River. As we made our way up the bumpy trail, his chalet-style house gradually came into view, a split-level architect-designed home with a balcony and wide sliding windows.

'Some tepee,' remarked Jane.

I stopped the Jaguar at the foot of the wooden stairs that led up to the house. Then I climbed out and squinted against the sun, looking for any signs of life. I blew the car horn a couple of times, and then one of the sliding windows opened and a small man in a plaid shirt and well-pressed slacks came out on to the balcony.

'Excuse me,' I called. 'Are you Mr Thousand Names?'

'I'm George Thousand Names. Who are you?'

'John Hyatt. And this is Jane Torresino. Ms Torresino made an appointment with you?'

'I'm not a dentist,' said George Thousand Names. 'You don't have to make appointments. But I remember. Come on up.'

We climbed the stairs that led up to the balcony, and George Thousand Names came up and shook hands. Up here, he looked even smaller – a delicate and diminutive old man with a face as creased and crinkled as a cabbage leaf. He stood very straight, though, and he had an inner dignity about him that immediately made me feel he was someone extremely special. Around his neck hung amulets and necklaces that looked ancient and potent and mysterious, but he wore them as naturally as if they were nothing more than decoration. On his wrist was a Jaeger-le-Coultre wristwatch, solid gold, with a tiger's-eye face.

'Your friends from Sausalito briefly mentioned that you were worried about some of our legends,' said George Thousand Names, leading us into the house. It was a calm, elegant place, built of polished pine, with Indian rugs and cushions all around. Through a half-open sliding door I could see a modernistic kitchen with a ceramic range and microwave ovens.

Jane gave George Thousand Names a pottery jar of tobacco she had bought that morning in Healdsburg. 'I've heard it's kind of traditional,' she said. 'I hope you like Klompen Kloggen.'

George Thousand Names smiled. 'I don't know why white people are always so apologetic in the face of tradition,' he said. 'Sure, that's a fine brand. Won't you sit down? How about some coffee?'

We sat around on comfortable cushions on the floor,

95

while a young Indian girl who was presumably George Thousand Names's maid percolated coffee for us. Just behind George Thousand Names's shoulder, the sun slid in through the wide window like a lance, and gave his aged head a brilliant halo of light.

George Thousand Names said: 'There is something in both of your minds that is troubling you greatly. You fear that you have no comprehension of what it might be, and that you will both be swallowed up by it.'

'How did you know that?' I asked him.

'Very easy, Mr Hyatt. It shows on your faces. In any case, white people don't usually consult Indian medicine men unless they feel they have exhausted every possible explanation that their own culture can offer.'

Jane said: 'We're not at all sure that this has anything to do with Indian legends, Mr Thousand Names. It was just a guess. But the more we find out about it, the more things that happen, the more it seems to point that way.'

'Tell me about it. From the beginning.'

I explained about my job at the sanitation department, and how Seymour Wallis had come in to see me about the breathing in his house. Then I described what had happened to Dan Machin, and next to Bryan Corder, and finally to Seymour Wallis himself. I talked about the pictures of Mount Taylor and Cabezon Peak, and about the bear-lady who was missing, and about the doorknocker with the hideous face.

George Thousand Names listened to all this calmly and impassively. When I'd finally finished, he lifted his head, and said: 'Do you have any idea what you're describing to me?'

I shook my head.

Jane said: 'The whole reason we've come up here is because we can't understand it. I work in a bookstore, and I looked up Mount Taylor and found there were all these stories about Big Monster connected with it, and the First One To Use Words For Force. I wouldn't have thought much about it, except that the First One To Use Words For Force was supposed to come back by the path of many pieces or something like that, and it somehow seemed to click. I can't even explain why.'

The Indian girl brought us coffee in pottery mugs, and fresh pecan cookies. She must have had a psychic sensitivity to my innermost thoughts, like George Thousand Names. Being served up with a plateful of fresh pecan cookies almost made up for having *Moon River* on the brain.

George Thousand Names said softly: 'Every Indian demon has a common name and a ritual name, like many European demons. There were, for instance, the Eye Killers, who were said to have been created by a chief's daughter abusing herself with a prong from a sour cactus. Then, as you say, there was Big Monster, whose real name was quite different, and the First One To Use Words For Force.'

The medicine man seemed to be choosing his words carefully. He bit into a pecan cookie with immaculate dentistry, and chewed for a while before he continued.

'The First One To Use Words For Force was the most terrible and implacable of all Indian demons. He was wily and cunning and vicious, and his chief enjoyments were causing hatred and confusion, and satisfying his lust on women. The reason we call him the First One To Use Words For Force is because his tricks and his savagery created in the hearts of men their first feelings of fury and revenge.

'As you may know, there are benevolent Indian gods and evil Indian gods. At the great council of the deities, the evil gods sat facing the north and the good gods sat facing the south. The First One To Use Words For Force, however, was so treacherous and malevolent that he was accepted by neither side, and he sat alone by the door. He was the demon of chaos and disorder,

97

and the Indians sometimes say that when he was asked in ancient days to help to place the stars, he tossed his own handful of stars up into the night sky at random, and created the Milky Way.'

George Thousand Names sipped his coffee. I said: 'Is this what we're up against? This First One To Use Words For Force?'

The Indian's face gave nothing away. He replaced his coffee mug on its saucer, and delicately patted his lips with a clean handkerchief.

'From what you have told me, Mr Hyatt, it seems more than likely.'

I didn't know whether he was trying to put me on or not. Knowing the dry sense of humour that Indians have, I guessed he could have been pulling our legs. I could just imagine him retelling the story of how the dumb white folks had come all the way up to Round Valley to ask his advice, and how he'd solemnly told them about a demon who threw stars up in the air, and how the white folks had gone away convinced they were up against some ancient redskin spirit, and the whole damned tribe would be busting their sides.

'*Likely?*' I asked him, cautiously. 'What's likely about a demon?'

George Thousand Names smiled. 'I sense your suspicion,' he said. 'But I assure you absolutely that I am not playing with you.'

I couldn't help colouring a little. In front of this medicine man, I felt as if I had a television screen in my forehead, giving a late late show on everything I was thinking. Whatever his sense of humour was like, he was a real astute guy.

He said: 'The First One To Use Words For Force was the only Indian demon to conquer death. He died many times – sometimes as false proof of his love for a woman – sometimes as the consequence of a punishment meted out by the other gods. But each time, before he went to the underworld, he made sure that he hid in the upper world the essential ingredients he needed to come back to life again. His breath, his heart, his blood, and the hair which he cut from Big Monster's head.'

The sun had now dropped behind George Thousand Names's back, and I could hardly make out his face in the darkness. I said, appalled: '*His breath, his heart, and his blood?*'

George Thousand Names nodded. 'That's why you were right to come up here, Mr Hyatt. From what you have said this afternoon, it seems that the First One To Use Words For Force has decided to return to life, through the medium of your unfortunate friends.'

Jane said; 'But I don't understand. How could a demon's breath and blood and everything be *there* – inside a house?'

'It's quite easy. The First One To Use Words For Force was banished to the underworld many centuries ago – long before any white man discovered this continent. In those days, medicine men were almost gods in their own right, and even if they weren't actually able to slay the First One To Use Words For Force, they would certainly be capable of sending him temporarily back to the underworld. From what you say, I expect that the demon hid his vital parts in a forest or in the ground, and when this house was constructed, it was unwittingly built out of trees or out of stones in which the First One To Use Words For Force had instilled his many pieces.'

'But what about all those pictures of Mount Taylor? The demon couldn't have put those up. And what about the doorknocker?'

George Thousand Names raised his hands. 'Of course the demon himself didn't put those artifacts there. But I expect that his influence in the house has been strong for years. Those people who have been unfortunate enough to live there have probably done many things quite unconsciously, to prepare the way for the demon's eventual return to life. I expect that the doorknocker you talk about is a likeness of the demon's face.'

'And the pictures?'

'Well, who knows?' asked George Thousand Names. 'But remember that the ancient Indians used to draw pictures of prominent landmarks from a whole variety of different angles so that they could locate hidden hoards of weapons or supplies, or underground springs. All those prints of Mount Taylor and Cabezon Peak could be a very sophisticated form of pictograph, and if you put them all together, you may find that they lead you to some spot where the First One To Use Words For Force has secreted something important.'

'Like what?' asked Jane. 'I mean, whatever it is, it must be *very* important.'

George Thousand Names smiled at her benevolently. 'I don't usually like to hypothesise, my dear, but my guess would be that those pictures lead the way to the shorn-off hair of Big Monster. The First One To Use Words For Force cut off Big Monster's hair because it had magical properties which made the wearer invulnerable to human and supernatural weapons. It was said to be as grey as iron, this hair, and as strong as a whip. From what I recall of the legend, the First One To Use Words For Force hid the hair in the New Mexico lands of the Acoma and Canoncito Indians, so that the twin gods who killed Big Monster would never find it. But it was discovered, and spirited away, and nobody knows where. Without that hair, the demon would be open to attack, and would never have the stamina he needed to remain in the world of men and living spirits.'

I sat back on my cushion. George Thousand Names was so calm, so self-possessed, that I could no longer consider he was joking. But what he was saying needed such an enormous stretch of the imagination to believe that I wasn't sure I could accept it even now, no matter how sincerely he had said it. If it hadn't been for Dan Machin and Bryan Corder and Seymour Wallis, I would have politely finished my coffee and left. But two of them were sick and the third was lying dead in the morgue, and what George Thousand Names had told us was the only explanation that anyone had given us so far.

Jane said: 'If the First One To Use Words For Force is the demon's ritual name, what's his common name?'

George Thousand Names raised an eyebrow. 'You've probably heard it,' he said. 'The demon is usually called Coyote. The dogs of the desert were named after him. It's a name that means cunning and cajolery and vicious trickery.'

I coughed. 'Is there any way we can tell if he's really around? Is there any sign, any giveaway mark?'

Jane said: 'Like poltergeists, which are frightened of fire? Or vampires?'

George Thousand Names said: 'Coyote comes in many guises, but you can always recognise him. He has the face of a demonic wolf, and he is always accompanied by signs of bad luck.'

'Like what?'

'Like thunderstorms, or sickness, or certain birds or animals.'

I felt that familiar freezing sensation around my scalp. 'Grey birds?' I asked the medicine man. 'Grey birds that sit there and never sing?'

George Thousand Names nodded. 'The grey birds are Coyote's most constant compànions. He uses their feathers to fletch his arrows, which is something no Indian warrior would ever have done. The grey birds are the birds of disaster and panic.'

'I've seen them.'

For the first time, George Thousand Names leaned forward, his face intent and pale. 'You've *seen* them?'

'Thousands of them, literally thousands. They're all perched on the roof of the hospital where Dan Machin and Bryan Corder and Seymour Wallis were taken. My own sanitation department was around there yesterday, trying to get rid of them, but they wouldn't leave.'

'They're actually there?' asked George Thousand Names, as if he couldn't believe what I was saying. 'You saw them with your own eyes?'

I nodded.

George Thousand Names looked away. His eyes, gleaming and bright in the folded wrinkles of his skin, seemed to be searching into some invisible faraway distance. He whispered, more to himself than to Jane and me: '*Coyote . . . so it's come to pass.*'

I licked my lips uncertainly. 'Mr Thousand Names,' I said, trying not to sound too much like a white tourist bartering for Indian blankets, 'is there anything we can do? Or is there anything you can do to help us?'

George Thousand Names jerked his head towards me, and stared at me as if I was losing my bananas. 'I? What can *I* do in the face of a demon like Coyote?'

'Well, I don't exactly know. But if *you* can't do anything, what the hell can *we* do?'

George Thousand Names stood up and walked across to the open window. It was around five o'clock now, and the sun was only a couple of hours above the treeline. He stepped out on to the balcony, and Jane and I glanced worriedly at each other as he stood there, gazing out over the hills and the rivers of Round Valley. I stood up, too, and followed him out into the open air. There was a fresh smell of pine and wood-smoke in the air, and from far away came the echo and re-echo of someone chopping logs.

'Someone has set this ancient evil working again,' said George Thousand Names hoarsely. 'Somehow, Coyote has come together again.'

'I don't follow.'

The medicine man turned and looked at me. 'The way the gods and the medicine men dismissed Coyote to the underworld was to make sure that he was split up into parts, and that he had no means of recovering those parts. The first four times he died, he hid a flint on his body, so that he could dig up his breath and his blood and his heart-beat all over again. The last time he died, the gods made sure that he had no flint, and no axe. All that could possibly have conjured him up again was the bear-maiden.'

'Mr Thousand Names,' I said. 'I don't like to seem ignorant, but these legends are pretty much beyond me. I mean, I find them all a little hard to swallow.'

George Thousand Names turned away. 'Of course you do,' he said, in a flat voice that was neither irritated nor indulgent. 'How do you think *I* felt when I first heard about Jesus Christ walking on water?'

Jane, who was standing by the open window, said: 'Tell us about the bear-maiden. Please.'

George Thousand Names tiredly pinched the bridge of his nose between finger and thumb.

'The Bear Maiden was a beautiful girl whom Coyote lusted after. He tried dozens of times to seduce her, but every time she resisted him. It was she who sent him off to the underworld the first few times, to make him prove that he would gladly die for her. In the end, however, she succumbed to his sexual advances, and he gave her a night of love that won her over completely.

'From that moment on, Coyote filled her mind with evil thoughts, and gradually she changed from a woman into a bear. Her teeth grew long, her nails grew sharp, and dark hair grew down her back. Her greatest pleasure from then on was snapping men's necks with her powerful jaws.'

'Not your fun Saturday-night escort, in other words,' I remarked.

George Thousand Names gave me a down-home look that meant he was a long way away from flippant jokes. 'It's quite possible that this man Wallis's statuette, the one he found at Fremont, was enough to provoke Coyote into life. It could have been invested with magic, like a small totem. Did he mention any problems or difficulties at Fremont? Any sickness or argument or inexplicable events?'

I said: 'Yes. They were building a pedestrian bridge in a park, and apparently the whole damned thing was confusion from beginning to end.'

'Then that's it,' said George Thousand Names. 'The statuette of Bear Maiden was more than just an antique curiosity. It was the original magical totem which could give Coyote the strength and the will to wake from his sleep in the underworld. And Seymour Wallis brought it into the house.'

'Do you think that was accidental?' asked Jane. 'I mean, it seems like a tremendous coincidence, him buying that one particular house.'

George Thousand Names shook his head. 'From the moment Seymour Wallis dug up that statuette, Coyote was working his influence on him. He told you he felt dogged by bad luck, right? It wasn't bad luck at all. It was the demands of Coyote, drawing him nearer and nearer to Pilarcitos Street. I'll bet you something else, too.'

'What's that?'

'Pilarcitos Street is the first turning after 5th Street off Mission.'

I nodded. 'That's right.'

George Thousand Names held up the fingers of both hands. 'Five plus one is six. Then you have the number 1551. One plus five is six, and five plus one is six. Three sixes – 666. The number of the greatest of demons, no matter what culture you're talking about. The mark of the beast.'

Out there on the balcony, I suddenly felt cold. Jane, in the doorway, shivered. I said: 'What are we going to do?'

George Thousand Names scratched the back of his

neck. 'Two practical steps to begin with. First, call up your friend at Elmwood Hospital and have him separate all three of Coyote's victims into different clinics or hospitals. That's vital. Second, get hold of those pictures of Mount Taylor and Cabezon Peak and see if you can work out where that shorn-off hair is located. If you can keep *that* away from Coyote, you might have half a chance. Third – and this more difficult – keep any nurses or female doctors or any women at all away from Coyote's different parts. Coyote has a hunger for women's flesh, and that's what he's probably after right now.'

I took a deep breath. However strange and far-fetched all this legendary stuff seemed to be, I knew that for my own peace of mind I was going to have to call Dr Jarvis and tell him. He was intelligent, Jim Jarvis, and he was open to suggestion, but I wondered just what he was going to say when I passed on George Thousand Names's instructions.

I said: 'Mr Thousand Names, do you mind if I use your phone?'

'Be my guest. Would you care for some firewater?'

'I sure would. How about Russian firewater and tonic?'

I walked across the polished wooden floor and picked up the phone. Meanwhile, George Thousand Names came back inside and told his maid to bring us some drinks. Then he sat down cross-legged on his Indian-patterned settee and opened up his jar of tobacco. There was a pipe-rack on the coffee-table next to him, and none of them looked much like a pipe of peace. There were a couple of expensive meerschaums and three English briars.

The Round Valley Reservation operator put me through to San Francisco, and San Francisco put me through to Elmwood Foundation Hospital. Dr Jarvis, for once, was free.

'Jim?' I said. 'This is John Hyatt. I'm calling from Round Valley.'

'Thank God, I've been trying to get you. It's all hell down here.'

'What's wrong?'

'The whole place is going berserk. Your friend Dan Machin woke out of his coma and he's locked himself in with Bryan Corder. We've tried breaking the door down, but no luck so far. Dr Cane has just called the police for cutting equipment.'

Again, the surge of fear.

'He's locked himself in? You mean, they're *together*?'

'That's right. I don't know what the—'

The connection suddenly broke off. I rattled the phone, but the line was completely dead. George Thousand Names said: 'Sorry, that sometimes happens. Is anything wrong?'

I laid down the useless receiver. 'I think there is. Dan Machin has shut himself up with Bryan Corder. The hospital staff can't get in there.'

George Thousand Names steadily packed his pipe with tobacco, and reached for his matches. 'It sounds as though it's started,' he said. 'Perhaps we'd better get down there.'

'We?'

The Indian girl brought the drinks, and George Thousand Names lifted his glass of bourbon.

'You don't think I'm going to let white men have the greatest Indian demon all to themselves, do you? This is something that red men are going to talk about for generations to come. Now, let's drink to the confusion of our enemies.'

I raised my vodka. 'I don't know about the confusion of our enemies,' I said dryly, 'but I know damn well that *I'm* confused as hell.'

We drove back down to San Francisco that night at over ninety miles an hour, with moths pelting our windshield, and our faces strained in the green glow from the Jaguar's instrument panel. Tyres squealing, we took the curves down the mountains, and then we hit 101 and snaked southwards through Willits, Ukiah, Cloverdale, and back down into Sonoma County. It was just after midnight when we crossed into Marin County, and it was only when I saw the glitter of San Francisco sprinkled across the darkness of the bay that I eased my foot off the gas, and cruised across the Golden Gate at forty.

George Thousand Names had been snoring fitfully in the back seat, but he woke up with a start as we turned off Presidio Drive and made our way up towards the hospital. He stretched, and said: 'The trouble with English cars, they expect you to sit upright all the damned time. What do they think I am, a country squire?'

'You didn't have to come,' I reminded him, as we took the Elmwood turn-off and bounced down the drive into the hospital forecourt.

'That's like trying to tell Custer not to go to the Little Big Horn,' retorted George Thousand Names.

'Are you that pessimistic?' asked Jane.

George Thousand Names blew his nose, very loudly. 'Pessimism isn't a particularly Indian characteristic. I consulted the day's omens before I left, and they seem okay, although I have to admit that there's a cloud on the horizon, no bigger than a man's fist.'

'There are the birds,' I said, pointing. 'It looks like the sanitation department gave up trying to get rid of them.'

Our headlights, as we swung down the driveway, flashed across the ruffled grey ranks of birds. Then I pulled the Jaguar up, and we climbed out, and George Thousand Names stood in the breezy darkness, staring up at the silent feathery witnesses to Coyote's rebirth.

I said: 'Well?'

He nodded. 'There is no doubt at all. These are the

rare birds we call Grey Sadness. They were seen gathering at Wounded Knee, and at the funeral of Sitting Bull, and when Rain-in-the-Face died. They are the birds of mourning and bad luck.'

Jane reached over and held my hand. Her own hand was very cold. She said: 'Do they really mean that Coyote is here?'

George Thousand Names lifted his head as if he were sniffing the wind. 'Can you smell something?' he asked us.

I sniffed. 'Not much. I have a sinus condition.'

Jane said: 'It's like . . . I don't quite know *what* it's like. It's like dogs. Dogs, when they get wet.'

George Thousand Names nodded. He didn't say anything more. I took Jane's arm and led her into the hospital doors, and he followed, glancing up now and again at the birds, the bringers of Grey Sadness, with his eyes as wary and fearful as those of a man who is brought into a mortuary to view his father's body.

There were two uniformed policemen from the SFPD standing guard by the elevators. One of them came across the tiled lobby as we walked in, and raised his hand.

'I'm sorry, sir. Nobody allowed inside right now.'

'I've come to see Dr Jarvis. He's expecting us.'

The policeman examined us suspiciously. 'That's too bad. I got strict orders that no one goes up.'

'What do you mean?' I demanded. 'Dr Jarvis telephoned me three or four hours ago, and we've come all the way from Round Valley.'

'Mister,' said the policeman patiently, 'I don't care if you've come from the planet Mars. My orders are, nobody goes up.'

The second policeman came across and said: 'That's right. Those are the orders.'

'Now hold on a goddamned minute—' I said, but George Thousand Names interrupted me.

'We have authority,' he told the cop quietly. 'Do you wish to examine it?'

The policemen looked across at him with mistrust. But George Thousand Names reached into his red windcheater and raised one of the golden amulets that hung around his neck.

'What's that?' asked one of the cops. 'A Wilkie button?'

'Look at it,' insisted George Thousand Names. 'Examine it.'

Somehow he caught the light in the lobby with his amulet and flashed it into the policemen's eyes. The policemen appeared to blink, and stare, and take a step back as if someone had elbowed them out of the way. I looked at George Thousand Names, and then I looked at Jane, but all Jane could do was shrug.

'We have authority to pass,' said George Thousand Names loudly. 'Do you understand?'

The policemen nodded. One of them, like a sleep-walker, turned around and opened the elevator doors for us, and we stepped inside. George Thousand Names told me; 'It's all yours, Mr Hyatt,' and I pressed the button for 5.

'Is that a kind of hypnosis?' I asked him, as we rose smoothly upward. 'The way you used that amulet?'

George Thousand Names tucked it back into his windcheater. 'We call it The Way Of Kindly Conquest. It is a kind of hypnosis, yes, but it has the advantage of inducing an obedient trance for just a few moments at a time – a few moments which the victim never recalls. You can't make it work on people who are openly aggressive, or on people who are determined to resist hypnosis. But it does work quite well on ordinary people whose minds are fairly relaxed.'

'But won't those policemen come after us?' asked Jane.

George Thousand Names shook his head. 'It's very doubtful. Right this minute they're probably standing downstairs shaking their heads, absolutely sure that something's gone wrong, but totally unsure what it could have been.'

We reached the fifth floor, and the elevator doors slid open. George Thousand Names courteously ushered Jane out into the corridor, and I stepped after them, looking for signs of the terrible panic that Dr Jarvis had called me about.

The corridor was silent. I listened for a while, but I couldn't even hear the normal sounds of a busy private hospital, like trolleys, and conversation, and intercoms calling for doctors. There was nothing but the *click-hum* of the elevator as its doors closed behind us and it rose to higher floors.

'I guess we'd better try Dr Jarvis's office first,' I suggested. 'If he's not there, he'll be down at intensive care.'

'Lead on,' said George Thousand Names. 'The sooner we get to grips with this monster, the better.'

Jane laughed nervously. 'You're making this sound like a Frankenstein movie.'

George Thousand Names stuck his hands in his jeans pockets and made a moue. 'It's worse than that,' he said pragmatically.

We walked along the soft red carpet until we reached Dr Jarvis's office. I held my breath, and rapped on the door. We waited, but there was no reply. George Thousand Names, his eyes as patient as a lizard's in his leathery face, said: 'I hope you told this doctor what he was up against.'

I opened Dr Jarvis's door and quickly checked his tiny room. It was neat and orderly, and there was even a polystyrene cup of coffee on the desk, left abandoned like the last lunch on the *Marie Celeste*. A cigarette butt smouldered in the crowded ashtray. The bottle of gin, almost empty, stood on the filing cabinet.

'Spooky,' said Jane.

'They must be down at intensive care,' I said. 'It's just along here, on the left.'

We began to hurry as we turned the corner and made our way towards the intensive care unit. I don't know why. The silence gave us a sense of urgency somehow, as if the longer it stayed silent, the more terrifying everything was going to get. All we could hear was our own breathing, and the rustle of our clothes as we walked quickly along.

I didn't bother to knock on the double doors of the unit. I just pushed my way in – into the gloom and the shadows and the blue twilight world where Bryan Corder was living out his unnatural life.

Dr Jarvis was there, and so were Dr Cane and Dr Weston and Lieutenant Stroud from the police department, and two baffled and burly cops. Dr Jarvis turned as we came in, and said: 'You made it. I was afraid you wouldn't.'

'What's going on?' I asked him. 'What's happening in there?'

Dr Jarvis took my arm and led me forward to the glass panel which looked into the depths of the unit itself. It was still illuminated with blue light, but somehow the light seemed dimmer and more restless, like the cold phosphorescence that crawls across the sea at night, or the uncanny glow of decaying fish. I could make out the shape of the couch, and around the couch I could still see the chromium stands with saline drips and plasma. I thought I could see the bone-white curve of Bryan Corder's skull, too, but on the couch itself there was an indefinable lump of twisted limbs and flesh, and it was too dark to understand what it could possibly be.

'Dan Machin's in there?' I asked Dr Jarvis. 'I don't see where.'

Jane said: 'Can't you get in?'

Lieutenant Stroud, tall and urbane as usual, answered: 'Ms Torresino, we're not standing out here for our health. We've tried six or seven times to get inside, and each time we've been repulsed.'

'Repulsed?' I queried. 'What do you mean, "repulsed"?'

'Try it for yourself,' suggested Lieutenant Stroud. 'The door's right here.'

I stepped forward, but George Thousand Names said, very softly: 'Don't, Mr Hyatt. It's not worth it.'

Lieutenant Stroud said: 'What do you know?'

George Thousand Names glanced at me through the gloom, and I could see that he was trying to suppress a smile.

'This is George Thousand Names, lieutenant,' I said. 'I brought him down tonight from the Round Valley Reservation.'

'You're still gibbering about this Red Indian stuff?'

'You can call it gibbering,' I put in quietly. 'But so far it's the only reasonable explanation. George Thousand Names believes that what we're witnessing here is the rebirth of an Indian demon from way back in time.'

Lieutenant Stroud looked at Dr Jarvis, then at the other doctors, then at his two flatfoots. Then he turned to George Thousand Names with a sarcastic, beatific smile, and said: 'A Red Indian demon from way back in time? Is that right?'

George Thousand Names was too old and self-possessed to be fazed by sarcasm. He simply nodded, and said: 'That's right. The demon's name is Coyote, sometimes called the First One To Use Words For Force. He is generally understood to be the demon of confusion, anger and argument, apart from his insatiable lust for women.'

Lieutenant Stroud laughed, short and harsh. 'The demon rapist?'

George Thousand Names smiled, but kept his cool. 'That's just about right, lieutenant. The demon rapist. There's an old Navaho song which tells how Coyote met a young woman on a mountain pass, and how he tricked her into lifting her dress for him. It's a charming song, in its way. But what it omits is that Coyote was the most fierce and fearsome-looking of all demons anywhere, and that once he'd seduced a woman he'd generally behave like less than a gentleman.'

'What do you mean – "less than a gentleman"?' asked Lieutenant Stroud coldly.

George Thousand Names said: 'There are ladies present.'

'None of the ladies here are going to worry about anatomical details, if that's what you're thinking.'

'It's not that,' replied George Thousand Names. 'It's just that if this demon does manage to bring himself back to life, then no woman in San Francisco will be safe, and I'd hate to frighten these ladies unnecessarily.'

'Spit it out, will you?' demanded Lieutenant Stroud. 'If there's something going on here, I want to know what it is!'

'Very well,' said George Thousand Names. 'Coyote first seduces his women, and then he treats them to what the Navaho used to call the Ordeal of Three.'

Jane said: 'My God. I've heard of that.'

George Thousand Names touched her arm. 'It was the strangest of all ancient tortures, and its history goes back far beyond the civilisation of the North American tribes. It is said by many of our wise men that it was Coyote's personal invention, but who can say?'

Dr Jarvis frowned. 'I've never heard of the Ordeal of Three. What the hell is it?'

George Thousand Names touched one of the amulets around his neck. He said, in a toneless voice: 'The Ordeal of Three involved cutting open a woman's stomach, and sewing up into her stomach a live reptile, like a Gila monster, and then cutting open a horse or a cow, and disembowelling it, and sewing up the woman inside the horse. The art of the torture was to keep all three victims – lizard, woman and horse – alive as long as possible.'

Dr Weston said: 'Oh, come on. You're just making that up.'

George Thousand Names shook his head. 'Check with your anthropologists if you have to. The skeletons of a lizard, a woman and a horse, one inside the other like a Chinese puzzle, were dug up at Lake Winnemucca, in Nevada, not six years ago, by Professor Forrester of the University of Colorado.'

Lieutenant Stroud pulled at his lower lip. Then he said: 'Okay, Mr Thousand Names. If you know what goes on around here, what do you suggest is going on *there*?'

He pointed through the glass panel to the dim and shadowy forms on the care-unit couch. Something was moving in there, some shape, bulky and dark, moving and twitching with that jerky, unpleasant twitching that characterises the first movements of insects as they work their way out of their chrysalis.

George Thousand Names said: 'The Grey Sadness was enough to show me. What you're seeing here is the coming together of Coyote, the foulest of Red Indian demons. When he was banished to the underworld, he concealed his breath and his blood and his heartbeat, and now he's managed to bring them all back together again in one place. He's coming to life, whether you like it or not.'

Lieutenant Stroud stared at George Thousand Names for quite a while, his eyes glistening attentively in the darkness. He said: 'So you really believe it. You really believe that's happening.'

George Thousand Names said: 'It's not belief, lieutenant. It's not an act of faith. I *know* what's happening. It's as plain to me as a flat tyre on an automobile is to you. It's a fact.'

Dr Jarvis said: 'Then what — then what's going on here?'

'Go get a flashlight and you'll see,' said George Thousand Names, rather too calmly for my liking. 'The breath and the heartbeat are joining together. Soon, all Coyote will need is his blood and his terrible face.'

'Jane,' I said, leaning over and speaking quietly in her ear. 'The doorknocker at Pilarcitos Street. Can you go and get it? Knock it off the door with a hammer if you have to.'

Jane held my arm. 'I don't want to leave you, John. Not now.'

I took out a ten-dollar bill and folded it into her hand. 'You won't be away for long. Take a taxi. But just get a hold of that doorknocker before anyone else does.'

Jane looked up at me with those wide china-blue eyes, and then she put her arm around my neck and kissed me. 'Maybe we should have stayed together, you and I,' she whispered, and then she slipped out of the room and made her way off to 1551.

Lieutenant Stroud was saying: 'We've tried flashlights. It's the angle of the glass or something, but they won't penetrate.'

George Thousand Names turned from Lieutenant Stroud to Dr Jarvis and back again. 'In that case,' he said, 'the great Coyote has gained more strength than I thought. He is powerful enough to absorb your light completely.'

Dr Weston, the black lady specialist, said: 'Absorb? What are you talking about?' She clearly didn't think much of George Thousand Names's ethnic folklore. She had enough ethnic folklore of her own.

George Thousand Names said: 'You haven't been reading your *Scientific American* lately. When an object has sufficient density, it can actually.prevent light from reflecting away from it. It attracts the light back to

115

itself by its intense gravitational pull. That's what's happening here. Coyote is a beast of the underworld. If you like, he's a living black hole.'

'You mean, he's going to be completely invisible?' asked Dr Jarvis.

George Thousand Names shook his head. 'Only when he desires it.'

Dr Cane put in: 'What about his blood? If his heartbeat and his breath are getting together here, shouldn't we try to isolate Mr Wallis? He's the vessel for this demon's blood, I presume.'

'Yes,' answered the medicine man. 'Try to get him away. But be careful of the birds, and be careful of any magical tricks that Coyote might try to pull to prevent you doing it.'

'Magical tricks?' asked Lieutenant Stroud sceptically. 'Like what?'

George Thousand Names said: 'Lieutenant, this may seem like a joke but it's not. When I say magical tricks, I'm not talking about lifting rabbits out of a hat or sawing ladies in half. I'm talking about death and injury and illusions like you've never seen.'

I put in: 'It makes sense, lieutenant. Everything that George has said so far – it makes sense.'

'Who asked you?' snapped Lieutenant Stroud.

Dr Jarvis said: 'There's no point in arguing, lieutenant. None of us has a better idea.'

'You don't think so?' said Lieutenant Stroud, turning around. 'Well maybe I've got myself a better idea. Maybe this whole damned thing is a hoax.'

'A *hoax*?' I said. 'You think we'd take the flesh off a man's skull for a hoax?'

'Well, all this damn stupid stuff about Indian demons—'

'Stuff!' said George Thousand Names, bristling. 'You call our demons *stuff*! Are you crazy? Do you know what Coyote can do? Do you have any idea?'

Lieutenant Stroud was taken aback by George

116

Thousand Names's ferocity. He said meekly: 'Well, you mentioned the Ordeal of Three . . .'

'That's *nothing*!' retorted George Thousand Names. 'That's what he does with the women he's played with and thrown aside! Coyote has powers beyond all human comprehension. Powers that made it almost impossible for all the good and evil gods combined to destroy him. And that's without the added powers he stole from other demons like Big Monster and the Loogaroos.'

'The Loogaroos?' said Lieutenant Stroud, in disbelief.

'That's what the French colonists called them, when they first came to America. It's a corruption of *loups-garous*, which means "were-wolves". Coyote took powers from all of them. He covers his back with the hide of a werewolf, and wears on his head the scalp of Big Monster, and with those he is almost indestructible.'

Lieutenant Stroud listened to this outburst, and then stood there silent for a long moment, while all of us watched his face, wondering how the hell he was going to respond. I thought at first he was going to dismiss everything that George Thousand Names had said as garbage, but then I saw his expression soften, and the lines around his mouth deepen, and I knew that the medicine man's conviction had almost convinced him.

He said: 'I want to know what's going on in there, inside that room. I want you to explain it to me.'

George Thousand Names stepped forward. The blue light that irradiated from the intensive-care unit made his eyes glisten, and painted the lines and creases of his face in ultramarine. He raised one shrivelled hand, his fingers decorated with silver rings and his wrist hung with bead bracelets, and pressed it against the glass, as if he could feel vibrations from the dark and twisted mass that was Dan Machin, or Bryan Corder, or both of them, or neither.

With his other hand holding his golden amulet, he said softly: 'It is almost time for Coyote to make himself live once more, to model himself out of the clay of human flesh. He needs blood but he can rise without blood. He is moulding himself from the bodies of those who possess his heartbeat and his breath. Look!'

All the time that George Thousand Names had his hand pressed to the window, he must have been mentally struggling against the powers of Coyote. Because when he said '*Look!*' the blue light rose and brightened, as if a dynamo had been suddenly turned faster, and in that brief and horrifying brightness we actually saw what it was that he had been trying to explain to us. We saw the beginnings of Coyote, the demon, the rapist and traitor, the First One To Use Words For Force.

On the couch, we saw limbs rising and falling. At first they looked like the arms and legs of people drowning in a lake of darkness; but then the contorted mass of flesh seemed to rise up, and stand almost upright, and all I could do was stare at what it was and feel a horrifying shudder all the way down my back.

In some unspeakable way, Dan Machin and Bryan Corder had been twisted together as one creature. It was almost eight feet tall, rearing blindly off the couch with Bryan's fleshless skull as its head, but with both men's arms and legs reaching out towards us. Their torsos were combined in a shapeless double-torso of knotted muscle, and Dan Machin's ghastly face appeared momentarily from inside the beast's stomach, pressed against the translucent skin with its mouth wide open in a hellish howl.

Dr Jarvis said: 'It's impossible!' and Dr Weston moaned as if she was hurt. But then the blue light dimmed again, and all we could see was the murky outline of that monstrous creature, and the white reflection of the emergency lamps from what had once been Bryan Corder's head.

Lieutenant Stroud, his voice dry, said: 'All right, Mr Thousand Names – what is it?'

George Thousand Names lifted himself wearily away from the window. 'It's Coyote,' he said simply. 'He takes on many forms, but this one more than most. It could have been a woman, or a deer, or even a fish. He is once said to have moulded his earthly manifestation out of a girl and a tarantula. But tonight he's lucky. He has two strong young men for his reincarnation, and downstairs in the morgue you have Seymour Wallis's blood.'

'Did you give orders to get rid of. that blood?' demanded Lieutenant Stroud.

Dr Jarvis said: 'Dr Cane's taken care of it. Seymour Wallis's body should be halfway to Redwood City by now.'

'Redwood City?' asked the lieutenant. 'What's at Redwood City?'

'Elmwood Foundation finances a cryogenic research centre at Redwood. We can put Seymour Wallis on ice for as long as we like.'

I said: 'What are we going to do about *that*?' and I pointed towards the bulky shape in the intensive-care unit. 'We can't just leave it the way it is.'

Lieutenant Stroud gave me an impatient glance, as if to tell me to mind my own goddamned business, but he went up to Dr Jarvis, and laid his hand confidingly on his shoulder.

'Doctor,' he said. 'Is that thing a threat to human life? To the lives of your staff?'

Dr Jarvis licked his lips. 'I don't have any evidence of that. So far I've seen nothing more than extreme physiological abnormality. It hasn't threatened us in any way at all.'

George Thousand Names butted in. 'Coyote's very

existence is a threat! Once he has his blood running through his veins again, he'll tear us to pieces!'

'You have some proof?' asked Lieutenant Stroud. 'I'm not doubting your word, sir, but that thing in there is kind of human, and I'm not authorised to shoot human beings unless I have reasonable grounds to believe that they may be threatening life or property.'

George Thousand Names stood stiff as the spine on a porcupine, his eyes blazing. He pointed with a rigid arm towards the intensive-care unit, and said: 'That, lieutenant, is Coyote, returned from the underworld! What more can I tell you? *That's Coyote!*'

Lieutenant Stroud looked across at his two officers, and one of them raised his eyebrows as if to suggest that George Thousand Names may not have all of his marbles.

'What do you think, doctor?' the lieutenant asked Dr Weston. 'Is that a Red Indian demon or not? Or is it just a medical freak?'

Dr Weston, although she was shaken by what she had seen in the intensive-care unit, said: 'It's a freak. It has to be. I've never seen anything like it, but we can't kill it.'

Dr Jarvis said: 'Supposing—'

'Supposing nothing!' interrupted Dr Weston. 'Jim, this thing is the strangest medical event we've ever seen. It's like Siamese twins being created in front of your eyes. We can't destroy it now. There's no way!'

I put in: 'Dr Weston, you didn't see Bryan Corder hurt. You didn't see Dan Machin when his eyes lit up like a devil's. You can't say that. Whatever it is in there, whether it's a demon or not, we've got to make sure it doesn't kill anyone else!'

Dr Weston was about to answer, but she never had the chance. What happened next was like a road accident – it blurred past my eyes so fast that it was hard to understand anything. I do remember one or two vivid and horrifying things, though, and I guess they're going to stay in my mind forever.

Dr Jarvis suddenly said: '*It's coming this way!*' and just as we turned to look at the intensive-care unit there was a blast of shattering glass, and thousands of fragments of the observation panel sprayed across the room in a razor-sharp hail. One of the cops dropped to his knees at once, his face like chopped liver, and the other one turned away with his hands over his eyes and blood running down his fingers. My own cheeks were slashed in the glittering, tumbling burst of glass; but it wasn't the glass that frightened me.

It was the apparition of Coyote, rearing up like a huge pale praying mantis, his skull grinning fixedly on top of its shapeless trunk, his four arms smashing the remains of the window aside without pain or hesitation.

And there was the heat. The appalling, scorching heat. It must have been two hundred degrees inside that intensive-care unit, and now a dry, roasting wind moaned and howled as it surged out of the broken window.

Lieutenant Stroud plucked his police special from his pants and fired twice at the monstrous Coyote. But the demon waved one arm towards him, and he was hurtled away across the room, cracking his back against the wall, his gun skidding off into the slush of broken glass.

Dr Jarvis shrieked: '*John! Hold him!*' But I knew that there was no way we were going to hold this thing back, and I wrenched open the door and shouted: 'Forget it! For Christ's sake, get out of here!'

George Thousand Names, his hands lifted to protect his head, scrambled out of the room as quickly as he could. Dr Weston followed him, and then me, and then Dr Jarvis. The cop with the bleeding eyes was trying to help Lieutenant Stroud, but the demon waved his arm again, and the cop shrieked, and staggered helplessly towards the door.

'*I'm burning!*' he yelled. 'Put me out! For God's sake! *I'm burning!*'

Dr Jarvis ran towards him, but then the cop opened his mouth, and a fierce gout of flame gushed out from between his lips. *He was blazing inside* – his stomach and his lungs were on fire – and every time he tried to cry for help, a monstrous funnel of superheated flames bellowed out. Dr Jarvis hollered: 'John! A blanket! Get me a blanket!' but it was too late. The cop rolled against the side of the corridor, and slid to his knees, leaving a trail of fiercely-burning blood on the wall. Then he collapsed and lay still, and in front of our eyes, to our overwhelming horror, the flames that were burning inside him gradually broke out, singeing and then setting fire to his uniform from inside, and then engulfing his whole body, until he lay on the carpet blazing like a ritual suicide.

There was another moan of hot air from inside the room, and we heard something like a grumble and a roar, the sound of a devilish beast that was determined to destroy us. Then – miraculously – Lieutenant Stroud came diving out of the doorway, rolling sideways towards us, and gasping for air like an athlete who's testing his threshold of pain.

George Thousand Names and Dr Jarvis knelt down beside him. 'I'm okay, I'm okay,' he told them, trying to stand up. 'My back's bruised but I think I'm okay. For God's sake let's get out of here. That thing's gone crazy.'

George Thousand Names said: 'Not crazy. That's his natural behaviour. He's going to destroy and devour us, and there's nothing we can do.'

Lieutenant Stroud painfully climbed to his feet, his eyes fixed on the dark doorway where Coyote was hiding.

'Well, maybe there's nothing that *you* can do, medicine man, but I know what *I'm* going to do. That

– that *thing* in there has declared war, and if it's war he wants, he's damned well going to get it!'

George Thousand Names reached out and held the lieutenant's arm. 'Please, Lieutenant. You're not dealing with the *Creature from the Black Lagoon*. Bombs and teargas could never hurt Coyote. All you can do is to—'

His words were drowned in a roar that shook the whole building. Pieces of broken door, ribbons of shredded carpet, fragments of plaster and a dry fierce heat that stank of animals and death came blasting over us. It was Coyote, coming out in search of his blood, coming out in search of his face, and coming out to slaughter us. It was Coyote, the demon of wrath and fear!

CHAPTER FIVE

I was hardly conscious. A chunk of door-jamb had struck me on the left side of the head, and my legs had given way beneath me. I was lying against the side of the corridor, shrouded in tattered carpet, and it seemed that the whole world was coming down around me. The hot hurricane howled and shrieked, and pieces of debris tumbled and flew down the corridor. Over it all, as Coyote approached us, I heard a noise like someone screaming down an endless echoing pipe; a hopeless dreary screaming that frightened me more than almost anything else.

Screwing up my eyes against the scorching wind, I tried to look up. I could see George Thousand Names sprawled against the opposite wall, and Lieutenant Stroud huddled beside him. Dr Jarvis was further away, his hands clutched over his gingery hair, but I couldn't see Dr Weston at all.

Then the very air itself seemed to darken, and out of the darkness came something that wasn't much to do with Bryan Corder and Dan Machin any more. It was a spectral manifestation, a ghost made of eerie density and contorted flesh. It had a kind of negative glow to it, the glow of deep shadows or gloomy rooms, and it glided darkly down the corridor, the skull with its hideous grin, and behind it a rippling and loathsome cloak of half-substantial flesh. The screaming grew drearier and louder as Coyote went by, but there was yet another sound which accompanied his passing. *It was the flap of dead skin*, like flacid tarpaulin on a deserted warehouse roof. It was almost more than I could bear.

The noise and the wind seemed to drone on for ever, but suddenly I raised my head again and I became aware that Coyote had passed us by without harming us. I looked up a little more, and turned round to check behind me, and the demon had vanished.

George Thousand Names whispered dryly: 'I think it's all right now, at least for a while. He's gone to search for his blood.'

'How do you know that?' asked Lieutenant Stroud.

'Because he would have killed us otherwise, and taken great pleasure in raping Dr Weston. He needs his blood to stay alive, and if he doesn't get it in one moon's rising and descending, he'll be banished back to the underworld.'

Lieutenant Stroud, clutching his back, stood up against the wall. 'Well, that's the first piece of good news I've heard all day. All we have to do is keep Coyote away from innocent bystanders for twenty-four hours, and that's the end of that.'

George Thousand Names brushed off his windcheater. 'I'm afraid not, lieutenant. Whatever you do, Coyote will make sure that he finds his blood.'

I said, 'What about his face? His face was on the doorknocker.'

'He'll go searching for that too.'

'But I just sent Jane off to get that.'

George Thousand Names stared at me, and his face was totally grave. 'You sent Jane to get the doorknocker? You mean that?'

I felt panicky. 'Well, sure, I just thought that if he didn't have his face—'

George Thousand Names said: 'Great spirit, preserve us. If Coyote catches her with that thing, she won't stand a chance.'

Lieutenant Stroud came forward and he looked impatient. 'I'm sorry to interrupt the ominous warnings, but what did you mean about the blood? That blood should be locked up at Redwood City by now — isn't that right, doctor? How's Coyote going to find it, let alone get hold of it?'

'Oh, come on, Lieutenant,' I said, equally testy. 'Coyote just burst his way through three inches of toughened glass.'

'I didn't ask you,' retorted Lieutenant Stroud sharply. 'I was asking our resident expert.'

'Well, the answer to your question is that Coyote is a dog-monster of sorts,' said George Thousand Names. 'He has a supernatural ear and a supernatural sense of smell. The old legends said that when Bear Maiden was hiding in a cave, Coyote was able to smell her through ten spear-lengths of solid rock, and he destroyed the cave and half the mountain to find her. That was supposed to have happened on Nacimiento Peak, more years ago than even the Navahoes can remember.'

Lieutenant Stroud looked grim. 'Thanks for the optimistic forecast.'

'What are you going to do now?' I asked him.

'The first damned thing I'm going to do is call in the SWAT squad. We're going to find that, whatever it is, and give it a dose of what it just handed out to us.'

'Lieutenant,' put in George Thousand Names. 'I thought you were a sophisticated man. At least, more sophisticated than most policemen.'

'What's that supposed to imply?'

The old Indian looked at the detective cold and level. 'Your massive firepower is useless. Would you hunt a fox with a tank, or try to kill a mosquito with a machine-gun? Coyote is too cunning for you, lieutenant, too powerful, too elusive. What you must do is track him down in the way that the ancient gods used to, by appealing to his lust and his vanity, and by coaxing him into engineering his own destruction.'

'Are you kidding?' said Lieutenant Stroud. 'When I have to make my report about this, I'm going to have to say what immediate and decisive action I took. I can just think what the commissioner's going to say when he reads that I appealed to the fugitive's lust and vanity, and coaxed him into engineering his own destruction. Now, if you'll excuse me.'

The lieutenant went across to an office close by, and picked up the telephone. He rattled the handset a few times, and then eventually got through. As he called up reinforcements, George Thousand Names looked at Dr Jarvis and me, and shrugged. 'You can never explain to a white man,' he said.

I said: 'What about Jane? Can we do something to help her?'

'Of course,' replied the Indian. 'In fact, the best plan for you and I right now is to go to this house on Pilarcitos Street and seal it off from Coyote with the strongest spells we can. If he hasn't got there already, he'll try to steal the doorknocker and he'll also try to get to those pictures of Mount Taylor and Cabezon Peak.'

'Why's that?' asked Dr Jarvis.

'Simple – he wants the hair that he cut from Big Monster. Once he finds it, his immortality will be assured. We will never be able to destroy or dismiss him then.'

'All right,' I said. 'What are we waiting for?'

As we left the front door of the hospital, the first of the SWAT trucks and cars were arriving, and the night was howling and warbling with sirens. We walked quickly across the carpark to Dr Jarvis's Monte Carlo, and Dr Jarvis held the front seat forward so that I could climb awkwardly into the back. As he stood there, he glance up at the roof of the hospital and said: 'The birds – they're gone.'

George Thousand Names seemed to take it all very calmly. As he eased himself into the front passenger seat, he said: 'Of course. They have followed Coyote. They hang over his head like a cloud of sorrow. Sometimes they seem to fill the air like heavy smoke, and other times they are almost invisible. Birds are very magical and strange creatures, Dr Jarvis. They have spirits of a supernatural kind that men can rarely understand.'

Jim Jarvis started the motor, and we drove out of the hospital gates and into the streets of midnight San Francisco. It was a warm, clogged night and the city lights sparkled and rippled through air that was almost unbreathably humid. Although it was late, it was Saturday night, and there were still plenty of cars cruising around, and couples walking down the sloping streets.

As we sped along 17th Street as far as Dolores Street, I suddenly glimpsed a girl in a red blouse and white jeans on the sidewalk. I yelled: 'Jim – that's Jane! I'm sure that's Jane! Pull over!'

Dr Jarvis swung the car into the kerbside, and then backed up. I looked frantically through the tinted back window, and Jane came into view. She was walking steadily and purposefully in the direction of Mission Street, and she hadn't even turned our way. Dr Jarvis bipped his car horn, and it was only then that she stopped, and frowned in a dazed kind of a way, and came over to the kerb.

Dr Jarvis climbed out of the car and I squeezed myself out after him. I went around the front of the car and took Jane by the arms and held her. She was pale, and her eyes had a moist, myopic look about them, but otherwise she seemed okay. I said: 'Jane – Jane, what's wrong?'

She smiled, but somehow she didn't seem to be concentrating. 'There's nothing wrong,' she whispered. 'Nothing wrong at all.'

'But why didn't you take a taxi? What are you doing here?'

'Here?' she said, raising her head and looking at me vaguely.

'This is 17th. You were supposed to be going to Pilarcitos in a taxi.'

Jane touched her forehead as if she was trying to remember. 'Oh, yes, Pilarcitos Street.'

Dr Jarvis pushed me gently away, and examined Jane with swift professionalism. He raised one of her eyelids with his thumb, and checked her pulse. While he was doing this, she stood there silent and passive, her only expression a faint frown, her eyes staring off into some private distance that I couldn't even guess at.

'Is she all right?' I asked him. 'She seems like she's suffering from shock.'

'It could be shock,' said Dr Jarvis. 'On the other hand, it could be a form of hypnosis, or trance.'

'Do you think Coyote—?'

'John, I don't know *what* I'm supposed to think. But the main thing is that she's safe. Let's get her into the car and get up to Pilarcitos Street. Then your Indian friend here can do what he has to do to keep Coyote out of the house, and we can get Jane back to hospital.'

George Thousand Names stuck his head out of the car window. 'Are we going to be long?' he asked me. 'The quicker we get to that house the better. If Coyote has gotten there already, we won't stand a chance.'

Between us, Jim Jarvis and I helped Jane to climb into the back seat of the car, and then we swerved off from the kerb and made our way towards Mission Street and Pilarcitos.

As we came up the sloping street, the house at 1551 looked as dark and brooding as it ever had before. The windows were like sunken eyes, and the scabrous paintwork seemed to have flaked even more. Dr Jarvis slowed the car as we came nearer, and as we stopped outside he switched off the motor and we sat there for almost a minute in silence.

'Do you think Coyote's in there?' I said, in an unsettled voice.

'It's impossible to say,' answered George Thousand Names. 'But if he is, we'll soon find out.'

'How?'

'He'll kill us.'

Dr Jarvis wiped his mouth with the back of his hand. 'But he may not *be* there, right? He may still be looking for Seymour Wallis's blood?'

'Of course.'

I looked at Dr Jarvis and Dr Jarvis looked at me. 'Well,' I said, wryly. 'Here goes nothing.'

We got out of the car and then went around to help George Thousand Names. Jane stayed where she was, silent and presumably shocked. The three of us crossed the sidewalk and stood by the front gate of 1551, looking up at the gloomy porch, and the scaley lintels.

'Is the doorknocker still there?' asked George Thousand Names. 'I find it hard to see without my eyeglasses.'

Dr Jarvis and I peered into the shadows. At first I thought it had gone, but then I caught the dark gleam of bronze, and I knew that Coyote was still off pursuing his blood. For the moment, we were safe.

We opened the creaking gate, and went up the steps. George Thousand Names stood for a while looking at the evil grinning face on the doorknocker, and then he slowly shook his head.

'If any Indian had ever walked past this house and seen this face, he would have known immediately what it was,' he said quietly. 'This is just as provocative as having an effigy of Satan on your door. Well, let's make sure that Coyote can never use it.'

He reached into his windcheater and lifted out an amulet. It was a small gold medallion, with a strange pictograph scratched on it. He held it for a moment in the fingers of both hands, and touched it against his forehead. Then he stepped right up to the doorknocker, and raised his hand.

'Evil Coyote, devilish one of the south-west,' he muttered. 'This likeness is forever bound by my spell, forever locked away from you. This likeness will burn

130

you, this likeness will freeze you, this likeness will blow like the winds of the north against you. You may never touch this likeness, never use this likeness, without the wrath of the great spirits falling upon you forever.'

There was silence. A truck banged and rumbled across a distant road junction.

Then, softly, I heard a hissing sound. It was like someone drawing breath. Someone about to speak.

A gentle, insidious voice said: *'Fools.'*

I felt myself shaking. I knew it was stupid, to tremble like that. But it was the doorknocker, the bronze doorknocker itself, that was speaking. Its wild eyes shone with a lurid light, and maybe it was imagination working overtime, but I *knew* this time that it was bristling with hairs, and that its teeth were as savage and sharp as any real wolf or dog.

George Thousand Names stood upright. It was clear that he was making a fierce mental effort to stay in control of the situation. He crossed his arms in front of his face, and then made a sweeping, dismissive gesture with both hands.

'Coyote is a dog that runs in the night,' he said. His voice was shaking with dignity and stern passion. 'Coyote is a sneak and a liar. The gods hear this, and the gods know this. They dismiss you, they dismiss you, they dismiss you.'

There was a chilling laugh from the doorknocker.

'Silence!' shouted George Thousand Names. *'I command you to be silent!'*

Again, there was that hissing, and another hideous laugh.

'You have no power over me, you dotard,' whispered the doorknocker. *'My master is coming soon, and then we will see.'* It laughed again.

The front door of the house suddenly jerked open by itself and banged shut again. Dr Jarvis said: 'Jesus.'

But George Thousand Names hadn't given up. He raised his arms again, and said: 'The frost of the north will enclose you, the frost of the north will crack you. Coyote of the deserts will feel your chill and retreat like the hound he is.'

I still can't really believe what I saw then; but I'd already seen so much that night that one more weirdness couldn't faze me all that much. George Thousand Names pointed directly at the doorknocker with a rigid index finger, and out of that finger came a visible spangling cloud of ice. The ice settled on the doorknocker, encrusting it with white crystals, and its hissing died away almost at once.

Still George Thousand Names kept his finger pointed at the knocker, and the ice grew thicker and thicker. I could feel the cold from where I was standing, two or three feet away. Then, abruptly, the bronze head snapped, and pieces of frozen metal clattered on to the floor of the porch.

George Thousand Names let his arm fall. He was sweating, and breathing in agonised gasps. But he had enough spirit left to kick at the fragments of doorknocker with his foot, and say; 'A dotard, huh? You chunk of scrap.'

Dr Jarvis let out a long whistle. 'That was amazing. I never saw anything like that. Mr Thousand Names, you ought to get yourself a job in the frozen food business.'

I took George Thousand Names's arm. 'You won one,' I said. 'You took Coyote on, and you won one.'

George Thousand Names shook his head. 'We haven't finished yet, and my powers are not great. Dr Jarvis – do you have space in your car for those pictures of Mount Taylor and Cabezon Peak?'

'Why, sure. But I thought you were just going to seal off the house with a couple of spells.'

George Thousand Names wiped his forehead with his handkerchief. 'I wish I could, Dr Jarvis. But fighting that likeness of Coyote has made me realise that I haven't the strength. I'm too old, too weak. We're going to have to do it some other way.'

I pushed open the heavy front door, and we cautiously stepped inside. The pictures were still there. I said: 'Right. Collect up as many as you can and stack them in the boot. Then let's get going.'

Working swiftly and silently, we unhooked the prints and drawings from the walls, and carried them down to the boot of Dr Jarvis's car. There must have been sixty or seventy of them, and by the time we had finished, the whole back of the car was weighed down with picture frames.

Jane, who was still sitting in the rear seat, looked up and said: 'Is everything all right? I feel very peculiar.'

'Don't you worry,' said Dr Jarvis. 'We'll take you right back to the hospital for a check-up.'

'Oh, no,' she said. 'I'm fine – honestly. I think I'm just suffering from shock.'

'All the same,' said Dr Jarvis, 'a medical once-over might be a good idea.'

He climbed into the car and started the motor. George Thousand Names said: 'We ought to find someplace safe for these pictures. Someplace small, that I can easily protect with spells.'

'How about my place?' I suggested. 'I have a real small apartment, and if you stood behind the front door with a baseball club, you could keep the barbarian hordes at bay for a week.'

George Thousand Names said: 'That sounds good. Can you direct us there?'

We drove over to my apartment building, and Sam the janitor eyed us with undisguised suspicion as we hefted all the pictures of Mount Taylor and Cabezon Peak into his elevator and took them upstairs. I unlocked my apartment door, and between us we stacked all the pictures in my small hallway, under the poster of Dolly Parton. I stood back and brushed the dust off my hands, and said: 'Right. Now what about the spells?'

George Thousand Names said: 'I'd like a drink first.'

We went through to my diminutive sitting room, and I opened up my black Formica cocktail cabinet with the gold spangles on it, and poured out four Hiram Walkers. I didn't really approve of bourbon made in Illinois, but it was all I had. All four of us stood there, tired and shaken, and swallowed it down like patent medicine.

George Thousand Names told me: 'I'm going to hang this on your door.' He took a small bone necklace out of his windcheater pocket, and held it up. It didn't look anything special. The bones were old and chipped and discoloured, and even though there had once been red and green paint on them, it had now mostly worn off.

'This is the necklace worn by our ancient hero Broken Shield when he climbed Leech Lake Mountain and defied the thunder gods. Historically, it's beyond price. It may be three thousand years old. But it was made to be used and that's why I want you to have it tonight. Keeping Coyote away from Big Monster's scalp is far more important than any relic, no matter how much it means to us. Coyote will not dare to touch this. If he does, he will invoke the anger of Gitche Manitou the great spirit himself.'

'I thought Coyote was the kind of demon who didn't mind defying anyone or anything,' said Dr Jarvis.

'He is,' agreed George Thousand Names. 'But like most vain and idle demons, he would rather live a quiet life, and the anger of Gitche Manitou would be quite enough to disturb his fun for the next five thousand years.'

'Fun?' queried Dr Jarvis, and shook his head in disbelief.

'Dr Jarvis,' said George Thousand Names. 'Just

remember that, to some of the fiercer demons, devouring a human is nothing more diverting than eating a bag of roasted peanuts is for us.'

George Thousand Names hung the necklace on the handle of my front door, and muttered a few incantatory words over it. Then he said: 'I expect we're all tired, and we want to be fresh for tomorrow. I suggest that we all get some rest. I had my maid make a reservation for me at the Mark Hopkins. Do you think you could give me a ride that way, doctor?'

'Sure,' said Jim Jarvis. 'How about you, Jane? Can I drop you off?'

Jane had been sitting by herself on my favourite wicker chair. She said in a flat voice: 'No, that's all right. If John doesn't mind, I think I'll stay here.'

'Mind?' I asked her. 'You have to be joking. I haven't had female company here since my Aunt Edith came up from Oxnard and brought me a seedcake.'

Dr Jarvis squeezed my arm. 'I'll believe you, John. Millions wouldn't.'

George Thousand Names came over and shook my hand, too. He said softly: 'I want to thank you for having enough imagination to see what was really happening. At least we stand some kind of a chance.'

He and Dr Jarvis were about to leave when my telephone rang. I beckoned them back inside, and picked it up.

'John Hyatt.'

It was Lieutenant Stroud. 'So you're back home, huh? I've been looking for you. Is that Indian with you?'

'George Thousand Names. Yes.'

The detective coughed, and then he said: 'We've had a little trouble on the Bayshore Freeway just past Millbrae. The ambulance with Dr Cane and Seymour Wallis's body in was kind of ambushed.'

'Ambushed? You mean by Coyote?'

Lieutenant Stroud let out a testy breath. 'All right,

if that's what you want to call it. The ambulance driver said he was driving along real normal, and suddenly this immense kind of a monster reared up in the roadway ahead of him. He was the only man to escape alive. Dr Cane, I'm sorry to say, is dead. Burned out like my patrolman.'

I put my hand over the telephone receiver and said to Dr Jarvis: 'I'm sorry, Jim. Dr Cane is dead. Coyote got to the ambulance just past the airport.'

George Thousand Names looked deadly serious. 'The blood,' he insisted. 'Did he get the blood?'

I said to Lieutenant Stroud: 'Mr Thousand Names wants to know if Coyote got the blood.'

Lieutenant Stroud coughed. 'Tell him that Seymour Wallis was found a half-hour later in the Bay. He was so sucked out that the guy who hauled him out thought at first he'd found a dead shark.'

All I could say was: 'That's it, then. What else can we do? Do you have any idea where Coyote is?'

Lieutenant Stroud said: 'We have an APB out, and the SWAT squad are checking every possible hideout. But if you ask me it's going to be hopeless.'

'Okay, lieutenant,' I told him, and laid down the phone.

In the first smeary light of early morning that seeped into my room, George Thousand Names looked tired and hunched. He ran his gnarled fingers through his white hair, and said: 'Let's hope we don't lose this one, friends. If Coyote gets loose, then I can't tell you what carnage there's going to be.'

Jane suddenly looked up, and smiled, and I can remember thinking how strange that smile was. What the hell could there be to smile about?

I made up a makeshift bed for Jane on the settee. I was too exhausted and shaken to think of seduction, and in any case Jane was acting so withdrawn and remote that I could have yelled 'Let's ball!' at the top of my voice and all she would have said was 'Pardon?'

She wrapped herself in a blanket and fell asleep almost straight away. I went around the apartment turning off the lights and drawing the curtains, but somehow I didn't feel much like lying down and closing my eyes. I went out into the hall and looked at some of the drawings of Mount Taylor. The glass in the frames was pretty dusty and stained, and most of the prints were badly foxed, but if you looked close you could see that someone had pencilled under each one '*Mount Taylor from Lookout Mountain*' or '*Mount Taylor from San Mateo*'. There were similar notations under the pictures of Cabezon Peak – like '*Cabezon Peak from San Luis*'.

I tiptoed across my sitting room and quietly took down my Rand McNally Road Atlas. Then I crept back into the kitchen, closed the door and spread it out on the table, along with as many pictures of Mount Taylor and Cabezon Peak as I could crowd around. I laid a sheet of greaseproof cooking paper over the map, took out my pen, and began to mark on the overlay the locations from which each of the views of the two mountains had been drawn.

To keep myself going, I smoked half a packet of cigarettes and made myself a big mug of black coffee, as the sunlight outside the kitchen window grew stronger, and eight o'clock chimed from the pine clock on the sitting room wall.

By nine, I had almost every viewpoint plotted, and I lifted the sheet of greaseproof up and admired the pattern of tiny Xs that I had marked all over it. I couldn't imagine what the hell they all meant, and there didn't seem to be any pattern to them that I could make out; but I guessed that George Thousand Names would probably be able to enlighten me.

I tucked the paper in my trouser pocket, and then crossed the kitchen to put the percolator on for another

mug of coffee. I switched on the small black-and-white
television that my mother had given me last Christmas,
and after a couple of messages for Sugar Frosties and
some kind of dumb plastic catapult for shooting Action
Man over your neighbour's hedge, I caught a news
bulletin about the ambulance that Seymour Wallis
had been abducted from.

The announcer said: 'San Francisco's SWAT squad
are still hunting for a ghoulish hijacker who ambushed
an ambulance on its way to Redwood City Clinic from
Elmwood Foundation Hospital and stole the cadaver
of former city engineer Seymour Wallis. The hijacker,
described by investigating detectives as "armed and
extremely violent", inflicted fatal injuries on Dr Kenneth Cane, who was accompanying the body on its
trip along Bayshore Freeway, and on Miguel Corrali-
tos, a twenty-seven-year-old hospital orderly. The
body of Mr Wallis was later found by an early-bird
fisherman in the Bay off Millbrae. So far police have
no clues to the hijacker's motives for purloining the
corpse, but they promise fresh bulletins shortly.'

After that, they went into some report about orange
blight in a fruit farm downstate, and I switched the
television off. So Coyote was still free, although I
couldn't imagine what kind of form he had taken on
now, or where he might be. What does a hideous
demon do in the daytime? He can't very well roam the
streets of San Francisco, especially with Lieutenant
Stroud and the SWAT squad tracking him down.
That's if he left any tracks.

My percolator started gurgling and popping, and
gave me quite a start. I lit another cigarette, and
looked out over the backs of the apartment buildings
around me. It was Sunday, and a pregnant girl in a
smock was sitting on a fire-escape brushing her hair
dry in the morning sunshine. I coughed and wished I
could stop smoking. Right now, though, there didn't

seem much point. If cancer didn't get me, Coyote probably would.

The telephone rang. I lifted it up and said: 'John Hyatt.'

It was George Thousand Names, calling from the Mark Hopkins. He said: 'Did you sleep okay?'

'I didn't sleep at all,' I told him. 'I spent the rest of the night charting those viewpoints of Mount Taylor and Cabezon Peak.'

'Does it look like anything interesting?'

'Well, it could be. But I think it needs an interpreter. I came second to bottom in trigonometry, and that was only because I kept my pencils sharper than the guy who came bottom.'

'Do you want to come over? As long as you leave that necklace on the door, your place will stay safe.'

'You're sure?'

'Sure I'm sure,' said George Thousand Names. 'In any case, Coyote will probably be resting up right now, absorbing his blood into his system.'

'I was wondering where demons go to in daytime.'

'Demons are things of the dark,' George Thousand Names told me. 'In sunlight, their powers are weakened. So you can bet that Coyote is holed up in some abandoned house someplace, or down in some culvert, or maybe he's even made it to 1551.'

'Isn't it worth trying to flush him out, now that it's daylight?'

'John—' said George Thousand Names '– when I say his powers are weakened I don't mean that he doesn't *have* any powers. If we go near that creature, we're dead meat. I mean that.'

'Thanks for the cheerful message. I'll come over in about an hour. I want to take a shower first. I smell like a pig.'

'Okay,' said George Thousand Names. 'Don't forget to bring the chart you made.'

I was just about to say 'you bet', when the words

died on my lips. The kitchen door had opened a small way, and there was something standing outside watching me. I could see the glitter of dark eyes, and an even darker shape. I felt as if the world had disappeared from under me, and every nerve in my body tingled and crept with fright.

'Did you hear what I said?' said the tinny, distant voice of George Thousand Names.

I said: 'Wait. There's something outside my door. I don't know what it is. Wait.'

'Which door?' he demanded.

'The kitchen door. The kitchen door, it's—'

The door slammed open so hard that splinters of wood and broken hinges flew across the room. I gave a high-pitched yelp, and pitched off my chair, scrabbling across the floor towards the sink. I kept my knives there, in a drawer, and what I needed right now was instant protection.

The beast came through that door like a tidal wave of black fur. It was a bear, a massive full-grown grizzly, nearly four hundred pounds of hair and muscle and vicious curved claws. It collided heavily with the kitchen units, and the television and percolator and spice racks clattered and crashed on to the floor. As the bear turned, it snarled viciously, and I wrenched open the kitchen drawer too quick and too hard, and let out a shower of knives and forks and bean slicers and apple corers all over the floor.

I ducked down, caught hold of my biggest kitchen cleaver, and rolled as fast as I could towards the broken door. The bear paused, and snarled again, and it was only then that I really looked at it.

It was more than a huge beast of shaggy fur and dark animal smell. It had a pale white face, pale as a woman's, but with yellowish teeth that were bared with every snarl and growl. I stared at it, trying to understand what it was, what it could possibly be. I was so shocked and horrified that I couldn't grasp it at first, just couldn't get my mind around the fact of this terrifying beast's existence.

It was Jane. Hard and ferocious though they were, those eyes were hers. That face was hers. The strange statuette on Seymour Wallis's banister post had come to life, and it was her.

I whispered: 'Jane . . .'

She didn't answer, just snarled again and moved implacably towards me, her hard claws scratching on the kitchen lino. Saliva dripped from the points of her teeth, and there was nothing in her expression but blind animal hatred.

'Jane, listen,' I said, in a croaky voice. All the time I was trying to back towards the door. I saw the muscles rippling under that coarse glossy fur, and I knew that she was going to run for me again, and this time she probably wouldn't miss.

On the floor, the telephone receiver kept saying: *'John? John? What's the matter, what's going on?'*

There was a brisk tattoo of sharp claws, and the bear-woman leaped towards me with the force of a huge black automobile. I know that I yelled out, but it was with aggressive desperation this time, the kind of *banzai!* scream they teach you in the army to pump your adrenalin up.

As the giant bear hurtled towards me, I swung back my arm and whammed it straight in the face with the meat cleaver. That didn't do very much to help me. The force of the bear-woman's leap banged me back against the wall, and we collided together on the floor in a ghastly embrace of blood and fur and claws. I think I was concussed for a moment, almost crushed, but then I managed to push some of the furry weight off my legs and hips, and roll the bear-woman over.

I thought she was dead at first. The cleaver had struck her in the left side of the face, chopping a deep bloody V into her forehead, and damaging her left eye. The velocity of her own leap had done the most harm, because there was no way that *I* could have hit anybody that hard. I knelt beside her, shaking and quaking, and almost heaving up my last few mugs of coffee.

She opened her right eye and looked at me. I twitched nervously and stood up, well away from those claws and those teeth. She smiled. A sort of sour, self-satisfied grin.

'*My master will want you now,*' she whispered. '*He has waited so long for his beautiful bear-maiden, and look what you have done. My master will track you down, and he will make sure that you die the worst death that anyone could ever imagine.*'

I said thickly: 'Jane?'

But even if the face looked like Jane, there was nothing in the bear-maiden's mind that remembered Jane or the way she used to feel about me. She lay there, panting and bleeding, but I knew that I hadn't killed her, and it was only a matter of time before she came after me again.

The telephone said: 'Hallo? Hallo? John!'

I picked it up from the floor, and said: 'I'm here, George. I'm okay for now. The bear-maiden's here. It's Jane. The bear-maiden's Jane.'

George Thousand Names told me: 'Get out of there, quick. While you still have the chance.'

'She's hurt. I hit her with the meat-cleaver.'

'That's not going to please Coyote. Listen – just get your maps and git.'

'*Git?* I haven't heard anyone say that since Hopalong Cassidy.'

'John, you're hysterical. Just get the fuck out of there.'

Still stumbling and staggering, I gathered up my Rand McNally and my wallet, and stepped over the bear-maiden's twitching legs to the door. She rolled her eyeball up to watch me as I passed, and she whispered: 'Coyote will get thee. Have no fear.'

I went out of the front door, made sure the necklace

was tightly fastened around the handle, and headed for the elevator with wobbly knees. It was only after I'd hailed a taxi in the street, and we'd pulled away into the traffic, that I felt the first surge of real nausea.

I tapped the driver on the shoulder.

'Yup?' she asked me.

'Excuse me,' I said. 'I think I'm going to puke.'

She turned around and stared at me, a cigarette hanging from her lower lip.

'Mister,' she said. 'This ain't no goddamned airline. Sick bags ain't provided.'

'What do you suggest I do?' I asked her, sweating.

She drove at forty miles an hour over a cross-street, bouncing and jolting on the taxi's suspension. 'Swallow it,' she said, and that was the end of that discussion.

Maybe Red Indians are self-disciplined and ascetic, but George Thousand Names wasn't so self-disciplined that morning that he didn't take my hand in both of his hands when I walked through the door of his room at the Mark Hopkins, and he wasn't so ascetic that he didn't pour us both a large Jack Daniels.

I said: 'It's a nightmare. The whole damned thing is a nightmare.'

He was wearing a red satin bathrobe, and slippers with beads sewn all over them. He looked as if he was starring in a cowboy movie financed by Liberace. He said: 'That's the worst mistake you can make, to think it's a nightmare. If you think that, you will close your eyes to whatever happens, and hope to wake up. But you *are* awake, John, and this is really happening.'

'But how the hell can a girl I know – a girl I used to love – dammit, a girl I *still* love – turn into a creature like that?'

The old Indian set his glass down on top of the television set. With the sound turned down, some golf star was mouthing the virtues of tooth polish.

I said: 'She was a *bear*, George. She had hair all

143

over, and there was only her face. And she didn't even recognise me. I couldn't say anything. She came right across that kitchen at me like a locomotive, and she would have killed me if I'd given her half a chance.'

George Thousand Names sat down on the edge of his bed. It didn't look slept in, but then I had heard that some well-trained Indians could sleep standing up. Maybe that was just an apocryphal story, but somehow I could just imagine George Thousand Names standing in the corner, arms crossed, snoring the night gently away.

He said: 'Between the time that you sent her to get the doorknocker, and the time that we found her on 17th Street, Coyote must have assaulted her.'

I took a fiery swallow of bourbon. 'Assaulted? I don't understand.'

George Thousand Names looked across at me with elderly concern. I was beginning to feel that if I could ever have had a choice of fathers this man would have been it. He was compassionate, and understanding, but he was also cynical and wise, and you knew that whatever he said was God's honest truth. Or Gitche Manitou's honest truth.

'Coyote is the most lustful of demons. He probably raped her. There is an old Navaho song about how Coyote meets a maiden on a mountain pass. It goes "One day walking through a mountain pass, Coyote met a young woman. What have you in your pack? she said. Fish eggs, answered Coyote. Can I have some? the maiden asked. Only if you close your eyes and hold up your dress. She did as she was told. Higher, said Coyote, and walked up to the woman. Stand still so I can reach the place. I can't she said, there is something crawling between my legs. Don't worry, said Coyote, it's a scorpion, I'll catch it. The woman dropped her dress. You weren't fast enough, it stung me."'

George Thousand Names had recited this song in a flat, monotonous voice. When he'd finished, he looked

144

up at me and said: 'You see? He is cunning as well as brutal. When I say "assaulted", I probably mean "seduced".'

I couldn't believe it. 'That thing – that thing we saw last night – *that* had sex with Jane?'

George Thousand Names nodded. 'Very probably. According to the legends, it was only after Coyote had filled her mind with the most evil ideas of antiquity that Bear Maiden grew hair and claws. I'm sorry, John, but if we're going to lick this thing we've got to face the facts.'

'Oh, sure.' I felt bitter and upset. Of all people, why Jane? If I hadn't been dumb enough to send her on that fool's errand, she might have been safe.

George Thousand Names went to the window and looked out over downtown San Francisco through the hotel drapes. 'John,' he said, 'I know you take this personally, but you must understand that we're struggling with a life-and-death situation.'

I tried to smile. 'It depends on whose life it is, doesn't it?'

George Thousand Names shook his head. 'Not *whose* life, but how many lives. There are people out there, John, thousands of them, and Coyote can turn this city into a dismal carnage. If he stays loose, these streets will look like a slaughter-house before you know it. Coyote is a mad, random killer, John. A maniac beyond all maniacs. The only way to destroy him now is to outwit him, and make absolutely sure that he can't find Big Monster's shorn-off hair.'

'But all the pictures are round at my apartment'

'You sealed the door with the necklace?'

'Of course.'

'Then Bear Maiden can't get out and Coyote can't get in. At least, I hope not.

I took out a cigarette and lit it. It tasted like a Hungarian steelworker's instep, but I needed something to steady my nerves. I said to George Thousand Names: 'What do we do now?'

He rubbed his chin. 'I think we ought to discover where Big Monster's hair might be,' he suggested. 'Then, we can go tackle Bear Maiden. She's ferocious enough, but I think I have spells that could hold her. After we've done that, we'll go looking for the big one. Coyote himself.'

'Well, I just hope we live this day out.'

George Thousand Names smiled. 'The Costanoan Indians used to live here in San Francisco before the Spanish arrived. They had a prayer which began: "When evening falls, give me the small darkness and not the great."'

I laid my road atlas on the table, and produced the crumpled greaseproof overlay that I had painstakingly marked out that morning. We arranged the overlay on the map, and George Thousand Names scrutinised it like a sceptical art expert. He sniffed a couple of times, and his lips moved in a silent whisper as he located places and villages and mountains. After a while, he sat back on the arm of the hotel settee and frowned in deep concentration.

'Well?' I asked him. 'What does it mean?'

He glanced back at it. 'I'm not sure. It's a very unusual arrangement of viewpoints – quite unlike the usual pictographs that Indians used to draw to locate waterholes. If you look here, you'll see that it's made of several symmetrical curves. Now, that just didn't happen when Navahoes were making their charts of the desert areas. Time was too precious, and the countryside was too inhospitable. You made your pictures where you could, and you didn't worry about symmetry.'

'So what does that prove? That it isn't genuine?'

George Thousand Names shook his head. 'No. We're certainly pointed in the right direction. The very fact that there's a pattern here is meaningful. What we have to work out is what the pattern means.'

'How can we do that?'

George Thousand Names held the piece of greaseproof paper up to the window. 'Well, I have the feeling that what we're seeing here isn't a regular map. Those pictures of Mount Taylor and Cabezon Peak had a magical significance because they were the home of Big Monster, but I'm beginning to wonder if Big Monster's hair is hidden around that area or someplace else.'

He crossed the room and opened his brown pigskin suitcase. Then he came back to the table with a small glass vial of something that looked like black dust.

'I hope the supernatural doesn't embarrass you,' he said.

'Why should it?'

'Well . . . you're a white man. And it's a long time since white men understood the supernatural for what it really is.'

Having taken a chance on Jane's one-off theory about Coyote and Big Monster, and having travelled through the night to bring George Thousand Names down to San Francisco, I felt slightly irked at the suggestion that I was just another white bigot. But all I said was: 'One day, the Indians are going to find out that not all palefaces are mindless barbarians.'

George Thousand Names raised an eyebrow. 'Those Indians who are still left.'

We left that particular argument where it was. With Coyote loose, this was no time to do a big Wounded Knee number. But I knew that one day, if we escaped this thing alive, George Thousand Names and I were going to have to sit down and do some pretty serious talking. What Coyote's gruesome reincarnation had made me realise for the first time in my life was that America wasn't *our* land, not white land, at all. The Spanish hadn't arrived in San Francisco until 1775, and before that, all those centuries before that, Indian lore and Indian magic had made this land what it was. There were demons and ghosts in them thar hills, but they weren't white, and they didn't take any heed of white man's effete magical powers.

While I watched, George Thousand Names opened his glass vial and sprinkled blue-grey dust on my greaseproof paper map. He blew on it gently, and whispered a few words. Then, right in front of my eyes, the dust shifted across the paper just like iron filings drawn into patterns by a magnet. In a few seconds, it had marked out a pattern of curves that connected up the pencilled crosses I had made from each of the original pictures.

George Thousand Names studied the pattern and then smiled. 'Well,' he said, 'wonders will never cease.'

'What does it mean?' I asked him.

He pointed to the pattern with a stubby finger. 'That is a very ancient symbol. When I say "ancient", I mean that it bears about as much relation to present-day Indian tongues as Middle English does to modern American speech. It is very difficult to express precisely, but what it means roughly is "the place you will one day see from the north lodgepole of the tepee of the beast."'

I blinked. 'I don't think I'm any the wiser.'

George Thousand Names looked at me carefully. 'It's really very clear. The tepee of the beast is 1551 Pilarcitos Street – you remember how it worked out as 666. The north lodgepole simply means the view from the top of the house facing northwards. Whatever you see from that vantage point, that is where Big Monster's hair is hidden.'

'Well, for Christ's sake,' I said. 'What are we waiting for? Let's get up there!'

'Give me three minutes to bathe and dress,' George Thousand Names insisted. 'Meanwhile, you might give Dr Jarvis a call and tell him where we're going. If he has the time, he'll probably want to come along.'

The old Indian went into the bathroom and ran the tub, while I sat down on the side of the bed and picked up the phone. I dialled Elmwood Foundation Hospital and asked to speak to Dr Jarvis.

The receptionist said: 'I'm sorry, sir. Dr Jarvis isn't here right now.'

'Is there any way I can reach him?'

'I don't think so. He left here about twenty minutes ago with a young lady.'

I sighed. 'Okay. Can you leave him a message? Tell him John Hyatt called.'

The receptionist said: 'Oh, it's you, Mr Hyatt. In that case you may know where he's gone. He left with a lady friend of yours.'

'What did you say?'

'A pretty-looking girl with long hair. Ms Torresino.'

For a moment, I couldn't think what to say or do. My mouth was very dry, and I felt distinctly bilious again, as if I'd been eating too many Japanese seaweed cocktail crackers. I put my hand over the phone and shouted: '*George!*'

The medicine man appeared in the bathroom doorway, wrapped in a towel.

'I just called the hospital. They told me that Jim Jarvis left about twenty minutes ago with Jane.'

George Thousand Names said: '*What?*'

'That's what they told me.'

He began to rub himself quickly dry. 'In that case, we have to move really fast. If Jane's gotten herself out of your apartment, then Coyote must know where to look for Big Monster's hair. All the pictures were there, right?'

I said: 'Thanks a million,' into the phone, and laid it down. Then I asked George, 'What happened? I thought the necklace was supposed to keep her locked up.'

George Thousand Names stepped into a large pair of floral boxer shorts, and then sat down on the bed to put on freshly-creased linen slacks.

'The necklace was no guarantee. She may have found a way to shake it loose, or maybe a cleaner removed it. Even Coyote could have come by, and persuaded someone to take it off.'

'But even so, George, she's a *bear*. How the hell can she walk the streets like a bear?'

George Thousand Names laced up his brogues and reached for a smart blue blazer. 'She's a bear, and she isn't a bear. The hair and the teeth and the claws are the physical manifestations of the evil that Coyote has put into her mind. But they don't have to show themselves all the time. The Bear Maiden is a kind of Jekyll-and-Hyde creature. She changes according to her needs.'

'You mean she probably looks normal now, but she could change back into a bear at any time?'

George Thousand Names nodded.

I let out a long, frustrated breath. Then I put my arm around George Thousand Names's shoulder, and I said quietly: 'Why don't we think about this, George. Think where they might have gone. Maybe Lieutenant Stroud knows.'

'You heard the news,' said George Thousand Names. 'The police are looking for a medical freak, not an Indian demon. Right now, Coyote is holed up someplace, waiting for nightfall, and laughing down his sleeve at all of us. Especially Lieutenant Stroud.'

'Do you think Coyote's gone up to 1551?'

'It's possible. In fact, if he's really managed to work out where Big Monster's hair is, I'd say it's a certainty.'

For quite a few moments, George Thousand Names and I sat and looked at each other, and both of us felt the fright and the burden of what we had elected to do. We didn't *have* to get involved. We could leave it all to Lieutenant Stroud and the SWAT squad, and take the next plane to Honolulu. But somehow we both felt that now Coyote had brought his evil into our lives, there was only one way to go. And that wasn't off to Hawaii.

'George,' I said quietly. 'Is there any way at all that we can wipe Coyote out? Is there any weakness anywhere that we can attack?'

George Thousand Names stared at the carpet. 'I thought the necklace would work, but it obviously hasn't. Maybe Coyote's gained some new powers since he's been in hibernation. His only real soft spot, or so the legend says, was for Bear Maiden; and that isn't exactly a weakness because Bear Maiden was always so devoted to him.'

'What about Big Monster's hair?'

'That's the greatest threat of all,' said George Thousand Names. 'Once he finds it, that will give him all the strength he needs, and immortality, too. If that happens, we might as well pack up our bags.'

'Supposing *we* found it first?'

The Indian shrugged. 'Even if we did, we couldn't do much with it.'

'Couldn't we wear it ourselves? Would it give *us* strength?'

George Thousand Names looked at me as if I was totally bananas. 'If a mortal man attempts to wear the scalp of a giant or a demon, he will be destroyed by what he sees. In other words, for as long as he could survive it, which wouldn't be long, he would become a demon himself, and his mind just couldn't take it. So the Hualapai Indians say, or at least they used to.'

I reached for another cigarette. 'Okay. We'd better get ourselves up to Pilarcitos. Doing anything is better than doing nothing.'

CHAPTER SIX

Clouds had begun to drift across from the ocean, and by the time we reached Mission Street, the day, which had started off bright, was humid and dull. The taxi let us off at 1551, and with a feeling of dread we stood on the sloping sidewalk and looked up yet again at that dead and dilapidated house that just wouldn't let us go. George Thousand Names said: 'Whatever happens now, I want you to trust my knowledge and my wisdom, such as it is, and do what I tell you. It could mean the difference between life and death.'

I gave a nervous laugh. 'You really have a way of putting things that uplifts the weariest heart.'

He looked testy. 'Just do what I say, right?'

'You're the boss.'

We swung open that groaning gate, and went up the steps to the porch. The fragments of doorknocker had gone, although there was still a mark on the old grey paintwork where it had been, and blisters from the freezing cold that George Thousand Names had used to break it. There was something else, too. The word 'Return' had disappeared.

I pushed the door and it seemed to be locked.

'Maybe the police locked it,' I said. 'The SWAT squad could have been round here at some time.'

I stepped back down the porch, and stared up at the house. It looked grim and photographic under the gathering clouds. There was a feeling in the air that something dark and unpleasant was going to happen, and I couldn't resist a shiver.

For a second, something seemed to flicker in an upstairs window. It was pale, and it only appeared for a brief moment. But I clutched George Thousand

Names's shoulder, and I said: 'I saw something. They're in there. I swear it.'

The old Indian turned, and there was an airplane thundering low across the sky towards SF International Airport. He said: 'It was just a reflection from the plane. You mustn't get yourself upset.'

'George, there's something *in* that house.'

He stared at me. There were forty years and two divided cultures between us, and I guessed nothing could really bridge that gap. But something was working between us, too, some kind of trust, and I was grateful for it.

We approached the door again, and George Thousand Names reached out for the lock. He muttered quickly under his breath, gestured three times with his left hand, and the door clicked and swung open. Inside, there was that same dusty, forbidding darkness, and I smelled again that stale smell which would remind me of 1551 Pilarcitos Street to the moment I went to my grave. George said: 'Come,' and we stepped in.

First we checked the downstairs rooms. Seymour Wallis's study, the dining room, the deserted kitchen. In the sitting room, gloomy behind closed shutters, we looked over the spooky dust-sheeted furniture, the gold ormolu clock silent under its glass dome, and the oil paintings of grotesque hunts across nightmare landscapes that were so dark it was almost impossible to make out what they were. The house was so silent around us that we held our breath, and walked with as little noise as we possibly could.

In the hallway again, George Thousand Names stood and listened. He frowned, and said: 'Do you hear anything? Anything at all?'

I stood still, and strained my ears.

'I don't think so.'

'I feel that someone's watching,' he said. 'Whoever

they are, whatever they are, they know that we're here.'

We stayed silent for a few moments more, looking around at the dingy wallpaper with all the faded marks where the pictures of Mount Taylor and Cabezon Peak had once hung, but the house stayed so quiet that I began to think we'd made a mistake. Perhaps it *was* empty, and all that I'd seen flitting across that window was a passing reflection. I sneezed a couple of times from the dust, and blew my nose.

As I was putting my handkerchief away, I looked up the stairs and I went cold. *There was a small face watching me from the top step.* A face that was evil and hairy, with red-lighted eyes, and a grin so wolfish and vicious that I couldn't move, couldn't speak, couldn't even reach out for George's arm to warn him.

It was the doorknocker. The living doorknocker. Back in one piece again, and even more hideous and terrifying than it had been before.

George Thousand Names suddenly saw that I was gaping up the stairs, and he looked, too. But before he could do anything, there was a loud crack, and the doorknocker broke into pieces of dull bronze, which rolled and bounced and clattered down the stairs.

The pieces came to rest on the hall floor. George Thousand Names looked down at them with a sober face, and said: 'That's Coyote's idea of a warning. He's just reminding me that whatever I can do, he can undo and do again.'

In a dry voice, I said: 'We're not thinking of going upstairs after that performance, are we?'

The Indian sniffed. 'I don't see what else we can do. Do you smell anything?'

I couldn't really, but I said: 'Dogs?'

'I think so. It's faint at the moment, but it seems to be coming from upstairs.'

George set a foot on the first step, but I held his

arm, and looked him straight in the face, and said: 'George, I have to tell you this. I'm shit scared.'

He was silent for a moment, and then he nodded. 'So am I,' he confessed.

Slowly, quietly, we climbed the first flight of stairs until we came to the landing. Just in front of us was the room where Bryan Corder had lost the flesh from his head. There was a window at the end of the landing, but it was so dirty and stained, and the sky was so cloudy outside, that only the weakest light could penetrate. Coyote, after all, was a lover of darkness.

We looked at each other. 'Shall we check the rooms?' I asked George Thousand Names.

'We'd better,' he said.

We went across to the first bedroom, hesitated, and then flung open the door. It was a silent, dreary room, with a dilapidated brass bed and one of those massive walnut wardrobes that looks as if it's veneered with strange feral faces. I could see myself in the dressing-table mirror, and I suddenly realised how rough and pale I looked. Two days of shock and tension don't do much for your outward glow.

'Nothing in there,' whispered George Thousand Names. 'Not unless there's somebody hiding under the bed.'

'Are you going to look?'

He managed a lopsided grin. 'Are you?'

I said: 'Forget it. We'll *both* look.'

We got down on our hands and knees, lifted the bedspread, and peered into the shadowy darkness under the bed. There was nothing there except dust.

'Okay,' said George Thousand Names. 'Let's try the rest of the rooms.'

One by one, we flung open doors and looked nervously inside. The bedrooms were silent, cold, unused. Depressing and run-down reminders of the people who had once lived in this house. They could

155

never have been happy, not with the evil presence of Coyote built into their walls and their cornices and their chimneys, not with the demon's haunted breath whistling under every door with the midnight draught; and their unhappiness showed in the sparseness of their furnishings and the incongruous attempts at gaiety in their pictures. On one wall, there was a painting of mimosa. On another, a drawing of children dancing around a Maypole. Somehow, all these pictures did was emphasise the chilling sensation of dread that soaked through every wall, the dank terror that must have made every night under this roof a carnival of nightmares.

George said: 'I guess we'd better try further up. There's one more floor, and then the attic.'

I took a deep breath. 'Okay, if you insist. But when we come to the attic, I think we'd better toss a coin for the privilege of going first.'

We stepped out on to the landing again, ready to go up to the third floor, but all of a sudden we heard voices. They were coming from downstairs, in the hall. A man and a woman. I froze for a moment, but then I leaned over the banisters, and saw Dr Jarvis and Jane Torresino standing in the hallway. Dr Jarvis was saying: 'They must have been here already. The door's wide open.'

Jane said: 'Maybe they were. But it doesn't matter. The main thing is that you're here.'

I turned back to George Thousand Names. 'It's *her*,' I hissed. 'And she's brought Dr Jarvis round here.'

George Thousand Names tugged me gently back to one of the bedrooms. He closed the door, and gave me a long, intent look.

'This means one thing. Coyote must be here, in the house. She's probably brought Dr Jarvis along as a sacrifice. A little wedding present from a Bear Maiden to a Coyote. Quite a succulent treat for a demon who's been dead for hundreds of years.'

I pressed my ear to the door. I could hear Jane and Dr Jarvis mounting the stairs, and talking in subdued voices. I whispered: 'What can we *do*?' but George Thousand Names put his finger to his lips, and said nothing but: 'Wait.'

Jane and Dr Jarvis reached the landing and walked along it towards the next flight of stairs. Dr Jarvis said: 'Are you sure John said he'd meet us up here? It seems kind of strange.'

'Of course,' asserted Jane. 'Isn't the whole thing strange?'

As they passed our door, George Thousand Names opened it, and stepped on to the landing. I came out after him, with my heart palpitating and my throat tight with fear.

'John! You're here!' said Dr Jarvis, and grinned. 'What's going on here? Hide-and-seek?'

George Thousand Names snapped: '*Don't move!*'

Dr Jarvis said, 'What?'

'Don't move! Stay right where you are! That woman you're with is dangerous!'

Jane looked at me and then at George Thousand Names as if she really couldn't understand what we were talking about. I said: '*Jane?*' but I saw that her face was unusually white, and that her eyes were as blank as two clams on the half-shell. There was no trace of the cut that I'd inflicted on her forehead, but then after all I'd seen in the past two days, I believed Coyote capable of healing and mending anything that he felt like.

'John . . .' said Jane, in a slurry voice. 'How nice to see you . . .'

George Thousand Names butted in; 'Don't answer. Don't talk. She's not human right now, and anything you say can help her destroy you.'

Dr Jarvis frowned. 'Not *human*? What the hell are you—'

157

'Shut up!' barked George Thousand Names. Then, quieter: 'Shut up, please, I need to think.'

Jane stood where she was in the dusk of the corridor, upright but very tense, and when I looked at her it seemed as if her face kept subtly altering and flowing, like a white drowned face seen through running water. I knew she wasn't Jane; not the Jane that I knew. But she looked so much like her that it was impossible for me to feel anything but affection. Almost involuntarily I stepped forward, but George Thousand Names was quick and he held my sleeve.

'I know what you feel,' he said softly. 'But have patience.'

Jane suddenly laughed and snarled at the same time. It was such a horrifying sound that Dr Jarvis, in spite of what George Thousand Names had told him, jumped away. In front of our eyes, Jane was melting and changing like one photograph overlaid on top of another, layer after layer, until I could see that dark hair was covering her hands, and her nails had become curved claws.

Dr Jarvis said: 'Oh, my God.'

But George Thousand Names had this lesser demon under control. He lifted one of his amulets, and Bear Maiden shied back against the wall of the landing, snarling and growling, her eyes blank and red.

'I command you to obey me,' said George Thousand Names. 'Bear Maiden of the south-west, sister of those who loved you, constant until Coyote beguiled you. I command you to obey me.'

Bear Maiden stood on her shaggy hind paws and roared, her eyes blazing like a devil. At her full height, she almost touched the ceiling, and I was far from sure that George Thousand Names could control her. The medicine man raised both of his hands and shouted: 'Your mind and your will are mine. I command you to obey me!'

Dr Jarvis was shaking his head in fear. 'I don't *believe*

158

it,' he whispered. 'That girl was round at my apartment. I was *kissing* that girl. We had drinks.'

For a moment, George Thousand Names faltered. I could suddenly sense his wavering control. I guess our combined nervousness and lack of faith wasn't doing much to help him, and the fierce strain of keeping a monster like Bear Maiden at bay must have been enormous.

'Don't speak,' he hissed. 'Don't speak, don't speak.'

'But I can't believe it,' said Dr Jarvis, in a hollow, frightened voice.

The control snapped. I could almost feel it go like a dam bursting, like a tidal bore. With a shattering growl, Bear Maiden launched her massive bulk at Dr Jarvis, and her jaws crunched into his neck with a noise that still makes me feel cold all over. He shrieked in an agonised falsetto, and then with one jerk of her massive head, she ripped the skin away from his neck and chest in one bloody rag. He collapsed to the floor, twitching, while she turned on George and me with her eyes blazing.

'*Stop!*' shouted George Thousand Names, lifting his arms once again. 'By the powers of the great spirit, by the powers of the woods and forests, *stop!*'

The bear-woman snarled and tossed her head. But then she gave another softer growl, and turned away, dropping on to all fours. George stepped forward with his amulet held in front of him.

'I command you to obey me for one night and one day by the unbreakable spell of the greatest of those who lived at Sa-nos-tee. I command you to obey me until the sun's second sinking, and you will not defy me. This I command you in the name of the Navahoes of old and the Hualapai of ancient times. Now, be silent and sleep.'

The bear-woman snarled once, and then sank down on her haunches. In a few moments, the red eyes closed, and she slept. I looked at George Thousand

Names, impressed, but I saw what a toll that spell had taken. His face was glistening with sweat, and he was shaking.

I knelt down beside Dr Jarvis. His eyes were still open, and he was rigid with shock, but he was still alive.

'Jim,' I said gently. 'How do you feel?'

He whispered: 'I think my neck's broken. Just get me to Elmwood and I guess I'll be okay.'

George said: 'There's a phone in that bedroom. Be quick, because Coyote's upstairs, and he's going to be aware of all this.'

While George Thousand Names waited impatiently and anxiously on the landing, I dialled Elmwood and spoke to Dr Weston. I told her that Jim Jarvis had been involved in an accident, and asked her to send an ambulance across town straight away.

She said: 'It's nothing to do with what happened last night, is it?'

I could see George beckoning me. I said: 'I'll explain later. I have to go. But, please, get that ambulance here fast.'

'Come *on*!' urged George Thousand Names. 'We don't have any time to lose!'

I said to Dr Weston: 'I have to go. It's going crazy down here,' and I slammed the receiver down. Then I followed George Thousand Names out on to the landing and said: 'What do you want me to do?'

'Just keep close. And whatever you do, don't panic. If Coyote's still up there, you're going to get frightened out of your brain. But hold on. Provided you keep yourself together, you'll survive it.'

I took a last worried look at Dr Jarvis, lying sprawled and bloody on the carpet, and the dark furry bulk of the slumbering Bear Maiden, and then I followed George Thousand Names along to the second flight of stairs. It was even darker and more forbidding than the first. Its treads were threadbare and scuffed, and from somewhere upstairs a stifling draught was blowing, a draught that even I could smell. A draught that reeked of dog.

George Thousand Names went slowly up ahead of me, pausing every now and then to listen. It was so gloomy up there on the third floor that we could hardly see where we were going, and all I had to guide me was the rotting banister rail on one side and the damp wallpaper on the other. The smell of dog grew thicker as we climbed higher, and when we reached the second landing, it was almost nauseatingly strong.

'Oh, Coyote's here all right,' whispered George Thousand Names. 'He must have hidden up in the attic until nightfall. But he's here all right.'

We paced along the landing, staring up at the ceiling to see where the attic door could be. George Thousand Names said softly: 'He knows we're here. You hear how silent it is? He's waiting to see what we're going to do next.'

I felt distinctly depressed and afraid. I said: 'If I had my way, I'd run like hell.'

George Thousand Names said: 'Ssh! Listen.'

I froze, and listened. At first, I couldn't hear anything, but then the distinct sound of *scratching* reached my ears. It seemed to be all around, but George Thousand Names lifted a finger and pointed towards the ceiling.

'What do we do now?' I asked hoarsely.

George Thousand Names beckoned. We walked a few paces further along the dark landing until we were standing under the attic's oak-stained trapdoor. There was a frayed cord dangling down the wall, and I guessed this was one of those traps you pull down, and a built-in ladder slides out.

'Well,' said the old Indian quietly, 'we have the demon bearded in his den.'

I coughed, and looked up at the trapdoor apprehensively. The scratching continued, soft and repetitive

161

and creepy, like the fingernail of someone buried alive scratching hopelessly at the lid of their coffin. I said: 'George, I don't really think I want to go up there.'

He frowned at me. 'We have to. Don't you understand who this is? This is Coyote! This demon is like every medicine man's Moby Dick! I could have his scalp on my balcony rail, along with the pelts and the snowshoes! The scalp of Coyote, the First One To Use Words For Force!'

'George,' I said, anxiously, 'I'm not in this for the scalphunting. I'm in this because innocent people are going to die if we don't do something about it.'

'You're not a saint, and it's no good pretending you are,' said George Thousand Names, and there was more than a dash of caustic in his voice.

'Maybe I'm not,' I told him. 'But I'm not a bounty hunter either.'

George Thousand Names said: 'We knew this was happening. At the last great council of the medicine men at Towaoc in the Ute Mountain Reservation, many of the wise men said they had seen and experienced warnings and omens. The grey birds were seen, and the old voices were heard on Superstition Mountain that haven't been heard since they laid Red Cloud to rest. And the coyotes and the dogs have been as restless as if a storm was brewing up.'

'You *knew* Coyote was coming? Why didn't you say so before?'

'We didn't know. We guessed. But there will be much honour for me in defeating Coyote. I will be seen for the greatest wonder-worker of any age, past or present; and I will then do something I have dearly wanted for years. I will unite the medicine men into a strong and powerful council, and bring back Indian magic to the glory it used to have, in the days long ago when the grasses were free and the tribes had dignity and strength. The signs said that Coyote would come in the Moon When The Geese Shed Their Feathers; and he has.'

I stared at George Thousand Names's face in the dim light of the landing, and I could see what he meant. These days, there was no way for a medicine man to prove his powers, no test worthy of his magic. What good was an ancient skill for mesmerising buffalo in a country where buffaloes only roamed in zoos? What use was the power to make a spear fly amazingly straight in a society of handguns and teargas? That's why George Thousand Names relished this conflict with Coyote so much. No matter how hideous and terrifying Coyote was, he was a match for George's frustrated talents.

'All right,' I said. 'We'd better get to it.'

George Thousand Names reached out and squeezed my shoulder with his old horny hand. 'If the great spirit sees fit to take us, my friend, then let us remember the good words and not the sour.'

'Okay, you're on.'

I tugged the cord which hung down from the trapdoor. It seemed to be stuck, but then I pulled it harder, and with a rusty groan, the door came shuddering open, and the lower rungs of the ladder sank unwillingly towards us. From out of the dark space above us came a hot fetid breeze, and a restless scratching and rustling, as if something or someone was waiting for us impatiently.

'Let me go first,' said George Thousand Names. 'I have the power to hold the worst at bay.'

'Don't get the idea I was volunteering,' I told him.

The medicine man took hold of the ladder, which swayed and creaked and finally came to rest on the landing floor. Then, rung by rung, he climbed slowly upwards, pausing now and again to listen and to look. His head and then his shoulders disappeared into the gloom. I said: 'For Christ's sake don't do a Bryan Corder on me.'

He said: 'He's here. He's in this attic. Is there a lightswitch down there? I can sense him. I can smell him. Give me some light!'

I looked around, and there was an old bakelite switch on the opposite wall. I flicked it down, and a weak dusty bulb suspended from the rafters inside the attic lit up.

George Thousand Names screamed. He dropped from the ladder, and his old body thumped awkwardly on to the floor. I thought he was dead for a second, but then he yelled: '*Shut the door! Shut the door! Shut the door before it's too late!*'

I seized the bottom of the ladder and tried to wrench it upwards, but it was jammed on one side against the opening in the ceiling. I quickly clambered up four or five steps, and tugged at it as hard as I could to clear it.

It was then that I saw Coyote. I didn't see much. He was at the far end of the attic, where the light scarcely penetrated, and the whole loft was alive with thousands and thousands of diseased grey birds, crawling and flapping and scratching their claws on the floor. It was almost impossible to see any kind of shape, any kind of form, but through the fluttering crowds of birds, the Grey Sadness, I could make out something dark and enormous, with demonic eyes that glowed in a bristling face, and a terrible beast-like presence that was more evil and more vicious than anything I could ever have imagined possible. On the floor of the attic, not far away from me, stood the statuette of the Bear Maiden, except that it wasn't a statuette any more, but a tiny living replica of the gigantic bear-woman which slept downstairs. The statuette turned and grinned at me, with bared teeth, and then she scuttled back towards the shadowy protection of her master, the demon Coyote, like a kind of rat.

I knew why George Thousand Names had screamed.

Coyote, his slanting eyes fiery with hate, was unfolding his body from his gloomy corner of the attic, and in the half-second I stayed at the trapdoor, I saw something unrolling from his sides, something greasy and pale and writhing like millions of maggots.

I came back down that ladder about fifty times faster than I went up it. My system was so pumped up with adrenalin that I seized the bottom rung and slammed the attic trapdoor upwards with one hefty bang. Then I picked George Thousand Names up from the floor, and half-dragged him back along the landing.

At the head of the stairs, the medicine man gasped: 'Wait. Wait – he won't follow us yet.'

'*Wait?* I'm getting out of this damned place as fast as I can! Did you see that thing! Did you see it?'

George Thousand Names resisted my tugging. 'John—' he said. 'John – you mustn't forget the hair. You mustn't forget Big Monster's hair.'

'So what?'

'John, it's the only way we can defeat him. If we find the hair first, we've at least got ourselves a chance!'

I let go of George's jacket and rested my back against the wall. Upstairs in the attic, through the thin ceiling, I could hear noises that didn't bear thinking about. Slimy, soft, scratchy, shuffling noises.

'George, I'm asking. Let's get out. I can take bear-people but I can't take that thing.'

'Wait. Remember what the symbol said. Look north from the lodgepole of the tepee of the beast. That's where Big Monster's hair is hidden.'

I lifted my hands in temporary surrender. 'Okay. So which way is north?'

George fumbled in his pocket and produced a small round box.

'What's this?' I asked him. 'Another magical trick?'

He opened the lid. 'Kind of. It's a compass.'

It took us a few seconds to locate which way was

north, because every time Coyote moved upstairs in the attic, the compass needle shivered and swung. But then we got our bearings, and George Thousand Names pointed along the landing to one of the dingy windows at the very far end. 'That's it,' he said. 'That's the north window.'

We hurried along to the end of the landing and looked out. There was a dull view of the backs of the houses on Mission Street, but beyond that there was one obvious prominent landmark. It stood tall and stately and shrouded in low-lying fog, its piers and wires glistening in the grey morning light. The Golden Gate bridge.

George Thousand Names breathed: 'That's it. That's where the hair is hidden.'

'The bridge? How can you hide hair on a bridge?'

He smiled at me triumphantly. 'They said in the legends that Big Monster's hair was as grey as iron and as strong as a whip.'

I listened uncomfortably to the noises of Coyote moving across the ceiling above us. 'What does that prove? That doesn't mean anything to me.'

George Thousand Names gripped my arm tight to keep my attention. He said fervently: 'Where would you conceal anything that was as grey as iron and as strong as a whip?'

'Listen, George. I really don't know. I think we'd better—'

'John, *think*!'

I wrenched my arm away. 'I can't damned well think! I just want to get the hell out of this house before that trap door comes bursting down and that demon comes down here and does whatever demons do. I'm not interested in scalps, George, and that's all. I want out!'

At that moment, a shower of plaster dust sifted down from the ceiling, and I heard rafters cracking beneath the weight of something unspeakable. The air was filled with the husky sound of fluttering wings, as the Grey Sadness clamoured around their abominable master.

'Think!' snapped George Thousand Names. '*Think!*'

'Don't play games!' I screamed at him. 'Just tell me!'

George Thousand Names pointed to the Golden Gate, and his eyes were cold and intense. 'Wire!' he told me. 'The Big Monster's hair must have looked like wire!'

'Wire? But the only wire on the bridge is the cables. You mean it's woven into the suspension cables? In the Golden Gate? George, you've got to be nuts!'

He tersely shook his head. 'It's the kind of joke the ancient ones adored. Maybe they did it to humiliate Coyote and make it impossible for him to discover where the hair had gone to. They could make jokes in the future as well as the past, so my guess is that they intervened in the building of the bridge, and had Big Monster's hair wound into it. Maybe some Indian worked at the cable factory, and had the orders passed down from generation to generation to do what he did. Maybe it was done by potent magic. I don't know. But I know enough about the ancient gods and what they used to do, John. And, believe me, that's where Big Monster's hair is hidden.'

'Oh, come on, George,' I said nervously. 'You're guessing.'

'No guesses,' he said. 'Look.'

What I hadn't seen before was a tiny symbol engraved on the glass of the window. It was the same symbol that I had drawn when I plotted out the views of Mount Taylor and Cabezon Peak. George said: 'Put your eye to that mark and tell me what you see.'

There was a rumble from the attic, and a long strip of plaster moulding, the kind of plaster moulding that Seymour Wallis preferred to fibre glass, dropped to the landing floor with a heavy thud, filling the air with dust. I looked at George Thousand Names worriedly but he said: 'Go ahead – look.'

I peered through the mark, and he was right. It lined up directly with one of the suspension cables on the seaward side of the Golden Gate bridge. Maybe George's guess was inspired, or maybe his magic told him more than he would ever admit, but right then I was willing to put money on what he'd said. That hair was right there – twisted and woven into the suspension cables of the West Coast's most celebrated landmark. From what George Thousand Names and Jane had said about Big Monster, he was one of the most evil demons of all south-west America. And the city authorities wondered why so many people chose to jump from that particular bridge?

'I know what you're thinking,' said George Thousand Names. 'And, yes, it's probably true.'

'George,' I told him, 'you're a damned sight more psychic than you look.'

But time was running out. Already the shufflings and the heavings from the attic were shaking the walls, and sending cascades of dry plaster down on every side. I looked up and saw long cracks spreading at frightening speed across the ceiling, and electric wires being tugged out of the walls like nerves being pulled out of flesh. Then, with a thunderous collapsing sound, the whole house began to fall down around us, and we were half-buried in an avalanche of dust, plaster, splintered timber and shattered laths. The grey birds came flapping and fluttering around us, and for one moment, glowering triumphantly through the skeleton of the ceiling, I saw those demonic eyes and that body that writhed and twisted like something putrescent.

'Get out!' I yelled at George Thousand Names, and together we slithered over the dust and the wreckage towards the staircase. The head of the stairs was almost completely blocked with fallen rafters, but we managed to heave two or three of them aside, and crawl through the small triangular space that was opened up. George went first, and I came after, with the Grey Sadness already beating their wings around me, and the hot dry blast of the demon Coyote scorching my back.

There was another fierce explosion of power, the same kind of explosion that had first concussed Dan Machin, only five times stronger. George Thousand Names and I were hurtled down the last few remaining stairs on to the landing, and I struck my shoulder painfully against the banisters. We picked ourselves up and we both looked like bedraggled ghosts – white with fear and plaster.

'Next time you call me a paleface, just remember what you look like now,' I told the old Indian, wiping grit and dust from my mouth with the back of my hand. George Thousand Names coughed, and almost laughed.

Above us, the ceiling began to shake again, as Coyote ripped 1551 apart floor by floor to reach us. We ran along the landing, and Bear Maiden was still there, deep in her trance-like sleep, while Dr Jarvis lay beside her with his eyes rolled up in shock and concussion.

'We have to get them out!' snapped George Thousand Names.

'For Christ's sake – we can get Jim out – but what about the bear?'

'Coyote wants her. He needs her. She's his love and his passion from ancient times. She's also his messenger – his closest helper. We have to get her away. Without her, he's much weaker.'

The walls of the landing began to creak and shake, and one of the bedroom doors was twisted off its hinges and banged flat on the floor with a sound that made me jump with fright.

'Come on—' insisted George Thousand Names. 'Let's take the doctor down first.'

Awkwardly, keeping our shoulders bent to protect ourselves from falling plaster, we picked up Dr Jarvis and carried him to the top of the stairs. George Thousand Names was panting now, and his eyes were red-rimmed in his dusty white face. I didn't know how old he was, but he had to be the wrong side of sixty, and running away from destructive demons wasn't particularly good for the heart. As the house rumbled and shook, we staggered down the last few stairs into the hallway, and out of the front door.

In the street, the ambulance was just arriving, its siren whooping and its red lights flashing. I could see police cars turning up Pilarcitos, too, and there was already a jostling crowd of staring faces on the sidewalk.

Two medics came hurrying across and took Dr Jarvis out of our hands. Two more brought a wheeled stretcher, and they lifted him carefully on to it.

'What happened here?' asked one of the medics, a small Italian with thick-lensed eyeglasses. 'Are you guys demolishing this place, or what?'

'This guy's been bitten,' remarked the other medic, in a puzzled voice. 'Something's bitten his neck.'

There were more rumblings behind us, and we looked around to see part of the roof collapse inwards. The brick chimney stack slowly toppled after it, and there was a crash of glass and timber. Through the murky windows on the second floor, we could see the dull and evil glow of the demon, flickering with malice and hatred.

George Thousand Names held my arm. 'We have to go back, John. The Bear Maiden.'

'The what?' said the Italian medic. 'The bare maiden?'

We were just about to go through the front door again, when a hard, familiar voice said: 'Hold it! Mr Hyatt – Mr Thousand Names! Just hold it there!'

Through the gathering crowd came Lieutenant

Stroud, followed by two patrolmen. He came up the steps with a face as grave as an undertaker, and said: 'What goes on here? I picked up the call from downtown.'

George Thousand Names brushed dust from the sleeve of his jacket. 'We've found your demon for you, lieutenant. He's upstairs, and he's fighting mad, and the sooner we get in there and rescue the Bear Maiden, the better. It's almost too late.'

'Bear Maiden? What the hell are you talking about? You guys are staying right here. We have a SWAT squad on the way.'

'Lieutenant,' I told him, 'we have to go. The Bear Maiden is Coyote's helper. She's vicious and savage, and she acts like his eyes and his ears during the day. Most of the time she's a woman, but she can become a kind of werewolf whenever she wants.'

Lieutenant Stroud stared at me as if he had a mouthful of lime and salt and no tequila to go with it.

'A *werewolf*?' he said, flatly.

Another siren howled in the street. It was the grey SWAT truck, swaying and bouncing into the kerbside. Three SWAT officers in combat uniforms clambered out of the cab and came trotting athletically up the steps. Their senior officer was a short, fit man with cropped silver hair and hazel eyes like the rivets on a pair of Levis. He saluted and said: 'You located your fugitive, lieutenant? What's he doing up there?'

Lieutenant Stroud continued to stare at me, but said out of the side of his mouth. 'It seems like he's tearing the place apart. These gentlemen say he has a woman accomplice.'

George Thousand Names said, in a trembling voice: 'Are you going to let us go in there or not? I warn you, lieutenant. I am the only one who can subdue the bear maiden.'

'The *what* maiden?' queried the SWAT officer.

Behind us, there was a hideous groaning and tearing

sound as Coyote brought down the ceiling of the second floor. Dust rolled in clouds down the stairs into the hallway, and broken windows shattered and tinkled through the plaster. The whole house seemed to pulse and throb as if it was a tortured beast, and through the gloom and wreckage we could see the malevolent light of the demon's eyes. Even the sky above the house seemed to thicken and grow darker, and the grey birds were fluttering and circling around overhead, silent and ominous as ever.

The SWAT officer didn't wait to hear what kind of maiden it was. He turned around to his team, who were busy assembling teargas launchers on the sidewalk, and rapped. 'Three and five, around the back — move! Jackson, you come with me!'

George Thousand Names said: 'Lieutenant, please, don't let them. I must go in there alone. It's our only hope.'

The SWAT officer took out his automatic. 'Will you just stand aside, please, sir. We have to get in there and deal with this maniac fast.'

George Thousand Names raised his arms, blocking the front door. 'You don't understand — you'll *die*! Please let me get in there! I beg you!'

'Will you *move*!' ordered the SWAT officer.

But as he came forward to push George Thousand Names out of the way, the old Indian reached into his open-necked shirt and produced his golden amulet. I saw it flash momentarily, and then I didn't seem to see anything at all. The next thing I knew, we were still standing on the porch but George Thousand Names had gone. The SWAT officer turned to Lieutenant Stroud and blinked, and they both turned and looked at me.

Lieutenant Stroud said: 'Where'd he go? He just vanished!'

A frowning SWAT officer called from the sidewalk: 'He just walked in there, sir. You let him.'

'I *let* him?'

'Yes, sir. You lowered your gun and let him go.'

The SWAT leader frowned at Lieutenant Stroud suspiciously, but then there was another rumbling crash from inside the house, and a sudden hot wind sprang up, howling and shrieking, and sending grit and dust spraying out of the door. All of us dived back from the doorway, and the SWAT officer took cover down behind the porch steps.

'Right!' he yelled. 'We're going in!'

There was another explosion, another burst of power, and I was sure that George Thousand Names must have been hurt. But there was nothing I could do except crouch down by the front gate and pray. Jane was up there, too – and, bear-maiden or not, she was the girl I used to love. I glanced up at the house, and the grey birds were turning and swooping excitedly, as if they expected a feast of death.

The SWAT team scrambled through the moaning wind into the hallway, and hit the floor with their guns held up towards the stairs. More splintered glass flew around them, and one of them cried out as his hand was cut open.

The leader raised his arm, ready to signal an assault on the stairs, but at that moment George Thousand Names appeared through the blizzarding debris, and he was carrying something on his back.

'Hold your fire!' bellowed the SWAT leader, although none of his officers looked as if they had any inclination to shoot.

I couldn't see what was happening very well from my position by the gate. Maybe the SWAT men saw better than I did, although they never admitted it. But I was sure that George Thousand Names wasn't *walking* down those stairs at all. There seemed to be a curious radiance around him, and he was *floating*. He was carrying Jane on his back, not as a were-grizzly, but as a girl, slumped and naked over his shoulders.

173

'What did I tell you,' muttered the Italian medic. 'A *bare* maiden.'

George came across the hall and I swear that I saw an inch of daylight under his feet. His head was raised serene and proud, the head of an Indian who had known magical days when the grasses spoke and the tribes were closest of all to the great spirit. He was sixty years old and more, and there was no way that he could have carried Jane like that, no way at all, down the stairs and across the hall, with his back so straight and his face so calm. At that moment, he was the holy vessel of the powers of Gitche Manitou, who looks after all his servants, even those who are deaf to his whispers in the prairie winds.

As George Thousand Names floated out of the front door, all hell broke out behind him. The house seemed to shriek in anger, and I saw the floorboards literally boiling upwards and the walls rush together in one hideous spray of plaster and wood. The SWAT men were caught right in the middle of it, and I saw one of them smashed through a solid oak door. The crowds in the street shouted and shrieked, and ran back in terror.

George Thousand Names knelt down beside me, letting Jane slide off his back. She was bruised badly, and there was a red weal across her stomach, but she was still in her deep trance, and still unhurt.

It was George who worried me right then. I looked up at him and he was shivering and sweating, and his face was blue.

'George – we'll get you a doctor,' I insisted.

He shook his head. 'There's nothing you can do now. I'm too old for that kind of trick. Too much out of practice. You need strength, you see, mental strength, and I suddenly realised how little I had. We've grown soft, you know, John. Even the best of us. There was a time when men could fly like eagles. But not now. I'm done for, John. I'm truly done for.'

'George, listen, you're going to be fine. Just rest right now and tell me what I have to do.'

He was breathing in husky, painful gasps. 'Take Bear Maiden with you. Until I die, she'll stay in that trance. Take her down to the Golden Gate. See if you – see if you can bargain with Coyote – but don't let him get the hair – don't let him–'

He collapsed, and fell to the side of the porch steps in a heavy coma. An ambulance team were already running across the road towards us, and I said: 'Quick – please – he's had a heart attack.'

I pulled one of the blankets off their stretcher and wrapped it clumsily around Jane's naked body. Then I dragged her out of the front gate, past the milling crowds of police and SWAT officers and bystanders, and over to a yellow Pinto that was parked across the street. The keys were still in the ignition, so I wrestled Jane's limp arms and legs and blanket-wrapped body into the passenger seat, climbed in myself, and started the motor.

I took a last look at 1551. It seemed to be quiet now – a collapsed shell of a house. But the grey birds were still circling around it, and as I signalled to pull away from the kerb I saw a dim reddish light penetrating through the dark clouds of dust that still rose upwards from its sagging roof.

Then, hanging in the grimy air itself, enormous and terrifying, I saw the evil wolfish form of the demon Coyote, his face drawn back in a savage grin, the same face that I had seen on the doorknocker but magnified beyond the realms of nightmares. He was cloaked in birds and darkness, and the ground shook and cracked under his malevolent power.

The street was suddenly clattering with the sound of running feet. The crowds were rushing down towards Mission Street, away from the sinister apparition that hung over the house on Pilarcitos, and they were screaming and shrieking and dragging their children with them. Even the police and the SWAT officers were running. I pulled the Pinto away from the kerb, and sped down to the corner as fast as I safely could.

I turned north on Mission, towards Van Ness and the bridge. I didn't have any idea what I could possibly do to prevent Coyote from stealing back Big Monster's hair, or how I could bargain with him, but that's what George Thousand Names had told me to do, and at least I was going to have a try. My heart was racing, and I was breathing like an Olympic runner, and all the time I was willing myself not to look back.

Mission Street seemed so completely normal that day that I couldn't believe that a thing worse than the devil himself was behind me. People were shopping, walking, eating, laughing, and I was driving desperately northwards towards the Golden Gate, not even sure if I was going to come out of the next few minutes alive.

The Golden Gate was even foggier now, and the outline of the bridge's stately structure was limned in spidery shadows. Cars were moving across it with their headlights on, and when I wound down the Pinto's window I could smell the chilly flat smell of fog, and hear the ships mournfully calling as they steamed slowly out of the bay towards the ocean. As I came down Lombard Street to the bridge approaches, the fog grew denser still, and despite my panic I had to slow down and crawl along behind a line of other cars.

I glanced at Jane. She was still slumped in her seat, her head back, and for all I knew she could have been dead. I said another prayer for George Thousand Names right then, partly because I didn't want him to die, and partly because the Bear Maiden would wake up if he did. The last thing I wanted to do was fight a supernatural grizzly in the confines of a Ford Pinto.

The car ahead of me suddenly stopped. I blew my horn a couple of times, but he stayed put. I opened my door and climbed anxiously out, and then I saw what the trouble was. Two policemen had halted the traffic, and they were standing around in the road, pointing upwards. I ran towards them, leaving Jane in the car.

'What's the hold-up?' I asked, trying to sound normal. All the same, I guess my voice came out pretty high-pitched.

'Some kind of disturbance up there. Some kind of structural disturbance. You see that?'

I peered up into the fog. The policemen were right. The suspension cables of the bridge were swaying alarmingly from side to side, and there was some kind of strange encrustation on them. When I peered harder, I saw what the encrustation was. The birds. The Grey Sadness. Coyote had gotten here before me, and was extracting the hair of Big Monster from the cables.

'That's real strange,' said one of the cops. 'You see that? Up there? Now, does that look like a kind of darkness or doesn't it?'

He was more observant than he realised. The darkness, which clung around the bridge's uprights like a stain in the sky, was the substance of the demon Coyote. He was in his shadowy, amorphous form, the form that he took when he travelled with the sandstorms of the desert and the hot winds from the south. Now, up there, he was taking the prize which he had won for himself centuries and centuries ago, when Mount Taylor was the home of a giant and Cabezon Peak hadn't even been created. *The demonic scalp of Big Monster, the trophy which guaranteed him invulnerability and immortality.*

One of the suspension cables sagged, and then swung downwards, frayed and broken. It must have weighed tons, but it fell over the side of the bridge and did nothing but lash backwards and forwards in the air, a frustrated steel snake.

Right then, I didn't care about the police or anyone. I knew that Coyote had the hair, and there was no way

177

that I could explain that to anyone. I cupped my hands around my mouth, and shouted out: '*Coyote! Coyote! Coyote!*'

The policemen looked at me pop-eyed.

'*Coyote!*' I bellowed. '*Come out and face me, Coyote!*'

One of the cops stepped forward and took my arm. 'Hey, mister, just keep it down a little, will you.'

'*Coyote!*' I screamed. '*I challenge you! Coward! Lecher! Treacherous murderer!*'

The cop said: 'What the hell—'

But then the sky darkened even more, and the bridge shook with a rumbling vibration, and when the policemen looked up they saw what I was doing. There was a sigh of surprise and fear from all the people around who'd gotten out of their cars, a moaning sigh that could have been the sound of mourners at a foggy funeral.

Around the upper reaches of the bridge's spires hovered Coyote's ugliest and most feral form. It squirmed and changed with every dull breath of wind, but the malicious eyes burned down at us, and the racks of demonic teeth glistened through the fog.

Motorists and policemen scattered. One of the cops tried to pull me away with him, but I shook him off. Behind me, I heard feet running down the roadway, and the sound of more car doors opening and more people dragging their wives and their children away.

'*Coyote!*' I shouted. I was bathed in sweat, and trembling. '*I have your Bear Maiden, Coyote!*'

The gruesome demon's form rolled and twisted, and grew clearer in the fog. Now I could see that around its horned head, the iron-grey hair of Big Monster was wound, a ghastly garland of primitive magic. The bridge vibrated under me, and there was a deep, shuddering sound like thunder over nearby hills.

'*Coyote! Give me the hair and you can have Bear Maiden back! Can you hear me, Coyote? Can you hear me?*'

There was another rumble. Fragments of steel and

concrete dropped from the top of the bridge on to the roadway, bouncing off abandoned cars.

I turned, and started to hurry back to the Pinto, glancing over my shoulder at the hovering demon as I did so. I kept imagining its devilish claws sinking into my back, or its teeth ripping my flesh off, and my body was so hyped up that I walked like a tennis player on the crucial edge of a major tournament. I had to wipe the sweat from my face with my shirtsleeve.

I reached the car. The demon's wind was beginning to blow – a scorching hurricane that blasted my ears and made my face feel as if it was raw. I wrenched open the Pinto's passenger door, and tried to lift Jane out of her seat and on to the road. I was sweating and cursing, and all the time the bridge was heaving under my feet so that I could hardly stay upright.

At that moment, three uniformed SWAT squad men came running past me with carbines. One of them slapped me on the shoulder and shouted: 'Okay, feller – just get out of here as fast as you can!'

I shouted back: 'I can't! I have to destroy it!' but the man didn't understand, and went running off along the bridge towards the horrendous dark form of Coyote.

It was only when the three SWAT officers ran into Coyote that I really understood what I was up against. One moment they were pelting along the roadway with their guns raised; and the next second the wolfish shape of the demon descended on them with a crackling of electrified air, and a thundering sound that made the Golden Gate bridge tremble.

The man in front was spun around; and as he spun round I saw that his front was cleaved open like meat in a supermarket freezer. Then all three of them were hacked to pieces in front of my eyes by some fearful invisible force that chopped away their hands and their heads and their legs and their arms, and knocked the pieces in all directions. I think I probably screamed.

Now the demon was rippling towards me, only a few yards off, and the full power of his hatred and malevolence was directed my way. I desperately dragged Jane towards the rail of the bridge, and then turned to face Coyote with as much defiance as I could manage, which wasn't very much.

'*Keep away!*' I yelled. '*Keep away or I push her over!*'

The demon kept coming, and now the terrible hot wind was searing my face and drying my eyeballs, so that I couldn't even blink. Everything around me was darkness and fear, and those evil red eyes were fixed on me with cruel intensity.

I heaved Jane up on to the rail. Below us, through the fog, the grey waters of the bay heaved and foamed.

'*I mean it, damn you! I mean it!*' I shouted. And in that moment of total panic, I *did* mean it. I willed myself to mean it. If Coyote moved any nearer, his beloved Bear Maiden, his passionate werewolf mistress, was going to go over the rail and die.

I saw a disembodied snarl in the turbulent darkness in front of me, a snarl of terrible phantom teeth. I saw, too, Coyote's head, with its crown of magical hair. But he paused for one second. He paused. And it was then that I gambled everything, and let Jane fall to the sidewalk.

It happened in strange slow-motion, like a nightmare of running in which you can never escape. As Jane slid down to the road, I dodged sideways, and made a run for Coyote himself. With one hand, I reached out for Big Monster's hair, and I forced as much strength and energy through my body as I possibly could, and more. All the same, it seemed to take for ever; and I could actually see Coyote beginning to turn towards me, and his teeth baring in animal hatred.

It was like throwing yourself into boiling water. The heat and the turmoil of Coyote's presence was unbearable. I snatched, missed, and snatched again, and suddenly I was tumbling and rolling back across the road with a handful of long grey hair that fizzed and buzzed like live electric wires. I was thrown right back against the wheel of an abandoned Plymouth, and I grazed my face and my arm, but I knew that I'd done it. I'd actually stolen the Big Monster's scalp away from the demon Coyote.

There was a shattering roar of supernatural fury. I thought the bridge was cracking, the sound was so loud. I pushed myself sideways between two cars, and then I had to jump even further back as those cars were lifted and smashed against each other in an ear-splitting collision. I dragged the hair around behind a Cadillac, and raised it above my head.

In that moment, I remembered what George Thousand Names had told me. *'If a mortal man attempts to wear the scalp of a giant or a demon, he will be destroyed by what he sees. In other words, for as long as he could survive it, which wouldn't be long, he would become a demon himself, and his mind just couldn't take it.'*

I said only one thing. It was a whisper against the scorching wind, but it was all I could think of. 'George, help me. Wherever you are, help me.'

Then, closing my eyes in dreadful anticipation, I wound the strange slippery hair of Big Monster around my head.

I didn't think anything was going to happen at first. I raised my head, terrified and disappointed. But then a feeling like a dark depth-charge went through my whole body, and I was suddenly aware of a strength, both physical and mental, that I had never imagined possible. It was a frightening, evil strength. It was the strength of all my most violent and carnal desires amplified a hundred times. But it gave me such a wild jolt of exhilaration that I shrieked out loud – not a shriek of fear – but a shriek of sheer joyous overwhelming malevolence. I felt lustful, and vengeful, and I felt swamped with urges to rape and wreck and destroy everything and anyone I came across. I stood up from behind the cars, and I seemed to rise to amazing heights, taller and stronger than any human being could ever be.

I saw Coyote then clearly. Not a murky shadow, or a turmoil of cloud, but the demonic beast himself, crouching over Jane's body with his robe of worms and coyote skins on his back. I knew, too, what he was going to do. He had a grey bird perched on one of his bristly shoulders, and an armful of guts and blood from the dead SWAT men. He was preparing to reward Jane for her failure with his most loathsome specialty; sewing a bird into her stomach and then forcing her into the dead intestines of the SWAT men. The Ordeal of Three.

I felt anger so far beyond human anger that I roared out loud. I saw Coyote for what he was; and I also saw that the air was curdled with other demons and spirits – the ghosts of the wind and the fog, the manitous of earth and fire.

'*Coyote!*' I bellowed. '*Coyote!*'

The demon turned, his jaws dripping with blood. I raged across the roadway towards him, and all the time I felt with black delight that I was fearless, that I was not afraid of him any longer. I seized him, and felt the coarse and revolting bristles of his body, the maggoty softness of his insides. He struggled and screamed, but it was Big Monster's hair that was giving me strength – strength far greater than Coyote could cope with.

I tore him open like a sack, and out of his insides came living things that crawled and twitched, smothered in blowflies. I seized his jaws and stretched them so far apart that they snapped, and then I put out those blazing eyes. There was no blood. Demons aren't made of blood. But there was a stench of evil that was centuries old, the sour and sickening smell of the dog-beast, Coyote, the First One To Use Words For Force.

I stood away from his ruined body, and his breath

fled with the wind. His heartbeat palpitated for a few moments, and then went still. His eyes dulled over. The breeze of San Francisco Bay tossed away the bristles, the crumbling bones, the leathery skin. Soon there was nothing but a fragment of hairy scalp and a scorch on the sidewalk. A scorch that – if you walk across the Golden Gate today – you can still see.

Right then, with Coyote dead, I felt as if something as black and as vast as a locomotive was rushing into my brain. I knew that I wasn't going to survive these minutes in my demonic form, but I didn't care. I was almost elated, as if the ultimate high was rushing my way to hit me.

In the back of my mind, though, I still heard the voice of George Thousand Names. Maybe he knew what my plight was, and he was making one last supreme psychic effort. Maybe the strength was my own. But I heard him say: 'If a mortal man attempts to wear the scalp of a giant or a demon, he will be destroyed by what he sees. For as long as he could survive it, which wouldn't be long, he would become a demon himself, and his mind just couldn't take it.'

With an agonised cry, I pulled Big Monster's hair from my head, and hurled it as far as I could into the dull waters of San Francisco Bay. It curled and unwound with the wind, and blew away. I felt a desperate sensation of loss and exhaustion go through me, and I sank on to my knees on the roadway.

It was then, through clouding vision, that I saw Jane. She was lying on the sidewalk, and for one fleeting moment, I saw claws and teeth and black hair down her spine; but as the last of Coyote's dust was whipped away, she opened her eyes and she was Jane Torresino again, my once and perhaps even my future love.

She reached out her hand to me, and said softly: 'John . . . oh, John. I need you . . .'

And then the sirens were warbling in the distance, and we heard the welcoming sound of running feet.

It was September, the Drying Grass Moon, before I could make it up to Round Valley Reservation again. I borrowed a slightly clapped-out Pacer, and Jane and I travelled up over the weekend, stopping the night at Willits, in Mendocino County. It was afternoon by the time we reached George Thousand Names's house, overlooking the valley, and we parked the car. We climbed the stairs to the balcony, and a stern, quiet, middle-aged Indian was there, Walter Running Cow, and he shook our hands ceremoniously.

We had some tea, and in gentle voices we told Walter Running Cow about everything that had happened at Pilarcitos Street, and the emergence of Coyote, and what George Thousand Names had done to help us destroy him. We told him, too, how George had succumbed to a massive coronary at the moment of Coyote's death. Walter Running Cow listened in silence, and nodded now and again, while the sunlight crossed the room and the birds called long and plaintive from the distant woods.

Finally, the Indian said: 'It was a brave passing for George Thousand Names. By modern standards, you know, he was one of our greatest magicians. Maybe he could never have flown like an eagle, as the wonder-workers did in days gone by, but he used his powers to their utmost, and I believe we can all be grateful for that.'

I said softly: 'I needed to tell someone who believed. In San Francisco, it was treated as a straightforward homicide. The official explanation is that it was all the work of a maniac, and in the end he leaped off the bridge.'

'Well,' said Walter Running Cow, 'I suppose that all cultures need their rationale. Even Indian magic has its blind spots.'

'Will Coyote ever return?'

He looked at me, and his face was quite serious. 'Not in our lifetime, maybe. But sometime. I am not deprecating what you did, but one such as you could never dismiss a demon like Coyote for ever. And Big Monster's hair still floats in the tides of the ocean.'

'Talking of hair,' I said, 'there's one thing I want to do.'

I opened up the plastic shopping-bag I'd brought with me, and took out the dried bristly scalp of the demon Coyote. Walter Running Cow looked at it for a long time with a mixture of apprehension and respect, and then said: 'It is good that you have brought it here. George Thousand Names will thank you for this, in the skies.'

We went out on to the balcony in the last light of the day, and I tied Coyote's scalp to the rail, along with the pelts and the snow-shoes. Then we stood in the vastness of the Indian evening, while the breeze ruffled the long grass and set the trophy that belonged to George Thousand Names spinning in the faded warmth of the year, in the Drying Grass Moon, the month after the Moon of the Demon.